THE COMPLETE
SHADOW DRAGON SAGA

Dedicated to

Sky and Hannah Cross
Monika Gotthardt-Marshall
Leanne Tempest

Shadow Dragon Saga
Curse of the Dragon Shadow
Legend of the Dragon Soul
Rise of the Dragon Sworn
Blood of the Dragon Throne
Reign of the Dragon Born
Secret of the Dragon Crown

First Edition
Published by Fairies and Fantasy Pty Ltd 2024

ISBN: 978-1-922390-96-7 (paperback)

www.selinafenech.com

SHADOW DRAGON SAGA
SELINA A FENECH
THE COMPLETE SERIES

CONTENT ADVICE

Coarse language: Rare/mild
Violence: moderate-to-high fantasy violence
Sex: References, kissing, off page sex

Contains references to or descriptions of:
Slavery, animal cruelty, torture, blood and gore, kidnapping,
scars, fire, ableism, corpses/undead, birth, murder, child abuse, amputation.

CONTENTS

Curse of the Dragon Shadow 1
Legend of the Dragon Soul 169
Rise of the Dragon Sworn 339
Blood of the Dragon Throne 533
Reign of the Dragon Born 727
Secret of the Dragon Crown 925
Glossary 1153

ELUNDRAE
EIGHT WINDS OCEAN
TAEN HIGHLANDS
Nord-Halfort
Treedart Wilds
Heithorn Estate
EYLE TAENESK
Eldisun Grove
The Great Wing
Vesland Plains
Longtail River
EYLE TAENUSH
Unicorn Va
Abandoned Quarries
(1)
Lorg Cornis
Eishowl Pea
WESTERN
ALDERKIN DEPTHS
(Ewess Deemfret)
Midsun Dale
(2)
Snowshimmer Ridg
Yeonard's Passage
Vasthome Reach
Stunnfell Peaks
Lorg Blessun
(12)
Lorg Nisk
(10
(16)
Sut Myrr
Tallesis Shores
EYERSUNN SEA

Dragon Keeps

1. Braigwenkeep (Trade Hub)
2. Nevrynkeep (Mining)
3. Ardahnkeep (Trade Harbor, Old Rolanian Capital)
4. Tjollaskeep (Mining)
5. Salixkeep (Fishing)
6. Ulfrenkeep (Mining)
7. Ylvakeep (Farming)
8. Leskakeep (Farming)
9. Pryshakeep (Farming)
10. Dastmyrkeep (Glass)
11. Tarrickeep (Mining)
12. Gerichkeep (Lumber)
13. Skaellakeep (Farming)
14. Idrakeep (Penal)
15. Hjelzahnkeep (Training)
16. Eslindekeep (Incomplete)

NORTHERN
ALDERKIN DEPTHS
(Nerrun Deemfret)
Nord Myrr
EYLE NORDCREST
(14)
(8)
Lorg Sesstra
(9)
Gris
Hofen
Seasong
Shores
(15)
Lorg Eldstrom
Lorg Draeka
Sunborn Range
Draeskull Crags
Mestra's Horn
EASTERN
ALDERKIN DEPTHS
(IlstDeemfret)
Stonewing
Crest
(4)
Starris River
DRAEKHAN'S REST
CENTRAL
ALDERKIN DEPTHS
(Luns Deemfret)
(7)
(3)
Etherflame
Plains
(6)
DRAEKHANHELM
Grand
Hofen
Bovin
Steppes
Unicorn Tears River
(13)
SKYBREAK SEA
(5)
Erst Hofen
The Red Cliffs
SOUTHERN
ALDERKIN DEPTHS
(Sous Deemfret)
Talon
Bluffs

ALDERKIN
DEPTHS
UPSLOPE
Relic
Lower
Wet
Descent
Whisperwind
Passage
DragonMaw
Descent
Stores
Upper
Flats
1.
The Curtain
2.
Relic
Upper
12.
3.
9.
The
Grand
Arch
11.
Flowstone
Steps
Delver's
Circuit
Crystalline
Reservoir
STONESHIELD
GATE
Livestock
Root
Farms

THE UNDERCITY
Mushroom Farms
CURSED DEPTHS
Orphan's Den
DOWNSLOPE
UNICORN GATE
FIRSTMAN'S PASS
1. Temple Tower
2. Grand Column
3. Frostwork Column
4. Dragonwing Tower
5. Satinstraw Tower
6. Slowflow Flats
7. Rimstone Flats
8. Shimmervein Tower
9. Grand Arch Markets
10. Downslope Markets
11. Curtain Markets
12. Sinking Stream Lake

CURSE OF THE
DRAGON SHADOW
SELINA A FENECH
BOOK ONE OF THE
SHADOW DRAGON SAGA

CHAPTER ONE

One big consequence of stealing a baby was having to then raise the thing. Riony Eyfarr had learned that lesson the hard way.

She was only ten the first time she acquired a newborn. She never intended to repeat the experience. Eight years on, her first charge was more than a handful already.

Riony glared at the simple room carved from limestone. It didn't hold much. They didn't have many belongings. It also didn't contain her adopted sister.

I told her to stay at home. So, of course, she's gone. Better if I told the little spitfire to go catch cave spiders with her bare hands, then maybe she'd be here taking a nap.

Riony had only been away a short time, trading for food at the mushroom farms, but Lyrrin played a game of doing the opposite of what she was told. The kid thought she knew everything and drew trouble to her like a magnet to dragon-forged steel.

Riony prayed to the stars that she wouldn't find her sister in too deep this time. There had been a lot of talk in the undercity lately of kids going missing.

Riony and Lyrrin's small two-room dwelling was in the undesirable highest tier of the Dragonwing Tower stalagmite, keeping the rent cheap. The immense limestone formation had been carved and hollowed into multiple homes by the previous inhabitants of the caves, but few humans enjoyed climbing to the highest rooms, including Riony.

So many stairs. That I just came up. Grumbling under her breath, Riony stepped back outside and pressed the stone button that rolled her front door closed. She eyed the twisting pathways at ground level far below. At least descending was faster than ascending.

Riony vaulted over the ornate stone railing and slid down the smooth slope until she hit the level below. She jogged along her downstairs neighbor's balcony, dodging some hanging laundry, then leaped across a gap to a lower flat-topped limestone formation below.

The surface was slick beneath her boots, wet by tiny drips from a craggy ceiling far above. Riony angled out over the edge to check her landing was clear, then dropped the short distance to the street level below.

Now, where did you go? Riony aimed for the small local market first. Lyrrin had no sovs to spend, but could sometimes use her big blue eyes to be gifted treats in sympathy. Riony grasped the hilt of her sword, the scale-patterned metal biting into her palm as she barged through the maze of crystal-lit pathways between rock-cut buildings.

The warm, earthy air was heavy in her lungs. It had been three years since she and her sister had fled underground and Riony still wasn't used to the bustling slums of the sprawling underground metropolis that was now her home.

Thousands of human refugees had made the Alderkin ruins their own, filling the expansive cavern to bursting. But only that cavern, the one closest to aboveground, as though the humans there still tried to be as close to the sun and sky as they could, even if they could never see it. There were other levels below, more than even the bravest of delvers had managed to map, but they felt too dangerous, too haunted, to be habitable.

Riony's skin shivered at the thought of the dark, cursed depths beneath her, both terrifying and thrilling. The delvers told wild tales of their scavenging adventures, and she hoped she'd soon set her own eyes on those treasure-filled spaces, both for her sake and for Lyrrin's.

They needed the money delving would bring in. Riony wouldn't mind the status it would bring either. She just had to convince the delvers to let her into their ranks.

Riony's gaze scanned the buildings and homes stacked up the huge stalagmites and cliffs, tracing every surface. The dwellings stretched right up to the distant ceiling, jagged with stalactites, like the toothy maw of some gigantic beast.

Tracking down a missing child in this mess was like finding a flea on a full-grown dragon. Riony pushed a flop of red hair away from her eyes and searched the crowd filling the small street market she'd marched into. An easy view from her vantage point of standing a head taller than most.

"Lyrrin?" she called, hands cupped around her mouth.

Nearby, a spice seller did a roaring trade offering overworld delicacies to add flavor to basic undercity fare. The scents of curry and cake filled the street. Riony's mouth watered as she passed his stall, and her empty stomach growled.

As she forged onward, her gaze snagged on the story seller's shop, offering up the newest serials in press-printed booklets brought in from the dragonkeeps. It had been ages since Riony had the sovs to spare to buy and read those romantic adventures. A pang of longing stabbed at Riony, but she ignored it and kept walking.

From the shadows of an alleyway, a hand struck out and grabbed Riony.

A woman with a motherly face and missing front teeth leaned close to her. "Got any need for silvernix? Only fifty gold sovs."

Riony tugged her arm free and shook her head. She moved away fast.

Unicorn blood that cheap? Who is she kidding?

She rubbed her thumb over her acorn pendant, its surface polished smooth from the worry-born habit.

Spotting a street vendor Riony sometimes took Lyrrin to for fried rope worm, she touched his shoulder in greeting. "Have you seen my sister?"

"Little hooded scamp? Ran off that way not long ago." He pointed, then held a sizzling tray of sausage-like meat cooked on metal skewers under her nose. "Got some good juicy worms today if you want—"

"You know I love the juicy ones! But can't. Sorry!" Riony rushed by, eager to lay eyes on Lyrrin again and confirm she was safe, so she could skin the kid herself.

She couldn't afford meat now, anyway. Her last sovs went to the mushroom jerky she'd just bought. She'd been doing what she could to earn enough to keep her and her sister fed, but selling herbal remedies was a tricky and wildly unreliable business when living underground.

If she could convince Master Brishan to take her on as a delver, she and her sister would never have to worry about going hungry again. Trials were coming up soon, and Riony had been training so hard she had aches in muscles she didn't even know she had. And she knew most of her muscles, very fondly.

She was strong enough to join, she knew that much. She just had to make a good impression on the other delvers and she'd be in. But until then, the situation was dire enough without Lyrrin running off.

The direction the vendor had sent her went right toward the orphans' den.

I should have figured she'd go there.

Lyrrin could generally be found either trying to turn some random animal into a new pet or at the orphans' den, seeking company with others her age who had lost their parents on their journey to the Alderkin undercity too.

The memory of ragged, ravenous skeletons, and the raw, final screams of her amma cut through Riony's heart. Clenching her jaw, she shook off the visions of her past and pressed on.

Glow crystals lit the crooked pathway through the caves, casting a soft cyan light over Riony as she barged past other comers-and-goers.

A man in ragged brown hides and layers of dirt sat sprawled at an intersection. Riony's gaze lingered on him for too long and he met her stare with a sharp, cunning look. His eyes were red-rimmed and marked around the left one with a badly healed burn scar. Bowing his head, he reached out a beseeching hand and mumbled desperate pleas.

Riony flicked her gaze away and marched on.

Everyone in the undercity suffered. Everyone here had lost. She couldn't help him. How could she when she had nothing? She had to focus on keeping herself and Lyrrin safe.

The glow crystal at the entrance of the orphans' den flickered dully, almost out of charge. A young man with bronze skin and a tumble of golden curls took it from its sconce and replaced it with another, tracing the carved rune in a single swift motion to activate it.

Bright light washed over him, filling the area, and he turned around, spotting Riony.

He greeted her with a friendly smile. Riony had met him a few times before, since he was one of the regular helpers for the younger orphans. She admired him for that, and also for how he always managed to be well dressed and presentable in neat, new clothes.

Not the sort of ragged hand-me-downs that were all Riony and Lyrrin could scrounge up. He had a genuinely happy smile and somehow seemed to find it more freely than others in the undercity. Riony wondered how he did it, looking after others and himself with such apparent ease and joy. Maybe she could ask him to give her some pointers one day.

"Hey, Zade. Have you seen—"

"I am NOT clumsy!" A piercing, shrill voice answered Riony first. "I can do anything you could do and better!"

Riony winced. "Aaand that'd be her. Sorry, she's not supposed to be here."

Zade juggled the old glow crystal and chuckled. "We don't mind. Happy to have her around if you need someone to help look after her at times."

Riony fought down the bristly feeling at the implication she couldn't look after her sister herself.

Offering a smirk, she waved the offer away. "You might have made it your mission to rescue every orphan you see, but it's okay, I've got this one."

"It's no trouble. The more the merrier. The other kids enjoy her company."

There was another squeal from Lyrrin, then the gruff mumblings of a boy.

"Sounds like it."

"Kids, right?" Zade shrugged. "Think you can manage the extraction?"

"Sure. I'll go and grab her. Listen for my screams, in case I need backup. Stars shine upon you!"

"And you!" Zade's smile widened, and he waved as Riony stepped into the dormitory.

The smell coming from the orphans' den twisted Riony's nose. Unwashed, unhealthy children from babes to working age filled the space beyond capacity. The wide, low-ceilinged cavern seemed more suited to housing livestock than humans.

Carers stepped gingerly between the little napping bodies crammed together on the floor, soothing where they could. The community came together to provide for the children, when possible, but that only helped to a point. There were just so many of them.

And that care couldn't replace the parents lost in the overworld to fire or slavers or shadow revenants.

"It's not my fault. It's the gloves." Lyrrin's voice carried across the room from the play area. Riony beelined for her.

A boy replied, "Then why are you always wearing them?"

As most of the smaller kids were resting, there were only two in the play area—an alcove to the side with a few patchwork dolls and games.

As they came into view, Riony's guts turned cold. She swore under her breath. The boy was Benjin, little brother to people Riony did *not* want to be on the bad side of.

Reaching them, Riony lifted her hands in a gesture of peace. "Okay now. Seems to me like a good time for making up and being friends."

Lyrrin shot a tempestuous glare from under her oversized hood.

Benjin ignored Riony, a smirk dimpling one brown cheek. "If your hands worked right, maybe you could look after those pets of yours better—"

Something squirmed under Lyrrin's shirt, and she clutched it protectively.

"—and stop them ending up in people's stew pots."

"That was you?" Lyrrin shrieked and threw herself fists first toward Benjin.

For the love of stars. Riony stepped into her path, greeted with a hailstorm of tiny, gloved hands pummeling her chest.

"It wasn't me! I'm trying to help you. You're just too tamebrained to get it." Benjin leaned around Riony toward Lyrrin as though he wanted a black eye.

Riony grasped Lyrrin's wrists, wrestling with her until she stilled, then shot back to Benjin, "Don't talk to her like that. The only dumb thing she's done recently is get into a conversation with you."

The moment she let go of Lyrrin, the child sprung into attack again and Riony had to push Benjin a few steps back to safety.

A voice whispered in a husky breath close to Riony's ear, "What, exactly, are you doing to my brother?"

Oh sparks.

Riony grabbed Lyrrin by the collar, then turned to see the young woman who had snuck up behind her.

There weren't many who could look Riony in the eye. Aishena barely came close, but somehow seemed to loom over her through attitude alone. She was made of all thin, rigid angles, her ashy-tan face curtained by steel-toned locks.

She had Taen features, in the sweep of her eyes and sharpness of her nose, but Taen normally braided their hair in intricate patterns, and Aishena left hers hanging free. The way it shimmered and glided around her added to her ghostly presence. She moved as though sound offended her and had a habit of lurking in the shadows like a vengeful spirit.

Sly, confident, effortlessly capable. In other words, totally hot. A shame she and her siblings were all ice-hearted bullies.

Benjin straightened out his tunic with a huff. "She pushed me."

Riony held her palms up innocently. "It was for his own benefit, I swear."

The promise of swift retribution was clear on Aishena's pouted lips. "What possibly benefit could anyone get from being manhandled by a thug like you?"

As much as Riony wanted to say, *ask your amma*, she managed to suppress the impulse. "If I can just explain—"

"What's going on?" A new voice boomed from across the cavern.

Riony's mouth curled down as Yoskar, the eldest brother, approached. His bulky muscles were mismatched with how he studiously pushed spectacles back up his nose. Like his little brother, his silver-gray hair was clipped close to his scalp, sparkling against his cool brown skin. Not a braid in sight.

Both he and Aishena wore dusty leather armor covered with straps, buckles, and harnesses. Their belts held the tools of the delving trade: cave-silk ropes, athames, multiple personal glow crystals, and more that Riony could never afford.

Not unless she became one of them.

Exhaling slowly, Riony spread a friendly grin on her face. "Look, the kids and I were ... playing a little game, that's all. How about we go and talk about it over a drink or—"

"If Benjin takes one of my pets again, I'll stab him in his sleep!" Lyrrin howled.

"I didn't!" Benjin whined back, and the flurry of tiny fists began again.

Riony sighed and pinched the bridge of her nose. *This child is going to kill us both.*

Aishena, unaware that Lyrrin was all bark and no bite, lunged one big step toward the girl, arm raised.

A flash of protective instinct flared through Riony, and her hands shot out before her brain could catch up. They slammed into Aishena's chest, thrusting her backward.

The delver drew a long, outraged gasp as she stumbled. Yoskar caught and steadied her, then held her shoulders tight when she tried to rush back at Riony.

"Aish," Yoskar snapped.

A chill fell over Aishena's expression. She stilled and stood at attention like a soldier.

The command in his words also stilled the two quarreling children, who froze, hands still entangled between them.

Yoskar looked Riony up and down. "I've seen you before, sniffing around Master Brishan. You think you're going to become a delver?"

"I *know* I'm going to become a delver."

"No. No, you're not. Not after assaulting my sister like that."

"Whoa, slow down a second. I didn't mean ..."

"Which is exactly why you'll never be a delver. Brute strength is nothing without the brains to back it up. Master Brishan might have been considering letting you take trials, but you'll never be one of us. I'll make sure of it."

A trickle of cold sweat raced down Riony's spine. "I'm sorry. Please ..."

His roving, disapproving gaze stopped, and he leaned close to Riony, lifting a hand toward her face. Then he lowered it again. His fingers lingered near Riony's neck and landed on the acorn she wore tied on a leather strap there.

No ...

"What even is this ridiculous thing?" Yoskar's words were slow and mocking.

"Nothing. An acorn. Just a small reminder of life above." Riony tried to back away, but Yoskar's hand closed around the pendant.

From behind her brother's shoulder, Aishena simpered, mockingly. "Why? Do you still dream of returning one day? Dream of seeing the sky and stars? Feel the sun browning your skin?"

"Only when I'm not dreaming about being a better delver than you." Riony tried to keep the tone light and ignore the lump in her throat at how Yoskar's grip tightened.

Aishena scoffed. "You should know by now that dreams are like the mushroom farms. Full of sh—"

"Could you try not being a complete ass in front of the littles?" Riony snapped.

Yoskar's eyes narrowed, and he jerked his hand, snapping the leather thonging. He flung his hand sideways, and the acorn clattered against the stone wall and fell into a dark corner.

"No!" Lyrrin yelled out.

Riony shot her a warning glance.

Body shaking and shoulders slumped, she spoke in a flat tone. "Did that make you feel better? You can pretend all you like that you don't dream, but look at you, still acting like overworld nobles. Yet here you are, hiding in the dark with the rest of us losers."

Benjin stepped over to his big brother's side, puffing out his chest. "We're not like you. You have no idea how important our family is. We're Hjelz—"

"Benj! Silence!" Yoskar snapped.

Aishena's eyes had widened, and she had one hand resting on the hilt of one of the many athames on her belt, ready to strike.

What the sparks did I do to deserve this? Riony put her hands up in a calming gesture.

"Is everything all right here?" Zade stepped right between the opposing sides.

Bravely, Riony thought, considering she and Yoskar were both slightly older and significantly bigger than him.

He tilted his head toward Riony. "You need backup?"

"Did I scream?"

"Well, no, I guess not. But ..." He looked skeptically between the two sets of warring siblings.

Riony sighed, then through gritted teeth said, "Everything is fine."

"Yeah. Fine. We were leaving." Aishena gave Zade a look of utter disgust, then wrapped an arm over Benjin's shoulders in a way that made him wince as she dragged him away.

Yoskar shot a final condemning look back as he pushed up his glasses again and followed after his family.

Lyrrin stared at Riony, her bottom lip quivering.

"Hush," Riony warned again.

She stood still and waited as the delvers disappeared from view. Zade offered only one concerned glance back before he hurried after them.

Then Riony bolted over to where the acorn had fallen. The flea-ridden cot there was empty, just a tangle of threadbare rags, and Riony clawed through it, patting the edges and raking her fingers over the surrounding filth until the smooth, hard shape pressed against her palm.

She held her breath as she brought the acorn up and brushed it clean. With a look over her shoulder, she held the acorn close, acting as though to retie the leather about her neck.

Instead, she carefully twisted the top of the acorn free and inspected the miniscule glass vial held within. It shimmered, a silvery rainbow, the glass unbroken, despite the markings scratched into the side.

Lyrrin skittered up next to her. "Is the uni—?"

Riony slapped a hand over her sister's mouth. "It's fine. Our precious *acorn* is safe."

Lyrrin reached out and touched the etched lines with a gloved finger. "I'm sorry I made the glass more fragile. I just wanted to make it pretty."

Tears glittered over her vivid eyes and Riony pulled her in close. Anyone who saw them in person would never confuse the two of them for real sisters. Riony, a brown-skinned, flame-haired tower of muscle, and Lyrrin, diminutive and pale, with black hair and eyes a brighter blue than a sky clear of dragon-smoke.

But in this place, where everyone had fled to from the perils of the overworld, there were many who ended up in families that weren't those they were born into.

Riony closed the acorn pendant and tied the cord around her neck.

Patting the hood over Lyrrin's head, she said, "Didn't I tell you to stay at home?"

Lyrrin turned her face up, her expression petulant. "I'm not useless. I can look after myself and can't sit around waiting for you all day. This is where all the kids are. It's safe here."

Riony squatted in front of Lyrrin and took the child's gloved hands in her own. The leather was worn and cracked.

"It's entirely the opposite of safe. Safe is with me, or when I have to go, safe is in our home which you should be grateful to have. Which we'll be lucky to keep if Yoskar follows through on his threat to stop me from becoming a delver."

Lyrrin's lips wavered. "I'm sorry I got in a fight with Benjin."

Riony stood and extended her hand. "Come, I'll walk you back home, and I want you to stay there this time."

Lyrrin wrapped both arms around Riony's offered limb. "Why, where are you going?"

"Up above."

"Nooooo. I don't want you to."

Lyrrin tugged back, but Riony pulled her along to walk beside her, heading down the dimly lit path toward their home.

"I have to go. It's the only place to find green-leaf herbs, you know. They don't exactly grow around here. And we need trade."

"Can't you get some other job?"

"I know herbs. And they might be hard to come by, but even just a very few pieces of the right kind of green is more valuable than most jobs down here."

"Except delvers."

"Except delvers." Riony sighed. "Maybe we'll get lucky and Aishena and Yoskar will fall into a bottomless pit or get eaten by cave spiders soon, then I might get a chance. Until then, I'm going to need to sell some more herbs and fast."

Riony had hoped that her last harvest would have been enough to get them through until after delver trials, but Lyrrin was going through a growth spurt and eating like a bovin.

"Don't worry though. I've found a new foraging place. Safer than picking around near where the breachers go scavenging."

The land close to the Alderkin depths exits had been scraped bare anyway.

"Where?"

"I've found a warm spot. Up high above the snow line. There's a meltwater stream and I saw some green but haven't had a good search yet."

Lyrrin leaned away but didn't let go of Riony's arm. "A warm spot? They say dragon's nest in warm spots."

Riony swung her captive arm back and forth, dragging Lyrrin with it. Each swing grew a larger smile on the child's face.

"Who says? Wild dragons are practically extinct. I'd be more worried about the shadow dragon."

Lyrrin's eyes widened.

"Don't worry, if it shows up, I'll punch it so hard it will disappear in a puff of smoke." Riony brought her arms up to flex her biceps, lifting Lyrrin from the ground. "The trip is worth it. Just a quick harvest will keep us going until delver trials. I think I saw some shillgrue up there, too. I can make some more leather conditioner with it."

"My gloves are getting stiff again," Lyrrin conceded, hanging in the air and giggling. With one big swing, she jumped back to the ground, and her hood fell from her head.

Riony brushed a hand over her dark hair, seeing a slight cyan sparkle along the scalp, then quickly pulled the hood back up. "And I need to find more hair dye, too. We're almost out."

Lyrrin thought for a moment, then nodded. "Just be safe, okay? Also ..."

"What?"

"I'm huuungry," Lyrrin sang mournfully, eying the rope worm merchant as they passed.

Riony felt a tight ache in her own stomach as well. On the long climb back up the stairs to home, she reached into the satchel at her side and handed over the hard strips of mushroom jerky.

"Just for you. Not for any pets." She eyed the bulge of Lyrrin's shirt just above her belt.

Lyrrin nodded and waited for Riony to open their door. Another reason their dwelling had been cheap was that the rolling, circular stone that formed the door often got stuck. The clever Alderkin mechanisms that made the solid weight slide easily were failing after decades without anyone with the knowledge to repair it, much like a lot of things in the depths. Lyrrin could squeeze through the gap, but Riony had to put her shoulder against the heavy stone and heave to get it open enough to go in herself.

Riony followed her sister into the two small rooms they called home. She grabbed a pair of gloves, then threw on an extra shirt and thick, fur-lined cloak over the sleeveless tunic she usually wore in the temperate caves.

She slung her backpack over one shoulder. "Now please, please-please-please, stay here for me? Kid snatchers have been around again."

"Yeah, sure." There wasn't even the attempt of submission on Lyrrin's face. "Just don't take too long, or I might get bored."

Riony pushed the front door open again, shaking her head. She was tempted to take Lyrrin along to keep an eye on her but couldn't put her in that kind of danger.

Glancing back, she saw a small, furry snout poke out of her sister's shirt to nibble on some offered food.

Riony ran a hand through her short, wild hair. "You live to defy me, don't you?"

Lyrrin stuck her tongue out. "We should always try to help others when we can. That's what Amma always said."

Yeah, and that's what got her and Pabba killed.

Keeping just herself and one child alive since then had been hard enough for Riony alone. That's all she could focus on, those two lives, one step at a time. Keep them housed. Keep them fed.

Make sure her next trip to the overworld didn't get her killed.

"Take care of yourself. I won't be long." Riony turned away with a brave smile, doing her best to comfort Lyrrin, but her insides churned.

Every time she breached the overworld, she risked not coming back alive. And in a world where coming back dead was entirely a possibility, Riony didn't like the odds.

Riony kicked at loose rocks along the crumbling tunnel and created a mental list of the herbs she hoped to gather on her trip. It helped to calm her nerves as waves of past trauma set upon her in anticipation of heading aboveground.

Corpsefoot and shillgrue should be around; they grow like weeds anywhere. Some hennan or tinctoria for Lyrrin's hair might be less likely. They grow more on the plains. But anything with some pigment in the leaves will do.

Anything is better than letting her natural color grow out. We'd be in trouble then.

The voice in her head sounded so much like her amma's, and she recalled her many times crouching in gardens or over a candlelit table strewn in leafy bundles as her mother told her how to identify each herb and its medicinal properties.

They would talk about which herbs were safe for expectant mothers, and which they were learning to use for wider purposes now that the cure-all silvernix was scarce.

It was important for midwives to understand herbal remedies since the use of unicorn blood on pregnant women had been prohibited for decades, due to it causing strange birth defects. They didn't know for sure, but Riony and her parents speculated that was why Lyrrin was the way she was.

"Learn your midwife skills well, and you'll always have good, secure employment under a dragonlord family," Amma had said, her voice full of hope and promise. "And with the knowledge of natural remedies we've kept while everyone else relied on unicorn blood, who knows what fortune our future might bring?"

Riony sniffed away the sensation of wetness in her nose and kicked at a larger chunk of stone, like a challenge between it and her toes.

The twisting path was separate from the major transit tunnels humans used to get in and out of the main cavern, and the carefully carved walls, decorated with organic swirls and knotwork patterns were dusty and cracking.

The tunnel was already picked bare of anything valuable by delvers long ago. Riony walked alone through the darkness, lit only by her personal small glow crystal hanging from a netted pouch on her belt.

Trailing her fingers along the intricate carvings on the wall, Riony felt the catch of tendrils of cave spider silk. She wiped her hand on her pants to scrub the gummy strands away.

Cave spiders were just one reason most humans avoided exploring the massive cave system and carved tunnels beyond the one inhabited cavern.

When the Alderkin realized they had lost the war and their home, they collapsed and destabilized whole areas, and scattered the remaining levels with traps, making venturing into the abandoned depths a risk only delvers took.

Riony had only explored this tunnel due to running around trying to recapture one of Lyrrin's escaped pets for her.

That little owlette had been determined to be free. Riony could relate.

The crumbling fractures in the walls grew worse as Riony continued higher, creating large holes in the stone. It was through one of these gaps that Riony had discovered a path into a natural cave system, which lead out to the overworld.

Reaching that gap again, Riony found it bigger than she'd last seen it. Debris lay across the ground around it, and Riony sucked air through her teeth and stared at the rocky ceiling. After making a silent plea that the mountain didn't collapse on top of her, she hefted one of the larger rocks out of her way.

Something glinted in the space where it had been. A short crystal blade half buried in the dirt.

"Whoa. Is that—?" Riony snatched it up greedily.

An Alderkin athame. She'd never held one herself. They were way too expensive—if they still held a charge.

It must have only been revealed by the crumbling walls since the last time anyone had been through. Riony brushed the silty dirt from the knife, holding it close to her glow crystal to see what sigil the athame was imbued with.

There was the standard harden rune that engraved almost all Aldkerin artifacts, to toughen the brittle crystal. Beneath it, a couple of curved lines, intersected by a third, were etched into one flat side of the dagger.

A cutting rune! Nice! Her excitement wavered as she racked her brain.

How does it go?

Riony hadn't seen this rune activated before. Spying on rune usage and trying to memorize all their activation sequences was more Lyrrin's thing. But with only three strokes, Riony figured it was worth having a guess.

She traced the lines with her finger, one, then another, then another. Nothing happened, so she tried a variation on the sequence.

Each line had to be traced in the right direction, in the right order, to activate an Alderkin sigil, and those wild inhuman people had never shared that knowledge. Anything humans had worked out how to activate had been through trial and error.

On her third attempt, the blade hummed briefly to life, glowing a dull yellow, then faded out before Riony could test its capabilities. She tried to activate it again, but nothing happened. She pouted and huffed. It was out of charge.

With an active cut rune, even a tiny blunt blade like this could slice through nearly anything. But without a charge, it was basically useless.

Sighing heavily, Riony dropped the athame into her backpack anyway. Lyrrin might like to see it, even if it didn't work anymore.

Riony climbed through the gap in the tunnel and marched through the adjoining natural cave. It held the musty smell of guano, but if any bats or owlettes made the rocky nooks and crannies their home, they were asleep now.

She put on her gloves as she went and pulled her heavy woolen cloak closed as icy wind whistled toward her. It grew strong, as though pushing her away, a warning that the overworld wasn't a place for her anymore.

Natural daylight filtered in, pale blue, through the curtain of frozen water that rose high before her. She traced the light rune on her glow stone to deactivate it. Glow stone charges lasted for ages, but she still tried to conserve its energy as much as possible.

A waterfall had frozen, forming a wall across the cave entrance, all rivulets and icicles, dripping with water that still ran in just a few places and tinkling like wind chimes.

The hole Riony had pushed out through last time had already begun to seal up, with lines of dripping ice like cage bars spreading across the gap. She tried to clear it away with protected fingers that already felt cold, but the ice wouldn't snap.

Ice was always harder than she expected. But she was strong, too. Wrapping her cloak around one arm, she cracked her elbow against the icicles.

It had been her time as a slave to the Heithorns that had made her strong. The work she'd been forced into, the weight she'd carried from such a young age. That strength had saved her life more than once.

Sometimes she felt like she should be grateful for that, except that she completely sparking hated every moment of that time.

With two more hits, she managed to clear away enough ice to squeeze through.

The sword hanging at her belt caught against the side of the hole and she had to readjust the scabbard midway. The ex-dragonguard longsword often got in the way, but she'd go skinny-dipping with carnivorous olm before she went anywhere without it.

Frosty wind gusted around her, meeting her face with a pinching chill. Her cheeks tingled as Riony crawled through the gap and stepped out into the overworld.

This high into the mountains, snow was all she could see. Her path led to a place between peaks, so she couldn't look down onto the rest of the land, to see the scarred and burning hellscape it had become. She couldn't see the dragonkeeps looming in the distance.

Up there, she could pretend the world was healthy, peaceful, not plagued with death.

But the ever-present scent of dragon-fire hung in the air.

The sky was relatively clear, just a soft haze of smoke lingered, dulling the brightness of the sun.

Riony stood for a moment, turning her face to its warmth, relishing the feel of light on her skin. Her years underground had turned her complexion ashy. She missed how the sun had browned her skin to a warm, rich sienna.

Riony stomped out into the crunchy-slick snow, following the slow drip of water until that flow grew stronger, warmed by a hot patch of the mountain's molten heat under the surface.

Soon, along that meager flow, the snow cleared entirely, and a narrow stream emerged, rushing down the steep slope, surrounded by lichen-encrusted stone and just a few weak yet resilient green-leaf plants.

Riony smiled. She loved that color, that life that crept between the cracks, in even the most impossible of places.

Careful to not end up with a foot dunked in the icy water, she stepped around from rock to slippery rock, inspecting the plants.

Corpsefoot and shillgrue—as expected. She pinched off a generous number of sprigs from both. The shillgrue she'd keep and make into a leather conditioner, and the corpsefoot had value among women who didn't want to fall pregnant, so she could trade it well, too. A little bit of it went a long way, and overdosing had unpleasant side effects.

Riony was surprised to also find a small tuft of carrowmy (culinary), a patch of trailing genjermint (for sleeping tea—good for trade, too), and … Hennen! Riony recognized the thin bronze leaves immediately.

But the plant was scrawny, far too small to provide enough to dye even just the roots of Lyrrin's hair.

Carefully, Riony scooped some extra dirt around the base of the plant, that had been exposed by the melting snow. Hopefully the next time she came back it will have grown large enough to harvest.

Riony stood from her crouched position and arched her back, stretching it out and rubbing her numbed hands together. Her breath puffed out in a cloud. She watched it with a smile, and as it cleared, up on the white ridge above her, something moved.

The hazy silhouette of something big, four-legged. A long, low howl carried to her on the wind.

A wolf? So far up here? Maybe it had been driven into the mountains by the shadow revenants and burning vengeance of the dragonlords like the rest of the mountain's inhabitants. Riony squinted at it, checking it wasn't headed her way.

She patted the hilt of her sword. *I won't bother you if you don't bother me, pup.*

Riony turned back toward the stream, when a larger, darker shadow flashed over her. Something massive, flying right above.

It could just be a bird. Don't panic.

Riony tensed, working hard to keep her footing as she looked up, terrified of what she might see.

Terrified that it would be the shadowdragon.

A leathery wing flapped, lifting snow crystals in gusts. A piercing scream burst into her ears.

It wasn't the shadowdragon. But it was a dragon.

Riony stood frozen, awestruck. A dragon, a huge one! Not one of the smaller steed-like crossbreeds the dragonriders mastered.

Riony's amma and pabba had held to the Rolanian belief that dragons were born from the souls of their ancestors that had fallen from their path to the stars, tragic creatures born to suffer and bring suffering.

But Riony wasn't so sure. That might have been some of her previous master's enthusiasm for dragons rubbing off on her, but Riony always thought there was something beautiful about the powerful beasts.

Riony shielded her eyes, trying to get a good look.

A seasong dragon, maybe, based on the size, although it was much paler than they normally were and farther from the ocean than it should be. There was no sign of a harness or saddle showing.

Another cry emerged from its wedge-shaped head as it lifted high into the air again, shimmering against the clear sky. It was immense, large enough to take Riony entirely into its mouth if it chose to.

Its snakelike neck led to a body that seemed unhealthily skinny and a long tail that was crooked and boney. Armored scales of silver with a few specks of black covered the beast, and Riony's breath caught as she watched its elegant swoop through the air.

A dragon. A true, wild dragon. Untamed. Unbound. It was beautiful.

And it was coming her way.

It changed angle midair, looping around and directing itself for her.

No, thank you. This is not the day I get eaten by a dragon.

Riony wasn't sure it had seen her yet, and she didn't want to wait and find out. She filled her lungs with frozen air and ran.

The dragon's shrill cry chased her as she crashed over slippery, slushy ground. Her boots skidded dangerously on the steep slope. She pushed on, faster, toward the safety of the caves.

The beat of the dragon's wings grew closer and a gust of wind knocked Riony off her feet, throwing her onto her side on the slick ground. She skidded like a sled, back the way she'd come. Spinning, she tried to slow her descent, but her hands only grabbed uselessly at loose snow.

She slid fast on her back, headfirst, down, down.

The ground disappeared beneath Riony. She grasped for anything to halt her fall. Her gloved fingers brushed against slick, frozen edges as she tumbled roughly into a narrow chasm.

The deep crevasse of ice swallowed her. She crashed against the hard walls as she fell. Screams were knocked from her burning lungs in a painful percussion.

Bones cracked.

She landed hard and faded away.

Chapter Three

Riony awoke to a deep, dreadful sense of cold.

A thick, heavy cold, so encased around her bones that shivering couldn't shake it free. She'd never been so cold. And there was something else there, too. Another withering sensation.

Pain.

Ouch. Wincing her eyes open, she looked up at the thin ribbon of sky showing between the glassy walls that enclosed her. A warm, golden light shone down.

Sunset, already? Riony tried to sit up, and agony jolted through her. Her right arm throbbed and hung uselessly.

Her eyebrows rose at how she seemed to have acquired an extra joint, a new bend between her elbow and wrist where one shouldn't be. She looked away before the bile that was rising could escape her mouth.

A dull ache filled the back of her skull, and her hips and legs felt stiff and pockmarked with bruises. And there she was, some hundred or so steps straight down in a hole in the ice.

Well, this situation isn't much fun.

She muffled a groan as she brought herself into a sitting position. The pain from her arm made her eyes water, and the tears seemed to freeze instantly to her lashes. With an extra grunt, she got to her feet and reviewed her surroundings.

The crevasse ran like a gash in the glacier, narrow and disappearing off to either side. The walls were slick, clear, solid ice, hard as any stone. Climbing out seemed impossible, a dumb idea to try even with two good arms.

"Of course, I'm going to try anyway. What am I? Someone who doesn't try to do dumb and impossible things?" she said to her reflection in the ice.

She put on a brave smirk, but it faded quickly. She had to get out of there, one way or another. She was going home, no excuses. She was going to get home to Lyrrin.

Riony held on to the ice with her functioning hand and tried to support her weight with it enough to bring her feet up into footholds.

She balanced there for a moment, then tried to raise herself again. Without her second arm to support her as she reached for a new grip hold, her feet slipped on the slick surface and she tumbled back down, smacking her broken arm onto the icy ground.

Her scream of pain echoed through the long, thin crevasse. Attempting to climb had not been a good idea. Dizziness threatened to take her away from consciousness again. She heaved in a deep breath.

Nope. Don't you dare pass out!

Riony sat up again, leaning her back against the sheer ice wall. She shook her head to clear it, her wild, red hair tumbling over her eyes.

Riony's good hand went to her neck, grasping for the acorn. Still there, not lost or damaged in the fall. She still had some luck on her side.

The temptation to use the precious, silver fluid the acorn contained was hard to resist. Although barely more than one drop, it would be enough.

It could be enough to save a life though. What was a broken arm compared to a life? That single drop of silvernix had been in her family for decades. How could she use it now?

I can't. It's too precious. I might need it one day, for Lyrrin, for saving a life. This is just a stupid little broken arm. Nothing I can't handle.

Also, how dumb would I feel if I fixed my broken arm and still couldn't get out of here?

Riony took stock. She still had her acorn—last resort. She still had her sword—another small miracle she hadn't landed on it. It was too long to splint her arm with, and the athame in her backpack too short.

She had a few handfuls of fresh herbs tucked into the pouches on her belt. No food. No water. Her clothes weren't suited for being out in the cold this long. She was supposed to have been home hours ago, but nobody knew exactly where she had gone.

She rolled her head left, then right, taking in the length of the crevasse.

There had to be another way out.

Up on her feet again, Riony found the way to the left quickly dead-ended around a corner.

She shuffled along the other way, through the thin crack between mountains of ice. If that orange glow over her shoulder was the setting sun, she was heading back toward the stream where she'd started.

She stumbled a couple of times, feet unable to grip properly on the satin-smooth ground. She slouched to her left, leaning her less painful shoulder against the wall for stability.

The crevasse narrowed into a sliver so thin that Riony had to shimmy through, panicking partway when she thought she was stuck. She considered using that narrower section to prop herself between the walls and edge herself to the surface, but it widened out too quickly above head height.

On the other side of the tight section, the crevasse opened up again, finishing at another dead end.

No. No, I refuse to go out like this. How lame and boring, to freeze to death in a hole in the ice.

She turned on the spot, looking up and around, hoping for a smooth slope, somewhere easier to make the climb.

The dead end itself was less ice and more crumbling chunks of dirty snow. Maybe she could climb there.

Riony pressed her hand toward it, testing for purchase. It shifted dangerously. A small avalanche smashed around her feet. She dodged back. Rocks and mud mixed amongst the snow, landing hard.

She could only try to climb up there if she was ready to be buried alive. Which she was not.

Riony swore long and loud. When the landslide had stilled, she stepped forward again to inspect the muddy mess. She must be close to the stream, where the solid ground emerged from beneath the snow, but where she stood, she stood on ice only, surrounded by ice left and right.

Bright, clear ice.

Riony ran her hand over the ice on one side, moving her face close to it. It looked thin, like a glass window. There was something behind it, the shadows and shapes of a hollow space, blurry through the wavy, frozen water. A snow cave? Tunnel? She had to hope it could be another way out of there.

Her body moved before her brain and Riony kicked at the thin ice. Her foot hit hard, sending shock waves through her. Every busted and broken part of her screamed with agony, and she wilted onto her knees, gasping with pain.

"Shut up, Yoskar! I can so think before I act. Sometimes. Sparks! Why do I always forget how hard ice is?"

Shaking off the pain, Riony wiped away tears. When she could see clearly again, she checked her efforts.

Not even a crack.

She put her face close to the transparent wall, angling side to side, trying to gauge the thickness.

Riony didn't know a lot about ice. She didn't know whether she was looking at something as thin as a dragonglass sheet window, or a wall so thick she'd be chipping through it for a year. The frozen water was deceptive in its clarity.

But she was sure there was a hollow on the other side.

It would still take work, but she couldn't think of another option with her broken arm making climbing impossible, and that climb remaining improbable even with both arms. She had to do something, and fast. As much as she pretended sheer willpower could fight against the bad blood shooting through her body from the injury, she was fading.

She had to break through.

Her longsword felt clunky in her left hand as she drew it. Weighing her options, she decided not to ruin the blade more than she already had by attacking the ice with it. She gave it a solid whack with the sharp pommel instead.

Happily, the ice chipped away. Unhappily, the impact made every part of her ache and her head spin.

The sword worked. It was her body that was the problem. If she could just deal with the pain somehow, she could chip through the ice easily, and hopefully crack right through.

She patted the pouch on her belt where she'd put the herbs she picked earlier, and a thought formed.

Okay, that's not a bad idea. It's more like the kind of idea that makes a bad idea feel good about itself.

Corpsefoot, when too much was taken, had the side effect of numbing an entire body. Along with also quickly leading to vomiting, organ failure, and death.

But if she took just enough, enough to work without pain but not kill herself outright, maybe she could get home in time to counteract the overdose.

And if not, at least she wouldn't feel herself die.

"This is fine. This is going to work. You're just poisoning yourself, just a little," she muttered, as she pulled the herb out with shaking, gloved fingers, and plucked one large fleshy leaf. No, maybe two? Definitely not more than two.

This is such a bad idea.

She placed them on her tongue, then chewed. Her lips twisted at the tart tang.

Then she sat and waited. If it worked, it wouldn't take too long. Then she could make her way back, use plumeberry tea to clear the toxins, and work on healing properly. She just had to stay awake. Stay focused. Not let the sick dizziness take over. Easy.

It was only a few minutes before the pain noticeably lessened, and soon Riony could move without any pain at all. She had to remind herself how damaged her arm was, unbandaged as it was, lest she risk damaging it further. She still couldn't properly move the hand on that side, but the numbing effect was all she needed for now.

The cold didn't bite at her anymore either and her shivering had stilled. Her eyelids felt heavy as she pulled her cloak off and wrapped it around the blade of her sword. Holding it at that point in her left hand, she swung it like a bat, smashing the hilt into the middle of the thin ice.

It jarred, shaking her whole body, but she felt nothing. White chips flew from the point of impact, and the pommel punctured the ice. A hairline crack spread from that hole. She struck again, and again, each blow chiseling away more ice, growing the hole larger, spreading the cracks out like a spiderweb.

She bared her teeth in a grim smile. She was doing it. She was going to get through. She felt no pain. Maybe she had taken just enough corpsefoot that she wouldn't—

Her stomach contracted, a violent sense of pressure without the pain, and she doubled over, vomiting onto her feet.

Oh no.

Sweat dripped down her forehead and she had to wipe it from her eyes. Maybe she hadn't taken just enough after all.

Riony turned back to the wall, sending all her strength into the swing of her sword, her eyes wide with fear. She had to work fast.

Again, and again, and then *crack*. The sword blade slipped from Riony's grasp as she tried to wrench it back for another swing. The hilt and pommel had broken through and stuck fast into the hole.

Riony stared at the cracking wall for a few deep breaths.

With a primal roar, she charged shoulder first into it. She felt the pressure of the collision, and then the ice gave way. It fractured and broke, falling in clear crystals around her.

She toppled through the newly created hole. Her sword, freed again, clattered at her side. She grabbed it with her good hand, clinging to it like a doll to her chest as she stood. Vomited. Fell. Stood again.

Keep moving.

The space that opened in front of her was vast, a smooth, curved cave of ice, with a solid rocky floor. The light of sunset filtered through the frozen water, mixing a rainbow into the cool blues. The cave extended off into the distance, past where Riony's rapidly blurring eyesight could see.

She stumbled through, desperately hoping for an escape. Her vision darkened, with spots and stars shooting through the murkiness.

Her body was so numb, she couldn't feel her feet moving underneath her, couldn't feel her tongue in her mouth. But her insides now felt both hot and cold, and twisted the wrong way as though wrung between unkind hands. Sweat ran down her chest.

For a moment, she couldn't remember where she was, just that she had to keep moving. Get home.

Something glinted in her path, tucked into a nook on one side.

She thought it was her imagination at first. Or maybe the glow of Alderkin magic. Maybe she'd made it back into the depths. *Where am I?*

But the shiny, metallic shapes were head-sized, oval, nested together in a pile of carefully arranged stones.

Eggs? What could make an egg that big? Not even the largest carrion bird. The answer seemed both impossible and so entirely clear at once.

Dragon eggs.

There was no time to be in awe, as sickness surged again through her, spilling the spatters of an empty stomach onto the ice. The world swayed.

Riony stumbled on. She followed a gust of air and shambled out like the living dead into the overworld again. Over one crest of deep snow, then another, unsure which direction she'd find home.

The final blood-red rays of the smoky sunset glared off the bright ground, blinding her.

Woozy and completely wrecked, she collapsed.

Her consciousness faded in and out.

Pain returned, shooting through her gut and chest, as though a giant had reached a hand into her rib cage and squeezed. Riony put every effort into standing, but her body only twitched and gagged in response. Her head felt clamped in a vise, ever tightening, bringing darkness with it.

No. I'm not dying here. Lyrrin needs me.

Her body moved again, and she couldn't tell if it was through her own effort or some other force. Was she still stubbornly moving forward, one step at a time? She couldn't make sense of anything. She felt like she was flying.

Then it became clear she was being moved, carried on something soft and warm. Fur tickled her nose. Then she was dumped, unceremoniously, onto rocky ground.

She managed to crack her eyelids open, gaze rolling loosely around, seeking her savior.

The wolf was there.

It spoke to her with a voice from her past.

"Don't ever come back here again."

Chapter Four

Lyrrin paced the claustrophobic confines of the quarters she shared with her sister. *Why hasn't Riony come home yet?*

There were so many perils aboveground that could have given Riony a reason not to return home. Lyrrin's stomach flip-flopped, and she shook her head, trying and failing to shove those intrusive thoughts away.

She squeezed her eyes shut, huffing out a grunt of frustration. She didn't want to think about *reasons*.

Instead, she pouted.

Lyrrin didn't grieve the absence of sky the way Riony and the older people in the undercity seemed to. Maybe it was because she hadn't had many years of it that she could remember and miss before moving underground.

She did miss playing, though. She missed playing with Riony, back when their parents were around to be the parents, and Riony wasn't such a fun-killing tyrant.

It's been ages. I'm so bored.

They owned no clock, and there was no sunrise or sunset in the undercity. Sometimes, when it was quiet enough, Lyrrin could hear the bell of their neighbor's clock downstairs, but the air was currently filled with the sounds of bats, marking the coming of night in their own way, chorusing a shrieking, chittering cacophony as they awakened and flew out to feed.

Lyrrin lay on her back on the floor of their bedroom, the few thick blankets and bovin furs that made their bed barely cushioning between her and the limestone floor.

She dragged her arm backward and forward, pinching a little strip of mushroom jerky in her fingers. Sir Butterfur Spelunkychunks chased it in lithe, pouncing leaps across the roughly knitted wool.

At least since coming to the depths there had been lots of interesting animals to play with. Like cave otters. Lyrrin loved how they moved, like slick, shiny ribbons, whether diving through the underground pools or skittering up rocky walls.

Sir Butterfur was a young one, only about as long as Lyrrin's leg, and a sweet pale caramel color, similar to their limestone surroundings. The adults could get as big as Lyrrin and plagued the markets and public baths in search of food like adorable furry thugs.

Owlettes were also high on Lyrrin's list of favorite cave creatures. She didn't like the bats, with their scrunched in, angry faces. Some cloud mice would be nice to have, though. But they were so fast.

If only there was more room in their home to keep pets, maybe she'd have more luck in actually *keeping* them.

She'd been secretly feeding Butterfur for weeks before she managed to lure him into having snuggles, but he still came and went as he pleased if she didn't keep him buttoned up in her too-large tunic.

There wasn't much space for anything in the quarters Riony had rented. Only two rooms, each so small Riony could lay lengthways across them and reach out and touch the walls. Lyrrin wasn't tall enough to do that trick yet, but she was still growing.

A moth-eaten patchwork curtain separated one room from the other, defining a living area and a sleeping area, both lit by a single dimming glow stone.

The Alderkin amenities built into the living area and small bathroom to the side still mostly worked too, which was good in a city where so many facilities were failing.

They had hot and cold ventilation, running water, and a little area they could cook over a crucible marked with a burn rune. The bathing area was broken though, so they had to go and use the public hot baths.

Lyrrin had filled their one large pot with warm water, hoping Butterfur might like to splash in it, but he didn't show interest in getting in.

"Go on. I'm not trying to cook you. I promise."

Some of the bigger apartments that the delvers got to live in had their own hot spring baths big enough to swim in. Benjin had bragged about theirs. If Lyrrin had something like that, Sir Butterfur Spelunkychunks could swim around all day without fear of becoming a meal.

What if Riony can't become a delver because I fought with Benjin?

Then she'd never get a home with their own hot bath for pets to swim in. Lyrrin pouted. Benjin was an infuriating brat though. And if she found out he was the one who ate one of her pets she held fast to her promise of vengeance.

Lyrrin lured Butterfur close with the treat, then pulled him in for a hug. He wriggled in her grip, pointy teeth gnashing at the hard jerky. He was always so hungry, like she felt lately. She'd eaten almost all of what Riony had given her already and her stomach still grumbled.

She got up to see if there was anything else to eat in their small dwelling.

The previous Alderkin residents of these rooms had carved shelving into the rock walls of both rooms, with beautiful, flowing curves and leafy patterns framing them, but Lyrrin and Riony had few belongings to store there.

Lyrrin checked through their supplies. One jar had a handful of root flour in it, but Lyrrin wasn't allowed to cook while Riony was out and wasn't very good at making flatbread anyway.

There wasn't much else. Some old cutlery and dinted metal bowls, their ratty, secondhand and ill-fitted clothes, plus some multipurpose rags. One shelf held a line of mostly empty glass jars that Riony kept her herbs in, and Lyrrin had some bottles she'd scavenged that she liked to play at potion making with.

She didn't have much to put in them, but liked to scratch pretty patterns and Alderkin runes on the sides and imagine they were magic. Riony had taken their backpack with her, the one that had carried everything they'd owned as they had escaped the overworld into the depths.

There wasn't much in it anymore, none of the cool ropes and tools like delvers had that could help on her journey, but Riony always took it with her when she went out scavenging for herbs. Not that she ever filled it. It seemed to be getting harder and harder to find green things growing.

On the highest ledge of the shelves sat a doll made of corn husks and fabric remnants which Lyrrin pretended she was too old for now. But sometimes she got it down and held it close to her nose so she could smell the way the earth above and time with family used to smell, before she'd lost them both.

A small anxiety brewed within Lyrrin as she stared at that doll. That loss could happen to her again.

No. Riony will be home soon. She's not late because of reasons. Not bad reasons. Some other reason I can be angry at her about.

Lyrrin tucked her worry down deep. Better to huff at the boredom and tease Butterfur with the last of her food than to think about how Riony should have been back by now. She sat down again on the blankets and tore another tiny strip to dangle in front of the otter.

Lyrrin considered returning to the orphans' den to play. It wasn't so late that she couldn't find a friend to spend time with. Zade never scolded them for playing into the evenings. It would serve Riony right for making her wait so long if she came home to find her gone again.

We have to be extra careful, because of how you're different. Riony's warning came to her. Because it was, at least in part, Lyrrin's fault she couldn't go and play, couldn't be with the other children.

The stories of kid snatchers were real. Benjin had told her all about some of his friends from the orphans' den that had gone missing.

He really liked to boast, even about awful things.

Lyrrin hated that because of how she looked she might be a more tempting target. Her unnaturally blue eyes did attract attention, and that was even with the effort they put in to keep her hands and hair disguised.

All because Lyrrin had been born different. A mix of distant races with a complexion and features not normally seen in these parts where Taens and Rolanians were the norm, and strange even beyond that.

So she should be grateful to have a private room, and she should follow Riony's guidance and rules. But it was all just *so unfair.*

"This is the place, up here!" A muffled voice came through the stone front door. It sounded like Benjin.

Lyrrin stilled to listen better. Butterfur tackled her unmoving fingers, pulling at them with his grabby little claws and nipping at the jerky with his pointy fangs.

"Ouch! Naughty!"

There was a thumping knock at the door, and Lyrrin sat bolt upright. She herded the cave otter into a corner and threw a blanket over him.

Nobody is eating you! Then she pulled her gloves on and hood up before going to open the door.

It only rolled halfway, sticking again, and without Riony's help, she couldn't push it wider.

Benjin stood there, bouncing from one foot to another, face flushed with excitement. The light of the glowstone glittered off the expensive trim of his neat, fitted shirt.

Lyrrin fidgeted with her baggy, rolled-up sleeves and turned her nose up at him. "What do you want?"

"We found something that belongs to you!" He grinned badly, lips shaky and more agitated than happy.

Lyrrin frowned, checking her gloves, then her pockets. She didn't have much she could lose. Only her handkerchief and a pretty rock she'd picked up, both still there. "What are you talking about?"

Heavy footsteps and heavier breaths drummed up the stairs.

"Right at the top? Of course this peasant lives right at the sparking top," a female voice muttered.

Benjin puffed out his chest. "It's your sister. Delvers found her, collapsed in a tunnel. She's real sick. My brother and sister are bringing her up."

Lyrrin's eyes opened wide as she took in Benjin's news. "Riony's sick?"

She should do something, prepare, be ready to help her. But how? She turned on the spot, trying to think about what Riony would do. She dashed about, straightened the blankets, grabbed some washcloths, then put them down again. Went to fill a cup with water and then put it back.

What do I do? Flushed and flustered, she turned back to Benjin again. There was nothing she could do but wait for Riony to arrive. Maybe it wasn't so bad.

"Stop looking so happy about it!" she snapped at Benjin.

"Hey, we're the heroes here today. You want your sister back or should I tell them to turn around?"

"No way I'm carrying this dead weight a moment longer." Aishena reached the top of the steps, carrying Riony by the legs. Yoskar followed behind, holding up the rest of her under her armpits. His glasses had slipped and were balanced precariously on the end of his nose.

Riony hung limp and bowed between them. Her red hair clung wetly to a face that was mottled mauve and yellow and she smelled like off meat.

Her sword was stuck crookedly through her belt and the tip scraped along the floor. The backpack she'd worn before was off and balanced in the bend of her stomach and lap, her cloak gone.

"Where can we put her?" Yoskar asked.

Feeling light-headed, Lyrrin stepped back, clearing the doorway. She pointed to the bedroom.

The delver siblings grunted and swore as they squeezed through the doorway and dropped Riony on the blankets in a not-gentle way. She groaned, dry retched, then stilled again.

"What's wrong with her?" Lyrrin asked in a small voice.

Aishena rolled her eyes. "Razed if we know. Don't know what she was doing up that disused tunnel. Only found her from her groans echoing out. Niskina thought she was an Alderkin ghost."

"Count yourself lucky we found her." Yoskar brushed himself down, then stood still, staring at Lyrrin.

When she only stared back, Yoskar sighed and gestured with upturned hands. "Generally, we get *paid* for the things we find when delving."

"*Yoskar,*" Benjin whispered, looking mortified.

The older brother gave him a reproachful glare. "This is how the system works and it's how we earn the money we need to survive. And keep you alive, Benj."

He turned back to Lyrrin. "We're owed something for carrying this cumbersome body all the way up here."

Aishena put her hands on her knees, bending over to take a few deep breaths. "Seriously, how does she weigh so much? And stink so bad?"

The flames of anger heated Lyrrin's neck. "You want me to *pay* you?"

"Of course," Yoskar said flatly.

"Well ... like Benjin said, my sister already belongs to me. You're just returning her, so I'm not paying you anything!" Lyrrin stomped toward them, trying to get them to back out of the doorway.

They didn't move, and she had to stop before her face ended up pressed against Yoskar's armor-covered stomach.

"Wow, is this really all they have?" Aishena craned her neck, taking in the rooms.

Yoskar ignored Lyrrin, looking over her head. "That sword she carries around is decent enough. I'd take that as payment."

"Get out!" Lyrrin pushed at Yoskar, an immovable wall.

Aishena watched the futile battle for a moment, then grabbed Yoskar by his shoulder. "Come on, leave them be."

Then in a voice Lyrrin suspected she wasn't meant to hear, she said, "Let the kid say goodbye."

Benjin must have heard too. His head whipped toward Aishena, jaw dropped.

"GET OUT!" Lyrrin shrieked, tears running now over her hot cheeks.

The delvers stepped back, and Lyrrin slammed her fist against the door's closure mechanism.

Benjin stared back at her, pale-faced, as the door rolled closed.

Yoskar's voice carried in, muffled by the stone. "We'll come back another time for what we're owed. A debt must be repaid."

Lyrrin drew two deep breaths, quelling the shakes that were building within her, then raced over to her sister.

CHAPTER FIVE

The delvers had dropped Riony on her side, and she lay there like a lifeless doll.

Lyrrin carefully rolled her onto her back, tucked a pillow under her head, and straightened out her legs, then arms. When lifting Riony's right arm, Riony cried out fiercely, startling Lyrrin and making her let go. The arm flopped to the ground and Riony groaned again.

"What is it?" she asked, but Riony only moaned, her breath rough and panting.

Tentatively, Lyrrin touched the arm again, and saw the hints of bruising peeking out from the cuff of Riony's long shirt. She moved the arm slower this time and saw there was something wrong with how it bent within the clothing.

"Shh, I'm sorry. I'll try to be more gentle."

Riony didn't respond. Her head lolled, sweat running in rivulets all over, and she smelled of vomit and worse.

Lyrrin touched Riony's forehead with the back of her forearm and found it hot. She'd had enough of her own fevers in the past to know how Riony had cared for her then, so she opened the vent in the side of the room that had cool air flowing through and brought the bowl of water closer, still clean, since Butterfur hadn't swum in it.

She dipped a strip of cloth in it to dab Riony's forehead with, and as she did, Riony's eyes fluttered open.

"Plmmmbriss." Riony shifted, her left arm lifting, then falling again.

"What?"

Riony grunted, eyes winced closed, and brought her hand up to point at the shelf of herbs.

"Plumeberries?" Lyrrin asked.

Riony nodded in a wobbly way. "Tea. Hot. *Now.*"

"For your arm?" Lyrrin frowned, she didn't understand. Riony had a fever, and something wrong with her arm, but plumeberries were for poisoning.

"Is broken," Riony murmured, mouth slow and slurred. Her eyes were bloodshot and yellow-tinted, unfocused.

"Broken?" Lyrrin's voice came out high.

"Mmm."

"What do I do?"

"Straighten. Bandage."

Lyrrin reached a hand toward the acorn around Riony's neck. "Should we ...?"

"No. Not ... me. Not so bad." Riony gritted her teeth, closed her eyes, and was silent for a long moment.

Lyrrin failed to suppress a whining sob.

Riony stirred again, but her eyes didn't open. "S'okay. You can do this. First … hot tea."

"Okay," Lyrrin said, grateful for instructions, but unsure as to how to follow through on them. The long-sleeved shirt Riony wore was a thick, stiff fabric and had twisted itself tight around the broken arm, making it hard to inspect. Probably not good for the fever either.

"Can you take your shirt off?"

Riony's head had drooped to one side, and she didn't answer.

I have to do it then. No! First tea!

Lyrrin skittered across to the cooking area and traced the burn rune on the crystal crucible. It lit up, red and hot, and she placed a metal bowl of water on the top.

Then she went to the herb shelf, grabbing and checking jars—dropping one, kicking the broken pieces to the side, eyes blurry with tears—until she found one with just a few hard, dry berries in the bottom.

"How many? Is this right?"

Riony didn't respond.

Lyrrin sniffed and swallowed as she dropped all of them into the heating water. Her chest burned and throat closed as Aishena's voice echoed in her memory.

Let the kid say goodbye. Say goodbye. Say goodbye.

She knelt back by Riony's side. Riony still didn't move, but her throat pulsed with a rough heartbeat and panting breath.

She's too hot. Lyrrin tugged on the sleeve of Riony's good arm, inching the long shirt off. She had to pull, then readjust Riony, then pull, then roll, bit by bit to free Riony from just one side. And the other side she'd have to do even more carefully. Lyrrin let out a small, frustrated whine.

By the time she'd stripped off the layer, she'd worked up a sweat, and the water on the stove had boiled over.

Lyrrin ran over, grabbed the bowl off, and deactivated the rune. The heat warmed through the thick leather of her gloves but didn't burn. She poured the hot tea into a cup, spilling half of it as she sobbed at the wrong moment. She set it aside to cool enough for Riony to drink.

Returning again to her sister, Lyrrin inspected the bared wound. The sight of it made Lyrrin's lips twist into a crooked line, as crooked as the forearm itself. The hand was swollen and purple. The fingertips had turned black.

She backed away, scooting into the corner of the room and pressing herself to the wall. For a long moment, she couldn't hold back her tears, and they came in messy, gulping sobs.

Say goodbye.

Butterfur popped out from among the blankets and came over to sniff at what was happening. She grabbed for him, cuddling him tight until he nipped her arm and wriggled free.

Say goodbye.

"No!" she screamed and rose back to her feet in a fury.

She wasn't useless. She chose to listen to the echo of Riony's words instead.

You can do this.

Lyrrin wiped her eyes hard. "Tea. Hot tea."

Holding the cup in one hand and squeezing Riony's mouth open with the other wasn't easy. Lyrrin squealed in frustration every time a splash of tea missed and dribbled onto Riony's cheeks and chin. But some seemed to go down. Riony's throat worked, swallowing. And soon the cup was empty.

What next? Straighten? Eeeewwwww.

Lyrrin winced as she touched the puffy red and black skin of Riony's forearm, grateful for her gloves so she wasn't making direct contact. Then, whimpering loudly, she squeezed, pressing the arm into something more like a straight line.

As she pushed, she could feel the edges of jagged bone under her fingers. She tried to press those pieces of bone together as well, but Riony cried out in a wailing howl.

She couldn't do it, couldn't hurt Riony like that. It would have to be straight enough.

Bandage was next. When she and Riony had first come to the Alderkin depths, Lyrrin had more than her fair share of twisted ankles from racing around the uneven tunnels. She'd seen how Riony bandaged her many times, but trying it herself now, it just didn't seem to work the same way.

In her thick gloves she just couldn't get the bandage to hold, and it would loop loosely round and round. Every attempt jostled the fractured arm around more than Lyrrin thought was good, too.

With a glance over her shoulder to double-check the front door was closed, she slipped off her gloves.

She stared for a moment at her strange fingertips, the blue-tinted nails too dark and thick. Too sharp. Some strange affliction of birth, better hidden away.

Lyrrin tried again. The bandage went on tight and held when she tied and tucked in the end.

Sitting back with her legs splayed beside her, Lyrrin breathed out in a long sigh. Butterfur came over and sniffed around Lyrrin's pockets, but when they proved empty of treats, he went back to the corner, burrowing around and making a nest.

What do I do next? Lyrrin was tired. Her eyes felt hot as burning crucibles in their sockets. Riony was supposed to look after *her*. This was too hard.

Lyrrin bundled her knees to her chest and hugged them tight as tears broke free again.

Riony slipped between the seams of reality and dream.

The few times she woke, she did so in pain. So much pain, she wondered whether living was really the thing she wanted to do.

But she would, for Lyrrin.

And every time she woke, Lyrrin would be there, bringing a bowl near her mouth to catch the endless rounds of sickness that spilled from her. Trying to get her to drink tepid, unstrained tea. Getting the bowl again when the tea inevitably came back up. Talking to someone … *Sir Butterfur Spelunkychunks?*

Then the agony would be too great, and Riony would fade away.

She tried to hold on, turning her mind to the task of remembering where she was, what had happened.

She'd fallen into the ice, broken her arm. Poisoned herself—not her brightest moment.

There had been a dragon. A mother dragon.

There had been dragon eggs.

Had that really happened? It felt like a dream from a lifetime ago. Eggs in the ice, a glowing cave, a talking wolf. No. Those must be dreams.

She slept and mumbled and remembered. Her parents were there with her, alive again, in a memory that felt as recent, as real as the others. They weren't happy that they had to flee, but the tiny, stolen bundle meant they couldn't stay.

The bloody sword in Riony's small hand meant they couldn't stay.

They weren't happy with her. But she was happy to see them. She tried to warn them of their future, as though she could travel back through time in her dreams and stop their deaths from happening.

Then she held them and cried.

Don't ever come back here again. The wolf spoke, startling her into consciousness.

That voice … another hallucination.

Riony lay still, eyes unopened, waiting for the wave of pain to hit. It rose, but didn't crash over her and overwhelm her entirely. She stayed still longer, relishing the unexpected experience of consciousness, as voices drifted to her.

"I said come back when she's better." Lyrrin sounded like she did when she spoke through clenched teeth.

"Better? Honestly, I can't believe she's lasted this long." It was Yoskar. "I'm not waiting. I want payment now."

"We haven't got any money."

"You must have something valuable in there."

Silence for a moment. "We don't have anything. Riony's really sick. Just leave us alone."

"What did she do to get beaten up like that? Slip on a cave snail?" That was Aishena, her voice an icy, elegant sigh.

Yoskar huffed. "Proves that she never had what it takes to be a delver. She went wandering around where she shouldn't have been and paid the price. The depths aren't a playground."

"She is so tough enough to be a delver! She's sick and hurt 'cause she faced a dragon! A real brooding amma dragon!"

What? Riony's eyes snapped open. What had she said through her sickness? What did Lyrrin know? And why was Lyrrin telling the delvers?

Riony rolled onto her side, groaning as she got her feet underneath her. Since Lyrrin's announcement, things had gone quiet.

"She's lying. She's always making things up." That was Benjin.

"No. No, the entrance guards said they saw something last week, too. Idiots said it was the shadow dragon, but whiter." Yoskar spoke again, low and thoughtful. "A wild dragon? A *mother* dragon? Brooding? You mean there are eggs out there somewhere?"

No reply.

Yoskar barked, "Where? Where did your sister see them?"

A squeak came from Lyrrin, and Riony moved faster, supporting herself against the wall as dizziness washed over her. Her legs moved waywardly beneath her, humming with pins and needles.

A grunt came from Yoskar as Lyrrin remained silent.

"Aish! Where did Niskina say they found her?"

Aishena replied, too softly for Riony to hear.

Yoskar said, "Because we can't let a wild dragon brood here. It could attract attention. Attention we don't want."

"But ... a wild dragon? I don't think I can—"

Yoskar sighed dramatically and ground out the words. "If we get rid of the *eggs*, we get rid of the *dragon*, and we don't have to worry about it."

Riony pulled open the curtain between the two small rooms and saw Yoskar standing in the half-open front door, grasping Lyrrin by the shoulder of her tunic.

Aishena spoke again, from somewhere outside, delivering a string of directions in some kind of delver slang Riony didn't understand.

Yoskar let Lyrrin go with a shove, and his gaze turned to meet Riony's. Fierce and predatory. "Thank you for bringing this to our attention. I'm pretty sure I know where to find the nest. We'll crush every last egg under our heels, and you can consider your debt paid."

"No, you can't!" Lyrrin's words matched those Riony spoke in her head, her mouth still too gummy and throat too dry to speak.

The delver turned away.

"Stop." The word came out of Riony as a gravelly croak.

Lyrrin turned at the sound, wide, crying eyes taking in Riony.

Yoskar and his siblings were already gone. On their way to destroy the eggs Riony had seen in the snowy cave.

Chapter Six

Lyrrin's bottom lip wobbled. "They won't really break the eggs, will they?"

Riony opened her mouth to say something comforting, but it would have been a lie. Most people in the depths hated dragons. They were the beasts the Taen dragonlords rode, using their power to turn the Rolanian people to slaves and their lands to ash. And Rolanians were the majority of the population hiding from that fate in the undercity.

Let alone the other draconic being that haunted the skies, the shadowdragon, bringing an undead blight wherever it touched the ground.

Whether from religious belief or personal experience, dragons meant death or oppression and everybody in the undercity had lost something to a dragon one way or another. Most would take any chance they got to remove a few from the world.

Aishena and Yoskar were more of an unknown quantity. They had the look and bearing of Taen dragonlords themselves, but it certainly sounded like they wanted to see the eggs destroyed. And it was just the kind of thing a lightless jerk like Yoskar and his spooky sister would take joy in.

Riony cleared her throat. It felt ripped and raw, and her stomach made some provocative noises. She couldn't tell if the ongoing sickness was the corpsefoot poisoning about to knock her off for good, or the plumeberries doing their job in removing those toxins. Either way, her insides sucked right now, and her outsides weren't a whole lot better.

Riony pressed her forehead to the cool wall beside her. "Maybe they won't find the eggs. But now they know …"

"I'm sorry. I'm sorry I told. I just didn't want them to think you weren't strong enough to be a delver."

Riony half smiled at that.

Fat tears splashed down Lyrrin's pink cheeks. "I didn't think they'd do something to the eggs. Can you stop them? Please? We can't let them kill *babies*."

Dispose of the newborn. It can't be allowed to live.

No! You can't kill a baby!

Old memories mixed like blurry dreams into reality.

Riony shook her head, more to try to clear it than as a reply. She was woozy and her arm felt wrong. The pain had lessened but it felt hot, tight, and crooked. Her fingers on that side wouldn't move.

That was my good hand, too.

"I don't think I can. If the mother dragon comes back …" Riony didn't hate that dragon or her unborn eggs enough to want them destroyed, even if it had scared her into falling down that crevasse.

It was wild and free, and there was something so beautiful about that in a world where most dragons were tamed into utter subservience, simple tools to be exploited for their power in every way.

But when Riony's whole body felt like it had been broken into parts and put back together by an overenthusiastic toddler with a toy hammer, she wasn't sure what she could do.

"They can't break the eggs. They can't hurt the babies," Lyrrin pleaded again.

Lyrrin, who had brought home an injured owlette and hid it in her pocket for days before it flew away, who had been devastated when another of her pets was turned into a dinner by some hungry undercity dweller.

Lyrrin who cared about every creature big or small—how would she handle bringing about the deaths of unborn dragon babies?

Riony at least had to try to stop it happening. She could talk the delvers out of it, lead them the wrong way, something. She had no sure plan, still too addled from the effects of broken bones and vomiting up more than her own body weight to think it through.

But she could try.

Not like she hadn't taken extreme measures in the past in order to save a baby's life.

She gave Lyrrin a single nod.

"I want to come, too. I want to help."

"Absolutely not." Riony grabbed her long-sleeved shirt and put it on. She had to bite her tongue to avoid screaming as she bent her bad arm to put it through the sleeve.

She noted the bandaging there. Nice and neat, but no splint, and not tight enough. Lyrrin must have tried so hard, though. Riony's cloak had been lost somewhere in her previous misadventure. She hoped she wouldn't be out in the cold long this time.

What else did she need? She couldn't think straight, and her vision clouded and swam. She had to hurry if she wanted to stop the delvers in time. "Stay here."

"But—"

"*Stay,*" Riony growled.

Lyrrin watched her with scarlet-tinted, tear-filled eyes as she turned away.

As the door rolled closed between them, a tiny shriek came through the stone. "I'm not useless!"

Riony took the stairs. She couldn't manage the fast way down when she could barely keep track of her own limbs. Her lucidity blurred in and out as she stumbled madly through the undercity tunnels in a haze of pain and fever, trying to catch up to the delver siblings.

More than once she had to pause, hold herself still and swallow back a swell of nausea. More than once, she failed, gagging up a disturbing pink foam from a raw and empty stomach. Her rib cage felt like it was on fire, slowly roasting everything within it.

It was easier to catalogue the parts of her that *didn't* bring her immense suffering. Currently: zero.

The cyan light brightening the pathways glittered off where she sweated right through her shirt, and people looked at her aghast as she barged around them.

The urge to just curl up on the cool cavern floor and sleep was overwhelming. Then she imagined Lyrrin's face if she returned having failed. She wiped her dripping forehead and pressed on.

Riony reached the tunnel leading to the frozen waterfall and hoped Aishena and her brother hadn't found the right way. All they knew was where she'd been found … wherever that was.

How she'd even gotten back and where she'd fallen, Riony couldn't remember, but it made sense it was somewhere along the same path she'd used before.

And Aishena and Yoskar were delvers. They knew all the tunnels of the depths and would know this one too. They had enough clues to give them some idea of where they were going. It wouldn't take them long to find the hole into the external cave.

How long have I been out of it?

If it hadn't been long, if it hadn't snowed since then, there was no doubt the delvers could follow her trail across the white plains back to the ice cave and eggs it held.

Riony picked up her pace through the rough, natural cave up to the frozen waterfall exit, and as she stepped out into the bright white of the snow-shrouded world, there were Aishena and Yoskar.

A moment of hope that she'd caught up, that they hadn't found the eggs, was shattered by the triumphant look on Yoskar's face as they walked back toward her.

Riony exhaled a misty breath. "What did you do?"

"We did what we had to do to keep our family safe," Yoskar said as he went by, then threw back at Riony, "That's what you do when you're worthy of being a delver."

Aishena followed right behind. She pretended as though Riony wasn't even there, just scowled and bumped into her shoulder as she passed.

Riony steadied herself, watching them leave. A bitter taste filled her mouth. To crush unborn eggs … did they really do it?

Riony had to see the truth with her own eyes. The snow, slippery and compressed from multiple passages marked a clear path for her and crunched as Riony plunged along the trail downhill. She tumbled like a twig in a stream all the way to the ice cave.

The entrance was large enough for a dragon, but obscured behind a drift of fluffy white that gathered as the wind buffeted more snow against it. Riony didn't feel the cold as wind gusted through her thin clothing, her body aflame with fury and sickness.

She hadn't had a clear look at the cave before, too ill and too rushed, and again it went by in a blur, nothing more than shining ice above and to her sides and crisp, frosty dirt beneath her feet.

Reaching the deepest part of the cave, Riony blinked and wiped at her burning eyes, seeking the dragon eggs.

Where the bright, metallic orbs had once sat, perfectly arranged in a nest of warmed stones, now there was messy carnage.

Shards of textured shell, coated in slimy red film, were scattered around three tiny, fleshy lumps. Barely on the cusp of being grown enough to be recognizable as baby dragons, and small, too small. They spilled lifeless from their smashed shells. The air had a coppery tang.

Riony dropped to her knees in front of the broken creatures, mouth open in disgust, and a heavy, unexpected weight of grief descended on her.

They had done it. They had killed them.

The delvers wouldn't even have needed to touch the dragonlings themselves. They looked too underdeveloped to survive the harsh world outside their nurturing eggs. All it took was cracking the shells.

It wasn't the most terrible outcome, having three less dragons in the world. They were awful, destructive creatures.

These weren't dragonlord dragons, tamed and bound to do their bidding. But it didn't mean they would stay that way. They were likely to be captured by dragonlords and enslaved too, just another tool of oppression. And even if they managed to remain wild, they could still kill and destroy.

It wasn't terrible that they were gone. They were just three dumb dragons, in a land full of them.

But if their deaths weren't such a terrible thing, why was Riony weeping so hard?

Her previous master had berated her for having a soft spot for dumb animals. But it was the Rolanian way. All creatures were siblings, all were to be treated with care and respect—all except for dragons. Them, and unicorns now long gone, stood apart.

But deep down, Riony couldn't shake the feeling that a life was a life, and it hurt her deep inside to see these tiny lives extinguished. And if it hurt her this much ...

What am I going to tell Lyrrin?

Riony bowed her head. She reached out her remaining functional hand and touched a broken egg. "I'm sorry I couldn't save you."

Her touch disturbed the tenuous pile. The remnants of shell cracked even more, and the contents flopped onto the ground, revealing a fourth, smaller egg beneath it. Also damaged, with large cracks running down the length, revealing a slowly leaking membrane. But not fully broken.

Riony's heart rate kicked up. She shuffled closer and rolled the egg carefully out from amongst the others, bringing it onto her lap. It was slippery with bright-red blood, but that seemed to be from the other eggs. The insides of this one still seemed fairly full, despite the leak. The egg still held its shape.

At the intersection of a few fractures was a larger hole where the membrane spread across, intact, like a fogged-up window. Riony peered at the softly churning liquids within.

Something squirmed, and Riony gasped back. The movement inside the egg sent a splash of gooey, clear fluid spilling out from the leak onto her hands.

More wriggling, then a slithery body pressed against the membrane window. Red-veined and translucent, the beat of a tiny heart could be seen, fluttering.

A heartbeat that slowed visibly, fading before Riony's eyes.

Chapter Seven

It's going to die.

It was a fact. A simple, unchangeable fact.

It's going to die like the others.

And there was Riony, stuck as a useless observer in that moment between life and death, staring at the tiny, fading heartbeat, and wanting that fact to be untrue.

She shuffled the egg carefully off her lap, placing it back on the warm patch on the ground. The mother dragon had picked that spot for a reason, the one warm place in a world of frost and ice. It needed to stay warm. But Riony knew that wouldn't be enough to save it, as another dribble of fluid leaked from the broken membrane.

She couldn't fix that torn, protective skin.

Her good hand lifted as though possessed and wrapped around the acorn tied around her neck. An unconscious action, but it brought a shock of possibility along with it.

"Whoa, no, no, no." Her head shook. She wasn't really considering it, was she? She couldn't.

She lurched unevenly back to her feet, pacing away, as though distance could remove her from the tragedy about to happen. Remove any responsibility for it happening ... or not happening. Her thumb rubbed the smoothed side of the acorn.

It's going to die.

No. The silvernix was precious, too precious to consider using. Not to mention that it was forbidden to use unicorn blood on animals.

Riony scoffed. She'd always thought that was a dumb rule. She'd had that argument before as a child, screaming in fury at her parents to save the barn cat at their master's estate, back when they'd still lived aboveground. It had been burned by dragon fire and suffered in its last moments.

She'd adored that cat. It hadn't seemed right, watching it die when they could have saved it. A life was a life, that was the Rolanian way.

Her parents remained firm that their precious silvernix was for nothing but one of their own lives. Not that it had saved either of them, in the end. But their rules still rang like an off-key bell in Riony's mind.

Pacing back toward the nest, Riony eyed the broken egg.

Can I really sit here and watch it die when I could save it?

She grunted and snapped at herself, "You're not even sitting, tamebrain. Just walk away. It died with the others. You were too late to save any of them."

Riony imagined delivering that news to Lyrrin. Riony remembered how she'd cried for weeks about her cat. *Sparks, I* still *cry about that cat.*

Her pacing stopped and she clenched her hand around the acorn.

She returned to the egg, kneeling at its side.

Her fingers shook as she put the acorn to her mouth, and carefully opened the top with her teeth. She extracted the tiny vial from within and blew out a cold, wispy breath.

The acorn pendant fell to the floor and rolled away.

Riony could only stare at the silvernix. She didn't know what was going to happen. Generally, only dragonlords even had access to silvernix—their term for unicorn blood. Few others had seen it in use or used it themselves. Riony never had.

She'd heard the stories though, and hoped it would be enough, that it was even still potent after decades stored in that tiny vial.

That's what the dragonglass was for though, to keep the potency of the precious contents. As long as Lyrrin's decorations hadn't affected that.

Riony's skin felt clammy as she held the glass up to her eye. She rubbed the etchings on the side with a cold finger, checking the glass and looking at the opalescent fluid within.

Am I actually doing this?

She looked at the still leaking egg, the weak motions of the underdeveloped dragonling within. That life, fading away.

A life was a life. And the silvernix had been saved for a life.

Yeah. I guess I'm doing this.

She held her breath and let the single drop spill into the crack of the broken egg.

The thin liquid glowed as it ran like a teardrop through the split shell. It swirled about, coating the inner membrane, then was absorbed, disappearing.

At first there was no change, and Riony chewed her lip, watching, waiting to see the membrane stitch itself closed, waiting to see the miracle of magic that was legendary in their land.

Then the tiny creature inside shuddered and jerked, twisting violently within the shell, forcing more fractures into the egg. Riony swore and tried to hold the egg together with her one good hand. She fumbled, hand too shaky, and the shell shattered under her fingers.

The dragonling stilled completely.

"No, no! Please, it has to work." Riony's face scrunched up painfully.

She'd wasted it. It didn't even work and now it was gone. She was so stupid. She should have saved the unicorn blood, for Lyrrin, even for her damned arm, *something* other than this.

What had she been thinking? She slumped on the ground, broken and in pain, with fever rising again even against the cold of the ice cave surrounding her. She heaved in aching breaths and covered her face with her hands.

A dim shimmer flickered.

Riony peered between her fingers. A light glowed from the egg, growing into a steady beacon, cool and bright. Inside, the dragonling moved again, straining and stretching.

Each motion broke the shell further until it split in half and the tiny thing, still wrapped in the slimy membrane, spilled out in front of Riony's knees. The glow dimmed again, merely an occasional sparkle from within the milky lining encasing the baby.

It struggled then stilled, struggled then stilled. Sharp points deformed the membrane, but didn't break through.

After the creature's initial burst of movement, it was already slowing again, exhausted by its efforts.

"Um, oh sparks, what do I do?" What midwife training Riony had from her mother didn't cover anything like this. The dragonling seemed like it was trying to hatch, maybe *needed* to hatch, but it seemed too early, too small. Its egg was gone though and while the membrane still held it, it wasn't the same protection.

The dragonling was coming out, one way or another.

Riony pinched at the leathery tissue, rolling it around until she found the punctured section. She couldn't tear it with just one hand, and her other was useless, so she shifted position to hold part of the skin down with the toe of her boot, then pulled with her good hand.

The membrane tore, and a pale, blood-spotted ooze dribbled from it, followed by a small snout. It opened in a tiny, tremulous whine.

"Okay, okay, little thing. We're getting you out."

There was a snuffle and a sneeze as it emerged farther, revealing two bulbous eyes, covered by eyelids not ready to open, and a forehead with a single horn in the center. It flopped forward, unprepared for a head too heavy for a world outside an egg.

Riony caught it, laying it on her lap as she worked to pull the rest of the membrane clear. It mewled in soft trills.

Something melted inside Riony. She scrubbed her face with the back of her forearm, as though she could rub her feelings away. *Stars, damn it. It's adorable.*

"Hey there, welcome to the world."

It lived. At least so far. She only hoped it would continue to, but that would be up to its mother now. As the last of the membrane was stripped off, Riony could see that it wasn't the same shape as its dead siblings.

Its moonlight-pale flesh had a soft fuzz to it and fewer scales. Where the others had an array of horn buds on either side of their scalp, it only had the single, central one, and floppy ears on either side. Its wings seemed more delicate and diaphanous and less leathery. Thin, gangly legs wobbled awkwardly, unlike the stout, sturdy arms of the others.

Changed. Different.

Did the unicorn blood do this? It wasn't meant to be used on mothers … were eggs the same thing? Riony remembered the looks of fear and disgust in the delivery room when Lyrrin was born. Changed. Different.

Riony touched a hand to the side of the baby dragon's face, feeling the velvety skin, still slick and damp. "You weren't ready to come out yet, little one. But you'll be okay. You're going to be just fine."

Heavy breaths moved the creature's chest like bellows as its lungs learned how to work. Eyelids squeezed, then slowly peeled back, revealing lilac eyes. It cried softly against

Riony's hand, and its cute, gummy jaws tried to suck and nibble at her chilled fingertips.

The thrum of its voice echoed in the ice cave.

Then it seemed to grow louder, louder, until it reached an ear-splitting roar.

Riony whipped her head around.

The mother dragon had returned.

Riony looked between the massive beast before her to the carnage of broken eggs beside her.

Oh sparks. She'll think I did it.

Did dragons care for their eggs? Did they feel about their families the way humans felt about theirs? From the way the dragon snorted jets of hot air and her eyes rolled wildly around, and the continuous growling shriek emanating from her throat, Riony guessed she must.

That was grief. That was dire, livid fury. And it was all directed at her.

"Listen, it wasn't me." She got up and held her hand high in a gesture of innocence, of surrender, but she knew the mother dragon didn't understand.

Huge claws stomped forward, talons squeezing and cracking the earthen ground. The dragon's horns and wings scraped the ceiling of ice, raining crystalline shards all around. Her tail whipped.

The one living dragonling tried to stand and flopped onto its side against Riony's foot. With one careful hand and one pounding with pain, she scooped it up.

"One lives! Here, one of your children lives!" She lifted it before her as the mother dragon's sword-like teeth stopped right before her face.

The beast stilled. Hot breath gusted from her mouth, engulfing Riony in a sulfurous mist. Shining silver and black scales made a shushing sound against each other as the dragon bowed its neck, dropping her chin to bring an eye as big as Riony's head close to the dragonling.

The pupil expanded and contracted within an icy blue iris.

She sniffed once, then again. Scaly lips rolled back over her deadly fangs and she growled. It was not a fond sound.

"It's yours, you must—"

The mother lashed out, sharp talons swiping at the strangely shaped baby.

Riony threw herself onto her back, taking the baby with her. The razor-tipped claws passed right over them. The dragonling shrieked. It writhed and wriggled free of Riony's grasp.

The mother roared.

Was it rejecting the baby? Because it was changed?

"No, please, it's your baby!"

The mother dragon ignored her, turning toward the scrambling infant. Riony pushed herself between them, standing to shield the dragonling's escape. The tiny thing skittered away, legs wobbling and scraping under it, dragging itself into a corner to hide between ice and rocks.

But there was nowhere for Riony to hide.

She reached to her side for her sword, but it wasn't there, left behind at home in her fevered rush. Not that it would have been much use, but Riony would have preferred to go down swinging.

The mother breathed in deep and opened her mouth, and Riony wondered what burning alive was going to feel like.

Seasong dragons don't flame. The knowledge drifted to her, in the same voice from her childhood that the wolf had spoken to her in.

Kess, that dragon-obsessed psychopath. Why was her voice the one that brought her comfort now?

And when the mother dragon breathed out, no flame emerged. But its breath filled the cavern like a wave, smashing into Riony and lifting her from her feet. She flew back, cracking hard against the wall behind her.

They have an air attack, tamebrain.

Thanks, Kess.

She didn't have even a second to prepare herself between slumping to the ground and having the dragon's claw close around her. It gripped Riony's entire chest and squeezed. Talons skewered through her flesh. Ribs cracked and all of the air was forced out of her.

Riony's eyes bulged, and she opened her mouth in a failed, breathless scream. The dragon replied, shrieking in her face, hot breath and pungent saliva flying. Then the claw released and Riony dropped like a sack of soup bones.

Riony wasn't sure how she was still alive.

Every breath wheezed and gurgled as her lungs collapsed, flooded with blood that spattered and spilled from her lips. Everything felt shattered and sharp-edged.

Burning might have been better after all.

The shining scales of the mother's tail whipped over Riony's face as the beast turned on the spot and left behind the cave full of the dead and dying.

CHAPTER EIGHT

Kess didn't think she'd ever see *Pony* again. Not since the servant brat and her parents murdered some dragonguard and ran away from Heithorn Castle before they could be strung up for their crime as they deserved.

That felt like a lifetime ago. A life Kess didn't care to remember much of.

The surprise of finding that the body lying passed out in the snow was once her slave was only overwhelmed by the surprise that Kess decided not to let the intolerable woman die there.

It had been hard work, dragging her floppy weight onto Griskin and dropping her off back in the tunnels the rat had emerged from. Kess had only done it to clear the area of other humans again, worried that Pony would spook the dragon mother.

Kess hadn't cared otherwise whether the ex-slave lived or died. She had bigger things to worry about.

But she cared now.

I should have buried you in the snow when I had the chance.

Half a year.

Half a year Kess and her wolf, Griskin, had been tracking that wild seasong dragon, following it from distant northern shores, learning its behaviors, carefully keeping her distance when it seemed ready to brood, and scaring any other humans away—not that there had been any up so high in the mountains, until Pony showed up—so the mother didn't spook and move on again.

And then, finally, payoff. Up in this blistering, frozen world, the dragon had nested. Four eggs—a good chance of at least one healthy hatchling from a clutch like that. She considered taking an egg early but knew that dramatically dropped its hopes of hatching successfully. She couldn't keep it warm like the hot patch in the cave could. So she bade her time.

It had taken her years before that to even find a wild dragon to track.

Half a year of anticipation, waiting for her chance, the best chance she'd ever had, the closest she'd ever come to the one thing she'd always wanted.

A dragon of her own.

After dumping Pony back into the underground tunnels and giving her a warning to stay away, Kess had taken up position again on a high cliff. Griskin's paws folded in front of him as he settled down in the snow on his belly, and they watched.

The mother dragon flew her normal patrol, as though unaware of the human that had just been near her cave and her eggs. Kess sighed in relief.

What was Pony even doing there, in the dragon's nest? It didn't look like she'd touched anything, wasn't trying to walk out of the cave with an egg herself. She seemed broken and half-dead of sickness, but not from dragon tooth or claw.

Moving the woman out of the snow probably lifted her chances of survival above zero, but not by much.

There weren't any other signs of life in the tunnel Kess had left her in. Nobody to help. There were rumors of an underground city in these parts, where refugees, ex-slaves, and other cowards hid beneath the earth. Maybe someone would find Pony in time.

Who cares though? Kess rubbed the dry skin on her lips and huffed out a cloud of white air. Seeing that damned redhead again had her rattled. As long as Pony died out of the way of Kess's goals, it didn't matter.

Kess settled in, tucking herself into the warmth of Griskin's charcoal fur, running her fingers through the soft undercoat, then rubbing his ears. He leaned into her fingers for a better scratch, back leg twitching.

"Good boy, Gris," she whispered. "Not long now."

They had spent so many hours like this, together, watching and waiting, only interspersed with hunting enough to keep them both alive.

Kess was hungry now, but not as hungry as the mother dragon seemed to be.

Is she eating at all? Kess wasn't sure. Seasong dragons generally lived at sea, hunting huge schools of fish for their primary diet. There wasn't enough food up in the mountains to sustain a dragon of that size, even if it had a breath weapon adapted to hunting in this terrain.

Kess wasn't sure what type of dragon the father was; she hadn't been around for that part. It must have been before Kess began tracking the seasong.

Dragons didn't always lay directly after mating and could hold the fertilized eggs until the right time. It was only in factory breeding that humans had worked out how to force them to lay immediately for faster production.

It was strange that the seasong mother had come so far inland to lay her eggs. Maybe the offspring were hybrids, and the babies would need this climate to survive. Or maybe this is the one place in a world where almost all other dragons were tamed where she'd felt safe to finally nest. Even if it meant going without food herself.

And all the better for Kess if she was weak when the eggs were ready to hatch. She was half tempted to try to tame the mother instead, but the hatchlings were a safer bet. *Not much longer now.*

It had been a couple of days after the run-in with Pony that Kess returned from a hunt and settled into the snow on the lookout with Griskin again to keep watch of the nesting cave. With her hands buried deep in the fur of Griskin's neck, she felt his skin ripple and twitch, even before she heard him sniff at the air and whine.

Kess bolted upright, squinting at the white glare below. A couple of dark figures moved about and met another, who ran toward the cave.

"Raze it! Come on, let's—"

Another shiver ran under her fingers, the tension of a muscle as an ear swiveled back.

Kess widened her eyes.

Grabbing the white blanket from the satchel at her side, she hissed, "Roll!"

Griskin was already moving. He knew the drill. He tipped on his side and rolled up small. Kess curled her chest around him and flung out the blanket to cover them.

They both lay frozen beneath the white sheet, breaths held, as the dragon passed over the top of them. The seasong mother hovered there for a long moment, breaking her normal patrol. And then she screamed.

Oh no, she must have seen the other humans too.

In a burst of air so strong it blew the blanket away, the seasong dove, speeding to her cave.

Kess followed her with her gaze, scowling as a flurry of snow landed over her. With a tap of a hand, Griskin rolled back to his feet, taking her with him as she clung to his back, feet strapped into the stirrups of her makeshift saddle.

They careened down the steep snow-laden slope. Icy wind tugged at her tangled hair, and she held her breath and closed her eyes against the bitter, whipping cold. With each stride, the wolf's strength and surefootedness propelled them swiftly toward their destination.

Finally reaching the entrance of the ice cave, Kess brought Griskin to a halt. She exhaled a billowing cloud into the frigid air.

Inside the cave, the dragon continued screaming.

Kess didn't dare follow in after her.

All she could do now was wait and grind her teeth and curse.

The dragon emerged, pale claws stained in steaming red blood. Her long head swayed as though drunk, and when she extended her wings and rose into the sky, she flew north. North, the direction of the sea she'd come from. Her wings worked hard like a drum beating in the air.

She flew fast over the horizon and didn't turn back.

Kess watched, staring with her mouth opened and hands shaking. No, she wouldn't leave. She wouldn't leave her eggs, unless ... Snapping her jaw shut, she leaned forward on Griskin. He took his cue, taking them on silent paws into the ice cave.

Kess's hands curled into fists so tight she cut her palms on her ragged nails.

Half a year.

All that time, all that cold and waiting and hoping, and she was back to nothing.

Broken shells. Broken bodies. And the only satisfying thing in this place of disappointment, a broken Pony.

Griskin sniffed and whined, looking to the corner of the cavern. Kess only had eyes for the bloodied mess of woman lying dead on the ground in front of them.

"I told you never to come back here," she muttered, wishing she'd made sure of that herself, that all her dreams didn't now lay crushed on the dirty floor because she'd had one stupid moment of sympathy. "You never could listen, even for your own good."

Pony wheezed and her eyelids popped open, scaring the shit out of Kess.

"Razing ... You're still *alive*?"

Griskin recoiled too, yelping and pouncing back a step. He knew as well as anyone that dead things that started moving again were a bad thing.

"Wha … talking … wolf …?" The words came out between coughs and sprays of crimson.

Griskin lowered his head and growled.

Kess patted Griskin, reassuring him.

"Not a rev," she whispered.

He whimpered softly but straightened up from his defensive crouch.

"Just the biggest idiot of an intolerable human you've ever seen." Kess edged Griskin closer, angling the wolf to the side for a clearer view of the bloodied body before them.

Pony stared up at her face, making confused eye contact until Kess scowled and turned Griskin around again. The woman had the most infuriating irises that were gray or green or blue around the edge and warm brown, or maybe yellow, in the center, but all the colors played against each other and shifted in the light, making it hard to label any of them.

"Of course … you. Always promised … watch me die." Pony gave a sigh, a laugh, and a whimper of pain.

Alive, and still stupid enough to manage her ridiculous smile as her body lay smashed to pieces.

All these years, and Pony had barely changed. She still wore her scruffy red hair all messy over her eyes with that dumb little pigtail at the back. She still filled Kess with the uncontrollable urge to blacken both her eyes, then have her whipped for not crying out loudly enough when she got hit.

"Hi, Pony. You've really razed everything this time."

Her face scrunched in silent agony. "Right?"

Kess stared with heavy eyes. Maybe alive now, but not much longer. It was probably only due to the seasong dragon being half-starved to death that Pony had survived the attack at all.

Her punctured chest strained and arched. "Can you … help … please?"

"Help you? You want me to help you?" Kess barked out a laugh. Fury seethed like dragonfire through her veins. "You are the destroyer of my every desire. Why in all of Elundrae would I help you?"

Pony didn't answer. The stupid oaf at least knew there was no good reason.

"I helped you before and look what I got for it." Kess swung a hand at the smashed eggs, although Pony's glazed eyes didn't track the movement. "Why did you do it? Did you kill them all just to stop me getting what I want?"

As though hit by a surge of pain, Pony clenched her teeth, panting between them. As the breaths slowed again, Kess held her own, expecting to witness her end.

But instead, hot tears spilled from the woman's eyes, and she wobbled her head. "Not … me."

Griskin growled again, sniffing the air. His skin bristled beneath Kess's fingertips. The scent of death all around had him troubled. Kess only felt a dull, heavy weight in her chest. She snarled in contempt of that feeling of loss.

Unlike Pony, this wasn't the end for her. She'd get what she wanted one day.

"Just hurry up and die already. Put us all out of this misery." Kess cringed at her words, so small and petty. But seeing Pony there, in the moment when her greatest goal was lost, took Kess back to a life where small and petty was all she was.

She had escaped that. She had almost become something more, become what she was meant to be, and it was all made nothing by an awful Rolanian runaway slave.

Kess wouldn't help her. She wouldn't be sad this part of her past died.

"Goodbye, Pony."

"Please ... my sister ..."

A hot flush raced up Kess's neck. "We were never sisters. We were never even friends."

Between the spatters of blood on Pony's face, tears ran, streaming from the sides of her eyes and soaking the flame-red hair at her temples.

Kess glared down at her for a long moment, then turned away, leaving her to die alone on the frozen floor.

Chapter Nine

Riony counted her regrets as she took her last breaths.

One, she wouldn't live long enough to find out whether she was actually still dying of corpsefoot poisoning as she suspected.

Two, she hadn't had a good comeback to throw in Kess's weasel face.

Three, she wouldn't be there for Lyrrin anymore.

That one hurt. That one hurt more than the physical wounds she was dying from.

Her last hope for survival just rode away. On a wolf. *So weird.*

Four, Riony regretted not finding out the story behind *that.*

Riony wasn't surprised Kess didn't help her though. The ashy-haired girl always was cruel.

She probably couldn't have helped anyway. There was only one thing that could revive a body as broken as Riony's, and she'd just used up the one precious available drop to save the broken egg.

Kess didn't look like she did back when she lived like a princess in a castle, when she might have had access to such things. In her early years, Kess had so much access to silvernix that her hair still held a telltale white streak from its use.

Now, she didn't look like she'd seen the ass-end of civilization in years.

Riony could only tell it was her from the unique constellation spray of moles—beauty marks, Kess would have screamed—across one of her cheekbones. That, and the contemptable way she drawled the nickname, *Pony.*

No, this strange, ragged, wolf-riding version of her old master couldn't have had any silvernix.

If she had, she would have used it to save her life, wouldn't she? Even Kess …

Cold.

The sensation drifted through her in a strange, distant way. Yeah, she was cold. Too cold. Not enough blood left in her system to warm her flesh, too far from the warm spot on the cavern floor.

Cold. Hurt.

Her mind felt muddled, sensations abstract and detached as she faded away.

A throbbing hum built in her ears as her heart squeezed and slowed, and her vision dimmed.

Something snuffled at Riony's ear. She turned her eyes—the only part of her body that she still had some control over—to the side. Something blurry, shimmery, and small moved near her.

The newborn dragon had re-emerged from its hiding spot and snuggled up to her, clinging to even the small remaining warmth that her broken body radiated.

Oh great. There's another regret.

Hey, little one, Riony thought groggily, no longer able to form words aloud. Even thinking hurt. Especially the sinking knowledge that this was the end and that she'd be leaving Lyrrin all alone. She didn't even want to leave the poor, abandoned baby beside her alone.

How could either of them survive without her?

She didn't want to leave at all.

She whimpered and agony shot through her, withering her consciousness away.

The dragonling mewled, tiny mouth opening wide. In the one clear spot between the darkness creeping in around her vision, Riony noticed it was injured too, a razor thin scratch straight across its snout.

Liquid shimmered there, pale and ... silver? Shimmering and opalescent in the same way the drop of unicorn blood had been.

Riony blinked, choking as her throat filled with hot fluid. She couldn't draw another breath.

Bleating again, nuzzling closer, the newborn's snout pressed against her cheek. The wetness of its blood tingled against Riony's frosty skin.

A wave of nausea consumed her, rippling through her body in an unsettling sensation that caused her very thoughts to falter and fail. Her heart clenched and stopped, her lungs unable to hold air, and her mind seemed to rush toward oblivion like a pebble tossed into a well.

Stars wriggled across her darkened vision and it felt as though she was tumbling, falling up into them to never return.

Then the sensations of death transformed. Pain shifted, still overwhelming, but now it swirled within her like a high and low tide meeting at the edge of the sea.

Riony's back arched off the frozen ground, and she threw her mouth open in a silent scream.

The shattered insides of her being, crushed and torn, mended and regrew beneath her bruised and ripped flesh. Bones straightened and stitched themselves together, lungs were patched of holes and cleared of blood, then even the tears and welts in her skin closed, repairing themselves.

The crimson rivers that flowed through her veins surged and felt replenished of what they had spilled.

The cave lit up, some light source brightening all around, and Riony distantly realized it was she who glowed, as though the stars in her eyes had flooded into her flesh.

The light faded, and Riony gasped back into herself, back to a body that felt whole, numbed of the pain that had moments ago been all-consuming.

Breath came easily. Her vision cleared. Even her broken and swollen arm felt whole. She held her right hand in front of her face, testing each finger one by one. Fresh and pink and perfectly functional.

A hysterical giggle burbled through Riony. She gave one quick look behind her, to make sure she hadn't actually died and was now only a spirit. That she didn't see her dead body there separated from her was a relief.

She had been saved. Saved by the tiny creature beside her.

Turning onto her side, she stared at the little being. The baby's horn, the shape of its body ... Unicorns had been extinct since before Riony was born, but the newborn had similarities to drawings, tapestries, and Alderkin carvings depicting them.

She saw it so clearly now but couldn't understand how. Had the drop of healing blood changed the still forming baby in its egg? Made it somehow more unicorn than dragon?

It seemed impossible, but Riony couldn't deny that the blood *had* just healed her. Brought her back from the precipice of death.

Nothing else could have.

Whatever it was that made Lyrrin the way she was hadn't had the same effect. There wasn't anything unicorn-like about her as far as Riony could tell, beyond her strange hair color. She bled red like everyone else.

But this ... This strange half-dragon, half-unicorn thing that pawed at her, limply trying to crawl into her lap, it had healing blood.

She helped the newborn up, scooping its shivering body into her arms and hugging it for warmth—hers and its. Brushing a thumb over its snout, it came away with the barest hint of shimmer that faded instantly. The baby's own wound that had bled the silver fluid had also closed, healed by its own blood.

Riony's head shook in awestruck denial. A baby dragon. With the blood of a unicorn.

And it looked at her with wide, innocent eyes as though she were its mother.

Oh no. Is this really happening again? Taking Lyrrin as a newborn was a rash decision that had led to a lifetime responsibility Riony hadn't wanted to repeat. But there she was, considering taking another baby into her care.

She'd originally thought she'd heal the egg and leave the dragonling to the mother, but if Kess was to be believed, the mother dragon wasn't coming back. The way she'd reacted to it, Riony feared she wouldn't let the dragonling live even if she did. The vulnerable newborn had nobody else. Nobody but Riony.

And this baby, this one came with even more potential consequences than Lyrrin had.

"By all the stars," Riony said in a hushed voice. The implications settled onto her like the weight of the ocean.

The single drop of unicorn blood she'd carried had been the most secret, most precious treasure she could have conceived of. And here was a creature the size of a small cat, filled with that miraculous blood.

Wars had been fought and races had been annihilated over such blood.

Even before unicorns had become extinct, what she had before her would have been a king's ransom of wealth. Now, with the last unicorn slaughtered more than thirty years ago, this bundle of velvety scales and floppy iridescent wings was unique in the world. Priceless.

Riony dropped her head forward with a deep sigh. "What in all the sparking stars are we going to do?"

Chapter Ten

Riony couldn't sit on the frozen cave floor, staring at the extraordinary critter forever. She had to get back to Lyrrin. She had to deal with this thing. This ... part-dragon, part-unicorn ... Dragicorn? Unidragon?

Riony wasn't sure what it really was. Or how she was going to keep it alive. Or keep it secret and safe or what should be done with it. The pressure of stress rose through her chest and she exhaled it in a long, low curse.

Cold. The thought came to her again.

Such a strange feeling, to notice her sensations in that odd, detached way. It was easy to blame those floaty, demanding thoughts before on a confused, dying brain.

Riony wasn't sure it was a good sign that they were still happening. She *was* freezing though, in just two thin layers of clothing, substantially ripped and soaked in blood, and no cloak.

Now that the rushing heat of fevers and adrenaline were leaving her system, she'd have to move fast to get back home, or have the immense pleasure of another brush with death before she knew it.

In Riony's arms, the unidragon had closed its eyes and seemed to be sleeping. It's shivery, sleepy sniffles melted Riony toward it. It was cute, in an awkward sort of way. Which Riony thought was the best way.

In slow, careful motions so as not to disturb the unidragon—assuming it would be easier to smuggle home asleep rather than awake—Riony lifted the bottom of her long-sleeved top and scooped the baby in close to her stomach.

There were holes in the fabric where the mother dragon's talons had pierced right through, and Riony wrung blood out of the hem. It wasn't a clean or dry place for a newborn, but there weren't any other options right now.

She belted the hem of the shirt underneath the unidragon, tucking it in so the baby was curled in there like a hammock. There, close to her skin, each of them warmed the other. Its small heart fluttering and the shiver of its breath tickled Riony's skin.

It was lighter than she expected. More skin than bone, and it folded up small, but would still be a noticeable lump on Riony's stomach.

Wary of her freshly healed body, Riony took her time bringing herself into a standing position, but there was no dizziness, no aches or twinges. She felt better than she ever had.

Oh sparks! I'm going to have to hide that my arm's better.

Yoskar, Aishena, and the other delvers knew it was broken. There was no way she could explain how her arm had returned to normal so quickly. She was going to have to feign injury for some time, on top of keeping the unidragon secret.

Between all of that and keeping Lyrrin safe, it felt like too much.

For a split second, Riony considered abandoning the unidragon. Leaving it there in the snow where it would expire naturally and no one would know it had ever existed. No more burdens, no complications. No risks.

She placed her hands over the fabric that held the newborn close to her belly.

She couldn't. It had saved her life—whether it had intended to or not, she owed it. She had to at least make an attempt at keeping the little thing alive.

Plus, it was awfully cute.

Glancing around the cave to take stock of all that had occurred, Riony noticed a dark patch on the ground, farther down the slope. The way she'd come through after breaking in from the crevasse.

Stepping closer, Riony cheered. *My cloak!* She must have dropped it there in her blind stumble to get home, after using it to hold on to her sword.

She snatched it up, shook it free of chipped ice, and threw it around her shoulders. It made her feel colder at first but would be worth it when she stepped out into the blustery mountain air outside the cave.

It would also mean she wouldn't have to walk all the way through the undercity showing off her blood-soaked clothing.

The march home was filled with internal debates and wary glances.

As soon as Riony reached parts of the undercity tunnels where others moved around, she felt as though somehow she would be caught out instantly, as though everyone would somehow know she had the most precious thing in the world tucked under her shirt.

Even if it were a simple, standard dragonling, trying to smuggle it into the undercity would be the folly of a lifetime. She kept her cloak hanging down all around her, to conceal her lumpy, reddened clothing.

She picked up her pace as much as she dared without jostling the newborn too much, skittering through the cyan-illuminated pathways until she reached home.

Rolling open the front door, she exhaled deeply in relief, but fears still shook her insides.

"You're back!" Lyrrin squealed.

All nerves, Riony nearly jumped out of her skin. "Hush!"

The door jammed and she pushed it with her shoulder wide enough so she could fit through without squishing her sleepy bundle. Closing it would be more difficult, and Riony looked to her right arm, still in the bandaging Lyrrin had done.

Could she reveal to Lyrrin yet that she'd been healed? And how? Her mind swirled with worries of every potential consequence within an uncertain future.

"W-what happened?" Lyrrin's face was puffy, with angry red splotches across her pale cheeks, accentuating her bright eyes.

"A lot." Riony sighed. "A lot of very bad things."

Lyrrin's lips pulled in and her eyes glistened. "You have blood on your face."

"Bad things, Lyrrin! Very. Bad. Things." Riony scrubbed her cheeks with a handful of her cloak.

"They broke the eggs, didn't they?" Lyrrin part growled, part whimpered.

Riony didn't answer, but her expression answered for her.

"I hate them! I *hate* them! They are horrible, cruel, sparking monsters!"

"Keep your voice down." Riony glanced back at the still opened door. She dropped her own voice. "They wouldn't have even known about it if you hadn't told them. You have to learn to keep a secret, especially—"

Lyrrin's gloved hands balled into fists, her hood-shadowed face scrunched up, and she squealed a whining roar.

Riony realized her mistake too late. "I'm sorr—"

With tears streaking her cheeks, Lyrrin barged past Riony and bolted out of their rooms.

"Lyrrin, LYRRIN!" Riony yelled.

Tiny, stomping footsteps didn't slow or return.

Riony chased to the front door, but Lyrrin had already disappeared down the long, winding stairway.

The unidragon baby squirmed against Riony's belly. She ran her hands into her hair, tugging at the tangled mess that flopped over her face and screamed at the volume of a whisper, venting every anger she held.

She screamed at the delvers who smashed the eggs, the mother dragon who rejected the baby, Kess who left her to die, and at herself for every stage along the way and for what was yet to come with the new burden she carried.

What am I going to do?

Untying the lacings at the top of her shirt, Riony peeked down at the baby. "Shh, shh. Go back to sleep, please." Then maybe she could go after Lyrrin, bring her back, work something out.

The unidragon mewled at her weakly.

Hungry. The sensation thrummed in Riony's head.

Riony frowned. Hungry? Yeah, she was. But that didn't feel like her. She was hungry like an everyday fact. This was a pleading, pitiable demand. The unidragon blinked lilac eyes up at her from the shadows inside her shirt.

"You? You're hungry?" Of course, it must be. Even newborn humans needed to feed soon after birth.

It trilled a soft whine. **Hungry.**

"Oh. Wow. Okay. This is weird."

Riony glanced around their mostly bare rooms. Another mouth to feed and they had no food. She had no idea what to feed it either. Where to hide it. How big was it going to grow, and how fast? Was it going to be dangerous? How was it putting its feelings into her *brain*?

One thing at a time.

She couldn't chase after Lyrrin, not still covered in blood and carrying a priceless newborn creature.

Riony swung her cloak off and dropped it on the floor, then carefully extracted the unidragon from under her shirt. Its pale velvety scales were dirtied by rusty smudges of blood.

"Just stay here for a moment, okay?" Riony placed it onto her cloak, then stripped off her two ruined shirts, throwing them into the wastebasket. Maybe she would burn them later to avoid questions.

Her mother's voice told her that one should be clean when handling newborns. Riony decided to assume some of the wisdom around human babies would apply to dragon hatchlings too.

Wetting a washcloth under some warm water, she wiped the drying blood off her face, neck, chest, and arms. Her fingers shook as her cleaning efforts made her confront the bloody mess she was in, the sheer, gory extent of it. Some of the crimson matter she wiped off was chunky in a way she didn't want to think about.

She frantically scrubbed at the sticky, staining red that was the only remaining evidence that she'd been moments from death.

Hungry.

"I know!" she snapped. *Sparks.*

The dirtied washcloth was hurled into the pile with the trashed clothing. Riony threw on a clean shirt and wet a new washcloth. Crouching before the unidragon, she carefully wiped the blood from it too.

Its heavy head wobbled and eyelids drooped every time she ran the warm cloth over its skin. When she brought the rag near its face, wiping its cheeks, it mewled and opened a gummy mouth, suckling at the wet rag.

"Ew, slow down!" Riony balked at the idea that it might take a liking to the taste of her blood. She reached for another clean cloth, but they were all gone, used up during Riony's fever and left in a messy pile across the room.

So she took a clean piece of Lyrrin's clothing from the shelf and dipped the corner in the water, holding the dripping edge to the unidragon's mouth. It turned toward the wet cloth and sucked on it weakly.

All Riony had to offer was water, but it seemed better than nothing. A decent drink of water might settle it down and help it feel full until she found actual food for it. She could scrounge up enough flour to make flatbread. Would it eat that?

Riony filled a bowl with water and placed it in front of the baby, but it made no attempt to lap from it as a cat would. She offered the soaked cloth again, but it seemed to have lost interest.

"What do you eat?" Riony thought out aloud, as though she could magically conjure up the desired food. Her whole world felt turned upside down. She tried to make a plan for the next few steps into the unknown.

Looking over at the bed, she wondered, if she tucked the hatchling into a corner there, wrapped it in blankets, would it stay still? Would it stay quiet? She had no confidence of either.

It wasn't unheard of for some people in the depths to keep pets, and Lyrrin sure brought home her share of strays over the years, but this was different. She couldn't risk leaving it alone. She would have to wait for Lyrrin to come back on her own.

I hope she isn't out there challenging Yoskar to a fistfight.

Now that the unidragon was cleaned, she scooped it up again. Kneeling, she pushed the baby out onto the bed area and curled the blankets around it, hoping the low, cushiony walls would keep it still and warm there. It rested its chin weakly on the edge of the nest and trilled.

Something else moved beside it, rustling under the blankets. Riony ripped the top layer back to see the same little furry snout that she'd seen Lyrrin feeding before.

"Um ... Sir Butterfur, ah, Spelunk-something?" Riony ventured.

The soft, caramel-furred cave otter twitched its whiskers at her in obvious annoyance and burrowed back under the covers again.

Lyrrin would be thrilled to find out their number of pets had doubled when she got back. Because she was going to have to find out.

Riony wasn't sure where else she could keep the creature other than here with them, and she couldn't do that without Lyrrin knowing about it.

And she would understand the importance of keeping quiet. Temper aside, she was a good kid and had done well with keeping secrets, at least up until blurting out about the dragon mother, and Riony hadn't been lucid enough to make it clear to Lyrrin at the time that it was something that should be kept quiet.

But Lyrrin had gone eight years without letting people see her hands, so she could be trusted with this new secret.

Once Lyrrin was in on their new charge, she could watch over the unidragon and Riony could get back out to hunt or trade for food. It wasn't too hard to catch a few cave spiders in the darker tunnels. Risky, but they had a decent amount of meat in their armored legs.

And if the unidragon didn't eat meat, she wasn't sure where to turn next. Trade with the compost farm for more mushrooms, or the root farmers for flour or baked goods, or maybe even a breacher for something scavenged aboveground, fruit or green vegetables, depending on the cost.

It had been eight years since her family had fled their previous dragonlord masters, and before that, Riony had never dealt with dragons directly, beyond hearing about them from Kess. She knew the big ones ate meat, but what about the younglings?

What about a dragonling that was part unicorn?

The unidragon's eyelids closed heavily, as though unable to keep them open any longer. Riony rubbed a finger gently across its snout where it had bled and it thrummed a soft purr.

The small vial of dragon glass she'd kept hidden within the acorn for so long had been lost in the dragon's den. Unicorn blood only kept in dragonglass—in anything else it spoiled within moments, but in dragonglass it seemed to keep indefinitely.

They had a few dragonglass bottles in their room, larger than anything silvernix was generally kept in, but they'd probably work ...

If she could bleed this small creature, even a drop could win her any trade she could want within the depths. She'd be richer than the delvers, richer than her wildest dreams.

Tired. Riony felt it again, more shared sensation than language. The unidragon's snout scrunched as it yawned and settled its cheek against her hand.

"Yeah, little one. I bet you are." Riony scritched its neck.

The thought of putting a knife to that soft, pearly skin made her stomach turn.

But could she, if it meant earning what they needed to stay safe? To keep it hidden? To get the unidragon itself the food it needed to live?

Would even attempting to sell unicorn blood out of the blue lead to this creature's existence being revealed? Or would people simply avoid her like that shady woman trying to sell fake silvernix that she saw recently? Riony didn't know. Everything was too uncertain, and she couldn't even take her next steps until Lyrrin returned.

Where was she?

She'd been gone for some time now. Even in her worst tantrums, she'd often cool off and come back quicker than this. Riony's stomach turned again and stress ached between her temples.

The unidragon had fallen asleep and the blankets wriggled beside it as the cave otter burrowed in close, seeking to share its warmth.

Staring at them, Riony questioned if she was having her best or worst idea in recent history. And that was comparing it to poisoning herself.

"Won't know until I try it." Riony grabbed her leather backpack off the floor and gathered up the top blanket from the bed around the unidragon.

Lifting them both, she lowered the newborn into the bag with the blanket tucked all around. It curled neatly into the bottom, just one claw sticking up askew over its head. A wriggle and snuffle, and it settled back to sleep again.

Turning to the bed, Riony chased the moving lump with her eyes.

She tried reaching around under the covers, but the cave otter was too fast, and she got no closer than brushing her grasping fingers against its silky coat. It skittered out, running up the wall with its grabby hands, chittering at her angrily.

Checking her belt pouches, she found the tiniest sliver of mushroom jerky. She held it on display in the palm of her hand, nice and still, until the caramel nose twitched, catching the smell.

"Yeah, that's right, it's a treat for you. You like treats?"

When the otter approached, Riony drew her hand closer and closer to the opening of her backpack, then tossed the crumb in.

Sir Butterfur pounced inside. Riony shut and tied the flap.

Lifting the animal-filled pack onto her back, she felt the otter test the exit a couple of times before it seemed to calm and curl up with the unidragon. At least it might help keep the baby warm, too.

Even though it was still marked with blood, Riony swept her cloak on over the backpack too, hoping to add an extra layer of obscurement.

Then she picked up her sword from where Lyrrin had left it beside the bed and slipped it into its scabbard, made a wish that she wasn't going to have to use it soon, and headed out into the tunnels.

Her first place to look was Delver's Circuit, the richer section of the undercity upslope where Aishena and her brothers lived. She could imagine Lyrrin had marched directly there to make trouble.

Riony passed through the Grand Arch and had barely finished climbing the flowstone steps when she turned an unlit corner and walked straight into Aishena.

Bouncing back, Riony stilled her once-broken arm quickly, reminding herself it wasn't to be used.

Aishena and her brother didn't seem to notice either way. The delver looked back at Riony fiercely as though the collision was an intended insult.

They didn't have Lyrrin in tow, so Riony ducked her head and tried to keep going, but Aishena blocked her path.

Her expression shifted slightly, still angry, but also concerned. "Hey, you seen Benjin?"

"We can't find him anywhere," Yoskar added more aggressively. "Checked the markets, orphans' den, usual places."

Riony stilled, taking a step away and looking back with matching concern. "No. Have you seen Lyrrin?"

Both heads shook.

Not at the markets. Not at the orphans' den. Not here punching Yoskar in the shins. More than one child missing.

Riony swallowed hard. If she'd lost her sister while trying to care for the strange creature in her backpack, Riony didn't know what she would do.

CHAPTER ELEVEN

"**Y**ou think it's kid snatchers?" Riony asked with a shaking breath. She cast her gaze around them at the other cave dwellers passing by, heading through the archways in the nearby Curtain, the long wall of draping limestone that walled off the upper slope area.

Nobody else showed signs that it wasn't any normal day, that they knew or cared that children were missing.

"No. No way. Not even kid snatchers would be dumb enough to mess with delver families," Aishena growled. "With *us*."

Yoskar removed his glasses, wiped at them, and returned them in a motion that seemed to be more based in habit than their need to be cleaned. "Although, Zade wasn't at the orphans' den, and it looked less crowded in there than usual. It's not just Benjin and Lyrrin that are gone. Looks like they hit bigger than usual."

"When was the last time you saw Benjin?"

"Not since we left him behind when we went ... you know." Aishena seemed almost ashamed, eyelashes lowered onto her cheeks.

"Smashing up dragon babies for funsies?" Riony asked.

Yoskar jabbed a finger toward her. "It had to be done."

Riony sniffed and took a step closer to him, looking right down her nose into his eyes. "Lyrrin was still in my room when I got back, but then she ran off. She was real upset about something. What was it again? Oh yeah, dragon babies being smashed up for funsies."

Yoskar rolled his eyes. "You want to stand here and fight over it until the kid snatchers are long gone? Or are you going to come with us and do something about it?"

"Come with ... you?" Riony stared, dumbstruck.

The delver siblings had already begun moving, Yoskar in the lead.

All the tension of pain and death and loss had built inside Riony and she was itching for a fight, as though punching something, anything, hard enough could bring Lyrrin back. But Yoskar made a good point. Annoyingly. They needed to move.

With a stifled groan, Riony hurried after them. "Where are we going?"

Yoskar kept up the swift march. "Back to the orphans' den. Somebody has to know something."

Riony tried to stay hopeful. "Maybe Zade's just taken the kids out somewhere for a day trip."

Aishena gave her a withering look. Her hands clenched and unclenched into fists. "If we can't find Benjin, I'm going to kill Brishan and the others. I can't believe they wouldn't help us look. If all us delvers had been out right away ..."

Riony bit her lip. Aishena had really expected her fellow delvers to help out? Without some form of payment in return? Riony eyed the backs of them, their custom-fitted leathers, stuffed packs, and belts carrying more wealth than anyone other than fellow delvers.

Long coils of rope hung by each of their hips with slim, sharp grappling hooks at the end. Aishena had a thick belt with a whole line of athames sheathed, like a row of teeth. Riony wondered whether they still held charges, and what they were charged with.

Yoskar had a long staff, made of real wood, strapped to his back. Along its length were different-colored crystal shards embedded into the timber. Riony had never seen anything like it.

Nobody had that much wealth without it coming at the cost of someone else. They were rich because they controlled access to the depths, charged a premium for what they scavenged, and left others to remain without. Delvers did nothing selflessly.

As much as Riony wanted to be part of those ranks, she wouldn't be like that once she was. Would she? She dreamed of being rich, of not worrying about where their next meal came from. But where did she draw the line as to how rich she could be while others still suffered?

Riony shook off the thought. She had enough to worry about right now.

They reached the tunnel leading to the orphans' den, and Zade was there, approaching from the other direction. He stumbled as he walked, mopping at a bleeding nose.

"Zade!" Yoskar barked.

He looked at them, then his legs folded, and he fell forward. His knees cracked on the ground.

Riony sprinted past the two delvers, catching Zade with one arm before his face could join his knees in the dirt.

He squinted at her. His normally smiling mouth was downturned, and his eyes were darkened by a bruise spreading out from the bridge of his nose.

"Are you okay?" Riony asked softly. "What happened?"

Before he could answer, Yoskar reached him and lifted him by the scruff of the neck. "Where are the kids?"

"I'm sorry ... the slavers ..." Zade winced.

"Back off! Let him go!" Riony stepped between them. There wasn't much room, with Yoskar still grasping Zade as though he was about to throttle him. They stood uncomfortably close, but Yoskar didn't budge.

Aishena prowled beside them. "Let him go? You heard him. Slavers. The kid snatchers have been snatching kids, and this piece of shroom-shit let them!"

"From the look of his face, I'm not sure *let* is entirely accurate."

Yoskar growled, "Did they take Benjin?"

Zade closed his eyes for a moment before looking right into Yoskar's. "Yes, they have him."

With an audible exhalation, Yoskar released his grip and stepped back, chest heaving.

Out of his grasp, Zade slumped forward again and Riony put the arm she wasn't pretending was broken around him.

He offered her a sad, half smile.

"And Lyrrin?" Riony's voice cracked.

Zade's lips twitched and he wiped at his bloody nose. "Yeah ... they got her too. I tried to stop them, the slavers. I noticed them luring the kids out, rounding them up. They moved so fast. One of them knocked me down when I tried to call for help."

He gestured at his swelling face.

Riony worked hard to keep the appearance of calm, speaking through clenched teeth. Her right hand, despite the ruse of being broken, wrapped tight around the hilt of her sword. "Where are they?"

"Already gone. They'll be aboveground by now—"

"Aboveground?" Riony stepped back from him, needing space to breathe. They took Lyrrin, the kid snatchers really took her, and they had her aboveground.

"Which exit?" Yoskar snapped.

"They headed toward Unicorn Gate," Zade said, leaning back on the wall since he no longer had Riony's support.

"It is the closest," Yoskar stared that direction as though he could see through stone and witness the slavers' retreat.

Riony leaned beside Zade, needing the support too, as though she'd been clocked right between the eyes as well. *Aboveground.*

Sure, she went aboveground herself. Rarely, and only where the risks felt lesser, and even then, her estimate of risk had recently proved to be outrageously wrong.

But Unicorn Gate led out into ashy wastes where revs and dragonlords clashed. It was the aboveground they had left behind to hide here in the dark. It was the aboveground where her parents had died.

Aishena was saying something, and when Riony stared, not following, Aishena slapped her cheek. "Get with it! You loaded up? Ready to move?"

"What? Now?"

"No, in four sparking days' time when my brother is dead, and your sister has been sold off to be a dragonlord's footstool. Yes, *now.*"

Riony turned cold all over. They were leaving now. She had every belonging worth taking on her already—her sword, her cloak, and her pack. A pack which held an impossible creature, newborn and vulnerable.

"I ... I have no food."

"Get to it then," Yoskar hissed, checking through his own packs and gear.

"And no coin. Or trade."

"By all things mighty ..." Aishena scowled as she reached into a pouch and handed Riony a fistful of sovs. It was more money than Riony had ever held. It would be enough for any food she wanted.

"Really?" Riony took the coins as though they were a trap about to spring and snap her hand off.

Aishena rebuckled her bag and hauled it onto her shoulders. "You can repay me by making yourself useful in getting our brother back."

"Lyrrin too."

"Whatever."

Zade cleared his throat, straightening up away from the wall. "I'm coming as well."

Riony threw him a look that was a lot more skeptical than intended.

Zade shrugged and turned his face down so that his golden curls flopped over it. "It's like they said. The kids got taken, and I let it happen. And it's not the first time. I wasn't able to do anything before. But if you're going out there, if you're going after them, I'm in too. I have to do something."

Aishena spoke to her brother as though nobody else was there. "No, I don't want that foppish creep coming along."

"Hey!" Zade protested.

Riony stepped in to defend him again. "Foppish, sure, but you know, in a harmless and not creepy way."

He wiped his red nose again. "Wow. Thanks, I guess?"

Yoskar eyed Zade. "The more hands the better. It makes sense to take along as much help as we can for what we may face aboveground. He can come if he wants."

"I do."

Riony reached out and put a hand on Zade's shoulder. Then she asked their small group, "Is there anyone else we should ask that can help too? Other delvers?"

Aishena turned away, growling at a wall. "They ... won't go aboveground."

Zade added, "The other kids that got taken, they have no one else."

Yoskar grunted, then said, "Get what you need. Be fast. We'll meet you at the exit."

Great. A team of dragon-baby smashers and a pretty-boy who faints at a bloodied nose. Still, Riony figured it had to be better than trying to get Lyrrin back alone. Which she would have tried, regardless.

With a nod to the others, she took her fistful of sovs and ran as fast as she dared to the Grand Arch markets. She held her arms behind her back, supporting the backpack as she moved so it didn't bounce too much.

Sheets of milky-clear stone hung like curtains beside towering stalagmites that ringed the cavernous market space. Some pillars were marked with Alderkin carvings, but no one knew if they were purely decorative markings or if they once held magic like other artifacts found in the depths.

Alderkin tools, scrounged from uninhabited lower levels by delvers, were on display at the first stall, a few activated ones glimmering in a rainbow of light.

Ducking to avoid a woman nursing a large shopping basket on one hip, Riony crashed against one seller's table and had to quickly steady a wide crystal box with a chill rune on it. It would have been worth her life if that thing broke. She propped it back up, gave a speedy apology, then dashed onward.

Behind the stalls that had light stones, crucibles, athames, and even rarer treasures, were others selling general groceries. The ones Riony needed.

Mushrooms and shroom-jerky from the compost farms, alcohol and flour from the root farms, loaves, cakes, flatbreads, and hardtack from bakers using the root flour.

The scent of bread made Riony's stomach growl, and she worried again about what to feed the unidragon, and how long it could survive if she couldn't feed it.

As though wakened by her thoughts of hunger, Riony felt it stir against her back.

Hungry.

There were too many people around to speak back to it out loud. Riony had no idea whether the little unidragon could hear her thoughts too but thought as loud as she could anyway.

Hush, hush now. Try to sleep.

Softly, she hummed the tune to the lullaby her mother once sang for her and Lyrrin. And in her head she sang.

Rest small one, rest ye in peace,
The dragons sleep, the dragons sleep.

There was no time to ponder what Alderkin treasures Riony could buy with the riches she held. She raced straight to the food stalls.

She hit a bakery first, breaking the coin there with one of everything they offered plus a stack of hardtack. The stallholder was surprised to see her buying with so much coin, but Riony didn't stop to answer questions or engage in small talk.

They'll dream of fire, food, and flight,
And won't wake until the morning light.
And lest they wake with fearsome roar,
Safe ye'll be behind closed door.

She bought a netted bag for her new supplies and added in filled waterskins, fresh and dried mushrooms, and even went to the dairy stalls.

Goats in the depths were fed on a diet of root off-cuttings, and their milk had a distinctive burned butter flavor Riony had never taken to. Lyrrin loved it, though. Riony hoped the unidragon would take some, or if not, she would find Lyrrin soon enough and it could be for her.

The stall also sold some goat meat, from stock that was too old to milk. A tough, leathery jerky, barely palatable compared to the mushroom version. She spent the very last of the coin on a few strips of it and a large round of stiff, dried cheese.

So close your eyes, and dream so deep,
While dragons sleep, while dragons sleep.
And in slumber, I'll guard you too,
As all the stars watch over you.

The unidragon's feeling-thoughts quieted in Riony's mind, and it seemed to have settled back to sleep.

Feeling as though she'd bought a year's supply of food in bare moments, Riony made for the Unicorn Gate exit.

The tunnel to the exit wasn't well used. A few guards were stationed there, mostly to fight off any undead creatures that tried to break in.

They didn't have any rules about letting people *out*, though. Not many people were that bold. Riony's passing warranted only a slight raise of eyebrows from the guards.

Were they in on it? They received only a meager salary from the community for this station, but they seemed far better off than that income would suggest. Taking bribes to let slavers pass by with a catch of children?

Riony gave them a sharp glare and silent promise to deal with them when she got back.

Yoskar and Zade were there at the exit already. Riony frowned, wondering why Aishena wasn't there yet too, when she emerged out of the shadows beside Riony.

Aishena glared at the netted bag Riony had hung from a loop on her pack's side. "Why are you hauling your gear like that?"

"Other pack's full," Riony said.

"With *what*?" Aishena hissed.

"With all my love letters from your amma."

Aishena's expression flashed from annoyed to murderous. Riony would have said there was a hint of fear layered in the tightness around her dark eyes, if she thought Aishena was capable of feeling that emotion.

"Enough. We're moving." Yoskar signaled the guards, and Aishena stalked to his side.

In front of them, two massive stone doors blocked the way. Each was made from limestone with streaks of calcite crystal sparkles, carved into a beautiful vision. Tall trees reached the full height of the doors, intertwining at the top, and between the trunks, unicorns frolicked.

Riony hadn't seen those doors since she came into the depths the first time.

There was a soft grinding sound, and the doors smoothly rolled open.

Staring out over the vast, open world before her, Riony actually felt glad to have the delvers and Zade by her side. The tortured landscape sent a shiver of fear up her spine as they stepped out together.

They were beneath the snow line here, and a river of ice runoff flowed nearby, down the barren, rocky slope until it was lost in a forest below, dark and mangled from repeated burnings.

There may have been some green there, but a steady, light fall of ash from the skies and ever-present smoke made everything seem orange and gray. The air was acrid and tangy on Riony's tongue.

In the far distance, the jagged remains of a destroyed village sat on a low hill, and even farther, the imposing silhouette of a dragonkeep was just visible in the sooty haze.

It was a land of fire and death. Slavers and marauders. Dragons and destruction.

And somewhere, out there, was Lyrrin.

Chapter Twelve

Like colossal tombstones, the doors to the undercity slid closed behind Riony. The thundering boom as they slammed shut felt like an ominous toll of a death bell. Separated from the sanctuary of their underground home, Riony's breath caught in her throat.

She sniffed away that feeling of rising panic. Lyrrin needed her, and nothing this blasted landscape could throw at her was going to get in her way.

"They definitely came this way." Zade pointed to where a clear trail of large and small footprints marked a path downhill.

The ground was barren and muddy, over-scavenged of anything worth feeding to humans or livestock that grew within sight and running distance of the safety of the Alderkin tunnels, making the footprints easy to spot.

"If we make haste we can catch up to them." Yoskar didn't even glance back as he broke into a run. He moved at a blistering, nimble pace, despite all his bulky muscles.

Aishena followed without a word or hesitation, an angular, gray slip in comparison.

"Okay, we're hoofing it." Riony took a moment to adjust the straps of her pack, tightening it as much as she could so it didn't flop around behind her. The speed they would need to move at was already going to be a rough ride for a newborn.

Was shaking bad for baby dragons, too? Riony's head hurt with worry.

The delvers slid down the rocky hillside, taking steep shortcuts that cut straight down across the slower, zigzagging trail.

Having little respect for the effects of gravity was part of their job, and Riony would have happily joined in the reckless human landslide had she not been carrying a precious newborn in her backpack.

She followed their path more carefully, sliding uncomfortably on her backside down the steeper sections to avoid falling and landing on her back. Loose rocks slipped and tumbled down in front of her and she locked her ankles, found her balance, and skated down with them.

Zade was neither delver nor aspiring delver. He was already breathing hard and scrambling to keep up with even Riony's cautious pace. He kept casting concerned looks between her and the increasingly distant delver siblings.

"Can't we just take the path? It's not much slower," he gasped between breaths as they hit another flat section of passing trail, then ignored it to go straight down the rubbly mountainside again.

"Not much slower is too much slower," Riony shot back.

"Going to be much slower again if we break our necks before we catch up to the kids. Hey! Hey, slow down! We have to stick together!" He yelled out to the delvers who increased the distance between them. He called out a couple more times, but they didn't ease their pace.

"Come on, hurry up. You're not going to let those delvers get to the kids first and steal the big heroic moment from us, are you?" Riony smirked at him.

"You know, I always have wanted to be a hero." Pushing the tumbling hair out of his face, he smirked back and burst into a faster sprint.

As the ground flattened, the trail of slaver and child footprints became clear again, heading toward the ragged remains of the forest.

Riony stretched her long legs into a smooth, loping run, keeping her chest bent forward and pack supported. The netted bag of supplies banged by her hips, and she grabbed it in one arm to still it. Zade matched her pace, a grim look of determination around his bruised eyes.

A low, faint howl drifted from somewhere far above.

A quick glance back up the mountain didn't show any sign of wolves. Or one wolf in particular.

Kess.

Despite being fully healed by the unidragon, there was a piece of Riony's insides that still stung. Hurt by the abandonment of someone she should have expected that or even greater cruelty from. Why was she even surprised?

There probably wasn't anything Kess could have done for her anyway. Did she actually expect Kess Heithorn to sit by her side and hold her hand as she died?

Probably lucky that she didn't, or I might actually be dead now, and that raging psychopath would have ended up with the baby dragon-thing.

In all that had happened since then, it had been easy for Riony to forget that Kess had ridden into that cave on a wolf and told her to hurry up and die. Riony could have been forgiven if she'd decided to believe the whole experience was some kind of pre-death hallucination.

How in the world is she out here? Riding around on a wolf?

Riony expected the girl to remain cloistered and safe and hidden away at Heithorn Castle, doted on by unwilling servants and protected by the dragonriders she obsessed over.

Although the Heithorns weren't royalty, they were high enough ranking dragonlords that Kess would have been assured a long and comfortable life. But instead, she was out here, back in Riony's life again, as wanted as an iron spike to the brain.

What caused Riony's teeth to clench was that Kess wouldn't even call her by her name, even now, so many years later, as she lay bloodied and near death.

Pony, Pony, Riony Pony.

There was nothing cute about the nickname. The wolf wasn't the only thing Kess had liked to ride around on.

Riony wondered if she whipped it, too.

The old scars on her back tingled, jostled and scraped by the heavy backpack and thoughts of the past.

Puffs of ash rose with each beat of Riony's footsteps.

"How are you holding up?" she asked Zade.

He huffed out his words. "Still breathing. Not used to running."

"Not my favorite thing either." She eyed the delvers, up ahead and showing no sign of slowing down. They talked tough, but it was another thing to see in action. She was begrudgingly impressed. "But we're going to keep running until the kids are in our sights. Then maybe take a quick breather before beating the spleens clear out of the slavers."

Zade smiled wryly and nodded.

A rough path wound into the charred forest, clear of obstacles besides the odd fallen trunk, blackened and cracked. Riony wanted to keep her mind on that path, on her destination, on saving Lyrrin, but Kess's presence stung at her mind like a poison.

There wasn't a lot Riony remembered about her younger years, before her time at the Heithorns, when her parents had been bondsmen to the Gyrsteins. She and her parents had been Uf'Gyrsteins until she was six.

She did remember when those dragonlords died though. The plague that swept through, the smell of burning bodies. They had once been rich lords, but obviously had exhausted any supplies of silvernix by then.

It was only Riony's amma's special treatment as a prized midwife, housed separately from their lords and other servants, that had spared them the same plague-born end.

After their masters' deaths, Riony's family was sold on, changing from Uf'Gyrsteins to Uf'Heithorns. Moved out of a dragonkeep to a rural estate where the lords lived richly, guarded by their own stable of dragons that the Heithorns themselves were proud riders of.

Lady Heithorn was the one who had the idea that, being as Riony was much the same age as her daughter, she would make the perfect playmate for her isolated child. She gave Riony to her like a gift.

And Riony had known just enough kindness in her life before then to be completely, naively blind to the suffering that Kess would inflict upon her.

Riony saw an instant friend, a pretend sister.

Kess had seen a new pet. Some loyal livestock. A living target to take out every spite and misery on with words and teeth and fists and whips.

Riony cracked her neck, rolling the muscles in her shoulders and feeling the strength in her legs as they pounded the ground beneath her.

She hated that Kess was the beginning of forging her into steel.

Riony's parents, Eylin and Farrad, always talked about the Uf'Gyrsteins as being good masters. Kind masters. But Riony didn't want to be Uf' anybody ever again.

When she and Lyrrin made it alone to the undercity, they decided to make their own new last name. Taken from the names of their lost parents. Eyfarr. Riony felt stronger, freer, having her own family name with no prefix of ownership attached.

Lyrrin had never known a life as a slave, and Riony intended on keeping it that way.

The woods Riony ran through were sparse, with most of the canopy burned away a while ago. Some trees, although blackened, had new life. Green leaves poked from tangled limbs, and fresh shoots of grasses and shrubs were scattered around the ashen ground.

If they weren't in a hurry, Riony would have loved to stop and browse the varieties of flora growing there. Maybe she would, on the way back, with Lyrrin.

As the plant life grew thicker, the trail disappeared. Zade and Riony caught up to Aishena and Yoskar who stood amongst the brushy regrowth, arguing.

"Tjollaskeep is the closest city. They would take the kids there. It should be due east from here." Aishena had her face turned to the sky, angling toward the brightest spot where the sun was obscured behind the haze.

Yoskar crouched down and studied the ground. "Not necessarily. There are other estates and factories within a few days march in other directions. A fresh batch of young workers could be sold off in many locations, not just the keep."

Catching her breath, a wave of dizziness washed over Riony. She hoped it wasn't a sensation coming from a faltering newborn, and instead considered that it could have been the stress of her recent brush with death, Lyrrin's kidnapping, or the fact she hadn't kept any food down since before she'd broken her arm.

Despite being magically healed, she probably still needed to eat.

Riony reached with her unbroken arm and pulled a waterskin from the net bag, taking a long drink. She had just taken a bite of flatbread when Aishena turned on her.

"Well?" she demanded, as though Riony could break the argument.

"I just need a moment," Riony puffed around her mouthful.

"She's so weak. She's going to hold us up," Aishena told Yoskar as though Riony wasn't even there.

"You didn't even think she'd still be alive a couple of days ago. She seems to be much better," he replied.

Riony pulled her bandaged arm closer to her chest. "Spite is like a fuel for my healing process."

"Still not sure we should have brought her along. She's a liability, with her arm broken and no brains to spare." Aishena reached out and jabbed her finger into what she believed was Riony's broken forearm.

Riony winced away, but the fact she didn't cry out seemed to win her some approval.

It felt like playtime with Kess all over again.

"Having another sword on our side could make the difference ahead." Yoskar stood back up, squinting into the distance.

Riony finished her bread and put her hand on the hilt of her sword, grasping it for comfort as she often did. She would have reached for her acorn if it hadn't been lost in the ice cave. Sure, she brought a sword into the mix, but she'd hate to have to admit she didn't really know how to use it.

She could swing it hard at an unmoving target, but that's about all the training she'd been able to do on her own. She wasn't so naïve as to think her opponent in a real battle would stand still for her to chop down like a tree. She only got that lucky once.

"There are some broken twigs that way." Zade pointed off to their left. "They must have passed through there."

"Dubious," Yoskar muttered. "There are broken twigs everywhere. What makes you think those broken twigs are any different to those over there?"

"Also, that's north. We're going east." Aishena pointed, clearly having managed to get her bearings. She muttered to herself about tamebrain creeps they shouldn't have brought along.

Riony had a go at squinting at the bright sky but didn't know how to turn that view into a direction, and as a slave, she never had a chance to study geography growing up. She was lucky her parents taught her to read.

So she looked back at the ground, to see if she could somehow tell the difference between twigs that had been snapped by marching children or some other force.

They all looked about the same to her. Although one thing stood out as she glanced around. Scratches in the burnt bark of a thick trunk, close to where Zade had pointed.

Stepping closer, it was clear the deep grooves weren't some random animal claw marks. They had been quickly and messily carved with the Alderkin rune for Return. A split diamond shape, layered over with an arrow and a cross.

Riony slumped into a crouch before the symbol, pressing her hand beside it.

Lyrrin.

"Over here! We have a marker," she called.

The three others gathered around her, staring at the deep gouges in the trunk.

"It's a rune, see?" Riony traced over it, although she didn't know the right sequence, and based on the way Aishena rolled her eyes she was way off.

Yoskar knelt next to Riony and touched the ground beneath the mark. He rubbed fragments of charcoal between his fingers. "Fresh. But this could mean anything. It could be from anyone."

"No, Lyrrin did this. I know it."

"How? Does she have a knife on her?" Aishena sounded hopeful, as though the eight-year-old could have contrived an ambush and slashed the throats of her captors by now.

"Not exactly," Riony mumbled. "But she loves runes. She's a clever kid. She did this."

Standing again, Riony turned on the spot and looked sharply through the nearby trees. "There's got to be another one. She'll mark a trail." *She knew I'd come after her.* "Over there!"

The direction of the second carved return rune led them north.

"I told you it was that way," Zade said, offering a lopsided smile. "Broken twigs."

"East," Aishena spat, practically hissing like a cornered cat, slim shoulders raised and pointy. "It's the clearest direction. North has no destination within a week's march that isn't ruined or burnt, and beyond that another week to reach Hjelzahnkeep." She shared a look with her brother. "We head for Tjollaskeep."

Yoskar rubbed the soot between his fingers again, staring between the two options.

"I'm following the runes whether you come with me or not," Riony stated.

Zade took a step closer to her, offering a nod of support. "The longer we keep arguing about this, the farther ahead they get. I want to catch up to the slavers sooner rather than later, and I'm sure you do too."

"Evidence suggests north," Yoskar said with a commanding finality.

Aishena's face paled and her lips puckered in as he moved over beside Riony and Zade. When he straightened up and stared back at her, she scampered over beside him like an obedient pup.

Yoskar and Zade stepped off ahead, as Riony took a moment to adjust her pack again, feeling a squirm of movement against her back.

When she looked up to move forward again, Aishena stepped in front of her, blocking the way.

She snarled and whipped her long sheets of silvery hair away from her face. "If you're wrong about this ..."

Aishena ran her hands along the row of athames at her belt and did her trick of looming over Riony despite being a head shorter.

"If you lead us in the wrong direction, away from Benjin, forget ever becoming a delver. If you stop us getting our brother back, we'll make sure you're never even allowed back into the undercity again."

Chapter Thirteen

Riony and the others took a slower pace now. Each of them was on high alert, casting their gaze wide in all directions as they pressed on. They had a rough heading, but if the slavers turned off a different direction and they missed Lyrrin's mark, they could go on too far the wrong way, get lost, lose precious moments backtracking.

But each time Riony fretted that the gap had been too large since the last sighting, another rune came into view.

Good work, Lyrrin. Keep it up. We're coming for you.

They moved with an intense purpose along the trail, rune after rune. The first time one was carved into a rock rather than ashy trunk, Yoskar had raised his eyebrows.

"Wow. Soft rock," Riony said.

The delver didn't say anything as he kept up the lead.

Yoskar and Aishena remained ahead of Riony and Zade, still acting like self-designated leaders, but not as far ahead as before.

Their path wound through the wooded descent of the mountain. The land felt twisted, cursed. Ancient trees loomed over them, blackened and tortured from being burned, attempts at regrowth, being burned again.

The ground was littered with the ashy branches and fallen trunks of those that couldn't cling to life.

Faster growing plants like vines took the opportunity to spring through the charcoal, shooting lines of vibrant green up black trees and draping across the thin canopy. The only birdsong was the shrill cry of an eagle, somewhere far above in the clouds.

Riony kept her ears pricked for the sound of a wolf's howl but didn't hear it again.

The air had a crisp chill, blown from the snowy peaks above them, and the two critters snuggled together in Riony's pack helped keep her warm.

Hungry. The feeling reached her again.

The initial run down from the Alderkin depths entrance had stirred the newborn creature awake. It wasn't moving much, only a few weak wriggles. Riony hoped that as it had only just left the egg, that it felt at home in the enclosed space. She also hoped the otter wasn't crowding it too much. But it didn't fuss or cry out.

Only the twanging intrusions into Riony's mind of its hunger kept her aware of its presence. Intrusions which felt more desperate and sad as they continued to march the trail downhill.

Riony would have pulled the pack open to try to feed or comfort the animal, but Zade remained close by her side.

"When was the last time you were aboveground?" he asked conversationally, as though small talk was the thing Riony needed most right now. Maybe he was making an attempt to distract her from their troubles, which was sweet in theory, but not even the best conversationalist could lessen Riony's weight of concern right now.

"I haven't been this far out since Lyrrin and I made it to the undercity a couple of years back." Truthful, technically. Riony didn't want him prying into her recent adventures.

Zade turned his face upward. "I do so miss the sky when I'm underground. How about you?"

"Yeah. I miss it lots." *I miss it, and a whole lot more.*

With a kind smile, Zade said, "The slavers can't be much farther ahead. And your sister is a tough one, clever too. Things are going to work out."

There was a pressure against Riony's back as the cave otter tried to force the bindings on the pack. She covered its movements by shrugging her shoulders and adjusting the cloak that hung over the bag.

Riony was worried its struggles might hurt the newborn. If she could just slip some food in through the top, at least it would be happy. But after a second brief escape attempt, it calmed again. It seemed content to curl up and share warmth with the unidragon, as Riony had hoped.

"More footprints here," Yoskar called from ahead.

The few sightings of the slavers' trail they'd had between rune markers seemed to have calmed Aishena down. But she still walked in a jangle of twitchy anxiety, as though itching to break into a sprint again.

Riony just hoped that their slowed pace was still gaining on the slavers. They couldn't be moving too fast while herding a clutch of children along with them. Riony couldn't get Lyrrin moving fast at the best of times.

Hungry.

Riony winced as the feeling ached through her mind, the demand growing more powerful.

Zade reached out and put a hand on her shoulder. He looked at her with concerned eyes, shaded by a cloud of warm blond curls. "Don't worry. We'll get you to your sister. I promise."

Riony swallowed awkwardly. "Uh. Thanks."

His intense expression was softened by a smile that tugged just one side of his lips.

Riony shook her head. Even now, as they chased slavers over a burned and blighted land, he managed to find a genuine smile. It warmed her with hope. "How do you stay so positive?"

"I just know that good things happen to people who deserve it."

Riony bristled and the warmth she felt a moment earlier fled her skin. "Sounds like a very Taen sort of philosophy. Does that also mean if something bad happens the person deserved it? Did the kids deserve to be kidnapped?"

Zade squeezed his grip on her shoulder. "Of course not. But I do think things happen for a reason. Things will work out, for everyone. Trust me."

His grin grew, and Riony found herself smiling back.

"What reason? The kids getting kidnapped doesn't make any sense." Aishena appeared like a wraith on Riony's other side.

Zade's expression soured, and he let go of Riony. "Kids have been taken before."

Aishena scoffed. "Loner kids. Orphans without anyone to care if they are gone."

Zade fixed her with a glare. "I cared."

"And what did you do about it? Nothing. And I bet you still wouldn't have if the slavers didn't slip up and take a couple of children that do have people who care enough to go after them." Tossing her silver hair over one shoulder, Aishena then rested a palm beside her collection of athames strapped at her belt.

Zade held the delver's stare but didn't reply.

Riony swallowed. "The way you two are sandwiching me right now is making me feel uncomfortable."

"Must you be so suggestive?" Aishena tsked.

"Suggestive? I said uncomfortable. You're the one who went there, not me. Maybe you're projecting your own desire for a three-way sandwich. But you're hotter than you are mean, so if you're offering, I might be convinced. If we leave Zade out of it. Sorry, Zade."

"This isn't the time!" Aishena growled.

"I don't mean *right now*. I'm okay with setting time aside after our perilous rescue mission is a success." Riony thumbed the straps of her backpack, trying to feel the optimism in her words. Trying to stay positive like Zade.

Aishena just shook her head as though the concept warranted no more attention. "I still can't believe the slavers took our brother."

"They probably just took advantage of us not being around at the time they were doing their snatch and grab." Riony's tone grew cold. "Maybe if you didn't decide to go and kill a bunch of—"

Aishena's hand shot out and grabbed Riony by the front of the shirt. Riony stumbled as Aishena yanked her in until she felt her hot breath snarling over her face.

"Stop messing around!" Yoskar snapped from ahead. "Get back up here, Aish. We need more eyes on the trail."

With a soft growl, Aishena snatched her hand back and stalked away to catch up with her brother.

Zade raised his eyebrows. "Kill a bunch of what?"

"Never mind."

With a shrug, Zade turned his gaze away to the woods around them. "She's just on edge from being aboveground."

"Yeah. I think we all are." Riony sighed and leaned into her forward march.

"Is that why you're excluding me from end of mission celebration plans?" He smirked, but almost sounded hurt.

"Oh. I was just joking around. Mostly."

Zade watched her with friendly eyes for a long moment. "Or maybe I just haven't charmed you enough yet."

Riony chuckled and gave him a warm smile in return. "I really don't think that's going to change my preferences but I'm always open to being treated with anything above pure contempt."

Zade gave a hearty chuckle. "And as for being aboveground, it's not all that bad."

"Yeah, right up until a rev pops out of the ground and bites your neck out."

Yoskar, clearly keeping his ears and eyes on everything, called back from ahead. "This area has been burned very recently. Unlikely we need to worry about revenants. Once burned, they stay dead."

Riony crushed some charcoal under her boot and it disintegrated in a puff. Yoskar was right, they had moved into an area where nothing had been given a chance to regrow again.

Pale ash powdered the ground, not yet washed into the soil by rain. Over beside a low cliff, the ground still smoldered, ghostly sheets of smoke gusting into the sky.

But Riony wasn't sure Yoskar was right about not having to worry about shadow revenants. Riony *always* worried about revs.

The charred forest continued to thin out as the slope grew steeper again, trees replaced by sharp outcrops of stone that formed a crumbling maze. A soft crunching sound startled the four of them, freezing them like deer.

A bovin pawed at the sooty ground, working to unearth anything edible beneath the burned surface that it could munch on. It was massive, the large hump on its shaggy back easily twice Riony's height. But it wouldn't be any threat to them.

The cud-chewing creature gave them a lazy glance from its hooded eyes before continuing its attempts at grazing. Riony's parents told her how bovin used to travel the plains of Elundrae in huge herds, in numbers so great that the odd member being taken by a wild dragon hardly mattered.

Now the herds had all been rounded up into farms to feed the ever-growing numbers of city dragons, riding dragons, and factory dragons.

The single, solitary bovin seemed so sad. Riony wondered where its family was.

The color of light changed as they continued on, a warmer glow washing through the smoky skies. Riony tried to get her bearings on what time of day it was. So much had happened since she'd woken from her fever, and she didn't even know when that was or how long she'd been out beforehand.

Had Yoskar said a couple of days?

Squinting at the sky, Riony pleaded with the sun not to set before she'd found Lyrrin again.

HUNGRY!

Riony stumbled, clutching her head.

"Are you all right?" Zade reached for her, then called to the others, "Hold up, something's wrong."

Riony brushed him off and straightened up, offering an awkward chuckle. "No, I'm fine. Don't worry. Just stubbed my toe."

Zade frowned at where she rubbed her temple. "Um ..."

"Because ... I was dizzy. Because I'm hungry. I just need a moment. Alone. Don't worry, you can keep going."

Forehead twisting further, Zade turned from her to the others, who continued walking. "Can you just wait?"

They made no sign of even listening.

"We've got to stick together," Zade grumbled. With an exasperated look, he chased after the siblings, calling them back.

The moment he stepped away, Riony pulled the backpack straps from her shoulders and placed it carefully on the ground. She hunched over the opening, both to block any view of what was inside and stop anything inside getting out.

The first thing she saw when loosening the ties was a furry caramel snout pocking out. "Go on, get back in there!"

Riony held the otter at bay with one hand as she fished around for food with the other. She hoped with her back turned the others wouldn't see her using her 'broken' arm. She thrust a piece of mushroom jerky at the bag opening.

The snout twitched, then vanished, replaced with a grabby paw that reached out blindly until it latched on to the food, then pulled that food back into the bag with it.

"What's going on?" Aishena yelled from ahead.

Riony cast a look over her shoulder. Zade had caught up to them, and the three had stopped, waiting just ahead of a large rocky outcrop. The trail they were on now was a clear goat track that ran through a narrow crack between the massive, jutting stones.

HUNGRY.

"Nothing, just taking a short break. I'll catch up," Riony yelled back. She could hear Zade and Yoskar arguing in low voices.

Riony quickly opened the bag wider, and drooping, weak eyes of the unidragon blinked at her. Riony waved a piece of goat jerky near its nose, but it didn't take it. She quickly tried again with a piece of cheese.

Hungry. The unidragon whinnied a pitiful whimper, but didn't take the hard lump from Riony's fingers.

"I'm trying," Riony whispered back.

The stomp of footsteps behind her made her heart rush as Aishena marched back her way.

Riony lashed her bag closed again, lifting it onto her back, but before she could turn around, the footsteps had stilled.

"Do you hear that?" Aishena had stopped mid-stride, head cocked at an angle.

Shifting the weight of her pack to hide any movement within it, Riony shrugged. "Nope, can't hear a—"

A gurgling scream interrupted her, punctuated by two more shouts.

"Oh, *that*," Riony said.

"Watch out!" Yoskar yelled, as a figure emerged from the narrow pathway between the rocks ahead.

The man tumbled in a shambling run, slipping and gasping. His dirty brown tunic was slick with blood, and he clutched at the oozing mess of his stomach.

Riony dashed forward, good hand on her sword.

The man landed face-first on the shaley ground in a clatter before she reached him.

"Rev?" Riony asked. She stepped back in shock as Yoskar approached the body and checked.

"No. Still warm. He was alive a moment ago."

Aishena reached them too, glaring at the path ahead, where more screams emerged.

Zade's face had paled and he shook his head at the recently dead before him.

"I'm going to see what's happening," Riony said, tightening her grip on the hilt of her sword.

"This man wasn't a rev, but *something* killed him. Something through there," Yoskar warned.

"And that man might have been one of the slavers," Riony snapped back. She pulled her sword free with her left hand, pointing at the rocks. "We might have caught up. That could be the kids on the other side."

Aishena was moving first, and Riony had to put on a burst of speed to meet her pace. The crevice was shaded and cool, cutting a crooked line that blocked their view of what was ahead until they rushed out the other side.

There, in a clearing of rock shards between massive boulders, three men brawled in a brutal fight. Riony tracked the figures as they tumbled and clawed at each other. Not three men. Two men, and a rev.

The shadow revenant had once been human, not reborn from the corpse of some other animal. It must have been a fresh corpse, too, as it still had flesh on its bones.

That set it apart from the ones who had killed Riony's parents. Riony would never forget their sickening yellow skeletons, the grasp of their rough, boney hands. The crackling sounds they made as they moved. The snap of their jaws.

Her stomach bottomed out and her grasp on her sword shook.

Yoskar and Zade caught up to her and Aishena.

Their movement drew the attention of one man, who had blood dripping down his face. He locked eyes with Zade. "Help us!"

"Where are the kids?" Aishena ignored the battle before her, scanning around as though the children were hidden behind the scattered rocks.

"We should help them," Riony whispered.

Yoskar pointed across to the continuing pathway. "The kids aren't here; this isn't them. We should get out of here before that thing turns on us."

Another man dropped limply to the ground before Riony could argue.

The rev launched itself at the remaining one who'd called for their help. A furious flurry of limbs and teeth, wrenching and gnashing at the man's face.

Riony found herself marching forward.

She knew Yoskar was right. They should get away, keep moving as fast as they could to find Lyrrin and the other children.

But her lips curled in anger and her knuckles turned white around her sword and her feet kept moving.

She was only halted by the man she intended to save collapsing into a bloody pile.

And the rev turned its attention to her.

Oh sparks.

Riony lifted her sword just in time as the revenant flung itself at her. A puff of ash burst off the creature as it collided with the metal. Riony coughed and swung blindly. She put all her strength into the swing, dragging the undead body along with the blade, pushing it away from her.

The clamor of movement caused the creatures in her backpack to buck and scamper about.

There was a spattering of curse words and arguments from the others behind her as she blinked her eyes clear. The rev charged again.

It moved faster than a living human, its sinewy arms and gnarled hands grasping stronger. One latched around Riony's upper arm, the sharp-nailed fingertips sliding into her flesh like a skewer through a rope worm.

Gritting her teeth against an emerging scream, Riony leaned away from the toothy jaw that snapped at her neck.

The unidragon and otter stopped moving, lying perfectly still again. Not in rest this time, but frozen in fear. The wave of terrified sensations from the newborn overwhelmed Riony.

She shook it off and tugged her arm to the side, readjusting as much as she could within the monster's grasp to bring her sword between them. She held her sword in her left hand, which she wasn't used to, and it was slowing her down. Making her clumsy.

But she wasn't sure yet if it was worth giving up the ruse that her right arm was still broken. As long as she could swing her sword, she wouldn't give up.

With a cry of effort, she sliced, then thrust, cutting into the chest of the rev, then trying to run it through. Her aim failed, unsteady, and she slipped to the right.

But the rev let go, forced back for a blink of a moment. Riony wasted no time, slashing again. Another puff of ash escaped from the strange, flaky flesh of the rev. It writhed under her blow but didn't stop, trying to straighten up and attack again.

Riony didn't give it a chance. She hacked at it another time. She had no fancy footwork, no special names for her movements; she didn't even know if she was holding the sword right. But the one thing she could do was keep chopping, landing blow after blow until her muscles burned and long after.

Blood dripped down her right arm, and she kept the already bandaged limb still and close to her chest.

She had the creature at bay, but it showed no sign of letting go of its twisted semblance of life. The cuts from Riony's sword sliced into the ashy skin, leaving huge gashes, but revenants didn't feel pain.

"Um, a little help?" she called out, keeping her eyes on the monster.

More swearing, and the gloom of the day seemed to brighten with warmth behind Riony.

"Get out of the way," Aishena hissed.

Riony dared a glance over her shoulder. Aishena strode forward, a burning athame in each hand. She clutched the hilts fearlessly as the crystal blades radiated scarlet light and licks of flame.

The rev's claw swiped right past Riony's nose. She dodged away, stumbling back.

With the path clear, Aishena vaulted in. With an elegant spin that put all of Riony's basic slashing to shame, she stabbed a flaming blade deep into the chest of the revenant.

Sparks she's hot.

The revenant jerked like a puppet shaken by its strings as the heat spread through its body, glowing through the ashy flesh, then it collapsed at her feet.

Riony opened her mouth to thank the delver but was silenced by a withering look.

"You have to burn them, tamebrain. That or completely smash them to bits. But burning is the only way to be sure."

Aaaaand there's the nastiness again.

"I mean, I do know that. I just wasn't given my free burn athame as a special welcome gift to the wasteland of the undead."

Rolling her eyes, Aishena deactivated her remaining athame, then stepped close to the corpse to retrieve her other one.

Placing a foot on its chest, she yanked the burning dagger free.

And the revenant surged back into life. Teeth snapping, limb flailing life.

But it couldn't be. Riony gaped, horror crawling through her veins. *It was burned. It should stay dead.*

Riony blinked hard, hoping the nightmarish vision would fade, that the rev would lie still again.

The undead monster still moved. It lashed out, wrapping a clawed hand around Aishena's ankle, trapping her in its grip.

CHAPTER FOURTEEN

The revenant growled, deep and guttural. It lashed a second hand around Aishena's ankle, twisting until a cry was forced from her throat.

For a moment, Riony could only stare in shock at the still-moving undead.

How? How was it still moving?

It was even ashier than before, still glowing and smoking from within its burned and hollow rib cage. It hissed and snarled like a wild creature as it tried to claw itself up Aishena's leg.

Yoskar ran in first, grabbing his sister from behind and wrenching her backward. The rev didn't let go. It dragged along the ground after them and Aishena kicked at its grasping hands with her free leg.

"Get off! Get it off me!"

Riony's petrified body snapped back under her control, and she shook herself, inhaled deeply, and prepared to fight the undead thing again.

Zade circled in, a sharp hunting blade in one hand and the pallid tint of worry on his face, but he must have known as well as the rest of them there wasn't much he could do with that small steel blade. He hung back, cursing.

With an aching left arm, Riony lifted her sword high and brought it smashing down with a roar. She hit true, right across the rev's forearms, and thankfully not Aishena's struggling legs.

The blade cracked straight through one arm, severing the rotting flesh, breaking through bone. The clasping hand, removed from its body, released Aishena, and its second arm recoiled too.

With the tug-of-war with the creature ended, Aishena and Yoskar stumbled backward from unburdened momentum. When Aishena put her foot down to steady herself, she cried out again, hopping and limping.

The rev was already back on its feet. It shook its dismembered arm at them as though in anger, a shimmer of ashes raining from it.

"Run," Yoskar yelled. "We have to get out of here!"

Riony nodded, her gaze shooting desperately around the area surrounded between towering boulders. There were a few paths leading out. She couldn't see any runes from here. "Which way?"

"That way!" Zade yelled, pointing to a narrow path at the back of the clearing.

But the rev rushed toward them, blocking that option. Aishena's injured leg collapsed under her as she broke into a run away from it.

Yoskar scooped her up and over one shoulder. "Away from the rev!"

"Yeah. Yeah, smart idea." Riony took the lead, sheathing her sword and moving at a frantic pace down a pebbly slope, away from the rev.

Zade puffed beside her, and Yoskar kept pace easily, even with the additional weight of his sister. Everybody's expressions were paled and grim.

Glancing over her shoulder, Riony flinched to see the rev still close behind, close enough to hear its bared teeth clattering. The clearing vanished over the crest as they part ran, part tumbled down the hill, and Riony's heart clenched painfully at the thought they were going the wrong way.

"We should stop and fight it," she gasped out. "We could—"

"It didn't die," Aishena snapped, bouncing over Yoskar's shoulder, her arms dangled down his back, still clutching her extinguished athames. Her hair hung all around her face like a shroud. "It should have died. If the burn didn't kill it, I don't know how …"

They skidded on a landslide of loose shale, then the ground flattened out again. Massive trees loomed ahead, and they ran for them. The snarl and clatter of the rev remained close behind, never slowing, never tiring. Breath burned in Riony's lungs like dragonfire.

Breaking into the cover of the forest, Riony widened her eyes, trying to spot anywhere to take shelter—a hollow trunk, a climbable tree, an abandoned hut. Anything they could block off or defend.

They couldn't keep running forever, but the rev could.

The forest was dark and claustrophobic, thick with new growth, unburned for much longer than the path they'd been on before. A thin fog clouded the woods, obscuring the trees and vines that writhed and twisted around them, heavy with the scent of decay.

The ground was slick with moss and the remnants of old ash and littered with fallen logs and jagged twigs, forcing Riony and the others to dodge and leap between them, sliding and stumbling.

Only a few thin streams of orange light broke through the canopy, and placed in the center of a larger beam were some blocky, unmoving silhouettes.

"This way," Riony gasped out.

The others veered along with her, flocking as though in formation. Growing closer, the silhouettes manifested into clearer forms. Immense crystalline standing stones, laid out in a circle between the trees.

In the middle was an additional stone structure, ancient and crumbling, but still walled on at least two sides, as far as Riony could tell.

The structure was familiar, and even one wall to put their back to was better than nothing.

Riony pointed. "Over there!"

Zade and Yoskar—still carrying Aishena—crashed ahead toward the standing stones. Riony forced another burst of speed into failing legs. The first stone passed by her side, then she snapped backward, caught by a hand on her backpack.

She grunted and bent forward, trying to tug free. The rev held tight. The straps of the pack strained against her shoulders. A couple of stitches popped.

"Let go!" She kicked out behind her with one leg.

Her boot made contact and the rev was knocked away, rattling back over twisted vines and fallen branches.

Off-balance, Riony fell hard on her side. She flipped around quickly, crawling backward like a crab across a ground slick with slimy, rotting leaves. The rev scrambled along the ground toward her, slithering forward in a disturbing, uneven motion on three limbs.

It watched her, locked on to her with hollow, blackened eye sockets.

A strange frisson of energy shivered up Riony's back, and just as the rev's remaining hand reached for her foot, it stopped. Twitching and snarling, it moved in strange juddering motions, backing away, almost as though in pain.

It lunged forward again, hissing and lashing its arm out, but some invisible boundary in line with the standing stones held it back.

Riony continued away from the revenant anyway, struggling back onto her feet.

"What's happening?" Zade asked as she caught up to him.

They both slowed then, eyes locked on the rev, who stalked the perimeter of the stone circle, grinding its teeth and hissing and throwing its whole body at the apparently solid air.

"I have absolutely no idea," Riony replied.

Yoskar also turned to see why the chase had ended. Frowning, he put Aishena down.

She hopped over to the wall of the central building, leaning there with a scowl as she stared at the revenant. "Why did it stop?"

"Again, I don't know." Riony turned to take in the ruined shrine. She'd seen Alderkin ruins like these before. They were scattered all over Elundrae. There had been one practically in the backyard of Heithorn Castle.

Whatever the shrine had once been to that magical race, the crystalline building was now mostly shattered, ornately decorated chunks spread among the overgrowth. Vines and lichens clung to its remaining weathered walls.

Intricate engravings and runes could still be seen etched beneath the plant life taking over, faded and worn away by time. Only the large standing stones, that could have been there thousands of years and probably last another thousand years, stood tall and strong.

Alderkin temples like this held no magic anymore, lost with the extermination of that race, but something was keeping the revenant from crossing the border.

Zade flinched as Riony took a step toward the prowling revenant. "Keep away from that thing!"

Riony nodded, but she still took another step closer.

The revenant howled and thrashed at the air, trying to claw at her, but unable to move close enough to fulfil its bloodlust.

Riony reached out and placed her palm against the standing stone closest to the revenant. The hairs on the back of her neck all jumped to attention, a shiver zinging up her scalp. Her forehead wrinkled.

What was that?

"There's something. Something about this place ..." Riony had touched Alderkin standing stones in the past, but they'd never felt like anything other than cold, lifeless rock before. And never heard even the whiff of rumor about them being safe from revs. That would be the kind of info people would talk about.

Yoskar moved beside her, right in front of the feral undead creature. He pushed his glasses back up his nose and eyed it warily. "It really can't get in?"

Over at the wall, Aishena grunted and slid down onto her backside. She brought her ankle up onto her other knee to inspect it and grunted again. "Whatever the reason, it seems stuck out there. And *I'm* stuck here."

Riony looked up, trying to catch a glimpse of sky. The canopy of tall trees growing inside and outside of the stone circle shadowed them, and no brightness could be seen through the rustling leaves.

The sun must have set. Riony's heart raced. "We can't be stuck here. We have to keep going, catch up with the kids."

"Did I say *we*?" Aishena asked.

Riony's hands clenched into fists. She'd never been apart from Lyrrin overnight. The thought that Lyrrin would spend a night without her, aboveground, under slavers' control, sent her into a blind panic. "I'm not waiting."

Aishena rotated her foot with her hands and inhaled sharply. Then nodding to herself, she stood back up. "Agreed. I'll distract the rev, keep it over to this side, while you all head out the other side and try to pick up the trail again."

Riony stopped mid-protest, mouth gaping, unprepared for that offer.

"No!" Zade snapped. "What haven't you understood yet about having to stick together? It's suicidal to split up."

Aishena just shrugged.

Zade threw his hands into the air, huffing a frustrated laugh. "Yoskar, you wouldn't leave your sister behind, would you?"

Yoskar's expression remained impassive. He cast a scrutinizing gaze around the ruins. "If she still can't keep pace in the morning, then yes."

Aishena didn't seem concerned by this statement at all. She nodded in firm agreement.

Zade shook his head, aghast. "She's your sister!"

"She is. And that's why I trust her to manage herself while I continue on for Benjin, who must be prioritized in this instance."

"Wait, what do you mean, in the morning?" Riony asked.

"We make camp here." Yoskar moved away from the prowling revenant, back closer to the shrine wall where Aishena and Zade had remained.

Riony stalked over beside him. "But—"

"The sun is down, and the slavers will have to make camp too. They probably already have, earlier than us, taking the stamina of young children into account. We will catch up tomorrow." He removed his pack, putting it carefully down onto the uneven, broken paving.

"We could be catching up now, get the kids out while the slavers sleep," Riony said, shifting from foot to foot. Her arm still bled and stung, and her whole body screamed for rest, but her mind, ever stubbornly deaf to her body's woes, wouldn't listen.

"You can do what you want," Yoskar said. Kneeling beside his bag, he unstrapped the crystal studded staff off the pack, then began digging through the contents. "Good luck lasting till morning alone out there."

Zade threw Riony a long, pleading look. "Please, can we stick together? I don't want you to end up like those slavers back there."

"Ugh. Fine. We stay. But the moment Aishena can hobble along again, we move on." Riony frowned at the delver, who stood with her back against the wall with a defiant look upon her face.

Riony was in possession of a remedy that could make Aishena be healed and moving again right now. Her pulse hammered in her ears and her head spun, unable to form clear decisions. Could she do that? Could she reveal what she carried to these three? She didn't trust them, that was for sure, but was she risking Lyrrin by not?

A faint, desperately pitiful cry of **hungry** washed over her thoughts.

The truth couldn't be fought any longer. They had to stop. Riony had to stop.

She hoped Yoskar was right about the slavers stopping too.

Aishena pulled her pack off and dropped it beside her but remained standing. Her athames were back in her hands, and she grasped them with white knuckles. "Brother, this place feels strange. I don't like it."

Riony raised an eyebrow, wondering if the spooky delver had felt the strange shiver of energy she had.

"We stay. If whatever is keeping the rev out holds, this is our safest option to rest. If it doesn't, we move on again regardless." Yoskar kicked at the ground, clearing an area on the smoothest section of ancient paving. Roots and tendrils wound their way around the broken stones, growing out of the cracks.

Riony paced around, still unable to settle. She glared back at the revenant that had chased them so far off their path, still growling at them from across the ruins.

"Who were those guys back there? The ones the rev made spare parts from. Just some random overworld crazies?" she asked.

"No. They were with the slavers. I recognized them from earlier when they took the kids," Zade said, a dark expression shadowing his face.

Aishena asked, "But why were they there? Do you think the rev attacked their group and they stayed behind while the others got away?"

Riony shuddered. If so, they must have been so close to catching up. The kids could have been just ahead of them. And now they were offtrack.

Yoskar shook his head. "The positioning of the event was the ideal location for an ambush."

Riony just stared at him.

"You didn't notice? Of course not. Just rushed right in without a clue."

"I noticed," Aishena muttered.

"Shut up. No, you didn't," Riony muttered back.

Yoskar sighed in a deliberate display of unsurprised disappointment. "I expect those three slavers were waiting there for us."

"An ambush? Why?" Zade asked.

Yoskar shrugged. "Probably a tail guard, left to take out anyone trailing them, just in case. That would be a clever tactic. Then they just got unlucky when the rev found them first."

The mention of the creature had them all turning to watch as it continued to tirelessly test the boundaries. It hadn't slowed its thrashing, ravenous attack at all.

"Did you see how strange it was?" Aishena asked softly. "Charred and ashy, even before I struck it with a burn athame."

The abnormal revenant growled at them from the growing shadows, its remaining arm beating and clawing at the air.

Riony remembered the puffs of soot that flew from it each time she struck with her sword. She'd assumed back then that it had just gotten dirty, rolling about in the charcoal-covered forests. Sparks, she didn't know what revs did in their spare time. She was pretty sure they didn't bathe though.

If it had been covered in that flaking soot for another reason though, a reason like maybe it had been burned already ... Riony shuddered at the implications, a brisk chill blowing through her that seemed to come from within.

Chapter Fifteen

There was something strange about this place. A zing of energy was building and thrumming under Riony's skin. She blew it off as caused by the stress of their mission to retrieve the children and the fear of the revenant still patrolling the invisible border between the standing stones that kept it from its human prey.

No matter what she felt about this place, it was where they had to rest.

Nocturnal birds chorused the fall of night, cooing eerily through the woods around the Alderkin ruins. Twisted and gnarled branches seemed to move of their own accord, as if alive and watching the intruders closely. The forest felt old and primal, a place where the shadows and the spirits of the dead still roamed. At least one still did.

Within the ruins, the once-grand entrance to the building beside them was now a gaping hole, covered in vines that obscured the way in. Riony poked her head through for a look.

The temple's interior was dark and silent. One standing stone stood within it, formed from a thick slice of an immense sparkling geode. Alderkin runes that Riony had never seen before marked around the edges. Elegantly carved reliefs of unicorns on the walls were obscured by lichen and moss, making the depicted creatures look ill and mangy.

The ceiling had caved in at the far end, taking part of the wall with it. Otherwise, the temple interior was bare, looted long ago.

It would be warmer and more sheltered in there than camping beside the exterior wall. But through some unspoken agreement, everyone settled for the night outside.

Yoskar quickly got to work on a campfire, breaking dead sticks into a pile on the uneven paving. Aishena remained leaning on the wall, hands still tight around her athames and eyes on the revenant.

Zade put his hands on his hips, taking in their campsite as flames licked to life, brightening everything with an orange glow. "No way. No way! Do you all see what I'm seeing?"

Riony had just begun unloading her bags and quickly reached for her sword again.

But Zade's face cracked into a wide grin, and he jogged over to a small tree tucked in beside the wall of the shrine. "Apples!" he shouted, far too loud for common sense.

"Apples?" Riony froze, dumfounded.

She didn't believe it as Zade reached into the foliage and plucked a round red fruit into his hand, holding it up for them to see.

"No way," Riony echoed. Her mouth flooded with saliva at the memory of their taste. She rushed over, and Zade tossed the apple to her. Bringing it to her nose, she breathed the sweet perfume in deeply.

"I can't even remember the last time I had fresh fruit of any kind!" Dried fruit was the main trade from aboveground that irregularly made it into the undercity, and even then,

Riony couldn't often afford it.

She cast her eyes over the branches, counting quickly. Most of the apples were ripe, or ripe enough she'd eat them anyway, and there had to be at least a dozen. She almost snatched at them with both hands at once, but quickly stilled her right arm.

It's broken, remember? As far as everyone else knows, anyway.

Zade laughed as he raced to pick the rest himself, gathering apples into the scooped-up hem of his shirt. Riony smirked back at him, leveraging her height to snap up a bigger harvest.

"I don't see what all the fuss is about," Aishena scoffed, glaring hard at Zade. "I had apples only a few months ago."

Riony cradled her bounty as she went back where she had left her netted bag next to the now roaring fire. "You don't want any of these, then?"

Pouting, Aishena limped from her position at the wall over to the fire as well, taking a seat on a chunk of toppled pillar. "I didn't say that."

Riony sat cross-legged on the ground, rolling the apples from her arms into her lap. She longingly stared at her treasure of ruby delights.

As much as she wanted to, she couldn't withhold them from the delver. Aishena hadn't hesitated to give her that much wealth and more to buy supplies with before they left. Even if it was probably pocket change to the delver.

She picked two apples and lobbed them over to Aishena, who caught them deftly as though snatching arrows from the air. Aishena nodded a stoic thanks. Zade, still grinning, handed a couple of his collection to Yoskar, then the two of them took seats around the fire as well.

Riony slipped out of her backpack straps and let it down gently onto the ground behind her, keeping it obscured by her body and cloak in case of movement from within. Then she picked the ripest of the apples and brought it to her lips.

The rush of tart juice and sweet crunch of flesh brought tears to Riony's eyes. It had been years. Her whole body sang with delight at the flavors dancing over her tongue.

As she savored each bite, she thought of Lyrrin. It seemed wrong to be experiencing something so blissful while Lyrrin was in danger.

Aishena must have felt a similar way, as she nibbled on the fruit with a dull expression, punctuated by soft, gruff sighs.

"We're going to get the kids back." A steel-hard determination settled over Riony. She knew what she was saying had to be true, because she knew she wouldn't stop until it was.

She picked up her remaining few apples, holding them in front of her. "And we can share the rest of the fruit with them when we do."

So they didn't get bruised in amongst her other supplies in the netted bag, Riony put the fruit away into a pouch on her belt. She couldn't put them in her backpack; the cave otter would surely demolish them. The backpack was just for animals now.

Riony remembered the out-of-charge athame she'd picked up on her trip out to the mountains. She never had a chance to show it to Lyrrin before. It must still be tucked away in her backpack, under the blanket cushioning the unidragon.

Another present for Lyrrin when I get her back, she thought, and returned to finishing the apple.

Nobody replied to her proclamation, but she noticed Aishena stash away one of her apples as well.

Zade smiled softly, his tumbling hair glowing in the light of the flames. "I used to live right beside a whole apple orchard once, just outside Tjollaskeep."

"Not far from here then. How long have you been underground?" Yoskar asked.

Zade shrugged. "A couple of years? I haven't really counted. It's not the sort of anniversary I like to celebrate."

Riony grunted an agreement around her full mouth.

"But my family, we were farmers before that. Hard work, but not as hard as it's been since. Not as hard as the kids in the orphans' den have it."

Riony paused her chewing and tilted her head toward him. "It's good of you, how you look after them."

She felt bad that she hadn't done more herself but found raising even one child to meet her capacity.

Zade beamed, and he looked back at Riony in a way that would probably have melted the right girl's heart. "Thanks. I'm proud of how I've been able to help the kids. I'm glad you can see how important what I do is."

"Real savior, aren't you?" Aishena rolled her eyes. "You don't know hard work until you've been a delver."

"Is that an invitation?" Riony replied. "Because I accept."

With a huff, Aishena threw the core of her apple at the roaming revenant. It snarled from the shadows beyond the glow of the fire.

"Wasteful." Riony clung to the remains of her apple, nibbling away until she'd eaten everything but the seeds. She shuffled around, stretching her legs out in front of her with her legs splayed out wide, letting the worn muscles rest and enjoying the coolness of the stone beneath her.

Zade stared at the revenant warily, as though the lobbed food scraps would be the thing that taunted it into breaking through the invisible barrier. When it still didn't approach, he turned his attention to Riony again.

"How about you? Been underground long?"

"Not long enough to forget what being a slave feels like," Riony replied and spat her final apple seed into the dirt.

"I'm sorry."

Riony sniffed, then smirked the pity away. "Weren't you a slave too, just on a farm?"

"I suppose. I guess it never felt like that though. I mean, the farm was owned by dragonlord masters, but we had a decent life. Hard work but satisfying. And they protected us from the revs."

A bitter, vicious edge twisted Riony's smile. "Of course, they protected you. Have to keep their livestock alive, after all, or who else will do all the hard work for them?"

Zade stiffened, and Riony knew she was going too far. But the threat of Lyrrin falling to that fate of slavery riled up her every nerve.

What if she ended up owned by a family like the Heithorns?

She stared at the dragonlord sword that lay beside her. "Protecting the land is one fine excuse to keep the rest of the population enslaved. To take what they want and kill who they want."

Riony expected Yoskar and Aishena to defend the dragonlord way. She was sure there was dragonlord blood in them. People didn't end up with that silvernix tinted hair from a peasant ancestry. Hair that pale was found most in families who had been exploiting unicorn blood for generations.

They remained quiet, though, staring into the fire with only cursory glances toward the others or between themselves.

It unsettled Riony that Aishena, at least, hadn't bitten back.

"You don't disagree?" she taunted the delver directly.

Aishena caught her eye for a moment before looking back into the fire. She readjusted her sitting position, wincing as she moved her swelling ankle. "We've lost family to dragonlords, too."

Riony drew quiet. Yoskar didn't add any further explanation, just glared at his sister over the flames which lit the glass of his spectacles.

"Your parents?" Riony asked tentatively.

Aishena's lips twitched. "Yeah."

Zade shook his head, turning away to stare at the ground.

Riony kept her eyes on Aishena. The harsh lines of her angular body and sneaky ghoulishness held a deep grief that Riony had never noticed before, beneath the bravado and venom.

"Hey," she called out. "See that purplish-leaved ground cover beside you there?"

Aishena's eyebrows twisted at the odd question.

"A poultice of it will help ease the inflammation on your ankle," Riony finished.

The delver's face remained confused for a moment before it softened. With a sharp nod, she plucked at some leaves and rubbed them softly onto her skin around the top of her boot.

"No, a poultice, a—for the love of stars. Let me show you." Getting to her feet, Riony strode over and knelt in front of Aishena.

The delver balked as Riony took the injured foot onto her lap and worked the boot off, but she didn't pull away or object.

The whole process was slow and clumsy, as Riony had to work with her left hand only. Aishena just stared at her with wide black eyes and darkening cheeks.

Pulling up a big handful of the wine-tinted foliage, Riony worked it between her palm and a stone paver beside her until the membranes broke down and it mashed into a soggy pulp.

"Like this," she said and gently applied it in a thick layer all around the ankle. "We just need something to keep it in place."

Still kneeling, Riony straightened up and ripped at the lower hem of her shirt, pulling a strip off right around the bottom. The removed length left more than a little of her stomach showing.

As she bent to tie the makeshift bandages, Aishena muttered, "You did that on purpose to show off your abs, didn't you? Just like you wander around the undercity in that ridiculous sleeveless tunic all the time. Can't resist showing off your muscles."

"Aw, you noticed!"

"That's not ... I ..." Aishena punctuated her stuttering with a grunt.

Behind Riony, the other two had begun laying out blankets for their bedding.

Then Zade called out, "Um, Riony? What's in your backpack?"

Oh sparks.

Riony spun around. Her abandoned pack wriggled on the ground where she'd left it.

Closing her eyes for a second, Riony took a deep breath, then strolled over to the bag. She knew she couldn't keep her secret for long.

"It's just one of Lyrrin's pets." Untying the pack, she reached in and grabbed the wriggling cave otter firmly from the scruff of its neck. She pulled it just close enough to the bag opening for the others to see.

There was no way she could keep a live animal hidden in her bag for long. That's why she brought along two. Sir Butterfur made the perfect decoy.

"That's what you had in there all along?" Yoskar raised his eyebrows.

"Why," Aishena said, more a mocking statement than question.

"Because I wanted at least one thing around here who appreciates me." Riony pushed the wriggling sausage of fur back into the bag and closed it up again.

Aishena's eyes turned to the poultice on her ankle. "You aren't ... unappreciated."

"Oh really?" Riony perked up. She held out her arm, displaying the mess of coagulating blood around the rev's claw marks. "Don't suppose you want to return the favor, then? You could come over and tenderly tend to my wound. Maybe we could even go and tenderly tend a bit more of each other over in a dark corner of the shrine there."

Riony jiggled her eyebrows up and down and tipped her head toward the empty structure.

Aishena's face scrunched. "Why are you *like this*?"

Riony shrugged. "Why are you *not* like this?"

Yoskar pinched the bridge of his nose and turned away.

"So, that's a no, then?" Riony asked. Without waiting for a reply, she picked up her backpack and netted bag in the same hand.

"Where are you going?" Zade asked, looking to get up from his blanket and follow.

Riony offered a wicked smirk. "I'm not going far. Just going to find a bit of privacy to go and tenderly tend to myself. Unless there are any takers? No? No? No? Okay, good night."

Swaggering away, Riony breathed out a sigh when nobody attempted to follow her through the entrance of the shrine. Her heart was racing.

She hadn't felt anything from the unidragon for a while now. No sensations of hunger. Even pulling the otter in and out of the bag hadn't disturbed it. *Please still be alive, little one.*

The interior of the shrine wasn't very large, and most of the rear end of the room had collapsed in, leaving a gaping hole to the night sky above and mess of crystal and stone piled on the ground.

Riony was happy not to venture any farther and tucked herself into the corner right near the doorway.

Activating her light crystal, Riony quickly dug through her supplies to retrieve a large piece of shroom jerky. Opening the pack again, she thrust it into the face of the ready-to-escape otter.

The silky-furred critter took a moment to rethink its plan, then grabbed the food and burrowed deep into the backpack. It pushed around the body of the dragonling, and Riony peered in, desperate for signs of life.

Jostled by the otter, the newborn weakly opened its eyes.

"Hey, hey there, little one," Riony whispered soft as a breath. She scooted down onto her side, holding the pack open close to her face. "I'm so sorry. I'm sorry I've been shaking you all about and haven't had a chance to feed you. We've got time now."

Sorting through her netted bag, Riony retrieved the skin of goatmilk first. The unidragon had drunk some liquid before, so she hoped this might sustain it.

But when presented with a corner of cloth soaked in the milk, the baby turned its snout away.

"No? You don't do milk?"

She tried goat jerky again. Surely it must eat meat. She took a big bite herself, chewing as she waved the remainder in front of the dragonling's nose.

Hungry. It looked at her with a pitiful sniffle.

Riony's heart twanged like a plucked bowstring. She tried some of everything she had to offer.

It took nothing more than a few suckles of water, dripped from a flask over her fingers.

In between trying to get the unidragon to eat, Riony gave her arm a swift wipe down and tied one strip of cloth around the deep scratches, tightening the knot with her teeth. In desperation, she even offered the rag with her blood on it to the hungry critter, but it didn't take it.

The otter poked its snout back out, trying to snatch at the tiny banquet laid out on the ground.

"Quit it, Sir Furrybutt Whatever-your-name-is." Riony tossed it some more food to keep it out of the way. "How does a rodent like you get knighted anyway?"

How was Lyrrin so good at this? She'd managed to bring in and keep alive all sorts of creatures, and there Riony was, failing at feeding the one most precious creature of all.

Heat burned in the back of Riony's eyes. She only knew one thing Lyrrin would do.

"Hey, little one. We're going to name you, okay?"

It blinked milky, translucent eyelids over its large lilac eyes.

"Little bit dragon, little bit unicorn. Okay, then. How about Dracuni?"

She reached out a hand, and the newborn nuzzled against it.

"Yeah. That's it. You're Dracuni. You know what that means right?" Riony settled down, curling protectively around the backpack and the delicate life inside.

"I've named you now. That means you aren't allowed to die on me."

Chapter Sixteen

The ground was hard and cold and Riony's restless mind swirled with worry.

She worried that Dracuni was fading from starvation before her eyes.

She worried that a lack of sleep would make her falter tomorrow and fail to save Lyrrin.

She worried that the revenant who continued to growl and pace too close for comfort would suddenly burst through into the shrine and devour them all.

How could anyone sleep through that?

She hoped Lyrrin was able to get some rest. That she and the other children were at least being kept safe and alive by their captors. She figured they would be, for the most part. The children were a valuable commodity for the slavers.

But Riony also had enough experience with people who treated other humans as a commodity to know that they didn't mind a little wastage.

Keep your head down, Lyrrin. Don't let them see you marking the trail. And try to sleep. You get super cranky when you don't sleep.

Riony sent her thoughts out into the dark night, as though she could connect with Lyrrin's mind the way Dracuni seemed to connect with her own.

That was unlikely. Riony had to console herself in the knowledge that Lyrrin was a tough kid. Lyrrin's mother had been strong, too. Riony knew that from being at the birth.

Riony had been Riony Uf'Heithorn, slave and whipping-girl to Kess, for years when Lyrrin's mother came to the Heithorn estate.

She and Kess had watched through a high window as the elegant, determined young woman arrived by dragon, along with her mother and a dragonguard big enough that he could have been a dragon himself.

The woman had the whitest hair she'd ever seen, a slight bulge to her stomach, and a steely look of defiance that glared down on every command she was given by her mother even as she followed them. Riony had never crushed so hard and fast on anyone before the way she did on that bold young woman.

She projected an instant kinship with her from that feeling, that rebellion in the face of obedience. She tried out mimicking the young woman's insolent expression that afternoon and got an extra-long whipping in return.

That evening, Riony had returned to the servants' quarters, to the small room her family shared, as she did each day after her duties with Kess. And she begged her parents to take her and run away from that place, as she did each day after her time with Kess.

And just like each day, her amma and pabba said no. The Heithorns weren't kind masters, but the world outside their protection would be even crueler.

"It couldn't be worse than this," Riony moaned as her mother applied an herbal ointment to the fresh wounds on her back.

Pabba had only just returned from his work in the fields and kicked his dirty boots off at the door. "You only say that because you've only ever lived under the protection of dragonlords."

Amma tsked. "I'm so sorry that spoiled child treats you this way. I know she has troubles of her own, but she's a right monster. We will get you out from under her control, one day. Your midwife training will continue, and soon our masters will see you are more valuable used elsewhere."

A scowl and pout were the politest things Riony could offer in reply.

"Did you see the young woman that came in today?" Pabba asked. He pulled up a simple, wobbly wooden stool beside where Riony leaned over the table.

Riony blushed. "Yeah?"

"She's come all the way from Draekhanhelm—"

"The capitol?" Riony perked up.

"Yup. All the way here to give birth because the Heithorns have such an excellent midwife on staff."

Amma smirked. "That's me, by the way."

"She's pregnant?" Riony sat up, mind taken off the stinging welts on her back. She pulled her shirt back down, feeling it stick to the wet ointment.

"A few months off the birth still. But I've already asked if they will allow you to be my assistant when the time comes." Amma wiped her hands clean, working the rag over the four plain steel rings she wore across her fingers.

"You think I'm ready to be at a birth?" Riony wasn't so sure, already cringing away from the idea based on just the knowledge and theory she'd been taught about the process. Plus, she was only ten, younger than others her amma had trained when they had started assisting in births.

Amma ruffled her hair. "We'll make sure you're ready, and we'll show them that's the place you deserve to be. A respected midwife, not a plaything to a monster in girl's clothing."

It was that hope alone that got Riony through the coming months. She was always on the lookout for the beautiful moonlight-haired woman. The mother-to-be roamed around the estate often, shadowed by her mother and mountainous dragonrider bodyguard. Riony kept her eyes on the woman's growing belly, counting the days.

Nobody seemed to know who the young woman was or spoke of her by name. She was simply referred to by all as "the guest." There was an air of secrecy around her entire existence that thrilled Riony, as though most of the estate pretended she wasn't even there.

The birth came early. And went long.

Riony wasn't sure she helped very much, but she followed all her mother's orders with all the speed and precision a ten-year-old in a highly stressful environment could.

The guest's mother paced around the birthing chamber the entire time, wringing her hands. The beast of a bodyguard had been left in the adjoining entry room just outside.

Hours and hours passed, intermittent with bursts of frantic efforts and periods of waiting with nothing to be done but listen to the guest's wailing screams.

Every time the young mother seemed to have been pushed beyond her limits, every time she seemed to wane and faint, she would come back, drawing again on some unknown reservoir of power. Riony was shaken with awe at her strength.

All through one long night the labor continued.

With one final push, Amma announced the babe born.

"Her color. I'm not sure she's breathing," she said softly to Riony as they worked together to cut the cord.

"What is it? What's happening?" the guest asked feebly.

"Let me see," the guest's mother barged in between them as Amma briskly rubbed the newborn down.

Riony gasped. "Look, she breathes!"

Amma lifted the infant, preparing to hand her to the sobbing mother, when the older woman snapped. "Bring it in here!"

Confused for a moment, Amma watched as the older woman headed over to the entrance chamber. With a frown, she quickly swaddled the newborn and carried her along as she followed, beckoning Riony after her.

They stepped out into the small adjoining chamber that led into the birthing room. The burly guard waiting there eyed their appearance, but his only acknowledgement was the twitch of his nose.

Riony hadn't been this close to him before. He looked like he crushed tree trunks between his thighs for fun. Like he could barely fit through a doorway without grazing his biceps. Riony glanced down at the small bumps of muscle on her own arms, aspiring to be that strong one day.

A small table stood in the center of the space, meant to hold gifts to mothers and their newborns, laid out as the woman was in labor. As the guest didn't seem to know anybody at the estate, there was only one small flower decorating the table surface.

The old woman tossed it aside. "Show me the baby."

Amma laid the swaddled newborn on the table. "Oh, she's still a bit blue. But I'm sure she'll be all right soon."

Amma frowned as she wiped at the infant's scalp. White mucus cleared away, but the blue coloring remained.

With very little care, the older woman unwrapped the newborn, leaving her cold and bare on the table. The baby squinted at her with the brightest blue eyes Riony had ever seen. Her tiny mouth opened, but she didn't cry.

"It's her hair," Riony said in amazement. "The blue color is hair."

The older woman sucked in a sharp breath and grabbed the baby's arms, inspecting the hands. Fingers so small that Riony could barely believe they were real were closed in tight fists. There was a blue tinge to the skin there too, and when the older woman forced the hands open, she gasped.

"Was silvernix used?" Amma asked softly. "Any time during the pregnancy?"

The older woman said nothing. She backed away from the table, her chin lifted and a hard expression growing.

Riony reached out, touching the newborn's strange hand. The baby wrapped her fingers in a strong grip around her finger. "Still, she's healthy. Especially for an early birth, right, Amma?"

The older woman shook her head and turned from them, speaking to the guard. "Dispose of the newborn. It can't be allowed to live."

Riony's eyes shot wide-open and she stepped in front of the table. "No! You can't kill a baby!"

Amma moved beside her, clutching her arm and trying to pull her away, hissing under her breath.

The older woman threw a disdainful look back toward them. "The witnesses too. Get rid of all of them."

The guard gave a rough grunt of agreement and drew his sword. The older woman left, returning to the birthing chamber. Riony could hear the young mother inside, questioning in a weak voice.

"Your child didn't make it. And I'm cleaning up the other loose ends of this mess for you."

A wail and weeping followed that clawed into Riony's soul, only distracted by the glint of the sword that approached, ready to end her life and her mother's and that of the tiny, special little being that had only just taken her first breaths.

"Please, please just let us go. We won't tell anybody anything," Amma pleaded with the massive man. She still clung to Riony, trying to drag her away from the protective position she'd taken in front of the newborn.

A deep animal snarl built in Riony's throat. She set her stance, refusing to move. It wasn't fair! They couldn't just kill the baby. She didn't want to die either, but she wasn't going to try to trade her life for another.

From the lazy smile and sickening look of pleasure in the man's eyes, Riony doubted he'd take any trade anyway. He seemed excited by the very concept of hacking down three defenseless victims.

A fire of defiance flared over Riony. She snatched her arm free from her mother and launched herself in a flurry of fists and teeth at the man. She wrapped her whole body around one of his arms, flailing and fighting as hard as she could.

Like a drowning kitten, she was grasped by the scruff of the neck and lifted away. The guard rumbled a harsh laugh as she continued to kick and thrash, futile against limbs that were as thick around as her whole body.

That laugh drove Riony mad. She contorted like a wild animal, and a foot finally connected. The clang of steel followed, the sword knocked free from the man's other meaty hand. With a grunt of annoyance, he dropped Riony as well, as though discarding a soiled washcloth. She landed hard on her knees and collapsed face down on the smooth marble tiles. And right in front of her eyes lay the sword.

She snatched it with the speed of zinging adrenaline and unsteadily jumped back to her feet. Her hands grasped tight around the pre-warmed hilt and the tip of the blade dragged heavily along the floor.

"What are you going to do with that, little girl?" The guard snuffled and snorted at his own humor as he smirked at her. "As if you're even strong enough to lift—"

The sword tip piercing through his chest left his words unfinished.

Riony had lifted the sword. She had been strong enough. Her hard-worked arms moved fast and she'd thrust the blade deep into the thick bulk of the man before either of them could think any longer on the likelihood of that action.

Riony put *everything* she had into that thrust. Every bit of strength Kess had worked into her, every shred of anger at the scars on her back, every tear shed on hopeless pleas to flee, to try for something more than *this*, every hope and desire that burned in her that she and her amma and the baby would live.

She and the guard stood like that, connected by the sharp line of steel, for a long moment, as though neither of them could believe what had happened. Then the man gurgled. Blood dripped from his lips. His hands shot out weakly, grabbing wildly at the air around the sword as though he couldn't see despite his wide eyes still staring down.

He stilled, then slowly toppled backward. Riony kept hold of the sword, tugging as the suction of his body fought against her. Her hands had locked around the hilt as though nothing could pry them open ever again.

She remained holding that bloodied sword as her amma tried to drag her away. As she was scolded for what she'd done, in a voice that held pride and fear in equal measure. As she refused to run without taking the newborn with them.

She held that sword as her amma wrapped the baby back up and they all fled together, out through a window and across the fields. As they scurried along the stone walls of paddocks until they found Riony's pabba tilling the earth as the sun rose.

He took the hoe in his hands and the sack that held his lunch and nothing more. Riony still grasped the dragonguard's sword as they left Heithorn estate behind for the undead wastelands beyond.

"That's how I ended up with a sister," Riony whispered to Dracuni, who whimpered soft sleepy sounds from within the backpack.

And now I have you, too.

Taking Lyrrin had been easier than taking Dracuni, in some ways. Riony still had her parents back then. They knew how to care for a newborn, and Lyrrin was a good baby, a quiet baby, who didn't cry once as their family hid under trees from the hunt of dragonguards sent out to retrieve them.

Amma knew how to feed Lyrrin, clean her, settle her to sleep. Riony learned over time, too, and helped as much as she could. She did, after all, feel somewhat as though Lyrrin were *hers*. Her decision to take. Her responsibility. Now Riony was alone, and none of her midwife training could have prepared her for this. Another newborn taken. Another responsibility so immense it felt like it could crush her. Now two lives depended upon Riony, and all she could think was that she was failing them both.

Chapter Seventeen

Riony groaned and shifted, her body bruised by the hard ground beneath her. She opened her eyes and blinked. A dim light filtered in through the gaping hole across the shrine.

The night had been spent not so much in sleep, as in simply waiting for morning to arrive. Riony decided that anemic glow was morning enough. She stretched out her whole body, then rolled over onto her stomach, pressing into a quick set of push-ups, as she normally started her days.

Once her body had built up a warm flush, she stopped and checked on Dracuni and Butterfur, offering them both some food—taken greedily by the otter and ignored by the dragonling.

Riony chewed ravenously on some dry cheese herself as she stepped out from the ruined shrine to see the other three already awake as well. They all looked like they had about as much sleep as she had.

Yoskar kicked out the remains of last night's fire, and Zade sat off to the side, a troubled expression in his gaze as he stared out into the forest.

"Morning," he said when he noticed Riony join them. The bruise the slavers had given him had settled in, dark purple around the bridge of his nose and yellow along his bottom eyelids, making his blue eyes seem a sickly gray.

"Where's our new friend?" Riony asked, scanning around the perimeter of the standing stones.

"We lost track of the rev sometime during the night. One minute it was there, then it was gone." Aishena stalked around the campsite like a cornered beast, collecting scattered supplies and checking her weapons. Her gait was uneven but steady. Her injured ankle was taking weight.

That was good news, at least. Riony wasn't sure about the rev though.

"Does anyone find it creepier that it left than if it had stayed?" she asked. "What is a rev leaving to do? What pressing business did it have that was better than waiting to chew on our tasty flesh?"

"Doesn't matter," Yoskar said. He strapped his pack closed, then hoisted it onto his back. "We should move on before it decides to come back."

Riony nodded, her nerves all sharp and jangly within from worry and lack of sleep. She ducked back into the shrine for her netted bag and pack and threw her cloak over the top. Stepping back out again, the others were all similarly loaded up and ready to go.

"What's the plan? Which way do we take from here?" she asked. They could go back the way they came and try to pick up the trail again from there, but that was a long way up a steep and slippery slope.

Riony looked to Aishena for an answer, but she only stood at attention and waited for Yoskar to speak.

Yoskar held out both arms at a right angle. "That direction"—he pointed with his left hand—"is where the rev ambushed the slavers and we went offtrack. If we extrapolate that path farther north, we'd end up crossing the low peaks that were in this direction." He pointed with his right hand.

Riony put her hands on her hips. "Extrapolate my ass. Your best plan is to aim yourself at a whole mountain range and hope for the best? How are we going to actually find them if we don't find any markers again?"

Zade squinted at where Yoskar pointed, as though he could see the mountains through the dense forest. "Stonewing Crest is that way. It's a bit of a climb, but there's a good view over the rest of the area from up there. We'll be able to get our bearings and hopefully even see some sign of the slavers."

"Aboveground expert all of a sudden, are we?" Aishena scowled.

"At least he's helping. And that sounds promising." Riony flexed her feet, ready to move. She liked the idea of being able to look down on the land and spot her sister. She longed for any way to see her again.

Riony gave Aishena and her ankle an evaluating look. "Are we all ready?"

With an awkward twitch of her lips, Aishena said, "I'll keep up. The poultice helped."

A smile broke on Zade's face. "Wonderful! Look at us, sticking together. We're going to make it."

His optimism did little to scratch the surface of fatigue and worry amongst the others.

All four of them were on high alert as they stepped out from the ring of crystalline standing stones. Nothing burst out from the tangle of trees at them, so they picked up the pace, eying the surrounding woods warily as they alternated between a swift march and a jog as the terrain allowed.

As the tree trunks thinned, the ground sloped upward again, and soon they broke out from the forest and onto an incline of wind-battered grasses and rubbly stones.

Still, there was no sign of the revenant. That left a cold jellylike feeling in Riony's stomach, as though the odd, ashy creature might jump out at them again at any moment. *Why hadn't it died when it was burned?* None of them seemed to want to mention it, discuss it, or even think about it.

It was probably just a fluke anyway. Aishena's burn athame might have been faulty or something. Too low on charge. Riony didn't know, but she knew revs died when you burned them so something else must have gone wrong this one time.

Larger outcrops of rock jutted out from the earth like teeth, and their path soon became a trial of finding their way around the large stones and climbing the low cliffs and overhangs they formed.

Riony's legs burned and sweat dripped down between her shoulders and her pack. She chewed on her lip as they walked, but Zade kept by her side, offering her reassurance whenever a frown overcame her face. Somehow, he seemed so certain they would find the kids again, and that sure hope kept Riony going.

He kept them on track, pointing upward to a high peak ahead. The ground grew treacherous as they went higher. Sheer drops and gaping crevasses shot through the steep mountain, causing the group to zigzag around them.

A shadow passed over Riony, making her flinch. A carrion hawk circled overhead on vast wings. Not quite as big as a dragon, but a healthy size, grown large from plenty of options to scavenge in this land of death. Riony chased away thoughts of the creature picking at her bones. She never liked birds.

As they edged along a narrow path, Riony looked over the drop and gulped. It had not been nearly long enough since the last time she'd fallen down into a deep hole and wasn't nearly prepared to do so again.

Not to suggest I would ever be prepared to do that again. It would take wild and impossible conditions to even consider it, like if throwing myself into a pit would get Aishena to date me.

The delvers didn't appear to care about the risk of falling or the strain on their muscles, setting a fast pace that Riony matched. Zade had more obvious signs of struggling but didn't slow them down. A couple of times Riony reached her hand to him to help drag him up a steeper bluff, and he'd offer a beaming smile in return.

Once, she reached her good hand to Aishena and was surprised when the delver took it. Riony quickly ruined the moment by winking and jiggling her eyebrows at her, making Aishena scowl and storm ahead.

After what felt like hours, they finally reached a large, flat outcrop that jutted out into the air. Surrounded by gorges on most sides, it looked out over lower peaks and a valley beyond. The view was clear right out to the east and north horizons.

Riony stepped up to the sheer drop and took in the view, scanning the landscape hungrily for any sign of their target. Aishena moved beside her, shading her eyes against the sun and peering out as well. Zade remained a few steps behind them, catching his breath, drinking from a waterskin and rummaging around in his pack.

The forest stretched out beneath Riony like a green carpet, and in the distance, she could see the glimmer of a river. Beside that river, a line of smoke slithered like a silver serpent up into the sky.

"There," she gasped out the word, her lungs still heaving from the climb.

Yoskar reached behind himself, pulling free the crystal-studded staff he carried. Holding it before him, he traced a rune on a smoky stone near the top. With a soft crackle of magic, the crystal cleared to a shimmering transparent glass. He held it to his eye and looked toward the smoke.

Riony stepped closer, hoping to work out what he was seeing. She didn't even know quite what he was doing, angling the staff around and staring through that cleared stone. Light glinted in the corner of her eye.

She hadn't seen an Alderkin artifact like that before but wasn't surprised the delvers were keeping all the best stuff to themselves.

"It's them," Yoskar said.

"Can I have a look?" Riony asked.

"No." Yoskar set the staff back down, holding it like a walking stick as he deactivated the rune. "Seems like a more permanent camp, defensive palisades, larger tents. And cages. Cages with kids in them."

Riony shivered, the sweat on her skin chilling as her body cooled and a wind blew over her. "Even if the new lot of kids they took isn't there yet, that's probably where they are going, right? But how many slavers are there? How are we going to go up against them?"

"We can work that out when we get a closer look. If we hurry, maybe we'll catch up to Benjin still along the way. And Lyrrin," Aishena added.

"Move now, think later. Easy. My usual plan, honestly," Riony said.

They turned back as Zade was packing his waterskin away, face still flushed from the hike.

"You okay?" Riony asked.

"Yeah. You all are so fast though. I'll do my best to keep up. We're close now, we can do this."

Riony found herself smiling in return.

There was a clearer path leading north, as though sometime in the past this had been a passage regularly taken by travelers, until people stopped traveling overland as much. It led them from the lookout toward a gaping gorge, strung across by a ratty-looking rope bridge.

Riony poked her toes at the first plank. "That looks like a whole bunch of *nope*, held together by dust and cobwebs."

"It's the fastest route," Yoskar said.

Aishena pushed Riony out of the way. "We can secure it with our ropes if you're too scared of something delvers deal with all the time. Feels sturdy enough to me."

Spurred by a surge of competitive spite, Riony was about to fight Aishena back for the chance to be the first to plunge into oblivion, when movement across the gorge caught her attention.

From behind a boulder, a large charcoal-colored wolf emerged. It strode on silent paws to the other side of the bridge, Kess perched on its back like a mangy gargoyle.

Riony's whole body went rigid.

"Is that ...?" Aishena peered with confused eyes across the gap.

Riony muttered, "One of the world's cruelest and most vicious creatures, riding on a wolf? Yup."

"Little Kessara Heithorn?" Yoksar finished his sister's sentence loud enough to echo across the gorge.

Even from a distance, the snarl on Kess's lips was clear. The midafternoon sun glinted off her bared teeth.

"You guys know each other?" Riony stepped back, eying the delver siblings. She'd never seen them on Heithorn estate, but there had been the odd occasion that Kess was taken away to a dragonkeep for some purpose or another.

But only very rarely. Her parents generally avoided revealing her to their noble peers unless forced to.

"Look who we've found," she drawled.

"Sorry, who is this?" Zade asked.

There was something decidedly more feral about this Kess than the one Riony had once known, and it wasn't just the fact that she was riding on a wolf.

Kess had always been on the smaller side, but now she was both small and sharp, all wiry arms and razor cheekbones and pointy chin. Her storm-gray hair was half-bundled on her head in a matted mess of unkempt braids and half-draping down in tangled locks, wilder than the creature she rode.

Just one streak of white marked the front of her tresses, evidence of the wealth of silvernix that had once been spent on her.

Back at Heithorn Castle, braiding Kess's hair had been one of Riony's duties. It looked like she didn't have anyone to do that for her anymore.

"What are you doing out here?" Yoskar called across the bridge, ignoring Riony's question. "What are you doing *on a wolf*?"

"Could ask you two the same thing." Kess and her wolf approached the other end of the bridge but didn't step onto it.

Riony cupped her hands around her mouth and yelled back, "They aren't on wolves, you unfortunate accident of meat and emotions!"

Zade snorted.

Riony had been lying in a rapidly chilling pool of her own blood the last time Kess crossed her path. That had made it hard to get some appropriately scathing digs in at an abusive master that wasn't her master anymore. She fully intended on catching up.

She moved to the front of her group, standing right at the edge of the bridge, hoping Kess would cross it so she could catch the wolf-rider's face with her fist a few times too.

Kess leaned forward and patted the wolf on its jowls. "Griskin here caught wind of a familiar scent, something interesting he wouldn't let me ignore. Didn't think it would be you. Not since your organs were more outside than in when I saw you last in that ice cave. You were as good as dead."

"Wait, wait. You're not suggesting your wolf can talk, are you?" Riony hollered back. "Is it a language only other dogs can understand?"

Kess stared back dully. "With your lack of functioning brain matter, I wouldn't expect you to understand anything."

"I understood your mother's body pretty well last time I saw her!"

Yoskar grabbed Riony's shoulder and turned her toward him. "When were you dying?"

Riony winced and tried replying with just an innocent grin and shrug.

Kess said, "That dragon mother she messed around with ripped her all to shreds. You can imagine my surprise that she's up and walking around."

Zade held up his hands. "Hang on, dragon mother? Ice cave? Internal organs on the outside? What has been going on?"

"After ..." Aishena's face paled. She turned to Yoskar. "We must have missed it by moments. That dragon could have gotten us, too."

"Ah, you were the other two intolerable wastes who were there as well. Pony's keeping secrets from you too? Something let her walk out of that ice cave. Something that left her without a scratch."

"Your arm?" Aishena stared at the bandaged right arm that Riony still had up near her face.

"Um, whoops?" Riony said, waving back with wriggling fingers and swinging the supposedly broken arm back to her side. *Guess that ruse is over.*

"You've been pretending *this whole time*?" Aishena spluttered the start of a few more words, as though calculating out the running and climbing and fighting Riony had all done with her left arm only.

"Enough!" Kess cried. She pulled a dagger the length of her forearm and held it threateningly above the rope holding up the bridge. "How did you get out of that cave alive?"

Riony froze. That bridge was her shortest path to reaching Lyrrin. She held her hands up in surrender. But there was no way she was going to surrender the creature in her backpack.

"Kess, don't," Yoskar said. "We need to go that way. Our brother is in trouble. Slavers have him. Her sister, too."

Riony shot him a dark look. She didn't want Kess knowing a thing about Lyrrin.

"Since when do you have a sister?"

"Since I last banged your amma," Riony threw back.

"Would you stop?" Yoskar stepped in front of her and addressed Kess again. "Ignore this oaf and her half-witted insults—"

"Kess is a half-witted insult," Riony said.

Yoskar spoke over her, giving Kess a more reasonable tone than she ever deserved. "You seem to have been aboveground for a while. Help us out. You must know this area better than us. Help us get our brother back, and we'll make it worth your while."

Kess lowered her blade a barely perceptible amount. "You can make it worth my while, by making her answer my question. I want to know how she was healed. A runaway slave like her wouldn't have silvernix. I want to know what it was that helped her walk out of that cave. Then I'll help get you where you need to go."

Riony shot a pleading look at Yoskar. "You can't trust her."

A closemouthed grin grew on Kess's face, and she lowered her dagger entirely.

Yoskar folded his arms. "Tell us. Tell us all how you survived."

"Survived what? Maybe she's the one lying about the whole dragon ripping me up incident."

Aishena stood beside her brother, creating a wall of interrogation. "Even without additional injuries, you've been remarkably healed compared to how you were before."

"Go on, Pony," Kess called.

Riony fingered the hilt of her sword, judging if she could throw it across the gap and skewer Kess to the cliffside instead of being forced to answer. She doubted her aim was that good, though, and didn't want to risk losing her sword into the gorge.

"Fine!" She flung her hands up. "I did have some unicorn blood."

Aishena pouted skeptically.

"*You* had silvernix?" she said, heavy on the *you*.

"Just one little drop. It was a gift to my grandmother for saving her master's wife during childbirth, ages back when silvernix wasn't as scarce. I've just been carrying it around since then, you know, waiting for the right time when all our insides were on the outside."

Everyone stared at her silently, as though trying to judge the likelihood of her statement.

Riony pulled her cloak away to show her bare neck to the delvers. "It was kept hidden in the acorn. That's why it's gone now. I used it."

Exactly *how* she used it, she didn't need to say.

Aishena and Yoskar looked at each other and shrugged.

Riony turned to Kess, who seemed entirely unsatisfied with the answer. "You saw how the dragon left me. How else would I still possibly be alive other than using silvernix? Think I put on a poultice, you abominable, ill-nurtured fart-face?"

"Careful, you'll use up all your big words, Uf'Heithorn."

"I'm not Uf'Heithorn anymore, and never will be again!"

"You two clearly have some history." Yoskar took a step forward onto the bridge. "But we made a deal. Riony gave you an answer. Let's move on, and you can help us find the stolen children."

Kess lifted her dagger. "You think we made a deal? You're almost as tamebrained as Pony."

She brought the blade down, lightning fast over the rope. It sliced straight through. The slackened tension of the bridge creaked and twanged, an explosion of ripples running from Kess's side to theirs.

Then in a sickening slow motion, the whole bridge swung free. Riony lunged forward, grabbing Yoskar and dragging him back onto solid ground as the planks gave way beneath him. They fell in a tangle together in the dust.

Scrambling to her feet, Riony considered again throwing her sword. The bridge clattered against the cliff wall beside her, dust rising and obscuring her view for a moment.

She screamed across the ravine, "There are two things I hate about you, Kess, and it's your face!"

Panic worked her lungs. That bridge was her path to Lyrrin. She growled in frustration as Kess casually rode away.

Chapter Eighteen

Aishena knelt beside Yoskar, fussing over him before he brushed her aside.

"This is your fault!" she snapped at Riony.

"Saving your brother's life? You're welcome." Riony stalked up and down the edge of the gorge, glaring at the other side.

Aishena grabbed her shoulder, forcing her to stop and look at her sour face. "Why did you have to keep goading her? If you'd kept your big mouth shut—"

"She would have done it anyway! That's what Kess does. Given any two choices, she'll always find a third that's even crueler. She was *never* going to help you. Even if there was something in it for her."

Riony turned her face to the gray sky, her neck muscles straining as she wanted to scream and curse with all her might. Only the knowledge that Kess could probably still hear her and take satisfaction from her misery blocked her throat.

Leaving me to die alone was one thing, but if this stunt of Kess's stops me from getting Lyrrin back, I'm going to make it my life's ambition to carve every bit of misery out of that wolf-riding snot-licker as I can.

"If Riony used to be Uf'Heithorn, she probably knows what she's talking about," Zade said gently.

Riony backed that up with a dark glower. "I've got more than enough scars to prove it, if any of you want me to strip off so you can take a look. It might turn into a special moment. I'll see the concern on your lips as you try to stay strong at the pain I must have suffered."

Aishena closed her mouth and stepped back, turning her eyes away.

Yoskar got to his feet and moved to where the bridge had fallen. "Regardless, that was our way forward." He fidgeted with the delicate but strong cave-silk rope coiled at his belt. "It's too far across. Maybe we can tie our ropes together, Aish, but even if we could get a strong hold on the other side, it wouldn't be easy getting across."

"I could climb down, tie a rope to the end of the bridge, then—"

"We'd need both to span the distance. We'd have to get you over to the other side first, then maybe we could try to bring the bridge back up for us."

Yoskar and Aishena huddled together, tossing ideas back and forth.

Riony bounced on her toes, desperate to break into a run. Lyrrin was probably just there, in the valley below. There was no way she could make the jump, but her legs tensed as though they wanted to give it their best shot.

Zade looked up and down the length of the gorge before them with a pained look on his face. "There's another way."

Everyone turned to him, waiting.

"I think I know another path. I used to live near here—"

"Tjollaskeep? It's farther to the east," Yoskar said.

"But I've been through here before, on my way to the undercity the first time. I came in at the bottom of the gorge and had to find a way up. There's a path, farther along that way. It's steep, but it will get us down into the valley in the right direction."

"And you think you can remember the right way?" Aishena's tone suggested she was skeptical about his answer already.

"Yes." Zade's voice was firm and he straightened up to stare her in the eye. "I want to catch up with the kids as much as you do."

"I doubt it," she hissed.

"We all want to get to the kids as fast as we can," Riony said. "You really think you can get us there?"

There was a steely determination in Zade's eyes. "I do."

"Lead the way," Yoskar commanded.

Aishena opened her mouth, but a look from Yoskar silenced her.

Riony gave Zade an encouraging nod, and he turned, moving at a swift jog along the side of the gorge.

They all followed behind, clumped together at first, but soon trailing one at a time as the path narrowed between a cliff on one side and the sheer drop into the canyon on the other. They had to slow down, placing their feet carefully on the unstable stones.

What looked like a dead end approached, but before Riony could question it, Zade took what seemed to be a step off the edge into open air.

He dropped about knee-deep, then stopped and began heading back toward them. Riony leaned over and saw the narrow path, switching back their way, then zigzagging down the cliff face.

Yoskar and Aishena reached out to each other and connected a link between them with a rope. They didn't offer to do so with the others, nor did Riony or Zade have the right connections to hook onto anyway.

Riony would have felt better with something tethering her from slipping down the rough, rocky slope, but she also didn't want to stop long enough to fashion some kind of harness like the delvers had built into their leather armor.

Progress was difficult, with the ledge sometimes becoming so narrow that they had to turn face-first toward the cliff and cling to it as they tiptoed along.

Riony worried they were going too slowly. Too slow to reach Lyrrin in time to save her. Too slow to reach Lyrrin in time so Lyrrin could help save Dracuni. There had been so few pleas of hunger in her mind that morning, and they grew weaker and weaker.

Each time she tried to speed up, the path narrowed again.

Sweat ran down her forehead into her eyes and her heart hammered. And then Zade dropped off the edge in front of her, disappearing from sight.

"Zade!" she cried out.

"Down here," he replied. "We've made it."

Wiping her eyes clear, Riony looked over the end of the ledge, at the ground just a body-length below.

With a huff of relief, she almost leaped the rest of the way as well, but instead turned and lowered herself carefully so as not to jostle Dracuni. The more the newborn could sleep, the more it could conserve its energy until it ate. She didn't worry so much about the cave otter. It had eaten itself into a stupor the night before and would probably sleep through anything.

Landing beside Zade, Riony punched him lightly on the arm. "Don't scare me like that."

He smirked in return. "Didn't think you scared easily."

"Aw, it's like you really know me."

Zade quirked his lips in a half smile at Riony. "Wouldn't mind getting to know you a bit more. Maybe you can tell me all about dragons and ice caves and almost dying once we get where we need to be."

Aishena and Yoskar dropped lightly beside them as one, then unclipped from each other.

Aishena gave Riony an appraising look. "You climb well. You might make a decent delver after all."

That sort of admission from Aishena was as rare as horn ivory. Riony wanted to say something cocky like, *I'd make as good of a delver as I would a lover*, but found instead that she flushed hot from head to toe and had to clear her throat and look away.

"Me too, right?" Zade asked with a wide grin.

Aishena recoiled and shut her mouth tight.

A shallow rocky creek ran along beside them, just a thin trickle of water.

Zade pointed up the length of the gorge the way the water ran. "If we head that way, it should curve around and come out not too far from where we would have been if we took the higher path. Then it's just up the river to the slavers' camp."

Riony's heart kicked up a notch. They were close. So close.

Aishena and Yoskar also seemed to buzz with nervous energy, and nobody said anything else as they broke into a run again.

Hungry. The voice was tiny, fading, barely edging through the pulse beating in Riony's ears.

But she couldn't stop now. Couldn't slow down. Not when the slavers were within sight. Each breath pelted Riony's lungs, and her legs still burned from the climb, but she couldn't—she wouldn't—slow down.

They followed the meager creek until another branched into it, then another. The walls of the gorge shortened from an imposing, claustrophobic height looming over them on both sides, down to a lower ledge, then again to just a pile of boulders and rubble.

Then the land opened out before them in a burned-out meadow. The river ran along their side, and the ground was marshy as they sprinted for the cover of a blackened copse ahead.

The smell of smoke was in the air, but not just normal smoke. Cooking. The char of roasting meat. Riony's stomach clenched, and she felt Dracuni plead with her again.

The proximity to the slaver camp kept them quiet, and they moved through the burnt trunks and rough brush in slow and careful movements. The odd sound of a cracking twig or shift of dirt set Riony on edge, and she shot warning glares to the others to be more careful. Only Aishena managed to remain entirely silent as she treaded the path.

Yoskar took the lead, and as the ramshackle palisades of the camp came into view, he snuck up a low rise around to one side. He motioned to them all to keep down, and they crouched and scurried between scratchy bushes.

They lined up behind a fallen log, and Yoskar put his finger to his lips and pointed over it.

They were high enough there that they could see down into the camp.

Riony popped her head up to look, and Aishena slapped her down.

"You're like a signal fire with that hair!" she whispered and grabbed Riony's hood, pulling it over her head for her.

Sneaking around was more Aishena's thing than Riony's, and she did have a point. Riony muttered a thanks, then looked again.

The palisades barricading the camp were more charcoal than wood. Within them were large tents made of crude leather and thin metal posts. Cheap, scrounged-up materials. Since the dragonforges burned day in and day out, and the dragonriders burned the land, timber was scarcer than steel.

More metal caught Riony's eye, and she spotted two large cages, not far from where a carcass was being turned on a spit over a smoldering fire.

The simple barred cages were packed with children, at least thirty or more crammed into the small space.

Some slavers were bringing a couple of final kids up and loading them in. They must have only just arrived. Riony scanned over the faces.

"Benj," Aishena gasped, pointing to the back corner of the closest cage.

Riony squinted and spotted him too. The ashy-haired boy stood there, his back to another child who was crouched low by the bars and shadowed by a large hood. *Lyrrin!*

Riony's heart was ready to fly out of her throat. Her sister was there, within sight. She just had to get her out, somehow.

Lyrrin seemed to already be working on that. Riony could see the pale ungloved skin of one of her hands, working against the corner bar.

Is she trying to cut through? Riony knew that Lyrrin's nails were sharp. They were sharper and stronger than they had any right to be. But would they be enough to cut through steel?

Riony felt a surge of pride in her sister either way. *Good girl for trying. I'm almost with you. Once I get through those slavers…*

Each tent was big enough to sleep at least five men, and as the sun lowered over the mountains, Riony counted ten milling about, seeing to cooking and chores. Over by the palisade entrance, another seven stood in a group, having some kind of meeting with …

"Sparking *Kess*!" Riony growled.

"What's she doing there?" Yoskar whispered.

"Selling our fine asses out to the enemy, what do you think?"

Zade popped up over the log to look too, silent counting on his lips as he scanned over the number of slavers.

"If she's warning them of our approach, we have to get in there right now before they have any chance to prepare or move on," Yoskar huffed. "It's not ideal, but if we hurry, they may still be distracted by dealing with her. We could head around the back, over there, and—"

A shrill, piercingly loud whistle cut him off.

Riony whipped around to see Zade with two fingers in his mouth. "What in this razed earth are you doing?"

He stood up and took a few steps back from her and the delvers as the bushes around them erupted.

Grizzled, armored men surrounded them, swords and crossbows targeted.

Slavers, all around, and Zade stood beside them.

Chapter Nineteen

"Zade." The word was a low, warning drawl from Riony's mouth. She scrabbled around from where she crouched and reached for her sword, but the closest crossbow shifted her way and she stilled, remaining on her knees. "What have you done?"

Zade offered a gentle smile, tilting his head. "I told you I'd get you to the slavers."

"You ..." Riony couldn't speak around the anger, as though it swelled in her mouth, thickening her tongue. He had. He'd led them all the way. Always helpful, always staying positive. Because he'd always known exactly where he was going the whole time.

A swell of disgust made bile rise up Riony's throat. She couldn't believe she had started to like the traitor, that she'd trusted him. Any fondness was gone now, replaced with seething vengeance.

Yoskar had his head bowed, shaking it as though his own hindsight was catching up to him too.

Aishena growled through gritted teeth. "You creep! You're dead, Zade. Dead."

"Aishena, you had me worried a couple of times. Thought you were onto me. But then I realized you're just naturally unpleasant to everyone." Zade smirked as he looked down at her. "This is for the best. Don't fight. There's no point in getting yourselves hurt."

Riony snarled, "Oh, I could think of a few good points. I can help drive them through your skull if you like."

Zade dared to flash one of his brightest smiles her way, as though they were still friends, joking around.

"All right, all right. Enough of all that." A tall and imposing slaver stepped forward. The man wore ragged hides but moved with the bearing and confidence of royalty. He swaggered up beside Zade and smiled at him, turning his face to reveal a large burn scar around his left eye.

A twinge of recollection shook Riony. She'd seen him before.

Zade's shoulders slumped as though a great tension had been relieved, and he grinned at the man. "Thank the stars you got my signal! Things might have gotten messy if they'd made it into camp."

"Yep, saw you flash us from up on the lookout cliff. Was a little surprised you weren't coming in with Hamric and the others." The slaver looked around, as though the men he mentioned might still be on their way.

"They didn't make it. Rev attack," Zade replied solemnly.

"The ambush?" Riony hissed. Not just a tail guard, after all, but men Zade was supposed to meet with. If it wasn't for that revenant, the slavers might have had her and the delvers captured much sooner.

Riony's body shook. She felt used, tricked, by the revelation she'd walked right along willingly into the slavers' trap.

"Shame. Quite liked that guy. Still, you made it here anyway." The scarred man moved closer to examine the delver brother and sister. He bent down, scratching his stubbly chin as he eyed them. "Yep. I suppose it does look like the ones we're after. Good job."

Zade beamed. "I told you if you took their little brother that would lure the other Hjelzahn siblings out from underground."

Hjelzahn? As in Hjelzahnkeep? If so, they weren't just dragonlords; they were direct descendants of the Dragonking.

Well, that explained their steel-bright hair. No doubt fourth or even fifth generation, but still with their own stars-damned dragonkeep. Riony stared at Aishena with questioning eyes, but Aishena didn't meet her gaze.

"Yeah, it was a good plan, kid." The man slapped Zade on the shoulder.

"You took Benjin on purpose? To get to us?" Aishena's words were thick with venom.

Zade's eyes brightened, as though he was proud of how everything had unfolded so neatly for him. "Your mother has a big bounty out to get her children back. I had wondered whether the missing kids were you lot. I mean, you sort of fit the descriptions and bounty portraits, but I wasn't sure until Benjin went and bragged about it."

"Our mother ...?" Yoskar's voice was shaky and timid. Riony had never seen him like that, normally so stoic and bland. Now, he looked downright terrified.

Zade brushed a bounce of curls away from his face. "I'm just trying to reunite a broken family. I don't know why you two were hiding out, but it wasn't right, taking Benjin with you. He's young and deserves to be with his parents."

Aishena moved in a flash, lunging a couple of steps toward Zade before she was brought to a halt by a wall of sword points.

A bounty set by their mother? Somehow hurt by the revelation of the lie, Riony whispered across to Yoskar. "You said you lost your parents."

He didn't look at her. "We did. We didn't say they were both dead."

Riony muttered in a low tone, "Sure, but you knew that was clearly a misleading use of words—"

"Is this really the time?" Yoskar turned and snapped.

Riony shrugged and rolled her eyes. "I have the capacity to be mad at all of you all at once."

The scarred man grinned at Zade around a mouthful of yellowed teeth. "This is excellent work, kid. Between double the number of kids as usual, and the bounty from the three Hjelzahns, you can buy your way into whatever dragonkeep you want."

Riony jolted at the man's words. *As usual?* You've done this before? Selling children's lives away?"

She suddenly remembered where she'd seen the scarred man before. In the undercity, begging near the orphans' den. Or pretending to beg.

She'd seen him there, the same day she'd broken her arm and found the dragon eggs.

Looking around the rest of the group that had them surrounded, Riony's skin crawled. They were a weathered lot, etched with the scars of countless battles, expressions hardened by the merciless tasks of their trade.

The one with the grizzled red beard and piercing ice-blue eyes, wearing the dinted chest plate. And the woman at the back, with a motherly face and missing front teeth, brown hair hanging in a thick, heavy braid. A scrawny man with frizzy yellow hair that fluffed out around his ruddy copper skin.

Riony had seen them, too. She'd seen those faces before in the undercity.

The slavers had been right there under their noses the whole time.

And Zade, working for them.

"You don't know what you're talking about," Zade shot back. "I'm saving the kids' lives. You know what the conditions in the orphans' den are like. That's no kind of life for children, alone and abandoned. I've been helping smuggle them out to the safety of the cities where they should be."

Riony raised her eyebrows and cooed. "Oh, I'm sorry. I get it now. It's all been done from the goodness of your heart! Not at all for the sweet cut that you're getting on the price of their lives as you sell them off to become slaves."

"Why'd you bring this loudmouth along?" the scarred man grunted.

Zade chuckled wryly. "Hadn't meant to, but her little sister caused a fuss so she got rounded up with the rest of them, and then this one insisted on coming along."

Riony snorted out a puff of anger.

Zade stepped closer to her, and the skin around his eyes wrinkled in concern. "I'm sorry you got caught up in this, Riony. We don't have to be enemies. We could use someone strong like you on our side. I thought we were getting along really well."

"Yeah, that was before I found out you were the disgusting creep Aishena said you were."

"We can work this out. I can help make sure you end up somewhere good, maybe even somewhere together."

Riony squinted at the sky, shaking her head. "Yeah, that'd be real nice. It would give me the opportunity to remove your head from your shoulders."

Zade smirked, still for some reason thinking she was joking. He reached out to her where she knelt. "Come on, this is your chance to do something more than hide like a rat underground. We'd make a great team."

Riony cringed back from his offered hand. "Yuck."

Zade's face twisted, finally catching up that she wasn't being flirty with her threats. "You're really going to turn down the chance for you and your sister to live comfortably in the safety of a dragonkeep? The bounty on the Hjelzahn children is enough to make all of us rich."

Riony stared at the sky again and sniffed. "Well, good luck spending your bounty, because we're all going to be dead when that shadowdragon comes down to rest here."

A few of the slavers jerked their eyes upward.

Riony scooped up a handful of ashy dirt and threw it in the face of the men closest to her, then threw herself at them right afterward.

She didn't even take the time to draw her sword. She just launched herself bodily at the nearest man, bowling him over and taking the slaver beside him with them. She crashed down on all fours on top of them. A crossbow bolt sliced through the air in front of her nose.

Aishena took Riony's cue and didn't hesitate to join the fight. Silver hair flew as she ducked and spun away from the swords pointed at her chest.

With the twitch of a wrist, an athame was activated and flung into the neck of a crossbow wielder. It whistled through, swinging around in a shining blue arc, returning to her waiting hand.

Return rune, Riony thought in awe. *Just how many active athames does that delver carry?*

In the initial burst of surprise, Yoskar stepped forward with his staff, already ablaze from a red burn crystal at the end. He swung it with his thick, powerful arms in a wide arc at the line of swords before them.

Men dodged back, crying out in alarm. Some weren't fast enough. Their swords clattered from their grasps as the tattered fabric of their sleeves lit up in flames.

Aishena fought like a creature possessed. Her arms flashed at a blistering speed, one throwing and catching, then throwing and catching the return athame. In her other hand was another crystal blade, lit up pale green, clashing blocking blows against any weapon swung her way. Two more men had dropped at her feet.

Riony reached for her own sword, hoping to knock down a few slavers herself. Before she could pull it free, a bone-shaking jolt cracked over the back of her head. She fell face down, landing on the squirming man beneath her again.

"In the back? Rude." Grunting in pain, she tried to right herself and face the cowardly attacker. She twisted to the side, wary of landing on her back and the creatures held there, and a foot came down hard on her wrist, knocking her hand off her hilt.

Bodies moved all around her, kicking and grasping at her. She tried to swat them away and stand up, but her wrist was held down firmly by the heavy boot.

"There's too many," Yoskar cried.

Aishena bellowed a guttural growl in reply. There was the sound of a falling body.

Riony roared at the man pinning her wrist down. "Come on, let me draw my sword. Don't you want a fair fight?"

The large scarred man loomed over her. He sucked air through his teeth and his foot shifted. Riony struggled her hand free, but the man's boot came up to kick her swiftly in the face before she could touch her sword. Her neck sprung backward, and dark spots filled her stinging eyes.

She shook her head and spat blood, scrambling to get back to her feet. Her arms were clasped by multiple hands on both sides, and she wrenched and struggled, throwing one man into the dirt.

But her wrists were drawn ever inward, and the harsh scratch of rope wrapped around them.

Her vision was still clearing as she was relieved of her sword. To her side, Aishena stood with a blade held to her throat as another man plucked at her belt, relieving her of athame after athame. Yoskar was on his knees next to her, blood running down one temple.

More ropes came out, and the delver siblings were bound too. With some more not so gentle kicks, the three of them were roused back to their feet and into movement, flanked on all sides by the slavers.

"Well, that was a bit of excitement for the afternoon," the scarred man grumbled. "Let's avoid any more. Get this lot back to camp and into chains."

Into chains. Riony's heart contracted in her chest, hollow, raw, and rattly against her rib cage. She tensed her wrists in front of her, trying to wriggle free from the rope. It held tight. She kept trying anyway, rubbing her skin raw.

Depths damn it all. This couldn't end like this. She wouldn't be a slave again.

"I told you not to fight it." Zade appeared next to her with a look of concern as he took in the blood gushing from her stinging nose.

Riony sucked that blood in and spat it in his face.

His expression twisted and he wiped at the mess with his sleeve.

"You're more savage than that brat sister of yours. You had your chance. You deserve what you get from here on out." He moved away from her side, blending in with the other slavers who surrounded them.

And Riony, Aishena, and Yoskar were marched, bound and bleeding, into the slavers' camp.

CHAPTER TWENTY

It wasn't the scratchy, tightly wound ropes tying her wrists in front of her that hurt Riony the most. Or the split lip and aching nose from where the boot had met her face. Or the throbbing lump on the back of her head.

It wasn't even how from her cage, Lyrrin watched her and the delver siblings being brought in through the palisade gate, and how her sister's bright expression of hope had dropped away. It wasn't even the feeling of a ticking clock, counting down until someone took her backpack and discovered what was inside it.

Riony was massively displeased to discover that the thing that stung her deepest, was that Kess was there, watching from her perch atop that large wolf, with hooded eyes and a satisfied smirk as Riony lost her freedom once more.

But if anything was going to give Riony the fire needed to put a halt to that outcome from occurring, to spite Kess was high on the list.

"I will not serve a master again," Riony grumbled to herself under her breath. "Not one like the Heithorns. Not *any*."

Aishena and Yoskar said nothing as they were herded along in front of Riony. Their expressions were shut down and locked tight, as though preparing for the worst.

Riony had no idea what the three siblings had been hiding from. Whatever secret made life in their dragonkeep home so unbearable they had run to the underground, Riony couldn't guess, and from the looks of the delvers, they were holding that secret close.

Aishena looked to her older brother for guidance a couple of times, and although his expression was racked with the wrinkles of thought, he shared no great plot for their escape. His glasses sat askew on his bleeding face, but he didn't raise his bound hands to straighten them.

Riony hoped he hadn't already given up. She could see in Aishena's tensed movements that every part of her still yearned to fight, so at least Riony would have someone on her side when there was a chance to make a move.

She cast furtive glances around the area, trying to gauge their chances.

The slavers' camp was a hive of activity, with scores of men and women in ratty clothing moving about their end-of-day tasks with the rowdy energy of triumph.

A lot of them wore beaten-up metal armor in mismatched pieces. Cheap and easy to find remnants from the past war, and the weapons hanging from belts and stacked beside tents seemed the same.

The slavers marching Riony and the delvers in were arguing about how to divvy up Aishena's haul of athames and how they worked. Riony's precious sword hung on the belt of the scrawny man with frizzy yellow hair. She yearned to have it back in her grasp. If only she'd had it ready to swing earlier, maybe they could have avoided capture. But she wasn't ready at all for Zade's betrayal.

A few slavers cheered as they saw the new batch of valuable older captives being marched in. Must be a great day for them. They'll probably have a party.

Sucks being one of those captives, though.

Riony scanned the faces of the slavers, her nerves rattled. Nobody chose to live aboveground, outside of dragonkeeps, for good, happy reasons.

Sometimes, they had no other option and survived by running some immoral grift—like kidnapping and slave trading—out of desperation. Sometimes they remained aboveground by choice. Those were the ones to be wary of.

It was a brutal life that attracted those with brutal desires.

The scarred leader who headed their little parade had that ruthless glint in his eyes.

A new man with a limp and body as withered as the revenant they'd fought yesterday came over to join the leader, walking with him through the camp.

Kess had followed them in too, her wolf padding silently alongside. Riony did her very best to ignore her.

"Got what we were waiting on, then?" the withered man asked.

The leader raised one eyebrow over the flame-scarred side of his face, stretching the wrinkled skin with it, as though the answer was obviously right before them.

"We ought to pull up stakes and get moving. Been here in one place too long."

The leader slapped a hand onto the slim man's shoulder. "Relax, Colber. We scored big today. Let the team celebrate. We'll move on in the morning."

Colber did not relax. He jittered disturbingly, eyes twitching. "Last watch from farther north reported what they thought was the shadowdragon passing over."

"Last watch from northern lookout drinks more than what's good for her."

Another man with a tuft of orange hair like a struck match tucked his chin toward Kess. "Wasn't this one asking about seeing a seasong dragon flying north? Was probably just that."

The leader gave Kess an assessing look. "Didn't you get what you were after? Why you still creeping about our camp? Get outta here before we put you and your pet in one of these cages too, girl."

Kess narrowed her eyes slightly and dropped back, but like the bad smell she was, she stuck around. Riony's shoulders tensed. What had she wanted, and gotten, from these slavers?

Colber stepped closer to get the leader's attention again. "Iarl, please—"

"We only just got the kids in the pens, and it's getting dark. We rest, we imbibe, we move on before bird's fart tomorrow." Iarl released his grip on the man with a rough shove, pushing him away and leaving him behind.

Iarl brought them over to a large firepit, which cast flickering light across the faces of those around it in the dimming twilight. A dripping spit roast crackled, letting off a fatty, savory scent.

Hungry.

Riony's eyes popped wide. *No, not now you aren't. Please, Dracuni, back to sleep.*

They were close to the cages, and Riony kept her eyes on Lyrrin, trying to reassure her. Sure, Riony was outnumbered and outmatched, but she was still standing, still breathing. So she would keep fighting, however she could.

Aishena seemed to have the same idea and made a break for it when she saw Benjin there too. She only made it two steps before she was tripped over by Iarl's extended foot.

With her hands bound, she smacked face-first into the dust. Heaving, she wriggled until she got her knees under her. She sat up and glared daggers at the man.

When he backhanded her, it set off a ripple of whimpers through the children in the cages. No doubt they all looked up to her. She was a delver, paragon of the undercity, and there she was, beaten down into the dirt. A few children began sobbing.

We're not done yet, Riony whispered silently to Lyrrin.

Riony doubted Lyrrin understood the words, but she must have understood her determined expression, because she nodded once, then ducked into the corner again, working her sharp nails against the bars. Without a word, Benjin shifted to stand in front of her.

A brusque female slaver with impressively wide shoulders gave Riony a shove, pushing her toward a cart that had manacles attached all along each side. The cart was simple and bulky, constructed from thick timber beams, chipped and gray in a way that suggested it could have predated the taming of dragons.

Some sections were patched with metal to reinforce the weathered frame. Worn by time and use, it bore the scars of countless journeys along rough terrain and smelled of old hay and older beer. Riony wondered how many slaves had been chained to those sides over the years, delivered to their fates.

"What are we going to do with this one?" the slaver woman asked, her voice deep and husky.

Riony felt movement in her backpack. She had to get out of there, and fast. She whispered desperately to the woman, "You could slip me out of this rope and back to your tent. Claim me for yourself and I'll make it worth your while."

"Right you will. Before or after you try and knock my brains in and run? I wasn't born yesterday, and it takes something far prettier than you to make me consider the risk." The older woman barked a laugh and clamped the heavy manacle around one of Riony's forearms. Beside her, Yoskar and Aishena were chained as well.

"You don't have to be hurtful about it," Riony muttered.

Iarl stepped closer and gave Riony an appraising look. "Not sure what we'll do with her. Much older than is worth bringing on as a slave. Much harder to break. Not impossible though, just takes a lot more work."

His eyes glinted at the final word.

"That one's no good as a slave." Kess, still lingering, decided to put her dumb opinion in. "I can tell you that from experience. Better to put her down here and now before she stabs you all in the back."

"Oh, baby, don't be jealous. You know you're the only one I want to stab in the back," Riony crooned.

"See how she treats her master?"

Riony opened her mouth to make Kess regret using the term master when a desperate plea of **Hungry** caught her off guard. Riony winced at the sheer anguish coming from the newborn as it squirmed again.

Riony turned her head down and softly hummed the lullaby she'd sung to Dracuni before, hoping to lull it back to sleep.

Iarl leaned away from her and gave her a worried look, as though she'd gone mad. Eying her arms, he said, "She'd probably only sell cheap for hard labor anyhow. Might be easier to waste her to the worms now."

"Tsk, you would be missing out by not keeping me around," Riony said. She needed to stay alive beyond the next few minutes if she was going to hit upon a chance to get herself and her loved ones out of there. "I've got skills. Midwife, herbalism. Plus, I'm superhot—despite what *some* people with bad taste might think. You'll get a great price for me. Promise."

"Hey, boy?" Iarl called over his shoulder. "Is this true?"

Zade appeared again from the crowd that had formed around to take in the new acquisitions. He didn't look at Riony, just kept his eyes downturned, shadowed under a flop of golden hair. "Well, she knows herbs at least. Got a nasty streak though."

"Only to traitorous foppish creeps who deserve it," Riony butted in.

Zade continued. "So she could be valuable, if you can break her."

Iarl's weathered lips lifted in a grim smile. "Oh, I can break her."

Kess scoffed. "Good luck with that. Better than you have tried and failed."

Shaking her head, the ghastly gremlin leaned forward, and her wolf turned away.

Zade looked up to Riony then, making eye contact. He still had a smear on his cheek from where she'd spat her blood at him. His expression was dark and cold. "Just do me a favor, Iarl. Wherever she ends up, keep her separate from that little one with the blue eyes over there."

Riony growled and lunged for him, held back as the chain between her arm and the cart snapped straight.

"You've got a very special death coming your way, Zade."

He stepped closer to her, nose to nose, with Riony straining at the end of her tether. He grinned his bright grin. "Maybe I'll take your sister with me."

She dug her heels into the ground and roared, tensing every part of her body, and the heavy cart behind her shifted. It barely moved at all, but it was enough of a jolt forward that Zade jumped back and had to wipe the terrified look off his face.

Yoskar snarled at her under his breath, "You're going to get your neck wrung if you don't quit it."

Iarl took a step forward, wide-eyed and frowning. "What in the stars has she got wriggling around in her pack?"

A few paces away on her wolf, Kess's head snapped around, shadowed eyes pinning Riony in their gaze.

Riony swore as her backpack jumped as at least one of the creatures within it bucked at the closure.

"... Sir Butterfur Spelunkychunks?" Riony said.

Iarl stared blankly at her reply.

Zade waved a hand dismissively. "Just some pet she's all protective of. Cave otter. Been carrying it all the way since before we left the undercity. We can add it to the dinner menu tonight."

Over at the cages, Lyrrin's head popped up again amongst the other watching children, horror stretching her features.

A keening bleat whimpered from behind Riony. *Shh, shh, please, Dracuni!*

Kess's back straightened, and she turned her wolf around again, prowling toward Riony.

Iarl folded his arms in front of him and glared. "Is that what cave otters normally sound like?"

"Yes, absolutely," Riony answered.

Kess turned her attention to Iarl, moving close to him. "You know, I think maybe I'd like to take that one off your hands for you."

Iarl didn't flinch at the proximity to the huge wolf and met Kess's calculating stare. "*You know*, I reckon we'll keep her. Seems you misjudged her value."

"I know what I'm talking about with that red-haired monster. If you don't believe me, that's your loss. But I've got a good few gold sovs to offer and that's far more than she's worth."

Iarl unfolded his arms and casually picked at his fingernails. "Why you so interested in taking her, then? I think maybe you've been trying to bargain us down from the beginning. Knew something we didn't and thought you'd bluff us out of our catch."

Kess's sudden interest in her drew a cold sweat out of Riony's skin. She couldn't let Kess take her, not with the way Kess was angling around, trying to get a clearer view of her backpack. She could not let that dragon-obsessed goblin get her hands on Dracuni.

Riony said, "She just hates the idea of anyone inflicting suffering on me other than her. She's definitely underbidding the value of the satisfaction she'll take in that."

"Quiet, Pony!"

"Look, she's acting like she owns me already, ordering me around. Don't let her get away with it."

Iarl stepped in between them. "Listen, girl. If the catch here really has got midwife training, knows herbs, and can pull a cart like a bovin, I reckon we're going to get some decent bids for her at market. Thanks to Zade, we also know pretty well how we're going to keep her in line."

He nodded over to the cage where Lyrrin watched with wide eyes under her hood. Turning from Kess to Riony, he tilted his head and his eyes sparkled. "We keep you and your sister together, you'll behave as you're told, won't you?"

Riony swallowed. "Yes. Anything."

"There we have it." Iarl smirked.

With a grunting huff, Kess plunged one hand deep into a pouch strapped beside her on the saddle. Metal clattered all around as slavers reached for swords, but she quickly withdrew her hand and held something tiny up into the air.

The glass glinted and shimmered, an opalescent silver.

The slavers went quiet.

"I'll trade. Silvernix for the slave," Kess hissed.

Iarl narrowed his eyes at Kess and sucked air through his teeth.

Riony blinked, trying to understand what she was seeing. Her breath came heavy. "How ... how long have you *had that*?"

Kess ignored her. "You won't get a better deal anywhere in Elundrae."

"Right you are about that," Iarl said. He reached out a hand, and Kess snatched the tiny vial back.

"The slave first."

Iarl looked from Kess to the crowd of slavers surrounding them. "Could just take it from you if we want."

"Not before I smash it on the ground and we all lose. Just be a good little scumlord and make the deal."

Iarl spent a moment thinking it over, then shrugged and signaled for the husky woman to unlock Riony's manacle. Riony's mind swirled and her body felt shivery and wrong for all the anger running through it.

The manacle released, but Riony's hands were still tied in front by rope, and the slaver woman lashed another rope around that and handed the end over to Kess like a lead on a dog.

Kess dangled the vial between her fingers, and Iarl snatched it up. He held it close to his eye, turning it side to side and inspecting the contents. Then a grin broke across his face.

"We really have had a good day, friends!" he called out over the crowd, holding the silvernix high. A cheer went up and they banged on metal in applause. "First good sale of many to come!"

Kess rolled her eyes at them and gave a tug of the rope. Riony refused the first, but moved slowly on the second. Looking back, she nodded to Lyrrin, trying to reassure her. Tears shined off Lyrrin's cheeks from under the shadow of her hood.

Riony had hope though. She was probably in the best position to escape as she could get, now. The moment Kess took her out of sight of the slavers, it wouldn't be hard to overpower the little goblin and get away.

The wolf might be an issue. But still better than being manacled to a cart in the middle of scores of crazed overworlders. Riony cast her eyes over the slavers and a warning chill of danger ran over her. She didn't like the way they continued to eye her and Kess, how Iarl and Colber whispered to each other. How Yoskar and Aishena slumped and looked away.

But yet again, what she found she didn't like the most, was the satisfaction on Kess's sly weasel face at taking ownership over her once again.

Chapter Twenty-One

Kess felt close, so close to having what she always wanted. That redheaded menace was carrying it, and now she had them both.

She steadied her breathing and cultivated an air of extreme apathy as she turned Griskin away from the slavers and led Pony from their camp. But inside, her nerves stretched taut, twanging with both anticipation and the fear that her dreams could again be crushed.

You can't fool me, Pony. I know you've got more in that backpack than you're letting on. The creature that wriggled and mewled in there sounded much like the dragonlings she used to watch back on her family's estate, newborns just hatched but not yet gone through their taming ceremony.

It made her remember the time her older brother, in a rare moment of sibling affection, took her down to the hatchery to see a new batch of etherdarts, bred for him to choose the dragon that would grow to be his steed.

Her jealousy that he got to own one of those beasts had been high, but the excitement at seeing the fresh hatchlings overrode that emotion. Born from etherflame and treedart parents, they were already large, fresh from their eggs, and glittered in deep reds, earthy browns, and dusky purples.

Kess beamed, reaching her hand to touch the still-soft newborn scales.

Her brother sat with her on the low stone edge of the hatchling pen. The hatchery air was stifling, warmed beyond comfort by an etherflame chained on the level below that had been broken in battle and was only good for heating now.

"Which would you choose, if you became a dragonrider?" he asked.

"I *will* become a dragonrider," she replied.

"Whatever. But which one?"

She answered without hesitation. "The purple one."

Largest of the litter and with a striking array of horn buds around its skull. Its eyes were already open wide, bright and alert in a way tamed dragons' eyes weren't. She could imagine how magnificent it would grow to be. She could imagine soaring in the skies on its back.

"Do you think, after you've chosen—"

"Shh, it's Mami and Fadda!" her brother hissed. He hid Kess in a dark corner behind a pile of hay bales—she was never meant to have left the castle.

When their parents arrived, Kess watched, silent and seething, as her brother selected that very same purple dragon to be *his* steed.

"What about the rest of them?" he asked.

"We only have silvernix to spare on taming one," Fadda said. "The rest are waste."

"Good," her brother had said, staring over his parents' shoulders at the hay bales with a dark smile. "We don't need more than one new riding dragon anyway."

Kess hated how her heart squeezed into a painful lump at the memory.

I'll show him. I'll have my dragon soon.

She wasn't sure how Pony had done it, saved herself and one of the dragonlings from that cave. Maybe she really did have some silvernix on her that she used to heal herself after Kess had left, then took a dragonling—from where? It must have been hidden when Kess was in the cave.

When had she hidden it and why? The sequence of events didn't make sense. The mystery of it all had been bothering Kess since that day in the mountains. She'd gone back into the ice cave to check if Pony was still alive, not long after leaving her to die, and found her entirely gone. Only a frozen pool of blood remained to prove she'd even been there.

The lack of Pony in that cave, dead or alive, confused Kess almost as much as why she'd bothered to go back into the cave herself. She hadn't changed her mind about saving the intolerable woman, not really. She did have the means to save her though, and *if* Pony *had* still been alive, maybe Kess would have considered making a deal of some kind for the silvernix she needed to survive.

Only if Pony had anything of value to offer. Only if there was something in it for her, to salvage the wasted situation.

Kess couldn't imagine what that could have been, but she hadn't really considered using the silvernix on *Pony* without some payoff, had she? The woman had deserved to die, especially after ruining Kess's chance at one of the dragon's hatchlings. And it was a rude shock to find out that she hadn't.

Kess had wondered whether the mother dragon returned, somehow unseen, and swallowed Pony's body whole. Then Kess saw the bloody footprints leading out of the cave. Kess couldn't believe Pony had walked out of there. Even if she had, surely she just walked off to die somewhere else.

When Griskin picked up her scent again down from the mountains, Kess sought the answer to how Pony had cheated death.

Silvernix was an obvious answer, but for a brief, yearning moment, Kess had hoped there was something else, some other healing magic those cave dwellers had dug from the Alderkin depths. Something miraculous that she could use. That was something she wanted almost as much as her own dragon.

At least now she had one of those things.

Pony walked painfully slowly behind her, a dull, sullen look on her dumb face. Before they were even halfway to the gates, the oaf planted her feet in the ground and yanked back on the rope connecting them, almost pulling Kess off her wolf.

Kess glared back at her and pulled the rope. "Keep moving, Pony."

The oaf tugged back, the rope drawing taut between them. She stared at the ground, her face hot and red, and her voice was low and flat. "How long did you have that silvernix?"

"That's what you want to know?"

"*How long*? Did you have it ... did you have it in the cave?"

Kess sighed dramatically and rolled her eyes. "Of course, I did. What, you thought I might have just stumbled across it in the last couple of days? Silvernix isn't easy to come by lately. And, of course, I would *never* have wasted it on a life like yours."

Pony breathed roughly. "You … I was dying! And you … you could have …"

"Aw, does that hurt your feelings?"

Stilling, Pony turned her face up and stared Kess down. "I don't even know why I'm surprised."

Kess's face flushed then, and she turned away, tugging on the rope again. "Don't know why you're angry. Clearly, you're fine. Seems to me that if I'd stepped in, I would have ruined your plan to steal a baby dragon for yourself."

Pony stumbled a step forward before renewing their tug-of-war.

Kess's grin grew. Pony's emotions were always as easy to read as a book. "So yes, I'm glad I never wasted silvernix on you. I'm not even going to let those dullard slavers keep what they have now. I'll be back for it soon enough. I'm going to need it to tame my new baby dragon, after all."

"You're wrong. I don't have one. It's just a cave otter. I'm telling the complete truth that I don't have a dragon in my backpack," Pony growled.

She'd never been a good liar either, but for some reason managed it then. Still, it gave Kess pause. She better not have set herself up for stealing silvernix back from slavers just for some cave otter.

No, it sounded like a dragon. It has to be.

"We'll see soon enough." Kess looked the brutish woman up and down, taking stock of what she might be in for once it was just the two of them. Pony had grown a lot since they were kids, and she'd been tall for her age then.

That felt like a lifetime ago. That other life, back when Kess lived in a castle, luxuries all around. She'd had many slaves back then. But when Pony and her parents deserted, it had felt like a very personal abandonment.

Kess knew abandonment well. Friends who would spend time with her, then mock her behind her back. Her own family, too ashamed of her to stay in a dragonkeep where others could see her, cloistering her away to an isolated estate.

Or the time she was taken out into the blighted wilds by her own blood and left alone to perish.

Pony, though, had been one constant of Kess's life for years growing up. Somewhere along the way, the fact that Pony was *forced* to spend time with her was lost. The fact resurfaced like an explosion when Pony had the chance to run and took it.

Kess thought she'd never see Pony again, and never wanted to. Kess knew she was better off alone. Just her and Griskin. The only one she could trust.

Thoughtfully, she mumbled, "Who'd have thought it would be you who helped me become the dragonrider I was always meant to be?"

Pony lifted her bound hands in front of her in a pleading gesture. "I'll go with you. I'll be your slave again. But please, will you buy my sister too? I won't leave without her."

Kess narrowed her eyes, scanning over the cages back near the fire. The slavers had dispersed, moving around in the dimming shadows of the camp. "Sister? Which one is she?"

Pony tensed, and her face made some ugly shapes before she seemed to make up her mind. "The little one in the hood. Bring her along, or I'll yell out right now that I've got a baby dragon in my backpack and see what the slavers think of that."

"Do that, and I'll kill the girl myself." Kess brushed her fingers along a row of slim bone throwing daggers kept in her bracer. "I have excellent aim, don't you remember?"

Beneath her, Griskin's fur shivered, and he growled a long and low warning. Kess leaned over and petted him, enjoying the wary look on Pony's face as she took in the huge wolf.

"Why do you have to be such an enormous asshole about everything?" Pony grumbled.

"Because nothing, not you, not your sister, *nothing* is getting between me and owning my own dragon as I deserve!"

A growly voice muttered from beside her, "Yeah, I don't know about that, little girl."

The heavy hilt of a sword clocked Kess on the temple before she could turn to see who spoke. Her teeth clattered and skull shook, the world wobbling in her vision as she tipped sideways.

Kess let go of Pony's rope and grasped out desperately for Griskin but had been pushed too far across by the blow. Her feet slipped free of the stirrups and the saddle disappeared from beneath her. She thumped into the ashy dirt, head ringing.

"Get the wolf!" someone commanded.

A dark web flew in the corner of Kess's spotty vision, falling over Griskin. He yelped and growled. She tried to lift herself, crawling forward on her elbows toward his struggling form.

There was more scuffling to her other side. Pony, hands bound, landed face-first like a toppled column, and the four slavers who knocked her down kicked at her where she fell. She rolled on her side, taking the hits to her stomach and face like an idiot.

"Traitors!" Kess shrieked at everyone around her. No matter that she'd intended to go back on their deal too. At least she had the decency to plan on slipping back in at night and taking the silvernix without an audience. Maybe even pop some of the cage doors while she was there. If she had the time.

The slavers snatched Pony's rope, dragging her along the dirt kicking and cussing back to the cart where the Hjelzahn siblings were still chained.

The man with the scarred face stepped in front of Kess, staring at her as she lay prone on her side.

Lightning fast, Kess reached for her throwing daggers. A boot came down on her hand, kicking it away from her weapons.

The rough, reedy man, Colber, chuckled. "Look, boss, she's real angry at you now."

Kess shook her head, trying to shake off the pain. Griskin was down, trapped under a heavy net of steel rope, the kind used for catching massive livestock or small dragons.

Across at the cart, Pony stood again, the manacle being re-latched around her arm. Pony stared back at where Kess remained sprawled in the dirt, her mouth a thin, flat line.

Don't you dare feel sorry for me. Don't you razing dare!

The leader grinned dangerously. "Real mad, aren't you? Come on, then. Get up and fight me, wild girl."

Kess's whole chest heaved as she panted angry breaths.

"I'll even give you one free shot. What are you waiting for? Get up."

Pony's voice drifted over the camp, piercing Kess like a knife in her back. "She can't."

Chapter Twenty-Two

"**S**hut your mouth, Pony!" Kess screamed from where she lay on her side in the dirt. If she could have murdered with her eyes alone, Riony would be halfway to rigor mortis.

Everything had turned around again, and Riony was freed from Kess's ownership again—yay—only to be back in chains—boo.

Sparks. I should have just left with Kess, knocked her and her smug face off that stars-damned wolf, then come back for Lyrrin with two arms free and swinging.

The revelation that Kess had unicorn blood with her when Riony was dying had knocked her around though, left her feeling strangely twisted up inside and punch-drunk, and she'd screwed up her chance.

Riony casually tested her newly reattached manacle, latched on one side just above where rope still bound her two wrists together. She slowly strained as though yawning, but neither the rope nor chain budged.

"What do you mean, she can't?" Iarl called back.

A jab of guilt jarred Riony's gut. She'd spat those words in spite, but as the slaver held her with a questioning glare, she felt wrong revealing Kess's condition to them. On the other hand, Kess was a traitorous goblin who had left her to die when she could have been saved.

"I mean she hasn't had the use of her legs since she was born. She's always found some other way to get around." Riony drawled the last sentence out, holding Kess's venomous glare.

A small crowd of slavers had formed around them again now. A couple laughed out loud as Kess pulled herself into a sitting position and reached for her knives again. A sword tip close to her neck stilled her hand.

Iarl tilted his head as he examined Kess. "Why didn't you use your silvernix on yourself? Reckon I would have preferred my legs working than to trade that away for a loud-mouthed and defiant slave."

"You're dumber than you look if you think I haven't tried unicorn blood before."

A grin spread on Iarl's face.

Oh, you idiot, Kess.

"Got a plentiful supply of the stuff then, have you? Thought as much. Nobody offers gold sovs up front for a slave, let alone a vial of silvernix. Not unless they have all that and more." Iarl winked slyly with his burn-wrinkled eye, then lifted his chin to Colber. "Search her. And the wolf."

The scrawny man grabbed Kess's shoulder and flipped her over onto her stomach. She scrambled her arms about, trying to press herself back up, as her legs remained motionless. Colber put a knee on the small of her back and patted her down.

Riony grimaced and looked away. Her teeth were clenched hard together, and every part of her body felt riled up in a way she couldn't quite place.

It seemed fine for Riony to fantasize about knocking Kess off her wolf, because she knew the monster Kess truly was on the inside. Seeing these shart-faced thugs push Kess around and laugh at her fired up something primal inside Riony that she didn't want to examine too closely.

"Aish, please tell me you've got some secret backup athame stashed on your person somewhere," Riony whispered across the cart to the delver chained on the other side.

Aishena turned her palms upward and muttered in heavy disdain, "Where exactly do you think I would be hiding one?"

"I mean, I have some ideas, but you've already turned down my romantic advances before so ..."

"Hey!" Iarl yelled at Riony. "Who are you to this wild girl, that she'd pay so much to get you back?"

Riony's gaze shot over to Kess, still pinned to the ground like a bug, then she quickly looked away. "I'm nobody to her but damned livestock. I told you, she used to own me and thinks she still does and will bring everybody into her stupid grudge against me. She'd trade you the moon itself if it means she can get just one more claw under my skin."

Iarl scratched at his stubbly chin. "Nah. Nah, I think you're both lying. There's something more going on. She's been looking for you, for sure, you're right there. I reckon it's why she showed up here in the first place, with her lame excuse of making trade."

Riony bit her lip and looked back over to where Kess was having her belt unbuckled and pulled off. The pouches' contents were emptied out onto the ground and searched.

She hadn't ratted them out to the slavers? Riony thought for sure that's why Kess was there. Coming through to do some trade while children were being sold under her nose was almost as coldhearted though, Riony had to admit. Just not the full extent of coldheartedness as she expected from the malicious goblin.

"'Course, she didn't hint at what wealth she was carrying then. Not until you showed up and she saw what she really wanted. Now we know the scruffy little thing's a rich bitch in disguise."

A few brave slavers approached the wolf—Griskin, Kess had called him—and were poking their hands through the netting to search the saddle and its attached bags. Griskin twisted and snapped his teeth at them, but the net held him back from snagging their flesh.

"Come on, there's got to be something!" Iarl yelled at them as they turned out clothing, cookware, and more and more and more bone throwing knives than anyone could have reasonably expected.

"Found those gold sovs she was talking about." A bald slaver with an eyepatch tossed a leather pouch over to his leader.

He opened it and his fingers flicked through the contents. A scowl remained on his face as he watched Colber finish his search with an empty-handed shrug.

Kess had stopped struggling and lay with her forehead pressed to the ground, her face hidden under a fall of her tangled charcoal-toned hair. Her ears had gone a violent shade of red.

A nasty feeling of heat crept up Riony's neck and cheeks too, and she had to look away. *It must be my body's reaction to the sheer joy of seeing Kess humiliated, that's all.*

Beside Riony, Aishena and Yoskar were whispering fast words to each other. Maybe they were coming up with an escape plan, some way to get them all out of this. Riony hoped they'd share it with her, too.

But Iarl was already wandering toward them. He had his eyes locked on Riony in a way that made her skin crawl. "You know what, search that one too. Maybe little wolf girl is obsessed with something she's carrying, rather than the livestock herself."

Riony's skin flushed cold, and she took a step back from the approaching husky woman who had chained her up before. Her backside bumped against the solid cart behind her, nowhere further to go. She raised her bound hands in surrender.

With a half-hearted smile, she said, "You sure you don't want to take me back to your tent? We could do a full strip search, all alone."

"You really think I have more lust than logic, don't ya, pet? That and you think mighty highly of yourself."

Riony gestured at her body. "I mean ..."

The woman let out a rough chuckle, then shot her hands out faster than Riony expected. Not that there was much she could do.

The woman stabbed her knife into the netted bag at Riony's side, cutting through and spilling the contents on the ground. She kicked at the wheel of cheese and strips of jerky. "Nothing in this lot."

Then the woman grabbed Riony by the front of her shirt and slid the sharp dagger down her bare arms, slicing right through the straps of her backpack. One side, then the other. Riony couldn't even flinch away without risk of that blade going into her arms.

Other hands grabbed the pack from behind her before it could fall.

Riony turned, and there was Zade, staring her down with a twisted pout as he squatted just beyond the length of Riony's tether. Which she tested aggressively.

"Something in there, for sure," Iarl muttered as he smirked at her futile struggles.

"Zade," Riony's voice broke in its battle between pleading and warning. She tried to speak soft enough that only he could hear. "What you find in there, don't tell them. You don't understand ... Just tell them you can't find anything. It will be worth it, I promise."

Zade laughed as loud as an actor on a stage. "She's still trying to bargain with me! As though a deserting slave's promise means anything. We'll have your precious cave otter for dinner, and we'll have whatever else you are hiding in there for ourselves too."

Across at the nearby cage, Lyrrin had stopped working on the bars and was standing, watching with a wobbly tremble to her bottom lip.

Riony had been terrified of the slavers getting Dracuni. That imminent outcome still made her stomach churn, but now a new fear unlocked that they might hurt Lyrrin's cave otter right in front of her.

Kess's attention had turned to the bag as well. Not even the dirty tear-smudged cheeks and reddened nose were enough shame to keep her from lifting her face to see what she thought was Riony's secret stolen dragonling being revealed.

Close, Kess, but not quite.

Zade worked the knotted closure free. As he pulled the opening wide enough, a bolt of sleek, caramel fur burst out and upward. The otter made a great, wriggly leap for freedom, launching itself out of the bag and into the air.

Zade toppled over onto his back, crying out an embarrassing yelp.

A ripple of laughter and insults rolled across the watching crowd as he scrambled backward from the skittering otter, batting it away with his hands. Sir Butterfur's snout twitched at the sky, his whole body snapping to stillness for one breath, before zipping away across the ground and vanishing.

Riony bared her teeth at Zade in a vicious smile. "No wonder you had to turn to selling babies as slaves. If you're scared of cave otters, you were never going to survive long in the undercity."

Zade snarled and threw a handful of dirt her way.

A harsh, choking laugh was building slowly, hysterically, from Kess's direction. She had gotten herself upright again, sitting slouched over and shaking her head with each dark chuckle.

"That's really what was in there all along? A razing cave otter?" Her head snapped up so fast it brought a second sword point out from a nearby slaver to warn her back.

Kess howled across the camp, "You cost me *everything*, Pony. You have ruined everything. I've clawed myself up from nothing before and I'll do it again, and then I will turn every part of my attention toward destroying everything of yours!"

A harsh shiver ran up Riony's spine as Kess rolled her gaze over to Lyrrin's cage.

"Wow, she's a bit overdramatic. I see what you mean now," Iarl scoffed.

"Told you," Riony replied, then tried again to bluff herself and her backpack's contents free from scrutiny. "She's just crazy obsessed with hurting me. I don't have anything valuable."

The slave leader's eyes narrowed on her, then he waved a hand at Zade. "Come on, get back to searching that bag. Unless you're scared!"

Zade brushed himself off and moved back to kneel beside the bag.

Dracuni had been very still for a while now, only the occasional pang of fear would thrum from the newborn's mind through to Riony, frightened by the yelling and probably the panicked signals Riony's mind must be sending back to it.

She couldn't break free from her bonds. She couldn't reach Zade and throttle him before he revealed Dracuni to a camp full of slavers. And Kess. She couldn't save Lyrrin or the other children. She was stuck, and her muscles burned with wasted, useless energy.

As Zade moved to peer inside her bag, Riony couldn't watch.

She turned her eyes to the sky, to the last edges of flame red from the fading sunset licking over the heavy clouds. She prayed to Amma Moon, for Dracuni's safety, for Lyrrin's, even for her own. For something, anything, to free them from this moment.

Through the clouds, something moved, darkening the sky.

It swirled, moving in languid gusts. The clouds dispersed around its massive, shadowy form. Two hot coals of red light moved together in the gloom. Eyes. Eyes that held death, destruction, pure evil incarnate.

Riony's whole body turned to ice.

Anything. Anything but *that*.

"Shadowdragon." The word stuttered out on Riony's breath, as though even it wanted to retreat into her body to hide. She couldn't take her eyes off it, the churning, wicked shadows that flew in the shape of a dragon.

From nearby, Iarl rasped out a laugh. "You're not tricking us twice, tamebrain."

But at least one slaver must have been curious enough to follow her gaze. There was a yelp of fear, and then a sharp curse, and then cries went up all over the camp.

"Oh, mighty moon," Zade gasped from beside her.

Riony dragged her gaze away from the creature of evil that descended upon them to see whether Zade was referring to it or whether he had gotten a good look inside her pack. She exhaled in rough relief when she saw him looking skyward as well.

Everybody had their faces turned upward now. Some were frozen like statues, and others had already begun to scoop up anything they could carry and run. But even in their frantic retreat, all kept their eyes on the shadowdragon.

Maybe it wouldn't land. Maybe it would pass by and curse the ground somewhere else. Riony strained again at her bonds. She cast her gaze over the sharp points of the burned palisade stakes and crude weapons stashed around the camp. Nothing was close enough for her to use to break herself and the delver siblings beside her free.

The dim glow of twilight faded suddenly as the shadowdragon descended from the sky with a ghostly grace. The sinuous coil of shadows and smoke that formed its body twisted and writhed in the air. A deep, mournful rumble emanated from its chest as it touched down onto the ground.

The closest people underneath the shadowdragon's path had run to avoid its touch, but it settled in over the top of the palisades and tents and fires as though they were made of nothing more substantial than air, or as though it was.

The ghostly dragon seemed to shift and warp as it moved, its edges blurring and fading into the surrounding darkness in licks of curling blackness. Only those burning red eyes gave it a sense of life and intent.

Sobs tore from Riony's throat and tears streamed down her face completely unhindered. Not from her own fear. But from the waves of mourning that seemed to wash from the ocean of shadow before them. Sounds of weeping came from all around, especially in the direction of the cages.

A deep sense of unease already had Riony in its grips, and then the shadowdragon opened its wispy jaws and unleashed a skull-piecing roar.

The ground shook.

The sound was a visceral assault on the senses, like the anguished wail of ten thousand lost souls.

As the roar reverberated through the air, the earth shook again, cracking and splitting open. Small and large eruptions burst across the campsite all around the immense shadowy monster.

Rotten flesh and bleached bones clawed out from those holes. The corpses of animals, from small rodents to large birds of prey, to an enormous bovin, all rose from the dead, drawn inexorably back to a twisted semblance of life by the dragon's mournful cry.

Even grubs and bugs and worms and flies, any that were recently dead, any that hadn't rotted away entirely, made the ground itself writhe as they twitched back into life.

A few human skeletons, ancient and worn, pulled themselves out of their long-lost graves as well. Their movements were slow and awkward, as though still in the grip of death as they shambled out of the earth. But as they turned their eyeless gazes on the humans cowering before them, they drew rigid with terrible purpose.

Riony had only seen the horrifying effect of the shadowdragon's presence in person once before. The day it had come to the secluded village she and her parents had been raising Lyrrin in after fleeing the Heithorns.

The founders of that settlement had said they'd cleared all dead things from the earth before settling there, that it was a safe place. And it was, for years. But the shadowdragon's call went deep, right into the heart of the earth itself and to the bones of anything that lay sleeping far below the surface for centuries.

And it turned them into revenants, mindless, withered creatures that seemed to want nothing more than to bring more death to the world.

The shadowdragon's nebulous wings flapped, causing no disturbance in the air around it as it lifted itself back toward the sky and left those on the ground to their fate at the hands of its curse.

Riony's tears stopped. She yanked at her chain again, her breath hitching. *Sparks, sparks, sparks, razing sparks!*

The slavers also reawakened from their shock and mourning as the shadowdragon grew distant. They scrambled for swords and axes, crossbows and flaming torches, anything to defend themselves as the dead rushed into their attack.

Beside Riony, Aishena and Yoskar's faces were grim as they braced themselves for the onslaught. No weapons, not even their own arms available to defend themselves with.

The first of the undead animals reached them. A dreer, only just as tall as Riony. It must have been a baby when it died, which made it all the more disturbing as it snarled and snapped at them, decaying flesh hanging from its jaws.

Riony kicked out at it with all her strength, her chains clinking. Her foot connected with the dreer's skull, sending it tumbling back with a sickening crack.

But there were more, coming fast. An undead boar raced past, almost knocking Riony off her feet as it charged toward another victim. Its thick hide stretched across its bones like a tough leather, crackling as it ran. Aishena and Yoskar grunted as they fought to kick away their own attackers.

Fear and pain shot through Riony's head like a knife. Not her own.

Scared.

Wide-eyed, Riony cast around and saw her pack, abandoned where Zade had been moments before, as combatants stomped all around. She lunged for it and Dracuni in desperation.

Brought up short by her chain, she toppled forward, feet slipping out from under her as she overextended. The bag remained out of reach.

Scared!

I know, little one. Riony slipped and stumbled back to her feet, Dracuni's terror overwhelming her. Every nerve in her body screamed to reach the newborn and keep it safe. It was all she could do to keep herself safe as the dreer returned, needing another sharp kick to knock it away again.

"Over here, keep these two safe!" Iarl called out.

A small wall of bodies emerged from the chaos, weapons readied, lining up before the three of them chained to the cart. The two valuable bodies of the Hjelzahn siblings, and the spare.

Zade hurried in beside them, burn athames glowing red in the gloom.

"Those are mine," Aishena growled low, trying to reach out and snatch them back or maybe wrap her tied hands around Zade's throat.

He kept just out of her reach. "Tell it to your amma when she comes to pay for you."

Across the camp, the massive bovin revenant charged straight through one of the tents, tearing through the leather and metal structure and upending slavers as it went.

Screams punctuated the clang of metal against bone and the thunder of pounding feet. Riony took a chance to turn and check on the cages and found herself grateful that Lyrrin and the kids were still inside them.

The children cowered from one side of their enclosure to another, dodging away from the human rev that was trying to grab them through the bars. The strong metal would give them some protection, at least for a while, but Riony had to get over there fast, because this number of revs wasn't going anywhere anytime soon. And if that stampeding bovin set its course in line with the cages ...

The sound of the shadowdragon's roar still echoed in her mind, the depth of its mourning sadness rippling in her chest, and Riony wondered if they were all going to die there. But she couldn't let herself give up—not now, not ever.

Children were screaming louder now. More revs surrounded their cages, snapping and reaching for them from every side.

There wasn't enough room for them to all huddle out of reach in the middle, and louder shrieks cut through the din when a child would be grabbed by a clawed hand, the rev trying to pull them through, then being wrenched back away by the other children.

Riony screamed in frustration herself, as she longed to run over to Lyrrin's side and protect her. And then a crackling bolt of **Pain!** withered her knees. From the corner of her eye, she saw the boot that knocked into her pack as a man raced by, kicking it and its precious contents across the ground.

Pain!

Dracuni! Riony almost yelled it aloud. She reached for the bag again, now closer, but still out of reach.

Her voice broke as she cried out, "Zade, free us! Get these depths-damned chains off us so we can help fight properly. You know we can."

Zade plunged one of the burning athames into the empty rib cage of a skeletal fox. "I wouldn't even be here still fighting these things if it weren't for the bounty. Those two are wanted alive, and we're not letting some revs take that from us, and we're not going to risk letting you run."

"Zade, none of us are getting out of this alive at this rate. There are too many revs. You can't protect us here!"

Zade sneered back at her. "I'm not protecting you at all."

A swarm of undead insects flew at Riony's face, clouding her vision, biting and stinging. They couldn't rend her flesh the way a larger revenant would relish in doing, but they creeped her out even more. She swatted at them with her bound hands and whipped her head side to side, trying to shake them off.

When she could see clearly again, her stomach dropped away and she forgot how to breathe.

The massive bulk of the undead bovin, standing twice as tall as any human, with bones as thick as Riony's biceps, was coming right at her. Its hooves beat like thunder on the ground, churning up dirt and dust in its wake.

As it got closer, the earth shook beneath Riony's feet. It was going to crush them all. She pulled herself as far as she could on the length of her chain, trying to separate herself from being squashed between the beast and the heavy wooden cart behind her.

"Look out!" she cried.

Only Zade seemed to pay attention, turning to the approaching beast. He dove for cover at the last moment, leaving her and the delvers and the other slavers at the mercy of the charging behemoth.

The bovin's solid horns were down and its heavy skull made contact with the cart, right beside Riony, and everything exploded.

Chapter Twenty-Four

The force of the impact was like the boom of thunder, and everything wrenched into the air. Timber tore and cracked. Splinters and bodies flew, strewn about in the wake of the massive, rampaging revenant.

Riony was yanked by her bound hands into a barrel roll, tumbling and smashing against the broken cart. For a moment she was upside down, and she curled her body in to brace for the inevitable return to the ground. Yoskar let out a gasping moan, and Aishena yelped as Riony collided with them.

A metal cartwheel flew in an arc past Riony's face and disappeared into the distance.

As the world stopped spinning, what was the cart now lay split in two, cracked right down the middle where the bovin had hit it and charged through. The two sides had folded over, landing on top of each other and bringing Riony through the air to land on top of the delvers.

"Are you okay?" Riony grunted as she rolled herself off Aishena's lap and took her feet off Yoskar's shoulder. She wriggled around to get her feet back underneath her. A hot graze stung all the way up Riony's bare left arm, the skin stripped and red raw. Splinters the size of toothpicks jutted from the edge of the scrape.

The delvers in their protective leather armor may have been battered but seemed to have remained untorn.

"Why are you so depths damned heavy?" Aishena pulled herself from the dirt. Dust clouded around them, kicked up from the bovin's hooves and impact. Screams still sounded all about them as the slavers and revs clashed.

Getting to her feet, Riony gave a tug of her bound hands, still tied in the middle and still chained to the cart. Or what was left of the cart. Her side had come cracking down onto the delvers' side, and when she pulled, it nearly toppled over on top of them.

Yoskar hissed at her efforts. "Don't pull it this way. Push it off, you tamebrain."

Riony snorted at the insult but gave the command a try anyway. She leaned into the splintered wood and metal wreck, and Yoskar leaned beside her. Her half of the cart was mostly just one slab now, the heavier, sturdy section of its base that had the manacles bolted to it.

With one big heave, it slid off the remaining part that the delvers were attached to.

It had fared less well. The wheel on that side was gone too, and the beam along the side of the base where the chains were attached had cracked, but not quite come free.

"We have to get out of here and over to the kids," Aishena said. She kicked at the splintered beam. "If I just had one single damned athame on me still!"

"You'll know to keep one hidden next time," Riony said. "I'll offer you some suggestions when we get out of this." Frowning at the split wood, Riony nodded to herself. "I can break that. I'm sure I can break that. Move over this way a bit."

She waved at Aishena to create a gap between her and Yoskar, then strained at the end of her chain to drop herself in between them. Crouching with her feet braced against the lower part of the cart, she leaned forward and hooked her fingers into the cracked section.

Bending forward like that, her manacle rasped against her skin, pulled as tight as it would reach. But if Riony pulled upward from there, it would slacken.

Exhaling, she clenched her fingers around the timber and heaved. There was a satisfying crackle of ripping wood, but it didn't come apart.

The growl of a rev grew suddenly loud. A human revenant cut through the dusty haze, backlit by the nearby campfire. Riony ducked as its skeletal fingers snatched at her, its teeth chomping the air at her back.

Aishena and Yoskar lunged forward in unison and kicked the rev, launching it back into the rest of the camp.

"You guys keep the revs off me, I'll get you off this cart. Then you can get me off."

"Do you have to say it like that?" Aishena groaned as she stomped her foot on something small and slithery.

"I didn't even mean it that time!" Riony readjusted her grip, tensed her shoulders, and hauled upward again.

Snap, snap, snap. The splintered timber tore. She released, gasped a few breaths, then pulled again. As she felt the wood lift and break, she kept going, crying out as she strained every muscle in her back.

One final splintery strand broke and Riony jolted as the beam snapped in two, right along the seam that the manacles were bolted into. She tumbled backward, then was caught by her own chain, spun back around toward the cart again.

Metal jangled as the delvers gave a final kick and tug of their own, and the manacles came free from the cart.

The cuffs were still clamped around the delvers' arms, but the other end of the chains now hung free. Aishena looked at the detached end in awe, then up at Riony.

Riony nodded to her, then turned her gaze back to where her manacle was attached. It wasn't already splintered like their side had been, but with all three of them, and their hands somewhat freer now, she figured they could crack it.

"Aish, come on," Yoskar said softly.

"But ..."

Riony whipped back around to them and found Yoskar was already moving toward the cages.

"No, no, don't you dare!" Riony gasped.

Aishena hovered, her lips pulled closed in a thin line.

"Come on!" Yoskar growled. "Benjin needs us."

He broke into a sprint. With the barest flutter of a glance back at Riony, Aishena ran after him.

Riony wrenched at her chained arm. Her muscles burned in agony all over. She released a long, primal scream into the sky.

With her face turned upward, she breathed though a shaking sob, then opened her eyes again.

A sharp shock of ice shivered through her as she saw the shadowdragon, still there, circling high above.

I have to get to Lyrrin. I have to get to Dracuni. Sparks! Raze both of those depths-damned delvers!

Glaring at the half-cart she was still attached to, she dug her feet in, wrapped both hands around her chain, and leaned backward. Her muscles shook and twitched from over-exertion. The timber groaned but didn't break, only shifting on the dusty ground.

Riony clenched her teeth and grunted, taking a step backward, and the half-cart came with her.

She could move it. She could move! Slowly, very slowly. Each step felt like a full days' workout, but she could move.

Riony took in her options. The cages were across on the other side of the campfire, which must have been smashed into by something during the fighting. It now lay spread out across the ground in a field of glowing embers.

Her backpack and Dracuni were a few steps away in the other direction.

Silhouetted bodies clashed in the darkness all around against the ghoulish undead. She couldn't see Zade anymore, and Kess seemed to be gone too, despite the wolf still being trapped under the net.

Hopefully some rev with very big teeth had dragged her off somewhere to have a good chew on her gristly bones. And honestly, good riddance.

For some reason, the revs seemed to be ignoring the wolf. Riony had noticed that before, that they seemed to only have a frenzied desire for human blood. She hoped the same applied to Dracuni. Since the backpack still lay mostly untouched, she assumed it did.

A body lay close to Riony's side, still and surrounded by a dark pool of blood draining into the dirt. The poor man who'd tried to convince the scarred leader to move camp earlier.

Poor fellow was right. A sharp stake of wood jutted from his stomach. And his short sword lay beside an open hand.

It wasn't her sword. Riony wasn't sure where it might be at this point. She'd do anything to get it back, but until then, she'd take any weapon she could. It was only a couple of steps away, and Riony heaved the half-cart toward it. Her back and arms dripped with sweat.

She dropped to the ground beside the fallen slaver and propped the short sword between her knees. Holding it tight, she sawed at the rope binding her wrists. The chipped, serrated blade made short work of the bindings and her hands came free.

Shaking out her sore arms, Riony grabbed the sword into her right hand and rose to her feet with a huff of determination.

With a weapon in her hand, she felt like her chances of survival were no longer zero.

She gave it one good swing against where the manacle bolted to the half-cart, but it showed no sign of breaking, and she didn't want to break the old sword instead.

Every part of her screamed to go to Lyrrin. She would drag the damned half-cart right across the field of embers and fire to get there if she had to.

But she could still feel the pang of Dracuni's fear, hunger, and pain hanging like a weight over her mind too. And Dracuni was closer.

Squinting through the hazy twilight, Riony sought out Lyrrin in the cages.

There was a flurry of movement in that direction.

The cage Lyrrin hadn't been in was now empty. The door hung askew, twisted open by who knew what. The children that had been in it were now skittering all around the campsite, screaming and trying to find their way free from both the slavers and the revs preying upon them.

Yoskar was there, lit up with the bright glow of red Alderkin magic. He'd found his staff again and was swinging the flaming end, knocking back attackers as he rounded up children behind him.

Aishena was beside the other cage that Lyrrin and Benjin were in. She had no glow of magic about her but swung her attached chain like the deadliest of weapons as she stood guard before the cage, and the children crawling out of it.

A small gap was broken through in the corner were Lyrrin had been working with her nails. The bar was cut cleanly in two places, just tall and wide enough for a small child to wriggle out on their belly.

They were sliding out, one at a time, with Lyrrin still on the inside, encouraging them through.

A rush of pride burst into Riony like a deep breath after almost drowning.

Even the damned delvers. Maybe they were right to leave her. The kids needed them. Outside their cages they were easy pickings for the revs.

"You'd better get them all out of here safely," Riony muttered.

Turning away from the cages still felt like the hardest thing she'd ever done, torn between her two responsibilities. But Dracuni was close, only a few steps away.

She had to get the newborn off the ground. Even if the revs weren't interested in the backpack and what it held, one misplaced foot could mean the end for the precious creature.

Especially with that massive bovin rev still charging around the place. It had just gone right through one of the palisades and was coming back into camp on the other side.

Riony tucked the slaver's short sword into her belt and dragged the half-cart toward Dracuni. Her arms shook and ached. One step there, and she had to stop and draw the sword again, swiping it at an approaching hawk-rev that swooped at her.

She knocked it out of the air with her first strike, and it took three more before the mindless thing stopped moving.

One more step and she was near her pack.

Crouching beside it, Riony placed her fingers at the opening. She held her breath as she looked in at the completely still body of the unidragon baby. Only a quick blink of its wide lilac eyes showed it was still alive. Only the slight shiver of fear rippling over its soft, scaled skin.

Riony's heart broke at the terror and sadness washing from Dracuni. The poor thing must have thought she'd abandoned it.

"It's okay. I'm here."

Dracuni's heavy head turned upward and made a weak mewling sound.

"Hang in there. You can do it."

The din of combat seemed to be slowing, but the growling of revs and cries of pain continued. The slavers had fought hard, but there were just too many revs, and as each human fell, they grew more and more outnumbered.

A figure stumbled in toward Riony and she drew the short sword from her belt again, shooting back to her feet.

Not a rev this time, but she wanted to skewer the man anyway.

"Zade! Come on. Prove you aren't the worst person ever and help me get this damned manacle off!"

A trickle of blood ran down his temple, and he looked at Riony, distracted, then looked at the half-cart she was still attached to. He blinked a few times and then waved a hand holding a burning athame at the broken timber.

"Where are the Hjelzahns?" He was already turning away, scanning around the gloomy camp.

Riony yanked on the chain, rattling it loudly. "Forget them and your stupid bounty! Is that really worth more than saving my life?"

Zade turned his eyes back her way. "So you can keep fighting against the people who were trying to help you? Who were trying to help those children? This is the world we're trying to keep them safe from!"

Zade gestured at the clashing humans and undead all around them. "If you can't see that, now, in the midst of all of this ... if you can't admit that we need the dragonlords to keep us safe, and repay them in kind, then you aren't worth anything at all."

"The kids were safe in the undercity! We all ... Zade, ZADE! Come back here!" Riony screamed at him as he sprinted away.

Do I just have the kind of face that begs people to leave me alone to die or something? Riony was starting to take it personally.

A gust of wind blew Riony's hair across her face. The sound of wings made her cringe, and she turned to seek the shadowdragon's form against the darkened sky.

It had remained, lingering above, but it wouldn't come back again, would it? There were at least a few newly dead bodies around, and Riony's mouth twisted at the idea of facing such fresh corpses.

But the shadowdragon's wings didn't stir the air and dust.

The pounding of massive hooves snapped her attention back to the ground. That bovin had her in its sights again, charging directly at her and Dracuni.

Oh sparks, not again.

Riony grabbed the strap of her pack in one hand and wrapped her other around the chain, trying to drag her half-cart out of the path of the rampaging beast.

Riony's surroundings brightened in a flash of warm orange, and she turned her eyes upward. Panic shot like lightning through her clammy hands and she bucked at her chains.

She was in no way fast enough. Not to get clear of the charging bovin rev or to avoid the massive ball of fire lancing down from the sky toward her.

Chapter Twenty-Five

Dragonriders.

Kess edged herself out from the gap between a tent and a woodpile she'd squeezed herself into when everything got razed. Heat touched her cheeks as the bovin rev went up in flames. It barreled on like a flaming boulder from sheer momentum, before it slumped into a burning heap on the ground, not far from the smashed remains of a cart.

A jet of white liquid flame splashed across the camp, and screams went up as a few humans were caught in amongst the mass of targeted revs.

A snowflame! Kess shimmied farther out, her eyes fixed on the sky.

Two dragonriders were within view, their majestic steeds hovering on vast, leathery wings. The dragons' vivid scales shimmered in the glow of the fires beneath them.

Two etherflames, one orange and one red. Basic. Solid fire-breathers for dealing with undead, which made them a dragonrider staple, but big and slow, hard to maneuver.

The riders shone as bright as their steeds, their armor forged from the very same scales. Lighter and more flexible, but so much stronger than the simple metal that had been favored for forging armor during the war and was so easy to come by now.

Only the worthy could wear dragon scale armor. Kess watched every movement and action of the two etherflame riders, her gaze ravenous. The tamed steeds could do nothing on their own. The heavy metal spike hammered into their foreheads made sure of that obedience.

Every action, every command, came from the rider. The way they angled their weight, squeezed their grip.

Kess's hands tingled, as she missed that same connection she had with Griskin. The way she would move her body and he would respond, always seeming to know what she wanted, what direction to move and how fast.

She turned briefly toward where he was netted, thankfully safe from flames, for now. She'd get back to him soon.

Griskin wasn't tamed, though. He was as wild as they came, but still Kess had mastered him as her steed. *Only more proof that I'm ready to ride a dragon!*

Sometimes, Kess wondered whether a dragon had to be tamed in order to ride it. She'd been underestimated her entire life. How those people would be humiliated if she became the first rider to fly an untamed beast!

First, I need a dragon, any dragon, tamed or not, to prove them all wrong. Maybe I'll get lucky and one of the riders will be knocked off.

Kess scanned the night air, trying to catch sight of the elusive snowflame.

A hybrid of a snowshimmer—sleek, solitary, smaller-sized mountain dragons—and the big etherflames from the plains. They'd never interbreed normally in the wild, but the breeders who provided the dragonriders with their steeds had worked out how to get viable offspring with the best features of both parents.

Smaller than etherflames, they were fast and nimble, and their breath weapon was without compare for clearing out revs. The only thing that made them rare was their very short lifespan.

Still, they were the kind of dragon that only the best dragonriders would earn. The kind she would have one day.

There! Kess craned her neck as it sped across the camp again, laying down another stream of white flames.

For a long moment, Kess couldn't tear her gaze away from the dragons and their masters, her heart pounding in her throat.

The air crackled as the dragons unleashed streams of searing fire that erupted from their gaping maws, engulfing the undead in a cleansing inferno.

The entire camp was going up in flames. The woodpile Kess hid behind, already half-charred, scavenged from burned forests, smoldered and sparked.

But she remained frozen, transfixed by the deep yearning she'd known her whole life, to become what she was destined to be, what every Heithorn should be. Heat licked her arms and face, and she imagined what it would be like to be up above the burning earth, riding among those fearless ranks. How it would feel to command the awesome power of those beasts, tamed and under her complete control.

Someday, she would join those ranks of dragonriders. Nothing would stop that from happening.

Especially not burning to death in this stinking slavers' camp.

Kess dragged her body across the scorched earth, her fingertips blackened by soot. She had half the camp to clear to get back to Griskin. She could get there, but not fast, and the fear that she'd get trampled, set upon by the undead, or hit with a jet of fire left her sheened in a cold sweat.

Intense heat radiated from all around, and the scent of burnt flesh and decay filled the air. The undead creatures withered and crumbled under the relentless assault, their faltering growls reverberating across the camp.

The dragonriders had turned the tide. Slavers who had fled or hidden were coming back, picking through the fire and smoke to gather anything they could of value that remained.

Mostly, that meant the escaping children scattered all around.

Nobody seemed worried about a small, solitary girl, edging her way along the ground.

Through the haze of smoke, Kess spotted a figure lying motionless ahead on her path. A warning of caution flickered in her mind as she crawled closer. She was right on top of him before she could identify the body as Iarl, the slaver leader.

The sun blesses me. With a wry grin, Kess sat up and reached out to search the man for her vial of silvernix.

She patted his chest, feeling a small bump to one side under his ragged jacket.

As she pulled the fur-lined fabric apart, the man's eyes flickered open, filled with malice and rage.

Kess hissed, scolding herself for not checking he was actually dead first. She'd already made that mistake with Pony.

"Trying to pillage the dead?" The slaver's hand shot out, grabbing around her reaching wrist before she could withdraw it.

A surge of adrenaline fired through Kess's veins as his clammy fingers squeezed her skin. Depending on how injured the man was, he could still easily overpower her. She opened her clenched fists, holding her palms up in surrender.

"No, sir, I was trying to see if you were still alive, if I could help you."

"Ha!" Iarl barked, then winced. He let go of Kess, both hands clutching at his side. As he squeezed there, blood pressed through the fabric and stained his fingers.

"Where have you got the silvernix? You can use it for your wounds, so you don't end up dead after all."

His eyes went wide. "Yes. The silvernix! Where …" Fumbling around with shaking fingers, he pulled Kess's coin pouch out from where she'd felt the lump.

Kess slowly brought her hands down and stared at the injured man. The flicker of fire shone off his sweaty forehead and his breaths came fast. As another burst of flame went up nearby, he cringed away from it. Kess held him in a steady glare.

"You're right. I wasn't going to help you. But I've changed my mind. I'm going to give you a swift death, which is more than a slaver of children like you deserves, and then I'm going to take what's mine."

"You, little girl? Ha," he grumbled, lips curled in a painful smile as he tugged the pouch open. Coins spilled out onto his chest as he groped inside. "What are you—"

Kess had a sharp bone dagger lanced into the man's heart as fast as lightning. "And no. Not even silvernix will save you."

He stared at her, mouth open and eyes confused as she leaned her body weight onto the blade, pressing the rest of the way in slowly, holding eye contact the whole time, until the light in his eyes went out.

Kess tsked. "People always underestimate what I'm capable of."

She left the dagger there—she had plenty and could always make more. Plucking the pouch from his still fingers, Kess checked inside. There it was, her bottle of unicorn blood.

She quickly scooped up what she could of the scattered sovs as well.

"Yuck." She grimaced, wiping the man's blood off them on the sleeve of his shirt.

Bringing herself upright again, Kess looked across to her target—Griskin. Without him, it felt like half of her was missing. Not just the ability to move faster, but the way she understood his body language, as though she shared his superior senses. She felt so much less without him.

Kess hiked her legs over the dead body of the slaver leader—just an obstacle now in her path—then crawled forward on her forearms.

Sparks and smoke gusted around as a dragonrider swooped low, scattering embers across the ground. Kess snarled as they singed holes into her leather bracers and gathered under her stomach, burning through her shirt, but she kept moving.

Movement rushed through the haze straight toward her and she froze.

A human rev, skeletal and engulfed in flames, stumbled before her.

The creature's charred bones crackled and glowed, its skeletal frame twisted and contorted in its final moments as it collapsed.

The heat radiating from its burning body seared the air, filling Kess's nostrils with the acrid scent of smoldering bone and seared flesh.

Flames danced hungrily across the creature's remains, devouring it with relentless fervor. The crackling of the inferno drowned out the distant sounds of battle, leaving only the roar of the consuming fire echoing in her ears.

She watched, a mix of fear and fascination gripping her, as the flames lapped at the creature's brittle form.

Her breaths came shallow and rapid, her body trembling with a mixture of relief and lingering dread as the revenant stilled, the false life the shadowdragon had given the corpse burned away in cleansing fire.

That scourge that the Alderkin cursed the land with—Kess could feel her hatred for the blight spreading being deep in her gut. Her parents had taught her the history of what Elundrae used to be like before the shadowdragon came into being, drawing the undead from the earth.

How the Alderkin had cursed humans with it when it was clear they had lost the war. How dragonfire was the only sure way to cleanse the undead, no matter the collateral.

And how they never allowed Kess to become the dragonrider she'd been born to be, so she could help to save their land, too.

A shadow passed over Kess, and she looked up, hoping for another view of the snowflame darting by.

It wasn't there. Even the etherflames had moved from their hovering position, backing away. Their job was all but done.

But the shadow over Kess deepened.

She rolled onto her back for a better view, and her jaw trembled and breath stuck.

The shadowdragon was descending ... again.

But why? There were some freshly dead that it could raise, but Kess had never seen nor heard of it touching ground in the same place twice so soon apart.

It's smoky, swirling wings flapped without sound or substance, and the bright spots of its eyes shone like red stars against its void-black head.

The camp went strangely, eerily silent as it came to rest on the ground. No cries or wails this time, only a mute, clenching despair from everyone who observed. A desperate pang of mourning speared through Kess again, as it did the last time the cursed being touched ground.

And the shadowdragon roared.

The sound shuddered through Kess's chest, rattling her heart within her rib cage.

A deep growl grumbled from behind her. Iarl's white-eyed corpse jolted and convulsed.

Kess hissed between her teeth. She really didn't want to have to kill him twice.

Then another more terrifying, crackling sound came from between her and Griskin.

She turned her head slowly, not wanting to see what the sound was coming from, because there was only one thing close enough, and it couldn't be. It couldn't …

The still smoking human rev that had collapsed before her twitched and juddered.

Kess could only shake her head at it in denial. It had been burned. It was burned and it should never be able to come back again.

All remnants of flesh had been scorched from its bones, leaving only a horrific soot-blackened skeleton. Ashes flaked from it and fell like snow as it clawed itself off the ground.

Now the crying and screaming began again, a cacophony of terror rising all around from the remaining humans. Because all around, the burned revenants had impossibly come back from the dead … a second time.

Kess wailed through clenched teeth, tearing across the ground away from the new and old revenant bodies she had found herself between. She had to find shelter, somewhere to hide again. But where could that be, with the whole camp aglow with raging dragonfire?

Where could that be, in a world where burnt revenants could rise again?

A deep, dark thought shook Kess to her core. The curse of the shadowdragon was worsening. How? And why? The Alderkin were all gone, their race and their magic destroyed entirely in their war against the dragonlords.

If they were the cause of the shadowdragon, why was it getting worse *now*?

Chapter Twenty-Six

The overturned half-cart that Riony had sheltered behind as the world went up in flames now felt like less shelter than a parasol made of cobwebs.

The dead had come back to life. Again.

Riony wished she was closer to the shadowdragon so she could punch the thing in its face. Had anyone even tried that before? Maybe it was the one thing that would end this depths-damned curse for good, but nobody had ever dared.

Riony would dare. She'd love to punch that shadowy serpentine cloud in the face right now.

As much as she hated dragonriders, at least they'd had the revs under control. Riony had time to catch a breath, time to try, and fail, to pick the lock on her manacle with the tip of the short sword she'd pilfered, as the revs burned to ash around her.

And now they were all twitching back into life again.

The shadowdragon took wing, churning like a living tornado of nightmares back into the evening sky.

If only the damn cart had caught on fire too, at least then I might be free of the thing. If a little singed.

Dracuni bleated at her from the open pack near her feet, and Riony eyed the ashy, smoldering revenants that shivered back to life before her. The bovin, for starters, but also a hawk and a human skeleton and Colber—the skinny slaver, not long dead.

Somehow, he disturbed her the most. Still too warm, too squishy, his dead white eyes not far enough removed from a still-alive human.

Riony stood, pushing her bag and Dracuni behind her, between her ankles and the solid wood of the cart. In desperation, she jabbed the sword into the joint where her chain was bolted to the broken timber, trying to cut or lever herself free. With a bright clang, the tip of her sword snapped off.

"Sparks!"

There was no time to find another weapon as the first revenant lunged for her. Her grip tightening on the hilt of her even shorter short sword, she wished for the reach of her dragonguard longsword as the quick moving skeleton's boney fingers clawed for her face.

Riony cracked an elbow into its bare skull, knocking the lower half of its jaw flying. Ash eddied in the air behind it.

It stumbled back only to be replaced by the hawk, tattered, smoking feathers barely giving it enough lift to fly. It flapped in bursts, withered claws and fractured beak angling for Riony's neck.

Getting the sword between them, she swung like a bat, sending the undead bird soaring across the burning campsite.

And still the attack continued, both Colber and the human skeleton together now, grasping for her in unison.

The bovin had roused itself too. The crumbling, ashy joints seemed to reform like a strange, dry clay as the massive skeleton pulled itself together. Shaking itself off in a wave of smoke, Riony had her first break when it charged off in a different direction.

But the other two revs in human form wouldn't stop.

The ashy skeletal one reminded Riony so much of the one that had taken down the slaver ambush yesterday. Had it been burned and revived too, at some point? How long had this been happening? And how could these reborn revs be killed?

Nothing Riony did seemed to do more than barely keep them and their bloodthirsty jaws off her flesh for more than a moment. And sometimes it didn't, and their claws sliced ribbons across her arms and chest.

She met them with fist and sword, elbow and knee, forehead and feet. The blade of her sword sliced through brittle bones and spongy flesh.

The clash of steel against bone reverberated through the air as Riony unleashed a flurry of strikes, parrying and dodging and trying to push the relentless creatures off her just long enough to breathe. A gust of smoke stung her eyes and she fought blindly, tears streaming.

The revs didn't stop, didn't slow. Her brawling limbs and broken sword weren't enough to put them to rest again, if anything even could.

Across the campsite in the direction of the cages came a shrill scream. A voice Riony knew too well. *Lyrrin.*

Between the snarling, snapping faces of the two revs that had her pinned, Riony looked out, trying to spot her sister.

When the dragonriders had arrived, the slavers had taken the opportunity to gather their scattering slaves, rounding the children up as Riony worked frantically to free herself and get to Lyrrin before them. She'd lost track of her sister then.

She spotted the two delvers first, standing near the gaping hole in the palisades that the bovin had charged through earlier. A smaller figure ran behind them—Benjin, probably—out through the broken barrier. Yelling and the clash of steel and the bright red of the burn magic in Yoskars staff cut through the din.

And even through the smoke, Riony could see the bloodless pallor of their faces, the whites of their wide eyes.

Aishena turned then, her gaze cutting right through the chaos and meeting Riony's. Despite her arms till swinging and muscles still burning, Riony felt time seemed to stop as they looked each other in the eye.

And then Aishena and Yoskar turned and fled.

Riony wasn't even surprised this time. Everybody of sound mind was running now. Riony would be too if someone had just taken a depths-forsaken second to unchain her.

Some bold slavers kept fighting and rounded up what remaining children they could into the cages. The big red dragon—etherflame, probably, but only dumb Kess cared about that sort of thing—had its claws clamped into the top of the cage and was lifting the children who had been stuffed back inside to safety.

The safety of slavery, at least.

Amidst the chaos, Riony felt the impact of bony fists and claws breaking through her defenses and pummeling her body. She gritted her teeth, fighting through the pain.

She heard a shriek again and Riony's head swiveled, pinpointing the sound.

Lyrrin!

A man with ragged golden curls had one of her sister's arms gripped in his, dragging her toward the second cage. *Zade.*

Lyrrin bucked and squealed in his grip. As Zade grabbed her around the waist to toss her in through the open cage door, Lyrrin's little arm shot out.

Her ungloved claws slashed across Zade's face. His roar of pain rose over the other wails and screams.

Riony's nose scrunched up. *Good girl, Lyrrin. Hurt him good.*

"I'm trying to help you, you little freak!" Still gripping the small child, Zade roared again and swung her small form against the metal bars of the cage. The steel clanged against Lyrrin's skull, and she went limp in his arms.

Riony's burning body went cold all over.

She fought in a frenzy, twice as fast, twice as hard, unaware of any pain or exhaustion or anything other than trying to clear her path to Lyrrin.

Riony's teeth clenched so hard she thought she might break her jaw, and tears ran down her face from eyes abused by smoke and pain.

Stupid. I was so stupid. I should have gone to her first. She glared at the bag at her feet that held Dracuni. She couldn't do it. She couldn't look after them both. One responsibility was already too much for her to handle and she was getting everything wrong.

Aishena and Yoskar had it right. Just help themselves and stay alive. She couldn't fault them, really, since they'd managed to get themselves and their brother out of there. And what had Riony done?

Riony's parents had died from trying to help too many people. She should have learned their lesson and just focused on herself and her sister. Then she could have moved faster. Then she wouldn't have had to make efforts to hide what was in her pack and get messed around by Kess.

Then she might have had Lyrrin back already, and that dead man walking, Zade, couldn't have *hurt her.*

Riony's muscles strained, her body dripping with sweat. She couldn't keep fighting much longer. Her body was ready to crumple in on itself and give up completely, no matter how much willpower she used to try to keep going. And still the two revs that had her pinned wouldn't stop.

Dracuni mewled up from the ground, seeming to match Riony's rising distress and Riony growled back at the needy thing.

Zade tossed Lyrrin's limp body into the cage with the few other children that had been rounded up again.

The red dragon lifting the first cage of children had them just off the ground now, and panicked slavers were running after it, trying to leap up and grab hold of the outside of the cage, to be lifted away from the revenants too.

As the first etherflame dragon cleared the way, the second orange one moved in, angling around on huge leathery wings to get its claws onto the top of the remaining cage. The one that held Lyrrin.

Riony grunted as she tried to drag the half-cart forward, pushing against the two revs to clear ground at the same time, to get herself across the burning camp to Lyrrin before she was taken away.

But her muscles felt more like sacks of water at this point, wobbly and watery and weak. There was no way she could drag the heavy timber all the way through the campsite battleground in time.

Bright-white light scorched Riony's eyes, and she twisted to the side.

A stream of scorching liquid flame burst around her as the snowflame dragon swooped by.

The two revenants tumbled away, knocked back in the wash of fire.

Riony smashed backward into the half-cart behind her. She crumpled to the ground, dangling from her chained arm. Drawing deep, gasping breaths, her lungs filled with heat as the very dirt in front of her burned.

Hanging from the chain, Riony's face pressed against the timber, close to the ground near her open pack that had toppled onto its side. Dracuni peered out from within. The bright flames glistened in its wide eyes as it whimpered, moved to climb out of the bag closer to Riony, then circled back in again to hide.

The white flames formed a wall around where Riony huddled beside the broken cart. The snowflame's fire licked close to Riony's leg, and she pulled her foot away before it could burn.

Riony thumped her free fist onto the ground beside the bag. Her arm shook as tremors racked her overused muscles. She didn't even know if she had the strength to stand again.

"I should have gone to Lyrrin. I should never have brought you home from that cave." Riony's voice broke, the words too wrong, too painful. But she was so angry and so hurt and so left behind and so not enough to save anyone, even herself, that the words rushed out of her.

Dracuni's eyes widened, and it bleated and backed away from Riony into the pack.

Riony scrunched her face up and sniffed away a sob. Opening her fist, she reached out and cupped Dracuni's cheek in her hand. "I'm sorry. I didn't mean it. This isn't your fault."

Waves of worried emotion pressed into Riony's mind, and Dracuni clawed at the pack, as though trying to dig out through the leather walls to escape out the other side.

Riony pulled the pack closer, curling around it. "Don't worry. The revs won't come for you. If you can wait it out, try to run at the end, when it's all over."

When I'm gone.

Dracuni blinked at her, then looked to where her arm hung above her head, manacle heavy on her skin. The newborn bleated louder and scrambled more desperately. Riony reached for it, and it licked her palm as it dug little claws against the blanket it was tucked beside.

A surge of worry came again.

"Me? You're worried about me?" Riony's voice rose into a squeak.

With a big kick of its back legs, Dracuni unearthed the athame that Riony had left in the bag to show Lyrrin, back before everything fell to the depths.

Dracuni bleated again, circled around on the spot, then stilled again.

Picking up the athame, Riony gave the creature a half smile. She'd forgotten it was in there. Whether Dracuni thought it could help or just wanted it out of the way to be comfortable again in its hiding space, Riony didn't know.

But it was something. An offhand weapon to use with the broken short sword. That might improve her chances a little. Or maybe she could pick the lock on the manacles with it, since it was slimmer and pointier than the sword had been.

For one moment, Riony wondered whether the blade was an offering from Dracuni, one to take some of its blood. Riony probably looked awful, bleeding from multiple gashes, but it was her insides failing her now. Would it heal her worn muscles? Riony wasn't sure that was something silvernix fixed.

Regardless, she looked into the lilac eyes and soft scales of the little creature and knew she wouldn't do it.

"I won't cut you, okay? I want you to know that. I won't ever cut you to heal myself. I promise." The vow felt easy to make. Whether it was because Riony had little hope of getting out of there with or without unicorn blood to heal her, she wasn't entirely sure.

Holding the athame near her face, she nodded at it, took a deep breath, and prepared to fight again.

"Shame it's out of charge, because this cutting rune would have come in handy right about now." Riony rubbed her thumb over the sigil, tracing it out.

And the athame glowed into life.

Riony startled so hard that she launched onto her feet and almost landed in the surrounding flames.

"What the sparks?" The athame had been out of charge, she was sure. It had sputtered out in front of her eyes when she first found it.

Alderkin relics didn't just start working again. Once out of charge, they were done. Only Alderkin had the knowledge of how to recharge them, and they were all dead and gone even if they could have been persuaded to share.

But the cutting athame glowed a yellow as bright as the sun.

Riony gulped, held her breath, and ran the tip of the short crystal blade across her chain.

It sliced straight through with a soft sizzling sound. The remaining chain clattered free against the side of the cart.

Riony's body zinged with energy at its newfound freedom, as though shedding the weight of the half-cart gave her a second wind.

She glanced around. The two revs growled, skirting the wall of fire between her and them, waiting for the flames to die down so they could renew their attack.

Riony tightened her grip on the cutting athame. She wondered how well it might slice their heads from their necks and whether that would lay the things to rest.

Across the camp, the orange dragon had secured its grip on Lyrrin's cage and pumped its leather wings. The cage shook as it inched off the ground and the children inside whimpered and screamed. Riony didn't hear Lyrrin's voice.

Bending, Riony righted her backpack, tucking Dracuni carefully in and lashing the opening closed again. "Thank you, little one. I guess it's lucky I saved you, after all."

The straps of the pack had been cut below the buckle, but there were still a few notches in the remaining length. Riony pulled the cut sections out and rebuckled them.

Hoisting the bag onto her back, Riony then grabbed the broken short sword in her other hand. She climbed onto the pile of timber that had been the cart. Tensing her legs, she said a small prayer to the stars and Amma Moon, then launched herself over the white wall of flames.

She struck out at the two waiting revenants, hitting one with the cutting rune and one with the short sword. She didn't slow to see what damage she inflicted, only needing to clear her path.

Her arm muscles had borne the brunt of the fighting and heavy lifting earlier.

Now it was her legs' turn. They still felt fresh enough to run. And she put everything she had into moving faster than she ever had in her life.

She just had to get to the other side of the burning camp filthy with undead before Lyrrin's cage was too high for her to reach and she lost her little sister forever.

CHAPTER TWENTY-SEVEN

Riony barreled across the campsite, vaulting over burning bodies and dodging away from skittering revenants. A skeletal horse galloped by, passing in the opposite direction, snorting flames and streaming smoke behind it.

The orange dragon flapped, beating its wings hard with the additional weight of the cage and the children it held. Wind gusted across the camp, blowing in Riony's face, pushing against her like a barrier trying to hold her back.

A dark, shadowy shape leaped onto the dragon's tail, scampering up its back like a bizarre parasite. The dragon screeched and faltered, wings twitching and pulling in as the creature crawled around and up its chest.

Riony squinted at the creature through the heavy smoke, her eyes stinging and raw. A rev. A bear, maybe? Something larger than human, more mobile, more bestial.

It didn't try to hurt the dragon. Instead, it went straight for the rider.

The cry of alarm when the dragonrider noticed the attacker's presence was female. The revenant crawled to the dragonrider's saddle, and metal sung as the woman drew a pair of gleaming swords.

Perched upon the dragon's neck, just above its shoulders and the muscles of its wings, the rider twisted in her seat, flicking a leg upward and swinging herself upside down from one foot to dodge the revenant's claws.

Riony watched in awe as the rider brought herself under and around her dragon's neck and up the other side, climbing its scales like a cliff face, and coming up behind the confused revenant. Her armor glistened in the same sunset tones as her dragon, and her swords clattered against the revenant's back.

Riony knew it wasn't the right time to be forming a new crush, but damn, the rider was impressive.

Without its rider in control, the orange dragon faltered, wings held in place and torso stilling.

Even amongst all the fire and monsters, the dragon had only a dull, glazed look in its sun-bright yellow eyes. It looked everywhere and nowhere, head bowed, the heavy metal stake punctured into its brain leaving it numb to everything but its rider's commands.

The cage clattered back to the ground as the dragon's wings no longer fought against gravity. The door popped open, and the children inside squealed and pulled it closed again as revs closed in on them. Lyrrin stirred, propping herself up in one corner.

Riony's heart rushed with the warm blood of hope.

As long as the rev kept the dragonrider busy, it was buying Riony time.

Flames exploded to her left, and she dodged right, trying to keep up her pace.

Her path was strewn in bodies and burning embers, and her eyes were drawn to one—small and still moving—crawling with a steely determination in the direction of the netted wolf.

Riony's pounding footsteps slowed.

No. It wasn't worth heading all the way across there to slit the goblin's throat, then stab her in the back for good measure. As much as it sounded like a fun time, she didn't have the moments to spare.

Riony wasn't far from the wolf, though.

Taking a slight veer toward the trapped animal, Riony's lips twitched and curled. She didn't like the feeling that was swelling inside her. It felt too much like pity, and that was something she would never have for Kess. She knew better.

But maybe, maybe it was because she'd regained enough hope to share it around.

Riony had gone out of her way, had sacrificed greatly, to save the little creature in her backpack, even when it had felt like a poor decision. And now freed from her manacle by the athame that still glowed bright in her hand, she felt as though that had been the right decision.

She was so brimming with hope and compassion that it was hard to fight against. Maybe she could go out of her way once more to help another creature.

Stars, I better not regret this.

Riony skidded to her knees in front of the metal netting that pinned the wolf down. He growled low and deep as she raised the glowing crystal blade.

"Do yourself a favor, pup. Ditch the goblin. She's not your friend. She doesn't even know what the word means."

Riony slashed the athame and it sliced neatly through the netting.

"Go on, get yourself out of here."

The wolf twisted, roused into action by the prospect of escape. Riony scrambled straight back up into a sprint as the wolf thrashed itself free, each of them dashing in different directions.

Up ahead, the dragonrider's swords clattered to the ground. The woman's back was pressed against the dragon's neck, her hands gripping the saddle straps beside her head. She curled into a ball as the bear revenant's body smothered her in a whirlwind of claws.

Riony held her breath as she leaped over a spread of embers. If the dragonrider died, what would happen to the dragon? It currently sat like a bird on a perch on top of the cage. Its weight was too much for the shoddy construction and the bars were buckling and groaning, threatening to crush Lyrrin and the others inside.

Then the revenant shot backward, as though blown from a cannon. The rider's legs were both straight out in the air, her arms still grasping the saddle straps at her back. She'd curled in and waited until she had enough leverage on the rev to boot it off her. *Damn, that was bold.*

Riony could begrudgingly see why Kess was so obsessed with dragonriders.

Glancing over her shoulder, Riony saw the tail end of the wolf disappearing behind a cloud of smoke, the silhouette of Kess on its back.

Riony wasn't sure how she felt about that. The wolf deserved better, but it had made its choice.

With the bear rev off her, the dragonrider was already back in her saddle and the orange dragon sprung back to life, wings flapping hard.

The crushed cage groaned and creaked as it lifted from the ground, drawn upward within the dragon's claws.

A couple of adult-sized figures jumped onto it as it rose higher. One clung tight, but the other grasped at a bent bar that sprung free. The man screamed as he tumbled back to the ground. The children inside screeched as the cage swung around, threatening to toss them out of that hole too.

Riony threw the broken short sword to the ground and deactivated the athame, stuffing it down the front of her shirt as her quickest storage option, to free up her hands.

She drew every last bit of energy she had for a final burst of speed. She dashed the last few steps, ran up the burning downed carcass of the bovin rev, still twitching and hot under her boots, using its thick spine as a staircase, and leaped into the air.

She clattered against the side of the cage as it lifted above head height and clung tight.

Her cheek pressed against a bar, and she gasped in relief.

Then a boot smacked into her rib cage.

"Are you *sparking kidding me*," Riony huffed out the words.

The foot shot toward her again, and Riony knocked it aside with one hand, looking up at her attacker.

Zade shuffled away from her, around the corner of the dangling cage. Heading toward where Lyrrin still sat in one corner, looking woozy and teary.

"What are you going to do, Zade? Hide behind a child so I can't break that nose of yours a second time?" Riony kicked her legs out, swinging herself fast around the cage in the way she'd seen the dragonrider maneuver around her steed's neck.

The cage rattled and swung wildly from her weight, and the few children inside screamed. She went around the other side, cutting Zade off before he could reach Lyrrin.

"Why are you still fighting us?" Zade yelled back over the gusting flap of dragon wings. "We need to get out of here! They'll take us to safety."

"You're the one who tried to kick me off! I'm not going anywhere with them and I'm not going anywhere with you!" Riony shouted back.

Zade roared and lashed a fist out. Riony knocked it away from her face with her forearm.

His foot slipped and his swinging arm went wide, pulling his bodyweight sideways. The bent metal bar he held in his other hand creaked and popped. And then it slipped free.

Zade's eyes drew wide, and his mouth gaped in a scream as he fell into the open air. His hands scrabbled forward, trying to grab the cage again, but he fell through the smoke.

He thumped hard on the ground beneath Riony, and the impact cleared the smoke away. He cried out, back arching in pain, but survived. They weren't too far up yet.

Riony turned to yank open the door of the cage when another harsh gurgling scream ripped from Zade below.

The bear revenant was upon him, biting and tearing.

Within seconds, Zade's screams ended, and Riony looked away. She'd wished the young man a special death, but that was a rough way to go.

All she could do now was hope she and Lyrrin didn't go that way too.

The cage swung crookedly again as she wrenched the door open.

"Lyrrin!"

The other children cowered in a corner, clearing the way between her and her sister.

Lyrrin looked up, her blue eyes red-rimmed. Tears stuck her dark hair onto her cheeks and her lips trembled. Both arms shot out for Riony, one hand gloved, one without.

Riony leaned in, scooping her into a hug. The warmth of her sister's small form, clutched close against hers, was a salve to every pain she suffered.

"I'm here. I'm here."

Lyrrin gasped and gulped through sobs. "I tried. I tried to fight the kid snatchers, and not stop fighting, because I knew that's what you would do."

Riony squeezed her tight. "You did so well. I've got you now. And we're getting out of here."

Lyrrin blinked and looked from the airborne cage at the burning camp below.

Riony followed her gaze. It was hard to judge how high they were now with all the smoke beneath them, but Riony figured they were at least two stories up. The dragon had enough clearance that it began moving away from the campsite.

It would only get higher and faster from there.

Riony separated herself from Lyrrin. Pulling her arms out from her backpack straps, she moved it around onto her front.

"We're going to jump, okay?"

"Jump?"

"It's okay, it's not too high. We'll be scared for a moment, but it's better than a lifetime as a slave."

Lyrrin's little mouth closed tight. She looked into Riony's eyes and nodded.

Riony reached her arms out to Lyrrin again, pulling her in near her chest beside the backpack with Dracuni.

"Any of you lot want to come with us?" Riony asked the other kids.

The few children remaining shook their heads and clung to the corner of the opened cage.

Riony frowned. She didn't like the idea of them being taken away to slavery, but she couldn't force them to do what she was about to do.

Riony heaved up to her feet on shaking legs. She lifted Lyrrin with her, held tight in one arm as she held the cage with the other and stepped to the edge of the open doorway.

Yeah. It's not too high yet. I probably fell farther when I broke my arm.

Riony couldn't see the ground at all through the smoke.

She hadn't been prepared before, to fall a great distance again, not unless it was for something very special, very important. Now she was. This was worth falling for.

She swallowed hard and angled out into the air. Lyrrin squealed and hid her face in her shoulder, her legs wrapping tight around Riony's waist.

Dracuni also loosed a keening sense of fear through Riony's mind. Riony gritted her teeth. She was getting both of them out of this alive.

"Hey, listen to me now. This is important. The most important thing I've ever asked you."

Lyrrin didn't look up but nodded her face against Riony's shoulder.

"Once we hit the ground … no matter what … don't worry about me. Just take the backpack and run, understood? If you only do one thing I've ever asked you to do, do *this*. Okay, little spitfire?"

Lyrrin held still for a moment as the dragon's wingbeats grew faster.

Then she nodded again, and Riony stepped off the edge.

Chapter Twenty-Eight

Riony's shirt and cape fluttered like feathers around her as she, Dracuni, and Lyrrin plummeted through the acrid air.

As soon as they were off the edge, Lyrrin was screaming and didn't stop. Riony whipped her head about, trying to get a sense of which way was up, her red hair flicking into her eyes. Her body turned in dizzying circles, tossed about through gusts of smoke and embers.

She brought her knees up, wrapped her arms in, and curled her whole body around the two babies she'd stolen.

She'd taken them on, taken their lives as her responsibility, and she intended for them both to survive. But as soon as she'd stepped out into the air, she feared she'd made the dumbest decision of her life, that she'd killed them all. They couldn't have stayed in that cage though, flown back to captivity in a dragonkeep.

That could only end in Dracuni being revealed, taken from her, and forced into a life Riony couldn't even guess at. Who would take ownership of the precious newborn, and what would they do when they discovered its priceless blood?

Lyrrin, with her unique hair, hands, and eyes, wouldn't fare much better.

So Riony had jumped and had to trust in a plan that consisted of only two things: one, hope they weren't really up too high, and two, be the first one to hit the ground.

Stage one already had her shaken. They seemed to be falling forever, with the flame-heated air rushing around them and Lyrrin squealing and Dracuni's ***scared, scared, scared*** beating her thoughts like a drum.

That probably meant that part two of her plan wasn't going to end well. Definitely not for her. She only hoped she could cushion Lyrrin and Dracuni enough with her body for them to walk away. And that Lyrrin, for once in her life, would obey her wishes.

Please. Just take Dracuni and run. Maybe Lyrrin would catch up to the delvers, have their protection, make it home, even if she was going home without her.

The crackles of fire and clash of fighting grew suddenly louder and Riony braced for impact. Tears flicked upward out of her eyes into the air. The fiery landscape below expanded, a tapestry of swirling flames and billowing smoke, becoming real and solid and all too close, too fast.

She made contact. Her body smacked against something flexible and leathery, scraping against her back as she kept moving. Hot licks of cinders stung the bare flesh on her arms and flew around her face as she skidded down the soft, burning surface.

They bounced, slid, bounced again, then Riony toppled in a sideways roll off the leather and walloped hard onto the dirt on her back.

All the air woofed out of her chest. Riony closed her eyes and lay still, her flattened lungs squeezed closed like too-tight bellows, refusing to draw breath again.

Come on. Breathe. Breathe! Tears squeezed from the corners of her eyes as she willed her body to keep working.

There was a squeal and sob above her, as Lyrrin wriggled around, and her small hands tugged at the straps of the backpack that Riony wore on her front.

The weight of the bag and Dracuni lifted off Riony. She opened her eyes to see Lyrrin clutching the leather pack in a tight cuddle and wavering.

Working hard, Riony's chest inflated again in the smallest of breaths. She rasped out her words. "Good work. Go, run! I'm right behind you. Keep going!"

With a nod, Lyrrin took off. Riony wheezed in more air, her compacted lungs struggling to take shape again. She cried out as she pushed herself into a sitting position. Her whole body was going to be one big bruise tomorrow.

She was alive, still alive! But also, *ouch*.

A section of her shirt had caught on fire and she swatted at it, hissing as her fingers sizzled.

Glancing behind her, Riony saw the smoldering wall of one of the slavers' leather tents, tipped to the side and pulled taut. It wobbled, already slackening and slumping after her collision with it, tearing where the flames were taking hold.

Thank all the stars. The odds of landing on that one soft spot in all this chaos must have been a miracle. Riony shook her head at it in awe.

Behind the sinking tent wall, a silhouette moved, obscured by bright arcs of fire and a gust of embers. Riony tensed, expecting it to be a revenant, bracing for it to pounce.

But it turned, moving the other way. It was hard to tell what it was through the haze, large and misshapen, humanoid in some parts, but also not. A shiver ran across Riony's scalp. There was something wolfish about the shape, and its silent, prowling retreat. Kess?

Why would she still be there? She should have turned tail and fled this place the moment she got her wolf back. The silhouetted figure was gone now, vanished into the distance.

Whoever or whatever they were, Riony couldn't know for sure. And she couldn't wait around to find out.

She flopped forward onto her hands and knees, coughing as her winded lungs drew in a big breath of smoke. First, she crawled, then she got her legs under her, moving into a stumbling crouch, then a wobbling jog, until her legs and body worked well enough again to run.

She raced through the burning camp after Lyrrin.

It didn't take long to catch up, since Riony's legs were so much longer than her little sister's.

"Keep going, as fast as you can. I'm with you," Riony whispered. She put a hand on Lyrrin's shoulder, encouraging her on. The open gate of the palisades was just ahead.

There were less sounds now, less screaming. No more sounds of steel clashing against bone. They had been replaced with more disturbing wet chewing noises.

A few revs still prowled through the smoke, but all their prey had fled or already been killed now, and many of the revs seemed to have rambled out into the surrounding wilderness seeking more human life to hunt.

Riony kept her and Lyrrin moving at a fast and quiet pace through the haze, hoping none of the undead would notice that some of their missing prey had fallen from the sky and returned to them.

Nearing the gates there was a glint of metal on the ground ahead.

"Keep going, right out the gate." Riony gave Lyrrin a small push and sidetracked toward the bright strip of steel on the ground.

Lyrrin kept going straight, and Riony flushed with pride. *She's doing so well, and by the stars, she's following my instructions!*

All it took was a long sequence of life-and-death situations. Maybe Riony just needed to replicate these conditions back at home now and then, to keep Lyrrin open to her suggestions.

Home. A destination that was finally feeling possible again. But still so far away. She just had to make it one step at a time.

Riony had hoped that the bright spot in the dirt reflecting the glow of fire was a sword. Honestly, a weapon of any kind would have been a blessing. There were still revs all around, and it was a long, long way home.

When it came within full view, she bit her tongue to avoid letting out a triumphant scream that would alert all the revs to her location. A small happy squeal wheezed out of her anyway as she loped forward, bending to scoop up the abandoned sword as she ran.

Her sword. The dragon-scale patterned hilt felt so familiar in her grasp, the weight of it as recognizable as family. She had her sword back. She had Lyrrin. And she had Dracuni, still alive, tough little newborn it was. Riony looked up at the stars and all the ancestors they held looking down at her and blew them a kiss.

She swerved back toward the gate, sprinting to catch up to Lyrrin, and they broke out from between the perimeter together.

Riony didn't dare stop running. They left the carnage of the slavers' camp in their wake. She kept her legs pumping and kept gasping out encouragements to Lyrrin every time she slowed or started to lose her grip on the pack.

They ran until they physically couldn't run any farther, and then they stumbled on stiff, wavering legs, blindly through the nighttime forest, through sodden grass onto rocks.

The harsh scent of burning wood and flesh—some of it her own—clung to Riony's clothes and had scorched her nose and throat, but the air now seemed clear.

The night around them was quiet, only a few crickets trilling and the soft gurgle of running water and Riony and Lyrrin's lead-heavy footsteps breaking the silence.

Riony's head spun, dizzy with the hum of exhaustion, but she kept pushing forward.

She hoped no revs had wandered out this far in this direction. She hoped no slavers had come this way either. She couldn't fight either off at this point. She could barely lift a finger.

She also hoped the direction they headed in was the right one to take them home. But even if it wasn't, it was something she could work out after she was no longer busy passing out.

Her body finally gave in, and she folded to the ground, face-first into the dirt.

CHAPTER TWENTY-NINE

A great splash of frigid water across her face roused Riony.

She spluttered, and all four limbs flew upward, ready to fight off the next wave of attackers.

"You're alive!" Lyrrin squeaked, stepping out of the way of Riony's flailing fists.

Riony froze, blinked, and took in her surroundings.

Lyrrin stood close, but not too close, to her side, clutching the sodden end of her cloak, wrung between her hands. The pack, still closed, had been left on a flat rock behind her, and behind that, a cliff rose into the night sky, creating a small overhang.

It was dark, only moonlight weakly highlighting the edges of objects nearby. Riony could hear the trickle of water through rocks but couldn't see where it came from through the gloom.

"You *doused* me?" Riony wiped her face with her palms and forearms.

"I thought you were dead! You have blood ..."

"Where?" Riony asked, rubbing at aching and stinging dark smudges on her skin that could all have been bruises, burns, blood, or soot.

"*Everywhere*," Lyrrin whispered, her eyes bright and round.

Riony batted a hand at the air. "I'm fine, just—ouch—have to ... *woof*. Nope. I'm going to stay sitting down."

Riony's body felt like she'd gone ten rounds with relentless undead opponents, then fell onto her back from a great height.

Oh sparks, I totally did though.

She didn't blame Lyrrin for thinking she was dead. She was amazed herself that she was still alive, and there was a weird choking sensation in her throat due to wondering whether Kess had some part of that outcome.

There's no chance. She wouldn't have. Would she? No chance.

Kess had left her to bleed out and die alone in a frozen cave when she had the means to save her. Riony shook her head to herself. No. Hitting that tent wall had been luck, and luck alone.

And if that had been Kess watching from the smoky shadows, she was probably only there to get the front row view of Riony going splat and was sorely disappointed.

But still the lump in Riony's throat remained, images of Kess and Griskin's silhouette swirling in her mind like they did through the ashy clouds.

Riony shivered, the chilled water dripping from her face and onto her chest, soaking her shirt. She wasn't sure if they could dare to get a fire going.

"No sign of revs?" she asked.

Lyrrin fiddled with the wet end of her cloak and looked around with worried eyes.

"Nuh-uh. Haven't seen anybody else. It's been really quiet."

Riony nodded. It did feel quiet. She looked over at her backpack, lying still on the rock, and felt no sensations coming from Dracuni. She took a deep breath and swallowed hard.

"Hey, can you bring my backpack over to me? I would get it myself, but ouch."

Lyrrin moved quickly to pick it up, without even an eyeroll or grunt. Riony's lips quirked. She could get used to this, but she knew it wouldn't last.

While Lyrrin brought the backpack, Riony pulled her glow stone from the netted pouch on her belt, activated it, then tucked it down between some rocks so its light didn't spread too far. Just enough soft, cyan luminance for her and Lyrrin to see by.

"I'm sorry I let the kid snatchers take me." Lyrrin meandered back slowly, clutching the bag and looking at the ground.

"It wasn't your fau—*wait*. What do you mean, *let them* take you?"

"'Cause I saw them grabbing Benjin when I was going to go and fight the baby dragon killers."

Riony held the bridge of her nose and sighed.

"And then I followed and saw Zade and some other people grabbing up a heap of kids. And I tried to stop them, 'cause that's what you would have done."

"You think too highly of me, kid."

Lyrrin poked at a loose pebble with her toes. "But you would have! I even punched Zade so hard! Just like you would have! But it didn't stop them. I'm sorry."

Riony coughed out a chuckle, remembering Zade's bleeding nose and blackened eyes he'd blamed on the slavers. "That was you? That was a nice hit."

Lyrrin looked up, beaming. She skittered across the rest of the way and handed Riony her backpack.

"I'm sorry, but that otter of yours isn't in here anymore." Riony shifted around so she could lean against the wall of the cliff.

Lyrrin nodded and a couple of fresh tears dropped. "I saw him run off. Do you think he'll be okay out there?"

"Oh yeah. That guy? Tough little thing will be running around pilfering food from every pocket he can get." Riony was far more worried about the other creature she'd carried.

Her fingers trembled as she worked on untying the closure to the bag. Her head felt quiet, abandoned, without the added feelings and sensations of the little creature that she was getting used to.

Please be alive, little Dracuni.

There was still no movement from within as Riony reached a hand inside to feel the bundle of velvety scales and floppy wings. She cupped Dracuni's head in her hand and felt a slight wobble as the skin around its large eyes opened.

The newborn let out a weak, dull trill.

"What is that?" Lyrrin asked.

Riony put her second hand into the pack too and scooped Dracuni out onto her lap. "So, what I didn't get to tell you before you ran off to punch delvers and slavers, is that the delvers didn't kill *all* of the baby dragons."

Lyrrin wheezed, inhaling so much, so fast, that Riony was worried she might explode.

"It's a *baby dragon*?" Lyrrin cried.

"Shh! And sort of. Not entirely. I'm not sure."

Lyrrin dropped down next to Riony, cuddling up to her side and cooing at the limp bundle of pale rainbow scales on her lap.

"Is it okay? What's wrong with it?" Lyrrin asked, reaching out her gloved hand to stroke the baby's cheek. Dracuni opened its mouth again, a silent, wobbly plea.

Hungry. It was so weak now.

Riony frowned, her heart heavy. "It's hungry. But I haven't been able to feed it."

"For this long? Since it was born?" Lyrrin scolded her harshly.

"I tried. I tried everything, but it wouldn't take anything I offered it. And I had so much food before, you should have seen it ..."

"Did you chew on it first?"

"Chew on ... the dragonling?"

"No, the food, silly! It hasn't got teeth yet. You've got to chew up the food for it, like an amma bird."

Riony planted both hands on her face. "Ugh! Of course! But I don't have anything left now, except ..."

Riony checked her belt pouch, and inside were three small bruised and cracked apples. "Stars, I wanted to share these with you. They're kind of wrecked now. I think I landed on them a few times."

Lyrrin gasped. "*Apples*?" She reached for one and plunged her teeth into the browned flesh. "Mmm, it's so good."

She chewed for a moment, then stuck a finger into her mouth, scooped a lump of mashed pulp out of her cheek, and offered it to Dracuni.

Eyelids drooped, then lifted, then drooped again as the dragonling's snout twitched. With a tiny bleat, it opened its mouth, and Lyrrin stuck her finger straight in. She giggled as the newborn suckled on her, slurping off the chewed-up fruit.

Dracuni's eating!

Riony huffed an uncontrollable laugh of relief. "That's gross."

"You're gross." Lyrrin giggled back.

"I want a turn." Riony bit off a big chunk of apple, grinding it between her teeth. She sobbed happily when Dracuni lifted its head to take the messy fruit off her fingers.

Hungry. More hungry! The thoughts came through loud and clear as the little creature's appetite and strength came back.

"You're going to be okay, little one. We've got you." Riony spoke as she chewed, preparing to feed the newborn again.

She and Lyrrin took turns, laughing and chewing and feeding the baby unidragon, and sometimes taking a bite of apple for themselves as well. The three small apples were gone too fast, and Riony regretted the wealth of food scattered on the ground back at the slavers' camp.

No chance she was going back for it, though.

Dracuni was now sucking on the wet hem of Lyrrin's cloak, eyes drooping into a contented sleep. It felt warm on her lap, and with Lyrrin tucked in beside her too, Riony no longer shivered.

She hadn't meant for her little family to grow, but she was happy that it had.

Lyrrin seemed to have grown so much, too, in the last couple of days.

Riony scratched Dracuni's forehead around the base of its single horn, and whispered to Lyrrin, "So, the really special thing about Dracuni—"

"Aw, that's such a cute name!"

"—is that it—well, she, I think she's a she—she has blood like unicorn's blood."

"What? How can that be?"

"I don't know. I used Grand-Amma's silvernix on Dracuni's egg because it was broken, and then ... then the little critter was just born like this. I found out when she healed me." Riony held up her once-broken arm, stripping off the tattered remains of Lyrrin's bandaging.

Her sister gasped. "You could heal yourself again now! You could be all better! Except ..." Lyrrin's excitement faded quickly, and her frown returned, eyes searching in thought.

Riony shrugged. "I sort of promised Dracuni that I wouldn't do that. Which, honestly, I'm kind of regretting right now. Even my bruises have bruises. But I just couldn't, you know? I couldn't hurt her."

Lyrrin nodded vigorously. "That's what I thought, too. Just after I thought you could be healed, I remembered that it was her blood that heals, and you only get blood when you get hurt. I don't want to hurt her either. She's too cute! And only a baby."

"That's why Dracuni has to stay our secret. Bigger secret even than your hair and your fingers, okay? We can't let anybody take Dracuni and hurt her."

Lyrrin lifted her hands in front of her, one glove missing, revealing the sharp blue-tipped claws. Her bottom lip trembled. "I'll try. I promise I'll do my best. But ... Some people saw ..."

Riony put an arm around Lyrrin and squeezed. "It's okay. You did what you had to do to survive. We found your markers; that's how we followed you."

"You did?" Lyrrin perked up.

"Yup. Sometimes taking action is more important than staying secret at the time. We'll work the rest out as we go."

"What was it Pabba used to say? Big dreams, bold deeds?"

A hot sting rushed into Riony's nose and eyes, and she sniffed it away. "Yeah ... something like that."

Lyrrin nodded, folded her arms in, and snuggled closer to Riony. Sighing a soft release, Riony let the tension seep out of her body as she relaxed back against the stone behind her and even dared close her eyes for a moment.

The slip of feet on pebbly ground clattered through the dark.

Riony shot upright. She slid Dracuni off her lap and back into her bag in one swift motion, then gestured for Lyrrin to stay quiet as she reached for her sword. She stilled and listened.

"Shh!"

"You shh!"

A small whimper.

"Would you all be quiet? Sparks!"

Riony got to her feet with a muffled groan, sword drawn in front of her and Dracuni and Lyrrin behind. She frowned and squinted toward the surrounding darkness.

"Aishena? Was that you?" she called in a loud whisper.

As though materializing from the black background, Aishena stepped out over the rocky ground toward them. "Yes, it's us. You can put your sword away, tamebrain."

Riony lifted her sword point higher. "I don't know if I want to. What if, and hear me out, what if I get to stab you once for each time you abandoned me?"

"Not everything is about you." Aishena held up her hands, the manacle and long chain still dangling from one.

"It felt a lot like it was about me when the abandoning was happening. Come on. Just one little jab. It will make me feel much better."

"We had to get out of there to save the kids." Yoskar's voice pierced through the darkness. He stepped forward, trailed by a huddled group of a dozen or so children.

Lyrrin scampered to her feet and squeaked. "Benj! Cammi! Leeu! You all made it!" She rushed forward into the group of children, hugging and gossiping.

Riony huffed and lowered her sword. "Sorry. Looks like you two did the right thing. I guess I'm kind of used to people *not*."

"Fair. We kind of just wanted to take Benjin, but they all came as a set together." Aishena rolled her eyes at the tight huddle of whispering children.

Riony watched as Lyrrin moved through them, checking the faces. She watched Lyrrin's joy as each teary, sooty, relieved face met hers.

Riony's heart ached for how she had scolded Lyrrin for not staying in their rooms all alone. How the child kept sneaking out to spend time at the orphans' den.

It was never just disobedience. These were her friends.

Yoskar leaned heavily on his staff as he moved in closer and propped himself against the cliff wall with a sigh. "Benjin said they wouldn't have gotten out of the cage to us if it weren't for Lyrrin. No idea how she managed to cut through those bars though."

"Yeah, I don't know how," Benjin added, his eyes locked with Lyrrin's.

Lyrrin's lips were pressed together, and she hid her one ungloved hand under her cloak as everybody looked to her.

Yeah, no idea, I'm sure. Riony winked at the delver's little brother and gave him a small nod.

She reached into the front of her shirt and pulled out the athame she'd stashed in there. She chucked it over to Aishena. "She had this."

Aishena held the athame up, angling it to get enough light to read the rune. "A cutting athame? That has charge? How do you two own something like this?"

Riony smirked. "We all have our little secrets."

Aishena stilled. "I suppose we do."

Smiling again now, eyes sparkling in the dark, Lyrrin stepped next to Benjin. "Benj kept watch for me, so I could work without the kid snatchers seeing me."

Benjin made a big *aw-shucks* gesture, and his eyes kept turning back to Lyrrin every few seconds.

"That's still ours, by the way." Riony snatched the athame back out of Aishena's fingers, worried about how the delver was practically caressing it. "But I can get those things off you, if you want."

Riony gestured to the manacles still weighing down the delvers' arms. Activating the rune, the area blazed with yellow light.

"Did you see where Zade ended up?" Aishena asked, eying the athame in Riony's hand.

"Yeah. I saw him again, after the shadowdragon touched ground a second time."

Silence fell over all of them as the questions and the horrors of the moment resurfaced.

Riony cleared her throat. "He didn't make it."

Taking care not to slip and amputate Aishena's arm—while also fantasizing about it a little—Riony sliced the manacle lock. The chain clattered onto the ground.

"I never did like him." Aishena rubbed the raw skin where the manacle had been.

"Yeah, I *did* notice the open hostility. Never thought you'd be the one with the well-refined instincts, though."

Aishena shrugged her angular shoulders, flinching slightly as she looked to Yoskar as though for approval, but he offered none.

"Sorry I didn't get your weapons back off his corpse for you. Could have made a nice gift. Maybe make you realize you're sweet on me, after all," Riony said as she turned to work on Yoskar's cuff.

"I've got plenty more athames back at home." Aishena huffed and rubbed her wrist. "It would take far more than that to win my affections."

Yoskar's manacle fell free, then Riony turned the magically sharpened tip of the glowing crystal toward the band of iron that still clasped her arm, despite the chain being removed earlier.

"So, you mean something a bit more like journeying through the perilous aboveground with you, saving you and your brother's life, breaking you free from your chains, not stabbing you after you abandoned me. Something like that?"

"Not even close." Aishena smirked.

"Wow. High standards. That's hot."

"But ..." Aishena's eyes softened, and she tilted her head. "Maybe it's enough for us to put in a good word for you with Brishan. Get you a head start when the next delver trials come up."

Riony's jaw dropped and she nearly slipped and cut her own arm off. The manacle fell away. Swallowing, she slowly and carefully deactivated the cutting rune. "You'd do that for me? Really?"

With the light extinguished again, the area seemed much darker, and Riony could only just make out Aishena's shrug. "I mean, you did okay. And yeah, we do kind of owe you."

"A debt must be repaid," Yoskar agreed solemnly.

"I would kiss you on the mouth right now, but I respect your boundaries."

"Gross!" Lyrrin scoffed.

"You're gross," Riony shot back, grinning toothily.

Aishena made a show of ignoring Riony now and herded the group of children into shelter under the overhanging cliff. She didn't suggest a fire, either, but the sheer number of bodies and the barrier from the breeze seemed to keep everybody warm enough.

"Oh. Also, we found this." Yoskar removed his backpack and rummaged around in it. When he pulled his hand back out, he held up a wriggling sausage of pale caramel fur by the scruff of its neck. "Or rather, it found us. Caught it sniffing for food."

"*Sir Butterfur Spelunkychunks*!" Lyrrin gasped, running in to snatch the cave otter. She cuddled him tight and giggled as he skittered through the opening of her collar and hid in her shirt, chittering angrily.

Benjin added quickly and ardently, "Which we *weren't* going to eat for dinner."

"Well ..." Aishena muttered.

"We weren't!" Benjin snapped back.

Aishena's eyes sparkled. "All these hungry children ..."

"I will stab you in your sleep," Lyrrin hissed.

Riony chuckled and settled her tired body back onto a rocky seat.

"Some food and some sleep. We've got a long way to go back tomorrow." Yoskar pulled a bundle of flatbread from his pack—the parchment wrapping gnawed through in one corner by the cave otter—and shared the food with everybody.

"Dibs not keeping watch," Riony said, her eyes heavy.

"I will," Aishena replied, still at attention at the front of the group.

Riony nodded and settled in as best she could on the uneven ground, her pack and Lyrrin tucked in beside her.

It would be a long trip to get back to the undercity with all the additional children in tow.

But once they were back, they would be safe again. That's what mattered.

Safe from that dispersed group of slavers, from dragonriders, from seeing Kess ever again, and from the revs, and whatever was going on with the revenants coming back to unlife a second time.

We will be safe again once we get back to the undercity ... won't we?

Riony shivered. The hard lump in her throat had remained, as though she'd breathed in part of the shadowdragon's smoky form, a piece of its curse now embedded in her, turning all her insides into fear.

Chapter Thirty

Griskin's fur reeked with the musky tang of smoke residue. Kess leaned into him, her scraped and burned fingers digging deep into his scruffy coat, holding him tight, as they prowled through the darkness, hunting their prey.

She didn't ever want to be separated from her wolf again. At least, not until she had her own dragon to ride.

Kess had come so close to losing everything. Her wolf, her silvernix, even every belonging she carried on her person and in Griskin's saddlebags. She nearly lost her life in that madness of returned-again revenants.

Most of what she lost she got back. And Kess seethed at the fact she had Pony to thank for that.

It didn't make sense. That Pony would help her, in any way. When the world was being razed every which way around them, why had the intolerable woman spared a moment to help her?

Technically, Kess supposed Pony hadn't helped *her*. She'd helped Griskin. Which only gave Kess what she needed by association. *Pony always did have a soft spot for dumb animals. Or basically anything in a helpless damsel situation.*

That Pony had only been helping the wolf was a much easier to stomach answer than any other option. Like that Pony had helped her out of some kind of pity. Or literally any other emotion. Yuck.

Regardless, Pony's actions put Kess in an awkward position. Honor demanded a debt repaid. Kess may have been exiled from her dragonlord home, but she still lived by that code.

Luckily, the moment presented itself sooner than expected when that ridiculous woman threw herself from the sky.

Kess considered them to be even now. Which was good, because her ex-slave wasn't off the hook for ruining her chance to get her own dragon. Kess intended to follow through on her threat to destroy everything in that redheaded monster's life in return.

Maybe she would start with the little brat that Pony called a sister. *There's no way they're related. I wonder where along the line she adopted the little runt. And why.* The very concept made Kess's lips twitch.

That was why—the only reason why—Kess had Griskin following their scent. The tightness in her throat and gut drove her on, a horrible, strange feeling, a maddening need for revenge.

It took some time after fleeing the slavers' camp to lose the bear revenant that got on their tail.

Kess's fault, that one. She'd lingered too long to watch and see whether Pony had survived the fall. She needn't have. Either outcome was good. If the falling woman survived, the debt was repaid. If she didn't make it, oh well, how sad.

The undead bear's feral, unyielding chase led Kess and Griskin crashing through the surrounding brushy woods. They skirted the remains of the camp, getting tangled and scratched in the sharp thickets before coming up against the river.

They raced downstream along the pebbled shore, the bear close behind, until they hit a sheer drop that the water tumbled over.

Kess and Griskin leaped from rock to rock, a dance of fleeting fur, in a moment Kess felt must be what flying was like.

The bear rev hadn't the mental capacity or agility to follow their precarious path. It crashed like a mad berserker into the white waters and was washed over the edge of the high falls.

Free to return to her goal, Kess turned Griskin around. He picked up Pony's scent again back near the camp and they avoided any other run-ins with remaining revenants as they followed that trail.

The moon was high by the time Kess heard the soft giggles from Pony and the little girl. Griskin licked his lips, his skin shivering beneath Kess's fingertips as they neared their prey.

"Shh, boy. Quiet and careful now."

Griskin's paws moved silently over the rocky ground along the path between the river and the mountains. Kess's eyes weren't good enough to see more than some vague movement ahead, under the overhang of a cliff, but Griskin froze, foot lifted, eyes locked.

"That's them?" Kess clenched her teeth. She wasn't sure she could take Pony on one on one, even with Griskin on her side, from what she'd witnessed that evening. The woman was a beast.

"What under the sun are they laughing at?"

Pony had the little girl tucked in close, under an arm, and there was something else there. Something moving on her lap.

The otter was long gone. So what was it?

Directing Griskin to the side, they climbed up through a jumble of boulders opposite where her old slave sheltered.

With a pat to his head, Griskin settled in, silently between the large rocks. The view from there was good, and a soft cyan light glowed around her ex-slave, giving Kess a better look.

The thing on Pony's lap was small, smaller than a cat, and in the cool-blue light, it shimmered with a soft iridescence. Not in the way fur might, but in the way scales did.

Kess's heart set off into a sprint. Could it be?

It was! It was a baby dragon.

The unblessed woman did have a baby dragon all along!

Kess almost threw all of her bone knives then and there, rained them down into the eyes and necks of the woman and girl. Her desire for revenge only grew, but she pushed it aside.

She was going to take that baby dragon, and she was going to take it alive. Whatever cruelty she paid out onto Pony would be an added bonus after Kess had what she wanted.

But for that, she was going to have to wait.

"Come on, go to sleep, you must be exhausted," Kess whispered, as though the wind would carry her words over and convince Pony to rest.

And once they were asleep, the dragon would be hers.

And maybe she could cut a throat or two at the same time. No, just one. Better to have the giant oaf wake up to find everything she'd tried to protect gone.

The tightness in Kess's stomach grew unbearable. This must have been it, the pull she felt, that gut instinct. It was telling her she was right all along about what Pony had hidden in her bag. That what she always wanted was right within her sights.

Griskin's skin trembled, and he sniffed the air.

Kess cursed, and the two of them ducked lower on their rocky lookout.

It took a few more moments before Kess could hear the footsteps Griskin had already reacted to. And then voices.

Those razing Hjelzahns. Kess looked between the approaching group and Pony, who scrabbled around now herself to face who approached.

Kess bit her lip and grunted. Maybe she should have acted sooner. Even with how soft-pawed Griskin could be, she doubted she could sneak into a camp of that many.

Leaning into Griskin's fur, she rubbed the side of his neck and whispered barely louder than a breath, "Never mind. We know now where what we want is. We'll get it, sooner or later."

A little longer wouldn't matter.

Kess tugged softly on Griskin's fur, and he lifted and turned, slipping them away into the shadowy night. She could bide her time. She was good at that. She'd waited her whole life already to have what she deserved.

Kess would have her own dragon, and she would have her revenge on *Pony* soon enough.

CHAPTER THIRTY-ONE

Riony's muscles hadn't hurt so much since their journey aboveground a couple of weeks ago. She trudged up the final couple of steps to their high-level rooms and sighed happily as their newly repaired front door rolled smoothly into the wall.

She hurt but was grinning like a fool. At least until she looked inside and found Lyrrin and Dracuni gone.

"Lyrrin? Lyrrin?" she called out once into the room, and once out of the room, over the steps and apartments below her that cascaded down from their level on the highest tier of the massive carved stalagmite. The glow stone in the living room, still activated, cast a cyan light over the unoccupied room, through to the small bedroom beside it.

On the messy, scrunched-up blankets, Sir Butterfur Spelunkychunks turned anxious circles, around and around in the middle of the sleeping area, but otherwise Riony was alone.

"Where are they?" Riony asked the cave otter in a worried whisper. Did Lyrrin go to see her friends at the orphans' den? No, she wouldn't have. She knew she wasn't supposed to leave when she was on duty looking after Dracuni, and she took that duty seriously.

She can, and did, spend as much time with her friends as she wanted when it was Riony's turn to look after Dracuni. The two sisters had come to some agreements when they got home, and Lyrrin was enjoying, and rising to, new responsibilities and freedoms.

But even if Lyrrin's judgment had lapsed and she'd left, where was Dracuni? She wouldn't have taken the little unidragon hatchling with her. Even if Dracuni wasn't getting too big to hide in a bag.

Riony grasped her hair and turned a full circle around in the doorway. "Sparks, *where are they?*"

A muffled, stifled giggle replied.

And then the blankets at one of the ends of the sleeping area were tossed into the air, and Lyrrin jumped out, cackling with mirth. "Peekaboo!"

At the other end of the bed, the blankets flicked up as well. Dracuni flung them off her head and bleated a soft, trilling roar. She bucked on her four claws like a baby goat and flapped her weak floppy wings.

Happy!

That was a new sensation Riony was getting used to feeling from Dracuni, after those first couple of days of only fear and pain and hunger. Happy was a nice feeling to share.

Sir Butterfur seemed in on the game too, leaping higher in his looping track and chittering at them both.

"Are you sparking *kidding me?*" Riony exhaled into a shout. "You guys scared the ... mushroom farm manure out of me!"

Lyrrin only chuckled more, pulling a blanket back to her face, dropping it up and down in front of her over and over as Dracuni bleated in glee.

"She loves it! It's her favorite game," Lyrrin said.

"It's … a little bit adorable," Riony begrudgingly admitted and pressed the square stone switch to close the door behind her. "Hey. I got you something."

Riony dropped her pack in the corner of the room, rustled around in it, and pulled out a still-steaming bundle. She unrolled the parchment wrapping and held out a fried rope worm on a skewer to her sister.

"We haven't had these in ages!" Lyrrin grabbed the stick, and chomped her teeth on the other end, slurping and licking her lips. "Ow, still hot! But so good."

Riony had one for herself as well. She smiled as she bit the end through the crisp fried skin to the tender, fatty, highly salted meat.

"I figured we deserved a treat," she said around a full mouth. "We have something to celebrate."

Lyrrin stopped chewing. The stick dangled from her hand as she seemed to remember where Riony had been that day. She inhaled sharply. "Did you *get in*?"

Riony grinned smugly. "You're looking at the undercity's newest delver."

Lyrrin squealed and bounced on the spot, setting Dracuni off as well into another round of bleating. The unidragon half galloped, half tripped across the messy blankets to be beside Lyrrin to be part of whatever this new game was.

Riony sat down, leaning against the wall and sighing into a stretch. The trials were hard, but mostly a bunch of climbing and weightlifting and working with ropes, making sure the new recruits had the constitution to deal with the rigors of delving. Which Riony had, in spades. Passed with flying colors and had a good word from the Hjelzahns put in for her on top.

The trials didn't even involve a single riddle or fight to the death with other contestants. Not nearly as exciting as Riony had imagined the trials might be. Although, it wouldn't make much sense to kill off new recruits before they even started. Delving was a risky enough job as it was.

She took another bite and grinned at her sister's excitement. "I'll be starting next week, once I've got some gear fitted for me. Going to get me some of those sweet custom-made delver leathers!"

"We're going to be so rich!" Lyrrin squeaked. "We can have fried rope worm *all the time*."

"We can have all the treats, all the time."

Sir Butterfur stood up on his hind legs at the sound of *treats*.

Riony kicked her boots off, watching as Dracuni circled Lyrrin, little snout chasing the smell of the meat on a stick Lyrrin had forgotten in her excitement. "It will mean more food in general, which will be good, with two growing mouths to feed now, and yup … there it goes."

Dracuni had Lyrrin's rope worm in her mouth, slurping the entire thing off the metal skewer.

Lyrrin gasped. "No! Bad Dracuni! Stop it." She tugged back, but only came away with a bare stick.

Dracuni's teeth had come in after her first week. Just needly little nubs so far, but enough to demolish a sausagey worm. The little unidragon was definitely omnivorous. As of that point they hadn't found much that she wouldn't eat, once they worked out how to feed her.

Lyrrin's shoulder's slumped. "Are there any more?"

Riony took another savoring nibble of hers. "You snooze, you lose, kid."

With a pathetic whimper, Lyrrin pouted toward Riony.

"Oh, all right. Only kidding. Here." Riony held out the remains of her fried treat to share with her sister. Sir Butterfur came sniffing around too, skittering between them as Riony handed the food over to Lyrrin.

Riony tossed the wrappers to him. Plenty of salty fat drippings on them to keep him busy.

Riony licked her fingers, then wiped them on her thighs. "More money, more food. But it's also going to mean more responsibilities. I'll be away working a lot, so you're going to be stuck here with Dracuni more often too."

"I don't mind," Lyrrin said, patting the unidragon on the neck as she tried to snap up the food again.

"That means less time with your friends, less time with Benjin."

"Oh." Lyrrin frowned a little, the pout returning.

"I mean, it's not like we can hire a babysitter. It's got to be one of us with Dracuni, all the time."

Lyrrin's expression firmed. "I know. And it's okay. Dracuni is so special, and she's so cute and lots of fun. I don't mind if I'm alone with her. I want to look after her and keep her safe."

Riony smiled, but her insides turned with a combination of pride and worry at the huge responsibility and sacrifice she'd placed on Lyrrin's tiny shoulders. It was hard enough of a burden for her to carry herself.

Lyrrin brightened. "Plus, it gives me more time here to keep working on my runes. I had an idea just this morning about trying out some different runes on stuff that is already charged, like a glow stone."

Riony worked on stretching out the sore muscles in her arms and sucked air through her teeth. "You be careful messing around with that stuff. I don't want you blowing our house up."

"We're going to need a new place soon anyway!" Lyrrin skipped over to the doorway between living and sleeping areas and pulled the curtain aside.

There were a couple of charcoal smudges on the doorframe there. Height marks from when Riony and Lyrrin first arrived at the undercity and rented these rooms. Then a couple more as they'd gotten bigger over the years. Now there were also a bunch of lower markings too, cut into the stone.

Riony leaned in and looked at the scrapes. "Because you're working on scratching our walls down?"

"Because Dracuni is growing so fast! This is how big she was when we got home"—Lyrrin pointed to the lowest mark—"and this is how big she is now!" Lyrrin pointed to one twice as high up the doorframe.

"Whoa." Riony reached out and ran her fingers over the carved notches. She hadn't realized Lyrrin was keeping track of Dracuni's growth. The care in that made Riony feel warm inside. But she also found her forehead creasing and tension running up her neck.

The unidragon had grown that much already?

She and Lyrrin had managed to keep the creature hidden easily enough so far. Neighbors just assumed Lyrrin had dragged some new cave creature home as a pet, and Dracuni had mostly only ate and slept.

Only in the last few days had Dracuni started getting active, trotting around their rooms, wanting to play, and to play hunt.

And if anything, she was only getting more and more hungry. Riony had scrambled and called in every favor she could when they got back to keep them in food.

To those who had the privilege to care, Riony and the delvers had come home as heroes for having saved at least part of the batch of stolen children, and she'd received some value from that too, a few gifts of thanks here and there.

Now that Riony was going to be a delver, she didn't have to worry about earning enough to keep them fed, but she did worry about how that much food was going to make Dracuni grow and grow.

Riony's dream of becoming a delver had come true, but she wasn't sure for how long. Could she and Lyrrin keep Dracuni, and the unidragon's precious blood, secret in the undercity for much longer?

It was still easy to remember Dracuni's mother very vividly. Riony had had a rather up close and intimate view of the seasong dragon as the creature had crushed the life out of her. She was sparking *immense*.

Just how big was Dracuni going to get?

LEGEND OF THE
DRAGON
SOUL
SELINA A FENECH
BOOK TWO OF THE
SHADOW
DRAGON SAGA

Chapter One

Kessara Heithorn had dreamed of flying for her entire life. She knew she belonged on the back of a dragon, soaring through the iron-gray expanse of sky, high above the cinders of the world. She yearned for it, right to the core of her bones.

So being underground, prowling through stony, lightless spaces, left every part of her feeling twitchy and irritated. The dank air caught in the back of her throat, the threat of suffocation trying to drive her from the caverns.

She and Griskin had been searching for weeks through this cesspool of cowards who hid from the perils of the world above.

What should have been an easy hunt was spoiled by the overcrowding of the undercity and because the underground disagreed with her wolf, Griskin, as well. There was something in the musty air, making Griskin a snuffly, drooling mess. His clogged nose was unable to pick up the scent of their prey.

Kess had to follow her own eyes and ears instead, hoping to catch a glimpse of the redheaded monster or the small girl with the bright-blue eyes that Pony called 'sister.'

Her hunt was also complicated by the fact she couldn't risk Pony knowing she was in the caves until she had her hands on the dragonling. And gossip of a girl riding around on a wolf was sure to spread.

Kess wasn't much less conspicuous when not on Griskin either. She had sat on a corner alone once or twice, face hidden, pretending to beg, trying to get some information that way.

But as just one of many beggars, few people had stopped to show her any kindness and certainly hadn't stayed long enough for her to ask questions.

So she had to keep herself hidden, mostly on rooftops and skirting around the shadows of the crowded slums.

The way the buildings were stacked on top of each other in flowing tiers, carved into clusters of stalagmites—some as large as mighty keeps—made it easy for Griskin to leap from one roof to another, staying off the streets below. The constant hum and bustle from the dwellings covered the sound of Griskin landing on their stone roofs.

Kess kept her body low, pressed close to Griskin's back, his fur fluffing out around her. The smoky scent of the world above hadn't yet left his coat. Kess's hood remained over her head to hide the bright sparkle of white streaking her dark hair.

Then if anybody saw them, they'd mostly just see Griskin and assume it was just another of the weird creatures that inhabited these caves beside the humans. Kess had already seen some shockingly large otters, feasting on scraps they had stolen from a marketplace.

The otter Pony had in her backpack back at the slavers' camp must have been a baby. And the intolerable woman had been so close to tricking Kess into thinking that was all she carried. But she also had another baby in her backpack that day, the one Kess intended on taking for herself.

Kess perched behind a row of thin limestone spikes, watching the ground level below. A natural archway of majestic proportions was formed between curtains of stone there, central within the vast cavern, and the main way to travel between the upper and lower areas.

It seemed to be a major thoroughfare, from what Kess could work out of the layout of the ramshackle community. She'd spent all of yesterday there, but an entire day of surveillance yielded nothing, despite the sheer number of people pushing through.

There were some possible sightings. But flashes of scarlet always turned out to be some other red-haired Rolanians. Tall brutes that caught Kess's eye, that matched the build she sought, were more often men. Never Pony. Perhaps she never even came through this part of the caves.

"Come on, Gris." Kess squeezed her fingers lightly against his neck, and he stood up. It was time to move on, try a new location.

Griskin sniffed and wheezed as he carried her on soft, silent paws.

Although the temperature in the caves was even and comfortable, Kess shivered. *What if Pony's taken the dragonling and moved on already? What if she isn't even here underground anymore?*

She'd tracked Pony and her group of liberated children back from the slavers' camp to here but couldn't go in the gated and guarded entrance like the others.

Kess had to climb back up the snow-capped ridges of the mountain above and sneak in through the tunnel that Pony had come out of before, when she screwed up all her plans with the mother dragon and the eggs.

That extra travel meant she lost track of her target.

Kess hadn't realized how big this underground community had gotten. She hated the place, but she could see the allure for people who didn't have the stomach or skills for surviving aboveground.

The refugees had adapted well to the Alderkin ruins, learning how to use their magic and technology that remained in the abandoned homes.

As Griskin padded across a flat-carved roof, Kess wondered at the magic of these caves, the way cyan crystals brought a pleasant, cool glow to the craggy cavern. Through a window across the way, she spied a family cooking over compact stone crucibles that lit up with the heat of a bonfire. The scent of spiced food made her stomach grumble.

Smooth mechanisms slid below as stone doorways opened and closed. It almost matched some of the technological luxuries found in dragonkeeps.

If it weren't for the overcrowding, it could be a very comfortable life, for people who could live without seeing the sky. Food was harder to come by down beneath the earth. But the refugees had worked out how manage a semblance of farming underground, everything from goats to roots to fungi to worms. People would eat anything when there were no other options.

Kess had even spotted someone eating what looked like fried giant spider legs. Kess shuddered. No, this place could never be comfortable for her.

I better not be wasting my time here.

She shook her head, disagreeing with her own fears. Pony would still be here, somewhere. She'd run back to hide underground again as fast as she could, as soon as she'd gotten the kid she called sister back. The only reason she'd leave was if she knew Kess was there looking for her, and Kess had been too careful for that.

Kess just had to *find* her.

The leap to the next rooftop was long, and Griskin slowed. A low whine came from the back of his throat, and he sniffled and looked back at her with weeping eyes.

"Keep moving." Kess squeezed her fingers to encourage him forward.

Springing off his hind legs, they sailed across the open air between buildings, like ghosts in the cyan light.

As they landed on the rooftop on the other side, a shape emerged from the gloom in front of Kess. A low-hanging stalactite, right in their path.

Griskin went under it. Kess tried to dodge, but there wasn't time.

The spear of stone clipped Kess's shoulder. The impact twisted her around and tossed her off Griskin's back. Her feet came free of the stirrups, and she reached to catch hold of her makeshift saddle.

She missed, toppling off onto the damp, cold stone of the rooftop.

The fall sent her rolling uncontrollably in a bone-jarring tumble down the slope. Kess clenched her teeth and twisted her torso, trying to right herself. They were a few stories up. She couldn't take that fall.

Scrabbling her arms out, she clawed her fingertips into the clammy limestone. Skin scraped raw and fingernails broke as they dug through the soft, silty layer of dust and into the rock below. Belly down, her fingers hooked into the stone, swinging the rest of her body in an arc from that catch point.

Her legs went out into the air. Hands tensed like steel around their hold. Kess skidded to a stop, right over the eave.

She was bent at the waist, chest on the roof and legs dangling down. With a great heave, she dragged herself up.

Kess rolled onto her back, taking in hard, shaking breaths.

Clutching her stinging hands into fists, she swallowed away the threat of tears.

Her voice was a hissed whisper of a scream. "Raze this whole place! This entire stars-damned, unblessed place!"

Griskin appeared beside her, whimpering between sniffles, his wet nose pressing to her cheek.

"Get away from me, you horrible beast!" Kess pushed his face away from hers. Her bruised shoulder twanged painfully, and she stifled a cry.

"How dare you drop me? You're a useless, worthless fleabag! I don't want you! I ..." Kess choked as tears burst in a hot wave from her eyes.

Griskin slipped around the shield of her hands, licking at her cheek.

"I was *born to ride a dragon*!" She tried again to thrust him away, but he remained beside her, and then her hands were around his neck and she was clinging to him with all her strength and pressing her shameful tears into his fur. Between sobs, her words caught. "Not you. Not you ... A dragon."

Griskin folded into her, paws lying over her lap and head nuzzling her chest. She held him like that as she fought down her tears. Whether from frustration, pain, or any other cause, she couldn't let herself be weak like that.

As her emotions calmed, Griskin tilted his head up again, lapping his tongue and wiping his mucus-dripping snout over her face.

"Stop! You're gross." Her lips twisted up, but she didn't push him away again. She leaned her forehead against his and scratched him behind the ear. "The sooner we find that dragonling, the sooner we can be out of this miserable place, and you'll feel better."

We'll both feel better then.

The tumble down the rooftop had knocked Kess's hips and knees too, leaving them feeling bruised. She'd once met a dragonrider who had lost the use of her legs after a fall and had lost the feeling in them too. But Kess felt everything.

She could move her legs too, only barely. She'd just never been able to stand on them, never been able to walk on them. Born that way, nobody could work out why or fix the problem.

And how her family had tried to fix her.

Kess knew she didn't need to be *fixed*. And if only she could get herself onto a dragon, she could show everybody else, too.

She shifted farther away from the roof's edge, then used her hands to move her legs into a better position to get herself back onto Griskin.

Soon they were dashing silently across rooftops again, searching for a new vantage point to hunt from.

Taking a turn south—or what Kess thought was south but worried she was too turned around without the sun as a marker to know—she headed into a new area she hadn't properly explored yet. One even filthier and slummier than the busy main market district.

The squeals of playing children drew her attention, and she nudged Griskin that way, slowing their pace. The buildings and pathways ahead were carved into the cavern walls rather than built up within open spaces or larger stalagmites. She wouldn't be able to stay above them when there were no roofs to be used.

But she could see well enough from the final high point she ended up at and watched as a group of children milled around and played. She recognized a couple of their faces. They had been behind slavers' bars the last time she'd seen them.

Children that had only made their way back here with Pony's help.

Kess patted Griskin and he lowered down onto his belly, then they settled in to watch. This was the closest she'd gotten to a connection to Pony. She could spend some time there, listening and watching.

Voices drifted up from the pathways below.

"No, *you're* in! I got you! Stop cheating!" a tiny voice growled.

Kess leaned to the side and reached into one of her saddlebags, pulling out the bundle of strapping she'd been working on and some leather tools.

A woman muttered softly, "Fifty more yesterday! A whole town. Stars know how they kept a settlement going so long up there, but their home's gone now."

Kess examined the makeshift muzzle and bindings. The dragonling looked freshly newborn when she'd seen Pony with it. Even smaller, since it had hatched sooner than it should have. It was a few weeks old now. Dragons grow fast, since they have a long way to go from their tiny starting size to full-grown.

Kess pictured in her mind how big a dragonling of that age might be and decided to punch a couple more holes into the buckle strap just in case. It was the offspring of a seasong after all.

A man grumbled, "I heard it's a lot worse up there now than it was when we last saw it. You should hear some of the stories. Revenants coming back a second time, they're saying."

"Oh, I don't believe a word of that nonsense."

Kess huffed. She'd heard that rumor aboveground too and hadn't believed it, until she saw the terrifying truth of it with her own eyes. *But if you can kill a rev once, you can kill it twice. And soon, I'll be able to burn them all with my own dragon.*

The woman added, "Don't know how they think we're going to fit any more orphans in here if they keep letting them in, though. Whole undercity is ready to pop. Maybe they should open up some lower levels."

Kess switched to her hunting knife and trimmed another strap of leather off a spare skin. Once she had the dragonling, she couldn't risk rushing the taming process. She'd have to get it out of there first, go somewhere quiet and do it right. The wild beast would need to be subdued until then.

The man guffawed. "You think anyone is crazy enough to go down lower? Whole place is cursed from the way the delvers talk. We're lucky they've cleared all the traps up here. Hey! Watch it! Go play over there!"

Giving the leather a tug-test, Kess felt satisfied it would be enough to bind a young dragonling's legs.

The muzzle was done too, and Kess checked the herbs she'd stuffed inside remained in place, careful not to inhale their scent. Having the dragonling writhing and whipping around as she carried it wouldn't do. But luckily, she'd learned a thing or two about herbs from Pony, back when they were kids.

She took the remaining skin and a leather needle and worked on creating mitts to cover the dragonling's claws.

A child peeped, "Yeah, Lyrrin's sister! The one who helped get Cammi, Leeu, and the others back from the slavers."

Kess's hands stilled.

"Na-ah. Mira said it was that delver Aishena who saved the kids, all by herself!"

"No, it was her, and her brother, and that other girl. The big one, with the red hair. She wasn't a delver before, but she's a delver now!"

Her head shot up, and she sought the owner of the voice. A stick-thin brat with a tumble of ruddy brown curls that were matted in tangles at the ends. The nearby glow stone cast a cool blue light over him as he continued boasting in his high, squeaky voice to a few gasping runts.

"Aw, I wanna be a delver."

"You're too scrawny to be a delver."

"You're too dumb to know what I can be."

Kess stuffed her leatherwork away and took in her options. She could just snatch the kid and make him show her where to find Pony, but that was too risky. Despite the unkempt appearance of the ragged children, at least a couple of adults kept an eye on them.

There was one unlit pathway across from where the children were playing. It would only be a couple of big leaps by Griskin across the street to get down there. There was a small risk of being seen, but Kess was tired of waiting.

Nobody called out as Griskin bounded off the roof and dashed into the shadows of the narrow pathway. Kess's pulse raced regardless, driven into a frenzy by the feeling of being close to her prey.

The kids were separating from their circle, and Kess whistled to get the boasting kid's attention. He turned to look, squinting into the dark alley with beady, uncertain eyes.

"Hey, kid, can I ask you something?"

"Umm ... I probably shouldn't." He looked to one of the watching adults, but their backs were currently turned, separating a nearby scuffle of squealing toddlers.

"I just want to have a little chat." Slipping a gold sov from her belt pouch, Kess held it up high, letting it glint in the light.

The boy's eyes widened.

"Yeah, it's all yours. I only want to ask a couple of questions." Kess rolled the coin around her fingers.

He stepped closer, into the shadows of the alleyway. He flinched when Griskin became visible, seeing that he approached not just a strange young woman, but one who rode on top of a wolf. Kess could see the war of desire versus flight in his eyes. But the piece of gold flicking between Kess's fingers kept him moving toward her.

That piece of gold was probably worth more than an orphan like him could dream of. He'd spill everything Kess needed to know for his chance at owning it. And it meant nothing for Kess to spend a gold sov on that.

Because Kess always dreamed bigger.

And for those dreams, she needed to steal a dragon.

Chapter Two

The explosion rattled the herb jars on the shelves and buffeted hot air over Riony's bare arms. Jagged pieces of burning hot crystal rained all around the room.

Riony grabbed Lyrrin, leaning over her as her sister leaned over Dracuni, sheltering from the hail of searing shards.

Loud! Scared! The unidragon curled into a ball, hiding her snout beneath a translucent, iridescent wing.

"Oops," Lyrrin said, as the pattering stopped.

"Oops?" A crystal chip burned the tip of Riony's ear as it fell free from her hair. She shook her head, swatting at it to clear her hair of any other embers, worried it was about to catch on fire.

"Oops? Lyrrin, it's *my first day*. Is oops going to clean this up? Is oops going to stop time for me? Because I cannot afford to be late."

Lyrrin didn't offer an answer. She had the intense, bright-eyed expression she often had while messing around with Alderkin runes. She stepped away from under Riony's shadow and huffed at the source of the explosion. "Okay, so I can't add a burn rune onto a light stone. I know that now."

"We're learning. Yaaaay," Riony muttered. She kicked glowing fragments away from Dracuni and checked the young unidragon over for burns.

Dracuni peeked out from under her wing and blinked large, lilac eyes. ***Was loud. Was scary.***

"I know," Riony replied quietly. Dracuni's thoughts, which somehow found their way into Riony's head, had been changing. No longer a simple rush of emotion alone, they started to have more nuance. Past or future tense. More range. Names.

Something more like language, which felt crazy to Riony considering everything she'd ever learned about dragons said they were ferocious, thoughtless creatures if they weren't tamed.

Although Dracuni wasn't a normal dragon.

"Not hurt?" Riony asked softly.

No hurt.

Riony patted the pale scales on the unidragon's neck.

"The crystal must overheat too much when combining those two runes." Lyrrin looked at the sharp claws on her fingers, moving them as though tracing runes in the air.

"Yeah, I'd say so." Riony smelled burning. She hissed as she flicked a crystal shard out from where it had stuck into the waist of her new delver leathers. A singe mark smoldered and Riony licked her fingers and tried to wipe it away. It remained blackened. Riony glared at it.

She had only just been fitted for the sleek, clever armor that delvers earned after their training. The soft leather was designed to be close-fitting and flexible for squeezing through tight gaps. The trousers and vest had a heap of useful straps and harness points, and most importantly, Riony was sure she looked extra hot wearing it.

And now it has burn holes before even starting my first official day. What worried her more though, was that the smell of burning was only getting worse.

Riony followed her nose, searching around the room for the source of the smoky scent.

Lyrrin's eyes were on the collection of out-of-charge artifacts and almost out-of-charge glow stones they had collected over the last few weeks. They were spread out across the carved stone counter, piled in the corners of the room, lined up in between clothes and kitchenware on the shelves. An abundance of worthless and soon-to-be worthless Alderkin relics.

When they had returned from their overworld adventure, Riony had sought out a couple of spent athames. They were easy and cheap to obtain since they were practically worthless without any charge left. She kept them with her, hoping to discover how to recharge them.

Her cutting athame had miraculously recharged, so she figured there must be a way.

Like maybe she had a special magical essence unique to her that switched the artifacts back on again when she carried them around for a while. But realistically, she figured it was probably Dracuni that was the special one.

But no matter whether she kept the athames with her or with Dracuni, none of them glowed back to life. Whatever had renewed the cutting athame, it wasn't something she was able to replicate again.

Then grateful orphans had noticed her collecting the Alderkin junk and had decided offering more as presents was a wonderful idea. Riony suddenly had an army of children picking through waste to bring her every tossed and worn-out relic they could find, and her rooms were now filled with the useless things and not one of them had recharged.

No new athames for Riony.

She'd really been hoping to show off a collection that could rival Aishena's on her first day at delving. Now she would just have to impress the other delvers with her good looks and wit alone. Aishena didn't seem into that, but maybe the other delvers had taste.

Lyrrin had been the one to benefit most from the supply of Alderkin crystals. Glow stones were plentiful and often swapped out before they lost their charge entirely, so Riony was gifted a lot of those as well. That was when Lyrrin saw her opportunity to start experimenting.

"I thought I put it over here ..." Lyrrin searched through the artifact collection.

Riony continued her own search for the source of the burning smell.

Where is it coming from?

Looking through the curtain to the bedroom, Riony's eyes widened, and she rushed over to their blankets-on-the-floor bed.

Crystal clinked as Lyrrin sorted through, reaching for something toward the back of the shelf. "Let me just show you the other combination I worked out last night. It's much better."

"Lyrrin. Lyz. My darling sister. Are you not seeing the fire? There is a *fire* in our *bed*." Riony grabbed handfuls of blankets, folding the coarsely woven wool over itself on top of the burning sections and smacking it with her hands to smother the flames.

"It looks mostly put out now."

"And even worse, I am going to be *late*."

"It will only take a moment. It's really great, I promise."

Riony stopped patting down the blankets and looked Lyrrin dead in the eye with an expression that slammed Lyrrin's mouth shut. "*You could have hurt Dracuni.*"

A silent *oh* formed on Lyrrin's lips. She solemnly slipped the carved crystal away into her pocket and turned to the unidragon. "I'm sorry."

Dracuni inhaled, then snorted breath out sharply twice in a row, nostrils flaring. **WAS LOUD. Hot loud. Scary loud.**

Riony winced and rubbed her forehead. "You still can't hear that?" she asked Lyrrin.

Pouting with the depth of how not being able to hear Dracuni's thoughts was the very worst thing in the entire world, Lyrrin shook her head.

"Dracuni forgives you," Riony replied.

Dracuni lowered her horned head and growled at the closest piece of shattered glow stone.

As though not wanting to be left out, Sir Butterfur Spelunkychunks popped out from under a corner of blanket that hadn't combusted, chittering angrily.

Lyrrin folded her arms. "I'm sorry, okay? But—"

"You're really bringing out a but? Right now?"

"*But* just listen to me! Can't you please trust me for once?"

"You just almost blew us up." Having thought she'd gotten the fire under control, Riony straightened out the blankets to inspect the damage and a glowing ember puffed up into flame again.

"It was an important experiment! It could have worked out really well. I had to try it. Like Pabba used to say, big dreams, bold deeds."

"Pabba didn't know about magical runes that could blow us up."

"And now I know what will happen next time I put those runes together."

"There will *not* be a next time." Butterfur pounced on Riony's hands as she returned to swatting out cinders, as though he were playing a game. To get him out of her way, she said, "Lyrrin has the treats."

The pale-furred otter zipped over to Lyrrin, who absentmindedly dropped a treat from her pocket into his mouth as she stared Riony down with an immovable glare. "I want to be able to help. I want to be able to make things to help protect Dracuni. And maybe not all my experiments are working, but you just haven't seen the good one yet. I worked out this new rune—"

"You're trying out new runes? I don't know about that."

"Just ones the delvers and other trades use but keep secret for themselves. It's good, trust me! And if I can work out one good one, maybe I can work out others even better, and if you just let me show—"

"I DON'T HAVE TIME!"

Lyrrin's eyes glossed over with tears in an instant.

Swearing softly to herself, Riony confirmed that the blanket was no longer on fire. Her nose still held the bitter scent of smoke, but it seemed as though nothing else was burning anymore and the shards had cooled.

Lyrrin glared, red-faced, as Riony checked her one working athame was in her belt pouch, then strapped on her belts with their ropes and pouches and her beloved dragonguard sword.

She went and knelt in front of Lyrrin as she did the buckles, then she took Lyrrin's hands in hers, giving them a small squeeze.

"I'm sorry. I'm sorry I yelled. But I have to go."

Dracuni perked up as Riony moved to the door. A wave of worry and longing washed over her and the unidragon mewled questioningly.

Go? Safe here. Stay!

Everything Riony had communicated to the unidragon since they had arrived back home was how the hatchling had to stay in their rooms to stay safe, and so Dracuni had developed a high level of anxiety at the idea of any of them leaving their home for the dangerous world beyond those rooms.

Poor little thing. How much longer are we going to be able to keep you couped up in here?

Apart from the logistics of keeping a growing part-dragon-creature alive and hidden, another worry had grown in Riony's head. The thought that maybe, once Dracuni was big enough to look after herself, she should be released into the wild. But that freedom would only come with other risks, of being hunted by dragonlords, tamed, and her special blood being discovered.

No. No way can I let that happen. Dracuni needed to be protected from them, and all dragon-obsessed psychos, including Kess. Riony had been on edge since running into the wolf-riding gremlin, but thankfully hadn't seen hide nor hair of those two beasts since getting home.

She waved to Dracuni and Lyrrin, a small ache in her heart at having to leave them, even for a short time.

"I have to go. This is going to be good for us. I'm coming home rich today, okay?" *As long as I don't get kicked out up front for being late.* Riony locked eyes with Lyrrin. "Clean up. No more experiments while I'm out. Look after Dracuni."

Lyrrin's mouth twitched but she didn't argue. She moved beside Dracuni and wrapped an arm around the unidragon's neck. With how small Lyrrin was, and how big Dracuni was growing, they were almost the same height standing together like that.

Even Butterfur was growing, able to reach up to Lyrrin's hips as he begged for more food.

Lyrrin grumbled barely audibly. "Of course I'll look after Dracuni, and Riony has the treats."

Riony watched the approaching otter, shaking her head at the creature that had been smart enough to train into this game but not smart enough to know Lyrrin still had treats in her pocket.

It seemed to think the sisters had a magical pocket that the treats traveled between, only existing with one of them at a time, when they both kept plenty of treats on them. At least for now.

The initial outpouring of goodwill from the community that had fed the three of them well after returning as heroes had all but dried up, and with it, their pantry stores.

They wouldn't have to worry about going hungry again after today though. Riony had achieved her goal of becoming a delver; now she was going to be the best delver there was.

She was already mentally spending all the riches she intended on unearthing. Good food, a real bed, a larger dwelling for a growing family that included a dragon that seemed to be doubling in size every time Riony turned around.

Maybe a place big enough to have a separate, strong-walled room just for Lyrrin's experiments.

More otter treats. She dropped one from the now ever-present collection of crumbs in her belt pouch into Butterfur's awaiting grabby hands.

Riony pressed the mechanism to open the door. It rolled smoothly. Fixing that sticky mechanism was one small improvement in their lives, but after today, they could have many more.

Butterfur twirled around her ankles, sniffling up at her hands.

"Lyrrin has the treats," Riony said, and he ran back the other way again as she stepped out the door.

Lyrrin called out, "Wait! Riony?"

She turned back.

Lyrrin frowned, pouted, then lifted her chin. "Don't be late."

Riony huffed out in exasperation as the door closed between them. "Are you sparking kidding me?"

CHAPTER THREE

Riony took the fast way down from their high-level dwelling. And she took it faster than she ever had before. She skidded down carved limestone and vaulted over rooftops at a frantic rate. Muscle memory took over, knowing each tilt of slope, each point to kick off, each handhold to catch her landing.

She still scared herself when the sheer momentum she'd built up barreled her right off a rooftop she intended to land on, her body soaring through the air, momentarily weightless, before landing onto the next level down.

Holding on to a decorative column to steady herself, she smirked, laughed off the near miss, and then took off again.

Riony's face felt flushed, her heart pounding in sync with the rhythmic beat of her footsteps. The underground city spread out beneath her, a labyrinth of narrow alleyways and makeshift dwellings stacked together between the stone-carved homes left behind by Alderkin.

The cavern echoed with the bustling of its inhabitants starting out their day, the dusty cave air thick with scents of mushroom-heavy meals cooking.

The familiar route down from Dragonwing Tower felt like an extension of herself, an intimate dance with the cyan-tinted undercity. And a strange sensation grew in her chest as a grin spread on her face. A feeling of belonging. A feeling that this place had finally become *home*.

The undercity. It had its own stark beauty, a starry sky of cyan lights spread over the rocky backdrop, made soft by all the inclusions humans brought to their life in the cave. Pennants, curtains, and tapestries brought splashes of color to the creamy-brown world.

Human refugees had only taken homes and tried their hands at underground farming in this one upper level of the Alderkin depths, but delvers had not yet found the end to how many lower levels there were. Some believed the Alderkin ruins burrowed right down into the center of the earth.

As Riony dropped off the final rooftop to street level, she thought she glimpsed some other shadowed form dashing over the roofs nearby, but she couldn't slow down to look again or question it. She raced on, propelled by a sense of urgency to not lose the thing she had long dreamed of and only just achieved.

She was a delver now. One of the brave few able to search the Alderkin depths for hidden riches. Riches that made life better for everyone in the undercity, who needed the glow stones and cooking crucibles and other Alderkin tools that made life underground possible.

Getting paid handsomely for providing those artifacts was just one of the perks. Perks Riony and her family desperately needed.

Ugh. I shouldn't have yelled at Lyrrin. But I can't screw this up.

The streets were more crowded than ever, but as she hurried through in her delver leathers, people took notice and moved out of her way.

In her haste, she caught glimpses of familiar faces—neighbors and friends she had come to know so well. The fried worm vendor, the baker with the crooked smile, the old lady who always had a kind word for her.

But there were many new faces in the undercity now.

More beggars took up residence on corners than ever before. Pained expressions were etched around their eyes. Wounds sustained during their flight to this sanctuary marked their bodies.

Wounds that had come both from the undead and the dragonriders' indiscriminate attempts to cleanse the world of those revenants through fire.

Every wounded or diseased person Riony saw felt like a stab of guilt. The anguished cry of a burned child, cradled in his begging mother's arms, seared Riony's conscience as intensely as if she stood before the full force of a dragon's burning breath.

Because she held a secret that could alleviate their suffering.

Because she guarded Dracuni and the unidragon's precious blood.

She yearned to share the miracle of Dracuni's blood, to offer solace and hope to those who suffered.

But how could she do that to Dracuni? How could she bleed that innocent creature to alleviate the pain of others?

That didn't feel like her decision to make, and the more she got to know Dracuni, sensing the creature's growing emotions and intelligence, the more she felt it was a choice the creature could and should make for itself.

Not to mention the utter chaos that could result in anybody discovering Dracuni and the existence of a living creature with unicorn blood. Riony was not prepared for an army to come knocking on her door to take Dracuni away. That didn't sound like a good time.

The decision that Dracuni must remain hidden, concealed from the prying eyes of those who might exploit her, still weighed heavy on Riony. Doubt gnawed at her, questioning the ethics of withholding something that could heal and save lives.

For now, though, Riony justified she had to focus on her own and her small family's lives. Honestly, Riony figured they were enough lives to be responsible for.

But still, when faced with the pain on the faces she passed, Riony had to look away in shame.

When I have plenty of riches from delving, then I can help those people out in other ways. Then I'll have enough to share.

The crowds thinned as Riony passed Curtain Market and went into the richer Upslope sector. The sound of the thin waterfall of the Sinking Stream pouring through the cave ceiling into the pool below echoed behind her.

At the far back of the cavern, the ceiling seemed much lower and the tunnel ahead was lined with thin, sharp stalagmites and stalactites—Dragon's Maw Descent, the deep-run access tunnel that was the planned starting location for today's delve. She broke into a full sprint then.

Dust puffed under Riony's pounding feet as she bounded down winding staircases, carved at a time long before Riony was born or could even fathom. The cool breeze that swept through the descending shaft whispered tales of forgotten ages, and excitement pulsed through Riony.

Rounding a corner, she saw teams of delvers lined up in groups of two and three. Pale-aqua light spilled around them from the bright glow stones held within netted pouches on their belts. Only about half the delvers Riony knew of remained, and another team split off and left as Master Brishan called out a location off his roster.

The head of the delvers loomed tall, even over Riony's height, a solid block of body draped in a thick cloak. One of the few Taens in the depths, his charcoal hair had a hint of silver, even in his beard, but Riony figured it was likely just due to age, rather than the use of silvernix in himself or his bloodline.

He didn't hold himself with the same royal arrogance as the steel-haired Hjelzahn siblings. But he did still braid his hair in the traditional Taen way.

Riony's breath caught, looking over the impressive sight of the delvers standing together. They ranged in age from those similar to Riony, up to a few grizzled veterans. Their entire vibe was built from well-defined muscle and pure grit.

All wore a similar set of leather armor, but those who had been in the profession longest had fitted theirs out with more accessories, more of the expensive cave silk ropes, finely crafted harnesses, Alderkin athames, and crystal artifacts.

Most of them had sleeves on their armor, but Riony opted for a sleeveless fit. A decision born from style rather than function, and the undying hope that Aishena may one day look at her with physical desire.

Yoskar was there with his stone-encrusted staff, Benjin close by his side. The younger brother was not yet a delver; however, he had remained with his older siblings regardless. Riony was starting to get to know some of the other delvers, but as she'd only just finished training, the proper delvers hadn't yet deemed it worth giving her the time of day.

Spotting Aishena and Niskina standing near the back of the group, Riony dashed forward in a crouch, skidding into place, then straightening up between them.

"You're late," Aishena hissed from behind a sheet of steel-toned hair.

Chest still heaving from her run, Riony shrugged. "I've been here this whole time. I'm honestly upset you didn't notice me."

Aishena sneered. "Maybe you should have been later. Or not shown up at all."

"You're cute when you're annoyed."

Niskina snorted.

"Hey." Riony winked at her.

"Hey," Niskina whispered back, beaming. "Am I cute, too?"

Riony leaned back as though to take in the large, curvy young woman beside her. Niskina was something of the odd one out in the group of sharp-edged, grizzled strength. More softness and pouty smile with playful golden eyes and waves of chestnut hair tumbling around a glowing face.

A mix of Taen and Rolanian features gave her a striking appearance. She wore delver leathers, new and not yet scuffed from use, and unfastened down the front, showing a white shirt decorated with fine lace beneath.

"Cute? Yeah. But really more drop-dead gorgeous. Straight up dream material. Do I want to be you, or do I want to be with you? It's not even a question. It's both."

Niskina tittered a hushed giggle. "You're good for a girl's self-esteem, Ri."

"I could be good for a lot more if you were into girls."

"I know. It's a tragedy, honestly."

"Must you persistently flirt with every woman you see?" Aishena grumbled.

Riony tilted her head her way. "Aw, are you jealous?"

Aishena turned her back on Riony.

"Here, thanks for the lend." Riony reached into her largest belt pouch and pulled out a bound wad of worn papers. She handed the *Rebel Riders* chapters she'd borrowed during training back to Niskina.

Niskina clutched the serial to her chest. "Did you love it? Did you love the scene between Rider Jaym and his soul mate in the hot springs?"

"I learned things I didn't even know I needed to learn."

Brishan sent away a team with Jonna, Caed, and Daymora. Caed and Daymora hadn't given Riony much attention yet. Jonna, a V-shaped chunk of man-chest with a strong jaw and button nose combination that made him rather adorable, had made an effort to get to know Riony very quickly though, until it was clear she wasn't interested in men.

He didn't mind and suggested his access to plenty of other options was another perk of being a delver that Riony hadn't yet considered. That opened up a world of heart-racing possibilities in Riony's mind. Possibilities that the books she shared with Niskina detailed and added to in ways that made her flush hot all over.

Because while Riony liked to talk game, her position as a kid's sole, full-time carer didn't give her much opportunity to act on those words.

The way Daymora's eyes longingly followed Jonna as they walked away gave Riony hope of romance within the delver ranks as well.

Niskina tucked the booklet away, then pulled out another, handing it over to Riony. "Just wait until you see what happens next."

Riony took the offered serial reverentially, blushing as Niskina made a gesture more lewd than even Riony would consider making in their current company. Niskina was quickly becoming her new favorite person.

The exchange lured Aishena's judgmental attention back to Riony. She kept her voice low as Brishan continued to send away delvers to their work locations. "Why are you late? I thought maybe you'd chickened out."

"Chickened out?" Riony gasped, appalled.

"Lost your nerve, gave up the ghost, bailed faster than a pirate with a chest of gold and a hole in their rowboat," Niskina clarified.

"My shock was based on the idea that I would be scared of this, not from lack of understanding the term."

"You should be scared," Aishena spat. "If you aren't, maybe you need to go back into training because clearly you didn't learn anything. It's dangerous down there. The Alderkin traps are one thing, then there are the cave spiders, giant olms, ghost snakes … And why did you bring that ridiculous sword of yours along?"

Riony patted her sword in its sheath and the end bumped against the wall behind her. "I don't go anywhere without my good luck sword."

"It's too big. It's going to get in the way."

"You'll change your mind when I'm chopping up those spiders and olms and snakes with it."

More delvers around them left for their allocated delving sites, thinning the group down even more. Brishan checked his papers, then looked over the remaining delvers. "Yoskar, you can be on cataloguing today with me, since you have Benjin with you."

Yoskar nodded solemnly, and Benjin, by his side, glowered over a puckered mouth. The Hjelzahn siblings hadn't left the youngest brother alone for a moment since his recent kidnapping. They moved from the remaining delvers over beside Brishan.

Glancing at the remaining few delvers, Brishan met Riony's gaze.

"Riony Eyfarr, glad you decided to join us."

"Very glad to be here, Master Brishan, and I'm very sorry for being late."

Brishan's lips twitched beneath his bushy mustache. "I noticed you still had time for trading those trashy stories with my daughter."

"I'm sorry, Mast—"

"Call my stories trashy one more time and you've lost any chance of me participating in this stupid job." Niskina folded her arms and pouted her full lips at him like pointing a weapon.

Riony's eyes widened. She knew Niskina was Brishan's daughter, and Niskina had made her rebellious dislike of being pushed into the delving profession clear during their training. But to see her talk back to Master Brishan so openly made Riony's eye twitch.

"They are dangerous propaganda. *Rebel Riders*? Riding untamed dragons?" Brishan scoffed.

"Riding untamed dragons *and* protecting their soul mates with the power of their chiseled chests," Niskina said.

"It's utter nonsense."

"That's it. I'm leaving."

"Nisk!" Brishan looked more embarrassed than anything. His cheeks reddened around his facial hair and he took a step toward her.

Riony averted her eyes. They were the last delvers left now, the Hjelzahn siblings, Niskina, Brishan, and Riony, but it still felt like too many people to be witnessing the standoff between father and daughter.

Niskina turned back. "It's not nonsense. It makes more sense to be up there fighting for something like the Rebel Riders, than hiding down here digging around in this cursed Alderkin grave to make ourselves rich."

Brishan folded up his papers slowly and put them away, his shoulders lifting, then sagging. He fixed his daughter with a firm gaze. "Niskina, you're on cataloguing as well with me today."

Niskina looked longingly toward Riony and Aishena. "Can't I at least—"

"No. Aishena, you're with Riony. Take Section Thirty." He pointed to a narrow tunnel just across from them.

"Yes, Master Brishan," Aishena barked, standing straight.

Riony echoed her a moment afterward, awkwardness delaying her tongue. She had done her best to study the delvers' maps but hadn't yet memorized the different locations in the confusing three-dimensional maze of tunnels and caverns beneath the undercity.

Although she *had* laughed for a solid half hour over finding out one of the delving tunnels was called Wet Descent. *Wet Descent.* Riony snorted.

But Section Thirty sounded promising. The higher the number, the more recently the area had been opened up to delving.

Niskina stared at her father for a moment, then leaned against a nearby wall, pulled out another booklet, and started reading.

Waving a dismissive hand at her, Brishan reached out and tapped Aishena's shoulder, then beckoned her and Yoskar away from the others. "A word before you go."

Riony pretended not to listen as he spoke softly to them. She only heard every few words. *Cousin … He … Brought … Dead … News … Heir.* Aishena's face paled, but she didn't seem surprised. Yoskar just nodded grimly and met Aishena's searching gaze.

"Back to work. We can talk later," Yoskar said, flashing a look at Riony's unsubtle eavesdropping.

Aishena nodded. She chewed her lip for a moment as she watched Yoskar return to Benjin's side, then came back to Riony.

"Is … everything okay?" Riony asked.

"Perfectly fine," Aishena growled. "Stop gawking at me. Get moving."

"Great. Love the energy. Excited to spend the day with you."

As Riony and Aishena stepped toward their allocated tunnel, a warm glow lit the stones before them. Then a buzzing sound echoed up the passageway.

"Glowflies," Aishena grumbled. She stepped back out of the way, leaving Riony in the path of the swarming insects.

The bright bugs fluttered past Riony like a rush of warm air, ignoring her in their apparent haste. Each golden glowing abdomen looked like a flying ember as they flew by, tangling in Riony's hair and butting up against her face and hands when she tried to ward them off.

The air was thick with them. Riony had to close her mouth and eyes to avoid the finger-sized insects flying into them. The critters were common enough in the depths, normally hanging around, unlit, on the rough ceilings of the caves. Riony had never seen so many, all flying together with some common purpose.

The humming eased and Riony opened her eyes to see the last few bugs zip by.

Brishan watched as the insects cleared out. "Scratch Section Thirty for today. You two head over to Section Three."

"Section Three?" Aishena practically whined.

Gaping, Riony asked, "What? Why?"

Without lifting her eyes from her book, Niskina said, "You never head down a tunnel glowflies are swarming away from. It's always a sign there's something down that way you don't want to mess with."

"That wasn't covered in training," Riony muttered.

"Section Three?" Aishena questioned again. "There's nothing in Three. We cleared it out ages ago."

Brishan leaned over her, raising an eyebrow. "Then clear it out again. Unless you and the tardy new recruit would rather sit out the next few weeks?"

Riony winced at the word *tardy*. And *sit out*. And *weeks*.

"We'll do Section Three, Master Brishan." Aishena grabbed Riony by the elbow and dragged her away down the tunnel in the other direction.

When they were far enough away that their voices wouldn't echo back to the others, Aishena grumbled, "Look what I get for vouching for you. Section Three? This is glorified babysitting."

"When you said cleared out, do you mean nice and safe from nasties but still filled with treasure?"

"I mean empty, bare, lucky to find a rock left to refill the ones in your head that you seem to use for thinking."

Riony's heart sank. She was supposed to come home rich today. If she came home empty-handed, it was going to be even harder to face Lyrrin after yelling at her.

She looked over her shoulder to see Brishan leading Niskina, Yoskar, and Benjin away into another nearby tunnel. "Then let's do Section Thirty. We just sneak back that way and—"

"Were you not listening, or do you just not believe that we could actually know something more than you? You *do not* go down a tunnel glowflies are flying from. You go down that tunnel, you don't come back alive, you ridiculous tame-brained lout."

"I'm so glad you warmed up to me and respect me so much more now after our life-threatening adventure together."

Aishena glared.

"Okay, okay. We'll try to make the most of Section Three then. There must be something still around there that we can dig up."

"This is such a waste of time." Aishena sighed but continued moving to their designated area. "At the very least we can show Brishan that you can follow orders and do as you're told. Then maybe next time he'll give you a better area, and me too if I'm stuck with you again."

"You think there will still be a next time?" Riony asked with more vulnerability in her voice than she wanted to display.

"Look, Brishan seems to like you. Stop preening! The sun only knows why he's taken a liking to *you*. But sort yourself out, because one more screwup and you're out. And he doesn't abide disobedience or risk-taking. So … good luck with that."

"What? I can be obedient and not take risks."

Aishena laughed bitterly. "Your *very first* impulse was to sneak around his orders and run down the tunnel of imminent death. Sparks, you're probably going to find some way to get yourself killed in the boring empty rooms we're stuck with."

"We *could* make the time in the empty rooms together more interesting."

"And it's probably going to be me that ends up killing you."

Faced with the threat of death on all sides, or even worse, the risk of losing her new job, Riony made her one smart decision of the morning and stopped talking.

Instead, she turned her mind to the impossible challenge of how she was supposed to follow orders, not take risks, but somehow miraculously not go home empty-handed.

CHAPTER FOUR

"**S**parks," Riony huffed. "I really am sorry I was late. Do you think if we go back to Brishan and beg—"

"Because Niskina has obviously left him in a good mood to be doing favors for us." Aishena gave Riony the driest of glares.

Section Three was as bare as Aishena's levels of tolerance for Riony's flirting. Surveying the space, a cold, hard lump built in Riony's chest.

There's nothing here. Although the walls of the interconnected chambers showed beautiful carvings that may have once been the framing of a richly furnished Alderkin dwelling, everything else had been cleared away.

Every sconce had been stripped of glow stones. All furniture, tapestries, rugs—gone. All shelves lay empty except for strands of dusty webbing. Not even enough of that to gather up and sell to the rope makers.

Riony ran her hands up over her head, turning to take in the barren space. They were only one floor down beneath the undercity, barely far enough away that Riony felt as though she'd delved at all. She could practically still hear Niskina and Brishan's arguing echoing down the stairs from above.

They'd quarreled during training too, as Niskina debated all the reasons why she didn't want to become a delver like her father, but it was worse today, now that Niskina had officially been made one regardless.

Niskina seemed to be quite smart, smarter than Riony considered herself to be, but on the other hand despised delving and loudly dreamed of returning to the overworld, so Riony couldn't entirely be sure if the girl was sane of mind.

Delving had been Riony's goal for so long that the current situation felt like being smacked in the face with her own dismembered hand—both painful and humiliating. The chambers around her were as simple and domestic as the ones humans had taken over on the top level. Not one bit of the treasures and adventure Riony had dreamed of.

Aishena had already done one quick turn around the sprawling interconnected rooms of what must have once been a grand dwelling, decided it really was empty and without even any nasty cave creatures to take her anger out on, then had dumped herself down on a raised block to sulk.

Riony had followed her, a few steps behind, taking in the flat stone surfaces of each room, hoping she'd see something new that had been missed before. There was only one closed door they didn't go through, which Aishena ignored, and all Riony saw besides stone walls, stone floors, and stone ceilings was the layer of dust over those surfaces.

As Aishena had said, not even a loose stone that Riony could have kicked in frustration. So she had to settle for pacing up and down in front of Aishena. She chewed her lip and looked sideways at Aishena. The Taen probably-Dragon King-heir really hadn't warmed up to Riony much after getting back to the depths. Yes, she and Yoskar had vouched for Riony with Brishan, but they had been more closed off than ever, the three siblings a silent, secretive unit. Riony tried to be respectful of their privacy but couldn't help being entirely curious ever since the revelation their mother was out there looking for them.

Maybe if she couldn't dig up any treasures that day, she could at least discover something new about Aishena.

"Sooo ... Brishan seems to like you and Yoskar, too. Does he know, you know, that you're a Hjelzahn—"

"Shut it!" Aishena snapped, eyes darting for unlikely eavesdroppers. "Yes, he knows. He used to be a grayglim, worked with my mother. But a very long time ago."

A grayglim? Riony stifled a *phwoar* sound. She had only seen one of those elite royal bodyguards once in her life back at Heithorn Estate. They were as good as ghosts, the kind you were only likely to see when it meant your own imminent death. If the Hjelzahns' mother was one, then Aishena's stealthy proficiencies made sense.

"Does he know why you three are down here?"

"If that's your awful way of trying to find out for yourself why we came to the undercity, then you're thicker than I thought."

"It is nice to know you think of me." Riony rested her hand on her sword, making the sheath swing behind her. "I guess I'm just trying to understand, you know, why you three would leave home? I know the delving life is pretty good—usually—but only if you're not already coming from something better."

Aishena pushed her hair away from her face and stood up to glare at Riony. "You have no idea what we came from. You have no idea and no reason to need one and no right to ask. We are not friends and you are not my confidant so just mind your depths-damned business. There's nothing for you to know."

"Got it." Riony held up her hands in surrender. Clearly, nerves were too raw to be prodded. "I'll leave it. But ... If you do ever need someone to talk to, I am here for you. And I can keep a secret. Sometimes it can be good to share the load."

Aishena turned away, taking her turn to stalk back and forth within the room. Riony watched the tight, high shoulders and tense neck of the delver and knew that whatever secret she and her siblings were keeping, it certainly wasn't nothing.

If they really wanted to remain hidden, they should have dyed their hair like I do with Lyrrin. Hair that color screamed wealthy lineage and was rare in the undercity. Aishena flicked her silky-straight silver hair over her shoulder so she could turn back and glare at Riony some more.

Riony desperately sought around for a rock to kick again. This was going to be a long, painful day.

"Hey," she called over to Aishena. "What about that closed door? What's the story with it?"

"Jammed."

Riony headed through to the next room where the closed door was located and looked it over, testing the opening mechanism and trying to give it a bit of a push. The stone didn't budge.

Aishena appeared beside her. "I told you, it's jammed. Which means it's been purposefully sealed and most likely trapped as well. Doors like that are better left shut."

Riony ran her fingertips over the large round slab. "You're telling me this has never been opened?"

"Because it can't be and it's too big of a risk to open even if it could."

"But there could be anything on the other side." The prospect of untouched riches practically had Riony salivating. She tried pushing at the door again.

"Yes. Exactly. Bad anythings. Trying to get that door open could trigger this whole place to collapse."

Riony shook her head, undeterred. She pulled her cutting athame from her belt. "Then we cut our way through."

Aishena rubbed her forehead. "I know training mostly just covers basic safety, survival, and knot tying, but you can't really think you could cut through there, even with your athame. That stone would be almost as thick as your head."

Riony held out her hands, measuring. "That's not that thick. Oh. Okay. Yes, very funny."

"So glad you're amused."

Riony sniffed, darting her gaze over the blocked doorway. "Look, it's not my fault. No mention at all about glowflies or jammed doors. How much else wasn't I taught?"

"Delving consists more of on-the-job training. Like getting to know the limits of your tools and that the athame would run out of charge before you cut something big enough to fit a normal person through. Let alone something your size."

"Been sizing me up, have you?" Riony smirked.

"Only in your dreams."

There was the slightest hint of red over Aishena's ashy-tan cheeks that may have just been Riony's wishful thinking.

Aishena shook her head at Riony and her continued investigation. "There are plenty of other spaces to search, when Brishan isn't choosing to punish us, rather than waste time trying to get through a jammed door."

"But I mean, we're here anyway …" Riony moved across to the side, feeling around on the hollow wall beside the door that the stone would slide into, if it opened. She thumped her fist against the cold limestone in a few places, listening to the returned sounds.

"What in the depths are you doing?"

"I managed to fix my sticky front door." Riony turned and grinned back at Aishena. "I just had to find where the mechanism was jammed and reach it."

"You really got it working again?" Aishena sounded skeptical.

"Yeah. It was easy. It just took some trial and error." Then Riony added in a quiet voice, "And almost losing my arm."

Riony turned back to the wall, then traced the cutting rune on her athame. It activated with a yellow glow, and Riony again marveled how the object had somehow recharged itself during their trip aboveground. She found her target site and pressed the tip of the crystal blade into the limestone. It sliced in as smooth as butter and slowly, Riony worked to cut a rough circle, just large enough to fit her arm into.

It took a couple of minutes, during which Aishena huffed and Riony fretted that the charge of her athame would be spent, but soon the line of the circle closed and Riony juggled the resulting plug of stone from the wall.

She gave Aishena a smug look as she deactivated her athame. Holding her glow stone up to the hole, she peered inside the hollow double wall.

The insides were a marvel of stone and crystal mechanisms, from fine, weblike cogs and wheels to solid counterweights and moving levers. Most had been marked with harden runes, used to make the limestone behave more like steel. Riony couldn't identify the other runes, but imagined they might be used to make the parts run smoothly together without lubrication or weigh more than usual, and stars knew what other Alderkin magic.

The runes didn't matter though, as clearly they weren't intended to be manually activated. Like the harden runes, maybe they never needed to be reactivated after the initial function.

"Yeah, there it is! It's basically the same problem I had with mine, but worse. I just need to ..." Riony wriggled her hand into the hole, getting it in past the wrist, twisted around, and pressed in up to her elbow, turned again, shuffled closer, and pushed until her shoulder was pressed against the wall and the cut circle cuffed tight around her biceps.

"I should have cut this a bit bigger. Didn't realize my arms had gotten larger. I've been training more lately, can you tell?" She looked hopefully back at Aishena.

Aishena pinched the bridge of her nose and looked at the floor. "Please get your arm out of there before you set off a trap and bury us alive."

"I've got this. This is easy and doesn't count as risk-taking at all." Riony felt around inside the hollow wall, squeezing her hand down through the complex carved stone mechanism. It was tight, and her fingers scraped and caught. "Certainly not a big risk, anyway."

"Riony ..." Aishena growled warningly.

Riony ignored her. She groped blindly down through the labyrinth of stone shapes, feeling for the piece she needed to adjust.

There was just one line of bearings that had been pushed off track, whether by accident or design of someone trying to block this path for good. Riony pressed her cheek against the cold stone, reaching farther. Her fingertips rolled over the smooth bearings, rounding them up and bringing them into the groove they belonged in.

The final one slipped into place and they rolled together down the line.

A harsh, scraping sound filled the room. The stone door rolled.

Very quickly, right toward Riony's arm.

"Riony!" Aishena cried.

"Sparks!" Riony tugged at her arm, hoping it would just slip right out, but it was twisted and turned down though the gaps of the mechanism.

Riony eyed the approaching stone as it vanished into the wall, right toward her stuck limb. She breathed slowly and worked on reversing the path she'd woven her fingers down through.

Her bicep scraped clear, and she twisted to adjust her elbow to bring it through too.

Aishena grabbed her other arm and pulled, causing her elbow to bend the wrong way and block up the hole.

"That's not helping!" Riony cried.

Aishena's face went gray, and she let go, running over to the rolling door and trying to grab hold of it there. Her wiry muscles and slim figure had no chance of anchoring the massive rock.

Riony felt the approaching stone brush the back of her hand, pushing against it. With one final yank that bent bones in her wrist the wrong way, Riony's hand came free from the hole, and she fell backward onto her bottom.

Riony examined the scrapes and reddening skin around her hand, then chuckled. "Told you I could get it open. And I didn't lose an arm! That's two-zero for me versus doors!"

Aishena didn't reply. She stood in the now opened doorway, staring into the room beyond.

Riony got up to her feet, dusting herself off and wincing at her aching wrist. "Okay, so it was a bit of a risk. Sorry. I was only joking before about losing an arm. My door back at home wasn't nearly that close a call. Losing an arm really isn't something I want to do."

Aishena still didn't reply. Riony stepped over next to her and looked into the revealed room. Her jaw dropped.

"I take it back. I would have happily lost an arm for this."

The modestly sized room before them was pristine, a perfect time capsule, preserving a window into the forgotten Alderkin era. Statues, paintings, and ornate weaponry adorned the walls.

Glittering jewelry and ancient tomes were laid out on shelves, and a large, low bed sat right in the middle of the room, embroidered blankets tossed back, unmade, from the last time the inhabitant of this space had woken up, never to return.

"I am going to be so stinking rich!" Riony crowed.

Aishena raised her eyebrows. "We. We are."

"Shut up. You're already rich and who risked their arm for this?"

"Delver hauls get split evenly and don't you dare mention anything to Brishan about risking an arm when this gets reported."

Riony huffed but couldn't shake the grin off her face. Even splitting the value of what was before them, she was going to be rich. She and Lyrrin and Dracuni, and even Sir Butterfur Spelunkychunks would have everything they needed, everything they wanted.

We're having fried rope worm tonight!

She took a step into the room.

"Careful," Aishena warned.

"Come on, let's see what we can carry out of here! Try to show a little positivity sometimes!" Riony rested her hand on her sword hilt and spun around to pull a face at Aishena.

The tension of something catching against the end of the scabbard then snapping was so slight, Riony almost dismissed it as her imagination.

Then the entire room trembled. Dust cascaded from the ceiling as a low rumble built through the chamber.

Panic flashed in Aishena's eyes. "We need to get out, now!"

Riony broke into motion, dashing back to the newly opened door. The ground tremored beneath her, and the walls groaned, and the thunderous slamming sound of ceiling hitting floor came from right at her heels.

The destruction didn't end at the threshold.

Dust and debris engulfed Riony and Aishena. They ran together back for the entrance through a landslide of crumbling stones.

The walls closed in on them, and Riony's heart pounded in her ears as loud as the falling rocks. She could barely see though the choking haze as they made a frantic scramble for the exit.

With a final, desperate leap, the two of them burst through the collapsing entrance, landing sprawled onto the stairs leading up.

Gasping for breath, Riony turned to see what remained. The rooms behind them were filled completely with rubble and dust, the ancient treasures entombed once more.

A million nasty, sweary thoughts raced through Riony's head as she stared at the destroyed chambers. She felt even worse when she saw Aishena's wrathful expression.

"Oops?" Riony muttered.

Aishena glared, open-mouthed, at Riony for a long moment before covering her face with both hands and lying back on the steps.

Riony wondered if it wasn't too late to throw herself back under the rubble and hope for a swift death. Her heart pounded from the race to safety, aching with each beat at what they'd just lost.

It wasn't long before the sounds of destruction brought the clamor of footsteps rushing their way. Brishan and Niskina, along with Jonna, Caed, and Daymora, raced down the stairs toward them.

"Is everyone okay? Any injuries?" Niskina was first beside Riony, checking her over in the cyan light of her glow stone. She touched gentle fingers to Riony's temples and neck. Even her beautiful, tender attention wasn't enough to console Riony.

"What in the depths happened?" Brishan demanded gruffly as he waved away the dust and stared at the collapsed chambers.

Riony winced. "We, aah, *I* opened a jammed door."

"What? How?"

"You just have to reach into the wall and jiggle things around and then pull your arm out in time once the door gets moving again." Riony demonstrated the actions with her arm, and Brishan's gaze followed the swelling redness on her wrist.

Niskina noticed too and grabbed it, pressing to check for breaks.

"Scratch that. Why? Why did you even open it?" Brishan swung his anger over toward Aishena. "Didn't you tell her that would be dangerous? Not to open jammed doors?"

"I did try," Aishena grumbled.

Riony shrugged off Niskina's attention, flushing hot from her ears to her collarbones. "It was fine, really, and it would have been worth it. You should have seen the room we opened up!"

"Except unfortunately the interior of the room was also trapped. Which I'm sure I also warned you about," Aishena added.

"It might have been mentioned." Riony finally found a rock to kick, one of many now, and pushed it off the stairs with her toe. Gently. Not wanting to set off any more disasters.

It was bad enough that Aishena glowered so disapprovingly at her, not to mention Niskina's pitying eyes and Brishan's gruff stare. But it was even worse to have the additional audience of the more experienced delver trio casting judgment over her too.

Jonna folded his arms over his chest and leaned toward Daymora as though gossiping. "Gonna take months to excavate all that out if we want to go through there again. Access to three other sectors, gone."

She shook her head. Brown hair, cut sharp at her jawline, swung like a hangman's rope. "A big sparking mess. Could also destabilize Section Twenty-One. It's right under here."

Caed simply turned his back on Riony, which felt like the harshest reproach of all.

"I'm sorry," Riony said.

Brishan grumbled incoherently and then crouched down in front of her. "Kid, listen, I know you're keen. But you've got to be more careful. You can't just deal with problems by throwing your body at them as though it's expendable. Because you'll spend it real quick down here. It's not worth it. And until you can understand that, I can't let you down here again. I can't have that on my conscience."

Riony's eyes glossed over as she locked them with his. "Master Brishan, please, I've already learned my lesson. I'll be so much more careful next time."

He shook his head and stood up, turning away from her too. "Go home."

Home. Home with nothing. Home, having lost everything she'd dreamed of. She couldn't.

Riony sprang to her feet beside him. "I need this. I can't... You don't understand how much I need this."

Niskina rose up beside her. She gave Riony a long look, as though pondering why someone would so desperately want this career she seemed to despise. Then she whispered softly, "Fadda, please?"

Exhaling a loud groan, Brishan turned back around and looked Riony over with a scowl. "Go home."

Riony's heart felt frozen solid.

Then Brishan continued. "Sort yourself out. And come back tomorrow. You've got one last chance. If you even slightly screw up again, you're out for good."

Chapter Five

Riony thought things couldn't possibly get any worse.

She moped her way home, sore inside and out, empty-handed except the weight of her shame.

Delving wasn't what she thought it would be. She'd imagined the delvers plunging through the ancient depths with brave, reckless abandon, snatching treasures from the grasps of great peril.

But her attempt to take a risk in return for the chance of a reward was met with everybody sneering at her as though she were the dumbest stack of rocks they'd ever seen. It had also almost ended with her and Aishena being flattened by a stack of rocks too. Which might have been less painful.

Riony's cheeks burned so hot they were probably the color of her hair.

Recklessly throwing her body at problems had served her well in the past, and it felt like a betrayal that it had failed her now.

She passed by Curtain Market, the richer, Upslope trading area where she could have sold the Alderkin artifacts she'd found, if they weren't buried under a mountain of stone. Where she could have bought every tasty treat the vendors sold, come home the hero with two fried rope worms each for her, Lyrrin, Dracuni, and Butterfur.

I have another chance tomorrow. I'll do it all right tomorrow. No risks. No mistakes. I'll even leave my sword at home. Riony didn't like the idea of that final thought. The weight of the dragonguard sword at her hip felt like part of her body. She felt safer with it.

Another sensation washed over her as she meandered down the Flowstone Steps and toward the Grand Arch that led to her home district. A jab of fear, distant and strange. She could feel it tug at her insides, like a pull in the direction of home.

It felt almost like Dracuni's fear, but Riony knew she was still too far from the unidragon to feel that now. She wrote it off as her own feelings of fear at returning home empty-handed.

Lyrrin is going to be so disappointed.

Riony paused, almost turning to head back to the markets. Maybe she should sell off her cutting athame and say that was what she'd earned that day? Then nobody at home would have to know how bad she messed up.

Unless she screwed up again and tomorrow was her last day of delving ever. Then they'd know, and know she lied as well. Riony didn't like being dishonest with Lyrrin and generally was awful at delivering convincing lies anyway. She just didn't have the face for it.

One of the many reasons she'd receive whippings back in her days with the Heithorns.

And what if the sovs she got from selling the athame were the last she'd ever get and she and Lyrrin and Dracuni would all starve? Riony didn't count Butterfur. The tricky little fur-sausage would abandon them in a second once the treats ran dry and would be fine on his own.

Another wave of emotion rushed Riony. More worry, but also a bone-deep tiredness. Riony's shoulders slumped. All she wanted to do was get home and curl up with Dracuni on their singed and smoky blankets and feel sorry for herself. She ran her hands over her face, and when she looked up again, there was Lyrrin.

The child, hood up and gloves on, was running straight toward her, Butterfur chasing after like a streak of caramel silk. Lyrrin's cheeks were pink, and a worried look widened her bright eyes.

"Riony!" she cried out when she spotted her big sister, then—

"Are you okay?" they both gasped together.

Riony shook her head. "Fine. What are you doing out here? You should be with *your new pet*. Is your new pet okay?"

Lyrrin nodded vigorously, her expression still anxious. "She's fine. Darris came, ran a message to me, said something happened at delving and that you were hurt!"

Riony scanned over the crowd and spotted the boy about a block back, watching from a street corner with pursed lips before he dashed out of sight.

Riony frowned. How did the gossip spread so quickly? Did everyone know? She worked her lips to force out the shameful truth. "There was an accident. I made a mistake, but I'm fine. Everything is okay." *As long as I don't screw up again.* "You didn't need to leave your pet. You should have stayed with her."

"Darris said it was bad, that you were hurt bad, and I had to come right away."

Butterfur stood up on his back legs, nipping at Lyrrin's gloved fingers and trying to reach his paw into her pocket. With an annoyed huff, she picked him up and dropped him inside her shirt, patting him through the cloth to settle him.

Confusion crinkled Riony's brow. "Well, he was wrong. And you still should have stayed home. Your new pet comes first, always."

A red tint flushed around Lyrrin's eyes and they glossed over. "You're my sister. You matter too."

Riony simply shook her head.

"Dra—"

"Shh! *Your pet*," Riony shushed, wishing she'd given the unidragon a less obvious name for use in public discussions.

"She's okay. She was sleeping anyway. Are you *sure* you're okay? You don't have to hide it to make me feel better." Lyrrin had her clever eyes on the red swelling on Riony's wrist.

It was Riony's turn for her eyes to water. She wanted to vent everything, to swear and cry and be told she hadn't messed up despite knowing she really, really had. But she didn't want that comfort from Lyrrin.

She wanted that from her amma and pabba who she could never see again. Who would never comfort her again.

Riony opened her mouth to again express her okay-ness, when a bustle of children from the orphanage raced by, giggling and gasping.

"No way you saw a wolf," one of them huffed from the back of the pack.

The leader called over her shoulder, "I so did! Let's find it! Let's hunt the wolf!"

Every nerve inside of Riony caught ablaze. Dread curled within her. The sensations from Dracuni, a fear so strong it had reached her all the way out here …

She and Lyrrin stared at each other for a long heartbeat.

And then they ran.

Riony forged a path through the crowds, breaking ahead of Lyrrin on her longer legs. Bystanders swore as her shoulders crashed against them, but she didn't slow down. Rounding one corner, then another, the stairs leading up and up and up to their home were in sight.

Riony bounded over them, legs burning as she leaped three steps at a time. She had ascended more than halfway up the huge stalagmite when Lyrrin cried out in alarm from back at ground level.

"There!"

Grasping the low stone balustrade, Riony leaned over, casting her gaze to where Lyrrin pointed.

A shadowy form prowled below, jumping from rooftop to rooftop. Passing through a lit section, the form of the large gray wolf became clear and so did his wretched rider, and the limp, bound form of Dracuni, lying across Kess's lap.

"No," Riony breathed the word.

The wolf's ears twitched, and Kess turned back. She smirked as their eyes locked, then her wolf pounced down again, out of sight onto ground level.

Lyrrin was already running that way, just a street off from where Kess went, from her closer starting position on the ground.

Riony vaulted over the low stone wall, off the steps, racing down the steepest part of the immense stalagmite structure. Her feet skidded, and she leaned back, sliding down in more of a fall than a run, her palms grazing against the stone as she steadied herself.

Her heart raced, worried she wouldn't catch Kess in time. Worried Lyrrin wouldn't catch Kess in time. Worried Lyrrin *would* catch Kess before her and it wouldn't end well for Lyrrin.

The shadowed shape she'd seen before on her way to delving must have been Kess and her wolf. If only she'd slowed to look then, if only she'd had time. Riony cursed under her breath.

The point Riony had left the stairs at wasn't her usual route down. The melted wax formations of stone bumped under her feet, threatening to buck her off and send her tumbling headfirst to the ground.

The slope plateaued below her where a natural limestone pool had formed and dried. Riony leaned into the rock, grasping at it to slow her descent before she hit the flat section. It came up fast, and her legs buckled beneath her when she hit. She rolled across it, missed catching the rimstone edge, and plummeted down to the ground level below.

The short fall ended quickly in a puff of dust and spores. She found herself in the back of a small goat cart, filled with mushroom waste headed for the livestock.

"Where in the stars did you come from?" the elderly woman leading the goat sputtered.

Riony shook off the fall, got her bearings, and took off again, not even sparing breath for an apology.

More voices went up as she left a trail of stinking brown dust in her wake. Teeth gritted, she ran on, ignoring the indignant stares and the ache in her jarred bones. Nothing mattered other than reaching Dracuni in time.

She was not letting that miserable goblin steal the unidragon. Because she knew exactly what Kess wanted, and exactly what that would mean for Dracuni. Riony wasn't going to let that happen, no matter what.

The way Dracuni was draped, bound and drowsy over the wolf's shoulders, Riony worried she might be too late. *No. Kess wouldn't need to tie her up if she'd already been tamed.*

Riony had lost sight of both Kess and Lyrrin by then, despite getting down from Dragonwing Tower faster than she ever had before. She dashed down the narrow pathways toward where she'd last seen them heading. It led to the back entrance toward the Orphan's Den.

Speeding down that narrow tunnel, Riony saw Lyrrin far ahead, running out the other end toward the mushroom farms.

I've almost caught up. I've got you, Kess.

She followed Lyrrin's path, through the gasping crowd that obviously just had a front row view of a wolf running by, and into Whisperwind Passage, the same tunnel that led up to the hole into the mountains.

As Riony reached the entrance, she could only see the barest glimpse of gray fur ahead in the tunnel, where it split in three directions.

Lyrrin pulled a glow stone from her pocket. The one she'd jammed in there before, that had some alteration to it that she'd wanted to show Riony.

Riony had almost reached Lyrrin as the girl stopped and traced over the two runes on that stone.

"What are you doing?" Riony gasped.

"We can't catch them! We have to slow them down." The glow stone shimmered to life with a hum of magic, and Lyrrin pulled back her arm to throw it.

"No! It might hurt Dracuni!"

"Trust me! Just close—"

"Lyrrin, don't! I can catch them!"

But the glow stone was already arching through the air.

Riony sprinted harder, heart ready to burst. She had to get to Dracuni before whatever those runes did went off. But the rounded chunk of calcite sailed through the air so much faster than Riony could move.

Kess turned back, frowning at the brightness coming her way. The crystal clinked on the stone floor, bounced, and rolled to a stop at the wolf's feet.

Lyrrin cried out at Riony's back, "Stop! You have to close your—"

Riony saw only white. She threw an arm up in front of her face a moment too late as the glow stone crackled with magic and filled the tunnel with a burst of light so strong it seared Riony's eyes, making them burn and fill with tears as though someone had carved them both out with a hot spoon.

She prepared to be hit with a hail of fiery cinders, but only the brilliant glow filled the air, pulsing again and again, each burst duller than the last, until the charge wore out and Riony was left in darkness.

It shouldn't be this dark. There should be light from my glow stone.

Somewhere nearby, the wolf let out an ear-splitting whine.

"What was that?" Kess growled. "Go. Just move, you dumb animal!"

Riony rubbed at her eyes, trying to clear them. She blinked and squinted around the glowing blobs that filled her vision. Blurry shapes moved nearby, and the wolf snuffled and whimpered. It was close, really close.

Riony lunged, trying to catch and grab the animal. Fur slipped through her fingers. Kess cried out.

"Razing … ugh!" Something glanced off Riony's waist. It skipped over the leather armor, then clattered on the ground. A knife? Kess didn't normally miss. She must be blinded too.

That was a small relief.

"She's to your right. Grab them!" Lyrrin called out, her small footsteps pounding up behind Riony.

Riony threw herself in a wide-armed grapple, stumbling into empty air and landing on her knees.

"Go, go!" Kess yelled.

The wolf growled, and Riony felt the flick of its tail lash by, heard the muted patter of its running paws, heard the impact as it stumbled into a wall.

"They're getting away!" Lyrrin said from Riony's side.

"And I can't see a sparking thing!" Riony snapped.

"If you'd just listened to me and closed your eyes, we could have caught them!" Lyrrin yelled back.

Riony curled her hands into fists. She turned her eyes side to side, trying to will the blurry splotches away. She found that when she looked directly at something it was nothing but a distorted shadow, but she was starting to be able to see around the edges, the very periphery of her vision clearing.

But that meant it could be clearing for Kess and the wolf too.

"Which way did they go?" She pushed back up onto her feet, wiping her still leaking eyes and trying to feel for where she was in the intersection.

"That way."

Riony could barely make out the small, wobbly shape that was her sister. "*Lyrrin!* I can't see."

"The first on the left." Her voice was small and wavery.

Riony exhaled a low sigh. Kess and the wolf had gone the wrong way, taken the turn into a tunnel that headed downward rather than up to the exit. She might still get a chance to catch them.

Riony's morning had left her with a renewed wariness of the depths. She had never gone far down the tunnel Kess had taken and didn't know what perils it may hold. But she knew people who would.

"Lyrrin, listen. I want you to go and find Aishena and Yoskar, tell them Kess is here and took something from us and that I need help."

"But *I* can help. You're just trying to get rid of me! I'm sorry the glow stone hurt your eyes, but if you'd just trusted me and listened, it would have worked."

"And if you'd listened to me and not thrown the thing, I could have caught up to them! They're getting farther and farther away with every moment."

Lyrrin sniffled and her voice caught. "It looked like you were too far away. I was just trying to help."

"You can help by going and getting the delvers. They'll be near Dragon's Maw Descent. My vision is clearing up. I'll stay here and make sure Kess doesn't get out of the caves. You go and get help."

The shadowy blur in front of Riony bobbed up and down. A nod. "I'm sorry. Be careful."

Riony reached out, feeling for the top of Lyrrin's hood, then down to her cheek. "It's okay. I'll get Dracuni back. No matter what."

Lyrrin whimpered, then disappeared back the way they'd come.

And Riony turned toward the dark hole before her and ran blindly into it.

CHAPTER SIX

Getting through the streets of the undercity was a battle for Lyrrin. The crowds trading in the Grand Arch Markets jostled her small body and blocked her path as she ran the very fastest she could run. She ducked and weaved through the small gaps between the meandering grown-ups.

Butterfur fussed in the confined pouch between the layers of her clothing, and she kept one hand on him and one holding the neck of her shirt closed in case he spooked and jumped out and ran away and she never found him again.

She didn't want to lose anyone she loved again. Not Butterfur or Riony or Dracuni or anyone.

Lyrrin had only seen Kess and the wolf she rode on from a distance, when they came into the slavers' camp not long after she and the other children had been locked in the cages. At first, Lyrrin had looked at her in awe. A girl, riding a wolf! There was more than a little jealousy.

She'd had no idea who Kess was to Riony. Lyrrin had never met Kess before that, but the way Riony had talked about her since then, she sounded like the worst person in the whole world.

And now she had Dracuni, all because Lyrrin had left the poor baby unidragon alone.

She held her bottom lip between her teeth and willed away the wetness in her eyes by blinking hard and often.

Because her legs were small and she still did her best, but she just didn't have the strength that Riony did, and what if because she'd tried to do something her way instead of Riony's way she'd messed up everything and now Riony couldn't see properly and they might lose Dracuni?

The flash crystal would have worked if Riony had just listened to me. It would have worked, wouldn't it?

Lyrrin had only tested the combination of the light and burst runes one other time before, and that first glow stone that she'd altered mustn't have had as much of a charge left as the one she'd thrown at Kess.

Her first trial had been bright, enough that it took a few long breaths to confirm that she hadn't permanently blinded herself, but then her vision cleared up quickly.

The one she'd thrown at Kess was much brighter. She didn't know that would happen, that the amount of charge left would affect the power, and that the rune combination seemed to use up every last bit of the charge remaining in its burst of light rather than having the same energy usage each time.

She hadn't tested enough.

And Lyrrin worried that was a mistake that was going to hurt them all.

Her lungs felt like crumpled paper bags by the time she reached Dragon's Maw Descent deep-run access tunnel. Riony had shown her some of the delvers' maps and Lyrrin could still see them in her mind, how the pathways twined around each other as they went up and down through the earth in different directions.

She kept running, although she had left the well-lit inhabited areas of the undercity behind. The tunnel grew darker and darker and Lyrrin didn't have a glow stone of her own. Not one she hadn't tampered with, anyway, and the rest of those were back at home.

The light had completely gone and a shrill zing of panic filled Lyrrin when she finally saw a glow up ahead.

A group of figures were silhouetted in the light, seven tall and big, and one small like her. The small one was talking enthusiastically and Lyrrin recognized Benjin's voice.

"Yoskar wouldn't let me bring it back. But it looked so cool. The rat bodies were all dried up like hard leather and their tails tangled in a massive knot. Cammi said she saw one like that once, but still alive! She called it a rat king."

"That is disgusting," said a woman with short brown hair framing her soft cheeks and large doe eyes. The repulsed expression twisting her lips was at odds with her pretty face. "I hope you burned it."

"I was about to, then all this mess happened. I'll go back and do it later today when Benjin is with Aishena," Yoskar said, because all things dead must be burned.

The group of delvers stood near a tunnel from which soft billows of dust were floating, catching in the cyan light. The occasional sound of settling stone also drifted up from that dark hole.

Lyrrin arrived, puffing at their side. She yelled in big gasps, "Kess stole … something important. Here in the undercity. Riony chased her! They went downward. She needs help!"

Everybody turned to her, expressions a mix of eyebrows up and eyebrows down. Along with the three Hjelzahn siblings, Lyrrin also recognized Master Brishan and his daughter Niskina from Riony's descriptions of them. She didn't know the three others, but they wore delver armor too.

Aishena scowled the fiercest. "She's here in the caves? Kess and her damned wolf?"

Lyrrin fretfully patted Butterfur though her shirt and nodded. "Riony's chasing them. She needs help."

"Sorry, what? A wolf?" one of the other men asked. He had shaggy blond hair that fell in tight spirals over his warm-brown skin.

Aishena ignored him and turned to Yoskar as though ready to pounce. "That unblessed maniac almost stopped us getting Benjin back. She didn't honor our deal at the bridge. This is our chance for payback."

Yoskar's mouth pulled inward, and he looked toward Benjin, whose eyes were glimmering at the prospect of a chase. "I'm not sure it's our duty. We need to focus on keeping ourselves and Benjin safe."

"I'm fine. I can help too," Benjin said.

"That's entirely what we don't want you doing," Yoskar replied.

Benjin scowled in reply. Lyrrin caught his eye, and they shared a knowing look.

Brishan lifted his hands in a calming gesture. "Okay, slow down, little one. What's going on?"

Lyrrin whined with impatience as she started again, "Kess—"

"Kessara Heithorn. A nasty piece of work that caused us some trouble up above on our way to get Benjin," Aishena clarified.

"I know of the Heithorns. Not a Kessara though," Brishan said.

Lyrrin raised her voice over them to continue. "She stole something really important of ours, and we have to stop her before she gets out of the depths."

"What would they even own that would be worth stealing?" a handsome dark-haired delver at the back said softly to the woman beside him, who chuckled behind her hand.

Lyrrin pressed her lips closed tight.

Aishena's pointy shoulders lifted higher, adding to her angular build. "Kess crossed our family. She's dishonorable and I'm happy to help Riony take her down. I'll go on my own."

"No," Yoskar said firmly.

Aishena's gaze dropped to the floor, and she took a small step back.

"Please," Lyrrin whined. "Someone needs to help her. We have to stop Kess getting away. We're running out of time."

It was in a small voice that Aishena added, "We owe Riony—"

"We've repaid that debt bringing her into the delvers," Yoskar countered.

"Fine, so she's a delver now, and delvers help delvers, right?" Aishena turned that question to the others watching the argument.

"You should help," Niskina nodded, turning pleading eyes to her father.

"Delvers look after each other," Brishan nodded. "And I suppose Riony is technically still a delver. We'll all go."

The other three delvers, despite a range of mocking expressions, stepped forward beside him.

Yoskar turned hard eyes to his peers. "You're willing to help other delvers, now? Daymora, Caed, Jonna? Where was that camaraderie when Benjin went missing?"

The woman, Daymora, met Yoskar's challenge with a steely gaze of her own. "That was different. That was a problem up above. This is a problem below. This is delver territory. We're in."

Lyrrin rubbed the gloved fingers of her hands and shook her head. "It's okay, we don't need everyone. We only need Aishena and Yoskar. We just need help knowing about the tunnel Kess went down."

"Which tunnel was it?" Niskina asked. "Can you describe its location?"

"It was the one right near the mushroom farms." Lyrrin thought back to the delver maps she saw. "Whisperwind Passage."

Brishan folded his arms across his wide chest. "It branches out a few ways, none of them particularly good. And after the morning we had, it would be better if we all go."

"No, it's really okay. Please, just Aishena and Yoskar is fine. I don't want to cause a big fuss."

"If there's a wolf-riding thief stealing from delvers, I want to see they are caught," Brishan replied. He turned to the others with a swish of his long cloak. "All ready?"

The delvers checked over the items on their belts, tightened buckles on their leather delving armor, and nodded. Aishena bounced on her toes as though ready to sprint. Yoskar still had a hard-lined frown marring his face.

"I'll see you all when you get back," Niskina said, twiddling her fingers in a light wave at the group.

"You're coming too," Brishan huffed.

Niskina folded her arms over her chest in a way that matched her father. "I mean, I love Riony, but I'm not sure I'm ready to die for her. I don't need to be involved. This is a delver thing."

"Yes, and you're a delver."

"Not that I want to be!"

"You're coming, and hopefully you'll learn something about duty and responsibility." The tension of keeping his voice level cracked around the edges of Brishan's words.

"You mispronounced *obedience*."

Brishan grunted, then his voice boomed through the tunnel. "We're all going. *Now*."

Niskina continued to glare at him but didn't argue again.

Yoskar finally offered a nod of acceptance. "Fine. We will help Riony. Benjin, stick close to me and Aishena. Aishena, keep an eye on him."

"Maybe he should stay behind," Aishena said uncertainly.

"Whose idea was it that he should stay behind last time? The time when we left him alone and he ended up kidnapped? He's coming with us."

Aishena's lips pulled in tight, and she looked away.

Benjin shuffled over close to Lyrrin and whispered, "I'm coming with you!"

He flashed her a bright grin, as though this was his best day ever. First finding some weird tangled up dead rat, and now getting to go hunting a thief with a group of delvers, he looked ready to split his cheeks.

Lyrrin could only grimace anxiously in return. This wasn't what Riony asked for. This was too many people to bring along, to find out what Kess had stolen.

But they were already moving.

Oh no, oh no. Lyrrin chased after them, sprinting to keep up with their long, running strides. Getting help was good, but if they did catch Kess, they might all end up seeing Dracuni. And even if they thought the unidragon was a normal dragonling, that was going to cause big trouble for them.

Riony must have decided she could trust Aishena and Yoskar with finding that out. Or maybe Riony thought she could get some information off the Hjelzahn siblings, then send them away again before they saw anything.

But all the others? And all determined now to catch the thief in their midst? Lyrrin clenched her jaw to try to stop the trembling there.

As they moved through the streets to the rhythmic pounding of the delvers' pace, crowds parted before them. People pressed themselves to the walls of the narrow passages to make room for the urgency of the delvers in a way they didn't even consider for Lyrrin's urgent flight on her own.

It made the return journey much faster. They crossed the bridge over the small stream feeding Moonmilk Pool, and the musty, heavy scent of the mushroom farms rushed in with Lyrrin's panting breaths. She checked her pocket for her handkerchief in case she started getting sniffly.

With the tunnel in sight, she tried to be hopeful.

Riony should still be there, at the intersection, standing guard until her vision cleared. She could say something, explain to everyone that they weren't needed. They might listen to her.

But when the group reached the intersection, Riony wasn't there.

The delvers came to a stop at the three-way split, looking to Lyrrin for direction.

She stared wide-eyed at the tunnels, willing Riony to reappear. "This, this is where I last saw them. Riony must have chased after Kess."

"Which way?" Aishena asked.

Lyrrin pointed, and Brishan tsked.

"It's a dead end, at least. If they haven't chased back out and into another tunnel already, we have the thief cornered. This whole section is dangerously unstable though. Riony better keep her eyes open and be careful down there."

If she can see at all. Lyrrin cringed and fidgeted with the leather of her gloves.

"Why didn't Kess follow the path to the exit?" Aishena asked, lifting her chin toward the middle tunnel. "She must have known about it to come this way. Why'd she go down instead?"

Lyrrin didn't think it would be good to share her rune experimentation with the delvers. She racked her mind. "They … they all got … dust in their eyes. Kess and the wolf couldn't see properly and went the wrong way. Riony got it in her eyes too."

Brishan dragged his solid hand down over his mouth and beard, covering a sigh. "Riony is down there, charging around blindly, chasing a thief and a wolf?"

Lyrrin nodded a tiny nod.

The delvers exchanged glances.

Aishena pulled an athame from her belt and adjusted her glow stone. "Then we'd better hurry."

Chapter Seven

Kess couldn't tell whether she was still blinded, or whether it was simply so dark she couldn't see anyway.

She didn't have one of those glowing crystals that lit up the main sections of the undercity. She'd considered stealing one, but she didn't know how to make them start and stop glowing like she'd seen others do and didn't want a bright beacon on her as she prowled around the shadows.

I should have grabbed one. Shoved it down in my pack somewhere out of sight. But Kess hadn't expected to be lost in some lightless tunnel.

There was a torch and tinder and a striking steel in her packs for light and fire that she used aboveground, but she didn't have the time for that while being chased.

She should be heading up, out of this awful, buried world, with her prize claimed. From the angle at which Griskin moved, Kess could tell they were headed downward.

Razing Pony and that damned brat. What did they do to us?

Griskin whimpered again, sniffling wetly, and bumped into a wall. His eyesight still hadn't cleared either. And Kess knew his eyes were so much keener than hers. And may have been hurt so much more by that bright flash.

A couple of times they slipped and tumbled down rough flights of stairs, Kess cursing all the way. But they couldn't turn back. Even with her human ears, Kess could hear that monstrous oaf storming after them.

"Kess! Where are you, you miserable …" The yell came from close around the corner Kess had just passed. "Turn yourself in, and I promise I'll treat you as nice as you treated me!"

Kess's back muscles tensed rigidly. She leaned over the dragonling and hissed into Griskin's ear, "Move!"

Griskin charged forward again, and again their path dipped, descending deeper into the mountain. The smells of the markets and fried foods, and even the cloying stink of manure and fungus that surrounded this passage's entrance were all distant now. The tunnels were cool and quiet and smelled of only dust and dried bone.

The dragonling stirred, wriggling weakly against Kess. She crouched low in her saddle, pinning it between herself and Griskin.

How was it shaking off the sedation already? It should have lasted at least until they got out of the caves. Of course, they should have been out of the caves by now.

Everything was going wrong.

Even the dragonling itself. There was something strange about it.

Kess had never seen a dragon like it.

The gangly creature was small, much smaller than what Kess expected from a seasong dragon mother. Even if the mother had bred with a different species—rare in wild dragons, but with so few left, it may have been a necessity—it would have been with a midsize variety, a snowshimmer or etherflame.

Treedarts were too small and hadn't had successful breedings with seasong dragons even in captivity. But based on the diminutive size of the dragonling, Kess couldn't rule it out.

The coloring didn't match that theory though. Even with the paleness of the mother, a treedart would introduce ochre yellows and rusty browns. Sometimes deep purples, like the dragonling she'd chosen as her favorite from the hatchery, the etherdart her brother claimed for himself.

There was nothing earthy about this dragonling's coloring. It shimmered in an unearthly iridescent rainbow, overlaying the pale, silvery sheen of its scales. And those scales were soft, almost velvety.

Kess supposed it was also possible the hatchling was smaller than usual because it should have only just been born. It had come out of its shell earlier than usual. From Kess's calculations, the hatching date would have been closer to now.

If she treated the creature as a newborn rather than one a few weeks old, it wasn't that much smaller than expected. But there were still oddities about it.

The flimsy wings, the strange, singular horn formation, the tufts of hair down the back of its neck and at the end of its tail were all things Kess had never seen on a dragon before.

That central horn is going to be a problem. That's where the taming spike should go. I might have to get more advice from a breeder or tamer before doing the ceremony. Why can't anything just razing work out?

There she was, finally with her hands on her own dragonling, and it was this weird and abnormal thing. Not at all the strong beast she'd dreamed of. Would it even grow into a dragon that could fly? That could be a worthy steed for a dragonrider? Or would it prove to be lame and useless after all?

Kess's heart felt as though it squeezed to a painful stop. She gritted her teeth and shook off the swell of emotion, fought away the deep ache that echoed through her insides as though they'd been scooped out and left hollow and bloody.

No. She had her hands on a dragon, and she wasn't letting it go, no matter what. She was going to see her dreams of flying come true.

She just had to get out of this razed and ruined cave. As soon as she was up under the sun's blessed touch again, she could do the taming ceremony. She had her vial of silvernix tucked away safe in Griskin's saddlebags, and she had her metal spike. She'd seen it done before. It looked easy enough, if done with care. She'd make it work, even if it wasn't the normal way.

By all accounts, the very first tamed dragon had occurred by accident, when the Dragon King's silvernix-coated spear pierced the brain of a wild dragon. A freak coincidence that changed the course of history, giving humans dominion over the fiercest of creatures and all others from there down.

Still, Kess didn't want to risk getting the ceremony wrong and having to start from nothing again.

The dragonling squirmed, getting stronger. The lids over its huge eyes lazily tried to open and a tiny, pitiful trill came from beneath the muzzle.

"I'm coming!" Pony yelled from somewhere behind.

Did she have such good hearing?

Griskin turned sharply, a moment too late. Kess's leg and shoulder bumped against a stone wall as Griskin's side collided with it. The wolf followed the wall along, close to his flank, then stopped and cornered again. He sniffled and lapped his tongue against his snout.

"What's wrong? Keep moving!" Kess ordered.

A shimmer formed in the darkness of her vision. An aqua glow, growing stronger. Thumping footsteps carried it her way.

Kess squinted against the light, her eyes scratchy and raw as though someone had rubbed a handful of broken glass into them. She could only make out the glow, and a tall, dark smudge that carried the glow. *Pony.*

There was a long, sheering sigh of metal being drawn. "Give the dragonling back. Now. And I might consider leaving your head on your shoulders."

Kess's hand whipped out fluidly, plucking a bone dagger from her bracer and sending it toward the light. It clinked off metal.

"Still can't see? Let me clue you in then. You're at a dead end. You're trapped. You're screwed every which way, like your mother last time I saw her."

Kess drawled, "You keep making these jokes about my mami, but I think we both know neither of us cared for the woman."

"You get my point though. Or you will, and feel it sharply, if you don't let the dragonling go."

Through blurred vision and dim light, it did seem as though Riony had a point. Kess seemed to be boxed in.

Maybe she could get Griskin to rush Riony, leap past her. But even without clear eyesight, the redheaded monster could easily gut Griskin with that stolen sword. Kess couldn't take that risk.

The carved walls surrounding her were shadowed and blocky in her vision, and she couldn't be certain one of those shadows wasn't another tunnel or some form of exit. Her way into the caves involved going through a broken hole in a wall, so she had to assume more were possible.

Kess shifted her weight, urging Griskin into slow movement. He edged them along the wall again, and Kess ran her fingers over the cracked and crumbly stone, hoping to feel for an exit.

"I'm still the one with my hands on the dragon, and I'm the one with the wolf, so I don't hate my chances." She spoke with a loud, laughing confidence to cover the sounds of her actions. "I'm also guessing the reason you haven't jabbed me with your sword yet is that your vision hasn't cleared up either."

"Except your wolf is blind, too." The blurry smudge that was Pony circled slowly, matching Kess's motion and angling closer. "Personally, I'm not minding the lack of sight so much. Means I don't have to look at your dumb face."

"Keep your distance. Griskin can still bite your throat out easy enough, blind or not." Kess's fingers pressed into a softer section of stone, and pebbles crumbled out around her hand. She drove Griskin toward it, hoping it was the edge of a natural gap they could escape through.

The barest low whine came from deep in his throat, but with another nudge from Kess, he pawed at the stone in a digging action.

Riony took a step forward.

"And if you try to swing on us, you'll hit the hatchling first." Kess pulled the weak creature up into her arms, holding its body against her chest like a shield. It mewled pathetically.

"Sparks, Kess! Please, just don't hurt her."

The tame-brain really had gone soft for the wild dragon spawn. Kess smirked. That was all the leverage she needed.

But then the pattering of many feet tumbled down the tunnel descent toward them.

Pony chuckled softly. "Listen to that. Here comes my backup."

Griskin growled at the loudening sound. He reared, digging at the wall with both front paws as Kess leaned close to him.

Far too many new blurry figures emerged into the space before Kess, bringing more light with them. She scowled and drew another dagger, holding it out as a warning with one hand as her other kept hold of the hatchling.

"When you said there was a wolf, I didn't think she'd be riding it!" said a man.

Another gasped. "What is she holding?"

Then a boy said, "Is that a … no way."

A sharp, clipped male voice barked, "What's the wolf doing? Get it away from that wall! The whole place could cave in." Yoskar Hjelzahn. She remembered his terse tone from the bridge.

Kess scoffed. She wouldn't be so easily tricked. Griskin must be close to a way out. She just had to buy time. "Everyone back off!"

A thick rectangle of a man stepped forward. "You have to stop the wolf from digging. This whole area is unstable."

"You're unstable if you think we're not getting out of here. You want us to stop digging? Then clear the path and let us go the other way."

"Fine, fine! Everyone move back!" the man ordered.

"No! I'm not letting her get away with what she's stolen," Pony bleated.

Figures moved around in front of Kess, stepping back and forward and into each other's spaces. She gritted her teeth, blinking furiously against the blobby dots that obscured them.

"We'll all be buried if she doesn't stop."

There was a genuine panic in the man's voice that rattled Kess. Griskin must have sensed it too, or something else, as he stopped digging and spun an anxious circle on the spot.

Kess's back hadn't been turned for even a moment, when a guttural cry cracked through her ears, and a shadow fell over her.

"No! Don't!" a woman screamed, too late.

A bulk of muscle and leathers collided with Kess's side, grabbing awkwardly at her middle. The thick arms bundled around both Kess and the dragonling, and all three of them tumbled off the back of the wolf.

Kess gripped tight to the dragonling, refusing to let it be snatched from her grasp, and she and her brutish attacker—Pony, no doubt about it—flew toward the wall.

Kess braced for the smack of her body against rock. On impact, it was the stone that gave way. The cracked wall smashed apart. Abrasive slabs and shards scattered around them. They broke straight through.

In a deafening tumble of dust and rocks, Kess prepared to be buried alive and wasn't prepared at all to be plunged into a rushing stream of frigid water.

Legs and arms and tied up dragon claws tangled and lashed as the three of them swirled about in the current. The thin channel plunged, taking them under.

Pony's grasp disappeared from her skin as the torrent tossed them mercilessly. But Kess kept her arms tight around the hatchling, refusing to ever let go, as the water took her under and down into a breathless darkness.

Chapter Eight

"Riony!" Lyrrin screamed. She ran, but her legs skidded beneath her as soft hands grasped around her shoulders, holding her in place.

Time seemed to move in a stuttering series of images. The moment Kess's wolf turned around. Riony, wiping her eyes on the back of her forearm, tensing to lunge. The tumble of flailing limbs hitting the wall. Dracuni's tail, flicking up between them. The unstable sheet of limestone, cracking like eggshell.

Riony, Dracuni, and Kess disappearing into the dark hole beyond.

"Riony!" Lyrrin cried out again.

"Whoa!" Niskina had Lyrrin gripped tight. Keeping her from running into that same hole or the snapping jaws of the panicked wolf.

The huge storm-gray beast yowled and yapped, turning side to side in clear distress. Its icy-blue eyes spun wildly, unfocused and weeping, and it sniffed at the air with panting desperation, causing it to cough and sneeze. The stirrups of the rough makeshift saddle on its back swung wildly, empty of their rider.

"Get that thing out of the way," Brishan ordered.

Aishena moved first, activating an athame with a dexterous tracing with her thumb. It lit up red and hot.

She approached the wolf, holding the blade before her like a flaming torch, the wolf backed up into a corner, growling. It could at least see something then.

It raised its head as it sniffed toward the hole again, then howled loudly.

Lyrrin felt a pang of guilt for the wolf, that she had blinded it and Kess and Riony, and now their loved ones were missing and Lyrrin wanted to howl too.

Brishan pointed to the other female delver and the man with the thick eyebrows and kind green eyes. "Daymora, Jonna, help keep that beast cornered."

The two delvers drew athames as well, although they didn't activate them, and moved beside Aishena.

"I always wanted a dog. Think I could keep it?" Jonna asked with a grin. He tentatively reached toward the wolf, who snapped, almost taking off his fingertips.

Daymora beamed back at him. "You're such an idiot."

With the wolf out of the way, the hole was clear, and Lyrrin stared at it, willing her sister to reappear, Dracuni in her arms. Only the rumble of rushing water emerged.

Benjin reached out and gently touched Lyrrin's arm. "It's okay. They'll find your sister. It's what they do."

"Then why aren't they doing something?" Lyrrin cried.

Niskina's grip on Lyrrin softened. She shook off Niskina and Benjin and dashed over to the still crumbling hole.

Yoskar's crystal-studded staff appeared in front of her face, a barricade barring her way.

"Stay back! It's not safe." His tone was gruff, and then quieter, he muttered, "As wild as her sister."

"Keep her out of the way," Brishan said. He leaned toward the break in the wall, staring in at the darkness beyond. He called out Riony's name, but the gurgles of rushing water were all that replied.

"Sparks and stars," he grumbled. "I know the new girl has impulse control issues, but to charge an obviously destabilized wall like that, she must have been blind."

She was. And it was my fault. Lyrrin bit her lip, and her nose went hot and sore. Butterfur ran circles within her shirts, matching the swirling sensation in her stomach. She wrapped her arms around her middle, trying to still them both.

She leaned as far forward as Yoskar's staff allowed, hoping to see signs of her sister returning, climbing back from that gaping hole.

Through the dust and trickle of crushed limestone falling like a curtain, there was only water. A massive, churning channel of an underground stream, coming in from above and disappearing below. No glimpse of red hair within the splashing liquid. No strong hands gripping the edges.

There were other grumbling, crackling sounds and the world felt off-balance, as the water roared and the wolf growled and Lyrrin's heart pounded in her ears.

"We have to go after them," she pleaded, meeting the eyes of the delvers spread through the dead-end room.

They turned away, unable to hold her gaze. Only Aishena kept her eyes locked with Lyrrin's, and Lyrrin didn't like the way her dark eyes stared back.

It was the same expression the delver had held back when she'd said *let the kid say goodbye.*

Yoskar lowered his staff and said flatly, "What we have to do is get out of this room. Those cracks are spreading."

"No!" Lyrrin pushed away the staff, ducking under it to get closer to the wall, and Brishan caught her at the edge of the hole. Her feet kicked out, catching the crumbling rocks, scattering them over the floor.

She squirmed within his grasp. "Let me go after them!"

Brishan held tight. His eyes softened as he looked down at her. "Listen to me. There's every chance your sister will wash through that tunnel to somewhere safe. We will go and check the maps and see where that might be, and we will send search parties."

It sounded like a plan, but also a slow plan. How long would that take? And what if Riony and Dracuni didn't have that time? Lyrrin stopped fighting, but Brishan kept a strong grip on her as his frown deepened.

"But there's just as much chance that she won't. And I'm not letting anyone else jump into a hole with a fifty-fifty chance."

Lyrrin's stomach churned. She studied the expression on Brishan's craggy face, both hard and soft, sympathetic, but firm. He wasn't lying just to scare her, and he also wasn't withholding the truth from her because she was a kid.

Lyrrin wasn't sure how she felt about that. Those weren't good odds.

She felt as though she had two paths split in front of her leading into her future, and down one of them her sister was already dead.

Caed loped over beside them to look into the hole as well. He sniffed and frowned. "Clean water, and cold. One of the melt streams rather than warm springs. Natural channel, not Alderkin carved, so it's unlikely it will be safe or come out somewhere we've mapped."

Lyrrin felt her future swing further again toward the path she didn't want. Her face scrunched up as she tried not to cry.

Niskina sighed loudly. She came over and pulled Lyrrin out of her father's grasp and put an arm around her shoulders. "Sparks, both of you! Could you use less tact? I'm sure Riony's going to be fine. She's tough as dragon scales."

Somehow, Niskina's words made Lyrrin feel even worse, and she gulped away a sob.

Caed simply shrugged. "Speaking of dragons, what was that thing the wolf girl was holding? Looked like a baby dragon to me."

Yoskar pushed his glasses up his nose and stared down at Lyrrin. "You said Kess had stolen something from you. Was that it?"

All eyes turned to Lyrrin, frowning and questioning. Benjin seemed outright hurt at the evidence Lyrrin had a very exciting secret that she hadn't told him. Considering he already knew one big secret of hers, she thought that was probably enough.

Lyrrin muttered, "No. I don't know what that was. She stole … something else from us."

"What did she take?" Yoskar asked.

"*Something*," Lyrrin murmured. She couldn't think of anything, a lie to offer, over the turmoil of worry inside her that was as loud as the rushing water. Her eyes kept turning back to the hole. It had grown larger, and a jagged crack split downward from it, running into the floor.

Had it been there before?

"The creature looked like a dragonling to me. Dragonlords used to have me working their breeding factory, so I know what they look like. Was an odd one though," Daymora said, keeping her keen eyes on the wolf.

"Aw, I've never seen one before. And I didn't get a very good look," Benjin pouted quietly.

Niskina said, "Where did that thief get a dragonling from around here?"

Aishena shifted just enough to meet Yoskar's gaze. Then they both looked at Lyrrin.

She could see them adding it up in their heads, the nest, the eggs they'd shattered, Riony being the last person in the cave.

"There was a dragon nest," Lyrrin blurted out before they could question her further. "Up in the snowy mountains. Riony found it, but Aishena and Yoskar went up after and broke all the eggs."

Benjin's mouth dropped and he looked at Yoskar the way he must have when he saw the Rat-King corpse. "You smashed baby dragon eggs?"

"I considered it a prudent course of action to deal with the eggs so the hatchlings didn't attract attention from people attempting to catch them. Especially the wrong people," he replied without a shred of remorse.

Benjin flinched a little, then grumbled, "But still … baby dragons!"

Brishan huffed beneath his beard. "Probably for the best. We don't want dragonlords coming around and deciding that the undercity is theirs."

"That doesn't explain how or why the wolf girl had a hatchling though," Jonna said, leaning into Daymora as their expressions equally demanded answers.

"Riony said Kess is obsessed with dragons. And Riony said she saw Kess up on the mountain too, because she was after those eggs. So she must have found another one that didn't get broken, and that's why she has it," Lyrrin finished, hoping she sounded confident and convincing.

"Why did she come into the undercity with the beast, then? What did she steal from you?" Yoskar frowned and leaned in close, whispering to Lyrrin. "Did your sister have more silvernix?"

That might have been a good explanation, but Lyrrin couldn't work out if agreeing or disagreeing would cause more problems. She just wanted Riony back.

Lyrrin balled up her hands and scrunched her face. "It doesn't matter! Can we please go and search for them now? They need our help!"

Yoskar gave her a long look like she was a particularly difficult passage in a book he was trying to understand. And still nobody sprang into action.

She couldn't understand how they were all standing around so calmly, as though the world didn't seem to be falling apart, as though her sister and Dracuni weren't gone and feeling less and less likely to get back with every second. As though they'd all already accepted the loss.

Aishena left her position guarding the wolf and crouched down beside Lyrrin. She deactivated her athame, and the absence of the red light left the room feeling chilled in the wash of cyan glow.

She seemed to struggle over her words for a moment, then said stiffly, "We can't go the same way your sister did. That's not a water channel that's safe for people. But we'll do what we can to get her back."

Aishena didn't sound even slightly convincing.

Lyrrin clung to Butterfur, hugging him through her shirt. She trembled with fear and grief and anger, and the earth seemed to shake with her.

The earth *did* shake with her. A thunderous crunching sound overwhelmed the roar of the water, and the floor they stood on lurched, dropping down a foot on one side.

There was a moment of silence afterward, as everyone steadied themselves, took in the new angle of the floor, and watched as newly forming fractures ran across the limestone like lightning.

Brishan bellowed, "Move! Get out of here, now!"

Everyone sprang into motion. The wolf was ignored over the larger threat of the floor breaking apart into loose slabs that wobbled and tilted.

Lyrrin remained still. She stared at the hole again. The channel that wasn't safe for humans.

Yoskar grabbed Benjin as Aishena reached for Lyrrin, snatching her wrist and dragging her into movement.

Lyrrin pulled back, slipping her hand from the glove and leaving Aishena holding the limp leather. She reached down into her shirt and pulled out Butterfur. She let him loose on the tipping floor, pushing him in the direction of the hole.

"Riony has the treats!" she cried to him, over the yelling delvers and splitting stone. The silky caramel otter skittered over the moving floor on sure, gripping feet. He sniffed at the air, snout and whispers twitching, then dove into the water channel.

Not safe for humans, but the natural habitat of cave otters.

"Back up! Back!" Daymora yelled. She grabbed Jonna by his shoulders as a wall of stone smashed down in front of them. The pathway out of the dead end was erased by the cavern closing in on itself.

The crumbling sections of floor under their feet felt like pieces of shattered ship on a sea, being drawn into a whirlpool, bumping into each other and sinking. With nowhere left to run, delvers pulled rope and tools and tried to lash themselves to something solid, but everything was crumbling away.

Lyrrin stumbled, falling onto her hands and knees. The slab of stone under her split in two beneath her belly, tipping her sideways.

The broken sections of floor tilted farther and farther, until they no longer had each other for support, and then they fell away entirely, taking everyone in the room with them.

CHAPTER NINE

I cy water rushed up Riony's nose as though it wanted to get intimate with her brain. The current seized her like a vengeful spirit. Desperate gasps for air yielded nothing but mouthfuls of water.

Of all the ways Riony thought she may die on her first day of delving, drowning hadn't even appeared on the list.

Even then, drowning would be the second worst thing to happen, because in the initial confusion of hitting water, the very worst thing happened—she had lost her grip on Kess and Dracuni.

Scared, cold, help, scared, hurt, screamed through her brain, churning together with the roar of the water.

Which meant Dracuni was still alive, still needed her. Riony just had to reach her. And not drown first.

Riony could only open her eyes for short bursts. Her vision was still damaged, but if anything, the washing of chilled water over her sore eyes seemed to help.

The walls of the tunnel rushed past in a blur of jagged rock, lit by the glow stone on Riony's belt, and the water's icy fingers clung to her, dragging her deeper. She couldn't see the others.

She struggled to orient herself in the rushing torrent. Her hands wanted to claw at the walls, end the relentless tumbling, pull herself up and out if there was even anywhere to pull herself up and out onto.

But she could feel Dracuni. Her pain, her panic, and she knew the unidragon was down, somewhere just ahead of her in the stream, still moving. She could *feel* her there, as though a string had been bound around each of their hearts, tugging Riony to her. So she let herself be dragged on.

Riony's chest burned and tightened from lack of air, but determination and sheer fury kept her from passing out. Because Kess had taken Dracuni and had tied her up, muzzled her!

Riony would come back from the dead to exact revenge on Kess for that. A little drowning wasn't an obstacle at all.

Tackling them had been Riony's mistake, but she'd been desperate and hadn't seen how fragile the wall behind them was. She couldn't have known it would plunge them all into this splashing vortex.

But still her heart constricted with the shame that she had again thrown her body at something and caused a mess.

And Brishan was there, watching too.

Riony had more to worry about than whether she'd still be a delver when she got home, but she worried regardless.

The water's pull grew stronger, and Riony's body felt like lead, growing heavy with exhaustion from the effort to not be smashed against the tunnel walls and the inability to breathe.

She dropped suddenly again, sliding down stone worn smooth from the flow. Then she was expelled in a spraying fall of water, splashing down and plunging into a deep expanse of both darkness and light.

Bright streaks of moonlight blue stirred into existence at the motions of Riony's hands and feet. And out in the deep well surrounding her, other things moved, lighting their path as they went. Small things ... and big things.

Chest bursting, Riony propelled herself in the direction she hoped was upward. She erupted from the surface in a spray of luminance, gasping for air.

She flicked her hair from her face and blinked the water free from her eyes. She could see clearly now except for two trailing blobs obscuring a small section of her vision.

Her heart pounded, a cacophony that echoed in her ears as she struggled to keep her head above water. The ropes and pouches and sword at her belts weighed her down. The cavern echoed with the rush of the waterfall she'd emerged from.

The current had eased in this larger body of water, no longer a crashing maelstrom. Only a steady tug now, dragging Riony away from a low shore she had almost washed onto, and toward an abyssal crack in the cavern ahead.

She exploded into motion, swimming toward that shore.

Because on it lay two shadowed forms.

And because one of the large things that moved in the water, brightening the luminescence in its path, was coming toward her.

Paddling wildly through the water and shooting glances behind her, Riony saw what hunted her. An olm.

The slithery, pale, legged eels had a nasty bite, even when small enough to emerge in the pools and reservoirs of the undercity. But this one must be ancient. It was huge, big enough to take most of Riony in its translucent maw.

And Riony did not have the time to be chewed on by a giant carnivorous water worm right now.

The creature lunged up at her, and Riony kicked out. Her foot met the slick skull and glanced off. Just enough to deter the olm, it turned the other way. But the kick also pushed Riony off course too.

The current fought against Riony, and she had never excelled at swimming. She had to grasp on to a semi-submerged stalagmite to stop from being taken away into the next stream.

If Kess and Dracuni didn't lie waiting for her on the shore, and the olm didn't circle back around toward her, Riony would have clung to that pointed peak of limestone for a solid day as she tried to catch her breath.

Instead, she lunged forward again through the water. With a steely resolve, she dragged herself out onto the crystalline rimstone edges of the shore, her hands snagging and scratching against the sharp edges.

Drenched and battered, she pushed herself to her feet, her eyes fixed on the prone body of a monster and the precious creature she'd stolen, lying upshore.

She put her hand on the hilt of her sword, confirming it hadn't come free from where she'd sheathed it before tackling Kess. She'd be livid if she'd lost her lucky weapon in the bottom of the olm pool. Her fingers tensed and released, then tensed again over the scale-patterned metal.

Kess was up on her elbows, face down, busy hacking up a lungful of water. Dracuni lay on her side, shimmering chest heaving and breath gurgling inside that awful muzzle. Her legs were still bound, two by two, her front claws trying to work together to scratch off the leather over her face.

Then she stilled, turning toward the light Riony brought with her. Dracuni trilled, and there was a surge of emotion that sounded painfully like ***RIONY!***

I'm coming! Riony stumbled forward in a desperate rush.

Kess moved just as fast. One of her arms looped around the dragonling, pulling her close, and in her other hand she held a dagger and pressed it against Dracuni's soft neck, angling it up toward her jaw.

"Better think twice about where you're galloping, Pony."

Soft calcite crystals crushed under Riony's sodden boots as she came to a stop.

She could take Kess in a one-on-one fight, easy enough, without a wolf involved. But whether she could do that before Kess stuck that dagger up into Dracuni's brain or threw it into Riony's heart, was another question.

The way Kess's gaze tracked Riony's every action, the adjustment of her footing, the tightening of the grip on her hilt, made Riony think her eyesight must have cleared too.

Kess confirmed that with, "And don't you dare draw that sword on me." Then "No, take your fat-fingered hand all the way off it." And "*Now*, Pony."

She pressed the dagger harder, and Dracuni yipped. Any semblance of language coming through in Dracuni's thoughts was overwhelmed by ***Scared, scared, scared!***

"Fine. No sword!" Riony lifted both hands up in a gesture of surrender.

Kess eased the dagger back, and Riony withheld her sigh of relief. She couldn't risk Kess even nicking Dracuni with that sharpened bone.

Because if Kess drew blood, the relentless psychopath would know she'd stumbled upon something far more valuable even than the dragon she'd always wished for.

Riony turned her hands palm upward, shrugging. "But let's just talk this through. How do you honestly plan on getting out of here alive?"

"I've gotten out of worse!" Kess's shrewd gaze flickered all around, regularly returning to Riony between taking in their shadowy, cavernous surroundings.

Riony took her chance to get her bearings too. The underground lake lay on one side, and the shore of crystal-veined limestone rose in shimmering tiers of ancient, dried out rimstone pools toward dark crevasses leading away in several different directions.

The ceiling of cracked and broken straws had fractures running through it too, small and large, mostly dry except for the one gushing water which had expelled them into this space.

It wasn't anywhere in the undercity or surrounding tunnels Riony had ever been before. It wasn't anywhere Riony could identify from her brief study of the delvers' maps either.

A shiver ran down Riony's back, chased by the water dripping off her leather armor.

She could find a way out, couldn't she? Her delver training hadn't covered getting lost somewhere like this. It was all about how to not get lost in the first place. But Riony figured she just had to head upward. And if up led to a dead end, find another way up.

First, she had to get Dracuni safely back from Kess. Before Kess lost it and did something stupid. There weren't many people who could tell that Kess was panicking. The flat glare on her pointy face, framed by the tangled, gray-streaked braids, and still hands didn't give it away.

But Riony could see the sharp breaths swelling her chest. The whites around her enlarged pupils. She'd seen Kess's panic before and seen her hide it.

She leveled Kess with a solemn look and took a slow step forward. "Just hand over the dragonling. You know you're out of options."

Kess adjusted her position, leaning on her side by the water's edge, with Dracuni pulled in close. "We'll go back in the water, wash out somewhere else."

Riony tilted her head at the blue swish of light circling in the pool close by. "And trust your luck with the olm?"

"It would treat me kinder than you."

"Don't pretend you know anything about kindness. You've got a startling array of lacking qualities, Kess, and of them all, the inability to understand kindness is your worst. But I know you're smarter than dunking yourself into underground rapids again."

"Flattery won't get you anywhere, Pony."

Riony bristled. No one could get under her skin like Kess, even with one word. She took a soothing breath. "Listen. There's no way to be certain the stream washes out of the mountain somewhere. You're more likely to get stuck and drown and take the dragonling with you."

"I'll take my chances." Kess shuffled closer to the edge.

"Stop!" Riony grunted, frustration shooting through her like fire. She pressed her palms to the sides of her head and squeezed, shaking it at the awfulness that was about to emerge from her mouth.

The words came out, tasting like vomit. "We can work together. Just stop. I'll help you get out of here. Just don't hurt the baby dragon."

Kess stilled, keeping her eyes on the rippling surface. "Why would I ever work with you?"

"Sparks, I don't know! Maybe because we're down, stars know where, under an entire mountain, in dangerous, cursed, trapped, and unstable, uncharted Alderkin ruins. *And I have the only light source.*"

"You're just saying that to get close to me, get a chance at snatching this hatchling back."

"OF COURSE I AM!" Riony bellowed. "But what's it going to be, Kess? We all die here in a never-ending standoff? Or you get to keep leveraging an innocent life to order me around as long as you can until you screw up?"

Kess smirked, shifting back from the water's edge. "I don't screw up. My plans just keep getting screwed up by other idiots. Namely you, Pony."

Riony cringed and swallowed bile. "Stop calling me that."

"I thought you said I could order you around?" Kess pressed into a more upright sitting position.

She pursed her lips as she looked Riony up and down with a thoughtful gaze, then shook her head. "I think it would be smarter if you just throw me that glowing crystal of yours and me and *my* dragon find our own way out."

"And how long is that going to take you? The olm aren't the only things creeping in the depths that would love to eat some unsuspecting prey. You aren't prepared. You never know what could burst out of the shadows down here."

Kess rolled her eyes lazily. "Stop overselling it. It's a cave. How bad could it be?"

A guttural growl from above answered her.

Riony's eyes shot up, searching the cavern roof for motion. A stream of rocks and debris trickled from one of the larger cracks. But nothing emerged.

She huffed and looked back at Kess.

Seeing how Kess regarded the ceiling with her widened eyes, Riony smirked and counted off her fingers, "Could be anything. Ghost snakes, cave spiders, stinging glowflies, diseased bats—"

"Revs?" Kess asked, eyes still turned high.

"Those are the one thing we don't have to deal with," Riony grumbled, annoyed at the interruption. "Kind of the whole point of living underground."

The growl emerged again.

Kess shimmied backward, dragging Dracuni with her toward the closest wall.

"Sounds like a rev," she muttered.

It did sound like a rev, but Riony was already exasperated from dealing with Kess and never expected a rev to appear in the depths. So she yelled, "It's not a sparking rev!"

Then a second later, the animated human corpse fell through the air and landed right in front of her.

CHAPTER TEN

The earth tried to swallow Lyrrin whole.

There was a moment of freefall. Her hood flapped around her ears and her stomach felt like it floated up to her throat.

Then just as fast as the falling started, it ended in a thunderous crash.

The shattered stone floor landed on the floor of the level below, flattening onto it like slamming a book closed. Lyrrin bounced and rolled, the extra layers of oversized clothing giving her some protection. She collided with Aishena, who caught and steadied her.

Yoskar waved the dust away from his face, and Benjin squirmed in his overtight grip.

"I'm fine, you can let me go!"

Yoskar didn't let him go.

Aishena also kept one hand on Lyrrin's shoulder, but lightly, looking the other way as the dust cleared.

The delvers moved slowly, careful of injuries, but the fall hadn't been far. When Brishan and Niskina stood up, the floor above was only a little higher than their heads.

Jonna and Daymora shared a chuckle of relief that spread through the whole group. They clasped hands, helping each other up.

"That was quite a ride," Caed said with a relieved sigh.

The wolf had come down with them and whimpered in the corner, turning circles of distress as it looked up and down.

The new area they'd landed in had beautifully tiled flooring in multicolored calcite—now broken and mostly hidden beneath the chunks of ceiling—and the natural columns had been carved with spiraling motifs.

"Everyone okay?" Brishan asked, while looking to Niskina.

Mutters in the affirmative came from all around.

"I don't recognize this area," Daymora said, eying the columns.

"Are we going to be able to get back from here?" Lyrrin asked, but her soft voice was lost under the continued rattling of loose stones pattering around them.

"Yeah, I think it's uncharted." Jonna grinned widely. "Well, that's one way to open up a new sector."

Brishan snorted. "Not the right way. We were sparking lucky that wasn't worse than—"

The ground shifted again.

There was a single heartbeat of time as Lyrrin held her breath, hoping the quaking motion was her imagination.

With a skull shaking crack, the floor went out from under her in the blink of an eye. The entire floor broke through, and they all were falling again.

There was another thunderous crash as the rocks hit the next floor down. Lyrrin tensed, waiting to hit it as well. But with the combined weight of two floors worth of stone, that floor didn't even slow the cascading rush of rubble that time. It smashed straight through.

Shattered tile and chunks of stone filled the air. Aishena fell near Lyrrin, and through a swirl of pale, flying hair, she reached out and caught Lyrrin around her waist. Bodies of other delvers twirled and tumbled through the air beside them, the light of their glow stones strobing through the dark pit.

Some of them screamed. Lyrrin's own fear escaped in short bursts of uncontrollable shrieking, punctuated by paralyzed breathlessness.

Again, the combined weight of the landslide hit another floor, and again pierced through. And again and again. The earthshaking rhythm boomed, boomed, boomed, with the crack and patter of smaller rocks and bodies ricocheting within. Gray fur flashed by. The wolf yelped and whined.

Aishena kept Lyrrin pulled in tight, and when larger slabs of stone caught against the rough wrought hole, threatening to block their path and bring them to a bone-jolting stop, she angled her body, kicked off, and rolled away from them.

She had a dim-green glowing athame in her hand, twice-hardened rune activated, and thrust it into any surface that came within reach. It slowed their descent a few times but didn't stop it.

Lyrrin held tight to the delver, looping her gloved fingers into the straps of her harnessed armor. Her other hand, glove gone, she tried to use the same way Aishena used her athame. Clawing at the walls or broken floors that flew upward beside them.

Her clothing buffeted around her, and it was so much more terrifying than the time she and Riony had jumped together into fire. Then, at least, she was with Riony. Then, she knew the ground had to be beneath them. Now, she felt as though they could fall into the center of the world.

Benjin had teased her about the dangers his siblings faced in the depths, including bottomless pits. Now, she was worried he might not have been lying.

The booming finally ended in a clattering earthquake. And it took Lyrrin a moment to realize that meant their fall would be ending too. And what that might mean.

Aishena seemed to work that out faster. She struck out with a mighty grunt one last time and sank her athame deep into the closest wall. It caught, slicing down through the soft limestone like cutting fabric. She and Lyrrin swung from the hilt of the dagger, wrenching violently from the sudden halt, and Aishena's grip slipped.

They fell again, clattering down a second later onto a steep pile of stone and smashed furniture and shattered crystals. Together, they slid in a rough landslide and came to a stop under a huge archway.

Dust filled the air thicker than smoke from a wet-leaf fire.

Lyrrin coughed and tried to sit up.

"Careful. Move each part of your body slowly. Make sure nothing is broken," Aishena choked out beside her. Then she cried out "Yoskar?"

Groans and skittering rocks came from all around.

"I have Benjin," came his reply from across the clouded space.

"I'm here. I think I'm okay," Niskina's voice came from nearby.

Brishan boomed the loudest. "Caed? Daymora? Jonna?"

The dust began to settle, and Lyrrin could see silhouettes moving within it. The delvers, and the shaggy form of a wolf, crouched at the edge of the landslide.

"Here," came Daymora's reply.

"Good enough," came Caed's.

And then nothing.

"Jonna?" Brishan called out again.

"Oh no. Oh no, no, no," Niskina gasped. "Keep the kids over there!"

"Stay here," Yoskar muttered.

"Mm-hmm," Benjin groaned from somewhere low down.

A few of the silhouetted bodies scrambled in Niskina's direction, bringing the lights of their glow stones together at one point. They looked as though they were moving through murky water, as the brown dust obscured all but light and shadow.

The delvers knelt down, keeping their voices low in a rush of whispers, pleas, and instructions.

Then Lyrrin heard Brishan say softly, "He's gone."

"No," Daymora growled in a slurred, drunken way.

Brishan muttered a few more soft words, sounding like a prayer.

"Gone?" Lyrrin asked Aishena in a trembling whisper.

"Just stay back there." Aishena gave her a soft push away from the landslide and toward the archway, then went to join the other delvers. She knelt down into the huddle of them.

In the archway, the air was clearer, and Lyrrin gasped it in with shaking breaths. Her whole body felt rattled and bruised, and even her tough claws were red-tinted with scrapes and grazes. Her heart was going faster than a hummingbird's wings.

She turned her face upward, and the hole seemed to extend up into an infinite void above them. They were so far down. And one of them …

Lyrrin couldn't look at the huddled team of delvers and the hole left between them. She turned away, looking instead at the space behind her, through the archway, and her breath caught.

Brishan's voice rumbled through the air. "Come now, up to your feet, all of you. We still have our lives, and the dead won't mind us doing what we must to stay that way."

Lyrrin turned back to them. All but one of the delvers stood.

"Get that wolf subdued!" Brishan ordered. "We can't have it running loose around us."

"On it," Aishena, Yoskar, and Caed replied together.

There was a scuffle nearby, and three bodies pressed the wolf against a wall in unison. The two larger bodies, Caed and Yoskar, kept it pinned there as Aishena's arms moved fast, lashing strong cave silk rope around the beast. It growled and whimpered.

A figure stumbled through the clouded air toward Lyrrin. The dust had settled enough to see faces clearly when nearby, and Niskina's was shaken, streaked with dirt and tears.

Brishan followed. Daymora remained unmoving, beside where Jonna had fallen.

Niskina took in Lyrrin's wide-eyed shock. "Are you sure you're okay, little one?"

Lyrrin's throat still felt clogged, so she could only point.

Through the archway, where the dust sifted like a low fog across the ground, there stood a vast, regal chamber, packed to overflowing with Alderkin riches.

Down there, in the heart of the earth, they had fallen into a place untouched by time or traps or plundering, where the air hung heavy with enchantment.

The vast room before them gave the air of both royal chambers and laboratory, a dwelling of a mad wizard from another race, lost to time and rumors, unknowable to those who now stood in their place.

Stone slab tables with legs carved into realistic animals were piled high in ancient tombs and scrolls and crystalline artifacts that gleamed beneath the soft light of the delvers' glow stones.

The walls were adorned with intricate carvings that danced with iridescent light, as if the very stones still resonated with ancient magic. In the center of the room, up on a tiered platform, an immense slice of natural geode stood upright, casting fleeting rainbows upon the surfaces around it.

The chambers held a sheer volume of Alderkin relics and tools that could double what was currently in use by humans in the undercity. Every artifact held the whispers of a past imbued with both grandeur and mystery. Every one immensely valuable.

And all of it felt hollow, because behind them lay a body. Because they had just lost a life, and the delvers all looked at each other and the gaping pit above them as though they weren't sure it would be the only one.

With the wolf downed, Aishena, Yoskar, and Caed joined the others away from the rubble, taking in the sight.

"Isn't that something," Caed murmured, wobbling as he favored one leg.

"It's the Alderkin mother haul," Niskina replied, but her voice was flat.

"What is it? I want to see!" Benjin called.

Lyrrin turned to see why he hadn't joined them yet and saw he was still lying where he'd been asked to stay near the edge of the mountain of fallen stone. He shifted, trying to sit up.

"Ow," he muttered, and then seemed to think again and howled a second time, "Ow!"

He slumped onto his back again with a high-pitched cry.

Yoskar was by his side in a flash. "What is it? Where are you hurt?"

"My ... my neck. My head."

Aishena's expression turned stony, and she ran to join them.

Lyrrin wobbled awkwardly across the unstable rocks a few steps behind. She hovered at the edge of the boundary of the tight circle formed by the siblings.

"What's happening? Is he hurt?" she asked.

Benjin lay flat on his back on a large broken slab. There was no sign of blood marring his finely made clothes, only dust settling over his white shirt and embroidered vest.

Yoskar had his hands on either side of Benjin's neck, touching with the gentlest motions. Aishena held her glow stone up near his face, staring into his eyes.

"Can you wriggle your toes? No, don't nod, you tame-brain!" Aishena scolded.

Yoskar added, "Stay still. Don't move anything. You can talk but try not to move your head too much."

"Okay," Benjin whimpered. "Is it bad?"

Aishena and Yoskar shared a long, silent look.

Niskina moved in beside them, kneeling next to Benjin. "If you can wriggle your toes, you're doing great. Falls can be really hard on your body, and breaks are far too common in delving." She shot a caustic look at her father. "But we're all here with you and it's going to be okay."

Benjin looked like he wanted to nod again, but after a glance at Aishena, he stayed still. He mumbled through a still mouth, "What do we do?"

"Is it his neck?" Aishena asked softly.

Yoskar nodded, glaring at her with unrestrained aggression. "You should have been with *us* during the fall. You could have helped keep him safe."

Aishena turned her face to the ground. "I'm sorry."

Lyrrin felt a pang of guilt too. Aishena had helped her, instead of her own brother. Whether that choice was made just based on how close they'd been at the time, or something else, it had cost Benjin. Lyrrin didn't want that.

She wished Riony was there with her, that Riony had been the one to help her, and that nobody had to have gotten hurt or fallen or died.

"I'm okay though, aren't I?" Benjin asked.

Niskina reached out and squeezed his hand. "You will be. We just have to get you safely out of here so you can get to work healing and get better."

Lying on his back, Benjin set his gaze straight, looking at the empty distance through which they'd fallen. The delvers followed his gaze.

Lyrrin didn't. She'd already seen how far down they were. With one lost already, and Benjin's neck broken, and Riony feeling so far away, she didn't want to look again.

Over beside Jonna's body, Daymora let out a single, chest-cracking sob.

And the tied-up wolf loosed a long, mournful howl that echoed up and up to the world that remained so far above them.

CHAPTER ELEVEN

Kess had only a fleeting moment to decide whether she should let the revenant rip Pony to shreds or make any attempt to avoid that outcome.

The hideous, shaggy monster—the revenant, not Pony—dropped directly in front of the oafish woman, and the fool didn't even have time to draw her sword before the creature was lunging for her with clawing boney fingers and yellowed teeth.

Unfortunately, Kess had to agree that finding her way out of this premature grave was going to be an exercise in frustration on her own.

With a curse on her lips, she sent a bone dagger flying. It hit true, skewering through the rev where the base of the skull met its neck. It had enough rotting meat still on its bones for the knife to lodge in satisfyingly.

Sometimes getting a hit there was enough to sever whatever cursed connection a revenant had to life. More often, it just seemed to make them angrier.

The once-human undead gargled and hissed, spinning around to turn its attention to what had stung it.

Angrier it is.

Despite its eyes being bloated, milky spheres, it locked on to Kess. Jaw snapping, it raced for her with ferocious, inhuman speed.

Kess drew and threw two more bone daggers from where she sheathed them in her bracers. One went right into the target, lodging between hip and thigh bone. The other hit location mirrored on its other side, but bounced off, clattering away on the ground.

Bone daggers didn't have the weight to slow the creature down or the capacity to cut it into pieces small enough to end it once again. But Kess had faced enough revs aboveground to learn some tricks. How she could spike them in strategic spots, disable them, slow them down enough so she and Griskin could get away.

But without her wolf's speed, and with only one dagger causing the rev to limp unevenly, it still approached too fast.

Pretty certain now that she'd made the wrong decision in helping Pony, Kess pushed her dragonling prize behind her and braced for the worst.

Claws up and jaw wide, the revenant froze in place as a steel blade skewered through its chest from behind with a loud *shluck*.

Kess exhaled roughly. "Finally got your sword drawn?"

"I really, truly, honestly wasn't expecting there to be revs down here!" Pony yelled from behind the rev. "Also, you're welcome!"

"Oh, we're counting who just saved who, are we? Because you're welcome first."

"Great to see you're still the spoiled baby I used to know."

Kess's cheeks flared. She was so much more than the person she used to be. That girl had died alone in the woods, and the woman who had crawled out of that grave on Griskin is something so much more, even if this worthless, intolerable woman couldn't see it.

"And don't think I'm dumb enough to think you were saving me and not this helpless hatchling." Kess shifted again, making sure her hostage wasn't squirming away.

Unperturbed by the length of steel through its gut, the revenant twisted and jittered on the horizontal sword. Its head flicked around, neck cracking as it turned entirely backward to face Pony.

Arms contorted, shoulder sockets popped, and the rev pushed itself farther up the sword to reach its sharp-nailed hands out for Pony.

"Ew, no! I don't like that at all!"

She balked at the disturbing, half-backward body but didn't release the dragon-scaled hilt of her sword. Leaning back, she kicked into the revenant, pushing it away and pulling the blade free with a grunt.

The rev clattered awkwardly to the ground, disjointed limbs and crooked elbows pointing in every direction. It landed far too close to Kess for her comfort, and she drew another dagger.

Its attempt to skitter across the ground toward her was halted by Riony swinging her sword with all the finesse of a lumberjack into the rev's side. The clumsy strike landed with a walloping impact, lifting the corpse off the ground and flipping it over in the air.

Kess flushed, involuntarily impressed at the strength behind that blow, then immediately disgusted with that emotion.

"Where did you steal yourself a dragonguard sword from?" she snapped.

"Pulled it out of my ass." Riony kept up the assault on the revenant as it rolled around, trying to right itself. "Seemed like a better time than ever seeing your face again."

"You're the one making a career of being a fool, a liar, and painfully unfunny all at the same time."

"Aw, thanks for acknowledging how multitalented I am."

Pony chopped the battered old sword down, straight through the rev and cracking onto the stone below. Kess cringed at the horrible abuse the once fine weapon suffered.

The swing severed through the living corpse between shoulder and arm, leaving that limb lifeless. But still the undead monster howled for their blood.

It wasn't one of the strange, ashy, re-raised ones Kess had seen recently, but without the use of fire, it would still take a great deal more dismemberment to put it down for good. Pony hadn't broken a sweat yet, but Kess wasn't certain she'd be able to put the monster to rest with that sword alone.

"Hit it into the water," she ordered.

"What?"

Kess pointed to where the midnight surface of the water rippled with blue glow as an olm swam beneath. "Knock that unblessed thing into the water!"

Finally catching on, Pony circled the revenant that skittered on three limbs like a demented spider, putting herself between it and Kess, and it between her and the water.

The monster took the opportunity to snatch Pony's ankle in its death-worn fingers.

Kess withheld a gasp when Pony went down, falling flat on her back as the rev scuttled up her. But the fool was smiling. She brought both legs up to her chest, pressed them into the revenant, and thrust them out together.

The stinking mass of skin and bones went flying, arcing high in the cyan-lit cavern, and then splashed down into the luminescent water with a bright splash.

"Saw a dragonrider do that once," Pony said.

Kess just scowled, her eyes on the rippling water.

There was a moment of stillness, with Kess and Pony's labored breathing seeming loud even over the rushing water. And then the water churned.

The cavern lit up, the strange, glowing water brightened by the splashing and writhing olm, tearing its meal from the bones of the undead.

And then Riony was back on her feet, and the point of the sword was at Kess's throat. "Let go of the—"

Kess flung the dagger from her hand. It sliced across the fingers Pony had wrapped around the hilt of the sword.

"Sparks!" she hissed, and her hand spasmed, dropping the blade. It clattered onto the crystalline floor and tumbled down, disappearing with a plop into the water.

"No, no!" Pony raced after it. She landed on her knees at the water's edge and plunged her hands in, splashing around, reaching deeper and deeper until she almost had her face in the water.

"I told you not to draw on me," Kess drawled and pulled another dagger. She adjusted her sitting position, pulled the dragonling back in front of her, and settled its squirming with the warning of the tip of the blade.

Pony continued to trawl through the water, lying flat on her stomach and angling out farther. "My sword ... I'm going to kill you if you've lost my sword!"

"You're the one who dropped it. It's just a sword. Let it go, unless you want to be second course to the rev."

A trailing blue glow headed through the water for Pony's reaching hands. She thrust herself out of the water again, rolling backward away from the snapping jaws of the olm. Smacking her soaking arms onto the surrounding rocks, she cried out in an echoing shriek.

"Wow. Who's being the baby now?" Kess raised her eyes.

"You have no idea, *no idea* what that sword means to me!"

"I'm sorry," Kess said, and Pony's eyes snapped to look at her with an intensity of skepticism that left Kess's lips curled. "It must be a hard loss. Almost like if someone had been carefully hunting a mother dragon for almost a year, then some imbecile stumbles in and destroys everything *I've been waiting my entire life for.*"

Pony pointed an accusing finger Kess's way, spraying an arc of water with it. Red droplets spilled from her knuckles. "As if you couldn't have just picked a different dream to follow from your lap of luxury instead of wanting the only thing in the world that was denied to you."

Kess's voice dropped, low and dangerous and with a great effort spent to not let it break. "If you think owning a dragon was the only thing denied to me, you never spent a day at Heithorn Estate with your eyes open."

Pony had the grace to shut her mouth then. Her cheeks darkened and she turned away, rolling over onto her hands and knees and staring at the ground.

In a land where the symbol of wealth was a miraculous, healing fluid, strength and power were the pinnacle of status to dragonlords. Having a weakness like Kess's was a dishonor her family did everything they could to fix, and when it couldn't be fixed, it was hidden away. And then disposed of.

Before shame could creep hotly up her own neck, Kess grumbled, "So I've lost my wolf and you've lost your sword. I'd say we're even. But I still have the hatchling, and you still have the light. And we're still stuck down here, wherever here is."

Pony still didn't look at her, just shook her head limply.

Kess continued. "I want you to know I blame you entirely for this situation. So you had better get me out of here, in one piece, or I'll make sure this baby dragon doesn't stay in one piece either."

Pony laughed, almost hysterically. "And how are we supposed to make that work?"

"I keep my hands on this hatchling. And you carry me."

Pony convulsed as though gagging.

Kess hated the idea too. She didn't want to be beholden to that intolerable traitor ever again. The thought of being in such close proximity to her for any length of time left a horrible, hot, acidic feeling melting away her chest.

The only thing the two of them had was a shared history of immeasurable cruelties. She couldn't trust Pony for a second, no doubt as much as the woman would trust her in return.

She wanted Griskin back. She hadn't thought she'd miss him so sharply. They hadn't been this far apart since they'd met. Every aspect of her existence since that day had been shared with him, and her experience of that existence changed through him.

The way his skin would shiver or his ear would twitch. The tensing of a muscle in his shoulder or the raising of a paw. The subtle differences in growl or whine or sniff, it all felt like a language between them, as though he and Kess shared the same heightened senses.

She felt numb without him, cut off at the ears and eyes and waist.

Wherever he was, somewhere up above, those other cowardly cave dwellers better not have hurt him.

Pony was still shaking her head. "I don't even know the right way out."

"Up, obviously," Kess snarled.

"I know that much. I'm not as dumb as you look. But how? Which way?" Pony shifted up into a kneeling position, gesturing to all the dark tunnels leading from the craggy cavern.

Kess glared at the options as though she could intimidate a sense of direction out of them. None seemed any more promising than the others. She looked up, the direction she hoped to go, frowning at the toothy limestone ceiling.

"That rev must have come from aboveground. The stream could have washed us down to a point where we are only just below the surface. That crack up there could get us out. If we could get up there."

Pony stood and looked at the hole above them. She ran her hands through her short tumble of fiery hair, sending droplets of water showering around her. She reached a hand up and seemed a long way from the cavern ceiling.

"Looks too high up even for a monster like you."

"I could reach it," Pony said.

Kess scoffed.

Pony bounced on her toes a few times and took a deep breath. Stepping onto the highest nearby point, she flexed her long legs and launched upward.

Fingertips scraped the cavern ceiling. One hand missed. The other caught, clinging by nails only to an outcrop at the lip of the crevasse high above.

Pony grunted and hung for a moment by one arm before swinging the other up to join it. Her leather armor was sleeveless, with just one strap around each bicep to hold the shoulder guards in place, which tightened and strained around her upper arms as she lifted her chest in a pull-up. Her head disappeared up into the hole.

Her voice echoed as she called back, "Not a lot of space up here. Can't see any sign of daylight. I might be able to climb out but couldn't bring anyone else with me. Not someone intent on using their hands to keep threatening a baby creature anyhow."

She lowered herself down, hanging by one hand again for a moment before dropping back to the ground in a fluid, effortless motion.

It took Pony winking at Kess for her to realize she was staring with her mouth open. She shut it promptly.

Getting out of this place with her is going to be a razing nightmare.

"One of these tunnels must get us out of here," she muttered.

"Are you going to pick? If we take the wrong one, we could be walking around in circles until we starve to death or strangle each other."

"I'm pretty sure what will come first."

"And," Riony continued, her voice rising in frustration, "there are no carvings or signs that any human or Alderkin has ever been down here before. This might be a dead-end natural cave that nothing but the occasional falling revenant and olm have ever seen."

She swung her arm back toward the water, where a slash of glowing luminescence streaked speedily toward them. It made no sign of slowing as it approached the shore.

"Those things don't come out of the water, do they?" Kess asked.

"This morning I would have said no, but then a rev fell from the ceiling, and I feel in uncharted depths now."

Pony's eyes narrowed and she reached for the empty sheath at her side. With a breathy, grunting curse, she raised her empty fists instead, as a slithery shape breached the water and launched itself at her.

CHAPTER TWELVE

The grown-ups spoke, making a plan and allocating tasks to get them out of the deep hole they'd fallen into. And Lyrrin was left by the side, hovering and hurting.

She and Benjin had gone through a lot together when they were taken by the kid snatchers. When they had been pulled from their underground home and had their lives and future threatened, Lyrrin had even shared her secret with him.

She had taken off her gloves and shown him the hard, sharp, blue-tipped nails she had at the ends of her fingers. They planned together how she could use those, cutting a trail of markings along their path for those who came to save them and sawing through the bars when they were caged.

And Benjin stood watch every time Lyrrin slipped off a glove to work with her sharp nails. And he hadn't shared that secret with anyone since.

He was still a braggart, but she liked being around him now, liked that they shared an interest in Alderkin runes and magic. He'd told her with sparkling eyes all about Yoskar's staff and all the cool things it could do, and Lyrrin didn't even tease him for boasting once.

Lyrrin wasn't sure what the neck injury meant but it sounded pretty bad. She also knew if she had never thrown that glow stone she had altered at Kess, they wouldn't be where they were now, hurt and lost and dead.

Daymora cried for a bit longer, then pulled off her scarf and laid it over Jonna's body. Lyrrin couldn't see him behind the pile of fallen rocks and was scared by even the thought of seeing him, so she stayed away.

While the delvers muttered their plan over to the side, Lyrrin took a step closer to Benjin.

"How are you feeling?"

Careful not to move his neck, Benjin turned his eyes up and as far from Lyrrin as he could.

"It really doesn't hurt that much. They shouldn't be making such a fuss," he said, but his eyes were red and puffy and his nose wet where he couldn't wipe it. His brown skin was coated in a layer of pale dust, except for a couple of places where scrapes from the fall had bled through.

"Is there anything I can do to help?" Lyrrin was starting to notice the sting of grazes on her bare knees and one bare hand. Otherwise, her oversized clothing, hood, and glove had protected her.

Even her ungloved hand only had a few minor cuts, the skin tougher there than most people's hands. She kept it hidden, tucked up her sleeve. Her other glove was probably somewhere deep within the pile of rubble.

"I'm fine. I don't need your help." Benjin still wouldn't look at her, and his mouth closed into a thin, firm line.

Probably because he also knew they wouldn't be down there, he wouldn't be hurt, if it wasn't for Lyrrin.

"I'm sorry. I know I made some mistakes, but I'm not useless. I want to help."

Benjin's golden-brown eyes reddened more. "Just leave me alone!"

"What's going on?" Yoskar snapped, glaring at Lyrrin. "Stop disturbing Benjin."

"Okay." Lyrrin backed away, and said again, even softer, "Okay."

"All right." Brishan clapped his hands together, and the group of delvers began to move apart. "Daymora, are you ready to give it a go getting out of here? I'm sorry to ask, but you're our best climber and in the best condition after the fall."

"I'd prefer to buddy with someone for a climb like that ..." She looked to Aishena and Yoskar, who both shook their heads.

"We're staying with Benjin," Yoskar said.

Niskina tried to step forward, but Brishan held her back, and Caed leaned heavily on one leg.

Daymora straightened her shoulders. "I'm sure I can make it on my own."

Brishan clapped a hand on her back. "The others might come looking for us eventually, but they're at the other end of the undercity right now. Some of the mushroom farmers must have heard the racket this made, but unless we hear someone hollering from above, we have to assume we're on our own."

Yoskar nodded. "We need to take action now. We can't risk a delay."

Brishan waved to the others. "And we'll do what we can to prep Benjin for transport from down here. With that Alderkin hoard, we might be lucky and find something with a float rune."

Lyrrin's ears pricked up. She hadn't heard of a float rune before, but she knew the delvers kept a lot of what they'd discovered of Alderkin magic to themselves, just as the Alderkin themselves had.

"Niskina, can you—"

She turned her back on her father, heading into the grand chambers. "I'm going to find something to brace Benjin's neck."

Brishan flinched, but grumbled, "Good, fine, do that. Caed, have you got bandage in your kit to wrap that leg of yours?"

"I'll sort myself out." The shaggy blond delver limped across to take a seat next to Benjin and gave him a lopsided grin. "Might have a few candies in the bag with me too."

"Did you hit your head too? Benjin shouldn't be chewing anything," Yoskar said coldly. He'd already moved through the archway and was ducking and checking the sides of furniture.

Caed popped something into his mouth and muttered around it, "Didn't say they were for him."

Lyrrin looked over the separating group, and the sulking wolf bound up beside the wall, and Benjin lying still and flat and refusing to look at her, then ran over beside Aishena.

With a deep breath and scrunched-up face, she said, "Can I help? What can I do?"

Aishena moved into the Alderkin chambers as well without looking back, but she responded with, "Help us find a float rune."

"I don't know what that looks like."

The delver paused, then squatted down over the dusty floor. Her shoulders were hunched and angular as she scribbled in the dust.

Lyrrin craned her neck, but Aishena kept her work hidden until she was done and sprang up to her feet again.

The shape she'd left drawn in the fine dirt was an upside-down triangle formed from a zigzagging line, with a couple more lines scratched across it.

Waving a hand back at it, she walked away. "It makes things practically weightless. Alderkin sometimes put it on larger objects, ceremonial crystal platforms to carry other things on, because the magic slightly affects items in contact with the runed crystal too, making them lighter."

Lyrrin memorized the shape of the rune. She hadn't seen how to activate it, even if Aishena had drawn it in the correct sequence, but Lyrrin had a knack for working out a rune's sequence. No one had shown her how to activate a blast rune either—a *four-stroke* rune—and she worked it out in only twelve tries.

There was an obvious pattern to how to trace the lines, a way that just felt right. The float rune was only a three-stroke rune. Easy.

Aishena ran her hands over a spike of orange crystal as long as her arm, brushing dust off. She muttered, "Imagine having all of that magic and using it to move furniture."

"Oh, they used it for plenty of other things too," Brishan replied from across the cluttered space.

Lyrrin followed after Aishena, looking at the crystal she passed by. No float rune on it. No runes at all, so the crystal probably had no charge either.

If there was something though, with a charge, anything big enough, maybe I could add the float rune onto it myself.

Lyrrin fidgeted the fingers of her ungloved hand around the hem of the sleeve she had it hidden up inside. But she'd never tried combining a float rune with another before and couldn't be sure what the recipe would do. She knew from experience that some combinations were explosive.

And even the result of her best experiment, the flash stone, had gone very wrong.

"A lot of this stuff seems half-finished, crystals and items being prepared for later use," Yoskar said from beside a set of shelves that were carved into the cave wall and filled with calcite rhombohedrons and prisms in pale blues, yellows, and whites.

"That geode slab is something," Aishena said, passing it warily. "A lot like the one in the shrine we camped in aboveground."

"Most Alderkin shrines aboveground have something like that in them," Brishan said. "Not so unusual. But there are a lot of relics in here I've never seen before. The Alderkin had trashed most of their personal belongings in the top level during their last stand. Even what we could salvage, it was never like this."

"Stop salivating, Fadda." Niskina stopped beside a table and picked up a thick ancient tome, assessing the binding. She wrenched the cover off, then tore it to pieces, pulling out some rigid strips.

Yoskar winced audibly, hissing in a breath.

Niskina didn't stop. "You'll get your chance to rob the dead later, once we all get out of here alive."

Brishan's face flushed red, even in the cyan light. "The work we do serves all the people of the undercity!"

"But you serve yourselves first. Always acting high and mighty that you aren't like the dragonlords, while you're doing the same thing, really. Making yourself rich off others. Others who often end up dead." She paused her destruction of the priceless relic to give her father a long, fiery glare through glossy eyes.

"I suppose you think a life aboveground as a rebel would be any safer?" He flung an arm up dismissively and turned his back on her.

"No, but at least then I'd be making a difference."

Lyrrin turned around, pretending to be searching along a low side cupboard. But a glint of light from the wall above caught her eye, and she looked up.

She had to move a few steps backward to take in and make sense of the flowing, carved shapes on the stone surface. And as she did, an image became clear.

"Whoa," she gasped.

In the corner of the room's shadowy depths, a mural sprawled across the expanse, a tapestry of realistic figures, carved in intricate detail and adorned with the shimmer of inlaid crystals.

At the center of the scene, a man on horseback reared, his arm poised in frozen action. His features seemed aflame with unyielding cruelty. A streaking arc of motion was struck through the stone, leading from his arm to a spear—a spear lodged into the skull of a dragon soaring above.

The dragon, wrought in tarnished gold and ruby reds, hung in midair, head bowed in agony, its serpentine form spiraling in anguish.

Poor thing was the first thought that came to Lyrrin. The injured dragon looked so deeply broken and sad.

"The leg's not too bad. Just sprained, I think." Caed hobbled into the room, catching up to the others.

"You should stay with Benjin. Someone needs to stay with Benjin." Yoskar headed back their way, converging with Aishena who made the same move.

"I ... I can," Lyrrin offered. She wasn't sure Benjin would like her company, but it was something she could do without causing more problems. Although, despite her offer, she couldn't take her eyes off the mural.

A pale section of satin spar below the horse's feet caught her eye, and she gasped. A fallen unicorn lay there, its elegant form broken and sullied on the ground, its eyes empty and vacant. Swirls of silver were inlaid into the ground beneath it.

And standing witness to the tragic scene were tall figures in a style of clothing Lyrrin hadn't seen before. They seemed human, but taller, narrower, with mournful expressions and large, somber eyes of bright, glistening gems.

Caed had reached where she stood and turned to follow her gaze. "Yikes, did you all see this?"

Aishena and Yoskar, already heading their way, stepped closer to look. Brishan and Niskina also turned from where they had been searching the largest table, continuing their argument in whispers.

Caed pointed up high, and Lyrrin tilted her head back, seeing the final part of the design that she hadn't noticed before from her shorter vantage point.

Behind the flying dragon, another ethereal form unfurled its wings.

Captured with inlays of a dark, oily stone that Lyrrin didn't recognize, a specter of shadow and smoke mirrored the pierced dragon. Wrathful and disturbing, its presence even in the mural seemed to merge with the very essence of darkness itself.

"It's the curse." Aishena's nose scrunched up and she took a step away from the mural as though it itself was the cause of all that plagued the land. "It's showing when the Alderkin cursed us all with the shadow dragon."

Caed shivered. "Stars, this whole place feels cursed."

Aishena turned to him, wide-eyed. "You don't think this *is* the source of the curse? Some magic in this image?"

A cold chill shuddered down Lyrrin's back. Scanning over the mural, she couldn't see any runes or other Alderkin symbols that suggested this was some kind of spell wrought from stone.

Niskina tsked and took a step closer, letting her gaze wander over the artwork. "I really doubt it."

With her voice low so Brishan couldn't hear, Aishena muttered, "You're just being contrary because you think it makes you seem smarter."

Niskina tucked her tumble of chestnut curls behind her ear. "I seem smarter because I think critically about things instead of believing whatever some old idiots tell me. And just look at this! This could be an accurate Alderkin record of the first tamed dragon. They could have *been there*."

Niskina pointed at the figures surrounding the rider.

Were they Aldkerin? Lyrrin had never seen images of them before. Anything in the undercity level had been destroyed, either by Alderkin themselves or the first humans to settle there.

Yoskar sniffed at the mural and those gawking at it once. He adjusted his glasses, then marched off. "I'll be with Benjin."

Caed raised his eyebrows at Niskina. "So you'd believe the old idiots that created this image instead, who were also our enemies?"

"They were only our enemies because the dragonlords were killing unicorns." She stared hard at where the magical creature in the mural lay with its life spilled out on the ground. She moved closer, reaching out a hand to touch it.

Everyone else at the mural tensed.

"Could you imagine, seeing one in person? Having lived while they still lived?" Her voice was soft, dreamy. She sighed sadly as her fingertips brushed over the image of the dead unicorn, but there didn't appear to be any other consequences, no trap or curse set off by her touch.

Emboldened, Lyrrin stepped closer too. She was fixated on the sparkling gemstone eyes of the Alderkin, in startling sapphire, emerald, and amethyst. They all wore hoods, and most stood gravely with their hands behind their backs. But one had his hand lifted, pointing at the tragedy before them.

And that hand had long, sharp nails. Not so much longer or sharper than a regular human's, on first glance. Only as long and sharp as her own.

The chill that had shuddered through Lyrrin now rattled deep in her bones.

Niskina huffed violently, making Lyrrin jump and hurry away from the mural. Her heart pounded furiously, and she clenched her ungloved fist, throwing furtive, confused glances at the mural.

Niskina said roughly, "We should have been on their side. We should have fought alongside them to stop the dragonlords draining the land of every drop of silvernix they could get. Now all the unicorns are gone and look at the world we're left with."

Aishena lifted her hands in disbelief. "Yeah, because the Alderkin cursed us!"

"And maybe we deserved it!"

"Enough bickering," Brishan commanded with a sigh. "Emotions are high. We're all grieving and haven't been given room for that grief while we're still stuck in this situation. So let's work together and get out of it sooner rather than later."

Niskina sorted the strips and boards she'd accumulated from destroying ancient relics in her hands. Nodding once, she headed for where Benjin lay.

"I still think this place is cursed." Caed sighed and limped over beside Brishan, helping search the overflowing table.

Aishena tossed a final glare at the mural, then shook her head once. "The shadow dragon didn't even appear until decades after the first taming. Probably because that was when the Alderkin cursed us, when they knew they were losing the war. This is all rubbish."

Everyone moved away, continuing the search.

Lyrrin felt glued to the spot.

In that moment, she didn't care about the shadow dragon and who cursed who, or why or when.

She'd never seen anyone else like her before. She'd never seen anyone who came out different at birth because of silvernix being used in the pregnancy. It wasn't allowed for that very reason. It was a rule only rarely broken.

Amma had said babies born in the time before people knew better had a whole range of strange features, so even if she did meet another silvernix baby, they probably wouldn't be the same.

So how was she now looking at someone who felt so much like her? Bright-eyed, sharp-clawed. She wanted to reach out and pull down the Alderkins' hoods of stone and see their hair.

Did she really want that though? She felt so desperate for connection, but the Alderkin were an extinct, reclusive race that had struck the humans and land with magical warfare for decades and then left it behind, cursed.

They were evil monsters, and humans had only moved into their haunted, abandoned, underground city in desperation.

So why did Lyrrin's chest tremor with an overwhelming, yearning sense of belonging that she'd never felt so close to touching before?

CHAPTER THIRTEEN

The surface of the water broke in a spray of blue light, and a slithery, caramel streak launched upward.

Riony opened her fisted hands and reached for the flying otter. She snatched him from the air as the open maw of the huge olm bobbed above the water, seeking another meal.

"Butterfur?" Riony tried to keep hold of Lyrrin's cave otter, but he skittered up her arm and circled around her shoulders a couple of times, chittering angrily at the luminescent pool. The olm circled and disappeared into the depths.

"Oh. It's that thing again," Kess grumbled.

"You sound so disappointed you didn't get to watch me flex my fighting muscles again." Kess scowled in reply.

Riony moved away from the water in case the olm really did decide to slither out to eat them. Sir Butterfur Spelunkychunks stopped nattering and sniffed a couple of times before climbing down Riony's chest and trying to break into a pouch on her belt.

Taking a moment to breathe and blink, Riony stared at the otter using her body as a climbing wall, wondering why and how he ended up there too.

"Did ... you come for treats?"

He snuffled, pressing his snout into the closure of the pouch and gnawing at the stitching with his pointy teeth.

"Okay, hold on!"

Riony dodged his bites as she undid the drawstring and pulled out a soggy piece of shroom jerky for the otter.

"Why did you come all the way here for treats? Did Lyrrin tell you I had them? If she did, and you found me ..." she said, mostly to herself.

Maybe he could help them find the right way back up again too, back to Lyrrin.

A tremor of heartache shivered through Riony.

Lyrrin must be so worried. At least she's safe up there with the delvers. I'll get back to her soon.

"I think I have a plan." She addressed Kess but looked at where Dracuni lay still and trembling in Kess's arms, knife to her throat.

Her lilac eyes were wide open now, and water dripped from the muzzle.

Breathing hard.

Riony spoke directly to the dragonling. "We're getting out of here. Butterfur is going to help us find the way."

"That's your plan? We're going to follow a cave rodent?" Kess asked.

"He's got good senses. He might be able to sniff out the right way. Better that than choosing randomly."

Riony knelt on the ground, pulling off one of her belts and a coil of cave silk rope and laid them out in front of her.

Butterfur jumped off too, sniffing around the items on the ground in case more treats were being put out for him. Droplets of water beaded off his silky fur.

Riony looked over to Kess, sizing her up.

Riony's leather delving armor felt gross and squelchy, and she hoped the plunge through the water channel hadn't ruined it. The vest section, which extended down like a harness with straps that looped around the upper thighs, was going to be too big for Kess, but it would have to do. Riony undid the buckles and stripped it off.

The air in the cavern felt cold through the damp, thin layer of her remaining undershirt. She tossed the vest over to Kess.

"Put that on and do it up as tight as you can get it."

"I don't know what sort of fantasy you're trying to indulge in right now—"

"It's to carry you, dumbass. You wear that, I'll loop my belt and rope through the attachment points, and I can wear you like a backpack. That keeps arms free for both of us, since I'm assuming you're not letting go of my dragonling yet?"

Kess picked up the nearby vest with one hand and inspected it warily, all the while keeping her knife to Dracuni's neck. "*My* dragon. And I'm not exactly in love with the idea of being literally tied to *you*."

"What, were you expecting me to princess carry you out of here?"

Kess glared back as she put one arm into the vest, then switched hands holding the dagger to put the other arm through. "Do you really think you can carry us both all the way out of here like that?"

"Physically, no sweat. Emotionally, time will sparking tell."

Kess had always been on the smaller size, and whatever she'd been doing running around outside her estate like some wild girl on a wolf hadn't put any more meat on her bones. Dracuni probably weighed as much as her.

Riony frowned at Kess's thin but wiry arms. "Are you going to be able to keep holding the dragonling the whole way?"

"Don't question my capabilities, Pony."

"Oh, I am loving the idea of being tied together for the foreseeable future as much as you are." Riony wiped the blood off her cut knuckles and approached Kess and Dracuni.

Kess tensed, keeping her dagger pressed to the dragonling and staring mutely as Riony adjusted the buckles even tighter and tied the rope and belt through the metal rings and straps on Kess's side and back.

Help, scared. Dracuni mewled, and Riony reached out a hand to comfort her.

Kess jerked the dragonling farther away. "Don't try anything."

Gritting her teeth, Riony turned around and pulled the makeshift straps over her shoulders, pulling her and Kess's backs together. Pulling the belt around her chest, she buckled it tightly.

She was going to get them all out of there, even if she had to bring Kess along too. Even if it the simple act of carrying her brought back flashes of trauma that left her sick to her stomach.

The scars on her back seemed to burn.

Giving a swift shake of her head, Riony huffed out a breath, pushing all of those emotions down. She tested the straps one more time, then pressed up to her feet. It took a moment to readjust her center of gravity, leaning forward to make up for Kess against her back and Dracuni in Kess's arms.

"You good?" Riony checked.

"This is so humiliating."

"You smell like wet dog."

"You smell like cave dirt. Can we get moving already? Quickly?"

Riony agreed with Kess on that. The less time spent like this, the better.

"Hey, furry worm." Riony clicked her tongue until Butterfur looked at her. "Lyrrin has the treats."

His whiskers twitched, and he stood upright on his back legs, turning his snout up and around. Then without hesitation, he wriggled off toward the second tunnel on the right.

And Riony followed. Her footsteps fell heavier than usual, crackling over the crystal rimstone, but once she built up momentum, it wasn't much of a strain carrying the extra weight.

"This had better work out, Pony."

"If I had a way to kill you now before you stuck that poor baby with a knife, I would do it."

After a quiet moment, Kess murmured, "I know."

Riony grimaced and clenched her teeth.

There had been plenty of times when Riony carried Lyrrin around. It never bothered her, not in the way carrying Kess had.

But Lyrrin saw her as her sister, not as livestock to be worked hard and whipped for the fun of it. There was one time, though, when Lyrrin was only five years old. Riony had been playing a game and galloping around with her, and Lyrrin called her Pony in a shriek of joy.

She'd had to set Lyrrin carefully down on the ground and then go and sit alone for a long while until the rampant shivers of old fury and fear calmed.

Lyrrin didn't understand. But she never called her Pony again.

The tunnel they followed the cave otter into was narrow, and Riony worried it would scurry through a tiny crack and leave them. But he remained just ahead, sniffing the air and meandering along the rocky slope.

Riony's glow stone dangled from where her belt was now strapped across her lower ribs, and the cave silk rope dug into her shoulders, but she kept a sure footing on the uneven ground and loose pieces of ancient, crumbled stalagmites.

The slope became steeper, and Butterfur scrambled up a pile of smashed rocks and through a hole above.

The loose debris shifted under Riony's feet, but she grabbed the ledge of the horizontal opening and pulled them all up through it, crawling out onto the level above. Kess and Dracuni flopped heavily over her back. Kess's tangle of messy braids tickled Riony's neck. Dracuni breathed roughly.

The ground there was flat. Unnaturally flat, and Riony looked up from her hands and knees to see a long tunnel with a paved floor and arched nooks and niches running up each side, carved into the stone.

Out of the natural cave system and into something else. That's progress, at least.

Turning to the niche closest to her, she found herself face-to-face with a humanoid skull.

Scrambling up to her feet, Riony checked the other alcoves. Ancient, cobwebbed skeletons lay in every one.

She held her breath for a long moment, waiting to see if they moved.

"They aren't revenants," Kess said, although her voice was hushed as though she still didn't want to risk waking them. "This may be some kind of burial catacombs?"

Riony also knew, from some talk of history somewhere in her past, that some races buried their deceased. But when burning the dead had been the only safe option for decades, the practice creeped Riony out in a wide range of ways.

Around the arched spaces, delicately twining designs of flowers and vines reminded Riony of the patterns sculpted around her shelving at home.

"The carvings look like Alderkin work. And I can't believe I'm saying this, but finding a tunnel filled with skeletons is probably a good sign. At least people have been here before, which must mean they had a way to get out again too."

Riony checked for Butterfur, who continued to happily trot along through the halls of the dead. He'd never had to worry about revenants in his life, lucky critter.

Kess shifted, her knobbly spine rubbing against Riony's. "We keep going then."

"You mean *I* keep going. And you get the unmatched joy of riding me." Riony pressed forward again. Puffs of dust lifted from the ground with each footstep, and strange sounds, barely audible, echoed all around.

"Do you have to say it that way? Besides, I'd trade you for Griskin any day."

"Yeah. About that ... How did you end up with a wolf as your mount of choice?"

"What, you want me to share my story? Like that's going to make me open up and get emotional and change my mind about getting out of here with my dragon?"

"No, it's just that when a jerk from your past rides in on a sparking wolf, you get curious, you know?" Riony gave a beleaguered sigh. "I just, I never thought I'd see you again. I thought you'd never leave your estate, and I sure as stars wasn't going back there either. The fact that you're here is doing my head in."

"So sorry to disappoint you."

An unpleasant warmth had built up in the wet layers between Riony and Kess's back. It made Riony itch and ache, as though the old wounds there were reopening. She gritted her teeth, trying to stay focused on moving forward.

An intersection came up, and Riony stepped onto a fallen slab of stone to turn the way Butterfur had gone. Unstable, it tilted and Riony pitched to the side, knocking the three of them against a wall.

Ow! Dracuni whimpered.

"I'm sorry, Drac— Sorry."

Kess hissed, "Be more careful!"

Riony tucked her thumbs in under the straps at her shoulders and marched on. "Or what? You're going to whip me?"

Her footsteps and harsh breathing crackled through the silence.

"I ... Only once. I only did once."

"And the other million times you just got someone else to do it for you!"

Riony didn't know why she even said it. She didn't expect an apology, and how the silence drew on, she knew she wasn't going to get one.

Kess wasn't lying. The whip had only struck from Kess's own hands once. But that somehow made it so much worse. That Riony had been so far beneath care, beneath being seen as a person or anything of any value, that she wasn't even worth being punished directly.

It was such a screwed-up, awful thought, and everything felt wrong and confusing in her head, and she hated that Kess's presence made it all come out again, that feeling that she was less than nothing.

That cruelest oppression of simultaneously being owned and unwanted.

Kess's back sagged against Riony's. Her voice was soft and even as she said, "I left Heithorn Estate ... My brother ... He took me for a ride on his dragon."

"Nice. Doesn't sound like him at all." If Kess had always been an amateur psychopath, Kife had a heart so lightless it put the darkest of the Alderkin depths to shame.

"Then he dropped me in the charred wastelands and left me to die alone."

Riony swallowed hard. She fought down the chilling emotion creeping through her chest. *No.* She would not, absolutely would not feel sorry for the miserable gremlin that even at that moment held a knife to Dracuni's throat.

"I always hated him," was all Riony could say.

She trudged along, Kess's legs bumping against the backs of hers.

Kess sniffed aloofly. "I figured as much from the time you spiked his soup with a sprig of morass mercy at the harvest moon feast."

"You planned that! You made me do it!"

"And you executed the plan with more glee than I'd ever seen you follow orders with."

Riony's lips twisted viciously into an uncontrollable grin. "The way he passed out, face-first, right into the bowl in front of everyone ..."

Kess didn't laugh, but there was a soft tremor or convulsion in her back, and then she stilled again and cleared her throat. "Now, I've told you how I ended up with Griskin—"

"You did not."

"How about you? Have you been hiding underground since your family decided to commit murder and go on the run?"

Riony tilted her head. She often wondered what rumors spread around the estate after their escape. It seemed as though Kess didn't know it was Riony who had killed the dragonguard with his own sword, or why.

Riony sorely felt the loss of her sword again. She let that sadness flood her senses so that she didn't fall into the larger grief of the loss of her parents.

She chatted lightly, "We actually spent several lovely years living in a nice village in an old quarry with a beautiful waterfall nearby, which was everything that murderous fugitives could wish for."

"More than the noose that was waiting for you at Heithorn Estate."

Riony palmed her forehead. "I knew there was another reason we didn't go back, other than never wanting to see you again."

Riony could almost hear Kess's eye roll. "And who is that blue-eyed kid that you almost gave your life to save from slavers? Where did you pick her up?"

"She's my sister." Riony bit her lip. She couldn't trust Kess, but Kess had been there, at the estate, when the pregnant guest came to give birth. Neither of them knew who the young woman was at the time, but in the period after Riony and her family had fled with Lyrrin, maybe Kess had heard something.

Maybe Kess knew who Lyrrin's mother was.

"She's not your sister. Any fool could see that. But still you risked your life for her." Kess's voice dropped, almost confused. "Her, and now this dragonling too. Why are you trying so hard to save it? It's like you're still a slave to others, giving your life for everyone around you."

Any softness Riony felt fled instantly. She growled, "At least it's my choice now."

"But why? What do you get out of it?"

Riony threw her hands up. "Helping the people I love and who love me? That's what I get out of it! Not that you could understand that."

"No ... No, I couldn't."

Kess didn't speak or move again for a long time. Riony kept up the path, following Butterfur as he led the way through a labyrinth of short, interconnecting corridors stacked with bones on either side. They reached some stairs and headed up them.

The ancient, dry limestone felt crumbly under Riony's boots. The new level opened into wider tunnels, with high ceilings and alcoves of a grander scale, columns and flourishes carved into the facades. With only a small pool of light to see by, it seemed as though tunnels led out into an infinite void in every direction.

A twittering, crunching sound came from down a side path, and Riony peered into the darkness. Shadowy, eight-legged silhouettes crawled over a still twitching corpse.

Bad bones, thought Dracuni with a whimper.

"So happy for us we aren't going that way." Riony turned sideways so Kess could look too.

"Is that another rev?" She shuddered. "More importantly, what are those things all over it?"

The revenant, something dog-sized and four-legged, snarled and gurgled as the spiders stripped the meat from its bones. Riony had seen the skull-sized critters before, generally only a couple at a time. But they swarmed en masse over the rev.

Carrion eaters were fairly common in the depths, scavenging on whatever they could get. But between the spiders and the olm, Riony was starting to wonder where they were getting all their food from down there.

She wondered how many revs had been falling from the ceiling.

It's probably something else. They're probably all just eating each other. Otherwise, there would be more bones around. Ones not neatly tucked into niches.

"Just cave spiders," Riony replied, relishing when Kess shivered again. "On the plus side, if we're down here long enough to get hungry, we know what we can eat."

"The *spiders*?" Kess balked. "You cave dwellers are disgusting. You probably eat worms."

Riony smirked and got moving after Butterfur again. "They're delicious fried. A bit of salt to bring out the flavor. So fatty the juices drip down your chin. Mmmmm."

"I'm not sure if I'm more worried about your diet or that rev back there."

"The spiders have it pinned; I don't think it's coming after us," Riony replied.

"No, you tame-brain." Kess leaned back, turning her head to whisper into Riony's ear, as though what she was saying couldn't be said too loud. "I'm worried that if there are revs getting in down here, but they aren't going up and attacking you worm-eating cave dwellers up above ..."

Oh. Riony's heart sank as she caught up. "That there might not be a way out."

Chapter Fourteen

"I think I found one!" Caed called out from a corner of the Alderkin chambers close to the archway. He leaned into a gap between the wall and some tall shelves, hopping on his good leg.

Lyrrin turned from where she had been pretending to search the low side cupboard below the mural but had really been studying the Alderkin images with hungry eyes, hoping for any other details or clues about why their hands looked so much like hers. Why their eyes shone bright like hers.

"What do you mean *think*? Either you found it or not." Aishena stalked toward the delver, an anxious menace to her step as though suggesting he better have the correct answer.

Caed extracted a large sheet of pale-blue calcite from a stack of shining stones. It was as long and wide as his torso, straight on three sides with a couple of natural points at the top, as though it had been a slice cut from the center of a huge twin crystal.

"I mean, it's a float rune, but the final mark isn't right," he said, holding it up for Aishena to see.

Lyrrin moved closer to watch as well, the allure of seeing a new kind of rune activated enough to draw her from her obsessive staring at the mural.

Aishena ran her hands over it, wiping off dust and some strands of cave silk. "Hmm, it's like it's been chipped off in that section."

"I already tried activating it, but nothing happened," Caed said apologetically. "This whole stack here seems to be damaged goods."

"Any news?" Yoskar called from beside Benjin.

Niskina looked up too, pausing from her work creating a neck brace to keep Benjin's head still.

Aishena shook her head. "No, it's no good. We'll keep looking."

Benjin's cheeks were red, and he stared up into the hole above them with a huffy expression. "I want to see. What are they doing?"

Caed moved closer and held the slab up high for Benjin to look at. "Sorry, buddy, the rune's damaged."

"Can't you fix it? We're spending too long down here when we should be helping Riony," he said, although he still didn't look at Lyrrin.

Brishan joined them in the archway and pulled a flask from his belt, taking a swig. "Don't have the tools. We've never successfully been able to carve our own runes. The crystal just doesn't seem to take to chisels or files. Not sure how the Alderkin made their marks."

Benjin's nose scrunched up as though in pain, then he blurted out, "Lyrrin can. Lyrrin could fix the rune."

Lyrrin's face flushed. She *had* been able to make those same marks. She had talked with Benjin about her experiments, and he'd even offered ideas for new combinations to try. But that was meant to stay a secret. "Benj—!"

"Please try. Don't you want to get out of here? Don't you want to go and help your sister?" His voice sounded rough.

"I do. But …"

"Can you really carve runes? How?" Yoskar got to his feet and stared at Lyrrin. Everyone stared at Lyrrin.

Her first impulse was to lie. She'd lied and told half-truths her whole life to keep her hands hidden. It had been the one rule her parents and Riony had always enforced, not to be broken, lest the worst happen. Lyrrin was never told explicitly what *the worst* was, but she'd imagined plenty of terrible things.

Then the slavers had taken her and Benjin and the other children and that had felt like the worst had already happened, and sharing her secret with Benjin seemed like something she had to do.

Even Riony had said to her, *Sometimes taking action is more important than staying secret at the time. We'll work the rest out as we go.*

Maybe she could fix the broken rune. Maybe she could do the one thing needed to save Benjin.

Lyrrin's ungloved hand trembled as she lowered it down from hiding within her sleeve. She held it up in front of her. "I just … I have sharp nails."

"Whoa," Caed gasped.

"Is that why you're always wearing gloves? I thought maybe you just had burn scars," Aishena said. She reached out an upturned palm and waited for Lyrrin to offer her own hand in return.

Lyrrin pulled her hand back closer to herself, bit her lip, and then extended it again to place it in Aishena's. Her skin tingled as Aishena brushed her fingertips over Lyrrin's clawed nails. It felt so wrong letting anyone see her hands, let alone touch them.

But Aishena offered a half smile and said, "It's like you've got your very own built-in daggers. I'm jealous."

A smile twitched on Lyrrin's lips too.

Brishan watched from above, brows set low over his eyes as he examined Lyrrin's hands.

"You can really cut crystal with those?" Yoskar ducked down beside his sister, the light of their glow crystals glinting off his glasses, lighting up his wide eyes as he studied her hands.

"Yeah. I've done it before."

"With runes? That worked?" Yoskar's tone was sharper than a knife.

"Uh-huh." Lyrrin didn't want to tell them all the details of the blast rune she'd added to the glow stone that had blinded Riony and led them to falling into this pit, so she chewed on her lip, hoping they wouldn't ask.

"Do you want to have a try fixing this up?" Caed asked, placing the sheet of crystal on the floor on one end and holding it upright in front of her. "It just needs this line extended down to here."

The glossy surface caught the light of the glow stones from the surrounding delvers. The float rune was carved large in the top center of the slab, surrounded by the usual hardening rune most crystal artifacts utilized to make the soft calcite more resilient and functional.

Lyrrin examined where a shell-shaped section had been chipped off, taking with it the end of one line. Another crack spread from that impact point, running through the middle of the rune.

With all eyes on her, Lyrrin took off her other glove. She worked better with her left hand. Tentatively, she pressed her nail firmly into the crystal.

The grating, high-pitched screech sounded like the crystal screaming as she re-carved the missing line.

Caed winced and shuddered from his position holding the relic. "Ow, my teeth!"

"That's it, that's the complete rune now," Aishena said, one of her eyes twitching from the effect of the sound. "I'll try ..."

Lyrrin was already tracing over the rune with a soft brush of her fingertips. She knew that the line she'd fixed would be the last in the sequence, from what Caed said. And it just made sense that the spiraling triangular line would be first.

She felt the stone hum under her touch as her fingertip danced across the etched shapes. And the slab of crystal came to life with a cool purple glow, lifting from the ground.

Then it pulsed violently, and with a smacking crack, split apart right along the fine fracture line.

Caed dropped the broken sections. "Sparks, it must have been too damaged."

Yoskar kicked at one of the broken pieces. "We almost had it."

"I'm sorry," Lyrrin said, looking up at the surrounding delvers.

"Not your fault," Niskina said. "You did great. That's a pretty amazing thing you can do."

Benjin coughed roughly from beside her. He was refusing to look at her again. Lyrrin didn't feel very amazing.

"Maybe we can find another one, less damaged, or hopefully not damaged at all. I'll keep looking." Caed limped off toward the back of the room.

Lyrrin tried to follow, wanting to distance herself from the failure, but a hand grabbed her shoulder.

"How did you know how to activate that rune?" Aishena asked. "I never showed you how to do that."

Brishan folded his arms, frowning at her as he waited for the answer too.

"I just guessed. It's only three lines, and Caed said which was the final one. I'm pretty good at guessing runes, and it's easy to know when you're right, because of how the stone sings to you."

"How the stone does what?" Yoskar had been walking away but turned back to Lyrrin then. His crystal-studded staff was strapped to his back and protruded over his shoulder as he leaned over her.

"You ... you don't feel that when you trace the runes the right way?" Lyrrin replied.

The delvers returned a blank stare.

Lyrrin tried to make herself smaller. "It's just a feeling I get. Not a sound really, just like a warm humming inside. I thought ... I thought everyone did."

Aishena looked at Yoskar, and Yoskar shook his head and looked to Brishan, who hadn't taken his shrewd eyes off Lyrrin. Niskina shrugged. Benjin made an embarrassed choking sound.

"There are a bunch of runes I haven't seen before on some of this stuff. Maybe she could help us figure some of them out." Aishena pulled her larger belt pouch open, showing a mass of crystal chunks jammed in there along with some wadded-up parchments. She must have been collecting as she'd searched.

Niskina's eyes turned toward the large standing stone in the middle of the chambers, then back to Lyrrin. "Or the runes on the geode slice. Do you think you could try to work some of those out?"

"We don't know what those runes might do," Yoskar warned. "On something so big, that's a risk."

Niskina tilted her head toward Benjin. "I just thought maybe they could be healing runes."

Aishena's eyes popped wide, and she turned, pleading and hopeful, to her older brother. "She could be right. We know Alderkin had healing magic, but they didn't like hurting unicorns, right? So maybe they had something else. Healing magic of their own."

She turned to Brishan. "Aren't there old stories from before humans worked out how to bottle silvernix, about how people would go to the Alderkin shrines to beg aid from the Alderkin when they needed healing?"

"There are," Brishan said. "And just about all shrines I've seen have one of these geodes in them, if they hadn't been broken already. But people went to the shrines to beg the Alderkin to get the unicorns to help them, from what I understand, and they rarely did."

Aishena wrung her hands, looking from Benjin to the large standing crystal. "We don't know for sure though. The Alderkin were so secretive."

Lyrrin watched and tried to work out how old Brishan was. He seemed very, very old to her, but a lot of grown-ups seemed very old to her. Even if he was only as extremely old as fifty, he would have been alive when Alderkin were still around, during the wars. She wondered if he'd ever seen one up close.

He bowed his head. "I don't know. Maybe it is worth a try."

"I can try," Lyrrin agreed. She wanted to do what she could to help, because Benjin was right. She wanted to get out of there, then try to find Riony and Dracuni. And she wanted to get out of there without anyone getting more hurt.

Aishena moved over to the geode first and gestured at the engraved lines at the base. "I think this is the main rune here. The other markings surrounding the ring"—she pointed at more than vast array of smaller designs all around the circular crystal—"don't look like normal runes. They look more like pictorial symbols, maybe just decorative."

Lyrrin stood beside her, staring up at the huge crystal. The massive geode was a silvery blue, its sharp-toothed points angling into the hollow center and rings of deeper and deeper blue surrounding outward.

The gap in the middle was almost as tall as Riony, and if Lyrrin stood in the middle with her arms out, she didn't think she could touch both sides at once.

"That's a five-stroke rune," Brishan said.

Lyrrin jumped, startled. She hadn't realized he'd followed them over too.

"You think you can work that out?" he asked.

"Maybe. I worked out a four last week."

He raised his eyebrows.

"Try. I'm going to keep looking for another float rune," Aishena said. Her voice had a sharp, anxious edge, and she slipped away like a ghoul into the shadows.

Lyrrin crouched down, ignoring how the scrapes on her knees pulled and split, and tried to take in the flow and pattern of the rune before trying to trace it.

"Riony," Brishan broached softly, kneeling down beside her. "She's not your blood sister, is she?"

"No?" Lyrrin replied like a question, wondering and a little scared that Brishan was going to suggest she start preparing not to see Riony again. That maybe them not being related by blood might make that easier.

"Do you know who your birth parents are?"

"My amma was a young dragonlord lady," Lyrrin replied confidently, because she felt it was best to tell the truth as Riony and her parents had told the story to her. "She didn't want to keep me because of how I was born different, probably because of silvernix used in the pregnancy, so Riony stole me."

Brishan raised his eyebrows, crinkling his forehead all the way up to his braided salt-and-pepper hair.

"They never saw who my pabba was, but he was probably an Elgarthian, considering my coloring."

"They do have your pale skin," he agreed, although he kept staring at her as though she was a puzzle to be solved.

He didn't say anything else as Lyrrin tried a few combinations for the lines of the rune.

It was definitely more complicated than any Lyrrin had tried before. The design was mostly symmetrical, with one asymmetrical section in the middle where the lines swirled to meet each other. Two brackets and a V-shape surrounded that middle spiral.

Lyrrin let her fingertips play over the design, listening for the hum of the magic, trying each line in turn, one way and then the other, until she found one that sent the buzz of enchantment thrumming through her. Then she worked until she found the second, then third.

Did nobody else really feel that same hum of magic? She wondered how anyone had worked out any of the previous runes without having been able to feel they were on the right line. They could be guessing forever and never know if they had any part of the sequence right.

It didn't help much having Brishan watching her every movement with narrowed eyes. A couple of times she forgot the steps she'd already worked out, just due to nerves. But within only about ten minutes, Lyrrin reached the fifth line and completed the sequence.

At first nothing happened. A small glow to Lyrrin's left attracted her attention, as one of the pictorial symbols lit up.

"Is that all it does?" Lyrrin reached over and touched the shining glyph. And then the entire geode flashed with a silvery light.

Between the sharp teeth of the crystal, the hollow center shimmered and swirled and then reformed to show a sparkling image of another place. Ruined walls, a broken stone ceiling. A stream of dull light piercing down to a rough leaf-strewn floor.

"What happened?" Yoskar came charging over.

"Did you get it working already?" Aishena asked, appearing in a flash as well.

"It's doing ... something," Lyrrin replied. Although, heartbreakingly, it didn't seem to be the something they needed.

"That's ..." Aishena cast her eyes over the huge geode and the scene glowing from within. She stepped closer, holding her hand near the rippling surface of light. "It looks like somewhere aboveground. There are plants, things growing on the walls."

"I don't think this is a healing device," Brishan said. "I think this is a gateway, magic to take you somewhere else. There were rumors the Alderkin had such magic, but only ever rumors."

"You mean this would actually take us to where the image is showing us?" Aishena asked. "If it could take us aboveground, we can get out of here!"

Brishan clapped a hand on her shoulder, as though worried she was about to step through. "But we don't know where to. Alderkin shrines with these ring crystals are all over Elundrae. That could take you anywhere in the land."

Caed limped over, his face lit by the silver glow as he stared agape. "You mean we could travel to different places without having to fight our way through the revs? This could mean travel and trade with the dragonkeeps!"

"You say that like it's a good idea," Niskina scoffed. "If we bring the dragonlords into our business, they're going to want to claim the undercity for themselves."

She came closer to look at the portal as well. The light glimmered off her dark curls.

"I should go through," Aishena said. She was already adjusting and checking over her gear, making sure she had everything in place. "Then I can see where it comes out to, work out that location, and if it's close enough to the undercity, come back with help. I found these maps as well, when searching before. I can track my way with them."

She pulled out a large square of folded parchment from a side pouch, opening it to show the others the sepia ink lines in the shape of the land.

"No," Yoskar said. "It's not safe. It could be a one-way trip, and you could end up stuck on the other side of Elundrae. We stick together."

"I just, I really feel like it looks like the shrine we stayed at. Only half a day's hike from the undercity."

"They all look pretty much the same, I'm afraid," Brishan said.

"Deactivate it," Yoskar commanded.

Lyrrin looked to Aishena, but the lean girl just nodded solemnly. She refolded the map and tucked it away.

Lyrrin dragged her fingers over the lines of the rune again, and the glimmering window flickered out in a flash, and the sense of hope she'd felt a moment before flickered out just as fast.

Through the archway, Benjin coughed again. What had sounded before like him clearing his throat in distaste, now came out as a wheezing gasp for breath.

Yoskar and Aishena bolted between the stacked tables and cupboards to return to his side. Lyrrin followed but remained a few steps back.

Benjin's eyes reddened as he sucked air through a whistling throat. "It's just the dust. I'm fine."

Lyrrin reached for the handkerchief in her pocket, wondering if it could help him, but it was more for dealing with sniffles. Benjin didn't seem sniffly. He breathed as though someone had grasped his throat in a choke hold.

"The break is inflaming the surrounding tissue." Yoskar growled at Aishena. He adjusted the straps of the brace Niskina had patched together. Where he loosened them, the skin of Benjin's neck looked hot and puffy.

"What does that mean?" Lyrrin asked in a squeak.

She remembered Riony's broken bone, how her arm had swollen, gone bad, fingers turned black as clean blood refused to reach them. If it hadn't been for Dracuni's blood, Lyrrin wasn't sure Riony would still have those fingers. And that was a break in an arm. Not a break in the bones of a neck.

"His skin is swelling up around his breathing pipe, closing it," Aishena replied flatly. "We have to get him out of here and find some way to treat him, before he loses the ability to breathe entirely."

Chapter Fifteen

By the fourth time Butterfur turned around, came back toward them, sniffed the air, then picked a different tunnel again, Riony was ready to take a seat on the cold, hard floor and join the skeletal masses around her.

Her damp pants chafed, and the rope cut into her shoulders, and Kess's horrible bony limbs kept banging into her, and her brain was a mess of painful old memories, tangled in with all of Dracuni's sensations of pain and fear.

It was only the hope of prying the dragonling from Kess's clutches and returning safely to Lyrrin that kept her burning legs going.

Sure, she had muscles for days, but carrying two bodies as far as she had was starting to hurt. She'd never admit that to Kess though, so she kept up the pace and channeled the heat from those burning muscles into a seething spite that helped her forge onward.

Even if it was starting to seem as though Butterfur was struggling to find a path back to Lyrrin.

Dracuni had looped her tail forward, wrapping it across the side of Riony's waist. Riony patted the soft scales and tuft of hair at the end.

Scared, the unidragon communicated again, but it was a sad, tired kind of scared. **Want home.**

"We're going home," Riony replied with a soft determination.

"I'm not sure your rat knows the way out," Kess said, as though she'd been spoken to.

"His name is Sir Butterfur Spelunkychunks, and that's how you shall refer to him."

"He still doesn't know the way out. If there is one." There was a dull resignation in Kess's voice.

That was what scared Riony the most. That the relentless goblin that had stalked a mother dragon for months, maybe years, to get what she wanted, sounded out of hope. And that it had been Riony's choice to trust their salvation in the cave otter that had ruined them.

"And what's your plan? Which direction would you like to go?" Riony thrust her fingers out angrily at their current four-way intersection, from which she could see the previous two intersections and more again up ahead.

The catacombs were a confusing labyrinth of interconnecting tunnels and twisting pathways. And it didn't feel as though they'd been going upward in a long time.

Kess didn't offer any new options.

Riony put her head down and kept walking. "I'm following the rat."

"I thought his name was—"

"Shut it, Kessara."

"You're not in charge right now, in case you forgot." Kess's arms moved, and Dracuni keened. The sound rattled and gargled in the soggy muzzle.

Why? Hurt why? Dracuni's breathing sounded labored, and Riony almost felt the press of the dagger herself with how the fear and confusion pierced into her head.

Riony had no way to explain to the hatchling that hurting things was how many people got what they wanted. And that everyone would want Dracuni if they knew what she was. Everyone might hurt Dracuni. Kess, as cruel as the goblin was, wasn't an exception there.

But she was the one with her hands on the hatchling right now.

"Fine, yes, you're in charge! I am your devout peon, your obedient bondswoman. Oh, Exulted One. Beloved Ruler. Glorious Mistress of Order-me-around-however-you-like."

"You always were the very worst at being servile."

"Hand me your feet so I might kiss them."

Kess tensed. "This is exactly the kind of behavior that got you whipped."

Riony's shoulders firmed up with a tension to match Kess's, pressed together back-to-back like two blocks of stone.

Riony grumbled out, "The point, that I lost somewhere along the way—"

"Because you just can't help running that giant mouth of yours."

"Is that you don't need to keep jabbing your knife at that poor baby to keep me in line. You've got me. You win."

"I don't believe that for a second," Kess said, but Riony could feel the pressure in her arms ease, and Dracuni snuffled a sigh.

Mouth trap, bad.

"Also, it would be super cool of you to take that muzzle off her as well."

"That sounds like a terrible idea."

"It's upsetting her and making it hard for her to breathe. If you want a nice, healthy dragon to steal at the end of this, you need to get that muzzle off her."

"She?" Kess seemed to consider this. "*She's* a wild, untamed dragon. She'll bite me if I remove the muzzle."

No bite. Want breathe.

"She said she won't bite you."

Dracuni mewled pitifully from within the confines of the leather.

"What do you mean 'she said'?"

Riony patted Dracuni's tail, soothing herself as much as the unidragon. "I can hear her. Her emotions and thoughts. I hear them right in my head."

She knew she was giving Kess more leverage against her, more insight into how and why she cared so much for Dracuni. But there was a part of her that also hoped it would make Kess realize the baby dragon was so much more than a dumb tool to tame and own.

Although she'd never realized that about Riony.

"Wow. You must have knocked your skull really hard when you jumped from the sky out of that slaver cage."

Riony remembered the silhouette in the smoke, watching as she miraculously landed on the taut tent wall. "You were there?"

Kess swallowed loudly. "I don't believe you can communicate with this wild beast."

"Yeah, well, if dragonlords weren't so keen to tame every dragon from birth, maybe they'd find all dragons were really chatty."

Riony walked them through the end of a narrow tunnel into a larger space. A natural cave with the addition of sweeping staircases, high platforms, and massive, elaborately carved columns, rising into the darkness above.

"That's nonsense," Kess said.

"Dracuni, nod once if you understand me and won't bite Kess."

Riony felt the pull of movement as Dracuni's head bobbed behind her.

Kess muttered a low, whispered curse. "I don't know what sort of tricks you've trained this creature with, but ... I'll take off the muzzle if that will stop your delusional spouting."

Elbows poked into Riony's back as Kess juggled Dracuni. Then the dragonling sucked in a deep breath and huffed loudly.

Better. Better!

"She says that's better," Riony relayed.

Kess scoffed. "What kind of name is *Dracuni,* anyway?"

"Umm ... My sister made it up," Riony lied.

"As ridiculous as Sir Butterfur Spelunkychunks. I'll think of something more suitable for the beast." Kess thrust her hand back, holding the removed muzzle toward Riony. "Put this away somewhere in case I need it again."

Riony took the muzzle, staring at the wet mass of mashed leaves inside. A heady soapy and peppery scent made her nose scrunch. "You put morass mercy in here? What were you thinking?"

"What's the problem? You were happy to use it on my brother."

"That was one tiny sprig, on one big monster. You've used way too much in here. No wonder she was having trouble breathing. You could have killed her!"

Kess shrugged. "I needed a way to tranquilize the hatchling. Although I expected it to last longer."

Riony dumped the contents of the muzzle out onto the floor with a splat and moved away from it quickly. The stuff was potent and dangerous. A strong hit of its scent caused rapid sedation, and prolonged use could have terrible side effects.

She tied the muzzle to a loop on her pants, but hoped Kess wouldn't ask for it back at any point.

Maybe it was something in Dracuni's strange hybrid makeup that allowed her to shake the effects off despite still inhaling the crushed herbs. Or maybe they'd had their potency washed away in the water. Either way, Riony hoped that also meant she wasn't suffering the headaches, hallucinations, and nightmares it could also induce.

Riony had learned about morass mercy in midwife training with her amma and shared the knowledge with Kess during a time when they had joked and plotted together about ways to torture her big brother.

And there was Kess now, using that knowledge to kidnap innocent creatures. Tension surged from Riony's clenched fists, up her arms, and into her gritted teeth.

"I should never have shown you even a moment of kindness."

Kess's body shuddered. Her voice was flat and emotionless. "You were the only one dumb enough to ever make that mistake."

Riony's feet stopped, as though they'd simply forgotten how to put themselves one in front of the other. She felt so tired, and a painful strain ached around her eyes.

"Keep moving, Pony. I don't want to die down here with you."

Inhaling deeply, Riony growled, "If you call me Pony *one more time,* I will become unhinged in a way you've never experienced before."

But she started moving again. Marching forward. Legs on fire and heart sore.

Butterfur picked a winding staircase that led up far out of sight.

Riony's heart sank at the sight of the stairs. But they did have to go up, so up she went.

The staircase seemed endless, a winding spiral that coiled skyward, unguarded to the drop on either side. Built into the edges and walls around them stood gargantuan statues of solemn people. Alderkin, maybe. They looked human to Riony, but even when formed from rock, somehow more elegant and ethereal.

Kess stayed blissfully silent, and Dracuni's thoughts had calmed too. Curious, almost content to be carried through new and interesting areas. Riony's steps echoed against the weathered stone, each footfall an effort in determination.

Riony had no way of knowing whether Kess still had a knife to the young dragon's throat. But she had no way to strike out at her now either with Dracuni in Kess's arms, and both of them strapped behind her, and a long way to fall in every direction.

So Riony battled upward. Sweat poured down her chest and neck, making the thin fabric of her shirt cling to her. Her heart pounded a raging beat when finally, the end of the stairwell came into view.

The soft light of Riony's glow stone filtered through a narrow opening ahead, painting the chamber beyond with its muted cyan radiance.

The somber room before them was awash in swathes of cobweb, hanging gray and tangled from the ceiling and covering sculpted murals on the walls.

Riony stepped carefully into the space, listening for the scurry of arachnid limbs, but could only hear the deep gasps of her own breathing.

Butterfur ran across the floor, jumping and dodging over the spread of dusty cave silk. He went straight for a larger tunnel but didn't continue along it. Only stood there, sniffing at the ancient air.

Three other passages led from that room, and Butterfur went to inspect them as well, dashing between each tunnel entrance.

While he was making up his mind, Riony turned her attention to the room around them. She had hoped they had left the halls of the dead behind when she saw no more alcoves stacked into the walls.

But in the center of the room, an imposing stone slab cradled the relics of a body long departed. Bones, weathered by time, rested upon tattered cushions, surrounded by the scattered remains of silver armor and crystal weapons. The tomb of a warrior.

And before that altar, veiled in cave silk, stood a massive crystal sword.

As if guarding its master's legacy, the sword leaned against the high platform. The sword's hilt spiraled upward, shaped like a unicorn horn. The skeletal hand of the body was stretched across from where it lay on the altar, holding the weapon even in death.

The blade, almost as long as Riony was tall, dully gleamed even below the layers of dust. It was thick, too, a wide and solid spike of glassy calcite, inlaid with sections of lilac and sky-blue stones down the fuller. And on the largest of those inlaid gems were Alderkin runes. Standard hardening runes, plus something Riony didn't recognize.

Riony's eyes were transfixed upon the weapon.

"Oh baby," she exhaled with a greedy longing.

She beelined for it, approaching with a slow reverence as she got close.

"The rat's that way. Where are you going?" Kess asked from behind.

"There's a sword here." Riony didn't turn around to help Kess see what she was seeing. "Other artifacts too."

She could feel Kess angling, trying to see around Riony's back. "Don't touch anything. They could be cursed, trapped, full of dangerous creatures. Isn't that what you told me?"

"I'm just looking." Riony already had her hands on a glow stone that lay at the edge of the altar. A spare could be crucial, if it worked. She shoved it quickly into a pocket, because Kess didn't need to know. When no curses seemed to be set off, she light-fingered a few other artifacts small enough to tuck away.

Butterfur skittered back to the largest tunnel and sniffed at it again. He turned an anxious circle on the spot, then moved a little farther into the mouth of the tunnel.

Seems like he's made his choice.

Riony turned to follow, but her feet remained planted. "I kind of want it though."

"Want what?"

"The *sword*. I need a new one, considering you made me lose mine. And it would be good to have a weapon other than one little athame." Riony twisted at the waist so Kess could see the sword in all its magnificence.

"That old thing? That doesn't even look functional. It's way too big to actually use."

Riony sighed. She should have known Kess wouldn't understand the rampant desire she was feeling for the weapon. Kess only got like that about dragons.

"I could swing it," Riony argued.

"It's *ceremonial*. And absolutely looks cursed to me."

Riony frowned at the weapon. She had never seen anything like it in use before, but it did have hardening runes on the crystal, so it couldn't be entirely decorative.

But with the previous owner's hand still gripping it tight, and the webs of cave silk enshrouding it, Riony did get a creepy, foreboding feeling about taking it. As sexy as it was, it probably wasn't worth it.

She turned away with a despondent sigh.

She was two steps away when Kess said, "The rat's getting away. Hurry up, Pony."

"Oh, *that's it*." Riony huffed and cracked her knuckles. She spun back toward the sword so fast Dracuni's tail swished behind her. "I'm taking it!"

Kess groaned, "By all things blessed. Stop!"

But Riony marched to the sword, hot air snorting from her nose and her teeth bared. She grabbed the section of hilt not occupied by the skeletal hand and tugged.

The blade came away with the soft snapping of webs, and the boney fingers fell loose, releasing their claim. The knuckles and joints of the desiccated hand toppled off the altar, bringing with them an arm, a shoulder, a skull. The rib cage smashed down the tiered dais of the altar.

Sections of silver armor followed, clattering across the ground and bouncing into webs which vibrated in a disturbing hum until the whole room seemed to shake with the din.

"What under the blessed sun have you done?" Kess rasped.

Riony hefted the sword in two hands. "Mmmph. I think I found my soul mate."

"No! Listen!"

Riony stilled, lifting her eyes from her new treasure and focusing out into the space around them. A rattling, skittering sound came from the webs, from the walls, from the ceilings. *Everything* moved. The stone itself seemed to bulge and creep.

A massive swarm of cave spiders rushed for the source of the clattering sound, right toward Riony, Kess, and Dracuni.

Chapter Sixteen

"We should go through the portal." Aishena moved close to Yoskar, looking right up into his face and whispering not quite quietly enough.

A harsh anxiety rattled her words. "At least then we'd be aboveground. We could look for a healer, a settlement, some of those herbs Riony used on my ankle to reduce swelling. *Something!*"

The words seemed to rattle in Lyrrin's heart as well. Aishena was right. They had to do *something*. Benjin's breath whistled roughly beside her.

Yoskar shook his head. "If we use that portal, we could end up all the way across Elundrae, on our own, in revenant-filled wastes, and all three of us could die there. It's not the right move."

"I can go alone, try to send help. Lyrrin can show me how to open the portal so I can come back from the other side, if that works, and bring help that way." Aishena glanced back and forth between the portal and Benjin.

"We stick together." Yoskar's expression was firm, but his voice remained calm. He put a hand on Aishena's arm. "His neck is braced. Daymora must be nearing the top soon. The other delvers will get ropes and pulleys set up. We just need to set up a stretcher for him now so we can lift him out, if no float runes can be found."

"And then what? How are we going to help him once we're back up there? Riony might have had some remedy but she's ..." Aishena noticed Lyrrin listening and dropped her voice lower, hissing in Yoskar's ear.

They moved a step or two away, continuing their argument.

Benjin finally looked at Lyrrin again, turning reddened and fearful eyes to her with a deep, wheezing sigh. He lifted a hand, just a fraction, angling his fingertips toward Lyrrin. She rushed over beside him and took his hand before his movement hurt him or he got scolded by his siblings for it.

"I'm here. I'm sorry," she said softly to him.

He tilted his head as though to shake it, and Lyrrin gave him a warning look.

He rasped a frustrated groan. "*I'm* sorry. Not you. Don't be."

"You aren't angry at me?"

"Not at you." His voice broke over the words as he tried to force enough breath into them. "At me."

"But it's my fault we're down here, I—"

"You tried to save your sister. You ... you're so brave, clever." He squeezed her sharp clawed fingers in his soft pink hands. "You're special, never useless. I'm the useless one."

Lyrrin leaned back on her heels, frowning. He was Benjin Hjelzahn, brother to some of the toughest delvers in the undercity, and most of the time he spent bragging, Lyrrin had to admit he had reason to be. Mostly. How could he think he was useless?

Benjin closed his eyes, and a tear squeezed from the side. "All I do … is get kidnapped, hurt."

"No. That's not your fault. And I got kidnapped too!"

"Only 'cause … punched Zade for us." His chest rose and fell sharply in incomplete breaths. He opened his eyes again and offered a lukewarm smile.

"Sorry … I told your secret." He held her fingers tightly.

Lyrrin placed her other hand over his. It was scary, having her secret out. Nobody but her family, and then Benjin, ever knew. So far no one had treated her differently, but she didn't know if things would stay that way. Brishan still watched her warily.

But she wouldn't let Benjin know her worries. Not now. "That's okay. I think it was the right thing to do. Anything that could help get you out of here, help you heal."

Anything? Lyrrin bit her lip. The words had come so naturally. But did she really mean *anything*?

Benjin's nose scrunched up. "Get us *all* out. Find your sister."

Lyrrin's eyes glossed over. She was more worried about Riony than she wanted to admit, because there were so many other things to worry about right now. She wanted her big sister back so desperately.

And if she could, if Lyrrin could find Riony, she could also find Dracuni. And the unidragon had the one thing in all the land that was guaranteed to save Benjin.

She wondered what Riony would do. They'd decided they didn't want to use Dracuni themselves. But what about when it came to saving someone else's life? Was keeping the secret worth Benjin's life? The only living creature with silvernix blood … maybe it was a secret too big to share, for any reason.

But Lyrrin didn't have to tell the others *everything*.

"It's going to be okay." With a final squeeze of Benjin's hand and a confident, close-lipped smile, Lyrrin stood back up and stepped over to where Aishena and Yoskar continued their hushed argument.

They didn't stop on account of Lyrrin's presence. So she took a deep breath and spoke over them in a fast rush of words.

"If we can find Riony we can save Benjin because Riony still has some silvernix."

The two delvers' mouths slammed shut and they swung to stare at Lyrrin.

"She has silvernix? How?" Aishena asked.

"Remember how she had some before, that she used when her arm was broken? She still has a bit more." Lyrrin felt wrong lying and had to look down at their shoulders instead of making eye contact.

Aishena angled her head up to look up the gaping hole above them as though ready to climb all the way back herself. "Could she have left it at home? Can we get it if we get back to the undercity?"

"No, it's definitely with her." At least Lyrrin hoped Riony had Dracuni with her still. "She always keeps it with her."

Yoskar kept his eyes on Lyrrin, studying her expressions. "This doesn't make sense. It's strange that she'd have any to start with, let alone enough for multiple treatments. Where did she get it from?"

Lyrrin did her best to face Yoskar and lock eyes with him. "It's real. It was a gift from a dragonlord to my grandmother because she saved their wife during labor." That much was true, although that wasn't the silvernix they had anymore.

Aishena turned hopefully to Yoskar. "We should go and try to find her. One of the maps I pulled is of the depths, and if we are where I think we are, this area connects through to catacombs that the water channel runs through. I think I could find the way down there. She might not be far away."

Lyrrin frowned. How long had Aishena been holding on to that information for? Could Riony be nearby? "Can we go and find her?"

Yoskar scoffed. "It's too fantastical. Silvernix? A gift? She's making things up because she wants to find her sister."

Aishena's mouth opened, but she didn't speak. She looked down at Lyrrin and snapped her mouth closed again.

"We stick to the plan. Help will come soon. I'm going to find something to support Benjin on the way up. Don't waste time chasing ghosts."

Aishena's face darkened with hot red patches. But she nodded firmly.

Shaking his head, Yoskar walked away.

Lyrrin expected Aishena to follow, as she usually did, but the delver ran her hands up into her silver hair, tugging it at the roots. Then she dropped down into a crouch, covering her face with her hands.

"I don't know what to do," she whispered.

"Aishena, please. Riony really does have silvernix."

The delver turned a skeptical, hard-edged face toward Lyrrin. "Even if she does ... I have to stay here. That's the plan."

Lyrrin clenched her fingers closed into fists as her nerves fired up. "That's Yoskar's plan. And maybe he's not right."

"He is. He looks after us. He does the right thing." The words seemed directed more toward herself than to Lyrrin.

"Did he do the right thing when he took you to smash the dragon eggs?" Lyrrin challenged.

Aishena winced slightly, then her face grew calm and stubborn again. "Yes. It was the right thing. For us." Her words held a bright, high edge. "He's the smart one. He's the planner. I can only follow well. Take action when told."

Behind her, Benjin's breathing grew louder, harsher. Niskina hurried over to sit beside him.

He needed silvernix, and he needed it soon.

"Why? Why can't you decide what you want to do?" Lyrrin pleaded.

"I can't," Aishena hissed. Her hands curled into fists and then loosened, and she stared at the open palms as though she hated what she saw. "I can't because the last time I didn't follow Yoskar's orders, I lost my father and my sister."

She crumpled forward, landing on her knees.

Lyrrin knew the pain of losing family that Aishena must be feeling, even if the delver didn't show it on her face. She simply sat on her knees, stony-faced, staring toward Benjin, but her eyes were distant, glazed.

"I'm sorry. I lost my parents too," Lyrrin said. But she didn't know what it was like to lose a sister. She didn't want to know what that felt like, when that was all she had left. "But your amma is still alive, isn't she? She was the one who put out the bounty for you."

Aishena's head shook slowly side to side. "Yes. My mother is still alive."

Lyrrin's heart hurt with a sudden strong wish that hers were too. "Why won't you go back to her?"

"It's ... we ..." Aishena struggled over her words, then her face scrunched up and she exhaled sharply. "You know we are Hjelzahn. My father, he was the one who was a Draekhan heir."

Lyrrin's eyes widened. Riony had once tried to explain to her about Yeonard Draekhan, the Dragon King, and all his children, and all their dragonkeeps and families and heirs. It was mostly just a lot of confusing and forgettable names to Lyrrin.

"So are you ... like a princess?"

Aishena laughed wryly. "No. We're still technically heirs, but way, way down the line of succession by many generations, from Hjelzahn the First, who is still alive himself, thanks to plentiful silvernix. And my mother ... She's a grayglim who served my father and was training me to be one too, as Yoskar trained under Fadda. Until things changed."

"What happened?" Lyrrin knelt down in front of Aishena.

"On a mission, a couple of years back, my mother was downed, knocked off her dragon. She wasn't responding, out cold, right when the shadowdragon touched ground." A shiver shook Aishena's wiry form. "She survived. But ... she was different when she returned home from that mission. Refused to ride her dragon. Secretive. Cold and distant."

Aishena's lips twisted. "Or at least, more secretive, cold, and distant than she had been before. But she was a grayglim warden, after all."

Lyrrin hadn't heard the term before, but just nodded as though she did, because she didn't want to interrupt Aishena and the flowing stream of words tumbling from her.

Aishena's voice dropped to barely a breath. "And then ... heirs started dying."

"Naturally? Or ...?" Lyrrin whispered back.

Aishena raised her eyebrows. "Nobody knew at first. And at first, nobody really cared. It started with new heirs. Fourth, fifth, even sixth generation. Still important people within their own family lines, but, well ... in the grander scheme, there are so many of us."

The rattling sounds of the delvers searching through the Alderkin chambers echoed softly out to them.

"Rumors were spreading, though, and then Tarric the First was found, murdered in his own bedroom. The Dragon King's own son. Then the hunt was on for the Heir Killer.

And then Yoskar, he told me he thought it was her. Our mami."

"Why? Why would she do that?"

Aishena lifted her shoulders weakly. "I don't know! I didn't know. And I didn't believe him. She was still training me, when she was home, and I trusted her, instead of him."

Aishena turned her eyes up to Lyrrin and reached out to squeeze her hands. Her eyes searched Lyrrin's face as though looking for something. Understanding. Forgiveness. "He begged me to leave. He told me she was dangerous, that our family were all at risk. And I didn't listen."

"And then one night … I found them. Fadda and Neif. Dead and bleeding in the library. Neif was … my little sister. I still can't understand. I don't know why … why would anyone …?"

Lyrrin shook her head and pressed Aishena's hands in hers, careful not to scratch her. She didn't know either. She'd seen terrible things, even in her short years. Terrible monsters and terrible actions by humans, and she could never understand either.

Because why would anyone turn to cruelty when they could choose kindness instead?

Riony once told her that it was because those who suffered cruelty became cruel in turn, but that didn't make sense to Lyrrin. She wasn't born yet when Riony and her parents were still slaves, but she knew that someone had been very cruel to Riony because of all the scars on her back.

And Riony was still kind.

"Do you know who did kill your family?" she asked.

"Yoskar said it was our mother. That she had changed, she wasn't really our mami anymore, and we couldn't trust her. That we had to take Benjin and run if any of us wanted to stay alive. And we did. We fled our home and came to hide here, and I make sure I listen to Yoskar now."

"It's not your fault. It would have been hard for anyone to believe. What happened to your father and sister, you didn't do that."

"It all sounded so crazy … I still don't know what really happened. But I could have *stopped* it happening if I'd acted on orders sooner. I am the hand and must act as the voice commands, not question it."

Lyrrin let go of Aishena and rose to her feet. She was barely taller than the kneeling delver but looked down at her with piercing eyes. "I don't know what happened then. But Yoskar *is* wrong now. Riony has silvernix that could save Benjin. And you said she could be close to where we are now. We could heal him!"

Aishena turned to watch where Benjin wheezed and choked. His normally bronze face was blotchy gray and red. Niskina brushed his forehead and muttered soothing words.

Aishena turned back and her shoulders sagged. She remained kneeling, as though she'd forgotten how to move, and was slowly turning to stone like the stalagmites that had been smashed in the landslide around them.

Yoskar yelled at Caed across through the archway in the Alderkin chambers, and Brishan chided them both. Dust still settled and filtered through the cool cyan light of the delvers' glow stones, and it felt almost as though they were all already ghosts.

"Please, Aishena. You can listen to your own voice, your own instincts. What do you want to do?"

Aishena pulled her hands up near her face, studying them as though the answers were in the dusty lines and knuckles. "Something. I have to do something. Waiting ... feels like we've already given up."

Lyrrin extended a hand to help Aishena stand up. "Then let's get the silvernix and help Benjin before it's too late, so you don't lose any more of your family."

The weight of the whole mountain above them felt as though it weighed down, crushing the air in the space, making it solid and flat in Lyrrin's chest.

They had to do something.

Before either of us lose any more family.

Chapter Seventeen

The pale, hairy legs of countless cave spiders skittered against the smooth floor, creating a nightmarish percussion in their multitude.

Little creatures? Dracuni seemed more curious than anything.

A star-filled sky worth of little creatures.

They wouldn't normally worry Riony when it was the odd one or two of them. But racing toward her now were so many it seemed as though the dull dusty stone that formed the room had burst into terrifying life.

Each scurrying creature was as big as her head. Their creamy shells gave them a ghostly appearance, and the cyan light glinted from the black, shining orbs of their eyes like fractured glass. Their strange mouths chattered and fangs twitched.

"Are you going to run or what?" Kess barked.

"Yeah, yeah, I think I will." Riony grasped her new sword tightly. It was heavy, far heavier than her old sword, and she didn't think she could even lift it one-handed. It certainly wouldn't fit into her scabbard. She hoisted it up and pressed it in a hug across her chest like a child carrying a doll. And she ran.

The point of the sword stuck up high over her shoulder, bouncing along with the two bodies on her back as she pounded across the room.

"Drop that thing, it's going to slow us down," Kess ordered.

"No way. Much like my undying hope that you will choke on your own vomit when you finally realize what an awful gremlin you have been, I will cling to this till my last breath."

"Can you for once in your ridiculous life shut your mouth and save your breath? You're choosing between a chunk of stone and our lives!"

"I'm choosing both, thank you very much, although your life is negotiable." Kess's demands only made Riony clutch the heavy weapon tighter. Rage still burned through her to the chanting echoes of *Pony, Pony, Pony.*

Grinding her teeth, she barreled for the largest tunnel that Butterfur had disappeared down.

The spiders flowed in from all sides around them, closing the gaps in which Riony slammed her feet down. She leaped through the vaulted archway of the tunnel as the floor disappeared entirely under the crowding arachnids.

The passage ahead was clear, although from beneath a shroud of webbing to her side came a soft growl that sounded like a revenant. Bones twitched out from the cave silk, as spiders stripped the monster of its flesh. She slowed to gawk at it, horrified to see another one succumbing to that fate.

"Ew, sparks. This is going to haunt me more than that time I saw you naked."

"They're still coming!" Kess cried.

Riony dared a glance back, seeing the creatures filling the tunnel behind them. The air reverberated with the cacophony of scuttling limbs. "Dracuni, if you could work out how to breathe fire, now would be a great time!"

Dracuni snorted. No flame appeared.

Riony continued her dash down the tunnel, desperately scanning for any sign of Butterfur. Cobwebs caught her face. An intersection passed in a flash, and she prayed the cave otter hadn't gone that way. Heartbeats thundered in her ears as her every muscle propelled her forward, trying to stay ahead of the wave of hungry scavengers.

"They're gaining on us!" A tremble laced Kess's words. She always did have a thing about spiders. If being eaten alive wasn't a real threat right then, Riony would have enjoyed the moment a lot.

She responded with a fierce grunt as she sprinted faster. The thought of those arachnid horrors closing in and hurting Dracuni was enough to ignite a burst of speed she hadn't known she possessed.

She wasn't too keen on being eaten by the creatures either.

The recollection of the rev, pinned down and being consumed alive—or undead—was still too vivid in her mind. They were taking every shred off its bones. Which may or may not actually kill the cursed undead.

The pale spiders raced after them with eerie agility, their hairy legs creating a clacking echo that built up within the tunnel walls like a horrific symphony.

They were right behind them, scratching at Riony's ankles, tripping up her feet. She caught the heavy crystal sword by the hilt again and swung the blade in a wide, low arc, taking herself around in a full circle.

The spiders scattered clear, only one getting caught up and hammered by the thick sword. The creature's abdomen broke like a cracking egg. Yellow ooze flicked up across the floor.

It was a slow swing, the weight of the blade dragging Riony's body with it and the tip scraped along the ground. She could barely bring it back up again on the other side as she spun around to continue running forward.

Her attack gave them only seconds of clearance before the spiders closed in again.

Kess let out a yelping scream, and Riony felt the smack of something landing on them.

Beast jumps!

There was a great wriggling and wrenching of bodies against Riony's back. She forced an extra surge of strength into her legs so the wrestling match tugging her shoulders didn't take them all down. Dracuni snarled, and there was a snapping, crunching sound.

Bit it! Dracuni thought with a strange surge of pride.

Good work, Riony thought back, even though she still wasn't sure the hatchling could hear her thoughts in return. But she didn't want Kess to think she was talking to her.

Kess sounded livid. "They can jump? You didn't tell me that!"

"Oh yeah. They can jump," Riony panted out between breaths.

"There's one on my legs!" Kess shrieked.

Riony pivoted, twisting fast so that Kess's legs swung out, smacking them and the spider into the tunnel wall. The spider cracked against the stone, and Kess bit off her own whimper.

"Sorry! Sparks," Riony instantly regretted the spontaneous apology. *She doesn't deserve your remorse. If you show weakness, Kess will consume you as completely as the spiders did those revs.*

Kess's back had tensed like it could snap. "Better that than the spider."

Riony almost tripped and stumbled at the begrudging gratitude in the words. Gratitude was not something that Kessara Heithorn *did*. Riony must have imagined it. Because a version of Kess that could show appreciation rattled Riony more than the horde of spiders nipping at her feet.

But it also made her wonder whether Kess really was that desperate.

Riony called over her shoulder, "Cut Dracuni's bonds; she can help fight them off!"

Yes! I help. I scratch!

"I won't—"

Another spider flew at them from a wall. Riony managed to sidestep it, avoiding it landing on her or Kess's shoulder.

"Tell the beast it better not dare try to run," Kess huffed.

"She *can* hear you."

There was a quiet grumble, then a shuffling of elbows and the snap of leather.

Free! Free!

Riony sighed inwardly.

"If the spiders come near you, kick them off! Don't let them bite you!" Riony called back. She couldn't risk Kess seeing any broken skin on the unidragon.

"You know I can't ... were you talking to the beast again? Wait, are these things *venomous*?"

A shadow flashed through the air on Riony's side. Sharp fangs flew straight for her, and a crackly cry nattered from the spider's mouth.

Then it collided with a sharp point in midair, a bone dagger, piercing right through the middle of its eyes. It dropped to the ground, swarmed over by the others.

"Nice shot."

"Always."

There was a swish as another of Kess's throwing daggers lanced out, and then the crack as it went through soft shell.

Through the flexible leather of her delver pants, Riony felt a scuttling presence that sent ice water shooting through her gut.

They were *on her*.

She glanced down, catching sight of two, maybe three of the arachnids. They clung tight with their creepy long limbs, pressing hooked paws through the leather as they clung to their bucking prey.

Riony flushed hot and cold, her sprint turning into a leaping, bounding gait as she tried to shake them off. They shook and bounced but held tight.

"Can you run smoother? You're ruining my aim!"

The sounds of more spiders falling to Kess's daggers echoed through the tunnel. One by one, they fell to Kess's skillful throws, but there seemed to be no end to their numbers.

"They're on my legs!" Riony yelled back.

There was a scrambling sound and a weak yelp. "I'm out of daggers."

"Already?"

"The rest are on Griskin! Only got a hunting knife left."

Which she'd no doubt continue to hold on to to keep Dracuni under threat.

Even if Kess could have pulled a few dozen daggers from various hiding places on her body—something that wouldn't surprise Riony—there wouldn't be enough for all the spiders.

With a breathy grunt, Riony angled the big crystal sword downward, smashing it against her legs, and more preferably, at the spiders on her legs.

The first splattered with a bile-inducing satisfaction right across Riony's shin. She lugged the weighty blade up and down again, jabbing and smacking, while continuing her attempts to move forward and away from being submersed under all the other spiders still chasing them.

A heavy, sharp pain surged into her thigh. Another burst of pain matched it at the ankle on the other side.

The walls on either side of them came to an end and the tunnel opened out. With one final surge of energy, Riony burst through into an expansive natural cavern beyond. The weights of the critters clinging to her legs disappeared.

"They've stopped! They aren't following us!" Kess yelled.

"What?" Riony turned to look over her shoulder but didn't dare slow down.

The cave spiders hesitated at the threshold, clinging to the shadows, some unknown barrier causing them to give up the chase and retreat.

Riony's relief was short-lived. The ground pitched steeply, falling away beneath her feet. She swung back around to see the steep slope ahead, sliding down toward a sharp edge and sheer drop.

Twisting her body just in time, Riony avoided toppling in a headfirst roll down that hill. Instead, she put herself face down onto the slick, silty stone as her feet went out from underneath her.

She let the sword fall free from her hands as she smacked down. It slid and clattered on the rock beside them, coming to a stop when it hit the remains of a broken stalagmite.

Riony, Kess, and Dracuni kept going.

Kess and Dracuni thumped down heavily on top of Riony's back as she fell, and the glow stone at her ribs jabbed into her chest, knocking the wind out of her.

They slid fast, feet first toward the ledge.

"No, no, no!" Riony gasped, digging her nails into the soft limestone slope, trying to halt their race toward doom. Her knees banged over the uneven surface and her shirt tangled and tore against her chest and dust filled her nose.

Her legs went out into open air as they hit the lip of the drop. Riony scrambled, arms clutching for any purchase. Her hands latched over the cliff edge and caught tight. Flying out into the air, her body jerked, then angled back, and with the smash of skin onto stone, they came to a dangling stop.

Riony let out a harsh whimper.

The pain of three bodies worth of weight shot like lightning into Riony's fingertips as she clenched them around the rock ledge. Kess's legs and Dracuni's tail swung behind her as they bounced against the side of the cliff. She stretched her toes out, trying to find purchase against the rough wall.

"Have you got Dracuni?" she bit out the words between waves of pain.

"I won't drop her," Kess replied. "Have you got us?"

"Mmmph."

"Then pull us up, tame-brain!"

Riony's arms trembled with the strain, and then she stopped, holding her body limply against the wall.

She pressed her forehead to the rough stone. Sweat poured over her heated skin. "I'm sorry. Maybe I regret taking the sword now."

"Really? Was it the imminent death by spider or the remaining chance to plunge to our deaths that finally inspired remorse?" Kess replied. *"Pull us up."*

"I can't." Riony rolled her head to the side, leaning it against her upright arm that clung for their life. A shaking, anguished smile formed on her lips.

"Kess ... I got bit."

CHAPTER EIGHTEEN

Lyrrin waited, hand extended to Aishena, who stared at her with dark, troubled eyes, the silence broken only by Benjin's struggling breaths.

Then Aishena lowered her gaze away from Lyrrin's, shook her head, and stood up without assistance. "I can't leave Benjin here and run off to gamble on gut instinct. I have to do what Yoskar says. The odds of finding Riony are ... too low."

Lyrrin folded her hand closed, tucking the pointy nails into her palm and fighting off the tear-prickling feeling like she'd just been smacked in the face. She wanted to get Dracuni back, to save Benjin. But she also really, really wanted Riony back too. She was more scared than she wanted to admit.

She needed her big sister. And nobody was going to help find her.

Aishena had taken a step away when she looked back and frowned at the emotion she must have seen reddening Lyrrin's face. With a sniff, she moved closer to Lyrrin again and pulled a folded wad of parchment from her belt.

"Here, look."

Lyrrin's eyes widened as Aishena unfolded the crinkly, dusty sheet. Scratched onto the surface in fine sepia ink lines was a complex mess of chambers and levels and interconnecting tunnels. It showed the insides of the mountain they were deep within in flat relief and also from multiple angles, as though cut through with a giant knife.

Lyrrin's gaze flickered around the map, trying to make sense of the major landmarks. The largest cavern at the top, with the sinking stream waterfall running through the center, was the undercity where they lived. But there were so, so many more caverns below, more than Lyrrin had ever imagined.

"This is the most detailed map of the Alderkin depths I've ever seen. We have plenty of partial maps, and what the delvers have been mapping out ourselves, but nothing like this. I haven't had much time to study it yet, but look at this." Aishena's fingers traced paths across the parchment.

"That looks like Whisperwind Passage," Lyrrin muttered, absorbed in the carefully inked lines. Had they been drawn with a hand that looked like hers?

"Correct. I think this is the water channel Riony went into. And see this mark?" Her voice was low, almost a whisper, and Lyrrin strained to hear. "That's where I think we are right now."

Lyrrin gazed hungrily over the drawing, trying to map where that rushing stream could have taken Riony. The mark Aishena pointed to was like the rune on the gateway geode. And below it was a gridwork of smaller hollows, spaced out between some larger natural caverns and mazelike tunnels.

The water channel ran through there, pooling in one cavern before continuing down into the earth. That was the only place the channel expanded out into more than a narrow tube.

"She could be right there!" Lyrrin clutched the sides of the map, pulling it from Aishena's hands and trying to trace a path from their location to that cave. It was complicated, a few levels down and through the labyrinth of smaller chambers. "I could go ... if you give me a glow stone."

It could be a long walk, even if it was the right way, even if Riony ended up there, and not somewhere else, or if the map wasn't accurate. And if Riony hadn't moved on to somewhere else. Or something else hadn't happened to her or between her, Kess, and Dracuni.

There were a number of routes leading away from that cavern too, and Riony could have taken any of them if she was trying to find her way back up again, which Lyrrin was sure she would be. Their paths might not cross at all.

There were just so many ifs, but at the same time it felt as though Lyrrin was so close to having her sister again, held back only by stone walls and darkness.

Hopefully Butterfur was with Riony and Dracuni too. It had been an impulsive action, sending the otter into the stream. The cave otters of the Alderkin depths were often found using both natural and Alderkin-fashioned water channels like fun slides though, and it took more ingenuity than the humans had managed so far to keep them out of the water reservoirs.

He would be okay. Because Lyrrin couldn't stomach the idea of losing him, and Dracuni, and Riony, at any point, let alone all in one day.

"No, it's too dangerous for you to go alone. And it's just speculation, just my thoughts. I could be wrong. Yoskar and the other delvers will have to look too and will know more. We can't split up right now, not with Benjin hurt down here. But as soon as he's safe, we'll start looking." Aishena eyed Lyrrin and the map with a frown but didn't try to take the parchment back again.

An ache twisted in Lyrrin's chest. She understood the logic, but she hated not being able to do anything. It made her feel so small and useless.

"Daymora must be nearly at the top by now too. She really is an excellent climber." Aishena looked up, squinting into the darkness. "There might already be help on the way. It shouldn't be long now."

Lyrrin nodded, but still her eyes filled with tears.

Aishena's shoulders twitched upward, and her mouth moved awkwardly without making a sound, and then she hurried off to continue helping the search of the Alderkin chambers.

A fat tear plopped down onto the ancient map, and Lyrrin rubbed it with her palm before it could soak in and blur the ink. She pulled the map to her chest and cuddled it, as her feet walked her backward into the shadows behind her, taking her to somewhere dark and private to cry.

She didn't want Benjin to see her tears, when he was being so brave, when he had said she wasn't useless. She sidled up the wall, out of the moving pools of light created around each delver, hoping to melt into the gloom and disappear.

A soft growl reverberated near her feet.

The wolf.

She turned warily, finding herself standing right between where the animal's bound legs lay in pairs.

Lyrrin had forgotten all about Kess's … pet? Companion? Mount?

Her body froze in place, expecting the gnashing of teeth to meet her flesh if she spooked the animal any further. She'd approached far more wild animals than Riony had ever been comfortable with and knew she had to avoid sudden movements.

The wolf lay on its side, motionless. The charcoal-gray coat was almost invisible in the shadows, and only its glossy eyes, wide and warily watching her in return, glinted through the dark.

Lyrrin's vision adjusted to the lower light, and she saw a lashing of silk rope kept its mouth closed. No worry of being bitten then.

Carefully folding the map and cringing each time it crinkled loudly, Lyrrin tucked it away in a pocket in her coat.

The wolf panted roughly through its shut teeth in a gasping, fretful way, broken by the occasional long snuffle through a running nose.

Lyrrin's heart immediately softened. "Oh … poor pup."

In slow, gentle movements, Lyrrin knelt beside the tied-up wolf. It recoiled from her, long snout turning away while its eyes remained locked on Lyrrin's position. Front paws, bound together, scraped at the dust and rubble, but it couldn't shift its prone weight.

"I'm not going to hurt you," Lyrrin said softly.

The wolf's snout twitched, and wet nostrils flared. Whites showed around the edges of its eyes.

"You're all sniffly, huh?" Lyrrin said softly. She wanted to reach out and pat its fur but could tell it wasn't ready for that yet. "I got all sniffly too when I first moved underground."

She fished around in the inside of her oversized coat, checking the pockets. "It's the fungus farms. They spread spores in the air, and they make some people and animals sneezy. I know it feels really awful, like you want to stick a scrubbing brush up your nose."

Her fingers found what she was searching for, and she pulled out an old handkerchief that had been folded into a bundle.

"I don't get sniffly much anymore, but Riony makes me carry this around all the time anyway in case it comes back." Lyrrin held it briefly to her own nose and took a deep breath, inhaling the minty-green scent that chilled her nostrils like an icy breeze.

Lowering it down, she pushed it along the ground tentatively toward the wolf's snout. "She made it for me. But it might work for you too. I hope it helps you breathe better. Because I can't undo the rope around your mouth, sorry. I think the others would be mad at me if I did that."

He didn't move, only continued to stare.

Lyrrin looked over the crudely stitched saddle and pouches strapped around the wolf's midsection. She had only seen Kess and the wolf briefly at the slavers' camp, but she had instantly envied the strange, wild girl with how the two of them seemed to move almost as one.

She sighed. "You're worried about Kess, aren't you?"

His tongue flicked out through the tiny gap at the front of his snout, licking anxiously. A soft, barely audible whine came from deep in his throat.

"I don't blame you for what Kess did, taking Dracuni. That's not your fault. You were just being a good pup, doing what your friend wanted." Lyrrin's voice held a gentle weight.

The wolf's eyes held a flicker of recognition. They softened, and in an achingly slow movement, he brought his snout closer to her, sniffing at where her fingers still rested, not far from the offered handkerchief.

She didn't move, didn't twitch, as its wet nose bumped against her. Then it turned to the herb infused handkerchief and smelled it. A wary sniff at first, and then a long, rattling inhalation. With a soft whine, it lay its chin flat onto the ground, with its nose right over the medicinal fragrance.

Lyrrin reached out, letting her fingers dust over the very tips of the wolf's thick fur. "I miss my sister too," she admitted softly. "I'm really worried about her."

"Someone's coming!" The cry from Niskina made Lyrrin startle.

The wolf winced, but didn't move, as Lyrrin scrambled back to her feet and headed away from the shadows.

Benjin had his eyes squinted closed, lips trembling with each difficult breath. Niskina got to her feet from where she had been sitting beside him and pointed up into the crumbling stones that darkened as they rose higher and higher.

Lyrrin squinted, only making out the barest of movements, the slightest sound of stone shifting.

"Who's there?" Niskina called out, frowning.

There was no reply. No calls of welcome aid being promised, no ropes being lowered.

Aishena jogged over, with Yoskar and Brishan following. Caed brought up the rear, limping heavily.

"Are the others coming down for us?" Aishena asked. "We're going to need ropes, pulleys, a stretcher."

"Daymora would have told them. Only, I can't see ..." Niskina continued to frown.

They all stood in a circle beneath the hole, craning their necks in hopeful search of approaching relief.

The shadows flickered, and swifter than a bird, a figure flipped down from above and landed on silent feet in the space between them.

The brown-skinned woman with cold, age-worn eyes balanced effortlessly on the unstable pile of fallen stones. She had hair the color of burned wood, braided in small rows up the sides, and thick knotted bundles along the top, leading to a long, trailing whip of hair at the back that swung as she turned to take in the delvers.

She wore close-fitting armor of smooth, dully gleaming scales the color of smoke, and rested her hands on the hilts of matching swords, sheathed at her hips.

"Ma—" Aishena choked on the word.

"Lady Hjelzahn?" Brishan said at the same time. His face scrunched up as he turned, entirely confused, to Aishena and Yoskar. "You told me your mother had passed away."

Is that ... their mother? Glancing at Benjin again, she found him with his eyes wide open, round as the moon. Only Riony and Lyrrin knew about the slavers' plot to get the bounty on the Hjelzahn siblings.

The other children returned from being snatched up hadn't heard the details, so they had been unable to spread the news. Benjin said that was the only reason he and his siblings hadn't left the undercity entirely.

"*Hjelzahn?*" Caed whispered from the back, searching all eyes around him for answers, but nobody replied.

The woman didn't give any visual or verbal response to the discussion. She remained with her hands on her blades, casting her gaze over each person in turn, eyes narrowing as they fell upon Brishan.

"What is she doing here?" Niskina asked.

Yoskar moved to the front of the crowd. "She's come for us."

Lifting his arms high, he grasped the end of the staff that had been stored on his back. He pulled it down in front of him and activated a burn rune on one of the crystals embedded in it in one swift motion.

The cavern lit up red as he held the weapon threateningly between Lady Hjelzahn and the group of fallen delvers and children.

The woman's eyes narrowed again, and she lifted her hands away from her weapons and into the air. "That's right. I'm here for my children."

An inexplicable shudder ran up Lyrrin's spine at the strange, flat tone to her voice.

"Yoskar," Brishan exhaled his name. "What's going on?"

"She didn't die." Yoskar didn't take his eyes off his mother for a second. "We left, we came here, to keep away from her, for the sake of our lives."

"Why under the stars?" The delvers' master turned to the woman for answers. "What does he mean?"

"I didn't expect to see you, Brishan. A fellow grayglim, keeping my children from me."

"Kverra, I'm not. I didn't know!" He took a step closer to her, but Yoskar warned him back.

Aishena seemed to have turned to stone. She was frozen mid-stride, with only her eyes turning frantically from Yoskar to her mother.

Lady Hjelzahn watched her daughter and Brishan closest of all. "Let me take them, and nobody has to be hurt."

"Why would anybody have to be hurt?" Niskina balked.

"We're not going anywhere with her!" Yoskar roared.

"I don't understand what's going on!" Caed cried and limped up to Yoskar's side.

"I thought we were getting out of here. How is she here? Where are the other delvers?"

Yoskar's grip on his staff wavered, then he lifted it high before him again. "How did you find us down here?"

Lady Hjelzahn tilted her head and stared dully back at him with cold, midnight eyes. "A slaver told me they'd found you in the undercity."

"No, *here*! Down here in this hole!" Yoskar's voice grew frantic.

"A girl. In a tunnel. She was looking for help for you." The woman took a casual step down from the heaping rubble.

"Don't move!" Yoskar yelled.

"All right, everybody calm down. We can talk this out," Brishan said.

Yoskar shook off the words and spoke in a low, dangerous tone. "Where's Daymora? What did you do to her?"

This seemed to snap Aishena out of her trance. "Why ... what would she do?"

"Kill her!" Yoskar snapped. "She'd kill her, because she wouldn't want any more audience down here than there already is. She would have killed us already too if she thought she could take us all on!"

"Yoskar!" Brishan scolded.

"Where are the other delvers then? Where's the help that should be rushing our way right now? If Daymora made it to the top, why aren't the other delvers here? Unless something happened to her."

Aishena's mouth opened wide and she turned pleading eyes to her mother, an unspoken 'no' forming on her lips.

Benjin whimpered, and Lyrrin skittered quietly over beside him, dropping to her knees to squeeze his hand.

Lady Hjelzahn took another step forward, eyes glinting in the red glow of Yoskar's flaming staff. "Is that what Yoskar has been telling you? That I'm the killer? Did he tell you that I was the one who hurt your father and Neif?"

She focused on Aishena, and the delver seemed entirely hypnotized by her attention.

"He's been lying to you. Yoskar is the one who murdered them."

Chapter Nineteen

"Bit? Bit by *a spider*?" Kess's voice went embarrassingly shrill. However, she was hanging from the back of a reckless idiot over a drop so deep she couldn't see the bottom. The rockface plummeted straight down into inky darkness.

"No," Pony groaned softly. "More like ... two spiders. Maybe three."

The leather and fabric between their backs was soaked through with sweat and felt as hot as iron laid under the midday sun. Kess could feel the muscles in Pony's shoulders tensing and shifting as she held their weight by her fingertips.

"What ... what does that mean?" Kess asked.

"You really don't know anything about cave spiders? You weren't prepared for the depths at all," Pony muttered.

"I hadn't expected to spend so long down here," Kess snapped back.

"It means that I don't know how much longer I can hold on. The poison, it's going to cause paralysis, spasms ... death, if the first two symptoms don't fling us off this cliff face first." Pony's voice was quiet and calm in the same way it used to be when she knew she was about to get a whipping, and it made Kess want to slap her.

Every part of Kess ached. The vest and straps holding her to Pony's back cut into her chest and thighs, and her core and arms burned from trying to keep a steady hold of the dragonling.

Now that she'd cut the bonds on the creature's legs, it had relieved some of the strain by actively clinging to her. It hugged close to her chest, front claws over her shoulders, and stomach pressed so close Kess could feel its heartbeat. And it hadn't attempted to bite her ... yet.

The intimate position left Kess questioning the instincts of the wild beast and left her feeling strange and disgustingly vulnerable.

It's still a dragon and is my dragon that I will tame and raise and ride.

If they didn't all die first.

Kess's heart rate spiked as she stared down into the abyss below her feet again. There were a couple of smaller projections in the rockface below and to their side, but otherwise it was a sheer drop into night-dark doom.

She could see Pony's hips and top of her legs too, see trails of glossy, red blood dripping from puncture marks through her pants. The dragonling mewled softly, and Kess found herself stroking its neck.

A few eyeball-sized bugs clung to the stone near them. Disturbed by the presence of dangling humans, the insects buzzed into movement, lighting up and flying away.

"Kess?" Pony's voice trembled in a way Kess had never heard before in her life.

Her throat dried up and closed and she couldn't reply.

"Kess! Listen. I need you to get Dracuni out of here, okay? You told me you could do it without me, and lucky you, now you get your chance."

I don't want to. The thought pierced too fast into Kess's mind. She gritted her teeth and gave her head a swift shake. She was being a baby. She was capable and strong. She could and she would get herself out of there and she didn't need Pony. Or anyone. Not for anything. She was always better off alone.

The sweat between them chilled as a drift of cool air puffed up from the darkness below their feet.

"Kess! Are you still alive back there or have you given up already?"

"I'd sooner acknowledge your intolerable self as the next rightful heir to Heithorn estate than give up," Kess hissed.

"There's the Kess I know. Right. You need to hurry. Help Dracuni climb up first."

"If this is some kind of trick ..." Kess tensed and wrapped her arms tightly around the hatchling.

Pony groaned breathily and it sounded like she headbutted the stone wall.

"Please don't be a stubborn ass right now. I need you to save Dracuni. She's special, you don't realize how special she is. Stop questioning and just help her up. Then I can help you climb up too."

"And you?"

"And then, if I can still move, I'll try to follow. Who knows, we might get a miracle, but you have no idea how my arms feel like dragonfire right now and I can't feel anything below my knees. *Please,* Kess!"

Kess wished for a second that her small vial of silvernix was with her, but she kept it in a pouch on Griskin.

"Don't you have some remedy? Some herbs to neutralize the poison?"

"Everything was ruined in the water." Pony readjusted her grip, jostling all of them. "If I didn't know better, it'd sound like you were worried about me."

"I'm just annoyed at how long it's going to take to get out of here on my own."

"It will take even longer if you're starting from the bottom of this hole with all your bones busted. I can't ... mmmph ..."

There was a skittering of dust and pebbles, and one of Pony's hands slipped free. She cried out, and Kess gasped as they swung freely for a moment. With a colossal grunt, Pony threw that arm back up again and caught the ledge.

"Okay, okay!" Kess brought her hands underneath the hatchling's chest.

It was already wriggling into action as Kess pressed upward, giving it a boost as it stepped on her shoulders, then head. Filmy wings flapped uselessly over Kess's face.

"Come on, Dracuni. You can do it," Pony encouraged.

Kess lifted her hands as the hatchling climbed. It pressed its back feet into her palms, and she boosted it up from below. Angling her head back, she watched as it clung to Pony's bare arms and scrambled upward against the rock.

Kess realized her temple was so close to Pony's they were almost touching as they both arched their necks to watch.

Pony murmured, "Kess, I know you probably won't, but I have to ask. Can you do me a favor? When you get out of here, find my sister and … just make up the most epic, ballad-worthy battle ever in which I died, okay?"

"You don't want me to tell her you died because you stole a cursed ornamental sword and made a mountain full of spiders angry?"

Riony's chest sobbed softly. "Yeah … it doesn't sound great put that way."

Kess bit her bottom lip, as the hatchling pulled itself up over the ledge, tail swishing as it disappeared over the top. "I'll tell her."

Pony sighed so deeply she seemed to deflate to half her size.

"Okay, how do I get up?"

"Going to have to cut you off."

"What?"

Kess held her breath as Pony let go with one hand. She hung from the other, turning sideways away from the cliff while grasping around at her waist.

Something lit up bright yellow. She heard a slicing sound, and then the belt secured around Pony's chest was slid free. The glow stone on it bobbed, light flickering, as she tucked it through her other belt still at her waist.

"Should … should I take that?" Kess murmured.

"Yeah. Yeah, probably." Pony's words sounded slurred.

She thrust the belt and attached light over her shoulder, and Kess reached for it. Checking the front of the vest Pony had given her, she found a couple of metal loops and tied the belt securely through them, so it hung close to her heart.

"Cutting now. You'll drop. Try to hold on, so you don't pull us both down, okay?"

"I'm ready."

Kess dropped startlingly as the first shoulder strap was severed. She yelped awfully and swung to the side still attached to Pony's lowered shoulder. Twisting, she grasped out, getting one arm around Pony's waist, before she jolted down farther.

The remaining rope between them tangled and pulled and Kess's momentum brought her spinning right around to smack face-first into Pony's chest.

The woman's shirt was torn, and her skin scraped. Rivulets of sweat ran red as they passed over ragged grazes. Over one of her shoulders, the edge of an old scar was just visible. Kess turned her eyes away from it as a stone formed in her throat.

Pony was breathing deeply and staring down at Kess as she hung from the cliff edge with one hand, and Kess clung to her. Her skin felt flushed hot under Kess's arms. The glow from the stone at Kess's chest shined up between them.

Kess stared back up into Pony's face, which used to be gaunt and square, but had grown into strong cheekbones and jaw. Her eyes still held that infuriating mix of indeterminable colors. It was still the face of the only person that had ever shown any kindness to Kess, no matter how much she'd been punished for it.

A tremor built up within Kess, and she couldn't fight how it rattled her teeth and hands.

Pony only stared back at her with a hard, determined gaze. Her free arm wrapped around Kess's shoulder on one side, pressing them in closer. Then she slipped the glowing stone blade between her skin and the rope and cut her free.

Kess's arms shot up around Pony's neck, clasping tight as her legs swung beneath her, her body no longer attached with anything but her own strength.

The yellow glow from the blade disappeared, and Pony reached down between their hips and tucked it away again.

"You need to let go now. I'll help you climb as much as I can." Pony licked sweat from her lips and winced as she grasped her free hand around a strong strap on the leather vest, holding Kess tight from that point at the side of her ribs.

It took all of Kess's strength to unlatch her fingers from around Pony's neck.

Pony pulled her in closer. Her red hair flopped over cheeks burned the same color from exhaustion.

Kess held her breath.

A small smirk emerged on Pony's face. "Wow, Kess. I never knew you were such a sucker."

Kess dropped.

She screamed roughly as she went down, caught, then swung on the end of Pony's arm. A small swarm of fire-bright insects around them took off again.

Banging against the stone wall in a rough arc, Kess lashed her arms out, trying to grasp on, and then she dropped again.

Kess never thought she'd be scared of falling. She was going to ride a dragon one day, and that was a fear she couldn't afford to have. But as the air rushed up around her, it felt as though all spirit and life rushed free through her throat as well, fleeing her body.

Then she struck stone faster than she should have. Breath whooshed out of her. She found herself on a narrow ledge, which only caught half of her, and she tumbled and almost went over again.

Scrambling, belly down, she clung furiously to the stone, fingernails digging in so hard they broke.

It took three deep, wheezing breaths to convince herself she hadn't died. Looking down, there was still a long way farther she could have gone. She had come to a stop, thrown like rubbish from Pony's grasp, onto one of the tiny jutting ledges she'd seen below them before.

Sounds of scraping rocks and pattering pebbles came from above. Kess angled up to see Riony pressing her forearms into the top of the cliff and lifting herself up with ease.

"It's okay, Dracuni, I'm fine. I'm here." The voice drifted down and stabbed Kess deep in her heart.

"What? What are you doing? You ..." Kess panted, half sobbing the words.

Riony faced away from the drop. Her shoulders sagged and she pulled a stone from her pocket. Tracing her fingers over it, the stone lit up a bright cyan.

She had a second light stone. But she ... she ...

"But you were bit! I saw it!" Kess shrieked.

"Yeah, it smarts, too." Riony touched her fingers to the puncture wounds on her hip, hissing as she made contact. "Lucky the spiders aren't actually venomous."

Kess turned cold all over.

Her voice was flat. "You tricked me."

"Don't take it too hard. No, actually do, you dragon-stealing gremlin. I mean, everyone in the depths knows cave spiders aren't venomous." Pony rolled her shoulders a few times and stretched them out. Bending down, she picked up the hatchling, and it curled up into her arms, tucking its head under her chin and trilling softly. "I've got you."

"And what about me? Are you going to leave me here?"

Pony cricked her neck and half turned. "Yeah. That's the plan."

"Go on then. Go!" Kess bit down the fury and tears in her voice.

The monstrous redhead didn't move. "You've got light ... You ..."

Kess rasped, "Don't worry, Pony. It's not like it's the first time I've been abandoned to die alone."

"Me either." Pony turned away again. Her voice echoed roughly through the cave. "I learned it from you, after all."

She walked away.

Kess rolled over onto her back on the tiny stretch of rock and screamed wordlessly into the darkness.

Chapter Twenty

Benjin's hand spasmed, squeezing hard around Lyrrin's fingers. Her knuckles cracked but she didn't feel the pressure as she stared at his mother, numbed from the words the grayglim woman had just spoken.

Yoskar was the one who killed the Hjelzahns' father and sister?

Lyrrin never liked the eldest Hjelzahn sibling very much.

He was terse and commanding and never once cracked a joke or a smile. Benjin always said it was because he was very, very clever, cleverer than anyone else in all the depths, and so he knew all the risks that other people couldn't even see. And he had the responsibility to protect his brother and sister from those risks.

Lyrrin had told Benjin at the time that Riony was like that too but wasn't mean about it. She didn't treat everybody else as though they were their enemy, like Yoskar did. Yoskar even thought unborn baby dragons were worth killing on the chance their existence could lead back to hurting his family.

Lyrrin never agreed with Yoskar's severity. Even his grim sister seemed lively and friendly compared to him.

Especially now, as he stood poised to attack, the red light of his burning crystal staff glinting in his wild, furious eyes.

Could he really be the one who murdered his own family?

Aishena's face was stony. She straightened her back, rolling her shoulders as though preparing for a fight. Only her dark eyes showed her emotions—fear, confusion, betrayal. She turned that vulnerable gaze between Yoskar and their mother in equal turn. "What does she mean? Yoskar?"

"She's lying, obviously," he snapped. "She's trying to turn you against me, trying to turn the odds in her favor."

Around the rubble-strewn space, the delvers held wary positions. Niskina and Caed whispered to each other, equally bewildered.

Aishena's earlier confessions had given Lyrrin a starting point for the conflict unfolding before her, but it was still all so confusing. Why would Yoskar kill some of his family, then put so much effort into protecting the other two?

It didn't make sense.

Yet all eyes were on Yoskar now, wary and assessing.

"Yoskar, lower your weapon," Brishan said in a soft, low voice.

Yoskar sucked air through his teeth and waved the staff, jutting it as he spoke. "She's lying! She's here to kill us and will happily kill every person here the very moment she thinks she has the advantage! Aishena ... You know, I would never hurt Neif. I would never ..."

A broken slab of stone shifted and crunched as Lady Hjelzahn took another step forward. "Look at him, he's ready to burn me alive, his own mother, here and now in front of you all. He's gone mad."

Lyrrin had to agree that it didn't look good. Yoskar was the only one with a weapon drawn, the only one threatening violence. Caed had circled around behind him as though ready to lunge in and take him down if needed. Niskina remained beside Lyrrin and Benjin, eyes locked on the conflict as she made comforting noises and patted Benjin's forehead.

His eyes were screwed closed, as though taking in just the words of those around him was too much, and he dared not even look.

Yoskar moved to match his mother's forward advance, closing the distance between them.

In a rush, Aishena leaped three big steps, positioning herself right in the middle of Yoskar and her mother's path. There was an athame clutched in each of her hands, not activated, but held so tight her knuckles whitened.

She lifted one and pointed it at Lady Hjelzahn, who halted her next step. "Why would Yoskar kill them? He's been looking after us, Benjin and me. He's done everything he could to look after us."

"Like I said, he's gone mad. Now why don't you ask the same of me? Why would I have killed my husband and child?"

Yoskar answered immediately. "She changed! You know she changed after her accident. You were the first to notice, Aish. You told me how she was so much colder during your lessons, that she didn't feel like the same person anymore. That's when I noticed the changes too; that's when I realized how bad it had gotten."

Aishena swung her attention from her mother to her brother, back and forth, mouth open and brows furrowed.

"Changed?" Lady Hjelzahn scoffed. Her eyes were still as black pools, staring her daughter down. "I am your mother and your master. Help me stop him, before he breaks our family apart even more. That's an order, Aishena."

She pleaded, "Mami—"

"Are you not still my prentice?" Lady Hjelzahn snapped.

"Mestra." Aishena bowed her head in a shimmer of steel hair. With a shaking hand, she lifted her other arm, pointing the second athame at Yoskar. But she didn't lower the one directed at Lady Hjelzahn. "I ..."

"Have you forgotten how to follow orders?" the woman in gray bellowed.

"Aish, she's lying to you! Don't let her get into your head. Take her down before she takes us down or move out of the way and let me do it!" Yoskar hissed.

Aishena winced and remained frozen, besieged by orders from both sides.

Lady Hjelzahn and Yoskar circled closer.

"Just hold on! Everybody stop for a moment!" Brishan growled.

"Maybe it was someone else!" Benjin yelled.

His sudden outburst startled Lyrrin. She grasped his hand, pressing his shoulder gently to keep him still as his body shook with harsh breaths, inflamed from his cry. He wheezed and squeezed his eyes closed as he forced air through his swollen throat.

Lyrrin's eyes widened as she understood him. "Benjin's right, it could have been somebody else who did it, not either of you! You don't have to fight."

Lady Hjelzahn's lightless eyes turned on Lyrrin, her face expressionless, unreadable. Lyrrin shivered, cowering closer to Niskina.

"Maybe … you could be fighting each other for no reason." Aishena's arms remained raised, the crystal tips of the athames shivering in her shaking grasp. "What proof do you have, Yoskar? How do you know it was her?"

"I didn't see … none, exactly." He pressed his glasses back up his nose and wiped his forehead with his free hand. In the hot glow of the burn stone, his skin glistened. "I saw other evidence, that she was a killer, that she was killing … other people, dangerous people to kill, for no discernible reason."

Heirs. That's what Aishena had told Lyrrin. That heirs had been dying, assassinated by some unknown killer. And Yoskar thought for some reason that it was their mother. That was why he'd asked her to leave the first time, but she hadn't believed him.

Whatever evidence he'd had at the time, it mustn't have been enough.

Yoskar glanced at the others in the room before looking pointedly at Aishena. He seemed to be wavering.

"You're being a fool, Yoskar. You're mistaking the signs of my grayglim duties for sinister plots." Lady Hjelzahn's voice seemed laced with ice, and the barest hints of a smirk raised her lips as she took another step forward.

"No! I took my suspicions to Fadda, to Lord Hjelzahn …" Yoskar squinted his eyes closed and shook his head once, as though berating himself internally. "It was right after that when he and Neif were killed. I think he went to you, and you killed him for what he knew, as you would kill us too."

Aishena's shoulders dropped. "That's not enough. It *could* have been someone else, all along … Fadda and Neif could have been victims of the heir killer. The *real* heir killer, out there somewhere, who was never our mother!"

Brishan grumbled at the term. "That's what I thought I was protecting them from. With all the news of heirs dying, with them telling me their parents were gone too, I thought I was helping to keep them safe from that, down here. Kverra, I didn't know you lived."

"I do, and I shall, as long as my son doesn't murder me. Trust I mean you no harm." Lady Hjelzahn grinned toward Brishan, but there was nothing warm in her expression.

"No, don't trust her!" Yoskar roared. "Please listen to me. If she's here for anything other than our deaths, then where is Daymora? Where are the other delvers? Where is the help that should have reached us?"

Lyrrin wasn't sure what was happening or who did what terrible thing to who. But they didn't have the time for accusations and arguments.

"Can you all stop fighting?" Lyrrin asked, pleading most with Aishena, still hovering stuck between her family. "You need to sort this out. Benjin's breathing is really bad."

He'd expended so much energy to call out and had gone limp since, just a low whistle of breath passing his ashy lips.

Niskina checked over the neck brace, loosening it from his swollen throat. "We really do have to get him help as soon as possible."

Lady Hjelzahn's gaze fluttered over the boy as though he was barely there. Brishan, Yoskar, and Aishena were all she seemed to care about, keeping her eyes on them.

"They're right. Enough of this fighting," Brishan said. He moved beside Yoskar and placed a hand on his shoulder. "Show us you aren't a killer and put the weapon down. We have to work together to get out of here."

Yoskar stared across at where Benjin lay panting on the ground, his face crumpled. With a grunt, he deactivated his staff, placing one end of it down, but still holding it upright like a warding shield.

"I'm not the killer," he said. "But I will do anything to protect my brother and sister. And I still don't trust her."

Aishena remained where she was, athames raised as a barrier between mother and son.

A soft growl caught Lyrrin's attention, and she peered through the inky shadows toward the wolf. A slick, slithery shape dashed past the bound animal, rushing toward her.

Lyrrin let go of Benjin and put both of her hands out in front of her, gasping. The damp, clinging cave otter scrambled up her legs and started reaching its paws into her pockets.

"Butterfur?" Lyrrin breathed his name in quiet disbelief.

Riony! Riony must be somewhere nearby, and she sent Butterfur back to me for treats! Lyrrin clutched the cave otter so tight to her chest that he squirmed and nipped at her arms. It worked. Her idea worked.

For a moment, Lyrrin held her breath, waiting and hoping to see her sister following the otter's path toward her. She didn't come.

But if Butterfur had been down the channel after Riony and then come back again to Lyrrin, Riony had to be close.

She held the creature up on display. "Aishena, please! Put the weapons down. Look! We could find Riony, help Benjin. We could all get out."

Aishena's nose crumpled, but she held her stance. "No. Something isn't right. I feel … I don't know who to listen to. I don't know who to believe."

"I'm your Mestra, first before any other," Lady Hjelzahn said. She held her arms wide and took a step closer. "You are the hand and will obey the voice."

"No! I know! But …"

Lyrrin got to her feet, moving toward Aishena too. "What do you want to do? Forget about following orders. You can decide. You were right about the map! If Butterfur made it back, you must have been right!"

"What does an otter have to do with this?" Caed muttered from behind Yoskar. He no longer looked prepared to strike his fellow delver down and just watched the situation before him with a wrinkled forehead.

"Don't get any closer," Yoskar warned the advancing woman, his voice still edged like a knife. "Everybody stay still!"

"And lower those blades, prentice!" Lady Hjelzahn commanded, stepping within reach of her daughter.

Aishena's arms dropped, and she gasped as though it was a surprise to even her, as though her limbs had followed the order without her agreement.

"No!" Yoskar howled. He bolted forward out of Brishan's grasp, charging at his mother.

The sing of twin blades rushing from their sheaths echoed through the cavern. Lady Hjelzahn moved in swift flashes of slate gray, drawing, lunging, slashing.

Yoskar was there, between Aishena and his mother.

The flurry of motion ended as fast as it began.

Niskina screamed.

It took a moment for Lyrrin to make sense of the shining length of steel emerging from Yoskar's back. It didn't fit there, jutting out crookedly, sheened in spatters of red. How had it appeared there so fast?

With a viscous, slurping whisper, it was gone again.

Then everybody was moving.

Niskina sprang to her feet, placing herself like a wall in front of Lyrrin and Benjin, pulling free a pair of her own athames. They lit up in a crackling burst of crimson.

Brishan crashed down on top of Lady Hjelzahn like a landslide. Legs kicked and tangled as they rolled. Their bodies danced across the shifting stones and Brishan came up onto his knees, pulling Lady Hjelzahn with him.

He pinned one of her arms, still grasping a blood-red blade, holding it tight around the wrist. The second short, curved sword was knocked free and clattered onto the broken rocks as he pinned her other.

The sudden movements and noise startled Butterfur and he dove into the safety of Lyrrin's shirt.

"What's happening?" Benjin rasped.

Lyrrin gaped, staring, unable to reply.

Yoskar turned a slow orbit, eyes flitting about until they landed on Aishena. His glasses slipped down, tipping off the end of his nose and clinking onto the ground. He opened his mouth, then fell.

Aishena lunged for him, trying to hold him up. His solid chest crashed into hers, taking them both down. She cried out, and Caed limped to her in a rush, helping to roll Yoskar off her.

"Yoskar? Yoskar!" Aishena scrambled upright and into a crouch beside him.

Lyrrin held her breath, waiting for Aishena to say it was okay. Waiting for Yoskar to sit back up. In the combined light of the two delvers' glow stones, a gaping hole in Yoskar's leather armor glistened. A hole in the front to match the one in the back.

The sword had gone straight through the middle of his chest. Lyrrin felt as though she'd forgotten how to breathe entirely.

"Sparks!" Caed hissed. He glared, teeth bared, across at where Brishan held the grayglim mother.

"Get off me, traitor!" Lady Hjelzahn growled, but Brishan kept her pinned beneath his weight.

"Caed! Quickly! Help me." Aishena's hands moved in a flash, pulling bandages and bottles from the pouches at her belt. Her chest heaved and her eyes were wild.

Yoskar didn't move as she pressed a dressing to his wound. He didn't cry in pain. He only stared with unblinking eyes.

Caed caught Aishena's hands, stilling them from their futile work. He leaned into her, whispering. She shoved him, pushing him back. He argued in a crackle of breath.

"No, no, no," tumbled in a silent flurry from her lips. Aishena stared down at Yoskar, then touched his cheek, his neck.

Lyrrin's hands were shaking, and she patted them over the bulge in her shirt where Butterfur lay frozen in fear.

Because she'd seen bodies of people who were no longer alive before. She recognized that absolute stillness.

Aishena screamed out a long, broken wail, rocking back on her heels and staring up into the cavernous hole above them.

"What happened?" Benjin cried again more desperately.

Aishena leaned forward, picking up Yoskar's broken glasses and cradling them in her hands before squeezing her fist tight around them.

She turned dark eyes streaming with tears toward Lyrrin and her brother. "He's … Yoskar's dead."

Chapter Twenty-One

Riony carried her precious Dracuni on one side and her precious replacement sword on the other and prayed to all her ancestors in the stars that she was heading in a direction that would save her from being stuck in these cursed depths forever.

Sir Butterfur was long gone. The cave otter had rushed ahead back when the avalanche of spiders fell upon them. Riony couldn't blame the critter. She would have run from the ravenous arachnids that fast too if she'd been able to. But it did mean she no longer had a compass to help lead her through the dark labyrinth of the Alderkin depths.

There was only one large tunnel leading away from the cavern with the deep pit—apart from the one full of spiders, which wasn't going to happen—so after picking up the sword and scrambling back up the slippery slope, she headed that way and hoped for the best.

She hobbled, making every effort to ignore the sharp pains of the bites in her legs, and the dull, shivering ache in her chest.

Her arms, at least, felt fine and strong and better for holding the weight of two things she loved.

Riony hadn't intended that taking the sword would help get Kess away from Dracuni. It had been a rash moment of unadulterated petulance that made her take the blade and not let it go. And there were moments when she thought she really had screwed everything up.

She was so sparking lucky there'd been a thin ledge just beneath her toes that she'd been able to stand on the whole time she put on her show for Kess.

And she'd been doubly lucky that paranoid goblin had fallen for the ruse.

Riony thus decided that the massive Alderkin blade was her new good luck charm. Unfortunately, the crystal weapon was far too big to hang around her neck the way she used to keep her acorn. It really was inconveniently large.

Dracuni fussed, wriggling about into a more comfortable position.

Riony dipped her head and pressed it to the soft scales at the dragonling's neck.

"I'm so sorry I let that monster get you. It's okay, you're safe now. We're getting out of here."

Other person? Dracuni questioned.

"What ... Kess?"

Where other person?

"She's not coming with us. She can find her own way out."

Dracuni rested her head on Riony's shoulder, staring back the way they'd come. She snorted, and her sense of confusion drifted through Riony's head.

In hole?

"She'll be fine."

Dracuni snorted harder.

"Okay, odds of her attaining a state of fineness are very slim. But I wouldn't put it past her. Plus, she kidnapped you, remember? It's better that we leave her."

Abandoned. Alone. To die.

The ache in Riony's chest shivered again. It was a horrible, sticky, guilty feeling that she had no time for. She willed the feeling away by summoning up memories of cruelty she'd suffered while under Heithorn ownership.

Only whipped by Kess's own hand once. Once. As if even once was forgivable. Sparks, Riony could take the beatings. It was the emotional and mental abuse that screwed her head right up.

And that one time Kess had taken the lash in her own hands, that had screwed her up most of all.

We both hurt each other beyond repair that day.

Riony's eyes washed over hot and wet, and she shook her head. She'd gone too far into her memories. Needed to rein it back. Just remember enough that she didn't feel bad about walking away.

"Kess is only getting what she deserves."

Dracuni didn't make a move or sound.

Riony huffed, forcing the breath out between her teeth. "Okay, fine! I know it doesn't feel good. Sparks! But what else can I do?"

Riony's mind and heart raced. She hated every outcome laid out before her. She didn't want to care about Kess's death. But she felt all kinds of awful about being the cause, that she was a horrible person for leaving Kess to die. *Abandoned. Alone.*

She also worried that if Kess *didn't* die, she would just keep coming back and being a problem for her and Dracuni.

And *helping* Kess? Riony would rather scratch a dragon's balls with a short stick.

"We have to get away from her. We have to look after us now."

Dracuni mewled and blinked wide lilac eyes at Riony.

"Don't look at me like that. You don't know Kess like I do."

But that was Kess from eight years ago. The spoiled brat who rode Riony around like livestock and had her whipped for looking sideways.

The hard-edged, determined young woman, riding boldly on the back of a wild wolf—that was someone different, someone new. Cruel still, in all new, exciting ways, but there was something else there, hiding in the dull pain buried under the venom in her words.

Something that made Riony's heart reach recklessly outward, the way it once had in the rare moments she and Kess had found joy in each other's childhood company.

But Riony had always been punished for it.

There wasn't one time she'd shown Kess kindness that it hadn't come back to bite her.

You were the only one dumb enough to ever make that mistake.

The aching shiver returned.

"Ugh. Stop it!" Riony grunted at herself.

Dracuni lifted her head from Riony's shoulder. The unidragon sniffed at the air, then turned and prodded Riony with her snout.

"No. We're leaving. We're going home to Lyrrin and we're never thinking about Kessara Heithorn ever again."

Dracuni became more insistent, turning her head down and poking Riony's cheek with the point of her horn.

"Ow! That's sharp!"

Danger!

Riony's footsteps halted. She could hear a dull buzz coming up the tunnel behind them.

For a moment, she half believed that Kess had somehow already tamed a giant ghost snake and was riding it up the tunnel after them for revenge. She wouldn't put it past her.

But then the tunnel lit up. Like a sun chasing toward them, the glow grew closer as the buzzing intensified.

Riony gasped and threw her back against the tunnel wall as the swarm of glowflies hit. They filled the tunnel, rushing through.

The cavern she'd just left had been full of the large bugs, clinging to the ledges and walls. A few had been disturbed by her climbing but had only lit up and flew to a new spot close by.

They fluttered and crashed against Riony, even as she turned and sheltered against the wall, shielding Dracuni behind her chest. Thousands and thousands of glowflies streamed through like shooting stars. Something must have disturbed every single bug in that cavern. Something big.

Over the buzzing, a gut churning chorus of roars rumbled.

You do not go down a tunnel glowflies are flying from. You go down that tunnel, you don't come back alive.

Riony was running. She was running before she had time to put thought into action, her feet pounding the ancient stones beneath her through some drive of their own.

She was running back the way they'd come.

Dracuni clung tight over her shoulder, and Riony hefted the heavy sword in both hands, and they crashed through the remaining stragglers of glowflies.

One final fiery insect flittered through the air in front of her as she broke through into the large cavern. She skidded to a stop there, careful not to tumble down the slope toward the pit again.

Riony cast her gaze down that rough hill of crumbling limestone, silt, and dried stalagmites to the ledge and drop beyond.

Kess had pulled herself to the top and was clinging there, hair stuck against a dripping face, eyes large, grasping and clawing at the edge. Her chest was up on the flat ground, legs hanging behind.

Then with a sudden jolt she slipped back again, just her chin and arms above the edge.

Her head angled up, and she made eye contact with Riony. Terror and something too painfully like hope widened her eyes farther and she opened her mouth in a scream.

"REEEEE-OH-NEEEEEEEEEEEE!"

Kess.

A gargle of hideous roars rose from the darkness below, followed by the scrabbling of hard edges against stone.

Kess's wiry figure bobbed again, as though being plucked from below, and she fell back, disappearing into the pit.

Riony's heart seemed to stop.

The light from the glow stone Riony had left with Kess dimmed, then brightened again, coming back *up* from the dark maw of the pit.

She came with it, upside down. Her small form dangled, brought up over the ledge, hanging from one leg in the grasp of a nightmare.

A sickening tangle of bleached white bones, gleaming against the cyan light, worked both with and against each other, wrenching and crackling. Skulls and legs and fangs and claws, stripped of all flesh, were jammed into each other until there was no sense of where one skeleton ended and another began.

The mess of arms and claws tangled against themselves, fighting over the screaming woman in their grasp, like a ball of ants fighting over a dropped candy.

The huge conglomerate of bones swayed in the air like a toppling column, swinging Kess wildly. She writhed, steel hunting knife in one hand, trying to hack at the amalgamation of bones that had captured her.

In a scattering of chalky fragments, Kess flew free. Her body arced through the air in a stream of cyan light, then crashed into a cluster of limestone columns, cracking through them and disappearing under a pile of rocks and dust.

"KESS!"

Riony skidded and leaped recklessly along the slope, beelining across the cavern to where Kess fell. Silty limestone sand slipped under her boots and rocks dislodged and tumbled down into the abyss, eliciting more roars from below.

In a final burst of speed, Riony fell onto her knees and skidded to a halt beside the pile of shattered stalagmites and the small figure poking out between them.

She placed her sword down on one side and Dracuni clambered off, circling around on the spot and sniffing back at the pit behind them.

Bad, bad things.

Riony nodded distractedly and reached a hand for the still form in front of her. "Hey, are you still alive?"

Kess grimaced in reply, her whole face crumpling up. Her chest and arms lay free on the rough ground, but her legs were hidden beneath a pile of broken stalagmites and drip-columns.

Squinting up at Riony, she gasped her words. "You ... came back. Why did you come back?"

"Because I never could be very smart about things."

"I didn't think ... you'd ever come ... for me."

"That's what your amma said last time I saw her."

"How can you joke," Kess winced as though in great pain, "at a time like this?"

"Poorly and with inappropriate regularity. I'm sorry. It's ... my way of coping."

"You joke *all the time*."

Riony averted her eyes. "Weird."

Kess closed her eyes and shook her head softly, and Riony couldn't tell whether it was from pain or annoyance.

"Okay, let's get you out of there." Riony put her hands beneath Kess's shoulders and pulled.

Kess screamed, a violent, gut churning cry.

Riony swore and let go.

Panting and whimpering, Kess said, "I'm stuck."

Riony got to her feet and started hauling the rocks. The pads of her palms were grazed as she frantically grabbed and threw, grabbed and threw, small and large sections of shattered limestone. The debris cleared away, leaving behind something that left Riony's heart chilled.

A section of naturally formed limestone column, longer and wider than Riony, lay right across Kess's legs. With a rough snort, she gripped the end of it with both hands, braced her legs, and lifted with her whole body.

It barely shifted. Kess screamed again. Behind them came a reply of a hundred roars at once.

"Sparks!" Riony stood back up and paced on the spot, breathing frantically. With a fierce shake of her head, she squatted to try to lift the column again.

"What are you doing?" Kess sobbed. "Just leave! Isn't that what you want? Leave and I won't be anyone's problem ever again!"

"I'm not sure even you deserve to die like this."

"I'm stuck!"

"I CAN GET YOU OUT!"

The column didn't budge.

"Why?" Kess's voice was the smallest, pitiful plea. "Why are you like this?"

A roar rattled the air around them, close this time, no longer filtering up from somewhere far below.

Riony turned slowly, scared to see.

A mountain of bones sprawled along the ledge, breaching over the top like a cresting wave.

And Riony could finally understand, in all its horror, what she was seeing.

Not just some strange, living pile of bones. It was a massive, moving tangle of revenants. Hundreds of them, human and beast and so broken she couldn't even tell what they once might have been, all picked clean to the white of their skeletons.

They must have come from above, like the one that had fallen on them.

And all had tumbled down there, into that pit, into a churning pot of cagey ribs and limbs that stuck into one another and knotted and bonded and held until they moved together as one immense, horrific creature.

The rat-king of revs.

And it was rumbling toward them on dozens of feet and claws.

It moved forward from three points, two armlike ropes of entwined revs on the sides, and the main mass of skeletons in the middle. There, three huge mouths roared again. Bears or boars or something else. Their blank, eyeless skulls were hard to identify.

But they formed a hideous three-headed face to the legion-born creature, with long, toothy maws snapping the air.

The conglomeration moved awkwardly, rattling and scraping as each of the hundreds of revs tried to act on its own within the confines of their bonded form. But they all moved with the same purpose.

To spill the blood of the humans.

Riony gritted her teeth and looked back up to the only tunnel that didn't lead to death by spider, now lying behind the approaching mountain of bones. She and Kess and Dracuni were cornered down in the lower side of the cavern.

Turning back, Riony found Kess panting and pale. Dracuni fretted, dancing on her claws and staring up with round eyes.

Bad, bad, many bad things.

"It's okay. It's going to be okay." Riony pulled the cutting athame from her belt and activated it. It lit up with a yellow glow—still with charge, thankfully.

Squatting down, she pulled Kess's hand up into hers, then pressed the athame into it.

"Cut through the stone with this. If you cut it here, the section on your legs should be small enough to push off. Then we'll see about getting out of here." Riony frowned at the way Kess's skin felt so cold and clammy, how her fingers curled weakly beneath her own.

"Dracuni, stay back with her. Stay safe." Riony chewed her lip, then glared at Kess. "And you, I'm trusting you to look after her."

Kess gave a pained laugh. "Why would you do that?"

"Not very smart, remember?"

Kess shook her head, closing her eyes in an agonized wince.

Riony grabbed the hilt of her weapon, then pressed back up to full height, rolling her shoulders and neck.

"Where are you going?" Kess asked.

"I'm going to try out my new sword."

Riony turned, facing the conglomeration of death scuttling toward them. She lifted the heavy crystal blade up before her, as the mountain of bones lunged to attack.

Chapter Twenty-Two

They're not coming back, Lyrrin. Amma and Pabba are gone forever.

Lyrrin didn't remember much of her earliest years, when her family lived on the run as fugitive slaves through the dangers of the aboveground. But she remembered the happy times in the safe village they'd found and made their home in.

She was young, and she didn't have much experience with death, until their safe village was no longer safe anymore. She hadn't been able to understand that Amma and Pabba weren't coming after them when she and Riony had run. That she wouldn't see them again the next morning.

She couldn't understand that they weren't just out of sight, just down the path, just around a corner, and would appear again with hugs and loving smiles at any moment.

I'm sorry, Lil Moon. I'm so sorry I couldn't save them.

And Lyrrin never did see them again. And Riony never called her Lil Moon anymore. That had been Amma's name for her.

By all accounts, Lyrrin had been an easy baby, calm beyond measure, never one to scream or fuss. But something changed the day Amma and Pabba died.

Tears and anger came fast to Lyrrin ever since.

As they did now, looking at Yoskar's unmoving body.

"Why? Why did you do that?" she shrieked at the cold, gray woman.

Her son ... he was her son!

"It was self-defense." Lady Hjelzahn lolled the words out lazily, still trying to wrench free of Brishan's grip. "He rushed me."

"Kverra!" Brishan said her name as a harsh admonishment.

"You didn't have to kill him!" Niskina growled from her defensive position in front of Lyrrin and Benjin.

Lyrrin tried to move in front of her and was pushed back. Benjin was paralyzed by the throes of breathless sobs.

"He was mad. It was the only way," Lady Hjelzahn said.

"Stop lying!" Aishena howled. She shot up to her feet and swayed on the spot, head hanging low and silver hair curtaining her face.

Lady Hjelzahn stilled, ending her struggle instantly. Her dark eyes glinted as she stared, taking in the wary stances of everyone around her, the blades held high, the faces wet with salt water. Hers remained dry as chalk.

Lyrrin watched as the woman kept her eyes on Aishena the most, unconcerned with anyone else in the room. Not a flicker of attention or pity for Benjin, her youngest child, lying in the dirt near Lyrrin's feet, choking on his own grief. A chill shuddered through Lyrrin, and she clutched at Butterfur's warmth within her shirt.

There's something very, very wrong with this woman.

"You drew first. I saw you. You drew on *me*." Aishena pressed her knuckles to her forehead. "Yoskar was right. He was right about you! I should have listened to him. Now ... What do I do now? What do I do?"

"She drew on you first?" Caed rasped. He had remained kneeling beside Yoskar's body. With a snarl, he rose to unsteady feet and pulled an athame as long as a short sword. It brightened a pale green as he ran his thumb over the runes.

Niskina frowned at her father. "What do we do? Can you hold her until help arrives?"

Aishena pushed something into her pocket, then redrew her athames as well. "Help isn't coming. *Yoskar was right.* Daymora is dead. Nobody is coming. No one is going to save us."

The corner of the grayglim's mouth lifted in a cruel smile, as though in confirmation.

"This is all sparking insane. We should tie her up." Caed gestured for Niskina to hand her cave silk rope over, as his and Aishena's were on the wolf.

Aishena laughed without any mirth. "She's going to kill us all."

"I didn't really want to." Lady Hjelzahn spoke flatly. From her motionless state, she twisted into sudden action. A foot booted out. A joint popped. Her arm slipped free from Brishan's grapple as though it had been held only by a wisp of web. An elbow cracked into his jaw.

He stumbled for half a heartbeat before he steadied and reached to grab her again. She pounced away from his swinging arms, landed near her fallen second sword, and kicked it up into the air. Her shoulders rolled and popped again as the blade flew, then was caught neatly in her hand.

She twirled the twin blades once. "It would have been so much easier if you'd let me take my children away to deal with elsewhere. Or if I could have removed the grayglim trained one from the mix before we started. But now I will have to deal with everyone the hard way."

Aishena remained slouched forward, staring down, as though unable to raise her eyes to anything around her. "I should have listened to him. I should have ..."

"Kverra, you don't have to kill anyone! What madness has taken you?" Brishan circled around the woman, bringing himself back near Aishena and the others.

"Whatever it is, she's the one that needs to be put down!" Caed said.

Lady Hjelzahn didn't even flinch, just kept her gaze steady on Aishena and Brishan.

As though Caed decided that lack of attention on him meant he could take the opportunity to strike, he rushed forward, limping crooked and fast at the woman, his blade out in front of him.

Aishena peered up through her hair with a gasp. "No!"

Niskina took his lead, charging forward too. She was snatched from her path by Brishan, who swung her in an orbit around him and threw her back toward Lyrrin and Benjin. "Stay back! She's too dangerous!"

Caed thrust his long athame toward Lady Hjelzahn's side. It clinked against flashing metal. Then leather tore, blood sprayed.

Lady Hjelzahn didn't even blink as she lowered her sword again, and Caed dropped at her feet. He gasped once through a bloodied throat and then stilled.

Lyrrin felt frozen in place, as though her spirit had already fled her body too, gone up to the stars to be with her lost loved ones, and her body had yet to awaken to that fact.

Her clawed hands were all that moved, flexing and closing, wanting action, but the rest of her could do nothing but stare with hot eyes at the lifeless bodies growing in number and the blood draining across the rocks.

This wasn't right. None of this was right! Lyrrin wanted to charge the woman too, join the fight against the remorseless monster. But she had no weapons beyond her claws, and they hadn't even been able to stop foppish Zade. And the grayglim woman was so much more. She fought like the touch of death itself.

Lyrrin wished she could fight like her sister, that she could swing a sword with strong arms and make a difference.

She wished her sister were here to do that for her.

But help wasn't coming.

There has to be something I can do!

"No!" Niskina's voice tore through the hollow space as she stared at Caed's body. She tried to charge again and was held back like a rabid dog on a leash by her father, feet scraping in place.

"We can take her. She can't kill us all!" she hissed at him.

"She *can*. You've never faced a grayglim, Nisk. Stay back and protect the kids. I'll handle this."

Lady Hjelzahn wiped the bloody blade against her thigh, staring coldly at them all.

Aishena shivered, shaking herself off and grimacing at Brishan. "You? You haven't been a grayglim since longer than Niskina's been alive. I will do it."

"You never finished your training," Brishan shot back.

"Then maybe between the two of us, we won't die immediately."

Brishan drew two athames of his own, lighting them up pale green, as Lady Hjelzahn strolled lazily toward them.

Lyrrin's heart pounded, willing her eyes to look away. She didn't want to see more. There was a cold, deathly finality in Lady Hjelzahn's dark eyes and unyielding approach.

She could kill them all.

But she hadn't. Not yet. And she hadn't tried to right away. She'd lied and waited until everyone had finally turned on her.

No ... that wasn't when. She'd struck as soon as she thought she could take Aishena out by surprise.

"Aishena! She's scared of you!" Lyrrin's words spilled fast and loud. "She wanted you gone first because you're her biggest threat."

Lady Hjelzahn swished a sword up to point at Aishena like a challenge. "Never once were you able to defeat me in sparring."

Aishena kept her eyes on her mother, but her eyebrows dropped, expression searching.

"But now, I'm all that's left to protect my family. All the family I have left. I never beat you in the past, but then I wasn't fighting for my life and his."

A new confidence seemed to surge in Aishena, straightening her spine and pulling back her shoulders. Tilting her head, she drawled, "And now, I have my athames."

She lifted her arms and activated the crystal blades, one hot red and the other cutting yellow.

There was a flicker of hesitation on Lady Hjelzahn's face. But she didn't slow her advance.

"Lyrrin!" Aishena snapped,

Startled, Lyrrin blinked her wet eyes clear and swallowed the lump from her throat, her body coming back under her control.

"Go. Go where I showed you on the map. Find that giant sister of yours and bring her back here. We need another sword on our side." Then more softly, "Say goodbye to Benj and *run*."

Lyrrin wanted to say no. She wanted to argue because it didn't feel like she was going anywhere to help anyone. It felt like she was being sent away to run and hide because she was the only one left who had that option.

Benjin couldn't move. He could hardly breathe. He gulped tiny, infrequent breaths, his face red all over, eyes scrunched shut and soaked in tears. Niskina hovered beside him, staring in horror at the standoff before her that could end at any moment.

Aishena was telling Lyrrin to say goodbye and run because she didn't expect the kid to get where she needed to in time to help anyone but herself.

Because she was too small. Too slow. Too useless.

But there was one more thing down there in the caverns that hadn't been counted on.

"I'll come back. I'll bring help," she whispered it, so quiet only Benjin would hear, if he could still hear anything. He didn't respond.

Plunging her hands into her shirt, Lyrrin pulled out Butterfur and placed him down on the ground. "Go. Go hide. Go home." *Just be safe, little friend.*

He sniffed at her once, then skittered up the cave wall, heading up the broken hole above them. Lyrrin was sad to see him go but didn't want to risk bringing him where she planned to go next.

Lyrrin ran across the rocks for the wolf.

She didn't know if it would help her. She only knew it wanted to find its rider as desperately as Lyrrin wanted to find Riony. And she knew it was fast.

Lyrrin crouched beside it in a rush. No time for careful movements.

It didn't flinch from her as it had before. It remained still, lying on its side, snout beside the laid-out handkerchief. Its breathing came clearer.

Good. It would need its sense of smell.

She held eye contact with the shaggy beast and took its front paws into her hands, then slashed clean through the rope binding them with a clawed finger.

The wolf exhaled in a huff and shifted.

The clash of metal against hardened crystal rang through the cave behind them.

Lyrrin reached for his back paws. Even as she tore through the ropes there, the wolf scrambled up to his feet, towering over her crouched form.

Light flashed through the cave—blood red, broken-egg yellow, sickly green. Colorful bursts mixed with dancing shadows. Rocks crunched and scattered. Metal sung and whipped through the air.

Lyrrin kept her gaze locked on the wolf, eye to eye. "We're going to find them. You're going to take me to find Kess." *And Riony.*

She reached out again and pulled off the rope binding his jaw closed. It could have stayed on. The wolf could have run with it on. It might have been safer for it to stay on.

But Lyrrin hoped that it would be the act of good faith that would win the wild wolf's trust.

As the ropes fell free, the charcoal-gray wolf whipped his head back. He straightened his legs, arched his hackles, and stared Lyrrin down.

She raised her hand tentatively toward the saddle. "Please, let me go with you."

The wolf bared its teeth and a long, low growl rumbled from deep within its belly.

Chapter Twenty-Three

That reckless, foolhardy idiot. That was all Kess could think as Riony ... Pony ... put herself between the churning mountain of bones and Kess.

She's only protecting the hatchling. She doesn't care ... Why did she come back? She came back. She left me. Idiot. She's going to get herself killed.

Kess's mind was a vortex of swirling thoughts, muddied with nauseous agony.

A chill ran through her, and she felt as though she were back in that ice cave, looking down as Riony lay bleeding, making the decision to leave instead of stay and watch her die. Instead of saving her life.

She'd gone back. With what intention exactly, Kess still didn't know, but she went back into that frozen dragon lair ... too late. Pony had already found her own way of saving herself and was gone.

Only Kess and Griskin and the acorn pendant tucked away deep in the wolf's saddlebags knew Kess had gone back.

Riony didn't know. *She had no reason to come back for me. She owes me nothing.*

A wave of darkness threatened to pull Kess's consciousness away. She bit her tongue to chase off the hollow feeling. She hardly felt that self-inflicted pain over the mind-scraping agony shooting up from her legs.

When she'd once compared herself to the fallen dragonrider who lost the use of their legs, she'd felt lucky that she at least had feeling in her lower limbs, even if they didn't work right for her.

Now, she wished otherwise.

Now, she almost considered taking the rock knife Riony had given her and using it to hack those legs off to be free. She might have tried if she thought there was a chance the dull blade could cut through. Surely it wasn't going to work on the massive column that had her pinned.

Getting up onto her elbows, Kess jabbed the glowing yellow crystal at the stone to make that point. She gasped as it sank straight in, slicing like dragon-forged steel through silk.

Blinking hazy eyes, she tried again, slicing a long line down through the rock. There was a smooth press of resistance as the blade slid along the stone, and the powdery dirt smell of crumbled rock.

Kess had seen how the humans of the undercity had used Alderkin artifacts, for lighting, for cooking, but she hadn't seen anything as powerful as this. This could cut her free ... one way or another.

A bolt of pain shot through her legs and Kess crumpled flat onto her back again.

Across the cavern, the revenant conglomerate roared, and Riony roared right back at it.

She'd scrambled up to the highest point of the slope, standing in the small globe of light from her glowing stone like a cyan star.

"Over here, you dumb jumble of body parts! Stars, you're ugly! If I wanted to see that many bones, I'd date men!"

Two of the three massive bear skeletons turned her way, gnashing at the air. They wrenched and pulled toward Riony, as the other large central creature continued to try to go the other way, toward Kess and Dracuni.

"That's right, up here! Come and get me!" Pony yelled louder, waving one arm high over her head. "Look at all these juicy bits you could be biting! I'm what you want! Come on!"

Her streaming shouts turned even more attention from the sentient individuals within the mass her way. The majority headed toward her now, moving faster with the joint effort. It clattered and scraped up the slope toward her.

Kess's eyelids grew heavy. She watched as the first long, ropey tangle of skeletons reached for Riony. She lifted the massive sword and swung, skimming it just under the main bulk of bones, swiping through the fringe of peripheral limbs and sending bones pattering across the ground.

Caught in a faint haze, Kess wondered how Riony could swing that huge blade at all. If she could keep it up, maybe she could hack that monstrous mass to bits. Maybe Kess could just rest ... just close her eyes for a moment.

But it was clear even by the second swing that Pony couldn't keep it up. The sheer weight of that crystal weapon was visibly tiring her, and fast. The third swing went even lower, scraping along the ground.

With a grunt, Riony dodged to the side away from the scores of grasping hands and claws, ducking between a cluster of thin, cage-like stalagmites.

Kess's head felt hot and heavy, and her body felt terribly cold.

The hatchling mewled behind her.

The hatchling. My hatchling. My dragon.

She was so close to everything she'd ever wanted. A dragon for herself, right there, within her grasp. She couldn't give up now. Nothing was going to stop her from achieving her goal. Nothing.

With a whimpering grunt, Kess pushed herself up onto her elbows again, leaning forward. Her arm shook and sweat streamed down her chest, and she pushed the glowing knife through the stone.

The crystal was short, only as long as her hand, and once she'd cut that deep, she had to change angles, slice in from the side to meet that first cut, pull sections out, widen the gap so she could reach in and cut deeper. Her stomach churned and ached from being curled to support her weight as she worked.

Acid rose in her throat as pain made her want to faint away and leave the agony behind. But she kept cutting, section by section, slice by slice.

Nothing—*nothing*—would stop her.

The hatchling moved anxiously around Kess, sniffing at where the stone rested on her legs, then stilling to watch the nearby battle, then clawing at the column. It baffled Kess that the wild creature hadn't turned on her, hadn't tried to eat her as she lay there at its mercy.

Kess had to push the hatchling aside twice so she didn't get too close to the magical cutting blade. She didn't want her prize hurt. *Until the taming ceremony.* Kess's face wrinkled as her chest clenched with confusing emotions.

"Are you through yet?" Riony yelled. Her voice was broken between deep, panting breaths. She weaved through columns and stalagmites, drawing the revenants after her. They smashed up against the rocks in their hectic efforts to grab her. Splintered bones rained onto the floor.

Kess opened her mouth, but only a painful grunt emerged. Her fingers bled as she scraped them at the cut rock, trying to pull the next chunk clear.

Riony jumped up to the flat top of a broken column, then skidded down the other side as a skeletal mouth snapped the air where she'd just been. "Not to hurry you, but playing keep away with this thing isn't as easy as I make it look!"

Kess nodded faintly. She was almost through. She could do this.

She was folded almost in half, trying to reach the furthest part of the stone to cut through. Her arm grazed the stone as she thrust it into the narrow split she had carved and ran the blade down the final length.

The heavy column shifted, and Kess cried out as the longer section, cut free, dropped the remaining height down from her legs beside her.

The small length left on her legs resettled, sending blinding stars of pain through Kess.

She took three deep breaths, her chest heaving, and then she folded forward again and pushed against that stone. It shifted a fraction, and Kess thought she would wither away to nothing from the agony that motion caused.

The hatchling moved in beside her, matching her efforts, pressing her small front paws against the rock.

Lips shaking, Kess wailed and pushed with every last bit of strength she had, and the hatchling pushed too, and the stone toppled and rolled away.

Given a clear view of her legs, or what remained of them, Kess let out a harsh yelp. The sight flushed every bit of blood from her veins and replaced it with ice.

Blood darkened the thirsty stone all around her. Her legs weren't the right shape. The leather of her pants bulged and split and a mess of skin emerged through them, punctured with spots of horrifying white shards.

They were broken, both of them, in a way that wasn't ever going to get better. Tremors quaked through Kess's whole body.

It's okay. It doesn't matter. They didn't work anyway. It doesn't matter.

Kess gulped down a rush of tears. Her head swam. Everything was filtered through an oozing veil of pain.

Her hands lay lifeless at her sides, the yellow-lit blade in her limp grip.

A soft trill came from next to her. The hatchling was there. Her hatchling. The unusual creature blinked those huge lilac eyes up at Kess, then pawed softly at her arm.

"We need to move. I know," she found herself saying in reply. Kess took an unsteady breath and pushed her palms against the ground, shuffling her body backward. Her legs followed, peeling and catching against the ground they had been pressed into.

A chest-racking scream sobbed from her as anguish fired through every nerve.

The rattle of revenants slowed their pursuit of Riony, turning to the noise.

"No, not over there! I'm here, you want me, you brainless bone bits!" Pony screamed even louder than Kess had. The mass turned back to her, like a field of wheat blowing in changing winds.

How am I going to move? How am I going to get us out of here? I have to get us out of here. She couldn't think through the pain. She wondered if she really should use the slicing blade to take off what remained of her legs. Whether that would hurt more or less.

The dragonling trilled again and bumped her arm with its snout.

"What do you want?" Kess whimpered. "I'm trying. I just need a moment ... then I'll move."

Talons tapping on the stone floor, the hatchling tentatively approached her legs, sniffing then growling softly.

"Don't touch them!" Kess snapped, waving the creature away.

It skittered back, lifting its chin and tilting its strange one-horned head side to side.

Dracuni. Did they call you that because of your horn? She was such a strange dragonling, and Kess couldn't make any sense of its action. It moved back toward her, pressing in close until her head was tucked against Kess's stomach.

Dracuni turned up to look at Kess and whined a low, keening sound, then licked at the tears she hadn't realized were dripping from her chin.

Those tears came harder, as though shaking up from the depths of her spine until they poured free from her eyes. What was this creature doing? Was it feeling sorry for her?

It pawed and fussed, and Kess could only gape at it. Dragons weren't like this ... were they? She'd only ever known tamed dragons, or hatchlings so new they had barely peeled their eyelids open for the first time, awaiting their imminent taming.

But she'd been told, she'd studied, she *knew* wild dragons were savage, cruel, monstrous beasts. This hatchling couldn't be showing her sympathy. Nothing made sense.

Pain surged through her and her consciousness toppled toward darkness.

A thunderous bang startled her alert again and left the cavern shaking, as a long arm of the revenant mass smashed across the ceiling, knocking down a huge stalactite. It hammered to the cave floor, cracking into an explosion of boulders and dust. They rolled and smashed down into the pit below.

Riony leaped through that cloud of debris a moment later, chased by the middle section and three huge maws of shining white teeth.

"On your left!" Kess screamed, as the other arm swiped in, running on a clatter of skeleton feet and the swinging momentum of a hundred undead bodies angling toward their prey.

Pony braced, holding the heavy sword in front of her body like a shield. The skeletal mass broke like a tide around her and the blade, bones flying in every direction. Riony went tumbling too, down the slope after the broken chunks of stalactite.

Kess's warning cry had drawn the conglomerate's attention, and it turned her way.

Riony hit the dried remains of an ancient rimstone pool and caught the edge before going over. Getting up onto hands and knees, she slapped the ground loudly. "I'm still here, you dumb sack of bones!"

Her cheek was bleeding, red as her hair, and she brought her sword up again just in time to take another hit. The very extremity of the mass's long arm whipped into her.

Riony turned the blade into it as it passed and smashed through, slicing the end clear off. A rolling tumble of bones flew like shooting stars through the air and crashed down onto the ground near Kess.

Most broke apart on impact, hailing across the cavern floor. Separated down into pieces small enough to end the shadowdragon's curse of faux-life that animated them.

But one larger cage of ribs, endless ribs and spine like a long whip, still twitched and turned. The skeleton raised the long-fanged skull of a serpent and turned to face Kess.

The massive snake skeleton curled and shook itself free of the remaining bones tangled within its splintered ribs, then rushed straight for her.

Chapter Twenty-Four

Through the hail of bone fragments, Riony almost didn't see the revenant snake become detached from the cluster.

She could hardly track its path, as the massive arm made of too many creatures swung for her again, blocking her view. And she definitely wasn't going to get to that boney serpent before it got to Kess and Dracuni.

Help!

"Sparks!" She ducked low, flattening her body to the ground and rolling under the rev-king. The clawed and hard-boned feet that drove the 'arm's' momentum kicked and tripped over her, heavy from the combined weight. Her ribs cracked and bruised.

Dracuni's fear pierced through her mind like lightning.

Breathing with pained difficulty, Riony tumbled up to her feet again on the other side and bolted toward the snake revenant. It was almost upon Kess, and still so far from herself. She considered dropping the heavy sword, currently resting over one shoulder, so she could run faster.

But it was the only protection she had from the flooding mass of bones throwing itself at her like a swarm of locusts on the last standing crops. She had those few random Alderkin crystals she'd pocketed, but she didn't know what they were and had only grabbed them as presents for Lyrrin.

The serpent reared, raising up, within striking distance. Riony could only see Kess through the cage of the creature's fillagree of ribs.

Kess pushed Dracuni behind her with one arm and raised the other, the bright-yellow glow of the cutting athame shimmering through the rev's pale bones.

It struck.

Kess slashed upward, crying out a high-pitched yelp.

Riony ran harder.

Kess and the snake collapsed in on each other. The serpent's skull lay on either side of the girl, sliced in two from the nape right up to its fangs.

The coiling length of its skeletal spine had lost all life, crumbling into pieces as the magic that had animated it and held it together was destroyed.

But Kess didn't move either.

"Kess!" Riony bellowed. She was a few long strides from the end of the snake's long tail.

Kess stirred, lifting her face. It was ashen, her eyes shockingly red against skin so bloodless it could have been as dead as the creatures they fought. Her head wobbled weakly on her neck, but she raised the cutting athame and sliced through that rev's skull again, for good measure.

She looks bad. Really bad. Not that she's ever looked particularly good.

The stone over her legs was gone, but Kess remained sitting where she was. Riony figured once she wasn't pinned, the stubborn goblin would have tied a leash around Dracuni and crawled herself out of there with her kidnapped bounty before Riony could stop her.

Riony could get them all out though. Now that Kess wasn't stuck, she could scoop her and Dracuni up and try to get past the conglomeration of bones. It was huge, filling half the rough slope of the cavern as it swung around trying to catch her, but they'd have a chance of breaking past it to the exit.

Riony might have one more good swing left in her, if she could get Kess and Dracuni onto her back again and keep her arms free. She just had to get to them.

The rev-king's whiplike appendage crashed down in front of Riony, overextending and hitting the ground between her and the others. Shards of bone shot out from the impact and Riony skidded to a halt, bringing her arm up over her eyes.

The revs in that section were shaken but still moving, trying to right their joined mass and turn on the humans again. And now they lay between two options.

With a growl, Riony lifted the huge Alderkin sword and let it fall down into the cluster of skeletons. It was more of a drop than a swing. The sword was ridiculously heavy, and even carrying it around like a shield left her arms aching.

The hardened crystal cracked down through the boney tangle, crushing a couple of revs within the mass under its weight.

Each blow she did manage destroyed some of the massive multi-monster, but she couldn't keep this up much longer. Riony had the awful feeling that Kess was right, and the sword was purely ornamental and that she was going to die like an idiot holding a decoration.

But for now, all she had to do was keep the creatures' attention on her, and that crunching blow did the trick.

The armlike tangle of revs pulled away from Kess and curved toward Riony, sweeping across the ground. She pulled the sword up by its hilt in front of her, the long blade tip scraping across the ground.

A skeletal claw slashed down her bare arm, drawing a scarlet line. Riony held her sword with one hand and punched that one particular rev in the skull with her other. There was a satisfying crack, but it and its joined companions didn't slow.

Riony dodged back, only to hear growling behind her. The triple-bear-headed central body of the conglomerate circled up behind her. It swept toward her from one side and the armlike section from the other, penning her in between them like a collapsing corridor of bones.

Riony ran up the slope between the two closing in walls of bone, trying to get to the end of them before they smashed shut around her. The bones clattered, grinding as the revs reached clawed arms and paws for her.

Lungs burning, Riony broke through the final fringes of bone as the two sides of the conglomerate closed up like a drawstring bag behind her.

A low, unseen stalagmite caught her foot and she tripped, going over and tumbling across the rough ground. Sharp limestone straws snapped under her and jabbed into her hips and arms. Rolling to a stop, she looked up.

Into the bared teeth of a huge gray wolf.

Oh, stars no, out of the rev-king's grasp and into the wolf's mouth is not how I expected my day to go.

"Riony!" The small cry came from behind—no, *on top of*—the wolf.

It angled around, and there sat Riony's little sister, dwarfed within the fluffy coat of the huge wolf.

Riony's jaw dropped.

"Lyrrin? What in this razed earth are you doing down here?"

"Stuff has happened. Lots of very bad stuff!"

Riony frowned and her heart stammered. She'd abbreviated tragedy to Lyrrin that way herself before and was terrified at wondering what had happened to Lyrrin to bring her here on this wolf.

There was no light on Lyrrin, no glow stone brightening her and her ride. Wherever she'd come from and why, she'd done so alone, just her and the wolf, through the darkest depths of the Alderkin caverns. Riony wanted to snatch her up off the wolf into a crushing hug.

The rev-king roared behind her. The two sides had knotted together when they crashed into each other, a writhing mess of undead. The confusion as the revenants tried to reorient themselves within the larger mass bought Riony some time.

"What is that thing?" Lyrrin gasped.

"Yeah, we've got a bunch of bad stuff going on here too." Riony hefted her sword back up onto her shoulder.

Lyrrin's eyes widened as she took in the weapon.

Riony turned to face the monstrous mess of bones again. "Can you ... are you controlling the wolf, or ...? Just try to get down to Kess and Dracuni. Get them on the wolf and get them out of here."

"Griskin?" The feeble cry echoed up the cavern.

The wolf sprang into motion, taking Lyrrin with him.

That answers that question.

The squirming cluster of revs had agreed upon a direction again, dragging their mass toward Riony. The wolf dashed, skirting the wall of the cavern to get around it, shooting like an arrow toward Kess.

Riony tried to chase after them but was brought up short by the second tangled long limb of the conglomerate looping toward her.

Riony's worn-ragged body rebelled, but she gritted her teeth, cricked her neck, pulled up the sword, and braced. As long as the rev-king's attention was on her, the others had a chance to get away.

The wolf reached the small pool of light from Kess's glow stone. It let out a low, mourning howl.

"Dracuni!" Lyrrin squealed, the sound echoing through the cavern.

Sister, sister! Dracuni thought with happy relief, ducking her head out from behind

Kess.

"How ... Gris ...?" Kess's voice was low and thick, barely audible over the grating bones lashing out at Riony.

"Oh no. I'm so sorry. Do you think you can get up onto Griskin?" Lyrrin asked.

There was such worried tenderness in her tone it made Riony's breath come fast. What was happening down there?

There was only a grunt in reply.

Her hurt. Her much hurt, Dracuni thought.

"I'll help lift. Three, two ..."

Kess screamed with such an acute howl of pain it made Riony bite her tongue bloody.

"I don't think she can move!" Lyrrin cried out.

Griskin growled, the reverberation mixing into the ongoing, echoing roars of the revenants.

"Hang on, I'm coming!" Riony bellowed back.

Heart hammering in her ears and nose scrunched from a war of emotions, she lifted her sword like a tower shield in front of her. Taking in the nightmarish swirl of bones before her, she tried to pick the thinnest section.

She ran for it, face-first, hoping she would plow straight through and come out on the other side with her sister and the others.

Sharp talons and jagged bones scraped up against her. It was like running through a thicket of thorns and twigs. It gave way to her and the blade, at first, until her momentum ran out.

No, no, no! Riony wrenched at the bones entangling her, pushing her feet hard into the ground as she tried to continue her charge, but she was stuck tight.

"Riony!" Lyrrin called out.

"Don't worry about me; just get the others out of here!"

A snapping, skeletal canine jaw wormed through the jumble of bones toward Riony's face. She grabbed it through its eye socket and smashed it up into a rib cage above, trapping it away from her.

"Use the sword!" Lyrrin's voice broke through the clamor of writhing bones.

"Don't you think I'd be doing that if I could? It's too sparking heavy!"

"You have to activate the rune!"

"I don't know how!"

"I'm going to tell you how if you just listen!" Lyrrin snapped back. "Up from the bottom of the triangular line—"

"What's it going to do?" Riony tugged her hand free from the clutch of grasping bones and ran a finger over the carved rune.

"It's a float rune. Aishena said it's used for moving furniture and things."

"Sorry, *what*?"

Teeth of some kind closed on Riony's shoulder. She bit back a cry.

"Then up the short line, then down the longer line!" Lyrrin continued.

It felt like the weight of almost the entire rev-king had piled in on top of her now. Dozens of jaws tried to reach through the tangle, aiming for her flesh. Riony went onto one knee, pressed down within the violent, living graveyard.

With a grumble of desperation, Riony finished the sequence.

The massive weapon lit up with a cool purple glow. Riony felt for a moment as though her arms had gone numb, no longer feeling the pulling weight of the sword. Until she realized it was the sword that no longer had weight.

The clamoring mass of bones seemed to chew on her entire body, as though every bone of every revenant within the whole was teeth that could consume her.

From her half-kneeling position, she took a deep breath, then burst upward.

Riony brought the long blade up with her with magical ease, blocking a gnashing skull angling for her neck. She twisted, continuing her arc of motion, spiraling the massive weapon in a wide, spinning swing.

Bone fragments went flying. The revenants shattered around her, leaving her in a clearing of crumbled skeletons.

"Oh, sparks yes!" Riony grunted the words intensely. *I could swing this baby all day!*

The ends of her curly hair tickled her cheeks as they floated up around her face as though blown in a silent wind, and she felt light on her toes.

The swarming bones readjusted themselves, pulling in again.

Riony turned to the lowest point and pushed the sword tip into the ground like a vaulting stick, hoping to just break over the top of the skeletal mass as she leaped.

With a gasp, she flew airily high over the revenants, landing lightly on the other side. She snorted out a breath, and then let out a hearty chuckle. With a daring smirk, she turned to face the rev-king.

The fight suddenly felt a lot more equal, and Riony was ready to crack bones.

In the whirlwind of the battle, the thinner lengths of the conglomeration that had swung about like limbs before had both become entangled into the main mass. That surging, seething sea of bones scrambled for Riony.

She struck. With teeth bared in violent glee, she hammered the huge sword through the conglomerate. A whole section cut free, a mix of human and reptile skeletons. It rolled around behind her as she smashed again into the larger mass.

The smaller section moved more spryly, coming at her back with a vicious growl. Twisting fast, she rammed the pommel into the largest skull of the group, then brought the rest of the sword around to half that section again.

The purple light glowed strongly and the sword swung easily, crushing the semblance of life out of the undead creatures.

But even with the new power of the activated Alderkin sword, it could take a hundred swings to take the monstrous mass apart, and a hundred more to finally put down all the individual parts.

Riony knew she'd try, knew she'd keep trying anything she could to get them out of there. But she wasn't sure she *could* keep throwing her aching body at the thing much longer.

Brishan's scolding voice came back to her.

Kid, listen, I know you're keen. But you've got to be more careful. You can't just deal with problems by throwing your body at them as though it's expendable. Because you'll spend it real quick down here.

Pure, reckless, relentless action had served Riony well in the past, but she knew her luck would run out one day. She had to be smarter … which sucked for her. She always was more of a hit-things-till-something-worked kind of girl.

As the rev-king shook off the broken pieces Riony had laid waste to with her sword, exposing the central three bears, she opened her eyes wide in realization.

Maybe she just needed to get help from the people around her that already were smarter.

"Kess, give Lyrrin your light stone!"

"No! Why?" came the paranoid goblin's reply.

"Just do it! Lyrrin, can you add a burn rune on that thing?"

"But that will—"

"Yeah, I know exactly what it will do! Add it on and throw it to me."

Kess made some objectionable noises. Muttered arguing. There were some scrabbling and scratching sounds.

"Done, are you ready?" Lyrrin called out.

"Throw it!" Riony jogged back from the rev-king, giving herself some space and putting herself in position to catch the stone.

"It might be bigger than last time! The more charge left, the bigger the reaction." Lyrrin hefted the stone with her small arm. It arced brightly across the cavern.

"I love it when you give me good news!" Riony caught it in one hand.

"Okay, you disgusting butcher's boneyard. You want to eat something? Let's go." Riony charged toward the heart of the monstrosity, going right for the largest bear maw.

She carried her sword lightly in one hand, trailing it behind her as she ran, and activated the new rune on the already lit up glow stone with her thumb as she clutched it in her other hand. It hummed with magic, growing brighter, and hotter, and brighter again.

With a thundering war cry, Riony leaped high. The three giant mouths of the bear skeletons snapped, and the hundreds of other claws and talons and boney fingers reached for her. She hurled the ever-brightening crystal straight down the throat of the largest bear.

The explosion shook the cavern, bringing down smaller stalactites. Burning fragments of bone sizzled through the air, crashing all around. The rev-king gave off a multi-mouthed roar as it crumbled in upon itself in a crackling bonfire.

Riony landed on the other side, half sliding, half running down the slope to throw herself over Lyrrin and Dracuni.

Boney limbs waved and lashed out from the flames, throwing embers. Chunks of stone and charred revenant bits pattered against Riony's back.

In a cacophony of mournful howls, the churning, sparking remains of the rev-king conglomerate tumbled down the slope and over the cliff edge, disappearing into the darkness below.

Underneath Riony's embrace, Lyrrin whispered in awe, "It worked."

A grin broke across Riony's face from ear to ear. She deactivated and dropped her sword, then lifted Lyrrin up under her armpits, holding her high and swinging her in a circle.

"You did it! That was amazing!"

A proud half smile didn't reach Lyrrin's worried eyes. She patted Riony's arms, pressing them down.

"We have to hurry. We have to get back to the others, fast," she said.

Riony put the girl back on her feet, a frown twisting her forehead. "Why? How did you even find us? Are we that close to the undercity? What's happening?"

Lyrrin's lips closed tight and she shook her head. With a deep breath, she said, "No. We fell too. Benjin is hurt really bad. Aishena and the others are fighting her mother who's a grayglim. Yoskar's dead. Jonna's dead. Caed too. Daymora, probably too."

"What? WHAT?!" Riony roared.

The rev-king suddenly felt like a million years ago. All the blood rushed from Riony's head. She grabbed her sword and turned to take up Dracuni too, ready to run.

Kess was propped awkwardly on one arm. The other held Dracuni around the neck, cutting athame shining yellow in her hand. She leaned heavily over the unidragon, breathing unevenly. Griskin pawed the ground next to her, growling up at Riony.

Her voice came out low and slurred. "I won't … I won't let her go. I have Griskin again now. The dragonling is mine."

Riony tightened her grip on the sword and prepared to pummel Kess close to death. It was only then that she got a good look at Kess's legs.

She already looked far too close to death.

Her hand around the crystal dagger shook.

Dracuni trilled a whimper. There was no fear coming from her, despite the magically sharpened blade near her throat. More worry, maybe even pity.

"Put the athame down. You're in no state for being such a stubborn, butt-faced jerk right now."

"No! I won't let you take the dragon. Then you'll leave me, leave me again." Kess's eyes turned, unfocused, lids drooping, despite how she kept her face angled toward Riony. Sweat dripped from her pale skin. "I need … I need the dragon."

"You *need* to calm down before you pass out and skewer yourself."

A spasm racked Kess's wiry form. She opened her mouth in a silent cry.

Riony took a step closer, crouching in front of her. Griskin growled softly but didn't move. Riony laid the sword down beside her and lifted empty hands for his inspection. His gaze flickered between Riony and Kess and Lyrrin, and his growl became a whimper.

"No," Kess's voice was a weak plea. "Let me have her. I'll treat her well, I promise."

"You're planning on taming her," Riony snarled, but the anger in her tone was tempered with a gut-churning feeling she couldn't place.

"I can still be good to her. I have to … I have to have her."

"Like you were good to me?" Riony scoffed. "You. Can't. Have. Her."

Kess's face scrunched up with pain, her eyes screwed shut as she exhaled a whimper.

Riony leaned in and plucked the athame from her limp grip like picking a flower. She moved to deactivate it, but it sputtered out, yellow light dimming to nothing as it ran out of charge. With a sigh, she tucked it into her belt.

Dracuni mewled and skittered across to Riony's side, bumping her cheek against Riony's shoulder. Lyrrin let out a sigh and patted the dragonling.

Kess's arm swung weakly, trying to pull the hatchling back, then she slumped forward onto her elbows, face hanging just above the ground.

Help? Dracuni trilled, looking at Kess.

Riony breathed through her teeth. "Sparks, Kess. Where's your silvernix? Do you still have any? Is it on you or the wolf?"

Kess's head wobbled. "I need that for taming. I can't use it."

"You idiot! You are, very best-case scenario, going to lose your legs entirely. And much more likely, you're going to take your last breath any second now. Where's the silvernix?"

"No."

Griskin whined softly, lowering down onto his belly in front of Kess and nudging her as though expecting her to climb on. She wasn't going anywhere. She leaned there, face down, legs twisted horrifically behind, all her efforts required not to collapse entirely flat onto the floor.

"You can't see anything past your one stupid goal! You aren't taming Dracuni. I'll never, *ever* let that happen. And you won't be riding any dragon if you're dead!" Riony groaned and dragged her hands down her face, bringing them away bloody from the gash in her cheek.

"You never understood." Kess's voice was so broken Riony had to lean in to hear. "What being a rider means. It's the only way ... only way I can be worth something. I'll never ... give up."

Kess's arm slipped and she dropped lower, her body trembling.

Help? Dracuni questioned again.

"I'm trying to help her!" Riony reached for the pouches and bags strapped over Griskin's back.

The wolf's snout swung around toward her, growling fiercely.

Riony growled back at the beast, frustration swelling through her.

I help. Same as helped you? Dracuni thought.

Riony paused, then looked down at the hatchling, stunned. "What? No. You can't."

"What is it?" Lyrrin asked.

"Dracuni ... wants to help."

Lyrrin's eyes widened. She whispered, "She *can't*! Then Kess would *know*."

"Stop pretending you can talk to the dragonling," Kess murmured.

Riony ignored her, shaking her head at the unidragon. "Kess and her problems, they're not your responsibility. She's got silvernix, somewhere. Maybe when she finally realizes she's not going to get any better without it, she'll actually use it!"

Kess's arm slipped, and she slumped lower. A long, low wheezing breath rushed from her.

She went down on one side, shoulder thumping onto the ground. Her head lolled, constellation marked cheek pointing skyward as her eyes stared, unfocused and watery.

"I'd treat ... her ... better ... this time."

Her body shuddered scarily.

"Kess. You dumb goblin ... KESS!" Riony yelled.

She didn't move.

"Kess?" Riony sprang up to her feet, her whole figure flushing with a horrible, gurgling energy. She paced hasty steps, eyes glued to Kess's unmoving form.

Her chest felt as though she'd swallowed one of Lyrrin's double-runed crystals.

"We need ... where's the silvernix? We need it!" she rasped.

Lyrrin made her own attempt to get close to Griskin, to search his bags, but he was on the defensive now.

But while he growled at Lyrrin and stared her down, Dracuni slipped closer to Kess.

I help.

"Dracuni ..." Riony's lips wavered, unsure what she intended to say next.

This moment ... It should have been like waking from a nightmare. It should be a celebration, to see the cause of her torment perishing. A sigh of relief that Riony and her loved ones would no longer be hunted.

But all Riony could see in front of her now was a girl who had suffered her whole life and was now dying in agony.

If Kessara Heithorn wasn't already dead.

Griskin seemed to have noticed a change and turned away from warding off Lyrrin. He whined and pressed his head against Kess's belly.

Riony fell hard onto her knees beside Kess and Dracuni. She couldn't say anything, didn't know what to do. Didn't know how to feel.

Dracuni bobbed her head once, then ducked it down low, bringing her horn sharply across her front leg. The sparkle of opalescent fluid spilled from the cut.

Riony chewed her lip and held her breath, as the unidragon pressed her bleeding leg against Kess's sweat-beaded forehead.

A soft sparkle of light glimmered where they met, and Kess drew a harsh gasp of air.

She convulsed, her body contorting in the grip of the unseen force. Her breath hitched and a brilliant light suffused the cavern.

The air itself shimmered all around her body, radiating out through her flesh, an otherworldly luminescence that cast eerie shadows across the rough walls.

Riony, Lyrrin, and Dracuni were bathed in the ethereal glow as they silently watched the unfolding magic.

Griskin loosed something between a groan and a whine and backed away from the glaring light.

Kess's back arched off the ground and her mouth and eyes opened wide and round. Her hand shot out, finding Riony's nearby. Kess's fingers latched tightly around hers as her eyes closed again.

Deep, disturbing sounds of mending permeated the air. Bones seemed to snap into place, flesh knitted back together, wounds sealed as if sewn closed by invisible hands, as shimmers crackled and bolted all over Kess's body.

As the light dimmed, Kess lay still, her chest rising and falling in a peaceful rhythm. The cave returned to its natural shadows, the magic of Dracuni's blood receding like a retreating tide.

Kess's eyes opened again, and she stared at the ceiling as she took a few long breaths. Then, scowling, she snatched her hand away from Riony's as though it were acid.

She launched upward, hinging at the waist into a sitting position. Grasping at her legs, she stuck fingers through the tears in her pants. With a wince, she adjusted her sitting position, and Riony saw a flicker of disappointment on Kess's face when her legs didn't follow the rest of her body on command.

Kess turned from her legs to those around her, gaping. "How ... did you use my silvernix?"

Riony only pursed her lips. A slow, heavy settling of relief combined with sickening concern weighed upon her. Because she knew it was only moments before the clever gremlin added things up.

Kess's shrewd gaze cast over Griskin's undisturbed packs, the lack of bottle or vial in anyone's grasp. Then it turned slowly to the hatchling beside her.

She lashed a hand out, grabbing Dracuni by the front leg, staring with wild intensity at the smudge of silvery blood there.

"Back off!" Riony had the inactivated athame in her hand and aimed at Kess in a flash.

Kess dropped Dracuni's leg, more in wonder than in obedience.

"You ... you said she was special. When you were pleading with me to save her, you said that. I thought it was part of your trick."

Shrugging, Riony muttered, "Had to add some truth into the show. Figured it would sell better."

"What is she?" Kess leaned toward Dracuni again.

Riony pushed her back by the shoulder. "She's not yours."

Dracuni skittered over to Riony, chin held up. *I help?*

Riony scooped her up into her arms.

"You did help. You did good." She murmured the words low, for Dracuni, but didn't know herself whether they were true. There was nothing good about Kess knowing Dracuni's secret.

"You really can communicate with it too, can't you?" Kess sighed out the words, as though they were the most tragic thing she'd ever said.

Riony nodded once.

"And you, you too?" Kess threw to Lyrrin.

"No, just Riony can." Lyrrin pouted.

Kess pressed her fingertips to her temples. "This ... how is any of this possible? Even dragonriders who have been with their steeds their whole life don't have that sort of connection. I've heard rumors ... but this ... and her blood! She bleeds silvernix!"

"I am aware of that fact," Riony said carefully. She kept Dracuni held tight to her chest. "That's why it's so important that she's protected. Why I have to protect her. If the wrong person got her ..."

Kess's eyes flittered, as though every thought passing through her head showed through them. Her forehead wrinkled and she gave a firm nod. "You're right. She has to be protected."

"I won't ... sorry, what?"

"You're *right*. This is huge, far bigger than me getting myself a dragon to ride." Kess clicked her tongue, and Griskin shuffled toward her, low on his stomach. He licked her under her chin, and she leaned into him for the shortest moment before her face hardened again and she climbed up onto his back.

Riony got to her feet as well, still cuddling Dracuni tight, wary of Kess, returned to full health and reunited with her dangerous steed. But the goblin didn't attack. She ran her hands up the wolf's neck, buried her fingers deep into his fur, and sighed.

"Can we go and help the others now? They need us!" Lyrrin bounced on the spot, distress making her small body jitter.

"Right, yes." Riony shook herself and reclaimed her crystal sword.

"Benjin really needs Dracuni, too. If Dracuni is okay with that."

"Dracuni felt it was worth saving this monstrous sack of bones, so I'm guessing she might be okay with helping your friend."

I help! Dracuni butted her snout into Riony's chin.

"Did I hear you say Lady Kverra Hjelzahn is there, fighting her children?" Kess asked.

"She's trying to kill everyone!" Lyrrin cried again with urgency.

Kess's face scrunched up. "Why?"

"I don't know! But she's so fast, and her swords—"

"She's a grayglim, the most elite of royal guards, spies, and assassins. We'll be lucky if anyone is still alive by the time we get there."

Lyrrin whimpered, and Riony shot Kess a withering look. "We're going, and we're going to get there in time to save everybody. Because that's what we do, right? Big dreams, bold deeds."

"Big dreams, bold deeds," Lyrrin repeated, her blue eyes sparkling.

Kess rolled her eyes. "If you do want to save anyone, we need to get back there fast. Griskin can do that. But he can't carry all of you."

She stared down at Lyrrin. "Honestly, I'm shocked he let you ride him at all. But I could take the kid again, and Dracuni. Get them out of this haunted hole and go help the Hjelzahn brats."

"I don't know ..." Riony steadied her stance, leaning from foot to foot, as though that could somehow steady the turmoil of her insides at this version of Kess in front of her, offering her help. What was even happening?

But there was no chance Riony was letting Kess ride off with the two things she loved the most. "Lyrrin could go on Griskin, take Dracuni back to Benjin to help him. I'll carry you again."

"No way am I letting you split me up from Griskin again. I'll take them. You and your heavy ass and heavy sword will have to catch up."

Riony hefted her newfound love up in front of her, staring at the facets of the crystal blade and the rune carved into it. She smirked.

"You know ... I think Griskin actually will be able to carry all of us."

Chapter Twenty-Six

"Do we even know we're going the right way?" Riony took up most of the makeshift saddle in the middle of the wolf's back.

She held her sword above her head, lit up and weightless. She sat lightly in the saddle, gripping tight with her other hand so she didn't float right off, but still took up the majority of the space.

"Griskin knows," Kess replied flatly. She leaned over Griskin's neck, squirming farther away any time Riony shuffled too close on the galloping wolf's back.

Griskin had raced along one long tunnel, turned into a smaller one, went through a broken wall into Alderkin chambers so rich they made Riony's mouth water, up two large flights of stairs, and was sprinting down a small corridor with multiple intersections and doorways.

Riony figured they must look ridiculous, all of them stacked onto the wolf's back like that. But it was also exhilarating. Griskin was fast and strong and pounced with agile precision through the Alderkin depths.

Even if Kess never did get her dragon, surely this was almost as good. There was a clear bond between Kess and the huge wolf. Maybe not the strange mind-speak Riony had with Dracuni, but still some kind of silent, mutual communication.

Riony's arms and chest remained tense, ready to strike Kess down at the first sign the goblin was turning on her, but part of her sparked with hope.

Kess could have tried to grab Dracuni again after she was healed. She could have ridden off on Griskin without Riony and Lyrrin, left them to run more slowly back to Aishena and the delvers. But she chose to let them ride with her. She chose to help them.

Riony's head practically throbbed with the conflicting emotions whirling in there. Could she ever trust Kess? Could she ever forgive Kess?

Why do I even care? All I have to do now is ride with her and hope that isn't a bad idea.

Riony would do what she had to do, as long as it got them where they needed to be in time.

"Are we close? We had better be close." Riony squinted into the long corridor ahead.

Lyrrin, clinging on behind her, with Dracuni pressed between them, said, "I'm not sure. It was dark on my way to you. But it didn't take long, so we should be there soon."

Bouncy! Dracuni thought.

"Someone's still alive and fighting," Kess said.

Riony frowned, confused how Kess had drawn that conclusion, until a few moments later the sounds of a frantic swordfight resonated toward her.

With a final, growling leap, Griskin burst into a cavern piled in crumbled debris and lit up with a rainbow of scattered athames.

The shear amount of rubble gave Riony pause. Her sister had come down through that. One of their number didn't survive that fall, and it was a miracle—plus some small testament to the delvers' skills—that number wasn't higher.

Dancing across that landslide of broken stone, Aishena and a woman in gray dragonscale armor traded blows almost faster than Riony could keep track. Dual swords of bright steel met glowing athames of red and blue in cracking blows.

Brishan stood a few paces beside the combat, stretching and rolling an arm that was dripping blood, then moved back into the fray.

In a twirling flick, Lady Hjelzahn disarmed Aishena of the blue athame, and it clattered across the floor. Aishena's belt, normally stuffed with a long row of the crystal daggers like a toothy dragon's maw, was empty.

With those three focused on their battle, nobody but Niskina saw the approach of the wolf and its riders. She crouched beside the small body of Benjin, one hand on his shoulder, one hand on an athame.

"Off," Riony whispered to Lyrrin. "Take Dracuni, take cover."

Kess turned her head to Riony's words but said nothing.

Her sister slid from the back of the wolf, the unidragon clutched against her chest. They were across the long room from Benjin and another large archway leading into a more decorated space, and Lyrrin pressed herself to the wall, creeping along it in the shadows.

Riony decided she needed to make a bigger entrance.

Letting go of the wolf, she let the weightlessness of her sword carry her. She crouched up onto the saddle, then leaped off into the center of the room, landing with a crash onto the pile of shattered rocks. She swung the massive glowing blade in a full circle in front of her, then pointed it toward the battle.

"Will all murderers in the room please drop their weapons, or do I have to break some more bones with my fine new sword? I'm honestly okay with either option."

The Hjelzahns' mother's scowling attention flicked toward Riony. Aishena grinned ferociously and in a move that won her a larger portion of Riony's heart, she took the advantage to slash her burning athame toward her mother's throat.

Brishan took his chance from the side as well, striking with a pale-green athame toward her shoulder.

Lady Hjelzahn threw herself into a vaulting backflip before either blade touched her skin. Landing out of reach, she raised twin swords in a guarded stance, assessing the additional threats that had appeared.

Kess and Griskin padded up from behind Riony, prowling forward to join the standoff. The wolf's head was low and his throat rumbled. Kess took in the space with narrowed eyes.

From her vantage high on the tumble of rocks, Riony could see the bodies lying all around. Jonna, body twisted and broken from a fall, face covered in a delver's scarf. Caed and Yoskar, left where they had fallen, soaking in pools of their own blood. Her lips curled into a furious snarl.

"Drop your swords now before I shove your eyes down your throat and make you watch as I jam every inch of this beautiful blade through your chest." Riony flexed, holding her huge sword in one hand only, and pointed it at the grayglim woman.

She clearly had no experience with float runes because she stared at Riony with a horrified awe. Still, she didn't drop the swords. She stood like a statue, only her eyes moving, face twitching, as she recalculated her odds.

"I can still take you all," she muttered, not even sounding winded.

Kess and Griskin stalked closer to the woman, and Riony opened her mouth to warn her back. She was getting too close, and those swords looked mean sharp.

But then Kess angled Griskin back around so that he was facing Riony, Aishena, Brishan, and the others.

"You don't have to take everyone down," she said in a hard, dull tone. "Because I'm going to help you."

Riony's blood turned to ice. She growled, "Kess ... what are you doing?"

Lady Hjelzahn tilted her head, taking in the wolf-rider. In a voice that gave Riony shivers, she asked, "What do you propose?"

Kess plucked a couple of bone throwing daggers from sheaths on Griskin's saddle and pointed them across the space to where Lyrrin and Dracuni inched along the wall.

"I'll even the odds for you and whatever your end goal is. And I get to keep that hatchling over there."

An overwhelming, reverberating hum built in Riony's ears, and her breaths shook through gritted teeth. After everything they'd just been through ... after everything!

"Kessara," Aishena gasped out her name. "She wants to kill us, all of us, that's her goal. Then she'll kill you too. You can't—"

"I can look after myself. I will get what I want, and this is my chance."

Lady Hjelzahn nodded curtly. "I prefer those odds. You have a deal."

The chill in Riony's veins reversed, flaring up with the heat of flowing lava. Every part of her felt hot, shuddery, ruinous with overflowing fury.

She couldn't even speak, couldn't even think of a single cutting word to hurl back at the awful goblin that could do nothing but hurt her and whip her when she was down. A curdled mixture of hatred and charred hope ground through her guts.

In a roar of rage, Riony threw herself and her sword at the girl and the wolf.

Griskin pounced to the side and the sword crashed down beside him, shards of soft limestone scattering from the warning blow. A bone dagger whistled through the air. Riony twitched back. The sharp blade skimmed across the side of her neck, leaving a sting. Kess wasn't playing. She was throwing kill shots.

This wasn't some ploy. Even in her fury, Riony had hoped, had wondered if Kess was lying, to get closer to the murderer in their midst. A trick to take that grayglim woman down.

When will I learn? When? She'll never be kind to you!

Riony bellowed, wordlessly, madly. Something broke painfully in her chest.

She swung again, scooping the blade from the ground in a hail of stones and sweeping it up to cleave Kess through the middle.

Kess wasn't the only one going for blood now.

The wiry girl ducked low against Griskin's back, the blade skimming across the tangled braids on her scalp. The wolf lunged, getting within arm's reach of Riony, snapping sharp teeth at her hands. She had to dodge back, give herself space to swing again.

Kess's throwing daggers rushed at her in a flurry of pale streaks. Riony deftly blocked two with her sword, but the next found its mark, sinking into the flesh of her upper arm. The slim blade remained stuck, protruding from her skin. Riony ignored it.

The pain only fueled her determination, her grip on her sword tightening.

How could you? How could you!? The words burned permanent scars of repetition in Riony's mind.

She thundered, "I'll never let you have Dracuni. You'll have to kill me first!"

"I know." Kess dropped the words, heavy and emotionless, into the air.

More throwing daggers sliced through the air. Riony met the flying blades head-on, sword raised as a shield, bones pinging off as they hit. The impacts reverberated through her arms.

Each dagger throw was a threat she couldn't ignore. Kess's onslaught forced her to pivot and dodge, every step a calculated dance of survival.

Another found purchase in her thigh, hilt jutting out awkwardly. The pain of it was no more than a fly bite compared to the uproarious turmoil shredding Riony from the inside.

Riony didn't slow. In the barest moments of reprieve as Kess sought more blades, Riony bore down on her with ferocious sweeps of her sword. It whirled in blinding arcs, a tempest of glowing crystal that forced Kess to remain constantly on the move. Griskin's swift footwork countered Riony's brute force, keeping them just out of reach.

Neither yielded an inch. They each fought furiously, for their very lives, for everything they wanted and cared for.

An unsteady slab of stone shifted under Griskin's paws and he had to dodge toward Riony instead of away to stay clear of the resulting landslide of rubble. She brought her sword hammering down, flat edge toward his snarling head.

Kess swung him around, taking the blow across one of her legs instead. The sword tip traced a line through the ragged leather covering her calf. Blood spilled from the wound, and Kess spat a curse.

Beside them, somewhere, somehow, came the singing clash of steel on crystal. Riony couldn't understand it at first because the only thing in the world right now was her blinding fury, and Kess, and Kess's imminent death.

Then Aishena's cry reminded her that other people existed. "Get to Benjin! Help him!" It was the cry of a sister, desperately trying to save her younger sibling.

"I can't!" That was Lyrrin.

Riony blinked, eyes clearing slightly from the red haze that had flooded them.

Across the cavern, Lyrrin and Dracuni were pressed into a corner, with Aishena and Brishan in battle with Lady Hjelzahn in front of her. Across the other side, Niskina stood over Benjin.

The fight with the grayglim was a whirlwind of motion, each movement precise and fierce as she clashed with Aishena and Brishan. It took both of them to even keep her at bay, and she still had time and attention to lash out toward Lyrrin every time the girl tried to edge closer to Benjin.

"Let me help!" Niskina paced, stepping forward and back from the flurry of blades.

Riony narrowly dodged Griskin's teeth on her wrist and turned her full attention back to him. Kess had only a single bone dagger in her hands now, clinging to it, making Riony think it might be her last. She pressed forward, aiming a blow for the traitor's head.

Kess rolled away, hanging sideways from the saddle before righting herself and bringing Griskin back around to attack again.

The flurry of the other battle moved closer, and a nearby squeak from Lyrrin proved she was being forced along with it.

"No, Nisk! Stay back!" Brishan cried.

"Stay with Benjin!" Aishena added.

"You're at a stalemate, but the three of us could best her."

A thunderously loud clash of weapons sounded and Brishan grunted. "You've never fought a grayglim, you don't know—"

"I can still do what's right!"

Through the corner of her eye, Riony saw movement as Niskina ran into the fray.

And then Brishan made the most horrific choice Riony had ever seen. He turned his back on Lady Hjelzahn to bodily push his daughter out of the battle.

He thrust out with both hands, slamming them into her chest and knocking her onto the ground, across where Benjin lay. Air whooshed out of her, and she lay there, winded, gasping for breath.

Lady Hjelzahn's twin blades met around Brishan's neck and scissored clear through.

The ringing of that steel upon steel turned into a piercing scream from Niskina that shook through the cavern. She wailed a long, sharp note of grief that cut Riony deeper than Kess's blades.

Every part of Riony tensed, and her face scrunched in on itself.

Brishan ... Master Brishan, who was going to give her one last chance to be a delver after her spectacular screwup. Who was going to be so impressed when she had come back the next day, followed orders, and done everything she could to be the perfect delver because it was all she'd dreamed of, all she and her small family needed to live comfortable and safe.

And Riony felt a venomous guilt to even think that, to see Brishan die and to feel the loss of her own dreams slipping away right before her eyes.

Niskina had lost her father, and Aishena had lost her brother, and all the other delvers' families had lost them, and Kess ... Kess remained. Kess could have changed things. Worked with them to stop the murderous Lady Hjelzahn.

But instead, she ruined everything in Riony's life, the way she always did.

In that fraction of a heartbeat, as Riony grieved for Brishan, and all the dead around her, and the death of all her dreams, Griskin lunged, jaws snapping shut around Riony's leg.

Pain radiated through Riony's body. She cried out, staggering on her other leg. Griskin tossed his head, yanking her with him, teeth closed like a vise through her flesh and grinding against bone.

He pulled Riony off her feet and sent her rushing to meet the ground. She cracked down on her back in a puff of dust, crooked shards of stone jabbing against her. The long Alderkin sword tumbled out of her hand. Bone daggers, still pierced in her arm and leg, jarred with agony at the impact.

The wolf's snarls echoed in the air, a victorious proclamation. Kess, panting and bloodied, glared down at Riony, one final dagger in her hand aimed for Riony's heart.

CHAPTER TWENTY-SEVEN

Griskin thrashed his clamped jaw, as though trying to pull Riony's leg clear off at the knee. She bit off a scream, breathing through the pain. Searing agony shot through Riony as his teeth tore through her muscle with each swing of his head.

Kess toyed with the slim bone dagger in her hand. Her lips curled.

"You don't have to die," she said. "Let me take the creature, and this will end."

Riony gave a feral growl. "Counteroffer—you drop dead and let the world be a better place without you in it."

Kess lazily rolled her eyes.

Brishan's body had only just crumpled, headless, to the floor. Aishena exploded into action, putting her mother on the back foot for the first time in her wild brutality.

Niskina lay where Brishan had pushed her, paralyzed by breathless sobs. When Lady Hjelzahn disarmed her daughter of her athames, Niskina's sobs stilled, her expression fierce. She threw crystal blades in to replace those dropped. Aishena fluidly plucked them from the air, still alit and glowing red hot.

There was still some life in each of them yet, and Riony would keep fighting until Kess sank that final dagger into her heart.

She twisted, throwing her arms out, trying to reach her dropped sword so she could swing it back in the wolf's face. She needed to detach its teeth from her skin.

The sword was out of reach, sliding away from the ends of her fingertips. Instead, she found Yoskar, lying nearby, eyes staring lifelessly back into hers.

A silent sob clogged Riony's throat, blocking her breath, as though her body was already preparing to join him in death.

But in death, the stern delver offered a glimmer of relief for Riony.

She wrapped her fist around Yoskar's crystal-studded staff, pulling it from his cold fingers and swinging it for Griskin's jaw.

Out of reach, Griskin kept her pinned as the staff whooshed through the air near Riony's knees, far shorter than the huge sword.

Movement behind the wolf-rider drew Riony's attention, and she glanced toward it. Lyrrin stood there, a few steps back from the wolf. Dracuni was down on the ground, curling anxious circles around Lyrrin's legs, as the young girl gestured with both hands in a grabbing motion.

Her lips silently mouthed, *"Throw it to me."*

Kess's head began turning to follow Riony's line of sight.

Riony shot her gaze back at Kess and clenched her teeth beneath a smirk. "What's the problem, Kess? You're about to have everything you wanted. Don't you have the stomach to finish this? Just like you didn't have the stomach to whip me yourself? Your parents aren't here to do it for you this time, coward."

"You always behaved as though you wanted to die." Kess snapped back to face Riony. Hesitation flickered over her pointy features. "I'm glad you're so eager. That will make this easier."

Riony swung the staff again, weakly and too far from reaching her target. But it was only for show, to keep Kess's eyes on her.

"Go on, then! Have the guts to follow through on one damned thing in your life, you self-serving, two-faced goblin. Kill me! You want your dragon, then you have to kill *me*."

On her third swing, Riony let the staff fly.

Kess dodged the flying weapon, scoffing at Riony's missed attempt.

And the staff landed where Riony intended.

She didn't know what Lyrrin was going to do with it. Something clever, probably. Add more runes onto one of the stones and make another flash bomb? Fire bomb? Riony braced herself for an explosion. She trusted Lyrrin to make it work. She should have trusted her all along.

But she was also prepared to go out along with Kess and the wolf if that's what Lyrrin had to do to keep herself and Dracuni alive.

The clatter of a hot, red dagger turned Kess and Riony toward it. Aishena's last athame spun across the floor, knocked from her grip.

Lady Hjelzahn's twin blades cracked through the air like lightning, chasing her daughter across the space with swing after swing. Unarmed, it was all Aishena could do to keep herself out of reach.

Kess nodded as though to herself, then glared down at Riony. "It's over. Wish I could say it had been a pleasure, Pony."

Her arm pulled back like a striking serpent, the bone dagger glinting in the cyan light.

And then a small figure came flying through the air behind Kess, bellowing a high-pitched roar like a miniature barbarian. Kess turned too late, and Lyrrin brought the crystal-studded end of Yoskar's staff down over the back of her head.

It hit with a thudding crack. Lyrrin landed in an awkward tumble by the wolf's flank, and momentum carried her all the way up to Riony's side.

Kess slumped, dangling down over Griskin's neck. The wolf growled gruffly, unlatching its teeth from Riony's leg and backing off. He lifted his head, bobbing it up and down as Kess's body lay limply over his neck, as though trying to stir her.

Riony pulled herself up into a sitting position and grabbed for her sister.

"What was *that*?" Riony asked in awe.

Lyrrin shrugged bashfully, holding the staff in a hug to her chest. "I asked myself what you would do. I was trying to be more like you, because normally you do the saving."

"Lil Moon," the long-unused affectionate term slipped out, hurting Riony's heart with its appearance. She swallowed and continued. "You don't have to be like me. You're so much cleverer. Bashing someone on the head with a stick should be your last resort."

"Maybe. But also, I didn't want to do something that might blow you up. Maybe we can both learn from each other."

Riony ran her fingers over Lyrrin's cheek, then patted her hooded head.

With a great, sighing groan, Riony got to her feet, leaning heavily on the leg that didn't have a dagger and teeth marks in it.

"Sword. Dracuni," she said, tucking her fingers in a beckoning gesture.

Lyrrin ducked to grab the weapon, eyes wide with excitement as she lifted it easily over her head to place it back into Riony's grasp.

Griskin snarled as Dracuni galloped past to join them. Kess's arms worked, trying to press herself upright, but her head flopped and she swayed.

As Riony lifted her glowing Alderkin sword his way, the wolf lapped his tongue nervously and backed into the shadows.

Hurt? Dracuni trilled and stood on her back legs, front paws reaching up to be held.

"I'm okay, I can handle this." Riony winced as she hobbled her first step. "Lyrrin, take Dracuni over to Benjin and Niskina. I'm going to help ... Aishena!"

The silver-haired delver was down on her back, her mother standing over her, blades raised and ready to strike.

"You always were too easy to disarm. You would never have made the grayglim ranks if you can't even keep hold of your weapon." Her voice was strange, filled with a cold flatness, at odds with the heart-racing battle she'd just ended. "You have to die, regardless. Every last one has to die."

"It's lucky, then, that I kept my hands on one more weapon." Aishena moved in a flash, tugging a long, thin athame out from her chest armor.

She didn't even activate it, just struck the sharpened crystal upward. It plunged through a gap between the scaled armor, deep into Lady Hjelzahn's gut.

The blow knocked the woman backward, and she folded, falling in a rumpled heap.

One steel sword then another fell, *clang, clang,* out of her hands.

Aishena spun her legs above her, then brought her body up with the momentum in a liquid motion. She snatched up the twin blades, pulling them back away from the twitching body of her mother as though worried the grayglim would strike out at her with them again.

Riony limped as quickly as pain allowed over to Aishena's side. "Are you okay?"

"For someone who just killed their own mother, I'm perfectly fine." Aishena kept her face down, shadowed by the fall of her hair.

"I thought you were done for. Nice trick with the hidden weapon."

Aishena tilted her head and shrugged. "I've been keeping one concealed on my person at all times since you suggested it while we were chained to that cart."

"Stars *damn it*, you're hot," Riony gushed.

Aishena flickered a dull look toward Riony, then turned her eyes again to the two bloody swords in her hands and the body of her mother lying before them.

Which continued to move.

No blood spilled around the athame lodged into her intestines. The woman twitched, then opened her eyes. One hand snatched at the hilt of the crystal dagger with terrifying speed.

With a great, spasming tug, Lady Hjelzahn pulled the long athame free from her stomach. It came out clean. The wound remained dry.

"Um … That isn't normal," Riony said.

Aishena was already stumbling backward, horror stretching her features.

Lady Hjelzahn rose to her feet.

"No, no!" Niskina screamed.

"We have to get out of here!" Riony stared upward at the ragged hole above them, leading up and up and up. She was in no state to climb. Maybe she could hold off the unsettling gray woman while the others did.

There was an archway behind them, opening into a shadowed, cluttered space. They'd have to go past Lady Hjelzahn to go for the other tunnel they had come from, even if they preferred to face the rev-king again instead of her. Riony was fifty-fifty on that.

"Lyrrin, the gateway! Activate it!" Aishena yelled.

"The what?" Riony asked.

Lyrrin was already running through the archway, carrying Yoskar's staff and Dracuni, who bobbed over her shoulder.

Riony raised her sword, prepared to square off against the grayglim woman, to buy time for whatever it was Aishena and Lyrrin were planning.

Lady Hjelzahn straightened, glaring down at the tear in her armor. Something that looked uncomfortably like intestine poked out through that hole. With indelicate fingers, the woman pressed it back in again.

"*Nope*," Riony muttered and hobbled speedily toward the archway.

The weightlessness of the sword helped carry her, and she jabbed the tip into the ground, using the length like a crutch as she hurried after the others.

Aishena was beside Niskina and Benjin. She lifted him with as much care as time afforded. "Come on! Snap out of it!" she scolded to Niskina, then hurried after Lyrrin.

Niskina remained, gasping sobs her only movement.

Riony detoured a few steps to grab the sobbing girl's hand. Then she continued on, dragging Niskina with her.

She limped through the archway into a room that would have been everything she'd wished and dreamed for a long time ago, that very morning.

Now all she wanted was to live and save the few remaining lives around her.

"Is there a way out through here? Where's the gateway?"

Riony could only see adjoining rooms, all dead ends.

Lyrrin was crouched on the ground in front of a huge geode slice that towered in the center of the Alderkin riches. She traced the complex rune at the base, and then another symbol to the side lit up.

Lyrrin touched it with ungloved fingers, and the inside of the geode shimmered with magic. The air contorted and changed, coalescing into a sparkling image that seemed familiar to Riony.

"Hurry! Go through!" Aishena commanded. She didn't wait for a response. She strode straight into the enchanted image, the touch of magic glimmering over her, and Benjin, limp in her arms.

"Are we sure … is this safe?" Riony gulped.

Glancing behind her, Lady Hjelzahn's legs juddered into movement, breaking into a run toward them.

And at her side, a charging wolf. Kess squinted, leaning crookedly as she rode.

"Sparks!" Riony growled.

Lyrrin, and Dracuni in her arms, both looked up at her, questioning.

"Go!" Riony nudged them toward the strange gateway. They twinkled through it, visible still on the other side through the veil of glowing magic.

Then Riony dragged her aching body and Niskina after them.

A frisson of energy washed over her, making her skin prickle in goosebumps. For a moment, she couldn't breathe, her head spun, and it felt as though a rush of wind blew straight up into her rib cage and out the top of her head, taking all her bodily contents with it.

She stumbled out the other side into the crumbling interior of an Alderkin shrine.

Riony's bad leg caused her to trip on the uneven floor and she fell. She let go of Niskina in an effort not to bring her down at the same time. Landing on her hands and knees, Riony flipped herself over as fast as she could, grasping again for her sword as she stared back through the strange glowing portal at the two deadly figures racing her way.

Lyrrin stooped beside the large geode they had just tumbled through, scrabbling her hands around in the leaf litter and dirt at its base.

In the water-ripple image of the room they'd just left, the wolf leaped.

Then the light went out.

CHAPTER TWENTY-EIGHT

Kess's head thumped with blinding pain, but she could still see her prey right in front of her. Everything was blurry, but the strange space between the huge, glowing crystal window rippled and whirled the most.

Still, she could see Pony down on her back. The brat who'd given her the cowardly blow from behind was there too, and behind them, Dracuni, the creature she'd do anything to claim.

Griskin was in midair when the light faded in a zing of magic, and Kess's quarry disappeared before her eyes.

She and the wolf went through the middle of the massive geode and landed alone on the other side.

Griskin whined, sniffing at the ground and finding nothing.

Searching with her eyes, Kess grunted, "Where are they?"

A wave of pain washed through her skull at the use of her voice. She reached her hand back, feeling the rising egg on the back of her skull. The kid hadn't hit her very hard, just enough to cost her everything that had been within her grasp.

It's your own fault too. You shouldn't have hesitated. You should have put Pony down, once and for all.

Kess scrunched her hand into her hair around the swelling wound, seething anger out in a long breath through her teeth.

It wasn't fair. How dare that ... that monstrous, traitorous, intolerable oaf have the one thing Kess always wanted? How dare *she* have a dragon, and at the same time something that was so much more than a dragon?

Dracuni ... Kess should have known from the name, from the strange, singular horn formation and coloring. But how could she have known such a creature could exist? She still didn't understand how it did.

She only knew she had to have it.

Kess spoke the truth when she agreed Dracuni had to be protected. Every blight-bitten fool in this razed world would be after the thing if they knew what it was. And if that unblessed idiot Pony couldn't even keep the secret from Kess, she was in no position to keep that creature out of someone else's hands.

Kess wanted the hands that laid claim to the priceless hatchling to be hers. More than anything. Certainly more than the crawling, awful sense of familiarity that had crept into her during her time spent with Pony.

The way they had fallen back into that strange semblance of their old relationship brought every childhood emotion back to Kess in an unwanted rush. The mutual torment, the shame ... the longing.

As a slave, Pony had never truly cared for Kess. Never could. And in a life where Kess existed knowing no care from anyone, she despised that sense of desire for care from someone so beneath her.

It would have been better if Riony had never been part of her life.

Now her target was gone, who knew where, and she had no leads or idea where to start next.

Why did I hesitate?

It was just a life, one life, that stood between Kess and everything she wanted. It should have been easy. Kess should have never allowed Pony's life to matter to her.

The soft crunch of a footstep twitched Griskin's ears, and Kess turned to see Lady Hjelzahn approaching.

"What happened to them?" She glared from the circle of crystal at Kess.

She'd lost her twin blades, but now held a long, thin crystal dagger.

The one that had moments ago been plunged into her stomach.

Kess shivered and backed Griskin away slowly. "They must have used some kind of magic."

"Invisible?"

"No, Griskin would smell or hear them if they were still here. I think they are … gone. Somewhere else. The view behind them through the crystal was a different place, an overgrown ruin. They might be there."

"Could they come back?"

"Would you?"

"Hmm." Lady Hjelzahn turned midnight-dark eyes toward the archway and the hole leading above. Then returned them to Kess, adjusting her grip around the crystal knife.

Kess eyed her hand. "We could continue to work together until we both have what we want."

"No, I see no value in that."

"We part ways here, then." Kess leaned over Griskin, spurring him into motion, gaze still locked on the approaching grayglim.

"No. You won't leave this place." Lady Hjelzahn moved to stand directly in front of Griskin, showing no fear for the beast whose shoulders stood almost as tall as hers. She ignored his growls, gaze locked on Kess.

"Whatever is going on between you and your children, whatever all of this was about"—Kess gestured to the bodies, sapped of their warmth on the floor of the caved-in area—"it doesn't have anything to do with me."

"I can't leave any witnesses." The grayglim burst into motion. Twisting past the wolf's biting teeth, she lunged the crystal blade toward Kess's chest.

Kess muttered a curse as it clipped up against one of the many steel rings on the harness-like vest she'd been given. The hard metal diverted the strike sideways. The force behind the blow bruised her ribs but didn't cut through.

"Gris, go!" Kess cried, and he bounded away from Lady Hjelzahn's second lunge.

Letting the wolf take control of their path, Kess turned back, eyed up her target, and let her last bone dagger fly. It sank neatly beneath one of the woman's collarbones.

The throwing daggers Kess carved from bones were small and thin, but punctured into a chest like that, they could still breach a lung, stop a heart.

Lady Hjelzahn plucked it out, clean and dry, and tossed it to the floor.

A gut-deep disturbing dread filled Kess. She leaned over Griskin, urging him on faster. They raced out of the rich chambers and up the pile of debris.

Footsteps pounded after them.

Reaching the summit of the landslide, Griskin jumped.

Lady Hjelzahn leaped after them, her fingertips brushing the end of the wolf's tail.

The nimble wolf landed on a small ledge, all that remained of the floor above.

He kept going, kicking off the wall there to bounce higher, scrabbling onto the next level, and then the next.

Beneath them, stones pattered down, disturbed by their climb.

Kess couldn't hear the grayglim, but a quick glimpse back showed the woman climbing after them.

She was fast, but Griskin was faster.

Floor after floor, he jumped from ledge to ledge. One gave way, crumbling beneath them, but his agile feet brought them pouncing safely to the other side and up again.

Kess held her breath and forced herself to look down. Neither heights nor depths should scare her. She could no longer see the murderous woman behind them in the dark pit, spotted with dimming crystal blades, scattered amongst the bodies far below.

Griskin's side bumped into a wall, and Kess hissed when the cut on her leg collided with the stone. The cut Pony had drawn with that ridiculous sword stung but wasn't too deep. It would heal on its own. She'd had worse. And maybe Kess could even entertain the idea of using her silvernix, since soon, she'd have it in plentiful supply.

Griskin brought them leaping up one more level, and above them, Kess found a solid ceiling. She recognized the room as the one she and Riony had broken through the wall of into the water channel.

The tunnel leading out was a mess of debris and crumbled stone, almost blocking the exit, but there was room enough to squeeze through.

Griskin led the way, and Kess rummaged through her saddlebags for any remaining weapons, shaken and worried the unnatural grayglim woman was still after them. Nothing turned up. She was going to have to replenish her supplies once they were out of this awful underground tomb.

Griskin's breathing was heavy, and she let him slow his pace as they moved through the shadowy tunnel. Lady Hjelzahn was long behind them in the climb. They should have a few moments to recover, and were almost out into the larger, inhabited cave. Reaching down, she pressed both hands into the thick fur of her wolf's neck.

Blessed sun, it's good to be back on Griskin again.

He trotted nimbly down the unlit passageway. Kess couldn't see anything, but she could feel the wolf's sure motions, the turns of his ears, the twitch of his snout, as his keen senses led them confidently through the dark.

Soon, the sounds and smells of the undercity were noticeable for Kess too, and they came out into a lit area near the pungent fungus farms.

She leaned forward and gave Griskin a pat on his jowls. It was then that she noticed the small parcel of fabric tucked into the strap collaring the wolf's neck.

"What's this?" She pulled out the soft, thin cloth and unwrapped it. Within, the crumbled remains of dried herbs sent a strong whiff of fragrance into Kess's airways.

Griskin snuffled and pawed at his nose.

"Is this why you're not as sniffly anymore?"

Kess took another tentative breath. The bright, minty fragrance shocked a nostalgic memory free. She'd smelled this mix of nose-clearing herbs before. Delivered to her by Pony, back when they were children and Kess was sickly, and Kess hadn't even asked that favor from the slave.

When Kess's mother found out Riony had given her peasant's herbs as a remedy, she'd been furious. Peasant's herbs, for a Heithorn! Not that they had enough silvernix to spare on common sniffles by that point or would have spent any more on Kess even if they had.

Riony had been whipped for it. Told she needed to understand her place.

Somehow, those lessons never stuck.

Kess learned. She learned to share less of her and Pony's activities with her parents. It didn't seem to slow the whippings though.

Kess wondered whether they were taking out the disappointment they felt toward her inadequacies as their daughter on Pony instead. That wild Rolanian slave who had all the qualities of strength and vigor a Taen dragonlord should display and their own child lacked. Pony was the perfect surrogate for all their spite.

And she ... she just took it.

Kess shivered and refolded the handkerchief and moved to tuck it into one of the saddlebags. Then with a scowl, she tossed it onto the floor. She didn't need it. Griskin didn't need it. They were leaving these caves for good, because as big of a fool as Riony was, she must know she couldn't come back here safely.

Kess turned Griskin toward the main thoroughfare of the cavern. There was no point now hiding her presence, slinking through the shadows as she'd done before.

The refugees of the undercity rushed to clear a path for her and the huge gray wolf she rode on.

The people muttered and stared at her passing, and a gaggle of squealing children built up behind her, daring each other to get closer.

Kess ignored them, pressing on toward one of the main exits.

She wasn't sure where she was going, only that somewhere out there was everything she wanted.

Dracuni. The creature may not have been the strong dragon she'd hoped for. Kess didn't really know what she was or how she would grow. Whether it would ever prove to be an effective steed.

But that didn't matter, because Dracuni was something far more valuable.

How ... how did Riony come upon this creature?

A living creature with unicorn blood.

The concept thrilled Kess beyond comprehension. Even if there were any true unicorns still alive, the value of each one enough to turn commoner into a noble, Dracuni would be worth ten of them. A hundred of them.

Never had a unicorn been able to be kept in captivity. They would wither and die within hours of being captured. They had to be bled and bottled as fast as possible to save every drop of the precious silvernix.

But that strange hatchling, it was living under a human's care, with them, possibly even bonded to them. Kept as easily as keeping a tamed dragon.

It had bled for Kess and still lived to bleed again another day.

Kess flinched at the memory of how the small critter had looked at her with some animal version of pity, had done that for her, to save her.

It didn't matter. She owed the creature nothing. Debts were not earned by wild creatures. The value it offered Kess came before anything else.

And she could do as she said and be a good master to it. She'd at least treat it far better than anyone else who got their hands on it. Maybe she wouldn't even have to tame it.

She could be good to the creature and still get what she wanted from it in return.

Kess could buy a whole hatchery of her own with even a fraction of Dracuni's blood. She could buy an entire dragon army.

When Kess arrived at the mammoth stone doors of the exit, she smirked at the carved unicorns adorning the stone. She shot a glare at the guards, and they hastily pressed the mechanism.

Stone ground against stone, and the smoky chill of aboveground air blew in. Kess rode out into the darkening night, as determination set inside her like molten steel plunged into water.

She would find Dracuni.

Then nothing would be out of reach. She could have anything and everything she ever wanted.

And if all it cost to get that was killing Pony ... she wouldn't hesitate again.

Chapter Twenty-Nine

Riony dropped her head back and it bounced on the broken tiles of the Alderkin shrine floor. "If somebody can confirm we have at least a few minutes before the next thing tries to kill us, that would be wonderful. My heart is ready to give up on me."

Dracuni nuzzled up at her side, sniffing at the blood dripping from the thin knife jutting out of her arm. She rumbled gently, low in her throat. ***Much bad hurt.***

"Yeah. Much bad hurt," Riony agreed.

Lyrrin stood above them, staring at the geode gateway, still deactivated. "I don't think they are coming through. They don't know how to work it. I think we're okay. Except for Benjin."

Groaning, Riony rolled to one side, then crawled up to her feet.

Aishena kneeled across the small space, beneath where a tumbled down wall and ceiling let moonlight in from above, the damaged ruin strangely familiar. She had Benjin in her lap and was staring down at him with motionless grief.

"It's his neck. It's broken, swollen. He's barely … I can't tell if he's breathing." She looked up at Riony, and although her face was still, her cheeks were streaked and shining. "Lyrrin said you had silvernix. She said you can help him."

Riony turned on Lyrrin. "You told her *what?*"

"Only … not everything … only that you could help. We have to help him, don't we?" Lyrrin fidgeted her hands, free from their gloves.

Secrets were spilling as freely as the blood had.

"How? How am I supposed to help? Without them knowing? And it's not even up to me." Riony took a stumbling limp closer to Aishena and her brother, hoping there would be some other way to handle this problem.

Oh, he looks really bad.

"What do you mean it's not up to you? Who is it up to?" Aishena asked.

Riony bent at the waist, groaning gruffly. She pressed fisted hands against her temples. This was all wrong; this was all too much. "Sparks!"

She hated this. She hated that she held the knowledge that could save Benjin's life, and she wanted to, so badly. But doing so meant trusting everyone here with Dracuni's secret.

A secret that had already been revealed to the most dangerous person possible. *Kess.* Riony seethed at the mere intrusion of the goblin's name into her mind.

That harm was done, and Riony could already feel the repercussions coming to kick her ass from down her path ahead.

But whatever the consequences, she couldn't let Kess live and Aishena's brother die.

Riony crumpled down onto her knees in front of Aishena and Benjin. She stretched her arm out, bringing Dracuni in by her side so the dragonling could see the injured boy.

"I can't help. But Dracuni can. If she wants to."

Aishena frowned, and silent tears rushed from her eyes again. Riony knew she must think her mad and her brother lost.

Hurt? Dracuni nuzzled Benjin's hand with her snout. He didn't respond.

"He is. He won't survive on his own."

I help?

"If you want to. Only if it's okay."

Aishena stared aghast at the one-sided conversation.

"Is she going to help?" Lyrrin asked softly as she joined them.

Dracuni bobbed her head and moved lithely, bending her long neck and bringing a claw up to her horn. There was the slightest scratching sound, harsh in the breathless silence as everyone stared at the creature. Even Niskina's sobbing had stilled at the bizarre tableau before her.

Aishena gasped as the shimmering blood became visible.

The unidragon pressed her bleeding claw to Benjin's hand.

Riony's shoulders slumped. It was done. There was no coming back from this. She remained there, kneeling before them, as Benjin's body flushed with the brightness of starlight.

Aishena held the boy tight as his body twisted and twitched, the healing magic rushing through his failing system, repairing what was broken. Her mouth hung open and dark eyes glinted with the magical glow.

Then Benjin stilled and opened his eyes. When he raised a hand, desperate and seeking Aishena's crying face, she wailed loudly and brought him up into a crushing embrace.

The siblings held each other, crying thick tears of combined relief and loss.

Riony took a shaky breath and wiped her eyes.

"What about you?" Lyrrin asked softly. "You look like a pincushion made out of raw meat."

Riony smirked. "I *feel* like a pincushion made out of raw meat."

She grabbed the narrow hilt of the knife puncturing her arm and pulled. It slurped out, tight from the suction. Riony saved her whimper for when it finally popped free. Staring at the sharpened length of bone, Riony scowled and snapped it in half.

She tossed the pieces into a shadowy corner of the ruins, then adjusted her sitting position to work on the one in her thigh. She hoped she still had a bandage in one of her pouches. Probably contaminated with olm-pool water, but it would have to do. They couldn't go back for other supplies. They had what was on them now and nothing more.

The second dagger dragged through her skin until it was out and Riony discarded it with disdain. Looking at the mangled lower half of her leg and the teeth marks through her boots, Riony figured she'd need more than a few bandages. Maybe one of the other delvers would have something she could use to bind her wounds.

Dracuni returned to her side, blinking lilac eyes as she tried to climb into Riony's lap.

Riony let out a low groan. "Just a moment, little one."

Hurt too?

Riony shrugged. "Nah, it's nothing. I'll be okay."

Dracuni's toothy mouth opened in a scolding warble.

A tear spilled from Riony's eyes. She pressed a hand to Dracuni's cheek and whispered, "I promised I wouldn't ..."

Snorting warm air near Riony's hand, Dracuni pushed her snout against Riony's fingers until she dropped them in her lap. And then the dragonling pressed her claw into it. The tiniest shine of silvernix remained there and absorbed brightly into Riony's palm.

Riony pulled the beautiful creature up into her lap as the ethereal brilliance enveloped them. She let a few hot tears fall against Dracuni's neck as her physical wounds healed, but the ache in her heart remained overwhelming.

"Thank you." She breathed the words near Dracuni's ear.

Aishena watched with pained eyes as the glow around Riony subsided. "I have so many questions."

"Yeah. I thought you might. And I'll get to them. Just ... let's take a moment to recover first."

Niskina slapped a hand against the ground and glared through puffy eyes. "A moment? To recover? We have _lost family_!"

Riony ran a hand into her hair and tugged at the red strands. "I know. I'm sorry."

"We've lost more than our families. We've lost our home," Aishena said flatly. "Again."

Riony looked at where the end of the ancient Alderkin shrine had collapsed, opening to the forest around it. "I don't think we're far away, though."

"We could be anywhere, anywhere in Elundrae. Yoskar said ..." Aishena choked on the words.

"No, I'm pretty sure ..." Riony stood up, bringing Dracuni with her, unwilling to let go of the hatchling that had signs of fatigue catching up to it fast. She stepped out the vine-shrouded doorway and looked around. "Yep. Apple tree. Remains of our fire. This is the shrine we stayed at, just down the hill from the Alderkin depths."

For some reason that made Aishena start crying again.

"If we want to go back, I think we can just use the gateway again. It might work from this side too." Lyrrin closed in on it, pointing to the rune she'd cleared off at the bottom.

"Whoa, no!" Riony said. "I'm not ready to face what might still be on the other side."

"We _can't_ go back," Aishena said. Benjin was squirming and griping in her hug now, but she refused to let him go. "That place, it won't ever be safe again, from _her_."

Riony knew Aishena meant her mother. But it was again Kess's name that stabbed at her heart.

She swallowed away the remaining shreds of fury and tried to think about what was ahead of them now. "Niskina could go back. There's no reason she couldn't go home. We can help her back to one of the entrances."

With a sob, Niskina turned her face toward the ruined stone wall. "I can't go back there."

The grieving young woman closed off again, staring blankly at the ground and coughing through her tears.

Benjin was whispering to his sister within their tight bubble, and she spoke hushed words in return, the only one Riony could make out, over and over, was *sorry*.

The energy of Dracuni's blood still zinged through Riony, but she also felt tired to her marrow.

She lowered herself down, sitting with her back against the doorframe of the shrine. Dracuni drooped, curling up on her lap with a snuffle.

Riony reached an arm out, and Lyrrin took the hint and hurried into it.

"How are you holding up? Today was ... intense doesn't quite capture it. Unreasonably hectic? Catastrophically tragic? Just plain shitty?"

Lyrrin coughed a small laugh. "You really can't stop with the jokes."

"Who said I was joking? Those were all fair descriptions. And I do want to know how you're feeling."

"I cried already. I'll probably cry again." Lyrrin took Riony's hand in hers, tugging on it so that arm that looped around her pulled tighter.

"That's okay. Cry as much as you need to."

"But I also feel good because I still have you and Dracuni." Lyrrin frowned over her small smile. "But also bad that I feel good when the others lost more. And ..."

"What is it?" Riony prompted.

"I left Sir Butterfur behind." Lyrrin's tears came again. She pressed her head into Riony's shoulder, thankfully now free from daggers or holes caused by daggers.

"That little furry menace? He'll be fine. The caves are his playground, and I'm sure he'll miss you, but he'll survive without us."

Lyrrin made a sad noise and buried her face farther.

"And you know what? He was how I found my way back to you. Or at least, most of the way, until you found me. You were so clever to send him after me. Sparks, I wouldn't have survived today without you. I'm so happy we're still together too."

Lyrrin's small body shook for a moment, then the sobbing slowed. Riony rested her head against her sister's.

"Riony?" Lyrrin's voice was small and hesitant.

"Yeah?"

"Did ... did my mother have hands like mine?"

"No. Why?"

"Never mind."

Riony's eyebrows twisted, but she didn't question her sister further.

She didn't have anything else to offer either. She hadn't had the chance to question Kess more about the guest who'd given birth at Heithorn estate to find out anything more about Lyrrin's mother's identity. She wished she could give the kid more answers.

Not that I could have trusted a word that came out of that horrible goblin's mouth anyway.

The ghost of Kess's weight on her back made her twitch. She shouldn't have gone back into that revenant-filled cavern. She should have left Kess to die, the same way Kess had done to her.

Riony grasped the muzzle tied to her belt, tearing through the soaked leather straps. She scrunched it in her fist, then threw it into a shadowed corner to join the knives.

Her throat burned dry from the embers of her fury. And from the utter shame that she had, for even a moment, thought Kess could act on something other than selfishness. And how there was part of Riony that bruisingly wanted that to happen.

Riony rubbed her knuckles over the middle of her chest, as though trying to massage the ache beneath her ribs. Everything felt broken. Everyone felt broken. Her, Aishena, Niskina, the kids.

Could she trust these crushed souls with Dracuni's secret? Could she even trust them to keep themselves in one piece in the dangerous aboveground life they'd been thrust into?

Maybe not, but Riony would do her best to keep them all alive.

They'd all lost too much. She didn't want to lose anyone else.

Except maybe Kess. That was one life she was ready to strike off.

The zealous greed in the wolf-rider's eyes scared Riony. If she'd been a threat to them before for wanting a baby dragon, what would she do now that she truly knew what Dracuni was?

Did she just hear a wolf howl? Or did she imagine it?

A shiver rattled her bones. "I'm not even sure if we can stay here overnight."

She was met with silence and sobs.

Riony looked at the ruined and crumpled faces around her. "I mean ... it's probably okay. One night. There might even be a couple of apples left for us. We can move on tomorrow, hit up what remains of that slavers' camp, see what we can salvage from there."

Aishena turned her chin up, as though expecting orders. "And then?"

"Then ... we take it day by day. We find a new home. We will."

Lyrrin cuddled close to Riony's side. Dracuni snuffled a soft snore, head on her lap. Everybody else—Aishena, Niskina, Benjin—looked to Riony with worn, anguished expressions.

"There must be somewhere out there that can be safe for us. For all of us, together."

For those of us who remain.

RISE OF THE DRAGON SWORN

SELINA A FENECH

BOOK THREE OF THE
SHADOW
DRAGON SAGA

Chapter One

Riony had thought the most perilous thing about living aboveground again would be the ravenous undead or the threat of Kess and Lady Hjelzahn hunting them or being caught up in indiscriminate burnings of dragonfire or attacks by ruthless lowlifes and slavers.

She never thought it would be Niskina's grief.

Although Riony had never imagined she would be traveling aboveground with Niskina and the two remaining Hjelzahn siblings in tow, all still grieving in their own ways. With Riony responsible for them all.

This was the third small sanctuary of life they had come across in the few weeks since leaving the undercity and the roughest of them all. Despite the relief of finding other humans to trade with for desperately needed supplies, they were in the locality equivalent of a rusty bear trap.

Riony's eyes darted in each direction, warily checking every ramshackle building and equally ramshackle inhabitant around her. Her fingers twitched, ready to draw the huge crystal sword strapped to her back. Aishena walked close beside her, her younger brother wedged between the two women.

"Where the stars did Niskina go? She was supposed to wait around the corner with the kids while we traded with that mockery of human sentience back there. Who skinned us for far more than we owed," Riony grumbled to Aishena while scanning down the dry dirt street for a sign of the other young woman.

Aishena's eyes remained on Benjin, as though if she could only stare at him long enough and hard enough, she could protect him from all harm.

She reached for Benjin's face, and he scowled and pulled back. Her voice was more worried than scolding as she said, "And you were supposed to be waiting with Lyrrin and Dracuni and Niskina, all out of sight and safe."

Riony looked toward where Lyrrin was keeping Dracuni distracted and hidden behind the broken walls of a crumbled building a couple of houses down. She couldn't see her sister or the growing hatchling, but at least that meant any eyes on the street wouldn't see them either. Still, she knew they were safe.

Catch. Catch good! Dracuni's cheerful narration of her game with Lyrrin was a constant, reassuring presence in Riony's mind.

The surrounding shambles might have once been a pretty village, but only three buildings remained intact, their walls blackened by fire. A few grizzly men, laden with scrappy, chipped weapons, sat leaning against a wall, gambling with dice. Despite their apparent engagement in their game, all eyes were on the newcomers.

"I followed Niskina to try to stop her. She went in there. Also, we're not just kids, and we don't need a babysitter." Benjin pointed to the largest building, a two-story structure of stone from which the sounds of rowdy carousing emerged, even though it was barely midday.

Riony turned her face up to the smoky sky and said a silent prayer. "Every time. Every sparking time."

If there was alcohol or a man anywhere within a dragon's flight, Niskina would find them and end up there, drowning her sorrows in both. Riony tried to be compassionate, but Niskina's behavior added exciting new risks to any run-ins with fellow humans, and Riony was feeling risked out.

"I didn't want to go in *there* after her," Benjin said.

"Smart choice." Riony juggled the ragged sack of food, waterskins, twine, and tools that she'd just traded for, eating up the last of the gold sovs that Aishena had had in her pockets when they'd left their home for good.

Aishena hadn't said a word of protest about paying for everything. She had been so fast to follow Riony's orders and suggestions lately that Riony had become scared of how that power might corrupt her.

The men who were gambling stood quickly, making Riony twitch. Her eyes locked on them and theirs on her. She could see them sizing up her and the sword she carried, and she lifted her chin to them in a dare to try her.

They moved past, swaggering into the crude tavern, leaving Riony and her companions alone on the street.

"Aish, would you go in there and drag Niskina out before she drinks away everything we own or gets into some other trouble?"

Aishena straightened as though at attention and nodded once.

"That wasn't an order. If you want …"

The silver-haired young woman had already turned and slinked away toward the tavern.

"I'll look after the kids then, I guess," Riony muttered.

"We don't need looking after." Benjin lifted his chin and extended himself to his full not-even-teenaged-yet height.

"Do you want to go back with the other … *sss*." Riony caught herself before using the word *kids* again.

Benjin still scowled at her. "What did you get from the trader? You should have let me come and haggle, since you did so badly at it."

He's sounding more and more like his brother every day. Hooray.

Riony raised her eyebrows at the boy. His short-cropped pale hair had grown into a thicker mat since leaving the undercity, sparkling in the grayed out light. The cool brown of his skin had warmed in their few weeks under the sun, even with its light filtering through ashy skies.

Riony's own skin was transforming too, from the ashy wan it had taken underground to a glowing sienna. Only Lyrrin seemed unaffected by their days aboveground, her pale tones denying the sun's influence.

"I got everything on our list except fishhooks, which they didn't have, and I did just fine with the bargain, thanks. This isn't the same as doing a trade at Curtain Market, little delver. Getting out of a trade with one of these lowlife overworld smugglers alive is the deal you aim for, and you should be grateful for anything else."

Every moment they lingered left Riony antsy. The sour scent of stewing meat emerged from a low building with half its walls lying on the ground in piles of loose stone, a makeshift stable and kitchen in one. Riony didn't want to know what they were cooking. She also planned to ignore any curiosity about the subject when eating the dried meat they had traded for.

Benjin grumbled, "Like you're an expert on living aboveground."

"Lived my whole life aboveground until two years ago, and not locked away behind dragonkeep walls like some."

Benjin flinched almost imperceptibly, and Riony regretted mentioning anything that related to his family and the past that had led him here.

"Weren't you kept by the Heithorns under their protection, too?" Benjin jabbed back. Aishena must have been telling him things.

It was Riony's turn to flinch. Anger rose like a boiling tide in her, and she willed it away. Her anger was all for Kess—not for Benjin. "Not since Lyrrin was born. We were on our own after that, for years, until we found somewhere relatively safe." *Until it wasn't safe either.*

Benjin harrumphed and reached for the sack, his face still a picture of disapproval. "Let me see what you got."

Riony handed it over with a sigh.

He riffled through, pulling out some of the dried meat and two of the waterskins and transferring them into his bags. He didn't take more than what would be his and Aishena's share, so Riony didn't argue.

They were still salvaging together enough supplies for survival on the run. They had been thrust out of the undercity without notice, with only what they'd had on their person. Riony, Niskina, and Aishena had their delving tools and armor—although Riony's chest armor had been left on Kess and lost.

Aishena had been disarmed of almost all her athames during her fight with her mother, but Lyrrin had sneakily picked up a couple of the dropped weapons amongst the chaos and returned them to Aishena afterward—something Aishena seemed very grateful for.

The twin blades taken from Lady Hjelzahn remained with Aishena too, although she refused to acknowledge or use them.

Aishena, in return, gave Lyrrin her spare glow stone. Lyrrin added it to her treasures with glee, along with the few random crystals Riony had snatched from the Alderkin warrior's tomb when she'd taken her sword.

She had a seeing stone like the one on Yoskar's staff, a small burn crucible, two matching stones that Lyrrin hadn't worked out the function of yet, and a crystal with a ten-stroke rune she couldn't activate, no matter the hours she'd been spending trying to crack the sequence.

After one night at the first shrine, they had moved on to the ruins of the slavers' camp to salvage what they could.

There wasn't much left amongst the charcoal remains—almost everything flammable was gone—but they had found one crate that had escaped the dragonfire. Within it, a few blankets, which were treated as a treasure more precious than silvernix after a chilly night on the hard ground with nothing soft for comfort.

Lyrrin had also found a sling, and Niskina a metal-handled poleaxe. Riony tried to find some armor to replace her missing delver vest, but although lots of metal pieces remained, the leather straps were burned away. She took a couple of bracers anyway and had been working on drying leather to repair them as they traveled on.

They'd been heading west since.

Despite having spent time in this ruined aboveground world before, Riony had to admit it felt far worse now than it did then. At least then she'd had her parents with her.

Along the dusty road that cut through the ruins, shards of charred bone scattered the ground. The remains of revenants.

There were no high stone walls around this settlement as there were with the dragonkeeps, bringing safety to the population and keeping the revs out. Only a few scrounged together barricades huddled around each of the standing buildings themselves, the windows blocked and barred.

But even settlements with walls weren't always safe. Riony knew that too well.

During the weeks between using the strange Alderkin gateway to flee from the murderous Hjelzahn mother, Riony and her friends had several brushes with revs themselves. But no more of the strange ashy ones.

Between Riony's beloved sword, Aishena's athames, and Yoskar's crystal-studded staff—now Benjin's—the odd lone rev was no longer much of a threat to them as long as it stayed dead.

Up the roadway, through the haze of old smoke and kicked-up dust, a cart rattled toward them.

It was drawn by a scrawny goat and led by a woman whose face was marred with dirt settled into worried wrinkles. Three other people rode behind, perched between bundled baggage.

The woman's eyes softened in relief as she brought the cart to a stop within a safe distance of Riony and Benjin.

"See? There are other children here," she called behind to her companions.

One of the three blanket-shrouded figures on the cart turned to look, revealing a small eager face. What should have been the puffy cheeks of youth were hollowed and the sockets of their eyes dark. Any visual signs of gender were lost to the ravages of hunger.

Riony's heart contracted as she moved forward, only a few steps separating them. "No, there aren't other children here. We're only passing through, as you should be too. This isn't a settlement for families. This is a hive of hornets lured to nest by a sweet drink."

As though on cue, a rousing chorus went up from within the makeshift tavern. What was taking Aishena so long?

A shaggy man emerged from the kitchen-stables and leaned against the doorframe, picking his nails. His keen gaze scraped over every inch of the cart and what it carried. Riony saw what he saw. No weapons in sight.

"You need to keep moving," Riony told the woman in a low voice.

"Is there food here?" the woman asked, ignoring Riony's suggestion. "We had to leave Tarrickeep. Any Rolanian not serving a dragonlord is getting forced out. I thought another keep would take us, but … We've been traveling, trying to find anything …"

Riony knew hunger. She knew that when forced to choose between starvation and danger, safety could be dismissed over the chance to eat.

Riony reached over to Benjin and took back the sack, pulling from it three wrapped bundles of food. "Take this. Keep moving. There's a safe refuge below ground in the Eishowl Peaks. Try to get there."

Riony gave them hasty directions to the undercity as Benjin glared at her.

"We need that food," Benjin snapped.

"You've got yours. I'll sort something else out."

The woman's eyes turned red as she took the offering and handed it over to the boney arms reaching from the cart. She looked so very tired as she muttered her thanks. Her gaze flickered over Riony's sword and physique.

"Are you … employable? For protection? Can you take us to this underground place safely?"

"I'm immensely flattered you think I'm some kind of hired muscle, but—"

"We can pay." Her voice was abrupt, desperate. She fumbled around the belt on her skirts and pulled a heavy coin pouch into view.

Riony slapped her hands onto it and hissed. "Careful! You want to get robbed?"

Riony checked the man who'd been watching and stepped to place herself between him and his view of the woman.

"But you … you seem …" She gestured to the food Riony had given them as explanation.

"Doesn't matter what I seem like. Everybody is looking after themselves out here. Don't forget that. And I've got enough to deal with looking after my own. I'm sorry." Not to mention that they couldn't be traveling with strangers—not without revealing Dracuni.

The unidragon had gone quiet, as though sensing Riony's tension.

In a voice Riony hoped was loud enough for her and Lyrrin to hear, she said, "It's okay." And then in a quiet, growling rasp to the woman, she continued, "But you have to keep moving. *Now.*"

The woman recoiled and her mouth curled as though to protest. But then she nodded and tugged the goat's leash, and the small cart rolled into motion again. Their figures grew smaller and smaller until they turned the corner behind a pile of rubble, out of sight.

The shaggy man at the stables moved as though to follow the family, but after a quelling glare from Riony he returned to loitering in the doorway. Benjin complained about the lost rations, and Dracuni returned to her game with Lyrrin.

Nobody but Riony could hear the unidragon's words, but still Dracuni chatted away happily as though they could.

Throw. Throw. Too high!

The door to the tavern burst open, and Aishena barged out, dragging Niskina behind her and bringing a swell of laughter and the scent of stale alcohol onto the street. Niskina stumbled as she was pulled down the building steps.

No wonder they'd taken so long. Riony should have known that a polite mention that it was time to leave wouldn't be enough to separate Niskina from her drink.

They arrived in front of Riony, and Niskina huffed, snatching her arm free. She tossed her tumble of chestnut hair from a face that was already reddening with alcohol and pouting fiercely.

Riony angled to get herself in line with Niskina's roaming, hazy eyes. "Niskina, with all kindness, could you please try not to drink dry every settlement we pass through within minutes of arriving?"

"Oh, they still had plenty." Niskina waved a floppy hand dismissively, as though that were the core of the problem.

Riony knew she was hurting. The death of her father was still so recent, but her behavior was a concern. Riony had worried at first that the feisty young woman might sell Dracuni out in her drunken state or in trade to fulfill some desire. But she, and the others, had all kept that secret close. So far.

A couple of men had gathered at the door of the tavern, pleading and jeering for Niskina to return to them. She grinned, turning back, and Aishena spun her around away from them again.

With a longing look over her shoulder, Niskina moaned, "Come on. Can't we just stay here one night? Or two?"

Aishena said coldly, "We're not risking all our lives so you can bed that lot."

Following the conversation, Benjin's eyes widened and his cheeks went the same color as Niskina's.

"But they're sooo nice," Niskina slurred.

Riony raised her eyebrows. "Them? They aren't even men. They're red flags sewn together into creepy man-shaped puppets."

"So what? What does it matter what they are or what I do?"

"Because we need to move on."

"Why? Where are we even going, anyway? Move on, move on, that's all you keep saying. What's the point? Move on *to where*?" Niskina glared, waiting for the answer.

Aishena and Benjin also turned, looking to Riony for answers.

Riony still wasn't used to that. Frankly, it unnerved her, considering how much lower in the pecking order she'd felt in the past. But she hadn't lost her father or brother in the escape from the depths. She'd continue to take the lead while the others managed their grief.

Not that she had any answers.

She ventured her thoughts out loud. "There were other Alderkin depths around Elundrae. Maybe—"

"All destroyed in the war, from reports I've seen," Aishena said. "At least all the entry levels completely collapsed."

"What about getting into lower levels?"

Benjin said, "How would we get into them?"

"They might have magical gateways too, like the one we found."

"The one we found only went between it and the shrine we'd been to before," Aishena said. "That might be it, for all we know."

Riony wasn't sure about that. The oval geode structures existed in shrines all over the land. They must act as gateways too. But Aishena was right that there seemed to be no signs of other gateways being functional. At least, not *yet*.

The map Aishena had taken from the Alderkin chambers showed there was one nearby this settlement that Riony hoped to go to, to test some theories.

Niskina sighed a puff of spirits-scented air. "No way we can waltz up to a dragonkeep or some dragonlord-ruled estate with the bounty on you two."

Aishena paled.

"That's not our fault," Benjin growled.

"We couldn't do that anyway. Not with Dracuni," Riony added gently.

Benjin still turned on her, as though everything was her fault. "You said you lived for years up here, that you found somewhere safe. What about that place?"

Riony's throat dried up. "I said *relatively* safe."

"Relatively is still better than not at all, which is why my vote is still to stay right here." Niskina eyed the tavern again.

"Where was it? Could we go there?" Aishena asked over Niskina.

Riony scrunched a hand into her red hair, grimacing. "It was a secluded village in an abandoned strip mine. The town leaders figured that all the earth had been removed, so it should have been safe from the shadowdragon raising any revs there."

"That does make some sense," Benjin said.

"Yeah, and we all thought we were safe because the shadowdragon never came, and we thought it never came because there was nothing there for it to awaken. But then it did come, and there were still bones that answered its call." Riony's heart raced and her breath came quickly.

She swallowed the feelings down. "Not many people escaped alive. I don't even know ... It's probably abandoned."

"We should go there, then," Benjin said firmly, sounding so much like Yoskar that Riony jolted.

"I just said it wasn't safe after all."

"Back then. But if the shadowdragon raised everything already, and that was a couple of years ago, then there mightn't be any revs left there now. And if it is still abandoned, even better. We can set up a hideout there." Benjin's eyes glimmered as he presented his plan.

"I don't —"

"Aish, what do you think?" Benjin turned to his sister for backup.

"There could still be revenants, plus the bodies of the population ..."

Riony's breath juddered to a halt, and she had to force her lungs to work again.

Benjin scoffed. "Tell them we should go there."

"We should go there," Aishena repeated.

Across the road, the man remained at the doorway to the kitchen-stables, watching their debate with narrowed eyes. Urgent unease trickled like icy water through Riony.

"Fine, we can ... head in that direction." Better than continuing west, anyway, which would lead them toward Heithorn estate. They just had to aim farther south instead. Still, the idea of coming anywhere near either location left Riony feeling cold.

Dracuni had grown quiet again. A sensation of worry came from the unidragon into Riony's mind, washing over her own feelings.

Hurt? Scared? Dracuni inquired.

Whatever the bond between them, Riony hadn't been able to get Dracuni to hear her thoughts as she heard Dracuni's, but the hatchling seemed to sense her emotions well enough, which Riony would have preferred not to share.

She gritted her teeth and breathed through her nose and put a smile on. "It's fine. Still, it's a long way to go. And I want to stop at that shrine nearby next."

She'd been itching to test out her theory about the Alderkin shrines since the morning after they had fled the undercity. She'd woken up to find that the cutting athame, used up the day before, was working again. Just as it had recharged during their journey to save Lyrrin and Benjin from the slavers.

It has to be the shrine recharging it somehow.

The bigger question was whether it was only that shrine. One of Benjin's glow stones had run out of charge during their weeks aboveground, so they could test that.

"The shrine isn't far, right? What if you all go and do that while I head back inside?" Niskina skipped a few steps away, out of Aishena's reach.

Riony ran to block her path, holding her arms wide like a barricade. "Nope, sorry, you've lost your do-things-alone privileges."

"Come on, Ri. I just want to have a bit of fun." Niskina slapped Riony's hand away, trying to step past.

Her sheer level of defiance made Riony grateful for Lyrrin's cheery contrariness. Sure, Niskina was hurting, but she was putting herself and the rest of them at risk.

"I don't know if you even care if you live or die right now, but I do, and I can't let you go back in there." Riony grabbed Niskina by the shoulders, stilling her.

Niskina's eyes washed over, glossy with tears. "If you really cared, you'd stop trying to tell me what to do with my life. Let me through and you can go and be boring somewhere else."

Anger flared in Riony, defeating her attempts at patience. "You're killing me here!"

Kill? Bad hurt? Dracuni's anxious call flooded Riony, then a cry from Lyrrin came from their hiding place.

Riony was ready to run for them when she saw Dracuni racing toward her.

"Come back!" Lyrrin whisper-yelled from behind the bounding unidragon.

Dracuni had grown enough in the weeks aboveground that she could no longer be carried. Not by Lyrrin, anyway. She was now the size of a large dog, and even stronger. If Dracuni wanted to go somewhere, it was hard to stop her.

Dracuni's frantic run slowed as she approached Riony, lilac eyes blinking. Her head tilted, horn shimmering in the glary light. *Not hurt?*

Riony groaned. "I was exaggerating!"

Dracuni didn't have any grasp on hyperbole or sarcasm though, and now there she was, standing right in the middle of the dusty street.

The tavern door had closed again, but the man at the stables remained. He straightened up, moving a couple of steps closer as he sucked air through his teeth. "Is that a dragonling you've got there? What is that weird thing?"

"It's your ass on a plate if you keep asking questions," Riony shot back at him with a leveled glare, daring him to try anything.

Lyrrin caught up after Dracuni. Her face crumpled. "I'm sorry. She just ran out."

Riony half nodded a response, but she kept her gaze locked on the man. He rubbed at his patchy beard, and Riony could see the calculations working through his head as his eyes narrowed and nose twitched.

Ownership of any kind of dragon was valuable.

Only three young women and two children stood between him and that value.

But one of them had a very, very big sword.

The man's chances of taking Dracuni depended upon whether he was willing to split that value with others or not.

As he lifted his chin and opened his mouth, turning as though to call for backup, Riony realized he'd decided. She reached for the buckles that strapped her sword to her back. "Get ready to run."

But before a sound emerged from the man's throat, something flew into it. It jabbed through the flesh, jutting out, bright white against the flush of blood that emerged around it. A slim dagger, carved from bone.

The man dropped.

Dracuni skittered behind Riony, who spun on the spot, looking for the source of that dagger, already knowing who she'd see.

A huge gray wolf prowled toward them down the dusty street. Atop Griskin, almost lost behind the thickness of his fur, rode Kess, more daggers already in her grasp.

"Pony," she drawled, her lips twisted in a sly grin. "Were you really about to let somebody else steal what is mine?"

CHAPTER TWO

S he found us.

Fury ignited inside Riony, aching in her chest at the sight of the traitorous goblin. The audacity of Kess to show her face again after turning on them, let alone continue to hunt them, was something else.

Dracuni peered out at Kess from between Riony's legs. ***Is friend?***

"Her? No. She isn't our friend," Riony muttered back.

But I helped?

"I know. I'm sorry. You can't trust her."

A wave of deep sadness and confusion channeled from the unidragon and she crouched lower behind Riony.

Riony had risked her own life, and Dracuni's, to save Kess from the revenant conglomerate. Dracuni had given her blood to save Kess. And Kess had betrayed them.

Riony still didn't know what had made her run back into that cavern.

She wished she hadn't. She should have just continued on and never seen Kess again, then maybe she could have helped the others beat Lady Hjelzahn. Maybe Brishan wouldn't have died. Maybe they'd all still be delvers, together, living safely underground.

But she had gone back for Kess.

Somewhere, in the depths of her mind, the way Kess had screamed her name—her *name*, not Pony or some other insult—still echoed, raising goosebumps over her skin.

It had felt as though Riony had seen Kess with everything stripped away by fear, and in that moment, Kess had cried out *her name*.

And then went right back to being an irredeemable, selfish assface directly afterward.

And she was still wearing Riony's delver armor!

Rude.

"When you say that guy was going to steal what's yours, did you mean a violent death at the end of my sword?" Riony questioned.

"Oh, stop your ridiculous posturing. Just hand over the dragonling, and I'll even let you and your ..." Kess looked over the rest of them—two defiant children, Niskina wavering on her feet, Aishena wavering in indecision. "Wow. Maybe I shouldn't let you all go. Seems like it would be a mercy to put this lot down."

"Sounds like something your brother would say." Riony's hand moved toward her sword.

Kess raised a dagger in warning. "Except I'm trying to do the right thing. Let me take Dracuni. You really think you and this lot can keep the creature safe? Look at you! You almost just let that scumbag call every lowlife here to see what you have, and what then? What happens when they find out what she is?"

"As though she'd be safe with you with a stake through her brain! You're outnumbered,

Kess. You can't have her. Either you leave or you die, here and now. Either way, sounds like a good time to me."

"You want to take her on?" Aishena whispered from her side.

Riony nodded. "We can beat her and the wolf. I'm sure of it."

"But Niskina is ... and the kids ... Kess dropped that man with one hit." Aishena cast worried eyes over the rest of them.

She had a point, but Riony and Aishena together should be able to win this. And every part of her wanted to fight. "We take Kess out now, and that's one less thing we have to worry about hunting us. We're doing this."

Doubt flickered in Aishena's eyes but she nodded anyway.

"You're really going to try to *kill* her?" Lyrrin stared at Riony, her bright-blue eyes wide, sparkling under the shadow of her hood. "Right here? And what about Griskin? You're not going to kill the poor pup too, are you?"

Riony huffed out a grunt. None of this was *ideal*. But what else could she do? "We have to do this. *I* have to do this."

Kess watched with a shrewd, amused expression, toying with her throwing knife. "You really do want me dead, don't you? And how many of your little group here are you willing to lose before you get to me? Hand over the creature, or you're about to find out."

Before Riony could tell Kess she was about to find out what having a fist down her throat felt like, the door to the tavern swung open, and two men stumbled out.

"Told you she's still here," a tall man with an eyepatch said, then his gaze landed on the dead body.

Riony pointed at Kess. "It was her. She did it."

The second man, wearing an impressive array of mismatched armor and age-worn weapons, glared at Kess and Riony and every newcomer standing over the body of someone that might have been a friend to him, or at least some kind of shady acquaintance.

"You killed Aldo." Then he yelled into the tavern, louder again, "Oi! These churls killed Aldo!"

"Not *Aldo*!" More than a few voices wailed back from inside.

Okay, maybe the thugs are closer friends than I gave them credit for.

There was a scuffle of movement from within the building.

Kess stared at Riony, and Riony stared back.

Riony's feet cramped with the tension of wanting to spring forward. Her arms burned with the desire to swing. Her teeth ground against each other with the swirl of emotions driving her to fight, fight, fight, to inflict pain upon Kess to match the hurt of her betrayal.

But more men spilled out, drawn by the call.

Riony ground out her command. "Run. To the shrine. Go!"

Aishena was the first to move, snatching Benjin by the arm and dragging him with her. "This way!"

Niskina broke into a dash after them, herding Lyrrin and Dracuni in front of her. The unidragon bounded in a glittering streak along the dusty road and around the side of the kitchen-stables. She could move fast now. Riony hoped it would be fast enough.

The tavern emptied, the rough men and women rushing out onto the street between Riony and Kess, yelling and drawing weapons.

After sending one final screw-you glare at Kess, Riony ran too.

The side street was in even worse repair than the rubble of the main road, with dead bushes and tumbleweeds tangling the way. Riony leaped and dodged around them.

Behind her, there was the growl of a wolf, the clink of metal, and the sound of one body falling, then another. More yelling, harsh and incensed, was followed by the pounding of feet.

Maybe the community of smugglers, thieves, and slavers would finish Kess off for them. That idea didn't bring Riony the happiness she'd hoped for.

She was even less pleased when she felt the sharp chink of a thrown dagger as it hit her sword, right near the back of her neck.

She didn't need to risk a glance behind her to know Kess was in pursuit.

Griskin was fast, but there was a score of pursuers after Kess as well, harrying her as she tried to reach her target.

Riony reached the edge of the ruined village, running right over the flattened remains of a cottage toward the tangle of burned forest ahead. She'd caught up with Lyrrin now, the others all farther away.

As though challenged by Riony's presence, the small girl put on another burst of speed, sprinting ahead again. They scrambled through an overgrown field then into the sparse woods.

A sear of pain along her upper arm made Riony catch her breath as another dagger sliced along it. Even with half a town chasing them, Kess wasn't letting up.

"Are you seriously still throwing knives at me right now?" she yelled back.

"This is your fault, Pony! You should have given me Dracuni!" There was a cry and a stumble, and a crossbow bolt whizzed past Riony's head. She spared a second to glance back, seeing the mass of people chasing them through the blackened trees.

Sparks! The shrine better be there, and it better work!

The ground sloped down, forming a small gorge, and up ahead, Riony saw a standing stone marking the wide perimeter of the shrine.

She skidded down the slope to where a trickle of a creek ran toward the Alderkin ruins, where the main structure sat upon a mound amid the tiny flow of water.

Benjin and Aishena reached it first, still far ahead of the others. They ran into the small temple of crystalline stone, and a few seconds later, Aishena yelled out, "It's not working! It's not activating!"

"Try it again!" Riony yelled back.

She bit her lip as she ran. If the gateway wasn't working, they were running into a dead end. They could try to fight back from within the cover of the shrine, but they were hugely outnumbered, and who knew which side Kess would fall on.

No wait, I do know. Her own side.

Griskin let out another vicious growl, and a man cried out. Riony winced. She knew what a bite from that beast felt like. Kess could also still be heard, hurling insults along with her knives.

Between Riony and Lyrrin, and the shrine farther ahead, Niskina had stumbled, and Dracuni was circling around her in an anxious trot.

Friend get up?

"Keep running!" Riony yelled back, but Dracuni remained by Niskina as she rolled forward and into a sitting position, her shoulders shaking.

"Still nothing!" Aishena called out through the shrine doorway.

Okay. Maybe we're fighting our way out of this.

Riony reached Niskina and grabbed her, dragging her up and into a sprint again.

The huffing breath of the wolf sounded right behind them.

"Eyes!" Lyrrin cried, swinging her sling about in one hand.

Riony turned away from it, squinting her eyes closed as much as she dared while still running.

"You aren't getting us with that again!" Kess yelled.

There was the sound of skidding leaves and stones behind them as Lyrrin's altered glow stone burst into a flash of blinding light. It was only a sliver of the larger crystal, cut down for smaller pieces in Lyrrin's experimentations.

The light it produced wasn't nearly as strong as ones she'd used before, but it was enough to make Kess stop for a moment to avoid it.

That gave Riony, Lyrrin, Niskina, and Dracuni the advantage they needed to break ahead of her again.

Dracuni moved the fastest, splashing through the trickling puddles and over smoothed rocks. The other three were right behind as they ran through the circle of standing stones, and a shiver of energy raised the hairs on Riony's neck.

"Try the gate again!" she yelled as she skidded to a stop at the shrine doorway.

Benjin was crouched at the base of the massive slice of jagged geode, and his fingers moved swiftly, tracing the rune there in the way Lyrrin had shown them all.

Symbols on the side of the crystal gateway brightened with the glow of magic. Benjin gasped loudly, "There's two! Two symbols have lit up!"

"Just pick one! We need to get out of here, now!" Riony turned her back on the approaching pursuers just in time for her crystal sword to shield her from another crossbow bolt.

"One of them is the same symbol as before," Lyrrin said, rushing in beside Benjin.

"Then do that one!" Riony looked back, as Kess and Griskin bounded toward them ahead of the army of Aldo's friends.

The circle of standing stones at the other shrine had kept a revenant out, and for a moment Riony hoped it would keep out all evil, heartless things. Unfortunately, Kess passed straight through.

A sparkling glow filled the shrine as the gateway activated, showing another place through the rippling air within it.

Benjin stood up straight beside Riony, Yoskar's staff held before him, the burn rune activated. "You all go through. I'll hold them off."

"I don't think so," Riony said, turning and giving him a push toward Aishena.

A knife plinked again off the wide sword shielding Riony's back, then Benjin yelped as it ricocheted into him, scratching across his cheek.

Aishena grabbed him bodily, and they were the first through the gateway.

Riony's head swiveled, watching her friends, her pursuers, her friends again.

Lyrrin went through with Dracuni. Niskina stumbled after. Griskin was within pouncing distance. Riony dove headfirst through the swirling magic.

She bit the dirt on the other side, rolling and yelling, "Close it!"

Lyrrin deactivated the portal.

For a long moment, the only sound was heavy breathing as they all drew breath back into overworked lungs.

Then Benjin turned a circle, scowling. "This is the shrine near the undercity. We're right back where we started again!"

Riony blinked at her surroundings, wiping dirt off her face. He was right.

"It was the same symbol as we used before, so it makes sense it's taken us to the same place." Lyrrin ran her fingers over the markings around the side of the geode slice.

There were dozens of symbols around it, some of them cracked.

With a dull voice, Niskina asked, "Do you think the other one was the gateway in the depths?"

"Maybe. Either way, we can't go back there." Riony looked at how big Dracuni was getting. There'd be no way to keep her hidden in the undercity for much longer. And if Aishena and Benjin returned, their mother would no doubt get news of it quickly enough. "I mean, Niskina could probably go back if she wanted."

"No. I don't want to see that place ever again." Niskina moved from a sitting position onto her hands and knees, crawled into the corner, and promptly vomited.

"You got hurt!" Aishena reached for Benjin's face and the fine red line marking his brown cheek.

"I'm fine. It's nothing."

"You can't go trying to take on enemies like that. You've got to keep yourself safe." Aishena turned to Riony. "Can we fix this? Can Dracuni heal him?"

Dracuni sniffed at the air, standing up on hind legs and looking at the cut.

Hurt. Should help?

"No, this isn't bad hurt." Riony winced as she leaned on her cut arm to bring herself upright.

Help you too? Dracuni tossed her chin upward at Riony.

"She seems to be happy to help," Aishena said.

"No! We're not bleeding her every time one of us gets a little scratch! Does that really sound okay to you?"

Aishena's eyes narrowed, and for a moment, Riony actually hoped for the return of the caustic, headstrong woman who seemed so absent now.

"I'm really fine," Benjin repeated, tugging Aishena's hand and making her look at him. "We aren't using Dracuni like that."

"Here." Riony got to her feet, rummaging in the pouches on her belt where she'd been collecting herbs on their travels. She handed over some short green sticks. "Squeeze the sap from these and rub it on. It should stop the cut from turning bad."

Lyrrin appeared in front of Riony, hands out for some of the weftweed.

"Did you get hurt too?"

"Nope," Lyrrin said, then went over to Benjin and wiped his cheek with her gloved hands.

Her sister's kind ministrations didn't stop Benjin from glaring at Riony as she dabbed some of the sticky clear sap onto her arm. "We should have run earlier. You and your grudge against Kess are going to get us killed."

"Kess is the one chasing us. I was just trying to stop her." Riony's nose wrinkled at the pungent tang of the sap. "Would I have taken some pleasure in stopping her? That's up for debate."

"I can't believe she found us, that she's still chasing us," Lyrrin grumbled.

"That's Kess for you. Stubborn to her core. And knowing what Dracuni is, what her blood is, well ... Kess wouldn't be the only person who would chase us to the ends of the earth for that." Although it appeared more personal for Kess than simply wanting Dracuni for the value of her silvernix blood.

There was a deep, hurting anger hiding in Kess's expression. That Riony, her ex-slave, was running around with the thing Kess had always wanted and more ... it must be eating Kess alive. Riony was surprised Kess had been as restrained as she was, that Riony wasn't the one lying back on that dusty road with a knife in her throat.

She's never going to stop. I'm going to have to stop her.

The thought of actually ending Kess's life sent an uncontrollable shiver across Riony's shoulders.

She had only really taken one life before, the guard at Lyrrin's birth, and that was in self-defense. Dealing with Kess was a form of self-defense too, but she kept recoiling from the idea.

She knew she could possibly order Aishena to do it, but that wouldn't be fair.

If it's going to happen, it should be by my hand.

"You were really mean to her though," Lyrrin said, pouting toward Riony as she finished dabbing sap on Benjin's cheek.

"I'm sorry, what?"

"The very first thing you said was that you were going to kill her. How is that going to solve anything? If you'd been nicer, maybe we could have talked it through and explained that we really are looking after Dracuni. And maybe she could help us and not try to take her away or tame her. She seemed to understand that, sort of, back in the caves. We got along for a little while."

"Yeah, and how did that turn out? How did that end? With her betraying us and siding with a murderer to get what she wanted."

Lyrrin inhaled in a way that scrunched up her nose, and she tossed the spent weftweed sticks into a corner of the shrine. "I just think there are lots of nasty things in this world already. You don't need to become one too."

Riony's shoulders slumped. She felt exhausted, worn thin physically and emotionally. "We can't make friends with everyone."

Lyrrin remained firm, staring up at Riony fiercely. "Doesn't mean we should make them enemies instead."

Riony broke eye contact first, turning her focus on the small weeds tufting through the cracks in the stone floor. Lyrrin didn't really understand how bad things could get, that Riony was doing everything she could to keep them safe. But then why did it feel like Riony was getting everything wrong?

Aishena fussed over Benjin, holding his chin to tilt his head and check what Lyrrin had done. She muttered, "We're just lucky that the gateway finally worked."

Niskina, who had cleaned herself up a little but still looked a shade paler than usual, rejoined them. "Why did it take so long?"

"It worked once Dracuni got closer to it," Riony said.

Me? Dracuni lopped across to Riony, leaning her chin on Riony's hand.

Riony's fingers scratched around the tufts of moonlight hair down the back of the unidragon's head. "I've been to other shrines before. There was one on the grounds of Heithorn estate. They've never felt like the ones I've been in when Dracuni has been with me. They've never had this feeling of energy and magic."

The others nodded their silent agreement that they felt it too. Niskina shivered visibly.

"Dracuni is the only difference. And I don't think it's the dragon part of her. I think it's the unicorn part of her." Riony pointed to the carvings that decorated the lichen-covered walls.

Five unicorns frolicked in a line, elegant and long legged, their manes and tails stylized into knotwork that swirled into the sculpted foliage around them.

Aishena moved closer to the beautiful relief, brushing a hand over it. "Unicorns gave the shrines magic?"

Am I unicorn? Like those? Dracuni looked between her scaly tail and the carvings.

"You're something else." Riony crouched down beside Dracuni, staring into her liquid lilac eyes. "And I'm just guessing. The Alderkin got their magic from somewhere. They must have had a way to recharge their crystal artifacts. All the gateway crystals across the land must have worked at some point."

"The magic could have been something else from the Alderkin themselves, maybe?" Lyrrin asked, her voice soft.

"It was since Dracuni came to this shrine that the gateway worked, and crystals recharge here. My cutting athame has recharged twice now. I think maybe the shrines were all working, back when there were more unicorns around."

"That would give the Alderkin another reason why they fought so hard to stop the unicorns from being killed," Aishena said.

"Like they needed more reasons than it was awful and wrong," Niskina cut in.

Aishena continued, ignoring the interruption. "If they needed unicorns to keep all their magic working, it would also make sense why the war turned so badly against them not long after the last unicorn was gone. They wouldn't have been able to recharge their war weapons."

"Pabba told me that once," Niskina said, eyelids low. "He said that they found glow stones and athames for utility and household items still with charge but rarely ever found any kind of weapon still charged."

"If Dracuni is making these shrines magical again, then we can keep all our things charged!" Benjin said brightly.

He pulled out the glow stone that had recently run out and activated it. It sputtered a little light, but they mustn't have been there long enough for it to be fully working again. Still, the small show of light encouraged Benjin's smile to grow.

"All the more reason that Dracuni is special. That she needs to be protected, no matter what." Riony turned to hold the gaze of each person around her as they nodded their agreement.

Special! Dracuni trilled.

"Do you think if we got some raw crystal and brought it to a shrine, whether it would work if I put a rune on it?" Lyrrin's eyes were sparkling now, too, with the same enthusiasm Benjin had.

"We should try to get some and give it a go!" Benjin replied.

Lyrrin had already been spending most evenings with her crystal experiments, Benjin watching along with rapt attention. She'd broken a glow stone down into half a dozen smaller slices but was disappointed when she realized that they all still seemed to be set to the light rune, even if they didn't have the rune directly on them anymore.

Lyrrin had said something about it being attuned to the first rune activated on it, as far as she could tell, so all the shards had to become light shards again, plus the addition of other runes that Lyrrin knew the effects of.

"We could use the Alderkin map to travel around to all the shrines and recharge them with Dracuni," Lyrrin said. "That way none of our crystals will run out of charge, and if we can get all the gateways working, we'd be able to travel all over Elundrae!"

"That's not a bad idea, actually," Niskina said. "You said that you stayed here once and a revenant couldn't get in?"

Aishena grimaced. "The thing was right across from us, howling and clawing at the air."

"But it didn't get in," Riony added.

"Then we've got a map that shows us places we can go that are safe from revs. We should aim for them as we head toward Riony's old village. Let's have a look. We can plan our route."

"The shrines won't keep us safe from Kess or ... Lady Hjelzahn," Aishena said as she extracted and unfolded the map. She held it flat between them.

"Kess is three weeks' travel from us now, even if she works out where we went," Benjin said, pointing to where they had last been and drawing a line with his finger to where they were now.

"Doesn't mean we can let our guards down. I get the feeling that both Kess and your mother are very much the 'strike when you're least expecting it' types," Riony muttered.

"Whereabouts was that village of yours?" Niskina asked.

Riony looked at the map, trying to get her bearings, remembering how they'd traveled there the first time, how they'd fled from there the last time.

She pointed and shrugged. "Somewhere around there."

"There's what, seven or eight shrines between here and there? More if we take a more roundabout route."

"A roundabout route sounds good," Riony replied. Her words stuck in her dry mouth, and she had to swallow mid-sentence.

Benjin took control of the map then, planning out a path for them, arguing with Niskina and demanding backup from Aishena.

Riony turned away from them, moving to the doorway for fresh air. They needed a plan to keep them all together and moving on, but the thought of their destination left a cold sweat across her back and a chill in her stomach.

Traveling around the shrines would be good. It would draw out their journey to her old home. Because Riony wasn't sure if she was ready to face those memories.

Chapter Three

The magical glow emanating from the crystal circle went dark just as Kess and Griskin reached it, cutting her off from her target.

With slight pressure from her fingers, Kess brought Griskin to a stop, whirling him around to take them back out of the enclosed shrine before they were cornered.

Razing, cursed Alderkin magic! Her eyes burned with caustic frustration, and she shrieked wildly. The rough men and women of the settlement that were pursuing her slowed down, recoiling from her outburst.

Then another close call with a crossbow bolt proved they hadn't yet given up their vengeance on Kess for the death of one of their friends.

That man had to die though. Kess couldn't allow him to take Dracuni or find out Dracuni's true value.

If Pony had been brighter, she'd have done the same thing too. But it was clear Pony wasn't capable of doing what was needed to keep the creature out of the wrong hands. And the rest of the group seemed to be even more of a useless mess.

Which was why Kess needed to get the unidragon for herself.

Kess wasn't sure she had even communicated her intention to Griskin when he burst into movement again, whether she'd shifted her body or pressed her fingers through his fur as a signal without realizing.

They were so often of the same mind, on where to go, and how to protect themselves and each other, that the wolf acted as she wished with no need for commands.

"Let's dust these chumps," Kess whispered, leaning low into Griskin's back.

He loosed a low growl, kicking out around the entrance of the shrine, then broke into a long, loping sprint through the burned forest. Clouds of ashy dirt flew up behind them.

He didn't run as fast or as straight as usual, and tension tightened the muscles under the pads of Kess's fingertips tangled in his fur.

"Come on. We've almost lost them."

They ran up the low gorge slope, over the rise, and down another valley where the trickle of water met them again, flowing into a larger creek. Kess held the saddle tight as Griskin jumped over the muddy stream. They landed on the other side, and one of her legs shook free of the stirrups and straps holding her in place.

She leaned around to bring it back into position with her hands, and her breath stuck in her throat. A crossbow bolt was lodged in Griskin's thigh. Blood made the fur around it dark and glossy.

Kess growled as rough and low as her wolf. "Those unblessed monsters!"

Back on the other side of the small creek, a man with a crossbow had stopped and worked on reloading.

Kess slipped the smooth, sharpened bone of one of her knives into her hand, exhaled, then sent the knife flying.

Her lips curled crookedly as the blade landed true, right into the man's eye. A cold, melancholy satisfaction shivered through her as he fell.

More yelling and curses came from behind her as she pushed Griskin on again, dashing along the side of the stream.

Kess winced with Griskin's every step at the rasp and whine of his breath. He was hurting. But they would both be dead if he stopped.

"It's okay. It's okay. Just a bit farther."

The forest grew thicker, less burned and dry and more a riot of fresh, tangling growth, vivid green and tender, sprouted from a hard black core.

The stream, too, grew clearer. The water there filtered into icy clarity over reeds and polished stones.

When Kess could no longer hear the murderous yells of her pursuers, she kept Griskin going until *he* could no longer hear those cries.

He slowed then, the tension easing in the muscles of his haunches.

Pulling at straps and buckles, Kess dropped the saddlebags and packs onto the ground. Then with a lean to the side, Kess urged Griskin toward the water.

Griskin whined and huffed.

"Don't be a baby. I know you hate baths, but we have to wash your wound." She pushed again.

After one more soft growl, Griskin relented, wading into the softly flowing stream. It came halfway up his legs, and the bolt was lodged in much higher.

With further urging from Kess, Griskin lowered himself down into the water, lying stretched out on his belly. Water rippled and ran around Kess's ankles.

Kess turned to inspect the wound, but no matter how she twisted herself around in the saddle, she couldn't get a good view or a good angle on the bolt. So she unstrapped herself from the seat and slid into the water beside the wolf.

The water instantly soaked through her pants and shirt, tickling around her with icy splashes. Shuffling along the slippery stones, Kess brought herself close to Griskin's side. He dwarfed her when she was next to him like that, even one of his hind legs seemed twice her size.

She placed a palm over the bloodied fur and her other around the short shaft of the bolt.

"Hold still," she ordered, and then pulled.

Griskin keened, and his leg twitched, claws scraping against Kess's thigh. They didn't break through the leather of her pants, but it stung.

Kess bit her tongue, inhaled through her nose as the pain subsided, then began scooping water over Griskin's wound.

"I'm sorry," she whispered, barely a breath.

She worked her fingers gently through the fur, loosening where the already dried blood matted it. She continued to wash water over the area until the fur parted and she could see the injury clearly.

It was a clean, deep hole, like a spot of night sky between the tufts of charcoal fur. Blood welled, dripping out, staining Kess's hands.

She couldn't bandage this, not around that high part of his leg—it was more his rump than anything. The fabric she had would never be enough to loop around it.

She needed something else.

It grows everywhere. People think it's a useless, gangly weed, but they just don't appreciate it for what it can do.

Something-weed? Wilt? Wild? What was it?

That time … Kess's face scrunched up at the memory.

Pony had tripped while carrying Kess through a field on the estate. They were never meant to be out that far, but Kess wanted to watch the dragonriders flying routines, and the southernmost paddock had the best view.

Riony tripped in a hidden ditch, and both of them had fallen hard, hit the low stone wall beside them, and come away bloody.

Riony just wiped herself off on her shirt, said it was nothing. But she'd seemed so worried about the deep graze on Kess's knee.

Probably because she knew what would await her if the lord and lady of the house saw her bring Kess home bloodied.

She'd found a twiggy green plant right beside them.

Kess had balked at the stinky, slimy sap it produced but finally allowed Pony to apply it. It didn't soothe the pain at all, but it slowed the bleeding and apparently helped avoid infection too.

Riony had been so careful with Kess's wound.

And when they'd returned to the estate, Riony was whipped that afternoon anyway. Because she'd allowed Kess to look dusty and unkempt. They hadn't cared about Kess's injury at all.

Kess scowled, and a hot feeling grew behind her eyes.

She shook it off. "There's got to be some around here somewhere."

Shuffling through the water, Kess brought herself up onto the bank in a section between the tall reeds and called for Griskin to follow.

The low shore of muddy soil was thick with growth, blades of thin, lime-green grass, patches of moss and clover, and thicker bushes of rangy weeds.

Griskin moved past her up onto more solid ground where the bags had been dropped, and his body exploded into a shiver, sending water droplets flying all around Kess.

"Careful!" She wiped them off her face. "You'll hurt yourself."

Griskin whimpered at her tone, sat in a curled position, and began licking at the bleeding area.

Kess scanned over the wild garden surrounding her, hoping to identify the plant from memory. It didn't take long to see something that might have been right. It had the same firm green stems and apparent disinterest in growing leaves.

Kess snapped off a section, and a clear sap spilled quickly from the break. The smell that hit her nose, an offensive, tart stench, was what made her sure she'd found the right thing. There was no forgetting that scent.

It took a great amount of shuffling to crawl up the marshy embankment to where Griskin had settled, but Kess didn't call him to her.

She pushed his licking muzzle away from the wound and squeezed the sap onto the area. Even if it didn't help much, maybe the offensive odor would stop Griskin from bothering it.

The bolt hadn't been in too deep, but even small wounds could turn a whole body bad quickly. Kess shivered, cold from her saturated clothing. She drew in closer to Griskin, tucking herself next to his warm fur.

They weren't going anywhere right now anyway, not unless the drunken thugs from the settlement had more persistence than she would credit them with.

After wiping the last of the sap off her fingers, Kess gave Griskin a scratch between his eyes.

"Don't worry. If Ri—" Kess's throat went dry. "If Pony's stupid weeds don't work, we'll fix you up some other way."

Kess still had silvernix, after all. If there was any sign of the wound turning bad, she'd use it.

Silvernix was required for a taming ceremony, but she'd never get to that stage if she lost Griskin first.

For a moment, she wondered—if she were forced to choose between Griskin and a dragon, which would she pick? But that was ridiculous to question. She would not choose. She would have both.

If she had to start again from scratch, she could obtain unicorn blood again. It might even be possible to use Dracuni's own blood. Would that work? Would the spike even stay in the creature? It seemed to heal quite quickly itself.

Maybe Dracuni didn't need to be tamed at all. Riony had managed to keep the thing under control without taming. But Kess had to admit there was some sort of bond between the two of them.

If someone took Griskin away from me and then expected him to behave for them in the same way, I'd call them a fool.

She didn't doubt Dracuni would be the same. Loyal to Riony at this point.

It would have to be tamed.

From this higher point on the bank, Kess looked over the unruly stretch of green to the stream below. It might be worth finding some swampland to harvest more morass mercy from too. It could come in handy.

It was a risk traveling into areas where it grew, as people had been known to succumb to the sedative scent and fall asleep there, drowning in the mud. She'd become dangerously woozy gathering what she'd needed the last time.

Maybe she could find a trader selling some instead. Traders out in the wastes were unscrupulous types that sold all sorts of terrible things. Finding some morass mercy should be easy enough.

And she had plenty of land to cover before finding Pony and the unidragon again, if her hunch about where they were was correct.

Kess pulled one of her bags closer, digging around in it for some food. She'd bought a couple of jars of pickled fish the last time she was on the coast before following the mother dragon inland to the mountain. She'd thought at the time she'd save them until she had her own dragon, to share as a meal with her first tamed hatchling.

"No hunting tonight. Let's rest." She cracked the seal on one of the glass jars. Using a large leaf as a plate, she tipped the contents onto it in front of Griskin.

Griskin slurped and inhaled the soft fish, bones and all, before Kess had even opened the second jar for herself.

She dipped her fingers in, picking at the flakes of pink flesh. It was buttery and salty on her tongue.

Closing her eyes for a moment, she tried to remember what she saw as Pony and the others had gone through the magical gateway. Riony's 'sister' had tapped a lit symbol on the side, the same symbol as when they'd escaped from the Alderkin depths.

Are they selecting where to go?

Why would they go back to the same place again? That was what it had looked like to Kess. But only two symbols had been lit up, so maybe they didn't have a choice, really, from what they were yelling. Maybe they could only go to places they had previously been.

That wouldn't help Kess get back to them faster though.

"If it weren't for those intolerable gateways, we would have had them. Twice, we would have had them! How are they doing it? How is that blighted Alderkin magic even working for them?"

Griskin replied with a soft whine as he sniffed at the jar in Kess's fingers, brine sloshing over the edges as her hands trembled.

Kess dumped the remains of her jar, barely picked at, onto Griskin's leaf-plate. Then she leaned back into him, closed her eyes, and worked on formulating their next steps.

Kess had been lucky the first time, coming across their scent at the shrine just down the hill from the undercity. She'd also found there the muzzle and some of her daggers snapped in half. There was no doubt Pony and the others had spent the night in that location. She'd been able to get Griskin to follow their scent from there, only a few days behind.

But now, if they'd gone back to that first shrine again, it would take weeks to hike back there, giving Pony a few weeks head start. It would be harder to follow their scent. And if they found another gateway from there, Kess could lose them for good.

There's no way I can keep up with them, let alone catch them, like this.

She needed something more. A faster way to travel.

She was going to have to get help. And it was going to hurt to ask.

Chapter Four

The sky was almost blue, and the sun was almost warm, and Riony almost felt a sense of calm until the howl of a wolf set her teeth on edge.

"Back to me!" she yelled to her friends who had drifted away from her through the abandoned village they'd stumbled upon.

A rabbit bolted from between tall tufts of grass ahead, and Lyrrin's voice carried through the air, swearing roughly. "You ruined my shot!"

Danger?

Dracuni's head popped up from within the ratty remains of what might have once been a neat hedge. Egg yolk dripped down her chin and she crunched bits of shell in her mouth.

"That sounded like a wolf!" Riony yelled back.

It had been a few weeks since Kess's ambush, but Riony had been on alert for the wolf riding gremlin to catch up to them again.

Only Niskina was nearby. She couldn't see Lyrrin or Benjin and Aishena. Last she'd seen, they were all together up ahead, sneaking about in a small hunting group. Lyrrin's voice had come from behind the broken stone wall of a ruined cottage.

Dracuni pushed through the twiggy, untended bushes and ran to cower around Riony's legs, almost bowling Riony over.

There were a few more mutterings before Lyrrin and Benjin stepped out into view. Aishena lurked behind them, scanning all around the weed-woven ruins with her dark eyes.

Niskina strolled toward Riony at an unbothered pace. "Relax. That wasn't your psychotic ex-girlfriend."

Riony flushed red with a riot of unpleasant reactions. Her words ground out. "She. Is. NOT—"

"Not dumb enough to go spoiling her ambush by letting her wolf howl at us along the way." Niskina wandered over to where a feral urchin cucumber, brown and half dead, hung from the roof of the cottage. She examined the misshapen, spiky fruit with a pout on her round face.

"Yeah, I suppose you have a point. But ..." Riony looked over her shoulder, checking for an ambush.

Farther along the overgrown path, Benjin pointed up to the sky. "Besides, it wasn't even a wolf. It was that carrion bird. Used to get a lot of them back home. They sound like that."

Riony turned her face to the sky to see the wide-winged silhouette of the monstrous bird circling above. Her face spasmed involuntarily. All the wild chickens running around between the broken buildings and overgrown fields were bad enough.

"What was that?" Niskina asked softly with a knowing grin.

Riony shrugged and cricked her neck. "What?"

"That look of utter terror I saw pass over you just then."

"I ... don't like birds. They creep me out," Riony whispered.

"Hold on, I'm sorry. Birds?" Niskina put a hand on her wide hips and looked Riony up and down as though seeing her for the first time. "Just the big ones?"

"Any birds. I don't like their beaks and beady eyes. I don't *hate* them—they just make me ..." Riony shivered uncontrollably again.

Niskina pouted and approached Riony with her arms wide. "Oh, sweetie. You fight revs as though it's playtime, but *birds* scare you? Let me give you a hug."

Riony sighed and stood stiffly as Niskina wrapped her soft body around her in a tight embrace. "Please don't tell the others."

"Never."

I like birds. Want to fly like birds. Dracuni fluttered her filmy wings.

Lyrrin walked over, Benjin close beside her like some kind of bodyguard. She handed a dead chicken, small and still warm, over to Riony.

"Did you get this with your sling?" Riony swallowed and hid her disgust as she took it.

"Yeah." Lyrrin didn't seem happy about it, looking at the chicken sadly.

She gave it a soft pat, gloved hands trailing through the feathers. "It'll be good to have some more meat since there's a lot to catch here. I'm going to try to get a few more for Dracuni."

"You're becoming a good shot," Riony said, and Lyrrin's expression brightened.

The unidragon sniffed at the bird. Her jaw opened, revealing a row of small but sharp teeth, and she inched toward the chicken until Riony lifted it higher out of reach again.

"We'll eat soon."

But hungry!

"You were just feasting on chicken eggs," Riony said.

Hungry, always hungry! Want meat but can't catch!

Lyrrin frowned at the conversation she was only half aware of. "Can we go back to hunting now without interruptions?"

"We've still got to be careful. Stay close and stay alert."

"We *are*," Benjin said. "Besides, we haven't seen the wolf rider for ages. We've lost them."

"No. We can't become complacent. Kess will never give up."

"She could. She might change," Lyrrin said.

Riony barked a laugh. "I know you like Griskin, but just because you made friends with him doesn't mean you can make friends with all ferocious beasts—especially Kess. And Kess is the one in control—don't forget that. Griskin is loyal to her."

Riony still hadn't forgotten the feeling of the wolf's teeth around her leg, how Kess had aimed for her heart. She shook her head, unable to look Lyrrin in the eye. "I'm sorry. Not everything in this world can be solved by being nice."

Lyrrin glowered, muttered under her breath, then marched away, Benjin close behind.

"Don't go too far!" Riony grunted. "Sparks."

Niskina sighed breathily. "Do you need another hug?"

"As much as I'll kick myself later for ever refusing a good hug, I am *not* in the mood."

Niskina watched with laughing eyes as Riony held the chicken by a claw between her thumb and forefinger. Riony thrust it into Niskina's hands and left it to be her problem.

Dracuni snuffled at the out-of-reach hen as though insulted, then a couple more chickens ran by, clucking, and she bounded after them. She hadn't been able to catch anything herself yet on their travels, despite trying.

She was growing fast and awkward on limbs that seemed bigger than she was used to dealing with. She still couldn't fly, her wings diaphanous and flimsy, and she hadn't breathed fire either.

Would she ever be able to do either, given what she was? Would she ever be able to look after herself if she had to?

There was a great clucking and flutter of feathers as Dracuni's pounce missed her target again.

Sparks!

Riony's eyes widened. *Between Lyrrin and Dracuni, maybe I need to be watching my language more.*

Turning back to her own task, Riony stepped over a low metal gate into a field to continue seeking herbs to dye Lyrrin's hair with. And Aishena's too, it was decided, after a bounty hunter had recognized her a few days ago.

The bounty on the Hjelzahn siblings was still active, their mother still seeking them. And the steel-bright hair of the dragon king's lineage was drawing too much attention to them.

Stepping between the tangles of weeds, Riony's foot came down on something brittle and crunchy. A quick look sent a shudder right up her spine. Chicken bones.

It wasn't the first animal carcass she'd seen in the village, and between that and the multitude of overgrown plants, it was clear the area hadn't been burned in a long time. Riony hated to think what could rise there if the shadowdragon landed.

Don't think about undead chickens. Don't think about undead chickens.

A few hasty steps away, Riony found the bronze-leafed herb she sought.

"Stars, it's all so depressing." Niskina sighed the words. She sat on the low stone wall of the field, watching as Riony pinched off the fresh growth of the hennan.

"You'll have to be more specific."

"All this." Niskina waved both arms around her. "This would have been such a beautiful village once. Now it's a ghost town. And everyone who lived here once, loved here once, are probably all dead."

"They could have made it to a dragonkeep."

Niskina snorted.

"Or the undercity."

Niskina tsked. "Don't we deserve to live under the sun and outside of walls?"

"We are." Riony spotted something shiny between the brushy leaves and bent to pick up the steel shoulder guard there. Yet another piece of the common trash leftover from the Alderkin war.

"Running for our lives from shrine to shrine, hiding from revs and our own families and your ex-girl—"

"Only finish that sentence if you're prepared for the consequences." Riony thrust the metal armor at her like a weapon.

Niskina rolled her eyes. "This isn't really living though, is it? It feels as though the whole world is already dead and we just haven't realized it yet. Why are we even still trying? Why bother going on?"

Riony stared at the steel in her hands, forged by dragon breath, cheap and flimsy. Disposable fodder in a war that only ended when two races were exterminated entirely. Unicorns and Alderkin, and with them, the magic of the world.

She dusted the dirt off it, tested the crackled leather straps, then began buckling it onto her shoulder, adding it to her growing collection of armor. She didn't want to let it go to waste. She didn't want to give up on the world just yet.

"We keep going for Lyrrin and Benjin and Dracuni," she said.

Niskina looked at her with such deep sympathy it almost broke her. "I wish we could make things better for them too. But it seems impossible. Everything … everything is broken. Stars, I could do with a drink!"

"Yeah, because that's going to fix anything."

Niskina glared back, a red flush tinting her eyelids and golden irises flashing.

Tucking the harvested herbs away in a belt pouch, Riony strode over to sit beside Niskina on the wall.

"You're a grown woman and you can make your own choices." Riony adjusted the shoulder guard, fidgeting with it instead of looking at Niskina directly.

The metal was dented and sat unevenly, pinching her biceps. "But I don't think throwing yourself at every bottle and every man we come across is going to make it hurt any less."

"What would you know? Give it a try and you might change your mind."

Riony gave a shrug and smirked. "Not even the end of the world is going to find me throwing myself at men. And unfortunately, the women I've thrown myself at equally aren't interested in return."

"Sincerest apologies for my part in that disappointment, although I never really knew if you were being serious anyway."

"Me? Not serious? How could you have gotten such an impression? If you ever decide girls are for you, I'll show you how serious I can be." Riony waggled her eyebrows and gave a bright smile.

Niskina elbowed her softly.

Riony's grin faded quickly. "At least yours isn't a personal rejection. Meanwhile, I have no clue what to think about Aishena."

Niskina's eyes narrowed conspiratorially, and she glanced over her shoulder to check they were alone. "She did date a fellow delver once. Male."

"Oh."

"Broke it off very quickly. And dated a girl right after."

"Oh?"

Niskina chuckled, shaking her head. "Again, briefly. Despite *much* wooing and desperate attempts to re-win her favor from both sides. You should have heard Pabba scolding ..."

Her shoulders slumped, and her lips turned down, and she swallowed hard.

High above, the carrion bird keened again, the wolflike cry echoing through air that smelled and tasted of old smoke.

Riony leaned in, pressing her arm up against Niskina's. "I'm sorry. I'm sorry about Brishan. I wanted to help. I thought we were coming to save you from Aishena's mother. Then I didn't do anything. I didn't get to help anyone because I brought a traitor back with me."

Anger turned Riony's breath ragged, shaking out her nose as she worked to unclench her teeth. Because of Kess, because she'd saved Kess, they'd lost Brishan. Niskina had lost her father. And Riony had lost her chance at the life she'd wanted for so long.

To be a delver, to be somebody who could earn a good life for Lyrrin and Dracuni and the caramel little rat they'd left behind, Sir Butterfur Spelunkychunks, and any other pets Lyrrin brought in. It had all been lost because of Kess.

"It's not your fault. That he died. It's mine. It's mine, and it was *his*." Niskina snapped her mouth harshly around the last word.

Her head bowed, a tumble of chestnut curls hiding her face. "I wanted to help too, and if he'd just let me do what I wanted, if he'd trusted me to do what I could, maybe I could have made a difference."

Riony's heart kicked against her rib cage and she relived the horror of watching Brishan turn away from his deadly combatant to push Niskina out of the fray. And the price he'd paid for that.

"But he didn't trust me. And then he was gone. And now we're here, doing nothing but ticking off another day we've remained alive. So yes, now, *now* I'm going to do whatever I want. Including all the ale and dubious men I can find."

Niskina's skin trembled between where their arms touched. Riony was about to ask about that hug again, or offer one herself, when Aishena appeared silently beside them like a ghost from the shadows.

"Sparks! Give us a little warning sometimes!" Riony gasped.

Aishena just shook her head and pointed across the village. "You have to come and see this. Now."

CHAPTER FIVE

Lyrrin took a step closer, enthralled by the view before her.

Benjin snatched her arm and tugged her back a step. "Careful. The stones are loose."

She nodded vaguely in return, eyes still stuck on the landscape before her.

From the rocky outcrop they'd found at the edge of the village, the valley dipped below them, winding between low mountains like the furrows of a messy blanket. A strange, dark area marred a point in the distance, but that wasn't what had attracted Lyrrin to the scene.

It was the unique pointed arch of the mountain to the left, the clearly defined jutting stones of the hillock beside it backdropping that dark area.

She'd seen this landscape before. She'd locked the shapes in her mind.

Dracuni made a sad trilling noise and sat beside Lyrrin, licking her fingers. Lyrrin wished she could hear Dracuni's thoughts but didn't need to know her words to know her intention. This was a very sad place, and Dracuni could feel it too.

A commotion of pounding feet and snapping foliage came from behind.

"What is it? What's wrong?" Riony ran up beside her, puffing deep breaths.

Niskina and Aishena followed close after, pushing through the branches that stretched across the goat track.

Lyrrin brushed off Riony's concerned hands. "Look. Do you recognize it?"

Riony looked all around them, a frown of confusion over worried eyes. "No? Recognize what?"

"This is it. This is where the first taming happened." Lyrrin pointed to the shapes in the landscape. "It's exactly the same as the mural in the Alderkin depths."

Riony squinted at the horizon. "Oh yeah, the mural. Something with a dragon and a unicorn? It flashed by as I ran for my life."

Lyrrin's heart sunk. She wanted her sister to have seen the full carving, to have seen the beauty and tragedy of what it showed, and to have seen the depictions of the Alderkin, with their gem-bright eyes and sharp, clawed hands.

She hadn't talked to Riony yet about it, how connected she'd felt, seeing those people who looked so much like her. She wasn't sure how to bring it up—not without Riony having seen it too. Maybe it had only ever been wishful thinking on Lyrrin's part that those people were like her. It seemed like a dream that felt dead before it even began.

Because even if, somehow, Lyrrin was part of the Alderkin race, what would it matter? It would only mean the same outcome that she already knew. That her family was dead and gone.

"We had a better look at the mural," Aishena said. "This is a pretty clear match for the landscape the Alderkin depicted."

"It would have been right down there." Niskina's voice was low and rough as she pointed to the dark area. "What do you think that is?"

Benjin brought Yoskar's staff up in front of his face and activated the seeing stone. The magnifying crystal flickered and cleared.

Peering through it, he hummed. "It's hard to see. It's just ... dark. But there are standing stones around there. I think it was a shrine."

"Can I see?" Lyrrin asked. She put away the sling that was still in her hands, looping and tying the ends around the strap of her backpack.

Benjin handed the staff over quickly, but there was a soft hesitation when she pulled it from his hands.

"There are also *a lot* of revs down there," Benjin said.

Lyrrin looked through the crystal, shining and clear, and it brought the distant landscape closer to her. It felt almost as though she could reach out and touch it.

The darkness surrounding the shrine spread as though night had fallen just in that area. All around and within those shadows, things moved. Skeletal, wasted undead from the tiniest rodent through to gigantic bovin and dreer shambled over blackened, cracked ground.

For a moment, Lyrrin thought she saw the shadow itself moving. She waited, looking harder, but saw no other signs that the shadow had life.

With a shiver, Lyrrin handed the staff back to Benjin. It slipped from her gloved hand before he had it and one end clattered to the ground. He snatched it up.

"Careful!" He pulled the staff close to his chest, clinging to it with both hands.

Niskina squinted at the view. "That means they were here, right? The Alderkin who made the mural. They were there. They saw the first taming."

"Doesn't mean the mural showed what really happened," Aishena said.

Lyrrin recalled the depiction of the shadowdragon emerging above the scene.

Riony put her hand out for a turn to look with the seeing stone, but Benjin ignored her.

Benjin continued. "I didn't see the mural. But the stories of the first taming shared by the dragonlords say that Yeonard Draekhan went to the Alderkin to heal his beloved, and they betrayed him, attacking him by calling a dragon with their magic. But he fought back mightily, and his spear struck the dragon between the eyes and tamed it."

"What about the unicorn, then?" Niskina asked. "The dragonking hid the truth for years, that his spear had silvernix on it. He tried to keep the secret of how to tame dragons to himself. Then it finally came out. So just think through the sequence of events. There had to have been a unicorn there. And he, at the very least, hurt it, if not killed it, like we saw in the mural."

"Why would he do that? Why kill it? If he was trying to save someone, he didn't need much silvernix." Lyrrin glanced down at Dracuni, and her stomach felt burbly and sore.

Aishena turned away from the view, staring at the ground instead. "Whatever happened with his attempt to have his first wife healed, I think it's safe to say it went wrong. All accounts say she died that day. There's a yearly day of mourning in the keeps on that date."

Riony counted on her fingers. "His girl doesn't get healed like he wants. So he straight-up murders a unicorn in return. Alderkin get angry and somehow summon a dragon—"

"Pabba said once there were rumors of Alderkin summoning wild dragons into battle during the war," Niskina interrupted.

Riony finished her thought. "Then he gets a lucky shot with his spear and tames his first dragon, then tells everyone what a big hero he was. Yeah, I could see that being the kind of unhinged thing a guy who has been keeping himself young off the blood of unicorns for eighty years might do."

"And making everyone call him *Draekhan*. Be for real," Niskina muttered.

The whole idea made Lyrrin's lips turn down. Killing another thing because something you loved died. It sounded awful.

She tried to imagine what she would do if Dracuni failed to, or chose not to, heal Benjin after he was hurt. Or if she refused to heal Riony if Riony was dying. Would Lyrrin lash out and hurt Dracuni in return? Kill her? Even thinking it made her feel sick.

She tried to turn away from those dark thoughts and instead look again at the darkened landscape.

"Should we go down for a closer look?" Lyrrin asked.

The others gave her appalled looks. Lyrrin puckered her lips and turned away. She could see the swarming revenants as well as they could. But it had also been a place the Alderkin had found so important they'd created that imposing mural about it.

And there was a hollow within her that desperately wanted to be closer to anything that could answer her questions about them, and herself.

"Can I see the map again?" Riony asked, and Aishena quickly retrieved it.

Riony unfolded the map and hunched over the parchment. "Whatever happened down there, the place looks the very opposite of safe right now. We're not going to that shrine. But there's another one nearby, across the other side of the village."

"Odd that there are two so close together. We haven't come across any others like that yet," Aishena said.

"Maybe the Alderkin made a new one after whatever happened down there," Lyrrin said.

She squeezed in beside Riony to look at the map as well. The next shrine they went to would be their fifth, and they had marked them on the map as they went. They had been traveling from shrine to shrine, and at each one their presence, or most likely Dracuni's presence, reawakened the magic there.

Their Alderkin crystal items recharged, and the gateway, if it was still standing, was activated. The large geode slices at a couple of the shrines they had passed were smashed and broken, and they'd crossed them off on the map. You couldn't travel through a broken crystal.

"Yeah, I know. I can feel it too," Riony said.

Lyrrin had gotten used to her sister seemingly speaking at random, so she watched and waited. Dracuni had tucked herself in between Riony's legs and rested her chin on her front paws.

"Dracuni says the shrine down there feels really sad, and she doesn't like all the bad things."

"Dragons flying!" Aishena snapped.

Out across the horizon, two tiny dots soared. They were a long way off, but Aishena was already herding Benjin back into the thicker bushes and away from the clear outcrop.

Riony folded up the map and gave Lyrrin a soft nudge as well. "Better safe than sorry."

"It's not going to be Mami," Benjin groaned, pushing Aishena's grasp off, but he still continued away from the open area. "She doesn't ride her dragon anymore. Not since she changed."

"We can't rule it out. She might ride again. She would do anything to find us. We're lucky she doesn't have a wolf's nose to track us down or we'd be dead already."

Lyrrin followed her sister down the goat track back into the village along with the others. Even the mention of a wolf made Riony's shoulders lift and tension show in the lines of her neck.

They had backtracked a couple of times in their travels, going from a new gateway back to a previous one to make it harder for Kess and Griskin to track them, but still Riony behaved as though the wolf and rider would jump from the bushes at any moment.

Riony cast her eyes over the cluster of chickens hanging from Benjin's belt. "We've got plenty of food. We should get moving onto the next shrine and get there before it's dark."

As they stepped back out of the overgrown outskirts of the village, there was a rumble on the road beside them.

Carts, moving faster than seemed safe, were drawn by a range of creatures. The smaller two were pulled by a horse and a goat, and one sizable wagon was drawn by a bovin. Its large head bobbed, shaggy mane hanging over hooded eyes. Heavy hooved feet thudded as it dragged the wagon over the uneven ground.

A crowd of people moved around the carts and wagon, rushing back and forward to drag debris off the ragged road where it lay in their path, crying to each other to keep moving.

Riony stepped to the front of their own small group. The eyes of the approaching crowd were already on them, watching warily.

"Dracuni, back up," Lyrrin whispered.

Dracuni snorted softly and circled back around to hide under a bush.

A bent woman with wild gray hair moved to the front of the convoy. "Children! Hurry, hurry with us."

Riony called back, "Why the hurry?"

A man who was more bones than skin hobbled by, carrying a sniffling toddler at his chest. He gave a wild wail. "Revenants. Hundreds. An army of them!"

Lyrrin's heart pattered, and she stood on tiptoes to try to see behind the crowd, to see if the undead were within sight, but couldn't.

The wagons had reached them where they stood beside the remains of a cottage on the side of the road.

The procession didn't slow, but the bent woman did, stopping before them. Worry crinkled the pretty wrinkles lining her eyes. "We had to run. Our home ... we saw them coming. We can handle a few revs, but this ... The walls would not keep them out. We took what we could, but they are still behind us. They will be here soon."

Each cart and wagon was piled high, each animal towing what seemed to be an entire village packed into baskets and barrels. A few smaller children were loaded between the belongings, and around them, scores of people hurried along.

Within the crowd, another older lady glanced over, and her eyes met Lyrrin's with what felt like the shock of lightning. Her eyes were the color of flowers, a lilac brighter than Dracuni's. The woman turned away quickly, her hands tight around a child on both sides.

Lyrrin's heart beat faster again. She stepped forward, trying to get a better look at those hands.

Riony gripped her shoulder, pulling her back beside her.

"We'd better move too," Riony said. "We know where we're going. Let's get there fast."

"Good luck, then," the gray-crowned woman said, turning back to her own flock. A girl, older than Lyrrin but younger than Riony, wobbled past with a flushed face and huge belly, and the older woman put a hand on her lower back, urging her on.

"Let's go," Riony said.

"What about them?" Lyrrin asked.

Mid step, Riony paused, chewing her lip.

"We should let them know where they can be safe. We should take them with us," Lyrrin said, heart in her throat. She still had nightmares about the few friends from the orphans' den that they hadn't taken with them from the slavers' camp, taken away in a cage by the dragonrider.

"What about Dracuni? They'll see her. They could ..." Riony shook her head.

"They'll just think she's a baby dragon. We'll keep her away from them as much as we can. But we can't just leave them all running from the revs. For how long?"

Niskina moved in beside Riony, tilting her head. "They're exhausted already. If the revs aren't far behind, they're already going to be moving faster than these people. If they don't go somewhere safe, they aren't going to make it."

"Sparks," Riony hissed. "I know. You're right. But is that going to be safe for us? For them?" Riony's eyes went over Lyrrin and Benjin and Dracuni, still tucked under the branches.

Aishena had a thoughtful scowl but said nothing.

"We'll find out. But we should try," Lyrrin pleaded.

"They're coming!" a child toward the back of the procession yelled, their voice high and cracked.

From the far end of the road, a skittering, rushing shape barreled toward them. First one, then another, then five more at once, bursting from the surrounding brush and charging their way.

"Stars save us!" the gray-haired woman cried, her hurried gait turning uneven on wobbly legs.

Riony let out a long, low groan as Lyrrin kept her fixed in a glare.

"Fine. Okay. Yes." Jogging out into the path of the crowd, Riony waved her arms in the air. "Follow us. We know somewhere safe. This way, now! Leave what you can't carry and run!"

Chapter Six

Home. What a dreadfully depressing place to come back to.

A home Kess hadn't returned to since the day she'd been unceremoniously jettisoned from it. She approached with caution, as though the place she had spent her childhood was a snake that could rise up and strike her without warning.

Coming to a crest, Kess paused to look down over Heithorn estate. The looming, fortified walls cradled the main cluster of buildings within. The grand central keep had the appearance of an old-fashioned stone castle, towering above the main hall, kitchens, stables, hatchery, gatehouse, and dormitories, with their newer, ceramic-tiled roofs and smooth, rendered walls.

"We came all this way. Let's see this through. Come on, Gris."

He moved with hesitation, as though he could sense her rising anxiety. His paws treaded softly, and he stalked, low and hunched, ears down, straight toward the estate.

Maybe she should enter through a back gate or a concealed entrance. Shouldn't she hide herself and her return with the shame her family would no doubt treat both?

No. I will not hide. There was no reason she shouldn't ride straight up the main road to the entrance gate. This was her home, her birthright. She was the daughter of the Heithorns, honorable dragonlords and riders. She wouldn't cower.

But she was also going to see family who had plotted her death once already.

Kess noticed the quiet first. An eerie silence, without any sound of human life making Griskin's ears swivel toward it. No smoke came from chimneys. No slaves worked the fields around the walls.

Strange. But the only person who needed to be there was her brother, with his dragon. That was who she was going to get help from, one way or another.

And it was without doubt going to be the most intolerable experience of her life, but Kess couldn't see how she was going to catch Dracuni without a dragon, and Kife was her closest connection to a dragonrider.

It was a last resort to even consider asking Kife for help. Kess was certain the chances he would kill her on sight were far higher than him helping her—just one reason she'd never returned for help or to attempt to get herself a dragon from there before. But now she had leverage.

Now she could offer a share in the most precious creature in all the land. That should be enough to keep even Kife on her side.

As she got closer to the estate, she realized it wasn't going to matter how she approached. The place looked entirely empty.

The solid front gates stood ajar. Through them, once manicured gardens sprung with wild vines and unruly foliage, chasing each other up the walls of nearby buildings.

Abandoned? How long had the estate sat empty? Kess had been gone for five years. From the looks of it, it could have been an equally long time since anybody had lived there.

Kife had always said they only stayed at the isolated estate because of Kess. Had they left as soon as she wasn't a problem anymore? Had they left the very next day?

Maybe they threw a party first.

Kess mused that she should perhaps feel grief or anger to see her family home in this state of disrepair. But all she felt was a dull, heavy sorrow that she wasn't at all surprised. Abandonment came easily to Heithorns.

It only hurt that she could imagine them now, living safely and richly in a dragonkeep, happy, as though she'd never existed.

Should I have come home sooner? Made my way straight back here from where Kife left me? Forced them to continue to suffer my existence?

A burning sob hit Kess's throat so fast that she almost toppled backward off Griskin in her attempt to breathe it away.

"Raze them all!" she rasped, then set her face like steel. "Let's see if they left anything valuable behind in their rush to be rid of the life I subjected them to."

Kess and Griskin circled the entrance courtyard. Everything was as Kess remembered it—the well with its woven metal roof, roses growing beside the portcullis, the whipping post—but with added layers of grime and weeds sprouting from every gap and corner.

Griskin didn't like going into buildings, but Kess still urged him up to the main hall, stroking his neck. "No one is going to catch you. Nobody's here."

The door was already open, and Griskin whined, sniffing at a lump of debris right behind it.

It took a moment for Kess's eyes to adjust to the dim interior light. Not just debris, but a body. Mostly bones and moldering remains of clothing. The bared teeth of the skull were open in a silent, endless scream. A couple of the limbs were farther away from the torso than they should have been.

Frowning, she turned back to glance over the walls and surroundings outside. No sign of burning. If there had been a revenant attack, Heithorn estate was protected by Kife and two other dragonriders. There would have been fire.

But now that she looked again with a keener eye, she saw the dull ochre of other old bones piled into corners, obscured beneath vines and grass.

Whatever had happened, there hadn't even been anyone around afterward to clean up.

A plague couldn't have taken everybody so quickly.

A bandit assault would have had less chance of getting past the dragonriders than revs.

A low growl echoed from one of the pathways between buildings outside, all too familiar.

I guess it was revs after all.

Kess watched from behind the door. The living skeleton of a horse wandered aimlessly into the courtyard, growled again in a way that a horse never should, then ambled away.

"What odds do you give that it's the only one?" Kess whispered to Griskin.

He lapped his tongue and huffed.

"Yeah, me too. Keep your ears open, and bolt if anything gets too close."

Kess and Griskin stalked silently through the main hall and up the carpeted stairs into the chambers above. Candelabras still lined the walls between paintings and tapestries. A few finger-sized bantam ferrets scattered in the distance, making Griskin twitch.

Lord Heithorn's office was open, and Kess led Griskin in. Papers and letters were spread on the desk, grayed by mold. Velvet upholstered chairs lay toppled to the side.

Two skeletal carcasses rotted in a jumble in the corner. Unlooted, untouched. The faded silver brocade dress on one body and the heavy gold chain on the other were all too familiar.

Mami. Fadda. Kess's lips curled, and she tried not to breathe in the dry scent of death wafting from them. *I guess you didn't leave after all.*

She hurt, unexpectedly, feeling their loss deep in her chest, and she hurt again feeling that she probably cared more for them in that moment than they ever cared for her. Sure, they had gone to great expense attempting to "heal" her, but Kess had never felt as though it came from a place of love.

It had come from a place of shame. From attempts to make their daughter worthy of the Heithorn name so that they would no longer have to stand the dishonor of having a child who wasn't a perfect physical specimen in a world where the rich should be able to heal anything.

Why had they stayed once Kess was gone? If she were the reason they'd lived far from the luxury of a dragonkeep, why were they still there? Had the attack come before they were able to leave?

And why hadn't the dragonriders fought the revs? Were her brother and the other riders killed before they could?

Kess blinked at her parents' remains, dry-eyed.

"I should burn them. That's the right thing to do." *And the safe thing as well.*

She couldn't bring herself to move closer to them. She couldn't imagine touching them, dragging them outside to burn on a pyre.

Whatever unkindness they had shown her, they were her parents. And now they were bones, and the sight of those bones shook something deep inside Kess until she had to turn away. Nobody should have to see their family that way.

Pretending her parents weren't lying dead in the corner, Kess took Griskin around the desk. She pulled the tattered curtains aside and peered out the window. There was movement below, at least three more revs, shambling aimlessly through the estate surrounds.

We're going to have to be careful getting out of here.

Revs didn't seem to target animals, only humans, and sometimes Kess remained unnoticed, hidden up on Griskin's back. But not always.

Maybe she should set fire to the entire place before she left.

But Kess wasn't leaving empty-handed. There had to be some value she could wring from these hollow walls first.

Bringing Griskin close beside the bookshelf lining the back wall, Kess reached in beside a heavy dragon-head bookend and pressed the lever there.

A soft click sounded from behind the wood and books, and Kess tugged on that section of shelf. It swung forward with a whine of old hinges to reveal the compact vault where her family stashed their wealth of silvernix.

She glared at it for a long moment before turning back to her parents' bones. She needed the key.

She almost turned and left without clearing any riches from that vault. She still had one vial of silvernix, and Griskin's leg was healing well so far.

But if there was any chance the lockbox held more, it was worth having. She had to toughen up and do what had to be done.

She brought Griskin beside the bodies and lowered him down onto his belly so she could lean over and reach within the clothing of her father's corpse.

The ragged fabric felt damp in a way that sent grotesque shudders through Kess's fingers, up her neck, and over her scalp.

When her hand closed around the key she wanted to jerk it back, but she held her mettle long enough to also take the gold chain and house crest beside it as well. Then she was able to turn away again and pretend the bodies weren't there.

She wiped her hands furiously on her saddle blanket. Two turns of the key and the vault opened. She reached in, rifling through a scattering of papers, opening a single velvet pouch which held fewer sovs than Kess carried on her. Not a single bottle, not a tiny vial, not a drop of silvernix.

Kess swallowed the acid in her throat.

All her family's wealth, gone. Her parents hadn't used it all on her. There had been a few dragons tamed, and a scattering of illnesses cured.

But Kess had counted at least five doses on her in the time she could remember, and no doubt there'd been more when she was younger, as soon as her parents realized she wasn't learning how to walk. As soon as they saw her legs didn't kick and move the way other babies' legs did.

How long had the Heithorns been out of silvernix?

Kess turned Griskin away. She didn't bother closing the vault or any doors behind her.

She still had her single drop of silvernix which she'd use for taming her dragon. As hard won as it was, she couldn't spare it on anything else.

She'd almost died for it, Griskin had almost died for it, and worse, she had killed for it.

After finding each other, it had taken a little while for Kess and Griskin to grow strong enough together to do more than simply survive.

Once they had, Kess had begun pursuing her goal of owning a dragon. She'd considered the ways she might obtain one and decided raising one from a wild dragon egg was her best option. And for that, she needed silvernix.

There were plenty of unscrupulous smugglers out in the wastes and Kess sought them out, looking for one that sold the precious liquid.

She'd been through almost a dozen smugglers, fleecing them of their gold and valuables after they'd lied to her about their ability to provide unicorn blood. It had satisfied her growing frustration and helped her to build her own considerable wealth.

But the news of the wolf-riding thief had spread, and when she finally found a supplier who really was trading silvernix, it turned out he already knew about her.

The guy was a monster. Kess had seen it from the moment she'd met him. From how he called himself *Shadowlord* to the decorations on his coat, made from fingers of those who'd crossed him. But Kess needed the silvernix, so she took his invite to meet at his hideout to make the trade. And walked right into his trap.

A literal pit trap that 'Shadowlord' had built into his den, dropping her and Griskin into a pit with the smuggler's own pet—a revenant wolf.

From the bodies down there, Kess knew she wasn't the first to have fallen victim to his trap. But she and Griskin were the first to fight their way out of it.

Kess had realized then that she should have killed all the smugglers from the start instead of letting them warn each other about her. She'd been too soft and almost paid the price. And so Shadowlord was the first she'd killed.

There had been many since then, but it never got easier. Her heart felt hatched with scars tallying all the lives she'd taken to survive. And voices spoke deep in her soul, voices that sounded like her family, telling her she didn't deserve to take lives to preserve her own.

Kess took the narrow servants' stairs down again and cut quickly across the courtyard to the hatchery. Heading in from the back like that, she passed one of the standing stones of the Alderkin shrine ruins that backed up right behind the hatchery building.

Heithorn estate was built almost directly over whatever the Alderkin had been doing with the land there before. Her family hadn't bothered demolishing the shrine and instead had used it as additional storage during harvest months.

It didn't take long to see that the hatchery was empty. Kess had hoped there may have been a dormant egg or abandoned dragon, but there was no sign of either, alive or dead.

The ever-present pile of hay in the corner had mulched itself down almost flat and writhed with beetles and worms.

It had been behind those bales that Kife had hidden her the time he brought her down to see the baby dragons. When he'd tricked her into choosing his dragon for him.

Then he'd left her there, alone and cold in the night air that she wasn't supposed to be out in, too humiliated and upset to try to make her way back to her room herself.

Riony had found her crying on the dirt beside the one tamed hatchling and the burning bodies of the discarded options.

Without a word, she'd picked Kess up and carried her out. And then she'd roared, running and swooping, pretending to be a dragon. Through a growing smile, Kess had hissed at the fool to hush.

But it was too late, and they were heard, and Pony was blamed for taking Kess out of her rooms at night, and it was Pony whose back was opened yet again at the whipping post.

Only months ago, there had been such fire inside Kess, so much drive while hunting that mother dragon, for all the time tracking and waiting. How come all she could feel now was this dull, bland weight of sorrow? What was wrong with her?

It's Pony. Seeing her again, it's mixed up everything inside me, making all these intolerable memories come back. That's all.

And even if Pony had been the only person to ever be kind to her, she didn't *like* Kess, didn't care for her. Given the nature of their relationship, Riony could only ever know hatred for Kess.

But still, Riony was kind, mostly, and that was more than even her family had mustered. And that kindness had kindled a brittle ember inside Kess that had wanted more, had wanted that kindness to become liking and caring.

How could it, though, when it was Kess's ownership of Riony? When it was Kess's family and Kess's very existence that kept Riony in constant suffering and torture? So Pony hated Kess, and Kess made sure she hated Pony in return because nothing else would be tolerable.

And now Pony stood between Kess and what she needed. If she could have Dracuni, that wealth, that power, would it be enough to make people finally respect her? Would it be enough to make people find kindness for her, or more?

Kess wasn't sure. But she had to follow through.

I have to achieve my dream. Otherwise, what am I?

Kess only narrowly dodged a roaming revenant on the way into the keep. It was a big risk spending any more time in the rev-infested estate, but there was one last place she had to check.

The dragonriders' rooms. Kife's room. They were in the upper levels of the keep, since the dragons themselves were often kept roosted on the battlements up top. She needed to find his body too, to know for sure that all her hopes had come to nothing, that she'd have to start planning anew again. This was one part of the estate Kess had never been allowed in, never managed to sneak into. Only dragonriders were allowed.

She followed the polished marble stairs up as they circled around the tower, checking rooms as she went. Empty. Empty. And empty again.

Finally, an immense pyre of emotion ignited within Kess.

Empty? No bodies, no belongings, no anything.

They might have packed up and left after the revs got in, after Mami and Fadda died. Kess knew she was kidding herself. There were no signs of burning because the dragonriders were already gone. Kife was already gone.

Kess grasped at the only remaining furnishing, a Heithorn crest banner, and tore it from the wall.

He was supposed to protect the estate! That was his job, their job, as dragonriders. I would have done it!

Kess's breathing slowed again, and her eyes narrowed, glaring at the room before her, stripped of all belongings, all furniture, everything her brother could take with him.

He had abandoned Kess, and then he'd abandoned the entire estate.

But that also meant that Kife might still be alive out there somewhere.

Kess just had to find him.

CHAPTER SEVEN

R iony ran. She had the toddler that the malnourished man had carried in one arm and the man himself slung over her shoulders.

Aishena and Benjin led the way, navigating through a thicket of dry brambles and scratchy twigs. Lyrrin, Dracuni, and all the other children and refugees filled the space between. High-pitched yelps punctuated the pounding of feet as the army of revenants closed in.

"Almost there. I see the standing stones!" Aishena called back.

Riony had one good look at the massive number of revenants before they ran, and it almost paralyzed her with hopelessness. She ran anyway hoping the shrine would work and protect them. Otherwise, they were all in for a very unpleasant death under an ocean of undead.

Not all the army of revs seemed to be chasing the people. They were moving with some purpose of their own. Unfortunately, it seemed to be in the same direction the humans were going, and as soon as any of the revs caught sight of them, they raced ahead to attack.

They seemed to be coming in from all sides now and were almost upon them.

"Nisk! Take her!" Riony tossed the toddler across into Niskina's arms.

Niskina cradled the crying infant and kept running.

Riony bent to the side and put the man back on his feet. "Go! It's just up ahead!"

He nodded, hobbling unevenly away, one leg not working as well as the other.

And Riony unbuckled her sword.

She didn't get a chance to activate it before the first revenant hit. A haggard goat of rotting flesh rammed its head at her, jaws gnashing.

Riony got the sword between them, knocking it out of the way with a heavy blow that strained her arms. Then she ran her fingers over the float rune, and the sword lifted weightlessly in her hands.

Riony swung and clashed against the ferocious undead as she jumped and jogged backward, holding them off from the remaining stragglers as they closed in on the shrine.

Sparks, it had better be safe. They'd had one other experience since the first time they sheltered at a shrine when a revenant hadn't been able to breach the invisible barrier. But that had been only one rev each time. Not dozens. Not hundreds.

Even activating the gateway and trying to flee that way would take long enough that the revs could take half the people there before they got through.

A full-grown dreer skeleton galloped toward her. All deer-like elegance it would have had in life was lost in the wild fury of its attack. It stood twice Riony's height, and its cloven hooves were cracked and sharpened by rot. It would only need to kick her as it passed by to have her saying goodbye to her intestines. And she really preferred that they stay where they were.

A glance over her shoulder showed the remaining refugees crossing the boundary of the standing stones. They huddled and pushed, trying to all fit within the shelter of the walled shrine within the ring of tall crystalline blocks.

Sister? Sister, hurry!

Riony turned her back on the approaching revs and sprinted for safe ground. A slithering bolt of patchy red fur hung over bones raced for Riony's feet. An undead fox, snapping and growling. Riony leaped, the float magic of her sword bringing her far higher than natural, and she came flying through the barrier between the standing stones.

She felt the small flutter of energy ripple over her skin, then landed firmly on both feet. Her eyes sought Lyrrin and Dracuni, finding them encircled by Niskina and the Hjelzahn siblings, backs to a wall.

Safe? Dracuni angled her head, watching behind Riony.

A great scream went up from almost every voice sheltering in the shrine as the wave of revenants crashed down upon them.

And then were held back, blocked by the invisible wall.

As the revenants clawed and roared from the boundary of the standing stones, people continued to scream and sob, but slowly, as eyes opened and they saw the revenants couldn't reach them, the cries dwindled.

"What is this? How is this possible?" The elderly woman who had given them warning before walked boldly right up to the invisible barrier, staring the gnashing revenants in the eye like a grandmother scolding a child for stealing dessert too early.

"We don't know for sure how it's happening, but we noticed some other shrines kept the revs out. Not all the shrines, though." Riony glanced again at Dracuni.

She didn't want them making any link between the unidragon and the magic of the shrines. But she also didn't want them assuming all shrines would be safe.

The woman turned again, assessing Riony with her gaze. She lifted a finger imperiously in the air. "Will it hold?"

Her accent was strongly Rolanian, and there were a few streaks of red hair amongst the gray.

"For now." Riony honestly wasn't sure how long the magic keeping the revs out would last, especially if and when Dracuni wasn't there anymore. For all she knew, it only worked when Dracuni was at the shrine since that was all she'd experienced.

The older woman gave Riony and her glowing sword one long, hard look, then lifted both arms in the air, tattered shawls hanging from them like wings, and she strode into the crowd, speaking in hurried words to this person and that as she went.

The people, a few dozen of them, murmured in low tones between themselves. They unloaded whatever filled their arms—baskets, bundles, babies—onto cleared space on the ground.

Riony deactivated her sword and leaned it against the wall beside Lyrrin, then dumped her packs beside it.

"Is this everyone? Did everyone make it?" her sister asked.

"I didn't see anyone behind me that wasn't made of bones and rot. Are you all okay?"

There were nods all around, and then Lyrrin sighed into a smile. "We won! We won against *them.*"

Her blue eyes flicked to the revenants amassing around the barrier. Her small face tensed. Her lips trembled, then returned to the smile again.

"Not really a battle, which is good because we would not have come out of that with all our insides still on the inside. But sure, I'll count it as a win," Riony said.

But safe? Safe here?

Riony sought Dracuni, who was curled between Lyrrin and Benjin's legs, face tucked under the hanging hems of Lyrrin's long coat.

Riony realized she'd never answered her before. "Yeah, the bad things can't get in."

Also safe from others?

Dracuni was looking behind Riony at the crowd of refugees. They had calmed now, a relieved energy spreading as they laid out cooking supplies and rugs on the ground.

Others are not-friends. Dracuni's emotions were a muddle of sadness and confusion.

"They aren't Kess. She's the not-friend. These people ..." Riony didn't know.

These people were desperate, and if they knew what Dracuni really was ... Riony hated the thought of having to protect Dracuni from them. But she would.

She patted Dracuni on the snout. "Just stay out of the way, okay? I won't let them hurt you."

"We aren't going to hurt any of you, child." The older woman approached them again, stopping a respectful distance away from their cluster. "But we would like the same guarantee."

Riony stepped up to meet her. "Because we lured you to safety here from the revs just so we could beat you up ourselves? Sounds exhausting."

"Plenty of folk in this world who offer safety provide harm instead."

"Can't argue with that. But no, we're not planning on hurting anyone." Riony held her hands up in a gesture of peace.

"And what is that creature you have with you?"

Lyrrin tucked Dracuni's head farther under her coat.

"Just a baby dragon," Riony replied.

Something else. Dracuni snorted softly but remained still as though tamed.

"And what are you? Dragonlords? Dragonriders?" Her words cut sharply from her mouth as she eyed their weapons, Aishena's steel-bright dragonlord-born hair, Niskina's mixed features.

"No, just travelers. The dragon is ... a rescue."

The woman's eyes roamed over all of them, the irises pale against her dark skin. She smirked when she saw Niskina, still clutching one of their children.

"Just a group of rescuers, then. Well, keep the dragon away from us. We've no love for the things."

A soft sigh of sadness blew from Dracuni. ***Not-friends.***

Riony couldn't reply then; nor did she know what to say. She wished it were safe for Dracuni to make friends, that the very blood in her veins didn't make her a target.

The woman tapped two fingers on her chest. "I'm Myrwa."

Riony introduced herself but left the others anonymous. She took a couple of steps toward the shrine entrance, seeing that the gateway there was still in one piece. "Listen, we'll keep to ourselves—"

Myrwa waved a hand. "I didn't say that. Just keep the beast away. The rest of you are welcome to join us. We're making some food and would like to share it with the people who saved our lives."

"Thank you, but what I wanted to say was we can split paths. You don't have to stay here. Amongst all of this." Riony pointed at the swarms of revs building around the barrier.

Their growls reverberated through the cooling afternoon air.

Riony hid a shiver. "Inside the shrine, there's a sort of magic doorway. We know how to make it work. You can travel straight to the Alderkin undercity, where it's safe."

"I'd scoff at such a thing, but I'm not quite blind enough to miss that giant glowing sword you were heaving around. Alderkin magic if I ever saw it. And I've heard of the undercity refuge. Let me speak with the others. Until then, come and join us."

Riony lifted a shoulder to her companions, questioning.

Niskina offered a halfhearted shrug in return and strode off to find someone to hand the sniffling infant to. And probably something to drink.

Aishena seemed less comfortable.

Myrwa was already heading away, so Riony asked the delver quietly, "Was it okay for me to offer them passage through the gateway?"

Aishena's expression dropped. "I... don't know. We couldn't send them *there*, could we?"

"Oh, oh no! Not to the gateway in the depths," Riony clarified, waving her hands to dismiss the idea.

None of them wanted to open the path back to where Brishan, Yoskar, and the other delvers had died. Where they may still lay, for all they knew.

"We'd send them to the one down the hill and give them directions from there. And we wouldn't show them how to use the gateway either—just send them through." Riony hoped her offer sounded at all sensible.

Aishena chewed her lip thoughtfully.

Lyrrin spoke up instead. "I think it's a good thing. We're helping them. That's important."

"As long as it doesn't bite us back," Benjin added in a flat tone that sounded like his brother. "We should take Dracuni now and leave in case any of them get curious."

"We don't know whether this place stays safe without Dracuni here though. What if we pop away through the gateway and the revs come crashing through onto these people?" Riony flicked an arm at the growling wall of desiccated bodies around them.

Benjin's jaw worked. "Maybe one night will be okay."

With less confidence than before, Lyrrin asked, "If we're staying, can I … go and meet them?"

Riony looked over the group of refugees. There were mostly families, all quietly settling in, trying to get comfortable with what they had managed to bring with them.

Niskina had found the thin, older man who'd carried the toddler before and another younger man with him who greeted the child and Niskina happily. Niskina leaned her curves into the conversation as she laughed at something the young man said. Riony found herself envious of how the girl could make the most of any situation.

There seemed to be no imminent threat from the people around them.

"Sure. Just be careful, and stay away from the hordes of ravenous undead. You know, the usual rules."

I stay, Dracuni huffed. She circled the ground, then sat and leaned against the wall of the shrine.

"I'll stay with Dracuni," Aishena offered and gave Benjin a look that told him he would too.

A large cooking fire was soon roaring, brightening the area as dusk fell with a soft blanket of fog.

The army of revenants had mostly lost interest in the humans they couldn't reach, but continued to stream past, parting the mist like ghosts. Riony shivered. Despite being safe within the shrine, it was super creepy. Where were they all going? And why?

Riony settled down at a clear spot near the fire and collected her harvest of hennan, setting it out to prepare for drying and grinding to make hair dye. It had to be processed properly before the soft leaves spoiled.

Pots burbled beside her and Lyrrin stood across the flames, offering one of her chickens to the refugees. There was a strange expression on her face, both timid and fierce at the same time, as she stared at the young woman she'd approached.

As that woman turned to the fire, taking a seat to pluck the hen, Riony noticed her eyes. Bright lilac.

"Know some of the old crafts, I see?" Myrwa took a seat beside Riony, nodding to Riony's fingers picking away gently at the leaves of their own accord. "Got some good skill there, not bruising the leaves at all."

Riony smiled softly. "This was how Amma taught me."

"Using it for dyeing?"

"Mm-hmm."

"Did she teach you that if you mix in a little shillgrue, the color will hold longer?"

Riony's fingers stilled. "No, she didn't. She wasn't around for long enough to teach me everything."

Myrwa nodded solemnly. "Well, now you know. Even with all my years, I still feel like I haven't done enough, haven't taught enough."

Riony put down the sprig of hennan she was working on and looked at the ground for a long moment. "Does that feeling ever change? I never feel like I'm doing enough … Like

I should be doing more. For my family, friends, people like you, for the whole sparking world. But what can I do? What can any of us do in the face of so much wrong?"

Riony pointed with her chin at the slow marching horde of undead surrounding them. Endless, undying horror. Relentless. Uncaring. Unyielding. The very sight of them seemed to drain the hope from Riony like water burbling down a drain.

She dropped her voice to a whisper, as though ashamed of the words coming out. But still they spilled. With Niskina intending to do whatever she wanted to do right up until the end she thought was nigh and Aishena unable to form a single opinion of her own, Riony had been feeling utterly alone in the burden of her responsibilities.

Faced with this woman, with kind, wrinkled eyes, and a willingness to share knowledge of herbs that felt so much like home, Riony's heart seemed to crack open and flood her mouth with words and worries.

"Things are getting worse. I've never seen anything like these numbers of revs before. If this is what the world is now … what future could we have? What future will the kids have?"

Riony sought Lyrrin in the crowd, still awkwardly trying to strike up a conversation with the purple-eyed woman. Nearby, the pregnant teenager winced as she paced. Benjin sat beside Dracuni, meticulously cleaning Yoskar's staff. The toddler in the ragged man's arms pinched at his beard.

"I've been fighting and fighting just to keep us all alive. But for what, in the long run?" Riony whispered, unable to speak her worries any louder.

Myrwa picked up the work that Riony had laid down, carefully plucking the small leaves from the stems. "You don't look to me like the type who gives up. You're doing just fine. And more than that, you are making change."

Riony huffed. "We've lost our home more than once. Lost family. All the changes in our lives recently haven't exactly been positive."

"I mean for us. Look what you did for us!" Myrwa tilted her head to the people around them. "You got us here. You brought us to safety. You saved our lives. Every single life here. And you've given us hope."

"You'll go to the undercity?"

A man approached and handed Myrwa a bowl of steaming food. She took it, then passed it along to Riony.

"No. I spoke with the others. They're tired. Tired of running. Tired of hiding. So we thank you for your offer, but we've decided that we are going to stay here."

"Here?" Riony raised her eyebrows at the ruined stones, scraggy bushes, and growling undead circling them.

"The revenants will pass by, and we're safe here from them anyway. We could start again. Go back and see if anything on the wagons is salvageable, reclaim our belongings. We could build something here." Myrwa waved to a girl across the fire then pressed her hand to her heart, keeping it there as she returned her focus to Riony.

"Safe from revs. Not reliant on dragonriders"—she paused and spat on the ground—"to protect us. No longer running. Free and aboveground. This place, it's the hope we've been looking for."

"That ... sounds nice." Riony's fingers warmed around the bowl she'd been given, and she sniffed at the food.

Rice, with a little carrowmy making it fragrant and golden. She hadn't had rice in years. It wasn't something that could be grown underground. But it had been a staple in the village they'd raised Lyrrin in. A rush of nostalgia hit her like a sword to the chest.

"You could stay here with us," Myrwa offered.

"I don't think that would work out." Riony didn't want to explain the multitude of ways they were being hunted or why.

"Think on it. Your little one seems very taken with Naya." Myrwa nodded over to where Lyrrin watched the young woman preparing the chicken to cook.

Lyrrin stared at Naya's working fingers, a small frown of disappointment on her face.

Naya's eyes had a brightness to them like Lyrrin's, but her hands had no sharp, clawed nails. Riony couldn't see any sign her hair, a mousy brown, had been dyed either. Larger than usual ears poked from that hair, pointed, with tufts of hair at the ends.

She broached the subject carefully. "Naya, her eyes ..."

Myrwa tsked. "Unicorn blood used while she was in the womb. She has the usual silvernix-birth changes. Lilac eyes, ear shape, a bit of fur here and there."

"Those are the usual changes? No changes to hands? Hair color?"

"Not that I've seen. There were a lot when I was young and before people knew better. Not sure the story with Naya's mother, why and how she used the cursed stuff, but Naya ended up with us when the family didn't want her."

"Cursed stuff? You don't like silvernix?"

Another bowl of food arrived for Myrwa, and she took a mouthful with pinched fingers. "Don't like where it came from. We are siblings to all life, and when we take life to sustain our own, we must do so with respect."

Riony nodded. That was how she'd been raised too, in Rolanian customs.

Myrwa continued, "There was no respect in the slaughter of the unicorns. To utterly destroy our eldest siblings, first born to Amma moon ... What person with a heart and soul would approve?"

Riony glanced over at Dracuni, snuggled up onto Aishena's lap despite getting too large to fit now, tail and back legs dangling off. "That leaves a lot of heartless and soulless people out there. Nobody seemed to care where it came from or who they hurt to get it if they could profit from it."

"Some of us cared. Back when people were running hunts, trying to catch and bleed every unicorn they could get. Some of us tried to stop it."

Riony stared at her food. She hadn't been able to bring herself to taste the rice, as though she would be eating memories. "I thought only the Alderkin fought to stop the hunting of unicorns?"

"Taens believe they are above all other life in our world—not a part of it. But many Rolanians were against it."

"Really?"

Myrwa shrugged, picking at her rice. "More people cared than you know since those who caught those unicorns then became dragonlords and shaped the world in their favor, pretending they had every right, that we were all on their side. But we protested, and when our protests were ignored, we fought. We were labeled extremists, traitors, and worse. But we tried anyway."

It warmed Riony inside to know that there were people who cared more about the creatures being harmed than the value that could be gained from them. She wondered what they would think if they knew about Dracuni. Whether they would still hold strong to their past principles.

She wasn't about to test that theory, but there was a subtle release of tension in her shoulders.

"Was it worth it?" she asked. "Fighting. When faced against so much? When fighting a losing battle?"

Myrwa put her bowl down and stared deep into Riony's eyes. "It was. Even if we didn't win. If only for the reason that when our children ask us what we did in the face of something terrible happening, at least we don't have to say *nothing*."

Riony looked over the somber procession of corpses slowly marching by. This world, with magic all but gone and undead dominating the land ... Was this the price all humans had to pay for the greedy few who'd glutted themselves on the deaths of unicorns?

Riony had only seen the mural of the murdered unicorn in the depths briefly as she'd fled past, but the others had described it to her. How it seemed to suggest the shadowdragon had been around since that first unicorn died, not since the end of the war as a final curse from the Alderkin.

But unicorns had been gone for more than thirty years, and Alderkin gone now too, so why was the undead plague only getting worse? More and more revenants, revenants that didn't die when burned, revenants that came back again and again. Revenants marching together with some united cause.

How was the shadowdragon getting stronger and stronger?

There was one other important moment depicted in the mural of the unicorn's death.

A human tamed a dragon for the first time.

And more and more and more dragons had been tamed ever since.

Despite the heat of the fire brushing a warm glow over her face, Riony shivered.

"Do you think the Alderkin cursed us with the shadowdragon?" Riony asked Myrwa.

Myrwa scooped the last few grains of rice from her bowl. "I don't think they needed to. I think we cursed ourselves." She stood with a soft groan and brushed off her skirts. "Eat your food before it gets cold. I have people to see to. I think maybe you do too."

Riony followed her gaze across the fire where Niskina had a half-empty bottle in her hands and was sitting between two young men.

They were laughing boisterously, and despite them feigning hushed whispers, Riony could hear their game of 'bed, wed, or behead' carry across to her. Just in time for Niskina to put Riony up for consideration to her new friends.

"If you declare your intention for any of those three to me, you'll be getting bed, wed, and beheaded by my sword instead," Riony snapped back.

"Oh, would you relax? It's just a game!" Niskina pouted.

She stood and gave Riony a challenging glare before pulling the two men up to their feet as well. Before she could lead them away, a whimpering moan broke over the soft chatters of the camp.

"Myrwa?" a young girl's voice called.

Riony traced it to the pregnant teen.

The girl's round-cheeked face was both pale and blotchy red, and she buckled forward, clutching her bulging stomach. "I think it's happening!"

Chapter Eight

Riony found herself on her feet as Myrwa chatted to the young woman in hushed tones. The old woman brushed the blond curls away from the girl's warm sienna face, then pressed a hand to her swollen belly. Wetness soaked through her skirt.

"Yes, love, I'd say it is definitely happening now."

"What is it?" The commotion had been enough for Niskina to abandon her potential partners and join Riony, craning to see.

"I think she's gone into labor," Riony replied.

There was a fluster and worry on Myrwa's face at odds with how commanding she'd been before. She ushered the pregnant girl away from the main group, eyes seeking, bringing her by Riony on the way.

"Is everything okay?" Riony asked.

Myrwa said softly, "We lost our midwife a few months back. Kellae is our first birth without one."

"Riony can help!" Lyrrin almost shouted in reply, having appeared in between Riony and Niskina.

Myrwa frowned at the ramshackle collection of armor covering the bulk of Riony's arms. "You're a midwife?"

Riony took a step back. "Oh no! No. Not really. I mean, I trained to be one. But only until I was sixteen. And I haven't even been at a birth in years. And I never did one on my own—only ever as an assistant. It's really … I couldn't …"

Kellae grunted out a scream, bending in pain so suddenly she slipped from Myrwa's supportive grasp. Riony lunged forward and grabbed the girl.

Gently lifting her back to her feet, she bit her lip as the girl met her gaze, her expression wildly pleading.

"If the pains are coming so close together now, it won't be long. This should be quick for you." Riony tried to sound reassuring and remove herself from her position of support, but the girl gripped back on to her fiercely.

"Amma died. She died giving birth. I don't want to. I don't want to do this."

You and me both, Riony thought, blood rushing from her face.

"Come on. We don't have anybody else," Myrwa said, grasping both Riony and Kellae and pushing them on.

They stumbled together like that around the side of the shrine where Aishena, Benjin, and Dracuni had stayed.

It was the quietest, most private area, as the refugees had given the unidragon space on the otherwise crowded safe ground.

Her hurt? Dracuni lifted her head.

"Her have baby. Sparks, I mean, *she*." Riony cleared her throat, pretending she was talking to Aishena. "She's having a baby."

A couple of other refugees, older women mostly, brought some blankets over but quickly stepped back again, hovering at a distance. Riony sent Lyrrin to the campfire for hot water.

"Niskina, swap with me?" Riony said, prying herself from Kellae's clutches.

The flush of alcohol seemed to have vanished from Niskina's face, and she wore a wide-eyed, awed look of terror, at war with her attempts to school it into something calm and confident.

She gave a wobbly smile to the groaning girl. "Hi. You can call me Nisk. Do you have any family you'd like brought over?"

Held up by Niskina on one side and Myrwa on the other, Kellae shook her head roughly, sobbing through her pain. "A brother. But he's ... a long way away. Slavers got him."

"Lower her," Riony said, and they brought Kellae down into a squatting position.

Lyrrin returned, sloshing a large steaming pot. Riony gave her hands a brisk scrub in the hot water, then checked on how far along the labor was.

Her finger shook, and she muttered about a million apologies, feeling clumsy and awkward, but her own mother's voice came through in her mind, reminding her, guiding her as it had when she was younger.

"You're really close. I'm going to ask you to push soon. Do you think you can do that?"

"How? How? It's too much. I can't do this!" There was a high edge of panic in Kellae's voice, and she was crumpling in Niskina and Myrwa's arms.

Riony was worried the girl was about to lose it entirely. "Listen, okay? Nobody likes to admit it, and it's going to sound gross, but it's the truth. You're going to push, just like you're doing the biggest poo of your life."

"Riony!" Niskina scolded.

Kellae's eyes widened, and then she coughed out something between a sob and a laugh.

"You can do that, right?" Riony gave her a casual smile.

Kellae brought herself a little more upright and nodded.

"Yeah, you can do this. You're already doing amazingly," Niskina added.

Riony showed the girl how to breathe with the pain, but the fear was still heavy in her eyes. Her breaths came out shuddering and soaked in tears.

Niskina drew her attention again, smiling encouragement. "Is the father around?"

Kellae bared her teeth and growled through another wave of pain.

Myrwa shook her head. "The father is a dragonrider. He ... took payment from Kellae for saving our village once. Two revs he burned, and half our winter stores as well, and still demanded *payment*."

A stone formed in Riony's throat.

"I'm so sorry." Niskina leaned in, holding Kellae closer and rubbing her back.

The fear had left Kellae's eyes, and they burned bright with anger. "They think they own everything!"

"Okay, I need you to push now!" Riony urged.

Kellae's hands fisted closed around Niskina's and Myrwa's, and her whole body tensed as she bellowed. "They won't own my baby. They won't. They won't!"

"Again, push again!" Riony's hands were slick, cradling the tiny head. She prayed silent wishes to the stars that the shoulders would follow, that the babe would breathe, and that Kellae would stop bleeding.

Kellae's legs shook violently, and she threw her head back in a wailing cry.

Riony caught the baby in her trembling hands.

And the baby breathed.

As the army of the undead growled and shambled at her back, Riony rubbed the baby down, marveling at the tiny hands, gasping lips, and the lift and fall of the chest, then handed the newborn to the mother.

She helped Kellae settle the baby down into her shirt, up against her skin, tucked in there almost the same as how Riony had carried Dracuni home from the ice cave.

Niskina and Myrwa lowered Kellae again, letting her lie down and rest as Riony cleaned up. Once the afterbirth had passed, the bleeding stopped as well, and Riony let out a long sigh of relief.

"Good work," Myrwa said, catching Riony's eye as Riony washed her hands again.

"I honestly didn't do a thing. It was one of the easiest births I've ever seen."

Myrwa's expression turned sad. "You do far more than you realize."

Kellae stared down at the new life on her chest in utter amazement, as though she couldn't comprehend where it had come from.

"How are you so beautiful?" she whispered.

Riony stood and wiped her hands dry on her pants.

Niskina rose as well and stared at the new mother and child for a long moment, then turned her eyes to the revenants surrounding them. She murmured, "That was ... that was something."

There was a brightness in her eyes for a moment, but then her face crumpled and she stormed off, swiping tears from her cheeks.

Riony picked up the pot of water, turning to empty it farther away.

"Wait! What do I do now?" Kellae called out. "I don't know how to look after a baby."

Riony tipped out the bloodied water and huffed a wry laugh. "You know, I was ten when I ended up with a baby to look after."

Myrwa seemed to do the math, looking over at Lyrrin, but Kellae's eyes remained on her baby.

"I didn't have to do it alone though, because my amma and pabba were with me, at least for a while. And you don't have to do it alone either." Riony nodded to Myrwa and then tilted her head to the other women hovering a few more steps away.

One of them was just finishing knitting some tiny clothing.

Myrwa gave Riony a long, knowing look, her pale eyes glossy.

Riony nodded to her, then strode on wobbly, tired legs over to the wall beside Dracuni and Lyrrin.

There was a bright, happy sense of amazement humming from Dracuni. She had her neck stretched long, straight up, watching over Kellae and the baby.

Riony settled down next to her, thumping onto the stone paving as the rush of energy within her waned.

Made baby! Dracuni thought. ***Her make baby!***

"You liked that, did you?" Riony asked.

Dracuni's body shivered in a strange, excited dance. ***New life, new life!***

"It was kind of more gross than I thought it would be," Lyrrin replied. "And I already thought it would be pretty gross."

"Yeah," Benjin agreed, cheeks gone ashy pale.

Riony rolled her eyes. "I think Dracuni gets it. It was kind of magical."

Baby! Baby life! Dracuni trotted forward on excited paws, but then backed up again after a wary look from Kellae and Myrwa.

Lyrrin moved in closer and tucked herself under Riony's arm. Since traveling with Niskina, Aishena, and Benjin, she hadn't cuddled up to Riony as much as she used to. Wanting to seem as grown and tough as everyone else, Riony figured.

"Was it like that when I was born?" Lyrrin asked.

"Not really. Your mother was in labor for far, far longer."

Lyrrin's eyes widened. "Like that? But longer? How long? An *hour*?"

"All night and then some. She was really strong."

Lyrrin was silent for a moment, then asked, "Do you remember anything else about her?"

"Just that she had this haughty audacity I admired. Serious attitude goals."

Lyrrin smiled, close-lipped. "Do you think now we're aboveground, maybe we could look for her?"

Riony's heart gave a lurch. "I never even knew her name. I don't even know where we'd start. We can't go back and ask the Heithorns. They'd kill us."

"Do you think ... she might be looking for me?"

"If she knew you were alive, I'm sure she would. She seemed to me like the type that would stop at nothing to get you back. But ... she was told you didn't survive."

"So she won't ever look for me, and I'll never know ... who she is."

Riony tried to pull Lyrrin in tighter, but Lyrrin pushed her away and sat up, moving back over to where she'd put her bag and blanket on the ground beside Benjin's.

A hot ache built behind Riony's eyes, and she closed them for a long moment.

She got it. She could understand entirely why Lyrrin wanted to know about her birth parents, but it also hurt. Riony had done everything she could to be there for Lyrrin, to be her family. Because they were the only family they had. Riony's own parents were gone. And they were never going to come back, could never be tracked down and found again.

Riony looked away from Lyrrin as well, only to be met with Aishena's cold, dark eyes beside her.

"You did a good job with the birth," she said.

"Yeah, I really sat there and waited for the baby to come out like a champion."

Aishena tilted her head. "I'm not coddling you. I wouldn't say it if I didn't mean it. You took control and helped the girl through."

"Well, you can go ahead and take control whenever you like too. And I don't mean in a sexy way. Although I wouldn't say no."

Aishena leaned forward, her mouth twisted in offense and eyebrows furrowed. Then that moment of fire vanished, and she backed down, staring at the ground. "I can't."

Riony sighed and rubbed her face with her hands. "Almost thought I had you back for a second there. I miss the old Aishena."

"The old Aishena got her family killed." She jolted up onto her feet, then stalked away, moving to the other side of Lyrrin and Benjin, closest to him.

Dracuni had settled down, her head laying on Riony's lap, still watching the mother and child curled up on their blanket across the ground.

Riony rubbed her soft ears. "Just you and me, then."

Dracuni trilled.

Although her bags and sword lay just nearby, Riony didn't unpack or even pull out a blanket. All her limbs felt like stone and her heart seemed to be solidifying to join them.

She leaned her head back against the shrine wall behind her, chest heaving with breaths to try to ease the pain in there.

More than anything, more than she had in a long time, she wished her amma was there with her.

She felt like she was doing everything for everyone and was exhausted through to her core and worried she still wasn't doing enough.

It felt good to have helped save the people there, helped bring the new life into the world, but it also felt so futile. How much longer would any of this last?

Does that even matter? We did good here and now. That's what's important.

And Riony liked the idea of doing more, of working toward a world that could be safe for Lyrrin and Dracuni and all the other people in her life and this land.

If I can just keep us alive, one more day, then another, and another.

Riony knew she'd keep trying. She wouldn't stop trying.

She just didn't know whether she'd break first.

Chapter Nine

Kess and the city wall guard stared each other down at the entrance to Skaellakeep. "Are you going to let me in or what?"

She sat atop Griskin before the solid iron gate, and on either side the dragonkeep walls rose boldly from the earth, towering into the sky and encircling the entire city.

The gigantic barrier was crafted from weathered stone that bore the scars of dragon fire and scraping claws, overlaid with sleek steel plating like protective scales, designed to keep the undead hordes out. Although scratched and mottled, the metal plates caught the smoke-filtered afternoon sunlight, flashing orange-gold like fire.

The face that had peered at her through the peephole in the gate turned away. "I don't know, Borab. Some wild-looking girl. She's riding on a wolf! You have a look."

The face disappeared and another replaced it, staring down his long nose at Kess. "What do you want?"

"I want to come *in*, obviously."

"For what?"

"To be inside?"

The guard slurped air through his teeth. "We're all full up. Not taking any more refugees and thieving scum. You'll have to find somewhere else."

"Do I look—?" Actually, Kess realized how she must look. Keeping her hair untangled hadn't been much of a priority in recent years. She was covered in ashy grime, and her clothing was a patchwork of mismatched leathers. Pony's delver armor, although too large, was the nicest thing she owned. It was too well made to waste.

Pulling the gold chain and family crest she'd taken from her father's corpse, she held it up high for them to see. "*Regardless* of how I look, I am a dragonlord, daughter of the Heithorn line, and I demand to be let in."

"How'd we know you didn't steal that from someone? Never met a dragonlord that travels by ground. Don't get much of anyone coming in by ground anymore. Either people travel by dragon or don't travel at all."

"Then congratulations, you've only ever met cowards. Listen, I've been told that my brother, Kife Heithorn, is in this keep, and he does have a dragon and would be happy to show it to you up close if you don't let his little sister in."

An embellishment of the truth, but they didn't need to know that.

The voice of the other man came muffled from behind the gate. "I've heard of that guy. He's with the city watch riders. Maybe we should let her in."

So the info she'd tracked down was true. Kife was here. She'd finally found him, after months of searching.

The face in the peephole grimaced. "I'm not sure ..."

"Standing there and opening the gate for anything that is still alive is literally your one job, you gutless bovin. And if you don't, I'll still find my own way in, and we can have words about your inability to do simple tasks while my wolf uses your balls as a chew toy."

"Okay, maybe we shouldn't let her in," the guy behind the door said.

"You just said we should!"

"Maybe we should check with the captain."

"I'm not bringing her into this! Look, I'm letting the girl through and she can go be someone else's problem!"

The peephole closed and gears ground, clunking and clattering, swinging the heavy gate open.

As she waited, Kess ran her fingers along the cool, smooth metal, craning her neck to absorb the full majesty of the keep's protective barrier.

It took Kess's breath away. She'd only been to one of these marvelous fortresses a couple of times in her childhood, when her parents were chasing down leads on a potential cure for her, some promise of new medical innovation that had proven to be a lie every time.

But she'd been as much in awe then as she was now. The sheer height of the dragonkeep cast an imposing silhouette against the horizon. The union of stone and steel, a marriage of tradition and innovation, formed an impenetrable bulwark, a solemn promise to the city's inhabitants that within those walls was a haven that the blight of undead could not touch.

And far above, majestic dragon silhouettes soared in the ashy sky, and Kess's chest felt both full to bursting and hollow at the same time.

The rattling ceased, the way forward open.

Griskin sniffed the air and growled softly but moved forward when urged. Kess gave a cold, hard smile to the two guards as she rode by. Then she was in darkness, the long tunnel spanning the thickness of the walls.

Even before she'd exited out the other side, she could hear the sounds and smells of the bustling city coming in with the beaming light.

The dragonkeep held every facet of human life cradled inside. Even the farms and factories were packed within the high walls. The road from the gate wound up through high-fenced fields with bovin packed shoulder to shoulder, braying in the sweltering heat. Their purpose was twofold—to sustain the dragon workforce and feed the ever-growing human population.

Kess smiled at the idea of buying a good meaty bone to treat Griskin with once they reached the city proper and the markets there. Even she hadn't had much more than rabbit or mouse deer in a long while.

The smell from the stockyards was intense and the heat far worse than it was outside the gates where a small breeze had been blowing freely.

Farther along, Rolanian slaves filled buckets of water from a tanker dragged into the fields by a tamed treedart dragon, sitting vegetatively as it waited its next command. Their crops looked dry, and an overseer yelled at them as though his volume could save the failed harvest.

In the distance, dragon-run factories belched plumes of smoke into the sky, forging steel, glass, and all the modern luxuries desired and deserved by those who kept the land safe. A fine ash fell in the air all around from some fire on the horizon.

Reaching the pinnacle of the road, Kess caught a view of Grand Hofen, the water a rich blue against the browns and grays of the city that butted up against it. White sails of ships shimmered bright in the glary afternoon glow, and a steamer, run by dragonfire, puffed past.

All of this. All this majesty Kess could have if she owned her own dragon. And how much more she could have if she owned the only creature in the land with silvernix blood.

As she and Griskin stalked into the more built-up areas, the keep wasn't quite as majestic as she remembered others being.

The precisely paved streets teemed with homeless refugees, gathered on blankets in the corners like debris blown in the wind. Some huddled in the small shadows of palatial residences, trying to find relief from the heat.

And those doors were adorned with an excess of locks that spoke of growing unease.

The skyline was a blend of bygone grandeur and contemporary innovation. Stone fortresses, their turrets and spires reaching skyward with a timeless grace, stood amidst modern structures crafted from steel and glass that glittered in the sunlight, reflecting more of that burned orange heat down onto the world.

The silhouettes of dragons crowned many of the buildings, sitting motionless, tame and unthinking, awaiting their master's next command.

The people Kess passed were wary of her and Griskin, but Kess didn't feel the need to hide. Let them see her. Let them see who she was, and let them remember her when she returned once more, triumphant, and more powerful than any eyes that currently watched her with fear or disgust.

I just need to find Kife. And make him help me.

It didn't feel like an easy goal, but that had never deterred Kess before.

Kess stopped by a street vendor, buying a few kebabs of bovin meat for herself and Griskin. She dropped an extra gold sov into the man's hand for directions to where the city watch dragonriders spent their evenings.

As the man rattled off the lefts and rights of the pathway ahead, Kess looked over the streets. A death cleaner moved by, sweeping up a dead rat from a corner. He lifted the canvas corner of his cart and threw it in. Kess glimpsed the fingers of a human hand in the shadows contained within before he covered it over again.

Nothing dead could linger within the city walls. Everything was destined for the pyres that burned ceaselessly.

The street to the tavern the vendor had suggested took Kess near a building with elaborately carved unicorn horns flanking the entrance. The scent of desperation was thick as sickly figures surrounded the building, lying in the street. A woman in stark white robes overlaid with an excess of silver jewelry strode among them, followed by two heavily armored men.

They're all sick. The beggars reached for the white-robed woman, pleading and crying.

Kess tried to make out what they were saying in the cacophony of wails. Were they asking for silvernix? She'd heard of silvernix charities, but never seen one.

The robed woman pointed to a Rolanian child, lying limp between surrounding family. The guards picked the girl up, none too gently, and took her away. The family cried their thanks and praise as the doors to the building closed between them and the child.

Kess frowned, uneasy. The child had bright-red hair in a tone that was too familiar. That was all that was making her feel on edge. They were going to help her, weren't they?

"Come on. I want to get out of this heat." Kess nudged Griskin on.

They had to divert from the provided directions when they stumbled upon a riot. A dozen Rolanian slaves threw stones, clashing with armored Taen guards.

What razing madness is this?

Kess and Griskin went around, looping the block, until the tavern was in sight. A lamppost burned bright beside a swinging sign with a draconic emblem on it.

Griskin lifted his snout, and a shiver rustled through his fur beneath Kess's fingers.

"You have a scent?"

He chirped a short bark. He'd had a good sniff around Kife's emptied rooms at the estate. He knew what Kife smelled like.

"Lead the way."

Griskin followed his nose down a side alley of potted flowers and barred windows until he reached the doorway of a tall apartment, ornate with carved stone and faux crenellations along the rooftop, four stories up.

The door was as overburdened by locks and bars as all the other fine buildings Kess had passed.

She considered knocking but didn't want there to be any chance of being turned away, especially in her current state of dishevelment.

A balcony on the top floor had bay doors standing open.

"Let's go see if brother is home."

The narrow side street was almost empty, and the only person wandering through, a gentleman wearing a ridiculous turquoise suit, gave Kess a fearful look, then hurried away.

She spurred Griskin toward the challenging climb. The wolf's powerful hind legs propelled them effortlessly from the ground up onto the bars of the pregnant window, the metal shaped into a bulging protrusion to allow those inside to lean out.

Kess tucked herself in close to Griskin's back, his fur tickling her cheeks as she hugged around his shoulders, making her body part of his. Kess's eyes, sharp and focused, scanned the architecture for the perfect trajectory, guiding Griskin with the gentle pressing of her fingers.

His paws barely whispered against the uneven stone walls as he pushed off again, twisting mid-leap to land upon the neighbor's lower rooftop. The wind tousled Kess's hair in a moment of suspension that made gravity seem a myth.

With a final bound, Griskin soared across the gap between buildings to the targeted balcony. They landed with a whispered thump between the open doors.

"What in the sunless shit?" a woman's voice cried.

There was the scrabble of moving bodies, and Kess raised herself up on Griskin's back, staring into the gaudily furnished living room.

A young woman, her finely braided hair tinted wine purple, had fallen backward off her chair. A man with the physique of an ancient statue, wearing only the bottom half of dragonrider armor, dropped a bottle on the floor. And a third, glass in one hand, fumbled to reach his sword with the other.

Kife.

"*Kessara?*" he yelped.

"It's a razing wolf!" The topless man seemed torn between grabbing a weapon too and righting the dropped bottle that was spilling out onto the fur rug. "Kife, why is there an entire living wolf in your house right now?"

Her brother had the humility to look shocked for a whole few seconds before he started laughing and leaned back on the lounge. He wiped some spilled liquid off the plush fabric beside him.

"Bryn, Vori, meet my baby sister."

Getting to her feet, Bryn tottered sideways as she attempted to seat herself back in the armchair. "Really? This thing on this wolf—this is for real? I thought you'd spiked my drink for a minute there."

"With how much you drink I don't need to." Kife chuckled.

Kess narrowed her eyes, fury growing inside her.

He laughed.

He'd left her to die, and now, seeing her again, he sat there, laughing.

He hadn't changed a whole lot in the years since she'd last seen him flying away on his dragon. Being six years older than her, he'd always appeared grown-up, and the addition of some neatly shaped stubble seemed the only difference.

His charcoal hair was even kept in the same style of braid he'd always worn, a thick central plait interwoven with smaller strands brought up from the sides, then hanging long down his back.

He wore full dragonrider armor decorated in the same colors as the flag that flew over Skaellakeep—blue and red.

Kess kept her anger in check. It wouldn't serve her. "I need to talk to you. Privately."

"Pssh, you just got here! Come and join the party! I'll find you a cup." Vori searched the table where flying goggles lay amongst empty bottles and plates piled haphazardly.

"I want to meet Kife's sister, the wolf-riding feral! You never even told us about her!"

"It's been a while since she's been around," Kife said, neatly leaving out why. He turned back and assessed Kess, then poured himself another drink from the mostly spilled bottle. "Did you come here to get revenge? Or just to embarrass me in front of my friends?"

Kess's reply was a rasp of hot air. "Embarrass you?"

Kife turned his sly smile to Bryn. "Blessed sun, Kess, we can smell you from here!"

Bryn chuckled in return, then pushed him away when he went in for a kiss.

The rage in Kess broke the dam, unable to be contained. "Don't you have *anything* you want to say to me?"

Kife raised his glass in a mocking toast. "I'm shocked and impressed you survived!"

"What did she survive?" Bryn asked, as though it were a fun tidbit of gossip.

"He left me in the wastes to die," Kess shot back.

Vori actually looked scandalized. "Your little sister! Kife!"

A smirk settled cruelly around Kife's lips. "Family, right?"

All three of them laughed.

"But why is she *riding a wolf*?" Bryn asked, as though waiting for a punchline.

"Those legs still not working for you, Kess?" Kife threw the question to her.

Vori looked Kess up and down. "I thought she was just trying to be cool and tough with her pet. Not that she was, you know ..."

Vori made a face that was an awful mix of disgust and pity.

Covering the cruel smile on her mouth, Bryn leaned away, as though Kess's condition was catching.

Freezing her own expression into stone, Kess kept her eyes on her brother, determined to prove that she wasn't hurt at all. "Kife. You will come and speak with me. In private. Right now. Or I will drag you out of here with my wolf."

Her tone must have conveyed how deadly serious Kess was because the laughter stopped, and Vori and Bryn both drew their swords.

Kife lifted one hand, finished his drink, and stood. "Relax, relax! I'll go and have a little chat with the baby sis and her pet. Then we can go back to having fun."

He beckoned for her to follow him, and they exited down a short hallway to a grand bedroom. Griskin padded in, head low and wary in the enclosed space. Kife shut the door behind them. The solid wood muffled the conversation and laughter from the others almost entirely. Private enough for what had to be said.

Kess's mouth went dry at the thought of telling Kife what she wanted, what she needed, and why, no matter how many times she'd rehearsed the moment in her head. Her hands absently ran through Griskin's fur as she tried to regain her voice.

Kife turned on her, his expression flat and annoyed. "What are you doing here?"

"I've come to ask you ... to join me in a mission of great value."

Kife's eyes widened, and he blinked a few times. "Wow, you're here asking me for *help*?"

Kess sneered. "No, to join me, in an offer that will make you richer than you ever imagined."

"Sure, very plausible. How about you run off to whatever filthy den you and this creature came from? You don't even have the honor to try to get your revenge on me." Moving over to the bed, Kife began working on unbuckling his armor. The shining blue and red plates of dragonscale shimmered in the soft light of oil lamps burning on the bedsides.

Kess brought the throwing knives in her bracer up to display. "You aren't scared that I would? That I could kill you right now if I wanted?"

"Not really. You never had the guts for something like that." Kife tossed his chest plate uncaringly onto the end of the bed. He glanced back at Kess again, shaking his head. "How you even survived ... *you*. And that you'd come ... I want to say 'crawling back,' but, well, wolf."

Kess stared at him for a long while. Maybe she should just leave, find some other way forward. But as much of a heartless jerk as Kife was, she knew him. She could make this work.

"Are you going to listen to me, or should I find some other dragonrider who wants to win their weight in silvernix?"

Kife paused mid buckle, eyes snapping up to Kess. "Who are you planning on robbing? Not many but Yeonard Draekhan and the firsts have that much silvernix left in stores."

"Not in stores. Alive."

"Sorry, what?"

"What do you think I need a dragon and its rider for? This is a hunt for a living creature with silvernix blood."

"A unicorn? You've found one?"

Kess made a noncommittal grunt. She knew it was a risk telling him about Dracuni at all, that he could easily leave her for dead and hunt on his own, so she would keep some details to herself for now. Still, she had to tell him enough to get him invested.

"Is this some kind of joke or trick? This can't be real." Kife had laughter in his voice, but the way he assessed her with keen eyes showed there was also eagerness there. He was interested.

Kess consciously let her emotion into her voice, baiting the hook again. "Do you really think I would have come here, come to you for help, if this wasn't real? If it didn't mean *everything*?"

"It *is* clear that you're desperate," Kife admitted with a smirk. "Okay, I'll hear you out and join your little mission. I want to see how it pans out. I want to see this unicorn."

"Good. Get your friends to leave. You can't tell anyone else about this."

Kife cracked the door open again. "I'm not an idiot! Bad enough we're splitting the prize."

Strolling out into the living area, he barked, "Okay, clear out! We've got family business!"

Kess watched from the shadows of the hallway as his two dragonrider friends grumbled, collected their belongings, and left.

Would I have friends like that one day? Kess snorted softly. Hopefully she'd earn better quality companions than them with the wealth and power Dracuni would provide.

Kife took a seat on the plush upholstered lounge again and patted a spot next to him.

Kess brought Griskin around, letting him sit in the breeze of the open doors where he could see the sky, and remained on him. "Speaking of family business, I'm not sure if you've heard, but our home in the west is in ruins and our parents dead."

Kife blinked once, then sniffed. "That ass-end-of-the-world place wasn't my home. This is where I belong—in a dragonkeep with other dragonlords, where the honor and the action are."

He leaned forward, jabbing a finger toward Kess over the cluttered table. Then he pointed around at the overly furnished chambers. "Couldn't even afford a nice place with what was left after our parents blew all their wealth on you."

Kess realized she'd shrunken smaller in her saddle, and she straightened herself up. "Were you there when—"

"I already heard about it, reports of their death. It's old news." Kife leaned back, arms extended on either side along the back of the lounge. "Tell me more about this unicorn and how we're going to catch it."

Across the room, a door opened, startling Kess. Not the main entrance, but a smaller side access. A boney Rolanian woman in a plain servants' dress stepped in, a metal cleaning bucket dangling from one hand.

"Not now. Go away," Kife snapped.

He still keeps slaves? Of course he does.

Kess waited for her to leave before continuing. "There's a group of intolerable fools protecting the creature, keeping it with them. And they are using the Alderkin shrines, using magic there to travel around the land. We'll need to start by locating all the shrines."

"No, we won't. We have that info already. They're marked on dragonrider maps from back during the war," Kife said.

Hope crept anxiously through Kess. "Does it show their unique symbols?"

"Symbols? No, just locations."

"Then we still need to visit and identify them." Kess reached for a roll of paper in her side pack and unfurled it to show the glyphs she'd drawn on it in charcoal. "I've seen how they are using the shrines to travel and how each gateway has a unique symbol. I think we can track them that way."

Kife didn't seem too sure. "You think we can track where they'll end up if they make their escape through one of these gateways?"

"Yes. That's how we'll catch them." Kess nodded firmly, despite her doubts.

It was only a theory so far, but it had to work. It was all she had left to try. Surely, on dragon wings, they would be fast enough to catch their prey.

But if she was wrong, she'd just sold out the most precious creature in the world to the man who had thrown his little sister to the wolves for less.

CHAPTER TEN

Kess dreamed of her brother stabbing her in the back, right through the heart.

She gasped awake, arms seeking Griskin, and panicking again when she didn't find him close.

It took a couple of moments to remember where she was. That she was lying on the bed in her brother's guest room. That Griskin had refused the strange, soft fabric and instead slept away from her for the first time, underneath an open window.

Kess pushed herself into a sitting position. The covers of the bed lay undisturbed beneath her. It had felt too unfamiliar to tuck herself into that comfort, and the room was already warmer than the cold ground she was used to.

Only a cool, dim glow came through the open window, the sun not yet fully risen, and there were no other sounds from the door to the rest of the apartment.

Kess tried to get comfortable again so she could be well rested for the day ahead and the beginning of the hunt. The mattress was the softest thing Kess had touched in years.

But Kess tossed and turned. She probably just wasn't used to this sort of luxury. But she had been once. She'd grown up with fluffy beds and full plates and clean clothes. It was so much more than many people had or she had experienced since.

So why was I never happy?

Sitting up again, Kess rubbed her face. Despite a solid night of sleep, she felt exhausted, her eyes dry and her chest heavy.

Stretching her arms wide, Kess got a whiff of herself. She really did smell.

She reached for the jug on the nightstand and poured water into the basin. Even the washcloth she used to scrub herself with was plush and velvety.

To live like this again ... Kess's shoulders slumped. She could. She could give up her hunt and just stay in the dragonkeep, find a home there with the gold she'd accumulated over the years and her Heithorn name. It would be easier, wouldn't it?

Kess wrung the cloth tight in her fists. She couldn't forget the way Kife's friends had looked at her. She knew the way dragonlords treated anyone with physical weakness. No, it wouldn't be easier.

She could never fit in among their ranks, never get the respect she deserved if she didn't have her own dragon and more.

That was why she was doing this—all of this. She'd never been happy back home and could never be happy until she was in a position that would command respect. And then ... then maybe even friendship. Or love.

She couldn't give up.

Besides, now Kife knows about Dracuni, there'll be no stopping him.

Kess was about as clean as she could get herself. She had no fresh clothing to change into and wasn't prepared to take Griskin into the bathroom with her and subject him to running water spouts. He'd never forgive her.

But her face was no longer smeared with ash and her fingernails no longer black-rimmed.

The dragonglass mirror over the nightstand gave her a view of herself in startling clarity, and Kess frowned at the tangle of her hair. She raked her fingers through it, breaking up some of the larger braids and redoing them. But she'd never been good at braiding her own hair. It had always been one of the slaves, or Pony, who did that for her.

In the end, despite her efforts, Kess felt just as scruffy as before—wild and disgraceful compared to the city nobles.

After calling Griskin over to the side of the bed, Kess slipped into the saddle, and they prowled out into the living area. The sun reached in, golden and warm through the open balcony, and the mess of the night before had been cleared away by silent hands during the night.

Why isn't Kife up yet? He's not taking this seriously at all.

As she glared at his bedroom door, it cracked open. The same boney servant woman from the night before slid out through the narrow gap and closed it again behind her. Her head was bowed, ebony hair falling around her face in waves. Her dress hung undone, and she worked to hurriedly button it as she skittered down the hall.

Kess's heart pumped into a riot and her skin went cold.

He'd done that back at Heithorn estate too, forcing any slave he wanted into his bedchambers. Kess hated it. But it had taken him showing an interest in Riony for her to take action.

I can't believe he's still doing that. Or maybe I can.

No matter that Kess had lodged a fine steel throwing dagger into the collar of his shirt, pinning him to a door. No matter that it was the only time she'd ever drawn his blood in one of their sibling scuffles.

Kife had wiped the nick on his neck and laughed. "There are plenty of better options than that boyish beast of *yours.*"

That was the moment Kess had realized Riony didn't feel like she was *hers.* That despite the awful ownership involved, there was no connection between them. Not in the way Kess wanted.

All Kess had achieved that day was keeping Kife away from Riony, not restraining his conduct or teaching him any lesson. And Kife had quickly taken his revenge in return.

Maybe Kess's mistake that day was throwing a warning shot. She could have finished him, then and there. But she was pretty sure that would have been the last straw in her parents' tolerance of her.

Now, Kess wondered if it would have been worth it. She should have stood up to Kife sooner, not just because he was interested in the person closest to Kess, but for everyone he'd hurt.

A hot flood of shame overtook her face as the servant reached the exit.

"Hey!" Kess called out, her voice rasping. "Come here."

The girl's whole body jarred to a stop, but she obeyed the command in a dull, unflinching manner.

"I mean ... please, wait a moment." Kess nudged Griskin forward, closing the gap between her and the servant.

Large eyes of sunset amber stared more at the wolf than at Kess, but the servant stood calmly before Kess as though ready and willing to be eaten alive.

One sleeve still hung from a shoulder, and soft pink scars crept over her dark skin. Fresh lash marks.

"Kife isn't going to be home for a while." Kess pulled her coin pouch from her belt. Most of her gold was tucked deep in Griskin's saddlebags, stitched into hidden pockets, but the pouch held more than enough. "Take this. Buy your way to somewhere else. Find work under a dragonlord who doesn't ... do what Kife does."

Were there any? Kess didn't know.

There was a skepticism in the young woman's eyes that reflected Kess's thoughts. If the servant hadn't been drawn thin from hunger, she would have been startlingly beautiful. No doubt Kife had bought her for that very reason. There was a stillness to her, a resigned submissiveness born of self-preservation.

She didn't immediately reach for the offered coins.

Footsteps and the clink of porcelain came from Kife's room.

Kess thrust the bag toward the servant again. "Just take it. Go somewhere else, or don't. Do whatever you want with it. I don't care."

The slave met Kess's gaze for barely a second. Then thin, long fingers snatched the coin pouch, and she hurried to the exit, not looking back once.

Kess watched the back of the door for a long time, trying to ease the turmoil in her gut.

"Good morning, little sister!" Kife strode out into the living area, buckling the straps of his armor at the wrists. He looked around the room, especially at the bare table. "Where's breakfast? Olan should have had it set out by now."

"We're skipping breakfast," Kess snapped, worried the girl may have gone that way herself on the way out.

"I'm not going on a unicorn hunt hungry."

"We've already wasted enough time with you sleeping off your booze! We should have gone last night."

"I at least need to grab some food from the kitchen."

Kess prowled Griskin up toward him. "There is a creature alive out there, with silvernix blood. How long until its existence is discovered by someone else? How long before we miss our chance? We leave now."

"You really expect me to head out, chasing around the wastes without any food?"

"I managed it when you left me for dead. Do you really think you'll fare worse than your poor little sister did?"

Kife's mouth pulled closed into a tight pucker. "Fine. We'll go."

He picked up his sword and goggles from where they'd been left on the lounge the night before.

"Do you have any spare?" Kess asked as he pulled the flight goggles over his braided hair.

"No."

Kess pressed her teeth together. That was going to make flying unpleasant.

Kife made a sharp beckoning gesture, then opened a door leading to a spiral staircase rising between the stone walls. The steps were narrow, and Griskin gave a breathy whine at the enclosed space. But he followed Kife in, and they wound around and around until they pushed through another door and out into the harsh sunlight scorching the flat rooftop.

Lying on the hot stone, a chain around his neck and food trough by his side, was the purple dragon Kess had once wished could be hers.

"You still have him," Kess said flatly.

"Oh yeah, it's been a fantastic beast. You picked well, sis." Kife strode up and unlocked the chain.

The etherdart's scales weren't as bright as Kess remembered. Now, they were a dull, smoky purple.

"Did you end up naming him?"

Kife scoffed. "Why would I name it?"

As the heavy chain released from the steel collar, the dragon didn't move. The padlocked chain was a ward against theft rather than to stop the dragon liberating itself. It blinked once, its wedge-shaped head lying on the ground, as large as Griskin from snout to jaw.

The saddle was already in place, scales beneath it worn and smoothed from the rub of ever-present leather over the dragon's shoulders.

Kife gave a soft whistle, and it lowered its wings to allow a clear way to climb up to the seat. Kicking his feet into the thick scales, Kife jumped up into the saddle in two swift steps.

Turning back to Kess, he gestured at her and Griskin. "What are we doing about this situation? Are we leaving the overgrown dog behind?"

"No!" Tempering her tone, Kess added, "We're not leaving him. I'll need him when we're not flying."

"I suppose I can get the dragon to carry the wolf."

"In ... his claws?" Kess looked at the talons, long and curved like scythes.

Kife made a grabby motion with both hands. "Your pet isn't going to get squished. The dragon is entirely under my control, sis."

Yeah, that's what scares me.

She couldn't trust Kife—not really. But at this point she wasn't sure what other choice she had. "It's going to be okay, Gris."

She urged him closer.

"How are you even going to be able to get up to the saddle?" Kife asked, one corner of his mouth lifting.

"Just fine." Kess brought Griskin sidelong against the dragon's neck, then gripped the angular scales running in a ridge over the dragon's shoulders and pulled herself out of Griskin's saddle.

Her arms were wiry but strong, and she could climb better than most. It wasn't the elegant mount Kess wished for, but she was up and seated behind Kife fast enough.

There was a moment when Kess considered pushing Kife off the dragon and claiming it for herself. But Kess only knew dragon riding in theory—not practice. She wasn't certain she could control the creature on her own.

And Kife already had the dragon moving, scooping Griskin up in its front claws. Griskin howled a high whine that pierced right into Kess's heart. She angled for a view of him and heard him whimper again. Scared, but unhurt.

But she took the message. She knew if she tried anything, Griskin would suffer first, and her suffering would follow on swift wings.

The dragon lifted from the ground. A strong surge upward almost threw Kess off its back, and Kife chuckled as she scrambled to hold herself in position.

Grabbing a spare belt from her waist, Kess used the steel loops on the delver vest to buckle herself safely to Kife's saddle. She wasn't going to fall or be pushed. She wouldn't be left behind, and neither would Griskin.

The dragonkeep spread out below them, growing smaller and smaller as they rose into the air. Wind rushed around them, stinging Kess's eyes, but she refused to close them. The world below was burned and gray, stone and steel, smoke and dust.

She hadn't flown for years. She hadn't flown since the last time Kife took her out on his dragon and never took her home.

Kess had made friends with death that day. Had fixed her one desperate goal onto her heart with the stab of a sharp blade—that she would become someone that no one would dare abandon.

Now, flying alongside her brother, she only hoped she could get what she wanted from Kife before he decided to leave her to the wolves again.

CHAPTER ELEVEN

Riony wasn't sure her father's motto of *big dreams, bold deeds* was ever meant to include brazen attacks on dragonlord properties.

"Are we really, literally, seriously, actually going to do this?" she asked.

In the shadows of a rocky outcrop, Riony squinted through Lyrrin's seeing stone, scanning the ore mine sprawled below. The gritty scent of dust hung in the air, drying Riony's tongue, and her words were punctuated by the faint clinks of metal echoing from the excavation site.

Aishena remained silent as though she wasn't the person Riony was most seeking advice from, and Niskina sharpened her poleaxe as though already decided.

Lyrrin snatched the clear crystal back. "That's Avri and Tamas down there."

Benjin nodded. "It's definitely them."

Riony squinted at the now much smaller children sitting on a mound of muddy rocks, sorting through the muck with their bare hands.

"We didn't save them when the slavers took them from the orphans' den. This is where they ended up. And all those other kids too. We owe it to them to help out now. We've got to save them." Lyrrin punched her small, gloved fist into the palm of her other hand.

"Okay, little spitfire, don't go charging in yet." Riony remembered the terrified faces in the cage the dragonrider had carried away, the one she and Lyrrin had jumped from.

Children she hadn't been able to take with her. She hadn't known them personally. But Lyrrin did.

And whether she knew them or not, whether she owed them or not for having failed to save them the first time, she wasn't sure she could see them kept there as slaves and then turn away.

She just didn't like the idea of risking her family to save them.

Every part of her existence had become about weighing lives against each other, and she hated it.

Dracuni lay low on her belly beside Riony, snout resting on the rocks as she looked down at the mine. Her lilac eyes were focused and bright as they followed all the movement far below.

Want to help.

Riony sensed her anticipation, both fear and excitement. Dracuni had grown so much in recent months, too big for even Riony to carry with any ease. But both flying and flaming were still absent among her skills.

"Even if we go ahead with this, you're staying out of it," Riony replied.

Air puffed from Dracuni's nostrils, disturbing the surrounding dust. ***Still want.***

She had learned more in their travels about *friends* and *not-friends* and why they had to be so careful nobody found out what she could do—what her blood could do.

That had scared her at first, but she'd also grown bolder. They had come across more groups of refugees as they'd traveled and had helped those people find safety at the shrines, too, or sent them to the undercity. And each group of people they met who didn't capture and bleed Dracuni only made her more excited to meet and help the next.

Even Myrwa's small community had come to accept Dracuni after a couple more visits. Dracuni hadn't yet called them *friends* but had started calling them *not-not-friends*.

Riony now thought of them as friends though. Seeing Kellae's baby grow happy and strong within the safety of the shrine had made their visits back there worth it. The shrines seemed to stay safe at least for a while without Dracuni's presence, but without knowing how long that lasted, their group tried to get back there regularly, bringing the magic with them.

And Myrwa always had a hot bowl of carrowmy rice available for Riony whenever they did.

Riony felt good about the people they had helped.

But this was the first time they'd considered outright attacking a dragonlord property.

Aishena, who had been sharing the seeing stone on Yoskar's staff with Benjin, continued to stare at the field of rocks and rubble below, chewing over her thoughts but not sharing any.

The dye Riony had prepared at Myrwa's camp and used for Lyrrin, Aishena, and Benjin's hair had run out in the weeks since, and Aishena's long locks had faded almost back to their normal silver. Just a hint of earthy red tinted the silky lengths.

Niskina didn't bother to get a better look with the magical Alderkin crystals. "Come on. Let's do this! This is it—our chance to help people, to be more than just idiots on the run. We can make change, like in the *Rebel Riders*."

"Those are just stories," Riony said.

Stories she'd missed since leaving the undercity. There were no chapter vendors in the wastes of the aboveground world. She doubted any of the overseers below would read that sort of fiction either, so turning up some booklets wasn't likely to be a fun surprise bonus to their guerilla ambush.

In the last chapter Riony had read, Rider Zeina had just kissed her true love on the Cradle Archway before being ambushed and Riony might *never* find out what happened next.

Niskina huffed. "They could be real. We've heard plenty of stories from people about some dragonriders fighting back against the dragonlords."

"Rumors. And a few outlaws making trouble isn't the same as it is in the books. It's not all honorable saviors and glistening chests."

Niskina stared longingly into the distance for a moment as though she were missing the chapters as well. "Stories or not, I don't care. There's still truth in stories."

"How often do the Rebel Riders win in those stories? How often are they triumphant in making the world a better place?"

"Most of the time."

Gesturing to the ashy sky and burned remains of bones lying in the dirt around them and the slaves down the hill, Riony scoffed. "Yeah, lots of truth."

Niskina rolled her eyes. "I'm doing something whether you're too cowardly to help or not."

Riony turned to her other side, putting her back to Niskina. "Aish, what do you think?"

"The plan is solid enough. I'll do as instructed."

"Our plan of walking in and hoping for the best? Yep, it's up there with the greatest moments in tactical history." Riony tugged at her tangled pigtail.

Her hair had grown and fell over her face. She undid the short braid, pulled her hair back, and retied it again. Still, a wavy red strand flopped across her eyes.

Lyrrin said, "The plan *is* good. We've seen the cargo dragons leave and return already, and we know we've got a couple of hours once they go again. We know how many overseers there are—one in the front watchtower, four down in the mines, and four up top. That's less than two each."

"I think you're miscounting because part of the plan was also that you and Benjin are staying out of the way with Dracuni."

"You, Aishena, and Niskina only have five to deal with before the ones in the mines come out, so my math is still good," Lyrrin shot back. "We've got to help them."

Riony couldn't say she hated the odds. Two against one felt like a treat compared to being chased by hordes of revs.

Benjin looked eagerly at Lyrrin, but then a frown came over him. "I think, if Yoskar was here, he'd say it's too risky."

"The cargo dragons are almost done being loaded," Aishena said.

"It would be less risky if you let us help," Benjin added.

"No," Aishena and Riony said together.

Riony leaned over to look down at the mine again. Slaves ranging from scrawny children to elderly men were bowed under the weight of baskets that they brought and dumped into canvas containers in front of the dragons.

Two seasongs, one green and black, one green and silver. Both tamed. They reminded Riony of Dracuni's mother. Although not as large as her, they were still some of the largest dragons she'd ever seen.

Behind them, toward the back of the mine, was another small tower that looked only half-completed, the top section draped in dark cloth.

The men on the dragons gave a signal and the canvas containers were lashed closed and attached with hooks to the industrial harnesses over the dragons' backs. The great leathery expanses of their wings stretched out, almost as wide across as the mine itself and the fortress wall encircling it.

The beating of those wings echoed like distant thunder as they worked to lift their burdens into the sky.

"Now or never," Lyrrin whispered in a rush.

Riony took in her sister's determined expression with a frown. "More like 'now or maybe another time soon after we've thought about it a bit more.' I'm still not sure this is a great idea. We would be putting targets on our backs."

Lyrrin raised one shoulder. "Well, Niskina is already gone, sooo ..."

"Sparks!" Riony jumped to her feet.

Niskina was gone, beyond the scree-strewn slope and approaching the mine gates.

"You three, stay here!" Riony gave her best, most commanding glare at Lyrrin, Dracuni, and Benjin. Then she took off.

She'd already removed her bags and left them with the kids, but the weight of the sword on her back made the stumble down the steep hill an exercise in stubbed toes and scratched hands. She cursed Niskina for adding this rush to their risks.

Niskina was almost at the gates when Riony caught up to her, panting and cursing.

"You were really going to walk in there on your own?" Riony scolded.

Niskina smiled sweetly back. "What do you mean? I knew you'd come and help me. You're too much of a softy."

"And thank you, so much, for exploiting that."

A male voice called from the stone watchtower beside the gate, "Someone approaches!"

"Revs?" another voice replied. They sounded right on the other side of the steel-plated door.

The man with pale skin and neatly braided black hair leaned out of the watchtower to take in the two women.

They both waved back politely.

"More visitors," shouted the watchtower guard uncertainly.

"Busy day. Let them in then. Let's see what these ones will pay us."

Riony whispered to Niskina, "Busy, do they get traders or something through often?"

"Yes, just hoping to trade," Niskina called back to the guard in her sweetest voice.

The solid gate swung smoothly aside, and as Riony marched across the threshold, she unstrapped her sword and brought it before her in her hands.

Niskina tucked her tumble of hair away from her face and drew her poleaxe.

All four aboveground overseers had come toward the entrance to see who the visitors were. They each wore clean and neat leather armor, painted gray and green. Only their boots showed any sign of the muddy conditions.

Two of the men had salt-and-pepper hair that matched their uniforms, but the other two were closer to Riony's age. All had lashes carried on their belts.

Heat rose through Riony, prickling over the scars on her back. Maybe she did want to fight these guys after all.

Her and Niskina's approach was met with a ripple of chuckles.

"What is this supposed to be? The feeblest ambush in history?" one of the older men waved a hand dismissively at them.

Riony put her sword tip down and leaned on the hilt casually. "This is your warning to get yourselves out of here. You're all going to run. Run back to whatever dragonlord owns this place and tell them the mine was lost to revs. That there were no survivors. You can run and tell them that, or you can stay and experience the 'no survivors' part yourself."

The four of them stared back, still chuckling.

The older man spoke again, his tone friendly and distinguished. "Don't be silly, child. If you want to trade, we can trade without violence. We have plenty in our stores, and I'm sure you two can find some way you can pay us."

The chuckles rose to laughter.

"And what would a stain on humankind like yourself charge to allow us to walk out of here with every slave?" Riony gestured to the children sorting ore from waste amongst the lode pile.

The overseer frowned at that. "More than any value you have, girl. If you refuse to be respectful about this, then we are done."

He lifted a hand in the air, flicking a finger at Riony. He held his hand like that for a long moment, then flicked it again, looking up toward the watchtower at Riony's back with confusion.

Riony turned as well, seeing the direct line from the window down to her and Niskina. There was movement within, a flash of glowing yellow, and a crossbow clattered out of the window and landed on the ground.

A moment later, the overseer in the watchtower followed it, groaning as he hit the mud below.

"How dare you attack us like this!" One of the younger men, someone Niskina no doubt would have been flirting with under better conditions, turned wildly around.

He looked to all the walls and shadows as though they had brought an army against them. "This mine belongs to Ulfren the First! We're supplying all of Ulfrenkeep and most of Elundrae with copper. They need this metal."

Riony lifted her sword again, activating the rune so that it lit up purple. "If they need it so much, tell them to come and mine it themselves."

The door in the base of the watchtower squeaked as it opened, and Aishena strolled out, cutting athame glowing bright.

"What is that she's carrying?" the other young overseer asked, his eyes wide.

"Alderkin magic." The old one spat on the ground. "These rats side with what isn't even human."

Niskina gasped. "Watch out! There's another guard."

Riony followed her gaze toward the covered tower. The man was up the long ladder on the side and tugged a rope. In a swish of fabric, a large, glittery disc was revealed.

A signaler. Riony hadn't seen one of those since the night her parents had died.

The guard began cranking handles beside the plate covered in facets of mirror, adjusting the angle.

"No, we do not want that." Riony ran for him.

Her sword made her footsteps light and she glided across the scrappy dirt and puddles. She prepared to leap up to the man, but it was too late.

The signaler caught the weak sun, magnifying it into a beam that lit up a patch on the blanket of slate-colored clouds above.

The older overseer said, "Let's see which side has no survivors when the dragons arrive."

Riony adjusted her hold on her crystal sword and continued toward the structure. "Not if I bring that whole thing down before anyone sees it."

The man up on the signal tower pulled a crossbow from his back, aiming it down at Riony. "Don't even—"

There was a soft *thunk*, and he stilled, then fell. A heavy pebble tumbled down with him.

Good aim!

Dracuni's thoughts came through clear, sounding close, much closer than where she'd left her. And she'd bet good money that stone had flown from Lyrrin's sling.

Riony couldn't see where they were and didn't have time to look. She had to deal with the signaler first, still angled and burning into the sky above them.

If the dragonriders on the cargo dragons turned back and saw, or any other nearby dragonriders caught sight of it, they'd be in big trouble. The nearest shrine to escape through was a half hour run from there.

Riony rolled her shoulders and lifted the huge Alderkin blade. Taking in the support structure beneath the signaler, she chose her target and brought her body around in a full spin.

The sword struck right in the joint between the metal struts. The impact jarred Riony's muscles, but the sword cracked through, separating the rivets and bending the structure. It toppled to the side. The disc separated from its supports, cracking with the screech of metal and rolling down onto the ground.

Shards of glass mirror clattered and chinked as the metal disc whined to a stop.

The slaves working aboveground scattered. The four overseers huddled closer together as they looked at Riony and her sword again with newly born fear.

But from a hut beside the mine entrance, four more men appeared, shouting at the destroyed signaler and their cornered colleagues.

"More of them? I thought we'd accounted for them all." Riony rejoined Niskina and Aishena.

The overseers drew weapons—lashes and swords—and squared up against the women.

Niskina muttered back, "Night shift maybe? They didn't come out all morning! I didn't know they were there!"

Riony rolled her eyes. "Maybe another good reason to have spent more than a few hours watching the place before we rushed in! Honestly, if you're relying on me being the voice of reason, maybe consider things aren't going well."

Drawing another athame which lit up burning red, Aishena looked from the mine entrance to the eight men before them. "We can't be sure the others in the mine didn't hear all this noise. They may be on their way too. The dragons might have also seen the signal and will return as well."

Riony sniffed and cricked her neck, gripping the hilt of her sword strongly in both hands. A dark, violent mood arose within her, and a desire to break the face of every man with a lash in his hand.

"Go," she growled. "You two go and get the slaves out of the mine as fast as you can, and I'll hold back the ones up here. And hopefully we'll all get out of this place in one piece."

Aishena gave Riony a concerned look but followed orders with a swift nod. She and Niskina made a dash for it and disappeared through the black square entrance into the earth.

Riony hoped Aishena and Niskina could deal with the four overseers in the mines. She hoped that once the slaves worked out what her friends were trying to do, they would join the fight, and the numbers would turn to their side.

She also hoped that, wherever Lyrrin and Dracuni were, they weren't planning on getting any closer.

But as the eight men edged around, encircling her and testing her boundaries, Riony suddenly felt very alone.

Chapter Twelve

All the air rushed out of Lyrrin's chest as the eight men surrounded her sister.

There weren't meant to be that many. Riony, Niskina, and Aishena were supposed to work together to incapacitate the guards up top before going down into the mines together.

But instead, it was her sister versus eight. Her sister, grinning and goading the men as though any one of their swords couldn't end her.

Lyrrin grunted fiercely. "I'm going down there."

"We're supposed to stay here," Benjin said. "Well, really, we were supposed to stay up there."

He tilted his head toward the slope and the higher vantage point in the rocky crags they'd left behind.

As soon as Riony and Aishena had hurried after Niskina, Lyrrin had followed to be close enough to gather up any fleeing slaves if they ran out the open gate so they could be led to safety. And close enough to be able to hear snippets of the conversation and know what was happening.

They were tucked on a small ledge behind some jagged rocks just outside the gate, a perch tall enough that they could see over the stone walls encircling the mine.

"I'm going anyway," Lyrrin said, sliding down the rocky edge on her bottom. "You stay here with Dracuni."

Dracuni snorted and stretched her front paws, revealing the talons there, then shifted forward.

Lyrrin raised a hand, putting it in front of Dracuni's snout. "No, you stay here. Stay with Benjin."

"Who said I was staying?" Benjin leaned on Yoskar's staff, using it like an extra limb to navigate down between the stones.

Dracuni opened her mouth and snapped it closed again, then pushed against Lyrrin's hand, moving past her and down the angular boulders.

Lyrrin wished she understood what Dracuni was saying the way Riony did.

"Well, they can't be angry at us for not sticking to the plan anyway," Lyrrin said as she jumped the last section to the road below. "They didn't either."

And Lyrrin was angry too. Angry at her sister for always acting like it didn't matter what happened to her, like she didn't need help.

The three of them ran for the open gate.

Through the entrance, the fight was a swirl of circling bodies, swords and lashes swinging.

Riony stood defiant at the entrance to the mine, wielding her massive sword to ward off the men. But even with the float rune activated, the crystal gleaming with otherworldly luminescence, the swings were slow. Powerful, but slow.

Especially compared to the eight guards with their slim steel blades and flicking leather, who dodged in and out, taking turns trying to skewer Riony. She caught the strike of one blade against the steel of her shoulder guard only to be met with a fist in the back of her ribs.

Riony roared as she hammered the sword in a horizontal sweep, catching up one man with the flat and flinging him across the yard into a pile of muddy stones.

Lyrrin gasped, and Dracuni trilled a whimper when the flick of a lash landed across Riony's face. They ran faster, through the gate, almost there.

Riony's breaths came in ragged bursts, and blood poured from her brow, but she didn't slow down, didn't yield. Steel clashed with crystal, reverberating within the stone-walled space.

Dracuni was ahead of the kids now, galloping in long, leaping strides.

"Dragon!" one of the guards yelled.

"What in the unblessed ..." Another turned as well, the two of them aiming swords at the unidragon.

"What are you doing? Get out of here!" Riony snapped in between blows.

Dracuni growled and gave her head a violent shake. She raised up on her back legs, chest heaving like bellows.

Is she going to flame?

Lyrrin skidded to a stop outside of the main fight beside piles of sorted stone, ore, and coal. She scooped a rock up into the cradle of her sling. She swung the leather straps in circles, taking her aim.

Dracuni's shoulders strained, and her neck shivered. Her mouth opened wide. The men scrambled to get clear.

Nothing came out.

"Get it! Get that thing!" one yelled as they ran back toward her.

Dracuni opened her mouth again, roaring with the hint of a whimper.

She dropped back onto all fours and lowered her head, her single horn angled right back at the guard's threatening weapons. She skittered left and right, jumping and pouncing toward the men, then backing away again, and nipping at their legs.

Lyrrin loosed her first stone, but it flew right behind a guard's back when he stepped forward in a lunge. She loaded another.

"Back off!" Benjin ran up beside Dracuni, Yoskar's staff alight with a burn rune.

The flaming red crystal left streaks of heat in the air as he swung it, scaring back the men trying to hit Dracuni.

Lyrrin sent a shot again, and again she missed. Everyone was moving too fast, dodging in and out unpredictably. Standard stones weren't going to knock any of them down—not if she couldn't hit them.

"Eyes!" Lyrrin shouted as she activated a flash stone.

She only had two left, and no one would let her slice up their remaining glow stones to make more. One left now as she sent the stone soaring into the fray. It landed at Riony's feet.

Dracuni tucked her face under a wing, and Riony and Benjin threw an arm up over their eyes as the burst of light went off. The guards stumbled and swore.

Riony held her sword before her like a shield against the blind swings of their weapons and barreled through them, stopping in front of Dracuni. "Go. You're clear—get out of here! What do you mean, 'make me!?' We are *having a talk* after this!"

The guards wiped at their eyes, slowing their assault as they regrouped. The flash stone had only bought them a moment. The men circled around the three of them, taking a few breaths, and stared at the new threats. The strange, snappy little dragon. The fiery blazing staff.

That red glow seemed to be holding their attention the most.

Lyrrin had also sliced the small crucible Riony had found her in the Alderkin depths into smaller shards. But all they had on them were burn runes, which wouldn't do much if she couldn't hit her target.

But maybe she could make them do more.

Lyrrin tugged one of her gloves off, shoved it in a pocket, and scrambled over to the pile of coal, grasping a large chunk. She quickly pressed one of her sharp-tipped nails into the stone, slicing a gash.

Activating one of the burn shards, she wedged it in. The black mineral sparked and smoldered, glowing from within. She dropped it into her sling and sent it flying.

It caught alight midair, soaring like a miniature meteor into the middle of the fight.

It hit a guard in the ankles, making him dodge back from the crackling stone, taking him out of a melee with Benjin. The guard's thick leather armor didn't catch, nor did the coal seem to hurt him, but he swore and stared into the sky as though it had begun raining fire.

Lyrrin prepared another, as large as she could throw with her sling. It came flaming down through the sky between two guards and her sister, making them scatter.

More accustomed to Lyrrin's explosive experiments than her opponents, Riony recovered fastest, pressing the men back with a slicing arc of her sword.

As Lyrrin continued to rain the field with fire, one man turned and fled, running into a nearby building and slamming the door behind him.

Riony had another guard on his back, and Dracuni and Benjin kept their attackers at bay with nipping teeth and burning crystal.

From the dark entrance to the mine, a clamor of voices and slapping feet emerged.

Niskina stepped out into the light, poleaxe in hand, herding a group of children ahead of her. "Straight out the gate, run!"

As the fleeing slaves streamed across the yard, more faces peered out from behind huts and rubble.

Lyrrin waved her hands above her head. "Come on! We're getting you out!"

Her friends from the orphans' den turned toward her, their eyes widening. Avri, Tamas, and a few others came running in a huddle, taking a wide loop around the clash of combat still centering on Riony.

A group of four young men came out of the mine after Niskina, guiding some of the younger kids and older slaves. They remained near the entrance, helping people through and sending them toward the gate.

The faces of those who came out of the mines were fearful, eyes bulging and cheeks hollow. Bare hands and arms were pale from spatters of dried mud, their feet and legs the same. They all looked one color, their skin, clothes, and hair all the shade of dust and stone.

One child who tottered past looked barely four years old.

"Get back to your stations! Don't you dare leave!" the older man who had led the conversation before rushed at the fleeing slaves, smacking his lash in the air. "We will find you! You'll all be dragged back and punished!"

A slash of Riony's sword forced his retreat.

"I think that's all of them!" Aishena stepped out of the mine with her athames glowing.

The group of four men nodded to her, grouping around her as they joined the others running for the gate.

"Lead them out, I'll be right behind you," Riony said.

Niskina nodded from up front, taking the first group through the exit.

Lyrrin raced across the muddy ground to Benjin and Dracuni just as Aishena reached them too.

Aishena gave Benjin a deathly cold glare. "Take Dracuni and get to the front with Niskina."

A guard swung his sword in a slash toward Aishena's chest. Without even seeming to look, she raised her cutting athame in a block and sliced the sword clean in half. The man stumbled back, swearing.

"We're done here. Go!" She grabbed Benjin by the shoulder and brought him into a run with her.

Two guards gasped in the mud, and one other had fled. The five remainders gathered close, arguing between themselves, wary of the slaves rushing around them freely.

Dracuni showed no sign of leaving Riony's side.

Lyrrin grabbed one of Riony's belt loops and tugged. "Come on. Let's go!"

"NO!" Riony barked.

Her arm was sliced raw from lash bites, and she swung it accusingly at the guards. Blood ran down the side of her face, dripping from her chin, and her expression was wild, ruthless, and anguished all at once.

"I can't let them go. Not after everything they've done. I can't forgive them for this! They don't deserve to live!"

The quiver of fury in Riony's voice terrified Lyrrin. "Come on, please. You're hurt. You can't keep fighting."

Dracuni whined a low whimper, circling closer around Riony's legs and nudging her with her cheek.

"I can, and I will!" Riony's eyes were red-rimmed and glossy, her words hissing out between bared teeth. "They kept them, all of them, as slaves. These children. They whipped them and beat them!"

"It's okay—the kids are out. They're going to be safe. We can go." Lyrrin tugged again.

"We're just doing our jobs!" one guard yelled back, spittle flying.

Riony roared wordlessly at the men, raising her sword high.

She's going to kill them. If she stays, she's going to kill someone.

She couldn't let Riony keep fighting and fighting and fighting. She was going to end up with blood on her hands, and Lyrrin didn't want that for her sister. Not again. Not for her or anyone.

No, I'm not going to let you do this to yourself.

With her breath held, Lyrrin stepped between Riony and the men.

"Stop!" She raised her hands up, one at her sister, and one at the guards.

Riony's chest pulsed with panting breaths, her attack frozen. "What are you doing?"

Lyrrin's face scrunched up with the sting of emotions, and she blinked tears.

Lyrrin turned to the guards, pleading. "This is your last chance. Run. Just run!"

Blood roared in Riony's ears like the rumble of an angry sea. She wiped her face with the palm of her hand, and it came away slick and red. A dull ache spread around her eye from an elbow that had connected with it during the scuffle.

Hurt?

"I'm fine!" She sucked at the air that hissed the words out, trying to bring them back in, soothe them.

Hot liquid trickled down her temple and cheekbone, and she swiped it away again. A tentative touch of the area revealed a wide split across her eyebrow.

At least it's going to leave an awesome scar.

"I'm fine," she said a second time, her voice softer, barely audible over the raging beat in her chest that wouldn't ease, no matter that they were no longer running. "Don't worry."

Dracuni looked up from beside her hip, her lilac eyes narrowed. ***Not fine. Do worry.***

The light of the shrine gateway spilled across the faces of all the people who had escaped the mine. From children to very old, almost all were Rolanian, but some of the young men had Taenish features. They looked at the gateway with shivering expressions and determined, thinly pulled mouths.

The first brave few had already stepped through to the other side.

"It's safe, see?" Lyrrin and one of her friends from the orphans' den did a pass through the gateway and back again.

She held the boy's hand—Tamas?—and as they came back to the starting side, his eyes lit up and a smile split his dusty face.

Letting go of her hand, he ran into the gateway and back once more, barking a laugh of wonder as he grabbed another friend for the next round trip.

"We do want to get everyone to the *other* side as quickly as we can, please," Riony called over the crowd.

She gave the kids a little push to suggest they stay where they end up.

She wasn't sure how much time they had before they were followed, before search parties were formed and dragons filled the sky, as they had done when Riony and her parents fled the Heithorns.

The guards at the mine had laid down weapons when faced with Lyrrin's ultimatum and Riony's fury. They'd left the men tied up, but it wouldn't be much longer before the carrier dragons returned and found the whole mine cleared out.

The freed slaves moved more confidently into the gateway after the children's demonstration. They knew they couldn't stay there, and as much as the Alderkin magic scared them, being recaptured was less preferable.

Niskina and Benjin had gone through with the first of the group, and Aishena remained beside the gateway, reassuring those as they stepped into the window of magic that would take them across Elundrae.

As the last few passed through the gateway, Aishena gave Riony a nod and followed. With a final glance at the sky, Riony pushed Lyrrin and Dracuni in front of her through the shimmering light.

Lyrrin deactivated the gateway on the other side and beamed up at Riony. "We did it! We helped them all get out!"

With her eyes on the crowd of both new arrivals and people from Myrwa's enclave, Riony spoke low. "*We* weren't all supposed to have been there. You shouldn't have come in! Those guards have seen Dracuni now."

"They didn't know she was anything other than a baby dragon," Lyrrin whispered back.

"Which we shouldn't even have! You think they aren't going to be telling the dragonlords they work for that there was a baby dragon running around with the people who are freeing slaves? What do you think they will want to do about that?"

Not little sister's fault. I choose. I go! Fight like big sister!

Dracuni stood tall on straight legs, her neck up and chin high.

She was getting big now but was still a baby compared to any of the massive, tamed beasts the dragonriders would hunt her with if they realized what she was.

Riony said to both Dracuni and Lyrrin, "What aren't you understanding about how dangerous that was?"

Danger for you also.

"I couldn't stop her, and I told her not to, and you were the one trying to take on eight guards at once! I could see just how dangerous that was. Could you?"

"I could have taken them!"

Lyrrin's mouth closed, and her lips and cheeks puffed out with air. "At what cost?"

Benjin came over from where Aishena had been fussing over him, and gave Lyrrin a big grin as though this was all their victory.

"Not at the cost of any of you three." Riony gave them all the hardest glare she could offer.

Lyrrin gasped, open-mouthed and insulted. "What about you?"

Benjin shrugged. "Aish is being like this too. As though I was going to stay out of it. I have to look after Aishena too because family looks after family."

Myrwa swept in beside them then, pulling Riony into a hug that shut her mouth and turned her from the three stubborn children.

"You've doubled our numbers, my friend," Myrwa said into her ear, then let her go, patting her shoulder and staring at her bloodied and bruising face. "We welcome these people. But I do wish you'd given us some warning."

"Some of them we will take to the undercity," Riony replied. "That's where they came from. We just wanted to get everyone somewhere safe, fast. Sorry."

Myrwa waved off the suggestion. "They can go if they want to, but they are welcome. Look, look who you brought!"

A mid-teen boy was on his knees in front of Kellae who was also kneeling and leaning into an embrace with him, her child pressed between them. Their faces were wet with tears and stretched with smiles.

Kellae leaned back, using one of the baby's rags to wipe the dust and saltwater from the boy's face, her mouth moving, saying so much so fast.

Riony tried to remember the night of the birth, the questions about Kellae and her family. "Her brother?"

Myrwa smiled in return. "All of these people are family now."

Outside the shrine building, all around, Myrwa's people brought the new arrivals in, and they in turn were coming back to life with relief.

The space had changed again since Riony's last visit, with small huts crafted from rugs and old, charred timber filling the space within the standing stone ring.

At least a couple of the huts were starting to look almost solid, as newly salvaged material was added to the structures. Patches of garden beds sprung with vibrant seedlings. Clean laundry hung in a line between two of the larger standing stones.

Pieces of broken pillar had been rolled into a ring around a central fire pit, where a sputtering collection of pots hissed the scents of roasting vegetables and stewed mushrooms into the dulling day. Seats were given to the newcomers and food doled out.

A warm glow fell through the surrounding woods as the sun dropped away, and as the light faded, voices grew louder with released joy.

Slowly, finally, the churning in Riony's chest wound down to a soft, anxious thud.

She sat with Dracuni at the edge of the celebrating people. She cleaned her wounds as she watched Lyrrin and Benjin play with their lost friends, doing some strange wide-legged dance with their arms in the air.

She ate a bowl of rice as one of the older women of the shrine enclave rolled a barrel out from one of the huts. There was a short argument about whether it was ready or not before the barrel was unstoppered and drinks were poured.

Niskina made a face and coughed as she had her first mouthful, and the four young men with her teased her before mirroring her reaction to the drink. They dragged Aishena, scowling, into their cluster and cheered as she downed a cup without flinching.

Riony wiped mud from her sword and boots as Kellae introduced her brother to Dracuni, their voices lost beneath the growingly boisterous crowd. The young boy reached a timid hand to pat the unidragon but snatched it back when Dracuni raised her snout to meet him. Kellae hugged her baby and laughed.

"What is it?" the boy asked, his eyes too large in his skinny face.

"Just a baby dragon," Kellae responded, giving the same reply Riony had always given them.

"I've never seen a baby one before."

"They normally raise them in factories until they are big enough to work. But this is how they look." Riony tried to give her words the weight of someone who knew everything about dragons and couldn't be questioned. Having grown up around Kess, it was easy enough to channel.

"Is it … tame?" The boy reached a hand again, clearly wary of how Dracuni tracked his movement and sniffed at his fingers.

No matter how Riony had tried to get the dragonling to act still and calm like a tamed dragon, she had become bold around people she knew.

Riony nodded. "The taming spike is under the horn. It's … decorative."

Most of Myrwa's people and the new group kept well away from Dracuni still, as Riony preferred it, but Kellae had taken to the unidragon and would give her small strips of meat and other treats when they visited.

The young men with Niskina were keeping their eyes on Riony and the unidragon as they toasted again.

Kellae and her brother wandered back to join the others.

Riony winced as she rubbed some weftweed sap over the cut on her eyebrow.

"Took a nasty hit there." One of Niskina's four young men sat down beside Riony.

Bronze-skinned and amber-haired, he looked as if he'd been dipped in honey. He gave her a smile that almost entirely hid his eyes.

She shrugged. "Me and lashes are old acquaintances."

"And what's this little fellow? Treedart?" He leaned forward, directing his gaze at Dracuni, on Riony's other side.

Riony leaned forward as well to block the man's view. "Yeah, treedart. Runt of the litter. Just a rescue we picked up."

The man whistled low. "Just a rescue, she says, as though having a dragon of her own is nothing. Pretty impressive, I'd say."

Riony placed a hand on Dracuni's neck, hoping she took the hint. Dracuni made herself small and still, behaving the most like a tamed dragon that Riony had ever seen.

You worry?

"Gotta do what we can to stay safe out here," Riony said, answering them both.

The man leaned back, smiling again. He was cleaner than most of the other slaves from the mine, in rough leather pants that had been scuffed and resewn in places.

"Riiiiiiiiiiiiiii!" Niskina squealed as though forgetting the rest of her name.

She dumped herself down on the ground in front of Riony in a burst of tumbling hair and flushed cheeks. Two more young men sat somewhat more gracefully on either side of her.

"We did it, Ri! Look what we did!" Niskina leaned over her legs and squeezed Riony's boot.

"Found some new friends?" Riony tried to raise her eyebrows, but it hurt.

"Oh! This is Renshy." She gestured to the man beside Riony. "And this is—"

"Eydon." A sandy-skinned man with dark hair pulled back into a long ponytail leaned forward to shake Riony's hand.

"Layle," said the man on Niskina's other side. All mousy-colored, his eyes kept darting, alert and wary.

"And Stets," Niskina said, looking behind her. When he wasn't immediately at her back, she propped herself up higher. "There he is. Stets!"

From over beside the crowd, a wall-shaped slab of man looked over the heads of others and nodded back. He returned to conversation with Aishena, an intense focus on her face and lips.

Good luck, friend, Riony thought as Aishena gave the man a glance up and down once, then maintained her usual, skeptical scowl.

"These lovely men helped us take down the guards in the tunnels," Niskina said, leaning into Eydon's shoulder.

Riony could smell the tart, bright tang of unaged wine on her breath.

"Happy to help out," Renshy said, taking a sip from his cup. "I mean, you were freeing us, after all."

"Been there long?" Riony said, eyeing their clothing, not caked in mud and dust the way the other slaves were.

There were weapons on their belts too, but they could have been taken from guards on the way out.

"Only just got brought in an hour before you lot showed up," Layle said with a hushed voice.

"Barely long enough for us to start plotting our own escape." Renshy laughed. "So we're very grateful that you dealt with that for us, because planning is not one of our strengths."

"Can't say it's ours either," Riony said. She gently pushed away an offering of Renshy's cup.

Niskina slapped both her hands down onto the ground. "I have a plan, though. That we keep doing this!"

"Drinking and flirting with more men than you have orifices?" Riony said.

Renshy spit his drink, choking.

Niskina only gave her a daring grin in return. "Saving people! We were like the Rebel Riders today. Fighting back, making change!"

Riony's mouth moved in small twitching shapes. "Okay. It was pretty great. Maybe not as great as the stories. But we all made it out alive."

Niskina's whole body seemed to soften, sighing out the fire of battle it held. "I used to hate it, you know, hiding underground in the depths. I never wanted to be there, forced into that awful greedy work that killed my mother."

Riony offered a sympathetic look. Niskina had told her once about the lively Rolanian woman who had won a grayglim's heart. It sounded so grandly romantic, how they ran away together, only to end in tragedy during a delving accident.

Niskina poked the dirt in front of her with one finger. "I've wanted to be up here, doing something good for the world, for as long as I could remember. I'm just sorry it took my father dying to get me out."

"I'm so sorry," Eydon said, leaning closer to her again.

Niskina's eyes glistened for a moment, but she shook her melancholy off, maintaining her smile. "It's not like how I thought it would be, up here. I had been so idealistic! But today ... today makes me feel as though we can help make the world into something better.”

"Our lives are certainly improved,” Renshy said and lifted his cup in a toast.

Music started up near the main fire, and Niskina grabbed the hands of the two men beside her. She rose to her feet, dragging them with her. “Come on. Let’s dance!”

Renshy offered a hand to Riony. “I’d love to dance with you.”

"Oh. Um. No, thanks. Not really in the mood.”

"For dancing? I can stay here with you if you’d like some company?” he replied.

Riony rubbed the back of her head. “Depends on how you define company.”

"I told you she wouldn’t be interested.” Niskina gave her a sly smile. “What she might be interested in is that lovely doe-eyed maiden over by the smokehouse that has been ogling her since we got here.”

Riony looked, catching the young woman’s gaze. Dark round eyes were rimmed in thick lashes that fluttered down over her cheeks, then rose again to hold Riony’s stare. The hint of a smile, bottom lip pressed between teeth. Riony had noticed her on a previous visit. Totally, sweat-inducingly gorgeous.

Heat rushed up Riony’s neck.

"Somebody needs to stay sober and on watch.” Her voice broke over the words. She swallowed hard and looked at the ground.

The gasp Niskina drew in sounded like it could have exploded her chest. “What is this? All the flirting and lecherous proposals that tumble from your mouth, and when presented with an opportunity for a *real* tumble, you’re going shy?”

"It’s not that. I just ... I’m—”

"Riony,” Niskina rasped, scandalized. “Have you ever even kissed someone before?”

The hot, squirming embrace of shame tangled around Riony’s chest as she remembered. “Of course. Plenty.”

Her first kiss ... she couldn’t forget that.

But since then? She’d never really gotten a chance to do much of anything since taking care of Lyrrin. It wasn’t that she didn’t want to—she just knew it would be too hard. Too hard to have a relationship like she really wanted.

Instead, she vented that with her big mouth, and when that turned people away? They wouldn’t have wanted her anyway. She couldn’t have been with them even if they did. It didn’t matter.

And now she had Dracuni too. She couldn’t think beyond caring for her charges.

"Plenty? I mean *real* kissing. Just like this.” Niskina grasped Eydon’s collar, tugging him in to meet her mouth.

He leaned into the kiss for a few passionate heartbeats, then both of them chuckled as they pulled away, eyes on each other.

"I’m perfectly aware of what kissing is. It’s what you can all do to my ass.”

Niskina tsked and tugged at the hands of the two men beside her, gesturing at Renshy to follow them as well. “Come on. Let’s go have some fun.”

Renshy stood up and offered his cup to Riony one more time before following the others away.

"Nisk?" Riony called out. "Just be careful, okay?"

Niskina blew a raspberry in return and skipped crookedly into the dancing crowd.

Riony leaned back against the wall, watching her go.

It was nice to see some fire in Niskina again, a reawakening of who she'd been before. But she was still being too reckless for Riony's liking. They'd gotten lucky today, in many ways. Things could have gone much, much worse.

But Riony wasn't thinking about the mine anymore.

She closed her eyes, trying to block out the words, the vision, the feelings. She didn't want to remember, but the memory had wedged itself into her head like an axe.

Sitting together on Kess's bed, staring out the window at one of the estate's dragonriders who was kissing a kitchen maid up against a shadowy wall in the courtyard. The way their bodies had moved and entwined with each other …

Mouth dry, Riony had asked, "What do you think it's like?"

"What?" Kess replied.

"Kissing someone?"

"It sounds gross. Kife said they put their tongues in the other person's mouth. Intolerably disgusting."

"Hmm." Riony leaned on her folded arms, eyes fixed on the couple below, her heart beating fast in her small chest as though thumping a signal drum she wished someone would answer. Not yet ten years old and only guessing at the new feelings within her.

Kess lowered herself from the window ledge back to the bed, leaning on the wall.

There was a pink blush, high on her cheeks, under the constellation of dark spots sprayed across one cheekbone.

She muttered, "But we could … I don't know … try it. If you *have* to know."

"I'm not going to kiss you even if you order me to. Even if you whip me." Riony ducked back down too, thumping onto the mattress in a way that made Kess bounce and scowl.

"I'm not ordering you! I was just offering, you ungrateful wretch—something *you* seemed to want. I don't *want* to kiss you!"

"And I don't want to kiss you! You're just trying to trick me, then tell on me to your parents!"

"Forget I offered!"

"You never meant it anyway!" Riony leaned forward, anger flushing her face.

Kess leaned in too, poking Riony with a pointed finger. "Neither did you!"

"Oh, really?"

"Yeah, really!"

"Fine! Kiss me then." Riony dared, heart in her throat, nose brushing Kess's.

And Kess did.

And for a startling, brief moment, it felt warm, and right, and aching.

And then Kess kicked Riony out of her room in a fit of tears and screams.

And then for a week she told all staff that she'd fallen ill and let nobody into her chambers.

And Riony didn't get whipped that week, and she had no idea what she'd done wrong. *Kess's usual psychological torture.*

The furious beating in Riony's chest kicked up again, as achingly fast as it had been when fighting the men with lashes. There was nothing quite the same as the burning sting of a lash.

Dracuni had fallen asleep next to Riony when Aishena appeared like a ghost at her side in a swish of silky hair.

She looked at Riony with heavy eyelids. "Did we do the right thing today?"

Riony frowned at the cloying fragrance of alcohol that had arrived with the woman. It wasn't like Aishena to drink. "The plan didn't exactly play out right, but we all made it out."

"I mean doing that at all, attacking the mine."

"It was risky, but I think we made a lot of people happy." Riony gestured to the partying crowd.

Aishena slipped as she sat down beside Riony, falling against Riony's shoulder and staying there. "I'm not sure ... I don't know if we did the right thing. I'm not sure it's what Yoskar would have done."

Her voice hiccupped over her brother's name. The flash of fire reflected on flat glass and the thin bend of wire held tight in Aishena's hand. Glasses. Yoskar's glasses.

Riony didn't have the heart to bring up that Yoskar didn't always choose the right thing over what served him and his family first.

"Are you okay? What did they have in that barrel?" Riony shifted to bring her arm out from between them and straighten Aishena up, and as she did, Aishena leaned into her more, bringing her face close.

"I heard Niskina telling one of the women that you were looking for someone to kiss."

"Okay, firstly, that's Niskina deciding what I want and who I want. And secondly, Niskina is going to be telling everyone the tale of how badly I beat her ass if she doesn't quit it."

Aishena's gaze remained lowered, not looking Riony in the face. "What do you want? Do you still want to kiss me? I know you did once."

A breath shook out of Riony's mouth. "Honestly? I'd given up on having anything more than begrudging mutual tolerance from you."

Aishena flinched. "I'm following commands. I'm trying to do the right thing and do what I'm told. That's what I'm supposed to do. You don't want that? You don't want me?"

"There's wanting. Trust me, there's wanting. But I kind of like seeing that there's some wanting in return, you know?" Riony tucked a finger under Aishena's chin, tilting it up to look into the young woman's eyes to see if there was anything there other than pain.

Gaze still turned away, Aishena lifted herself toward Riony's lips.

Riony gently pushed her away. "Whoa. Hey. I don't think this is the right time to turn any wanting into doing, okay?"

Aishena's face crumpled. "What do I do? Just tell me. I have to get it right. I have to do what I'm told. What do I do? Tell me what to do, and I'll do it."

Riony had never seen Aishena like this, her words slurring and eyes unfocused, chest heaving into inconsolable sobbing. Niskina had always been the one for breaking down into drunken tears and venting all her grief and fury. Aishena had remained solemn and guarded in her mourning as she did in all things.

Where their bags had been piled together near the wall, the glint of metal showed, poking out the top of Aishena's. Her mother's twin blades, that had ended so many lives, that Aishena carried the weight of.

"Nothing." Riony looped her arm around Aishena, bringing her close to her chest and holding her as her body shook. "You don't have to do anything."

Grief poured from Aishena in waves of whispered wails and shuddering sobs, and Riony held her, watching the night and the fire and the dancers and the dusty children and the sleeping baby dragon and the stars far overhead who were watching them in return.

As the heaviness of Aishena's grief soaked into her, Riony's eyes filled too. Which of the stars overhead were her own parents? Her own family lost?

Against the ebony blanket of sky, a bright spark burst, shimmering and flying like a falling star but bright and close.

Blinking her eyes clear, Riony tried to make sense of what she'd seen, but it had already passed.

She wanted to believe it was some message in the sky from her ancestors, but her heart only knew messages of fear and loss, and raged within her again like a cornered animal.

Chapter Fourteen

"We lied to you." Renshy's expression was flat, guarded, as he and his three friends stood squared off with Riony, Niskina, and Aishena.

Aishena's hand drifted to the athames on her belt, and Riony brushed her arm with her fingers in a message of patience.

"Lied about what?" Riony asked.

Her eyes were still bleary from a restless night, but despite waking to this confrontation, she could still spot Lyrrin, Benjin, and Dracuni nearby, and all seemed well around Myrwa's camp.

"About why we were at the mine, about who we are. We're sorry, but we needed to know we could trust you first."

Niskina's eyes sparkled, and she pulled her lips in, sealing her mouth tight.

"I didn't think you looked much like the others at the mine." Riony again catalogued their weapons, trying to gauge whether she should be drawing hers. "And do you trust us enough now to stop being vague weirdos?"

Stets, the big one, laughed in a deep rumble.

Renshy smiled in that way that hid his eyes and gestured to the refugees and liberated people resting in the cool morning air. "I think we know enough about you now."

"Come on. Tell them," Niskina hissed.

"Do you know what they are talking about?" Riony asked.

Renshy grew solemn again. "We were in the mines on a reconnaissance mission, for the rebellion. And we want to invite you to join us."

Letting out a squeal, Niskina bounced on the spot. "They told me last night!"

"Rebellion, like … the Rebel Riders?" Riony asked, trying to imagine the men in front of her like the characters in those stories without blushing.

Three of the men looked back blankly, but Layle replied softly, "Not quite. No dragons. Not so much romance. We just organize and do things like what you and your friends pulled off yesterday."

"And with your help, we could do more," Eydon said, snaking his arm around Niskina's waist.

The way she giggled and cast lazy, longing looks over his mouth made Riony wonder what they'd gotten up to the night before.

Riony's neck still felt sticky from Aishena's dried tears.

Aishena had awoken that morning to her usual cold, bristly self. And had refused to do anything more than apologize for her 'misdirected outburst' then ask that they never speak of it again.

Riony got it. She knew Aishena was just seeking comfort. That she needed it. After so long holding it together. She needed someone there for her when she broke.

She hadn't wanted Riony. Not really.

Sighing, Riony tried to focus on what the men were saying. It seemed important, after all. Riony just felt like there were too many important things to keep track of.

"Sorry, what are you asking? Are you inviting us to join your rebel group?"

Renshy lifted his hands. "It's not our group. We're just a part of something bigger. But we can give you an introduction to people that run the show. They have a base not far from here, in the old glass factory."

Niskina grabbed both of Riony's hands in hers. "This is it! This is our chance to help more people, to really change things!"

Aishena took a step back, bringing herself close by Riony's shoulder.

In a hushed voice, she said, "Our actions yesterday will have drawn attention. I'm not sure if seeking more rebellious associations is a good idea. We have too many enemies after us already."

"I haven't forgotten," Riony replied.

She still flinched at anything that sounded like a wolf howl, even though it had been half a year since they'd last seen Kess.

Aishena's voice was firmer than it had been for a long while. "Then we should lay low. At least for a while. Maybe it's time we finally go to our planned destination."

Their planned destination—Riony's old village. A shiver tugged at her flesh as though it were trying to drag her forward, make her run. That was the feeling she always got when thinking about that place. Even the thought of it made her want to run the other way.

Niskina gave Riony a pleading look.

Shaking her head, Riony said, "It's just a meeting. We should at least go and hear what they have to say. Maybe they can help us stay hidden better, have somewhere even safer for us to go."

Aishena opened her mouth, seemed to think again, then nodded. "As you say."

"Yay!" Niskina cheered.

Renshy clapped his hands together. "Fantastic. Gather up your things, and we'll take you after breakfast."

It didn't take long to pack as none of them had really unpacked after the party the night before.

Myrwa joined Riony to discuss plans for the new arrivals as she chewed on some day-old flatbread. They stood together, looking over the small community within the ring of standing stones.

Children lay wrapped in blankets on the ground in small clusters, but some of the older newly freed were up and talking with the settlers, helping with cleaning and cooking.

"They've all decided to stay," Myrwa said.

"Even the undercity kids?" Riony replied, trying to identify them amongst the sleeping children, but they were all identical dusty-haired bundles of fabric and limbs.

But then a flash of Lyrrin running by drew her gaze to a few children who were awake and playing near the makeshift huts. There were hugs shared and waves of goodbye-for-now, then the children went back to their game, crawling around on the ground.

"They said they don't have anyone waiting for them underground. They want to be in the sunlight again."

Riony could see it in their faces as they wriggled on their bellies like worms, touching the grass that sprung up around the paving with giggling awe. There was joy there and hope, like she'd never seen on their faces when in the orphans' den.

"Is that okay for you? I didn't mean to have you look after everyone."

"I'm not. We all look after each other here. And it's only for now. Some seemed excited by the idea that other shrines are safe and settled as well. That they could travel and start their life again at the closest shrine to their original homes. But we can help people move around more on your next visit, yes? I can see you're off again already."

"Yeah." Riony frowned as she adjusted the pack on her back and the sword strapped beside it. "Do you know anything about an old glass factory nearby?"

Myrwa nodded. "A couple of braver types have been there when out foraging. Good place for it. It's not far."

"Haven't seen anyone else around that area?"

"I haven't been myself. My legs don't run fast enough to risk getting caught outside the shrine. But no, nobody has mentioned anything."

When Riony told this to Niskina on their way out of camp, Niskina just scoffed. "It's a hidden rebel base. They're going to stay hidden if they don't know the people poking around."

"I guess so."

Myrwa's group had been at the shrine for months now. If these rebels were good people, wouldn't they have made some effort to introduce themselves, being so close by? Maybe do something to help the new settlement grow and stay safe? Or even trade with them?

Or maybe Niskina was right and they just needed to remain secretive to protect themselves and what they did. Still, Riony checked her access to her sword, undoing one of the straps so she could draw it faster if needed.

They had only been walking a short time when the forest ended abruptly, replaced with low scrub that had recently been burned, leaving it brittle and blackened. And ahead, beside a quarry scraped clean to the bones of the earth, was the remains of the factory.

Renshy led the way toward it. "The entrance is inside the main building there."

A couple of smaller side houses seemed to cower in the shade of the larger one. They leaned against the massive walls of metal beams and charred masonry that formed the main building, like ducklings beneath their mother.

Almost the entire top half of the largest structure was made of glass, but those windows were high and fogged with soot. The walls were solid and unbroken, and Riony couldn't see inside.

Their steps crunched through the tangle of twisted roots and scattered leaves, kicking up the scent of smoke and sulfur.

An uneasy tension knotted in her gut. Her footsteps faltered as she gazed at the tall steel door, standing ajar before her.

Aishena made a small sucking breath sound.

"What is it?" Riony whispered to the woman at her shoulder.

Aishena met her gaze, her eyes worried. But then she shook her head. "Nothing."

"You don't like this either, huh?" Riony had hoped it was just her being paranoid. But as much as Aishena refused to admit it, she'd had excellent instincts in the past.

"The kids and dragon should wait out here," Riony said.

Whatever they were walking into, she didn't need to bring them with her on the off chance this was going to be safe. She didn't want whoever was in there to see Dracuni yet either.

As long as Renshy was telling the truth that they didn't have any dragons, then Riony and Aishena could deal with a few thugs if they were about to get robbed.

Lyrrin pouted. "You're leaving us out again!"

Dracuni, who had continued doing her best ever performance of playing tame, rose up tall as well. ***Not want to stay.***

"This is just going to be a boring grown-up chat, okay? Stay out here and keep watch for us. That will be more exciting."

Benjin stamped Yoskar's staff on the ground in front of him. "We should get to meet the rebels too. We should get to have a say in what's going on."

Renshy held the door open as Niskina and Eydon went in. "I'm sure it's fine for us all to go in. The people we're meeting don't mind having kids around."

Riony held her little sister's glare, pleading with her to acquiesce. "The kids and dragon stay out here. That's final, or we're turning around right now and Niskina will never get to live her dreams."

"Fine. It looks smelly in there anyway," Lyrrin said, sneering at the moldy darkness around the base of the walls.

"Layle," Renshy said. "Stay out here with them. Make sure they stay safe."

The man gave a casual salute, alert and stern as he turned to watch over the children and Dracuni.

Aishena gave Riony a grateful nod, then stepped with her into the building, with Stets at their back.

Riony's eyes adjusted to the gloomy interior.

The huge space was divided in two by a half-length partition wall, and the area they entered first had rows of cages along one side, lined up and aimed toward domed furnaces.

Checking them with a focused stare for signs of prisoners or signs that those cages were their intended destination, Riony realized they had been cages for dragons.

A couple of the narrow stocks still held the lifeless bodies of the dragons who'd worked there, squeezed into the space and draped in chains. The desiccated corpses didn't look very old, scales and draped skin clinging tight over their bones.

Were the dragons just left there to die when this place closed down?

Riony shivered. The whole building seemed to have been left to ruin without any care for what had been left behind. It should have at least been burned, to get rid of the corpses that the shadowdragon could raise.

The carelessness infuriated her. But she'd seen it before. It infuriated her *because* she'd seen it before.

Stacked across the other side, piles of old wooden tools and baskets burst with the rippling shapes and round caps of fungus in vibrant oranges and dull browns. The air was thick with their cloying, earthy scent.

The skitter of movement caught Riony's alert eyes. Dozens of tiny mouse deer grazed amongst the fungus on their stick-thin, dainty hooves. A few startled at the presence of humans, dashing away into a maze of rotting crates and barrels. Others sniffed the air, then put their slender heads down again.

Shattered glass refuse littered the floor, glittering and sharp like all the stars had fallen out of the sky. Above them, the ceiling was all glass, a few panels broken, but that didn't account for all the shards.

It must have been wastage from the factory itself. Jagged edges dug through the soles of Riony's boots as she stepped inside.

Stets closed the door behind them.

"This is it," Renshy called out.

"Where's the entrance?" Niskina asked. "Are they going to come out and meet us?"

There was a long, soft sliding sound from behind the partition. Something large, in motion. Shadows shifted and glass crunched and from behind the wall, the head of a huge, purple dragon emerged, snarling at them, fire flickering between its teeth.

And beside that dragon, Kess rode in on her wolf.

Chapter Fifteen

Basic thugs, Riony could handle. A secret rebel group who might have decided they weren't on the same side, she could handle.

But Kess, with a dragon? Kess, and the person who was *on* that dragon?

A clammy, chilled sweat rushed over Riony.

Movement fluttered all around as the little mouse deer made themselves vanish into any nook available.

"What's going on?" Niskina asked, turning to Eydon beside her, as though he might say this was some mistake, that he didn't know these wolf-and-dragon-riding ambushers.

Instead, he lunged forward, grabbing her arms and pinning them behind her.

There was a scuffle to Riony's left as Renshy grabbed Aishena.

Riony's hand was halfway to her sword when Stets had her pinned as well, locked in his massive arms.

"What are you doing?" Niskina cried, struggling and wrenching against her captor.

"We're getting one hell of a bounty," Eydon said, close to her ear but loud enough for everyone to hear. "We were looking for someone else in the mines, then you lot landed in our lap—in more ways than one."

Niskina stilled and went pale. "You left. You left during the night. Is this where you went? To plan this? How could you!"

"Pretty easily, actually," Eydon replied. "It didn't take much to get you away from the Alderkin gateway to somewhere we could grab you. Rebels, ha!"

Renshy swore, and there was a flurry of limbs as Aishena broke free from his grasp.

"Give it up before I burn you on the spot." Kife leaned forward in the saddle of his dragon, and the beast directed its mouth her way.

Kife. His presence made Riony's stomach churn.

Riony had always wished that he wasn't still plaguing the world with his presence, that some deadly accident had befallen him on a dragonrider mission long before now. But there he was, still alive, looking far too excited by the idea of burning a human alive.

What had Kess told her twisted brother? About Dracuni? About her blood? Keeping away from Kess and Griskin was one thing, but now that she'd teamed up with a psychotic dragonrider, it was going to be so much harder.

Riony cursed herself. They'd gotten too complacent. Things had been going so well and they hadn't seen Kess for so long, hadn't had bounty hunters recognize the Hjelzahn siblings for so long. Riony had walked into the factory half expecting trouble but believing she could handle it.

And then there was Kess, bringing a dragon to a knife fight.

Aishena stilled, lifting her hands back off the hilts of her athames.

"You can't burn this one." Renshy yanked the coil of cave silk rope from Aishena's belt and pulled her hands behind her back to bind them. "Remember the deal."

"You made a deal with *these two*?" Riony laughed at him. "And I thought I was dumb."

"Nobody is disputing that, Pony." Kess had the kind of triumphant look on her face that made Riony's hand itch to slap it.

"After all this time without you around, I thought you'd given up, Kessara." Riony tested Stets's hold on her, finding no give. "Is this what you've been keeping busy with? Selling us out to *him*?"

Riony flicked her chin at Kife, who simply seemed amused by the scene.

Then she gave Kess the most shaming look she could muster. "I mean, you've done a whole load of dumb and evil things in the past, but this is on a whole new level of idiotic malice. Congratulations on the personal best, but you know he's going to kill you, right?"

Griskin gave a grumbling moan, his eyes and nose weeping. Kess leaned forward and petted him casually. "And wouldn't you be happy if he did? Saves you the trouble."

Renshy finished tying Aishena, cut the rope, and threw it across to Stets. The bulky man began wrapping Riony's wrists behind her back.

She kept her chin up, an uneven smirk across her bared teeth. "I've got the feeling I'd be dead by that point and unfortunately wouldn't be able to celebrate. This is the guy who tried to kill you already. What are you thinking?"

Despite the triumphant sneer on Kess's face, somehow she seemed smaller than usual. She hunched close to Griskin, almost hidden in his fur. "Don't pretend you care. I told you I'd do anything to get what I wanted off you, and so here we are."

Kife clapped his hands together, the slap echoing through the large space. "All right, now where is this creature she's supposed to have?"

Still outside. Still with a chance to get away. Riony hoped Dracuni and the kids had heard Niskina's earlier cries and were already gone, but she could still sense Dracuni nearby. There were no spikes of fear yet, just a low edge of concern, as though she was picking up on Riony's stress.

Riony breathed deep to belt out a warning.

Stets slapped a meaty hand over her mouth and pressed a sharp length of metal to her throat.

Riony stilled. With her pack and sword still strapped on her back, her arms were bent at a painful angle to where her wrists were tied together. She tried to shift them and rub the rope against the blade, but she couldn't get the angle right.

"Don't worry," Renshy said as he pulled a leather pouch from his pocket. "Your critter is just out there with a couple of kids. Layle can handle it. You'll have your bounty in a moment."

"Those kids are little savages," Kess replied. "Don't underestimate them."

"I'll go and help bring them in," Eydon said, finishing off the knot around Niskina's hands.

Her shoulders were slumped, but she turned toward him fiercely when he let her go.

She kicked him in the back of the knee as he walked away, making him stumble.

"Watch yourself!" he growled back as he steadied himself. "We've got no bounty to collect on you, so we can go either way on whether we keep you or not!"

"Bounty hunters? Is that all you are? I should have known you were such cowards. You handle a woman's body like one." Niskina leaned into the words, spitting them in fury, but there were tears on her cheeks.

Sparks, she wanted this to be real so badly. And now we're all screwed.

Aishena, hands tied and held tight in Renshy's grip, said, "Whatever bounty is out on me and my brother, I'll pay more. We can work it out. We—"

Renshy pressed the pouch he was holding over her mouth and nose. Aishena gasped and wheezed, fighting for a moment before her eyes rolled and she slumped, leaning into Renshy's hold. Her legs buckled beneath her.

Morass mercy? Riony glared daggers at Kess. Had she given it to them?

Renshy juggled his grip on Aishena, keeping her pinned to his chest like a precious trophy. He grinned at Kife. "All right now. We brought you the redhead with the strange dragonling, all as agreed last night. I'd like to see that payment we also agreed on now."

"Get out there and get us the dragonling first!" Kess ordered. "I'd do it myself but I have to keep my eyes on this one. She's trouble."

Riony winked at her over Stets's hand.

Kife narrowed his eyes as he looked between the two of them. "Relax, little sis. We can deal with these three, then go grab the others ourselves. It's a couple of kids and a hatchling. What are they going to do? Even if they run, we can catch them. It'll make it more fun too."

"It's *not tamed*, brother. Have you ever met an untamed dragon before?"

"Hold up. It's not tamed?" Renshy barked. "Eydon, leave that one and go help Layle bring the others in."

Seeming hesitant to let go of Niskina again, Eydon sneered then stepped back from her quickly, dodging the boot she stomped at his shin.

"Come on. Let's wrap this up," Kife said, pulling a jingling pouch from the bags on the dragon's saddle. "You'll get this when we have the dragonling. And you can keep the Hjelzahns too, for whatever they are worth. The other three can be disposed of."

"Eydon seems to have a soft spot for the pretty one," Renshy said, and Eydon gave a noncommittal grunt as he crunched across toward the door. "But might as well get rid of the big one now. Do it, Stets."

Riony winced as Stets's grip around her mouth tightened and he rumbled a low chuckle.

Run. Run. RUN! She closed her eyes and screamed inside her head as loud as she could, hoping Dracuni could hear, trying to pierce the distance with her thoughts.

There was a shimmer of feeling in return, a ripple of confusion and worry.

Then Stets shoved Riony hard from behind, toppling her forward.

She landed on her knees and gasped as shards of glass jabbed through the thick leather of her delver pants. The tip of her sword, strapped to her back, hit the ground too, sending her forward again. She went down, hands tied, unable to stop the face-first fall onto the glass-barbed ground.

She turned her chin and gritted her teeth as she landed. Sharp points of agony sprang up all across her chest and cheek. Riony tried to bite off her cry, to not give Kess or Kife any pleasure in seeing her hurt, but it felt as though she'd been struck by a hundred daggers, slicing and needling their way into her skin.

She whimpered, and the opening of her mouth scraped more shards over her chin and lips as she worked hard to draw breath.

"Riony!" Niskina yelled and charged forward, shouldering Stets.

He brushed Niskina off, sending her stumbling, careening sideways in an effort to not fall into the glass herself.

"I like that one's spirit," Kife said, jingling the coin pouch. "Maybe I'll buy her too."

"You couldn't afford me!" Niskina spat back, setting her feet firmly and looking ready to charge.

Behind them, Eydon hovered near the door, seeming unsure whether he needed to get Niskina under control again or continue outside as ordered.

Riony squirmed, trying to get her knees under her and push up off the biting ground, and every movement cut her more. Before she could even twist onto her side, Stets's foot struck out, cracking into her ribs. He worked the point of his toes between her and her backpack and pressed down.

Glass fractured beneath Riony, grinding through her shirt into her skin. A racking wail of pain came unstoppable from her chest.

"Come on, Stets. Stop mucking around," Renshy said.

"Hmm, fine." He grunted.

The boot was removed, then was replaced by the crushing weight of Stets's entire body as he straddled Riony's back, sitting on her backpack. He leaned over her, chuckling softly every time his movements made the glass beneath them crackle.

Fingers wrapped into the hair on the back of Riony's scalp, then squeezed tight, wrenching her head off the ground in a painful arc.

Niskina gasped, a flurry of cries and prayers coming from her mouth. She stepped forward again, but a turn of the dragon's head toward her kept her in place.

Slivers of glass clattered as they fell from Riony's face, stinging as the heavier pieces slid free. Blood dripped into Riony's eye and she tried to blink it out. She stared across the ground, wanting to scream at Kess, to spit and spite her, to say something so devastating that it could take some of this victory away from her. But Riony couldn't even breathe.

Kess stared back as Stets pressed his dagger again to Riony's throat.

Then Kess flinched and averted her eyes.

It was the smallest thing. The briefest flicker of humanity, the kind of slip Kess never usually made, like screaming *Riony* back in that revenant-filled cave. It was the closest thing to a kindness Riony would ever know from her.

And she tried to accept that in the moment before she died. But it didn't feel like enough.

"Wait!" Kife snapped. His eyes weren't on Riony but on Kess. He smiled, and there was no kindness in his expression.

Stets remained in his crushing position. Riony desperately tried to drag in some air around the blade at her neck.

"This is no good," Kife said. He leaned back in his saddle, folding his arms. "We can't let some random thug kill an Uf'Heithorn. It just doesn't feel right, don't you think, sis?"

"What are you talking about?" Kess replied in a jittery, scathing tone.

Riony felt no comfort from Kife's words. Whatever he was planning, it wasn't going to save her. He was going to find a way to make this hurt even more.

"I mean, she was your pet, after all." Kife's eyes glittered mischievously, and he gave Kess a mocking, doting look. "*You* should be the one who gets to put her down."

CHAPTER SIXTEEN

Lyrrin thought she heard something from inside the building. A crunching sound, a cry.

"Did you hear that?" she asked.

Benjin turned his eyes upward. A carrion bird circled high above and warbled a howl, echoing the sound.

"Ugh." Lyrrin squinted into the morning light at it, willing it to leave so that its wolflike howls didn't set Riony off into overprotective mode again.

Although she's still leaving us out anyway.

Dracuni sat still and calm, watching Layle pace in front of them, with only a flick of her tufted tail betraying her impatience.

Lyrrin ran a hand over one of her soft ears. "Shouldn't be much longer. They'll probably come and get us once they decide it's safe."

Dracuni huffed softly.

Benjin stood with his back to the building, Yoskar's staff held before him, staring out across the scrub toward the forest, at least making an effort to be on guard. But Lyrrin knew Riony had only left them outside to keep them safe.

It made sense. They shouldn't be letting too many people see Dracuni, if they could help it. But it still annoyed her that if something wasn't safe to start with, why was Riony going in at all? Or why go in with fewer people to help?

A rough snort came from Dracuni, and she rose in a start onto her hind legs, eyes wide.

"Hey! What's your dragon doing? What are you telling it to do?" Layle said. "Move away from it!"

He put a hand on Lyrrin's shoulder, giving her a shove to the side so he was between her, Benjin, and the dragonling. "I don't want to get burned by kids mucking around with a dragon."

"She's not going to hurt you." *Unless you deserve it,* Lyrrin thought, cringing at the place the man had touched her, pushing her like she was a piece of furniture. "I think she's worried about something."

A cry, muffled by the wall of the building, came from behind them.

It was Riony. Lyrrin knew it. And Riony never screamed like that. Not unless she was really, really hurt. Lyrrin's heart raced into a gallop.

"What's—?" Benjin's mouth clamped closed again, his question answered before he asked it.

The mousy man had drawn his sword in a swish of steel. His ever-roaming eyes narrowed, darting between Benjin and Lyrrin. "Come on then. Time to head in with the others. Go on, you two."

"What about our dragon?" Lyrrin said, refusing to move. "What are you going to do with her?"

Layle didn't even glance back at Dracuni. "It will come along as commanded too. Does it do voice commands yet? Tell it to go inside."

"I'm not telling her to do anything for you." Lyrrin glared at the man from under her hood.

The man tsked and stepped toward her, sword raised. "We don't need you, girl. Only the Hjelzahn boy and the dragonling. I'll work out how to make the tame-brained thing move without you."

Lyrrin pulled a face at him and said, "Except that our dragon isn't tamed."

Layle only had a moment for realization to hit him, to try to turn back and put his eyes on the dangerous creature behind him, but it was too late.

Dracuni snapped her jaw closed around one of his ankles.

He cried out, hopping and trying to pull away.

With a flick of her snout, Dracuni tossed the man onto the ground in a puff of soot and dust.

Wood and sparkling crystal swung through the air and Benjin thunked the end of Yoskar's staff into the man's head where he lay. Layle lolled to the side, unmoving, but still breathing.

Dracuni growled, giving her head a shake before letting the man's ankle go.

"Sparks, these guys *were* leading us into a trap!" Benjin grumbled. "Aish thought so. She told me on the way, but I didn't believe her."

"Come on. We need to see what's going on in there." Lyrrin scanned the area.

They couldn't go through the front door without immediately being seen. Beckoning Benjin and Dracuni to follow her, she ran over and climbed up a couple of old wooden crates and onto the roof of one of the small buildings leaning against the large factory.

They were at the level of the first row of sooty windows there, and Lyrrin hurried to the first broken one and peered through.

The first thing she saw was the dragon. It was huge. Bigger than the ones who had come to the slavers' camp and tried to carry her away in a cage. A heavy purple beast with a wide chest and dark wings.

It had a rider, propped casually on top, and beside them was Kess on her wolf.

Benjin leaned next to her. "This is bad. Really bad."

"They always leave us out, and then we have to go and save them anyway!" Lyrrin replied.

One of the young men who had brought them there was holding Aishena, only partially upright, in his arms.

Niskina had her wrists tied, standing off to the side, cringing away from the sharp teeth of the dragon's maw hovering near her.

And in the middle, the biggest man leaned over Lyrrin's sister. He grabbed her by the back of the head and her bound hands, lifting her up off the ground, then dropping her onto her knees.

He kept one hand clasped at the back of her head, holding her up by the hair like a puppet and making her face Kess, who stalked toward them on Griskin.

The wolf had leather wrappings around his four paws, protecting him from the glass that was spread all across the floor. They'd clearly had plenty of time to plan this ambush.

Even from a distance Lyrrin could see blood, and lots of it, dripping from Riony's arms and face and soaking the front of her shirt.

Dracuni let out a quiet whine.

Lyrrin felt it, too. She wanted to moan and scream and run in there throwing fists, but there was a *dragon*, a full-grown dragon and rider. She put a hand on Dracuni's neck to still them both.

Kess pulled a throwing knife, and her voice echoed up from the expanse below. "I'll finish it fast for you. Where do you want it—eye, neck, or heart?"

"You left out the best option," Riony replied. "Up your own ass."

The third man was near the exit, pausing to watch for a moment, his hands on the door.

"We've got to do something, fast." Benjin leaned forward, checking the gap between the jagged pieces of the broken window as though seeing if he would fit. More crates were stacked up and covered in fungus just beneath them.

Lyrrin nodded but backed away from the window.

She whispered, "What can we do? There's a dragon in there! I only have one flash stone left, and it's really small. I could maybe hit Kess or the guy holding Riony, but that doesn't deal with the dragon."

"You don't have to take out the dragon," Benjin said. "It's tamed. You only have to take out the rider!"

Lyrrin looked again, taking in the high walls and glass ceiling and Kess pulling her arm back to throw the blade that would kill her sister. They needed a distraction and a way to disable the dragon.

Lyrrin got her sling into her hand, a stone from her pocket loaded into it, then she slid forward on her belly through the broken window so her whole top half was hanging out into the air.

She spun the sling and let the shot fly.

A sheet of glass above the dragon shattered, cracking like sharp thunder, then falling in a jingle of bells.

Her aim was slightly off. The shards hailed down over the dragon's tail.

"What in the razed earth?" The rider turned in his seat, sheltering his eyes with a hand as fragments bounced near him. He craned his neck up, searching for the cause.

"Watch out!" Kess held her throw as Griskin sniffed the air, his nose wet and snuffly.

Lyrrin had another shot on its way, and it landed true, directly above the dragonrider.

Glass fell like crystal daggers. The rider dove from his saddle and tumbled under a wing to take shelter.

The dragon didn't flinch, didn't move as glass plinked and scattered from its scales. No longer controlled, it sat numb and dazed.

"That's it!" Benjin cheered. He grabbed Lyrrin's hand as she turned around on the windowsill and lowered onto the crates below. "Go!"

Lyrrin landed in a puff of spores and dust, stinging her eyes and nose, but she kept moving, climbing down the stacked boxes and barrels.

There were two thumps behind her as Benjin and Dracuni followed, wobbling the rotting wood.

Without the threat of being bitten in half, Niskina was first to move, charging the big man holding Riony. She crashed into his side, hard.

His grip on Riony must have slipped because in a roar, she thrust up onto her feet.

Turning back from watching the falling glass and de-seated rider, Kess swore and sent her knife whipping through the air.

Riony bent at the waist, ducking low as the knife flew toward her neck.

In a soft thud, it stuck deep into the flesh of the man behind her, right below his Adam's apple.

Blood spurted, and the man clawed blindly for the blade, tried to press against the freely flowing blood and hold it all in. He dropped down onto one knee, then toppled like a felled tree onto the ground in a crunch.

"Stets!" The man holding Aishena almost dropped her as he fumbled for his sword.

Benjin came in swinging, Yoskar's staff lit up red with a burn rune. "Let my sister go!"

The staff cracked against the sword, sparks flying in the dim, dusty light.

Niskina was at his side, hands still bound behind her back. The man who had been going outside must have seen that the reasons he was going out were all inside now anyway and rushed toward Niskina with his own sword drawn.

Lyrrin reached Riony's side. A curved sliver of glass jutted from Riony's cheek, and all over her chest and shoulders, fragments glittered between flowing crimson. Lyrrin shuddered and her eyes went hot. She scrunched up her nose to fight off tears.

"Cutting athame!" Riony hissed.

"This is faster!" Lyrrin already had a glove off and clawed one of her sharp nails down through the rope around her sister's hands. It tore and snapped, the frayed, blood-stained sections falling free.

With a moaning sigh, Riony stretched her arms. She tried to reach for her sword, but Kess already had more daggers drawn.

Then Kess lifted her head in a scream. "You wild monster! Get off me!"

Dracuni was there, snout snapped shut around Kess's toes.

Griskin circled, trying to turn back and bite the dragonling circling around behind him, teeth locked on Kess's boot.

"Dracuni!" Lyrrin cried.

"Free the others." Riony gave Lyrrin a short, worried glance before she ran headlong at the wolf and his rider.

She cleared the distance and leaped forward as Kess aimed a dagger at the unidragon, tackling Kess off Griskin's back and sliding across the floor in a jangle of glass shards.

"I should have killed you the second you stepped into this building!" Kess screamed, gurgling with fury.

Riony had her pinned, straddled over her, hands holding her arms down. "Then why wait for your sadistic brother to order you to do it?"

Lyrrin hurried to Niskina and Benjin, who warded the two men there away with Yoskar's staff.

There was a snarl and a growl as Griskin pounced, trying to get to Kess, and Dracuni blocked his way. The glass beneath Dracuni's claws shimmering with spots of opalescent blood. Lyrrin bit her lip and it trembled between her teeth.

The dragonrider remained under the dragon's wing, picking shards off his armor almost casually. He made no effort to rush back into his saddle, a moment Lyrrin was hurrying to beat as she sliced Niskina's bonds as well.

Instead, the rider glared out over the combatants and shouted, "Fire!"

The dragon's purple jaw dropped open, its chest heaved, and golden light burst from its throat.

A ball of fire shot out, roaring across the room. The dragon hadn't aimed, hadn't turned its head toward a target—just loosed the fireball directly the moment it was ordered. It flew past Lyrrin and Niskina, barely an arm's reach away. The searing heat was gone in an instant before it collided with the row of cages across the other side of the room.

It hit like an explosion, setting fire to everything around it. A stampede of tiny deerlike animals emerged from hiding places and rushed for a way out.

"Sparks! He's going to kill everybody!" Riony rolled off Kess and onto her feet.

She glared between the rider and his dragon, as though trying to gauge how to take either of them down while also keeping watch of Kess, gasping for breath where she'd been left.

Riony drew her sword, activated it, and stood over Kess, and for a moment, Lyrrin was sure she was going to bring that sword down and finish off the wolf rider once and for all.

Then Dracuni was there too, looping around Riony's legs and mewling.

"I have to!" Riony barked back. "If we run now, they're only going to keep chasing us! Forever!"

With a powerful huff, Dracuni rose up on her hind legs and pushed Riony back with her front paws.

As the dragonling's iridescent silvery claws touched to Riony's chest, she gasped, "No!"

And then she lit up. As though flooded with moonlight from within, Riony glowed.

Everybody stilled, drawn to the strange sight.

There was a *tink, tink, tink* of glass shards sliding free from her healing skin and dropping to the floor. Freely bleeding gashes closed. Riony stared back at the dragonrider and the young men who'd brought them there with a terrified fury.

"Raze it all, Kess. You were telling the truth!" the dragonrider crowed, wide-eyed as he raked his gaze over Riony and Dracuni.

"That thing, it bleeds silvernix?" Renshy's head was shaking as he looked at the trail of immeasurable wealth Dracuni's bleeding claws had left behind her. "Eydon! Come on!"

Renshy let Aishena fall limp from his grasp. Whatever she had been worth to him before was nothing compared to Dracuni.

Niskina rushed in and managed to catch Aishena's ragdoll body before she hit the glass too.

"You're not getting anything from us!" Benjin growled, swinging the staff at the men as they tried to push past him.

Renshy brought his own sword clashing down against it, striking hard, no longer trying to capture Benjin, no longer playing it safe. Eydon dodged through beside them, running toward Dracuni.

They knew about Dracuni's blood now. All of them. The rider, these men. They would all want the unidragon. A knot of cold fear tangled in Lyrrin's chest. Kess was back on Griskin and the rider was redirecting his dragon's head with taps on its jaw.

Panic crept like frost over Lyrrin's skin. They needed something, something big to get out of there.

Lyrrin shouted, "Eyes!"

Benjin stepped back, covering his face as Lyrrin's final flash stone landed in front of him and went off.

Renshy swore and stumbled back, still swinging his sword wildly.

"Give me Yoskar's staff," Lyrrin cried, arms reaching out.

"What? What for?" Benjin pulled it back closer to himself.

"Fire!" the dragonrider shouted again.

A crackling sphere of fire hurtled right toward them.

Lyrrin and Benjin threw themselves down in a crouch. Eydon, between them and the dragon, wasn't fast enough, and the flame passed right through him. He screamed for only a moment, then fell, still burning.

Benjin hissed as one side of his head caught alight, the short hair getting singed. Lyrrin patted it out with her gloved hand, gasping at the acrid smoke.

"Please, the staff," Lyrrin said again. "Trust me. We have to do something to stop the dragon and rider long enough to get away from here."

Benjin, frowning and teary, handed Yoskar's staff to her.

With one hand still ungloved, Lyrrin worked quickly, scratching additional runes over the ones already there in the crystals embedded in the wood. She added burn onto light, and burst onto burn, and return onto cut, using every combination she'd tried before and many she hadn't, and activating every sigil as she went.

The staff hummed with power as half a dozen crystals activated at once with even more runes.

Getting back to her feet, Lyrrin hurled the staff across the room.

"What are you doing?" Benjin gasped.

Lyrrin's heart pounded as she watched the staff clatter to a stop at the feet of the dragon. "Saving us, I hope, or blowing everything up. Come on. Run!"

The first explosion was bigger than Lyrrin had expected. There was a whomping boom that seemed to lift and throw everything in the room for a split second, then a gust of air rushed all around as Lyrrin and Benjin ran for the door.

A flurry of curse words came from the dragonrider as the staff shot up into the air, popping and flashing and zipping around, and then another larger burst went off, loud as a lightning strike.

Above the dragon, every window shattered and fell.

The dragonrider and Kess, on Griskin, ran for cover beneath the dragon's chest. As the shining slivers rained down, carnage cascaded across the ceiling, section after section breaking and falling, chasing Riony and Dracuni across the room.

Riony caught up with Niskina and took Aishena from her, scooping her into her arms as they ran.

Lyrrin pushed the door, holding the heavy metal open. "Come on!"

Dracuni ran out, followed by the others.

Benjin turned back, his face red and twisted as he watched the staff crackle and snap into pieces, burning and blasting apart, then he ran out too.

Out in the burned scrub, they kept running, feet pounding until they hit the forest.

Benjin stopped there, breathing so hard his body shook all over.

"You destroyed it! Yoskar's staff, it's gone!" Benjin yelled at Lyrrin.

"I ... I'm sorry." Lyrrin's mouth went dry. She had; she'd destroyed Yoskar's staff. She hadn't really thought about what that meant, in the heat of the moment, only that it might save them. But Benjin looked at her with such fury it cut right to her heart.

"We have to keep going. We have to get to the shrine!" Riony shouted back.

Aishena hung heavy and still in her arms.

Niskina gasped, her eyes on the glass factory behind them.

Lyrrin turned to see Kess and Griskin emerge from the door. The wolf and rider raced their way.

CHAPTER SEVENTEEN

Kess pulled a splinter of dark blue glass from the leather of her bracer as Griskin navigated them through the woods at a caning pace.

She was lucky it hadn't gone through to her skin.

She'd seen exactly how ripped up someone could be by those broken shards.

There was so much blood—so much blood on her.

Kess saw flashes of Riony—Pony—kneeling on that glittering ground, swathed in red. Then of her lying on the frozen floor in the cave, washed in a scarlet sea. Flashes of her bloodied back, struck by a lash.

The intolerable woman treated suffering as a sport. And when the dragonling had pressed her bleeding paws to Riony, she hadn't ordered it, hadn't asked for it—instead she'd said *no*. Was she not using the creature for healing? What kind of unblessed fool was she?

And what kind of fool am I for not putting Pony out of her misery sooner?

Why, when Riony knelt on the floor in front of her, cut through with agony and even still defiant, why did Kess's heart achingly contract? She had no room to feel anything—not pity, not compassion, not doubt—when it would block her from her destiny.

Still more fragments of glass scratched against Kess's back, caught in the thick vest armor. She'd have to deal with them, and her traitorous emotions, later.

Now, she had to catch her prey. They were just ahead of her through the trees, but they'd almost reached the shrine settlement.

She'd stalked around the edges of it the evening before but couldn't see a way to get in and take Dracuni with so many people around, partying through the night. So instead, she and the bounty hunters had made a plan to lure those they wanted out.

A rock whizzed past Kess's head, slung from Pony's "sister." Where had Pony picked up that little feral?

With the standing stones in sight, a cry went up amongst the settlers at the incoming chase. Some fled and hid, but more stood their ground, bringing Pony's group into them.

Pony skidded to a stop before the wall of people. The Hjelzahn girl was cradled in her arms the way she had once carried Kess. Kess shuddered at the memory of those same arms around her, and she sneered.

"Help her through." Riony handed the limp weight of the woman to a person in the crowd.

Then Pony turned to face Kess, glowing sword ready to swing.

Griskin came to a halt too, growling at the crowd blocking the way.

"Want to rumble, Kess?" Pony asked with a smirk, angling her sword so it glinted in the late morning sunlight. "I'll have you on your back again in no time."

"Not before I stick you with my knives." Kess prepared to throw one of the thin bone blades, but an older woman stepped in front of the monstrous redhead.

She said over her shoulder to Pony, "Leave, child. Be safe."

Through a gap in the people Kess saw the gateway light up. She cursed, angling to get a better view of the glowing symbols.

Pony gave her one more look, lips twitching, then disappeared through the crowd as well.

"Coward!" Kess screamed, her voice breaking over the word.

Another rock clattered down beside Griskin's booted paws. Not from Lyrrin's sling, but from a different child, hurling it with their hand.

"Go on, girl. Get out of here. Whatever your reason for chasing them, you won't find understanding here." The old woman stood boldly before Griskin, the shawl over her arms swaying as she made a shooing motion.

Another rock landed close. Barely a pebble but enough to make Kess flinch. The way they were looking at her, glaring shame with piercing eyes ... as though *she* were the bad guy.

They never could understand. They didn't know she was doing everything, anything she had to do to become someone who could do good for the world. So she could be a dragonrider, to help save people just like them.

She was doing what she had to in order to become a hero. Wasn't she?

Kess couldn't think of anything she could say to make them understand that, not fast enough. Not when they were already on Pony's side for some unblessed reason.

They didn't know Kess was trying to do the right thing. Yes, she wanted to be a dragonlord again, and a dragonrider, for respect, but also to do the good work that dragonriders do.

The light of the gateway within the shrine went out. Pony and the dragonling had escaped again.

But Kess smiled. Because she heard the approach of beating wings.

Now these people would see that she was on the side of a dragonrider! That she was on the right side, the good side.

Faces turned upward as the sound grew clearer, and Kess watched them to see the awe in their expressions she felt when she saw a dragonrider fly.

But as the dragon's shadow passed over the people, they shrieked and ran. Some fled into the flimsy huts, others into the stone structure of the shrine, and a few out into the dangerous woods. Only a handful remained rooted in place, terror on their faces fighting with a furious determination.

"He's on your side," Kess whispered, more to herself, as she gaped at their reaction.

Why were they running? Why were they scared of a person who had probably saved hundreds of people just like them from the revenant plague? Weren't they grateful?

Kife brought his dragon down. There wasn't enough clear space to land on the ground so he perched up on the arched roof of stone and crystal covering the shrine. The stone creaked and crumbled under the dragon's weight, and the people inside wailed.

"Where are they?" Kife called down.

"Already gone. But I saw where," Kess replied.

Kife punched the front of his saddle. "This was a mess! And the last time we're going with one of your awful plans."

Kess said nothing in reply, tonguing the inside of her teeth to keep from biting back.

"Hurry up, then!" Kife snapped. "Let's go so we can catch them at the next stop."

He turned away, fuming, as Kess jumped Griskin up onto the shrine roof beside the dragon. She had to run the wolf past some of the braver people to get there, getting an eyeful of the older woman's utter disdain on the way.

Kife pressed his hands to his dragon's neck as Kess climbed up behind him. "We should blast this place. Destroy the portal and stop them using this one again."

His dragon's flame crackled around his teeth.

"There are people in there." Kess buckled herself to the saddle behind her brother.

"So? They're protecting criminals. We should start destroying all the shrines as we go, get rid of all escape routes."

"We won't let you!" the old woman called up from below.

The numbers around her had grown again, others coming back to join her, daring the dragon and its riders with their expressions.

Kife laughed. "And what do you think you could do to stop me?"

A rock flew from the old woman's hand, glancing off Kife's leg. He swore and directed his dragon's head to aim at her. "I'll burn the lot of you!"

"Kife, stop it." Kess shoved him in the shoulder.

He glared back, and despite the rushing turmoil inside making her shake, Kess gave him the dullest eye roll of sibling contempt possible. "You'd really dishonor yourself with something as low as burning a pathetic old woman who hurt your feelings?"

Kife twitched the shoulder she'd shoved, as though cringing off her touch belatedly.

"We're wasting time," he said, and the dragon's wings flicked out in a clap of leather.

They lifted from the shrine rooftop as a hail of pebbles and jeers chased them from below.

Griskin gave a soft whine. He'd gotten used to being carried in the dragon's talons, but he didn't like it. Kess didn't blame him. She hoped none of the stones reached him.

Kess checked their map, identifying the symbol she'd seen lit up on the gateway against the ones they'd recorded, then pointed a heading. The dragon's wings beat hard, pushing them fast through the air.

It wasn't far. They would be on their target again in no time with the swift flight of the purple etherdart.

She looked back at the shrine disappearing in the distance. Her face heated, shame at her brother's behavior like poison burning her skin. But that was just Kife. He'd always been awful. Other dragonriders weren't like him. Surely.

"A sun-razed glass factory," Kife scoffed, his voice barely carrying over the roar of wind around him. "What were you thinking?"

"It was the only building big enough nearby," Kess yelled back. The only place to lure Pony where they could hide Kife's dragon inside until they could spring their trap. "It would have worked if those bounty hunters had brought everyone in at once and believed me when I said not to underestimate the kids."

"What would have worked was not having a saddle full of glass I had to clear off before making chase. Anywhere else and I could have caught them."

"Is that what took you so long? Scared of a few bits of glass?"

"Not scared—just not stupid enough to cut my ass into pieces." Kife made a show of dusting off the saddle again. "That and making sure those bounty hunters were done. Couldn't have any of them surviving after learning about that little silvernix dragonling."

Kess had to admit that was important. They had seen Dracuni's blood with their own eyes. She should have thought of that too, should have done something about it before chasing off. Was she slipping so much?

Maybe she'd just hoped she could have caught Dracuni without any more blood on her hands.

"You screwed that up in every way, Kessara."

"I did? You're the one who delayed things. You should have let the bounty hunter finish off ..."

Pony. The slave. Riony. Her pet.

Every word felt wrong now on Kess's lips. "Finish *her* off. It should have been fast and easy, and her death would have broken her group and let us take the dragonling."

Even if the fungus-filled space had made Griskin sniffly again, Her plan should have worked. Even with the shattered glass all around, it should have worked.

But Kife always had to bring cruelty into everything. He could never allow something to be easy when it could be cruel instead.

"It was a gift to you, sister." He seemed taken aback, hurt she hadn't appreciated it. "You're the one who took too long dealing the death blow."

She couldn't deny it. A shiver ran over her, the chilled wind blasting through her leather garments. Riony kneeling, covered in blood. It should have been fast. It should have been easy.

Getting Dracuni was everything Kess had ever wanted, wasn't it? At any cost?

Kife turned in his seat, glaring down at Kess from behind his flight goggles. "I shouldn't have let you take the lead on that plan. My contribution has been the only thing that has worked so far. Getting those signal flares out to bounty hunters across the land. *You* have been useless."

His shifted angle brought a gust of smoky wind over Kess, and she grasped the buckles holding her in place, checking they were connected tight. A fire burned below, and Kess imagined herself falling, falling into that burning forest, pushed from her seat. But her brother didn't try to kill her. Not then. Not yet.

And the flares had been a good move, but she wouldn't concede that aloud. The time and expense it had taken to get those flares out to as many bounty hunters as they could had delayed the hunt, but seeing one light the sky the night before had made it all worth it.

Having the extra eyes on the ground looking for Pony and the dragonling had paid off, and the flare had worked as intended, getting to them fast.

They didn't want the bounty hunters trying to capture the bounty on their own and discovering what Dracuni was.

Kife sniffed. "That weed you gave the bounty hunters to subdue the grayglim-in-training worked well though. We should get more of it, use it on the lot of them next time. Was it the same thing you used on me that time you slipped something into my soup?"

"It was Pony who did that," Kess replied fast.

"Sure it was. The pet acting without the master's command. You never did train the wild beast well. Learning about this sedation herb is the one thing she was ever good for."

A dreadful desire to defend Riony caught in Kess's throat. But it was just a symptom of wanting to defy her brother. Whatever he said, she felt the urge to argue. He could say the sun was hot and she'd feel the urge to debate that it was made of ice. That was how they'd always been and had nothing to do with Pony, or what she had or hadn't been good for.

Still, Kess found she had to say something. "You and our parents seemed to think she was plenty good at being whipped."

Kife laughed, huffing in time to the dragon's wings. "The kid deserved it every time! That whole family were mad. We should have gotten rid of the lot of them before they decided to murder a dragonguard and steal a baby."

"Sorry, what?" She was unsure she'd heard him over the deafening rumble of flight. "A baby?"

"The baby. The guest's baby. Those criminals stole it."

Kess straightened in the saddle, her mind rushing over what she'd remembered of when Riony had abandoned her and fled. All she'd been told was that they'd killed someone and run.

But it did line up to the time when the guest, that mysterious young woman who had haunted their estate like a ghost during her pregnancy, had also left. No longer pregnant. But without a child. After Riony and her mother had been at the birth.

"I thought the newborn died?"

"That's officially what happened. Our parents didn't want anyone knowing what their slaves had done. But they were seen with the baby during their escape. I was told since I was part of the main hunting party for them." Kife seemed to take pleasure rubbing those words in.

That he had information Kess wasn't privy to. That he always had a higher standing than Kess ever had, ignored and locked away most of her life.

But she knew something he didn't. She knew that Riony called one of the kids she traveled with 'sister,' despite it being clear that she wasn't. And the child was just the right age to be the stolen baby.

It didn't mean much—not to her hunt for Dracuni. But it did mean that somehow, for some reason, Pony and her family had stolen that baby and raised her as their own, and Riony called her sister and was loving and protective of her in a way she'd never been to Kess.

"Do you know who the guest was?" Kess asked.

"Some dragonlord lady," Kife said confidently, providing that he knew no more about the woman than Kess did. "Not someone I've ever met since—not at Skaellakeep. I haven't exactly been able to rub shoulders with the upper class as I should, with the Heithorn name as tarnished as it is. Thanks to you."

"Of course," Kess replied flatly. Of course that would be her fault. Everything was.

"Chin up, little sis." Kife reached back and squeezed her roughly on the knee. "Once we have this silvernix beast, all will be forgiven. Incredible how you were able to find such a unique creature. I can't even fathom it!"

"I didn't know what it was when I first found the eggs. I had only hoped for a dragon of my own to ride." A weight was filling Kess's chest, like a slow trickle of molten lead.

Visions of blood. A stolen sister loved more than a Heithorn daughter. She turned away from staring at her brother's back and squinted narrowed eyes at the huge expanse of the dragon's wings keeping them in the sky, and her heart hurt.

"And how were you even going to raise a dragon? Or tame it?" Kife scoffed. "You never could think things through."

"I was ready!" Kess snapped. "I have what's needed."

"Really?" Kife drawled the word, as though it were a sound of triumph. "Where under the sun did you get silvernix from? Our family had been out for so long."

"There was a lot that our family was lacking," was all Kess offered in explanation.

Kife's words drew cold, stabbing like icicles. "And you know why. You know why we moved into isolation, why I was taken away from the life and honor I deserved. And even after you were gone, nothing changed!"

After I was gone. After you left me to die. "Is that what you'd hoped to achieve? By getting rid of me?"

"Don't take it personally, Kess. I'm sorry about what I had to do, but it was for the best for *our family*. For the Heithorn name! But nobody understood, and your damage had already been done. Our parents refused to leave the estate, mourning their poor lost daughter."

"Did they—?" Kess's voice was small and lost in the wind.

"That's what they told everyone. But really, they were too embarrassed to move back to a keep because of how poor we'd become."

They hadn't mourned her. Nobody had missed her at all. Abandoned by everybody. Kess wasn't surprised.

Rushing air pummeled Kess's eyes, making them water. She closed them for a moment, trying to give them some relief, but they continued to burn and sting.

Kife continued, pummeling her with words as hard as the wind. "I refused to let that be the fate of the Heithorn name, fading out of history in squalor. I took the other dragonriders with me to get work at Skaellakeep, to regain some of the wealth and honor you took from us. And while I was gone, revenants overtook the estate."

There wasn't a hint of remorse in his tone. "I lost my parents because of you, little sister. Because you broke them. Because they couldn't face the world in their shame, they remained trapped in that place to die."

Kess shook her head, wanting to argue. Wanting to say that it was Kife who had abandoned his family, left them unguarded. But it did all come back to her. Her very existence, and how nobody could just accept her as she was, had cursed their family into its demise.

And now the only person who had ever been kind to her was the life she had to end to gain the acceptance she'd never had.

The heaviness in her chest had filled right up into her neck and behind her eyes, wanting to burst out between her ribs in an ugly flood. Everything had been easier before Pony came back into her life. Everything had been clear. Get a dragon. Become a rider. One dream, strong and honorable and inevitable.

And now, here she was, letting her hateful brother's words slide like knives under her skin as cruelly as the glass had sliced Riony. She was having rocks hurled at her like a common criminal and questioning how far she could go for her dream.

I should be stronger than this.

"I think I should hold on to the silvernix, sis," Kife said. "That and the taming spike. You can't be trusted to handle anything. You ruined the ambush—ruined our family. I don't want you to ruin the taming of this creature too."

Kess felt for the pouch at her side that held the items for the taming ritual. She'd taken them off Griskin to keep close when she thought they'd have Dracuni that morning.

Her voice was weak. "I can do this."

"Have you ever tamed a dragon before? No. I have. I know what to do."

Kess's hand reached into the pouch and closed around the parcel. "Fine. Take it."

She thrust the leatherbound treasures forward.

"Raze it, Kess! Not now!" Kife snatched the parcel quickly, securing it in front of him. "You could have dropped it! Absolutely hopeless."

Kess only blinked the water from her eyes and moved to buckle her pouch closed again. A thin length of leather flapped at the closure, caught in the wind. She narrowed her eyes and tugged the thonging free, revealing the acorn dangling at the end.

That stupid, simple pendant that she'd found in the icy cave when she'd returned after leaving Riony to die from her injuries. When she'd gone back and found her missing, only her frozen blood and the pendant remaining.

It must have been tangled around the other items when she'd taken them from Griskin's bags and ended up in her belt pouch.

Kess squeezed it in her hand and tucked it into a pocket in her vest. A token to keep her focused on her target. To keep her on track to achieve her goal.

But the focus didn't come. She felt more confused than ever. She knew she was losing all her cards to Kife, but somehow she couldn't seem to care.

All she could think of was the way Riony had looked at her when she'd seen Kess standing beside her brother. Not with fear. Not even anger, really. But concern.

Riony knew as well as Kess that it was only a matter of time before Kess was abandoned again.

Chapter Eighteen

Kess had a dragon. She had a dragon to chase them with now and with that dragon came Kife.

"Oh sparks, we are so screwed." Riony let the words drop like an unwanted weight from her mouth.

She knelt on the stone floor of the shrine they had arrived at, old leaves and vines tangling beneath her. There was no roof left on this Alderkin ruin, and dark pieces of ash drifted down like snow from a nearby fire.

The air was thick and tangy with smoke. Riony filled her chest with it anyway, dragging deep gulps and letting the acrid sting on her tongue reassure her body it was still alive.

Stars, it was so close.

Riony had been sure for a few moments that it was the end. She could still feel the ghostly pressure of the knife to her throat. The sensation of glass under her skin. How Kess had turned away. Riony's shirt was still saturated in sticky blood.

Yup. She was definitely having nightmares tonight.

I can't believe Kess brought her sadistic brother and his dragon into this. What was she thinking?

Still, thanks not at all to Riony herself, she and all her loved ones had escaped. Having Dracuni, Lyrrin, Aishena, Niskina, and Benjin all there and mostly unharmed helped the air return to her tight lungs.

Then the relief Riony felt at having escaped curdled inside her. Myrwa and the others … Kess wouldn't hurt them, would she? Would Kife?

Riony scrambled to stand. The floor of this shrine was cracked and sunken, tilted to one side, making Riony feel unstable on her feet.

Should she go back? Myrwa had told her to leave. As long as Riony wasn't there, there should be no reason for Myrwa's people to be harmed. But Kife loved to do cruel things for no reason.

"Are you okay?" Lyrrin looked up from under her hood, blue eyes bright and wide. Dracuni stood beside her, tail flicking.

Riony wavered, caught between pacing toward the gateway and worry for those with her there. Her sword was still in one hand, glowing and light as a cloud but feeling like a weight regardless. "Are you?"

You answer. You answer little sister. Dracuni's eye ridges lowered, and her nostrils flared.

Riony shook her head, whether as the answer itself or the refusal of one, she wasn't sure. It didn't matter. She dropped the sword without deactivating it. She didn't have to worry about it running out of charge. Not here.

She checked Lyrrin with her hands, tsking at the singed edges on her gloves. "You weren't hurt?"

"We're fine."

Big sister hurt most.

Riony reached for one of Dracuni's front paws, lifting it to check under the claws and finding it already healed, no sign of glass splinters.

But Dracuni had still bled. "That was so reckless, coming in like that!"

Lyrrin's face scrunched up fiercely and her lips popped, ready to argue, when Riony grabbed her, pulling her close to her belly and squeezing her tight. "You saved me, Lil Moon. You saved us."

Helped too, Dracuni huffed.

"All three of you," Riony added, nodding acknowledgment to Benjin.

"Effess um emmums arress agth," Lyrrin said, muffled.

"Huh?" Riony gave her some space.

Lyrrin said again, "I guess you making us stay outside helped. I mean, if we'd all gone inside at the same time, we'd all have been trapped by that dragon."

Riony wanted to smile but it didn't come. She crouched down to Lyrrin's height. "I'm so sorry I'm stuffing everything up. You should never have had to do any of that."

"Should never have destroyed Yoskar's staff," Benjin said, scowling. The brown skin across one side of his head was an angry, dark plum, the hair scorched away.

He knelt next to his sister who lay on the cracked paving, haloed in dry leaves. He watched her with a worried frown as she stirred but didn't wake.

Niskina knelt opposite. "We should never have been there at all. I was so stupid to think I could ever do something more. To ever trust this blighted world."

She pressed her palms hard into her eyes and screamed once, long and strangled.

Aishena's arm twitched, lashing out clumsily to grab an athame from her belt. Her eyes peeled open, fluttered. "What ... what happened?"

"It's okay. We're okay," Benjin replied.

After one false start, Aishena bent at the waist, leaning smoothly up into a sitting position. Her mouth opened in pain, and she grasped her forehead in both hands for a moment before her expression returned to its usual steely calm.

"Careful. The morass mercy has a nasty hangover." And probably didn't mix well with the actual hangover Aishena had done amazingly well at hiding that morning, Riony thought, but didn't pile on.

Aishena kept an admirably composed expression, but her words came slowly. "We were ambushed ... Kess. And ... that was her brother, wasn't it? On the dragon? I could see, for a while, but I couldn't move."

Aishena had told Riony about how she'd met Kess, only once, at Hjelzahnkeep. But once had been enough to make an impression. There weren't many dragonlords with disabled children.

And Riony's experience with Lyrrin's birth had taught her why. Children who were born different often didn't survive their first day.

She didn't know Aishena had met Kife too, but the way she said *her brother* made Riony think he'd made an impression as well.

Riony replied, "Yup. Kess, Kife, and a dragon. We're absolutely boned in the worst possible way."

Aishena had turned her attention to Benjin, fussing over the singed area across his temple.

"I'm fine. It's just soot." He pushed her hands away. "The fireball barely touched me."

"*Fireball?* That Heithorn set dragonfire upon children?" Aishena's eyes glinted with the desire for murder. "Why were you in there? You came in, didn't you? You should have followed orders and stayed out!"

"Maybe you should have not followed orders and followed your instincts for once and none of you would have walked into that ambush." He growled back. "And maybe Yoskar's staff wouldn't be gone. It's gone forever now!"

"I'm sorry," Lyrrin said softly.

"Gone?" Aishena clutched at a pocket on her chest. "But we got away. Somehow. Somehow, we got away?"

"For now," Riony said. "Map?"

Aishena nodded and drew the folded parchment out.

Riony took the map and laid it flat on the ground. "We're here, the gateway we activated before going to the village where we met Myrwa."

Aishena's eyes narrowed. "You couldn't have moved us farther from our now-airborne hunters?"

"Sorry, that was me. I just hit the first symbol that I could," Lyrrin said.

"Maybe you should have thought for a second before doing it, then," Benjin hissed.

Riony held up a warning hand. "It's fine. We're safe here for the moment. I'm just worried about how close that fire is. And whether it's going to flush any revs our way. We should pick our next location and move on from there."

Niskina, who had been watching everything with dull eyes since her scream, flicked the corner of the map. "Move on where? Why?"

"To safety," Riony replied.

Niskina scoffed and turned away.

Riony gave her a long, hard look. Niskina seemed completely crushed, but Riony didn't know how to manage that right then. Immediate risks of danger had to be dealt with first.

"Aish, what do you think about where we should go? If you were a couple of raging monsters with a dragon and scent hound, where would you *not* go looking for your prey?"

Aishena frowned, bending over the map as well. Her fingers traced a few locations, then she mumbled, "I don't know."

Drawing a sharp breath, Riony cricked her neck, then let the air out slowly in an effort not to hit something.

Behind her back, there was a rasping whisper from Benjin again. "I can't believe you did that. You told me to trust you, and you destroyed the last thing I had of my brother."

Lyrrin's voice had the high, growling edge it took on when she was trying not to cry. "I didn't think—I'm sorry. I just needed something, fast."

"It was Yoskar's! And you blew it up without even caring!"

There was a strangled shriek and the stomp of a foot. "I *saved* us!"

"Did you have to do it that way?" Benjin stalked away to the shrine entrance, glaring out at the smoke-gray surrounds.

Riony was halfway turned to call Lyrrin over to try to calm her down when the light of the gateway illuminated the hazy space.

She whipped around fast, expecting another ambush, that somehow Kess had unlocked the activation of the gateway rune. She couldn't have—she had no idea how to use even basic runes. And they hadn't taught Myrwa or any of the others how to do it either.

Instead, she saw Lyrrin there, stepping away through the light.

Sister? Dracuni galloped toward her, and Riony scrambled to her feet, chasing after. "Lyrrin!"

But the light went out. And Lyrrin was gone.

"Did anyone see where she went?" Riony ran to the tall slice of crystal geode, scrambling to trace the sigil.

"I didn't see," Aishena said, brow furrowed and lips thin.

Benjin moved in stumbling steps toward his sister, staring at the empty space where Lyrrin had disappeared. "I didn't mean ... I didn't want her to go."

"Nobody saw which symbol she used?" Riony growled, frantic as the rune sequence finished.

Around the edge, all the location markers that they had been to before lit up. Between them were the ones they had not yet visited, and the ones which had cracks through them.

There was silence behind Riony and she grunted louder again, smacking her hand on the closest symbol to Lyrrin's height.

The gateway lit, sparkling with the vision of the shrine near the rough smugglers' settlement. Riony half stepped through, looked, called, came back.

She deactivated the rune, fingers shaking, then tried again.

Their first shrine, back near the undercity outskirts.

Nothing.

"Sparks! Why would she do that? Where is she?" Riony closed the gateway again.

Dracuni stood close to where Riony crouched over the Alderkin carving. **Sister coming back?**

Riony's fingers slipped over the rune, tracing the wrong line, ruining the sequence. She clenched her hand into a fist and choked on her breath.

And the gateway lit up again on its own.

Lyrrin appeared before Riony, her face firm and determined.

In a scooping step, Riony grabbed and lifted her as she got to her feet. "What was that? Where did you go? Don't do that to me!"

Lyrrin jangled in her arms, pokey and pointy lumps pressing between them as Riony squeezed her. With a stern snap, she said, "I went for supplies."

Sister came back! Dracuni circled around Riony's legs and Lyrrin's dangling feet.

Riony put Lyrrin down again before the three of them tangled up and fell.

The 'supplies' Lyrrin had gone for were sticking out of every one of her pockets and balanced in a clinking pile in her folded arms. Calcite spikes and spars, glassy and shimmering.

"You got crystals?" There was only one place Riony knew from their shrine locations where she could have gotten them.

From the looks on the faces all around her, they knew it too.

Lyrrin nodded. "I'm going to make a new staff for Benjin. I needed these. I had to go."

Somewhere none of the rest of them had been willing to return to. Riony's throat went dry, and all the strength seemed to leave her body. She leaned against the crystal of the gateway.

"You went back to the Alderkin depths," Niskina said, stepping forward. Her chin was up, and her chest heaved visibly up and down. "Was ... What was it like?"

Lyrrin's head tilted, and she spoke gently. "It's been cleared. Ropes and pulleys set up. There were large candles, melted down where ... where your family were."

Aishena put a hand on Niskina's back, turning her so they faced each other. "The delvers have seen to them. They've been honored. They've had their final light."

Niskina sobbed and pulled Aishena into an embrace, crying into her shoulder. "But we weren't there. We weren't there for it."

Benjin swiped the back of his hand across his cheek and nose, still staring at Lyrrin.

"Did you see anyone?" Riony asked.

"There was no one there. Almost everything was taken, but they must have left all these behind since they were unruned." Lyrrin shuffled the crystals in her arms to steady them.

Raw crystals. They would have been useless to any delvers, but Lyrrin might be able to work with them. Riony just shook her head, unable to think through the rights and wrongs and risks and fears, and Lyrrin in trouble, and Lyrrin gone, and was any of this worth it?

"You're really going to make something with those? For me?" Benjin asked, mostly to the stone floor.

"I'm going to try. I know it's not a replacement, that nothing can replace what is gone. But it's the best I can do since it was my fault."

Benjin took some of the crystals from Lyrrin, helping her empty her full arms. "It's okay. You did save us. And Yoskar ... Yoskar's gone. Keeping his staff safe seemed so important before, as though I was keeping part of him alive. But it was more important that you saved everyone still here."

Lyrrin sighed, silent but visible in the deep droop of her shoulders. She and Benjin started sorting the crystals from her hands and pockets into bags.

Niskina still sobbed, arms wrapped around Aishena, who stood considerably still but didn't return the embrace. In the delver's hand, Yoskar's glasses were held tight.

Riony hadn't really seen how much Aishena was hurting. Not until last night. But she should have known. She should have known how much all of them were hurting, having lost their family and their home.

Riony had felt it all herself before. She still felt it every day.

She let her back slide down the gateway crystal until she hit the ground and sat there, staring over her small, sorry group. All broken. And Riony doing her best to keep them together but making all the wrong decisions and nobody listening to her anyway.

And horribly, at that moment, the person that Riony most wished would listen to her, would just hear reason for the first time in her life, was Kess.

The dreadful gremlin was obsessed. Obsessed with getting a dragon, and now obsessed with getting Dracuni. That was all she'd ever cared about.

Riony knew that, but still, the lengths Kess had gone to left her rattled.

Back at Heithorn estate, Kife had taken and enjoyed his share of whipping duty, when Kess's own parents or the estate master delegated out the torture. Riony knew Kess didn't care about that, but she should care that her brother had also been the cruelest of everyone to Kess as well.

Had she forgotten? Had she forgotten that he was the one who'd taken her from her home and left her to die?

Kess and Riony had almost, *almost* been friends at times. And still Kess had chosen to betray Riony without a second thought and turn to her ruthless brother instead. It felt like a knife to the heart, and Riony was furious she even cared.

She was also keenly aware she could have had a real knife in her heart, one that Kess didn't throw.

Kess had plenty of time to skewer her in the glass factory. But still ... had there been hesitation? Riony shook her head and rubbed her aching eyes.

Big sister is bad hurt. Dracuni bumped her arm with the tip of her snout.

"I'm fine. You healed me already. This is old blood." Riony wiped her cheek clean, showing the smooth, repaired skin beneath.

Bad inside hurt.

Wetness rushed over Riony's eyes, and she blinked it away. "The smoke is making my eyes sting."

Dracuni huffed but sat down without any more thought words accusing Riony inside her own brain.

Riony remained resting there, trying to slow the race of her heart, still raging from her visit to death's door and following escape. Trying to make Dracuni sense that her insides weren't bruised or battered by everything that had happened.

She waited while Niskina cried and Benjin and Lyrrin made plans for their crystals, and Dracuni curled up beside her and said nothing more in her thoughts but thrummed a soft, purring sound.

Yet even after some time, Riony's pulse still beat in her ears and it only seemed to be getting louder.

"What is that?" Aishena asked, pressing Yoskar's glasses away into the pocket of her vest.

Dracuni stood on her hind legs, ears twitching toward the open ceiling of the shrine. ***Dragon. Flying dragon.***

"Dragon!" Riony repeated aloud for the others. She scrambled forward and grabbed the map, still lying on the ground. She folded it roughly, patting down the misaligned mess. She was panicking for no reason.

Dragons were fast—*even etherdarts, although they're built more for combat than speed.* Kess's voice offered the information through a memory—but it couldn't be them. How would they know to come for them here?

"I see it," Aishena said, standing alert and staring skyward.

The faint silhouette of a serpentine body and wide, flapping wings was grayed out between gusts of smoke blowing through the sky. It tilted and dove straight toward them.

"Go. Get the gateway open!" Riony barked.

"To where?" Lyrrin asked, crouching over the activation rune at the base.

"As far away as possible!"

Air rushed around them as the leathery expanse of wings seemed to wrap the shrine itself right above them. A dull purple. Front talons carrying a wolf.

Riony scooped up her sword and pushed Dracuni first through the lit gateway. The others followed in a rush, Riony at the back as the dragon landed behind her, snapping at the space she'd just vacated.

The gateway closed, cutting them off from their pursuers.

"Sparks, how did they get to us so fast?" Riony glanced again over her shoulder, scared that they might still somehow come through behind her.

There was a cracking rumble like a mountain collapsing on itself. On the side of the geode gateway, the symbol for the shrine they'd just been at split through the middle, fine fractures spidering out.

"You don't think ...?" Lyrrin asked.

"They destroyed it," Riony rasped.

Getting away through the shrine gateways was one of the few advantages Riony had to keep herself and her loved ones safe.

But their hunters had found them and had been fast enough in the skies to reach them before they'd even had time to recover.

And if they destroyed the shrines, there would be nowhere left to run.

Chapter Nineteen

"Careful!" Kess scolded as Griskin whined and bucked in the dragon's claws. The blowback from the fireball that had destroyed the shrine was uncomfortably hot even up on the dragon's back. Kess leaned as far out from the saddle as she could to check her wolf's fur wasn't singed. He looked back up with deep, mournful eyes.

I'm sorry, Gris. Not much longer now. I hope.

"What are you complaining about?" Kife pressed his hands and weight against the dragon's neck in a combination of motions, similar to how Kess moved when riding Griskin.

The dragon responded, stretching its wings again to fly. "That's one less place for those rats to scurry to next time. Did you see where they went?"

"Yeah, but it's a long way off." Kess showed him on their map.

"Nah, no problem at all. We'll be on them again before dark."

And the dragon lurched quickly into the sky in a motion that left Kess's stomach behind.

She wanted to enjoy flying, to relish these moments in the sky, being where she always dreamed that she'd belonged.

But she was with Kife. On Kife's dragon.

And all it did was make her remember the first time they'd flown together.

"If this is for my birthday, you missed it by a week," Kess had said from where she'd sat on her bed, picking at food that seemed flavorless.

It had been a few years since Pony had abandoned her, and although there had been other slaves that managed Kess's everyday needs, there was no one who'd replaced Riony. Kess spent most of her time in bed.

Kife ushered a large servant in and had him pick Kess up without even asking first. "A week ago? Yes, I'm very sorry about that. That's why I wanted to make it up to you."

Kess tried to get comfortable in the slave's hold of her. He wasn't at all used to carrying her, not the way Pony had been. He pinched and squeezed her legs too tight.

"Just what is this surprise you have for me?" Kess was skeptical it could be anything good.

She checked for her pair of steel throwing knives she always kept on her, worried that her parents, finally sick of their bedridden daughter, would smother her in her sleep. They were tucked neatly away under the tight sleeves of her velvet dress.

They stepped out into the courtyard, and there was Kife's purple dragon, awaiting patiently, mindlessly.

Kife waved his arm at it. "I wanted to take you flying. I know you've always wanted to."

All the air left Kess's chest, and she devoured the shining scales and elegant wings of the beast with hungry eyes.

She spoke breathlessly. "Mami and Fadda won't allow it."

"Do we care what they will or won't allow?" Kife climbed up into the saddle in a couple of long, acrobatic steps.

He reached down as the slave lifted Kess up and Kife pulled her onto the saddle in front of him, passing her around like a parcel.

Small for her age and not yet a woman, thirteen-year-old Kess was speechless with awe as she ran her hands over the dragon's neck.

"Watch it!" Kife said, smacking her away. "It's trained to take orders from touch. You could set it off to burn this whole place down."

"Sorry." Kess sat back again, pulling her hands in and tucking them folded around her middle.

She should have known. She'd studied the entire theory. But she'd never been on a dragon in the rider's position before. And it was overwhelming and magnificent. It felt right.

And when they took off, Kess thought her heart was flying as well.

Rushing air tugged at Kess's finely embroidered day dress and lifted her hair, and she suppressed the rising giggles of pure joy. Heithorns didn't giggle.

Although Kife controlled the dragon, Kess felt every sweep of its wings and all the strength of its grace as though she were one with it. And below her, everything seemed so small. A land and its people wrought into a distant painting, insignificant.

All that existed was Kess and the sky and the beat of powerful wings. It was everything she'd ever wanted.

They had been in the air so long that Kess's back and stomach hurt from the effort of keeping upright and stable against the gusts of wind, and her uncovered eyes stung and watered, yet she could have stayed up there forever.

But it had been a long time, hadn't it? Why were they traveling so far?

The dragon descended, circling on still wings and lowering toward a forest clearing below. A blackened patch amongst the green, where something had recently been burned.

Were they near home? Maybe Kess hadn't realized they'd turned around at some point. She scanned the area for landmarks or signs of the estate buildings but saw nothing she recognized.

"Why are we landing?"

"The dragon needs a short rest. We'll be done and home soon."

It was as they landed that Kess couldn't suppress the short trill of a giggle at how purely beautiful the creature beneath them was, how incredible its motions as it carried them. She turned, willing in that moment of happiness to sincerely thank her brother for this gift, when his hands grasped her shoulders and threw her from the saddle.

The fall to the ground was swift and shattering.

Every part of Kess turned cold and heavy from brutal shock. Brittle ashes crunched beneath her, wafting a bitter scent all around. She winced at the bend in her wrist and the crunch of her hip she'd landed hardest on.

"What was that for? You idiot!"

Kife wasn't smirking or laughing through cruelly twisted lips as he usually did when he pulled such pranks on her. He rolled his jaw, sniffed once, and said, "Goodbye, Kessara."

"Goodbye?" Kess laughed, bemused.

"It's time our family moves on. Without you. You've held us back long enough."

He turned from her and flew away without another word. Kess screamed at the empty sky until her voice was gone.

In that clearing of leafless, thorny brambles and burned bones, Kess remained, staring at the sky until the sunset. It had to be a prank. Or even if not, he'd change his mind. He'd come back. Someone at the estate would find her missing, and her parents would be informed, and people would come looking.

Her first night alone was spent in tears and sobs made silent through fear and aching cramps from a hungry belly. She curled up, right where she'd been left. Waiting. Waiting for someone to find her and take her home. Waiting for *something* to find her and end her suffering.

She awoke with leaves stuck in her hair, her dress wet from dew, and shivers raking through her due to the cold she had no protection from. And by the time the sun had risen high enough in the sky to warm the life back into her, Kess knew nobody was coming for her.

She wanted to scream again but her throat was already torn and dry.

So she cursed her brother silently. If he'd wanted to kill her, he could have at least done it quickly. She might not have even fought him.

But now, now she was angry.

She must have survived on fury alone for her first few days.

Although the trees of the forest had some green shoots in the canopies, the understory had recently been burned. Kess crawled through the ashes, finding no berries, no game, not even the common weedy grass shoots that Pony had shown her could be pulled up whole and the sweet inner stems chewed on.

Kess drank from muddy puddles, and she ached with hunger and her mind felt foggy and almost gone when she finally saw a lone soot-darkened rabbit.

Low to the ground as she was, it hadn't seen her yet.

Kess's hands shook around her throwing knife. On a good day, she'd hit it no problem. But this wasn't a good day, and if she missed, she doubted she'd have the strength to ever throw a blade again.

The knife flew straight, and with a short piercing cry, the rabbit stilled.

She collected her kill, leaned her back against a tree trunk, and fought back the bile in her throat as she held the still warm, velvet-furred body.

The initial swell of triumph Kess felt at the successful hunt was swiftly quashed. She didn't know how to dress a rabbit. She didn't know how to start a fire. She didn't know how to cook.

Turning her eyes up and away from the blood on her hands, she saw two eyes shining back at her from behind thin, charred scrub.

Kess froze, rabbitlike herself in the face of the massive predator.

A low, rumbling growl reverberated, the wolf lowering its head.

It didn't approach, but it didn't leave either.

Kess remained still, not wanting to provoke it, wondering whether her small daggers would do anything against the giant lupine.

They remained motionless, locked in each other's gaze for so long that Kess grew bold. She growled back at the creature, frustrated. "Why aren't you trying to eat me?"

No reply—not that she expected one.

She dared to move closer, crawling around it in a wide arc. She took her rabbit with her, worried the wolf was just waiting for her to leave it so it could steal her catch. Not that she knew what to do with her kill anyway. Her arms shook beneath her as she pulled herself over the rough ground, weak and exhausted.

The full length of the wolf came into view as Kess moved around the dead bushes. It still didn't move. It couldn't. It was caught in a trap.

A tangle of snare wire wore bloody lines around the wolf's front leg and neck. It was ragged, the charcoal-dark fur matted, and body thin beneath.

Kess shifted closer. The wolf tried to back away, but the wire tugged against it, and it twitched and whined, stilling again.

In the soft dirt all around the trapped creature were dozens of other footprints, matching the tracks pressed into the ground beneath the bound animal. Wolf prints, of all different shapes and sizes, circled around the area.

Kess listened, waiting to be set upon by the pack, but nothing came. How long had this wolf been stuck there? She checked the tracks again, seeing them trail away.

"Your pack abandoned you?" Kess was no tracker, but even she could see the prints surrounding them were old, softened with rain and wind. "Of course they did."

Kess wondered for a moment if she could kill and eat the wolf. But she didn't even know what to do with the small rabbit she'd dragged over with her. She knew she would only waste the wolf's life in her failed attempts to preserve her own.

And if either of the two of them should be put out of their misery, Kess wasn't sure it was the wolf.

The shadowy animal licked its lips as the gamey scent of blood wafted around them.

In a fit of hopelessness, she flung the rabbit toward the wolf's head.

"Go on. You have it." She shuffled closer, knife in hand.

It remained still as stone, eyes on her as she cut the thin snare wire free. "You can eat me too for all I care."

The last section of twined metal snapped and Kess sat back, staring into the face that would end her. Those icy blue eyes regarded her. The jaws snapped.

The wolf snatched the rabbit in its teeth and ran.

A rough, hysterical laugh burbled from Kess's empty chest. Maybe she always was destined for a slow and painful death.

She tried once to move on again, but her arms crumpled beneath her.

Lying in the remains of the snare wire and wolf prints, Kess wondered how long it would take for her to die.

It wasn't within the next few hours, as she watched the sun pass overhead, stinging her dry eyes and cracking her lips. She was still alive when she heard the faint sounds of padding paws approach.

She lifted herself up to see the shaggy dark wolf return. "What are you doing back? Couldn't find your family? I told you, they left you to die!"

It moved closer, head low and wary.

"Come to fill yourself on more meat? Go on then!"

The wolf opened its snout, giving a soft, grumbling *oorf*. It turned, flanking her, then began moving away again.

"Are you going to eat me or what? I'm done! I can't ..." Tears spilled in a rush from Kess's eyes.

The wolf paused, looked back, took another step, and waited—almost as though it wanted her to follow it.

Kess crumpled, dropping to her elbows and pressing her forehead on the ground. "I can't."

The press of warm fur at her side made her cringe, but she didn't fight it. There was a scrabble of paws, and Kess wobbled as the wolf burrowed its head beneath her chest. Then she was being lifted into the air.

She grabbed tight, hands clutched around fur in surprise, as the wolf got underneath her and stood with her draped over its back.

It was awkward and uncomfortable and the wolf smelled of old meat and rot, and Kess pulled herself closer to it and held it tight and cried.

And the two of them survived. Together.

"Stupid beast!" Kife snapped, bringing Kess back into the present. "We aren't going to make it by sundown."

"You flew your dragon hard already on the last stretch. It's tired."

"It's not working hard enough! Dumb thing is getting old. I'd have replaced it by now if I could afford it." Kife adjusted his seating and the dragon began its descent. "Today has been a complete mess. We're making camp. We'll pick up the trail again tomorrow."

The dragon settled them down in an old field, more rubble than weeds. Kess would have never chosen such an exposed place to camp when traveling alone with Griskin, but the threat of revenants attacking in the night was less with a dragon around.

Back on the ground, and back on Griskin, Kess hunted their dinner and cleaned the game and set the fire as Kife lay on his blanket, picking his nails.

On her way to her own bed, Kess passed by the purple etherdart and paused. She had been so enamored by the creature once. But after having spent so long tracking the wild seasong mother dragon, after having met Dracuni, there was something so sad and pathetic about this tamed creature now.

The thing she'd always longed for, and it just seemed ... broken.

She reached a hand up to the scales of its cheek. It remained stone still beneath her touch, neither flinching away nor leaning into her hand. There was no brightness of life in its eyes as there was in Dracuni's, so alert and emotive. Only a dull stupor.

Its head was lowered, and Kess stared at the steel diamond of the taming spike, stuck there between its eyes. The imprint of the hammer on the end was still visible.

"Get away from my dragon," Kife muttered.

Kess did because it was his dragon, and she couldn't bear to look at it any longer. She and Griskin curled up on their blanket together as they always did.

He was the only one who'd ever really cared for her. The only one she could trust.

There was a moment, in the depths of those unblessed caves, when Kess had wondered if maybe she could have trusted Riony too. Riony, who had come back for her. Who hadn't let her die.

But it was a mirage of hope. A shimmer in the distance that Kess hadn't dared look at lest she crawl toward it only to be left dead for wanting what it didn't provide.

And even if there was a real chance it had existed, Kess had then broken any trust with Riony in a way that could never be fixed. It wasn't worth considering.

Kess glared across the fire at where her brother snorted and grumbled in his sleep, her eyes on the pouch by his side where he'd put the silvernix and taming spike.

She couldn't trust anybody. She was alone. Always.

Chapter Twenty

Griskin nipped at Riony's heel, teeth gliding over the leather of her boot. Riony lunged away. She wheeled around, sword drawn.

The gateway closed, blinking out before her eyes and leaving them adjusting to the absence of light. Another close call, one of many.

The beat of dragon wings echoed like a nightmare in Riony's head—a sound she was now constantly on guard for and heard far too often.

The shrine they'd arrived at was dark, empty. Cyan light flared as Aishena activated her glow stone.

Watching the symbols around the geode gateway, Riony held her breath. There were refugees sheltering at the shrine they'd just fled, as there were around many of the Alderkin ruins now.

The symbol didn't crack. Riony let the breath out slowly through pursed lips. Hopefully it meant nobody there had suffered Kife or Kess's wrath at their escape.

Riony was honestly surprised that, so far, they hadn't destroyed any of the shrines where people had settled. Or destroyed those people. They only destroyed shrines without communities around them, which there'd been a few of.

Maybe Kess was reining in Kife. As far as the lesser of two evils went, at least Kess was never one for wanton destruction. She was more about personalized cruelty and psychological torment. She knew her strengths and stuck to them.

They'll probably destroy this shrine when they get here and don't find anyone.

It was the first time they'd been to this location since activating it, due to it being high up craggy mountains that were a pain to travel around on foot.

But they wouldn't be leaving on foot again. They couldn't risk getting more than a short sprint away from a shrine anymore. If they were caught out by the dragon with nowhere to run, it would be over, and with Griskin able to track them traveling on foot, it left few options.

Aishena already had their map out and was muttering calculations softly. After weeks of relentless pursuit they had a good idea of how fast Kife's dragon was now.

"If they head straight here, we have about two hours."

It was mostly guesswork, since they didn't have a timepiece with them, but 'two hours' translated roughly to 'enough time to catch our breaths and get comfortable before having to run again.'

Lyrrin groaned, dumping her backpack on the ground, then dumping herself down onto that. "I want to sleeeeeeeep! You said we could sleep!"

Riony winced, exhausted too. "Sorry. They don't normally keep coming at night. I thought it would be okay to stop for the day."

Benjin held a blanket, hurriedly gathered in his arms. They had just been preparing to settle in for the night when their hunters caught up to them again.

He had the same thoughtful look that his brother often wore. "They must be getting desperate."

"Or just pissed off from this stupid game of dragon-and-mouse," Niskina said.

"Either way," Benjin continued, "they're choosing to prioritize the chase over getting a good night's sleep or resting their dragon, like they did before."

"Maybe they just didn't feel sleepy tonight?" Riony shrugged.

Benjin rolled his eyes. "Or maybe they thought changing up their actions would catch us off guard, and it almost did. It's time we start changing things up too. We should be fighting back! Setting a trap! Finding some way to stop them coming after us."

Dracuni, eyes wide and sending shoots of excited anxiety through to Riony, pounced backward and forward on her claws.

Fight back! I can bite!

"Not going to happen." Riony gave the unidragon a quelling glare.

Although around the same size as Kess's huge wolf, Dracuni's scales were still soft compared to a normal dragon's, and her teeth not as long, and her talons not as hooked, no matter how fierce she'd been acting lately.

Aishena pulled Benjin protectively to her side as though he were about to leap into combat right then. "It's too dangerous. We just have to keep away from them."

"We should fight. Yoskar would have done anything, *anything*, to keep his family safe," Benjin said.

Aishena put a hand to her chest as though clutching at her heart and it came to rest over the pocket which held her brother's glasses. "That's what I'm trying to do for you—trying to keep you safe."

"That's not enough!" His words cut hard, landing in a swell of silence like an ocean.

The words slapped Riony in the cheek, even though they weren't directed at her.

It *wasn't* enough. Running and hiding and barely living, existing in a way that could hardly be considered life—it wasn't enough. Not for Lyrrin, not for Dracuni, not for any of the people in her care. And she couldn't work out how to make it better.

Aishena's face flushed, and although her lips formed shapes, she didn't reply.

With a sigh, Benjin said, "It's not enough because our family is bigger than just you and me now. It's everyone here."

Aishena brushed a hand over the place where Benjin's hair had been singed by dragonfire. One of the burns had gotten weepy and still wasn't fully healed. She nodded but didn't seem entirely convinced.

The words didn't comfort Riony either. It was a nice sentiment, but her shoulders sagged as though an additional weight had been laid upon them. Because he was right. They were all family now, and Riony was responsible for all of them.

Lyrrin and Dracuni and Benjin all stared up at their elders with fiery gazes, as though they really thought they could take on a full-grown dragon.

"We can discuss war plans later," Riony said, mostly to placate them. "For now, we take a moment here before we move on again, and hopefully we can sleep at the next stop. We'll go before they get here so they don't see where we end up. That will buy us maybe a day. But first, rest."

That seemed to settle things, and bags were unloaded, and seats taken on the dirty floor. Niskina shared flatbread, still warm from the fires of the settlement they'd just left. She didn't keep any for herself, and instead unstoppered a brown bottle she must have also received and took a long, steady swig.

Aishena remained on her feet, moving to take a guarding position at the door, and the two kids laid out Lyrrin's blanket, then lined up Lyrrin's remaining collection of crystals on it. Dracuni crouched with her chin on the ground, watching as Lyrrin tested and worked on the shining stones.

Everyone looked exhausted. They'd realized early on that Kess and Kife must also know where all the shrines were. And had somehow worked out how to tell which gateway Riony and her friends were traveling to if the terrible siblings caught a glimpse of the symbol activated.

How do they know which symbol takes us where? Knowing Kess, she's probably mapped every shrine in Elundrae, even ones we couldn't have reached and activated yet, just to rub in how much better she is at strategy than us.

Riony didn't bother unpacking anything. She just sat on the cold cracked tiles of the ruined shrine.

They'd worked out a few tricks to buy time, jumping back and forth between multiple gateways so their hunters wouldn't know which one they were at. But having refugees at the shrines was a blessing and a curse.

More than once the settlers had been threatened into revealing what symbol had been illuminated. None of Riony's tactics had delayed the swift dragon long. And there were only so many shrines activated, all fairly close together since they'd had to get to them all on foot the first time.

Maybe Benjin is right. We need a plan. And we need someone better to come up with that plan than me.

"That's the last one," Lyrrin said, holding the newly carved staff close to her face and flicking at the crystal embedded there, as though checking it wasn't going to fly out.

"It's amazing!" Benjin beamed, gave Lyrrin a quick hug, and then moved away to show Aishena the finished staff.

All of Lyrrin's new crystals had been expended upon that staff, except for one that she'd turned into a cutting athame for Aishena, since they all agreed that might come in handy in case they were captured again.

Some of the crystals broke in the making, simply too fragile or flawed to stand up to carving, but everyone remained in awe that any of the crystals carved fresh by Lyrrin had worked at all.

All Lyrrin had left were the two matching stones and the crystal with a ten-stroke rune from the Alderkin tomb Riony had taken along with her sword.

Dracuni shuffled closer to them until her front claws were touching the shining stones. ***Rocks pretty.***

"Still haven't worked those ones out?" Riony asked.

Lyrrin huffed, wiggling a finger in the air in frustrated motions. "Ten strokes! I just can't keep them straight in my mind. I've tried marking them down, but after about five strokes, I don't feel the crystal singing as strongly, can't tell if I'm still on the right track. And these ones ..."

Lyrrin picked up the matching stones, shaking them in paired fists. "They activate, but they don't seem to do anything!"

Riony reached a hand to take one of the crystals from her. It was a flat slice of hexagonal calcite that fit in the palm of her hand. "You don't have to work every one of them out. You've already done amazing things. If we were still in the undercity ..."

Riony's throat dried up and she swallowed to fix it but her words had dried up too.

Dracuni's sadness also reached her. ***I miss brother Butterfur.***

Yeah, I miss the slithery rat too. Riony tilted her head toward Dracuni, but didn't say anything aloud, since any mention of the cave otter made her sister burst into tears.

Unaware, Lyrrin continued, "But this could be it! One of these crystals could be what we need to keep ourselves safe." Lyrrin ran her finger, ungloved, over the rune on the paired stone. A soft rosy-pink light glowed.

Dracuni lifted her head. ***Pretty, pretty rocks!***

And the slice of crystal in Riony's hand pulsed. "This seems to be doing something. I don't know what, but something."

"What?" Lyrrin took it back, staring. "It's not doing anything. It's not even activated."

"It did something. I felt it. Yours didn't do anything?" Riony swapped to take the activated rosy stone.

Lyrrin's eyes went wide. "What? I can feel something. It hasn't done that before! It feels like a heartbeat."

"Activate that one too," Riony said. Lyrrin traced the sigil in a liquid motion. And the same pulsing beat she'd felt before thrummed under Riony's fingers.

It *was* like a heartbeat. Small and faster than her own, a heartbeat she knew well from years curled up sleeping together. "It's your heartbeat."

"Do you think so?" Lyrrin shuffled in and pressed her ear toward Riony's chest as she held her own crystal.

She gasped. "This one matches yours! In time and everything!"

"Have you ever had someone else hold one before?"

"No, I just tried one on its own. I just thought they were two of the same. I didn't think they were paired together like this."

"Dracuni, hold still for a moment," Riony said.

She balanced her crystal onto Dracuni's snout.

"It changed!" Lyrrin said, passing her stone over to Riony again to feel.

It had changed to a heavy, solid pulse, slow and rumbling.

Nose tickles, Dracuni sniffed, eyes smiling.

The incredible magic the Alderkin had, and to have created something like this with it, left Riony's own heartbeat stuttering.

She said a silent apology to the person whose grave she'd stolen these from. At the time, she hadn't thought of them *as* a person who had a past and experiences and loves and hopes. She'd only seen treasure that she could take.

But that warrior who'd lain there with their sword and their belongings, and these stones ... had they taken one into battle with them so a loved one back home could feel that their heart was still beating?

How far away from each other did these work? If the gateways could take people all the way across Elundrae, Riony wouldn't be surprised if these stones allowed them to feel their lover's heartbeat all the way across the world.

"Heartbeats ... this is the most romantic thing I've ever seen," Riony whispered, pouting.

"Ew," Lyrrin grunted. "They're useless! I doubt I could even make them explode if I tried!"

She took back the crystals and deactivated them with a huff.

"Not everything has to explode to be valuable," Riony said.

Lyrrin replied with an eye roll.

"Says the woman who thinks hitting things with her sword is always the best answer," Niskina grumbled.

She sat cross-legged, the bottle on the ground in front of her and gripped in both hands.

"Shush, I'm trying to make this a learning moment!" Riony replied.

"You know what I've learned? That we should never have tried to be heroes." Niskina pushed the bottle out of her hands and it rolled, clinking and empty across the uneven tiles. "That stupid stunt at the mine ... thinking we could actually be rebels ..."

"We still did the right thing though?" Lyrrin's voice went up at the end, as though she asked a question.

Aishena turned as though to say something but remained silent.

"We helped a heap of people. That was something." Benjin returned to sit beside Lyrrin. He sounded tired, questioning as well.

Niskina leaned back against the wall, rolling her head from side to side. "And *we* paid for it. We got betrayed. We're the ones being hunted."

"Bad people screwing things up doesn't negate that we did do a good thing," Riony said, trying to sound confident and comforting and failing.

"We never should have tried to change anything. We should have just gone straight to that secluded village of yours and hidden from the world as long as we could." Niskina locked her gaze on Riony, and it was cold and brutal. "But you've clearly been avoiding taking us there. Why? Does this place even exist?"

"It's not like that. I just ..."

Aishena's back straightened just as her face fell. "Does it exist? You haven't been lying to us, have you? Just to give us a place to hope for?"

Everybody looked to Riony then, a sea of tired and broken faces. Even Lyrrin, who knew the place they'd grown up in was real, seemed confused, worried, as though maybe that life had all been a long-lost dream.

This family Riony had gathered were all looking to her.

She firmed her insides, pushing down the fear and doubt. "It's real. And we can go there. We will go there. But now, without being able to get too far away from the shrines, I don't know how. It doesn't have a shrine very close by. We could be tracked and found too easily."

"More excuses," Niskina muttered, turning away.

"I think I have an idea about that," Lyrrin said, patting Dracuni beside her. "I think we can shake off Griskin's scent so he can't track us on foot."

"Really?" Riony's pitch rose weirdly as she tried to hide her disappointment.

Excuses, Niskina's voice echoed in her head.

Because Niskina was right.

She had been avoiding going back to the place where she'd watched her parents die. And all her excuses were running out.

Chapter Twenty-One

Lyrrin had felt good coming up with a plan. Like she was clever and contributing as much as the bigger kids. But then everybody's lives depended on her plan working, and that left Lyrrin in a constant anxious sweat.

It was a big responsibility, no matter how much Riony encouraged her that it was a great plan, that it was working.

It's been weeks since Kife and Kess have found us. It's going to be okay. It's going to be okay.

After collecting what they needed, they covered every gateway they had activated with fungus from the glass factory, they'd headed off on foot as stealthily as they could. They'd started from a shrine where there were no witnesses to point their hunters in the right direction, even if it was farther away from where they were going than others.

They didn't go straight to the village. They zigzagged, activating a couple more shrines along the way but not using the gateways, including, finally, one that was only a couple of hours walk away from their old home.

Our home.

Lyrrin didn't remember a lot from her time growing up there. And those memories were warm, fuzzy, sunlit fragments of smiling faces and games with dolls.

The sloping, crunchy ground of slate and rugged boulders was familiar in a way that felt like she belonged there. The warm orange tones of the rocks and the trees with fresh-scented, needlelike leaves brought Lyrrin a nostalgic joy she hardly understood.

But she knew it meant they were close now. Would she remember more when she was there? Would she know which home was hers if it were still standing? Would she remember her parents' faces again?

Riony hissed, holding up a hand, and everyone stilled. Lyrrin couldn't hear or see anything, and after a moment of silent, stone-still waiting, Riony shook herself and gestured them forward again.

There was one sound—the low burble of water from ahead.

"The river!" Lyrrin gasped.

She hurried to the head of the group, leading the way. The modest stream came into view, tumbling along over flat slabs of stone. "Is this the right one? Where's the waterfall? Wasn't there a waterfall?"

"This is it." Riony nodded, her face as hard and level as those rocks. "The waterfall is over on the other side of the village."

Wasn't she excited, too, to see their home again?

Dracuni stopped for a drink, and they all filled empty waterskins, bobbing and keeping watch like deer, then they followed the stream out of the thick woods.

A wide, empty stretch of rock lay ahead—a canyon stripped bare to hard, orange stone glowing in the warm afternoon light. Concentric tiers looped around the flat base, carved into the surrounding slope like giant steps.

And in the middle, tall, spiked-log palisades were ringed around a clutch of cottages.

Lyrrin pulled her seeing stone and Benjin lifted his staff, activating his own as well.

"I can't see any movement inside," Benjin confirmed first.

Lyrrin looked a little longer, her eyes raking over the buildings. Stone walls and straw-thatched roofs were drooping and green with weeds. Raised garden beds spotted the solid stone ground, some in thin rows, and some wider rice paddies layered in tiers, all overgrown and brown.

It was there, hazy in her mind, the memory of all these things. Like watching a play performed of a story she'd once been told. It resonated within her, like a fairy tale coming to life.

But the way her sister looked at those houses reminded Lyrrin that it was a dark kind of fable—one that had ended in horrible death.

"Seems clear to me too," Lyrrin said.

Riony looked up at the last fluffy tree shading them overhead. "Maybe we should wait a little while undercover before—"

"I'm going to check it out," Niskina said, marching forward.

Benjin and Aishena followed. Lyrrin took a step, then turned back, waiting for her sister.

With a small nod, Riony walked with Lyrrin toward their old home, Dracuni at their heels.

The gated entrance hung open, the orange stone beneath it stained and dark. As everyone walked ahead, right through, Lyrrin noticed Riony frowned and walked around the darkest patches.

"No bodies," she said, barely a mumble.

"Maybe there were some survivors? Maybe the bodies were burned before the last people abandoned this place?" Lyrrin offered.

They ambled farther into the walled-in village, but there were no remains of pyres—only one large scorch mark beside a mostly destroyed town hall.

"Or maybe the shadowdragon visited again," Riony replied, her lips thin.

Riony didn't need to finish her thought—that all the humans who had died there had gotten up and walked away. Lyrrin shivered.

From up ahead, Benjin said, "There are no signs of revs. Unless they're all hiding in buildings, but that's not like them."

Aishena moved from door to door, pushing them open and peering inside, checking just in case.

"Stick with me," Riony said to Lyrrin and Dracuni.

The unidragon ruffled her wings, the thin, iridescent film over them shimmering.

"Because it could be dangerous still."

There was another gap of silence as Dracuni stared up at Riony.

"I know we came here to be safe, but we have to check it *is* safe first."

Lyrrin tried not to be jealous of the conversation she couldn't really be part of, but it didn't work.

Riony strode with purpose, beelining for a building ahead. The high thatched roof was punctuated with a solid stone chimney. Was that home? It didn't seem familiar to Lyrrin, no more than any other cottage around them.

"Stay back," Riony said. Taking one deep breath at the already ajar door, she pushed it open.

Lyrrin watched her sister's face, the flickers of emotion over it unreadable.

"What is it?" Lyrrin asked.

"Nothing. There's nothing here." Riony stepped away, wobbly for a moment. She put a hand against the wall before rolling her shoulders and moving on.

Frowning, Lyrrin peeked in to see what Riony was looking for. Inside the dark space, a heavy anvil and barrels lay toppled on the floor. Half-formed weapons and bars of steel lay scattered amongst pliers and hammers.

What was it about this building that had drawn Riony to it? What didn't she find?

Lyrrin looked up, following a shaft of light that shone in through a hole in the ceiling, making dust motes dance.

High above the messed-up workspace, solid wooden beams created triangles and struts, holding up the high roof around the large central furnace.

The flicker of memory tugged at Lyrrin, and a pain filled her chest.

She'd been up in those rafters. Hiding. Crying. She didn't remember much though. Her eyes had been covered the entire time.

She'd only been told afterward that her parents were gone.

Was this where they died? Right on this stone floor?

Lyrrin didn't want to look too closely for fear she'd see the stains of their blood.

Dracuni trilled, a questioning sound, then circled behind Lyrrin, herding her away from the haunted space.

She moved on, following the others through the ghost town.

Two more houses along, and Lyrrin's heart jumped into her throat.

That was it—their home.

She didn't need to see Riony freezing before the modest cottage to know. Her sister reached up to her neck, clasping around her collarbone for the acorn pendant that was no longer there.

Does she even realize she still does that all the time?

Lyrrin knew Riony missed their parents so much more than Lyrrin did. Lyrrin missed the absence of *parents*, of having an amma and pabba, and the few clear memories she held close. A lullaby sung at night. A grazed knee wiped clean by Amma. Wrestling with Pabba on the soft rug of their living room as stew bubbled away on the hearth.

Riony must have so many more memories. So much more of them to miss.

"Should we go in?" Lyrrin asked.

"Sure. Why not?" Riony replied flatly.

Riony went through first, pushing the heavy door. It groaned loudly, scraping a protest across the floor. The three of them winced, but after a moment where nothing rushed them from the shadows within, they stepped inside.

Dracuni sneezed softly at the dust stirred up by their entrance.

"It's our ... it's where we grew up," Riony said, as though in reply.

Dracuni's head rose up, eyes wide and curious. She trotted over the rug, mildewed and moth-eaten and barely there. Lyrrin tried to remember what colors it once was. She'd been six the last time she'd seen it. She felt like she should remember more, but so much felt locked away.

Through the side door, Lyrrin found their bedroom.

Two small beds, side by side, lay flat on the ground without frames. The mattresses were split and spilling old straw turned to sawdust by beetles and rodents.

"That one was yours. Do you remember?" Riony pointed.

There were no headboards, but the stone wall that butted up to the heads of the beds had rough carvings of flowers and stars scratched into it.

"Oh!" Lyrrin's chest swelled, happy and sad all at once. "I remember! I got in so much trouble for doing that!"

A couple of time-grayed blankets remained strewn across Lyrrin's bed, and on the pillow lay a straw doll.

Lyrrin gently picked it up, but it still cracked in her fingers, as though the straw and tiny woven clothes would turn to dust in her hands. It matched the one that she'd taken with her into the undercity, right down to the bow tied around its waist.

She rubbed her thumb over the ribbon. Blue.

The one they had left behind in the undercity was red.

More memories stirred. "I always thought ... I thought my doll had a blue ribbon. But you said I was mistaken. You said it was red. Always was red."

"I ... I'm sorry. I lied." Riony stared at the ground.

"Why? Why did you trick me?"

"I didn't have time to take both dolls. We had one each. Matching except for the ribbons. But that night ... I only grabbed one."

"You grabbed yours."

Riony nodded.

"And then you told me it was mine. You gave your doll to me."

Riony finally lifted her gaze to meet her sisters. "It was just a doll ... I didn't need it. And you'd lost so much ... I'm sorry I tricked you. I'm sorry I didn't get your doll."

Lyrrin put the toy down again. It belonged right there, left behind in this home they'd fled like the other doll remained back in the undercity. Was it still there, in their rooms?

Two homes lost.

It felt like reawakening bones in a grave, being there amongst these long-lost moments, disturbing them, returning to reclaim them.

No wonder Riony didn't want to come back.

Flinging herself around her sister's waist, Lyrrin clung tight. "It's okay. It was just a doll."

Dracuni circled around their legs in the dim, dusty light until finally, their embrace broke.

Riony's nose wrinkled, and she stared up at the ceiling. "Come on. Let's check on the others."

Back outside, Benjin ran up to meet them.

"Everything seems to have been left behind, untouched. There's so much stuff," Benjin said in awe, gazing greedily over the houses filled with belongings.

Lyrrin tried to imagine living there, in the houses people had left behind, with their belongings. There would be plenty of what they'd need.

At the lowest point of the quarry, a dam of deep blue water created a reservoir, filled by rain. Some of the garden beds had the wild remains of vegetables, growing in tumbling messes, reseeded randomly wherever there was dirt to grow. There was even the faint cluck of a chicken from behind a building.

Despite being overrun with weeds, and ghostly in the absence of life, it was almost pretty there. It felt peaceful. Maybe it would work out.

"Wasn't there ... did we have a swing?" Lyrrin asked.

A faint smile came to Riony's lips. "Yeah, there was. Just down here."

There were no trees within the quarry boundaries, not enough soil anywhere to sustain plant life beyond the raised garden beds. But down closer to the water, a frame of logs had been built, with a row of swings hanging along it.

Lyrrin ran over and tested the frayed ropes with a strong tug before lowering her weight into the flat plank seat.

She wobbled her body to and fro, but the swing didn't move more than a jiggle.

Benjin grabbed the one beside her. "You've got to do it like this."

After a couple of sways of his body, the swing picked up.

"You never did learn how to get going on your own." Riony chuckled and gave Lyrrin a push from behind.

The hood blew back off Lyrrin's head as she swung through the air.

That was another familiar feeling—the rush and dip of her stomach and press of warm hands on her back. Her eyes prickled with tears and her mouth split in a grin.

Dracuni ran beside her, nipping playfully at her legs as they pointed skyward.

There was a crash of sound from nearby, and Riony grabbed the rope, stilling the swing in an instant.

Niskina leaned halfway through the shutters of a building nearby, feet dangling out behind her. "Yeah, there's heaps inside. Bottles, barrels, food and drink for days!"

"As long as it hasn't all gone bad by now," Aishena said from her side of the wall.

"Be careful over there," Riony called, flinching as Niskina shimmied back out of the small, high window, knocking one of the shutters down with her.

The crash echoed softly through the rocky walls of the surrounding canyon.

"Relax!" Niskina called back, far louder than Riony had dared. "This place is deserted."

"It won't matter if you're loud enough to draw in everything from the horizon!" Riony had tried to push the palisade gate closed again, but it was only propped up in place.

"Come on. Use your athame to cut the lock," Niskina told Aishena, her voice like an order.

With a brusque nod, Aishena had the glowing yellow blade in her hand.

"You don't have to do what she says!" Riony began marching toward them.

Aishena cut through the locked handle of the door, and Niskina pushed the heavy wood, and the entire door fell inward, flat onto the stone within.

The crack that sounded was like a boulder split by lightning. It echoed around the quarry, reverberations swirling for long moments before vanishing to silence again.

Even the surface of the water rippled at the sound.

Lyrrin stood up from the still swing, staring at that deep, dark blue.

Something was moving beneath the surface. Rising pale-yellow domes dripping with strands of rot emerged. Skulls. Dark, hollow eyes. Melting, waterlogged flesh.

"Revs!" Benjin shouted first.

Five of them, all human.

"We can take them," Niskina yelled. "It's not too many. We should just take them out, then we can stay here."

Lyrrin nodded. It made sense. If there were only five of them, they could handle it. They had before.

But Riony wasn't answering. She wasn't drawing her sword. She wasn't running. She wasn't moving at all, other than with great shudders that shook her body.

She was staring at the rev in the middle.

Afternoon light glinted off the rev's skeletal hands beneath the drape of ragged sleeves.

Silver rings. Four of them, one across each finger.

Amma.

Chapter Twenty-Two

A mma.

Riony knew she should move. She needed to get to Lyrrin and Dracuni. She needed to keep them safe. She couldn't move. Her whole body felt encased in suffocating ice.

Four silver bands. They stood out, glistening against fingers that were dark with decay. Mottled, leathery skin was wrought tight against the bones beneath.

But those were her mother's hands.

Amma.

Nothing else about the body was familiar. There were no green eyes left within the sockets to search for comfort within. There were no lips to cover teeth that used to only show when her daughters made her smile. Now those teeth were laid bare, a gnashing cage for the growls in her throat.

The wine-red woolen gown that matched her hair was a blackened, torn net. Bones were visible where once there'd been soft skin.

It was her. It wasn't her. Amma. She was dead and gone. She was there.

Amma and four other revenants crawled free of the blue-tinted reservoir, locked eyes on their prey, and rushed into attack.

Down near the swings, Lyrrin, Benjin, and Dracuni were the closest.

Get to the kids. Get to the kids. GET TO THE KIDS.

Words screamed through Riony's head. Maybe she even screamed them out loud because Aishena and Niskina bolted past her on either side, running in to meet the ravenous attackers.

But still, Riony's body remained stuck in place, turned to stone. Shattered, cracking stone, falling to pieces. If she couldn't hold herself together, there would be nothing left.

Amma.

The last time Riony had seen her mother, she'd lain twitching on the floor, flesh pulled free from all the soft parts of her and eyes staring blankly upward to where Riony clutched Lyrrin, hiding in the rafters. Amma had already been dead then. Riony hoped she'd already been dead then.

Either way, it had taken longer for her to die than Pabba. The revs had left him alone once he was still, but Amma still twitched, driving the undead into a frenzy. Why wouldn't she stop moving? Wouldn't it ever end?

It had lasted forever, until the stars had fallen from the sky and Riony's hands had grown ancient and cold, covering Lyrrin's eyes and ears, and Riony had forgotten how to breathe from holding in her screams. Had she died too? Why wouldn't Amma stop twitching?

Even now, her corpse refused to lay still.

Riony's breath was coming too hard, too fast, burning through her body and clouding her head. Her eyes dimmed at the edges as a deep, painful terror overwhelmed her.

With athames glowing in red and yellow, Aishena downed one rev with deadly precision as she moved herself in front of Benjin. There was a squabble as he tried to push back in front again, barely missed by a clawing hand.

Niskina had her poleaxe out, taking strong swings at the rev closest to her as Lyrrin and Dracuni both dodged back, trying to create some distance between them and the undead.

Move. Move. Move, Riony pleaded with her bones, teeth gritted and eyes watering.

With a strangled grunt of effort, she drew her sword. Her fingers trembled uselessly across the rune, rattling beyond control, unable to activate it.

One rev split free from the brawl near the water, knocked aside by a blow from Benjin's staff. Scrambling up from the ground, it caught sight of Riony.

A rev with silver rings. Her rotted jaw unhinged with the ferociousness of her howl. She charged, arms and legs flicking in a hideous, convulsing gallop.

Amma.

Riony couldn't move. She could only hold her heavy—too heavy—sword in front of her.

The rotting corpse of her mother smashed into that sword like a ball against a bat. But it wasn't the ball that gave way, flying off again. It was Riony that crumbled.

She landed flat on her back, sword crushing down over her chest and cheek, and the squelching, putrid flesh of the revenant—*Amma*—landed on top.

All the air left Riony's chest in a *whuff*. Even if she could draw breath, she didn't have time before the body on top of her flailed again into attack.

Those fingers with those rings had once been a source of comfort. Those hands that had once balmed her back when she'd been whipped, that had tucked her unruly hair behind her ear. Those fingers with those rings, one for each generation of midwife in their line, that were one day meant to be passed down again.

Those fingers scraped across Riony's scalp, pulling free a fistful of hair.

"Ri? We need you and your big-ass sword! What are you doing?"

Those fingers dug into uncovered arms between bracers and shoulder guards, squeezing and cutting deep between the muscles.

Riony's mouth opened, gasping, but she couldn't even scream.

Amma. Please.

Teeth gnashed and growled above the sword and Riony's face, turned and pressed into the hard ground beneath.

"Riony!"

"Someone get over there!"

Pain lanced into Riony's stomach, a skeletal finger, sharp like a dagger, pushing deep. Her breaths were frantic, bellowing. She was sobbing, out of control. She couldn't move, couldn't move, couldn't lift one finger gripped white-knuckled around the hilt of the sword she couldn't raise in defense.

Sister!

"I can't get away from this one!"

"Lyrrin, look out!"

Boney knees and long-nailed toes scrambled over Riony's legs, shredding through leather pants to the skin of her thighs.

Amma. Stop.

The finger in her stomach curled like a hook, pulling free with a bloody pop before stabbing in again.

Stop hurt! Stop, bad thing!

Pale, iridescent scales danced across the ground in front of Riony's paralyzed face.

Dracuni's jaws snapped, closing on air as the revenant continued its clawing frenzy, arms and legs lashing faster than Dracuni could bite.

Stop.

Stop.

Her thoughts and Dracuni's thoughts overlapped.

The shadowdragon-risen body of Amma ignored the unidragon entirely. It only cared to extract its vengeance upon humans. It only wanted Riony's blood and was taking plenty of it.

Maybe there was something of her mother still in there too, seeking revenge for having been allowed to die, to die so painfully, as her daughter did nothing but watch.

I'm sorry. I'm sorry. Amma, please.

Dracuni snapped again, moving in closer, her feet beside Riony's face. The small dragon bucked and growled, and the rotting body bucked and growled in return, trying to reach past the stabbing horn to the soft human.

A finger dragged across Riony's ribs and finally a scream emerged, rattling from her throat. On the inside, Riony no longer pleaded to make herself move. She just pleaded for it to be over.

"Why isn't she moving?"

"This rev won't stay down! I can't ..."

The bang of an exploding crystal cracked through the quarry.

Amma's fingers raked down the side of Riony's neck and collarbone, almost a tender motion, drawn too deep into the skin. Riony twitched with agony. She couldn't even move enough to curl up into a ball—only jolt and jerk at each stabbing nail into her flesh.

This is how she must have felt. This is how Amma felt as she died.

Stop, creature, stop!

Dracuni fretted, dancing on her talons. Her snapping jaws and jabbing horn only slowed the tearing apart of Riony's body and soul. Both felt shredded to ribbons.

With one big push from Dracuni, the revenant rolled off Riony. There wasn't even a second before the living corpse turned to attack again.

With a high, desperate roar, Dracuni rose up on her hind legs. Her chest swelled. Her mouth opened. Rows of short, ivory teeth glistened.

And she breathed.

A bright, shimmering flame gusted out of the unidragon's throat. It didn't touch

Riony as it passed over her, catching the revenant right in the face. Flames like wafting moonlight rippled over the rev.

And it didn't burn. But it did change.

Spine arching and limbs twitching, the revenant of Riony's mother rolled onto its back. The silver flames flickered all around its bones and rotting skin, and beneath that bright light, flesh reformed.

Soft and pink at first, then deepening to bronze, muscle and tissue grew over yellowed bones. The revenant gurgled and howled as the empty section at her stomach closed over, organs plumping out beneath the skin. She curled up, then stretched out as though in agony, raising up onto her knees, knees that were now whole again.

She was being healed. Every part of her was changing beneath the iridescent flames from corpse to living flesh.

Deep-red hair sprouted from her scalp and eyes bulged wet within sockets, and as the throat regrew, Amma gave the most dreadful human scream Riony had ever heard.

"Amma?" Riony rasped, her chest convulsing with ragged breaths.

Finally, she moved, without any order given to her limbs, without deciding first to do so, one hand detached from the hilt of her sword and reached for her mother.

Her mother, there, made whole again.

Could it be? Was she healed? Riony shifted, her sword sliding off her to the ground. Her body moved, responding to the sight of her mother, trying to draw her closer.

"Amma?" The shrill, desperate cry didn't come from Riony.

Her mother's scream juddered out to nothing. She hung there, kneeling on the ground, face turned up and arms dangling, and there was no more movement. No rise and fall of her chest. No pulse at her neck.

The body—*Amma, Amma!*—went still then fell in a slump.

"Amma? No, no. No*!" Not again. Not again!*

Riony couldn't bear it. She wished the revenant's clawing hands had ended her because she couldn't take seeing her mother there before her, watching her die a second time. She crawled, sobbing over the body, perfectly healed and untouched, and perfectly lifeless.

She wrapped her arms around the body of her mother and screamed wordlessly.

The body before her, as whole as it looked, as beautiful as it looked, was empty. All the flesh had healed, all the blood and bone and nail and hair restored. But not her soul—that had fled into the stars long ago. Not her life.

There were footsteps all around Riony now, rushing, cursing bodies.

"Sparks, what was that? Did you see that?" Benjin gasped.

"Amma?" Lyrrin's voice was broken by sobs. "It was … it was …"

"Help her up. Get her away from … that." Aishena's hands came underneath Riony's armpits, dragging her off the body.

Riony tried to fight her, tried to hold the body of her mother just a little longer. But all her strength was gone.

She was up on wobbly legs, pressed between two people.

"Oh no, oh no, Riony. Are you okay? Hey, can you hear us?" Niskina moved close to Riony's face.

Dracuni remained silent.

Aishena's voice was hushed. "What do we do?"

Riony blinked, trying to regain her vision through thick, sticky tears. Blood dripped down her arms and from the tips of her fingers, over her stomach, pooling at the hem of her pants.

She couldn't. She couldn't do this. She couldn't do anything. She wasn't okay. She didn't know what to do.

She thrust the clinging hands off her, and she ran.

CHAPTER TWENTY-THREE

Kife hurled a stick into the campfire, making it spark up. "Another dead end! This was your last chance, Kess. And there was nothing here."

Kess dodged away from the flying cinders. She'd just kindled those flames and she scowled at the scattered embers, struggling to stay lit. They'd set down in the clearing around midday after finding no sign of Riony in the village within the quarry, and from how Kife had settled in, it didn't seem like they were moving on anytime soon if they even knew where to go next.

"It was worth checking. It matched what Riony said about where she lived after leaving the estate. But there could be other similar villages. Maybe it's not the right one, or maybe they haven't arrived—"

Kife lay back on his blanket again, as he had been for hours, hands folded behind his head. "Or maybe they're hiding underground somewhere like rodents and we're never going to find them flying from one side of Elundrae and back again every day! You've ruined all our hopes of capturing them. You and your dumb dog have lost the trail."

Kess petted Griskin on the ear. "The fungus stuffs up his nose. He can't help it. I didn't know those fools would be smart enough to use that against us."

She remembered the parcel of herbs wrapped in a handkerchief that someone had tucked into Griskin's collar when in the caves. She should have worked out what was in it before discarding it. But she'd never imagined Pony would use the fungus as a way to mask their trail.

"So you're both useless then."

"And what have you done?"

"If it weren't for me and my dragon, we never would have even gotten close to catching them the few times we did." He rubbed his temples. "I need a break to clear my head, work out a new plan. Somewhere that's not a filthy patch of ground!"

Go home then. Kess seethed.

She regretted bringing her brother into this at all. And she'd always known she would, but she'd thought any suffering he inflicted upon her would at least be balanced by how useful he and his dragon were. But they were no closer, at all, to her goal. And she still needed his wings.

She said, "It will be dark soon enough, so this filthy patch of ground will have to do for the night."

Kife grunted. He grabbed a leather pail from the stack of bags beside him and threw it at Kess. "Go and get some water for my dragon."

Kess caught the bucket made of thick hide, riveted together. She wanted to tell him to do something for himself for once, but at least heading down to the river would give her a reason to be away from him for a while.

"Try to keep the fire going," she said and turned Griskin away.

They meandered through the dense forest, weaving between the towering trees shrouded in slivers of gray-green foliage. The earthy scent of damp soil mingled with the crisp, refreshing aroma of needlelike leaves scattering the ground, crushed under Griskin's paws.

The river ran close to the village, and the distant murmur of flowing water grew louder until Kess could see the whitewater rush of it over the sharp-edged boulders.

Before they stepped free of the tree line, Griskin's ears pricked up. His nose twitched.

"What is it?" Kess whispered.

Tension prickled through the muscles down the back of Griskin's neck beneath her hands. She turned her own face toward the light breeze blowing over the water from upstream.

The wolf released a rumbling growl.

Kess tightened her grip and pulled herself low into his fur, a surge of anticipation coursing through her veins as she urged him to follow the scent.

Keeping to the long afternoon shadows of the thick trunks, Griskin skulked swiftly on silent paws, chasing his nose. Kess wasn't sure what had gotten him so riled up, whether he was leading her to their dinner or something else.

But nothing could have prepared Kess for what she saw as they rounded a bend in the river.

A thin waterfall sprayed down between tall rocks into a round pool below, gurgling and glugging. On the shore, pieces of armor and clothing lay strewn, and a bloodied, bare body stood in the stream of water. Strands of vibrant red hair looked like fire within the flowing water.

Pony?

Kess flinched and pulled Griskin back behind the bushes that ringed the tumbling stream, making sure they weren't seen.

She took a breath and dared to look again.

It's her.

Kess's heart kicked into a racing beat. She was right. They had come here. It was the right village. She'd found them.

And there was Riony, alone, defenseless, not even the clothes on her scarred back to protect her.

Kess's face flushed hot, and she almost turned away again, ashamed of looking. But this was who she'd been hunting. Her prey—that was all. Just an obstruction between Kess and what Kess really wanted.

There were no signs of anyone else, and Griskin sniffed the air a couple of times but didn't direct her onward.

Where are the others? Where's Dracuni? What happened?

A softer, more feminine sound echoed amongst the splashes of the waterfall.

Kess listened closer and heard it again.

Deep, gulping sobs mixed with the burbling of water. Riony's body twisted to the side, and the water flowing over her ran red.

The breath in Kess's throat caught.

She was injured. Badly injured. Even the constant spray of water wasn't clearing away the blood that continued to flow freely from long scratches and punctured holes across her arms, stomach, neck.

Riony's back curved and shook with the intensity of her grief, and she clutched the rocks beside her in support but still fell onto her knees.

Kess had never seen her like this. Never. Not after being cut by whips or glass or daggers or swords. She wasn't sure she'd ever seen Riony cry.

And this wasn't just crying. This was a soul-deep, broken wail.

She wasn't even trying to stand anymore and had curled against the back wall of the falls, letting the water hammer over her.

Kess's own eyes suddenly felt wet, and she widened them in horror and refusal of the sympathetic urge.

Turning away quickly, Kess tried to slow the furious pace of her breaths.

Whatever had happened, whatever was happening, it was wrong to be a spectator there. Even her enemy deserved privacy in such a vulnerable moment. It wouldn't be honorable to take advantage of it.

Even if it would have been a good idea, even if it got her so much closer to claiming Dracuni as her own, the thought of doing anything to Riony then caused an aching pressure in Kess's chest.

Kess led Griskin silently back down the river. She filled the bucket, wondering whether that water held Riony's blood, and her hands shivered. She returned to camp.

The fire was out. She scowled, dropping the bucket with a splash beside her brother.

"Watch it! What took you so long?" Kife sat up, flicking droplets off his chest.

"Nothing." Kess lowered herself off Griskin to her blanket and thumped down on her side. Her pulse and breathing were still frantic.

"Why do you look so flushed?"

"It's nothing!" Griskin lay down beside her, and Kess turned her face away from her brother, hiding it in the wolf's fur.

"Did something happen?" There wasn't any concern in Kife's words—only the edge of blame.

"No. Shut up. I'm going to sleep."

"It's not even dark yet. And the fire is out. And you haven't hunted."

"Then do it yourself if you aren't too dumb to manage it!"

Kife grumbled, kicking around behind her in a drawn-out show of annoyance as he worked on the fire.

Kess curled up tighter, trying to calm the raging pounding in her chest. She closed her eyes but only saw the body, the blood, the water.

What had happened? Why was Riony alone? Had she lost the others? Had she lost

Dracuni? A stab of coldness dug into Kess's gut at the thought that the little dragon had been hurt somehow, that Riony hadn't been able to protect it.

No. Riony had told Kess she'd die before letting something happen to Dracuni, and Kess believed her.

But if the unidragon was still around, why didn't Riony use it to heal herself? Even in the glass factory, she'd tried to refuse the healing blood. Did she care so much about the creature that she'd suffer herself rather than harm it?

Kess could feel the truth of the answer. She knew Riony well enough that she couldn't deny it.

She always had been the kind of person who put her suffering last.

Kess closed her eyes again, haunted this time by a different vision. A thin line of blood across a cheek. A lash in her hands. Fingers around her throat.

It had been Kife's revenge.

The evening after Kess had warned him off Riony, with a dagger thrown close to his neck, Kife had sat at dinner and proudly told their parents just how excellent Kess had gotten with her aim.

"Really?" Her mother wiped her downturned mouth with a napkin.

"Wouldn't it be fun to have a demonstration?" Kife asked, eyes twinkling.

Her father placed his metal goblet on the table. "Yes, I would like to see this myself."

He muttered the words as though he couldn't believe his daughter could be good at anything.

Kess's lips twitched, and she pushed the food around on her plate. "My aim is coming along just fine, but it would be crass to draw weapons at dinner."

"No, let's!" Her mother clapped her hands together. "A throwing demonstration it is. I want to see my daughter's excellence as well."

All three of them beamed sly smiles, like predators whose prey was her humiliation.

"Hmm, how shall we do this?" Kife picked a small apple from the overflowing fruit bowl, tossing it and catching it a couple of times.

He stared over Kess's head to where Riony stood still behind her chair. "Come here, you."

"Kife!" Kess hissed a warning.

He only smiled as Riony rounded the table to stand in front of him. He gestured for her to bend down to his seated level, then jammed the apple in her mouth.

"Go on now, back over against the wall. All the way. That's it." Kife leaned back in his chair, grinning at Kess. "You can hit that target, can't you, sister?"

"*Easily*," Kess rasped.

The blushed red of the apple matched Riony's hair as she stood stock-still, eyes on Kess without reprimand or judgment. Only waiting. Only a terrible feeling of acknowledgment that both of them were the victim in that situation.

Kess turned away, glaring at the family portrait above her father that only showed three people. "You should have picked a harder target for me. Shall I show you how I can hit right through your eye in our family portrait there?"

"The apple, Kess. Go on," Lord Heithorn said. "No need to destroy artwork."

Kess looked down at the table, not wanting to look again at the target. Her fingers trembled as she closed them around a dull serving knife.

"No, no. One of your fine throwing knives. They're so lovely and sharp," Kife said.

Everyone stared at her, waiting. Could she refuse? She would be humiliated either way, whether she took the shot or not. Riony would be punished whether she took the shot or not. The only way out was to throw the blade and throw it well.

She shifted around in her chair, drew one of her thin steel blades, and tried to steady her hand and breath.

She could do it. She could hit such a target. But normally her targets weren't so very close to the eyes and lips and cheeks of someone ... someone she ...

If she missed ... *if she missed.*

She wouldn't miss. She sent the dagger flying.

Riony didn't even flinch.

The knife stuck into the apple, inelegantly, askew.

Kess stifled a shuddering sigh. "Done. Happy now?"

"She's bleeding!" Lady Heithorn sounded scandalized but a smile still bared her teeth. "Your pet is bleeding, Kessara. Poor form."

Turning back, Kess saw it too, a thin trickle of blood from where the knife and apple and lips all met in the corner of Riony's mouth.

With a hard, glimmering sneer, Kife stood and patted Kess on the shoulder. "Aw, better luck next time. Looks like you need more practice."

Her father said nothing at all. Just sniffed and left the table. Lady Heithorn and the serving staff followed him out.

Kife gave Kess's shoulder another tight, rough squeeze before leaving as well.

Nothing was said as Riony removed the apple and wiped her mouth with the back of her hand. It only smeared the blood, making it seem even redder. She picked Kess up and carried her back to her room.

Kess stared at her bloody chin the entire way back, unable to look away. An uncontrollable, awful turmoil of anger and shame curdled her stomach and burned her ears.

As gently as ever, Riony set Kess down on the side of her bed. On the bedstand lay a lash, gifted by the lord and lady in case Kess wanted to discipline her slave herself. She never had. She glared at that thick fringe of knotted leather.

"Do you ... need anything else tonight?" There was a softness in Riony's voice that infuriated Kess.

"You moved!" she snapped, her eyes stinging. "You moved and ruined my shot!"

Riony shrugged. "It's okay. The cut isn't bad. The kind of thing that might make your blight-born brother cry, but I've had worse."

The anger in Kess expanded in a rush, like flames under bellows. Was the tame-brained slave actually trying to comfort her? Trying to make her feel better?

How dare she? How dare she be the one, standing there bleeding, and still she pities me?

How dare she be the one who is hurt over and over and still she pities me?

"Turn around!" Kess barked.

"What? Why?" Riony did anyway.

"Get on your knees!" Her voice was a broken shriek, and her hand wrapped around the handle of the lash.

She knelt. "What are you …?"

Kess struck, bringing the lash across the thin fabric between Riony's shoulders.

The girl hissed, spine arching. She sounded more surprised than anything. "Kess!"

"You humiliate me! Every day!" She struck again, harder. Blood welled through the pale cloth. "Your very existence shames me!"

Riony's shoulders rose and fell as each stroke cut her skin, her breath snorting and ragged, and then with an animalistic cry, she thrust back to her feet and flew at Kess, knocking the lash from her hand with the sweep of an arm. Her face was red and wild with ferocious emotions, skin stretched around bared teeth, still marked with blood.

They both screamed and clawed and Kess fell back onto the bed, and then Riony was upon her, fingers closing around Kess's neck. The grip was vicious but not enough to crush, and already softening as Riony's eyes widened, searched, as though she were coming back to herself.

"Do it!" Kess scraped the words free. Sobs clogged her throat as much as the squeeze of Riony's hands. "Do it! Get rid of me and be better for it! Get rid of me!"

Riony released her grip, stumbling backward.

"You want me dead! I know you do. Do it! Nobody will care if I'm gone!"

Kess had never forgotten the look of horror on Riony's face as she fled, leaving Kess alone with her guilt and her tears.

The girl she tormented had refused to grant her mercy, even if that mercy was for both of them.

And still, even now, it felt like every drop of Riony's blood spilled was Kess's fault, that Kess's presence still caused her suffering, and it no longer seemed to matter that it was for the cause of something greater.

Kess had always justified every cruelty. She'd needed her Pony to get around. She'd needed to get herself a dragon and would go through anybody to get it. She needed to capture Dracuni, and it didn't matter who was hurt in doing so.

But Kess could feel the truth worming through her veins like hot wire. She could no longer ignore it, no longer lie to herself.

It did matter.

Now Kess just needed to work out what that meant for what she did next.

CHAPTER TWENTY-FOUR

R iony wasn't sure how long she cried beneath the waterfall. It was definitely at least one eternity, maybe two.

She cried until her bones ached and her throat was raw, and every time she tried to pull herself together—because how could she have *run away?*—she only cried harder again.

No longer could she tell the difference between the sobs shaking her body and the water pounding down over it. She curled up on a smooth worn stone beneath the cascade. Maybe the water would wear her down too, wash her away to nothing, and it wouldn't hurt anymore.

At least her wounds would be clean. The thought of those putrid hands, her mother's hands, digging into her flesh had driven her to strip off and stumble into the falls. She wanted to wash everything away.

Despite the crimson threads still spilling from her lacerations, they didn't bother her. She could handle physical pain. It was the only thing she'd ever really been good at. What a talent to have.

But she couldn't handle loss. She couldn't handle seeing those she loved die, or want to die, or come back from the dead only to die again. How could she survive that? It was clear that she couldn't.

It's too hard. Everything is too hard.

And even then, she knew the others still needed her, and she'd abandoned them. How could she go back, where they were, into the village where she'd lost her mother twice?

I'm not strong enough.

Everything felt broken, and Riony knew it could never return to how it was before. Everything she'd lost was gone forever. Everything had changed. Even this waterfall felt so much smaller than she remembered.

She'd lost so much, and she was so tired.

Her heart ached for her friends, knowing how much they had lost too. She had to pull herself together, for them.

Lifting her head under the spray of water, she let it rush over her eyelids and cheeks for a moment, cooling them before she stood and opened her eyes. She flicked wet hair off her face.

Over at the tree line, a rustling of leaves caught her attention. She made herself small and still behind a boulder. Nothing leaped out at her after a couple of moments waiting.

"Lyrrin? Aish?" she called softly, not wanting to draw attention to herself.

There was no reply.

"Niskina?"

It wasn't Dracuni either. She couldn't sense the unidragon nearby. She could barely sense her at all now that her own mind had stilled enough to listen.

In a rush, Riony squeezed her pants back on over wet legs. Her shirt went over her head in a tangle of torn and sticky fabric, and she scooped up her armor and boots. The metal clattered in her arms as she scurried over the rocks to where she'd seen the movement.

Scanning through the surrounding forest, she couldn't see any sign of motion beyond the dappled, late afternoon light streaming through the swaying trees and the odd bird flitting about.

Then she looked down. Tracks. Imprinted into the soft soil, leading up to this position and away again. The prints of a large wolf.

"No, sparking *no!*"

Riony ran. Barefooted over sharp sticks and bristling leaves, flashes of branches and trunks either side, she hurled herself at a breakneck pace through the forest.

The air rushed across the torn parts of her skin, stinging the scratches as they dried and puckered. The deeper holes spurted blood with each pounding step, and Riony pressed a hand tight over her stomach in an attempt to hold it in.

Ducking through the broken gap in the palisade she had escaped through, she scraped her back and dropped a shoulder guard but didn't slow down.

Up ahead, Lyrrin sat on the flat stone ground, right where Riony had left her. Her sister had Dracuni beside her, the dragonling's head lying limply across her lap.

Riony came skidding to a stop beside them. Dracuni didn't stir.

"What happened? What did Kess do?" Riony dropped her remaining armor and reached for Dracuni.

"Riony! You're back!" Lyrrin said at the same time. Then, "Kess? What do you mean?"

"She ..." Riony looked all around them.

There were no sounds of fighting.

There were no revs left, no ... bodies nearby. Benjin rustled around in a garden bed, and Niskina and Aishena were down near the water, stacking logs and sticks.

There was no sign of Kess or Kife or his dragon. "I saw tracks ... wolf tracks. I thought Kess had found us."

"We haven't seen her."

"Then what's wrong with Dracuni?" Riony scooped a hand under the unidragon's chin, lifting her heavy head.

Dracuni blinked lazily. Her thoughts were soft and muted. ***Very tired.***

Just tired? Not wounded or sedated by morass mercy. Riony shook her head in disbelief.

They had been wolf tracks, hadn't they? Riony had only looked at them for a moment before running. Even if they were, and not some other animal, it could have been a different wild wolf.

It couldn't have been Kess.

If it were Kess, Riony would have been floating in the river with a knife through her back. If it were Kess, the Heithorns would have been here by now, stealing Dracuni away.

Riony's skin was clammy and a shiver ran down her back. She was still expecting the wolf-riding monster to burst out from between the cottages.

Lyrrin patted Dracuni's neck. "She just seems to be feeling weak."

Released from Riony's hand, Dracuni's head flopped back down on Lyrrin's lap, and her eyelids fluttered closed again.

"Aishena said it can happen with young dragons when they are learning to flame. She said a dragon's flame uses up their blood—that she didn't realize what that meant for Dracuni until ..." Lyrrin choked up.

Until Dracuni breathed healing fire.

But the body she'd healed was one already long dead.

Leaning over Dracuni, Riony pulled Lyrrin into a hug. "I'm sorry. I'm sorry you saw that. I should have made it all stop sooner. I couldn't move. I—"

"No. It's not your fault. You didn't want to come back here. We all made you. We made that happen to you." Lyrrin squeezed Riony and sniffled. "I was so scared for you."

Riony winced at the pressure against her wounds but didn't let go.

Lyrrin seemed to notice though and pulled away, eyes on the smears of blood. "Were you hurt badly?"

"Not at all," Riony whispered.

Lyrrin gave her a dry, knowing glare. "You're allowed to say you got hurt. You're allowed to be scared sometimes too. You don't have to always pretend you're okay."

In the time since they'd left the undercity, Lyrrin had grown so much. Riony had felt protective of her ever since the moment the newborn was given a death sentence for looking different. And even more since Riony's parents had sent her and Lyrrin into the rafters to hide, telling her that she had to look after her sister.

It was her job, her responsibility alone. Because they were gone.

She'd never stopped to question who, then, would ever care for her in the times when she was broken. She'd just tried her best to never *be* broken, no matter what. Until everything came crumbling down.

And there was Lyrrin.

A soft, guttural sob escaped through Riony's aching throat, and she hung her head. "I'm not okay."

"Me either." Lyrrin reached for her hand, and they sat together in silence for a while, quiet tears running.

When she spoke again, Lyrrin's voice sounded younger than usual. "I thought, maybe for a moment, that we might have Amma back. Alive again."

Riony's chest sagged. "Yeah. Me too."

Dracuni's eyelids fluttered. ***Tried to burn. Tried to help. Didn't know who body was.***

"It's okay. You stopped *it* hurting me. It wasn't really our mother."

Still sorry. Still bad. Dracuni remained unmoving, her thoughts muffled. She seemed so very weak, barely able to move.

Running a hand over Dracuni's snout, Riony said, "I'm sorry I didn't come back sooner."

"She just needs rest. There was nothing you needed to do. Aishena and Niskina are handling everything." Lyrrin looked over Riony's shoulder.

"They are?" Turning, Riony saw then what the two other young women were doing with the branches and logs they'd dragged down near the water's edge.

They were building a pyre.

It wasn't neat, created from stacks of dried brambles and straw, overlaid with already half-burned timbers that had been part of the destroyed town hall. Lying on top was a body shrouded in blue cloth.

Aishena caught sight of Riony and strode up the quarry slope. There was a firmness to her steps that had been missing since they'd left the undercity, and despite the pained expression on her face, she stood tall.

"I only know Taenish funeral customs, but Niskina said she remembers blue was the color used for her mother."

Jogging up to join them, Niskina took a deep breath, wiped her eyes, and smiled. "I hope it's okay. We wanted this to be right for you."

"For me?" Riony swallowed.

"Lyrrin told us you didn't get to say goodbye properly last time. And it's hard ... not getting to say goodbye. It doesn't matter how long it has been," Aishena said.

She pulled Yoskar's glasses from her pocket and held them in a tight fist at her chest. "That doesn't excuse that we've been so caught up in our own grief that we have been making you carry us for so long."

Riony tried to reply, but her throat felt gummed closed.

Niskina knelt in front of her. "We're going to do better. I'm sorry. I've only been thinking about myself, and you're always so strong, I never saw your pain. But we're here for you."

Riony felt as though she should be mortified, humiliated that everyone was seeing her at her weakest. Instead, she felt warm and cared for and lighter than she had in a long time.

"Blue is perfect."

"These are the best I could find." Benjin ran over, flushed and panting with dried leaves stuck in his hair.

He handed Riony a bouquet of stringy stems, spotted with a rainbow of modest flowers.

"Thank you." A soft smile grew on Riony's lips.

It looked like he'd picked every flowering plant he could find, and in doing so had, he collected herbs and weeds that Riony had learned all the names and properties of from her mother. Placing flowers on a pyre was a Taenish custom, rather than Rolanian, but it seemed right.

"Are you ready?" Aishena asked, head bowed.

Riony groaned up to her feet. "We'll find out soon."

Lyrrin didn't follow. Her hood was off, and the bright blue of her natural hair sparkled along her hairline. Both of her gloves were off too, and Riony realized how comfortable she had gotten around the others, how nice it was that Lyrrin could show herself to them and be accepted.

"Are you coming?"

Lyrrin shook her head. "I think I'll watch from here. I want to stay with Dracuni. Yes, I'm sure."

I rest. Dracuni whiffled.

It wasn't far to where the pyre was built, near the water's edge farther along from the swings. Lyrrin and Dracuni would still see everything, hear everything. Riony would have liked to have had Lyrrin by her side, but at the same time needed the space for herself.

Aishena said quietly, like an apology, "The others are in there too, underneath. So they can all be burned."

Riony nodded. That was important. The dead must be burned. She tried not to think of them as revs sharing in her mother's funeral. They were likely other people from her village. Riony hadn't looked at any of them long enough to try to identify them. She refused to speculate on who they were. But they'd all been people once. They all deserved a funeral too.

Riony placed the bouquet over the blue-draped body, and Aishena stepped forward. With a look to Riony for approval, she placed Yoskar's glasses atop the pyre.

Riony gave her a single firm nod, and Aishena let out a long breath.

Beside them, Benjin had the burn rune on his staff lit and held it out, waiting for Riony to take it.

She hesitated, unsure whether they should light the pyre, whether it might attract attention. But fires were common in Elundrae, and she could see that she wasn't the only one who needed this funeral to move on.

Taking the staff, she thrust the brand-hot crystal into a tuft of straw and watched it light.

They all stood in silence as the flames licked around the edges of the blue fabric, growing stronger until the pyre was ablaze in brilliant heat.

"I don't remember enough from my mother's funeral to know what to say," Niskina whispered. "I could speak delver rights, if you like?"

"That's okay. I know what to say." Riony's mouth felt dry. She didn't remember the exact words, but she knew the meaning of what to express deep in her core.

Sunset had only begun to tint the horizon and the sky above had turned a deep cornflower blue. A single star pricked through the smoky expanse, shining down early.

Riony didn't have a candle to hold as she spoke, so she pulled a thin stick from the fire's edge, holding it upright so the small flame flickered before her.

"My love to those who rise to find their way home. The candles will guide you, the bright points in the sky, held by our ancestors, our family gone before. My love to you as you hold your own candle in the sky and wait for us, those you've left behind." Riony stuttered over the words and tears spilled from her eyes.

She looked into the light of the burning stick she held, then up into the sky. "Keep your candles burning bright. We will be together again."

"That was beautiful." Niskina sniffed and wrapped her arms around Riony.

Even within Niskina's tight embrace, Riony felt as though she was breathing easier than she had in a while.

They stood together for a long time as the fire roared and crackled and then stepped back as the heat grew too intense.

Aishena stood at attention, the flames reflected in her glistening dark eyes as she stared at the pyre.

She blinked slowly, then turned to Riony. "We thought we would stay here tonight, but we can move on again tomorrow if you want."

"Move on? Where?"

"Anywhere that's not here if you don't want to be here. We'd understand." Looking back up the slope to where Lyrrin cradled Dracuni, Aishena continued, "We could have left tonight if Dracuni was up to it, but she's too big to be carried now."

From the dreamy, calm sensations Riony was getting from Dracuni, she could tell the young dragon was already asleep. And she clearly needed the rest.

Riony had a vague memory of Kess telling her how some types of dragon had flammable blood, and it was that blood they breathed, spraying and igniting from their mouths. It was why snowflames had such a short lifespan, with their concentrated liquid fire.

That worried Riony.

"We'll stay as long as Dracuni needs to recover fully. And then ..." Riony looked up over the cottages, the untended gardens spilling over their raised beds, the tall palisade walls.

There were painful memories there, both old and fresh, but also a sense that this was home. And maybe it could be again.

"We'll see if we can make a home here. There don't seem to be any other revs. We can fix the palisade. We could be safe."

"You don't have to stay here for us. Only if you're okay with it," Aishena insisted again.

Riony smirked. "I'd be more okay with it if you decided we could share a cottage together. Maybe a bed? I'm in tremendous need of comforting."

"And there she is again." Aishena rolled her eyes, but a small smile shifted her lips. "It's good to have you back."

Riony shrugged bashfully. "It's good to be back."

And for a moment, Riony felt it, that promise of safety, a place where they could stop running, a place that could be a home, and her heart itself seemed to sigh.

And then the sound of dragon wings filled the air.

CHAPTER TWENTY-FIVE

Riony closed her eyes for a single second, hoping it was only her imagination. Or the roar of fire. Distant thunder. An oversized bird. She'd even take the shadowdragon itself, although she knew its wings made no such sound.

Please let it be anything—anything other than that purple dragon.

She looked up, and there it was, swooping down toward them. Kife's dragon, holding two riders and the wolf in its front claws. Gusts from the dragon's wings stirred up the pyre, sending sparks skittering across the rocky ground.

It felt like a nightmare after having just woken up from one. They had nowhere to run. The nearest shrine was hours away. There were no trees to block the dragon from landing. And it was heading directly for Lyrrin and Dracuni, sitting together on the clear ground.

"How did they find us?" Niskina cried. She turned from side to side, searching as well for a sanctuary that wasn't there.

The wolf prints. It must have been Kess at the waterfall. But she would have had plenty of time and opportunity to have killed Riony then and come right here afterward. Why did it take so long?

Why would Kess choose not to take her advantage while Riony was so vulnerable?

She couldn't understand, but she could go crazy trying to understand that nasty girl's motivations. Maybe she chose not to end Riony then so that Riony could be witness to Kess's success in capturing Dracuni now. That didn't seem like Kess, though. She was driven, selfish, but not necessarily cruel.

Perhaps she'd spent too long with Kife, and he'd twisted away any humanity she had left.

Either way, they were there now, and they were going for Dracuni. Riony glared up at the tiny figures riding high upon the dragon's back, silhouetted against the dusk.

You don't have her yet.

They had nowhere to go. But they could still fight.

Scanning her eyes across the ground to the place where she'd dropped it, Riony couldn't see her weapon anywhere. "Where's my sword?"

"Beside the swings!" Aishena barked, breaking out her athames, her eyes on the approaching giant.

While it was still far higher than seemed safe, the dragon's front claws snapped open, releasing the wolf. He whined as he dropped through the air, and there was a cracking thump as he landed behind the overgrown gardens. Voices rose from the dragon's back, lost in the wind and thwumping beat of wings.

Riony found her sword with her eyes, leaning up against the triangular struts of the swings, and she ran for it as the dragon curved around in a tight banking turn, one wingtip touching the ground.

The purple beast straightened up again, claws out, diving at Dracuni and Lyrrin.

"Come on! Come on!" Lyrrin was on her feet now, bending over Dracuni with her arms around the unidragon's torso, trying to lift her.

Dracuni's legs slipped weakly against the hard ground, unable to stay upright.

Riony snatched up her sword without stopping, dragging it as she raced on. The heavy edge clattered and chipped along the rock-hard ground. She traced a finger over the rune without looking, eyes ahead as she tried to ignore the stabbing pains in her stomach and sting in her arms.

She had to get to Lyrrin and Dracuni in time. She was too far away and the dragon too close.

Aishena got there first. "Let go!"

"No!" Lyrrin screamed back.

Aishena was stronger, pulling Lyrrin down into a tackle, rolling beneath the sharp talons that cut through the air. The wide purple wings thrust outward, slowing the dragon's dive.

Dracuni bleated, snout drooping, paws scrambling weakly as the purple etherdart collected her into the cage of its huge claws.

Sister, help!

"Dracuni!" Riony's bare feet slapped over stone.

She had no armor on, and as her sword glowed into life, lifting weightless in her hands, the purple light shimmered across a fresh spill of blood from her waist. Cold sweat broke out over her forehead and neck, and she bit her tongue as though that could help her ignore every other pain.

They had Dracuni. They had her. She couldn't stop.

The dragon banked around again, hovering low across the ground as its wings worked hard to raise it into the air. From the saddle, Kife grinned down, clapping his hands in a slow rhythm as though in appreciation of a performance.

Riony expected to see the same smug expression on his sister as well, but she only looked pale and small, crouched behind Kife.

They were still close enough that Riony could see a deep frown etched between Kess's brows. Still close enough to reach.

With a mighty cry, Riony launched from her sprint into a flying leap. She put every bit of strength she had into her legs, her feet, springing from the hard ground. The magic of her sword carried her, higher and higher than she'd ever been able to jump on her own.

She angled the sword as she flew, ready to direct it into a slashing cut across the dragon's front legs. She would make it drop Dracuni. Maybe she could bring it down entirely.

But then the dragon beat its wing and it swept through the air, blocking Riony's soaring path. The sword stuck into the filmy leather, slicing a thin slash and tangling into the tissue.

Riony hit the thick, muscular structure of the wing across her middle, bending in two from momentum, and lost her grip on her sword. She screamed at the impact against her already aching wounds.

Then the wing lifted in a powerful motion, flicking Riony and her sword free.

Riony tumbled in the air, a heavy weight bound to gravity with no magic to soften her fall. Before she could even tell what side was up or down or think *oh sparks, I'm falling, how far am I—*

Her back hit the ground. The impact shuddered up through her spine and her head lolled back, cracking on the bare stone of the quarry.

Riony gasped through the daggers that filled her chest and the darkness that filled her eyes. Her head throbbed and swirled, and acid stung her throat.

Her sword clinked lightly down somewhere behind her.

The dragon beat its torn wing, rising slowly, awkwardly, higher and higher. It flew up into the sky above and the candle-lit stars that sprinkled through the dusk, and it took Dracuni with it.

When smoke rose from the direction of the village, Kess's stomach dropped.

She'd been lying on her back, feigning sleep despite it being too early, despite the war of emotions in her head keeping her starkly awake.

Maybe Kife wouldn't notice. Maybe …

"Hey, do you see that?" He sat up from his reclined position, hand over his forehead as he squinted into the sky.

"It's probably just a nearby rev burn." Kess's heart beat too fast, and her voice caught.

Her decision not to get rid of Riony at the waterfall would amount to nothing if the idiot had gone and lit a massive fire. Kess didn't want to go and find out what was burning. It couldn't be good.

"It seems to be coming from the village. I'm going to check it out."

He was up and climbing into the saddle before Kess could object.

"Wait for me." Kess scrambled, hugging Griskin as the wolf pulled them both up off the ground in a fluid roll.

She raced Griskin over to the dragon's side. Kife already had the dragon's wings stretched and beating as she clambered up into the seat behind him, gasping at the effort.

"Don't leave Griskin!"

"We're not going far."

Kess was about to buckle herself to the saddle but instead made a show of reaching for one of her knives. "Bring him."

Kife rolled his eyes as he brought his flight goggles down. "Yeah, yeah, I'll bring your smelly mutt."

They flew, and as they soared over the forest and the village came within sight, it was clear what was burning.

"It's a funeral pyre," Kess yelled over the wind.

For whom? Who'd died? Who had Riony lost that had left her so broken?

Would anyone ever feel that way if they lost me?

"Who cares? There's the creature!" Kife pointed.

In Kess's wind-blown eyes, the figures below were blurry smudges, but she could see the silvery rainbow scales sparkling in the firelight.

Kife aimed the dragon down.

"What are you doing? We can't attack now. It's a funeral!" Kess hissed. "Where's your honor?"

"We can have all the honor we want after we have the silvernix-bleeding creature!"

And then they had her. They had Dracuni in the dragon's clutches, and it was over.

Kess's breath came in short, desperate pants.

Kife had dropped Griskin from far too high. Riony had struck the dragon's wing—*the fool! Why did she throw herself into the air like that? Against a dragon?*—and had hit the ground hard.

But they had Dracuni.

But it didn't feel right.

But what could she do?

They had Dracuni but it felt like everything she wanted was being lost.

"You can't … You can't leave Griskin behind!" Kess cried out.

The dragon hovered for a moment just above the ground, torn wing working hard.

"The wolf? It doesn't matter. We don't need the dumb dog anymore." Kife smiled over his shoulder, then turned halfway around in his saddle. "And now that I think about it, I don't need you anymore either."

No. Kess scrambled for the strap holding her to the saddle that she hadn't done up in their brief flight.

With a sweep of his arm, Kife shoved her and she tumbled off the dragon's back.

Again. Thrown away by her brother again, but this time it came as no surprise. She'd expected this betrayal from the start. And as she rolled down the length of the dragon's outstretched wing, she felt as though it was everything she deserved.

The wing lowered, and Kess clawed at the leather through sheer self-preservation, then slid off the wingtip.

There was a moment of free fall before she rolled across the ground, elbows and hips knocking in the tumble.

The dragon lifted into the sky, taking Kife and Dracuni away with it, and leaving Kess at the mercy of all those she'd betrayed in turn.

She didn't even bother lifting herself from the ground.

There was crying, yelling. The kid Riony called her sister was fighting with the Hjelzahn girl. The younger brother tried to hold her back. The pyre still burned.

It wasn't long before an imposing length of glowing crystal was pointed at her.

"You did this!" Riony stood above Kess, her face pale and twisted with ferocity. The sword wavered in her grip then steadied.

"I know," Kess replied.

Riony shook her head, wincing her eyes closed for a long moment.

"You ..." She grunted. "Why didn't you ... You were at the waterfall?"

"I'm sorry," Kess said.

"Sorry?" Riony sounded like she'd been told trees grew gold.

She flicked her head again, as though she were trying to shake water from her ears. "I told you! I told you he would do this. You're only getting what you deserve."

"I know."

"Stop saying that!" Riony roared.

There was a low growl nearby and more shouting. "Keep it back!"

Kess turned her head from where she lay. *Griskin.*

He pounced from side to side, snapping at the glowing blades and crystal-studded staff holding him at bay. He favored one side, hurt but alive.

He'd survived. That was all Kess needed to know. And he would continue to survive, and he'd be better off without her.

"I'm sorry," Kess said again, eyes on her wolf.

She would have liked to have said goodbye properly, told him to leave and get away before he was also punished for her mistakes. But those two words would have to be enough.

"He took Dracuni!" One of Riony's legs went out from beneath her, and she pulled herself back up again quickly.

The falter brought the tip of the sword right up against Kess's neck, and she swallowed.

This was it. This was what all her dreams and scheming and battles had come to. Never destined to fly. Never deserving, for all the pain she'd caused along the way in pursuit of what she'd thought was owed to her. How did she ever think she belonged in the sky?

It seemed right, after all, to die at Riony's hands. At least it wasn't Kife who'd ended her.

"Do it," Kess said. "Do it and be rid of me. Do it, *Pony.*"

Riony screamed, and it came out as a harsh scratch of air. Her hands around the sword tightened and the blade lifted.

The bright-eyed, pale-skinned child was there. Not Riony's real sister but loved more than Kess ever had been.

She grabbed at Riony's arm. "Don't! It won't fix anything."

Riony's head swayed from side to side, lolling freely on her neck. "She'll never stop, Lyrrin. She'll never ..."

"You're bleeding!" Lyrrin's voice was high and crackling. "Put the sword down, please! Just stop."

Kess saw it then too. Twin dark trickles, running down Riony's neck from her ears. The thick bloom staining her shirt at her waist, growing rapidly larger.

Riony shook her head again as though refusing, denying the reality of everything around her, and the sword lowered in her grip.

Then her eyes rolled back to whites, and she folded into a limp pile on the ground.

Chapter Twenty-Six

Kess couldn't see whether Riony was alive or dead as her body was immediately surrounded by four others. Kess tried to move forward, but the fear that she would see Riony lifeless and gone locked her joints, and the cold grip of death seemed to wrap around Kess's own heart.

"What happened?" The woman that Kess didn't know the name of blocked the view with her curvy back.

"She hit the ground really hard. I heard her head crack," Lyrrin said in a high, whining pitch. "And she's bleeding, a lot."

Through a small gap, Kess saw the Hjelzahn girl pressing splayed fingers across Riony's neck and skull. "Oh no, oh no."

"What is it?" the boy asked.

"It's not good." Aishena laid Riony's head carefully back onto the rocky ground again, then straightened her body into a more comfortable position and pushed the large sword to the side.

As she lifted the bottom hem of Riony's shirt, her chest heaved up and down. "She's tough though. She could make it. She's going to make it."

Still alive then. But maybe not for long.

"What do we do? We don't … we don't have Dracuni." The curvy girl whispered the last part despite everyone being close enough to hear.

A soft snout brushed Kess's ear, her own chest heaving with ragged breaths as well. Drawn like a lost traveler to a guiding light, Kess reached her arms around Griskin's fur in a subconscious reflex while her eyes remained locked on the others. The wolf's body was low to the ground beside her, and she hefted herself up into the saddle.

"We should have kept some, bottled some of Dracuni's blood, just in case," the Hjelzahn boy said.

"Riony would never have allowed it." Aishena's eyes flitted across the multitude of scratches and flowing wounds, and she had her fingers clutched around one of Riony's wrists. "We have bandages, herbs. We can try … to make her comfortable."

From her raised position on Griskin, Kess could look down at those kneeling on the ground and the motionless body of Riony between them. Still and far too pale. The blood from her ears had smudged into a red streak across her cheek from Aishena's hands. She wasn't responding to the little sister's constant calling of her name.

Kess brought Griskin a step closer.

The curvy girl snatched Riony's sword, still glowing, off the ground and waved it in the air between them. "Get back!"

"I can—"

"What? Gloat? Betray us again? Which of us are you going to kill next?" She advanced, swinging the sword with each thrust of her words.

Griskin dodged back. "I'm trying to—"

"Nisk! Bandages. We need them now if we're going to stop this bleeding!"

Nisk grunted fiercely at Kess, a final warning, then turned and ran for a building nearby where a few packs were piled together.

Kess reached into the small hidden pouch under the front of her saddle and moved around toward the gap that Nisk had left. "I have—"

"Stay back, Kess! We don't have anything left for you to take from us." Aishena glared up at Kess and Griskin, unflinching despite her proximity to the wolf's mouth. "Be grateful that we don't have time for you or the vengeance you have coming your way."

Yellow light illuminated in one of her hands, a glowing knife, like the one Kess had used to slice through stone. She and Griskin dodged back again.

This was ridiculous. Riony was running out of time. Bandages and herbs weren't going to do anything. Kess had seen a guard fall from the walls of Heithorn estate once, seen the bleeding ears, seen the soft spot on the back of his head. He'd been dead before they could even debate if it was worth opening the family vault to save him with silvernix.

Nisk returned with a bundle of gauze, and she knelt across from Aishena, shuffling around the others to get closer to Riony's middle.

The sister stood up to give Nisk more space, and with a huff of desperation, Kess spurred Griskin into a pounce.

In a flash of fur, she had the child pulled up against the side of the wolf, a slim bone dagger to her throat.

"Stop and—"

"Let her go! Don't you dare hurt her." Aishena sprung from the ground, tracing her feet across the ground into a fighting stance.

"I'm not going to! I'm trying to get you to listen so—"

"Let go of me!" The girl shrieked and wriggled. Her hands lashed at Kess's grip.

The tips of her fingers dug and sliced into the thick hide bracers around Kess's forearms, snapping free the throwing daggers held there. They clattered onto the ground.

Razed earth, how are her fingers so sharp? Kess hissed but didn't let go.

Nisk circled around behind Griskin, Riony's glowing sword held high. "What cruel trick are you trying to pull now? Did your brother leave you behind to finish the rest of us off?"

She was being surrounded, and Riony was still bleeding.

Raising her voice over the accusations and interruptions, Kess bellowed, "I have silvernix!"

A silence followed, dark glares and confused faces all around until Kess held the tiny vial up for display.

She was glad she'd stolen it back from her brother late one night. Even then, she knew he'd betray her, so it only made sense to betray him in advance and take back what was hers.

"Hand it over," Aishena commanded.

"Not going to happen." Kess closed her fist back around the miniscule bottle.

She wasn't trusting anybody else with this. She couldn't.

Aishena's face became more furious than before. "I hope you're ready to trade your life for it then because we have nothing left you'd want to trade."

"The only thing I want is for you to *get out of my way!*" Kess pushed the child free from her grip and marched Griskin forward.

It seemed as though Aishena was determined to play chicken, holding her ground until the last second before swearing and stepping aside.

Riony still hadn't moved. Kess's chest clenched like it was being squeezed with a dragon's claws at the thought it might be too late. She slid down off Griskin and sat beside the wounded woman.

"What if she's just getting close to finish Ri off?" Nisk asked. "This has to be some kind of trick."

Aishena circled around, keeping a close eye on Kess. "Don't try anything."

"If I wanted her dead, all I'd have to do is wait." Kess touched two trembling fingers to Riony's neck and found a struggling pulse. She sighed shakily.

"Well, if you were going to help her, you could have just said so," the sister glowered.

"If any of you had listened to me, maybe I wouldn't have had to point a knife at a child." Kess glowered back and carefully cracked the seal on the tiny vial.

"I'm still not sure I believe you are going to help her," Nisk snarled.

Kess ignored her, turning her face to Riony's. She wasn't entirely sure she could believe it either.

But sacrificing her silvernix for this felt like only a trivial loss amongst many when Kess already had so little left. No dragon, no wealth. No hopes, no dreams, no goals. No family, no friends, no love.

Saving the life of the only person who'd ever shown her even the dawning light of kindness or caring was the least she could do, after every suffering Riony had taken on her behalf. After all Kess's mistakes.

Kess tipped the vial, letting the single, glistening drop of iridescent fluid spill onto Riony's lips.

The bickering and threats turned to silence as everyone watched and waited.

A flush of starlight glow glimmered over Riony's bronzed skin. Her eyes remained closed, but her mouth opened in a silent gasp and then a roaring wail.

Her back arched up suddenly and her chest collided with Kess, still bending over her. Kess pressed her hands onto Riony's shoulders as she bucked and writhed. She wasn't strong enough to keep the larger woman pinned, so she slid her hands beneath Riony's head to stop her from cracking it on the hard stone ground all over again.

Kess knew that the pain of being pulled back together by that magic was almost as great as the original wound.

Brilliant light shimmered all around them, pulsing through Riony's flesh as the unicorn blood mended every scratch and gaping hole, every bruise and fracture.

With her hands scooped around the wild hair and small pigtail at the back, Kess was close enough to see the few strands of silver spreading through the red.

How many times had Riony come close to death and been healed by silvernix now? In the dragon's nest cave, in the glass factory, now … Any other times?

Enough that it was starting to show just as Kess's hair was streaked with the stains of her parents' attempts to fix her.

Too many times.

Slowly, the light dimmed, and Riony stilled.

Kess suddenly found she was terrified, shaking and sweating and far, far, far too close to this woman who only moments ago had been going to kill her. A woman who could probably snap her in half if the desire took her.

But before she could back away, Riony's eyes snapped open.

Taking in Kess's close proximity, Riony's expression was of pure horror. "What in the starless depths is going on?"

Kess sneered. "You idiot. You almost killed yourself. You always act too ready to die."

"What? Why do you care?"

"Because *you* have people who don't want you to die." Kess shifted her weight off Riony and gestured to the four standing around them.

There was a rush of agreement and then a flail of limbs as the little sister flung herself in first, right onto Riony's lap, toppling her back down again as she tried to sit up. Aishena and Nisk helped pull Riony upright again, then wrapped their arms around her in a hug as well.

The boy patted Riony awkwardly on the knee before she grabbed him by the scruff of the neck and dragged him into the huddle too.

Kess turned to Griskin, her only anchor to life, and pulled herself into the saddle.

There was a flurry of low voices behind her, blending into one long string of sound, half the words lost under others.

"Kife took Dracuni."

"I know. I remember."

"Wasn't sure. Your head—"

"You should have treated the other wounds earlier."

"—brain is still feeling weirdly squishy. What did Kess—?"

"Lucky she had some—"

"Did you force—?"

"No, it wasn't like that."

"Then she grabbed me but—"

"You're kidding me. Why?"

Kess looked over the rocky ground, turning lilac and gray with the falling light. The pyre still burned down near the shore, and Kess wondered again who it was for since everyone she knew that had been traveling with Riony was there, alive still.

All except for Dracuni. She was long gone now, in that dragon's clutches. And everything felt over.

Kess leaned toward Griskin and whispered, "Come on. Let's go."

"You trying to make me regret not dying?"

"It could be the only—"

Riony and her little sister argued in hushed tones.

"It won't—"

"It could!" the small girl pleaded.

There was a low, disgusted grunt and then chasing footsteps pounded toward Kess.

Riony stopped in front of her, expression closed, eyes roaming as if searching for the answer to questions she hadn't asked. "Where are you going?"

"Away."

Blood still marked Riony's face like stripes of war paint, and Kess found she couldn't look at it for long.

"If you're going after Dracuni again—"

"I'm not. I'm done. It's over."

"You're giving up? Now?" Riony laughed without any humor. "Why? Because you got your feelings hurt? Betrayal stings. We both know that, and I *warned you* ..."

Kess leaned away from Riony's words as though they were blows from a sword.

"And now your malevolent turd-breath brother has Dracuni, and you're just going to roll over and let him win? Who even are you? Not Kessara Heithorn, that's for sure."

"What else do you expect me to do?" Kess urged Griskin to continue toward the gate in the palisades.

Riony matched their pace. "What you always do, you relentless, selfish gremlin! *Go after Dracuni* and don't stop until you've got her back!"

"Why would you want that?"

Riony gave a long-suffering sigh. "Because what I was going to say before you interrupted me was if you're going after Dracuni again, we're going with you."

Kess and Griskin stopped.

She couldn't form a response, could hardly comprehend what Riony was saying.

The sharp-clawed sister, the Hjelzahn siblings, and Nisk joined them, flanking Riony with wary expressions.

"With me? Why would you trust me?" They couldn't. They shouldn't. And she couldn't trust them either.

"We don't need a reason." The small girl lifted her hood up to cover her head, and Kess saw her hands more clearly, the sharp, long nails almost as blue as her eyes. "We're just choosing to."

Riony's voice was a low grumble, her eyes averted. "And you saved my life. You didn't have to do that. It earned you ... something. One last chance. Don't sparking blow it this time."

It felt like a trap. Kess could see the wire of the snare laid bare and glinting before her but couldn't turn away. The bait had her transfixed.

One last chance.

For what? What exactly was on offer here? The increasing race of her heart beat a rhythm of hope, but she knew the truth. It was one last chance to be used by this group of people to retrieve the prize, the same as she'd been used by her brother. And then discarded.

"That only sounds fair," Kess muttered.

"So will you help us, then?" Lyrrin asked, almost brightly.

"We have more of a chance of getting Dracuni back with you. Help us save her." Riony looked like she was swallowing a spinerat covered in manure. "Please."

That one word shook Kess. She knew Riony was desperate to get her dragonling back, but why all of this? Why was she even standing here, asking Kess for help instead of charging off like a battering ram?

The young girl's eyes flickered down to Griskin, giving him a gentle look, much kinder than the way any of them looked at Kess.

Kess's heart seemed to turn to stone and drop into her stomach. That was it. They wanted Griskin. Only Griskin. They needed a way to move faster. A way to track. They didn't want her.

It didn't matter. But it still hurt with a sharp, all too familiar pain.

"Fine. I'll help," Kess agreed, knowing she was answering on behalf of her wolf.

And they would help. They'd both do what they could.

But even with Griskin's speed, how were they going to catch up to a dragon?

CHAPTER TWENTY-SEVEN

Riony was filled with more emotions than she knew what to do with, and they were each screaming for her attention.

Her mother's body still burned in the dwindling embers of the pyre.

Dracuni had been taken. She was already too far away to hear her thoughts, but Riony could still *feel* her and her panic, like a string tied between their hearts pulled taut.

And Riony had almost died. And although that didn't seem very novel anymore, it was still freshly terrifying each time. She'd thrown herself bodily at her problems again and been swatted by a dragon. She should have known better. Her luck was going to run out at some point. But *Dracuni was taken.*

And it seemed somehow, in a complete slap in the face to reason, that it was Kess who had saved her, and through all the other noise in her head, Riony couldn't work out the angle. Did Kess just think she needed Riony to achieve her goals and no doubt also revenge on Kife? Just as Riony now awfully needed Kess if she wanted a chance of saving Dracuni?

But even with the wolf on their side, a rescue seemed hopeless.

"What do we do? How can we catch up to a dragon?" Lyrrin asked, as though voicing the same concern.

"It depends where they will be heading. Where would your brother go?" Aishena snapped at Kess like an interrogation.

"He has a home at Skaellakeep."

Benjin took Aishena's map, checking their shrine locations. "That's the other side of Elundrae, and we don't have any gateways open near there yet."

Riony cleared her throat menacingly as Kess tried to look at their map.

Returning her dull gaze to Riony, Kess said, "But I don't think he'll go there. He couldn't get there in one trip—not with the dragon's wing injured. That's going to slow him down."

"Where then?" Aishena asked.

"He's going to want to tame Dracuni as soon as he can and then probably hole up somewhere, make plans on what to do with his new wealth and work out how to protect that wealth as he builds up a supply of silvernix."

Riony's heart clenched, and she narrowed her eyes at Kess. That must have equally been Kess's plan. "So how can we get to him before he can hurt Dracuni? He could land anywhere and do it."

He could be doing it right now.

Kess shook her head, and a glint of her usual guile showed. "He can't. He doesn't have what he needs for taming. I took the stake and silvernix off him."

Riony and Kess's eyes met as the unspoken words hovered between them—that was the silvernix that had saved Riony's life. Kess looked away first, and Riony stared a moment longer, trying to understand.

Aishena rubbed a finger over her bottom lip and paced. "He may not need silvernix, not with Dracuni, but he will need a stake. He'll try to find somewhere to get one, within flying distance on an injured wing."

"Wouldn't he"—Lyrrin swallowed, her face paler than usual—"use Dracuni's blood to heal his dragon?"

Kess scoffed. "No. He wouldn't even think of it. He doesn't care about the dragon at all. He'll probably keep flying it until its wing is shredded before considering healing it for his own convenience."

"And how long would that be? Where can he get to in that time? Where is he *going?*" Riony's voice grew louder and faster, frantic with everything taking too long.

She picked up her dropped belongings from the ground and pulled her boots on, trying to be prepared and at the same time feeling as though there was nothing she could do.

"He has maybe a few hours' flight. And there's one place he could get to in that time where he might find taming stakes—a place that he knows is otherwise abandoned." Kess kept her eyes averted from Riony's and continued. "Heithorn estate."

"Abandoned?" Riony whispered to herself as she strapped on a bracer.

"Where is that?" Benjin held their map, with its markings and notes on the shrines they'd activated or had settlements at, right up close for Kess to see.

Riony sucked in an annoyed breath but they had to do anything that could hasten retrieving Dracuni, and consequences could be dealt with later.

"There's a shrine right there!" Benjin nearly shouted.

"But we haven't activated it," Lyrrin reminded him.

"Oh. Yeah."

"I suppose it might make sense he'd go that way." Aishena continued her thoughtful ramble.

She took the map herself, narrowed eyes darting over it. "He couldn't risk going to a keep, trading outpost, or smugglers for a taming spike with Dracuni in tow and untamed. He'd be seeking somewhere isolated. But it's still a big assumption. He could equally go somewhere like the glass factory, keep Dracuni in a cage while he sought what he needed."

Riony glanced over the map too and tried to get her bearings, turning herself in the direction of the estate.

It was the direction the dragon had flown. And it was the direction she could feel Dracuni's weakening sense of panic pulling from.

Riony stilled as Niskina helped her to buckle the final strap of her remaining shoulder guard. "We should try the estate, as much as I'd rather pull my eyeballs out and vomit on them than go back there again. But he could be there in a few hours, and it would take us days to get there on foot from the nearest gateway. We'd be too late."

"Just how close is the shrine to Heithorn estate?" Aishena stopped pacing, her brows furrowed deeply over her dark eyes.

"Directly behind the hatchery," Kess answered.

Riony threw her hands up. "It doesn't matter how close it is. It's not activated."

Aishena held up a finger to Riony and kept her interrogation of Kess going. "Would he go to the hatchery to find a taming spike?"

"Probably. Why?"

Aishena turned to Riony then. "Because the gateway could *become* activated."

"Oh." Riony sighed out the word.

Because Dracuni activated the shrines, and Dracuni was being taken to the shrine. Or at least, close enough to it that it might work. The larger Dracuni got, the farther away her effect on empowering the shrines seemed to be.

"That's it then," Aishena said firmly. "We'll split up. Kess will get you to the nearest shrine as fast as possible. Then you'll know soon enough whether Kife is at the estate with Dracuni. And you can travel through and save her."

Kess's eyes narrowed, but she didn't question the hows.

Riony had plenty of questions though. "Me and Kess? Kess and me? You're coming too, right?"

"I've tried to look at this from all angles. My gut is telling me that speed is the most important factor for this mission. It doesn't matter how many of us get there if we get there too late. We need our strongest to get there as fast as possible, and that's you, on the wolf, without any extra weight. The only faster way would be if Kess didn't—"

"No," Kess cut in.

"As I thought." Aishena gave her a sharp glare. "This is the best plan I can think of. Unless there are other ideas, if anyone else wants ... No, I think this is it. We should do this."

Riony took in the hard edges around Aishena's mouth, the tight lift of her shoulders, the worried flicker in her eyes. Aishena, who had distrusted Zade from the start. Who'd known the glass factory was a mistake. Who'd questioned her ability to lead or make decisions despite having the best instincts of all of them.

"It's a good plan. And if you think it will work, it's going to work." Riony took one of Aishena's hands and gave it a squeeze.

Kess made an ugly, unimpressed sound.

"Do you have a better idea?" Riony snapped back. "No? Right. Then we're going. Now."

Lyrrin dashed over, blocking Riony's path to the wolf. "But why? Why does it have to all be on you? More of us should go."

She turned to Aishena, pleading. "I know she's strong but it's too much. We're not supposed to put everything on her anymore, remember?"

"It's not all on Riony. It's her and Kess," Aishena said. "They are both our best options for fighting a dragon and rider. It's not just Riony and her strength and her sword that have a chance of beating Kife. It's also Kess's knowledge of the estate, insight into her brother, and her aim."

Everyone turned to stare at Kess then, and the wolf-riding miscreant seemed unsure whether to shrink and hide in Griskin's fur or show them just how good her aim was.

Lyrrin stepped in front of the wolf, closer than Riony approved of, and glared up at Kess. "You'd better actually help. It's up to you to bring my sister and Dracuni back safe. And if I lose either of them, I will personally make you regret it."

Kess stared down for a long moment before she nodded once. "I don't doubt it."

"Okay, go, and go fast," Aishena said.

Niskina handed Riony's sword to her, still glowing. "We'll keep the kids safe—don't worry. Go and get our Dracuni back."

Riony left the sword activated and strapped it to her back. Griskin lowered down for Riony, and she threw a leg over to slide into the saddle behind Kess. The wolf raised back up, his strong legs tensing and ready to run.

"Wait!" Lyrrin said and raced to Riony's side. She pressed a pulsing stone into Riony's hand. "So I know you're okay. And can you at least *try* not to almost die again?"

"Promise." Riony held her sister's hands in hers for a long breath as she took the paired crystal from her, feeling the beat of her sister's small heart.

Then she tucked the crystal down her shirt so she could keep feeling that thumping rhythm.

"Don't worry." She tilted her head toward Kess and pulled a face. "At least one impossible thing has already happened today, so we've got that on our side."

Then, without a command from Kess that Riony could discern, Griskin burst into motion.

They were at the palisade gates before Riony knew it, and she glanced back one last time at the home she'd lost then returned to, and was leaving again. The fiery glow of sunset lit the cottages as though each of them was a pyre. And she found she was no longer sad—only determined.

She'd lost what she'd lost, and it was the people she loved amongst that loss that mattered, and she didn't want to lose any more. She was going to do anything to get Dracuni back, and the very fact she was on this wolf and riding into battle behind Kess was proof enough of that.

She didn't trust Kess as far as she could throw her, although she enjoyed wondering just how far that might be for a moment.

But Griskin was fast. Even with how he seemed to be favoring one side of his body, he dodged and weaved through the trees faster than Riony could have run. With Riony's sword activated, her weight on the saddle was practically nonexistent. She only had to hold on as Kess sped them toward the shrine.

"Could you maybe scooch forward a bit more?" Riony asked in Kess's ear.

There was no response, but from Kess's silence and the hard angles of her back, she seemed as comfortable with this whole experience as Riony was.

The dwindling thread of panic coming across a great distance from Dracuni kept Riony on edge, but it also settled her. Despite knowing the plan, it felt like they were going in the wrong direction, away from that tugging string. But the sensation also meant that Dracuni was still herself, still thinking. Not yet tamed.

"If this isn't working, I could ride in front. It will make it easier for you to stab me in the back when you're ready," Riony offered.

No reply again. Not even a bite. That disturbed Riony almost as much as the rest of the situation.

Then Kess said, "Duck," and it took Riony almost too long to work out why, barely getting under the low branch that flashed by. They were already out of the woods of thin, straight trees and into a grove of drooping branches and prickly, waxy leaves.

She doesn't really care whether I get a log to the face. She just needs me to open the gateway, to distract her brother while she runs off with Dracuni.

Riony would be ready for the betrayal this time. She wouldn't be blindsided like she had been in the Alderkin depths.

But the way Kess had lain on the ground where she'd been pushed from the dragon's back, the way she'd seemed so ready for death—that had felt real.

Riony leaned close, muttering into Kess's ear, testing, "How did it feel when Kife left you behind again? Did that hurt more or less than knowing I was right about what he'd do to you?"

Again, nothing, even from words so cruel Riony's stomach churned at saying them. There was an almost imperceptible increase in tension across Kess's shoulders, maybe, but it could have been imagined.

Even Riony was furious Kife had left Kess to die a second time. He'd coldheartedly left her in the hands of her enemies to do with as they wished.

Nobody deserved that. Riony hadn't been thinking clearly at the time—half her head had been mashed to pulp, after all—but if she hadn't almost died, Kess would have suffered from her brother's betrayal at Riony's hands.

And Kess hadn't seemed to care.

Once, when they were kids, Riony had snapped. Gotten Kess by the throat. Even if she'd thought she could have gotten away with being a slave that murdered the Heithorns' only daughter, she hadn't really considered *killing* Kess. She'd just been angry and dumb.

And then Kess had told her to do it. She'd almost begged her to do it.

That lapse passed as quickly as it came. Both of them were somehow so horrified at those few moments of wild, brokenhearted fury shared between them that there was an immediate, unspoken agreement to pretend it had never happened.

This time seemed different. The girl riding in front of her on the wolf seemed like an entirely unknown entity. Riony had never known Kess to be without a persistent, driving goal to win no matter what, by her own means, to her own ends.

Riony didn't push her again. They rode in silence as night darkened the world around them. Griskin foamed and panted, stopping once by a small stream to drink before racing on. Kess leaned forward a couple of times, brushing encouraging hands over his ears in a way so tender that Riony again wondered who this person she rode with was.

Their way was brightened only by the glow of Riony's sword, but Griskin moved with confidence. It felt like both mere moments and an eternity passed as they rode. Still, that far away sensation of Dracuni's emotions called out across the distance, giving her hope. And Lyrrin's heartbeat pounded next to hers.

And then the standing stones of the shrine came into view and then the crumbling building within.

Griskin leaped between the tall pillars of crystal-streaked stone and into the central structure. The geode stood before them.

Riony slid off the wolf and crouched over the rune, tracing it quickly and out of sight of Kess. The gateway shimmered to life, all the symbols of other gateways they'd unlocked before lighting up around the ring.

And no new ones.

"What if he went somewhere else?" Panic clutched Riony around the throat.

"He might not be there yet. We made good time." Kess brought Griskin closer on soft paws.

Riony flinched away, but with an expressionless face, Kess pointed to a sigil halfway up the geode. "It would be this one."

"How do you know?"

"Each shrine is marked with their symbol." Kess looked at her like she was an idiot. She pointed to the doorway where, above the archway, the symbol for this gateway was carved in amongst etchings of unicorns and lilies.

Riony felt like an idiot. She'd never noticed. No wonder Kife and Kess had been able to track them so easily.

"Then we wait for that one to light up." Riony focused back on the geode, as though if she stared hard enough, she could will it to activate.

"If it doesn't soon, we should consider our next—"

"It will." Riony paced, turning her head to keep her eyes locked on the symbol. "Aishena is right as often as she's hot."

"Never?"

Riony threw her a sardonic look. *That* got a bite out of her?

She was going to see how deep she could rub that salt, but when she turned back to the geode again, her breath caught.

The symbol flickered, then lit with a glow as bright as the others.

"Yes! I told you!" Riony crowed and slapped the symbol. Light washed over her and the view through the jagged oval changed.

Heithorn estate.

Riony stepped one leg through. Kess didn't join her.

Frowning, Kess patted Griskin's ears again. It seemed like a subconscious action, as comforting to her as to the wolf. "Is it safe?"

"You've seen me go through plenty of times."

"You choosing to do something isn't a signifier that it is safe."

"Would I have taken Lyrrin and Dracuni and the others through if it wasn't?"

Kess seemed to chew over that like a piece of gristle, then moved to follow Riony through the magical portal.

They stepped out together on the other side.

Griskin sniffed at the air and gave a low growl.

"They're here. Can you make that ridiculous sword less bright? We should approach carefully," Kess said.

Riony pulled her sword into her hands and brushed her finger over the rune to deactivate it, and the purple glow faded away to nothing.

The Alderkin shrine on Heithorn estate was much like Riony remembered it. The simple stone building had shelving against every wall, packed with old farming tools and moldy canvas.

The back wall of the hatchery ran right up against the Alderkin structure on one side, the entryway opening out onto a small field within the estate's walls.

"Are you as excited as I am about the harm we're about to inflict on Kife?" Riony whispered as she followed Kess and Griskin, prowling carefully around to the hatchery entrance.

"Shh!" Kess scolded, then looked her up and down disapprovingly. "Can't you move any quieter?"

As they rounded the corner, it didn't matter how quiet they were being. Kife was being loud enough to cover any approach.

The dragon-sized front doors to the hatchery stood wide open. Riony and Kess slid into position beside them, daring quick glances around the edge.

A fire burned in a brazier in the center of the barn, creating a flickering dance of light and dark.

Kife had his back to them. He pulled a drawer out of a storage cupboard and tipped the contents onto the ground, then tossed the drawer after it, the timber smashing.

Swearing loudly, he swiped an arm across a shelf, searching and clearing as he went, knocking metal canisters and feed bowls down in a clanging chorus.

His dragon loomed over him, a foreboding backdrop staring blindly toward the door, and at its feet lay Dracuni.

She was on her side, legs and snout wrapped roughly in old rope.

Kife turned, and Riony ducked back behind the wall again.

I'm here. I'm here! Riony tried to force her thoughts through to the unidragon.

Sister? The returning thought was weak, but it came through. It was a reply. Dracuni had heard her.

You'll be safe again soon. *Somehow.* Riony hoped Dracuni didn't hear that last part of her thought.

Hurts.

Riony edged around to look again.

And she saw it—two knives lodged into Dracuni's front leg at opposing angles, spreading the skin beneath them, and a glass bottle tucked into the rope beneath them, slowly filling with shimmering liquid.

Riony's own blood turned cold. Dracuni was already weak from flaming. She couldn't take this. There was no way Kife could know that, but to bleed the dragonling at all drove Riony into a frenzy. She didn't even realize she was marching forward until Kess grabbed her by the shirt and pulled her back behind their cover of the wall.

"He'll see you!" Kess hissed. "There's too far to go. He'll see you before you reach him, and if he orders his dragon to flame, we're done!"

"He's bleeding her!" Riony rasped back. She glanced quickly around the open door again, seeing the dragon aimed directly for them.

Kess snatched her hand reflexively away from where it was still clutching Riony's shirt. "We need to do something about the dragon first while Kife's not on it. He hasn't found a stake yet. We've still got time to work out a plan."

"Aha! Finally!" Kife bellowed. He pulled a thin spike of shining steel from a wooden crate and flipped it in the palm of his hand.

Lifting a mallet from a pile of tools on the ground, Kife strolled toward Dracuni, whistling a Taen anthem of triumph.

Riony drew and activated her sword. "We just ran out of time."

R iony had seen a taming ceremony before, and there wasn't much *ceremony* about it. A steel stake was hammered into a dragon's skull, and that was that. Dragonlords only called it a 'ceremony' to make themselves feel special about the barbaric process.

And Riony only had however long it would take Kife to walk from one side of the hatchery to the other to work out how to stop him from doing that to Dracuni.

Kife on his own didn't worry Riony. He was a fair swordsman but was only human. It was the purple etherdart, sitting idle and tame, awaiting his orders that was the problem.

She and Kess were about as far away from the dragon as Kife was.

At least they had the element of surprise. Kife had no reason to believe they could get there as fast as they had. He remained completely casual and unalert as he pulled a bottle from his pocket and doused the end of the stake in iridescent liquid.

Staring at Dracuni, Kife muttered, "You're such a weird and ugly little dragon. It doesn't matter, though, when your blood is so very beautiful."

He'd already filled another bottle? *Dracuni, I'm so sorry.*

Riony gauged the distance between her and the unidragon and the way the big dragon was aimed right at them and could burn them the second Kife spotted them. She could race to get to the dragon first. But what then?

Riony had an idea that made her question how well silvernix repaired injured brains.

But she was out of time. She had to act, now.

"Sparks, this is the worst idea I've had in my life. Are you ready?" Riony reached over and wrapped one arm around Kess's waist, lifting her off Griskin's back into a close hold against her chest. She adjusted her grip on the glowing sword in her other hand.

"What ... what are you going to do?" Kess balked, going rigid in Riony's hold.

"I'm going to give you everything you ever wanted."

Riony turned away too quickly to know for sure whether Kess's cheeks flushed a deep red. And she had no time to consider any horrific ramifications behind that reaction. She burst into motion, bringing the two of them into the hatchery in a dash.

Kife's stroll became a disjointed stumble as he spotted them. "How in the razing ...?"

Riony ignored him, sprinting toward the purple etherdart. Then, with a roaring cry, she kicked off the ground with a strong thrust of her legs, and she and Kess flew. The magic of the sword lifted them, and they sailed in an arc through the shadowy hatchery.

The moment of confusion passed, and Kife sprung to action. "Fire! FIRE!"

His dragon's chest and neck convulsed, and its jaws dropped open. The crackle of fire rushed forth as it spewed a blazing sphere straight ahead.

Riony pulled her knees up, bringing Kess's legs with them, and the flames licked across her toes as they hurtled over the blaze. At the barn doors, Griskin whined, ducking low, and the fireball shot over him and out into the night.

Riony and Kess sailed over the dragon's head, and in a clatter, landed unevenly on its back. With her hands full, Riony braced her thighs around its scaly spine to stop them from slipping right back off again.

Then she lifted Kess and placed her into the dragon's saddle.

Kess made a face like an owl. "You ... you want me to ...?"

"You *can* control it, right? Oh, sparks. Don't tell me you've wanted a dragon all this time but don't know how to ride one!"

It was a risk, a huge one, giving Kess control of a dragon. If Riony had the first idea how to control it herself, she'd be the one in the saddle, snatching Dracuni and flying off without either of the terrible Heithorn siblings. But Kess in the dragon's seat was infinitely better than Kife.

The thin bridge of Kess's nose scrunched, and she spat, "Of course I know how!"

"Then congratulations. It's all yours. Please don't kill me in return." Riony flung her leg over from where she'd straddled the dragon's back and slid down the scales of its shoulder, landing with a soft thunk at its feet.

Dracuni was only a few steps away. Kife flung the stake and hammer down and raced toward the dragonling. Riony ran to beat him there. He drew his sword. Riony blocked his path with hers. Metal clanged against hardened crystal.

Kife's face was distorted with fury. "How did you even get here?"

"Easy." Riony shielded a strike toward her heart with the flat of her sword. "I just rode here on your mother."

Kife faltered, staring at her like one would a rabid bovin.

Riony only had a split second to glance down and check on Dracuni. The unidragon lay on her side, wings twisted and pinned uncomfortably beneath her, and chest heaving up and down. The bottle strapped into the bindings of her leg beneath the knives was overflowing. Sparkling blood soaked the dirt floor. Her lilac eyes fluttered.

"You're as mad and disgusting as you ever were, slave."

"And you continue to lack any sense of humor. Just one way you're worse than your sister."

Kife struck again, a thrust to the left, then the right. He was fast and precise, flicking the length of steel like lightning around Riony's cumbersome weapon.

Unbalanced from the flurry of attacks, Riony didn't expect Kife's boot to hit her ribs, and she stumbled back across the floor.

"Fire!" Kife bellowed again.

Riony spun around to see the dragon's head aimed right at her and golden light erupting up its throat.

Then its neck swayed, swinging the other way, and the fireball exploded against the far wall of the hatchery. A mound of grayed straw caught in a flash of sparks and smoke.

"Too close, Kess! Can you get that thing out of here?" Riony checked to make sure the back of her shirt wasn't on fire.

The dragon stepped a full circle on the spot, its tail smashing into shelving. Griskin had slunk inside as well, prowling and dodging around the dragon's feet.

Kess's voice growled in frustration. "I don't exactly have a lot of experience! I'm trying to make it work."

Riony smirked and angled the tip of her sword toward Kife. "That's exactly what the girls say you cry during sex."

Kife came at her, swinging wildly. "You think my useless sister has any chance of controlling that dragon? I should have smothered her in her sleep instead of leaving her to the revs."

Despite it being Kess he spoke of, a defensive streak flared inside Riony. "Sparks, were you born evil or was it being less desirable than dragon farts that drove you there?"

"Left, left! Fire!" Kife snarled. He disengaged, leaping backward.

The dragon's head swung left, bringing it in line with Riony again, then kept swinging. The fireball whooshed over Riony's head and spilled its flames across the thatched ceiling.

"You're going to burn this whole place down if you don't shut your mouth!" Kess leaned forward in the saddle, hands on the dragon's neck in the same position she held them when she rode her wolf.

"You've no right to be up there!" Kife yelled another command and Kess pressed her own through touch, and the dragon strained, legs moving one way and neck going the other.

Its tail swept a low arc across the barn, knocking down the brazier and scattering coals across the floor. The searing rocks skittered beside the tied up unidragon.

"Watch out for Dracuni!" Riony tried to get to the unidragon again, but Kife blocked her path with a swift jab toward her throat.

"Gris!" Kess gave a low whistle and pointed to Dracuni. "Get her out of here before this whole place goes up!"

The wolf bounded in, sniffed at the ropes and bleeding wound and Dracuni's blinking eyes, then wrapped his teeth around her tied up back legs.

A jolt of the unidragon's fear knocked Riony sideways.

"Careful!" she yelled.

But the wolf seemed to be as careful as he could be, pulling from the lashed rope. He could only drag the unidragon a little at a time, since she was limp on the ground and almost as big as he was. Dracuni bumped through the still red coals, and the larger dragon's claw came down right where she'd been a moment before.

Above them the thatched roof burned, filling the air with smoke. From some command of Kess's or Kife's or the dragon's sheer confusion, it beat its wings once, cracking into the ceiling above it and fanning all the flames.

They needed to get Dracuni out fast, but Riony didn't like that the dragonling was at the wolf's mercy. And as soon as he had her outside? Kess would take that dragon out as well and leave Riony without them.

Distracted, Riony only saw Kife's lunge of his sword too late. She turned her shoulder toward the blow, forgetting that her guard on that side had been lost and left behind.

The blade cut in. It seared through muscle and nicked bone. Riony snarled, breath hissing out through clenched teeth.

Kife grinned, admiring the color at the tip of his sword. "That's just first blood, slave. I'll have you strung up and bled out soon enough."

Riony had been swinging the sword with both hands but released her grip and let her right arm hang. She blocked his next attack clumsily with her left, then swung her sword in a wide arc, making Kife give ground.

She kept up the onslaught, backing him up across the burning floor.

Even when faced with the sweeping might of the huge, glowing chunk of magical crystal, Kife didn't slow down, dodging and striking between the gaps.

He no longer shouted 'fire'—there was plenty of that already—but he yelled other things. Down. Up. Sweep. Bite. Each was a command Kess had to counteract.

Riony tried to angle around, following Griskin as he dragged Dracuni out, but Kife kept her trapped as much as she kept him busy.

As relentless as his bloody sister.

There was a desperation there, too, that concerned Riony, and the back and forth between them had already wounded her. Smoke stung her eyes, and the blood dried and cracked on her arm under the searing heat.

She'd promised Lyrrin she'd try to not almost die this time and she already felt off track in that goal. She had to attempt something new. What would Lyrrin do? What would Lyrrin want her to do?

Groaning a short sigh, Riony offered, with all her sincerity, "Put your sword down, Kife, and we can all get out of this alive."

"Are you getting tired with that stupidly big blade of yours? Because I'm not stopping until your whole body is the color of your hair and that sister of mine is off my dragon. Sweep!" he yelled again.

The dragon was no longer bucking and twirling, the thump of its footsteps stilling behind Riony.

Has Kess finally worked out what she's doing?

Huh. So that's what relief and utter terror combined feel like.

"Come on, Kife," Riony offered again, because the only other option was continuing to throw herself into their deadly battle. "You're outmatched, and this place is a bigger burning trash heap than your life. Give it up."

He lunged again in a forward thrust of his sword, and Riony cut back, knocking him stumbling into the wall behind him.

And yet he smiled.

"Fire!" he screamed rabidly.

And Riony saw the dragon's teeth right over her shoulder.

In the moment it took her to gasp what might have been her last breath, the purple head lifted, and the fireball thundered past her ear, singeing her cheek.

It erupted against the wall around Kife with so much force that the stones shifted and tumbled. The roof came down with it, crashing in a fiery tide of sparks and embers right where Kife had been.

Right where Riony would also have been if she'd gone and engaged him in battle again.

I bet you're feeling my heart racing now, Lyrrin. And it's still beating, thanks to you.

The hole in the roof grew larger, cinders raining down. Dracuni and Griskin were still only halfway to the door.

After quickly strapping her sword to her back, Riony dashed across the room to their side.

"Let's get you out of here." She knelt behind Dracuni.

Griskin stared up at her with piercing eyes from where his teeth were still tight around the ropes.

Riony stared directly back. Somewhere between a sigh and a challenge, she said, "Don't make me fight you, pup."

Through the roar and spit of fire came a soft whistle, and Griskin let go.

He vanished on soft paws toward the purple dragon as Riony scooped her arms under Dracuni's limp body and neck. She hadn't lifted the dragonling in weeks, maybe months. But there was no way under the stars she was leaving her there.

"Okay. On three. One, two, THREE!" She heaved, arms burning, bringing the deadweight of the unidragon up to her knees, then waist, then over her shoulder.

She stood on shaking legs and took a step toward the doors.

Then the huge teeth of the purple etherdart filled her vision.

From her high perch on the saddle, Kess glared down with a fierce intensity.

Chapter Twenty-Nine

Riony sat with her back against the cool, flat edge of a standing stone, staring at the remaining ribbons of smoke tangling their way into the brightening sky, and wondered how she was still alive.

Dracuni lay half in her lap. Still. Sleeping. Riony stroked a hand down her long neck, the velvety scales warm and steady pulse beating beneath.

"It's okay. It's okay. You'll feel better soon."

Lyrrin would be feeling the unidragon's heartbeat too, with the paired crystal lying on Dracuni's chest. It was Riony's way of sending back a message to the others. *I have Dracuni. We're safe.*

Riony could still barely believe it, hours later, as the darkness of night yielded to a lilac luminance so much like the unidragon's eyes.

Safe. And as of yet, no more betrayal.

Dracuni was desperately weak from blood loss but seemed stable.

Riony didn't want to move her too far. She *couldn't* move her too far and refused to let Kess carry Dracuni with the dragon.

Kess had offered to when Riony had been struggling to lift the young dragon, and the offer had felt so much like a trap that Riony refused.

But Kess hadn't pushed, hadn't tried to take Dracuni from her despite how Riony had stumbled out of the burning hatchery, barely keeping herself and the growing dragon upright. Kess had only put the dragon's wing out above Riony, sheltering her and Dracuni from the fire and falling building.

Riony had stopped just outside the shrine, just far enough away from the fires that were rapidly spreading to every building of the estate, and there she and Dracuni had remained ever since.

With a fountain of apologies and fumbling fingers, Riony had removed the blades that had been pinned into the dragonling's leg to keep the wound open and bleeding. Dracuni's wound had closed quickly then.

Riony had stoppered the bottle of silvernix Kife had filled, glowered at it, and put it away. Despite the unforgiveable reason it existed, even Riony couldn't consider wasting it. And Riony's arm had been healed, too, when she couldn't avoid getting that magical blood on her hands.

Not far from them, across in the open ground between still smoldering buildings, the purple dragon sat idly, seemingly unaware of anything going on around it, with no rider in the saddle to give it commands.

Riony shook her head at it. *I can't believe that selfish goblin didn't roast me and fly off on her new dragon already.*

Kess didn't even stay on the dragon.

Once she'd maneuvered it outside, she'd slid down from the saddle and back onto Griskin without a word, and the two of them had skulked away.

As the stars wheeled overhead, Riony remained watchful, eyes locked on the dragon, wary that Kess could return at any moment and take Dracuni.

Why wait? Why not take the advantage with the dragon? Why did she leave? Why, why, why?

The questions alone kept Riony awake all night. Then as the sky brightened, she spotted the silhouette of Kess and Griskin high atop the stone walls that encircled the estate, watching as it burned.

A couple of times during the night, overcooked revenants shambled out of the flame-gutted buildings and collapsed.

Abandoned, Kess had said.

Abandoned to revs, much like Riony's village had been. A twang plucked at Riony's rib cage as she stared at the silhouetted wolf girl.

Now, finally, as the first bright rays of gold pierced the smoky air, most of the buildings were ashy rubble. The Alderkin shrine, made of solid stone and crystal, remained.

"It worked. This must be it!" Lyrrin's voice came from the interior of the shrine.

It roused Dracuni, and Riony turned and saw the glow of the gateway shining from within.

"We're out here!" Shifting Dracuni's head off her lap, Riony tried to stand only to find every one of her muscles had cramped from so long holding the same position. She grabbed her sword and used it to prop herself up.

Aishena came out first, athames in each hand at the ready.

"We're okay, I think." Riony groaned and stretched her back.

Lyrrin pushed through from behind Aishena and ran to Riony's side across the long grass, ash and dew smattering her legs. "You didn't almost die!"

She hugged Riony, then pulled back and gave her a questioning side-eye. "Did you?"

"I kept myself a very reasonable distance from imminent death. You would have been so proud."

"We came as quick as we could, on foot as we were, kids and all since they refused to stay behind," Aishena said, warily putting her athames away.

"What in Elundrae happened?" Benjin stepped out of the shrine along with Niskina, both turning to take in the idle dragon, the burning estate, Dracuni blinking awake, and the distinct lack of Kess.

Riony tried to summarize. "Fire, mostly. Kife is somewhere under all that char and ash. Dracuni is okay."

Hungry, the unidragon thought sleepily.

"And hungry." That seemed like a good sign.

"What happened to the awful wolf-girl? Did you have to—" Niskina made a squelching sound with her mouth and drew a line across her throat with her finger.

"The awful wolf-girl is still here," Kess muttered, emerging from a foggy drift of smoke.

Griskin padded up beside the purple etherdart, keeping a decent distance from the others.

Lyrrin gasped, then whispered, eyes sparkling, "She didn't betray you?"

"Not yet anyway," Riony murmured back.

Eying the wild girl and her wolf, Riony leaned on her sword and called over, "Are you going to take your dragon and go? Or do we have a problem?"

Aishena and Niskina flanked Riony, the kids and Dracuni behind them, standing opposed to Kess and the dragon.

"It's not my dragon."

"It could be," Riony offered, warily.

Aishena leaned in, whispering, "Is this the deal you came to? Are you sure it's a good idea letting her have a dragon?"

"If it means she's satisfied and leaves us alone forever, she can have the dragon *and* three of my teeth if she wants," Riony said.

"No," Kess exhaled the word. "I don't want that."

Riony pointed at her mouth with a frown. "They're good teeth, and I don't have any other body parts I'm willing to give you."

Kess closed her eyes in a slow, long-suffering blink. "The *dragon*. I don't want it."

"You don't *want it*? I'm sorry, *what*?" Riony's voice rose dramatically, and a hysterical burble built within her.

Maybe she had broken her head irreparably because she couldn't understand a thing coming out of Kess's mouth. Where was the girl who had spent every waking moment of her life working toward having her own dragon to ride?

It was only the awkwardly sincere contortions of Kess's face that stopped Riony bursting into manic laughter. She waited for Kess to say she wanted Dracuni instead. She waited for knives to be thrown. But Kess remained still, staring at the small flurries of ash swirling across the ground.

"It's Kife's dragon, and it just feels ... wrong. Broken. Riding it ... it wasn't what I'd thought it would be like. It felt like riding something already dead, like a primitive machine. It was nothing like ..." Kess's hand rubbed up through Griskin's fur and over his ear. "I didn't like it."

"You still can't have Dracuni if that's what you're angling for."

Behind Riony, the unidragon snorted agreement.

Kess shook her head and said nothing.

"You really don't want it?"

"After everything I've seen, no. I don't want a tamed dragon." Kess looked at Dracuni then with a hint of longing that made Riony grip the hilt of her sword. But she said, "I don't think being a dragonrider is what I'd thought it would be. What I wanted it to be."

Riony smirked. "A sport for the violently psychotic? It's perfect for you."

Kess met Riony's gaze, the icy blue-gray of her eyes flashing like a wolf's in the rays of sunrise, then she looked away just as fast.

Riony's smile dropped. There was something so lost, so shattered in that brief glance that it made Riony's heart stutter and mouth go dry.

Kess really had given up. Riony believed it now.

And she had no idea what it meant.

She frowned, taking in the lumbering weight of the etherdart sitting before them. "Soooo ... what do we do with this, then?"

Aishena paced around the dragon, inspecting the stationary beast. "We can't leave it here alone. It would die of starvation without being provided for."

Riony raised an eyebrow. "Can *you* ride a dragon?"

"I've had training, yes. But I don't think having a full-grown dragon with us is a good idea. It will attract more attention than it's worth."

"If reading *Rebel Riders* taught me anything," Niskina added, "it's that the dragonlords really don't like rebels having their own dragons."

"That's what you got from it? I was reading it for the sex," Riony whispered back.

"Can we—" Kess spoke up, seemed to choke on her words, swallowed, and started again. "Is there any chance we could free it?"

"Free it? Free the dragon?" Riony asked.

Aishena shook her head, confused at the question. "It can't survive on its own. You know that."

Kess placed a hand on the dragon's shoulder. "I mean, is there any chance we could *untame* it. Reverse the taming. *Free* it."

Riony's eyes widened. She sought the glint of metal amid the purple scales on the etherdart's forehead. "Reverse the taming?"

"Would that even work?" Lyrrin asked.

"I don't know if it's ever been attempted before," Aishena said.

Big dragon could think again? Dracuni lifted her head, neck wobbling.

"I suppose we could try," Riony said. "Would we just ... take the taming spike out?"

"Might need silvernix to heal the wound again. Otherwise, it may not survive the process," Aishena replied, tilting her head toward Dracuni.

I help. Want to help big dragon friend.

"I've got silvernix. Kife ... collected some, and I have it," Riony said, and then thought, **No more helping for you, Dracuni. You need to recover.**

Dracuni huffed and laid her chin back on the ground again.

"Let's try it!" Lyrrin practically squealed.

"It might not work, and it could be dangerous." Riony gestured at the huge creature's talons and teeth. "I didn't love my last run-in with a wild dragon."

"It deserves to be free," Kess said flatly. "Will you help or not?"

Everyone was in favor of attempting to untame the dragon.

They made a rough plan. Aishena cut the dragon's saddle, harness, and bags free, dumping them on the ground out of the way. She used her cutting athame to carefully remove the heavy steel collar around its neck.

Then she took the bottle of silvernix and waited for the moment it would be needed. Niskina, the kids, and Dracuni moved into the shelter of the shrine, just in case.

Kess tapped the dragon's shoulder, getting it to bring its head down low to the ground.

Moving around to get a position with good leverage, Riony ended up with one knee on the dragon's snout. The steel spike seemed so small compared to the bulk of the dragon's head, stuck there between its brow ridges since it had been a dragonling.

Riony cringed as she worked the tips of her fingers beneath the flat head of the spike until she had a solid grip.

She looked down at Kess. "Last chance to keep it for yourself. Are you sure about this?"

Kess brought Griskin around beside Riony, staring up with sad eyes at the dragon. "I will not shackle another life to mine without its consent."

Riony's fingers slipped from the hammered end of the spike, and she had to get her hold on it again. *Sparks! I'll deal with whatever* that *was about later.*

"Okay, let's do this." Riony pulled.

She braced her knee against the hard skull of the dragon's snout and tensed her back, every muscle in her arms straining. Her fingers locked around the stake, the metal biting into them as she refused to let her grip slide a second time.

Slowly, slowly, the spike eased out from between the scales and bone it had melded into. Then, as the thicker section detached and only the tapered end remained, the rest came free in a rush and Riony toppled backward, landing on the ground in a puff of ash.

Aishena stepped in with the silvernix, placing a few drops on the resulting hole and thick, dark blood that spilled from it.

There was a sizzle, and a flicker of light from between the dragon's dusky scales. The hole closed over.

And the dragon didn't move.

"Is it okay? Did it work?" Lyrrin took a step out of the shrine.

"Stay in there." Riony warned her as she got to her feet, brushing off the soot, but she was so covered in blood and ash it really didn't matter. Standing again, she was far too close to the dragon's teeth for comfort and she backed away, watching for movement.

Aishena joined her at the doorway to the shrine. "Maybe it's had the stake in too long. It might not recover."

Kess remained at the dragon's side, stroking its cheek. Gusts of smoke from the smoldering buildings drifted by.

And then something else, dark and smoky, fluttered in the air around them. Like a trail lifting from an extinguished candle but in reverse, a black, shadowy substance drifted down from the sky and into the dragon's healed wound.

And the dragon shivered.

"What in the stars was that?" Riony hissed.

Even Kess backed away from the beast then. "I've seen that before, sort of. In tamings. When the spike is hammered in, there's a sizzle and rise of dark smoke."

Riony and Aishena nodded, having seen it too. Riony had assumed at the time it was literal smoke, that the stake and silvernix somehow burned.

But this? They were seeing it happen now in *reverse*.

If that shadowy substance was just smoke, why would it *come back?*

Riony didn't have time to think about it as the dragon shook itself again, eyes rolling in their sockets. Hot air huffed in ragged pants between great swords of teeth.

It loosed a deafening, pained roar that ended in a whimper, then raised its head high, glaring down. It wavered side to side, eyes on Kess, its mouth opening.

Riony's toes tensed against the ground, ready to tackle the stupidly immobile wolf-girl away from a fireball or the snap of teeth.

The dragon roared again, and a great wash of emotions flooded forward—questioning, accusing, confused—and the group gasped as it hit.

Is everyone feeling this?

Then massive purple wings, all healed, snapped outward and pressed down. Kess and Griskin crouched low to the ground as a torrent of air rushed over them, swirling their clothes and fur, and the dragon lifted into the sky. As though learning again how to fly, its motions were stiff and awkward.

But it was free.

Chapter Thirty

Have I made the biggest mistake of my life?

Kess watched the purple etherdart fly away until it was nothing more than a smudge of memory against the shell-pink morning sky.

There were cheers and celebratory embraces and happy waves of goodbye from the others. A dragon freed. Perhaps it was a thing to celebrate, but Kess couldn't stop shaking.

I had a dragon. The thing I always wanted, all I ever wanted, and I let it go.

She'd wanted to let it go in the end.

While tracking Dracuni's mother, Kess had seen the unfettered glory of a free dragon. While hunting Dracuni, Kess had seen the compassion and loyalty of a free dragon.

A tamed dragon was a lame, faded substitute by comparison. Kess could find no honor in owning such a creature. And now, all Kess's goals and dreams felt equally diminished.

Want felt like a distant concept, and even further removed again from *having* that it would be simpler to ignore the possibility of either.

"Do you think it will be okay?" the Hjelzahn boy asked.

"It seemed to come back to itself and was able to fly unaided. Hopefully it will be able to hunt and stay safe too," his sister said.

"What was the weird smoky stuff that went into it?" he asked again, full of questions.

"Yeah, that was weird, right? It looked ... are we all thinking what I'm thinking, or have I lost it?" Riony replied.

"You know what it reminded me of?" Lyrrin said softly, almost too low for Kess to hear from where she remained separate. "The shadowdragon."

"So it was clear to people without head injuries too. Good to know."

Kess had thought so too. The swirling darkness, the faint sense of mourning that had emanated from it. She'd seen the shadowdragon enough for it to have felt familiar.

"I've been wondering about that lately. Since seeing the mural in the Alderkin depths. Since seeing the site of the first taming ..." Niskina turned her face to the sky, shaking her head as though unable to voice the end of her thought.

Riony finished for her. "That the shadowdragon isn't an Alderkin curse? That the shadowdragon is the result of taming dragons? Yeah, I've been wondering the same thing."

A long silence followed.

Kess stared at the taming spike, lying discarded on the ground. Dark, tar-like blood coated the end from where it had been lodged deep in the dragon's brain.

Could it really be the tamings that had created the shadow dragon? She imagined how many dragons there were across Elundrae with similar stakes in their skulls, the wisping smoke from every taming, rising into the sky, joining together into that one malevolent entity.

"We should clear up and get Dracuni out of here, go someplace where she can recover," Aishena said. "Somewhere safe, in case all of this has drawn attention from the living or the dead."

The unidragon lifted her head to Riony, and Riony whispered something back. Kess's lip twitched and she looked away.

There had been a moment, hidden between the flutters of her heartbeat, when she'd hoped that maybe, maybe once freed, the dragon would choose to remain. That it might choose her.

A truly ridiculous thing to hope—that anything would choose to be with her. Only Griskin ever had, and that was more than she deserved.

"Where should we go then?" Nisk asked brightly. "Where do you want to go, Ri?"

"Anywhere I can wash all this smoke and blood out of my clothes and sleep for a week sounds good to me."

Kess fussed with her saddlebags, checking the contents, pretending she had any reason to remain a moment longer.

Nisk slung an arm over Riony's shoulders. "We don't have to go back to your village. Any of the shrine enclaves will have us at least for a while. They feel like they owe us for helping get them somewhere safe from revs."

Kess frowned. Was that why people were congregating around the shrines? Were those ruins somehow protected from revenants?

And Riony had been helping people get there—saving people, all over Elundrae. While all Kess had done was chase and terrorize her, Riony had been the hero that Kess had always wanted to be once she got her dragon.

"How about Myrwa's?" Aishena said, her gaze casting over Riony with a tenderness Kess hadn't seen from the grim young woman before.

"Yes, please. That would be really nice." Riony sighed.

There was so much relief in her voice that it stung Kess to the bone.

"I want to see how big Kellae's baby is now!" the sister squealed. "And I want to keep helping people. Do you think we can? Keep traveling around and making more shrines safe for people?"

Riony pushed the girl's hood down and brushed her hand through her hair. "Yeah, that sounds pretty good to me."

"Let's move then," Aishena said. Her brother went into the shrine, and the glow of the magical gateway lit from within.

All of them were filled with joy and peace because they weren't being hunted anymore. Because the suffering Kess had inflicted upon them had ended.

Nose stinging and eyes hot, Kess nudged Griskin, leading him away along the smoky path through the rubble of her family home.

Behind her, there was a squabble in low voices between Riony and her sister, then Kess rounded the corner of what remained of the hatchery walls and could hear no more.

"Hey, butt face!" Riony loped over. A thick gust of smoke blew up around her as she stood, eying Kess with a crease between her brows. "I'm still waiting."

"For what?"

"The vicious betrayal."

"So sorry to disappoint." Kess pushed Griskin on again.

Riony called after them, "You really were just going to leave? No more games, no tricks, no treachery? No final shot at stealing Dracuni?"

Kess glared over her shoulder and said nothing.

"Where are you even going?"

Kess tensed, the squeeze of her fingers halting Griskin. Where was she going? She had no idea. She growled back. "Does it matter? What's with all the questions?"

"I'm curious, okay? Consider me confounded. I thought I knew ... *you*. But nothing is making sense anymore. Why did you help save Dracuni if you weren't doing it to take Dracuni for yourself afterward?"

"Dracuni saved my life. I repaid the debt."

Riony's shoulders lowered, and more quietly, she asked, "And why did you save me? You used your silvernix. You didn't owe me—you had nothing to gain. What possible reason could you have had for that?"

Kess snapped, "Maybe you're just *worth saving*!"

The words shocked them both to silence. Their eyes met through the smoky glare. Heat flushed up Kess's face and she turned away, swallowed by shame.

There was a mumbling of curses, and then Riony called out from behind her, "You don't have to go."

A long, rattly shiver ran up Kess's back. Had she misheard?

"You don't have to be alone anymore. You could ... come with us." Riony's words were strained, but real.

Want resurfaced within Kess like verdant new growth from beneath melting snow. She tried to shake the wanting away, but it clung with aching force to her bones. "Did your 'sister' put you up to this?"

"Nooo. Okay, yes. Sort of."

"Tell her I don't need her pity."

Riony ran both hands through her tangled red hair, tensing the muscles in her arms and looking at the sky. "It's not ... *just* her."

"I don't need yours either."

"No, I mean ... *sparks*." Riony turned around, staring back the other way, then she hung her head. "I'm tired, Kess. I'm tired of fighting, tired of loss and pain, and worrying that is all we can have from life."

Kess turned Griskin around, watching Riony's back as she took deep breaths between her words. She remembered Riony's back, scarred and washed in blood and the water of the falls, and how she'd cried those deep, mourning sobs.

And Kess knew exactly what Riony meant. She was tired too.

After another long inhale that lifted her shoulders, Riony said, "I just want people to be nice to each other, help each other, because that's what makes this blighted world livable. Even good, sometimes. And I know it might be a stupid dream, but maybe we can start making it real. We could start with the two of us."

"Us?" Kess repeated in a whisper. Griskin growled a soft warning, but she didn't react, unable to look away from Riony.

Riony turned her head to the side, still not looking back, almost as though she was too scared to face Kess. "What do you think?"

Kess didn't know what she thought. Half her insides were screaming this was a trap, to run, to strike first, and the other half *wanted* in a way that eclipsed any want she'd ever known before.

Kess tried to calm her breathing enough to reply as a waft of smoke puffed around her again. The heady scent burned through her nose, different to before, overwhelming, a soapy and peppery fragrance.

Kess's eyes widened in recognition.

Morass mercy.

She tried to call out, but her throat had gone numb, and she gave only a rough grunt.

"I don't mean you have to stay with *us* exactly." Riony shrugged, head hanging forward again.

Griskin slumped beneath Kess, crumpling in a limp puddle of fur. Kess fell over him, arms flailing weakly, slipping, losing all control.

"We could take you somewhere you want to be—one of the shrine settlements. Anywhere."

Kess slipped off the saddle, landing on her side on the ground. A figure stepped up, looming over them in the thick smoke.

Kife?

Kess's head swirled as she looked up at the ghost of her brother. Except a ghost wouldn't need a scarf wrapped around the bottom half of his face to block the smoke thick with sedative.

He survived. He survived. Riony!

Kess wanted to scream, but darkness tugged at her and all she could do was fight to remain conscious.

Riony mumbled, "Or if you did want to travel with us, maybe it wouldn't be absolutely awful."

Kife's eyes smiled as he dumped a burning pile of morass mercy in front of Kess, then leaned down and pulled one of her bone-throwing daggers from her bracer. Kess's fingers twitched, trying to stop him, fight him. Her throat croaked in protest.

How did he survive?

Kess's whole body seized. Silvernix. He'd had a bottle of silvernix on him when the fireball had knocked half a building down on top of him.

No.

They should have checked. They should have dug him up and made sure he was gone.

Was he going to kill her now with her own dagger?

After one long, hard look at Kess, Kife stepped away, rushing on silent feet down the stretch toward the woman with her back to them.

Riony. Riony!

"Kess, are you going to say *anything*? I'm trying ..." Riony groaned, starting to turn around.

Kife grabbed her by the shoulder with one hand and with the other, plunged Kess's dagger hilt deep into the center of her back.

Kess felt as though her own heart stopped.

No. No. Come on, Riony. Fight back. Fight. Scream. Call for help. Come on!

Riony took one stumbling step forward and then fell like a stone, face-first onto the ashy ground. The dull white of the dagger sticking from her back was stark against a growing spread of blood.

Horror flooded Kess, and she couldn't scream, couldn't cry. She couldn't even blink or turn away.

Kife stalked back up the long path to her, dusting off his hands.

"Wasn't that a bit of fun, little sister? This is just the first of the suffering I have planned for you to repay you for what you did to me." He grabbed her by the wrists, pulling her the rest of the way off Griskin.

"Although you did do one favor for me—leaving my saddlebags behind when you *let my dragon* go. At least that let me get to my supply of this wonderful herb." Kife kicked away the last of the fuming morass mercy.

Kess was barely listening to her brother's tirade.

Riony. Move. Move. Please.

She didn't move.

"You're coming with me. And you're going to watch as I get myself a new dragon, and then I'll get the silvernix-bleeding creature again and get everything back that you took from me. And we'll make sure every one of my triumphs hurts you as much as possible."

One thin, gritty tear spilled from Kess's frozen eyes. Darkness encroached from every side.

A low rumbling built into a harsh growl, and Griskin surged back to his feet. Wavering, legs buckling and wobbling beneath him, he swung his snapping jaws at Kife.

Too slow, too dazed. Kife stepped back with ease, then lifted one leg and thrust his boot into the wolf's flank. Griskin went stumbling, crashing through a gap in the tumbled-down walls of the hatchery and falling in a puff of ashes beyond.

Kife followed him in, stepped over the prone wolf, and picked up a rock, lifting it high.

"Say goodbye to your dumb animal."

Kess prepared for her heart to be shattered beyond repair, hoping only that the damage wouldn't be survivable, hoping it would be the last time.

A voice floated from around the corner. "This is taking too long. I'll go check."

Kife snarled and let the rock drop on the ground. He rushed back to Kess, snatched up her wrists again, and dragged her roughly along the ground. The world twisted and warped in Kess's locked eyes and she drifted in numbness and gloom.

They were just around the next corner when a cry rang out.

"Riony!"

"What did Kess do?"

"Help me lift her. Go, go! To the gateway!"

There was a long, wailing moan.

"She's not breathing. Aish, she's not—"

And all the light in the world went out.

BLOOD OF THE
DRAGON
THRONE
SELINA A FENECH
BOOK FOUR OF THE
SHADOW
DRAGON SAGA

CHAPTER ONE

Kess lay on her back on the damp stone floor and shivered as Riony paced the claustrophobic cell.

"Could you have possibly, even if trying, gotten us into a worse mess than this?" Riony thrust both palms against the wooden door holding them inside.

Too solid. It didn't budge, didn't even rattle.

Kess blinked, slow and sluggish, staring at the dark stain marking the back of Riony's shirt. "I'm sorry."

Kess had done her best to investigate every corner of the room she could through hazy, doubled vision and with limbs that refused to move.

More a disused root cellar than dungeon, chilled and musty, it had been chiseled deep into solid stone and closed off with a door neither rodents nor thieves could penetrate.

Shelving lined two sides of the room, empty of anything except the curls of old onion skins and cobwebs. Only the floor was storage now, for strewn bouquets and Kess's limp body.

She needed to focus, find a way out, find anything she could turn to her advantage. But her eyes kept returning to Riony, to the rusty color marring the fabric of her back.

Riony spoke over her shoulder, keeping her back to Kess. "This is all your fault."

"I'm sorry." Kess's head pounded.

Searing points of pain ached throughout her skull, and shame hurt her even deeper. *She won't even look at me.* Kess didn't blame her.

How long had they been in there? She'd tried to mark the days at first, in her brief moments of waking and lucidity. Soft scratches in the dust of the disused shelves. The tally lines doubled, tripled in her blurred vision. Days, weeks, months, she couldn't count the crookedly marked lines.

A dull beam of natural light reached in from a narrow ventilation shaft in the ceiling high above, the only thing marking day or night which seemed to turn from one to the other every time she blinked. She spent most of her time lost and paralyzed in nightmares, as the morass mercy carpeting the floor oozed its soapy, peppery scent into her lungs.

Days and nights and days and nights, all filled with nauseating visions of a blade, her blade, slicing deep into Riony's back. Clasped within her fingers as she plunged it in.

That didn't happen. It was just a dream. Riony is here.

"I can't think straight. Can you help me? Move me away from the morass mercy, please, Pony." The old name slipped out over Kess's numb lips.

Riony loomed in the space, monstrously tall between the walls closing in on all sides. "I'm not your Pony and I'll never carry you. Ever again."

Kess's eyes closed, too heavy, for too long. Tears squeezed from the corners.

She was small again, in a fine dress of embroidered silver velvet, upon a bed of soft down and plush cushions.

On her lap, she held a broad-paged book filled with illustrations of all the breeds of dragons, both naturally occurring, and hybrids bred by humans. A childish picture book, simple in its descriptions. She'd read other far more complicated texts on all aspects of dragon riding and breeding.

But she had a soft spot for this tome and its naturalistic depictions of dragons that were so much more fluid and powerful than the stiff technical illustrations in her other books.

"One day I'll have my own dragon." Kess said it as a promise, a truth held deep in her fluttering heart. "An etherdart maybe. I'd like something fast, though."

Sitting cross-legged beside her, Riony dutifully looked over the page Kess presented. "I thought snowflames were faster?"

Kess tsked. "Yes, obviously, but they burn out fast too. I need a dragon who will stay with me, be my companion in combat and honor as long as possible. The Dragon King's steed is his original and been with him over eighty years!"

She turned the pages slowly, a strange churning of nerves in her stomach as she shared her beloved book with Riony, as though she were sharing some deep, dark secret. A ridiculous feeling. She was only sharing her future.

"I'm going to be a great dragonrider. One of the best. They'll write ballads about my adventures!" Kess leaned back against the headboard and turned her face upward as though she could see the sky she would one day soar in.

"Those are some big dreams."

Kess closed the book with a pout. "Not just a dream. It's my future. Don't you have plans for your future?"

Even before she'd finished the sentence, Kess could see the deep, scalding shimmer of sadness and fury in Riony's eyes.

That was the moment Kess had realized, through all her designs for her own destiny, the person she was closest to had no future beyond what her masters set for her. All her churning worry turned solid and settled hard in her stomach.

"You'll probably still be with me anyway. I'll still need you, even when I have a dragon." Which was the second stupidest thing Kess had said within minutes.

Riony opened her mouth to speak, and blood dripped from the corner of her lips, staining her shirt.

Kess's whole body shook, a chill rattling through her uncontrollably, and her eyes peeled open. She was confused to find herself lying on a floor surrounded by bundles of smelly herbs.

It felt so real. Where am I?

"Try to stay awake, would you? This isn't the time to be dozing off." There was a tenderness beneath Riony's terse words that Kess didn't deserve.

"I'm sorry." Kess's lips barely parted around the words, her voice hoarse. Pain throbbed behind her eyes.

"Is that all you can say to me?"

There was so much more Kess wanted to say. "I'm sorry."

For everything. So many things. Too many things.

Riony dropped onto her haunches beside Kess, glaring critically. "Your apologies don't mean anything. It's too late now."

All tenderness in her tone had fled. Since being stuck there together, she'd had none of her usual smirking, obscene humor. No carefree bravado. Her words now only held a deathly finality that made Kess shiver.

She held her breath for a long moment as though it could clear her lungs and head of the sedative permeating the room, then pushed her words out in a rush. "A promise then. That I won't call you Pony, ever again. I know you hate it, that you always hated it."

"And you kept on using it anyway. Nice."

Kess's throat clogged, and the words rattled around within her head.

Because it was a good way to ensure you hated me in return. I'm sure you did anyway, how could you not? But it was better to make sure. Then I'd never had reason to hope for anything more.

Riony stood up again, irises of enigmatic hue scowling down. "Promises are also useless. It's too late, Kess."

It's too late.

A pain like a dagger to the heart choked Kess and she sobbed out the words, "Can I ever make it up to you?"

It's too late.

Footsteps echoed down, muffled through the solid door, and they both turned to the sound.

A jangle of keys, the click of a lock, the creaking whine of old hinges, and Kife stood in the threshold.

He held a scarf over his mouth and nose, forehead wrinkled as he glared down at Kess, and Kess alone.

Riony was gone.

Of course. Because she's dead.

"What a disgusting mess." Kife reached down for Kess's ankle as she wept soundlessly against the filthy ground.

He dragged her out of the room, pushing the door loosely closed behind him to separate them from the pungent herbs. Grasping her under the arms he hefted her roughly upward. He propped her up on the steep stairs, a couple higher than where he stood so they were almost eye to eye.

"Hey, wake up!" Kife slapped her across the cheek, as though the addition of physical pain would do anything to ease the effects of the morass mercy.

It only added spite into the swirl of emotions and nightmares blurring Kess's thoughts.

Kife was pacing the short length of his step, shouting, but Kess couldn't quite make the sounds turn into coherent words.

Something about silvernix. Expenses. Running out. Kill those guards if they ask for a bribe again. Crooks, everywhere.

Kess's eyelids drooped again but didn't close. Out there on the dark stairs, the air was clear, and slowly the edges of reality firmed themselves in Kess's perception.

The sting on her already bruised cheek was real.

The weak ache in her joints and long bones from a body wrought motionless and underfed for too long was real.

And Riony was really...

"I can't get an audience! Not even with one of King Draekhan's advisors, or any of the Firsts." Kife's words became clear as a ringing bell.

Good. Kess knew what would happen once he had the ear of the Dragon King, what Kife had planned.

Her memories cleared too, reminding her of how her brother would appear at irregular times to throw her scraps and abuse her for all his failures.

Memories of how she'd been entombed in her prison.

The flare, set off from the discarded saddlebags of an untamed dragon. A rider finding them, offering a favor to a downed fellow rider to bring them to the capital. Kife telling those they met along the way that Kess was unwell. How nobody questioned a dragonrider bringing a restrained and senseless girl into the city with him.

Kife threw his arm out in frustration and Kess flinched away from it.

"It's utter disrespect. How dare they turn away a Heithorn?" He still wore his dragonrider armor, red and blue, the colors of Skaella the First.

A finely crafted sword and collection of daggers, all with the Heithorn crest on the pommel, were on display along his belt, as though his presentation as a lordly dragonrider would grant him access to the king himself.

Kess closed her eyes for a long moment, wishing Riony would appear again, would come back to her, and wondering what Riony would do if she were there, and not gone forever.

Riony wouldn't give up.

"So, you're a reject as usual." She smirked at her brother. "What do you expect me to do about it?"

"As if you could do anything. It's your fault to begin with. You put such a stain upon our family name that I'm not being taken seriously by anybody."

"Then get rid of me if I'm such a thorn in your side." Kess bared her teeth, baiting, willing him to step closer.

Kife continued to pace. His long braid of charcoal hair swung at his back. The smaller side braids leading to the larger central one that ran down the top of his head weren't as neatly done as in the past and the stubble over his jaw was no longer neatly trimmed.

"Oh no, little sis. I'm keeping you around until you can see me in possession of a dragon once more, until you can see me capture the unidragon, so you can watch as I get everything you could never have. And once I have claimed every dream you once had as my own, then, maybe, I'll put you out of your misery."

Kess rolled her eyes at him. "So much melodrama. Only the dishonorable would need to gloat to a captive audience. But you never understood honor."

Kife stilled, turning on her with knife-thin eyes.

Kess rasped her words through a jeering grin. "Even our parents could see that. I wasn't the only child they were isolating away from the eyes of nobility."

Kife stalked to her in two swift steps and leaned down, his finger jabbing forward and mouth opened.

Kess didn't wait to hear whatever he planned to say. As soon as he was within reach, she threw her arms up as fast as she could.

Blessed sun, they're so slow.

Her joints cracked and muscles ached at being forced into action. They lolled more than struck, one aiming for Kife's throat, the other aiming lower.

If she could have killed him right there, she would have. For herself. And for Riony. But her body barely responded to her demands.

Kife hissed as she clawed weakly against him. There was a brief flurry of limbs as she grasped and scratched, and he kept her fingernails off his neck and eyes. Then he caught her by one wrist and threw her down the few steps to the landing.

Kess smacked onto her stomach, one hand pinned beneath her, fist closed tight. Bitter triumph shot through her aching heart.

Kife stomped down to her. "Don't push me, Kessara, or maybe I'll simply forget that you are down here."

He grabbed her by the ankle and dragged her back into her prison.

As he closed the door and locked it, Kess remained face down, resting her forehead against the floor and breathing hard. The cloying spice of the morass mercy invaded her again.

A slow, dully echoing clap filled the space. Riony crouched beside her. "Great work. Very effective. You know he's going to miss it as soon as he takes his belt off, if not before."

Kess rolled over onto her back, revealing the slim dagger clutched to her chest. "Hopefully that will be too late."

Kess knew she was speaking to a ghost, or some figment of her broken mind, but she didn't care. She didn't blame Riony for haunting her. If anything, it was a comfort she didn't deserve, to not be alone.

With senses already swimming, Kess groaned into a sitting position and shuffled over to the door. The lock—or *locks* in her blurring vision—were just above head height, and it took three tries to get the dagger into the right one.

"What are you even going to do if you get that open?" Riony folded her arms, eyebrows raised skeptically. "Going to go try to get yourself a dragon again?"

Her one dream, all she'd ever wanted. Not anymore. "No. Dracuni is still out there."

"So you're going to keep hunting her instead?" Riony was suddenly much closer, a wrathful spirit.

Kess's hand slipped, and she almost dropped the dagger. She tried to focus on working the lock. "No. I mean she's out there, without you to protect her."

"So you're going to?"

"If I have to. If I can." If it was too late to do anything else for Riony, for any apologies or promises, the one thing Kess could do was continue to protect the unidragon in her stead.

Although Kess doubted Riony's remaining companions would let her anywhere near them. *They must think I did it, that I killed her.*

Sweat beaded up all over Kess's chilled skin at the sheer exertion of simply keeping her hands up above her head. The lock refused to give.

Somewhere from high above, the howl of a wolf filtered down through the earth to her.

"Did you hear that?" Kess's hand jiggling the blade stilled, and the dagger slipped free of the lock.

"I didn't hear anything." Riony turned her face up toward the narrow ventilation shaft, the faint light setting her red hair aflame.

Was the air clearer up there? Is that why the morass mercy wasn't affecting Riony? *No. No. She's not really here.*

Was Griskin really there, or was that a desperate dream as well? It wasn't the only time she'd heard him call. Had he followed her? Found her? Couldn't reach her?

She hoped he was okay. That she hadn't lost him too.

Kess tried to lift her arm with the dagger back to the lock again, but it rolled droopily against the wall. She gritted her teeth, her eyes hot with defeat.

"I can't do this, not with all the morass mercy in here."

The weedy bouquets had lost some potency since she'd first been thrown in there. Faded enough that she could stay awake, but still messing up her ability to function, physically and mentally. Kess grasped at the nearest bundle of leaves and limply flung it to the other end of the room.

It wasn't far enough. But there were no windows or holes to dispose of the sedative foliage through. She pushed away another posy. Her efforts seemed to only stir up the scent even more.

Kess held Riony in a pleading gaze. "It's too much ... Too hard. I don't know if I can take any more."

Riony smirked in reply. "I don't want to hear the details of your love life, Kess."

Kess coughed out a laugh that quickly devolved into heaving sobs. "What am I going to do without you?"

Riony didn't offer an answer. She lowered down to sit cross-legged in front of Kess, watching dutifully as Kess decided her future.

And Kess knew exactly what she was going to do.

"I'm going to kill him. I'm going to kill Kife."

In revenge for what he did to Riony.

To stop him before he told anyone about Dracuni.

And before he killed her first.

CHAPTER TWO

Zarram Dragonhold was the largest dragon breeding, raising, and housing facility in the capital, with over two dozen breeders stabled and hatchery facilities large enough to raise over thirty hatchlings at a time.

But there was one dragon Dashiel Zarram cared about more than any of the other stock. Their stomach churned at the thought that very soon, the bond they had developed with that dragonling would be severed for good.

Dashiel skipped to keep up with their father's thunderous stride. "If I can show you the progress I've made with training Shiff, you'll see—"

"No. This little ... *experiment* of yours has gone on long enough." The giant of a man, built like a fortress tower, solid and grim, wiped his forehead and continued marching.

The stockyards sweltered in the midday heat as the Zarram siblings followed their father along on his daily inspection. Bovin lowed, jostling against each other in the tight pens.

Across on their father's other side, Vance gave Dashiel a gruff *told you so* expression. Their older brother had a build as equally intimidating as their father's, broad-shouldered in a way that threatened doorways and with a jawline cut from a wood block.

Dashiel refused to be intimidated, despite being the smallest and slimmest of the family. "Shiff isn't just an experiment. I really think there is intelligence within her. And emotions! That feel almost human, and it's like I am connecting with them."

Their father heaved to a stop then and rounded on Dashiel, looming over. "Intelligence? Emotion? Dragons are savage beasts. And your pet must be tamed before she becomes a threat."

"Pabba, please."

Their father raised a stern eyebrow.

"Fadda," Dashiel corrected themselves, switching to the Taen term.

Despite being Rolanian themselves, their father pushed them toward Taenish culture in all ways. As the only Rolanian dragonlords in the city, they did their best to fit in as their station in society rose.

All three of them wore their hair in intricate Taenish braids that made their natural curls less obvious. Their father and Vance had matching earthy-brown locks, streaked pale from silvernix usage, a signifier of their wealth and station. Dashiel kept their loose caramel curls shorter, a flop of gold standing upon their head, corralled by a few braids along each side.

Vance was in all ways his father, but Dashiel had always been a neat blend of both their parents. Sharp angled yet pretty. Shoulders wider than most women, but more curves than most men. Dashiel was the youngest too, at twenty-one. There was a good eight years' gap from Dashiel to Vance. They had a few sisters between them who had left for marriages designed to strengthen the Zarram name, but Vance and Dashiel remained at home.

Dashiel looked up into their father's eyes with a pleading determination.

The man scoffed and turned away, heading toward the dual-gate vestibule that led from the stockyards into the hatchery.

Dashiel tilted their head to Vance, mouthing, *Can you talk to him?*

"Because he listens to me when? This is up to you." Vance huffed a wry laugh and patted Dashiel on the back in a way that made them stumble forward three steps.

The siblings caught up as their father waited for the guard to open the interior gate. The solid steel barrier rose slowly into the recess above as the guard cranked the wheel. Lord Zarram tsked at the grinding gears. Something had gone wrong in the mechanism a while ago, meaning the gate only stayed open with direct intervention, so they had to have a guard on staff there at all times.

Dashiel knew the expense frustrated their father, but they hadn't been able to find anyone with the skills to repair it.

Vance closed the outer door behind them, cutting them off from the burned orange heat and smelly haze. Only a thin stream of light shined through a barred grate above.

As the inner gate screeched slowly upward, Lord Zarram turned to Dashiel. "Your investment into the king's riders is coming up. Your shimmerdart is a fine creature. The best of the current generation to raise for your steed. We can't waste her on these dangerous ideas of yours."

Dashiel had picked the hatchling for that very reason. She was glorious, large for her kind, bright and curious right from the egg. She should have been tamed on her day of hatching, but the newborn had looked into Dashiel's eyes with such knowing and fear that Dashiel couldn't bring themselves to hammer the spike.

They separated the dragonling from the others, worried it could become dangerous, and then they spent all their free hours together in the weeks since then, only to find the dragonling to be gentler than they could have imagined.

And the idea of taming the creature hurt more than ever.

The gate was fully opened and Lord Zarram turned to leave.

Dashiel grasped his arm. "I can't. Fadda. I can't do it. Please don't make me tame her."

Their father's mouth twitched and he looked away. "You can have until your investment. You will tame her then, alongside the other new recruits taming their chosen hatchlings."

The man strode away, waving one hand dismissively to signal that the discussion was over.

"I think that went as well as could have been hoped," Vance muttered.

Dashiel gave him a flat look. "Yes. Fantastic. I'm thrilled."

Vance leaned to one side, rubbing his thigh with a soft groan. "Come, Dash. You've a bright future. You made it through trials and into the king's own dragonriders! You'll be training with the best after investment."

"Not the best. You won't be there."

Vance let go of his leg and straightened up again. "I had my chance and lost it. I'm stuck here with Pabba now. But you ... You know how the other dragonlords look at us, even when the king himself favors our broods. It's up to you now to destroy their expectations."

The guard waited, straining slightly to keep the gate opened until the siblings stepped through. He cleared his throat softly.

They got moving again. Dashiel hated walking under the drop-gate, always worried the guard might let go and the solid metal would come rushing down and crush them. They took a hurried step to the other side.

A birdlike cry of steel rushing closed followed the siblings as they wandered through the hatchery. Servants sorted and turned eggs on their warming beds. They would be hatching soon, bred specially for the king's newest recruits to select from.

Vance and Dashiel reached the stables for the full-sized dragons. They lined a long hallway, with a fight deck opening into the sky at the end. The siblings stopped in front of a beautiful golden etherflame, dully chewing at a slab of meat in its trough.

"You know ... I didn't want to tame Viska either, at the time." Vance stepped into the stall and placed a hand onto the bright scales of the dragon's cheek.

It didn't respond.

Dashiel raised their eyebrows. "I did *not* know that."

"I didn't take as long as you have to get around to it. Only a couple of days. I fought Fadda over it, questioning why it had to be done, whether we could try another way. I had all these wild ideas. I think it was Eslinde's influence, really."

Dashiel grinned. "I bet."

Vance gave them a quelling glare. "But there's no other way. If you want a dragon that can be flown, that follows orders without question, it must be tamed."

Was it the only way? Dashiel reached a hand to the stake in Viska's forehead. She was such an incredible creature, mostly etherflame, but with just a little snowshimmer in her line a few generations back that made her sleeker and faster than usual for that species. What could she have been if all her autonomy hadn't been taken away by that sharp metal in her brain?

"The Rebel Riders don't tame their dragons," Dashiel said.

"The Rebel Riders are stories." Vance leaned against the stable wall and folded his arms. "Should I have left home to go and become a fictional character to save one dragon from taming?"

"There are rumors that they're real. Eslinde used to believe it." Dashiel mimicked Vance's pose, across on the other side of the stall, trying to look as imposing.

"And that's exactly the kind of influence I was talking about. She always had such rebellious stories and ideas." Vance shook and lowered his head, a soft smile across his lips as he stared at the floor. Then his eyebrows lowered. "But things change."

"You ever find out why she stopped coming around?" Dashiel asked gently.

Vance rumbled a growling grunt.

"It's been, what, five years?"

"Eight." The word jumped from Vance's mouth. "Doesn't matter. I'm sure she's busy.

I wouldn't expect her to indulge us with her company like she did when we were young."

Dashiel had always wanted to know what had stopped Eslinde from visiting. It was strange that she didn't even come around to check on or fly her dragon. It was kept a few stalls down, a fine snowshimmer. Eslinde would have had the resources to stable it herself, so it was an honor that she trusted the Zarrams with the keeping of her dragon.

Servants moved around, loading bovin meat from a cart into feeding troughs, and a few people walked in from the entrance.

Dashiel raised their eyebrows. "You wouldn't like to see her again?"

"It's not something I think about."

A grin split Dashiel's lips and they straightened up. "That's a shame, because she's coming up behind you now."

"How dumb do you think I—"

"Oh, Viska is so big now!" a wispy feminine voice exclaimed.

The woman and her grayglim and handmaiden attendants stopped at the entrance to the dragon's stall.

Vance shot forward from his leaning pose, almost stumbling as he righted himself.

Dashiel subdued a chuckle and moved to greet Eslinde. It had been so long since she'd visited the dragonhold, or been seen at all, that Dashiel was taken aback by how different she looked now.

She must be around thirty years old, but time seemed to have treated her badly. Her skin was sallow and pale, and her austere gray gown, sparkling with highlights of decadent gold, hung on a narrow frame. Hair like a silver beam of moonlight was tied back from her face in a simple braided bun, highlighting sunken cheeks and shadowed eyes.

She was a ghost of her past self.

"What are you, umm, why ... grace us with your presence?" Vance cleared his throat after the stumble of words and shot Dashiel a look of murderous intent.

She gave a wan smile. "I came to congratulate Dashiel on their upcoming investment."

"Me? I thought you might have come to visit—"

Vance slapped a hand over Dashiel's shoulder and squeezed.

"Your dragon," Dashiel coughed the words out.

A slight frown passed over her face and she shook her head. "I'm sure you are looking after her well."

"Always," Vance replied.

Eslinde placed one hand across her chest and gave a slight bow. Earrings of spiraling silver and glass swung as she straightened up again. "Congratulations, Dashiel. I heard you had the highest scores of the current recruits, highest of any since your brother."

Dashiel bowed in return, lowering from the waist far deeper than Eslinde had. Then with a bright smile, they asked, "Will we see you at the ceremony?"

Eslinde lifted one shoulder. "Perhaps. Perhaps I will come along. It has been a while. Maybe it will feel different now."

"You never did like watching the tamings. You don't have to attend." Vance shot

Dashiel a look, his tone defensive.

Eslinde waved one hand limply, her fingers skeletal. She looked up at Viska's taming spike, the end of it exposed between golden scales. "I used to watch, make myself watch and wonder how it must feel. A metal stake, right through into the brain. And I did feel it, so deeply."

Dashiel shivered, swallowing hard.

Shaking her head, she toyed with one of her earrings. "Now ... now I look at the spike and pretend it's just jewelry there on their forehead. Nothing terrible. Just a decoration over their scales. And I no longer feel it."

A deep, sinking sadness washed over Dashiel. From the silence all around, they wondered if Vance felt it too. The young woman who had once influenced them both with her fiery, rebellious heart was utterly gone. *What happened to her?*

The awkward silence expanded and then cracked as Eslinde muttered, "I'll see you there, then."

Turning, she strode toward the exit, her gown trailing behind her and attendants in tow, all silent and gray, like a procession of spirits. Vance exhaled audibly.

"Don't be down, brother. It looks like you'll be seeing her again soon," Dashiel teased.

"Yes. At your investment. Where you'll be taming your dragonling. Good times for all," Vance growled back.

Dashiel's playful tone dropped. "Thanks for the reminder."

"I'm sorry. She's just ..." Vance paced a small circle on the ground. "She doesn't look well, does she?"

Dashiel pulled their lips in. "No, she doesn't."

Eslinde looked as unwell as somebody with a wealth of silvernix at their disposal could look. An unwellness of the heart, a wasting away of a soul that the magical healing fluid couldn't repair. The Eslinde they used to know would never turn away from trouble, never pretend a cruelty was something lesser to protect herself.

Just jewelry there on their forehead.

Dashiel's eyes widened as the idea hit. "Oh. Oh!"

"What is it?" Vance turned expectantly toward the entrance of the stables, as though Eslinde was returning.

"I've got to go. There's something I need to try." Dashiel bounced with excitement, bounding away down the hall backward, grinning at their brother on the way.

Vance took a few steps as though to follow, then gave up. "Try what? Is this some new wild experiment?"

"I'll show you soon. If it works." They turned and waved over their shoulder.

Vance called out, "Are we going to regret this?"

Dashiel's exuberant jog slowed then. Would they?

It was just an idea, for now. A concept they could toy with to avoid facing a fate they didn't want. But if it came to following through, if Dashiel pretended to tame a dragon but left it wild and was found out, it could destroy everything the Zarrams had built as a family.

CHAPTER THREE

The door burst open, clattering against the empty shelves. Kess would have flinched, but her body was paralyzed by hunger and the morass mercy. She blinked up at the shadowed wraith filling the doorway.

"Still alive?" Kife snarled. "Could have done me a favor and passed away quietly, but you can't even do that one thing right, little sis."

It had been an eternity since he had last visited, last thrown her the crusts of old bread or left a bucket of water. Kess was as surprised as he was that she still lived. She was sure she'd joined Riony's ghost in an endless limbo of nightmares long ago.

He didn't come inside or try to drag Kess out.

Does he know I have his dagger?

Do I still have his dagger? Kess couldn't feel her own fingers, let alone the weapon she had tucked into the waistband of her pants during a dream long ago.

Does he even care if I did? He hadn't tried to take it back, hadn't called her out. Why would he need to? She was no threat. She was lucky to have enough strength to roll her eyes at him.

Which she did. Maybe if she taunted him enough, he'd try to finish her off once and for all. If Kess could summon the strength to stab him back at the same time, she'd call it a win.

From the way he stalked back and forth in the landing beyond the doorway, whiplike braid swinging, and sword drawn, maybe that time had finally come.

"I'm done with this whole razed affair! It's time to start fresh, without bad luck jinxing my every plan." He leveled the sword her way.

A trickle of fresh air flowed through the open door to Kess, and she tried to suck it in, help her body reawaken from the stupor it had been in.

"Giving up? Can't blame you. If I had your face, I would've given up long ago," Kess slurred.

Sitting behind her in the corner, knees up and legs splayed cavalierly, Riony chuckled.

Kife slashed his sword through the air but remained outside the small chamber. "I'm not giving up. I just feel like killing you might brighten my mood."

"I'm sure it'll help greatly. Good plan. Go ahead, then."

Riony laughed again, a soft rustle of breath. "Subtle, Kess, very subtle."

"Shh!" Kess frowned, then shook her pounding head. "No. Doesn't matter. He can't hear you."

Riony was only there to haunt Kess.

"That's exactly the problem," Kife said, as though she were speaking to him. He spat the words, jabbing his sword as though at imaginary enemies. "What good is this knowledge of the silvernix creature if I can't get the ear of the Dragon King? No way will I share it with anybody else. If I just had a dragon again, I could go after it myself, get proof ..."

"Proof?" Kess turned her head toward him, and it wobbled, skull pressed against the stone. Maybe she wasn't ready to die, not if she could conceive a way out of her cell. A sly smile spread over her lips. "Then you might as well kill me. I'll never tell anyone what I know. You can't use me for leverage to get your way in."

Kife's pacing ceased, and he glowered at Kess. She worried she'd gone too far, too unsubtle again for the outcome she desired.

But Kife was as familiar with subtlety as a blunt axe.

"You'll do whatever I need you to do." He lunged forward and grabbed her around the ankle.

Kess's throbbing head ached and swirled as Kife dragged her across the ground. Dried bundles of morass mercy rustled around her, kicking up their scent.

"Are you really taking me out of here?" There was a desperation in Kess's voice, and she twisted it around into a snarl to hide her hopes. "I won't say anything, even if you do get us in front of the king."

Kife's grin was viciously triumphant. "You keep your mouth shut all you want. I can still use you as *leverage*. I'll tell them you're a criminal, a traitor to the kingdom, who I caught scheming the king's downfall. *That* might get me an audience. Any way I can get in front of the king is worth it."

And anything that gets me away from the morass mercy is worth it.

"Even if you leave me behind?" Riony's eyes glinted like sharp knives from the shadowed corner of the cell.

A juddering shiver shook through Kess's chest. She rolled droopily, arms flopping in a weak attempt to reach for the ghost. "No, I won't!"

Kife laughed at her futile struggling. He got her out of the room and kicked the door closed behind him.

She was out. Kess closed her eyes and tried to think clear thoughts and breathe clear air, but the lingering effect of the sedative was drawing her under again. Her body didn't feel like her own.

The sway of Kife lifting her swung her whole world into dizziness and her head felt fractured and disjointed from her body. "You razing stink, Kess."

She sank away into a dark hollow. Swallowed into nothingness, only brief snatches of reality filtered through to her.

A stairwell, damp and slimy like the throat of a monster. Daylight. *Daylight!* A glare that burned her eyes and forced tears from between her lashes.

Rattling, bumping, thumping. Kess awoke sprawled on the hard bench of a carriage. It beat her back like a wooden bat and the motion stirred sickness in her shriveled stomach.

Stay awake.

Kife was right across from her, turned to the window. There was a jagged press of metal beneath Kess's clothing. The dagger was still there. She fumbled for it, eyes on her brother, on his neck, trying to calculate whether she could draw fast enough, whether her hands still knew how to throw, and exactly which of the three blurred copies of the man to aim at.

A large bump made Kess's whole body lurch and head flare with pain. She grunted and Kife turned to her. Turning her eyes quickly away, she stilled, and pretended to be squinting out the window instead of focusing on him. The buildings they passed by had wreaths of dried wheat and gold ribbons hung on their doors.

Summers End? It's been months ... I missed my eighteenth birthday.

A dry, rasping sob crumpled within Kess's throat as grief hit her. Not because of the birthday or the duration of her imprisonment, but how for some of that time she'd heard the distant echoes of a wolf howling. He'd been there, trying to find her, reach her.

But she hadn't heard Griskin for a while now. She worried at first that something had happened, whether a city guard had captured him or worse. But she knew the truth. He wasn't going to wait for her forever.

Griskin has abandoned me too.

"It's what you deserve," Riony said, sitting shoulder to shoulder with Kife across the carriage like best buddies.

Riony would never.

Was any of this real? Had Griskin ever come to Draekhanhelm and called to her through the night?

Even so far away from morass mercy, Kess's head still felt steeped in the stuff. It had soaked through every fiber of her and left her stained forever. She tried to stay awake, tried to draw the small dagger and carve it into Kife's flesh, but she slipped away again.

"You're such a dead weight, Kess." Kife dumped her unceremoniously on the floor.

She gasped as pain shocked her into consciousness. Her eyes swiveled, trying to orient herself in the space. A coolly lit chamber, expansive, with a vaulted ceiling and ornate columns, all in a pale marble, shot through with silver.

Lamps flickered with a pale-blue light from sconces. Fine wooden chairs, glassy with polish, lined the wall, as though this were some kind of waiting parlor.

Or audience chambers.

Kess frowned, worried her brother had gotten closer to meeting the king than she'd hoped he would. How long would she last if presented as some kind of assassin plotting Yeonard Draekhan's death?

Kife hadn't bothered putting Kess down onto a chair, although they were all empty. She had been dumped in the middle of the floor on the cold marble. He strode over and pushed a set of double doors open.

Then he swore and kicked at the threshold. "It took the last of my silvernix to bribe my way in, and the King isn't even here?"

Glancing over the unoccupied chairs again, and through the opened doors ahead into a grand chamber with dais and throne all cold and bare, a smile cracked Kess's lips. The whole place was empty. No king, no audiences, no guards. Just an empty space that was otherwise closed except to an idiot who spent silvernix on a guard to get in.

She chuckled. "That's probably the *only* reason you got this far. What a joke. Better luck next time, brother."

Kife dropped into a chair and folded his arms like a displeased infant. "No. This is going to work. We're staying right here until someone, anyone, arrives who will listen."

Kess managed to roll over onto one side and lift her head, a feat so impressive by recent standards that she took courage. Maybe she would take her revenge that day. "I have never heard a dumber plan in my life. Could you be more desperate?"

His sharp eyes locked on her. "I should have kept some of the morass mercy around to shut you up."

"Because you're too useless to shut me up yourself."

"I'm serious, Kess, close that mouth of yours or—"

"What? You're pathetic. You couldn't even defeat a Rolanian slave in a sword fight." Kess let a mocking giggle roll from her mouth and reached one hand to her waist.

"Shut up!"

"I so greatly enjoyed watching from atop *your* dragon as she beat your ass up and down."

"Enough!" he roared and was on his feet, storming across the floor her way.

Kess wrapped a hand around the hilt of the dagger, warmed from her body.

Kife bent down, grasping her by the straps of the leather vest that was once Riony's. He dragged her up off the floor, face-to-face with him.

Pulling the stolen blade free, Kess swung. It glanced feebly off the scales forming Kife's dragonrider armor. Her fingers were too numb to maintain their grip, and the blade slipped free and clattered on the tiles. Kife kicked it away and it spun across the glossy stone into a corner.

Kife raised an eyebrow and smirked. "If I thought you had any chance at all of hurting me, I would have taken that off you when you stole it. But it was far more fun to see you think you had hope."

He released one hand and then slapped the back of it hard across Kess's face. The crack of knuckle against cheekbone echoed around them.

In reply, a high, outraged voice struck through the air like a bell. "What are you doing to her?"

Whether he'd intended to all along or was startled into it, Kife dropped Kess. She collapsed hard, like a pile of bones.

A gasp of indignation followed, then the same voice again snapped, "Yensen!"

A flurry of motion appeared at Kife's side. A grayglim warden, clad in armor of smoke-colored scales and silk, had Kife locked in a grapple from behind before Kess could even shake off the stun of failing her strike, of being thrown to the ground.

Four others had also entered the room. A woman in a sweeping gown of gray and gold rushed toward Kess, before being pulled back by an older man at her side.

"Careful, this may be some sort of trap," he said in a tone that suggested he was actually excited by the prospect.

"She's hurt, look at her!"

There were a couple of handmaidens behind them as well, but Kess could only stare at the woman with the starlight hair, pulled into a tight, braided bun.

She looks like 'the guest.'

The mysterious visitor to Heithorn estate for the months leading up to the birth of her child. A child that was stolen and took everything good from Kess's life with her.

But she also looked so different, Kess wasn't sure. It may have been that age had narrowed down her cheeks and all the roundness of youth and pregnancy she'd had was replaced with a boney fragility. But there was also something so different in how she carried herself. None of the haughty attitude of the young woman awaiting birth. Only a grim chill of despair and apathy.

"Let me go. I can explain." Kife at least had the dignity to not try to escape the grayglim's hold. He remained still, chin raised.

The woman looked between him and Kess, assessing, as she tapped a finger to the corner of her mouth. "And what explanation could you have for this display of barbarity? I'd expect far more from a Heithorn."

It is her.

Kess glanced at her brother. Had he realized yet who she was? Just some dragonlord lady. That's how he'd described the guest when Kess had fished for any information he might have. And from the confused look on his face, he had never taken much notice of the guest.

"I'm sorry, do I know you?" He huffily jostled one constrained arm.

"Clearly not. But you are the Heithorn son?"

"Finally!" he groaned out the word. "Yes, last remaining of a noble family. It's wonderful to meet someone who recognizes it! You don't know how long I've been trying to speak to someone with some power around here."

The woman inclined her head, very slightly, and made no order to her grayglim to loosen his hold. Instead, she turned back toward Kess, stepping free from the gentle hold of the elderly man beside her. He muttered and grumbled warnings again.

She waved him off. "It's fine."

"Do beware, Milady," Kife said. "That girl is dangerous. A traitor to the kingdom."

"I'm not. Please, he's lying to get his way," Kess countered. Her eyes rolled back, and she shook her head, trying to stay conscious.

"This girl? She's too weak to stand." The guest leaned down, grasping Kess by her hands and tugging. "I can tell a person who has been abused and imprisoned for a long time. And I can tell when someone is trying to feed me lies."

When Kess made no attempt to get her legs under her, even with assistance, the woman frowned. "Jillisa, Olva, come and help me, please."

"If you'll just let me explain." Kife's voice rose louder, snapping in frustration. "I have important secrets that I must share with the king himself. If you can arrange an audience, you'll be rewarded, I promise!"

Kess tightened her grasp around the woman's fingers, still within hers. She couldn't let Kife get to her, get to the king through her.

The handmaidens bent down on either side, lifting Kess from the ground and bringing her over onto a chair. Kess kept her hold on the woman, meeting eyes as pale and silver as her hair.

As the handmaidens stepped back, Kess pulled the guest closer and whispered, "I know something too. About somebody you once lost."

Those ardent eyes snapped open.

Kess rasped, "But you have to make him leave. I won't tell you unless you make Kife leave."

"Someone I once lost?" The look the guest gave Kess was so intense it rattled her.

Kess nodded.

"What is she saying?" Kife leaned forward in the grayglim's hold. "Don't listen to anything that comes out of that girl's mouth."

The guest addressed her grayglim. "Yensen, could you escort Lord Heithorn out, please?"

There was hesitation then, a faltering of the man's impassive expression. "You aren't to be left unprotected."

"I'm well accompanied here." Eslinde gestured to the three others in the room. "Do as I say."

The man nodded once, a strand of long ebony hair falling loose over his face.

"You can't just … How dare you!" Kife screeched as Yensen muscled him toward the door. "I'll have you pay for this one day, when I get—"

"You threaten Eslinde the First so freely, boy?" The elderly man stepped forward, his gray robes swishing.

The *oh shit* expression on Kife's face would have brought Kess great joy in a normal situation. But she was too busy reeling herself.

Eslinde the First was the guest? The youngest of the Dragon King's first generation of heirs was the woman who had been hidden away at their isolated estate to give birth in secrecy?

That meant … Kess's head drooped and bobbed as a hysterical chuckle burbled from her.

Oh Riony, it wasn't enough to have a live pet with silvernix blood. You had to have a stolen heir as your sister as well?

Over Eslinde's shoulder, the redhead smirked in return. "Guess I'm just lucky? If only that luck kept me alive."

When the grayglim had Kife out of the room, Eslinde the First muttered, "Such a dreadful man. What has been going on between you two that he has treated you like this?"

Kess shrugged and almost slid off her chair. "This is pretty normal, actually."

"And all you deserve," Riony added cheerily.

"I know we never met formally, but …" Eslinde reached out and helped stabilize Kess, frowning deeply. She looked down at Kess's legs. "I remember you now. And I am interested to hear what you remember of me and those I may have lost."

The child who became Riony's sister. If this woman, the guest, had been any other dragonlord lady, Kess could have told her, could have assumed it wouldn't come to anything. Who had the resources to be chasing a single child across the wastes of the rev blighted world? Kess and Kife had tried and failed already.

But one of the Firsts would have all the resources required to reclaim their child.

Riony sat down in the seat beside her with a prolonged sigh. "And you're going to hand my sister over to this woman? Thanks, Kess. You just keep on hitting new lightless depths, don't you?"

Kess flinched away. She didn't want that. She didn't want to hurt Riony again, alive or dead. "I was mistaken. You aren't who I thought you were. I can't … I don't know anything."

Her words were an unconvincing stumble, but her head drummed with agony and she couldn't think.

Eslinde straightened to her full height away from Kess.

She blinked dully. "Really?"

"Your Highness." The older, robed man shuffled closer, although he kept some distance between himself and Kess, wrinkling his nose at the state of her.

Wisps of white hair trailed down each side of his head from a shiny bald top. "What with all this excitement, shall I cancel your meeting? Or will you still be able to meet with Lady Hjelzahn?"

A shiver jolted Kess's back against the chair. There were a lot of Hjelzahns, generations of them, since Hjelzahn the First. But there was one Kess never wanted to see again.

Kess choked on her words. "Lady Hjelzahn? Kverra Hjelzahn?"

"The same." Eslinde shrugged, keeping assessing eyes on Kess as she spoke to the man. "Well, Falden, it all depends on whether this girl has anything to tell me or not."

"Here? You're meeting her here?" Kess asked breathily.

Eslinde replied, "What does that matter to you?"

Because that grayglim noblewoman who seemed immune to pain would no doubt kill Kess as soon as given the opportunity. Because that woman seemed intent upon killing her own children, who both Lyrrin and Dracuni were likely to still be with. Because every part of Kess's drugged and confused mind screamed in fear at the thought of seeing that strange, cold woman again.

"You can't. Don't meet with her. We have to go before she arrives, please."

"Why? What do you have to tell me that gives me a reason to listen to any of this nonsense?"

There was only one thing. The only leverage Kess had to offer, to gain Eslinde's favor and keep herself away from Lady Hjelzahn, away from Kife. And she grieved for what consequences saying it might bring.

Kess reached out and grasped Eslinde's hands again with every scrap of her remaining strength, dragging her down so their faces were only a breath away.

She whispered, "Your daughter is still alive."

Chapter Four

Kess expected the revelation that her child was still alive might have caused some joy or relief in the princess.

Instead, Eslinde's expression was one of naked fear.

Worried the woman had misheard her somehow, Kess raised her voice. "She isn't dead, your—"

"Quiet!" Eslinde pressed her fingers over Kess's mouth and gave her a sharp look, before checking over her shoulders to see how close her entourage were.

The two handmaidens—one with skin aged like the bark of an oak and a stoic, motherly air, and the other young and wide-eyed as though everything around her were new and exciting—were a respectful space back, hovering in readiness to respond to any need that arose.

The older man, Falden, in his noble robes, also maintained a distance, eyeing the utter state of filth Kess displayed with thinly veiled disgust.

Eslinde remained frozen in position with her fingers shushing Kess for a long moment. Her eyes darted as though working through a multitude of thoughts.

The door clicking closed made both her and Kess jump.

Kess leaned sideways to see whether Lady Hjelzahn approached, but found instead the princess's grayglim, Yensen, returning. Whether he had ejected Kife from the palace onto the street himself or handed him over to other guards to expel, he'd returned with an eager speed.

Kess wondered if she should have asked for more, had Kife thrown in a dungeon. But she also didn't want to push Kife into sharing his knowledge of Dracuni in desperation.

There was concern on the grayglim's face as he took in Kess and her proximity to Eslinde. His dark eyes also fell on the dagger which lay in the corner.

"All's well?" he asked.

Eslinde's eyelids fluttered as she side-eyed him but otherwise didn't acknowledge the man.

"We need to go," Kess urged again in a whisper.

"Yes, some privacy is required." Eslinde nodded once and rose up tall, away from Kess. "Olva, Jillisa, help her to my chambers."

They bobbed a curtsy in time together, then each took Kess by an arm.

Their first attempt to assist Kess from the seat left her hanging like a spent scarecrow between them. They moved in closer, propping themselves under a shoulder each.

"Oh goodness, goodness, goodness," the older handmaiden said, turning her nose away.

"Falden?" Eslinde waved the man closer. "Would you wait here and give Lady Hjelzahn my apologies that I won't be able to meet with her today."

"Of course, Your Highness. Unless you need some assistance with this ... situation?" He gestured to Kess, forehead wrinkled.

"Oh, it's nothing. She's an old friend come upon hard times, that's all. Something of a misunderstanding."

"Hmm, quite." Falden settled himself into one of the chairs with a soft groan. Boney knees poked from under his robes.

As she turned to leave, Eslinde paused, then addressed him again. "And could you also check on what records or information we have on the Heithorn family, please?"

His eyes sparkled and thin lips pulled into a smile. "Always happy to assist."

Eslinde nodded, then broke into a long, elegant stride, leading the way out of the audience chambers.

Following behind, Kess tried to keep her head up as she was jostled between the two handmaidens. But her arms ached from the strain of hanging in their grasp and it felt as though her skull had been hollowed out and filled with hot lead.

The grayglim remained close at their heels as their procession wove through the corridors of the palace.

Kess took in what she could of the grand space. Surfaces of glossy marble and obsidian were brightened by flickering lamps and colossal windows of clear glass and steel. Dark wood furniture was made decadent with golden accents and silver upholstery.

Guards in dragon scale armor were posted at regular intervals as Eslinde led them down a long hall, through a tiled courtyard with precisely trimmed hedges, and into a labyrinth of corridors, carved out with large niches, each holding lifelike statues of ancient heroes.

A few other servants rushed about, all Rolanian and all wearing a uniform similar to the women carrying Kess—neat tunics and kirtles in charcoal gray.

Kess tried to keep her bearings, to work out how she could follow this path back to an exit if she had a chance, but a few turns along, her head whirled.

They ascended three flights of stairs, handmaidens huffing and muttering under their breaths, and their journey came to an end in what seemed to be a poorly managed library.

The chamber was of the same, stark glossy stone as the rest of the palace. The only thing that added color and texture to the room were the bookshelves that lined the walls, filled so completely that the books were wedged in at odd angles in every gap and spilled onto the floor in towering piles.

The vast space only held a few pieces of furniture, their black and silver forms reflecting on slick dark tiles, and all piled in a mess of books.

"Put her on the lounge," Eslinde said and then paced, chewing on a nail as the handmaidens moved aside a few leatherbound tomes and sat Kess down.

Kess's eyelids were drooping and she screwed them shut, then forced them open again to refresh them. The plush cushions beneath her were so soft against her body—that had forgotten any feeling other than hard and cold—that she almost broke down. It was only Riony's steady glare from the armchair opposite that kept Kess composed.

"I'm sorry I told," Kess whispered.

Eslinde spoke over her, tone commanding. "She needs food, clean clothing. Now please, both of you."

She herded her handmaidens back out through the door they'd just come in, then ran up against the grayglim as though hitting a wall.

"Wait outside too, Yensen."

He tilted his head, almost apologetically. "I can't leave you alone with her, Your Highness."

Eslinde drew herself up straight, barely coming to the man's shoulders. "You can and you will. She deserves some privacy and dignity in this moment. Or are you going to give the poor child a sponge bath?"

He frowned awkwardly under thick eyebrows, high cheekbone twitching. "The Heir Killer is still unknown and becoming bolder. This could all be a ruse. This girl could be a threat."

"Her?" There was laughter in the princess's voice. "She's no Heir Killer. And from the looks of things, she's been held captive right through when Skaella was assassinated last week. She's nothing but bruised skin and bones and has no weapons and can't even walk. What do you think she's going to do?"

A breathy, sobbing laugh broke from Kess and she slid down onto her side. She'd been underestimated her whole life but had to admit the princess's estimations felt crushingly accurate in that moment.

A deep, stubborn inner voice that had driven her on her whole life revived from within the shadows of her mind.

I'll show them. I'll show them all.

Eslinde continued her rant, jabbing a finger into the man's breastplate. "And you, you're nothing more than a jailer acting under my parents' orders."

Yensen looked pained. "Your Highness, I'm not—"

"Prove it then! Go on, get out!"

Yensen cast a concerned look toward Kess, then the princess, then Kess again, and then stepped out of the room.

Eslinde closed the door behind him, none too gently, then hurried back to Kess's side.

She knelt before the lounge, and her pale eyes looked deep into Kess's, searching. "You are the Heithorn daughter, aren't you? They kept you away from me as much as they kept me away from you during my stay. What was it ... Kessara?"

Kess wobbled a nod.

"And my child ... a daughter too? How, how do you know she lived?" Despite the closed door, Eslinde still kept her voice barely above a whisper.

Kess blinked, confused for a moment. Did she know for sure? It was just a guess really, based on age and circumstance. However, looking into the princess's face, she could see the same almond shape to her eyes as Lyrrin had, the same pouting, petal lips.

"I know. I've seen her."

"Recently? She's grown?" Eslinde's chest heaved with labored breath.

Across in the armchair, Riony leaned forward, resting her elbows on her knees and locking on Kess with an accusing glare. "Go ahead. Tell her. Let her know aaaaall about my sister and her unnaturally blue eyes and her strange, clawed hands. The Dragon King's daughter is going to love that. I'm sure she's going to make sure Lyrrin stays safe and well."

Kess pulled her lips in and kept them closed tight. She turned her eyes away, staring at the blurring floor beneath her.

Eslinde grasped Kess's wrist, pulling her attention back again. "Is she still at Heithorn estate? Where is she? What happened to her?"

The hammering of questions made Kess flinch, her head about to crack like an egg.

"If you tell her anything, you might as well stab me in the back again," Riony snarled.

"It wasn't me. Riony, I didn't ..."

Eslinde glanced over her shoulder, following Kess's eyeline. She frowned. "What are you talking about? Who's Riony?"

Kess crumpled into a gasping fit of hysteria. "A ghost. She's haunting me, for all I did to her."

Eslinde raised an eyebrow. "A ghost?"

A light rapping echoed from the door and Eslinde rose back to her feet, brushing her dress down. "Come."

The older handmaiden returned, a neatly folded stack of clothing balanced in her hands. "I've a selection for the child, should be some that fit."

Yensen peered in through the opened door, but Eslinde strode over and closed it on him. "Olva, could you check over her, please? She's behaving oddly. Speaking of ghosts. Could she be unwell, beyond her physical injuries?"

"Ghosts, you say?" Olva placed the clothing down on a low table wrought of black metal and glass beside a stack of books.

She moved close to Kess, pressing her face tight within her gnarled fingers and pulling her eyelids back. "Hmm, yes. I thought I noted a familiar scent ... beneath the *other* smells. Been a long time since I've worked with herbs myself, but there are some fragrances you'll always remember."

Eslinde drifted behind the woman, clasping her hands together. "An herb? Has she been drugged somehow?"

"For certain. It's a nasty sedative that healers only used if they couldn't get their hands on anything else. Terrible side effects. Prolonged headaches, withering, hallucinations."

Eslinde's nervous fidgeting ceased and a dull sadness washed over her face. "Hallucinations?"

The handmaiden released Kess from her tight grip. "Some silvernix should clear any long-term effects right up, though. Shall I fetch some?"

The corner of Eslinde's mouth twitched and she stared down at Kess for a long moment. "So be it."

As the older handmaiden went out, the younger came in, hefting a silver tray filled with steaming bowls, bread rolls, and fruit.

Once the door was closed to the grayglim again, Eslinde scrubbed her face with her hands and muttered, "It wasn't even real. Just hallucinations."

"Pardon, Your Highness?" The handmaiden placed the tray onto the table beside the clothing with a soft rattle of crockery.

"It's nothing." Eslinde peered at Kess as though she were a piece of trash she was eager to dispose of.

She will. She'll get rid of me if I can't provide enough information for her to believe me.

In a moment of panic, Kess blurted, "The redheaded girl and her family, they took the b—"

"*Bath!*" Eslinde practically shouted. "Jillisa, go and draw one, please."

The handmaiden had frozen with a serving lid held high in one hand. Blinking a couple of times, she curtsied and vanished into a side room. The burbles of running water emerged soon after.

"Careful!" Eslinde hissed near Kess's ear. "Nobody knows, nobody is to know there *ever* was a child! Only my parents and those from the Heithorn estate who didn't know my identity."

Kess nodded vaguely. Of course it was a secret. Why would a first heir travel all the way to the middle of nowhere to give birth? The Heithorn midwife was good, but the Dragon King himself no doubt would have had better.

"Not the biggest secret out there," Riony said. "Once this woman starts searching for Lyrrin, how long do you think it will be before she finds out about Dracuni? You might as well tell her now and get it over with."

"I won't tell," Kess mumbled to the ghost.

Or hallucination. Is that what she was? She seemed so real. Or maybe that's just what Kess wanted, for Riony to still be real.

The world all around her appeared like a view through a twisted mirror and Kess's whole body felt turned inside out.

"Could it be true? My heart feels taut like a bowstring." Eslinde kneeled beside Kess again, elbows on the lounge and palms on her forehead. "The redheaded girl ... there was one there, at the birth. The midwife's daughter and assistant. But no, they were all killed, weren't they?"

Kess opened her mouth to reply, leaned forward, and dry heaved over the side of the seat.

Eslinde jumped away, then when she realized Kess had nothing inside her to expel, tentatively returned. She brushed a hand gently over Kess's cheek where it was still hot and thrumming from being backhanded.

In a gentle voice, she said, "It's alright. We'll have you fixed up soon."

Tears welled up in the corners of Kess's eyes at the small act of kindness.

And then Eslinde continued. "And then you will tell me what you know. This isn't just some sickness. I can sense you are hiding something from me, and I will have the truth from you. All of it."

A chill rushed down Kess's spine as Eslinde strode over to the bathroom doorway.

Jillisa met her there, sleeves rolled up as she wiped her hands.

"This girl, Kessara, will be my guest for a while. Prepare the spare room for her and ..."

Eslinde swung back around to Kess. "Do you have any belongings to fetch?"

Nothing that wasn't on Griskin, somewhere far across the land. She hoped he would find a way to rid himself of the saddles and bags he no longer needed weighing him down. She hoped he would be okay without her.

He would be. He'd probably be better.

"No. I have nothing," Kess said, tongue thick and voice heavy.

Reality slid away from Kess again like an avalanche down a snowy mountain. There were murmurings from the princess about keys and locks as Kess was hauled into a steaming tub and scrubbed brusquely.

The water sloshed and hot wafts of soapy fragrance made Kess sure she was back in her cell again, surrounded by morass mercy.

The next Kess opened her eyes, she was dried and dressed in a soft nightgown and being lowered onto something soft. A cushion strewn daybed in a smaller room that was filled with even more books than the last.

Eslinde brought a blanket up around her and whispered, "I'll be keeping you near, to make sure you and your information remains safe. What you know ... it's very dangerous information to have. People have been killed for that knowledge in the past."

And then, despite the new faces and clean clothing and washed body, Kess was aware enough to realize she'd traded one prison for another.

The older handmaiden arrived, flanked by four guards. She held a palm-sized coffer. When she handed it to Eslinde, the guards bowed and withdrew from the chambers.

Eslinde clicked the latch and pulled from inside a single tiny vial of opalescent fluid.

The royals must still have a plentiful supply if they're willing to spend some on me.

Riony lay on the daybed beside her, hands behind her head and taking up most of the room. "Perhaps you'll waste the last of the kingdom's supply just as you wasted the last of the Heithorn wealth."

Had Riony ever been that cruel? Maybe she wasn't real, but she seemed so tangible, like Kess could reach out and touch her. But maybe she was just a hallucination.

A hallucination born from the ailment she was about to be cured of.

Panic spiked through Kess and she thrashed her arms weakly, trying to pull herself up and away from Eslinde's approach.

"No, no I don't—"

"It's okay, this will make you feel better."

I don't want to. I don't want to lose her again.

But the single drop of silvernix wet her forehead and the room lit with the glow of it streaming throughout her body, casting shadows from the towers of books. All the turmoil within her head seemed to retract like the tide of a stormy sea, all of the aches and confusion washed away as the healing light flowed through her veins.

She rolled to her side, arms reaching out, trying to touch the body that she was sure had been right beside her on the daybed. There was nobody there.

As the shimmer sizzling from her flesh dulled, Kess pulled herself upright, staring beyond the princess and handmaiden in front of her, checking every corner of the room for the familiar face, the smirk, and the tumble of red hair.

Nothing. Riony was gone.

Even the drug-twisted, cruel visage had been the only steady piece of Kess's existence these last months, and the real Riony ... Kess could feel the truth. Riony was the only good thing ever in Kess's life. The one truly good person. And she was gone.

Something cracked apart in Kess's core and she slumped back onto the bed, chest heaving and great clumps of tears rushing from her eyes.

"Did it not work? What's wrong with her?" The handmaiden shuffled in and pressed a crepey hand to Kess's forehead.

There was a long silence, and the princess's words came through muffled by the hum of Kess's cries. "She's grieving."

There was a deep sadness in her tone. A *knowing*.

"Your Highness?"

"Come. Give her space."

The click of a lock followed them from the room, and Kess was alone.

Thin streams of morning light woke Kess. Her eyes peeled open, puffy and sore, and her head ached dreadfully. But for the first time in months, it wasn't from the effects of morass mercy. It came from a night spent crying uncontrollably into a soft pillow.

She hadn't cried like that since Kife abandoned her in the wilds. Since the day Riony had first abandoned her, fleeing Heithorn estate with her family.

She's gone. She's gone. The thoughts that had tormented her all night continued repeating in a way Kess couldn't banish. Whether Riony had been a ghost or hallucination, it didn't matter. Kess couldn't bring herself to believe Riony lived. With the effects of the drug expelled from her system, she remembered everything clearly now.

The knife in Riony's back, right into her heart. The way she had fallen and not moved again. The cries of her friends, *She's not breathing, she's not ...*

Grunting fiercely, Kess squeezed her head between her palms and refocused.

She's gone ... So, what are you going to do about it?

"I'm getting out of here. And I'm going to kill Kife," Kess growled the pledge to herself.

Shifted into a sitting position, Kess took stock of herself and her surroundings.

The silvernix had healed all her ailments, but she'd lost weight and muscle while lying wasted and starved on the cell floor. She brought a leg up and began going through the motions of her exercises, her tendons feeling stiff and tight.

From her disjointed memories of the night before, and the number of books filling the space, Kess assumed this was Eslinde's spare room. There were a couple more bookshelves, although far more books on the floor than in them, a wardrobe, side tables, and the low daybed.

Beyond that, the room was shadowed. There were unlit lamps on each wall, but they contained no oil reservoir. Instead, each was topped with a bulb of glass.

Kess had heard stories of such an invention, illumination powered by the collected lightning breath of snowshimmer dragons. She imagined that destructive energy flowing through those lamps and balked at the idea of touching them.

One wall was split by a section of floor-to-ceiling glass. Morning light came in between crisscrossed, tightly spaced metal bars, and Kess could see a balcony beyond.

She made her way over to the doors, running her hands up to the handle, but it didn't turn. It seemed locked, completely and firmly, but there was no keyhole visible. Kess pressed her face against the glass to get the most she could from the view.

It was a long way down to the courtyard below. Too far to risk jumping even if she could get onto the balcony.

Beyond the courtyard were rooftops of the rest of the palace and all of the capital dragonkeep below. The sky seemed filled with dragons, transferring people and goods across the city or to other keeps. There was one gap in the aerial traffic, and Kess's breath caught as another wave of grief washed over her.

This time, not hers. It came from the colossal, shadowy mass that descended upon the city below.

The shadow dragon.

All riders and fliers gave it distance, but there was no urgency or worry in their movements. And Kess knew too, that as the shadow dragon roared its mournful cry, it would find no dead within the city's fortified walls to raise.

Still, every part of Kess recoiled from the sight of it, and she turned away, continuing her investigation of the room.

The solitary armoire, glossy with dark enamel, stood beside a matching dresser. Elegant knotwork surrounded the mirror with a single ring of gold around the edge.

On the tabletop was a glass pitcher of water, one stack of unfamiliar clothing, and another of the mixed leathers and garments Kess had arrived in, cleaned and folded. A small object glinted on the top of the stack.

Kess moved closer, lifting herself into the seat in front of the mirror, pointedly avoiding looking at herself. She could feel that her hair had been washed, but not combed or braided. She'd been cleaned of the filth and lingering scent of morass mercy and she didn't really care otherwise how she appeared.

She could only stare at the item lying on the armored vest Riony had given her.

The acorn pendant. She must have had it in her pocket the whole time. She reached for it tentatively, worried that it wasn't real. It was silky soft under her touch, polished by its previous owner's fingers.

Kess's hands trembled as she fastened the pendant around her neck.

Touching the quality hide of the armored vest, Kess considered putting it on too. But if Eslinde the First and her grayglim decided they no longer needed her, Kess doubted the leather armor would save her.

She had no other belongings there worth taking, no weapons, and she couldn't see much within the room she could easily fashion into a blade.

Kess was halfway across the room toward the only other doorway when raised voices pierced through from the room beyond. Something smashed, and a woman screamed.

Chapter Five

Kess froze, casting a look around the room again for anything she could use as a weapon.

Then a woman shrieked, "Eslinde! You're being unreasonable!"

"*Unreasonable?* You've lied to me for eight years! Tell me the truth!"

"There's nothing to say. Put that down! Don't you—"

Another crash and jingle of breaking glass echoed.

Kess moved to the doorway between her room and the argument and pressed her ear close.

"Stop this nonsense! How dare you treat me like this?"

"What are you going to do? What else do I have that you can take from me?" That was Eslinde's voice, although high and fierce with none of the restraint she'd had the day before.

"Who has been filling your head with these ideas?" The second woman's voice was much like Eslinde's, with only a slightly deeper warble differentiating them.

"Wouldn't you like to know? I'm sure you'll find out through one of your spies soon enough, Mother."

Kess tried to imagine the second woman from her memories of her time at Heithorn estate so long ago. The mother who had trailed the guest around as surely as their bodyguard. Short, pink-skinned and fine-boned, with a sweep of long black hair streaked white down the front, and apparently no older than her adult daughter.

That lack of age gap made some sense now. As the Dragon King's wife, the woman was surely being kept young on regular doses of silvernix just as he was.

The Dragon King's wife. Queen Vellira. Razed earth. Kess worried at her lip, hoping she hadn't made an enemy of one of the most powerful people in Elundrae.

"Enough of this, Eslinde. Whoever it is, they're lying to you."

"You're the liar. You took my baby away. You told me she was dead when she wasn't. You ... you *expected* her to be dead. You didn't just order the deaths of the midwife and her assistant, did you? You ordered hers, too."

There was another rattle of crockery and a gasp.

"I only did what I had to do to keep you safe."

"Just admit it!"

"Fine!" The word rang through the air, leaving a silence behind it. "I lied about the baby being dead. That useless guard was supposed to dispose of it and the witnesses—which was *required* to clean up the mess *you* made—but somehow the fool got himself skewered and the midwife ran off with the child."

"How could you?"

"How could I? Easily. I was protecting you!"

Stomping footsteps punctuated the words. "You were protecting yourself. If you had any love for me, you would have let me keep my daughter."

"Oh no. Don't pretend you're so naïve. You *know* that was never a possibility," the mother's words huffed with a cold, dry humor.

"Something, *something* could have been arranged."

"Exactly. I tried to arrange the best outcome for all of us out of an awful situation. My only mistake was bringing some thuggish dragonrider as our guard. But who would have thought the midwife had it in her to kill the man? I should have brought a grayglim along instead but needed someone ... more disposable."

"Disposable? I can't believe you. Those were people's lives. All those people ..."

"Don't blame me, you spoiled girl. If it weren't for me and what I did, you'd be among those bodies."

A long silence followed, then voices too soft for Kess to hear. She held her breath, listening closer and hearing only a few thumping sounds.

The door at Kess's ear opened too quickly for Kess to back away. She caught herself before falling to the ground and looked up at Eslinde.

"You were listening, then?"

Kess lifted a shoulder. "Obviously."

Eslinde's face was tight and jittery with emotion as she glared down. The room behind her was empty, the mother gone. The princess ran her hands down her silver silk gown as though smoothing wrinkles that weren't there, squared her shoulders, and turned away.

"Come on then. There is food."

She strode away toward the table where a small feast had been laid out, notably missing a couple of glasses that lay shattered across the room.

Halfway there, she stopped and glanced over her shoulder. "Do you ... require assistance?"

"No." Kess scowled as she pulled herself across the polished stone around stacks of books.

The long nightgown caught beneath her as she moved, making the entire process painful. She missed Griskin so much, for so many reasons. A flush of heat rose over her cheeks as the princess watched her climb into the chair opposite her at the table.

Then Kess saw the food and realized how hungry she was and didn't care anymore what the princess thought of her. Light streamed in through the window beside them onto plates piled with crusty bread, surrounded by chutneys and pickles, a side of smoked fish as long as Kess's arm, fresh fruit, and toasted nuts. The selection overwhelmed the small table.

A wheel of soft cheese large enough to feed a family had a dainty knife stuck into the top, and other vessels with lids steamed, filling the air with aromas of honey and spiced meat.

Eslinde didn't touch the feast. She stared at the closed door her mother had recently passed through. "It's true. Blessings from the sun, it is true. My daughter is alive and ..."

Kess spread a slice of creamy cheese over the still warm bread. She took her first bite with her eyes closed, letting it melt in her mouth before rapidly demolishing the rest.

Eslinde's attention turned to her, a soft line between her eyebrows. "Where is she?

Which dragonkeep?"

Kess chewed the last bite of bread as she opened the lids on one metal pot after another, peering inside at the stewed meats and creamy oats. "She's not in any dragonkeep."

"Another dragonlord's estate, then? Where did the midwife take her?"

Kess shook her head as she spooned a bowl full of a bit of everything, buying time. She had to be careful not to share too much, only enough to stay in the princess's favor without providing enough to allow her to actually find Lyrrin, and then Dracuni.

"I'm not sure exactly where she is. She's traveling Elundrae."

Eslinde shot from her chair. "On *foot*? Out *there*?"

Mouth filled to bursting, Kess just nodded.

Grasping the sides of her head in her hands, Eslinde paced. "What am I going to do?"

Keeping one eye on the woman's back, Kess rearranged the plates and cutlery before her, moving things around to cover her actions.

The heady scent of spiced milk tea sent Kess's nostalgia spiraling, and she reached for the metal teapot. After washing down another greedy bite, she slowed down, giving the panicking woman a thoughtful look.

"You are Eslinde the First, right? What can't you do?"

Eslinde stilled and gave Kess a withering look. "Travel outside this city, fly my dragon, even leave this room without spies and guards surrounding me."

She flung a hand toward the entrance, and Kess imagined the grayglim on the other side.

A piece of Kess's crumpled heart softened toward the woman. She put down her spoon, despite the food she'd eaten so far only awakening her appetite more.

"But you're Eslinde *the First*," she said again, fidgeting with the long sleeves of the nightgown. "Why would you be treated like that?"

Eslinde returned to her chair. Her silver hair hung loose, not yet braided for the day, and swung around her narrow face.

She rubbed her forehead again with boney fingers, then sighed. "Do you know that I was never meant to be born? There were meant to be no other first-generation heirs after Ylva."

Kess raised her eyebrows. There were a couple of decades between Eslinde and the heir prior to her, but nothing had ever been said publicly about the reasons for that. Most assumed it was because the previous queen had fallen from favor, and it took a while before Yeonard Draekhan took a wife again.

Eslinde held a slice of the crusty bread and picked at it, popping one shred into her mouth for every other few she tossed onto her plate. "My siblings decided fifteen of them was enough, especially once they started having their own children, and those children had children. There were worries about inheritance becoming complicated, *if* Father ever passed away."

"That's so unlikely?" Kess asked.

Eslinde barked a single *ha!*

"So what happened?" Kess hadn't been born yet when the Dragon King remarried and Eslinde was born, but from all she'd heard in the stories that reached Heithorn estate, it seemed as though both those events had been widely celebrated.

"My mother happened. Yeonard Draekhan's first wife, reborn! Or so he believed. He's absolutely besotted with her, so anything she wants, she gets. She wanted an heir, she got one. Only I wasn't the perfect child she'd hoped for." Eslinde's lips twisted into a smile so sly and rebellious it looked entirely out of place.

It vanished again and her voice became somber. "So when I got pregnant young to the wrong person, my mother had all the resources she needed to make it go away."

"That's why you came all the way out to the middle of nowhere to give birth?"

"An isolated estate of a reclusive, minor dragonlord family—"

"Minor?" Kess bristled.

"—where it was unlikely anyone would recognize me. It was perfect. The lord and lady knew, but they were well paid to keep the secret, even from their own children, which it seems they did."

Eslinde chewed on a crumb thoughtfully. "What happened to your parents? Neither you nor your brother were meant to leave your estate."

"Yeah ... Long story." Kess jabbed a spoon into her bowl of mixed foods and filled her mouth again to avoid saying more.

"Regardless, you brought me news that my mother wasn't able to make everything go away, and I'm grateful. Now we must make sure nobody else finds out. You heard my mother. She wasn't wrong. It's only thanks to her privilege that I'm only paying for my mistakes with my freedom, and not my life."

Kess continued eating, as though her curiosity was only casual. "Just from an unwanted pregnancy? Who was the father?"

"It doesn't matter. He's dead." Eslinde's lips drew thin, and she stared at her plate, scattered with a confetti of bread crumbs. "I have shared with you. Now tell me about my daughter. I want to know everything."

Kess looked over at the shards of glass glittering between piles of books across the room. "She's a lot like you in some ways."

"Is she healthy? Safe?"

Kess imaged the Hjelzahn siblings and Niskina and Dracuni, and how they all looked after Lyrrin and each other. And how Riony had cared for the girl, had run across a burning slaver camp filled with revs to leap onto a cage held in the air by a dragon to save her.

Wondering whether there was any chance Riony was still there looking after the princess's daughter only made Kess's eyes water. She blinked the threat of tears away.

"It's been a while since I saw her, but she was as healthy and well protected as could be hoped."

"How long has it been?"

Kess shrugged. She hadn't bothered for years to keep track of the days or dates other than by having a rough sense of seasons passing. All she knew was it was summer before and it was Summer's End now. "Weeks? Months, maybe?"

Eslinde's shoulders sagged, and she stared out the window over the city. "Anything could have happened out there since then."

Kess found it hard to swallow the spoonful of soft oats she'd just taken. "She's a tough kid, just like … the people who raised her."

"The midwife and her husband?"

Kess thought on that for a moment. When she'd stolen Dracuni from Riony's small rooms in the undercity, there was no sign of the parents. She hadn't really considered much of it then, too focused on her own all-consuming goal.

When did Riony lose them? And how? Kess didn't have to wonder whether it hurt Riony more than Kess's loss of her own parents.

She muttered, "I don't think the parents are around anymore."

"Gone?" Eslinde pressed a hand to her heart. "I'll never get to thank them for saving my daughter."

Kess sniffed and cleared her throat. "They called her Lyrrin."

"Lyrrin," Eslinde repeated in a whisper. Then she leaned forward, hands splayed on the table and an eager brightness in her eyes. "How do you know all of this? Did you spend time with her?"

Kess dug through the food in her bowl, mixing it into a pasty slop in her nervous motions. "I saw her around sometimes."

"Were you friends?"

"Sure."

Leaning back away from Kess, Eslinde gave her an appraising look down her nose. "Don't lie to me, Kessara."

Kess's shoulders tensed, and if she could have marched away from the table, she would have. She wanted to hide from what she'd done, the suffering she'd caused. But she had nobody to make it all go away.

So she faced it and spoke the truth. "I know what I know because I spent most of last year hunting your daughter and her group across Elundrae."

"*Hunting* her? Why?" Eslinde shot to her feet and snatched a sea-green teacup from the table with a look on her face that precisely matched Lyrrin's expression before the child threw one of her exploding rocks.

"Not *her* exactly."

Eslinde's arm lowered. "Not her? Then who?"

Kess knew she was getting dangerously close to truths she needed to keep hidden. She skirted around them again. "A bounty. I thought … I was doing the right thing. Something important. I was wrong. I was only hurting … everybody."

"At least you're being honest now." Eslinde's steely gaze was so intense that Kess had to turn away.

She shrugged. "Yeah, well, I just wanted you to know that if I couldn't catch her, she's not going to be easy to find."

"You might have given up, but I won't."

Kess recoiled, lips twisted in a snarl.

Hands trembling, the princess thumped the teacup back onto the table again, then swept away to the chamber exit.

She paused at the door, running her hand over the decorative stone archway at the side. There was a strange chorus of clunking metal around Kess, from the main door and the barred window beside her and through passages to the other rooms.

Kess caught a glimpse of the grayglim at the door as the princess stepped outside. After the door closed, the percussion of clicks sounded again.

"I have *not* given up," Kess muttered to herself.

Giving the window a skeptical glare, Kess tested it. Again, there was a handle, but no keyhole and no give at all in her attempts to get it open. Spurred on by spite, Kess worked her way around the entire collection of chambers, through the living room, the bathroom, changing room, a small office, Eslinde's bedroom—sheets and blankets strewn in disarray and dotted with books—and back to where she started.

Every exterior exit was locked shut in some way Kess couldn't comprehend or affect.

With a sigh, she settled again at the table. She wasn't giving up. She hadn't. Things had just *changed*.

At least she was awake and lucid again now. She could plan her escape, and revenge, and then ...?

Kess's face wrinkled and her chest ached, still too hurt in a way that silvernix hadn't repaired. She couldn't imagine a future anymore beyond the immediate.

There was nothing left for her out in the world. Griskin had left her, which was for the best. Kess couldn't even bring herself to care about owning a dragon anymore.

Kess's hand wrapped around the acorn hung at her neck. Even if Riony had survived, it didn't matter to Kess's future. Any offer Riony had been making to Kess, Kife had destroyed the chance of Kess taking.

She would hate me more than ever.

But if she was alive ...

Kess refused to entertain the idea, but still it stoked an ember within her, renewing her energy.

Kess removed the cheese knife that she'd tucked away into her nightgown sleeve. She'd hidden it, expecting all the cutlery to be cleared away, to not allow Kess a single option of weapon. But clearly Kess wasn't considered any threat.

With how dull and round the cheese knife was, they were probably right.

The windowsill beside the breakfast spread had some rough-hewn stone, contrasting the polished marble around it. Kess moved her chair closer and began working the metal of the blunt blade against it, slowly working it toward a point.

She still had one goal. To kill Kife. That was enough to keep her going for now.

The hard metal worked much more slowly than the bone Kess was used to sharpening. She gazed out the window as she worked, trying to get a sense of the layout of the palace.

The window looked over the same courtyard as the one in the spare room Kess had awoken in. A parade of at least a dozen grayglim were passing through in two neat rows, flanking three white-haired men within their ranks.

Kess had never seen Yeonard Draekhan, the Dragon King, in person herself. But she'd seen enough depictions of his unique, dragon tooth-shaped crown, of his hawklike profile stamped onto the backs of sovs, to identify him immediately.

It was hard to believe it was him, despite the evidence. He looked remarkably young for one hundred and twenty-something. Not much older than Kess's parents last time she saw them. Not much older than Eslinde.

Hair as white as snow hung in an intricate tapestry of braids down to his waist, over an ornamental breastplate and shoulder armor in gold. Silver robes spilled from beneath.

The men on either side of him were also obviously heirs as well, based on the milky shade of their hair, but Kess didn't know which. She had always been more interested in studying dragons than the history of the royal line.

The flash of movement drew Kess's eye to another window across the open space.

And a woman's cold eyes stared back. Kess shivered and pulled herself quickly out of sight.

But she knew in her chilled stomach that Lady Hjelzahn had already seen her.

CHAPTER SIX

"It's not going to work," Vance said, inspecting the fake taming stake.

"It will." Dashiel tried to reclaim the device they'd spent so long crafting.

Vance held it out of reach. "And what if it doesn't? What then? If something goes wrong, if it's found out that you faked the taming of a dragon, that you are *keeping* an untamed dragon, that would be the end of your dragonrider career."

Hunt? Catch?

Beside them, the shimmerdart lifted her head from the stone floor of her stall, watching Dashiel's grasping jumps with bright eyes. Almost a month old, she was growing fast, already hound-sized, with a mottled pattern of icy blue and earthy purple scales.

The stall was built for a full-grown flamesong dragon, and despite being large for her type, the dragonling seemed tiny in the space. But Dashiel refused to put her in the battery cages with the tamed dragonlings being raised.

Shiff needed room to move, and the difference in how strong she grew compared to those confined to only moving when told to do so in training was significant.

The modern stalls upstairs for full-grown dragons had no doors—there was no need with tamed beasts—but these older ones in the lower, underground levels had heavy drop-gates of solid steel, from when their family used to breed flamesongs.

The unstable combination of seasong and etherflame were massive, with extraordinarily powerful dragonfire, but had a nasty habit of spontaneously combusting and taking out everything around them. Some breeders still raised them for industry, but Zarram Dragonhold focused on riding dragons these days.

The stalls were mostly empty, only used for long-term storage, and hiding untamed dragonlings.

The eagerness in Shiff's eyes stung Dashiel. They hadn't had as much time to spend with her while preparing for investment, and although they'd left a range of blankets and ropes and balls on the stone floor of the stall to keep the dragonling amused, they could feel how much she missed them.

Dashiel stilled and folded their arms. "I know it's a risk to our family, faking the taming. But I can't do that to Shiff, I won't. She's like family too. I can feel her thoughts, her emotions."

Vance scoffed, relaxing his raised arm.

Dashiel took the bait and leaped for the taming spike, just out of reach again.

Shiff growled and circled around the siblings, fluttering her still-forming wings.

Dashiel grunted at their brother, pointing at the stake vehemently. "It's either this, or I take Shiff and we try our luck out in the world where no one will force me to stab her in the brain and leave her senseless."

Vance gave the small dragonling a gruff look that bordered on sympathetic. "Where would you go? The dragonling is still growing. How would you feed her, or yourself?"

"We could head out into the wilds. Hunt together."

Vance's eyebrow inched up dramatically. "You'd really try that? What do you know about hunting?"

"I'd work it out!"

"Yes, I suppose you probably would. You somehow manage to work most things out." Vance sighed and brought his arm down, holding the stake out. "I think I would prefer if you stayed and worked out how to keep your dragon out of trouble here, where I can help keep you *both* out of trouble."

Dashiel took back the taming spike, inspecting it to be sure their brother hadn't damaged the fragile construction. "Thanks."

"It looks well made. If it works how you propose, it should go smoothly. But you're going to have to swap it out for the real stake at some point too without anyone noticing."

"I've been practicing. Watch." Dashiel picked up a chewed splinter of old bone from the floor around the same size as a spike.

Dashiel wore their full rider armor in the king's colors—silver and red—prepared for the ceremony. Steel bracers at their forearms were two sizes too large, taken from Vance's collection, with a tight layer of leather beneath to shield their skin. Dashiel tucked the spike into one bracer, then did a quick swap, hiding the bone away in the other bracer and drawing the fake.

Mine! Shiff huffed, standing up on back legs and clawing softly at Dashiel's thighs.

With a short whistle from Dashiel, the dragonling stilled again, sitting as neat and still as a tamed hatchling. Smiling, Dashiel redrew the bone and tossed it across the stall. Shiff trilled as she chased after it.

Vance sighed. "I suppose we're lucky nobody will be standing too close."

"It wasn't that bad." Dashiel pushed the fake spike carefully back into their bracer, wary not to crush the soft metal. "I've thought of everything. There's even a bundle of ash inside, to simulate the smoke from the seared wound."

Clapping Dashiel on the back, Vance said, "Well, let's go and see whether today is the last day for Zarram Dragonhold's respectability. Collect that wild beast of yours."

The dragonling gnawed on her bone with a feral growl.

Nerves hit Dashiel like a wall. "Is it time already?"

"You're about to become one of the Dragon King's riders."

It took a couple of worryingly long minutes to convince Shiff to relinquish her bone, then Dashiel scooped the bundle of silky scales and leather into their arms.

The dragonling's claws wrapped around Dashiel's arm, a companionable touch, but still tight enough that the growing dragon's strength was evident. The tips of her talons pressed between the scales of Dashiel's armor like pincers.

A shiver of nerves washed over Dashiel, then came back mirrored from the dragonling. *Worried? Why?*

"It's going to be okay," they said to both her and themselves.

The Zarram siblings walked in silence up the cold stone stairs into the upper levels. When they reached the hatchery, the other new riders being invested that day were already there, eagerly pawing over the newborn hatchlings on offer.

It was one of the great honors bestowed upon those who succeeded in passing rider trials. The opportunity to choose their own dragon.

They didn't truly own the creature. It was bought by the Dragon King and the silvernix required for its taming provided by the Dragon King and it and its rider would serve the Dragon King.

But still the new riders' excitement was clear as they squabbled over which hatchling they considered best. They would be spending the next year with those dragonlings, training the tamed beasts to react to their commands, until they were large enough to fly.

As each rider made their selection, a servant took it away to prepare for the ceremony.

One of the Zarram servants approached Dashiel to take Shiff, wary of how much larger the dragonling was compared to those that had hatched that day.

Dashiel swallowed and whispered close to the dragonling, "Remember what we practiced. Calm and still."

Calm and still. Shiff agreed, but there was a begrudging tone to her thoughts.

Stars, I hope this goes well.

"That's a big beast you've chosen there." Jurge, one of the new recruits, watched as Shiff was taken away.

"Nepotism in action." Zyla approached on Dashiel's other side, her smile teasing but warm on her umber face.

Of the ten other riders being invested that day, Dashiel liked the two of them best. Although just out of her teens, Zyla's braided hair was the salt and pepper of a Taen dragonlord line, while Jurge's hair was all midnight, never touched by a heritage of silvernix usage.

He was a smaller pale-skinned man who had worked his way up from a common Taen family through sheer grit. Zyla, on the other hand, was the fourth rider for the Dragon King among her siblings.

"Like you can talk, Zee," Dashiel teased back.

At the entrance to the hatchery, a woman with arms and thighs like tightly packed bedrolls cleared her throat.

The nervous chatter ceased and the dragonrider recruits stood at attention.

Mestra Lerris looked over them with a glimmer in her eye, that from experience could have been either pride or a joyful readiness to beat obedience into her fresh squad.

"Today you become dragonriders, of the highest order," she barked.

Dashiel was surprised by even that level of rallying support.

Turning on her heel, Mestra Lerris ordered them in line behind her with a sharp snap of, "But you still have a long way to go. Don't embarrass me."

Wide-eyed like a hunted rabbit, Dashiel sought their brother.

Vance leaned on a wall across the hatchery, beyond the discarded broken shells and unwanted dragonlings on the raised platform the new riders had chosen from.

He lifted his chin, wry humor on his lips as he mouthed, "Good luck."

Marching alongside Zyla and Jurge, Dashiel tried to settle their nerves.

Their path to the parade grounds led the group up to the next level and along an exterior corridor with archways open to the view of Draekhanhelm dragonkeep beyond.

The late afternoon sun cast orange light over the city, unusually warm for early autumn. A waft of smoke rose from the Rolanian quarter down the hill to the west. Dashiel could hear the echo of a hundred voices chanting but couldn't make out the words.

Jurge craned to look. "Another riot?"

Zyla kept her eyes forward and tsked. "Can't go a week lately without either the penniless criminals or sun-touched religious nuts making a mess of our streets."

Or both at once, against each other, Dashiel thought. There were plenty of middle-class Taens who believed the Rolanians and their sinful ways were somehow behind the undead blight growing worse.

Even with the king's favor, the Zarram family had been on the receiving end of threats for not having been "born blessed" like the Taens believed themselves.

Dashiel had learned enough of his peers' religion to fit in, how they believed they were chased from their ancestral home by demons freezing the land to ice. But in their hardship to escape across the sea, they were blessed by the sun and delivered to new homelands where all the abundance that existed was a gift for their use.

A homeland that had before been Rolanian, but as the Taens learned first how to tame dragons, Rolanians became yet another resource the Taens had the privilege of owning.

When revenants began appearing across Elundrae, it wasn't long before those who considered their mythology to be fact saw it as the return of demons, come to punish the unworthy.

A Taen must be honorable to be worthy of the sun's blessings, and any who fail in life thus were never honorable or worthy, and Rolanians didn't even start out with a chance.

"Maybe I should have joined the city guard, they seem to be getting more action these days," Jurge said.

Through the smoke below, the dark silhouettes of small treedarts dashed from building to building, through the narrow streets and across rooftops toward the unrest, carrying armored soldiers. A crude and simple steed, barely larger than a full-grown wolf, they suited in-city use for policing people rather than revenants.

The new dragonriders' march turned the corner away from the sight, up one more wide set of stairs and out onto the vast flat rooftop of Zarram Dragonhold.

The stone was baked hot underfoot. Marble columns with sleek shafts and capitals carved to form swooping dragons lined the long parade grounds. Crowds of dragonlords, the families of recruits, and older troops of dragonriders filled stands behind those columns, sheltered from the blazing heat by a fluttering silk canopy.

Gold and black pennants with Zarram's crest alternated with silver and red pennants along the top and swirled in the hot wind.

Behind the stands, neatly ordered rows of unmoving dragons sat, saddled with ornate palanquins, the means of transport for all the guests in attendance.

Down the center of the parade grounds, there were ten pedestals, each with a squirming dragonling chained on top and a steel mallet beside them.

Dashiel took a long deep breath and took up position beside Shiff.

She was being good, still and calm. Perhaps too calm compared to the other as-yet-untamed dragonlings, but at least she wasn't drawing attention. Dashiel snuck a training treat from their pocket and gave it to her.

"Good work," they whispered.

A man Dashiel didn't recognize, wearing long ceremonial robes of silver satin, strode down the line, followed by two armored guards. He carried an embossed metal chest and handed taming spikes to each new rider.

Throughout this, the king's proxy delivered a speech. Dashiel had heard it all before, the tale of the first taming, the honor and glory of being a king's rider. Dashiel was too focused on the taming spike being handed to them to listen properly.

A sweat broke out over the back of their neck. Holding that sharp blade of metal, the tip glistening in silvernix, and standing before all those eyes staring down, Dashiel's fingers felt clumsy, their plans miserably ill-conceived.

Are they going to see?

Dashiel cast their gaze over the crowd. They were far closer than Dashiel had thought they would be, and in the front row, sitting straight-backed on velvet cushions, sat Eslinde.

There was no comfort from the familiar face. She was the Dragon King's daughter, after all. What would she think if she saw Dashiel refusing the ceremonial stake provided by the king himself for something they'd snuck in?

The Eslinde they'd once known, wild and rebellious, would cheer, but Dashiel wasn't entirely sure she was still like that.

Eslinde's gaze had a brightness to it that Dashiel hadn't noticed the last time she visited. As though some fire in her had awakened again. Beside her, off the end of the stand in her own separate wooden chair, sat a girl closer to Dashiel's age. A narrow, pretty face was pinched with a shrewd gaze, glaring at a point in the opposite stands.

"Rider Targe!" An announcer's call rang across the grounds, and the first rider raised their mallet.

Rider Targe pressed the tip of the stake to the dragonling's forehead and struck.

The blow was clean, the spike sinking straight down to the cap in one swift motion.

Dashiel had seen tamings gone wrong, where the spike turned crooked or had been hammered in slowly, the hatchling crying all the while. But even this made them sick to the marrow of their bones.

A shimmer through the scales of the silvernix taking effect was followed by a rise of dark smoke. The dragonling slumped, lifeless but not dead, as the announcer called on the next rider.

Dashiel looked away, unable to watch as rider after rider hammered the sharp metal into the hatchling's brains, trying to settle the surge of acid in their stomach. They had to act fast, swap the stakes, or Shiff would suffer the same fate.

Fingers trembling, Dashiel shifted position as though standing at attention with both hands clasped before them. As their hands joined, they shoved the provided stake up into the gap of their bracer.

But they pushed too fast, too hard, nerves overtaking their control. The sharp tip of the spike sliced through the leather between it and their skin, and then through their skin as well.

Dashiel's eyes shot wide. *It's over, I've messed it all up.*

Gulping through panic, Dashiel watched their hands, waiting to see the bright flash of light sparkle from their skin as the silvernix met it, the sign that would give away to everyone in attendance that something strange was occurring, that the rider before them had used the precious silvernix the king had provided on themselves instead of the intended purpose.

But nothing happened.

"Rider Brellson!" the announcer called.

Beside Dashiel, Jurge drove their spike neatly into their dragonling's head. Dark smoke twisted skyward.

Stars, stars, I'm next!

Dashiel rushed to draw their fake spike from their other bracer, their hands rattling like a sand serpent's tail. Hot liquid trickled within the torn leather of their other arm from the stinging wound.

"Rider Zarram!"

Dashiel turned pleading eyes to Shiff and whispered, "Hammer, strike, sleep."

She tilted her head, round eyes reflecting the clear sky above. ***Boring game, again?***

Dashiel placed the fake spike against her forehead and raised the mallet. "Yes, again, like we practiced. Hammer, strike, sleep, until you are back in your stall, and you win."

Please let this work.

Dashiel landed a blow with the mallet, making it look strong. But only a little strength was required.

The stake they'd created folded into itself on impact, telescoping down as the soft metal squashed into itself, leaving only a flat round lump beneath the cap. A few short teeth around the edge of that cap bit down into the dragonling's scales, too shallow to pierce through, but enough, hopefully enough, to hold.

Just a piece of jewelry, decorating the dragonling's forehead.

The puff of ash was less convincing than Dashiel planned, bursting out, then sinking rather than rising skyward, but it was done.

The dragonling slumped, a close approximation of the other hatchlings around them.

Hammer, strike, sleep. Shiff's thought came through as a whisper.

Dashiel exhaled a long sigh. "Good girl."

Nobody cried foul. Nobody rushed to inspect the deception they'd committed, but

Dashiel continued to shake anxiously, their arm stinging.

The final two riders repeated the taming process, with only one fumbling their strike. Their dragonling squealed, and Shiff opened one eyelid, their emotions flaring with concern.

Hammer, strike, sleep game?

Dashiel's heart hurt. They whispered, "Yeah. They aren't ... playing as well as you."

She closed her eye and lay still again, as though in competition with the others.

Dashiel wondered whether they could have saved every dragonling there that day, what lengths that would have taken.

There was no way. I'm lucky to still have Shiff.

As the ceremony completed with another speech, servants came along and unchained the newly tamed dragons, taking them away. As one unlocked Shiff, Dashiel reached forward and collected the dragonling themselves.

"I'll take her, thanks."

The final announcement ended with a polite applause, and the audience rose, shifting to either leave or spread down onto the parade grounds to congratulate the new recruits.

Dashiel didn't linger like the rest of their squad, instead rushing with Shiff back to the stairs to the hatchery below.

Vance waited there, leaning in the shade of a column. "I can't believe you pulled that off."

"Shh! Come with me!"

Dashiel led the way, hurrying down the long corridor and to the levels below and Shiff's private stall, Vance close behind.

Dashiel placed Shiff, still acting convincingly limp, onto a blanket. The second she reached the ground, one eyelid cracked open, and then her eyes sprung wide.

She stretched, flexing her claws on the rough woven wool. ***Game finished?***

Dashiel nodded.

Hate hammer, strike, sleep.

"It's okay, Shiff. We won't have to practice that one ever again." Dashiel patted her forehead, checking the cap of the fake spike was firmly attached.

"What is it? Did something go wrong?" Vance grumbled as he closed the gate behind them. "We should be up there celebrating with the others. We'll be missed."

"This went wrong," Dashiel said, pulling the real stake from their bracer with a wince.

"What?" Vance leaned closer, peering at the metal, and then his eyebrows snapped together in a frown. "Is that *blood*?"

Dashiel unbuckled the bracer and held out their arm, showing Vance the torn leather beneath. "It went right through."

"No, it mustn't have. Otherwise ..." Vance reached for the stake. "Give me that."

Holding it close to his face, Dashiel's brother tentatively touched the remaining silvernix at the pointed end.

Nothing happened.

"What in the stars light?"

"Could it be fake?" Dashiel asked. "Or ... I don't know, expired?"

Vance shook his head. "It couldn't be ... not if it's the same silvernix used for the other tamings. They all worked. Without silvernix, there would have been nine dead dragonlings up there."

"Just mine, then? Some kind of sabotage?" Dashiel took the spike back.

There had to be some mistake. They rubbed their hand over the iridescent coating again more thoroughly. Maybe contact with more of the substance would force it to work. But still the silvernix had no effect.

But the rubbing action over the spike caused the steel there to roll and ripple. Looking more closely, Dashiel scratched their thumb over the area, and a thin leafing of metal peeled away to reveal what seemed to be a smoky crystal beneath, glowing dully.

"Umm ..." Dashiel said, holding it to Vance to see, speechless.

Vance's usually passive face was twisted in fierce confusion. "What is that? What's the symbol carved there?"

"And why is it *glowing*?" Dashiel shook it in emphasis.

The mechanism for the gate clicked, and it rolled upward.

"Shiff! Sleep!" Dashiel hissed and hid the strange taming spike in their remaining bracer.

Their dragon huffed, but quickly curled up on a blanket.

White-faced, Dashiel turned to find their father at the door.

The man huffed. "Don't look at me like that."

"Umm ..." Dashiel said again, unable to say anything else. They swallowed, trying to process too many worries at once.

Lord Zarram's eyes had the soft hint of sympathy beneath bushy eyebrows. "I know that was difficult for you, what you did up there. But you did the right thing today, and I'm proud of you."

Dashiel coughed. "Right. Yeah. The right thing. That's what I did."

Vance and Dashiel exchanged side-eyed looks.

Brightening, Lord Zarram said, "Plus, I've heard the king is very happy with this brood and their riders, and the other dragonlords are hearing it too. We'll have our most profitable year ever from this."

Ah, yes, Pabba's main concern as always.

"Come on, enough sulking down here in the dark. Come and celebrate in the sun with the other blessed souls." Lord Zarram put a heavy arm over Dashiel's shoulders and dragged them toward the stairs.

Dashiel tried to pull away from their father's grip. "Actually, I think maybe I might stay down here ..."

"You will come and celebrate, and you will be seen behaving as you should." Lord Zarram squeezed Dashiel's shoulder a little tighter. "As fine as today has been, we must still be careful. The higher we rise, Rolanian blood into a Taen world, the further we can fall. Any scandal could ruin us."

CHAPTER SEVEN

Kess measured out the distance across the parade grounds with her eyes, gauging whether she had a chance of hitting her brother.

He sat in the stand opposite, glaring back at Kess with equal animosity, as though each of them could kill the other through force of will alone.

Even with her best throwing knives, even when she was at her peak, she would have been lucky to bridge that distance and land a killing hit. Since being held prisoner by Kife, her once strong arms had been left weakened.

Over the last few days spent in Eslinde's chambers, Kess had continued to refine the point on her stolen cheese knife and practiced throwing it at the back wall of the opened wardrobe. Whether the unfamiliar blade or wasted muscles were the cause, her aim was currently abysmal, only hitting her target once in every few throws.

The dropping sun hadn't yet delivered any relief from the heat. The rooftop was sweltering, a hot breeze blasting in with the ever-present tang of smoke. Kess fidgeted with the heavy skirt of the gown she'd been given. She'd worn her own leather pants beneath, feeling more secure that way, but regretted it now as her legs swam in sweat.

The braids done by the handmaidens that morning, far more intricate than she'd ever worn, with layers of swooping thin plaits intertwined with thicker weaves and glittering beads, was pulled too tight, leaving her temples aching.

Still, Kess had let them dress her like a doll for the chance to leave the palace. She'd hoped for an opportunity to slip away and escape, but a shot at getting rid of Kife was even better.

He doesn't seem too happy about seeing me again.

Every day Kife was alive and angry increased the risk of him telling somebody about Dracuni.

Kess twisted in her seat, looking over her shoulder at the grayglim watching Eslinde from a few paces away. Yensen, who remained by her side every day, every moment the princess stepped out of her chambers.

He wore the typical smoky-gray armor all of his rank wore, with a high-collared breastplate of dragon scale, lose silk sleeves between well-fitted shoulder guards and bracers, and leather boots so soft Kess could hardly hear when the man moved.

He seemed the same age as Eslinde, with long narrow eyes and silky black hair, held only in two plain braids on each side of his head.

Maybe I can ask Eslinde to send her shadow to go and kill Kife for me.

She'd need a good reason, though, and one that wasn't, 'Because he needs to die before he tells anyone there's a living creature with silvernix blood.'

She could tell the princess Kife was a threat to Lyrrin, but that was only in a roundabout way, and Eslinde was very good at sniffing out half-truths.

Anyway, Kess still hoped to be the one to spill Kife's blood herself. She'd wait for her chance.

It was unlikely Kife knew Kess would be at the dragonrider investment. Maybe he thought the Dragon King himself would be in attendance, but Yeonard Draekhan had sent a representative for this ceremony, as Eslinde assured Kess he did for most minor affairs such as this.

Eslinde was only attending herself because she knew one of the riders being invested that day. And she insisted Kess should stay with her.

"Ah, there they are!" Eslinde fanned her sweat-shimmered face with a hand.

The new recruits marched down the center of the rooftop parade.

Eslinde pointed to one with golden tanned skin and a mop of caramel curls. "That's Dashiel Zarram. Their family owns this dragonhold. And their brother ..."

Eslinde craned her neck, looking around the stands. She muttered, "Their father is over there. No. I can't see Vance."

There was a soft note of disappointment in her voice.

Kess squinted through the hot light at the rider, who waited through the opening speech beside the pedestal with their dragonling. A *big* dragonling.

The rider seemed nervous. Their features, angular jaw, full lips, and eyes lined with thick lashes, kept twisting between an awkward frown and solemn composure. More interestingly, they were clearly Rolanian.

Kess had known of some Rolanians who had risen into roles of dragonriders, back in her life at Heithorn estate. She'd sought out stories about them, telling herself it was for no real reason, just curiosity, and hadn't shared any of that information or the hopes behind it with Riony. Those stories were still too few and far between.

But if the Zarrams owned this dragonhold, they weren't just riders, but dragonlords. Owners of their own dragons. And plenty of them, from the size of the facilities.

Rolanian dragonlords?

The princess's eyes were still seeking the missing brother, and Kess gave her an appraising look. "How do you know the Zarrams?"

"Through breeding, mostly."

Kess's eyebrows rose.

"*Dragons*, Kessara." The princess sighed. "The Zarrams are some of the best breeders and trainers in Elundrae, and they've always had excellent stock. My family would often visit to trade. Vance, Dash, and I became friends young. Although I haven't seen them much lately."

Kess turned back to the proceedings right as the first rider struck the stake into their hatchling.

Unprepared, she gasped a loud intake of air.

Eslinde turned fully her way. Kess slowly let the air out again as casually as she could until the princess's eyes were off her again.

As the next rider, then the next tamed their hatchlings, a hot sickness rose in Kess's throat.

The rider would raise their mallet, and Kess could feel Dracuni clinging to her in the cave filled with spiders, feel her heart beating against her chest.

The mallet would strike down, and Kess remembered Dracuni trying to comfort her, help her, as her life bled out of her broken legs.

The newly tamed hatchlings fell still, one after another.

Is Dracuni still safe, out there, without Riony to look after her?

Kess's eyes stung and she willed away the wetness forming there.

Dracuni must be getting big now. Soon enough, she'd be able to protect herself. At least from a single human hunter, a single rival dragon. Not from the full might of the Dragon King if he knew she existed.

There had been no news or rumors in court yet about the existence of a silvernix-blooded creature, from what Kess had heard from Eslinde, so that at least was a good sign.

As the tamings continued, Kess noticed Eslinde's gaze wasn't on the riders and dragonlings before them.

The princess watched the sky. Kess's eyes followed, seeing only the wisps of swirling darkness rising from each taming. It was better than seeing the taming itself, but a heavy weight of grief filled Kess at the sight.

Was that dark smoke really the essence that formed the shadow dragon? Had each hatchling tamed that day strengthened it more?

How many other dragons were tamed that day, for other riders, or industry, in other dragonkeeps, all across Elundrae?

Only one hatchling didn't send a curl of black mist skyward. Dashiel's. There was a puff of a smokelike cloud, but it passed quickly and didn't rise as though there was a destination it sought.

Kess tried to get a better look at Dashiel's dragonling, but the ceremony ended, and the audience were on their feet, descending the stone amphitheater and mingling in the central area.

A number of dragonlords in decadent gold-embroidered finery swarmed upon Eslinde, which in turn drew her grayglim close to her back.

Off to the side in her separate seat, Kess quietly brought her hands to the wheels attached to the wooden chair and rolled herself away.

Eslinde had provided the mobile chair for Kess that morning, announcing that she had the finest engineering minds in the capital develop it.

The best Kess could say of the contraption was that it moved. The wheels turned clunkily when she pushed them, and considerable effort was required to get even a short distance.

Maybe that's just my wasted arms.

Kess would work on rebuilding her strength. And begrudgingly admitted the chair would help. There was none of the touch and response fluidity she had with Griskin, but at least she was moving and not on the floor.

And she could see her target. Kife lurked beside a column on the other side.

I just have to get close enough to kill him.

She figured at least he wouldn't expect it, here and now, so she'd have that advantage. Kess didn't care about the witnesses or consequences. It didn't matter what happened to her as long as he was gone too.

But getting close wasn't going to be easy.

The crowd parted and reformed around her, switching places as people went from greeting one acquaintance to another, cutting off Kess's slow moving progress.

Servants appeared with trays of chilled drinks, the glasses glistening with condensation. Kess swallowed a dry mouth and pushed on. A man with skin like uncooked pastry exclaimed in loud insult as Kess's rolling chair butted up against him.

"You stepped in front of me," Kess hissed, trying to readjust her angle and go around where the human equivalent of dough remained planted in her path.

Hushed whispers went up all around Kess as she tried to maneuver through the crowd. The looks of disgust thrown her way were far louder.

Almost every head of hair on that rooftop was brightened by the use of silvernix. All people who lived with every benefit that wealth offered. Straight-backed, strong, and youthful.

In a land where money bought health, and only the dishonorable were poor, Kess's body made her a visual target of shame.

Kess smirked as her eyes landed on Kife, not far away.

I'll give them something to really gossip about.

Leaning forward, Kess lifted the hem of her skirt, seeking the knife hidden in her boot. Before her fingers could close on it, a long-legged body stopped in front of her.

"It seems Eslinde has a new friend. I don't believe we've met."

Kess straightened, taking in the man in front of her. He had a long diamond-shaped face spotted with coal-dark eyes, pure-white hair braided into a thick rope down his neck, and a grayglim at his back.

Another First?

"No, we haven't met," Kess replied.

"You make it sound as though that's by design." The man gave a self-deprecating laugh.

Kess didn't miss the sly glint in his eyes. She'd spent the last five years in the wilds with lowlifes and snakes and recognized danger in human form when she saw it.

Kess tried to roll past the man. "Excuse me, I—"

"Haven't a moment for Ulfren the First?" He shifted in front of her and offered an almost imperceptible bow.

Kess attempted a polite smile with lips that were pulling into a cringe.

Not just any first heir, but first in line to the throne. Kess opened her mouth to introduce herself in return but wasn't sure it was the best idea. Beyond Ulfren's waist, Kife moved, getting farther away in the crowd. Kess swore under her breath.

"Your Highness. I'm sorry, I'm really nobody important and need to go."

"Nonsense! You seem terribly important to Eslinde. Where in Elundrae did she dig you up from?" The man peered down at Kess, making no effort at all to bridge the gap between their heights.

"Oh, just some smelly hole." Kess stuttered out a laugh, but her hands had gone rigid around the wheels at her sides.

Ulfren's black-hole gaze assessed her again.

Kess tried to do the math at what true age Ulfren was based on her knowledge of the Firsts. Ulfren wasn't the firstborn of the heirs, but the eldest brother had died of natural causes some time ago.

Ulfren looked older than his own father, but not the seventy or so years he probably was. More middle-aged. His loose-fitting gray trousers and coat had a metallic green trim of geometric knotwork sparkling around the hems and collar.

"And now that you've been dug up, what relationship do you have to Eslinde?"

Kess tried to draw herself taller in her chair. She played her tone off light the way he was. "Are you so curious of all her friends?"

"She hardly has any these days, which is why you are a curiosity indeed." Placing a long-fingered hand across his chest, Ulfren tilted his head in a show of sympathy that read as utterly fake.

A shiver ran down Kess's back under his dark gaze.

Ulfren's voice dropped low. "I just want to be sure she's not getting herself into any trouble. Again."

Chapter Eight

Again? Does Ulfren know about the pregnancy? Kess's mouth went dry. Her world was falling far too quickly into a sea of secrets and scandals she hadn't nearly enough knowledge of.

"What sort of trouble do you mean?" she asked innocently.

"Knowing Eslinde, it could take many forms." Ulfren rubbed his chin, shaking his head softly. "What she really needs, poor thing, is somebody who will keep an eye on her. For her own good."

Kess raised her eyebrows, although still attempting to peer past the man to keep an eye on her brother.

Ulfren continued. "Perhaps, if you're spending so much time with her, you could be that person. If you could get any information back to me on trouble Eslinde might be falling into, I would reward you well for helping me keep my sister safe."

That got Kess's full attention. A reward? She wondered just how big of a reward was on offer—assassinating a problematic brother, for example—and what she'd have to do to receive it. But if it was one First asking her to spy upon another, she assumed the reward involved had to be substantial.

Either that or Ulfren the First would have me quietly disposed of after I'm no longer useful. That's the more likely outcome.

Before Kess could respond, Eslinde swept in beside them. "Ulfren, lovely to see you. I heard you're staying in the capital for a while."

"Not as long as your stay has been." Ulfren rasped an unfriendly chuckle.

Eslinde only smiled courteously in return. "Might I steal this lovely girl from you now? We have people to see."

"Of course. It was an honor to meet Kessara Heithorn." Ulfren gave her a mockingly low bow, eyes locked on her as she flinched at her full name tumbling from his mouth.

He knew all along? What spies does he already have?

Eslinde's hands gripped the back of Kess's chair. "May I?"

"Sure. Yes," Kess said, eager to be away from the man too.

The offended glances Kess received as Eslinde pushed her through the dwindling guests were muted compared to when the princess wasn't at her back and grayglim trailing behind.

"What did my brother want from you?" Eslinde asked once they'd crossed to the other side of the rooftop.

"I didn't really speak to him for long."

Eslinde tsked under her breath, then in a brighter voice said, "There they are!"

"Eslinde, you made it!" Dashiel hurried toward them in a loping jog, the stemmed glass in their hand spilling a sparkling liquid along the way.

"Congratulations again, Dashiel." Eslinde leaned into a polite embrace which was offered enthusiastically but awkwardly, a fumble of long limbs.

Eslinde's grayglim gave Dashiel a reproachful glare, as though he could force Dashiel a respectful distance away with his eyes alone.

A much larger man followed at a slower, uneven pace. The structure of his face was similar to Dashiel's, but with any soft feminine curves removed from the lips and cheeks, and darker hair tumbling in loose braids over his outrageously wide shoulders.

Eslinde's smile widened. "And Vance. Good to—"

"Nice to see—" he said at the same time.

"—again so soon."

"Your Highness." He cleared his throat and leaned back as though wary an awkward embrace was in his future as well.

"This is Kessara." Eslinde stepped back behind the wheeled chair.

"Kess is fine," she said, fussing with her skirts as though they could hide the fact she wasn't standing to greet them.

Dashiel beamed at her. "A new friend? Is it you who has brightened our princess's mood so much?"

"Oh, I don't think that's it, exactly." Kess glanced back at Eslinde, who had seemed somewhat more lively compared to when they'd first met.

Keen to change the subject, Kess said, "I liked your dragonling selection. A shimmerdart? Large one too."

"You could tell all that from the stands?" Dashiel's throat worked as they swallowed hard.

"I ... umm. I like dragons."

Dashiel laughed and rubbed the back of their head. "Yeah. I like dragons too. We have some really special ones at the moment. Oh! How about a tour of our stock?"

Kess looked over at the stairs leading down from the rooftop grounds. Her wheeled chair was clunky enough on a smooth stone surface. She wasn't ready to test it on steps. "I don't think I can."

Dashiel had already begun leading the way and turned back. "Eslinde will come along too, right?"

Eslinde's gaze fluttered over Vance before replying, "I have time. Let's. It's far too hot up here."

Vance grumbled, eyeing the wheeled chair pointedly, "I don't think that's what Kess means, Dash."

"Oh. I see."

Kess waited for the flicker of revulsion over their expression, but it didn't come.

Dashiel put their glass, still mostly full, down on a passing servant's tray. "We can help you get down the stairs. If that's okay?"

A sneer twitched on Kess's lips, but as all three awaited her reply, she nodded.

It took a few mortifying moments at the top of the stairs discussing the best way to manage their descent. There were offers to carry Kess, but she worked out she could carefully roll the chair down the steps one at a time as long as she had someone assisting to make sure the chair didn't run away on her.

Dashiel volunteered, and they traveled down three long flights of stairs that way before they reached a flight deck lined with rows of stalls. The difference in temperature from the rooftop to there was shocking and the sweat over Kess's skin chilled. Her arms shook from the effort and it had been a slow process.

Kess struggled to meet any of their gazes as she clunked down the final step. "Sorry. I'm not used to this yet."

Vance leaned close and bent as though to adjust his shoes. His voice was low and gruff. "I don't show many people this."

He lifted the hem of his pants, revealing a metal joint where his ankle should be, connected to a carved wooden foot and shin. Their gazes met, and Kess sought answers in the intensity of his look.

He shrugged and straightened back up. "Sometimes things are gone in a way even silvernix can't repair. And that's not our fault. It'd be a better world if everyone understood that."

Kess's mouth popped open, but words refused to be formed, so she closed it.

Eslinde's eyelids fluttered again, as though looking at Vance and trying hard not to look at him at the same time.

Half her mouth lifted in a sad-looking smile. "He's still one of the best dragonriders in Elundrae, regardless."

Vance just grunted and gave Dashiel a shove on the shoulder. "Go on, go show off your dragons."

Smiling radiantly, Dashiel took them across to the first stall where a glistening green and black seasong dragon filled the space.

As beautiful a specimen as the dragon was, Kess found herself more interested in the furtive glances being passed between Eslinde and Vance. One would stare at the other, then quickly away when the other would look at them.

There was an almost tangible chemistry between them—one neither seemed to want acknowledged. Something far more private, even forbidden.

Could he be Lyrrin's father?

A Rolanian amputee getting a First princess pregnant would be a scandal. Eslinde said Lyrrin's father was dead, but she could have lied about that to protect the identity of the man.

And if it was Vance, did he even know there was a pregnancy?

Eslinde had arrived at Heithorn estate to be sequestered until the birth when she was only just showing. She said only those at the estate and her parents knew. But Kess couldn't trust the princess was telling the whole truth.

She couldn't trust anyone around her, not Eslinde, not the Zarram siblings. No matter how kind these dragonlords seemed, everyone had their own secrets and motivations. Kess's meeting with Ulfren was only a reminder of that.

They moved along to the next stall, where a dragon with scales the color of a golden sunrise curled restfully.

"Viska here has a little snowflame in her background, but we've been breeding back in more and more etherflame, for the size and extended lifespan." Dashiel patted the dragon on its crown of horns.

"She's beautiful. Her fire, is it more a liquid flame or fire blast?" Kess wheeled herself closer, taking in the size of the dragon's talons and thick leather of her golden wings.

"Fire blast, hotter than usual for a purebred ether, but it doesn't seem to weaken her as fast as snowflame's breath does," Dashiel replied.

A soft smile reached Kess's eyes, imagining the powerful creature in action. "And does the presence of snowshimmer in her line make her fast?"

"Does it ever." Vance smirked. "You're as keen on dragons as Dash, aren't you?"

Kess's smile faltered. "I wanted to be a rider ... once."

Wanted it more than anything.

Kess could only find a hollow inside her where that desire once was. She pushed her chair back away from the dragon.

Vance had his eyes on Eslinde again, then returned them to Kess, frowning softly. "How about you take Viska out for a fly? Dash can show you how fast she is."

"That sounds amazing. Although ..." Kess looked to Eslinde for an answer, expecting the princess to protest the offer that would take Kess out of her control.

But Eslinde shared a similar soft frown as Vance.

Raze them both, is that pity? Kess's nose crumpled.

"I suppose Dashiel could bring you back to the palace. We will meet you at the upper flight deck," Eslinde said.

Her grayglim had flown them both there, boxed into a palanquin on a slow, old etherflame. Kess hated flying that way, sitting locked in a container as the air rushed by around them, out of reach. Even if the journey back to the palace was short, Kess was excited at the idea of flying the incredible golden creature before her.

Still tamed, but in so much better condition than Kife's dragon had been. Viska was clearly well cared for, evident in that she'd even been given a name.

Dashiel had a grin splitting ear to ear and was already in the process of saddling up the dragon. They shared knowing looks with Vance, that Vance pointedly ignored.

Was the princess trying to get some time alone with Vance? That wasn't possible anyway with the grayglim always lurking at her shoulder.

It was only once Kess had been given a set of goggles and climbed up into the saddle behind Dashiel that the thought hit her that Vance and Eslinde's looks of concern weren't pity, that this wasn't a scheme to allow the two of them time together, but something more malicious.

Panic rose within Kess, her mind serving images of being thrown from a dragon's back again and again.

"Perhaps I shouldn't," she called down. "What about the chair?"

Eslinde flapped a hand. "Yensen will carry it back."

Yensen gave her a flat look that suggested he didn't think that was part of his job description but didn't argue.

"Don't worry, this will be fun. Have you flown in the saddle much before?" Dashiel settled into the seat in front of her.

"A bit."

The saddle was longer than Kife's had been, designed to allow more than one rider. Dashiel had selected it from a range along the wall.

"Those could be a bit tighter. May I?" Dashiel reached for Kess's flight goggles.

She nodded numbly and they adjusted the buckle on one side.

"Anything else you need?" they asked.

"My legs, they aren't strong enough to grip. I need to be strapped in." And she wanted to be strapped in.

If they were taking Kess to be tossed away, she wanted to make it as hard for them as possible.

Nobody argued or made a fuss though, and Vance tossed her a harness from the range of tack. Although designed for some other purpose, Kess fastened it over her dress and found enough points of connection between the leather strips and buckles to the saddle to feel secure.

Then they were moving. Dashiel had full control of the massive creature beneath them, leading it out of the stall and toward the open flight deck at the end of the long space.

Kess turned back, eyes on the princess, trying to ascertain her motivations in allowing this. Had what she'd assumed to be flirting between Eslinde and Vance actually been some silent communication of their plan to take Kess away and kill her?

They could have arranged it after the ceremony while Ulfren talked to me. I should have refused this offer.

But then the length of the flight deck ended, and the dragon's wings clapped out on either side, and they were in the air.

Kess's stomach bottomed out as the dragon rose sharply, leaving the city behind in the blink of an eye.

She is fast!

Dashiel called over the rushing air, "All good?"

Kess ran a hand to the top of her boot, feeling the knife still there. If they thought they could get rid of her easily, they were mistaken.

Her fingers shook. "Fine."

"Ready to go full speed?"

Kess balked. "She goes *faster*?"

Dashiel's laughter mixed with the gusting wind and whoosh of the dragon's pumping wings.

Lowering themselves closer to the dragon's neck, Dashiel barked voice commands and tugged a twin set of reins.

If Kess hadn't been strapped in, she would have been left behind in the burst of speed that drove them hurtling through the sunset-tinted sky. The golden scales scintillated under the hot sun like sparks of fire with each motion of the dragon's muscles.

Below them Draekhanhelm was a dark spot on the land, between charred wastes on one side and a sparkling sea on the other. Dashiel turned the dragon, taking them out over the water, and the scent of ocean salt and a cooler breeze hit Kess.

They dove, bringing the speeding dragon down to skim the waves before swooping back up into the clouds so fast Kess felt she'd left her soul behind amongst the seafoam.

Her heart raced, in awe of the dragon's speed and in anticipation of Dashiel's upcoming attack.

Dashiel leaned sideways and called over their shoulder. "What do you think?"

Kess kept an eye on Dashiel, making sure they weren't turning all the way around to face her. "The dragon? She's incredible. But she's still ..."

"Still what?"

The trembling anxiety and sense of imminent death within Kess left her bold, so she said, "Still tamed."

There was a long silence. "What else could she be?"

Kess didn't know how to explain to a dragonlord what a dragon could be. How Dracuni had been so lively, so loyal, so kind. How even Kife's dragon, when freed, hadn't destroyed everything around it when it so easily could have. The way Dracuni's mother had flown from her home in the ocean to starve in the mountains in an ill-fated attempt to keep her eggs safe.

Creatures with their own minds, unfettered by the control of humans.

Kess replied, "Something whole. She could be something whole."

The dragon slowed, gliding in air cleared of smoke by the sea breeze.

Dashiel shifted suddenly, leaving Kess's heart shuddering and hand reaching to her boot. The rider twisted to face her, then with one hand holding the reins taut, they stood up in the saddle.

"What are you doing?" Kess snapped. The person was going to get themselves killed rather than her.

Dashiel balanced upright on the saddle and grinned. "Do you want a turn in control? Shuffle up."

"Are you serious?"

"Have you ridden before?"

"No. Not really. Not *airborne*."

"It's fine, I'll talk you through it." Dashiel stepped over her to the back of the saddle, leaving Kess no choice but to move forward or have nobody in control of their steed.

There was enough give in her harness straps for Kess to pull herself forward into the empty rider's position. Dashiel handed down the reins and dropped casually behind her as though they weren't high in the air.

And Kess was in control.

Raze it all, I'm flying a dragon.

Already overwhelmed, Kess flinched when Dashiel pressed up close behind her. But there was no following attack. They reached forward and showed her how Viska had been taught to respond to motions from the two sets of reins and how to apply pressure against the dragon's neck for additional maneuverability.

"Vance doesn't use the reins at all, but since he doesn't fly much anymore, it's good to have rein training available for others who ride her," Dashiel said.

It was nothing like trying to get Kife's dragon to follow her commands through touch alone. The reins did make it easier, but also simple in a way that had none of the joy of riding Kess dreamed of.

Once she felt more confident that they weren't about to plummet from the sky, Kess held the reins in one hand and reached for the dragon's neck, pressing her hand to the warm scales.

It only took a few minutes for Kess to pick up the basics and get a feel for how the dragon responded. The thrilling connection of action and reaction felt so much like how she rode with Griskin that it made Kess's eyes water beneath the goggles.

Only, the dragon had no choice but to respond. A servitude rather than a partnership.

Having Dashiel behind her kept Kess on edge, and she kept waiting for the tip of a blade to pierce her back or the slice of a knife that cut her attachments and left her tumbling into the ocean below.

I could strike first. I have my knife. I could slash the rider's throat and take this dragon and be free.

But to murder and steal unprovoked was dishonorable. Kess couldn't bring herself to act against the apparently cheerful young dragonlord. No. She would wait for their false show to end. And when they sprung their trap, she would be ready.

Dashiel leaned close, calling in her ear over the wind, "Come on. No way you've never flown a dragon before. You're a natural!"

"Only once. Sort of. But it's a lot like my wolf."

"Your *what*?"

"I ..." A strange rush of both shame and pride tangled in Kess's chest. "I used to have a wolf that I rode."

"Really? Stars, that might be the coolest thing I've ever heard!"

Dashiel's enthusiasm almost cracked through Kess's worry, but her hands shook more than ever.

"There's the palace flight deck." Dashiel's chest pressed against Kess's back as they leaned to point past her. "Think you can bring Viska in to land?"

The palace below was a silhouette of angular gray blocks and spires against the rainbow hues of the setting sun.

The tremors hammering through Kess were getting worse. *When will they strike? They're running out of time. Why haven't they made their move?*

"No. You should."

She wanted them in front of her again. She was too vulnerable this way. They were going to kill her, throw her away … any moment. Any moment now.

"Okay, switch." Dashiel pressed their hands on Kess's shoulders to help themselves up, then stepped over her in the saddle.

Kess slid back, hands gripping tight around the harness straps. The angular blocks of grand fortresses and apartments of the dragonkeep rushed up toward them.

Dashiel brought Viska into a slowing spiral, drifting round, then round, as the looming steel and ashy stone walls of the palace came up on all sides.

They came to a stop on the upper flight deck, a smaller aerial entrance reserved for royals.

Kess found herself gulping air, her heartbeat thundering in her ears louder than the wind had.

Where's the trap? It never came. It has to. What are they going to do?

She roughly pulled her goggles off, and they dropped from her rattling fingers and hit the floor with a crack. The sound echoed through the cavern-shaped space.

A few dragons were chained to one of the walls, but otherwise, they were alone.

Maybe they intended to finish her off here.

Dashiel turned to her. "You're shaking. I'm sorry, was that too much? Are you okay?"

No. They were going to kill her. Betray her. Abandon her. There was no other explanation. Panic burned through Kess and she fought with the buckles on the harness, tearing at them to get free.

"It's alright. Slow down." Dashiel frowned, reaching to help.

Kess got the last connection undone and pushed herself from the saddle. She slid sideways, skirts tangled.

Dashiel caught her arm. "Careful!"

"Let go of me!" Kess shrieked, swinging in their grasp.

She wrenched her wrist free, clinging to the dragon's side. Her fingers slipped against the dragon's scales, weak from the unstoppable tremors.

She tumbled past the dragon's front leg and landed with a thump on her back.

Dashiel leaped down beside her, staring down as she lay prone and vulnerable, easy to kill.

"Do it!" she spat.

"Do *what*? What's going on? Are you alright?"

The care in their voice blocked Kess's throat and her words came out between sobs. "Why aren't you … why aren't you trying to kill me?"

Dashiel froze in place, face twisted in confusion. "Was I … expected to?"

"Yes!" Kess roared, the cry reverberating around them. "It's what everybody does! I haven't been in a dragon's saddle that I haven't been thrown from."

Dashiel's eyes went round and they stepped toward her.

Kess pressed up into a sitting position but couldn't find the strength to try to escape. Tears flowed as uncontrollably fast as her body shook.

Words gasped from her as though in a need to explain, to convince the person before her that they couldn't possibly be expected to do anything *other* than kill her. "Nobody,

nobody has ever been kind to me without it being a trap."

Dashiel came down slowly, tentatively, kneeling beside Kess. "It's okay. I'm not going to hurt you."

"You are! You will. Somehow. If not now, later."

"Stars," Dashiel whispered. "What has the world done to you?"

Somehow those words of compassion hurt Kess more than any hidden blade the rider could have gutted her with. And they disarmed her utterly as they wrapped arms around her, pulling her shuddering body into a tight embrace.

A choking, gasping wail broke from Kess's mouth like a death cry. She remained limp in their hold, unable to process a single thought or force her body into fight or flight.

Then she brought her arms up and clung back, crushing the rider's body into hers as though the pressure could stop the waves of tears and rattle in her bones.

But they kept coming, a release of every pain and humiliation Kess had suffered throughout her life.

Dashiel said nothing, just held her there on the floor beside the motionless talons of the golden dragon.

As finally some control returned to Kess's body, a shadow shifted near the entrance of the flight deck, and Kess lifted her head, peering over Dashiel's shoulder through tear-heavy eyes.

Down the long, dark room, a woman approached. Slowly at first, but once Kess lifted her face and met hers, the strides became fast and determined.

The grayglim armor could have been any royal guard in the palace. But the long whip of hair swinging behind the woman and the twin blades, one in each hand, could only be Lady Hjelzahn.

Kess's whole body went cold.

It might not have been Dashiel intending to kill Kess that day, but it didn't mean she wouldn't die.

Chapter Nine

Kess pushed Dashiel away and snatched the sharpened cheese knife from her boot. "Whoa." Dashiel held their hands up. "Sorry, I thought we were having a moment there."

"Get on the dragon, quick. Get out of here!" Kess urged, shifting forward to face Lady Hjelzahn.

"Why?"

"She's going to kill us!"

Dashiel turned to see the woman striding swiftly down the length of the flight deck. They folded their arms and pouted. "Really? Or is this part of the whole 'everyone wants to kill me' thing?"

The grayglim was close enough now that Kess could see a contemptuous smile twisting her lips at the sight of Kess's makeshift blade.

Kess knew she had practically zero chance of hurting the woman with it. She'd been skewered more than once by much sharper blades back in the underground and it hadn't slowed her down. But if Kess could just buy a chance for the dragonrider to escape, she'd take a shot.

There wasn't enough time for Kess to get onto the dragon as well. "Listen to me now and believe me later! Get onto the dragon!"

"Why would a grayglim be after us?" Dashiel remained still, glancing at Lady Hjelzahn again. There was enough threat in her advance that they frowned.

"She's after me and won't care that you're in her way."

The grayglim had her hands on the hilts of twin blades. Not the same ones she'd been disarmed of underground. Not nearly as finely made. But surely as deadly in her hands.

And then her advance halted and she scowled.

Kess dared a look over her shoulder, following the woman's line of sight. Two dragons flew in, landing beside Vance's golden etherflame.

Each had a grayglim rider on the front, and elaborate enclosed palanquin balanced lower down the dragon's back. One of the riders whistled loudly, and from the end of the flight deck, a half dozen servants appeared, wheeling mobile staircases over beside the dragons and lining them up to the palanquin doors.

Eslinde emerged from one, along with Vance, having managed their private moment after all, and looking only more awkward and unhappy from it. From the other came Ulfren, along with an additional two grayglim that had ridden in the enclosed seating with him.

He's serious about his protection. And probably for the best.

Kess narrowed her eyes on Lady Hjelzahn, waiting to see what she would do. The woman's expression left Kess chilled. There was something so lifeless and dark in her gaze as her face twitched, eyes darting over the appearance of the four other grayglims. She casually sheathed her swords.

As Eslinde approached, Lady Hjelzahn bowed low.

"Your Highness. A lucky chance meeting you here. We've yet to reschedule our meeting."

Eslinde blinked at the scene before her, Lady Hjelzahn addressing her in formal normality, Dashiel looking utterly confused, and Kess on the ground, face swollen and wet.

Kess tucked her hand holding the scrappy piece of sharp metal behind her back.

Eslinde stepped forward, Vance on one side.

"Kverra. Lucky indeed. I was so moved by the sad story of your missing children. How goes the search?"

Lady Hjelzahn straightened. "It continues. I hoped connections in court might have brought me news of them."

Yensen followed not far behind the princess, wheeling Kess's chair to her.

Dashiel helped her into it, and while they were close, whispered, "Okay, that was weird. I admit it. I saw the murder in her eyes."

"Pretend you saw nothing. Take Vance and go," Kess whispered back.

Ulfren and his grayglim milled about near their dragon, and Kess wondered whether they were trying to eavesdrop. She didn't care as long as they stayed nearby. She was certain it was only the safety of their numbers that stopped Lady Hjelzahn from killing them all as she'd attempted underground.

Eslinde's voice was soft with care. "Any useful leads so far?"

"Some gossip about a group seen around old Alderkin shrines including some that match their description."

Kess inhaled sharply.

"Although there are too many contradicting stories." The woman's void-like eyes turned on Kess. "It can be hard to know what to believe when some people enjoy sharing harmful rumors. But I am undeterred by such hindrances."

Kess glared back. The grayglim could take her thinly veiled threat and stuff it into one of the holes left behind from their last fight. If the woman wasn't prepared to reveal her murderous intent in front of everyone there, Kess wasn't prepared to be cowed by her words.

Unfortunately, it seemed as though Ulfren had decided nothing interesting was forthcoming from this meeting and was marching away, taking his three grayglim with him.

Kess inched her wheeled chair toward Eslinde.

The princess inclined her head. "Well, I'm sure you will find your children soon. As a grayglim, you must make short work of uncovering secrets."

In a low, icy voice, Lady Hjelzahn said, "I know many secrets. A kingdom's wealth of them."

Kess shivered.

Then the woman's voice softened. "But nothing is more important than getting to my children."

Kess brought her chair beside Eslinde, angled so her back was to Lady Hjelzahn. Ulfren and his guard were almost off the flight deck.

Kess looked up and whispered, "We have to go. Now."

Eslinde's eyes passed briefly over Kess, and she smiled beatifically at Lady Hjelzahn. "I'm afraid we're running late to another appointment. But if there is anything I can do, please let me know. Speak with Olva or Falden to arrange another meeting."

Dashiel moved next to their brother and grasped his arm, tugging him toward the golden dragon. "We've got to get back home, too."

"Do we?" Vance grumbled.

"Yup." Dashiel continued to drag him away, waving with their other hand. "Hopefully we'll see each other again soon."

"I hope so too," Eslinde replied.

"And I," Lady Hjelzahn said with a low bow.

Kess turned her chair and led the way out of the flight deck as the Zarram siblings lifted off on their dragon.

Eslinde walked in long strides to keep pace and whispered, "Why the hurry? What has upset you?"

Kess glanced back. Lady Hjelzahn remained motionless in the middle of the vast space as servants bustled about to secure the newly arrived dragons and return the mobile stairs.

Kess pushed faster, to get her and Eslinde closer behind Ulfren and the protection of his grayglim, but not close enough that the forward group could hear their whispered conversation.

"Lady Hjelzahn is dangerous. She isn't trying to find her children to reunite with them. She wants them dead and has tried to kill them already."

Eslinde scoffed. "For what possible reason?"

"I don't know, but I know Aishena and Benjin are keeping away from her on purpose."

They wove their way from the flight deck through corridors of ash gray and lightning-blue lamplight.

Eslinde's brow furrowed. "What of the eldest brother, Yoskar?"

Kess eyed the grayglim over Eslinde's shoulder, knowing he would hear everything said. "There was a fight between the family when I saw them in the Alderkin undercity. Yoskar was already dead by Kverra's hand when I arrived. I didn't witness it myself, only ... the aftermath."

Although traveling as fast as she could, every time there was even a small step or threshold in their path it slowed Kess down, and soon Ulfren and his men had disappeared ahead. Kess tossed worried glances over her shoulder, expecting Lady Hjelzahn to ambush them again at any moment.

Would the strange, cold woman dare attack a first heir? She had watched both Eslinde and Ulfren with a calculating gleam in her eyes.

They reached a short flight of stairs and Eslinde gestured for Yensen to help Kess down them, her frown deepening. "I can see Lady Hjelzahn has upset you greatly, but you couldn't be mistaken? There could have been some miscommunication."

Kess's body bumped as Yensen eased her wheeled chair down each step. She didn't want to explain that her splotchy, swollen face and remnants of tears were from an entirely different upset.

"No, I don't think so." The way Lady Hjelzahn and Aishena had battled throughout that crumbled cavern in furious flashes of steel and crystal held no hesitation in their attempts to end the other's life.

"Lady Hjelzahn wanted her children dead and was willing to kill everybody else around them to do so."

"But for what reason?" Eslinde pleaded again, a hand at her chest and face distraught.

Kess's tongue went dry, words sticking in her mouth. "Unfortunately, I was too busy betraying the Hjelzahn kids and their friends for my own interests to get the full story."

Eslinde tutted. "Quite the tangled history you have, Kessara."

They came out into the courtyard Kess had begun to recognize from her few trips through the palace and then up into the statue-lined hallways leading to Eslinde's chambers.

Eslinde paused at the base of the steep flights of stairs, giving Kess a long, assessing look. 'Do you mind if Yensen carries you up? I want to be in my rooms as fast as we can. We can collect your chair later."

Kess nodded. She wanted to be able to speak with Eslinde privately, to tell her more. She'd been so focused on Kife, and what threat he could pose to Dracuni, that she hadn't considered that Lady Hjelzahn's filicidal ambitions could be an even bigger threat.

But doing anything to stop her was going to mean sharing even more information with Eslinde. Kess decided then that she was willing to take a risk on one cloistered princess over an unstoppable grayglim.

When they arrived in Eslinde's chambers, Yensen placed Kess on the lounge and Eslinde swiftly sent him out again with the order, "Go back for her chair, and send for Falden."

Yensen hesitantly crossed the threshold, leaning back toward them and giving Kess a wary glance. "Given the situation, it seems prudent I remain on guard rather than distancing—"

"Work it out," Eslinde snapped and closed the door on him. She ran her hand over the wall beside it, fingers drifting in a nervous fashion. Soft thunking sounds echoed around the chambers.

"There's something else important I have to tell you," Kess said.

"I'm sure there is." Eslinde spoke with a hard clip.

The sun outside had dipped below the horizon and the chambers were gloomy, barely enough light to see. Eslinde marched to one of the wall lights and flicked a toggle beneath it and it sparked to life with a soft *zzzt*.

Kess flinched. "The remaining Hjelzahn siblings, they are who your daughter is traveling with."

Eslinde froze with her hand resting over the next lamp's switch. "Lyrrin? She's with Aishena and Benjin?"

"And ... some others."

Back in motion, Eslinde flicked the switch carelessly and then rubbed her thumb over her lips. "The girl, she was in grayglim training with her mother before the kids vanished from Hjelzahn keep."

"You knew them?"

"I knew *of* them. They're my great-great-something, great-niece and great-nephew, after all. Still, this is good. You said Lyrrin was well protected, and even a young grayglim is fine protection indeed."

Another soft *zzzt* as the next light illuminated.

"What's less good," Kess said, adjusting her skirts and seating from how Yensen had placed her down, "is that Lady Hjelzahn is a danger to her children and, therefore, also to Lyrrin."

"She'd go so far as to murder an eight-year-old bystander?"

"Without a doubt." Kess pulled a stray book out from underneath her and tossed it onto the low table nearby. The pitcher of water and glasses Eslinde kept there clinked, and Kess leaned across to pour herself a drink.

Eslinde meandered across the room toward the unlit lamps closer to Kess. "What about you?"

"What about me?" Kess lifted the glass to her mouth.

"Is Lady Hjelzahn a threat to *you*, if you know all of this about her? If she knows you know?"

Kess paused there, glass at her lips, and thought about how the woman pretended she never intended even a harmful word once more witnesses showed up. *Whatever her game, she doesn't want to reveal herself when the odds are against her.*

"She already tried to kill me once for what I saw. Whether she's still keen to snuff me out I would have known for sure if you hadn't arrived at the flight deck when you had."

"How can you be so flippant about it?" Eslinde rounded on her, mouth agape.

"Pretty easily." Kess gulped some water, trying to cool the hot flush crawling up her neck from how she'd just moments before cried into Dashiel's arms because the burden of fear of death and betrayal from every angle had become too much. "My question is, what can you do about her?"

"Without proof? Nothing much, I'm afraid."

Kess swung around to stare over the back of the lounge at the princess. "Nothing? I'm proof. I'm telling you she's a murderer."

"And who is going to believe you, or even me, without some form of evidence? Kverra is both an heir and a grayglim. And my brother Hjelzahn the First would not take kindly to me accusing any of his heirs, or the grayglim wife they took. He already doesn't like me."

Eslinde flicked the final lamp switch. There was a loud, crackling pop and it didn't illuminate. Kess startled at the sound, choking on her water. The remains in the glass sloshed over her fingers.

Eslinde sighed. "It's fine, they do that sometimes."

Kess's eyebrows crept up as she wiped her hand dry on her skirt.

Eslinde strode to the lounge, shaking her head. "I noticed you haven't been using the ones in the guest room. They're perfectly safe. Just ... don't touch the switches with wet fingers."

Kess continued planning to not touch the switches at all.

Eslinde reached the lounge and stopped in front of her, one hand out expectantly. "Now, speaking of safe ... I'm afraid I can't allow you to keep it."

"Keep what?"

Eslinde wiggled her fingers. "The knife, Kessara."

"If I *did* have a knife, wouldn't you be worried I'd use it on you if forced to hand it over?"

"Please," Eslinde mocked flatly.

She swished her skirt sideways to reveal a long slit pocket access, reached in, and withdrew a brilliantly polished length of steel. An exquisitely crafted epee with narrow swirling cross guard. With an equally liquid motion she thrust it back into its hidden scabbard.

"Right. Okay then." Kess pulled her dully pointed cheese knife from her boot and placed it in the princess's waiting hand.

Eslinde brought it close to her face to examine it, shaking her head and muttering.

"It wasn't meant for you," Kess added, mortified. "Although clearly it wouldn't have mattered if it was."

Eslinde snorted softly and tossed the makeshift weapon onto the low table amongst the stacks of books and glasses. "Us Firsts have to keep ourselves well protected. But mostly it's from each other. Why do you think Ulfren keeps three grayglim with him?"

Kess shrugged. "Desperate paranoia?"

"Accurate assessment of risk. My siblings, they've been quietly assassinating each other or scheming to remove our father from the throne for decades. As the youngest it doesn't mean much to me, although there has been a worrying increase in murdered lower generation heirs recently. And a few Firsts."

Kess remembered how Eslinde had laughed at the concept of her father ever leaving his throne, willingly or otherwise. "You're not worried someone will succeed in removing the king?"

Eslinde straightened her skirts and lowered herself elegantly onto the lounge beside Kess. "Not at all. As much as the heirs like to plot, my father will remain safe. He protects himself by being the only person who knows where his store of silvernix is kept. If he dies, it likely all goes with him."

"And you're not worried about yourself? If Firsts are being assassinated ..."

A coy smile lifted one side of Eslinde's lips. "Have you found any way out of my chambers yet? During the times I've left you locked in? Yes, of course you've tried."

Kess grumbled begrudgingly, "No. I haven't found any way out."

"Then suffice it to say there's no way in either." Eslinde stared at the entrance door, a strange sadness in her eyes. Then she shook her head softly. "Plus, there's my ever present grayglim bodyguard. I don't trust at all that he isn't acting on my parents' orders rather than my own, but he does protect my safety. And he is *very* good."

A loud rap on the door had Eslinde on her feet again.

A familiar woman's voice announced Falden had arrived. Eslinde hurried to let him in and greeted him warmly at the door. Olva followed, the elderly handmaiden carrying a wide tray with a dinner spread. Glistening dishes held a large rolled roast of dark meat, steaming vegetables coated in golden spices, and glass carafes of sunshine-yellow wine.

"I've brought you that information you were after, Your Highness," Falden said, his voice croaky with age.

"You have?"

"About the Heithorns?"

"Oh, yes." Eslinde beckoned him to the table by the window, away from Kess.

Falden took a seat and waited for Olva to place the tray down. Although Kess was sure it had been intended to be her and Eslinde's dinner, Falden took a glass and held it up to be filled.

Taking a sip of the pale wine, he smacked his lips. "Yes, yes. The Heithorns. A minor dragonlord family who chose to live in a walled estate far out to the west, which unfortunately was destroyed, the lord and lady amongst the dead, survived only by their son."

Kess scowled and called over from her place on the lounge. "Not only their son."

The younger handmaiden appeared as well, face red and breathing hard as she pushed the heavy wheeled chair over to Kess's side.

"Well, yes, there was a daughter too. One with ... aah ..." Falden blinked his pale eyes at Kess as she worked to move from the lounge to the wheeled chair. "A particular obsession with dragons. That was the impression those few who met her had."

"Oh, I'm sure," Kess muttered.

That was the impression. Where was this guy getting his information? Or did he simply find it too distasteful to speak the truth.

"But she's been missing and presumed dead for many years now."

Eslinde waited as her glass was filled, staring at Kess. "Quite a tragedy, by the sounds of it all."

Kess settled into the hard seat of the wheeled chair but didn't attempt to move it closer to the others.

Eslinde gave the older man a pitiful look and said, "I'm afraid I have another tragedy to turn our attention to now, though."

Falden took another sip of his wine and perked up.

Eslinde continued. "You must have heard of Lady Hjelzahn's attempts to find her missing children."

"I have, I have. Terrible matter. Has a bounty on them and all, and still no luck."

Olva worked to lay out the remaining food and serving plates, but Eslinde shooed her away. She went and joined Jillisa by the door where Yensen remained at watch.

Lowering her voice, Eslinde said, "But there's some gossip that the children might have been seen near Alderkin shrines? What do you know of that?"

Falden tugged the white strands of hair at the side of his head. "It's very worrying. Blasted criminals and cannibals of the wilds have been congregating around the old Alderkin structures for some reason. I pray for the sun's blessings those poor children aren't trapped in such a place."

"Are they so dangerous?" Eslinde glanced to Kess.

Kess rolled her eyes and shook her head.

Falden nodded vehemently. "Oh yes! Dreadful! They are pits of evil, filled with monsters worshiping cursed Alderkin magic, that are causing the shadow dragon's blight to get worse."

Eslinde's lip twitched and she drew a long sip of wine. "Surely, they are simply desperate people who've been unable to seek shelter in a dragonkeep. Perhaps they can be reasoned with, convinced to stop any dangerous activities?"

She swirled the liquid in her glass and set it back on the table. "Or if the Hjelzahn children are kept there, that they could be released? If I were to draft some messages, could they be delivered out to some of these shrine settlements?"

"You have a kind heart, Your Highness, but those animals can't be reasoned with."

Eslinde reached across the table to take Falden's hand in hers. "There are so few I can trust these days. You've always been my favorite advisor, always ready to assist me. Couldn't we at least try?"

Falden's lips jiggled between a prideful grin and attempted humility. "I suppose communication could be attempted. I could arrange that for you."

"And keep me informed of where Lady Hjelzahn is whenever possible? So any news we might receive about her children can be passed on." Eslinde got to her feet, offering a wide armed gesture that Falden should join her.

"Of course." He hastily put his glass back down as Eslinde herded him away from the table.

"You are an absolute treasure," Eslinde said as she whisked the old man back out the door again. With a word to her handmaidens that she needed nothing else that evening, the door was closed again, followed by the echoing sounds of locking.

When the princess turned back her way, Kess clapped slowly and quietly. "Masterful."

Eslinde offered a tiny bow.

Pushing her chair around the lounge, Kess headed for the dinner spread. "You know, if those messages do reach the shrine settlements, and then get to your daughter and her friends, they're only going to think it's some kind of trap."

"Possibly. If they even realize the messages are for them. I'm going to have to be so subtle with my language ... But I have to try." Eslinde joined Kess at the table but didn't serve herself any food. She seemed deep in thought as though already composing those coded messages in her mind.

Kess reached for the roasted meat. A long carving knife rested beside it, almost as though in mockery of Kess's previous effort to arm herself. Kess sliced a thick slab, dumped it on her plate, and stabbed the blade back into the remaining roast.

Kess picked at the juicy meat. *Griskin would love this.*

Eslinde's attention returned to her. "Now, you obviously already knew about these shrine settlements. And more. You have been open with me, but I know there is much you're holding back."

Kess munched on the meat. "I know plenty of things. You'll have to be more specific about what you want to know."

Eslinde's shoulders dropped, and the regal fire in her tone vanished. "I must play games with everyone in my life, Kessara. Please don't make me play them with you as well. You have brought a treasured truth into my life. But you are keeping a secret from me, something you're holding tightly to, something I know is important."

Kess's insouciant chewing slowed. In the lightning-hued glow of the lamps, Eslinde's face was drawn thin, sharp lines between her pale brows. A war of rebellious hope and learned hopelessness visible in her eyes.

I have to give her something. But I can't give her Dracuni.

"It's not the shrines or the people around them that is worsening the shadow dragon curse."

Eslinde waited, unmoving.

At the precipice, the words felt like treason, but Kess forced them out. "We think it's caused by the taming of dragons."

She remained still, waiting the princess's reaction, eyeing the carving blade, just in case.

"Is that all?" Eslinde seemed disappointed.

"Is that *all*?" Kess repeated in disbelief.

"It's not new information, I'm afraid." Eslinde reached for a carafe and refilled her glass, still avoiding the food. "I've known for quite some time."

Kess's words coughed out. "You ... what ... how?"

"I was initially shocked too. And I tried to spread the information, back in my rebellious phase. Back before all of that was crushed out of me." Eslinde's eyes fluttered and she took a long drink of her wine. "Nobody believed me, of course. Who would believe silly little Eslinde over the lies Yeonard Draekhan has been spreading for decades about it being an Alderkin curse?"

"The ... the Dragon King ... he knows too?" Kess could only stutter words out. How many life-threatening secrets was she now privy to? She reached for the carafe of wine and filled a glass for herself.

"I understand it must have been a big revelation for you, but as you think it through, what does it really mean? Not much. What could we do? Dragons are here and they are tamed, people aren't going to stop using them. They need them, for almost every aspect of our society." Eslinde gestured to the humming lights along the wall.

"But it's ... the tamings are causing the shadow dragon blight. We could end it, reclaim the land from the undead."

"Yet we need dragons as well for protection from those revenants. We are in a bind." Kess took a long drink of the sweet wine, inviting the heavy effect of it flooding her veins. What could they do? Was there no solution?

"No. It doesn't have to be this way." Kess thumped her glass down again. "There are other ways to live. Without dragons. They don't use them in the Alderkin undercity. And the settlements around the shrines. There is a magic there, but a good magic. It keeps the revenants out, and the people there are living peacefully."

Eslinde paused at that, raising her eyebrows. "Really, what life could they have without the assistance of dragons, out there?"

Kess remembered what she saw, as she'd chased her prey from shrine to shrine, of those small communities thriving within the standing stone rings. "It's a simple life, but they seem happy. And maybe people in the keeps could be too, without dragons. They could start small, untame a few—"

"Sorry, untame?" Eslinde leaned closer, eyes round.

"The dragons. They could be untamed." Kess watched the princess's stunned expression. "They can be freed, made wild and independent again. You didn't know?"

Eslinde was breathing heavily, pale eyes glimmering in the cool light. "No, Kessara. That is new information to me. And that is something I want to see for myself."

Chapter Ten

Dashiel jittered with nerves as they waited at the street level entrance of Zarram Dragonhold for Eslinde's arrival.

The racist slur that had been painted upon the wall beside the grand iron gates didn't help. It wasn't the first time, but was the biggest and boldest. Singe marks blackened the stone beneath it.

"Stars, did someone try to start a fire?"

"Good thing Zarrams don't burn so easily," Vance replied.

He'd been out waiting even earlier than Dashiel. He gave the wall a dark look. Servants hastily scrubbed to remove the crude message before the princess and her guest arrived.

That strange, wounded girl.

Dashiel hadn't been able to stop thinking about her since their flight after the investment ceremony. That had been a crazy day, and weeks later no answers had surfaced for the strange taming spike, fake silvernix, murderous grayglim, or what pain Kess's history held that had her so broken.

Dashiel could guess at some of it. Their brother hid their prosthetic leg from most people for a reason. Maybe the visit today would provide more answers, although Eslinde's communications had been vague in the extreme.

Still, Dashiel found themselves wanting to know more about Kess, wanting to help her see that not all the world was cruel.

She was a natural in the saddle, too. Imagine what she could do with some proper training.

Perhaps that was what this visit was about.

A black carriage approached down the cobbled street. Elaborate silver filigree accented the edges of the doors and windows, but it was the forest-green treedart drawing the carriage that identified it as one coming from the palace. Only the royal family had silvernix to spare on taming dragons for tasks that other livestock could perform.

"Here they come," Dashiel called to their brother.

Vance grunted at the unfinished cleaning work and moved to stand by Dashiel's side.

The carriage rolled to a stop.

Eslinde emerged first, gliding down in an elegant step. Her shoulders were back, chin lifted in a fiery countenance that had normally accompanied her when she was younger and she'd visit to talk about the most rebellious ideas.

She even smiled, very slightly. More in her eyes than her thinly pressed lips. She pointedly remained turned away from the half-scrubbed paint on the wall.

"Thank you for accepting our company today. I hope we aren't taking time from your training." She offered the siblings a shallow bow.

Dashiel returned the bow deeper. "Not at all."

They didn't elaborate as to the great pains they had gone through to skip training that day. But their mestra's great disapproval was nothing compared to missing out on seeing what had to be two of the most interesting people in the city.

Kess appeared then at the carriage door. She had the skirts of her courtly gown bundled up near her waist, revealing well-worn leather pants beneath, the kind a hunter or guard might wear. She kept the fabric out of the way as she shuffled right to the edge of the bench.

The grayglim Yensen moved about the back of the carriage, then brought the wheeled chair around beside the door.

Dashiel was about to offer assistance when Kess neatly climbed down and lowered herself into the seat. After straightening out her skirts, she rolled the chair over more smoothly and swiftly than she'd managed before.

Dashiel bowed down to her eye level. "It's good to see you again."

Kess leaned away from the words and fussed with her skirts some more, eyes averted. "You too."

Vance gestured to one of the nearby servants to direct the driver on where to park the carriage.

"Go with the carriage, Yensen. You can await our return there." Eslinde didn't look toward her grayglim as she commanded him.

"Your Highness." Yensen's eyes passed over the remaining graffiti, then Kess and the Zarrams. "I cannot allow you to wander such a facility unaccompanied."

Vance stepped forward, looming over the warden.

His voice held a low growl as he said, "I can guarantee Eslinde will be safe with us in the dragonhold."

Stepping between them, Eslinde said, "Oh, I'm sure he's far more worried that I'm the one who's going to steal a dragon and fly away and leave him to explain to my father how he lost his unruly daughter."

"Your Highness," Yensen said again, pained.

"I'm not going to run away. I'm visiting friends and you aren't required. Unless of course your true intentions are to spy upon me?" Eslinde turned toward him then, keeping him held in her icy stare.

He swallowed visibly, jaw twitching. "I will wait with the carriage."

Eslinde turned on her heel, triumph on her lips, and led the way inside, leaving the rest of them to follow.

Kess kept up easily with the swift march but allowed Dashiel to assist when they reached steps.

"Now, I'm afraid our visit isn't strictly social," Eslinde said.

"I hadn't assumed so," Vance replied.

"Where can we speak with utmost privacy?" Eslinde said, eyes on the numerous staff and servants moving about the corridors.

"This way." Vance took the lead.

The entry level of the dragonhold was largely for administration, meetings with trade partners, and services for the humans within the hold, as opposed to those for dragons. It was all gleaming and gilt with the finest furnishings the dragonkeep capital had to offer.

The squeaking of Kess's chair echoed down the hall.

Dashiel leaned toward her. "So … Has anybody tried to kill you lately?"

Kess flushed red. "No. Although I may feel the need for murder if you bring that up again."

"You'd murder me for my curiosity? Maybe you could look into that reaction as a place to start if you don't want everybody trying to kill you."

Kess gave them a dull glare.

Dashiel grinned in return, pressing a hand innocently to their chest. "I just want to know what the deal with that strange grayglim was."

"Oh. That's all?"

"What else?"

"The … crying?" Kess hissed under her breath, turning even redder.

They reached a short flight of stairs, and Dashiel took the back of Kess's chair. "That? That was nothing. You should see me when I witness someone who's a better rider than I am. Tantrum central. Lock myself in my room and cry for days."

Kess scoffed.

At the bottom of the stairs, Dashiel leaned over Kess from behind. "It's lucky it's been a few weeks since our flight together. I only emerged tear-free yesterday."

Kess gave them a flat look, but there was a softening in her shoulders and eyes as they searched Dashiel's face, the smallest hint of smile. "You needn't coddle me."

"Wouldn't dream of it." Dashiel beamed.

"Yes, this will do." Eslinde inspected the room Vance had led them to from the doorway, then entered.

Vance's office. Letters and leatherbound folios were stacked to one side of the modest desk—paperwork Vance had fallen behind on, as usual. Vance was many things, but he wasn't made for doing paperwork, despite how much Lord Zarram thrust upon him.

There were no windows, and the small room was farthest from the rest of the offices. Once an old storage room for the nearby hatchery, it had been converted when Vance's accident changed his career path.

The Zarram siblings had initial hopes that Vance would fly again, that the office space was only temporary, but their father had other ideas.

Vance struck an oil lamp alight, and Dashiel closed the door behind them.

Patting the heavy stone, Dashiel said, "The walls are thick here. It must be quite a secret you have to share, considering how keen you were to get rid of your grayglim."

Vance offered Eslinde the one chair in the room, but she shook her head and remained standing.

"Yes, well, asking one's friends to attempt to untame a dragon does feel like a thing that requires secrecy," she said.

Dashiel choked. "Sorry … *what* do you want to do?"

"Kess can perhaps explain the process better, but she believes—"

"She has witnessed," Kess clarified.

Eslinde continued. "Kess has *witnessed* a dragon's taming being reversed. And it is something I wish to witness for myself. Which is why I've come to ask those I trust the most whether they would attempt to untame their dragon for me."

Kess gave them a description of the process, and Eslinde confirmed that she brought the required silvernix with her.

Dashiel took the sole seat in the room then, dumping down into it with a sigh.

"Taming can be reversed?" They leaned their head into their hands, laughing.

"What's so funny?" Kess asked.

"It just would have been nice to know a few weeks ago, would have saved me the trouble of faking Shiff's taming." Although, Dashiel conceded, they wouldn't have wanted to ever drive that stake in, even if they knew it could be reversed.

"Dash," Vance growled in warning, too late.

"If Eslinde trusts us with this request, I trust her to know that I never tamed my dragonling."

"I suppose that means we can't use her to test the process then," Eslinde said, eyebrows raised, but offering no other judgment. "I was hoping for something small."

"Apart from Viska, every other dragon here is allocated and owned by someone who will notice if it suddenly becomes wild again," Vance said.

Dashiel leaped out of the chair again. "Then we try with Viska! You said you regretted having to tame her. This is your chance to undo it."

"Regretting that doesn't mean untaming her now is a good idea. What would happen to her?" Vance folded his arms and directed his questions at Kess.

She shrugged.

"Would she still heed commands? Would she listen at all?"

"Hard to say."

"Would she be dangerous?"

"Likely."

"How can you be sure she'll survive the process?"

"I can't."

"What do we even do with a dragon once it's untamed?"

"The other one flew away," Kess offered.

"Flew away? No. We can't do this," Vance said. "How are we going to explain even Viska's loss from our stables? I'm sorry, I can't take that risk."

Kess lounged back in her wheeled chair, giving Eslinde a look. "Maybe you were right. We can't even convince your friends to give up a single dragon."

"You did make it sound so appealing," Eslinde chided.

"I was being honest. Thought you'd appreciate it."

"Well, luckily there is one other dragon in your hold that won't be missed." Eslinde circled around the desk, bringing herself in front of everyone. "Mine."

Kess gave the princess a long, assessing look. "You'd give up you own dragon?"

"Of course. He's been idle for years anyway since I haven't been allowed to fly. And this is important."

Dashiel turned to their brother. "Her dragon is a good pick. Only those on the feeding and cleaning rosters might notice his absence, and you could adjust the paperwork to cover for that."

"Great, more paperwork," Vance muttered.

Eslinde moved around the table to stand directly in front of him, staring up into his face with a tilted head. "Please, Vance. For me. I have nobody else I can turn to with this request."

A growling grumble came from low in Vance's throat and his nose twitched. "Fine. For you."

Even with the agreement, Vance continued to try to find reasons not to, or to delay, but only helped them solidify their plan.

What if the dragon tried to get away? They would chain it down first.

What if the dragon was dangerous? They would do the untaming in one of the old flamesong stalls where it could be contained.

Why were they even risking it? Eslinde promised to tell them more, if it worked.

Down in the lower levels of the old building, Dashiel took Kess into Shiff's stall while Vance handled bringing Eslinde's dragon into another nearby.

"You really didn't tame her?" Kess asked, approaching the wild dragonling without any fear.

"You don't mind?" Dashiel asked.

"I ... I knew another dragonling that hadn't been tamed. She made tamed dragons seem so much less interesting." Kess held her hand out.

Still and calm? Shiff sniffed at Kess and her rolling chair warily.

"No, at ease." Dashiel patted the dragon's snout, then smiled back at Kess. "Wolves, wild dragons, legions trying to murder you ... You make my life feel so boring."

Kess shrugged. "You try living alone in the wilds for five years and I'm sure you'll also have plenty of tales to tell."

"Is *that* where you came from?" Dashiel could hardly imagine it.

They'd flown a little way out over the lands around Draekhanhelm but had never landed beyond the walls. They wanted to ask Kess so many questions, like whether she'd ever seen a rev close up, but didn't want to admit to the fierce young woman that they hadn't.

Shiff slithered to her feet, prowling forward. She scratched at the wheel of Kess's chair.

"Shiff, back." Dashiel swirled a finger at their side. "Sit."

The dragonling skittered over and sat at attention.

"You've trained her too?" Kess's eyes sparkled.

"Vance doesn't think it's going to hold as she gets older, more independent and savage. I guess we're about to have a full-grown wild dragon to test my training skills on soon."

"We're ready!" Vance called from across the hallway.

"Shiff, come." Dashiel clicked, and the dragonling followed at his heel.

They figured having the dragonling around might help communication efforts once Eslinde's dragon was untamed. Inside the next stall, Eslinde and Vance waited, looking over the medium-sized dragon before them.

Dashiel always liked Eslinde's snowshimmer. He was a blue the color of a smoke-free sky, and it had been an honor to keep a First's dragon stabled, even if it seemed a formality for a dragon that had for all intents and purposes been retired.

Vance worked on hauling a second set of chains across and locked them around the dragon's neck. "Just in case."

Eslinde patted the dragon's cheek. Dashiel didn't know why she no longer flew or whether she'd named her dragon. It was young when it had been stabled with them, eight years ago.

Kess talked them through the process again, and Vance found some pliers.

"Once the spike is out, it might take a while for the dragon to come back to itself." Kess placed herself just inside the opened doorway. "It did the other time. You'll see why."

"I certainly hope to." Eslinde moved around, lighting a few extra oil lamps to brighten the solid stone chamber.

"I just hope we aren't making a terrible mistake." Vance paused with the pliers around the end of the spike.

Dashiel elbowed him and said softly, "But you're going to do this anyway. It's for Eslinde."

Vance growled and grumbled under his breath. Then he pulled the taming stake.

It was a slow, torturous process, but the dragon didn't react. Finally, the stake slipped free, and Vance threw it and the pliers on the ground outside the stall.

Dashiel had the princess's silvernix at the ready. As they let the drop fall onto the wound, they held their breath.

What if the silvernix is fake again?

But then there was a shimmer of light, glowing between the dragon's scales.

Vance and Dashiel joined the other two at the doorway.

"So we just wait?" Dashiel asked.

Kess's eyes were on the air above the dragon's lowered head, and she nodded.

"There!" Kess said.

Eslinde gasped, and then Dashiel saw it too. Dark wisps of smoky mist, descending through the stone ceiling toward the motionless snowshimmer.

"What is that?" they asked.

But then the dragon was moving. Moving without a command or a rider. Slowly, at first. The twitch of an eyelid, the turn of a neck. Then the chains rattled as the dragon's whole body snapped to life and he roared.

Eslinde clutched her forehead and cried out, "He's screaming! Screaming in my head!"

What happens? Dragon talks!

Dashiel frowned. Could all dragons communicate normally if they weren't tamed?

Poor Shiff. What a strange, silent world where every dragon around her was mute.

They didn't know how to explain why that was.

"Can you communicate? Try to calm it," Kess ordered.

Eslinde's knees buckled, and she leaned against the doorframe. "He's so angry!"

The dragon thrashed again, tail whipping behind him. One of the chains locking him in place snapped like rock candy.

"Whoa!" Dashiel dodged a piece of flying metal. "Is the other one going to hold?"

"I'm not sure," Vance replied. "The chains are designed to stop people stealing the dragons, not to hold dragons down. There isn't usually a need."

Blue scales shimmered in the lamplight as the dragon's body convulsed, swaying and arching, eyes rolling wildly.

The second chain cracked, metal groaning as it tore free.

"Out! Get out!" Vance bellowed.

Dashiel raised their hands toward the snowshimmer. "We just have to calm her down, communicate—"

The dragon's head swung around, locked sights on Eslinde, and its mouth opened. A sparking blue glow built at the back of its throat.

Oh no.

A jagged streak of lightning shot out. Dashiel froze, the scene searing into their eyes in the harsh glare.

Vance dove, pulling the princess into a rolling tumble with him. She fell out of his arms as the beam caught up with him, and Vance howled.

"Vance!" Dashiel's feet were fixed to the ground.

"Go! Move!" Kess hissed, pushing into Dashiel from behind with her chair.

They stumbled together out of the room.

The snowshimmer snarled, eyes turning, taking in the solid walls on every side and only exit ahead.

Stop. Sit! Still and calm! Shiff rose onto her back legs, wings outstretched like a shield in front of the humans and her chest puffing.

Dashiel grabbed for the emergency release on the wall. "Shiff! Come!"

The dragonling darted from the chamber with the snowshimmer snapping at her tail. The moment Shiff was out, Dashiel pulled the rope, and the heavy drop-gate slammed down.

Dull roars echoed through the solid steel. Then scratching and the thud, thud, thud, of the dragon trying to batter his way out.

"Vance? Are you hurt?" Eslinde crouched over Dashiel's brother, hiding him from view with a curtain of silver hair and satin gown.

The parts of Vance that were visible had a faint twist of smoke rising from them.

Dashiel rushed over. "Is he okay?"

Vance groaned. "My whole mouth tastes like copper."

"Alive then, at least." Dashiel laughed in relief and helped pull Vance to his feet.

Vance stumbled, and Eslinde caught him under the shoulder.

"Careful," she scolded. She helped him cross to a wall so he could lean there.

Vance grumbled. "I'm fine. It's just …"

He leaned forward, pulling the hem of his pants up. The metal joint of his prosthetic leg smoldered, fused solid. "Raze it."

Eslinde jabbed him in the side with her fist. "That was reckless, moving in front of the lightning like that."

"You're welcome." Vance coughed.

Eslinde stepped in front of him then, brushing fingers over a singed piece of hair near his cheek and berating him in a long string of accusations.

Dashiel smiled softly and stepped back.

"Is he going to be okay?" Kess asked.

Dashiel squatted down beside her, taking a few deep breaths of recovery. "Oh yeah. I'd say so. He's probably loving this."

"Why would he?"

Leaning onto the armrest of Kess's chair, Dashiel whispered, "Vance has loved Eslinde for most of his life. Although he'd gnaw off his remaining leg before he'd ever admit it. Even to himself."

Kess blinked once, and for a moment, there was such a devastating clarity of pain in her eyes that Dashiel was worried she'd somehow been hurt by the dragon and was about to die in front of them. Then she blinked again and her face turned stony.

Before Dashiel could question it, Vance said, "You've definitely done what you set out to do. That's a wild dragon in there."

The snowshimmer continued to roar, the sound reverberating through the solid door.

"Will that hold?" Eslinde asked.

"It's designed to block an exploding flamesong, so I'd say so," Dashiel answered. They stepped up to rap on the door, but considered the snowshimmer might use its lightning breath and thought better of touching the metal. "Although I'm going to have to work out a way to feed it … Maybe it will calm down, after a while."

Very angry, Shiff thought.

Eslinde stared at the door and shook her head softly. "It really worked."

"I did say it would." Kess shrugged.

"Are you ready to tell us what this is all about now?" Vance asked.

Eslinde laced her fingers together and brought them up in front of her lips, took a deep breath, and then explained.

She'd already spoken vaguely to Dashiel and Vance in their childhood about how she didn't believe the shadow dragon was caused by an Alderkin curse. But to hear the truth of it left Dashiel shaken.

But also excited. "How many? How many dragons would need to be healed to stop the shadow dragon? If we did all of ours—"

"Dash," Vance warned. "That's not going to happen."

"Why not? If it was enough …"

"I doubt it would be enough," Eslinde said softly. "You have a few score dragons in your hold, but there must be hundreds, thousands across Elundrae. Each one is making the shadow dragon stronger."

"So each one must weaken it. We should at least stop taming more or ..." Dashiel's words shuddered to a stop and their mouth went dry. Frowning, they jogged over into Shiff's stall.

"What is it?" Kess asked.

"You've got to see this," they called out as they removed the loose paving stone. They retrieved the bundle from the hollow beneath and returned to the others. Dashiel unwrapped the cloth, explaining about the fake silvernix from the taming ceremony.

The strange crystal taming spike no longer glowed.

Dashiel held it out to show Eslinde and Kess. "This is strange, right? Like maybe someone else is doing something to the tamings. What do these markings mean?"

Almost in unison, Kess and Eslinde replied, "They're Alderkin runes."

Kess shot Eslinde a look. "When have you seen Alderkin runes?"

Eslinde's eyes narrowed, and she took the stake from Dashiel. "In study. You know I read a lot."

Shiff came to sit at Dashiel's feet, disturbed by the echoes of the snowshimmer's attempts to free itself.

Dashiel reached a hand down, patting her neck, imagining what might have happened if they'd used that strange spike. "But why—?"

"I'll look into it," Eslinde said and dropped the spike into a hidden pocket in her gown. "Don't tell anyone else about this or about the untaming. At least for now. We're flying into dangerous skies."

The snowshimmer roared through the barrier of its cell, a long, echoing cry that eked out into a high whine.

Dashiel shivered. Eslinde's expression suggested that having a full-grown wild dragon caged in their basement was the least dangerous thing they might face soon.

Yeonard Draekhan. Dragon King. Tamer of dragons. The ever youthful. The man who could no doubt have Kess killed off on a whim if the desire took him, regardless of anything Eslinde said. Somebody that Kess really didn't want to be in the same room with. Let alone presenting evidence that directly challenged the Dragon King's source of power.

"I don't think you need me for this," Kess said, gripping the wheels of her chair to slow down.

Eslinde kept up her swift march, pushing Kess along with her. "Nonsense. You are a vital witness. I know he's turned us away already, but I'm not taking no for an answer anymore."

Grand double doors lay ahead, inlaid with golden filigree forming the design of a massive dragon's head. From the center of its forehead, swirling lines and beams shot forth like a sunrise. A palace guard stood on either side.

"His Majesty has not requested your presence," one of the guards said in a confused, boyish voice.

"You must be mistaken. Yensen? Get the door." Eslinde didn't slow her pace.

Kess worried that the princess would use her and her chair as a battering ram, but her grayglim moved faster, pushing the double doors wide for their passage before either of the guards could react.

The two men were left stuttering in their wake as the grand doors swung closed again.

Inside the private advisory chambers, all heads turned their way.

Kess straightened in her chair and tried to straighten her expression as well, which was twitching into an anxious sneer.

She recognized Eslinde's mother, Queen Vellira, a brazen beauty with a glare so icy it could have taken the spark out of dragonfire. Falden, the old advisor who had visited Eslinde, sat alongside her, plus another half dozen elders Kess didn't recognize.

Ulfren the First was there, along with another white-haired man, the same Kess had seen walking with him in the courtyard weeks ago, hovering at his left. They leaned over the central table where a map of Elundrae was spread. Some tokens and figurines were spread around the central range of Eishowl Peaks, where the Alderkin undercity was.

On their side stood Yeonard Draekhan.

"Eslinde. Your presence is unexpected." Although speaking softly, his voice seemed to boom and echo through the coolly lit chamber.

The Dragon King's eyes were dark and piercing, with bright, glinting middles, almost as though the iris and pupils had been reversed. Kess found she couldn't look at them for long without shivers racking through her.

Eslinde seemed to have no such trouble.

"Well, we are here now regardless. Continue. I can wait my turn." Eslinde slowed her pace, pushing Kess to a respectable distance from the table and stopping there.

The princess remained standing, and her grayglim had become a shadow along the wall where other similar shadows lurked.

Craning her neck, Eslinde peered at the map. "Planning another incursion into Elgartha?"

Ulfren scowled and scooped the pieces off the side of the parchment, then roughly rolled it up. "We were done."

Eslinde raised her eyebrows and smiled politely. "I'm sure if anyone had managed to smuggle living unicorns off Elundrae, and somehow kept them alive in captivity, there would have been news of it by now."

Yeonard strode around the table to Eslinde and Kess's side. Floor-length robes of watery-silver fabric hung straight from elaborate shoulder guards of gold and gemstones, forming a high-necked collar in the center.

He clasped fingers laden with heavily ornate rings in front of him. "And what are you doing toward finding solutions for the silvernix shortage?"

So even he is worried about silvernix running out? Even with how free a supply Eslinde has had access to?

Kess wondered how much there still was in the Dragon King's hidden stores. But she knew no matter how much it was, someone like him would always want more.

He can't find out about Dracuni.

The ageless man stood in front of her. Kess frowned, turning her eyes to the polished floor, her breath quickening at the nearness of the Dragon King.

Kess hated the roiling feelings within her. She hated being someone who could be cowed.

What would Riony do, if she were here?

Probably say something inappropriate. Kess's lips lifted, picturing the fiery giant throwing a joke at the Dragon King about his amma.

Dashiel's words echoed within her. *Vance has loved Eslinde for most of his life. Although he'd gnaw off his remaining leg before he'd ever admit it. Even to himself.*

Kess's frown returned, pinned down painfully as though by knives.

Could Kess admit it, if there was such a thing to admit? It didn't matter anyway; there was nobody to admit anything to. She clutched the acorn at her neck.

But she also raised her head, locking eyes with the nigh-immortal ruler of their land. And it was he who turned away.

Eslinde's voice remained pleasant. "I do have news, actually, which is in a way relevant to our supplies and use of silvernix."

Kess hissed under her breath, "Now? Shouldn't we—"

"Everybody here knows the true cause of the shadow dragon already."

Ulfren scoffed again, pointing the rolled map at her like a weapon. "True cause? You've no proof. Must we listen to these delusions again?"

Yeonard Draekhan tilted his chin upward. "I had thought you'd grown beyond your tendency toward conspiracy, dear daughter."

Eslinde's fingers entwined in front of her. "Is it conspiracy that the shadow dragon curse is worsening? No. We've all seen the reports of burned revenants rising a second time. Of revenants congregating in great numbers. My companion here has seen it with her own eyes."

"You can't take the word of some peasant from the wilds on these issues," the other silver-haired man said.

"*Peasant?*" Kess grumbled.

"Hjelzahn, I understand you must struggle with trust while there is so much happening within your family line." The sympathy in Eslinde's tone sounded almost real.

Kess eyed the man. He had looked vaguely familiar. Kess had once in her life been in the same space as the Hjelzahns, back before she'd been cast out of her noble home.

Yoska, Aishena, and Benjin were a number of generations removed from Hjelzahn the First, though. Even Kverra wasn't related to him by blood and had given her children her darker skin. Hjelzahn the First was pale like his father, silver hair in only two braids at the front and loose at the back, and a single plait in the center of his small beard.

Eslinde strode forward, leaving Kess behind as she approached the table. Reaching into her pocket, she tossed the tarnished spike that had been pulled from her snowshimmer onto the surface.

"But I can trust Kessara's word because she has brought me information that I've been able to test and confirm myself. That tamings, the cause of the shadow dragon, can be reversed."

"Reversed?" Ulfren choked on the word.

"Reversed," Eslinde confirmed. "In a similar process, with a drop of silvernix, we can take back from the shadow dragon that which is strengthening it. We could end its blight once and for all."

Kess held her breath as she waited for the reactions of those who could make or break all their lives, those who had the power to change all of Elundrae, be its salvation or downfall.

There was shocked silence at first and then quiet mutterings shared with those nearest. Falden and Eslinde's mother leaned close, whispering to each other.

"So your news of silvernix is how we can spend it twice as fast, for no reward?" Hjelzahn eyed the spike on the table like it was a venomous snake. "Why would we use a precious resource to reverse something we've already invested in?"

"Because it would liberate our lands and our people from the curse of the undead," Eslinde replied.

Yeonard Draekhan's eyes glittered. "All the abundance we've brought to Elundrae, all our trade profits from metals and glass with other lands, all our technology and innovation has come from leashing the power of dragons. You would have us throw all of that away?"

Eslinde opened her mouth, but the Dragon King continued over her. "For what? So some peasants in the wild don't have to worry about revenants? They should be serving in the keeps anyway."

"The dragonkeeps remain safe, as always," Hjelzahn agreed.

Kess sneered. They had everything in their hands, here in their castles, kept safe by dragons, from a plague caused *by* dragons. All the while forcing those without dragons to enslave themselves to those with for protection.

"So you'll surrender the surrounding lands forever? Allow everything outside your walls to be razed to ruins?" Kess asked, her voice a low rasp.

Eslinde gave her a warning glance, then addressed the room again. "If we could simply stop taming new dragons, at least ..."

"You still bring us no proof. Some rusty old spike means nothing. The shadow dragon is a curse caused by the Alderkin and is growing worse due to the sins of the unblessed and dishonorable." Ulfren made a gesture that Kess had only seen Sunblessed Monks and Taen holy leaders make in the past. A draw of his hand from the sky to his heart.

"That's ridiculous," Eslinde said.

Ulfren smacked the rolled map down on the table, disrupting the figurines and tokens. "We should have expelled all of the Rolanians from this land when we rose to greatness upon the backs of dragons under the mighty sun, not allowed them to serve us."

A murmuring of voices rose in the room, no doubt shocked by the concept of no longer having either Rolanians or dragons around to serve them.

The Dragon King raised both arms into the air, and all voices in the room silenced.

"There is nothing useful left to say here. This audience is done."

"Your Majesty," Eslinde pleaded.

"Enough, Eslinde. You will stop pursuing these outlandish ideas. I thought you had learned your lesson last time." Yeonard placed a hand on her shoulder. His voice was almost kind, but the edge of warning in it was cold and sharp as a sword.

Ulfren glared at the closeness between his father and sister.

The elder advisors Kess didn't know moved first, clearing out of the room in a stream of swishing robes and white hair. Ulfren and Hjelzahn followed, shoulder to shoulder and in close conversation.

Eslinde's mother remained, eyes on her daughter.

Kess caught Eslinde's eye, trying to indicate she was ready to leave as well, but Eslinde gave an almost imperceptible shake of her head, and her lips pouted.

"Is Hjelzahn here looking into his missing heirs?" She placed her own hand down over her father's, holding it in place on her shoulder.

"One of the matters he's come to address, yes." The Dragon King moved to turn and withdraw.

Eslinde held tight. "I am so moved by Kverra Hjelzahn's search for her missing children. I want to assist, personally. Would you allow me to leave the city? Take a small team and a few dragons to find those poor children?"

"Eslinde. What are you playing at?" His voice rumbled.

"I only want to help. The Hjelzahn children are my family too, as they are yours, and—"

"Stop it! You expect me to give you the rope you need to hang yourself? You'll remain in Draekhanhelm, in the palace, until you can prove you've grown beyond your wild inclinations. Today has only been proof of the opposite."

Eslinde's carefully polite expression crashed down, and she flung his hand off her.

Kess had to push fast at her wheels to keep up with the princess as she marched from the room. Behind them, Eslinde's mother had her eyes on Kess, Falden whispering in her ear.

"Yensen," the Dragon King's voice grumbled, and the grayglim that had been following turned and went to him instead.

Eslinde didn't slow, storming out through the doors.

"Your grayglim?" Kess asked.

She glanced back. Yensen stood at attention for the Dragon King, who paced before him. They spoke in a snapping to and fro in voices too low to hear.

"He's hardly mine. He is the king's man."

Are any of them on Eslinde's side?

Kess had assumed a first heir would have more power, or at least more freedom. But Eslinde couldn't leave the city, wasn't listened to, wasn't respected.

How did one pregnancy lead to all of this?

Outside the chamber, Eslinde's pace slowed, and as the doors swung closed, she halted entirely.

Her breath snorted out. "The undead blight is growing worse, and our world is dying, and all any of them can think about is their ... their ... razing trade profits!"

It had been eye-opening for Kess. She'd thought there would be objections to untaming dragons, from those who were attached to their beasts, who needed them for vital work.

She didn't expect the rulers of the land to know exactly what was at stake and see it as a way to continue profiting from making the rest of the world so unlivable that people had to shelter and serve under them.

Eslinde sighed, eyes turned up to the ceiling. "Things have to change. They have to. With Lyrrin out there ..."

Kess sought for any last scrap of hope within her. Even in her darkest moments, she'd always found a way in the past. She just needed to know her next steps.

"So, what are we going to do about it?"

"Do?" Eslinde laughed wryly. "What can we do?"

"Everybody already seems to be blaming me for awakening your rebellious side again, so let's go all in. We could steal a dragon, fly off and find your daughter, and—"

"Even your plan relies on a tamed dragon." Eslinde shook her head. "And the vast majority of dragons are within the keeps. How can we untame enough out there to make a difference?"

Kess's mouth slammed shut. She didn't know. It seemed impossible. They'd tried to convince the most powerful people in the land to help, Eslinde's own family, and failed.

And in the process, all they'd done was make everyone in that meeting look at Kess as though she were the source of all Eslinde's problems.

CHAPTER TWELVE

It was the most terrifying thing Kess had ever faced. Her skin was clammy, her throat dry and stinging from rising acid. She grasped at her thighs, wishing there were weapons strapped there beneath her gown and finding nothing.

"Oh look, there's cloud cake!" Eslinde said brightly.

The ballroom before them was like a gigantic glasshouse, with vaulting walls and ceiling made entirely of sparkling windows, arching high above. Outside, the darkness of night cloaked them, so the panes reflected the glittering party beneath like a mirror.

Kess's last experience in a building with a glass ceiling hadn't been pleasant, but it wasn't the threat of shattering glass that scared her.

It was the people. Hundreds of dragonlords milled about the space.

Hundreds of dragonlord eyes to look upon Kess and find her wanting with one glance.

"I could have waited in your chambers," Kess said.

"Why ever would you have wanted to? We've both been cooped up in there too long. This is our chance to find some allies for our cause." Eslinde plucked a crisp swirl of pastry from a passing platter.

It had been weeks since their meeting with the Dragon King, and both were becoming frustrated by a lack of progress on all fronts. No ways to untame more dragons. No news of the Hjelzahn siblings, and thus Lyrrin, coming in from the outside world. No information of the group at all, of who traveled with them, of who was still alive …

No way to get to Kife and no weapon to kill him with even if Kess could.

Kess and the princess had spent most of their time reading and sulking.

But Eslinde had decided the ball might present opportunities.

Kess glared at the extravagantly decorated space, glittering with strings of gold that hung from the glass ceiling like sunset-struck rain. Yensen and many other grayglim bodyguards stood like statues around the perimeter of the space.

"Is this for some special occasion?" she asked.

"Oh no, just a regular gathering." Eslinde wriggled her fingers in a wave as Vance and Dashiel approached.

Like the majority of the guests, they wore shades of silver and gold, the Taen fashion. Vance's suit was on the silver end, unadorned but well tailored with a high collar, and Dashiel's on the golden end of the spectrum, a jacket of free-flowing silk over a suit designed to replicate the cut of armor.

Kess fussed with the gown Eslinde had provided her. Darker than the lustrous silvers around them, it was the gray of a tumultuous sky, shimmering with an overlay of thousands of tiny gems. But it didn't matter how fine the clothing, how close she fit into the surrounding fashion.

The other guests still stared at her and her chair in a way that made Kess feel naked.

She'd never been to anything like this before. She was rarely invited even to family dinners with her parents and Kife by the end of her stay at Heithorn estate, let alone been allowed by her family to be seen by society.

"You look great," Dashiel said, offering Kess a formal bow.

Kess scowled in return.

"No, really!" Dashiel laughed. "Don't you think so, Eslinde?"

Eslinde gave her an appraising look. "I suppose she has rather handsome features, when she isn't puckering them all together."

Kess's lips drew tighter.

"You look like you're wishing there was someone trying to kill you right now," Dashiel murmured with a sly smile.

Kess's face went hot and she hunched over in her chair. "Would you stop perceiving me already?"

Vance elbowed Dashiel out of the way and bowed low before Eslinde.

Eslinde's gown looked as though it had been spun from starlight. It clung to her narrow frame and spilled onto the ground in a glittering train. Although the gown was sleeveless, Eslinde wore dozens of silver and gold bracelets stacked up her arms that rattled together when she moved her hands. Her earrings, however, were the same ones she always wore.

Do they have some personal significance to Eslinde? A gift from someone special ... Lyrrin's father?

Kess watched Vance closely, hoping to see some tell in noticing those earrings, but his stoic expression gave nothing away.

Straightening, he said, "Our princess's beauty this evening leaves all my other senses envious of sight."

Eslinde's eyebrows went up, and she offered a slight bow in return. "How long did it take you to think up that line?"

"It came to me right then." Vance smirked.

Dashiel shook their head and whispered to Kess, "He's had that one saved for years."

A mischievous smile grew on Eslinde's lips. "I hope you'll find plenty of flattery equal to that while speaking with the attendees tonight."

"To business then?" Vance asked.

"Yes." Eslinde turned away, rising up on her toes and looking out over the sea of nobles. "Ylva should be here tonight. She's always been the kindest to me of my siblings, so I hope she'll be willing to listen. I'm going to do a round and see if I can find her. Go and mingle, all of you, and see who we can find that may support our cause."

Dashiel moved away first. "I'm going to mingle with some snacks first. See you all soon."

"Must we all go separately?" Kess asked.

"Divide and conquer," Eslinde replied.

Kess looked out over the crowd as though it were a pack of ravenous wolves. As Eslinde slipped between the bodies and vanished, Kess recognized a familiar face.

She reached out and grabbed Vance's arm, pulling him back as he moved away. "Does the Dragon King ever attend these evenings?"

"Often, although only briefly. Why? Planning to try to convince him again?"

"No, I'm hoping that the Dragon King doesn't attend, actually. Can you see that man through there?" Kess pointed to Kife, who had yet to notice her in return.

"Who is he?" Vance asked, narrowing his eyes.

"He's trouble. Could you do me a favor and keep an eye on him? Don't let him get anywhere near the king, if he does arrive."

Vance leaned over Kess, frowning. "That's not what we're supposed to be doing tonight. Eslinde—"

"It's important. I can't explain why right now, but it's very important, for Eslinde." Kess held his skeptical gaze.

Then Vance nodded and moved into the crowd, tailing Kess's brother.

Kess took a moment to calm her nerves. Already on edge, seeing Kife had shaken her up.

She wasn't lying to Vance, not exactly. If Kife got to the Dragon King and told him about Dracuni, it would affect Lyrrin, and thus Eslinde. But more than that, Kess needed time to decide what she was going to do.

Could she attempt to kill Kife tonight? She had no weapon anymore—Eslinde had been careful to check all cutlery since her first theft.

On the day of the taming ceremony, Kess had been ready and hadn't cared about the consequences of murdering someone in broad daylight.

But now, Kess couldn't imagine stabbing her brother in front of all these people. Now, when Eslinde was treating her almost like a human being, and was doing all she could to find Lyrrin, and to alter the course of the shadow dragon curse, to change the world …

The stakes were too high.

Kess couldn't let herself be taken out of the picture for revenge. She had to wait and be smarter.

Alone now and faced with the prospect of *mingling*, Kess found her courage and rolled slowly from her place near the wall. People parted for her as she pushed her chair between them, and yet she passed unnoticed, unacknowledged, as though invisible. All eyes turned away from her as she approached.

How am I supposed to talk to anyone if they're all ignoring me?

Shame flushed her face, and she almost turned around and left.

Then a small face appeared in front of her. A boy of no more than ten years old, wearing a suit like a miniaturized grown-up, stared at Kess and her chair with wide-eyed amazement.

"You have wheels! On your chair!" he said through a smile of missing teeth.

"Yes?" Kess replied.

"That looks like fun. Can I have a turn?"

"I don't think—"

"Get away from her," a gravelly voice hissed.

A man snatched the boy's hand in his and dragged him backward away from Kess as though she were plague-ridden.

A plaintive cry of "Faddaaaaaa," disappeared with them.

Kess's face screwed up tight.

How had she thought she would ever be accepted by these people? That if she had her own dragon and was a dragonrider and dragonlord again, it would make people like her?

There would still have been times when she wasn't on her dragon. What then? Would she have ridden around events like this on Griskin? Kess cursed her foolishness under her breath.

She still wished for Griskin. She missed him with a deep ache in her bones. She wished to be stalking the shadows, unseen and unheard on his back.

Still, at least if the nobles were all set on ignoring her, she was unseen and unheard enough. She could listen in to the surrounding conversations, see if she could identify anyone who may be sympathetic.

It only took a few snippets of conversation to leave Kess disheartened. She wasn't sure this was the right place to be seeking allies for their cause of freeing dragons. Everyone there was living the high life at the exploitation of others.

Dragonlords spoke with Elgarthan traders, negotiating a raise in prices for upcoming metal and glass shipments due to lower production. The Elgarthans weren't interested in excuses, as though the silvernix shortages were something the dragonlords had fabricated to get more money out of them.

They settled upon a slight increase, with the dragonlords agreeing to buy enough new human slaves to replace the dragons in their factory and keep up production.

Kess eyed the Elgarthans with fascination. She hadn't seen any of the seafaring traders in person before. Their skin was pale as milk, their eyes long and sweeping, and hair a deep blue-black, puffing out in a bundle of spirals. Their robes, in vibrant reds and purples, were the sole point of color in the ballroom.

Could Lyrrin's father be Elgarthan? She had a similar complexion.

One of the traders asked the Elgarthans jokingly about rumors they smuggled unicorns to their lands. The Elgarthan promised that if they had, they'd be doing a roaring trade for them by now.

Another dragonlord joked about smuggling themselves out of Elundrae, before the shadow dragon curse became any more dire. Kess wasn't sure he was entirely joking.

She turned to move on to another conversation, when Ulfren the First blocked her path.

"Kessara Heithorn. A pleasure to meet again."

Offering the politest smile she could, Kess bent over her knees. "You honor me again with your company."

When she rose, Ulfren moved behind her and began wheeling her to the side of the room.

"Come," he said, as though she had any choice in the matter. "There are some people I'd like you to meet."

Kess attempted to slow the chair by gripping the wheels, but her palms were slick with nervous sweat. "I really need to be getting back—"

"Here we are." Ulfren brought Kess to where a few men huddled in conversation.

Each wore the sunshine-yellow robes of Sunblessed Monks and had a chain of golden beads about their neck for each year of dedication to their faith. Kess had never mixed much with the devout, those who took Taenish mythology as law in all aspects of their life.

She nodded awkwardly to them.

At least Ulfren didn't drag me off somewhere to be killed.

"This is the most interesting young lady I had mentioned, who by some accounts is said to have spent time out in the world beyond dragonkeep walls. Is that true, Kessara?"

"It's true," she murmured, wary of the fervor in Ulfren's eyes.

A man with windswept ebony hair, square jaw, and dozens of golden chains looked down upon her. "Have you seen them, then? The Alderkin ruins. Do they stir once more into cursed power as the troubling rumors suggest?"

"Umm ..." Kess wasn't sure what to say.

She'd seen the gateway crystals working again, but apart from helping Dracuni escape her during her hunt, there didn't seem to be anything cursed about them. They were keeping the revenants away.

It seemed the men didn't require her answer, though.

An older monk clutched at his beaded chains. "More signs the curse is worsening. Something must be done."

Kess sighed internally. That is what she was there for that night.

"Actually, about that—"

"You surely don't hold to my sister's sacrilegious imaginings?" Ulfren interrupted. "You appear to be a clever young woman. Don't let her delusions draw you in. The cause is clear. Sin and dishonor are rife within our land, and it must be remedied."

The monks at his side bobbed their heads vehemently.

"And it is with great pain that I tell you that Eslinde is among those sinners. The Dragon King, blinded by her manipulations, favors her. But you must see that she defies all that is honorable with her behavior, spreading blasphemy and associating with Rolanians playing at being dragonlords."

A shiver ran up Kess's spine, and she cast a look back toward the main crowd for the Zarram siblings.

She shook her head. "It's not like that with Eslinde. The king doesn't favor her."

"No other heir is given a home under his wing, ever by his side. Not even myself, next in line to the throne." Ulfren's hand fisted closed and he slammed it into the palm of the other.

"My resplendent father is the savior of our people, bringing us into the sun's glory and power we deserve. But even he is not immune to a sinner's manipulations. We cannot allow someone like Eslinde to gain power."

Murmurings of assent came from the monks around him, all watching with zealous enthusiasm.

Kess chewed her lip. "I know I'm new around here, but I really don't think that's something you have to worry about, from what I've seen."

"And what have you seen?" Ulfren leaned in.

Kess stiffened. "Not much, really."

Ulfren sighed and crouched down before her. "Kessara, please rethink your loyalty to her. The numbers of our Taenish brethren who are turning back to the blessed sun's touch is growing every day. With my full backing and funding, we will be able to flush the sinners from the dragonkeeps and hold the curse at bay."

"And will your sister be among those sinners?"

Ulfren's face twisted in righteous sorrow. He put a hand on Kess's knee, squeezing firmly. "If she must. And any assistance from you would be a great boon. If you can help us to remove Eslinde, from the king's favor, of course, you will be rewarded greatly, both by us and the blessings of the sun."

Kess placed her hands on the wheels of her chair. Even for followers of the Taen religion, these people were extreme. She could imagine the lengths to which they would go to flush the sinners from the land. She pushed, rolling herself backward out of Ulfren's grip.

When he didn't immediately reach for her again or try to follow, she pushed back again.

"I'll ... I'll think about it." Kess knew that was the truth. The messy political corner Kess was feeling forced into was almost all she could think about.

Ulfren took a step as though to follow, but a grayglim appeared at his side, whispered briefly, and Ulfren hastily followed the woman away without another glance at Kess.

Beelining for a servant with a tray of cakes, Kess parted the crowd around her. All of the royal sibling infighting and politics had given her a headache and the need for something sweet. She took a cake in each hand and didn't bother to be polite about stuffing both in her mouth at once.

"Are you okay? You seem rattled." Dashiel had appeared at her side, helping themselves to the same cake tray.

Kess swallowed. "I just had a charming conversation with Ulfren the First and his sunstruck monks."

"Aah," Dashiel said, as though they knew exactly what that entailed. "What did you do that for?"

"Didn't really have a choice." Kess brushed crumbs off her lap. "How about you? Any fruitful conversations?"

Dashiel nibbled the corner of a sugar-crusted pastry. "No. Trying to broach the subject carefully has been a nightmare. Nobody is understanding. I just want to grab them by the ears and shake them until they realize what's at stake."

"If you thought that would actually work, I'd happily join in."

Dashiel finished their dessert and sucked crumbs from their fingers. "If I could get Eslinde's dragon to cooperate, then I could prove that dragons don't need to be tamed to still be useful. That would change minds."

"He's still angry?" Kess asked.

"Furious. I mean, I feel as though I would be too, in that situation. But there have been some inroads. Shiff has been helping me to communicate with the snowshimmer, and he's clearly intelligent, even more than I'd imagined. It gives me hope that Shiff can remain untamed long term as well."

Kess smiled at the mention of the dragonling. "I hope she can, too."

Dashiel stepped closer to Kess as a white-haired woman bustled by with a grayglim beside her. "I think, if the dragon we had untamed was one I had more experience working with from birth, then I'd be able to settle it down much faster. I was thinking of untaming another—"

"Oh no, you weren't." Vance slung an arm over Dashiel's shoulders. "No more untamings. We've enough of an issue with what to do with the snowshimmer."

Kess's eyes darted around, and she spoke softly. "What happened to the man I asked you to follow?"

Vance whispered in return, "Don't worry, I still have my eyes on him. Although he seems more interested in you than anything."

Vance flicked his chin, and Kess turned around to see Kife lurking not far behind her. She exhaled roughly. How long had he been there?

The conversation in the room changed pitch, from boisterous conversation to a low murmur, spreading through the room like a wave. Another pale-haired dragonlord was ushered away speedily by a grayglim.

"What's going on?" Kess asked.

"I'll see if I can find out." Dashiel stepped away, heading toward a cluster of nobles in the center of the space.

Yensen prowled through the parting bodies, on a mission. Kess wondered if he was looking for Eslinde, when a voice at her back whispered a little too loudly.

"Ylva the First, she was found dead, dead in a private room!"

Kess wasn't the only person to have heard, as the crowd surged suddenly, barging toward the exits.

"Eslinde," Vance growled and charged off in the other direction.

Gowned and robed bodies swished by Kess in a flash of gold and gray and she tried to push her chair out of the way. She couldn't maneuver as fast as the fleeing guests, whose focus was more on continuing their gossip as they left than on the girl in the chair they were flooding around.

After a few cursed words and rough pushes, Kess made it to the side wall. The glass panel reflected her wide-eyed face, hovering over the dark glitter of her gown. And then another face was reflected above hers.

Kife.

He grasped the back of her chair and spun it toward him. "What was that talk back there about *untaming* dragons?"

""You must have misheard." Kess's hand went to her thigh, to the backs of her forearms, out of habit, reaching for knives that weren't there. She put her sharpest edge on her words instead. "Couldn't you have enjoyed the party without following your little sister around? You've only grown more pathetic since you lost me."

The crowd had all but gone, leaving only Kess and Kife in the ballroom now. He lashed out at her, grabbing her by the shoulders and wrenching her from the chair.

"I know what I heard. Is that what you did to my dragon? Is that how you made it fly away without a rider?" Kife shook her and thrust her back against the glass wall.

The pane rattled and cracked.

"It just didn't want to be around you anymore." Kess slashed a clawed hand at his face, hoping to gouge an eye or split his cheek.

But Kife was taller, his reach longer. He leaned away from her attack and brought the hands pinning her to her neck.

Kess gasped for air as he crushed her windpipe under his grip.

"No, Kess. The one nobody wants around anymore is you."

Chapter Thirteen

The glass at Kess's back crackled and strained as Kife pressed her into it, hands tight around her throat. Pain shot up her neck, through her skull, and her eyes watered.

She couldn't breathe or speak or spit out any of the curses her brother deserved. She wished her legs would work for once in her life just so she could kick him.

Spittle flew from the corners of Kife's lips. "I should have killed you when you found me at Skaellakeep. I should have killed you instead of leaving you in the wilds. I should have killed you when you were a baby, before you ruined the Heithorn name!"

Gritting her teeth, Kess glared back in defiance.

The edge of a blade caught the light, flashing in Kess's eyes as it appeared by Kife's collarbones.

"Let her go." Dashiel held the end of the dagger.

They circled around, keeping the point against Kife's neck as they came around beside Kess.

Kife grunted. "Stay out of this."

Kess's vision dimmed, spotting with floating lights.

"How much clearer do you need me to be?" Dashiel pressed the dagger forward.

Kife hissed, releasing Kess and scrambling backward. His hands had been the only thing holding Kess upright, and her legs folded beneath her.

Dashiel's arm looped around her waist, pulling her back up and into their side.

Kife spat on the ground. "Rolanian scum. Don't you know who I am?"

"I really don't," Dashiel said dully.

Kife's face twisted in rage. "I'm someone you don't want to cross."

Kess swallowed, her head spinning and throat aching. She clutched Dashiel for support, leaning her head against their chest for a moment as she worked the breath into her lungs.

Her voice came out in a painful, soft crackle. "Your dagger. Let me throw it into his eye."

Dashiel glanced at her. "Your aim is that good?"

Kess put a hand out expectantly.

The moment Dashiel placed the blade into Kess's grasp, Kife turned and bolted from the ballroom.

Kess raised her arm, intending to take a shot at his fleeing back. But a wave of dizziness washed over her and the dagger dropped from her trembling fingers.

"Easy. Are you okay?" Dashiel adjusted their hold on Kess, bringing them face-to-face with one arm behind Kess's back.

They ran gentle fingers over her neck, inhaling sharply at what they saw there. Kess could feel the bruising with her every swallow and strained breath.

"I'm fine," she whispered. "You can put me down."

Dashiel's full lips moved as though preparing to refuse, then they carefully lowered Kess into her chair. As they bent over, arms still around Kess, their cheeks touched briefly, and Kess flushed with heat.

Only one other person in her life had ever held her so gently.

She gulped and her eyes watered again. *You can't go soft for every person who shows you even basic kindness, fool.*

Dashiel remained bowed over her, a soft smile emerging under their frown. "Okay, so that's two people so far that I've seen who want you dead, but I'm still not willing to think it's *everybody*. But just so I'm prepared, how many more are we talking about?"

Kess's throat throbbed with pain, so she just raised a hand and pretended to count the numbers on her fingers.

Dashiel chuckled and straightened up. "Popular, aren't you? Come on, we need to get somewhere safe. There's at least one more assassin roaming the palace tonight."

"Ylva?" Kess choked out.

"Yeah, seems as though the rumors are true." Dashiel ducked to snatch their small dagger from the ground. Sharp and well made, but barely longer than a palm of a hand.

Kess raised her eyebrows as they tucked it away again into a hidden pocket.

Dashiel moved behind her and pushed her chair, speeding them out of the ballroom. "Yeah, I know I probably shouldn't have it here. But I always carry it with me, ever since a few years back when I got jumped by a bunch of Taens who didn't like that I'd attended their party."

A few nobles milled about in the courtyard outside, but an equal number of palace guards spread through the area, moving people along and questioning others. Dashiel dodged around them, heading for the corridor that led up to Eslinde's chambers.

"Another one of the Firsts, gone," Dashiel said softly, as though they couldn't believe it.

"Another?" Kess asked.

They turned a corner and were confronted by a wall of guards, thrice the usual number on patrol. They had to explain who they were and where they were going, but a few of the guards knew of Kess and allowed them to pass.

Dashiel muttered, "In just the last few years we've lost Leska, Tjollas, and Nevryn. Skaella a few months back. And now Ylva. And here, within the king's city, within the king's own palace! Whoever is doing this has grown bold."

Dashiel and Kess worked together to get her and her chair up the long flights of stairs to Eslinde's chambers, and as they approached, the two grayglim at the door shifted, alert.

Yensen waved the second grayglim at ease as he recognized them and rapped at the door.

The sounds of clicking locks was followed by the door swinging open. Eslinde stood there, face pale.

"I'm so sorry, Kess. I wouldn't have left you, but ..." She glared at the grayglim.

When her eyes returned to Kess, they drifted down to her neck and she gasped. "What happened? Quick, come in, come in."

Dashiel brought Kess inside, explaining the situation, as Eslinde locked the door after them.

"It was Kife," Kess added in a rasping voice.

"Your brother?" Eslinde snapped.

"Your *brother*?" Dashiel echoed, aghast.

In the large central chamber, Vance sat perched on the edge of an armchair, and two handmaidens milled about doing busywork, shuffling piles of books around and dusting, their eyes more on Vance than their tasks.

Vance stood up at their approach. "Is that who you had me following? What was that about?"

Kess winced as all eyes fell on her. She gestured at her neck. "Just wanted ... keep him away."

"And for good reason, I'd say," Dashiel said.

Eslinde stared at Kess for a long moment.

Can she tell I'm not telling the whole truth? Kess gave a pathetic cough and looked away.

Sighing, Eslinde said, "I'll do what I can to make sure he can't get close to the palace again. Although after tonight it's going to be difficult for anybody to get close to the palace for a while."

Vance cleared his throat. "Speaking of which, now that you're safe, Dashiel and I should be on our way, before we cause a scandal of some kind or another by remaining."

The handmaidens swiftly turned their backs as though there had been nothing to see.

Eslinde nodded and placed a hand on Vance's arm, murmuring a soft thank you.

Dashiel held Kess's eyes, their gaze full of questions, but they simply smiled and said, "Always so much excitement when you're around. I'll see you next time."

Eslinde saw them both out the door, and then with a sharp order, sent the handmaidens on their way as well. They seemed happy to go now that the princess wasn't alone in her chambers with a man. There was a question of whether any silvernix was to be requested for Kess, but Kess shook her head.

Once the door was locked again, Eslinde brought her hand to her chest. A handkerchief was crumpled within it.

Eslinde had said she was closest to Ylva of any of her siblings. Given the animosity between some of the others, Kess didn't know how close that was, but redness marred the lines around Eslinde's eyes and the point of her nose.

"You ... okay?" Kess whispered awkwardly.

A gloss of tears washed over the princess's eyes, but she smiled. "As well as can be hoped. Oh, Kess, the night had been going so well. There was news! News of Lyrrin!"

Kess's breath caught in her crumpled throat.

Eslinde swept over and took a seat in the armchair across from where Kess remained in her wheeled chair. She reached for the pitcher of water on the low table and poured a glass, handing it to Kess.

"Sip it slowly. And yes, well, not Lyrrin exactly. But it could have been the Hjelzahn siblings, from what you described."

"Who ...?" Kess choked on the water.

Eslinde's eyes were full of hope and fire. "The rider said they'd heard of a group with two young women, two young children, and a dragonling, helping the people gathering around shrines, very recently. Just as you said, Kess. It must be them!"

Kess's nose wrinkled. "Two?"

Two young women. Only two.

No third.

She's gone. Riony is really gone.

All the physical and emotional pains inside Kess spiked, slicing through her. Her face pinched inward as she tried to fight tears, but they spilled out. The glass shook in her hand, spilling water on her lap.

"Kess?" Eslinde shifted closer.

Kess shook her head in reply.

"What is it?"

"Nothing."

"It's not nothing." Eslinde reached out and placed a hand on Kess's knee. "I recognize grieving, Kess. I've mourned enough to know it. I mourn my sister now, and I've mourned my daughter, thinking her dead, and I've mourned her father."

People Eslinde loved.

Is that why? Is that why it hurts so much?

Kess struggled to speak, throat aching from the clog of tears as much as the injury. "Lyrrin's father ... Not Vance?"

Eslinde leaned back. "What? No. Why would you think that?"

Kess tilted her head.

Eslinde blushed pink and stuttered, "No. Lyrrin's father is ... Don't change the subject! Tell me. Was there someone else you were expecting to hear of in that group? Who is it that you've lost?"

Nobody. I never had anybody to lose. It doesn't matter.

Every time Kess tried to open her mouth and throw out some flippant response, her lips pursed, pulled closed by sobbing pain in her chest.

Who had Riony been to her? An enemy. The thorn in her side at odds with everything Kess had wanted, and it had been too late, too late that Kess realized she'd been wanting the wrong thing.

Worse. She'd known, deep down, what she really wanted all along.

It had never been the respect of people who'd only care about her if she owned a dragon. It only ever mattered what one person thought of her. The only person who'd been kind to her. Who had come back to save her in the caves. Who even after every horrible thing Kess had done, had stood there and offered Kess one more chance.

And now she was gone.

"I ... I loved her." It was all the truth Kess could offer.

She didn't have the words to explain the violent tangle of their past, the awful power dynamics of ownership and cruelties suffered. And the loss, the loss, the loss Kess felt in every moment even when Riony was in her life because she knew she could never have Riony in a way that was real.

The weight of that truth, spilling from her lips, could crush Kess.

Eslinde shocked Kess dumb by leaning out of her armchair and wrapping her in a tight embrace.

"I'm sorry," she whispered.

And she held Kess for a long silent moment as sobs racked through Kess and her tears poured.

It was that act of kindness, something Kess would never have expected from a first heir of the land, that drew her out of the depths of her pain. Eslinde, the Zarram siblings, they did truly seem to care. Part of Kess still anticipated a blade in her back, but she fought that feeling down.

Eslinde had shown Kess kindness and respect, and Kess vowed to return the same, as much as she could without revealing Dracuni.

"Sorry too. For Ylva," she whispered.

Eslinde pulled out of the embrace and dabbed at her eyes. "Thank you. Of all the heirs we've lost, she is the only one I will miss."

Out at Heithorn estate, Kess had been isolated from court gossip and news. She hadn't realized how many were gone.

Wiping her eyes, she looked to Eslinde with concern. "Are you in danger?"

"Not in here. Nobody can get in here. Although if anything were to happen to me..." Eslinde sat back into her armchair and worried at the kerchief in her fingers.

"Nothing will. I'll make sure," Kess said like a vow.

Eslinde half smiled, her gaze flickering to Kess's throat as though she doubted Kess could even look after herself.

They all underestimate me. If only I had a weapon, if I had Griskin...

Kess knew there were parts of her that would never work the same as for other people. She just needed certain things to function as well as she knew she could. The chair was something, and she was growing used to it, but it wasn't *her* things.

Eslinde rose to her feet. "Since we have confided so much to each other, there is something important that I want to share, just in case. I can't have this secret be lost with me."

She walked toward the door, beckoning Kess to follow.

Kess slowly rolled after. She wasn't entirely sure she wanted to be the keeper of yet another secret. She seemed to know more than enough that many would be willing to kill for already.

"Why tell me?"

"You brought me the truth about Lyrrin. I think it's fair that you understand more about my daughter." Eslinde came to a stop beside the door, but she didn't reach to open it. Instead, she reached for the ornately carved panel in the doorframe that she often touched as she came in and out of the room.

"See here?" Eslinde pointed to a circular section that was a smoother stone than the dark granite surrounding it.

Eslinde ran a swift fingertip over the design there, and the sound of locks clicking echoed around the room.

"Alderkin rune?" Kess asked. Is that how she's been magically sealing her chambers?

Eslinde nodded and pried her fingertips into the edges of the circular section. She pulled and out slid a long shaft of crystal, glowing softly but darkened by paint at the ends to match the surrounding stone. Within the center was a cavity where a vial of silvernix lay.

"How?" was all Kess could say.

Eslinde slid the crystal back into the wall and activated the locking rune again. "It was provided to me by an Alderkin man who wanted to be sure I remained safe."

Kess shook her head. Eslinde was only around thirty years old, and not just in appearances like some of the heirs, but in actual age. She would have only just been born when the last Alderkin were killed in the war.

The words hurt Kess's throat, but she rasped them out anyway. "You're not that old. Not possible."

Eslinde smiled sadly. "It is. Because not all of the Alderkin are gone. My father has kept some prisoners of war in a secret prison below the palace."

"Alive?" Kess gasped.

Living Alderkin, still in Elundrae? There were always rumors some had escaped to other lands at the end of the war, but to know some existed still, below where they were now, shook Kess.

Eslinde brushed her hands over the disguised crystal again, as though stroking the cheek of a lover. "And one of them was Lyrrin's father."

Kess lay awake in the daybed in Eslinde's chambers, unable to sleep from the recent revelations.

That Alderkin still existed. That Lyrrin's father was one.

That Kess had loved Riony.

That she still did, but it seemed more certain than ever that Riony was gone.

Only two young women, the rumors had said. Certainly, something could have happened to Aishena or Niskina, making them the missing number of the three, but that was wishful thinking on Kess's part when she'd seen exactly what had happened to Riony.

At least Dracuni seemed to still be with the group and well.

And two children. Lyrrin was okay then, also. Riony would be happy to know that, and Kess noted that she wanted to find a way to continue honoring what Riony would have wanted.

Eslinde said there had been no replies yet to her messages, her attempts to communicate with Lyrrin.

Lyrrin ... who was half Alderkin.

Kess's brain continued to spiral when a sound beside her bed made her sleepless eyes snap open.

Eslinde stood there, finger to her lips.

"What under the sun ..." Kess hissed.

A few days had passed, and her throat still ached, but had been healing well enough that she didn't require silvernix to repair it.

"Come on, quickly." The princess ghosted toward the door. Her night dress was covered with a sweeping satin robe, and she carried an oil lamp in her hand. "No time to get dressed."

"Are we in trouble?" Kess's eyes darted as she shuffled to the edge of the bed where her chair sat.

The night outside the windows was pitch, no sign of morning light, and only a few stars sparkled through an ashy sky.

"No, we have an opportunity." Eslinde glided to the entrance and unlocked it.

Kess hurried to catch up, swinging her legs off the bed, then hoisting herself into the wheeled chair. Her nightgown was thin, and the autumn air was chilly. A robe would have been nice both for modesty and comfort, but Kess guessed her clothing was the least of her concerns.

Kess rolled to Eslinde's side as she pushed the main door open. Outside in the hallway, an unfamiliar grayglim slumped near the door.

Kess's heart pumped hard in dread until she heard a soft snore rattle from the older man's throat.

Eslinde placed a finger to her lips and spoke softly. "Yensen has to sleep sometimes. And this grayglim who took his shift tonight isn't the most reliable. I had Olva offer him a nightcap that may have had a little something extra in it."

"Why?"

"Because it's time I go somewhere I haven't been in a long while. Somewhere a grayglim would surely block me from reaching." Eslinde moved behind Kess's chair to assist her down the stairs.

"I don't think it's safe to be going anywhere without someone to protect you," Kess said.

They reached the final landing and Eslinde moved beside Kess. "I have you."

Kess snorted. "Like there's much I can do."

"Your preference is toward throwing knives from what I've gathered. Correct?"

Kess kept pace with Eslinde, rolling along the quiet, unlit corridor. "They've worked well for me in the past."

Eslinde stopped suddenly, thrusting an arm to stop Kess as well. Up ahead, a guard crossed the intersection, a warm globe of light traveling with them. Once they were gone, Eslinde turned to Kess, holding her gaze.

"I can trust you, can't I?"

Kess balked. "Can I trust you?"

Eslinde sighed and reached into the deep pocket of her bedrobe. She withdrew a stamped metal case and tossed it onto Kess's lap. "I just want to know one of those won't end up in me."

Kess raised her eyebrows as she clicked the book-sized case open. Inside, on plush black velvet, lay three exquisite throwing blades.

"They're beautiful," Kess's words rushed out on a breath.

"Yes, indeed. Please use them with discretion." Eslinde marched ahead again.

Kess pushed the wheels of her chair hard to catch up. As the chair rolled freely along the glossy floor, Kess hid one of the thin blades up each of her sleeves and the third down between the upholstery of her chair seat.

They took a corner into a bare, dead-end room, then Eslinde pushed against the wall, which swung smoothly in an arc away from her.

"Where are we going?" Kess asked.

Eslinde held her oil lamp high against the darkness of the rougher stone tunnel ahead. "To visit the Alderkin."

"Oh. Good. So not only can I know the information about them which is probably enough to get me killed, but we're going to go and break into the secret dungeon where they're kept?"

Eslinde gave Kess a sly smile in return. "This is the sort of trouble I used to get myself into all the time."

"Why? Just an inner need to be rebellious?" Kess muttered.

The tunnel curved sharply, then dropped down a steep slope. Eslinde helped Kess from having her chair run away with her.

"Curiosity, at first. I was always interested to know everything there was to know in court and managed to discover that Fadda was keeping Alderkin prisoners. Those strange, savage people who had waged war with humans for decades with their terrifying magic. I had to see them for myself."

"Why?" Kess asked again.

She felt no such compulsion to see them, even now on their way to meet those prisoners. She disliked the tunnels more than the undercity caves she'd hunted Dracuni in. The ceiling was low and claustrophobic, and the air was dank and filled with a rotting smell like sewage.

"I needed to face them, to prove to myself I was stronger than them. Better than our enemies." Eslinde let out a long sigh. "Instead, as I spoke with them, all I heard was sense. Sense I didn't hear anywhere else in court. They were so humble, so wise, and the more I learned their stories, the more rebellious I became. And then I fell in love."

"With an Alderkin?" Kess had never seen one herself before.

She had no idea how human they were ... or weren't. She knew Eslinde had said Lyrrin's father was one, but she hadn't elaborated on the technicalities.

"Alleem. He was the youngest of the four, by Alderkin standards at least. Oh, Kess, he was so beautiful. Inside and out. A soul of pure radiance, he could make anything sound like poetry and had eyes that made you feel both worthy and humble in a single glance."

A wry smile formed on Kess's lips as she thought about the kinds of things that came out of Riony's mouth.

Poetry indeed. To each their own, I guess.

Eslinde pressed one hand to her stomach. "I never thought ... When I became pregnant, I tried to hide it, but the truth came out. My mother worked it out first, and then the Dragon King had his spies reveal the whole story. Allem was killed. Almost everybody who knew anything about it at all was killed."

Kess had wondered how a single pregnancy could lead to a first heir losing their freedoms, and almost their life. But it made sense now.

They rounded another corner and came to a wider section where a guard, the regular palace variety rather than a grayglim, sat slouched in a chair, chin nodding against his chest. The only thing different about his uniform was a crown-shaped badge upon his shoulder.

"Did you drug him too?" Kess murmured.

The guard jolted, snorting back awake and squinting into the light Eslinde carried.

"Your Highness? You're not allowed to be down here." He stood up and straightened his leather armor and sword belt.

Eslinde gave him one of her coy smiles. "And you're not supposed to be sleeping on the job. But perhaps we can ignore both transgressions."

Clearing his throat, the guard stepped in front of the steel grated door he'd been snoozing beside. "You'll have to forgive me. But there were rumors. That the last lot on guard down here who let you through were all executed."

A flicker of concern pulled at Eslinde's brow, then she drew herself up tall. "Then we will have to be sure that nobody finds out that I was here. And if you don't let us in, then I will make sure the wrong people *do* find out that I was here and that you allowed it."

The guard looked over his shoulders, as though checking for any other eyes on them. But it was only him, the princess, and Kess in the empty early hours of night. He swore three times under his breath, then unlocked the metal grate. "Nobody will find out, right?"

"Not a soul." Eslinde tapped him on the nose as she strode by him into the opened passage.

Kess followed Eslinde through, marveling at how adept at manipulation she was. Ulfren's warning about Eslinde manipulating the king, about her being delusional, echoed in her mind.

But she's been honest with me, hasn't she? If anything, too honest. And she was leading Kess to proof of her words that very moment. Kess checked her access to the knives in her sleeves, just in case. Knives Eslinde had gifted her. But old habits of distrust were hard to bury.

Beyond the metal gate, a short corridor came to an end in front of them, with a few doors on each side. Although the doors had barred windows, no light came from within.

"Yrik?" Eslinde called softly.

A rustle of motion came from Kess's left, bringing with it wafts of stomach-curdling stench.

A face appeared through the bars, then a husky woman's voice. "Eslinde? Is that you?"

Kess squinted through the darkness, but in the low light the face was just a pale oval.

Eslinde rushed to the door and reached her free hand to the bars. "Priyune! I'm sorry, I'm so sorry it has been so long. Is Yrik ...?"

With Eslinde's lamp brought closer, the face became clear. High, knife-edged cheekbones swept down from eyes too large and too bright to be human. They sparkled like emeralds, matching to hair just as green, although matted and tangled around the woman's forehead and pointed ears.

The Alderkin woman's hand reached back through the barred window to hold Eslinde's, and Kess withheld a gasp. The fingers were long and came to sharp, angular points.

Just like she'd seen of Lyrrin's, when the wild girl had scratched through Kess's bracer.

A voice as low and gravelly as an avalanche came from the same cell. "I still live. Shael also."

The first Alderkin, Priyune, withdrew and a man came close to the bars. He too reached a hand to Eslinde, tipped with long blue claws and marred with a hatched mess of scars and untended wounds.

"Who has been hurting you?" Eslinde cried.

Yrik only grumbled in response, turning his face to the side and eyes low. Blue hair tangled long down his neck.

"I should have come back sooner. This is awful." Eslinde clutched his hand, squeezing hard. "When was the last time someone cleaned down here? Are they feeding you well?

Why are they torturing you?"

Yrik stared out the small hole in the door, brilliant blue eyes hooded and dull. "The slayer of unicorns has found a use for us, and he uses us as and when he sees fit."

"The Dragon King?" Kess asked. "What use would he ..."

Eslinde seemed to have worked that out already. She reached into her pocket and withdrew the fake taming spike the Zarrams had given her. She held it up to see.

"Are you making these for him?" she asked without any condemnation.

The man stepped back out of sight into the dark cell, and his voice was low. "He forces us. He brings crystals, and we must create with them what he wishes. We tried to deny him, at first, but ..."

"It's not your fault," Eslinde said.

"But it is our shame. He wanted another way to tame dragons, for when he had no sacred blood left. More dragons, each one growing the curse of the lost souls, and at our hands."

"Could the king be so short on silvernix?" Kess asked.

Eslinde scoffed. "I don't think so. He probably just wants to reserve all use of it for keeping himself immortal. And if everybody runs out of silvernix, he will have the only method in Elundrae to tame dragons. As he always wanted. He never wanted that power shared."

Kess shook her head. "A way to tame dragons without silvernix ... we can't even wait for it to run out then, as a way to stop the shadow dragon curse, because he'll keep taming dragons anyway."

Eslinde's hand squeezed tight around the crystal spike. "He won't be able to let the silvernix run out entirely. The Alderkin crystals need to be imbued with magical charge, which they can get from being kept close to silvernix."

So that's why she kept a vial of silvernix with her locking crystal, Kess thought. She'd considered at first that it was just a convenient place to stash some extra.

Yrik's face reappeared at the bars. His features drooped as though exhausted. "Are you and your friend here plotting something, dear child?"

"Not quite. Only hoping for change, as ever. But these new crystal spikes will make things more difficult."

"We have submitted to making them because we must, to survive. But we only persist because we are the last and it seems we must strive to not vanish into the earth's embrace." The man's blue eyes glistened. "But if coming to our end gives you some chance to put a stop to the curse on the land, we can accept that."

"No, no, no." Eslinde grasped for the bars again as though she could break them apart in her hand. "Don't say that. The land needs you. I need you. And ..."

Eslinde turned then to Kess. She moved behind her and pushed Kess's chair closer to the cell door.

"This is my friend, Kessara."

Friends? Is that what we are? Kess's lips pursed.

"Kess, Yrik is Alleem's grandfather. Yes, I know he seems young, but Alderkin age much slower than humans." Eslinde moved back to the bars, and the lamplight flickered in her glossy eyes.

She tilted her head and took a deep breath. "The reason I stopped coming, the reason my father had Alleem killed, is because I became pregnant, with Alleem's child."

Two other faces pressed in beside Yrik's then, all three vying to peer through the small window. The emerald-toned Priyune, and the third, Shael, with hair and eyes the color of an ice-melt stream, a shimmering pale aqua.

"A child?" Priyune said.

"Could it be possible?" Shael asked.

"Did it survive?" Yrik exhaled in a rush.

Eslinde clutched at the fingers that reached through the bars to touch hers. "I didn't think so. For years I thought she was gone. But Kessara brought me news that she still lives."

"A child!" Priyune said again.

"A child of Alleem's." Yrik's face dropped and he turned away from the bars.

"So young. Alone in the world," Shael cried.

"Not alone," Eslinde reassured them.

Kess gave an encouraging nod.

"Alone from her Alderkin people, separated from us. We must go to her. We must find a way!" Shael said. Then she reached a hand through the bars. "The crystal! The one you brought. Let us have it."

"It's already runed." Priyune tsked.

"Still, there may be something we can do with it, some compatible runes we can mark it with. The slayer of unicorns won't allow us charged crystals. Any crystal could help us find a way free of this prison." Shael's fingers flexed.

Eslinde held the crystal up. "I think it still has some charge. But it's not safe to leave. Not yet. We still don't know exactly where the child is."

Then she placed the crystal down into the awaiting hand. "But as soon as I know, then it will be time. And I'll do what I can to get you out."

Kess held her breath as she watched the exchange. Was the princess truly reckless enough to attempt to free these people, clearly the most valuable prisoners the king held?

It would be a good move, though. If the Alderkin were gone, they wouldn't be able to make more taming spikes for the king, and the dragonlords would run out of silvernix faster. They could cure the land of the shadow dragon curse.

Kess bit her lip. When had she ever had designs upon saving the world? *Raze it all, Eslinde is getting into my head!*

Eslinde paced, talking through a plan. "If I can find a way for all of us to leave, we could try to go to the Rebel Riders for asylum."

"Wait, the Rebel Riders?" Kess had been reading some of the chapters of those tales during her time in Eslinde's quarters. "Those are just fiction, aren't they?"

Eslinde smirked. "Not entirely. I was in the beginnings of communications with them before everything went wrong with the pregnancy. They hadn't trusted me enough at the time to offer their location, but perhaps I could attempt to reopen communications."

Kess wrinkled her nose, unable to believe it. The stories she read were outlandish fantasies. Romance like that never happened in reality.

"We could work alongside them, find and destroy silvernix stockpiles, keep the Alderkin away from the Dragon King. Stop people taming any more dragons. We could do this."

Yrik reappeared at the window beside the two other Alderkin. His sharp cheeks were streaked in tears. "You let us know when, dear child, and we will be with you."

Eslinde beamed at them all, the fire in her eyes brighter than the flickering flame of the oil lamp.

Fight the dragonlords, free the prisoners, destroy silvernix, save the world.

Kess's head and heart ached. It was too much, all too much. How had she gotten caught up in all of this?

Her goals were once so simple. Become a dragonrider. And even after that, when they'd changed, it was only to take revenge on Kife and keep Dracuni safe.

What would the princess do if she discovered Dracuni was a stockpile of silvernix in and of herself?

Would she need to be destroyed too?

Kess had gotten in too deep with Eslinde and her rebellious plans, which felt more and more like they would only ruin Kess's own.

Maybe she should consider Ulfren's offer. She had more than enough dirt on Eslinde to pass along.

Kess fidgeted with the fabric of her sleeves, feeling the knives beneath.

Could she really betray Eslinde, who had put so much trust in her? Even if it was to keep Dracuni safe, the last thing Kess could ever do for Riony?

CHAPTER FIFTEEN

Dashiel didn't like having to steal. As much as they justified they were only taking what belonged to their own family, it felt wrong to be sneaking around Zarram Dragonhold like a common thief.

But Dashiel needed the silvernix, and if he asked anybody for it, he'd have to explain what it was for, and it would never have been allowed. Not even by Vance.

He should understand how important this is.

Dashiel had been raised from birth to be a dragonrider. And a dragonrider's core purpose was to serve Elundrae in the fight against the shadow dragon's revenants. That was the war they fought.

But what if they could do something to end the war once and for all?

The Zarrams still had a reasonable supply of silvernix, which they used primarily for taming dragons, or the most extreme of illness or injury only. Although even when Vance had his accident, their father erred on the side of frugality, deciding that it was too late to save the leg anyway.

Dashiel thought they should have tried regardless, but that silvernix dose was one more dragon that could be tamed within their collection, to continue growing their wealth.

And now, Dashiel decided that the one dose of silvernix he'd just stolen was what should have been spent on their brother's leg.

It wouldn't be missed. Not immediately anyway. At the next accounting day, the loss would be noticed, but Dashiel hoped by then he would be able to show everyone proof that he could retrain an untamed dragon.

Dashiel was sure they just needed to start with a dragon they'd already worked with. One they reared and trained and already had a connection with.

Moving through Zarram Dragonhold, Dashiel often received surprised looks from the staff and workers at the dragonling slinking along at their heels. As far as they all knew, Shiff was tamed now and acting under verbal commands.

But there were often mutterings about how they'd never seen a hatchling take to training so quickly. It normally took months or years to get a tamed dragonling to follow verbal orders.

"That's Dashiel for you, though. One of the best trainers I've seen," an older feed manager told their assistant as Dashiel strode by.

"I still don't like how it looks at me," the assistant whispered back, just loud enough for Dashiel to hear.

One day, Dashiel would be able to reveal to all of them that Shiff was well trained because she was able to think for herself. One day soon.

Shiff was a few months old now and getting big. Her thoughts came through clearer than ever, and there were times she challenged Dashiel's commands, making them worry they were losing control over her. But even if Shiff didn't want to follow orders every time, Dashiel could feel they'd developed a bond, a relationship beyond master and servant.

All the other dragonriders invested at the same time as Dashiel trained their dragonlings together. Dashiel had been provided special dispensation to train Shiff alone, being as they lived at the dragonhold that housed the hatchlings and had trained dragons before, and because Zarram training methods were proprietary information.

At least, that's what Dashiel told their mestra.

Dashiel led Shiff down toward the bottom levels where they had stashed a red etherflame that had recently been taken out of breeding rotation. She had looked like strong stock, but her offspring continued to be born with malformations, so she was going to be sold on to industrial use.

But while the dragon wasn't being bred and wasn't yet sold, she wasn't being paid much attention to and was Dashiel's best option to untame.

It was a rest day, and there were only core servants working. As Dashiel and Shiff went down the final flight of stairs into the disused flamesong stalls, Dashiel thought they noticed the shadow of someone behind them, but when they looked back, there was nothing.

"Vance?" Dashiel called.

No reply. Their brother was the only other person who came down there, but only when Dashiel brought him down to see Shiff. Dashiel had taken over all care of Eslinde's now untamed and increasingly furious dragon.

The snowshimmer's roar echoed through the heavy steel barrier, and Dashiel eyed the rope and pulley system keeping the door weighted closed. Only once so far had Dashiel dared lift the door even a little to throw in food. Luckily, mature dragons didn't need to eat regularly, but it couldn't be helping the dragon's rage.

Hurting. Shiff narrowed her eyes at the door. ***Wants sky.***

"Let's hope the next one is a bit more understanding," Dashiel said.

Another? Shiff's forked tongue darted out, and Dashiel could sense her eagerness.

It had been largely due to Shiff's questioning and urging that Dashiel made the decision to try to untame another dragon. They'd noticed Shiff lingering near the door holding the snowshimmer captive, and at times, Eslinde's dragon calmed at her presence.

Shiff often came away from those encounters with a strong mix of conflicting emotions. Dashiel greatly wished for the small dragon to have another of its kind that it could speak to in a positive way.

They reached the stall right at the end where the etherflame waited senselessly.

A big dragon. A fire-breather. But one Dashiel had helped raise, had always treated well. Would she remember?

"I think it's going to work. How about you?"

Shiff flicked the end of her spike-tipped tail.

Dashiel had taken as many precautions as possible this time. The dragon was muzzled with a makeshift contraption made from harnesses and straps. The chains holding her in place were thicker than those used on Eslinde's dragon. Ones used for locking in special guests' dragons, in a show that the Zarram stables were especially secure for their customers.

The collar was even stamped with the Zarram crest, a dragon holding a star on a shield, to make sure their customers remembered where they were. Dashiel's father always put great consideration into appearances.

The dragon's breath puffed out in a steady rhythm, smelling like the remains of a forest fire.

She really is a big one, Dashiel thought, swallowing their fear.

"This is worth trying," they said aloud and left the door open behind them in case they needed a rapid escape.

Snatching up the pliers they'd left there earlier, Dashiel approached the dragon, commanding her to lower her head.

She did so in a smooth, instant response.

It took a couple of tries to get the pliers around the end of the spike, and tugging it out was far, far harder than Vance had made it seem. It seemed suctioned in, and Dashiel was panting and sweating from strain by the time it even budged.

And then it slipped free in a swift, slurping motion.

With fumbling fingers, Dashiel dropped the spike and pliers on the floor and hurried to apply the silvernix to the open wound.

As the magic spread its light through the dragon's body, sparkling below its scales, Dashiel imagined the dragon's brain knitting itself back together, repairing itself in a way it had never been able to before because of the steel stake within it.

And as before, the spiraling ribbons of dark shadow drifted down through the ceiling and into the dragon. And the dragon awoke.

"Easy, easy," Dashiel said in a soft voice.

The etherflame's eyes snapped wide open and neck pulled up. Chains snapped taut. Eyes went wider again. Her mouth strained against the muzzle. One leather strap tore.

Angry also, Shiff thought, body lowered as she skulked away from the bigger dragon.

"Yeah, yeah, I noticed, thanks."

The etherflame bucked against the chains clamped around her neck, and in a swift and easy stretch, the chains broke.

Far easier than the stockyard chains they'd put on Eslinde's dragon. The etherflame wasn't that much bigger or stronger, but the chains had snapped like a dry twig.

A piece landed near Dashiel's foot, and they could see that although the chains were thicker than the others, they were made of cheap, friable metal.

All just a show for the customers, hey, Pabba? That was like so much of how their father had gone about making their fortune. They should have known.

The dragon reared back, eyes whirling in their sockets, taking in the corners of the dark, enclosed space.

Scared. Scared.

The voice in Dashiel's head wasn't Shiff's. It came from the etherflame, more a surge of childish emotions than words or language, the way Dashiel had felt the connection when Shiff had been newly hatched.

Sparks flickered from her nostrils.

"It's okay. You're safe," Dashiel urged, unsure how much the dragon could understand.

Safe. Safe, still, and calm, Shiff added.

Dashiel lifted both hands in a calming gesture and kept their eyes on the dragon's.

A few huge breaths pumped the dragon's chest like bellows, and then she turned wild eyes to Dashiel. And her breathing slowed.

She remembers you.

"Really?" Dashiel's voice cracked, too high-pitched. "In a good way or ...?"

Red scales across the dragon's shoulders shivered and twitched, but her eyes stayed on Dashiel, lids lowering.

The hot glow around the dragon's muzzled snout dimmed.

Dashiel let out their own long exhalation. "That's it. You're good. You're going to be okay."

A flash of metal passed by Dashiel's eye, followed by a harsh, scraping thunk.

Dashiel frowned, unable to understand what they were seeing. The handle of a dagger, sticking out from between the etherflame's chest scales.

"What in the stars?" Dashiel spun around, searching for the source. A shadow fled up the corridor behind them.

Muted by the muzzle, but no less filled with fury, the dragon roared.

Dashiel didn't have time to turn back around.

Free of her chains, the dragon lunged forward. Dashiel raced her, trying to get outside of the door before she did. She stampeded through, knocking Dashiel out of the way with her flank.

Dashiel tumbled, crashing into the doorframe, barely missed by stomping, taloned claws. The etherflame galloped out of the stall, smashing an oil lamp on her way.

Flames flickered from the spilled oil and Shiff hissed at it, dodging back into the now empty stall for shelter.

Scrambling back to their feet, Dashiel didn't worry about the small patch of fire. The floor and walls were stone and there was little else to burn.

They were far, far more worried about the panicking, untamed etherflame charging up the wide stairwell into the rest of the dragonhold.

"No, no, no. Come back!" Dashiel raced after it.

The dragon moved faster, tail disappearing in an elegant swish around the corner ahead.

Stars, what do I do?

Even if Dashiel caught up to the dragon, could they calm it down again? It had been going well, hadn't it?

Who threw that dagger?

A scream came from up ahead and Dashiel sped into the chamber beyond, where a couple of servants had their backs pressed to a wall as the dragon bore down on them.

The muzzle suppressed the fiery breath, but more straps strained and snapped, sending the workers fleeing in terror. The creature's bloodred scales gleamed ominously, neck straining against the heavy collar around it, broken chains dangling and clattering like off-tune windchimes.

She forged on, her colossal form hammering down storage barrels and shelves in her path as she continued upward, as though sensing her path to freedom.

She's heading to the flight deck.

"Close that door!" Dashiel yelled through the chaos.

The workers beside the wide double doors froze, gaping at the dragon, uncomprehending. Dragons didn't just *move* on their own.

The etherflame plowed forward. The passages within the dragonhold were designed for the passage of large beasts, but in the dragon's wild rush, she smashed her sweeping tail against the doorframe, shattering the hinges and crumbling stone.

A woman was knocked aside, a trickle of blood on her forehead. Panic spread among the servants, their shouts blending with the dragon's roars.

With each step, Dashiel's heart raced. They felt the pulse of the dragon's emotions, a chaotic blend of fear, anger, and an innate longing for the open sky.

The flight deck opened out before them.

"Stop! Please!" Dashiel cried, breathless.

"What in the stars is going on?" Vance appeared, running beside Dashiel in a lopsided stride.

Dashiel gave their brother a pained look.

"You didn't!" Vance growled.

They both ran harder.

On the precipice of the open flight deck, the behemoth of flaming red spread her wings wide. The muzzle couldn't stifle the determination burning in her eyes.

Dashiel slowed their pace, holding their hands out, pleading. "Don't go. Please. You can be safe here."

Dashiel could feel the lie on their tongue. Now that the dragon had been revealed, could she be safe anywhere?

A wave of emotion returned, roiling and shifting but mostly **hurt, hurt, hurt**.

Like the crack of a whip, leather bands snapped around the straining jaw. The torn scraps fell free and the dragon opened her mouth in a deafening roar that echoed back through the flight deck.

With a powerful beat of her wings, the dragon swept off the flight deck ledge. Uneven at first, as though still finding her ability to move her body freely, but strong and determined.

The creature soared into the sky above the capital city.

Vance ran a hand down over his face and growled, "We are utterly screwed."

Chapter Sixteen

Dashiel stared at the retreating etherflame for a few heart pounding moments. "I can fix this. If I can recapture her ... or bring her down outside of the city or ..." Dashiel wasn't exactly sure how to fix this.

Had any rider battled with a full-grown wild dragon since the early days when humans hunted wild dragons instead of breeding them? Dashiel's chest contracted trying to imagine what they were about to face.

But still they turned and ran back toward the stalls.

"I'm taking Viska," Dashiel called back.

"You razing aren't," Vance replied, hobbling after. The run up through the dragonhold would have been hard on his missing leg.

Dashiel reached Viska's stall. The golden dragon wasn't saddled or harnessed. There was no time to do either. Dashiel climbed up her shoulder and settled into the bare scales at the nape of her neck, above the powerful muscles of its wings.

They had ridden bareback before, but never on a ride like this.

Vance blocked the exit to the stall, standing firm with arms crossed.

"Let me do this. Pabba can punish me all he wants for this mess." Dashiel gestured to the broken stalls and shocked servants. "But if I can do something to stop the etherflame before anyone else realizes what's going on, I have to try."

"Not without me you aren't." Vance stepped forward.

Dashiel adjusted their seating. They'd flown Viska plenty of times, but nobody knew her like Vance.

Still, they hesitated. "This isn't on you."

Vance blew out a low whistle, and Viska dropped, lying flat against the ground. Moving around beside the dragon's shoulder, Vance reached a hand to Dashiel.

"Fine." Dashiel reached back, helping their brother up onto the dragon's back.

Vance settled in front, and the moment he leaned over the dragon's neck, pressing hands against her scales, the dragon burst into motion.

Powerful legs scrambled beneath them as the dragon launched out of the stall, scaring the nearby servants again with the rush.

Down beside the stall entrance, Shiff trotted closer, looking around, confused, having finally caught up.

Going?

Many eyes in the area turned to the dragonling, roaming apparently on her own, then to Vance and Dashiel's hurried launch.

Dashiel cursed. "Get back to your room, now!"

Fly?

"No!"

They were almost to the edge of the flight deck, but the hurt from Shiff still came through as the dragonling turned and left.

Dashiel kept their eyes turned behind them at the wreck of the stalls and flight deck area, as Vance kept his forward, preparing the dragon to fly.

As Shiff exited the space, Lord Zarram entered, cheeks flushed red and chest heaving.

"What under the blessed sun is happening in here?" he roared. "What happened? Where are you going?"

Dashiel turned away, teeth gritted, and Viska took flight.

Air slapped Dashiel in the face as Vance pushed the golden dragon fast right off the deck. They hadn't even taken long enough to grab goggles.

Searching the sky with squinting eyes, Dashiel saw a blur of red.

"Above and to the right."

Vance turned Viska, soaring toward the heavy clouds.

The red dragon hovered still in the sky on massive wings, looking over the city. As dragons of the plains, etherflames had the widest wingspan of all breeds, built for hovering above the herds of the grasslands, picking their prey.

Dashiel whispered a quiet prayer that the red wasn't picking something from the city below as her target.

As they got closer, the dragon's emotions encroached into Dashiel's, a high level of bewilderment and panic. Freed jaw hanging open and eyes wide, her head swiveled, seeking escape in the open sky.

"Why isn't she leaving?" Dashiel yelled in Vance's ear.

But then they saw it too, so ever-present that they hadn't at first noticed.

A sky full of dragons. There were always at least a few, gliding over the dragonkeep. Dragonriders on patrol, or slower steeds transporting civilians and cargo. It was an everyday sight to Dashiel.

But to a wild plains dragon, it must seem like threats all around.

Viska was almost upon the red, and Dashiel's heart raced, unsure whether it was their own panic or the dragons.

"Slow down!" they yelled at their brother. "Don't approach so fast."

But the red etherflame noticed Viska then, shooting toward her, and brought her wings snapping back into her sides. She swooped in a swift dive away from them.

Vance sent Viska into the chase.

Both etherflames, the gold was faster than the red, through her mixed breeding, and Vance brought Viska down like a dart toward the fleeing dragon's back.

Viska's talons touched against the red's spine, and she snarled, spinning into a roll, belly up. As her head turned a full circle beneath the Zarram siblings, she loosed a long gust of fire.

The flames spiraled, scorching the air around them. Vance swore and turned Viska so sharply that her wings cracked like thunder.

Banking hard, Vance slipped from his seat, prosthetic leg kicking out as he tried to regain grip. Dashiel kept their thighs tight around Viska's spine scales and grabbed Vance by the back of the shirt, pulling him back into position.

They circled out and back around toward the dragon again, closing in fast.

But the massive burst of fire above the city had drawn attention. Four riders brought their dragons speeding their way.

The red etherflame beat her wings hard, aiming toward the dragonkeep walls and freedom beyond, but one of the city guard riders came back toward her, head-on. Blasting another short puff of flame, the red changed course, dipping lower, penned in.

"Try to direct her out of the city!" Dashiel yelled.

"It might be too late for that." Vance growled back.

Two more riders came in from the left.

Another moved in close enough to Dashiel and Vance to call down to them, "Has that thing got no rider?"

"Just let her go out—"

"Keep back, we'll handle it," the female rider waved her hand above her head in a series of signing motions, and two nearby riders saluted back.

The red put on a new burst of speed, aiming out toward the sea. The city guard riders barreled in toward her on their smaller, faster steeds, flanking her on both sides and forcing her to turn around again.

She swiveled her head, snapping at the air around the pursuing dragons. A rider on the shimmerdart to the left sent a shot of ball lightning blazing back toward her. The red dove under, dropping lower to the city again.

Dashiel kept their hands on their brother's back, keeping him steady as they pushed faster. Vance maneuvered Viska down into the small gap between the shimmerdart and the red escapee, then turned toward the dragonrider, forcing them to back off with the bulk of Viska's golden body.

But as they dropped back, the rider on the red's other side pushed their attack, bringing their snowflame down onto the red's wing, clawing at the leathery membrane.

The red etherflame keened as her wing tore, and she tumbled in the air. Turning and turning, she spiraled faster and faster toward the rooftops. Wings continued trying to flap but were tangled around her body in the twisting fall.

Scared. Hurt. Scared.

The terrified scream the red cried chilled Dashiel's spine and made their fingers clamp tight around Vance's shoulders.

Fire burst out around the dragon as she flamed and flamed again, desperately trying to burn her attackers, until the red etherflame looked like one giant fireball, plummeting toward the earth.

The riders pulled back, regrouping high in the sky.

Vance dove hard, one last time. Dashiel held their breath. If they could get to the red in time, catch her in Viska's claws, slow her descent …

The red hit a tall, spired building in a crashing explosion of stone and glass and fire.

She smashed straight through, catching everything flammable in her wake, then demolished a smaller warehouse with the slide of her huge body. She came to rest in a wide square, surrounded by fire and debris.

Screams echoed from the streets and buildings below. Vance shot Viska's wings out, catching the air and bringing their speeding descent jarring to a stop to avoid hitting the rooftops themselves.

Dashiel stared at the scene below, speechless with horror.

"We should get out of here." Vance leaned to turn Viska around.

Dashiel could sense the fallen dragon's pain and fear surging through their veins and couldn't leave the creature, not like that, not alone to her fate.

Reaching both arms around their brother's waist, Dashiel pressed the commands for landing and yelled them aloud for good measure.

"What are you doing?" Vance pushed back, trying to recover control, but Viska was already level with the rooftops and a second later skidded to a stop on the cobblestones of the square.

The red lay twisted and broken and panting before them. Dashiel leaped down from Viska's back.

A group had gathered, pulling bodies from the destruction of the burning warehouse. Dashiel could feel the rising heat on their back, and the flames glistened over the scuffed and torn scales of the red etherflame.

Screams and shouts surrounded them, and Dashiel moved fearlessly toward the downed dragon.

Tears streamed down their face as the red's chest lifted sharply and compressed, lifted again, then all the smoky air inside her wheezed out in a long, final breath.

"I'm sorry. I'm so sorry." Dashiel put a hand against her snout, still hot from the remnants of dragonfire. "This was all my fault."

Dashiel's face twisted, fierce with frustration and anger.

But it wasn't only their fault. It wasn't their actions that had led to this moment, not entirely.

Pushing past the dragon's slumped neck, Dashiel stepped over strewn bricks and smoldering timber to the dragon's chest. She lay belly up, exposing the wide underbelly scales and the dagger stuck between them.

Vance stumbled up beside them as Dashiel grabbed the handle and yanked it out.

"What is that? Did you do that?"

"Would I have done that?" Dashiel glared back.

"Then who?"

Dashiel opened their fist, staring at the knife in their hand. A finely crafted blade, larger than those designed for throwing, but serving the purpose well enough. On the pommel, a solid letter *H* was stamped, surrounded by a ring of thorns.

Heithorn?

Smoke gusted around them from the roaring warehouse fire.

"Sabotage?" Vance growled.

Dashiel clutched the dagger tight again, bringing it flat against their chest, lips twisting with fury.

It might have worked. Without the sting of this blade, keeping the untamed dragon calm and safe might have worked.

But now Dashiel would never know. And a dragon, and any number of people Dashiel couldn't bring themselves to turn and see, were dead.

Through the surrounding smoke, large shapes rushed in around them. City guards on small treedarts. They barked orders to the remaining citizens gawking at the downed dragon and some split off to manage the fires and shattered buildings.

"You should go," Dashiel said heavily.

"*We* should go," Vance snapped back.

Dashiel's eyes lingered over the heavy collar on the dragon's neck, stamped with the Zarram crest. "Someone needs to stay and claim responsibility. I'll do what I can to keep our family from feeling the consequences of all this."

Vance rested a hand on Dashiel's shoulder. "Not without me."

A squad of six guards approached cautiously, eyes on the siblings and the stationary bulk of Viska behind them. Too late for any escape that didn't add more guilt to the scene.

If Dashiel had thought that their standing as acclaimed riders and dragonlord nobles within Draekhanhelm was going to shield them from punishment, that hope was quashed by the glee on the lead guard's face as they took in their dark, tanned skin and Rolanian features.

"Zarrams?" the pink-skinned Taen man asked, a twang in their tone mocking of a strong Rolanian accent.

"Yes," Dashiel said, straightening up and staring up at the guard in his saddle.

Looking over the body of the red etherflame, the branded collar at its neck, and then up into the sky to make clear they'd seen everything that happened, the guard's grin widened. "Wild dragons? Is that what you keep in your unblessed dragonhold?"

Dashiel firmed their jaw and remained silent.

The head guard pointed to the riders at his side, and they climbed off their steeds.

"I don't know what tricks and cheats you Rolanians have been up to in your hold. But it's all come crashing down now."

The two guards on foot approached, manacles in hand. There was nowhere to run, surrounded by treedarts and fire on every side.

Dashiel sought their brother's eyes. He returned a look, solid and determined, and nodded once. Zarrams didn't run. Zarrams didn't burn. Zarrams would face their fate with honor.

Dashiel still shivered, scared for Shiff, all alone, and Eslinde's dragon, and Eslinde herself if the truth of untaming came out, as the heavy steel was clamped about their wrists.

Chapter Seventeen

Kess was drenched in sweat by the time she, Eslinde, and the princess's grayglim reached the audience chambers. She'd worked hard to keep up with the racing pace Eslinde set, charging down through the palace from the moment the news arrived that the Zarram siblings had been brought in shackled with chains.

A guard at the ornate doors opened his mouth at their approach.

"Don't you say a word," Eslinde commanded without slowing. She swung the double doors wide and marched in.

An angry hum of voices filled the chamber. Everyone was on their feet, hands flailing with emphatic gestures. Only the grayglim wardens guarding with their backs to the walls remained still.

Lord Zarram was there, red-faced and towering. "What trouble have you brought down on us? It's only by the graces the Dragon King has bestowed upon us that you aren't in a noose already."

Dashiel and Vance stood shoulder to shoulder in front of their father, hands clasped and locked in heavy iron before them. Dashiel's golden hair was dulled with ash and their face hanging, drawn long and pale. Vance held his chin high.

Neither responded.

"I don't know what ... How did you ...? Where ...?" Lord Zarram sputtered.

Across the room, Ulfren the First and Hjelzahn the First stood with a flock of Sunblessed monks like a spill of yolk, bright in the coolly lit room.

They listened, muttering horrified exclamations and prayers as a guard gave them a report. A number of the elder advisors in darker robes listened in from the fringes.

Eslinde stepped between the Zarram siblings and their father. "Perhaps I could have a moment with them. It seems something terrible has happened, and I would be honored to offer what aid I can to the Zarram household."

"Your Highness," Lord Zarram bowed deeply. "I am most honored and can assure—"

"A moment with them *privately*." Eslinde smiled pleasantly.

Frowning, Lord Zarram backed away. "Of course."

He wandered over as though to join the group headed by Ulfren, but from the looks he received in return, he pivoted and moved around to fidget with the corner of the table in the center of the space.

Kess moved in close beside Eslinde, forming a tight group with Vance and Dashiel.

Ulfren glared at their huddle from across the room, especially at Eslinde.

Eslinde wiped a finger across Dashiel's cheek, smearing a smudge of ash.

She spoke softly, "A wild dragon from your dragonhold attacked the city—that's all I have heard. Was it mine? Did she escape?"

Vance grunted. "No."

Kess eyebrows went up. "You untamed another one?"

"I did. Alone. Everything that happened is my fault." Dashiel's hands squeezed and released over and over in front of them. "Everything except ... It was *working*. The dragon was calm, was listening. And then ..."

"They were sabotaged," Vance growled.

"How? Who would?" Eslinde gasped.

Dashiel's eyes met Kess's for the first time since they came in. "There was a dagger, thrown at the dragon while it was confused and vulnerable. A dagger with an *H* surrounded in thorns."

"Heithorn." Kess crossed her arms, grasping at the wrists where two of the knives the princess had gifted her were hidden, as though doubting herself whether it could have been her.

She hadn't been there. The knives she had now had no crest. Yet it was so like the betrayals and cruelties she'd committed in the past that the doubt came easily. But she knew who it had to be.

Kess snorted out the words. "Kife. My brother."

Dashiel nodded, eyes still locked on Kess's. There was no judgment in their expression, only regret. It stabbed Kess deeper than if she'd betrayed Dashiel herself. She didn't need to throw the blade herself. Her mere presence in their lives brought tragedy.

"Why? What is that man's problem?" Eslinde snapped, nostrils flaring.

Kess flinched away. The princess knew she was still withholding secrets from her, but there was still one she refused to tell. "He's angry at me, and he's determined to do anything to take his revenge on me and anyone around me. Dashiel saved me from him after the ball."

"You think he wanted to get back at me?"

"No doubt. I also think he overheard us discussing untaming dragons."

Vance's shoulders lifted and rolled, and his face worked through a few dark expressions before he said, "And then he saw proof and took a chance at making a mess of everything."

"But he's your brother?" Dashiel shook their head.

Kess looked at the two Zarram siblings standing shoulder to shoulder, and her nose stung.

What would it feel like to have a brother who treated me with that kind of love and support? She couldn't answer, only turned her head down and rolled her chair back just a fraction, out of the tight group.

"Remind me to tell you how Kessara and I met, and then you won't be confused any longer at the state of the Heithorn siblings' relationship. But for now, do you have the dagger? Perhaps we can use it to our advantage," Eslinde said.

Dashiel lifted their empty hands upward. "It was taken off us. I don't know where it is."

"What other proof do they have? Explain to me everything and—"

"Enough colluding!" Ulfren pushed in between Eslinde and Vance, sweeping his arms to break up their group.

The back of his hand knocked Eslinde's chin, and Vance stomped a step forward.

Head still tilted back, earrings swinging, Eslinde gave him a warning look and he stilled.

She said, "I'm only comforting our family friends over what must surely be a misunderstanding."

Ulfren's long face turned to her, his dark eyes fierce. "Don't treat me as a fool. You last were in this room asking for us all to untame our dragons, and now what has been set upon the people of this keep? A savage, untamed beast. Is this the blasphemous world you hope for?"

"She didn't have anything to do with this," Dashiel said.

Kess wasn't so sure of that. Eslinde was the one who shared with them the possibility of untaming, and it was Kess that knowledge first came from.

Ulfren's voice dropped, deep and dangerous. "No. I know where the blame lies and where punishment must be served."

Hjelzahn stepped up behind him, nodding fervently. Around the other side, one of the elder advisors shuffled in, voice warbling in distress. "Let's not accuse so freely. There are still so many unclear details as to who was behind this and how it transpired."

Dashiel stepped into the middle of the building crowd. "It wasn't her, it was m—"

Vance elbowed them and spoke over the top, saying not much of anything, a grumbling philosophizing about the nature of dragons and guilt.

Ulfren's voice rose again, and Lord Zarram returned, defending the honor of Zarram Dragonhold more so than his offspring. And soon everyone was speaking all at once as voices grew louder and louder.

Kess's chair rolled backward. Slowly at first, and she clutched the wheels, worried somehow that it was rolling away on the perfectly flat floor. But the chair continued, backing up, then turning. A grayglim had taken control of it and was swiftly wheeling Kess toward a side door.

"Excuse me!" Kess exclaimed.

The grayglim said nothing.

Turning as fully as she could in her chair, she looked back toward the others, all so deep in argument that they hadn't noticed Kess being slipped away from beneath them.

Should I raise my voice? She wasn't sure they'd even hear her, and surely she was making a fuss over nothing. The grayglim wasn't Lady Hjelzahn and Kess was fairly certain she was the only one who wanted her dead.

As they reached the side door, another grayglim opened it and Kess was pushed through. "Where are you taking—?"

Before her, Dragon King Yeonard Draekhan turned from the floor-to-ceiling window to greet her with a steely expression. The small room was bereft of furniture, the glossy stone floor and walls decorated only by glowing lamps and silver and red pennants of shimmering silk.

Eslinde's mother stood motionless in a shadowy corner, dress draped about her like an elegant statue.

Kess swallowed a dry mouth, and the grayglim closed the door behind them.

The Dragon King took a single step closer, placing himself in the center of the room. "Do you know, Kessara Heithorn, how many people died today in my keep?"

Dropping her eyes down and bowing as best as she could from her chair, Kess said, "I do not, Your Majesty. But any number is too many."

He hummed. "True indeed. It is fortunate that it was a rest day, so few were in the warehouse that was destroyed. The reports make it clear what happened. All that is left to decide is who will take the blame."

A shiver ran up Kess's back, and she kept her eyes low. "Have you made that decision?"

And why did he bring me to him as though I could help make it?

The king moved closer, pacing languidly before Kess so her vision was filled with the sweep of his silver embroidered robes swishing back and forth, reflected in the tiles beneath.

"Perhaps it needn't be my decision to make. The Zarrams' trouble, alas, affects my daughter, which in turn affects me."

Kess couldn't fathom the entirety of the political fallout from what had occurred. But even what she could imagine seemed dire.

She tried to keep her tone even, logical, not pleading in panic. "Then blame nobody. Make it go away. Say it was a wild dragon only and an unfortunate accident that it was brought down over the city."

"But the people are angry. And they need a target for their fury." The Dragon King's voice echoed in the small space. "Look at me, child."

Kess turned her eyes up, breathless. "Your Majesty."

The Dragon King's dour face was framed between the ornate, twisting metal collar of his robes and the sharp pointed crown upon his head.

Kess felt a little relief that there was no anger in his expression. If anything, he seemed bored and annoyed that this issue had been brought to him at all.

He sighed. "Eslinde had been doing so well recently, before all of this."

Had she? Kess bit the thought from escaping her mouth.

The Eslinde Kess had first met was a living ghost, wasted away and wan inside and out.

It had been months since then, and Eslinde was only just regaining color and softness to her body, although the fire inside her returned much faster. But clearly that fire was all her father cared about and wanted extinguished again.

His strange, darkly bright eyes settled on Kess. "She had been doing well, before *your* arrival."

She held the Dragon King's gaze. "You believe it's my arrival that has affected her so?"

"You and the information you brought with you. Spurring Eslinde into illicit activities."

Kess's lips drew tight.

"Yes, I know about it all." His sparkling eyes narrowed, glinting like stars.

A terrible, cold sense of courage rushed through Kess. The kind of vibrating, anxious daring she used to feel in the wilds when facing death. She folded her arms, clutching at the hard metal beneath her wrists.

The Dragon King turned away from her then, striding to the window.

"My daughter is beloved." He cast a glance across to Eslinde's mother, still motionless in a shadowy corner. "The Zarrams are valuable partners. And you …"

Kess could hear all the possible endings to that sentence in her mind. She was nothing. She wasn't important. She was a shame and embarrassment to even have around.

She was expendable.

Through the massive expanse of crystal-clear glass, the sky was a tumultuous swirl of dark clouds, curdling over the roofline of the city. Smoke rose from a district to the east.

Kess released her grip on her forearms and the knives hidden there. There was no point in fighting.

Her life was already over.

"You," Yeonard Draekhan said thoughtfully and turned back to her. "You could admit that you were the one who freed the wild dragon to frame the Zarrams. Given your unique history, it will be understandable that you craved revenge on the dragonlords and riders who refused to let you fly with them. We even have a Heithorn dagger covered in dragon blood for proof."

Kess lifted her chin. "Is this what you've decided?"

"Oh no. This is your decision, Kessara Heithorn. You can confess, and I can make everything better for the Zarrams and Eslinde. Or choose not to, and the punishment for the crimes committed can be spread far and wide."

The sweat dampening Kess's gown from their rush to the meeting had cooled now, and Kess shivered.

Her attempt to keep her voice stable failed. "And what would happen to me?"

"You will go away to prison. I have a number of places to put people where they will never be seen again. For that you should be grateful, that you won't face the direct wrath of the populous. I may not be able to be so generous in swaying the outcomes for the others."

The Dragon King raised a hand then in a swift wave, and Kess was moving again. The grayglim had her chair under his control and rolled her back out into the audience chambers.

The king clearly felt no need to await an answer from Kess.

Did he not really care? Or did he already know the outcome?

The arguments within the room continued on. Her presence, or lack of it, went unnoticed.

The grayglim released her and Kess pushed herself slowly back to Eslinde's side, weighing the decision within her.

Kess had always wanted a dragon. To be a dragonrider. But that had always been the means to an end. To have the power to do good in the world. To gain respect and friendship and love.

Did she have any of that from Dashiel, Vance, or Eslinde? Maybe. Sometimes it felt as though she did. The flickering connections of friendship, the considered actions of respect … Love? No. Not love.

But they definitely had that for each other, and if Kess didn't do something, they were all going to be ruined. They seemed as close to good people as Kess hoped to find. They were important—to Kess, to each other, and the world.

And me ... I'm not.

She didn't matter. Even Griskin had given up on her.

And the person she most wanted to matter to was dead and gone.

The Dragon King strode into the room then, silencing the raised voices.

Folding his hands together, he showed far more concern than he had moments before in the privacy of the side chamber. "We've all heard what must be heard on this matter. Now, we must hear directly from the source of this trouble and decide upon the consequences."

Ulfren practically frothed at the mouth with glee.

To one side of Kess, Eslinde's eyes darted, calculating and troubled. She gave Kess a nervous smile.

To the other, Dashiel had a fierce and sickened expression on their raised face, and Vance hissed commanding whispers in their ear.

Dashiel shook their head once and opened their mouth.

Kess yelled into the room, "It was me. The plot to release a dragon upon the city was mine."

Chapter Eighteen

Kess sold her guilt as best she could. Offering up the tale of revenge and feigning delight at the destruction it wrought, as though her plot had played out exactly as she wished, and she simply couldn't contain herself any longer from letting everyone know from where that wrath had come.

Eslinde, Dashiel, and Vance, of course knew she was lying, and of all the expressions of surprise in the room, theirs were the most shocked.

"What are you doing?" Eslinde spat from the corner of her mouth.

Dashiel tried to raise their voice over Kess a couple of times, but Vance kept them quiet. Kess lifted her chin high and bared her teeth.

"I would have had every one of you burn in dragonfire if I could have, but because these cowards"—Kess glared at the Zarrams and Eslinde—"wouldn't be drawn into my plans, I was only able to free a single beast. But even still, I wanted you to know it was me who burned your city."

Kess found it remarkably easy to fill her words with spite. She put into them all the hurt and torment she'd ever suffered, and from the horrified stares of the elder advisors, she'd hit her mark.

Ulfren, however, gave Kess a withering glare. "This is ridiculous. How could she have done any of this?"

The Dragon King gestured to one of his grayglim, who brought forth the Heithorn dagger, holding it up on display.

"This was found with the downed dragon, and we have the girl's full confession as to how and why and that despite her evil influence she was unable to gain any collaborators." The Dragon King offered Kess an almost imperceptible bow of the head. "That seems to me all we need to know."

Lord Zarram pressed a hand against his chest. "And my children? Zarram Dragonhold?"

"Both free to leave. If there were damages to your property, we can discuss reparations at a later date."

With one wave of the Dragon King's hand, two grayglims approached and released Dashiel and Vance from their shackles.

"This isn't right," Dashiel murmured, dark brows low over pleading eyes as they looked at Kess.

Seeing them freed, a lightness came over Kess, and she breathed easier.

She offered a wry smile and whispered back, "It might be the rightest thing I've ever done. Let me do this."

"Kess." Her name sounded like heartbreak on Dashiel's lips.

Bowing repeatedly, Lord Zarram wished every blessing and honor upon the king, then forced Vance and Dashiel swiftly from the room.

Kess stared at the door they left through, a spike of emotion twisting her face. The thought that she may never see them again hurt, but she stilled herself, transforming the lines of her grief into a dull glare.

Eslinde looked pained enough for both of them. "And what of Kessara? What is her fate for … for what she's done?"

Playing along now too, are we? Kess wasn't surprised. She was the perfect scapegoat.

"Into custody and transported to permanent imprisonment tomorrow. Someone like her cannot be allowed to return into society." Yeonard Draekhan looked over the elder advisors and Sunblessed Monks as though seeking their say on the matter, although Kess knew it was already decided.

There were quiet mutterings of approval from them all.

Except Ulfren. "There are still—"

"The matter is concluded," the Dragon King boomed.

He turned to leave, but Eslinde fluttered in a rush to his side.

She spoke brokenly, as though finding her thoughts as the words tumbled from her mouth. "Allow me … Tonight, let me be responsible for Kessara's custody tonight. Her final night of freedom."

Yeonard Draekhan turned, frowning softly. His voice was warning, but gentle. "Eslinde …"

She reached out and clasped his hand. Whispering, but still loud enough for all to hear, she said, "I know she's done a terrible thing and I … want to be sure she receives what she deserves, personally."

Pulling his hand free, the Dragon King sighed. "She's your responsibility for the night. See that you remain responsible."

Eslinde nodded, steel in her eyes, then rushed back to Kess. The Dragon King turned the other way, heading to the side chamber.

Ulfren snarled, chest heaving with seething breaths. "Your Majesty?"

The king didn't slow, and the door closed behind him, blocked by a grayglim.

Turning to Hjelzahn instead, Ulfren hissed, "I won't stand for this blatant favoritism."

"Move, quickly," Eslinde whispered to Kess, then walked fast for the exit.

Kess followed, Yensen at her back.

"This can't be allowed! I know the truth!" Ulfren yelled at their backs.

They were two corridors away, where no one else was around, when Eslinde dropped back to walk beside Kess instead of leading.

Her narrow white eyebrows pulled together. "Oh, Kess. Why?"

Plenty of reasons came to Kess, of how she wanted to help, of how she was the one link in their chain that wouldn't be missed, but only one reason needed to be communicated, and urgently.

"The king, he knew, *everything*, and—"

"Lady Eslinde!" Falden rushed toward them from the corridor ahead. "I was looking for you. I have news!"

"Falden?" Eslinde slowed her pace, openly surprised for a moment. "Is this about the Zarrams?"

The advisor hadn't been at the meeting with the others, but he bustled toward them with red-faced urgency. "Zarrams? What about them? Did something happen?"

Kess coughed out a laugh.

Eslinde resumed her march toward her chambers, gesturing for Falden to follow. "Never mind. Tell me what your news is."

"As you know there have been plenty of rumors circulating about the Hjelzahn children. After a great deal of trouble, I managed to track down an eyewitness from an attack on a smelting factory. I wasn't sure it was relevant at first; however, this guard has quite the eye for faces." Falden patted about his body, then extracted a few sheets of parchment from a pocket.

"I believe we've been having trouble tracking the children because they've been dyeing their hair and disguising themselves. I can't understand why. Almost like they don't want to be found! But look at these faces. Surely it is them."

Falden thrust two of the sheets out, and Eslinde took them. She held them up so both she and Kess could see.

The guard had a good eye indeed. The sketches of black charcoal and white chalk captured Aishena and Benjin's faces perfectly. But unlike the steely-toned hair they'd had in the undercity, their locks were now dark.

Eslinde continued walking as she glanced back at Kess for confirmation.

Kess nodded.

The parchment trembled in Eslinde's hands as she asked, "And who else was with them? I want all the details. Perhaps they are being coerced."

Falden shuffled the other loose sheets, trotting at Eslinde's side. "Ah, there was a mixed-race young woman and a big redheaded Rolanian, an odd-looking dragon, and another small girl."

Eslinde snatched the final sheet from his hands, staring intently.

But Kess's eyes had glazed as though streaked with grease. She choked out the words, "When? When was this?"

Falden replied, "I spoke with the guard just now and came directly."

"No. The attack on the factory. When?" Kess rasped.

"The attack? It's not recent, I'm afraid."

Kess's heart turned sluggish, refusing to beat properly. "*When?*"

Falden counted upon fingers. "Summer's end, a bit more than three months ago."

Kess went rigid, her chair stuttering to a standstill.

"Although not current, the information that the Hjelzahns are disguising themselves is very useful. Thank you," Eslinde said.

Eslinde and Falden strode ahead, continuing the conversation, until Yensen cleared his throat from behind.

"Kessara?" Eslinde returned to her and crouched in front of the chair. "What is it?"

Kess's whole body struggled in a war between laughing and crying, relief and pain.

Three months. *After* she'd been locked away in Kife's cellar. After she'd met the princess. After Kife stabbed Riony in the back. *After.*

"She's alive?" Kess couldn't believe the words on her own lips.

Eslinde's information from the contact at the ball had been more recent, telling of only two women. Kess couldn't know what that meant. But Riony hadn't died from Kife's blade, and that awoke in Kess a startlingly painful hope.

When Kess gave no further explanation, Eslinde frowned and stood back up.

"I'm afraid my friend has had quite a day." She reached for the remaining drawings. "May I keep these?"

Falden released his grip reluctantly.

They had reached the base of the stairs, and Eslinde gestured for Yensen to help Kess up them.

Eslinde took a few steps herself before turning to Falden. "Thank you for this information. Hopefully we can use it to bring those poor children home. You haven't shared it with anyone else?"

"I came straight to you with it."

She offered him a respectful bow. "I would appreciate it most sincerely if it stays between you and me. Now, please excuse us, we are retiring early."

"Your Highness." Falden bowed in return.

They had reached Eslinde's chambers by the time Kess could breathe again.

Eslinde closed the door on Yensen but didn't lock it. She strode in, eyes still on the parchments, on the hooded face of a young girl looking back from the sheet on top.

Then her gaze fluttered to Kess, all too knowing.

"You have the look about you of someone who has discovered a person they grieved has come back to life." She smiled softly. "It's familiar."

Kess couldn't reply. She didn't know what to say. Of everything that had happened that day, a scrap of information which mightn't mean anything shouldn't be what affected her the most. She was now a criminal to the crown and tomorrow would be locked away forever.

Eslinde kept the portrait of Lyrrin and tossed the remaining sheets onto the low table in front of Kess.

And there was Riony, looking back at her. The guard had made her look fierce but still captured the ever-present smirk at the corner of her lips. For her portrait alone, they'd added color. Vibrant red for her flaming hair.

And Kess found herself explaining everything.

How she knew Riony from her past, when she was only Pony to her, but had become so much more. Of how she'd hunted them, but still Riony came back for her, gave her another chance, and another, when she deserved none of them. And of how she'd believed her dead by Kife's hand.

She explained everything except for Dracuni.

Shaking her head, Kess moved closer to the table, eyes locked on the portraits. "But I still don't know that she's alive now. What you heard at the ball ... there were only two young women with the group then."

Eslinde sat down on the lounge opposite and gave Kess a look so intense it engulfed her like a wave. "That could mean anything. You've told me before how you feel about her. What's most important now is deciding what you will do with your feelings. If she is alive, what would you do?"

Kess confronted those emotions within her, trying to name them and draw out answers. The fear of seeing Riony again and facing up to her crimes and betrayals. The way her heart had cracked open and changed forever when she saw Riony crying under the waterfall. The guilt for every pain she'd caused. The ache, ache, ache of impossible love.

Anything. I'd do anything to make amends for everything I have done.

Kess shook her head. "There's nothing I can do. Not anymore."

Eslinde brought Lyrrin's portrait up to her chest as though embracing it.

"I never ... because of my views and ideas, I never had close confidants before. Other than Alleem and the Alderkin. You and Vance and Dashiel, I want you to know what it has meant to me, having people around me who believe as I do and feel how I feel about the world. And now I fear I'll lose everyone. Again."

"You won't lose Dashiel and Vance," Kess said.

"I don't want to lose anyone." Eslinde stood up and marched toward the entrance door.

Stopping beside a cabinet, she rummaged in a drawer and pulled a dark metal key. She dangled it from the ring with one finger.

"I need to leave for a while. There are plans to make with this new information. Yensen will be with me, and ... I will manage my sadness if you aren't here when I return."

"I can't leave," Kess said.

"You might not find it so impossible as usual. I know you are capable. I know you've survived worse."

"It would mess everything up. I'd be hunted."

Eslinde smiled. "Sounds like that would be a change, for you."

Kess coughed something between a laugh and a sob.

"Best be fast about it, then you'd have until morning before anyone starts looking for you." Eslinde opened the door, then glanced back at Kess with eyes sparkling with tears and said, "You've gotten me closer to reuniting with what I've lost than I ever dreamed possible."

Then she closed the door behind her.

The sound of the key sliding into the lock and turning was so different to the usual chorus of clicking and thunking of magical closures.

The princess had left Kess with only a normal lock as the barrier between her and freedom.

She could leave. She could escape.

Kess turned her chair and rolled into what she'd come to think of as her room.

The wheels squeaked softly on the polished marble, and Kess brought herself beside the window.

Although one of Eslinde's piles of books obscured some of the view, the capital dragonkeep spread out into the distance before her, shrouded in bruised clouds and pattering rain.

Often when Kess gazed out that window, she would see the shadow dragon, futilely descending upon the keep where there was no dead for it to raise, and she would feel the cursed creature's mourning presence.

It wasn't there that evening, but the torment inside Kess felt the same.

Although it had left her shaken, the hope that Riony may still be alive meant nothing. Because tomorrow Kess was going away forever.

Because she would do anything for Riony. And Eslinde and Dashiel and Vance and this was what she could do for them all. She could save them by giving herself up. She would be saving Lyrrin's mother, and if that was one thing she could do for Riony, that would have to be enough.

Kife hadn't killed Riony. He'd stabbed her, yes, and Kess still wished a death of a thousand flaming humiliations upon him for that alone, but if that's what someone who stuck a blade in Riony deserved, Kess deserved it ten times over.

And if Riony was still alive, she'd still be able to protect Dracuni. So Kess wasn't required there either.

Kess settled into her chair and listened to the thunder breaking across the lightning-streaked sky and prepared to wait for morning.

Through the low grumbles of the storm, another sound turned Kess toward the main chamber. A soft sound again reverberated from the entrance door.

Was Eslinde back already?

The sounds at the door weren't the same as before. A harsh scratching and clinking of metal.

Kess had decided she wasn't going anywhere, but somebody was trying to break *in*.

CHAPTER NINETEEN

The door to Eslinde's chambers swung open and two pale-haired men stepped inside. Kess's breath hitched, and she pulled herself in behind the stacks of books, folding at the waist to lower herself enough to be hidden.

"I told you they wouldn't be here yet. It must take them a terribly long time bringing the chairbound girl up the stairs." Ulfren the First swept into the chambers he expected to be empty. "The route we came up will give us plenty of time to do what we must."

Kess felt for the knives hidden in her sleeves, considering for a moment dispelling his gross underestimations of her. How much more trouble could she be in, after all?

Although assassinating two first heirs may lead to a swift execution rather than a life in prison. Assuming she could trust that was where she was going. Maybe the place the Dragon King hid prisoners who held no value for him was in a pyre.

Does it matter either way? If I'm gone, I'm gone, and I'll be gone soon enough. What hope am I lingering on?

Hjelzahn followed his brother in, more cautiously, casting his gaze about the space. As he stepped to the door of her room, Kess ducked lower, away from the gap she was watching back through.

"If anyone was here there'd be a guard on the door," Ulfren said.

"There may be servants," Hjelzahn responded.

"They would have greeted us. Stop worrying and let's be quick about this. I loathe being without my grayglim for this long."

Hjelzahn's footsteps echoed as he walked away, and Kess looked through the opening between stacked books again.

"Then you should have brought them." Hjelzahn picked up a book from the low table in the sitting area, scowled at the cover, and tossed it back again.

Probably one of the Rebel Rider collections Kess had been reading.

Kess returned the man's scowl from her hiding place. The stories weren't *that* bad. The romance was intolerably unrealistic, but she liked the part when the characters raced dragons through a narrow chasm.

Ulfren scoffed. "We can't have any witnesses for this. Not even grayglim can be trusted, not by anyone who isn't the king. They all belong to him, in the end."

Well, you're going to have one witness for whatever you're plotting. Kess pushed her chair a fraction forward for a better view.

"Then let's hurry, as you say." Hjelzahn reached into a pocket on his embroidered robes and removed a thin vial the length of a finger.

Kess's mind turned to silvernix, but the substance within the glass didn't shimmer. It was a clear, ghostly green as Hjelzahn held it up into the light.

Hjelzahn uncorked the vial and held it out toward Ulfren. "She won't smell or taste it until it's too late."

Poison. That could be solved easily enough. Kess just had to remain hidden until they were gone, and then she could warn the princess before any damage was done.

Ulfren took the vial, giving it a tentative sniff for confirmation. "Good. There'll be no mess on our hands and the death will be blamed on the Heir Killer."

"A shame whoever has been ending heirs hasn't gotten to her already. Would have saved us the trouble." Hjelzahn stepped close to Ulfren's side. "No new leads on their identity?"

"None, unfortunately. As you say, an alliance with them could be fruitful indeed." Pushing aside a couple of books, Ulfren collected the water pitcher from the middle of the table and unstoppered it. With steady fingers, he tilted the vial over the opening.

Hjelzahn said, "Just a few drops will do."

Both Kess and Eslinde drank from that water while reading, the way they spent most of their days and nights confined in those chambers. If she hadn't been there, bent down in the shadows when Eslinde was expecting her to escape, both of them would have been dead by morning.

If she'd made her escape alone, Eslinde would have been dead without her.

"Check for any other pitchers. I want this ended tonight," Ulfren said.

The two first heirs stepped farther into the chambers, beyond what Kess could see from her hiding spot.

"What is Eslinde doing with all these books?" Hjelzahn muttered.

"No doubt reading them," Ulfren replied. "She must have something to occupy herself with when not plotting violent conspiracy with those Rolanian sinners."

"And how the king still favors her!" Hjelzahn said, and there was the slamming sound of book against book. "Eight years now of this special treatment, keeping her here with him in the capital. He's clearly grooming her for rulership."

Kess shook her head. If only they knew the truth, would they think more or less of their sister? Find her death more or less necessary?

It wasn't worth the gamble. Better to stay hidden and wait till they were gone in order to fix their assassination attempt.

Ulfren's voice was a low grumble from the far end of the chambers. "It was outrageous even when the king began constructing a keep in her name. At least he abandoned that."

Hjelzahn gave a grunt of agreement. "She was born after the first heir cut off and shouldn't be considered a legitimate heir in any regard."

"But to see our father putting her needs first, protecting her from her obvious crimes ... He must have more planned for her."

"We can't allow her to take the throne from you." Hjelzahn sounded livid.

"No, we cannot. For our land and our honor, we cannot. And it will be seen to this night." There was the clink of glass, then Ulfren said, "Here's another. I'll check this bedroom. You check that side room."

Kess sucked in a breath and pulled her head out of view as Hjelzahn appeared in the doorway. She was thankful her wariness of the lightning-powered lamps had meant she'd left them off when she came into the room and hoped the shadows would cloak her.

But there was a pitcher of water in that room with her, on the side table nearby, and if Hjelzahn approached it, Kess's hiding place would be revealed.

She reached behind her to where her third knife had been tucked down into the upholstered gap between seat and backrest of her chair. If Hjelzahn saw her, she could down him easily enough ... Then what? Ulfren too, or attempt to escape?

Kess pursed her lips. She'd work it out as she went, but she was ready to do whatever she had to, to keep Eslinde alive, for Lyrrin, for Riony.

Hjelzahn's footsteps plodded into the room. He must have seen the pitcher, or Kess herself, as he picked up his pace.

Then Ulfren's voice came through from the main chamber. "Who's there?"

The footsteps turned, squeaking on the tiles, and went back the other way.

Kess blew a soft sigh, then lifted her head again to see who had entered. Worry shook her that it might be Eslinde and that this was about to get bloody.

But instead, a grayglim walked alone into the space. Their shadowy armor reflected the cool light of the few lit lamps.

"Kverra?" Hjelzahn said, greeting her with all the warmth of a distant family member.

Kess's body went rigid, and her breath seemed caged in her lungs. Not Eslinde, but perhaps even greater potential for things getting bloody. Kess glanced over the thin barrier of books sheltering her and pulled the skirts of her dress closer to her from where they spilled on the floor beyond her cover.

"What are you doing here?" Ulfren asked.

The grayglim didn't reply. Turning to take in the space, Lady Hjelzahn's dark eyes held a chill that made Kess shake all over. The woman's daughter had inherited those same almost black irises, but they somehow seemed warm and bright in her face. On Lady Hjelzahn, there was nothing but abyss and void behind them.

In a tone so casual even Kess found it hard to believe he was busy poisoning their sister a moment ago, Hjelzahn said, "I had been hoping to speak with you, actually. But you've been rather difficult to pin down for a meeting."

Huffing, Ulfren approached as well, brushing a braid of white hair from his shoulder. "Perhaps you can arrange that now, elsewhere?"

Yes. Leave, leave, Kess urged silently.

Nodding slightly, Lady Hjelzahn said flatly, "I have been hoping to meet, too. I've just been waiting for the right time."

Drawing close, Hjelzahn held out an arm to direct the grayglim toward the door. "And how is now for you?"

"Are we alone?" Lady Hjelzahn asked, unmoving.

Hjelzahn raised his eyebrows. "We are ..."

"Then this moment is perfect."

There was one drawn-out heartbeat of a moment when Kess wanted to feel relief as the two first heirs moved toward the door. But only dread filled her, whispering the truth Kess hadn't seen.

The reason Aishena and Benjin hid from their mother. The reason Yoskar died.

It was only as Lady Hjelzahn drew her twin blades in a flash like liquid metal that Kess wondered, and then knew.

Heir Killer.

The man from whom Kverra had received her last name when she married his great-great-grandson died so swiftly it was likely he never even saw it coming.

Hjelzahn the First fell back, head tilting up and falling faster than his body, severed at the neck in a spray of streaming red.

Ulfren had enough time to sputter curses and confusion and to draw a sword that had been hidden beneath his robes before Lady Hjelzahn launched herself upon him.

There was no contest. Ulfren swung wildly, connecting at times with the blur of Kverra's precise blades, but more often those blades cut through his defenses, slicing into arms, thighs, cheeks, soaking his silver robes with dark blood.

"What are you doing? Why? Why?" Ulfren gasped between painful groans.

Kess pushed her chair into motion, then thought better of it. She couldn't help save the man, even if it was a good idea. She remembered how the strange, icy grayglim woman had plucked blades from her unbleeding body as though they were less than thorns.

With a final slash, Kverra had Ulfren down on his back. She strode languidly over him, straddling across his prone form as she stared down.

She disarmed him with a flick of her boot. "Because every one of you must die."

Both her blades swung down in mirrored unison, and a sound like tearing cloth was followed by a bloody gurgle of final breath.

Kess's body seemed to sympathize, feeling cold as death all over. *Every one of who? The heirs?*

She stilled her breathing, trying to remain as silent as possible, hoping the Heir Killer would leave now that her murderous work was done.

But the woman did not. With swift and sure motions, Lady Hjelzahn hauled the bodies from the room, one after the other, dragging them into the bathroom. She returned with towels and soaked up the blood until the living area appeared, at least on first glance, as though it hadn't been touched by murder.

And then like smoke becoming one with shadow, Lady Hjelzahn slipped into a gap between a bookshelf and a curtain and disappeared.

Kess bit off the curses building in her mouth,

She's laying a trap. She's lying in wait for Eslinde. Three first heirs in one night. Wouldn't the Heir Killer be proud.

Kess gritted her teeth. Not three. She wouldn't let the Heir Killer take Eslinde's life any more than she'd allow Ulfren to have taken it.

But she couldn't simply wait Lady Hjelzahn out. Eslinde would come back at some point, come right in and close the door to Yensen as she always did, and Kverra would have one of those blades in her.

Even if Kess came out as quick as she could and yelled a warning, it would be three of them against the Heir Killer, and Kess wasn't entirely certain the woman could be killed.

She had to warn Eslinde before she returned. The only question was how.

Glancing around the room, it was clear Kess couldn't make it back into the main chamber and out the front door. She'd be spotted immediately.

Especially in this chair.

Kess tucked her third knife away into her sleeve with the other. She didn't often feel useless. She'd always preferred to claw and spit and fight through anything in her way. But that had been so much easier when Griskin was with her. She had certain limitations, and without her wolf, speed was one of them.

Bent forward as she was, Kess slumped, putting her face in her hands.

What would Riony think if she were alive and found out Kess had let Lyrrin's mother die?

Riony never gave up. When faced with a dragon or cave spiders or a mass of revenants the size of a house, Riony had never given up.

What would Riony do now? Kess pondered, hoping for inspiration. She smiled wryly.

Probably throw herself from a great height ...

Kess's eyes turned to the window beside her, unlocked for the first time, and took in the great distance down to the courtyard below.

She was going to have to jump.

With painstaking slowness, Kess crept her chair closer and closer to the window. Even slightly too fast and it would squeak on the polished floors. Her heart thundered in her ears as loud as the storm outside.

She hated every second. She was too slow. She pictured over and over in her mind Eslinde returning and being slaughtered before she'd even reached the window. How long was Eslinde planning to stay away? Long enough for Kess to escape, however long she assumed that to be.

Kess reached the end of her book tower shelter. Anxious energy urged her faster. Turning her chair to go around the side table which held the pitcher of water, the wheels loosed a long, low whine against the stone beneath.

Holding her breath, Kess swung around to check through the door behind her.

And Lady Hjelzahn, marching out from her own hiding place, locked eyes with her.

"Raze it." Kess pushed the wheels faster, but Kverra was already at the door.

Shifting her center of balance, Kess spun her chair around to face the woman and grasped at the glass pitcher. She eyed the unlit lamps.

No wet hands? Let's see what this does.

Kess flung the glass vessel across the room, aiming for the toggle switch closest to the door. The pitcher shattered against the wall around it.

An arc of blue light shot out from the dripping toggle.

Kverra dodged back, as crackling spread through the room, running within the walls and exploding out from the lamps. Their glass shades shattered, and blue sparks streamed from them like horizontal waterfalls.

Kess had to rush back as the lamp nearest to her exploded, and she came up against the glass with the back of her chair as the blue embers caught fire to the books they landed on.

Pulling the handle to the balcony door, it clicked easily, unlocked for the first time.

Kess rolled out backward, eyes on the burning, sparking room, and Kverra, striding toward her through the flames and smoke.

As the back of her chair hit the balustrade, Kess glanced behind and down.

That's a long drop. It was farther than she'd thought seeing it from inside.

Whispering under her breath, Kess said, "If I am worthy to ride a dragon, then I am unafraid to fall."

With gritted teeth and shaking arms, Kess pulled herself out of her chair to sit atop the balustrade.

Riony would jump.

And she had. When she'd jumped from the rising cage over the burning slaver camp, the drop had been farther. But Kess had been there, and without even knowing why she'd done it, she'd had Griskin stretch out the canvas of a tent to catch the foolish redhead's fall.

Kess smirked wryly at how much she had lied to herself all that time. She'd always known why, deep down. Why she kept going back, why she held her throws or missed her shots, why she kept doing what she could to keep Riony alive and in her life.

She could no longer deny it any more than she could deny the fall that awaited her.

And there was nobody waiting below on the hard stone of the paved courtyard to catch Kess.

A spike of panic froze her in place.

Then Lady Hjelzahn reached the balcony door and Kess leaned back and let herself topple from her ledge into the open air.

Air rushed around Kess, dragging at the skirts of her dress that fluttered around her. She turned and tumbled, and then the fall ended with the harsh crack of bone.

A wheezing scream burst from Kess. She breathed roughly through clenched teeth, her head swimming with agony. She tried to identify the pain, catalog it: in her chest, her wrist, her leg—the most. But also *everywhere*.

Kess cried out again as she pushed herself from her crumpled tangle onto her back and stared up at the thundering clouds above, triumphant.

Because pain meant she was alive.

Rain spotted all around her, growing heavier, and from the balcony far above, Lady Hjelzahn glared down.

Kess returned a toothy, bloody grin.

"Go on," she growled. "Follow me if you dare."

The Heir Killer turned and disappeared from sight.

"Coward."

But no doubt a coward that would be rapidly heading her way down a safer route.

Kess groaned as she brought herself up to a sitting position. She felt around her sore wrist with the other hand, where bruising was rapidly darkening. Sprained, but intact. Her ribs were tender to the touch, but she could breathe without any telltale spray of blood.

Her leg, she could tell it was broken at a glance.

But beyond the pain, she could move as well as usual.

Icy rain pelted over Kess, soaking quickly through her clothes. She'd been wearing her leather pants beneath her dresses every day as the weather had grown cooler, and she was glad for it as she pulled one of her blades and cut the tangled skirts of her dress off. She'd move much faster without dragging all that weight behind her.

She just hoped it would be fast enough.

Kess pushed hard, getting herself across the paving of the courtyard and in through the nearest entrance. It was a relief to be out of the storm, and Kess felt hot and cold all at once from exertion and feverish aches and frigid rain.

She left a trail of water in her wake as she slipped up the corridor, trying to get her bearings. The courtyard she'd thrown herself into wasn't the same they often passed through going to and from Eslinde's quarters, but it too led into the labyrinth of corridors marked by grand statues of heroes standing vigil in niches along each side.

At the next intersection, the sound of marching feet pulled Kess back. She flattened herself low to the ground, lying against the wall below the shadow of a tapestry as a troop of guards marched by.

Their eyes didn't turn from their path as they crossed hers.

When the corridor was empty again, Kess turned to look left and right to choose her path but couldn't recognize either as a better option. She leaned against the wall for a moment to catch her breath and her leg throbbed, pain robbing the air from her just as quickly as she caught it.

Trying to imagine the layout of the palace and where she was within it, Kess headed left. She had learned well how to navigate the burned wilds of the world, how to get her directions from the sky and landmarks and find her way.

But the corridors of the palace left her feeling lost in a maze. Every space was made of the same dark polished stone and gold accented carvings.

Around one more corner, Kess recognized the grizzled face and braided beard of the statue before her. One more intersection along and she'd be in the corridor Eslinde usually took to her chambers.

A guard stood watch up ahead.

Getting as close behind the man as she dared, Kess pulled a metal button from the collar of her dress and flung it down the opposite hallway.

The guard turned but didn't leave his post to investigate. Taking the next button down, Kess tried again, and this time the man meandered down to check on the noise.

Kess bit back a whimper as she pushed to cross the intersection as fast as she could. Her sprained wrist crumpled under her, and she screwed her face up against the pain and pressed on.

She'd just reached the shadows of the next hall along when the guard's footsteps returned behind her.

She glanced back to check, but the guard didn't look her way. She'd dried enough now that she wasn't leaving a telltale trail behind her.

Sweating and shaking, Kess made it around the final corner.

"Eslinde had better come back this way," Kess whispered to herself as she climbed up into the niche behind a statue of a glorious woman warrior with a thick mane of white marble hair.

Kess pulled her legs in tight to her body. She winced and tears prickled the corners of her eyes as she drew the broken one in. She felt faint and overwrought all at once.

Her hiding place wasn't perfect. If anyone paused to look at the statue she hid behind, she'd be obvious. But without knowing where the princess went, it was the best place she could hope to wait for her. She only hoped she hadn't missed Eslinde already.

Kess spent the next short passage of time doing her best to rest while not succumbing to unconsciousness, as a woozy agony built within her.

Then the mumble of low voices and footsteps approached.

Kess remained still and hidden, not daring to peek her head out to look. It was only when the people were directly in line with the niche that Kess could identify them.

"Eslinde! Here!" Kess hissed.

The princess, flanked by her grayglim, handmaidens Olva and Jillisa, and advisor Falden, stopped abruptly.

Falden blanched and pointed a crooked finger. "Fugitive!"

Clearly, he had been caught up on the events of the day.

Eslinde moved in front of him. "Kess? What under the sun?"

Kess hated how Eslinde looked disappointed in her, as though Kess hiding there was the result of her escape attempt gone wrong.

"Just listen," Kess snapped. "Lady Hjelzahn is the Heir Killer. She came to your room and has killed Ulfren and Hjelzahn the First."

Gasps rose from Falden and the handmaidens. Yensen took a step closer to the princess and placed a hand on his weapon.

"What? Why were they there?" Eslinde's expression remained shrewd.

Kess shook her head in response. She moved to the edge of the niche. Once in the light, Eslinde also gasped as she looked over Kess.

"You're hurt! Did she do this to you?"

Kess longed for the healing touch of silvernix, but they didn't have time to send for it from whatever stores Eslinde had access to. The hairs on Kess's neck bristled, imagining the murderous grayglim launching upon them at any second.

"I'm fine, I'll manage. But Lady Hjelzahn saw me escape. She knows I'm a witness. She was waiting to kill you too, but now she's probably more interested in getting me. Even more than before."

Eslinde's lips drew in and she nodded once. "Then we can't keep you here."

Falden sputtered, "How can we know any of this is true? The girl may be lying to escape the consequences of her actions."

"Will you go and check?" Eslinde asked her grayglim.

"I will not leave your side at this time, Your Highness." Yensen remained planted where he was, eyes flickering to the ends of the corridor on constant guard for approaching movement.

"Of course, it wouldn't be that easy." Eslinde tsked, then sighed. She stepped away from her grayglim, standing beside Kess, her back to the statue looming over her.

She didn't look to her grayglim, but rather her handmaidens and advisor as she said, "I am sure Kessara is speaking the truth. She's not nearly as good a liar as she thinks she is. Which means it's time to leave. For all of us."

"Your Highness?" the older handmaiden folded her hands together and drew up straight.

"Ulfren and Hjelzahn the First have both been killed. In my chambers. With only someone already convicted of terrible crimes as a witness. This is all going to come down on our heads." Eslinde gestured to Kess and herself.

Kess shook her head. "It doesn't need to. I only escaped to warn you. If I'm already taking the blame, perhaps I could—"

"No, Kessara. It's time. We're leaving. And I hope there are some loyal to me here that will assist us and remain by my side." Eslinde looked to Falden.

The elderly man took a step back and blinked glossy eyes. "Our king has made it clear you're to remain here under his eye, Your Highness."

Eslinde turned to her handmaidens.

The younger bowed silently, then stepped away.

Olva lifted her chin. "Her Majesty, your mother, will hear about this!"

Eslinde straightened up, but Kess could see the hurt in the crinkled tension around her eyes. "I'd feared one of you had been disloyal all along, but it seems it was all of you."

Reaching into the slit pocket of her gown, Eslinde drew her fine epee. "Well, Kessara, I had been hoping we'd have some assistance in escaping my grayglim, but it seems it's just you and me."

Kess tilted her head and drew in a long breath, steeling herself against her pain and the fight to come.

At least this grayglim seemed entirely human, but two versus one still weren't odds Kess would favor.

She drew a throwing knife into each hand as the grayglim drew his sword.

CHAPTER TWENTY-ONE

The rumble of thunder echoed ominously through the corridor and Yensen's approach was like a gathering storm, his gaze piercing and his movements calculated, sending a shiver down Kess's spine.

She adjusted her grip on the throwing knife in her uninjured hand. She didn't really want to kill the man. Perhaps she could pin him in his joints the way she did with revs, slow him enough to get away. Or perhaps there was still more that could be said to persuade him from the fight. Kess opened her mouth.

Before any words could be exchanged, Yensen halted, his steely gaze on Eslinde.

"Why would you assume we'd need to fight, Your Highness?" His voice was low, filled with a restrained intensity.

Eslinde's brow furrowed, her gaze flickering between Yensen and Kess. "I ... I thought ..."

Her words trailed off as Yensen's attention rounded abruptly onto the others in the corridor.

Falden's hands shot up in front of him, guarding from the sword now pointed his way. "What are you doing? What about the king's orders?"

Yensen circled around them, opening a side door as he kept his sword pointed at the trio. After a quick glance inside, he waved the sword threateningly at the advisor and handmaidens.

"In," he commanded.

Kess raised her eyebrows at Eslinde as Yensen herded the three of them into what appeared to be a small office. Eslinde shrugged in return.

Once Falden, Olva, and Jillisa were inside, the grayglim closed the door on them, then pulled a short strip of metal from a pouch at his belt and jammed it into the lock.

Outraged cries came from within, and thumps rattled the door, but it remained sealed.

"You ... aren't against me?" Eslinde's voice was barely above a whisper, and she kept her sword before her.

Yensen's gaze softened, a rare glimpse of vulnerability crossing his features before they hardened once more.

"My duty is to remain by your side and keep you safe, Your Highness," he declared, his voice unwavering. "And I will fulfill that duty for as long as it takes."

"Oh." Eslinde only seemed more confused, a blush of color over her cheeks.

"Sooo ..." Kess slipped her knives back into her sleeves. "Are you going to help us get out of here or not?"

A small smile lifted on the grayglim's lips. Sheathing his sword, he approached Kess, awaited her approval, and lifted her into his arms.

"Where to, Your Highness?" he asked Eslinde with a bowed head. "Carriages?"

The princess kept her sword drawn, her fingers white around the grip, a war of emotions on her face.

"Follow me," she said and swept back down the corridor at a swift pace.

After a few turns, Kess knew where Eslinde was leading them.

This is going to test Yensen's loyalty once and for all.

Kess wasn't sure she liked that she would be at the grayglim's mercy when that time came.

Cradled in his arms, Kess winced as the journey jostled her broken leg. Twice they needed to backtrack or hide while guards marched by, and once Eslinde stopped, heading into a side room where she rustled around for a moment, then emerged with a pile of dark fabric draped over one arm.

When they reached the small, bare room and Eslinde opened the secret door to the dungeons, Yensen stopped.

Kess could feel his tension in his hold on her.

"We should be leaving," he said, low and warning.

"I'm not leaving without them," Eslinde challenged in return.

The grayglim looked like he had more he wanted to say, but he only nodded and followed as Eslinde pressed on, down into the rough tunnel.

He's really going to help?

From where she was pressed against the man's chest, Kess looked up at his square jaw, twitching in the corners. She wondered at that level of loyalty. To follow someone into any danger, to do anything they asked, to give themselves completely to that person and their cause.

Clearly, Eslinde still had her doubts, which left Kess on edge as well. But after a lifetime of betrayals and abandonment, Kess *liked* the idea of that kind of loyalty, of giving oneself. She wanted it to be real.

Riony's voice filled her mind.

I know it might be a stupid dream, but maybe we can start making it real. We could start with the two of us.

And then all of Kess filled with the kind of *wanting* that she hadn't known in a long time, back when she would have burned the whole world down to have a dragon for herself.

Her eyes stung with the intensity of it, wetting at the corners in a way that had nothing to do with the physical pain she felt.

The steep tunnel was dark since they didn't have a lamp with them, but up ahead light glowed brightly.

In the guard station where they had encountered a single, sleepy sentinel on their last visit, now there stood a dozen, heavily armored and alert.

At Eslinde's approach, they shifted to form a barrier between them and the cells behind. Each wore the badge on their shoulder marked with a pointed crown.

"Turn away, Your Highness," a grizzled older woman said with a voice like grinding rocks.

All manners and manipulation were gone from Eslinde as she lifted her sword and replied, "Turn away yourself. I'm going to get what I came for, one way or another."

Yensen grunted softly, glancing side to side as though seeking somewhere to put Kess down.

Whispering up at him, Kess said, "I can maybe take three. How about you?"

"More. Not enough," he grumbled back. Then slightly louder to Eslinde, "There are too many."

"Yes," replied the lead guard. "Even with your grayglim, you aren't getting through. We won't have any part in your treason. We won't be punished for your actions again. The king knows all about your visits and has made it clear you're never to go in there again."

Eslinde relaxed her stance and sheathed her sword. "That's fine then. Because I'm not planning on going in. They are coming out."

The guard rolled her head back in a scoffing laugh.

And Eslinde yelled, "Yrik! It's time!"

A muffled voice replied, "We are ready. Stand back."

Eslinde smiled and stepped away.

"What are you planning?" The lead guard's eyes widened, and she barked to the man beside her, "Get in there and see what they're doing!"

The man fumbled his keys, rushing toward the steel gate behind him that led to the hallway of cells. He swung it open with a clang, and then the air erupted into a deafening explosion.

Air blasted out, filling the space with dust, and then sucked backward again, howling through the tunnel.

Kess's unbraided hair whipped around her face, and the wind pulled against her so strongly she felt she might be ripped from the grayglim's grip.

The solid door to the Alderkin's cell cracked off its hinges, crumpling up into itself and vanishing into the deep hole of darkness that had materialized there.

Guards scattered, knocked off their feet and clawing at the ground to keep from being pulled in themselves. An unlucky few lost their grip and went hurtling into that dark, whirling space, their screams cut short as they vanished.

A deep, primal fear filled Kess, and she clung tightly to the grayglim.

The Alderkin created this terrifying magic from a single, small crystal? Kess had heard stories of the brutal war between the Alderkin with their magic and the might of riders with their dragons. But now those stories seemed so much more vivid and horrifying.

The wind eased, and Yensen moved fast, placing Kess beside a wall, then moving through the messy crowd, knocking down any guard still on their feet.

Eslinde held tight to the opened gate, white hair flying around her face and a grim smile baring her teeth. "Quickly now!"

The dark magic ended as suddenly as it began, and the three Alderkin emerged from their broken cell. They looked worse off than beggars in ragged and soiled rags, their bright hair darkened with filth and bones showing prominently through tight skin.

But they moved with purpose and strength, running over the downed guards, only a few of which still had enough sense to try to reach grasping hands at their ankles.

Eslinde stomped those hands aside, then followed the Alderkin out of the room.

Yensen quickly picked up Kess again and gave her an assessing look when she moaned at the pain shooting through her.

"I'm fine, hurry!" she snapped.

He did, chasing Eslinde and the Alderkin back up the steep tunnel.

When they emerged back into the palace, Eslinde was handing each of the Alderkin one of the dark cloaks she had taken from a room earlier.

"It was the best we could do with the crystal you gave us. It was already runed with magic to heal and stop a hole from closing," Yrik said as he pulled the hood up over his bright blue hair and long ears.

"We added runes to make a bigger, more explosive hole. We haven't done something like that before. It's lucky it worked," Priyune added.

"I'd say it worked well enough," Kess said, still rattled by the effect.

"Indeed," Eslinde said, throwing the final cloak around her own shoulders. "Now we just have to get us all out of this palace and out of this keep."

Eslinde moved to the doorway, but a shout and clamor of heavy boots sent her hiding within again.

"Could they have heard what happened below?" Kess asked, angling to see who approached from her position in Yensen's arms.

A troop of guards rushed by the doorway, jogging two abreast, grim-faced and set on the path in front of them.

At the very back of the troop, a young man whispered to the guard at his side, "First Ylva, now two more?"

"Prepare for a rough few days. They're going to take this out on all of us," their friend replied.

Kess sucked in a breath. Once the guards were gone, she shared a look with Eslinde.

"How long until the whole palace is locked down?" Kess asked.

"Not long enough for us to make it to a flight deck." Eslinde took another glance out the doorway, then turned back to the others. "If they have found Ulfren and Hjelzahn dead, they'll secure those escape routes first. Let's try for a carriage. Then make our way to the Zarrams' and fly from there."

Eslinde moved to step out into the corridor, when another figure pressed in toward her, thrusting bare hands against Eslinde's shoulders.

"Mami?" Eslinde gasped.

"You undeserving troublemaker! Of course you're here! I knew it!" The queen screamed at the pitch of a whisper.

She scurried farther into the room, pressing Eslinde back with each step. No grayglim or guards followed the woman in, and she looked harried and enraged, a flowing robe thrown on over a crumpled nightgown.

"After everything I've done for you, to keep you out of trouble, and here you are again seeking it out." She pointed violently toward Kess and then to the three Alderkin.

"I'm doing what has to be done," Eslinde said, although her voice held none of its usual strength.

The queen laughed bitterly. "You've been a fool your whole life! What lies have these animals told you to turn you to their side?"

The next thrust against Eslinde didn't push her back, her stance and jaw set firm. "Don't speak to me of lies, Mother."

"Grayglim!" the queen shrieked. "Put *that* down and get these prisoners back in their cells, then maybe we can clean all this up before anyone else knows anything happened."

Kess opened her mouth to throw an insult back at the woman, but Yensen spoke over her.

"I'm not beholden to your orders, Your Majesty." He offered a mocking bow of his head, then turned to Eslinde. "Would you like me to do something about her?"

"No," Eslinde said. "She's my mother."

The princess's arm came up fast like a striking snake and her fist cracked against the queen's nose.

The woman fell flat on her back, blood streaming from her nostrils. She wailed pitifully, but Eslinde was already moving, stepping over her body and leading the way for the rest of them.

"Nice hit," Kess said.

Eslinde shook out her thin fingers. "Well, I am the troublemaker, after all."

They raced down one corridor and the next, Kess biting her lips closed against the pain the frantic pace cost her. Then they paused, backs pressed flat against a wall as more troops of soldiers ran by, a flurry of sun-yellow robes gathered within them, wailing and growling words of fury.

News of the first heirs' deaths was spreading fast, and people were taking it as well as Kess had thought they would. The fallout would be no doubt as murderous as the inciting act itself.

"Almost there," Eslinde called back as they turned another corner, went out through a diamond-cut glass door, and rushed across an open garden.

Rain smacked against them, and their feet splashed through building puddles. One of the Alderkin stumbled, blue hair spilling from under the hood. The two women by Yrik's side lifted him back up, breathing heavily.

They weren't in condition to be running so far. Even Kess, not having to run at all herself, felt on the verge of passing out as the shattered long bone in her shin twisted and jabbed into her muscles at each of the grayglim's steps.

Then they reached the carriage house, and inside, it was clear of guards. Clear of anybody, except for one figure, moving toward them.

Lady Hjelzahn.

Chapter Twenty-Two

Within the cavernous flight deck of Zarram Dragonhold, an oppressive silence hung heavy, broken by the patter of building rain and thunder from outside. A few servants moved around, glowering and wary as they worked to clear up the wreckage from the dragon's escape.

Dashiel paced, feeling a churning, hot sickness through their stomach. At least none of the dragonhold workers had been hurt, but there had been people down in the city who were injured and killed because Dashiel had chosen to untame a dragon and hadn't been able to keep it under control.

But the person they were most worried about at that moment was the young woman with the dark, lightning-streaked hair and even stormier eyes.

"We shouldn't have let Kess do that," they said.

Vance moved about Viska's stall, circling his golden dragon and checking for injuries. "It was her choice, and we're lucky for it."

The dragon had come away from the aerial chase with a few burns. More for Dashiel to feel guilt over.

Thankfully, Viska had been returned to Vance's ownership, and the Zarram family returned home together on the dragon. Lord Zarram had taken control of the flight and hadn't said a word to his children the whole way, simmering and stern. The moment they'd arrived, he'd stalked off, calling servants to his side and barking orders.

"But why? Why did she do it? This had nothing to do with her." Dashiel tugged at their blond curls.

Vance rubbed at a mark of soot on Viska's leg, then straightened up again. "Maybe she felt responsible, given her brother's sabotage."

Dashiel kicked at a splintered piece of wood left over from the dragon's escape. "If anything, that was my fault for making an enemy of him when I stopped him from strangling Kess."

"Sounds to me more like his fault for being an irredeemable asshole. But regardless, the reason why isn't important. We must honor her choice by making the best of what she gave us."

There had to be more reason to it than that. Politics and machinations Dashiel could guess at but not confirm. All they knew was that it didn't feel *right*.

"She gave us her *life*, Vance. She will never see freedom again. We can't just let that happen."

Vance folded his arms and growled. "We can and we will. What else are we to do? I'm not going to allow you to give your life instead, nor would you let me."

"No, but—"

"Should it be Eslinde, then? Who else could take the fall for all the damage that was done?"

"Why not the Heithorn brother? We should find him and make him answer for what he's done, make him take the blame." Dashiel turned a full circle, staring into the dark shadows between flickering oil lamps that lined the stone walls, suspicious that the man could still be lurking somewhere nearby.

"Dash, look at it logically. We barely know the girl—"

"And yet look what she has done for us, to save me from my mistake. Raze logic!"

"And yet," Vance echoed, "she is one person. If we are blamed for what happened, we risk losing all of this! The Zarram name would be ruined, and any chance of any other Rolanian becoming a dragonlord would become even worse. You know how they already hate us."

Dashiel knew well. As they had returned to their dragonhold from the palace, a swarm of protesters had been building in the streets around the Zarram property. Even with the blame officially on someone else, there would be repercussions from this, because it had been a Zarram dragon; it had been Dashiel and Vance who were first seen at the site of the devastation. And because the Taenish nobles and dragonlords hated them simply for who they were.

Vance's face softened. "Kess's sacrifice wasn't just for us, but for our father, all our family, for those we employ, for Eslinde, for Viska and Shiff. She will save us all."

Dashiel dropped down onto their haunches and put their face in their hands. "I feel like I'm going to be sick. I hate this. I hate all of it."

"Then perhaps you shouldn't have done what you've done!" Lord Zarram boomed, as loud as the thunder echoing in from the open end of the flight deck.

Dashiel shot back up to their feet.

Their father stalked forward, red-faced, eyes gleaming. He waved his arms and the few servants who had been milling about fled the area.

Lord Zarram came to a stop in front of Dashiel. His gaze flickered disapprovingly to Vance for a moment before returning his full wrath on Dashiel.

His lips curled as he said, "How did you do it? The red etherflame? How did it become wild?"

Vance gave Dashiel a warning look.

"It just ... did?" Dashiel shrugged.

"Don't test me!" Lord Zarram held up a piece of metal. "I've just been to the old flamesong stalls."

"You've been down there?" A shiver of fear rattled Dashiel's words.

Lord Zarram threw the metal at Dashiel's feet. The taming spike that had been pulled from the red dragon.

Dashiel tried to formulate an excuse. What could they say? That maybe the spike had fallen out on its own? But before they could speak, their father held up another smaller piece of metal.

"I have. And look what I found." Lord Zarram threw the shiny disc at Dashiel's chest. Dashiel caught it and held it in the flat of their hand. They swallowed hard.

The fake spike cap that had been hammered onto Shiff's forehead.

He knows. Dashiel looked at Vance in panic, and their brother stepped closer by their side.

Lord Zarram turned then, pacing before his children. "I went there straightaway because I had a terrible notion. I wanted to believe it was all a plot by that broken girl, but no. No. Don't think I hadn't noticed your sneaking around. But I never thought …"

Dashiel said, "Please, I can explain—"

Lord Zarram cut them off with a fiery scowl. "My own blood has betrayed me! Lying and keeping secrets. Refusing to tame their dragon as ordered! I should never have let you keep your dragonling separate from the others. I thought that would be all I found in the old stalls but instead I find two wild dragons kept within my dragonhold!"

"You didn't open the other stall, did you?" Dashiel gulped.

"And let loose a second dangerous beast upon the city? Of course not." Lord Zarram stopped pacing and pointed a finger at Dashiel. "What have you got locked up in there? Is it Eslinde's dragon?"

"It is, but Eslinde—" Dashiel tried to answer, their words lost beneath their father's tirade.

"I'd noticed the snowshimmer missing, but I thought you'd moved her for training or exercise. What a fool I've been. I cannot even trust my own offspring."

Lord Zarram rounded on Vance then. "You've been part of this too, haven't you?"

Vance didn't cower, only lifted his chin. "If you take a moment to listen, perhaps you will understand, for once, our reasons, rather than expecting your will to be followed without reason. Not everything in this world is profit and prestige. But you forgot all your values long ago."

Lord Zarram sputtered, "You dare?"

"Anything he did, he did to support me and try to keep things safe," Dashiel said, stepping between the two.

Throwing his hands up, Lord Zarram turned his back on them. "I can't trust either of you, not anymore. Not to help me run this place. To think I had hoped to hand over control … What am I going to do now? I have so much more work to do to manage this disaster."

Dashiel knew Vance had never really wanted to take over the dragonhold from their father, but after his accident, it was Vance's only option. Dashiel couldn't bear to see their brother lose that too.

"I'm sorry for what happened. But please don't let everything be ruined from this one mistake. It was me, alone, who untamed the red etherflame. And it wasn't violent, not until it was attacked."

"Like Eslinde's dragon, roaring and howling and scratching at the door, isn't violent?" Lord Zarram scoffed. "I'm going to have to dispose of it now, and how do I then explain to Eslinde the First that her dragon had to be killed?"

"You don't have to do that. It's not hurting anyone. I will look after it, please, Pabba,"

Dashiel said, reaching a hand for their father.

Lord Zarram pulled away. "You can't be trusted to deal with anything! You couldn't even do what had to be done in taming your own dragonling!"

Dashiel squeezed the fake spike cap in their fist. "You didn't do anything to Shiff, did you?"

"Not yet. Not yet. But that is my next stop. I'm going to get a spike and silvernix and tame that blasted beast myself, once and for all!" Lord Zarram lifted a hand and signaled back toward one of the entrances of the cavernous space. A group of guards emerged.

"You can't, please. Shiff isn't dangerous. She's clever and listens to me."

"For now, maybe. But when she's as big as the etherflame that rampaged through the city today? What then? How will you keep her controlled? That red dragon killed people today, Dashiel!"

The guards brought chains with them, and for a moment Dashiel wondered if the chains were for them. But instead, they approached Viska.

Vance stood firm, blocking the guards' way, but with another order from Lord Zarram, they stepped around him and began chaining the golden dragon.

Dashiel's breath came out in angry snorts, the guilt burned away by fury. "Of course, the red etherflame was angry! It had gone its whole life enslaved with a spike in its brain! Can't you see the cruelty of that? No, of course you can't. You can only see the profit it brings you."

"Wealth it brings our whole family. You're so spoiled you can't even see the privilege all my hard work has given you. Why do you think that girl took the blame for your mistakes? Because the king himself asked her to, for us, because of the respect he has for me."

Dashiel's mouth squeezed closed. Was that why? Was Kess pressured into it by the king himself?

Vance grumbled, "If the Dragon King was protecting anything, it was his own interests."

He stepped away from the guards shackling his dragon and spoke in a rough whisper. "He knows who untamed the dragon, and he also knows why. He knows that it's the taming of dragons that is causing the curse of the shadow dragon and that the curse could be removed by freeing them."

Lord Zarram took a step back, staring at his son as though he'd gone insane. "What is this nonsense? The curse is the fault of the Alderkin. Everybody knows that."

Vance laughed without any humor. "It's a lie. It's all lies, and Yeonard Draekhan has known for years. Eslinde herself told us so."

A flicker of uncertainty crossed Lord Zarram's eyes.

Dashiel seized upon it, pleading. "Consider if for even a moment that it is true, Pabba. What would you do? If freeing our dragons could stop even some of the curse, wouldn't it be the right thing to do so?"

Lord Zarram's face went even redder, head shaking as he looked from Vance to Dashiel. "It's not something we could do. We've too much invested in this. You expect me to throw it all away? We'd have nothing. We'd be beggars and slaves like every other

Rolanian in the keep."

Dashiel's voice rose. "Maybe we wouldn't need to be locked away in a dragonkeep if we could end the undead curse! If we could set an example, show other dragonlords ..."

"You're fools, both of you. If we lose our dragons, then we are weak, and weakness has no place in this world. If you cannot understand that, then you are no kin of mine."

The final locks clicked onto Viska, and one of the guards came over and handed the key to Lord Zarram. He put it away in a pocket. All uncertainty had left his face now, and he narrowed eyes upon Dashiel and Vance.

"You will have no access to your dragons until I decide so. No access to silvernix. You will not leave this dragonhold. You will not speak your treasonous lies to anyone. And Shiff will be tamed. Tonight."

With a flick of his chin, the guards formed up around Lord Zarram and they all turned and marched away.

Dashiel lunged to follow after their father, but Vance grabbed their arm, pulling them back.

"I can't let him hurt Shiff. Please!" Dashiel clutched Vance's arm in return, needing the support.

"We won't," Vance said in a whisper. "But there's no point arguing with him. It wasn't enough to save my leg; it won't be enough to save your dragon."

"I have to do something." Dashiel glared at the space their father had left in the room.

"And we will. He'll need to go and get silvernix. We can get to Shiff first." Vance squeezed his grip around Dashiel's arm and nodded.

Dashiel gave him a wavery smile. "Thank you. For everything. Although I know at least some of your choices have been made to please Eslinde rather than myself."

Vance grunted. "Don't push it or you're on your own."

Huffing a laugh, Dashiel nodded in return, and the two of them made a dash for the stairs.

The windows they passed by were lashed by rain. Outside, the storm had worsened. The wind howled like a vengeful spirit, driving the rain sideways with its force. Lightning rent the sky asunder with jagged streaks of white-hot fire.

On the streets below, the angry crowd had only grown larger, despite the drenching torrent. Flaming torches and lanterns sputtered against the deluge and shouts rang out in competition with the lightning.

One point of light caught Dashiel's attention. A runner, coming down the hill street from the palace. They reached the crowd and were engulfed within it, and a riotous roar was unleashed at whatever news the runner had brought.

Torches and weapons were lifted into the air, and for a moment Dashiel wondered if they had brought news of Kess's supposed guilt, that they were appeased and would now leave to their dry homes.

But instead, they seemed only more enraged, raising their weapons against the gates of the dragonhold.

"What's going on down there?" Dashiel muttered.

"I don't know. As long as it stays out there, though, we're okay," Vance replied.

They hustled fast down the rest of the steps, and as they moved through the ground floor to the next descent, a panicked servant was hurrying in the other direction, muttering under his breath.

Vance put out an arm, stopping the round, older man.

"What is it? Do you have some news?" he asked.

The man bobbed his pale face. "From the palace! A tragedy has struck. Two heirs have been found dead, slain by the fugitive who unleashed the wild dragon."

"Two heirs? Which ones?" Vance growled.

"Ulfren! Ulfren the First. The other, I don't know. First heirs, though. Both of them. That's what people are saying."

Vance released the man, who bowed, then ran on to share his gossip.

Dashiel's blood turned cold. Was that the same news the runner had brought the mob outside?

Two heirs dead.

Vance's chest heaved and his forehead twisted as he said, "Eslinde."

Dashiel's own chest constricted. "Kess."

Chapter Twenty-Three

There was no surprise in Lady Hjelzahn's expression at seeing the group that had arrived before her.

She must have known we were coming, tracked us here.

Kess looked around the carriage house. One carriage stood by the gate, already prepared with a treedart dragon ready to pull, but no sign of who it was prepared for. Not a single servant, driver, or guard to be seen. Had Lady Hjelzahn sent everyone away—or worse—to avoid any witnesses for what was about to happen?

With eyes as cold and dark as a lonely midnight, Lady Hjelzahn stared at Kess and Yensen holding her. Resting her hands on the hilts of her twin swords, the grayglim woman addressed Eslinde.

"Your Highness. Move away from Kessara Heithorn. She is a dangerous fugitive."

Eslinde reached a hand down into her pocket where she kept her sword concealed beneath her gown. "And as agreed with the king, she is under my custody tonight. She is well under my grayglim's control, and I don't require any other assistance."

Lady Hjelzahn seemed taken aback by that. Did she even know about the untamed dragon and judgment placed upon Kess for it? Perhaps she didn't and had simply taken the opportunity to remove two heirs when she'd seen them without any guards.

The unnatural woman shook her head. "She has murdered two first heirs."

Kess raised her eyebrows. "You're going to pin that on me? I'm just the perfect scapegoat for everyone today."

"No, I don't believe Kessara did that," Eslinde said forcefully. And then her voice softened and grew cunning. "But for my safety, being a first heir myself, let us pass so we can leave to a more secure location. We do not want to face the true killer tonight."

Eyes narrowed, Lady Hjelzahn looked over the group—the princess, the grayglim carrying Kess, and the three hooded figures—as though weighing the danger of each of them.

She took a step closer, blocking their path to the carriage. "I'm to assume then that you all know who the true killer is?"

"They don't know anything," Kess blurted. "You only want me."

Lady Hjelzahn wasn't even looking at her. She gave Yensen an assessing glance and then turned a gaze of utter, disgusted hatred toward Eslinde.

With a threateningly lazy shrug, Kverra Hjelzahn said, "It may be a challenge, but you aren't the only one I want."

One more step and Lady Hjelzahn was almost in striking range.

"Eslinde?" Yensen asked softly.

He changed his hold on Kess, and she feared he was about to hand her over to Lady

Hjelzahn.

"Do what you must," Eslinde gasped back, as the ring of twin swords being drawn echoed through the carriage house.

Then Kess was airborne, thrown out of Yensen's grasp. Her mouth went wide in a gasp and she braced to hit the ground, but instead collided with another warm chest, and arms wrapped her, catching her fall.

Kess's broken leg swung and hit hard against the new body, and she cried out, eyes blurring and dimming from the surge of pain. Through her blindness came the sounds of clashing steel, a flurry of blades singing and scraping against each other and clattering against dragon scale armor.

Blinking her eyes clear, Kess saw she was held by Eslinde herself, who circled around the battling grayglims toward the carriage.

Yensen held his ground against Kverra, driving her back to clear the path. She didn't seem concerned at all, relentlessly striking back with already bloodied blades.

Was that from Ulfren and Hjelzahn the First? It seemed too fresh for that. Yensen wasn't bleeding yet either, at least not for how much blood covered the swords.

"You're in pain," Eslinde whispered down to Kess, eyes staying on the battle.

"That's what happens when you jump from a balcony to get away from a murderous grayglim."

"Kess!" Eslinde gasped.

"Just worry about continuing to get away from Lady Hjelzahn."

"Yensen has her. He'll bring the killer down."

Kess could only hope so. The battle between Aishena and her mother hadn't been as fair. Aishena had some grayglim training but was far too young to have completed it nor be as experienced as Lady Hjelzahn. Perhaps a full-fledged grayglim would have a chance.

Yensen was getting some hits in already. But Kess could see they weren't slowing the strange woman down.

"We need to get to the carriage," Kess urged.

"Go, quick!" Eslinde hissed to the Alderkin, who made a dash toward the awaiting coach.

One split off to open the gate. A flash of bright-green hair identified Priyune.

Thunder cracked from the sky above at the same time as Yensen's sword met the gray scale mail on Kverra's chest. He sent her stumbling back, cutting into the vulnerable joints of her armor as she went.

"I told you he was good," Eslinde said, cheeks flushed.

Kess's lips pursed. "It's not going to be enough."

As Yensen slashed again, slicing a line into the leather connection of the armor on Kverra's elbow, it seemed to dawn on the grayglim what Kess had already seen. Lady Hjelzahn wasn't bleeding.

Her sword shot out toward his frowning face, and he turned away from it at the last moment. A thin line of scarlet bloomed on his cheek, and Kverra's advantage became all too clear.

Teeth bared, Yensen doubled his efforts, moving faster and striking harder than before.

He was expending all his energy on one brutal assault, and when his sword struck into a gap between Lady Hjelzahn's chest armor near her waist, his bared teeth turned into a victorious grin.

The grin faltered when his sword came away clean. "What under the sun …?"

A boot hit his chest, sending him floundering backward.

And Lady Hjelzahn turned her fury toward Kess and Eslinde.

Kess clutched her throwing knife, but her eyesight was still swimming as the woman raced toward them, long braid of hair swinging like a whip behind her. Neither of Eslinde's hands were free to draw her weapon either, although Kess doubted she'd be a more capable swordsperson than a grayglim.

Lady Hjelzahn brought both her swords into the air and twisted her body into a spin, bringing the blades toward the pair of women with a momentum that could slice clear through both of them.

Then a dark swish of fabric blocked Kess's view of her imminent death, and a woman cried out. A twang of snapping metal was followed by the clatter of a broken length of blade against the ground.

In a reprieve of stillness, the figure turned slowly around to Eslinde and Kess. Priyune, the green-haired Alderkin woman, stared over them, her large emerald eyes unfocused.

One of her clawed hands was raised, clasping Lady Hjelzahn's sword by the broken blade. But the jagged end of that blade was lodged in her shoulder.

She stumbled onto her hands and knees in a puddle of rain and blood-soaked fabric.

"No!' Eslinde screamed, and her grasp on Kess loosened, but she didn't drop her.

"Watch out!" Kess cried, as Lady Hjelzahn's remaining sword slashed their way.

It pulled back at the last moment as Yensen threw himself upon the woman, grappling her from behind.

"Go! Get out of here!" Yensen yelled.

Yrik and Shael rushed to Priyune's side, lifting her and carrying her into the carriage.

Eslinde hovered, and Kess understood her unwillingness to leave. Their chances of escape, of surviving whatever their next location would be, were so much lower without a grayglim with them.

Yensen wrestled the unyielding woman, holding her from behind as she struggled to get her arms free, both of them facing back toward Kess and Eslinde.

Kess squinted, focusing her wavering sight and then lifted her throwing knife.

Hold her still, just for a moment, she willed silently.

Kess sent her dagger flying, and it struck true, deep into Lady Hjelzahn's eye.

"Oh my," Eslinde gasped.

The murderous grayglim stilled, going limp in Yensen's grasp. He held her for a moment longer, as though wary of ruses, then angled around to see the cause.

Then he let the woman go and hurried to Eslinde's side, limping slightly.

But still as she was, Lady Hjelzahn didn't fall. She remained there, swaying on her feet.

And then she slowly lifted her head to glare at Kess through her now lonesome eye.

"*Oh my*," Eslinde said again.

"That's not going to stop her," Kess snapped. "It's time to go!"

"Get in." Yensen took Kess from Eslinde.

Eslinde climbed hurriedly into the carriage, and Yensen none-too-gently dropped Kess inside as well, before slamming the door.

The sounds of him climbing into the driver's seat came through the dark timber and metal of the carriage walls, and then they lurched into motion.

The interior was dark, lit only by the frequent bursts of lightning that brightened the world outside the windows. The three Alderkin sat along one bench, Yrik and Shael seeing to Priyune's bloody wound.

Eslinde sat along the other bench, and Kess lay on the floor between them.

The pain from her leg had her feeling shivery and feverish, so she remained there for a moment, lying on her back and catching her breath.

Eslinde turned to look out the back window for a long moment, and Kess worried that Lady Hjelzahn was there, chasing them down on foot. But the princess turned back with a relieved sigh.

"How is Priyune?" she asked, her fingers fidgeting with one of her earrings.

Yrik muttered in his deep, gravelly voice, "She will survive this. The bleeding has stopped."

The hood had fallen back from Priyune's head, her green hair vibrant in the flashes of lightning. She leaned back, her eyes closed, but a smile spread on her lips. "I feel no pain, for we are free."

Eslinde's smile in return was thin and flat. "We're not quite free yet. Not until we're on a dragon and out of this keep. And even then, with the deaths of two heirs and running off with father's prisoners and scapegoat ... well. We'll see."

Kess pressed a palm to her forehead, wanting to laugh and cry. "Have we just become the most wanted fugitives in Elundrae? Because I thought I was going to hold that honor on my own."

Eslinde leaned over her, looking down at Kess from her seat.

She tutted. "Only if you had fled when you had the chance. Why were you still in my chambers when Ulfren and Hjelzahn were killed there? You had time to leave. And on that, why under the sun were my brothers there?"

"They'd come in to poison you."

"Poison?" Eslinde pressed a hand to her chest, sitting back in her seat again. "And here I had been feeling sad for their loss! Poison? Why?"

"They thought you were going to be named the Dragon King's successor. Because of all the special treatment you get." Kess lifted herself up onto her elbows, slowly shifting into a sitting position while checking on the parts of her that ached.

Eslinde stared at Kess for a long moment before bursting into laughter. "Special treatment?"

Kess chuckled too, a laughter of relief taking over as she tried to get her words out, explaining their plot, how Kess had heard it all. "I really hope nobody investigating the crime scene decides to have a glass of water."

Eslinde wiped her eyes, her face a mix of mirth and anguish. She reached a hand for Kess to help pull her up onto the seat beside her.

"Lady Hjelzahn ... *What* was that woman?" Eslinde shivered, rubbing her bare arms against the cold of the stormy, late autumn night. "She didn't bleed, didn't die. How?"

"I wish I knew. It's a trick I'd like to pull sometimes." Kess stared at the window, almost opaque with the amount of rain pelting against it.

Yrik turned their way, face shadowed by the hood still covering his head. "The woman has been touched by the shadow curse. Infected and yet still alive. I've seen it once before, during the war. A fallen human, not quite alive, but not quite dead when the shadow dragon cried its dark magic. The man went mad, still in part themselves, but driven by the shadow dragon's command."

Kess could only shake her head, believing and yet not wanting to. "So that's how you get a fully trained, unstoppable grayglim who seeks the death of all Dragon King heirs."

"And those who know her goal," Eslinde added. "You told me she wanted to kill you, but the unstoppable part would have been nice to know."

The carriage rumbled, careening around a corner so fast it skidded, water splashing up around the windows.

Kess said, "I would have mentioned it before, but the last time I saw the woman get stabbed was in a dark cave in a mess of fighting, and I wasn't sure of what I witnessed. I'm pretty sure now."

Eslinde stared flatly at her. "She had a knife through her eye, Kessara, and she didn't fall. Yes, I'd say it's pretty sure there is something strange about her."

Kess edged one of her remaining two knives out from her sleeve and rubbed a thumb over it in appreciation. "I was a bit worried I'd lost my touch."

"I'm not sure if I'm glad or not that I gave you those knives, Kessara," she said. "You're rather terrifyingly good with them."

"I'm not giving them back," Kess said, sliding the knife away again.

The carriage hit a bump, and Kess's leg knocked against the bench seat hard enough that she whimpered.

Eslinde gave her a firm look. "What is it? We have time now, so stop deflecting."

"It's just broken, I can—"

"*Broken*? Kess!" Eslinde moved closer. "We can—"

The carriage shuddered to a halt so fast that Kess and Eslinde almost slid right off their bench seat.

There was still no visibility out the window, the rain even harder than before. A moment later the door was flung open, and Yensen stood there, soaked to the bone, water streaming down his face.

"The way is flooded, Your Highness. If we're going farther, we're going on foot," he said.

The princess nodded, checking with the Alderkin who nodded their readiness in return. "Take Kess," Eslinde ordered. "How far are we?"

"A couple of streets. We can take the narrower alleys," Yensen replied, lifting Kess into his arms and pulling her out of the carriage.

Brown water churned around his legs, almost knee-high. Eslinde lifted her gown, bundling the skirts in one arm as she climbed down into the rushing water.

While they were waiting for the Alderkin to emerge, another group of people splashed past, oil lamps flickering through the rain and weapons in their other hands.

"More unrest, even on a night like this?" Eslinde tsked.

She took the lead, wading as fast as possible through the water. The next street wasn't as flooded, and the group broke into a run. Up ahead, there was the group that had passed them before, oil lamps burning like red eyes in the dark.

They're going the same way. Kess's face pinched with worry.

Around one more corner, the familiar walls of the massive Zarram Dragonhold came into view. And at the base of those walls, hundreds of people swarmed, breaking anything that could be broken and pounding at the gates. There were no Rolanians that Kess could identify through the rain and darkness, but the large group of bright-yellow robed Sunblessed Monks were easy to spot.

Eslinde slowed. "I'm not sure we're going to be able to use the front door. Those people don't look happy."

The smaller group moving just ahead of them turned back then. Holding their oil lamps high, they muttered between themselves.

Although the Alderkin were disguised, Kess felt a cold chill at the realization of how recognizable she and Eslinde were. Far too recognizable.

If news had gotten out of the palace about Ulfren and Hjelzahn's deaths, of who was with them when they died ...

"That's her! The Heir Killer!" a man in yellow robes yelled.

Safe to say they know.

A score of men broke off from the larger group. With one look at Kess, they charged toward her, weapons held high.

CHAPTER TWENTY-FOUR

Eslinde took a step forward, in front of where Yensen held Kess and cried out toward the approaching rioters. "It wasn't her. You're mistaken."

Whether they didn't know who she was, too muddy and bedraggled to be seen as a princess, or they knew but didn't care, the mob didn't slow their aggressive advance.

"I don't think these tamebrains are going to listen," Kess said.

She wanted to laugh at them calling her the Heir Killer. She'd unwittingly stolen Lady Hjelzahn's infamy. But there was nothing funny about the murderous rage directed her way because of it.

The mob was halfway down the street toward them, sloshing through a deep stream of flooding water.

Eslinde retreated to Yensen and Kess's side. "Ulfren and his unblessed extremists! He'd had them all riled up already, and getting himself killed has gone and pushed them all right over the edge."

Kess blinked water from her eyes. "That, and a wild dragon destroying a city block, all of which I'm apparently guilty of."

Eslinde pointed to the larger mob, still hammering at the front gate. "Seems they're plenty angry at the Zarrams as well, regardless of your attempt to take the blame."

Yensen said, "We need to go. Find some other way out of Draekhanhelm."

Face grim, Eslinde shook her head. "We can get in the back of Zarram Dragonhold, through the livestock pens. This way."

She still had her skirts bundled in one arm and the tall leather boots beneath were dark from muddy water. She led them back along the street they had come, then turned and took them up a steep alleyway between the dragonhold walls and a neighboring estate.

Rain pattered down all around them, mixing with the cries of the rioters at their back, chasing them down. The wind gusting through the street sounded like the low howl of a wolf and Kess's heart ached.

Yensen kept a tight grip around Kess, pressing on with stern determination, but she could feel a limp in his gait, smell the sour tang of blood from his wounds. Yrik and Shael followed close behind Eslinde, supporting the third, injured Alderkin between them.

With half of their group already bleeding and broken, Kess didn't like their chances.

As they reached the peak of the hill, the stone walls gave way to a tall fence of solid iron bars. A gate of ornate wrought iron featuring the Zarram crest at the top already hung open.

Eslinde pushed it closed behind them, the metal whining and clanking.

"The lock's broken," she called through the rain.

"Here." Shael pointed to a heavy cart, loaded with sacks of animal feed.

She and Yrik rolled it across to block the gate, and then with a strong swipe of a clawed hand, Shael knocked the pin from the axel and the wheel slipped off, the loaded cart tipping to the side.

"Watch out!" Eslinde grabbed Shael, pulling her away from the gate.

A few of the rioters had reached them, arms stretching through the bars for the hooded Alderkin woman. She slipped just out of their fingers.

The mob yelled and pushed at the gate, but the barricade of broken cart and grain bags held firm. A couple began attempting to scale the barrier. One man threw a flaming torch at Kess through the fence. It landed in a puddle at Yensen's feet, fizzing and sputtering.

"Keep moving. Go!" he commanded.

Eslinde took the lead again, down through the path between the livestock pens.

The pungent scent of wet earth mingled with the sharp tang of animal musk. Bovin brayed, disturbed by the storm, churning the mud and muck beneath their hooves. It overflowed from the pens onto the path, squelching as the group ran down toward the dragonhold building.

The clamor and cries of fighting came back toward them.

Four men wearing rich leather armor, with strips of bright-yellow cloth tied around their upper arms, had a fifth man, a Rolanian wearing a guard uniform, pinned against the wall beside the dragonhold entrance. They each took turns beating the guard.

"Stop them," Eslinde gasped.

Kess's fingers twitched for her knives, but before she could draw them, Yensen handed her into Eslinde's waiting arms.

With a fluid grace, he darted forward, his sword gleaming in the faint light as he closed in on the rioters.

Only at the last moment did they notice his approach. They turned from the guard they'd been using as a punching bag, letting him drop to the ground behind them.

The first rioter lunged forward with a bright short sword. With a deft flick of his wrist, Yensen parried the blow and delivered a swift strike to the man's jaw. The rioter crumpled to the muddy earth.

Without missing a beat, Yensen spun to strike the next man, knocking the hilt of his sword against the assailant's temple, sending him stumbling backward into the third. They collapsed together into a heap, and Yensen followed through, skewering his blade through both their torsos in a single motion.

The final man, faced with the fury and prowess of a grayglim warden, made the smartest choice of the lot of them and ran. He vaulted over a pen fence and disappeared amongst the bovin.

Kess had to admit, Yensen was good at what he did.

Eslinde took slow, heavy steps as she carried Kess closer. "Is the guard—?"

"Dead." Yensen shook his head.

"Inside then, quick!" Eslinde didn't hand Kess back and marched determinedly through the open entrance of the dragonhold. Once they were all through, Yensen closed and barred the solid gate behind them.

Inside the vestibule, the world quieted. The relief from not being directly under the relentless hammering of rain and thunder left Kess feeling deaf and numb. Her torn dress and leather pants were soaked through from the icy rain, and she shivered in a way she couldn't stop.

Only a small circular grate in the ceiling allowed a thin stream of lightning-highlighted rain in. They all stood around the edges of the chamber, avoiding the running water, but unable to progress farther in. A second solid steel door blocked their way.

"How do we get that open?" Kess asked.

"Over here," Eslinde headed to a large crank jutting from the stone wall.

An empty chair sat beside it, with a tipped over flagon leaking a still steaming drink onto the paved floor.

Yensen turned the crank, and the heavy gate raised slowly into the ceiling above, screeching all the way.

Once it was up high enough for them to pass under, the Alderkin stepped through to the other side, looking about warily.

"Let me carry Kessara again," Yensen said, and let go of the handle.

The steel door came slamming down at an alarming speed. Yrik cried out, jumping out of the way only just in time.

Like the ringing of a gong, the sound of the fallen gate echoed through the small space.

Eslinde startled, shaking Kess and sending a jolt of pain up through her broken leg. She gritted her teeth and groaned.

"Sorry," Eslinde said, then placed Kess gently down onto the chair, as though worried she'd hurt her again.

Then she yelled toward the closed gate. "Is everyone unhurt?"

Muffled murmurings from the three Alderkin on the other side came back through.

Sighing, Eslinde turned to Yensen. "What happened?"

"I don't know," Yensen replied.

He turned the crank again, and the gate rose as it had before. He let it up only a small gap this time before releasing the handle, and it slammed closed again.

"It only stays open with someone on the crank. Is that a security mechanism?" Kess asked, thinking of the dead guard outside and the empty seat she had taken.

Eslinde turned from the door to the crank, squinting at both. Her silver hair had fallen loose from the bun and was plastered to her head and cheeks with water. "I don't think so. It wasn't this way before. It must be broken. Is there a way to open it from the other side?"

Yrik's voice came through the steel door. "There's a crank, but it does nothing."

A cold, still calmness settled inside Kess beneath her shivering skin.

She asked Yensen, "Do you think you can get through after letting it go?"

"Not even I'm that fast," he replied.

Kess nodded as she looked at the distance, expecting the answer. The crank was all the way across the room, and the steel gate came slamming down as fast as a guillotine. Even if she had Griskin, she didn't think she'd make it through without being crushed.

"Someone has to stay behind," Kess said. "Someone needs to keep the gate open for everyone else."

Eslinde's face turned ashy. Her voice wavered and she said softly, "Yensen?"

"No," both Yensen and Kess replied together.

"No," Kess said again. "You'll need him."

After seeing the grayglim in action, Kess knew he was the group's best defense against any other threats they might face.

"Then I'll stay behind," Eslinde said, lifting her chin. "Whatever punishment will come will be lesser for me, as a First. I will stay and see it through."

Kess laughed wryly at the princess's foolish bravery. "No, you won't. For starters, good luck getting your grayglim behind the plan. And secondly, you're the princess, someone who people might listen to, to start fixing this blighted world. We can't risk losing you. Also, you're Lyrrin's mother, and saving you is at least a small part of the debt I owe."

Eslinde tilted her head, eyes watering. "Then ..."

Kess leaned away from her, pressing into the back of the chair and shrugging as nonchalantly as she could. "I'm staying. Obviously. You need Yensen, and the Alderkin all have to be freed as well. I'm the only one here who doesn't matter. It was clear when I took the blame for the Zarram siblings, and it's clear now."

"No." There was no command in Eslinde's voice, only a pained plea.

"It's our best option, Your Highness," Yensen said softly.

He gave Kess a single nod of appreciation and began urging Eslinde toward the closed gate.

"No!" Eslinde said more forcefully. She pushed past the grayglim and knelt on the ground before where Kess sat. "Kessara, you do matter. Please believe that. You've mattered to me. So much."

A loud thump came from the exterior door, startling them both. The shouts of the angry mob followed. *They've made it through.*

Kess turned back to the princess. "I can matter by saving you. Now get out of here!"

Eslinde's face scrunched up, pushing a tear from her glossy eyes. She reached for one of her earrings, tugging it free. Holding it out, she placed the skin-warmed silver into Kess's palm.

"For your leg, or anything else you need it for. To help you survive. Please survive, Kess."

Yensen returned to Eslinde, grabbing her by the arm and lifting her back to her feet, getting her moving.

Kess looked at the earring in her hand. The long, spiraling design ended in a small cap that unscrewed. A tiny vial. Kess didn't have to open it to know what it contained.

Eslinde has been keeping an emergency supply of silvernix on her this whole time.

Tucking the precious treasure away in a pocket, Kess leaned across and grasped the handle for the gate. She began turning, putting her whole body into cranking the gate open from her seated position.

"I'll see you again soon," Eslinde called back as they stepped through the opened gate, joining the Alderkin on the other side.

Her voice was scratchy, the strain of impossible hope pulling it so taut the sound brought tears to Kess's eyes.

"Sure. See you soon." Kess smiled, and let the handle go, slamming the solid gate closed between them.

Kess took a moment to inhale a long, deep breath to settle herself for the end.

The mob outside had grown louder and larger, hammering at the barred exterior gate.

And Kess was alone, with two knives and one vial of silvernix.

She considered using it then. Her whole body was ragged with pain and without a sustained effort of willpower, the tug of unconsciousness was an ever-present threat.

But whether or not she had a broken leg would mean nothing when the angry rioters got through that door. Maybe it would mean she could down three of them rather than two before she died herself, but Kess never doubted the end result.

She'd always expected, or even hoped, she would die gloriously in combat upon the back of her dragon.

I suppose this is as honorable of a death as I deserve.

But still, she found that she really didn't want to go. She didn't feel ready.

She would never know whether Riony was still alive. She wouldn't know whether Eslinde would find her way to Lyrrin. Whether Riony would be grateful for Kess's part in that. Whether that would be enough for Riony to ever think of Kess as anything other than a source of cruelty in her life.

The cacophony of voices outside rose louder. The tone changed, from righteous anger to incensed outrage. The clamor of weapon against weapon followed.

Kess stilled, listening closer.

Are they fighting amongst themselves? Or fighting someone else.

As the voices dwindled—downed or fled, Kess didn't know—it was clear the mob was up against an opponent that could easily dispatch a whole crowd.

Even Kess's slim hopes of survival dropped away.

An opponent like an unstoppable grayglim, determined to destroy her targets.

The sounds of fighting outside ceased, and Kess slipped off the chair, pressing back along the wall into the darkest corner of the room, praying for the sun's blessing that whoever had cleared away the rioters outside would leave again.

Then the exterior gate shuddered and clanged with the force of a heavy blow.

And then another. And another.

The hinges of the gate rattled and bent as the gate was pounded with the force of a battering ram. With each earthquaking strike, Kess drew and held a breath, expecting it to be her last.

Her fingers traced her collarbone, looping around the string of leather there and drawing out the acorn pendant. She clutched it tight in her fist.

And the door groaned, hinges snapping as it was beaten free. The slab of metal slammed down flat at Kess's feet, and she turned to face her death.

CHAPTER TWENTY-FIVE

"You don't think Eslinde was one of the two heirs that was found ..." Vance's eyes were dark under low eyebrows, and his shoulders rose and fell with strained breaths.

Dashiel shook their head, even though they couldn't be sure. Two first heirs dead and the blame on Kess. They didn't believe that part but knew it would be easy for others to believe, especially after the guilt Kess had already claimed that day.

Whoever had died and how, it was going to mean trouble.

No wonder the people outside are riled up.

Ulfren wasn't just one of the first heirs, he was first in line for the throne. Nobody really expected the Dragon King to pass it along anytime soon, but Ulfren's murder would cause chaos.

If all that blame was going to land on Kess, what would happen to her? Would she even make it to a prison?

Lightning flashed in through a window. The storm raged, rain sheeting the sky.

Vance looked back up the way they'd come from the flight deck. "If we could get to the palace ..."

Dashiel's eyebrows rose. "The palace will be locked down. Going to charge your way through the grayglims and castle guards to see if Eslinde is okay?"

Vance grunted. "Maybe."

Dashiel placed a hand on their brother's shoulder, turning him around again. "We don't even have a way to get there. Not with the mob outside. Not without stealing a dragon. And I think we're already in enough trouble."

Vance's shoulders slumped. "Look at you, being the voice of reason for once."

"I know. Wild, right? Listen, I'm worried about Kess and Eslinde too. But right now, I'm thinking about the other trouble we're about to get into. I need to stop my dragon being tamed."

"Right. Yes." Vance got moving again, hurrying down the long corridor.

"But that also leaves us with the question of what we do after we save Shiff." Dashiel caught up to their brother, stomach churning as they watched the stern angles of his face. "I think maybe you shouldn't have any part of this. Pabba is angry now. I don't know if he's going to forgive the person who directly defies him again."

Vance's uneven pace slowed and then resumed again. "I've found, in recent years, I'm less interested in that man's favor or forgiveness."

Along the corridor, portraits of the Zarram family hung. Their father, regal and imposing, in every one. A few showed their sisters—married away in trade deals—and their mother, who had died during Dashiel's birth, refused silvernix even in the late stage lest her baby be born physically different.

The wealth the Zarrams had accumulated over the years hadn't kept their family either happy or whole, but Dashiel didn't know any life besides this and hated thinking he was dragging his brother away from the protection of their wealth too.

"If you help me, he might cut you out of the business entirely. You'd be losing all of this."

"Oh no, Dash. Don't make me choose between paperwork or my sibling." Vance smirked. "Besides, isn't our end goal to free all the dragons? I'd be losing it all anyway. And it would be worth it."

A world without the shadow dragon. Could it really be possible? Dashiel hoped it was and that it would be worth it. But they had already seen the consequences of taking steps down that path and how many people would stand against them.

Dashiel released a long breath and clutched at their stomach. "Did I mention how much I hate all of this?"

"I can't imagine it's going to get much better anytime soon."

They reached the old stairwell down into the underground flamesong stalls. Rivulets of water trickled down them, coming in from leaks in the old building.

Vance gave Dashiel a wry, assessing glance. "Besides, if I don't go with you, what will you do?"

"Might be time to put that run-away-and-live-in-the-wilds plan into action after all? Shiff is older now. Bigger. It could work."

Vance huffed. "You haven't really thought about it, have you?"

"No. Kind of. I did wonder whether I could let Pabba go through with it. Let him tame Shiff, let things settle down, and then find a chance to reverse it later on. But what trauma would that leave Shiff with? What if she became angry and volatile like the other dragons we untamed and I lost her forever? I don't think it's worth it."

"Even if you lose everything else?" Vance leaned forward and rubbed his amputated leg before heading down the steps. The older, more functional section of the keep didn't have glass on all the windows, and the chill of the storm blew in. Torches guttered and flickered in niches along the wall.

"Says the person ready to be a one-man army against the palace to check in on his 'old friend.'" Dashiel smirked. "I only know I have to get Shiff somewhere safe, then deal with the consequences later."

At the bottom of the stairs, Dashiel paused for a moment and let all the thoughts and worries and fears inside them settle beneath the truth that had been picking at the edges of their mind. Vance stopped too, waiting.

Dashiel lifted their hands, looking at the palms, then clenching them into fists.

"I don't think I can stay here any longer, anyway. Pretending everything is fine, knowing what we now know. How can we continue on with our lives, continue letting our father and the other dragonlords destroy the world one dragon at a time?"

Vance's jaw worked. "No, I don't think I can either. I'm with you."

They held each other's stare for a moment, then without another word moved on together again. They passed by the stall that held Eslinde's dragon, first in the row.

Dashiel wondered if they should free it too, but it was too risky. Dashiel ached at the thought of the lives that had been lost in the city that day, no matter where the blame lay. They couldn't set another angry dragon loose.

And the snowshimmer seemed angrier than ever. She roared and scratched against the solid door in a wild rage. Disturbed by the storm or something else, Dashiel wasn't sure.

Until they felt Shiff's fear as well.

Captured! Need help!

Breaking into a run, Dashiel reached Shiff's stall. The door was open, and a guard stood in the threshold.

Behind him, the small dragon lay on the ground, a chain clasped about her neck and a muzzle strapped around her snout.

"I'm here, Shiff," Dashiel gasped out the words.

"You can't go in." The guard squared up in the doorway. He had a face like a lump of sandstone and arms limbs like gnarled logs.

Shiff got to her feet, moving forward, but was brought up short by the chain.

Captor has chained me. Chains tight! Anger edged in on the fear now that Dashiel was with her again.

"I'm sorry," Dashiel said to her, then turned on the guard. "Let her go. She's too small to cause trouble, and the chains are hurting her."

The guard pulled himself up straighter, rolling his shoulders in a way that made him seem to double in size. "I'm under orders from your father. Nobody touches the dragon until he returns to tame it."

Putting on their most threatening tone, Dashiel said, "Move out of my way."

The guard sniffed lazily and drew a wide short sword.

Dashiel reached for their belt. From the point of untaming the red etherflame, through its escape, to returning home, they hadn't had a chance to arm themselves with a sword.

All they had was the small push dagger they normally kept on them. Hardly longer than the palm of a hand, it was useful for scaring off bullies. Not so much in a sword fight. They drew it anyway.

"I guess we're doing this." Vance grunted and lifted both fists up in front of his chest.

Death to the captor. Shiff's chains rattled as she bucked to join the fight.

"Easy" Dashiel said, both to her and the guard. "You aren't going to skewer Lord Zarram's heirs, are you?"

The guard took a step backward, herded by the approaching siblings. "Just stay back and you won't have to find out."

"It's two against one."

"But I'm the only one with a weapon. A real one, anyway." The guard gave the sword a casual swirl, lip twitching. But still, he stepped back again, unsure.

"We don't need weapons." Dashiel took a long, bold step forward into the guard's space.

The guard startled, backing up again.

Shiff growled through the muzzle.

"Because we have a dragon," Dashiel said.

Shiff pounced. The guard, now within reach of the chain, went down face-first into a puddle as the small dragon collided with his back. He cried out, screaming as her talons dug in.

"Don't kill him," Dashiel told her, as a spike of emotion disconcertingly like bloodlust and vengeance swept over them.

Why? The pale blue and purple dragon stilled, but their thoughts were a violent challenge.

"He's only following orders. And you'll just make people think those orders were justified if he dies." As much as Dashiel sympathized with the desire to extract revenge.

Vance knelt on one knee beside the guard and pinned him down.

Pain to the captor, then.

Shiff tensed her claws one more time before very begrudgingly removing them from the man's flesh and stepping away with the rattle of chains.

The guard groaned as Dashiel patted him down until they found a key in his pocket.

"Come here." They beckoned to Shiff, and the dragon moved closer, still growling and sulky.

Dashiel pulled the muzzle off, cutting the straps with the dagger, and then unlocked the padlock holding the collared chain around the dragon's neck.

Shiff shook herself from snout to barbed tail.

Freedom! the young dragon seemed to bellow in Dashiel's mind.

"We're not quite free yet. Come on." Dashiel reached a hand for Vance, helping him back up.

The guard cursed and groaned but didn't get up as the three moved away at a jog.

They were out of the old section and moving into the main building when another group of five people ran their way down the corridor.

Dashiel still held their dagger in hand, and their fingers clenched around it.

"Vance! Dashiel!" a woman's voice, high and regal, called out.

"Eslinde?" Vance picked up his pace, running with a swaying gait. "What are you doing here? What happened at the palace?"

They met at the intersection of the hallway and stairs. Eslinde reached both hands for Vance as he drew close, and he grasped them in his.

"Too much to tell right now. We need to get out of the city. Most especially the three people I have with me here. Can you help us? Can you give us a dragon?"

"And you? Are you leaving too?" Vance asked.

Eslinde tilted her head. "Yes. I can't go back. This is my chance to be free."

Dashiel caught up. They took in how wet and muddy the princess and her grayglim were. The three people with them were tall and draped in dark, hooded cloaks that obscured most of their features. Bright eyes sparkled out from the shadows.

They seemed wary of Shiff at first, and when the young dragon moved naturally, coming to sniff at the hems of their robes, they muttered between themselves.

Dashiel looked behind them, down the corridor, hoping for one more addition to the group.

"Where's Kess?" they asked.

Eslinde's face scrunched, then drew out long. "We had to go in through the back gate. The guard there had been killed by the mob, and Kess ... she stayed to hold the gate for us."

"She's down there? Now?"

Eslinde nodded. "We went through only moments ago. But ..."

"Then we need to go and get her," Dashiel said.

"We couldn't get the gate open from the other side."

Dashiel wiped the sweat from their forehead and prepared to run again. "There's a trick to it, but it can be done. We'll go and get her, and then we'll all get out of here together."

A loud crash punctuated their final word, and a roaring cheer of screams came from the direction of the main entrance. A percussion of stomping feet and smashing objects followed.

"They're inside," Eslinde gasped.

Flickers of torch flame and long shadows emerged at the end of the hallway Eslinde had just come down. The way that also led to the broken vestibule gate.

"There are too many of them. We won't be able to get through," Vance said in a growl.

"Then how do we get to Kess?" Dashiel asked, but they already knew the answer.

"We have to get to the flight deck. We have to get out of here. I'm sorry." Vance grasped Dashiel's shoulder, turning them toward the stairs on the other side.

The first rioter stepped into sight at the end of the corridor, yelling a hunting cry at the sight of their prey. A clamor of footsteps followed.

Vance reached for Eslinde, but the grayglim stepped between them, helping her race up the stairs. Vance grunted and jogged after. Dashiel hesitated another moment, as the rioters charged down the corridor and Eslinde's three companions went up the stairs.

Burn and claw? Shiff asked almost gleefully as she watched the approaching mob.

"No. Run. Quick." The words dropped mournfully from Dashiel's lips. They turned and bolted up the stairs toward the flight deck with the dragon at their heels.

As the group spilled out of the stairwell and into the cavernous space, the booming voice of Lord Zarram competed with the storm drumming through from outside.

He stood in the center of the space, all remaining guards of Zarram Dragonhold around him. He barked orders, splitting them off into groups that went running one way and another to deal with the invasion.

"What is this?" he roared as the siblings and followers ran in.

"Princess Eslinde came to us for safety and needs a way out. We need Viska. Give us the key to my dragon." Vance stopped before the man, holding his hand out.

Lord Zarram stepped back. "You cannot trick me into treason. I know the Dragon King has a rule about how and when the princess is allowed to fly."

"Can't you hear what's going on? The rioters are in the dragonhold. We have to leave."

Dashiel held their father's gaze, pleading. "Come with us. It's not safe here."

Lord Zarram scoffed, chest shaking into a laugh. "Not safe? Our guards will have it all under control soon enough. I won't leave everything I've ever worked for because a few idiots kicked our door in."

Vance raised his voice. "Haven't you seen how many there are? They will overwhelm our guards in no time. You've only sent those men to their deaths."

"If there are so many, then the Dragon King will send assistance. He will assure our protection."

"I doubt it," Eslinde said. "If he were going to, he would have already. You raise fine dragons, my lord, but there are plenty of other dragon breeders he will happily turn his favor to."

Lord Zarram's cheeks turned red and his head shook violently. He backed away from their group, glaring at the dragonling skulking at Dashiel's heels. "I will not leave. And I will give you no key. Help will come!"

"Pabba," Dashiel called out.

With a narrow-eyed glare at the Rolanian word, Lord Zarram turned and stepped into a side room, and the loud click of the door locking behind him echoed out.

"Raze it," Vance growled. "I don't think he chained the other dragons, but I really didn't want to leave without mine."

"Show me the chains," one of the robed figures spoke. A woman, with a deep, musical voice.

"Over here," Vance said, frowning but leading the way.

At Viska's stall, the golden dragon waited in vegetative stillness. The robed figure stepped up to the dragon without hesitation and grasped the chain. The hand that reached out of the robe was tinged a pale, icy blue, and the fingertips ended in dagger-sharp points.

Dashiel shared a wary glance with their brother, but no explanations were offered.

The woman reached those sharp fingertips between the links of the chain, squeezed, and pulled. There was a screech of tearing steel as the chain link cut and snapped against the woman's strange hands.

And Viska was freed.

"No time to saddle her. Will you manage?" Vance asked.

"I'll be fine. I'm not sure about my friends," Eslinde replied.

"Not once in our long lives have we ridden one of these great beasts," a deep, gravelly voice replied.

Dashiel turned on the spot, checking the other stalls. "The orange etherdart there is saddled for multiple travelers. I can take them and Shiff on it. You take Eslinde and her grayglim."

With nods of agreement, the group split off, mounting the dragons.

Vance pushed Viska out of her stall first, golden scales flashing. Dashiel took a longer moment, helping the three strangers onto the dragon's back and getting Shiff into a secure position.

Own wings should fly, Shiff thought petulantly.

"You're not quite there yet. We need to be fast and travel far," Dashiel said, then commanded the orange etherdart out of the stall.

The rain hit hard as they swept into the air from the end of the flight deck.

Viska circled above, only a little over the dragonhold rooftop parade grounds. Dashiel brought the etherflame in front of Viska and yelled over the rain, "I'm going to check the back gate!"

Vance signaled back an affirmative, and Dashiel curved their flight path down and around the building. Rain poured over the walls and out of dragon skull-shaped spouts like waterfalls. Bovin in the livestock pens bleated and moaned.

Dashiel couldn't get too low, but they could still see enough.

Exactly what they didn't want to see. The exterior gate had been broken through.

A few bodies lay outside it. Perhaps Kess had fought back. Or maybe the guard there had. Dashiel wasn't sure. But there had been rioters there, and they had gotten in to where Kess had been trapped, alone.

Dashiel's fingers felt numb and their heart cold as they brought the orange dragon back up beside Viska.

Eslinde covered her face in her hands as Dashiel reported back with a silent shake of his head.

"Dragons, rising from the palace," the grayglim yelled.

Vance caught Dashiel's eye and signaled for them to follow.

Dashiel nodded back, grateful that the soaking rain hid the tears running down their cheeks.

Viska took off at speed, a golden streak through the glistening rain, and Dashiel followed, flying away from their home and all they'd ever known.

CHAPTER TWENTY-SIX

Lightning flashed through the open, destroyed doorway. Purple radiance filled the vestibule, and Kess squinted into it, seeing the monstrous figure there, holding a glowing blade.

"*PONY?*" The word squealed from Kess's mouth.

Shaking rain from her red hair, Riony stepped into the shelter of the room, stomping over the fallen door.

"Sparks. I thought I'd regret this, but I didn't realize I'd regret it quite so quickly."

Kess clasped a hand over her own mouth at the slipup, the name Riony hated. She'd promised never to use it again, swore it to what she thought was a ghost. Now, she wondered if somehow her mind had broken again, seeing the woman impossibly standing before her.

"I'm sorry. I'm ... what ... how ... *HOW?*"

"We came to find you, you dumb gremlin." Riony hoisted her huge Alderkin sword and rested it on her shoulder.

It clinked against the shoulder guard. She wore an almost complete suit of mismatched plate armor, glistening from the raindrops dripping off it. Only her upper arms were bare.

"We?" Kess's other hand remained clamped around the acorn at her neck, and her body trembled.

From behind Riony, Griskin padded forward out of the stormy night.

He sniffed at Kess, whined, and then shook the water from his coat. It rainbowed in the glow of Riony's sword, and then the wolf jumped in one swift leap to Kess's side.

"Gris?" Kess's voice was strained and high, unbelieving as her wolf licked at her cheek.

She wrapped her arms up around his neck, the fur wet but warm. A choked, laughing sob escaped her throat and her fingers shook.

Turning back to Riony, Kess gaped. "Am I dreaming?"

"Ew, gross. Don't make this more awkward than it is by suggesting that you dream about me." Riony wiped the water dripping off her chin with the back of a hand. "I know I must be looking unrealistically hot right now, but I am real, and so is the wet pup. You can't dream a smell like that."

Kess's face scrunched up in painful relief and confusion. She pressed her forehead to Griskin's and held him in a grip that denied any prospect of ever letting go again.

He lowered himself down onto the muddy floor beside her and panted joyfully. He still had her saddle and bags strapped on, and she checked the buckles, making sure they weren't rubbing against him badly. The soft touch of the leather and earthy scent of the wolf's fur felt like home.

All Kess's pains were forgotten, and her head was light and woozy from a rush of emotions.

"You ... came to save me?"

Riony lifted her sword again and gestured at Kess with it. "Who says this is a rescue mission? Maybe I followed your hairy mutt to find you for revenge. You left me hanging after I was all emotionally vulnerable, and it hurt my feelings."

Kess stared at the ridiculous woman and her heart ached. "That's what you'd seek vengeance for? Not for being stabbed in the back?"

Riony shrugged. "What's a knife in the back between traitorous acquaintances?"

Words burst from Kess in a pleading rush, and she leaned forward, drawn toward Riony with the intensity of them. "It wasn't me. Please, I need you to know it wasn't me who did that to you. It was Kife."

"Yeah. I kind of figured." Riony's eyes flickered down to the acorn at Kess's neck, and she frowned. "If it was you, you wouldn't have missed my heart."

The words reverberated in the space as though taking up all the air, and for a moment, Kess couldn't breathe. Tears and wonder and confusion warred through her, and she could almost smell the morass mercy again, scared she'd never left her nightmare-filled cell and everything, everything had all been a dream.

And if it was, she'd welcome it for this moment. To have Riony back.

Then Riony continued yammering, big mouth filling the void in a way that also held the yearning ache of home and felt so real.

"Of course, I had a dagger in my back so what could I know? I was never really sure what happened: why I got shanked, where you went, why you weren't appearing around every dark corner to steal Dracuni. Unsolvable mysteries everywhere."

Riony kicked at the fallen door, scowling at the rain blowing in onto her back. She moved farther into the space, not really looking at Kess as she spoke. Turned to the side, a dark pattern was visible on one of her biceps.

A tattoo?

"But then the wolf showed up. Alone. Clearly trying to get me to follow and help. That's when I put the pieces together. Realized the only other person who'd have fun playing backstabbing games who was there that day, and I figured Kife had taken you away and ..." In the soft purple glow, Riony's cheeks darkened. "I didn't like the idea of that."

She cleared her throat. "Plus, when a wolf comes to you for help, you don't turn it down."

"So ... you did come to save me?" Kess confirmed, uncertain.

Riony winced and rubbed her temple. "Do we have to say it out loud?"

She hates me. She clearly still hates me, but she came to save me anyway. Kess stared up at Riony over Griskin's shaggy fur. She stood with her sword resting effortlessly in one hand, armor gleaming, every inch the hero Kess had always dreamed of becoming herself.

The one thing Kess wanted. Like she'd never wanted anything else.

She bowed her head and spoke with a sincerity she hoped wouldn't be misunderstood.

"I'm sorry. For everything. I may not have wielded that dagger, but I brought Kife into the hunt. It was still my fault that he hurt you, and I thought you were dead, and ..." Kess's throat closed up.

And even if Kess thought Riony was alive, she never thought anyone would come to help her. She'd been sure that even Griskin had abandoned her.

But it seemed as though he hadn't. He'd gone to find help. He'd gone to the person who had saved him from the net in the slavers' camp. Who had reunited Kess and Griskin in the caves.

The one person who always tried to help Kess, even when Kess never deserved it.

"Clever boy," Kess whispered into his fur.

He whined and licked her chin some more.

"Listen." Riony's shoulders lifted and fell, jangly and awkward, her eyes averted. "You helped save Dracuni, and you saved my life. I owed you. And you never did reply to my offer, so it still stands. One last chance."

Kess leaned back against the wall and scrubbed her face with her hands, an almost hysterical laugh burbling from her lips.

"One last chance? After all I have done to you ... every cruelty and betrayal ... you return and walk into the burning ruins of my heart as though you could not catch on fire."

"I mean, you don't have to be so dramatic about it."

Kess did laugh then. "You ... you followed a wolf across Elundrae ..."

Riony groaned. "I didn't think it would be such a big deal. Would have been much faster and easier if the pup could have pointed out which gateway to travel through, but nooooo. Sparking *weeks* of walking."

"On foot?" Kess gaped. "And broke down a door ...?"

Riony lifted a hand palm upward, as though confused why Kess was questioning it. "Pup wanted insies."

Kess's face tensed, caught between laughter and tears. Riony appearing there felt like *everything* to Kess, but she could see, for Riony, it was just another day. It was simply what Riony did. She saved people, any people, without once questioning the pain or hardship it cost her.

Stupid, beautiful fool.

"And like I said, you don't say no to a wolf." Riony turned, squinting through the rain at the few bodies scattered through the livestock area, groaning in the mud. "Plus, like, *everybody* is out there smashing stuff tonight. What under the stars is going on in this dragonkeep?"

Kess couldn't work out where to start so she simply said, "Trouble."

"Fantastic. I'll fit right in. Aish says if trouble was a currency, I'd be the richest person in the land."

There was a fondness in Riony's voice as she spoke of the Hjelzahn girl and Kess refused to let the way that made her feel show on her face.

Then, suddenly worried, she asked, "The others, Lyrrin, Dracuni, are they okay? They aren't in the city, are they?"

"They're fine and far away. I know I'm not the smartest, but you're the dumbass if you thought I'd bring them on this mission with me."

Kess released a relieved breath.

Riony continued. "I was still fifty-fifty that this was all some elaborate trap you'd set to lure me to my painful death. And then Aish, Lyrrin, and Dracuni all declared my death upon return as well if I let you hurt me again. So I'd be dead four times over. A record, even for me."

"But still, you came," Kess said. She shook her head, laughing mirthlessly. "You always were a glutton for punishment. You don't still think it's a trap?"

"After seeing that dull look of acceptance in your eye after I knocked down the door, I'm pretty sure you really did think you were about to die. Also why were you holding my pendant like that, and how the sparks do you have it?"

Mortified, Kess clutched the acorn again as though hiding it in her hand could make it disappear. Her first impulse was to lie, to say it was nothing, meant nothing, wasn't Riony's at all.

But she owed Riony more. "I found it. It ... brought me comfort. I want to keep it."

Riony raised an eyebrow and muttered, "We'll see about that."

Shouting in the distance drew a line of tension down Riony's neck. "But how about we get out of here first? Get on your wolf. I've cleared the way out through here. For now."

Kess shifted into a more upright position and retested the current pain levels of putting her broken body into motion. Still witheringly high. She inhaled deeply and prepared to lift herself onto Griskin's back.

"No, we're not going that way," she said. "We've got to get through this door here. Or at least, you do."

"Umm, why?" Riony stepped closer, eyeing the solid steel door.

While her gaze was turned away, Kess took the opportunity to hoist herself up. She gasped a silent scream as her bruised rib cage twisted and as she pulled her broken leg over the top of the saddle, then folded over and sobbed without a sound into Griskin's fur.

"Kess?" Riony's voice came softly from beside her.

Lifting back up again, Kess schooled her face. "The door ... It only stays open when someone holds the crank. That's why I'm here. I stayed to let some important people through. People you need to catch up to."

Up the path that was now more a muddy stream than paving, torches flickered through the rain near the livestock yard entrance. More rioters moving around.

"I'll keep the gate open for you. Go and find them. You'll know them when you see them."

It hadn't been long since Eslinde and the others went through. Riony should be able to find them.

"And you?" Riony glanced at the growing crowd up the hill, frowning.

"Don't worry about me. I have Griskin. I'll work it out." She could run now, with her wolf. Hopefully fast enough to evade an entire city who thought she was the Heir Killer.

Riony gestured up and down toward Kess's body. "Sorry. I thought I had found Kessara Heithorn. Who are you?"

Kess held Riony's gaze. "Somebody who has learned from her mistakes but will still do anything I have to do for what I want. And I want you ... to get through this gate."

"Don't go getting all self-sacrificing so quick. I'm good with doors. Let me have a look."

Riony checked the handle, giving it a few pumping turns, then letting it go. The heavy gate boomed down. Humming, Riony assessed the solid steel structure.

Dropping her sword, she took two leaping steps toward the gate and kicked up to grab the high mantle. Hanging by one hand, she wedged herself into the corner between door and wall and angled her head to stare into the gap above.

A solid backplate, stamped with an embossed design of fire-breathing dragons, covered the triangle of Riony's back where the knife had so easily pierced before.

Kess stared, part of her still unbelieving. "When Kife stabbed you ... How did you survive?"

Riony turned back and gave Kess a dumfounded look. "I literally have an entire dragon friend made of silvernix."

"But you fell. You fell and didn't move, and they said you weren't breathing."

"Yeah." Riony chuckled as though remembering an old joke as she reached her arm into the gap where the gate slid into the ceiling above. "The dagger missed my heart, but it hit something vital inside. Blocked me up real good. But once Aish pulled it out, the silvernix did its job."

There was a grinding sound, then a click, then Riony dropped back to the floor. "Try that."

Kess turned the handle, lifting the gate knee-high, then letting go. It slammed closed again.

Riony swore, then pouted back Kess's way. "You really thought I was dead?"

Kess could only nod and try not to cry.

"Exactly what form of celebration did you choose for the moment? Cake?"

"I mourned you, you intolerable oaf!" Kess snapped.

"You always have such sweet and kind words for me." Riony stooped to reclaim her sword. "As much as I'm loving this moment more than the last time I loved your amma, it's time for us to move, one way or another."

Riony pointed her blade out through the broken door. Lightning flashed, and dozens and dozens of torchlights glowed through the storm, moving closer.

A horde of rioters trudged down the slick ground through the livestock pens toward them.

CHAPTER TWENTY-SEVEN

"I don't think we're getting back out that way. Not both of us, anyway. I'll open the gate for you," Kess said, getting her hands onto the cold steel of the crank wheel again.

Riony gave her a shrewd look, then nodded. "Okay."

Something small inside Kess crumbled at Riony's willingness to leave her. She'd wanted more time. But Riony had done what she'd come there for, reuniting Kess with Griskin, and Kess had to do the right thing for Riony in return.

Kess's strained wrist ached as she turned the handle as fast as she could, racing against those marching their way.

"Stop it there," Riony called back when the door had lifted to just under her chest height.

She slid in underneath it, pressing her back to the doorframe and one shoulder against the base of the door.

"Okay, release it, just a little."

Kess kept her knuckles tight around the handle. "What? No! It'll crush you."

"That's why I said *a little*, tamebrain. I'll see if I can hold it before giving it a chance to turn me into jam. Just do me a favor and do as I say for once in your life."

Kess bit her lip and let the wheel reverse freely half a turn, keeping her hands close in case she had to catch it.

The heavy gate came down on Riony's shoulder and she braced, knees bending and legs shaking. A huff of air exhaled from her. Steel groaned. The crank stopped spinning on its own.

"I've got it. No problem." Riony wheezed. "Let it go and come through."

Kess grabbed the handle fully again, taking the strain off Riony. "What? No! Just get out of here. Or … or at least use your sword to keep the door up."

"And risk shattering my baby? I'd rather invite all our new friends there to take turns rearranging my face." Riony flicked her head toward the rioters almost upon them.

The men and women at the front of the crowd had spotted them now, turning from where they'd been smashing through gates and freeing livestock.

"We don't have time. Do it!" Riony snapped.

Kess let the wheel turn freely, her hands loosely around it as it spun in case she needed to halt the door's fall.

But it only moved a fraction, then stilled. Riony let out a groaning roar. The armor on her back screeched as she slid down the doorframe, then held again. Her sword lay on the other side of the gate and she pushed both hands up against the heavy metal, arms shuddering from the strain.

"Would you stop gawking and *get through the door already*?" Riony howled.

Nodding, Kess pressed Griskin into action, and they flew on swift paws, ducking under the low doorway.

The moment the wolf's tail was clear, Riony grunted and released the weight, diving clear in a clattering roll.

The gate slammed down like a landslide. Riony lay panting at Griskin's feet.

Kess stared down at her. "You didn't have to do that."

"Oh, really? Sparks, well, let's get this door open again and I'll just pop you back on the other side where you were." Riony remained on her back for a moment and screwed her eyes up as she cricked her neck and stretched her arms.

Closer now, the tattoo on Riony's sweat-sheened bicep was clear. Four rings. Two blades. One candle. Kess didn't know what it meant. She shook her gaze free from it and swallowed.

"I mean … thank you." Kess leaned over in her saddle and extended a hand.

Riony gave her a look like she'd just been offered a sack of squirming eels. "What was I going to do? Come all this way, then say, 'Oh well, have fun dying to flames and pitchforks'?"

Angry screams and the pounding of fists and feet came through the steel. The rioters had reached the chamber.

Riony didn't take Kess's hand. She rolled over, reclaimed her glowing sword, and rose to her feet. "Let's get moving. That charming gathering is going to work that door out in no time and have plenty of people to keep it open."

On cue, the door lifted, and great cheer went up from the crowd on the other side. Then it slammed down again to the sounds of boos and jeers.

Kess cast her eyes about the space. It wasn't the wilds she was used to tracking in, but it wasn't hard to spot the wet and muddy trail left by Eslinde and the others.

"This way."

She took off, keeping Griskin at a pace that Riony could keep up with. The wolf didn't whine or resist traveling down the enclosed corridor. He still panted happily, tongue lolling as he ran.

Kess rubbed his ears. Her chest filled with air in a way it hadn't for a long time. She was whole again.

"What's wrong with your leg?" Riony asked, almost casually, in a huffing breath from Kess's side.

When did she notice?

"It's broken," Kess said, and when Riony gave her an expectant glance, she continued with, "It's a long story."

"I bet. Are you good? Not going to pass out? You're looking peaky."

"I'm fine. I'll manage." Kess pressed a hand to Eslinde's silvernix in her pocket.

If they had a chance to stop soon, or when they caught up to the others, she could use it and relieve all the aches and agony shooting through her. But not yet. Not until they'd seen their way clear of the danger. It wouldn't do to heal herself only to be stabbed again before they got out.

And the rumblings of the mob still chased after them.

The trail of muddy footsteps was enough to get Griskin going, but once he had the scent, Kess didn't need to watch the path or keep her eyes forward, trusting him to take them where they needed to go.

Instead, she found she couldn't keep her eyes off Riony.

How had Kess ever believed that washed-out hallucination she'd shared a cell with was real? Her morass mercy visions were a pale substitute for the vital vibrance of the real thing.

Wild red hair hung wet over her face and was twisted at the back into that same single short braid she'd always worn. Her lips turned up in a smirk as though running from a revolting horde was a good time. The purple glow of her sword lit her eyes.

Riony. There and real and alive.

If Kess was going to pass out, it was from how her heart hammered in her chest every time her eyes turned Riony's way.

More shouts and the crash of breaking furniture came from all around in halls and rooms they passed as they sped through a more modern portion of Zarram Dragonhold.

The rioters must have gotten in through the front as well.

Through the shouting, a familiar voice broke through.

"What I know will smooth everything over. It's worth enough that everyone will be back on your side."

Kess brought Griskin to a stop.

The path that Eslinde took split off, going up the stairs, but Kife's voice came from ahead.

"Is that who I think it is?" Riony said, bringing her sword up, her knuckles tightening around the hilt.

Kess eyed their two paths. "I don't think he's told anyone else about Dracuni yet, but—"

"But maybe I want to see how he feels about getting a blade in the back, regardless? I feel like it would be a good way to keep him quiet."

"For once we agree." Kess turned Griskin, taking him at speed along the corridor.

Portraits lay knocked from the walls, frames cracked, and canvases slashed.

"Just give me one dragon. I'll take what I know to the Dragon King and then send help," Kife said.

Kess scoffed. *Sure he will.*

"I don't know what it is you think you know, boy, but Yeonard Draekhan will send aid regardless. It must be on the way already," the booming voice of Lord Zarram followed.

The hall the two men stood in was narrow, lit by one lamp still attached to the wall and another fallen and cracked on the ground, flame sputtering over a pool of spilled oil, encroaching onto a woven rug.

The glow of Riony's weapon flooded over the scene, overwhelming the small flames. Lord Zarram and Kife turned to see who approached. The light flickered over the gold trim on Lord Zarram's elegant storm-gray jacket.

Kife reached for the sword hanging from his hip below his blue-and-red dragonrider armor.

He glared from Kess to Griskin to Riony and back to Kess. "What are you doing here?"

Riony answered first. "I'd say I came all this way to kick your ass, but that'd be a lie. It's just a nice little side bonus."

Kess lifted her chin, catching Lord Zarram's eye. "Did you know this is the man who set off the etherflame who attacked the city? He sabotaged your family."

Frowning deeply, Lord Zarram's eyes moved more intentionally over Kife, assessing his face, the sword and daggers on his belt, and the crest stamped into their pommels.

He moved away from the dragonrider. "I can't trust any of you."

"You haven't even met me," Riony cried after him as he scuttled off in the other direction. She turned to Kess. "Do I look untrustworthy to you?"

"You look like someone who should be dead," Kife spat.

"Did I ask you?"

Fuming, Kife drew his sword. The metal sang. "You've been begging me to put you in a pyre since you first plagued Heithorn estate. This time I'll make sure you stay dead."

Riony grinned. "To the death it is, then. I was going to offer you a battle of wits, but you're clearly unarmed."

Leveling his sword her way, Kife growled, "How I look forward to silencing that mouth of yours forever. Again."

The confidence in his tone concerned Kess. Faced with both of them, she thought he might run. But the corridor was too narrow for them to take him on at the same time.

Kess readjusted her seating, grimacing as her broken leg bumped Griskin's flank. She nodded to Riony. "I'll let you rough him up first if I can finish him off."

Riony's eyebrows went up and she cooed, "That might be the nicest thing you've ever said to me."

The slice of Kife's sword ended the conversation. Riony brought hers up to counter just in time. The clash of metal meeting crystal burst around them.

She swiped his blade to the right, taking the chance to jab him in the ribs with her left fist.

"Careful," Kess hissed, barely a whisper.

Riony left herself open with that punch, and Kife's sword slid down the length of the crystal blade as he pulled back and thrust into the gap. The lightning-fast lunge seemed clear to hit, and Kess held her breath.

But Riony readjusted just as fast, parrying with the long unicorn horn-shaped pommel of her Alderkin weapon.

Kess watched as the parry, thrust, parry of the fight picked up, and her smile grew. Had Riony actually learned how to use a sword?

Catching Kife's latest lunge in her cross guard, Riony also caught Kife's face with her fist, splitting the skin under his eye.

The knock back put Kife against the wall. He bumped into a hall table, and the vase on it fell and smashed.

Kife spat blood. "Don't look so cocky, slave. I survived a one-on-one with you before. I'm sure I'll win this time."

Riony twirled her massive sword once and moved into an elegant fighting stance. "That was before I had sword training from Elundrae's hottest grayglim."

Kess's smile faded a little.

Beneath her hands, Griskin's skin twitched. It had been so long without feeling those sensations beneath her fingertips that Kess almost missed it, almost forgot what it meant.

Griskin sensing something, far earlier than Kess could.

Griskin sensing trouble.

Kess strained to hear, and faintly over the clash of the swordfight, there it was.

Footsteps, and a lot of them, coming their way.

She pulled one of the fine, sharp knives Eslinde had gifted her from her sleeve. "Enough, Riony. We need to finish this."

"Just ... one ... more ..." Riony punched Kife three times in the stomach as she held him pinned to the wall.

There was a cracking sound with the fourth. "That was for bleeding Dracuni."

Griskin growled. The footsteps were clear now. Flames flickered from the end of the hall.

They were going to get cut off from Eslinde and the others if they didn't leave now.

Kife slumped in Riony's grip, and she had a wild, feral sneer on her face. She pulled him back up to her level and got the edge of her sword against his neck.

"And this is for stabbing me in the back and framing your sister for it."

"Enough!" Kess couldn't get a clear angle on Kife with Riony in the way, and she wasn't throwing a blade anywhere near her direction. Never again.

Riony spun around, angry at first, but then her expression cleared. Then she looked over Kess's shoulder.

"Oh sparks. Go, do it!"

Riony dropped Kife and broke into a run back the way they'd come.

Kife fell slumped and groaning against the wall. Kess's eyes narrowed, and she breathed to steady her shot.

But then Griskin was moving beneath her.

"Wait!" she growled.

He grumbled a growl back, turning them both around and bounding down the corridor after Riony.

Oh no. The rioters were far closer than Kess had thought. Middling noblemen wearing strips of yellow cloth around their arms were led by Sunblessed Monks, chanting in the name of Ulfren, their lost leader.

The stairs Eslinde and the others had taken were in the middle of the corridor, and both groups raced headlong at each other from each end.

Kess judged the distance. She knew how fast Griskin was, relishing in the speed as they broke ahead of Riony. They could make it there first.

Riony's heavy steps thumped, falling behind. Her breathing, already labored from the swordfight, came thick and fast.

We can make it. But she can't.

Kess cursed. Pushing her hands into Griskin's fur and twisting her torso, she skidded him to a halt, pivoting him around.

"Back the other way, quick!"

"We can … Nope, we can't!" Riony yelled, turning herself as well.

The mob passed the stairs, blocking their access to it entirely and continuing to charge.

Kife had just gotten himself halfway to sitting upright when they barreled back his way. He curled up in a fetal position. Griskin growled as he leaped over the top, and Riony hit him with a glancing kick on her way.

Hopefully the mob will finish him off. Not nearly as satisfying, but still a job done.

Kess and Riony were herded forward, keeping just out of reach of the rioters. They hit some steps, slick with water flooding in, and hurried down. Kess recognized where they were now. She recognized the older, rough-hewn stonework and musty scent.

They were heading into a dead end.

CHAPTER TWENTY-EIGHT

Griskin's paws splashed down the muddy steps toward the old flamesong stalls. The rough descent jarred Kess's broken leg and she gritted her teeth. Water pooled and flowed down the stairs, trickling in from holes in the old stone walls.

Kess whipped her head around, checking if there was a chance for them to still turn back before being cut off down there, but the first few rioters were already there, blocking the way.

"Raze it," Kess hissed. "We might end up having to fight our way out of here. There's no other way through."

Riony hit the bottom of the stairs first, frowning as she took in the short hallway and the end in sight. There were eight dragon stalls down there in total, some with doors open, but one important one still had its door closed.

Eslinde's dragon raged from within.

Riony turned again to face up the stairwell. "Sorry I spent too long punching your brother. But also not sorry."

Kess swung Griskin around to meet their fate.

The very act of the two young women—one with a very large, glowing sword, and one with a wolf—turning around to face the rioters, made their pursuers hesitate at the top of the stairs.

"I'm sorry," Kess replied. "That you had to come here and get caught up in this. And for before that."

Riony brought her sword up, pointing it threateningly at the growing mob. "You're going to have to be more specific."

"For everything." Kess turned and held Riony's gaze. "Everything."

Riony frowned as though she couldn't comprehend at all what Kess was saying.

"Heir Killer!" a haughty woman cried down the steps.

Riony raised her eyebrows. She pointed to herself, then Kess, mouthing, "Me or ...?"

The first few brave souls charged down the steps toward them, the others hanging back.

"Hey." Riony turned to Kess and winked. "Check this out."

Riony brought one hand off the hilt of her sword and traced it over a carving on the crystal blade.

The cool purple glow flared, bursting brighter in hues of vivid magenta. Pink-and-red-tinted flames rushed up the blade, crackling and swirling.

"Lyrrin worked out an upgrade for me."

The few rioters rushing down the steps halted in their tracks. One slipped, skidding a couple of steps down through the water, then hastily clambering back up again. There were additional gasps and rumbles of muttering from the mob, and although edging closer, they remained wary of the burning blade.

The heat from the weapon radiated out, warming Kess's cheeks that felt too cold from a rush of dizzying pain.

"You couldn't have done that before?" she asked.

Riony whispered back, "This is kind of designed for revs. I don't actually want to burn real living people, and I didn't know you were leading us into a dead end!"

"Add it onto my debt. Think you can scare these idiots off?"

Riony shrugged, then took a couple of steps up the stairs, swinging the flaming sword in front of her. The rioters at the front of the crowd cringed backward, but there were too many people behind them who couldn't directly see the blazing carnage coming their way for the path to clear.

"For Ulfren!" a man bellowed in a deep voice, and a flash of silver flew through the air.

Riony shielded herself behind the thick width of her blade, and there was a soft clink as the dagger glanced off, followed by a wet thunk and string of increasingly more obscene curse words.

A dagger had wedged itself into Riony's inner elbow.

Her flaming sword lowered as she kept ahold of it with her injured side and reached for the hilt with the other hand.

"Don't pull it out!" Kess snapped.

Riony grimaced. "You think I want to leave it like that as a souvenir?"

"That's going to bleed, and a lot, the moment there's nothing wedged in there."

Even with the blade stuck into the flesh, blood swelled around the wound with every small motion, running thick over Riony's sienna skin.

Riony pouted at the jutting hilt but retracted her hand without touching it.

"I will make them bleed in return." Kess rifled through Griskin's bags, sighing when she found a supply of bone daggers. Five, without a more thorough search she doubted she'd be allowed time for.

Riony got her sword back into her good hand and stepped clear of Kess's aim. "Aw, are you jealous somebody else got a knife in me?"

Kess sent the knives flying, one after another, a hailstorm of pointed bone. One, two, three, four, five rioters fell, screaming and clutching their wounds.

It wasn't enough to dissuade the others to give up though.

Having drawn Riony's blood, the crowd at the top of the stairs surged and grew bolder.

Kess's own stomach surged seeing the red staining Riony's skin. The blood dripped down onto the sodden ground.

Kess narrowed her eyes at the rioters and the stairs, all soaked from the storm.

"Listen. I have a plan to get out of here. But it's risky. Reckless even."

"I love it. Let's do it."

"I haven't even told you what it is!"

Riony shrugged. "As long as it gets us out of here, I'm open to anything."

The front line of the mob pressed forward again. Kess nodded and eyed the surroundings, calculating whether they had any chance at all. She considered the thickness of the rope and pulley and weight attached. The one small dry patch of shelter.

Their chances were low.

"Get up into that niche." Kess pointed to the carved-out section of wall where a torch flickered.

"Okay?" Riony deactivated the magic on her sword that made it flame, returning it to its cool purple glow, then lightly jumped up into the narrow space.

She hung out over the edge while she pulled the torch from its sconce and threw it away so she could fit in without burning herself.

Kess prepared Griskin to follow. "And make room for us."

Riony's forehead wrinkled, but she pressed herself as far into the gap as she could.

Griskin leaped, back paws scrambling against the wall beneath the niche as he tried to fit onto the too-small ledge before he found his balance. The three of them pressed together on the small shelf, barely covered by the wall on each side. Riony had to duck to avoid her head hitting the arched top.

The mob approached, still cautious, but without the flaming sword blocking them they edged closer.

Kess drew one of the fine blades Eslinde had gifted her. She lined up her shot.

Riony's voice was close to Kess's ear. "I sure hope that's some kind of secret magical weapon that fells a hundred foes with one blow, but you know you're not even pointing the right direction, yeah?"

The knife flew through the air, nicking the rope beside the closed gate, but not severing it.

Kess only grunted.

Riony's eyes followed where the knife went and then in a slow voice asked, "Kess, what's behind that door?"

Drawing her final remaining weapon, Kess exhaled slowly. She had to cut the rope with this shot. But the rope was thick, and the angle from where they sheltered in the niche was bad.

Still, she threw. The rope split, frayed. But held strong.

"No!" Kess grunted. "I'm out of knives."

She searched hastily through another of the saddlebags but nothing came up. The mob was growing bolder and was almost on them.

"Umm. We have one more." Riony held out her arm, the dagger stuck in it on display.

Kess's heart clenched. She didn't want to see Riony hurt. But she had silvernix. As long as they could get somewhere safe and Riony didn't bleed too fast, it might be okay.

She nodded once, lips thin.

Riony yanked out the blade. A spray of arterial scarlet followed, and Riony folded her arm, pressing the wound closed. Still, blood flowed far too fast.

Riony groaned, "Make it count."

Kess took the warm blade from her. Her heart hammered. "The angle isn't good. I need to be farther out."

She tried to lean out from her saddle, but almost slipped off Griskin's back entirely, and then he almost slipped off the shelf of the niche.

Riony grasped Kess's free arm with hers, each clasping the other's wrist. Riony whimpered as she used her wounded arm to hold the empty torch sconce to steady them both, and Kess winced as Riony squeezed her sprained wrist.

But it steadied Kess, and she leaned out at an almost horizontal angle.

That was it. A clear line of sight. She stared from the blood on the blade to the frayed rope and ignored her pain and the angry mob at her back and threw.

The blade slipped through the last strands of the rope. The counterweight fell, the gate rose up, and the bright, furious eyes of Eslinde's snowshimmer glittered from the dark space within.

"Pull me back in!" Kess gasped.

Riony did, and they pressed against each other, chest to chest in the small space, eyes wide and drawing fast breaths as an earthshaking roar filled the stairwell.

Blue-white lightning streaked through the air.

The dragon's attack lanced out, hitting a burly man at the front of the assault. The crackling energy dropped him and then leaped across the wet ground, arcing to the people beside him. It shimmered over their soaked clothing, their bodies tensing, jerking, then falling as well.

The effect rippled out and up the stairs and scores of twitching rioters fell to the ground.

Riony's words breathed over Kess's ear. "Sparks. That's what you were planning? You weren't playing around."

There was a mad scramble of remaining bodies and their screams almost overwhelmed the dragon's next booming roar.

"That was the first half of the plan. The second half is praying we don't get eaten."

Griskin whined. Kess reached back and tucked his tail into the niche to make sure as much of them as possible was hidden in the crammed space.

Eslinde's dragon emerged from its cell. Cautious at first, head swinging side to side, eyes taking in everything. It sniffed the air, then broke into a run. Its claws scraped and stomped over the paved floor, building speed as it reached the stairs.

When its head was level with the niche hiding space, the dragon loosed another bolt of lightning. Kess flinched back, pressing her cheek to Riony's shoulder.

More screams followed. A cacophony of footsteps and crashes reverberated down as people scattered, and the dragon gave chase. Its barbed tail flicked by, glancing over Kess's leg like the brush of wind, and then it was gone.

Kess leaned back as far from Riony as she could, a hot flush over her cheeks. "Come on. Let's try to get out of here before our luck runs out."

Riony flicked the acorn at Kess's neck and said, "I'm feeling lucky."

She pushed past and jumped down first. Her sword glowed in one hand and she kept her bleeding arm folded and close to her chest.

Kess urged Griskin to follow. Once out of the niche, they moved into a sprint up the stairs.

The acrid, fatty smell of smoking bodies made Kess screw up her nose. Most of them still groaned and twitched, stunned but alive. Only the burly man who led the charge and got hit directly seemed far too charred to have survived.

Griskin understood their path, and Kess turned back to check on Riony. Despite keeping her arm folded, blood streamed from her elbow and her face was turning ashy.

"Not much farther!" Kess called.

Hopefully they'd find Eslinde on the flight deck, and her grayglim could protect them while they saw to Riony's wound. Kess checked her pocket again, the silvernix still there. She blinked pain-bleary eyes.

Riony stumbled over the top step onto the flight deck, and Kess and Griskin bounded ahead.

There were a handful of rioters who had made it there, piling up anything flammable they could find onto a growing bonfire. Kess launched Griskin at them, scattering them with a growl.

Then she passed an empty stall and her heart sank. Viska was gone. Eslinde and the others were already gone.

"We're too late." She snorted a breath.

Riony leaned against the entrance of the stall, her chest heaving and eyelids drooping. "Sorry. Kind of felt like the faster I ran, the more blood squirted out of me."

The blood covered Riony's armor in a crimson flush and dripped from her clothes. Her gaze was unfocused.

Kess chewed her lip and looked around her for options, feeling pain blurred and heavy with disappointment and worry. All she could think was she had to get Riony to safety.

"It's okay. We're still getting out of here. We'll take a dragon," Kess said.

Riony ambled closer in an uneven stumble. She pointed with her sword. "Snowflame? They're fast, right?"

It was a pretty beast with ice-blue scales and gold-tipped wings and horns.

Kess raised her eyebrows. "Yes. They are. I'm surprised you know that. I thought you didn't care about dragons."

"I just remembered it was the one kind of dragon you didn't want to own, and I've got to get my digs in somewhere."

Kess huffed a laugh but turned Griskin toward the snowflame. It was already saddled with a small single saddle. The snowshimmer/etherflame hybrid was medium-sized but should carry them all. As long as Kess could command it.

Moving closer, Griskin whimpered.

Kess rubbed his ears. "Don't worry, boy. No claws for you anymore."

She maneuvered Griskin toward the back of the stall and had him run up the dragon's lowered tail and to its shoulders. Griskin's claws skidded on the scales, but he managed to balance there. Kess lowered him down onto his belly across the saddle.

"Get on behind him," Kess called down to Riony as she slipped off Griskin and onto the dragon's neck in front of the saddle.

She groaned as she slid her legs down and she leaned forward to catch her breath.

The brightening of the purple glow announced Riony had joined her. "Are you okay there?"

Kess nodded. She looked around from their perch and for a moment, there was peace. All the screaming was at least muted and distant, for now.

She reached into her pocket and blinked heavy eyelids. "Let's get you fixed up before we move. The princess gave me silvernix."

Riony shuffled in her seat behind Griskin and the saddle, her head wobbling. "I think maybe I have lost a lot of blood because I thought you just said a princess gave you silvernix."

Kess held it up, fingers fumbling as she worked to unscrew the earring vial.

"Hold on a second." Riony leaned out of Kess's reach. "If anyone is using it, it's you. You look like you're about to pass out, and I don't want that to happen while we're airborne. I have no idea how to fly a dragon."

"And you look like you're going to bleed out, and I need you to hold Griskin in place. I'm not losing either of you again."

"I'm fine," Riony protested, and then she slumped forward, armor clattering. Her chest flopped over Griskin's back and head bumped into Kess. Then she shot back upright again.

"I'm *fine*," she repeated more firmly.

"Fine," Kess sneered back. "Just hold on to Griskin for me as best you can."

She held up her own hand and made a show of tipping the silvernix toward it.

Riony smirked and nodded a lolling head. She reached one arm over Griskin's shoulder.

Kess let the drop of silvernix fall into her own palm. And then lashing out, she grasped Riony's outstretched hand in hers.

Riony jerked back, but Kess held tight, and the opalescent fluid pressed between them.

Light sparkled out between where their hands met, and then with a flush of moonlight glow, the illumination washed outward, engulfing them both entirely.

Kess cried out as the magic churned and worked on the broken and cracked bones beneath her flesh. Riony's jaw tightened, and her eyes remained locked on Kess's face, but she didn't make a sound.

It was a gamble, trusting there was enough silvernix in the dose to heal them both.

But as the light cleared, Kess sighed in relief at the absence of pain. Riony shook out her injured arm, still slick with blood, but no longer flowing freely.

Shaking her head, Riony pulled her hand free from Kess's.

"You're such a sneaky pain in the ass, Kessara."

"You're welcome, *Riony*."

Kess only got a glimpse at the reddened, dumbstruck look on the woman's face as she turned around. A thrum of nervous delight filled Kess at the thought of surprising Riony again. She could imagine the expectations Riony had for her, and she planned on shattering them all.

All the relentless determination she'd put into getting a dragon of her own, all the grit and single-mindedness she'd put into hunting Dracuni, were all turned now toward a new goal.

Repaying an impossible debt.

Kess's heart beat firm and steady as she leaned forward and pressed her hands onto the dragon's neck.

The snowflame reacted instantly, standing up and moving forward in a slow stroll. Out of the narrow stall, Kess leaned and adjusted, testing the motions.

"You've got this, right?" Riony asked nervously.

Kess grinned to herself and pushed the dragon into a run.

It galloped up the cavernous space toward the open flight deck. Screams and gurgling cries followed them, closer now.

They were at the edge when Kess glanced back.

Dashiel and Vance's father, Lord Zarram, ran up the length of the room, panting and stumbling. A horde of rioters followed at his heels.

Kess swore, trying to adjust, but the dragon's talons were already over the drop and into open air.

The change in Kess's motions left the dragon confused, and for a moment they dropped.

"Kess?" Riony yelled in an increasingly higher pitch.

Kess refocused. The dragon's wings snapped out, pumping at the air around them. They lifted, shooting forward into the darkening night.

Kess turned the dragon, taking it back to pass in front of the flight deck exit. She could no longer see Lord Zarram. Only a messy swarm of raging rioters.

Too late to go back.

The storm had eased. An odd flash of lightning brightened the blanket of clouds above them, but the rain had stopped, and Kess brought the snowflame high above the city, hovering there for a moment as she caught her breath.

From the back exit of the dragonhold, Eslinde's dragon burst into the sky with a roar and soared out toward the ocean.

And beneath them, Zarram Dragonhold burned.

CHAPTER TWENTY-NINE

Kess circled once, twice, her breath held as she tried to decide their heading, tried to spot any sign of where Eslinde had gone. The dark sky and city below were clear and sparkling, washed clean from the storm. Only a couple of other dragons flew since the rain had stopped. But they mostly moved around near the palace, on guard after the trouble of the day.

"What are we looking for?" Riony asked.

"A golden dragon, five-to-seven passengers." Kess hadn't seen Vance or Dashiel anywhere in the chaos of the dragonhold. She hoped they'd gotten clear. With Viska gone, she assumed at least one of them did. She hoped they both did.

Riony sheathed her sword over her shoulder and pulled a palm-sized crystal from a belt pouch. Invoking the Alderkin magic, the milky crystal turned glass-clear, and Riony held it up to her eye.

"There." Riony pointed southwest.

Kess narrowed her eyes at the gloomy horizon. Far in the distance, under a burst of storm-light, golden scales glittered—Viska, and another dragon, speeding away.

Kess's heart raced in turn. She adjusted her position on the dragon's neck and pushed it into pursuit.

She took it gently at first, getting a feel for the control and speed. Dashiel had taught her so much on their flight together, but this was a different dragon. And their seating was precarious.

Kess was wedged in between the dragon's neck and saddle. She wasn't tied on at all, and even the slow turn left her worried she was going to slip right off. Griskin's fur was warm at her back, and she could feel the tension in his soft whines. Behind them, Riony was off the saddle as well, hanging on to the straps with one hand and Griskin with the other.

Once Kess had the dragon pointed in the right heading, she pushed it faster.

"All good back there?" she called over her shoulder.

"Yeah." Riony's voice was muted by the rushing wind and a thickness of some emotion. "Sparks. I think I might get why you were obsessed with this."

Kess's chest rose and fell with a soul-filling breath, and she pushed the dragon faster again.

If Viska was going full speed, she doubted they'd catch up. But the others didn't seem to be moving too fast, whether due to the second dragon's abilities or the passengers. The sleek and smaller snowflame gained on them.

Out past the dragonkeep walls, the sky cleared. A bright moon shone down between clouds onto the plains below, turning them patchwork with light and dark.

A gust of wind buffeted them from the side, and Kess slipped from her seat. But a hand grasped the damp clothing at her back and held her in place.

As they came up behind the two dragons, the moment they were spotted was clear. Viska maneuvered abruptly, twisting away from their flight path and circling out and around, coming up behind the snowflame so fast that if Kess had been an enemy, she suspected they'd have been burned from the sky before she could blink.

She was proud she could keep a dragon in the air and on target at all. Could she ever dare to dream again of becoming a dragonrider with that sort of prowess, after all her misplaced ambitions?

Whether the rider recognized the Zarram dragon, or Kess herself, their fiery end didn't eventuate. Instead, Viska came up alongside them, flanking wingtip to wingtip.

The second, orange dragon slowed and leveled out with them on the other side.

They were close enough that faces became clear in the moonlight. Kess waved, filled with relief.

On Viska, Vance, Eslinde, and the grayglim signaled back with varying levels of enthusiasm. On the second dragon rode Dashiel and the three Alderkin. They'd made it. All of them.

"These are your friends?" Riony called into Kess's ear.

"Yeah. They are." The words warmed Kess as she said them.

People who had been kind to Kess, who offered her respect and friendship, even when she had no wealth or dragons or anything to her name. People she was proud to call friends.

Kess had only ever studied dragonrider technique in books, and it had been years ago. She did her best to make the correct hand motions to indicate the others should follow them. Vance and Dashiel each replied with a sideways pump of a fisted hand, affirmative, and Kess began bringing her dragon out of the sky.

Blessed sun, I hope I can land this thing.

"If we're heading down, I want to be near a shrine," Riony yelled. "Kind of still want an escape plan. No offense."

"Okay, let me find one." Kess slowed the dragon, gliding over the dark ground below, getting her bearings. From the mapping and tracking she'd done with Kife, she was fairly sure there was a shrine just over the low hills ahead.

"Really? No argument?" Riony asked.

"Really."

They came closer, and within a valley of twisted trees, a ring of standing stones glowed in a shaft of moonlight. There was no settlement around it, and the shrine building within the center was almost entirely collapsed, exposing the crystal ring standing within the crumbled walls.

"Is that one any good?" Kess asked.

"Yeah, it's activated," Riony confirmed.

It wasn't one that had been working before when Kess chased them across the land, and it was a fair way on foot from where most of those ones had been. Riony and the others had been busy.

"Time to see whether I can land."

"Sorry, WHAT?"

Kess already had the dragon at a slow glide. In theory, she just had to slow it down more, angle it right, and get it in the correct landing position. All things Dashiel hadn't covered on their flight together.

There was a clearing around the shrine, and Kess aimed for it. Despite pulling the dragon back slower, and slower again, the ground came up fast toward them.

The hand at her back appeared again, clenching into what fabric there was left of Kess's dress.

Leather wings clapped as they filled with air. The sound punched into Kess's eardrums, then they hit the ground. The dragon skidded, falling forward onto its chest, and Kess bounced from her seat, hanging beside the dragon's shoulder by Riony's hand.

They came to a stop with a final bump. Cloth ripped, and Kess slipped down and landed on her back.

Staring up at the sky and the two other dragons elegantly coming in to land, Kess laughed.

Griskin let out a ruff and jumped down beside her, licking her cheeks. She wrapped her arms around his neck and let relief fill her to every tingling extremity.

Riony climbed down from the snowflame, groaning as she got her feet on the ground. "Sorry, I didn't mean to drop you. Although if I knew you'd find it that funny, maybe I would have done it on purpose."

Kess wiped her face, still chuckling. "I'm just happy to be alive. That we're all alive."

Riony eyed the descending dragons. "And who are these special people we risked our lives to catch up to?"

Kess's laughter faded, overtaken by nerves. She hadn't wanted to tell Riony before who they were following. Whether she'd said Lyrrin's mother or a first heir or escaping Alderkin, it was all too complicated to have dealt with in the moment.

But that moment was upon her now.

"You'll see." She climbed up into Griskin's saddle and waited.

As Viska and the orange dragon landed in a soft rush of air around them, Riony's face twitched, and she moved to put her back to the gateway crystal. Reaching to her belt, Riony swiped her finger over a stone in a netted bag there. It illuminated the clearing in a bright glow of cyan light.

Dashiel was the first off their dragon. They ran for Kess, then hesitated at the looming wolf beneath her.

"He's safe," Kess said.

Dashiel raised their eyebrows, but still moved closer and wrapped her in a hug. "I thought we'd lost you. I'm so sorry we left, and you ... you took the blame for me, and ... Raze it, Kess."

They squeezed her harder.

Kess raised timid arms to hold them in return. "I'm sorry, Dashiel. Your father ..."

She explained in a rushed whisper what they'd seen as they left. "The mob, they were there for me, because they thought I was the Heir Killer. If it weren't for me ..."

Dashiel shook their head. Their voice was thick. "No. That's not the only reason. Those people had been waiting for any excuse to destroy us."

"I'm still sorry."

Pulling away, Dashiel's eyes were red, and they gave Kess a small nod before turning toward their brother. The siblings moved to the side together, speaking low and holding each other. Shiff was also there with them, Kess was happy to see, and the young dragon curled at Dashiel's feet.

Eslinde approached Kess next as though she were going to rush in for an embrace as well, but then her eyes locked on Riony.

And Riony's in turn were stuck to Eslinde.

Eslinde's eyes flickered briefly to Kess and over Griskin. "How? What happened?"

Kess patted her wolf, but her eyes were also on Riony. "They came to find me."

Eslinde nodded, her head tilted and expression softening.

"It's her," Riony said, as though to herself. She'd gone pale again like she'd been when losing blood.

"You recognize me?" Eslinde ran her hands nervously over her damp dress, the silver fabric darkened with mud. Her moonlight hair hung loose, wispy as it dried.

Riony rubbed the back of her head, a soft color over her cheeks. "The person I stole a baby from? Yeah, you kind of made a lasting impression."

Eslinde's back straightened. Yensen stood on guard beside her shoulder, and the three Alderkin were behind him, shadowed by cloaks and ominous. Vance and Dashiel simply exchanged matching nonplussed looks.

Riony took a step back and held both hands out in a calming gesture. "Also, really sorry about that, by the way. I can explain ..."

"No need. I understand. I know what happened. Although I hope to hear it in your words one day, too. But now, please tell me, is Lyrrin safe?"

Riony shot Kess a look as the girl's name emerged from Eslinde's lips.

"How much did you tell them?" Riony snapped in a whisper.

Kess gave her head the smallest shake. "Only what she deserved to know, about her daughter."

Riony flinched but nodded.

Eslinde moved closer, her voice strained. "Tell me, please, is she safe?"

Giving the woman a long assessing look, Riony sighed. "She was, as of a few days ago when I last checked in."

"Checked in?" Kess asked.

"It's not like I was going to abandon them all for the entire time I was chasing a wolf across Elundrae. We have a system. The others let a trusted friend know where they are, in code, whenever they moved locations. So anytime me and Griskin were near a shrine, I could go back and find them. Make sure everything was okay."

Eslinde pressed her hands to her chest. "And where is Lyrrin now? Can we go to her?"

"Whoa. Hold on. Beyond being the woman who gave birth to Lyrrin, I don't even know you, let alone trust you." Riony made a point of looking over the seven figures standing across from her in the clearing.

Frustration flashed over Eslinde, but she pulled her lips in and said, "Introductions, then."

Kess couldn't understand exactly how the two women before her felt. A mother who had missed the first eight years of her daughter's life, faced with the person who had been there for all those moments. And the person who raised the child as family, faced with the person who could claim a bond of blood.

But she knew emotions would be high.

She moved Griskin in between them and spoke in a slow, careful tone. "Riony, this is Eslinde. Eslinde the First."

"Oh." Riony grasped both sides of her head with her hands. "Oh shit."

She took another step back as though ready to activate the magical gateway and flee.

Eslinde mirrored Riony's earlier gesture, palms forward. "Please. I only want to meet my daughter and have no intention of harming you or any of the people who kept her safe."

"What about Lyrrin?" Riony stilled, and her expression grew dark. "How do I know you aren't planning on getting rid of her, to finish what your mother started when she ordered the baby, me, and my amma murdered."

"I wouldn't. Please tell her I wouldn't." Eslinde turned to Kess, expression pained and pleading.

Kess shrugged. "If you think she trusts me any better, you're out of luck."

"Yeah, I'm afraid you're going to need something more than the word of this traitorous goblin."

Eslinde glanced behind her, then gave Riony a long, hard look. Her silver eyes glittered in the cyan light.

"You can trust I mean my daughter no harm because I know exactly who she is. And why she was born different." She beckoned to the three cloaked figures.

They stepped forward and, at her urging, drew back their hoods.

Riony let out a rush of air. "That's … something alright."

Her eyes roamed over their bright-blue and green hair, vibrant eyes, and long clawed hands. Especially the hands.

The Alderkin each stared at her in return, at the glowing stone on her belt, and the hilt of the crystal sword showing over her shoulder, faces equally questioning.

"These are Alderkin," Eslinde said softly. "As was Lyrrin's father."

Her eyelashes fluttered as she glanced with flickering brevity across to the Zarram siblings. Vance frowned, but there was a softness of compassion in his eyes.

"Alderkin," Riony breathed the word. "Sparks. It makes sense, but also … how?"

"That's a far longer story, for later." Eslinde drew up straight. "Now, I have trusted you with the biggest secret in all of Elundrae."

"Yeah. Biggest. Sure." Riony choked.

"And also my own greatest secret. I have extended that trust to you, midwife daughter. And all I ask in return is to see my child who I believed dead, whom I mourned and missed every day."

Riony dragged her attention away from the Alderkin.

She swallowed visibly as she frowned at Eslinde. "Okay. Maybe I could take you, you alone, to go and meet her. No grayglims or dragonriders."

Her eyes narrowed on Yensen, Vance, and Dashiel as she spat the terms.

Vance moved up beside Eslinde, but Yensen spoke first. "Eslinde isn't going anywhere with you alone."

The princess tsked, but Vance gave her a quelling look.

"I am free of the palace and my parents but still you restrict me? I only want to meet my daughter! Why must you all make this difficult?"

Riony shrugged. "Sorry, princess. Let's tally up how many times we've each been literally stabbed in the back and maybe it will explain the trust issues. But ..."

Eslinde's shoulders slumped, her mouth opened as she waited on Riony to finish her thought.

Riony's shoulders lowered as well. "But this isn't really my decision to make. It should be Lyrrin's."

The two women stared at each other in silence for a long moment as owlettes hooted from the surrounding trees.

"I'll go and tell her you're here. Then the rest is up to her." Riony turned away.

Eslinde cried, "How long? How long will you be?"

"Shouldn't be long at all." Riony bent down to the base of the geode ring, then rose back up as the symbols all around the edge lit up.

Gasps came from the Alderkin, and they muttered between themselves. Kess only caught a few fragments.

"How does she know ...?"

"Shouldn't be possible ..."

Kess's eyes remained on Riony as she stepped toward the glowing magic.

There were so many more symbols illuminated now than Kess had last seen. Almost all of them.

Riony tapped the one Kess recognized as the settlement near the glass factory.

Without saying anything else, Riony stepped through, and the gateway closed behind her, taking the light and all the air in the world with her.

Kess's chest ached. She wanted to have gone with Riony, stayed by her side, never left her side again. But if Riony had wanted that too, she'd have invited her.

If she didn't intend on returning, would she have said goodbye?

Without the cyan glow of light, the night was so much darker. Kess shivered and leaned into Griskin. Somewhere in his packs there would be a spare shirt she could replace the remains of her gown with, but for now, Kess only wanted the warmth of Griskin's fur.

"I missed you so much," she whispered.

He groaned a low whine in reply.

Eslinde appeared at their side, ghostly in the moonlight. She approached confidently, but when Griskin sniffed at her, she stopped and took a step back.

Looking to the geode, she asked, "Can we trust her? Will she do as she says?"

With all the revelations just dumped upon Riony, she may decide it was safer to take her adoptive sister and flee Elundrae entirely. Especially with Dracuni in the mix.

Kess wasn't sure what she'd do if the gateway didn't open and bring Riony back to her.

But even the one time Riony had tricked her and left her for dead, hanging from a cliff over a monstrous mass of revs, she'd returned.

"I trust her. I don't know if she'll come back. But I hope so."

A soft smile played out over Eslinde's lips. "I can see why you like her."

Kess scowled in return. "It isn't some childish crush. I owe her my life. I owe her repayment for years of blood and torture and cruelty. I owe her a debt so large I could spend my lifetime giving my body, heart, and soul to make amends and not come close to being what she deserves."

Eslinde's eyes glittered. "But it is clear you're ready to try."

Looking at the unlit gateway geode, Kess prayed to the blessed sun that Riony would give her that chance.

Eslinde moved closer, reached for Kess's hand, and squeezed it in hers. "Thank you, Kessara, for getting me this close, so close, to fulfilling dreams I'd thought long dead."

With a final, melancholy smile, the princess left and joined the Zarram siblings. No doubt they'd have questions for her. The Alderkin kept to themselves in a small huddle, gathering crystal shards from the broken shrine and strappy weeds, and seemed to be using both in some kind of ritual on the injured Priyune.

And Kess settled in on Griskin, facing the gateway, and waited.

After a while, Eslinde paced, then fumed, arguing with Yensen and blaming him for losing her only chance at meeting Lyrrin as he worked on a small fire to keep them warm.

Kess remained apart from the others. Her fingers shook and grew cold. Griskin's fur had dried and was warm beneath her, and although the few twisted trees around the standing stones were naked of leaves for winter's approach, it wasn't the chilled air that affected Kess.

It was the worry that Riony wouldn't come back, but also, if she did, what was going to happen next between them. What Kess had planned.

But Kess had waited for what she wanted before.

It was hard to tell how much time passed. The moon and stars hadn't moved much overhead but it seemed like an eternity.

Then the gateway shimmered into life, and Kess sprang upright in her saddle.

Cyan light rippled over the magical surface, and Riony stepped through, brightening the area.

And from behind her, hiding near her hip, a smaller body followed.

"Lyrrin?" Eslinde ran forward, stopping a respectful distance away. She covered her mouth with both hands.

"That's her," Riony said softly, a hand on Lyrrin's shoulder. "That's your amma."

The girl stepped out from Riony's shadow, lifting her face. She had her own glowing stone and a range of other crystals along her belt. Her hood was off, showing a strip of blue along the roots of her hair, and no gloves over her hands.

The Alderkin approached then too, Yrik falling to his knees and Priyune and Shael crying and smiling into each other's shoulders. Lyrrin's eyes went round as the full moon when she saw them.

And then the gateway rippled again.

Yensen tensed as more bodies followed.

Aishena stepped through, her face grim and her hands on the crystal daggers sheathed at her belt. Her hair was roughly cropped at the chin and darkened with dye. Then Niskina, almost as heavily armored as Riony, her expression firm but eyes bright with emotion. And Benjin, holding a glowing staff and standing a foot taller since the last time Kess had seen him.

But larger again was the final shape pushing through the magical space. Dracuni's head emerged, high off the ground and large like a horse's. Her singular golden horn had grown long and sharp like a blade, and as the rest of her body followed between the sharp ring of crystal, she had to push and shimmy to squeeze through.

"You didn't say they had a dragon," Yensen hissed to Kess.

"I didn't think they'd bring her," Kess shot over to Riony with a concerned look.

Riony flinched and shrugged. "Everybody wanted to come. And does it look like I can stop her doing what she wants to do now?"

From farther to the side, Dashiel murmured, "She's not tamed?"

"No, but she'll stay friendly as long as you and your dragons stay friendly," Riony replied.

The Alderkin watched the unidragon as well, with an intensity to their bright eyes that made Kess worry.

Dracuni snorted, an almost embarrassed look in her lilac eyes as her back hips got stuck, then she finally popped the rest of the way through the crystal ring.

Then her attention shot straight to Shiff and the other dragons. The larger three, all tamed, made no response. But Shiff perked up immediately.

Riony tilted her head. "Looks like you've got a little untamed one too."

Dashiel crouched down and stroked the forehead of the pale-blue and muted-purple dragonling. "She wants to meet your dragon, closer up. Is that okay?"

"You can hear her?" Riony grinned and jabbed a finger in the air toward Dashiel. "Oh, we are having a chat later."

Dracuni was clearly communicating with Riony as well, and she nodded the go-ahead for the two young dragons to meet.

Shiff was half Dracuni's size, but far bolder. They edged closer, and Riony's jaw was tight with tension, until each young dragon trilled happily.

Eslinde stood still and patient across the clearing, her eyes never having left her daughter.

Riony sighed, then with a gently push to Lyrrin's shoulder's, she whispered, "Go on."

As Lyrrin took a couple of hesitant steps forward, the princess knelt to the ground, her muddy-hemmed gown pooling around her. She outstretched her hands, then took no further action, waiting for Lyrrin.

The girl moved slowly but finally lifted her own hands and placed them in her mother's. The long blue nails were quickly engulfed in the woman's embracing fingers and Eslinde beamed, tears trickling down her cheeks.

Mother and daughter spoke to each other in low, cautious voices, and a smile grew on Lyrrin's face as well.

Riony watched, chest rising and falling in heavy breaths. Then she turned away with an expression of a multitude of emotions. One that sought comfort. And she turned straight to Aishena.

The two of them clasped hands together, tight between their chests, and Riony leaned in, pressing her forehead to Aishena's. They whispered softly to each other, and there, on the Hjelzahn girl's forearm, Kess saw a tattoo. Four rings. Two swords. One candle.

Matching to Riony's.

Oh. Kess's heart shuddered weirdly.

As long as she's happy. All that matters is that she's happy.

Kess waited for the tender moment to pass and then moved so she could speak to Riony without Eslinde or the others hearing.

"I didn't tell them anything about Dracuni. She could have remained away, remained secret."

"Dracuni isn't so easy to keep hidden these days," Riony murmured back. "Generally, nobody has had any reason to think she's anything other than a dragon. We just try to be careful and hope we can trust people."

The unidragon was bigger than a horse now. Around the size stories told that unicorns once were. But there was still a playful frolic in her step as she engaged with Shiff.

Dashiel and Vance seemed fascinated by her, and Kess could see them speculating about her breed already. Dashiel's eyes were bright with an enthusiastic smile.

"These are good people. I think you can trust them," Kess said.

"And what about you? Can I trust you?" There was an edge to Riony's voice, something akin to exhaustion and vulnerability and worry all at once that left the words clipped.

Kess held her gaze and then turned in her saddle, lowering herself down to the ground.

"What are you doing?" Riony balked. "Is this some weird revenge plan to stab me in the toes?"

Kess's body shivered with nerves. She couldn't quite kneel. Not neatly, not formally. So she prostrated herself on the ground, bowing low at the feet of the woman who was once her slave.

"Riony ..." Kess hesitated. No longer an Uf'Heithorn, she didn't know how best to address her. But the effect of even using that name rather than the old, hurtful pet name was enough.

She swallowed a dry throat and went on. "By all my honor, I pledge my life to you and your cause. For whatever good it can provide you. However you wish to expend it. My life, my hands, my blades are under your command. It is the least you are owed."

Kess tried to imbue her voice with every fiber of sincerity she had. "I don't ask any forgiveness. I only ask that you let me serve you."

Her words came out broken and scratchy. "I am yours."

Kess remained there, forehead to the dirt, waiting. No reply came.

Turning her face upward, Kess felt a small amount of satisfaction that for the first time in her life, Kess had rendered Riony speechless.

EPILOGUE

The world blurred back into focus in a whirl of pain and nausea. Kife wrestled weakly against the hands that grasped his arms.

They continued to drag him forward.

Kife groaned and slumped. Only a thin slit of vision was present between swollen eyelids and hot liquid tickled as it ran down his temple.

"Where ... where are you taking ..." Kife's tongue was thick and tasted tangy and metallic. He'd lost a tooth somewhere along the way.

The mob had beaten Kife to the last breath of his life, but he'd held tight to that breath. Now he feared he'd been rounded up with the criminals to be punished again.

This is Kess's fault. How many times must the wretch ruin my life? I'll kill her. I'll kill her and her Pony and everybody who'd ever raised a hand against me.

Polished floor skidded by under Kife's limp feet as he was dragged along. And then they stopped.

"Advisor Falden and two handmaidens have been found in a chancellor's office, all dead in the same manner as Ulfren and Hjelzahn," a man's voice spoke in a low, confidential voice from nearby.

"More dead? Under my own roof!" A deeper voice boomed in a way that seemed to rattle Kife's aching ribs.

"Why can none of you tell me where my daughter has gone? Or find who killed two more of my sons?"

Only a murmuring of apologies and excuses followed.

Then, "Who is this you've brought me?"

Kife was pulled forward a few more steps.

"We found him in Zarram Dragonhold. He has Heithorn crests on his weapons."

"Heithorn? Are you part of this plot, along with Kessara?"

The blurred form of a silver robe stopped in front of Kife.

Kife lifted his pounding head.

The draping fabric led up to a wide chest covered in golden scale plate armor. Silver hair spilled down in long braids around a familiar face, one Kife knew from the profile stamped on every coin in Elundrae.

His split lips bled and cracked ribs ached as he grinned wide, laughing silently.

REIGN OF THE
DRAGON BORN
SELINA A FENECH
BOOK FIVE OF THE
SHADOW
DRAGON SAGA

CHAPTER ONE

Riony's heart raced in time to the heart stone lying against her chest—Lyrrin's pulse fluttering as she met her mother—and it felt like the world was ending.

She used to imagine what horrors might herald the end of days. Stars falling from the sky, birds crying like babies, rivers running with blood.

Nothing prepared her for what was surely the true harbinger of the end of the world which lay before her.

Kessara Heithorn … pledging her undying loyalty.

What in the deepest cursed depths is going on?

Riony was still damp from the thunderstorm they'd flown through to escape the capital of Elundrae, still smelled the metallic tang of her blood that soaked her almost as thoroughly, her body still flushed with the energy of the silvernix Kess had used to heal them both.

Completely, sincerely, what the sparks?

Riony stared down, open-mouthed, at the nasty gremlin bowing at her feet.

She looked like she had been dressed as finely as she used to be at Heithorn estate, but her dress had been torn apart and muddied, her neat braids pulled and fraying, releasing windswept streaks of charcoal and white hair.

Kess looked up, and Riony snapped her mouth shut and stepped away. Of all the things she was prepared to handle when she set off with a wolf to find her old tormentor, she wasn't even slightly prepared to deal with *that*.

Riony turned away, only to be faced with the sight of Eslinde and Lyrrin, crouched together, talking tentatively, their intent expressions so, so similar.

Or that.

Riony turned again, pacing madly between the stars-damned *princess of Elundrae*, her grayglim, far too many dragons, a couple of dragonriders who looked almost as confused as her, and also a few living Alderkin.

Not prepared for any of that either.

A hand against her cheek stilled her, and she turned again to meet the warmth of Aishena's dark eyes.

"Slow down, take a breath, and then tell me why you have so much blood on you. Is it yours?" Her tone was flat and scolding.

"It might be?"

Aishena clicked her tongue and began searching for the wound.

"I'm fine, it's okay."

"Is that 'Riony fine' or *not*-just-about-to-die fine?"

From nearby, Niskina snorted a laugh.

Riony took Aishena's searching hands in hers to still them. "I mean really fine. Healed by silvernix again, by *her*."

They both glanced at Kess, and Aishena raised her eyebrows.

Riony flicked her chin at the crowd of powerful strangers surrounding them. "And right now, more worried about all of this."

Aishena withdrew her hands and rested them on her athames. Her eyeline targeted the grayglim. "It is ... concerning."

Lyrrin's heartbeat still pattered rapidly, but she also smiled in a way that tore Riony's insides in three directions at once.

"I couldn't *not* reunite them, though. Even with the risks. Could I?"

Aishena's shrewd gaze softened, but she didn't answer, still looking over the strangers. Her sharply cropped hair, dyed a dark brown, swung at her jawline. She kept an eye on her brother, who in turn had taken up position as a guard, watching the skies with his seeing stone.

The cyan of Riony's glow crystal shimmered over Dracuni's moonlight-toned scales as the unidragon rested her head on Riony's shoulder.

Little sister is happy. You brought lots of good things back with you. Maybe you should follow wolves more often.

Riony huffed and patted the silky tufts of hair between the spikes on Dracuni's neck. She whispered, "We still have to be careful, with you. We don't know who we can trust."

Wolf girl said a lot to you. Is she a friend now?

Kess was upright again, sitting beside Griskin and leaning into his fur. At least she hadn't remained bowing to the ground, waiting for some kind of response. Riony's cheeks flushed hot, utterly mortified at the idea.

Kess had said a lot. The words still echoed through Riony.

I don't ask any forgiveness. I only ask that you let me serve you. I am yours.

Riony sighed out a long breath. "I *really* don't know what she is now."

You're the one who went off to save her.

"Only because she ... I mean ... I didn't think it would ... I just ..."

"Dragons! Incoming!" Benjin jumped off the stump he'd been standing on and ran their way. "Two at least."

Riony swung toward Kess. "What's going on? Is this some kind of trap? Did you say ... all of that *stuff* just to delay until the other dragons got here?"

Pulling herself up onto Griskin, Kess frowned. "If there was any trap being set, why would we wait for more dragons? We already have three."

The younger blond dragonrider jogged over beside them. "Umm, why would we be setting a trap on them? We're the ones with the princess and Alderkin. How do we know these people aren't setting a trap on us?"

"I'm sure *nobody is setting a trap*," Eslinde said, exasperated. "If there are dragons coming out of Draekhanhelm, they are coming after me because I stole the king's most valued prisoners."

Riony's mouth twisted. "I suppose that makes sense."

"The dragons are still a ways out." The older dragonrider eyed the sky, squinting at what was only a few small dots so far. "We have time to mount up and get ahead of them before they reach us."

Eslinde nodded firmly and began pointing between their party. "Dashiel, take the Alderkin again on the orange. Kess, take the snowflame and as many of the others as you can, their dragon is too small for all of them. Vance, I'll be on Viska with you and Yensen. We can take Lyrrin too."

Riony stepped between the princess and her sister. "You won't take Lyrrin. Also, Dracuni doesn't fly."

The younger rider, Dashiel, had already begun moving toward the orange dragon when they stopped and turned back. "What do you mean?"

Lyrrin pushed in front of Riony's guarding stance. "She can't fly. We've got to take her through the gateway."

Dashiel eyed Dracuni. "She's so big. She should have been flying after a few months of age. Even Shiff can fly already."

The little ice-blue and muted-purple dragon puffed her chest and flapped her wings in response. Dracuni snorted, her head drooping and diaphanous wings tucking in tighter to her body.

"How have you been training her?" Dashiel asked.

"I've been training her to roast the asses of people who question her training." Riony put her hand on Lyrrin's shoulder, keeping her in place. "Lucky for you we don't have time, because those dragons are getting closer and we're going through the gateway with Dracuni."

"Our dragons won't fit through the gateway," Eslinde said.

"Then we're going to have to split up," Riony replied.

"Nooooo. Not now." Lyrrin looked up at Riony, her bright-blue eyes pleading.

Eslinde's lips pulled thin and she straightened up, barely up to Riony's shoulders but as imposing as a giant. She smoothed back her white hair.

"No. Your sister is right. We will split up. Those riders are coming for me and the Alderkin. We can lead them away. Dash and Vance are some of the best riders there are. I'm sure we can lose those two riders and meet up again soon."

Riony gave her a single, firm nod. "Fly southwest. There's a shrine at the end of the river in the Valley of Unicorn Tears. Find it, we'll be there."

The incoming dragons were now close enough that the beat of their wings through the air could be heard. Eslinde and her grayglim warden claimed the orange dragon, and Vance mounted the brilliant gold beast.

"Kessara, do you want the snowflame again?" Dashiel asked.

"No. I'm going with the others through the gateway." Kess moved Griskin to stand behind Riony's shoulder. "As long as Riony agrees."

"Sparks. Why me? I guess?" Riony's insides felt jumbled.

She was not equipped or willing to be the master of another human, let alone someone who used to lord over her.

"Are you sure?" Niskina asked. She had cold eyes on Kess and hadn't loosened her grip on her pole axe.

Riony wasn't at all sure. She'd saved Kess, but had done it more for Griskin, who was a very good boy, and for a chance to inflict pain upon Kife. Maybe also for that small glimmer of hope, brought about by Kess saving Riony with her silvernix after she'd cracked her skull open, that Kess might make some good decisions in her life for once.

But Riony still didn't like the idea of Kess being *around*.

Having Kess at her back sent a shiver running through Riony, reliving the sensation of a bone dagger sliding deep in between her shoulders.

She knew it wasn't Kess who had stabbed her, and had for a while, but at the time, when her body wouldn't move, wouldn't breathe, and she felt death entwining her in darkness, she had believed it was the cruel wolf girl who had ended her, for no reason more than spite.

She'd been able to believe it all too easily. If it happened again now, she wouldn't be surprised. Only disappointed.

"Can we just get out of here and work the rest out later?" She herded her people toward the gateway, which Benjin had already activated.

"Should we take Lyrrin with us?" Yensen called from beside the orange as Eslinde climbed into the saddle.

"No," Riony snapped.

"No," Eslinde repeated. "It won't be safe for her in a chase. Will you look after the Alderkin for us, too?"

Riony nodded.

"And Shiff?" Dashiel asked from atop the snowflame.

"Sure, but if you don't catch up with us quickly, fair warning, Lyrrin will claim your dragonling as her new pet."

"Quickly now," Eslinde cried.

The incoming dragons were almost upon them, as their own three dragons spread their wings and one after another rushed upward into the sky.

The small campfire crackled as wind gusted it out, spreading embers like glowflies through the air.

"Everybody through, fast," Aishena called from beside the glowing gateway.

Benjin and Niskina stepped back to allow the cloaked Alderkin through, then followed.

Lyrrin made a soft, whimpering sound as Riony pushed her toward the gateway, her eyes watery and on the sky. "What if they get caught? What if they can't find us? What if I lose her again, already?"

Riony swallowed her feelings, trying to come up with comforting words.

A voice at her back spoke first. "Eslinde's grayglim will protect her, and the Zarram siblings are excellent riders with excellent dragons. They'll be okay."

Kess, offering words of assurance.

Riony blinked at the awful girl three times. Could she have really changed? Riony's lips twisted in disbelief.

Do dragon's piss fire?

Giving Lyrrin a gentle push, Riony said, "Go on, go through. Your amma knows you're alive now. I'm sure she won't stop trying to find you."

Lyrrin pouted but stepped through the gateway.

The untamed dragonling looked to Dracuni, then the sky where her owner had gone, and went afterward.

"They're almost over us," Aishena called out, gesturing Dracuni through next.

Riony glared at the incoming dragons as they swooped low in the sooty sky. Two lilac shimmerdarts, small and swift, shot past, and a massive red etherflame trailed behind.

Riony held her breath as they went overhead, releasing it as they followed Eslinde and the others.

Dracuni was halfway through the gateway, glimmering light spilling around her as she wriggled her shoulders through.

"Do you need a hand?" Riony thought the words loudly as well, unsure whether Dracuni would hear her with her front half already in another location.

I can fit! Don't push me. The crystal is sharp.

"The dragons are turning!" Kess snapped.

"What? Why?" Riony turned her eyes upward again.

The faster two dragons did a loop over the exposed gateway, the riders looking down at them. And they must have seen something because they signaled the big red back toward them too.

Only Riony, Kess, Aishena, and half of Dracuni remained. Aishena's murderous mother still hadn't flown out to find them, so Riony scratched the idea it could be her seeking her children.

"Could they be after you?" she asked Kess.

Kess winced. "Maybe. There might be some people who think I killed a few first heirs. I'll go, see if I can lead them off."

The large red was over them now too, diving down from the dark sky, heading their way. Kess spurred Griskin into motion, running him up onto one of the broken walls of the shrine, pausing there in open sight before dashing away along the clearest stretch of ground.

But the red dragon remained on target, coming straight for Dracuni.

"It's not changing course!" Aishena yelled, drawing athames.

Kess and Griskin skidded to a stop.

Riony swore, reached back, and unsheathed her sword. The clearing lit up purple as it activated. She placed herself between Dracuni and the red etherflame's seeking talons and braced. A gray shape darted in the corner of her eyes, then Riony's vision filled with scarlet scales, spikes, and teeth.

At the last moment the dragon swerved, head jerking awkwardly. A cry of alarm came from the rider as a wolf came pouncing up the dragon's spine and slammed into him.

The dragon banked sharply, revealing its back to Riony as it swooped around. Griskin loosed a feral growl as his jaws closed around the rider's shoulder, and Kess slipped from her saddle in a fluid motion, hunting blade in hand.

She caught on to the rider and wrapped herself around him in a grapple, slicing in swift motions through his scale mail armor.

Riony gaped as the dragon flew unevenly away over the tangled woods. She was stunned stone-still by the sheer ferocity of the attack and the horrifying thought that followed.

That maybe, all the times she'd faced Kess and Griskin, they'd been pulling their punches.

What's happening? Dracuni shifted within the gateway, backing out slowly.

Riony shook herself and focused. "I think the dragons are coming after you. As for everything else, I'm understanding less and less with every second. Watch out!"

A smaller shimmerdart landed in a whoosh directly on Dracuni's tail. Its talons clasped around the scaled length and wings pumped as it caught and pulled the unidragon.

Sensations of pain and fear rushed from Dracuni through Riony, and she launched herself at the dragonrider, crashing into the flank of the smaller dragon.

Batting it with the full length of the crystal sword, Riony dodged swiping talons as they detached from Dracuni and turned on her. Dirt swirled all around as the shimmerdart pumped its wings, the rider directing it away from Riony's attack.

The second shimmerdart dove to join the fray, curving its path away from a glowing blue return athame thrown by Aishena. Then two more larger forms overshadowed them.

The gold dragon and snowflame crashed down over each of the smaller shimmerdarts like an avalanche of shimmering scales. Vance and Dashiel, the dragonriders that had come along with the princess, showed no hesitation in clashing against their attackers in midair.

The gold dragon caught their shimmerdart neatly, wings and rider pinned together within clasped talons as Vance swept the dragon onward, away from the shrine. Blasts of flame and crackling energy followed.

The second shimmerdart had more time to react, and the rider turned the dragon over in a corkscrew maneuver, face-to-face with the similarly sized snowflame. The dragons tangled, claw to claw, turning over and over as their wings beat against each other's.

The orange, with Eslinde and her grayglim, hung back.

A burst of ball lightning shot from the shimmerdart and Riony ducked as it flew overhead.

Kess and Griskin raced into the clearing. A smudge of blood marked Kess's face below the constellation of moles on her cheekbone.

"The red is downed. What can I ... Dash, no!"

The shimmerdart had a claw around the snowflame's neck. Dashiel hadn't commanded their dragon to breathe yet, something Riony found a respect for, knowing how it shortened a snowflame's life, but no matter how they twisted and turned their dragon, the shimmerdart wasn't shaking loose.

A stream of liquid fire spilled from the snowflame's mouth, pouring over the shimmerdart beneath it. Splatters of burning dragon blood rained around the clearing. Riony hissed as a drop splashed over her arm.

The shimmerdart burned, its rider fallen, but still it didn't let go, unable even in its dying moments to take action without a command. It crumpled, falling, and was taking Dashiel and the snowflame with it as it plummeted to the earth.

Kess's wiry body tensed, leaning close to Griskin, and the two of them launched toward the falling dragons. Then a flash of gold passed overhead.

Vance brought Viska in and plucked Dashiel from the fiery comet of dragons. A moment later, the shimmerdart and snowflame crashed down. Deafening cracks sounded as trees split and flames went up all around.

All the incoming dragons were down, and Vance brought the gold dragon in, dropping Dashiel off lightly before landing himself. Eslinde and her grayglim came in to ground beside them.

Are you okay? Dracuni had backed all the way out of the gateway, looking sadly toward the plume of smoke rising from the woods nearby.

Riony's heartbeat hammered in her ears. She wasn't the one who was injured.

"Those poor dragons!" Lyrrin was also through.

Then all those who had gone through the gateway returned, weapons readied and eyes searching for the fight. Except the Alderkin, whose bright eyes were all on Dracuni.

Eslinde dropped down from her saddle and approached. "I don't understand. They should have come after us. Unless they saw the Alderkin, but still, they should have …"

Riony kept her sword raised, lifted toward Eslinde and the dragonriders.

"What is this about? Why are you drawn against us?" Then Eslinde's gaze went over Riony's shoulder and landed on Dracuni as well.

In a ring around Dracuni's neck and shoulders, scratched through her scales by the gateway crystal, iridescent silver blood shimmered.

Chapter Two

Lyrrin had spent so many hours of her life imagining the moment she and her birth parents were reunited. But she'd never imagined it like this, with Riony pointing a sword at her mother. A low whine built in her throat, and she swallowed it away.

Eslinde took a step forward, drawn to the sight of the silvernix bleeding from Dracuni's scratches. The droplets gleamed like moonlight in the cyan glow.

"Stay back," Riony growled.

Eslinde's grayglim and the older dragonrider, Vance, moved to flank Eslinde.

In response, Aishena, Niskina, and Benjin formed up into an opposing line beside Riony.

Lyrrin remained frozen between.

Taking a respectful step away, Eslinde gestured for the two men at her side to remain still. Her eyes remained on Dracuni. "What is that? It can't be …"

"It's nothing." Riony shrugged but kept her sword level. "We could all agree it's a trick of the light and go about our business as though this had never happened."

Behind Lyrrin, the Alderkin murmured between themselves in a melodious, susurrus language.

"That is silvernix, isn't it? That's …" Eslinde turned narrowed eyes to Kess, who stalked up behind Riony and took a guarding position at her shoulder.

A flash of something between hurt and pride twisted Eslinde's pale brow. "You knew! Didn't you? This is what you were keeping from me all that time."

Lyrrin noticed Riony flinch as she turned to see Kess behind her. Riony and the wolf girl locked eyes for a long moment, and Kess said nothing.

Eslinde tilted her head. "I understand your loyalties, but I think it's clear, whether you confirm or deny it. This is … this is …"

Riony sighed. "Yeah. You and your Alderkin may not have been the biggest secret in Elundrae after all. I had been hoping to keep this one a bit longer, though."

Dracuni bowed her head and Riony whispered, "It wasn't your fault."

Eslinde muttered under her breath, staring round-eyed at the bleeding dragon. The wounds were already closed, the shimmer of silvernix starting to fade.

Behind Dracuni, the gateway remained open. Riony glanced toward the unidragon and it, then back to the princess. "I'd like to know that you aren't going to do anything evil and stupid, now that you know what you know. The last thing I want is anyone attempting to one-up Kess's efforts."

Lyrrin's face twitched and crumpled with a flurry of emotions, and she stepped closer to her mother. "It's okay. You're not going to hurt Dracuni, are you? We don't have to fight."

Eslinde shoulders dropped, and she batted her hand again at Yensen and Vance, pushing them back. "Of course not. Lyrrin, I won't ever hurt you, your sister, or your … dragon?

I don't understand how this could be possible, though."

Lyrrin tried to respond, tried to reassure Riony that her mother could be trusted, or that at least she desperately wanted to believe her mother could be trusted, but her sister spoke over her.

"You don't need to understand; you just need to keep to your word and understand that I'll do *anything* to make sure you do."

"That, I can confirm," Kess added.

The Alderkin with hair the color of Lyrrin's removed his hood and bowed his head. "You have our word that we will not harm Dracuni and will do all we can to prevent others from harming her too."

Lyrrin was awed every time she looked at Yrik. Her grandfather, Eslinde had said. She had also told her that her father had died before Lyrrin was born.

Lyrrin had always known that was a possibility. Growing up in this world, many people lost family one way or another. Lyrrin tried to be happy to have found any family, to have had her theories confirmed about how similar she was to the depictions of Alderkin in the depths.

But it still hurt, as well, to know the truth.

Riony didn't look entirely convinced by the Alderkin's declaration, but still turned the tip of her sword toward Vance and Dashiel. "And what about you two dragonriders?"

"We're with Eslinde, however she commands," Vance said.

Dashiel exhaled through a lopsided grin. "Honestly, I just want to know how you bred her! She's amazing, I mean, apart from that she can't fly. Is that part of her breed too? What is she? Did you choose not to tame her or did the taming not take because—"

Vance put a heavy hand onto Dashiel's shoulder, stilling the flow of questions.

Sighing, Eslinde straightened her expression and her muddy dress. "I understand you barely know us and that we may seem intimidating to you—"

"Actually, I sort of think they're beating us in terms of intimidation." Dashiel gave a wry smile toward the glowing array of Alderkin weapons wielded by the other group.

"However, we must work together now to keep your special dragon safe. Because it seems to me somebody else out there knows about Dracuni."

Riony groaned and glared at Kess.

"Kife," they said together.

"Your brother?" Eslinde asked.

Kess nodded, her lips twisted in disgust. "That's why I was trying to keep him out of the palace, away from meeting the Dragon King. He knows, and he was determined to share that information with just one other person."

Eslinde turned her face up and eastward. "Considering the three riders who attacked were all in my father's colors and that we have more dragons incoming again, I would hazard a guess that your brother finally got his wish."

Riony lowered her sword but left it activated. She ran one hand over her face. "Sparks, I was really hoping he didn't survive the mob. Why did I have to be the idiot that left him alive?"

Niskina's dark glare was directed solely at Kess. "If your brother told the Dragon King … if the Dragon King knows …"

Riony turned toward the dark spots flying in on the horizon. "There may be nowhere safe in Elundrae for us now."

"We could move shrine to shrine, like we did when Kife was after us on his dragon," Lyrrin suggested.

Aishena shook her head. "The Dragon King has enough riders that he could keep multiple on watch at every shrine."

Lyrrin shivered. It had been scary when it was just one dragon chasing them. She asked hopefully, "Undercity?"

"I can't see how we'd keep Dracuni fed and hidden there," Riony replied.

The unidragon bowed her head and Riony gave her neck a comforting pat.

"We could steal a boat, leave Elundrae, and live as pirates," Benjin said, eyes twinkling.

Aishena batted him softly on the back of the head. "That isn't funny."

"I wasn't joking."

Lyrrin turned on the spot, taking in all the people around her. Her sister, looking ready for battle but also like she hadn't slept in weeks. Her mother, so new in her life. Aishena and Benjin, still with a bounty out from their mother. Dracuni, too big to hide and too small to fly. Niskina, giving Kess murderous looks while Kess only looked at Riony. And all the new people and dragons they'd somehow have to hide and keep alive too.

Lyrrin slipped her hand into Riony's. "What do we do?"

"I … I don't know," Riony whispered.

Eslinde cleared her throat. "Actually, I might know somewhere safe."

It took a lot of convincing to get Riony to agree to Eslinde's suggestion. She challenged all the minutiae of their plan, and it hurt Lyrrin to see how much Riony didn't trust her mother.

Do I trust her? She's the Dragon King's daughter.

Lyrrin only knew that she wanted to trust her. She wanted her mother to be someone who could also be family.

Their group had to split up again, with Dracuni unable to fly, and the two remaining dragons too big for the gateways. Riony refused to allow the two dragonriders to go alone on those dragons, in case they flew off to spread the knowledge of Dracuni.

Aishena volunteered to fly the orange dragon—Ambri, the riders called him—with Dashiel taking Viska. Vance preferred to remain with Eslinde.

Eslinde hesitated before the glowing gateway. "You're sure it is safe?"

Yrik raised his eyebrows at her.

Lyrrin offered her a hand to hold as she went through. "It's fine. We use them all the time."

Eslinde took her hand, her thin fingers cold and stiff. "I don't mean the Alderkin magic. I mean the encampment you're taking us to. Reports to the capital say they are filled with marauders and cannibals. And I'm sure that's an exaggeration, but how well can we trust anyone outside of dragonkeeps?"

Lyrrin raised her eyebrows then, matching her grandfather's expression. "Like us?"

"Oh no, not like you. I meant people who choose to be out … here." Eslinde eyed the twisted and bare trees nearby, as though expecting revenants or criminals to burst from the shadowed forest.

Lyrrin smiled softly. Although she'd grown up in an aboveground village until a few years ago, she had still been terrified when she was taken aboveground again after years of safety in the undercity. Taken by slavers, attacked by revenants, dragonriders, and the shadow dragon itself.

Everything she'd feared had come to pass. But she survived. And she'd since learned that not everything aboveground was monstrous.

"You don't need to be scared."

Eslinde looked down at her, silver eyes glittering.

Most of the others had gone through. Riony remained, waiting on Lyrrin, with Kess and Niskina at her back. Yensen and Vance in turn waited on Eslinde.

Riony stood beside the gateway, her eyes on where Eslinde and Lyrrin's hands were joined. "It will be a quick visit. We need to let our friends know what's happening, that we won't be around for a while, then we can get where we're going."

"Come on. You're going to like it." Lyrrin tugged at Eslinde's hand, and they both stepped through the wavering portal.

On the other side, the Alderkin remained hooded and within the shrine building, close to the gateway. Dracuni sat by the doorway out, and Lyrrin gave her a pat on the neck as she took Eslinde through.

Myrwa's enclave was calm and quiet. A few people moved around as the final cooking for the day was being shared, but many had already retired for the evening to their makeshift homes.

Soft cyan light filled the sanctuary within the standing stones—glow crystals, provided by Lyrrin, hung like stars between the fabric and hide huts. The path between the homes wound between vegetable patches, vibrant with an abundance of winter greens and rampant beanstalks.

A few children giggled and chatted near the communal fire, men stood nearby, singing as they wove netting on a hanging frame, and some women sorted through a jumble of torn fabric, stones, and metal poles.

"It's nice, isn't it?" Lyrrin looked up expectantly.

Eslinde blinked as she turned around, taking it in. "Are they all like this? The encampments around shrines?"

Lyrrin shrugged. "Not really. This one has been here the longest and has the most people. But they're all nice in their own way."

Myrwa stood up from a seat near the fire and pulled Riony into an embrace, her long shawl swaying around them, faded crimson like her graying red hair.

Then as she stepped back again, her expression turned cold. "Back again? Who is this you've brought with you? Last I saw that wolf girl, she seemed intent on murdering you."

Kess, hovering near Riony's shoulder, quietly moved Griskin a few steps back.

Riony spoke softly, "Don't worry, I'm keeping an eye on her."

She had Aishena's pack and began pulling bundles from it. She handed them to Myrwa and others who came to take the items their group had been collecting on their travels. Tools and crafts from other enclaves mostly.

If it were a normal day, they would take back trade from Myrwa's camp with them. But it wasn't a normal day, and Lyrrin didn't know when they'd be visiting the other shrines again.

"What about these other folk?" Myrwa sucked at her teeth as she glared at Eslinde's silver hair and her uniformed grayglim lurking nearby. "They look a lot like dragonlords and riders to me. Didn't think you'd mix with that type."

Her scolding expression made Lyrrin's chest ache.

"Come over here, you can warm up." She pulled on Eslinde's hand, dragging her out of earshot of Riony and Myrwa's conversation.

The grayglim followed closely, eyes wary and alert. Vance also kept his eyes on mother and daughter, but from a distance that made Lyrrin more comfortable.

She wondered what Eslinde's life must have been like, growing up as a princess in a palace, under guard and with everything she wanted.

Eslinde the First. Lyrrin could still hardly believe it.

Does that mean my name is really Lyrrin Eslinde? Like Aishena and Benjin and all their family get their last name Hjelzahn from Hjelzahn the First?

Lyrrin wasn't sure she liked that. She liked being Lyrrin Eyfarr. The name she and Riony had chosen for themselves together, when they were no longer owned by anyone, a name that reminded her of the parents who raised her.

As they approached the fire, a willowy older man, Haled, stood up and offered them a couple of bowls of steaming vegetables and flatbread. Eslinde reached into a pocket of her gown and pulled out a small purse.

"Will this do?" She held a silver sov on the palm of her hand.

Haled waved her away with a twiglike arm, chuckling to himself as he returned to rolling out dough.

Lyrrin flushed. Even a silver sov had been more than she and Riony ever had in the undercity. She hadn't seen currency at all since traveling aboveground.

"You don't need to pay," she said in a hush, then a little louder, "Haled, we aren't staying long. Can we have some food to take with us, please?"

Haled reached for a nearby basket and began filling it with stacked freshly cooked bread, jars of preserves, and bundles of fresh, snakelike beans, tied with string. "Of course, Lil Moon."

Once, only once, Riony had called her that in front of Myrwa, and now everyone there used the nickname for Lyrrin. It both warmed her heart and hurt it at the same time.

Eslinde put her coins away and bowed her thanks.

Under her breath, she said, "He's very kind."

Lyrrin chewed on some soft, smoky bread. "Not really. We all share out here."

Eslinde nibbled on the end of a green stalk from her bowl, watching as Benjin and Niskina also moved about the camp, doling out items from their bags.

"And they have no dragons at all here? How do they survive?"

Lyrrin pointed toward the large ring of towering crystals at the edges of the shrine enclave. "It's safe from revenants within the standing stones."

"What about dragons for other uses? Hard labor, manufacturing, protection from enemies?"

Myrwa drifted in beside them, making Eslinde jump when she snapped, "Only enemies we need to worry about are the blighted dragonriders. They come by every now and then, yelling at us and our 'rebellion,' before smashing something and seeing what they can take from us."

She flicked her chin at where Riony had joined the women picking through the broken hut. Riony hefted a large metal beam while the others propped it up again. Kellae stood to the side, bouncing her baby on her hip and chatting.

Eslinde frowned. "It's clearly a misunderstanding. I'm sure if the riders knew what this place really was—"

"Ha!" Myrwa shook her head and wandered away again, muttering about marauders and cannibals.

Eslinde's pale cheeks went as red as Riony's hair.

Lyrrin bit her lip. She had wanted this to all go differently. In all the times she'd dreamed of meeting her mother, she'd never imagined it would be quite so ... embarrassing.

"It's okay. I'm sure there are lots of things I don't know about where you lived, too," she said.

Eslinde smiled down at her with watery eyes.

Over near the central shrine building, Riony whistled softly and signaled it was time to go. Their group gathered up again, and Eslinde offered her gratitude with royal formality as she took the basket of food from Haled.

Back near the shrine, the grayglim stood close, watching as Benjin traced the activation rune. Giving the man a sharp look, Benjin leaned further over it, obscuring his work from view.

Eslinde turned back to the people waving goodbye. "The others here, do they know how to use the gateways too?"

Lyrrin's lips pursed. "We haven't taught anyone else how to. I think we should.

Sometimes revs hang around the boundaries for too long, making it hard for people to go out hunting and foraging. And sometimes the dragonriders hurt people."

"I'm sorry," Eslinde said, sounding as though it were directly her fault.

"We move around the shrines, visiting them all as often as we can to help out." Lyrrin dropped her voice low. "But the others say it's too dangerous to let anyone else use the gateways too. Because of Dracuni."

The gateway illuminated, and one after another, they all stepped through.

The shrine on the other side had no encampment around it. Perched on a barren, rocky hillock and blasted by the frigid winds off the southern coast, it hadn't been used for more than temporary stops in their travels. Lyrrin pulled her hood up and her gloves back on.

Benjin took the lead, trying to strike up a conversation with the Alderkin just behind him, but they remained quiet.

Dracuni trotted along beside the dragonrider's hatchling, both deep in some silent, enthusiastic conversation.

Eslinde and Lyrrin had split up along the way, with the princess assisting the dragonrider who's gait grew more and more pained the farther they walked.

Kess and Griskin wove back and forth along the group, sometimes scouting ahead, other times guarding the rear. Niskina kept her eyes on Kess and her hand on her pole axe, using it as a walking cane. Her mouth was drawn down in a scowl.

It was a long walk, and Lyrrin was yawning and shuffling her feet when their destination still wasn't within sight.

"Big day, huh?" Riony said.

She moved up behind Lyrrin, scooping her under the armpits and lifting her onto her shoulders.

"Whatever do you mean? Pretty normal, really." Lyrrin slouched, leaning on Riony's head.

"Speak for yourself! I got chased by a rioting mob, found out Alderkin were alive, and had one of the worst people in the world pledge themselves to me. I'd say it was fairly eventful."

Lyrrin yawned again as she bumped along on her perch. "That was weird, what Kess said."

"Right? What do I do with that?"

"I think she likes you."

"Dear sister, why would you say something so hurtful to me?"

Lyrrin smirked and sighed. Her sister's hair smelled of smoke and blood. Even with Riony checking in with them as often as possible, Lyrrin had been worried the entire time her sister had been gone with the wolf.

"You know, I thought you were the biggest tamebrain ever for going to find Kess."

Riony shrugged, making Lyrrin lift and drop. "Fair. But also, you were the one who was all 'you're being so mean, give her a chance!' after Kess helped us save Dracuni. I blame your influence."

"Fair. But still, I'm glad you went and found her."

Riony's hands were warm where they held Lyrrin's shins, and she squeezed her gently. "How is it? Being around your amma?"

"She seems really nice. You know, for a dragonlord."

"Yeah, I think so too. Just … Don't get too attached. Just in case. Bonds of blood don't always mean you can trust someone." Riony's head turned toward where Kess rode on Griskin, not far ahead.

Lyrrin shivered.

The moon cast its color-stealing light down over them and the cold of the winter night seeped into Lyrrin's bones as their destination came into view.

The looming walls of a dragonkeep.

CHAPTER THREE

Walking into a dragonkeep set every nerve within Riony on edge. Even if the place was only partially completed, abandoned to weeds and rodents. The immense walls encircled only halfway around where a city was meant to be, craggy and unfinished along the top.

Rising against the night sky, the wall seemed to bare its teeth at them, turning Eslindekeep into a shadowed monster in the night.

"Aishena and the other rider should have been here by now." Riony's jaw ached from tension.

Eslinde led the way around the outer wall until they could pass it. Within, a smaller temporary wall that had probably protected the builders undulated, its still standing and crumbled sections curving up and down, serpentlike. Loose stones shifted under Riony's feet as they climbed in through a broken gap.

"There," Kess said, pointing upward.

Benjin had the seeing stone on his staff activated before his face, following Kess's direction. "I can't see anything."

Riony squinted into the night sky but saw no winged shapes moving against the stars. She nudged Dracuni beside her.

Can't hear any other dragons except Shiff. Shiff likes to talk a lot.

Kess stared as well, then shook her head. "Sorry, I thought I saw a dragon."

Niskina gave Kess a cold look. "Did you or not? If it wasn't Aishena and Dashiel, we might have a problem. More of a problem than *you* already pose to us."

Benjin, by her side, nodded fiercely.

They all paused, watching the sky, but nothing more moved above them.

Eslinde said, "It might have been a great owl. They get very big around here, almost treedart size."

Riony shuddered. She could barely handle a pocket-sized owlette. She'd never told Lyrrin she was secretly glad when that pet got away.

"And there's plenty around for them to be hunting." Eslinde nodded toward the abandoned construction, where bantam ferrets scurried across the brushy ground between roads that went nowhere, empty foundations, and piles of rusting steel.

Gasping, Lyrrin shifted her weight on Riony's shoulders, indicating she was climbing down, and Riony bent over to help her.

Lyrrin went chasing over to a stack of cut stone where a flurry of furry forms escaped into the gaps.

She crouched and made kissy noises, trying to reach her fingers in. "They are sooo cute!"

"No more pets," Riony snapped.

They moved forward again, more hesitant now, over the uneven road. The cobbled paving, having never seen use or maintenance, had shifted over the years, pushed out of place by burrowing creatures and roots. It took them through the outlined edge of the unbuilt city toward a flat structure on a low peak in the center.

Vance grunted softly and bent to rub one of his knees.

Riony turned to him. "I haven't seen many Rolanian dragonriders before."

"Rolanian *dragonlords*," he corrected.

"You say that as though it's somehow better. And yet my estimation of you just dropped significantly."

Straightening up, Vance looked her in the eyes. "Or at least we were before we disobeyed our father, refused to tame Shiff, and fled the burning remains of our dragonhold."

"Okay, that's sounding better again."

Vance huffed, but his eyes were sad. "You don't like dragonriders?"

Riony returned a humorless smile. "Never met one I would trust not to skin me alive if I blinked at them wrong. Aishena had better get here safely."

"Same for Dashiel."

Turning back to them from up ahead, Eslinde tutted. "They're probably just being careful, flying low to avoid being followed. I'm sure both are safe and will be here soon."

Riony wanted to stay positive, but everything around her felt like a trap. The way the Alderkin continued to stare at Dracuni, conversing in low tones in their own language. The grayglim trailing after Eslinde like a bound spirit. The dragonrider, keeping as much of an eye on Riony as she was on him.

And Kess, at her back.

"Would you stop lurking behind me?" Riony rasped.

Kess's shoulders lifted, and sadness flashed over her eyes before her expression set calm and firm again. "Of course. Whatever you wish."

Griskin trotted faster, moving ahead of Riony.

She ran a hand up into her hair, scrunching the red curls in her fist. "And just in case you were wondering, yes. You have made things exceptionally awkward and weird. Things haven't been this awkward and weird since the last time I bedded your amma."

Riony waited, but there was no bite in return.

She sighed. "So ... thanks for that. I might have preferred it if you'd stayed mean."

Kess half turned and quirked an eyebrow. "Do you want me to be mean to you?"

Heat rushed up Riony's neck. "No. Stop it. You're taking things even further in the weird and awkward direction. I just want you to be yourself again, doing whatever selfish thing you want to do."

Kess's ice-blue eyes held Riony for a long moment, then she nodded slowly. "The selfish thing I want to do now is look after you. Good luck stopping me."

"You're failing to understand the meaning of selfish!" Riony snapped.

The slightest smirk rose on Kess's lips as she turned away, prowling ahead like a guard on patrol.

Riony was relieved to be distracted from the wolf-riding gremlin when Eslinde brought them to a stop at the base of solid, sprawling foundations.

"This is what was to be my palace." Eslinde stared dully at the stone wall before them, marked with archway niches all along the base, the flat top spreading across the crest of the low hill.

"Would have been nice if it had a little something more. Like walls or a roof," Riony said.

"My keep had been under construction before Lyrrin was born, but unfortunately all progress on that front ceased when my parents discovered my pregnancy. They decided that me having my own dragonkeep was no longer a good idea."

Riony searched the area with her eyes. There were certainly enough building supplies left about to set up a somewhat protective area, set camp, but with all trees cleared during construction and only a few smaller ones sprouting through, they would be very exposed.

"And why is it a good idea for us to be here? We're open to rev attacks, and wouldn't the first place the Dragon King looks for you be your keep?"

"They won't look for us here because they would also assume it's not a secure location, but that's because they don't know about this." Eslinde reached into the niche before her, pushed a stone aside, and pulled a lever.

The wall within the archway swung aside, revealing a gaping tunnel within. It sloped smoothly down into the earth, solid stone on every side and large enough for even their biggest dragon to enter.

Vance chuckled softly. "You and your rebellious ways. What have you got down there?"

Eslinde smiled softly in reply, her silver eyes sparkling.

Riony planted her feet and folded her arms. "Whatever is down there, we can wait until the others arrive to find out. I'm not going in there until I know Aishena is safe."

Benjin climbed the nearby slope to get up on top of the foundations, above the open tunnel, watching the dark skies. "They're coming now!"

Flying in from the south, the gold and orange dragons approached fast, as though in a race.

"Nothing on their tail?" Kess asked in a growl.

Benjin squinted through the seeing stone on his staff. "Not that I can see."

As the two dragons passed over the half-made outer wall, Viska put on another burst of speed, breaking ahead. Riony tensed, one hand reaching up to wrap around the hilt of her sword at her shoulder.

Then she heard laughing.

The gold dragon came to a sliding halt along the road nearby, talons scraping across the stone. Dashiel leaped down, grinning and panting.

"I told you I'd win!" Dashiel yelled up at the orange that glided in to land beside them.

Aishena brought the dragon to an elegant stop. She remained in the saddle, peering down. "Considering I had the lesser dragon and haven't flown for years, I wouldn't be so cocky about winning by such a small margin."

Dashiel beamed. "Maybe I went easy on you."

"Maybe I went easy on you," Aishena replied.

The tension across Riony's back eased at seeing Aishena there, in one piece, and even enjoying herself, despite her ever-blank expression. But with all the time they'd spent together since leaving the undercity, Riony could translate even the smallest flicker of emotion from the stern young woman.

Although Aishena required no assistance, Riony moved beside the dragon and caught her about the waist as she climbed down from the saddle.

Gently lowering her to the ground, Riony grinned and murmured in her ear, "Took your time. Run into some trouble, or were you just too busy flirting?"

Aishena pressed a hand to Riony's arm, her way of offering unspoken gratitude. She spoke back equally low. "We went out over Eyersunn Sea to lose some riders that were after us. Also, as I have never flirted in your presence, I'd be surprised if you could recognize it."

"There was that one time you got super drunk and tried to kiss me."

Aishena's hand around Riony's arm squeezed and released. "And I do enjoy being the better person for still being friends with you despite how you keep bringing it up. But I certainly hope that you don't think *that* is how *I* would flirt."

"It honestly took me far too long to realize you weren't flirting with me every time you glared my way."

Aishena offered a rare smile. "You've grown so much."

"So you weren't flirting with the pretty blond dragonrider?"

Aishena shrugged and took her pack which Riony had carried for her when they split up. "I didn't say that. I'll just point out that some of us can flirt and stay on task at the same time."

Across the paved area, Dashiel's laugh rang out, from something either Vance or Kess had said to them.

Riony wasn't sure either Kess or the stoic dragonrider could say something that would make someone laugh like that, but they were the only options in proximity.

It seemed everyone was happy to have the riders and dragons back.

"Come on then, now we're all here. Inside, everybody." Eslinde gestured to the tunnel. "Some help with the torches, Vance?"

Vance led his golden dragon into the tunnel, then brought her head to an alcove at the side that Eslinde directed them to.

The etherflame breathed a rush of fire into a channel on the wall, and all the way along the length of the tunnel small puffs of flame flickered from gaps beside the torches, setting them alight.

Despite the abundance of lighting, the passage still seemed stark and cold compared to the underground world Riony was familiar with. The undercity, with its glow stones, and luminous, waxy limestone flows, and ever-present scent of spiced mushroom or roasting rope worms.

A pang ached in her chest. She hadn't realized just how much she missed it.

Vance and Dashiel led the two tamed dragons in first, followed by Eslinde, her grayglim, and the Alderkin.

Kess kept ahead of Riony now, closer to Dashiel's side, chatting amiably in a way Riony found disconcerting.

Riony kept her group with her—Lyrrin, Aishena, Benjin, and Niskina, with Dracuni behind them, in case they needed to get out fast. Riony clenched her teeth as the heavy doorway sealed behind them.

Dashiel's dragonling remained trotting along at Dracuni's side, watching the unidragon with an awed expression and no doubt also chatting away.

Eslinde spoke from the front, her voice echoing between the hard stone walls. "Every first heir designs and oversees construction of their own dragonkeep. And I had such big plans for mine."

She paused, showing them a hallway of smaller rooms and private dormitories to one side. "I was in complete control over construction, and it was before my parents became suspicious of my motivations and kept me monitored, so I'm certain they're unaware this exists."

They passed another hallway with rows and rows of bedding, a barracks, stretching far into the darkness. The next room was stacked floor to ceiling with metal crates.

"Arms and armor," Eslinde said.

The spaces were eerie, unused, a fine layer of dust lying over every surface and making the air dry and grimy on Riony's tongue.

"Luckily, the underground section was completed and sealed before my pregnancy was discovered and construction ceased. I doubt my parents had any reason to suspect what I built here, that these foundations contain anything other than the usual basements and dungeons."

They passed a vast mess hall with long bench seating, and the adjoining kitchens, with multiple ovens, each as large as a room in the stalagmite apartment Riony once called home.

Within the kitchens and the bathing room they passed next, metal water pumps jutted from the ground, their curved handles the most decorative thing in the stark spaces.

Eslinde came to a stop at an intersection to another tunnel as tall and wide as the main one. She gestured inside. "Housing for dragons."

Vance and Dashiel led the tamed dragons in. Riony stepped in after them, checking the space. The huge square-cut room looked ready to stable scores of dragons, with walled bays furnished only with troughs. More water pumps stood at the end of each row.

Riony tried one, giving the handle a couple of quick pumps. Water splashed out at her feet. There must be an underground reservoir.

Shiff galloped in, sticking her nose into a trough, then snorting loudly.

"She's hungry," Dashiel said while settling the orange dragon into a stall.

Eslinde shook her head. "I hadn't reached the stages of stocking food stores, I'm afraid. And even if I had, it would have spoiled between then and now."

Dracuni had followed Riony in and inspected one of the stalls with a huff. *No blankets?*

"I'll find you a blanket." Riony patted her on the nose. "Food is something we're going to have to work out—if we stay here. Dracuni's a big eater still too."

"But we can stay here, can't we? It's so good!" Lyrrin asked, having run the length of the stables and back.

"You're just hoping to catch one of those bantam ferrets," Riony accused.

"Maybe."

Eslinde raised her voice over the growing chatter. "I know it's late, but we still have a lot to discuss. Find a room you prefer to be yours, settle the children and dragons in, then join me in the meeting chamber up ahead."

Riony eyed the tamed dragons, left still and unmoving in their stalls. "I'd feel better if Dracuni stays with me."

"Unfortunately, the hallways ahead are only designed for humans. Dracuni will have to stay here with the others." Eslinde gave an apologetic look, then swept away with her grayglim behind her.

Lyrrin and Benjin, smiling and wide-eyed, raced off to claim the very best room for themselves.

Kess followed, stalking out on Griskin.

Riony's gaze trailed after, and as the girl and wolf disappeared around the corner, a worried shiver rocked Riony's shoulders.

Niskina shared a grim look with Riony. "Don't worry, I'll keep an eye on her. I know she saved your life, but I don't trust her."

Hands on weapons, Niskina and Aishena left the stables.

Dracuni moved into the same stall as the dragonling.

I can stay here. Shiff is nice, I trust her.

"It's not Shiff I'm worried about," Riony whispered. "If someone tries to hurt you, you can't exactly flame them."

Dracuni lifted her shoulders in an almost human shrug. *Shiff says Dashiel and Vance are good. That they didn't tame her, even though it got them in trouble.*

"But they still have two tamed dragons with them."

Dracuni looked over at the gold and orange beasts, her lilac eyes shimmering and sad. *They are silent, as though not even there. Shiff says she's never gotten to speak with another dragon much before. They're all silent where she came from.*

A breath sighed out of Riony at the thought of growing up alone amid beings who were only the ghosts of the real thing.

Dashiel appeared beside Riony, startling her. "Tamed dragons ... I know. I wish we could untame all of them. Kess showed us how. Amazing, right?"

"Yeah ... amazing," Riony muttered.

"Maybe we could untame Viska and Ambri soon and—"

"I can't see that being a good idea." Vance stepped beside his sibling, folding arms across a wide chest. "Having a couple of dragons that can fly and fight is too valuable to lose right now, when we're out in these rev-blighted wastes with the Dragon King's forces after us."

Dashiel winced. "It's something we can at least think about."

Vance slapped a hand down over their shoulder, directing them out of the room.

"Maybe one at a time? I'm sure Viska will still like you ..." Their voice drifted away as they left the stables.

Dracuni snorted softly. *See? Nice people.*

"They're still dragonriders and dragonlords." Riony sighed.

She adjusted a strap on her bag and fidgeted in her armor, feeling the weight of them. She was looking forward to putting it all down and resting. It had been a long day.

"Are you sure you'll be fine in here?"

If I need you, you'll hear me. Dracuni pressed her cheek against Riony's.

It took a few more moments before Riony was willing to step away, and as she moved out into the hall, she was met with the haunting vision of the three Alderkin, tall and cloaked, standing in wait.

Her hand went to her sword on instinct, and their eyes followed, glinting in the torchlight.

"Where did you get that blade?" Lyrrin's grandfather spoke in a voice like crumbling stone.

As tempted as Riony was to give him the same answer she'd once given to Kess when asked how she'd acquired a weapon, she figured it was too early to be making ass jokes with an ancient and magical race who were the last of their kind.

"I found it. In the Alderkin depths. In a tomb," Riony winced, apologetic. "I only took it because I needed a weapon, because I was lost and shackled to a monster who was *really* getting on my nerves, and I didn't think at the time ... I'm sorry."

Riony held her breath, praying to her ancestors in the stars that the Alderkin wouldn't take her sword off her.

Priyune nodded, her eyes soft and glittering green. "The tomb of one of our greatest warriors, a mighty protector of unicorns from another war with humans, centuries before the dragon enslavers came."

Shael traced a mysterious shape in the air and bowed her head. "It was said she flew above the world and tore lightning from the sky to cast at those who sought to capture unicorns for themselves."

Yrik moved closer, assessing Riony with eyes the precise color of Lyrrin's. "It is a sword worthy only of one dedicated to protecting the sacred lifebringers. And it seems, although the unicorns are gone, the dragon you call Dracuni is of the same blood and magic."

"And I'm dedicated to protecting her," Riony said.

Yrik's eyes narrowed. "Are you? How long did you travel away from her to find the wolf-riding girl? How long did you leave Dracuni unguarded?"

"I ... She wasn't unguarded." Riony's mouth went dry.

There was no one she trusted more than Lyrrin, Aishena, Benjin, and Niskina to keep Dracuni safe. But she had felt guilty every moment she was away. She'd questioned every step she'd taken following Griskin. Even now, she wasn't sure it had been worth it.

Having Kess around left Riony's insides constantly churning.

She'd meant what she said, before getting stabbed in the back. She wanted the world to be better, to live kindly, to start by finding peace between herself and Kess.

But now, even with the apologies and promises Kess had vowed, Riony wasn't sure she could ever trust her.

Bringing Kess in had brought so many others with her, all of which now knew about Dracuni, all of which could be a threat.

Yrik held Riony in his sapphire gaze as though he could read every doubt passing through her mind. "Nothing is more important than keeping Dracuni safe. Nothing. If you wish to be worthy of wielding that sword, you need to accept that."

Chapter Four

Kess hadn't even found a room to settle in before she was ambushed.

Niskina stomped the end of her pole axe on the ground and then leaned against it. She tossed her tumbling curls back and glowered thickly at Kess. "I don't know what you think you're going to achieve from this game you're playing with Riony."

The clank of the weapon against stone echoed down the long corridor. Aishena was there too, standing coolly at ease and all the more threatening for it.

Kess turned Griskin slowly to face them. "I feel I've made my intentions clear. Embarrassingly so, apparently."

"Then let me make something clear to you." Niskina stepped fearlessly beside the wolf. "Riony might have decided to give you another chance, but I haven't. Your actions, your betrayal, led to my father's death. I won't forget that, and I won't ever forgive that."

Kess turned cold, as though plunged into an icy lake. "I know, I'm sorry, I—"

"I don't want to hear it. I don't trust it, and I don't believe you won't do worse again. You're only alive right now because Riony, for some depths-cursed, inconceivable reason, wills it." A full-body shudder of revulsion shook Niskina as she held Kess's gaze.

Then, as though she was unable to stand her presence a moment longer, she spun and left.

Aishena remained, a casual stillness to her like she was a statue of a soldier.

"Are you going to threaten me too?" Kess asked.

"Indeed." A glint flickered in Aishena's dark eyes. "Because Riony is a better person than all of us, in allowing you here. So, if you hurt her again, in any way, *any way*, you can expect that pain returned upon you tenfold."

Kess wanted to argue that she wouldn't hurt Riony, that keeping her from ever being harmed again was what she wanted more than anything. But she was also scared that she would fail. That through the simple fact of who she was, who she'd been, that she would be the cause of more pain.

Kess smirked off the rattle of fear. "Did nobody listen to what I said before? Was I too low to the ground? Could you not hear me?"

"*Everybody* heard you. *Nobody* believed you."

"So, it was both mortifying and futile. Wonderful." Kess's fingers twitched to hold a dagger, to have a weapon in hand, ready to defend herself.

She fought off the instinct. She refused to be cowed or give the grayglim-trained young woman a reason to strike.

Sighing, she steadied herself. "But my intentions are the same, whether you believe it or not."

"We'll see." Aishena remained statue-still, holding Kess in her dark gaze for a long moment before she vanished into the shadows.

Kess shrugged off the ache in her chest.

Griskin turned his head back to Kess and whined softly.

Kess leaned into his fur and rubbed his ears. "It's okay. Even if it's still you and me against the world, it's okay."

She held him for a long moment, inhaling the smoky musk of his fur and listening to his breaths as he panted nervously. She still could hardly believe he had come for her, had brought help for her, hadn't abandoned her. He was the only reason she was alive, a hundred times over.

And he made her feel like remaining alive was something she wanted, maybe even deserved.

She wrapped her arms around his neck in a hug. "I missed you so much. I'm sorry that I was ever cruel to you. You're one of the best things in my life and I owe you everything."

Kess decided not to bother finding a room to make her own. The most she could do anyway would be unpack some bags from Griskin, but it seemed better to keep everything on them.

A time would come when the others would decide they were done with allowing her to stay, with tolerating her presence, and she didn't want to have to leave anything behind when she was expelled.

Griskin padded down the expansive corridor, ghostly quiet. He didn't like the echoing tunnels and stone walls. At least the air was free of fungus spores.

They were the first to join Eslinde and Yensen in the meeting room.

Torches flickered along the walls, and an imposing granite table sat heavily in the center of the space.

The princess was pale with exhaustion, her eyes rimmed in pink, but she met Kess with a warm smile.

Kess found her lips turned upward in response. "Secret underground chambers? Seems as though you learned some things from your father."

Eslinde scoffed. "I'm sure the Alderkin's claim to secret underground chambers predates Yeonard Draekhan by centuries."

Kess pulled Eslinde's earring from her pocket and handed the now empty vessel to the princess. "Thank you, for this, and for ... caring whether I survived. I wouldn't have made it without you."

And if I wasn't healed enough to fly, Riony might not have made it either.

Eslinde's fingers closed around the earring and around Kess's hands, holding them. "I noticed your leg no longer troubled you. I'm glad you rejoined us, Kessara, not only for what you brought with you."

"What I brought?"

"My daughter! And not only that, but this unidragon creature they have! Such a resource. This ... this gives us hope."

Kess pulled her hands free from Eslinde's. "Dracuni isn't a resource. She's a living, feeling creature."

Eslinde tilted her head. "Of course. But we have to consider what can be done now with her, that we couldn't have done before."

Lyrrin jogged in then, jostling the large basket of food. "It's good we stopped at Myrwa's. I'm starving!"

"Same," Benjin followed close behind, and snatched a handful of green beans and a flatbread the moment Lyrrin put the basket down on the meeting table.

Riony and her friends came in next, with the Alderkin, Dashiel, and Vance following.

Eslinde gestured a little awkwardly to the children. "I thought, perhaps, they might need to sleep by now? This should be a meeting for grown-ups."

Lyrrin gaped, then pouted.

Riony had removed some of her armor but left the harness on for the sword on her back. She unsheathed it to sit down, and Kess noted how, even though the magic wasn't activated, Riony hefted it easily as she leaned it against the table beside her. She noticed how Riony did it in a way like she wanted people to notice.

"Everyone's hungry," Riony said. "I'm not sending them kids to bed on an empty stomach. And they should be included. They're some of our best strategists—don't look at me with pity! They're better than a lot of adults. They have good ideas."

"Like becoming pirates?" Eslinde muttered.

"It wasn't necessarily a *bad* idea." Riony shrugged and chewed on some bread covered in pickles passed to her by Lyrrin.

Aishena and Niskina took seats on either side, and Riony leaned into Aishena, whispering, then offering a bite of her food which Aishena declined tersely, which only made Riony grin wider.

Niskina reached over and pinched some of the bread, and Riony elbowed her, chuckling.

Kess wasn't clear on whether Riony was in a more romantic relationship with either of them—or both—but the familiarity and depth of care they each had for one another was obvious, and it left Kess feeling brittle and aching.

In all the years she and Riony had been confined to each other's company, they'd never had that sort of easy closeness. There had been closeness, but the kind that hurt them both more than it brought any comfort. And Kess knew why. She understood exactly why, and that only hurt more.

Eslinde cleared her throat from where she remained standing at the head of the table. "I wanted to speak with you all tonight, because I hope we can all be allies in our important cause moving forward."

Riony leaned back in her chair. "And what cause is that?"

Eslinde gestured to Kess. "I've heard from Kessara that you have suspicions about the true cause of the shadow dragon curse."

Riony also eyed Kess. "Tamed dragons?"

Eslinde nodded. "Consider your suspicions confirmed. Which then leads us to the bigger question. What are we going to do about it?"

Kess slid from Griskin into her chair, and he curled up behind it. "We're going to try to do something about it? With the Dragon King himself hunting Dracuni? Seems risky to do anything more than stay hidden and safe right now."

Eslinde had found a moment to pull her tangled hair back into a tight bun, but she shook her head with such vehemence that silver strands escaped around her face. "We must do something! The alternative is the ruination of all of Elundrae."

Niskina put together her meal, then passed the basket of food along. "What do you expect us to do?"

"You untamed one dragon. We could untame more. Enough to put an end to the curse."

Riony downed the last of her bread and leaned forward on her elbows. "Hold on. It's not all that easy. We haven't exactly got dragonriders lining up saying, 'oh please, turn my faithfully mind-wiped steed into a wild beast.' Even your friends here won't give up theirs."

"You really want to be out here without any dragons to protect us?" Vance growled.

"Managed it well enough so far." Riony picked her teeth. "Besides, even if we did have a supply of dragons to be untamed, you need silvernix."

There was a pause as Eslinde hesitated over her words. "Yes, and I had thought we'd have to find a supply, perhaps steal some."

Kess shot a look at Eslinde's remaining earring. She assumed it contained another dose. One wasn't enough for her plan, but still, she didn't share the information.

Gesturing back toward the stables, Eslinde said, "But with Dracuni—"

"*Nope.*" Riony rose to her feet. "And that's where I'm out. Typical that your very first thought is to use Dracuni for her blood."

"Even for the greater good? Even if it could heal our entire land? We would be sure to bleed her humanely—"

"And that's an even bigger *NOPE.*" Riony grasped the hilt of her sword.

Lyrrin straightened in her seat, but her chest was still level with the tabletop. "What Riony means, is that only Dracuni gets to decide what happens with her blood. Not us. We all agreed that's how it should be."

"This is also how it was with the unicorns." Yrik bowed his head to Lyrrin.

Benjin tapped his fingers on the table, stirring up dust. "How many dragons are we talking about? How many would need to be untamed to make a difference, to stop the shadow dragon from raising the dead? Ten? A hundred? A thousand? All of them?"

Aishena gazed at him thoughtfully. "We saw a mural in the Alderkin depths—that was one of our first clues about the true cause—that suggested the shadow dragon manifested even from the very first tamed dragon."

"This is true," Priyune replied. "I had the tragic misfortune of being witness to the event."

"The first taming? That was over eighty years ago! You don't look that old." Benjin's eyes narrowed.

"Alderkin age differently. We grow slower but live much longer."

Lyrrin grasped the edge of the table fervently. "Does that mean I'm going to get *taller*?"

"You're fine at any size, little spitfire," Riony said. "I think the more important part was that Priyune here has been alive the entire time the shadow dragon has."

Priyune offered Lyrrin a sly wink, then continued. "We saw the first dragon spirit enslaved, saw its tormented soul separated from its body. But it was decades later before humans began replicating that event in large numbers."

Eslinde nodded confirmation. "It was fifty years ago that my father's method of dragon taming was leaked, dragonglass was in wide production for storing silvernix, and everyone who was able tried to capture and tame their own dragons, and then began breeding them. That is when the first stories of the shadow dragon raising dead began."

Kess didn't know a lot of the wider history, but she knew tales from the Heithorn line. Her family had been some of the first Taens who hunted and tamed full-grown wild dragons.

It was what they had become famous for, and they considered those who sourced their dragons through breeding as dishonorable.

Until those who bred their dragons gained a financial edge over them, and the Heithorns began breeding dragons the same as all other dragonlords.

Yrik held his hands in front of him, staring at his blue-clawed fingers. "The Alderkin tried to understand it, tried to find our own way to stop the curse. But it was too powerful. The use of the life-giver's magic to subjugate such powerful souls ... Each broken spirit has only made the shadow dragon stronger, all merging into that single mourning, vengeful entity."

"How many dragons were around back then? Before everyone started taming them?" Benjin asked.

"Only the king and his heirs had them before that. A few dozen, definitely less than one hundred," Eslinde replied.

Vance puffed his cheeks and blew out a breath. "There's no way we can untame that many, to get the numbers even close to that low."

Benjin chewed his thumbnail. "But maybe we don't have to. If we can even get the numbers down to what they were a year or two ago, back when revs stayed dead when you killed them, that would make a huge difference."

Eslinde's mouth opened into a neat *O* shape. "That ... that might be feasible."

Riony folded her arms and smirked at Eslinde. "Told you. The kids have good ideas."

Benjin lifted his chin smugly. "So, how many would that be?"

Eslinde tipped her head side to side, lips moving silently as though counting in her head. "Tamings have slowed down a lot in recent years. Many minor dragonlords have run out of silvernix, but the greater households and heirs have not, and each is still taming dragons for riders and industry. Reports are that around eighty dragons were tamed in the last two years. I have been keeping an eye on numbers."

Benjin's smile dropped. "That's a lot. Even if we did have silvernix for them all."

"Which is up to Dracuni," Riony reiterated.

"But it's not impossible," Lyrrin offered. "And if the dragonlords saw the difference that made, maybe they would voluntarily untame their own dragons."

Kess scoffed under her breath.

Eslinde smiled thinly at her daughter. "Maybe they would."

"What other options do we have?" Dashiel brushed crumbs from their hands. "Couldn't we just wait for all the silvernix to run out? Then there would be no new tamed dragons."

Eslinde sighed and finally settled herself down into her chair. "My father has already found a way to tame without silvernix. Although I have removed that option from him, for now."

She gestured to the Alderkin. "I wouldn't put it past him to find a way again. And besides, he still has a vast store of silvernix, by his account. Enough to last decades. And then if he were to ever capture Dracuni ..."

"We're not going to let that happen," Riony said in a low, hard voice.

"Can't we tell everybody about the curse? Spread the truth?" Lyrrin asked. "If everyone knew, they'd do something, wouldn't they?"

Kess remembered their time in the palace, trying to persuade dragonlords to join their cause, to offer even a portion of their dragons up for untaming to attempt to weaken the shadow dragon curse.

But none of them wanted to hear it. None of them would give up the conveniences and luxuries dragons brought them, no matter the cost.

Even now, with two tamed dragons under their roof, there was always a reason why it couldn't be done. Always an excuse, even as all the world was blighted by fire and the undead.

The hopelessness of it all left Kess feeling hollow and numb.

Eslinde's shoulders drooped. "I've tried for years to share the truth, until people thought me and my ramblings mad. My father is entirely in control of the narrative, the silvernix, the power."

Drawing herself back up, Eslinde took a slow breath and looked about the room, holding each person's gaze in turn. "If we cannot untame enough dragons, the only other option I see to make a difference in the world, is to remove the Dragon King himself."

Chapter Five

A silence fell over the table.

Kess rubbed her tired eyes, her head shaking. "You're suggesting we overthrow the king?"

"No," Eslinde said with a sad finality. "I'm suggesting we kill him."

Murmurs of shock rippled around the room. Lyrrin, particularly, paled.

Eslinde offered her an apologetic look, then continued. "He is the only person who knows where his silvernix stores are held. If nobody else can find it, and nobody has, then without him, it is as good as gone."

Aishena raised her eyebrows. "No more silvernix, no new tamed dragons."

"I would estimate less than a year before all other sources are used up, give or take." Eslinde tilted her hand side to side in the air.

Kess cringed at what she was about to say, but it needed considering. "Dracuni counts as another source, potentially as large, or larger, than the king's supply, as she grows bigger."

Riony's expression in response could have melted the skin right off Kess's bones.

"All the more reason to end Yeonard Draekhan." There was no love in Eslinde's voice as she spoke her father's name. "I doubt he would have shared Kife's information to anyone else. If we can remove both the king and your brother, only the people in this room know about Dracuni's silvernix blood, yes?"

"As much as I adore the idea of seeing Kife lifeless on a pyre, making any attack against the Dragon King himself feels too reckless. Even for me. Which is saying something." Riony returned to her chair.

She looked tired as she leaned forward, scrubbing her face with her hands. "It's going to be hard enough to stay safe and hidden with the king's riders out there after us. It's more important right now to keep Dracuni safe as best as we can, not rush out on some kind of royal assassination mission."

The Alderkin all nodded in agreement.

There was worry in Riony's eyes as she looked over them, her lips pulling in.

Lyrrin leaned toward where Riony sat across the table, as though drawn that way. "I'm not sure I like the idea of aiming to kill people either. Protecting the people we care about is what do, helping people get to the shrine enclaves, building those communities. And it has made everything so much better."

Kess shivered. She hadn't yet changed from the remains of her ripped gown, and Eslinde's underground was chilled in a way that the undercity hadn't been. But the rattle in her bones had nothing to do with the cold.

Riony and her friends had been doing all those heroic things while Kess had hunted them. How did she think she had any place now among them?

Protecting people we care about. I can do that. At least I can do that.

"We only fight in self-defense," Benjin added. "Choosing people for death feels icky."

Riony waved a finger around the room, pointing at everyone. "Also, as glorious as we are in battle, I'm not sure our little group is really up to the task of taking down the immortal king of all of Elundrae."

"Perhaps not," Eslinde agreed. "Which is why I had planned to bring the Rebel Riders in to help us. Or at least hope to, once I can gain their trust enough to receive an invitation to meet."

Silence again, as Riony and her friends exchanged glances.

Eslinde sighed. "I know you may believe them only to be from stories, however—"

"It's not that," Riony said almost bashfully. "It's just, we *have* received an invitation from them."

"It says they were impressed by what we've been doing around Elundrae!" Benjin puffed out his chest.

Kess felt a twang of jealousy. If she hadn't betrayed them in the caves, if she hadn't brought her brother into the hunt so he could stab Riony in the back, maybe she also could have been the kind of person who received invitations from heroic Rebel Riders.

She asked, a little roughly, "So, you've met with them already?"

"No. We haven't followed it up yet," Niskina said, pouting.

"The invitation seemed entirely suspicious!" Riony waved a dismissive hand at her. "Remember what happened last time we accepted an invitation to meet up with rebels? I never want to see broken glass again in my life."

A wash of red flashed through Kess's memory. Riony covered in blood. Riony in pain. Pain Kess had caused. She flinched and tried to make herself small and invisible in her chair.

Riony frowned her way, then sniffed. "Besides, the invitation was sort of weird and vague anyway. Along with those other dodgy messages coming into the shrine enclaves, trying to lure us out, I wasn't trusting any of it."

Eslinde raised a hand timidly. "Oh, those messages were from me. After Kess told me about Lyrrin, I was trying to get in contact with you, but without arousing any suspicions."

Kess smirked. "Told you they'd think they were a trap."

Eslinde pinched the bridge of her nose briefly before regaining composure. "I would still like to follow up on the Rebel Rider invitation. It's somewhere to start."

Riony huffed and leaned into Niskina. "Looks like you'll finally get your wish."

The curvy young woman frowned over a soft smile. "Maybe not. As much as meeting Rider Jaym in person, or whoever the Rebel Riders really are, sounds like a dream come true, I made a decision a while ago. While you were away, Ri. I decided that once you were back, I would leave."

"Nisk?" Riony lowered her voice, but not enough. "Is this because of Kess?"

"No." Niskina's gaze flickered over Kess as though over a stinking carcass. "Not entirely."

Raising her voice, Niskina addressed her friends, despite the larger audience. "It's because it's time for me to stop being selfish. I've been thinking for a while about what more I can do, for everyone. And my thoughts keep going back to the Alderkin depths."

Aishena's hard gaze softened ever so slightly. "You want to go back there? I thought you hated it, that you only stayed because of your father making you?"

Niskina's smile in reply was sharp-toothed and wry. "Yeah, well, maybe my pabba had the right idea after all. That place is worth working on, to make it better for everyone. There's so much I can do there, sharing produce and supplies between the undercity and the shrines."

Benjin leaned halfway over the table with enthusiastic momentum. "The crystals Lyrrin has been sharing have made a huge difference to the people at the shrines. Imagine if you could share even more!"

The Alderkin muttered between themselves at this.

Niskina's eyes twinkled. "Exactly. Also bringing items from the undercity to the shrines will recharge them. This is what I want to go and do. I have the strength and knowledge now to really make a difference."

Riony's jaw worked, and she gave Niskina a pained look. "We won't be able to go with you. Not the Hjelzahns, not Dracuni, or any of these royal fugitives. Are you sure?"

"I am. I never wanted to be a delver. Pabba fled his grayglim duties to marry my Rolanian amma—"

Yensen's eye twitched at this revelation.

"—only to take her to die as a delver, and I rebelled against him every moment since. But now that I know I don't have to be a delver to do what needs to be done, I want to go back."

Riony reached both arms around Niskina, murmuring to her softly. The tattoo on her arm, four rings, two blades, one candle, disappeared under the tumbling fall of Niskina's curls.

Kess turned away, finding her eyes had flushed hot and teary.

All the mistakes she'd made. All the cost others have had to pay for them. She wasn't sure if anyone could ever forgive her. She wasn't sure whether she could ever forgive herself.

"Well," Eslinde said softly into the quiet room. "It seems we have come to a plan. Rest well, everyone. Tomorrow, we begin."

Kess didn't rest well. Despite it being long into the early hours of tomorrow's morning, despite the yesterday that felt as though it had spanned a year, despite having Griskin with her again, curled beside her in a way that felt perfectly like home, Kess couldn't sleep.

Instead, she decided she would continue her own plan of protecting Riony. She stalked Griskin silently along the cold tunnels of the base as the torches guttered away the last of their fuel.

All the others had found their own rooms, and those who had belongings unpacked them. A lot of the private room doors were closed. Kess didn't know which one Riony was behind. Maybe one along with Aishena.

Eslinde had kept Aishena and Benjin aside after the meeting, telling them about their encounter with their mother, explaining what they knew of the possession. The two Hjelzahn siblings listened silently and at attention, but the edge of tension was visible on Aishena's neck and jaw.

Would Riony be comforting her now?

Kess's chest felt heavy, and she rubbed tired eyes.

Movement up ahead set her every nerve alert. The large shape of a dragon, being led toward the exit as quietly as one can lead a dragon.

Picking up her pace, Kess snuck up to identify who had the dragon under their command and why.

Yensen. He turned quickly, having heard Griskin despite how soft-footed they'd approached.

"Kessara. You're still awake?" he said.

"Thought I'd do a patrol."

He nodded. "I had the same idea. To keep an eye on the skies."

He had the reins of the orange dragon, Ambri, in his hand. A good pick, much less recognizable than Viska.

They hadn't left any signs of their passage around the entrance aboveground from what Kess could see, but if anyone did come checking, Kess didn't like the idea of getting trapped down there without warning.

"Good idea. Tomorrow we should set up shifts, keep someone on patrol all the time."

Yensen only nodded again, his silky black hair shining like a pool in the darkness.

Kess smirked. "And if anyone spots you, don't lead them back to us."

He returned a twist of his own lips. "Of course not."

They went their separate directions. Kess headed to the stables, hoping that if she could see that Dracuni was still safe, that would give her the reassurance she needed to rest.

The vast room housing the dragons was dark, only one torch sputtering at the entrance. Kess and Griskin stalked silently along the stalls. In the closest, Viska slept, with Shiff curled near her neck. Ambri was gone with Yensen. Kess passed stall after stall down the cavernous room, her heart rate building as each remained empty.

Until she reached the final stall, in the darkest end of the stables, far out of reach of the single light source.

The moment Griskin stepped in front of that space, a bright-purple glow flared in Kess's eyes.

She held a hand across her face to shadow it until her sight adjusted.

In the stall, Dracuni lay curled on her side, sleeping.

And sitting on the ground in front of her, awake and alert, was Riony.

"Thought I heard someone moving around. Have you come to steal Dracuni in the night?" Her voice was low, with a biting edge of disappointment that stabbed right through Kess.

Rushing the words out, Kess stuttered, "I came to check she was safe."

"And aren't I glad I decided to make sure she was safe, too." Riony had her sword, activated and bright, lying on her lap, with one hand on the hilt. "I thought to myself, I'll sleep in here, just in case, but surely none of my honorable new companions will try anything. I was trying to be sooo trusting. I even took my armor off."

Riony had a blanket over her shoulders and beneath wore only a tattered undershirt and braies. "Armor or not, I'll do whatever I need to do to protect Dracuni. Although I really don't want to have to fight you in my underwear."

"It's not what I want to do with you in your underwear either."

Riony's eyebrows crept up her forehead.

The air was warm from the bulk of sleeping dragon, and Kess swallowed a dry throat.

"I mean ... I don't want to fight you at all. I still intend what I said, even if nobody believes me. I am pledged to you and your service." Kess reached a hand to her neck, feeling the smooth wood of the acorn there.

"Feels like the kind of thing you might ask a girl if she even wants first?"

Kess clenched her teeth, trying to keep her chin up and still. "I know you don't want me around, that nobody does, but I can be valuable to you."

Riony muttered some curse under her breath. "Your *value* isn't the issue."

Kess tugged sharply on the acorn's string, pulling the knot at the back free. "Here. You should have this back."

She tossed it gently, and Riony snatched it one-handed.

Frowning, Riony checked the pendant over. Kess had found, in the time she kept it, how the top could come off and there was a carefully hollowed space inside. But whatever it once held was gone.

Riony tied the leather string around her neck next to another, then rubbed the acorn again with her thumb. "So ... How long after you left me for dead did you go back into the ice cave again?"

Kess shrugged. "About as long as it took you to come back to where you'd left me dangling on a ledge above a gargantuan mess of revenants."

"So many fond memories." Riony cooed, but not even her usual smirk brightened her face. "Now, turn around and leave already. This is going to be a long enough night as it is without having to spend it with you."

Riony settled back in against Dracuni's stomach but didn't close her eyes or deactivate her sword. And Kess skulked away on Griskin, exhausted and heart aching.

Chapter Six

Standing outside the entrance to Eslinde's underground base, Riony felt like the farmer in the old riddle her father used to tell her. The farmer had a bale of hay, a lamb, and a wolf, and had to take them all across the river, but the boat could only fit two.

If the farmer left the hay with the lamb, the lamb would eat it, and if the lamb was left with the wolf, the wolf would eat the lamb, and the farmer had to be clever to make sure everything reached the other side safely.

Watching the gathering of family and strangers separated out before her, Riony hoped she wasn't leaving any lambs with wolves.

Or that she wasn't the unsuspecting lamb.

"Be careful out there." Aishena grasped Riony's hand between their chests and pulled her in close.

Then she turned and farewelled Niskina the same way.

Riony and Niskina stood alongside Eslinde, her grayglim, the two dragonriders, and Kess.

Aishena, on the other side, with Lyrrin, Dracuni, Benjin, and the Alderkin.

Riony whispered to Aishena, "Keep an eye on Dracuni and Lyrrin. I'm not sure the Alderkin would do anything, but I'm sure they'd have the power if they chose to."

Riony had spent the last few days trying to get a feel for all the new people around her. But the Alderkin remained ominously secretive, and everyone else had spent most of their time resting, recovering, and for the Zarram siblings, grieving the loss of their father and home.

Which made Riony feel bad for pressing Vance on his dragonlord identity. She hadn't added up before that the burning building filled with rioters had been their home. That the man swarmed by the mob as they left was their father.

Eslinde, who knew all of that, still wanted to take action toward her goals right away. But the Rebel Rider invitation specified arriving only during a certain phase of the moon—just part of its frustrating ambiguity—which required a few days' wait.

There was a lot of tense debate about who would leave and who would stay, but then they all began digging into the supplies of arms and armor Eslinde had stored, and the mood lifted.

Aishena's delver armor had been worn beyond repair during the last year, but now she stood in gleaming gold dragonrider scale mail with blue accents. "You've got the riskier end of the bargain, I fear. Kess, dragonlords, and a grayglim warden."

All of them were also now out of their muddy clothing and wearing varying levels of armor in Eslinde's colors. Yensen, however, remained in his shadowy uniform.

Riony said, "Are you worried about having a grayglim around? Because I'm ready to go with your instincts if we need to lose him."

Aishena frowned, then shook the emotion off. "I don't like him. But I'm not sure I'd like any grayglim at this stage. Just ... watch your back."

"Much prefer you watched it for me." Riony grinned. "But unfortunately, I need you keeping Dracuni safe."

Even now, the Alderkin gazed at Riony with disapproval for leaving. But with Eslinde taking both their full-grown dragons on her mission, Riony refused to not have somebody keep an eye on the away team. It would be all too easy for the dragonlords to fly off and bring an army back to take Dracuni away.

Lyrrin, who had just said a somewhat awkward farewell to her mother, moved on to hug Niskina goodbye, then gave Riony a quick squeeze too. "Don't worry, I'll keep Dracuni safe, since you're running off on us again."

Riony ruffled Lyrrin's hair, seeing the blue sparkle near her scalp. "You know one of the reasons I'm going is to make sure your mother stays safe. Besides, I won't be long this time."

Lyrrin swatted her hand way and pulled her hood up. "I was just teasing. My grandfather said he would talk to me about Alderkin magic while you're gone, so you can stay away as long as you like."

"Love you too," Riony called after her sister as she headed back into the tunnel.

While Niskina continued her goodbyes, Riony turned to the orange dragon. Vance was flying Viska and wanted Eslinde with him, which meant Yensen too. So Riony got stuck with Kess on the dragon Dashiel would fly.

Because wherever Riony went, Kess apparently was going too.

Yay. Maybe Kess realized this was actually the best way she could torture me.

Before Riony reached the dragon, Eslinde came to her side. She wore the same dress as she had left the capital wearing but washed clean of the mud that had darkened it. It was a fine suede-like velvet in silver-gray, hemmed in elegant gold embroidery.

She had put on gleaming gold pauldrons over the long-sleeved gown, more as some sort of display of power than for utility. Her hair was wound up in a neat braided bun.

For the first time since they had met, she truly looked like royalty.

Eslinde placed a soft hand on Riony's arm. "I haven't had a chance to say it yet. But thank you."

"For?" Riony swallowed.

It was so strange to have the ethereally beautiful woman, who was Lyrrin's mother and also a first heir, there with them. The rebellious attitude that had endeared Riony to her while she was the guest at Heithorn estate made sense now.

"For raising her. So well." Eslinde's silver eyes fluttered to Lyrrin.

Flashes of memories punctured Riony's thoughts. Her mother, teaching Riony about the wetnurse herbs she was taking in order to feed the infant they had run away with. Her father, sitting on the floor and singing counting rhymes to a clapping toddler.

Memories of both of Riony's parents, bringing Lyrrin into their family as though she were their own.

Riony sniffed. "I can't take much credit for that. It's only been the two of us for a few years. And she's been acting fully grown since she was five."

"She has?" Eslinde smiled beneath glassy, distant eyes, as though she were trying to imagine it. "I've missed so much."

"I'm sorry. If there had been any way we could have stayed and given your baby back without losing all our lives, we would have. But none of us thought the Heithorns would have taken kindly to me walking back in saying, oops, sorry I killed the guest's bodyguard."

"You?" Eslinde cocked her head, blinked at Riony, and then sighed. "No, it's not your fault. Even after your escape, my mother kept up the lie that you had all died. I had no reason to think otherwise until Kessara came to me."

"I'll have to hear that story someday."

They separated again, each moving to their dragons.

Wait. Dracuni fussed, trotting back and forth at the entrance of the base.

"You need something?" Riony called back.

They had already said goodbye earlier, but Riony felt Dracuni's nerves build the closer Riony got to the orange dragon.

I want to come too. I should.

Riony began her climb into the saddle. "You should do no such thing. You're the one the Dragon King is hunting."

Viska and Ambri had been saddled to fit them all, and Kess had developed a combination saddle and harness for herself and Griskin.

As they mounted up, Dracuni stepped out from base entrance, stretched her wings, and flapped them determinedly. The diaphanous webbing fluttered, gusting the wind around her, but she didn't lift from the ground at all.

Shiff chased after her, bouncing and soaring in small flapping jumps around her.

Riony couldn't tell if the dragonling was trying to encourage or tease.

Sparks! Dracuni hissed through her teeth and dug her claws into the paved ground, cracking the stone beneath her.

"It's okay. You'll work it out soon. But you have to stay in the base until we're back."

Dracuni continued to swear richly as she spun around, her tail flicking, and retreated into the tunnel. Shiff and Lyrrin both ran in after her.

Dashiel reached a hand down to Riony and helped pull her up the rest of the way. "I can help, if you want. Some dragonlings need a bit more guidance than others finding their wings."

Settling into the seat farthest back, with Kess and Griskin between them, Riony gave a thin-lipped smile as she pulled her flying goggles down. "Thanks."

A moment later, they were off. Niskina rode on Viska as they detoured to deliver her to the closest shrine. When they arrived, Niskina activated the gateway to the depths, put on a steely expression, and stepped through.

They hadn't opened the gateway directly to the Alderkin depths since the time Lyrrin went to collect crystals. Anytime they helped people travel there, they sent them to the shrine down the hill, where a small enclave had grown that helped people travel to the undercity.

But Niskina had made it clear where she wanted to go.

Riony waited beside the glowing portal, and a moment later, Niskina returned.

"There are still ropes and climbing gear in the hole leading up to the undercity. I think the delvers are using it as an access to new areas. I'll be able to make my way up."

"Are you sure?" Riony leaned in, taking Niskina's hand in hers and holding it tight between them. "You could come with us instead, meet your sexy Rebel Riders."

Niskina chuckled and rested her forehead against Riony's. "Don't tempt me away from doing something good. You know I'm easily tempted."

Riony took a deep breath, breathing in all the scents and being of the woman who was now as much her sister as Lyrrin. "No, you're easily one of the best people out here. Go on. Say hi to the rope worm guy for me. Warn the delvers about the revs in the pit. And stay in touch."

She stepped back, and Niskina nodded, then disappeared through the gateway. The rippling glow faded out.

Niskina's absence already left a hollow in Riony as she climbed back onto Ambri. She was glad they'd agreed to a contact system and would leave messages by the gateway regularly for each other.

In front of Riony, Kess had a dark expression on her face and her eyes had a flush of pink around them. "Her selflessness is ... inspiring. Those dark depths need somebody to do some good there."

"This isn't about your love life, Kess."

From the front, Dashiel snorted, and then they were in the air again.

It wasn't long before Riony spotted other dragons in the sky, blocking their way east. Patrols and hunters, spread regularly across the horizon. Riony, holding Lyrrin's seeing stone, pointed them out to Kess, and Kess passed it up the chain to Dashiel who signaled to the other dragon's riders.

After a sequence of hand gestures, both dragons banked steeply, heading south at speed. The winter air, already chilled, grew bitter and howling as they reached the Eyersunn Sea and glided out over the waves.

Riony was glad there had been plenty of goggles in Eslinde's supplies. She could imagine the icy air biting at her eyes without them. Even with a number of layers worn beneath her armor, the metal felt frozen.

She hadn't taken any of Eslinde's armor. It felt wrong wearing the armor of dragonriders and dragonlords. But she regretted it now, seeing how Kess and Dashiel, in theirs, weren't being frozen to the bone. The dragon scales didn't channel the cold the way steel did.

Riony leaned a little closer to Griskin, unashamedly stealing his warmth.

They flew until the coastline was a gray smudge on the horizon, then went east, following the line of land on their left until the ruddy heights of the Red Cliffs became visible.

Back over land again, the dragons flew higher and more cautiously, keeping watch for any other wings in the sky and for the destination described to them in the invitation.

Within three days after a dark full moon, meet us behind the staircase spire, where the clouds rise from the land.

Riony rolled her eyes.

Who talks like that?

Speaking in riddles didn't endear Riony to them. She preferred people who said what they meant. She hadn't been sure about chasing down the vague location in Snowshimmer Ridge before, and she wasn't sure about it now.

If the Rebel Riders were real, if they were anything worth finding, why didn't we ever hear more stories about them and their deeds outside of the books?

Stories of them actually helping people?

From their vantage point in the sky, it didn't take long to find the towering outcrop of stone, chipped away into even steps.

Would've taken us months to find on foot. Did they expect us to come in on dragon?

Maybe they assumed Dracuni could fly.

One short loop around the spire confirmed gusts of steam rising into the frigid air, and Vance and Dashiel brought them down into the cover of vapor.

The dragons landed with a soft splash, ankle-deep in pools of clear aqua water. The edges of the pool and surface of the mountain were limestone that had formed as slick and white as ice, and the air was cloyingly warm.

Riony scanned the small plateau. "Nobody here?"

"Anybody see anything?" Dashiel called across to the others riding Viska.

The gold dragon walked a circle through the warm water.

Eslinde called back, "Nothing. No signs of life, no symbols, or entrances. Maybe this isn't the right place?"

The spire loomed above them, the sun behind it, cutting its staircase shape in a clear silhouette. And the hot springs at their feet, defrosting Riony with their warmth, also brought to her a memory that flushed her from the inside as well.

She cleared her throat. "You don't think these are *the* hot springs?"

"What do you mean *the* hot springs?" Kess asked.

"I mean from the stories. Where Rider Jaym and his true love did things that I'm still not convinced are physically possible." And just to make sure it was clear, Riony added, "Sex things."

Kess's ears went red.

Dashiel shrugged. "I've only read a chapter or two of the stories. And I'm not entirely sure any of it was or could be real."

"Even if it was, what would it matter?" Kess asked.

"Well, for starters, I'd be both impressed and inspired by the passionate possibilities." Riony enjoyed seeing Kess's discomfort as her ears darkened further, to a deep maroon. "But more importantly, maybe this is supposed to be some sort of clue?"

Eslinde called across from Viska, "A clue? How?"

"You read the invitation. I bet this is some sort of test and the invitation is just the first step. Only people who've read the stories, who are really into the *Rebel Riders*, will be able to spot the markers and know what to do next."

Riony squinted through the mist. "Can you move us closer to that edge?"

Dashiel nodded, and Ambri sloshed through the hot water to the limestone crust that surrounded the pool.

"Look, down in that valley." Riony pointed over Griskin.

Between two close cliff faces, a bridge of stone dipped down, then up, an inverted archway.

"Do you know what that looks like to me? It looks like the cradle archway, where Rider Zeina kissed her true love for the first time. But then it ended on a cliffhanger and I didn't get the chapter after that to see if it went further." Riony sighed with deep lament.

"Are all of the scenes in these stories about sex?" Dashiel asked.

"All the best ones," Riony replied.

"Fine. Let's take a closer look, I suppose. Unless anyone has any better suggestions?" Eslinde asked in a resigned tone.

There were none. The two dragons spread their wings, gusting swirls of mist around them and water streaming behind as they launched out of the hot springs.

Riony's stomach flew up into her throat as they dove toward the archway. The closer they got, the more Riony was sure this was the same cradle archway from the story.

Although it had only been words on a page, the landscape of limestone white and rusty-red earth, cracked down the center by a sharp gorge, was a vivid memory in Riony's mind, and matched perfectly to what she saw now.

And Rider Zeina was her favorite character, so she remembered the scene well.

"Where next?" Dashiel yelled back.

As they flew over the top of the archway, Riony cast about, unable to see their next heading. "I don't know."

Kess's shoulders sagged, and she pointed off to their right. "That zigzagging chasm. There was one like that in the books."

Riony's eyebrows popped up. "I haven't read that one. *Interesting* that you have."

Kess slouched farther over.

"And which character had an intimate encounter there?" Dashiel's lips turned up as they looked over their shoulder at Kess.

"They raced their dragons through there." Kess's voice sounded like it came out through gritted teeth.

Riony nodded sagely. "Sounds like something they'd do. But I bet you anything I know what they did afterward."

She took Kess's thick silence as an affirmative.

Dashiel's face lit up, and after a few hand motions toward Vance, they took off.

Apparently keen to recreate the entire experience, the two riders took them shooting downward into the chasm. The narrow walls were just wide enough to fit the dragons one after another, the outstretched wingtips barely fitting as they glided through.

The chasm cut sharply left, then right, and Riony held tight to the saddle and Griskin in front of her, who whined slightly as they dipped and turned in the air.

Darkness grew as the chasm went deeper into the earth, shadowed by the overhanging cliffs on each side.

Anticipation grew within Riony, imagining the entrance to an underground base up ahead as they went deeper.

Then Dashiel leaned back and Ambri's wings struck out, catching the air and slowing them abruptly. A moment later, they were on the ground.

Riony leaned to the side, trying to see what lay ahead.

"Dead end," Dashiel called back.

Vance brought Viska in to land behind them at a slower pace, having apparently decided not to join in the race.

"Nothing?" Eslinde called out, her voice high and clipped. "Any other clues?"

Riony couldn't see anything. "You're more up to date than me, Kess."

Kess pulled her googles up, squinting up into the sliver of light high above and frowning deeply.

Riony followed her gaze. They were a long way down with sheer walls cutting up from the ground on three sides.

She shivered. They were boxed in, cornered.

"We should go. We need to get back into the air, now. This is—"

A shadow flickering over them cut off Riony's voice. Dragons. Five dragons, descending upon them.

This was a trap.

CHAPTER SEVEN

Lyrrin clutched her chest where the paired heart stone hung on a string. It thumped wildly with her sister's thundering pulse.

Biting her lip, she tried not to be scared.

"Don't worry, lots of things make my heart race, not just bad things," Riony had said before she left.

And that meeting the Rebel Riders was probably going to be one of those things. Riony didn't explain exactly why meeting the people from the stories she read was going to be so exciting.

All she said was to only worry if the heartbeat stopped.

Taking a deep breath, Lyrrin tried to relax. She adjusted her seating on the padded floor. The cold seeped up through the fabric beneath her. Extra blankets had been dragged into the dragon stables to create a comfortable, soft nest within view of Dracuni and Shiff.

The two young dragons seemed locked in some eager conversation nobody else could hear. Shiff would flutter her small wings, followed by Dracuni, followed by more silent back and forth and shaking heads, and then flapping wings again.

The room was lit with the cool cyan light of the glow stones, since the torches were out of fuel and Aishena had yet to find more in the vast stores of crated goods warehoused in the base that everyone had been helping themselves to.

Benjin danced across the floor in front of Lyrrin, wearing a too-large set of dragonrider armor, his staff clashing against Aishena's unlit athames.

They had been training together for a while, but Benjin had yet to land a blow on his sister. Generally, he came away happy as long as she hadn't knocked him down too many times.

Aishena had also been training Riony on better sword fighting technique, although Riony seemed to enjoy it when Aishena managed to toss her onto her back.

With a monosyllabic bark from Aishena, Benjin froze mid swing. Aishena stepped in, adjusting his stance, rotating his torso with her hands and tapping his feet into position with her own.

"Huut," she barked again, and they swung back into motion as though time unfroze.

Lyrrin watched, jealous. She'd been given some basic instruction on how to wield a dagger, but she didn't have the reach or physical strength deemed worthy of learning more advanced melee fighting.

But she had her crystals.

A range of them were scattered on the blanket in front of her now, and in front of them lay her belt, stretched out long and straight. She worked on fixing a couple more pouches onto the belt.

She liked to keep a collection of the runed stones at hand, as easy to reach as possible. A glow stone, a couple of flash stones, and burst bombs.

She had one little crystal with float and burn runes on it, like Riony's sword. It had been the test she'd done before her sister allowed her to touch her beloved blade. She used the flaming crystal now for getting fires started.

There were a few crystals with combinations that hadn't worked out that she should probably discard, and the ten-stroke rune Riony had taken from the warrior's tomb which she still hadn't worked out, that she carried in her pack normally, but had in front of her now while she was organizing.

She was frowning at it when the Alderkin approached.

"May we sit with you, child?" Yrik asked in his voice like a gentle earthquake.

Lyrrin's breath hitched, and she squeaked, "Yes?"

It had been a lie when she'd told Riony that the Alderkin were going to teach her magic. Or maybe wishful thinking. They hadn't at that time made much of an effort at all to speak with her.

Now that they had come to talk to her, Lyrrin tried to contain her excitement.

She shuffled over on the blankets to make more room for the three Alderkin, an attempt to be respectful, or wary, or whatever she was supposed to be at that time. She wasn't sure.

But as Yrik, Priyune, and Shael joined her on the padded floor, sitting so close Lyrrin could smell the earthy autumn-rain scent of them, all Lyrrin could do was stare.

They were Alderkin, and so was she. At least in part. Their hands matched hers, as did the brightness of their eyes and hair.

It had been a while since Lyrrin had dyed hers. It hadn't seemed as important since leaving the undercity. There were less people around that she felt she had to fit in for, and the people of the shrine enclaves didn't seem to care. So they saved Riony's hennan harvests for Aishena.

There was an almost finger-length growth of blue from Lyrrin's scalp now, before older remnants of dye dulled the lower strands to a muddy gray.

The Alderkin's ears were different than hers, long and pointed. That seemed to be something Lyrrin had retained from her human mother. Her face was softer too, less hard angles and sharp planes.

"You work with crystals?" Priyune leaned in, brushing fingers like blades across the stones laid out before them.

The forest-toned woman seemed to have recovered greatly since their arrival at Eslindekeep. The Alderkin had kept to themselves during that time, and there had been worry Priyune may succumb to her injury. But the Alderkin rejected any notion of using silvernix, even when Dracuni offered.

Lyrrin stuttered shyly, "I've loved them since we first got to the undercity. To the ... Alderkin depths?"

"Luns Deemfret." Yrik bowed his head. "That is our name for it."

"Do they sing to you?" Priyune asked, tapping the corner of a rune.

Lyrrin nodded, and Priyune gave her a twinkling smile in return that made Lyrrin's chest feel full and warm.

"You know more than a few runes, and you are mixing them. How did you learn?" Shael, who seemed the youngest, barely an adult by human standards, leaned in close.

Lyrrin knew she must be much older than she seemed, if Priyune, who had only the faint lines of wrinkling around her eyes was over eighty, and Yrik, who looked as though he could be her father, was really her grandfather.

"By myself, mostly. And with a few accidents," Lyrrin admitted.

"Careful with these ones." Shael pointed to the flash and burst bombs.

"Oh yeah, we worked that out." Lyrrin chuckled nervously.

She reached over to the ten-stroke runed stone and lifted it in her hands for them to see. "I can't work this one out, though. Could you ... would you show me how it works?"

Yrik stared at it for a long moment. "No. No not that one. That is special magic only for Alderkin."

Isn't that what I am? Lyrrin couldn't voice the question out loud.

In a softer voice, Shael added, "If it was to work for you, it would sing to you."

The fullness and warmth inside Lyrrin vanished, replaced with a clenching, hollow chill. She may have Alderkin blood, but clearly, she wasn't Alderkin *enough*.

Having spent all her life growing up as not *human* enough, to find out the Alderkin didn't consider her one of them either made her feel like she'd swallowed one of her burst bombs.

Yrik's angular face remained emotionless, but his blue eyes shimmered. "And the humans, they know and use our magic too. Did you teach them?"

"They already knew, mostly. People in the under ... in Luns Deemfret, they've been working runes out for a while before we got there. I worked out the gateway rune, though. But we haven't taught anyone else that one."

The Alderkin shared looks between each other, and Lyrrin hoped it was in approval. She suddenly felt as though her every word and action was being judged.

Aishena and Benjin's combat had slowed, and it was clear Aishena was keeping as much of an eye on Lyrrin as she was the sparring.

There didn't seem to be any aggression or threat from the Alderkin, though. If anything, they seemed sad.

Are they disappointed with me?

Then she saw the way they eyed Aishena and Benjin, training in front of them. With crystals weapons in their hands.

Lyrrin spoke softly. "You don't like humans using the crystals?"

She felt stupid as soon as she said it. Of course they wouldn't like it. Why would they? Their magic, in the hands of the people who had destroyed their entire race.

Without waiting for an answer, she rambled on. "We're only using the magic to help us protect Dracuni. Mostly. And to protect each other, but that's important too."

It wasn't true, though. They had also been using the magic and sharing the magic to improve their lives in the blighted, undead infested landscape of Elundrae.

Was that so wrong? Lyrrin felt all mixed up inside, and the Alderkin had gone quiet.

There was so much Lyrrin wanted to ask, about her father, about where they had been all this time, what their lives were like before, but she felt small under their timeless gaze.

So she turned back to the sparkling stones in front of her. "Was it the unicorns that gave crystals their magic?"

Priyune inclined her head slightly. "It was their magic. It flowed everywhere, through the earth, and our people learned how to create sacred spaces in the locations the unicorns visited the most, and ring those areas in standing stones to contain and amplify that magic. To use it for ourselves."

Lyrrin glanced over at Dracuni and her long golden horn. "We worked out the crystals would charge at shrines, and we thought it had something to do with Dracuni, too."

Shael smiled, eyes twinkling. "Yes, your creature with the blood of magic. She has been bringing life back to the land she has traveled on."

Each of the Alderkin had changed out of the stinking rags they'd fled their prison wearing, now in clean, simple military uniforms. The flat gray fabric seemed so plain against their gemstone features.

But as they all turned to look at Dracuni, there seemed to be an energy in the air, humming and singing through Lyrrin the way the crystals did as she traced their runes.

A harmonization.

Something Lyrrin desperately wanted to be part of. But all she could do was say, "Yeah, Dracuni is pretty special. We hoped that just having her around would be enough to keep things charged, but we did need the shrines too."

Keeping her eyes on Dracuni, Shael said, "There's only one way that works without—"

"Shh!" Yrik snapped.

Lyrrin flinched.

Shael tutted and snapped back, "Her mother knows already. Alleem worked it out for her, to keep her safe. He would want that extended to his daughter."

Yrik shook his head, silky blue hair shivering in the cool light. "Alleem shared too much, and we've all suffered for it."

The two Alderkin locked eyes. Priyune leaned away, as though avoiding the argument entirely.

Lyrrin pulled her lips in tight, fighting off the hot swell of tears.

In a tiny voice, she asked into the tense silence, "Alleem, my father ... What happened to him?"

"He was killed by the unicorn slayer!" Yrik's head whipped toward her, his expression still sharp.

Lyrrin's voice trembled. "By ... Yeonard Draekhan?"

By my other grandfather. Lyrrin felt as though she should be torn in two.

Then Yrik blinked, as though remembering who he was looking at, and his eyes softened, drooping deeply. "I'm sorry. He ... My son. It was hard to lose him, after we'd already lost so much."

Movement shifted in front of Lyrrin. Aishena and Benjin had stopped entirely, and Aishena was pushing her brother toward the door. With a knowing look to Lyrrin, she nodded once and left them to privacy.

Priyune leaned back in then. "He was taken away, around the same time Eslinde stopped visiting us. Which we now know is when she was growing you. We thought he had been taken and killed immediately, but some months later he was returned to our cell."

"Mortally injured," Yrik moaned the words. "Tortured beyond all sense."

"Shh yourself," Shael snapped softly. "The child needn't know—"

"She will know what happened to her father," Yrik responded. "How the unicorn slayer brought him back to us to die, declaring that he had fulfilled his part in some bargain in returning Alleem to his family. No matter that Alleem did not live to see the next day."

Lyrrin tried to imagine the man she had never known, to feel for him the way she'd felt when Riony had told her that the parents who raised them were never coming back.

There was a tight ache in her chest, but the sense of loss was different. It was the loss of something she'd never had. What ached the most was having seen the pure heartbreak in Eslinde and the Alderkin's eyes when they spoke of Alleem. Seeing how much he had been loved by others.

Lyrrin asked, "Do you think he knew about me?"

"None of us did, until recently," Priyune replied.

"No, don't you remember?" Shael folded her icy clawed fingers in her lap and closed her eyes.

Her voice was the low hush of old memory. "When he came back to us. His final words ... ramblings about gateways, about how he wouldn't show the slayer their ways, even for the child. We thought he meant the slayer's child, for Eslinde, that something had happened to her."

Pale-blue eyes popped open again. "But he could have meant his own child. He could have known about you. It seemed the slayer did everything to pry our gateway magic from Alleem. But he said he never shared it. He found some other way to be brought back to his family."

To die. Lyrrin shivered, and a fat tear splashed from her eye.

"We haven't told anyone else, either," she felt the need to say again.

The Alderkin bowed their heads solemnly.

"That was wise." Priyune reached over and clasped Lyrrin's hand. "To keep Dracuni safe, to keep you safe, to keep our ways safe."

Lyrrin tried to smile, but she still felt bad for not sharing. She knew it would make life so much easier for so many.

In a flurry of marching steps, Aishena returned to the stables. "I stepped out to check for signs of the others returning and saw a dragon flying over."

"Was it them?" Lyrrin wiped her face and stood up.

"No. Just one dragon, high up. I couldn't identify it. It's gone now, but ..." Aishena glared dark eyes at the walls around them. "The entrance to this base is solid, impenetrable, but I don't like the idea of being trapped down here if our location is found. We don't have enough food for a siege."

The Alderkin rose to their feet around them as well.

Lyrrin frowned, thinking through their conversation. "Would it be possible to bring a gateway stone here? Would it still work if we moved one?"

Their hesitation was clear. The gateways and how they worked were something they would die to protect. But there was something even more important.

"If we had a gateway in here, with us, it would make it so much easier to make sure Dracuni stays safe," Lyrrin added.

"It would still work," Priyune said. "But without being within the standing stones, it would run out of charge at some point."

Aishena gave them all a shrewd look. "The one in the depths didn't have standing stones around it."

Shael nodded. "Deemfrets do not usually contain gateways, for that reason. That one was moved into Luns at the end of the great massacre, to evacuate out who we could. I'm surprised that stone still had any magic left in it."

"Some Alderkin were evacuated?" Lyrrin asked.

Luns Deemfret, the central Alderkin ruins, was the last holdout of Alderkin fighting at the end of the war. But if some got out ...

Could that mean there are others out there? Somewhere?

Aishena's jaw moved as though chewing over the thought. "Even if we had a gateway in here with us, if we are trapped, only the humans could get out through it. The dragons are too large, except for Dashiel's little one. Even Dracuni won't fit soon."

Dracuni snorted.

"Still," she added, "it would buy us time. We could bring food in for the dragons, find some way to break the siege. It would give us options."

Options were something. Better than no way out. Lyrrin had spent most of the years she remembered living underground, but the Alderkin ruins felt like home. The cold square-cut tunnels of Eslindekeep felt like a trap, even without enemy dragons at the door.

She said as firmly as she could, "We should do it. One of the dragons could carry the gateway here. We would save its magic to only use in an emergency."

Then she added, a little pleading in her tone as she looked to the Alderkin for approval, "And we won't share how to use it with the others, the dragonriders."

Hesitation again, but then the approval came.

Lyrrin knew, beyond anything, they wanted to keep Dracuni safe. As did she and her friends.

But Lyrrin had also only just gotten Riony back, after weeks with only infrequent visits. Lyrrin had only just found her mother and the people she was descended from.

She thought those things would bring her some peace, but she felt more in danger than ever. And she had more to lose than ever.

CHAPTER EIGHT

It was too late to fly out of the chasm. They were down deep with nowhere to get a running start. All Riony could do was wait as five dragons descended upon them.

"Is this who we're looking for, or do we have a problem?" Dashiel asked.

Riony held up Lyrrin's seeing stone again. "The riders aren't in dragonlord colors. Whether or not that means we have a problem we'll find out shortly."

"Is that a razing *flamesong*?" Kess hissed, eyes locked on the largest black and gold dragon.

"The ones that spontaneously explode sometimes?" Riony watched it too, as it flew in behind the others, one red, one white, one aqua, and one bronze.

"And someone is riding it," Dashiel said, awed.

Kess's voice was low. "I thought it was an exaggeration, in the stories, saying one of them rode a flamesong. Just how much of the stories are real?"

Riony reached for her sword and brought it into her lap, activating the float rune in case she needed to move quickly. The dragons came within flaming distance, but didn't immediately roast them, which Riony considered a good sign.

They landed in a rush of wind and dust, their wings sending out whirling eddies that danced along the ground.

As the air cleared, the five dragons, ranging from a small shimmerdart to the massive flamesong, faced them from a wary distance away, cornering them against the cliff wall.

A gruff voice carried across the gap. "Riony? You're the one we sent an invitation to meet to. But it seems as though you've brought along more than a few uninvited people as well."

"Yeah, and it seems like your invitation has led us into a nice little trap," Riony yelled back.

The man on the bronze etherdart had a sharp jaw edged with a neat beard and handsome features that were weatherbeaten and marred by the wear and tear of battle.

He moved the dragon a step closer. "Just a little something we do to test for threats. We keep watch of the hot springs, and then if we decide those we invited weren't worthy after all, well ..."

He eyed the sheer cliff face behind Riony's group and the dark marks on the stone there. Scorch marks.

"At what point do you decide we're worthy or not?" Riony asked.

He shrugged lazily. "How about we start with introductions and go from there."

Eslinde shifted then, climbing nimbly down from Viska. Both Vance and Yensen attempted to stop her, but she batted their hands away.

She moved herself between the two opposing lines of dragons and spoke with a clear voice. "Eslinde the First."

From atop the bronze dragon, the man's eyes narrowed.

Eslinde continued, gesturing to the others. "My grayglim and two trusted riders accompany me."

A pale Taenish woman with neatly braided black hair moved her shimmerdart closer. "And who's that one? And why do you have a wolf?"

Eslinde hesitated, as though unsure how to describe Kess and her place there.

Riony sighed and climbed out of the saddle, then jumped lightly to the ground beside Eslinde.

Riony rested her sword on her shoulder. "Look, you invited me, and I brought these people along. And I brought them for a good reason. If that's a problem, I'd love to stop dancing around it and start knocking people off their dragons."

The man's eyes narrowed again, but from over on the aqua dragon, a woman chuckled.

"Stars, she really is how the stories say she is!" Warm golden eyes looked down at Riony from a face so striking it made Riony's heart flip-flop.

The woman wore minimal armor and clothing despite the cold weather, showing off blushed sienna skin and a musculature that made Riony feel desperately inferior.

A thick scar twisted the skin near her full lips, accentuating their shape as she smirked.

That scar … Riony had read about one like that.

Her mouth went dry. "You … are you …?"

The woman's eyes squeezed into sweeping lines as she smiled. "I'm Zeina."

Riony's hand shot out, grasping Eslinde's arm for support. "*Rider Zeina?* And she … she's heard stories about *me*?"

Zeina's face brightened again with amusement, and she blinked slowly before trailing her eyes leisurely up and down Riony.

Tearing her eyes away from the beautiful woman, Riony looked over each of the other riders. "Wait, if she's real, I mean, if the stories are really based on you, then …"

The man on the red etherflame had sun-kissed golden curls that fell in tousled waves around a tanned face, younger than Riony expected.

"Rider Jaym?" she guessed.

He offered her a winking salute.

Oh, sparks. Niskina would have loved this. Riony felt a little faint.

On the flamesong, a giant of a man sat still and solemn. Short-cropped brown hair had a sparkle of gray at his temples. He fit no description other than that of the bold steed he rode.

"Rider Samor?"

He sniffed and lowered sad eyes.

The man on the bronze dragon who first greeted them, and the Taen on the shimmerdart …

"I don't know these two," Riony said with a shrug.

"Our noble leaders won't let me write them into the stories." Jaym's tone was one of utter heartbreak, despite his cheeky smile. "Probably because they are already coupled up and don't have anything exciting to include."

"*You write them?*" Riony's grip on Eslinde tightened.

The princess patted Riony's fingers. "It's called propaganda, love."

"Thallan," offered the man with gruff reluctance.

"Norallei," added the woman.

Kess appeared by Riony's side, having stalked up silently on Griskin.

"Hold on. I've heard of this one too." Zeina lifted her chin as she assessed them. "The wild wolf girl who's been giving smugglers trouble for years."

Riony pouted and side-eyed Kess, trying not to be put out that Rider Zeina had also heard of her. A blooming hint of begrudging respect was also quickly tamped down.

The Zarram siblings and Yensen offered their names from their seats, and Kess grumbled hers, leaving off the Heithorn part. The full round of introductions were complete, but the Rebel Riders all remained on their dragons, and tension remained in the air.

Rider Jaym had his eyes on the sky, and Samor had a dagger in his hands that he cleaned his nails with. Only Zeina seemed unbothered, cracking nuts in the palm of her hand and popping them in her mouth.

In an unfriendly rasp, Thallan said, "Now that we're all friends, perhaps you can tell us why you've brought a First heir and her entourage with you?"

Before Riony could answer, a keening shriek pierced the air and the flutter of feathers rushed past her.

Riony startled and cringed again as the pocket-hawk circled her, then came to rest on Jaym's extended arm.

Sparks. Jaym didn't say anything about his pet in the stories. Breathing hard, Riony made every effort to not flinch away from the beady-eyed creature that preened its outstretched wings.

Thallan still awaited her answer.

Flustered, Riony couldn't take her eyes off the bird. What if it flew at her again?

I'm going to humiliate myself in front of the Rebel Riders. That's what.

Then a dark shape moved into Riony's vision. She refocused, finding Kess there. The girl and the wolf had taken a single step forward, putting themselves between Riony's eyeline and the hawk.

Kess knew of Riony's fear of birds. She'd teased her mercilessly about it when they were kids.

What is she doing?

Kess didn't turn or acknowledge the action at all. She remained straight-backed, angled to block as much of Riony's view in that direction as possible.

I pledge my life to you and your cause. For whatever good it can provide you.

Deep within Riony something cold and hard softened.

Blinking rapidly, she tore her eyes away from Kess and turned back to Thallan and the riders. She cleared her throat.

"Eslinde and the others came to us for a number of reasons, which all put together mean I'm fairly certain we can trust her and trust that she isn't going to go running back to Pabba," Riony said. "At least, half half-certain."

Eslinde fidgeted her fingers and seemed to be actively fighting to keep her mouth closed.

Riony huffed. "Yeah, you should probably take over. I never said I was some kind of diplomat. I'm just here to hit things with a sword in case it turned out there was something that needs hitting."

Offering a small smile, Eslinde stepped forward. "I am here because I have defected, and I come to you with the aim of joining forces to bring down the Dragon King."

Norallei scoffed. "Want to take your fadda's throne for yourself? We're not getting caught up in any of that nonsense."

Unbothered, Eslinde said, "Then you should know I'm last in line and with no designs upon that power. We aim to assassinate Yeonard Draekhan as part of our goal to end the shadow dragon curse."

It only took Eslinde a few moments to succinctly sum up their knowledge of the curse and how they hoped to defeat it.

Definitely for the best I let her do the talking, Riony thought.

The Rebel Riders remained silent for a while, then Thallan scratched at his stubbled jaw. "If it's all true, it could work. That silvernix stash is hidden well. Or at least well enough we've never found it."

"You've been looking?" Eslinde asked.

Thallan's mouth twisted bitterly. "We've been after it for years ... spent far too long searching the capital, and even got into Draekhan's Rest a couple of times, chasing rumors. Don't think we've ever gotten close to finding it."

"You managed to infiltrate the king's private estate? Impressive," Eslinde conceded.

"But you didn't actually find anything." Riony frowned at the aged armor and heavily laden saddlebags of the riders before her. "So, what have you been doing all this time? Other than failing to find the king's silvernix? Is it all just sleeping with each other and writing stories about it?"

Zeina's eyes crinkled, and she spoke through a full mouth. "It may be a large part of what we do."

"You don't believe the other parts of our daring tales?" Jaym sounded hurt.

Riony didn't attempt to look his way again. "I generally believe what I see, and in all my time aboveground, I haven't ever seen you all before, daring or otherwise."

The warm rush of having met the heroes of her favorite stories had worn off as Riony wondered again why she hadn't heard of them outside of those booklets. They'd heard of her exploits. They'd even heard of Kess.

But from all the people Riony had helped and met across Elundrae as they set up shrine enclaves or liberated slaves, none had mentioned stories of the Rebel Riders doing the same.

Thallan said, "We put our efforts mostly toward skirmishes with other riders, trying to keep the worst of them grounded. Making sure they don't think they are the only rulers of the sky."

Jaym sighed dramatically. "We used to harry dragonkeeps, just for the fun of it! But we lost some of our group, a while back ..."

He glanced across at Samor before continuing. "We've mostly been lying low since then, doing what we can to keep ourselves and our dragons alive while fighting off the ever-increasing number of revs."

Riony brought her sword down off her shoulder and deactivated it, letting the tip fall heavily before leaning on the cross guard. "So ... the same thing *non*-rebel riders do?"

Zeina's cool smirk faded, and she threw a nutshell at Jaym. "You're making us sound terrible."

Jaym muttered, "She's not wrong, though. We haven't done more than look after ourselves for years. Very dragonlord style behavior."

From the flamesong, Samor spoke up, his voice deep and soft. "*We* don't enslave people."

"You do enslave dragons, though," Kess said, a low tone of disappointment in her voice as she stared up at the bronze etherdart and white shimmerdart.

Riony noticed it then too. She'd been so fixated on the people she hadn't paid much attention to the dragons.

Trust that Kess did.

Both of those dragons were motionless and solemn, unmoving without their rider's commands. Both had the cap of a steel spike visible on their foreheads.

The other three, Zeina's, Jaym's, and Samor's, were alert and mobile, taking in their surroundings and observing the conversation, and, Riony guessed, in their own silent conversations with their riders.

It sure was something, to see those three riding real wild dragons, but it was a disappointment that they didn't all give their beasts that freedom.

"It's necessary," Thallan growled. "It takes years to raise a wild dragon and bond with it. It makes more sense to steal tamed dragons from our downed foes."

Riony remembered the three dragons that had tried to catch Dracuni after their escape from the keep.

Apart from the Zarrams' snowflame that died in the fight, all of the king's dragons had been left downed where they were. Alive, but unable to fend for themselves. They didn't have time to try to take them too and assumed they would be reclaimed by others.

Should we have kept them ourselves? Had more tamed dragons to fight on our side?

Riony felt a worming sick feeling inside. She was glad they didn't. It didn't feel right at all to take on more tamed creatures, the weapons of those that oppressed them and the very thing cursing their land.

"Besides, your dragons are no more free than mine," Thallan added, flicking his chin toward Viska and Ambri.

Riony said, "The princess and her entourage are fresh from the palace. I feel as though the *Rebel Riders* are the ones I expect more from."

Zeina threw a nut in the air and caught it in her mouth. She crunched it thoughtfully. "She's right. We could be doing more."

Shoulder to shoulder with Norallei, Thallan growled, "*We* have been more than willing to return to battle. It's you three who haven't been ready."

"If you do want to be more involved again, if you do want to make a difference, you can join us," Eslinde's voice rang out. "You and ... are there more of you? I expect you didn't all come to the meeting location. Are they back at your base?"

"We don't really have a base," Zeina said wryly. "We keep on the move."

All of their saddles were stacked with bags and bundles, cooking pots and blankets.

"So this is ...?" Eslinde gestured to the five of them.

"This is all that's left of us." Samor's eyes were rimmed red. "There used to be more."

Jaym added in a singsong voice, "I may have exaggerated our number in the stories, if that's what you're going by."

"There are two other groups to our name, on the move as well." Thallan gestured to the sky. "But only a handful in each, like us."

"Oh." Eslinde slumped a little.

Riony leaned in, whispering not at all quietly, "This is fine, right? Five more dragons is definitely enough to take on the immortal king of all the land and his, what ... few dozen dragons?"

"Eighty-two riders under his direct control, another forty-five in lower-ranking city guards, his own private stable of thirty-three, which he allows use of to his grayglim when necessary. Not including factory dragons. Not including each heir's dragons and riders the king could call on. As of last count," Eslinde rattled out.

Riony smirked. "Sure. Easy."

Zeina winked at Riony. "I'm in if you are."

Riony didn't reply, sure that if she opened her mouth, she'd stumble her words as she focused on not spontaneously combusting, flamesong style.

"From what I understand, if your goal is to end the curse on our lands, there could be other ways." Thallan looked around at all the dragons there.

"We're pretty good at taking on other riders. What if we focus on bringing down as many as we can, in smaller skirmishes? Does a dead dragon work the same as an untamed one?"

"You'd just kill every tamed dragon you come across?" Kess hissed.

Griskin growled softly, taking a step forward, but with a slight glance over her shoulder toward Riony, Kess moved Griskin back where he was.

Eslinde lifted both hands in front of her. "We don't know for sure it works that way. Their deaths might not lessen the curse."

Thallan didn't seem convinced. "Well, we don't have any other way to get rid of a heap of tamed dragons. Not unless you have your own massive stores of silvernix somewhere."

Riony shot Eslinde a look, and Eslinde returned it with a subtle nod.

"No, we don't," the princess said. "But these are all details we can work out as we go. All we need to know for now is whether our goals are aligned. Whether our mission is one you want to join."

Thallan grumbled gruffly, but before he could speak, Jaym spoke over him. "Helping to save the world sounds good to me. It'll give me lots to write about."

"Getting to know our new friends better sounds pretty good to me, too." Zeina popped another nut between her lips in a slow, sensual way that made Riony gulp.

"We decide together." Thallan gave a long-suffering look toward the two youngest of his group.

They excused themselves to discuss the matter in private. The Rebel Riders marched their dragons along the chasm until they were out of earshot, but the conversation didn't take long.

Not even long enough for Riony to raise her own fears that maybe they shouldn't be bringing these people in.

Harrying dragonkeeps for fun, fighting other dragonriders, and considering killing dragons en masse ... These were people who lived by violence.

And Riony knew that sometimes violence was justified, but she didn't want it to become their first choice, their normal.

The riders returned with their answer. They were in.

Putting her fears aside, Riony aimed for optimism.

Plus, she wouldn't mind getting to know Zeina a bit more either.

Rider Zeina. Sparks. And she winked at me!

Their group returned to their dragons, and soon they were flying back over the mountains toward the sea, leading the Rebel Riders back to Eslindekeep.

The ground below moved strangely, and it took a while for Riony to work out what she was seeing. It could have been old ash, juddering and swirling in the winter winds. It could have been a landslide.

But the gray, undulating mass below, covering the landscape, was a horde of revenants.

Bigger again than the one that had chased them and Myrwa's people to the shrine.

Riony shivered.

Could they really get rid of the revenants? And what would they be willing to do to achieve that?

The revenants knew nothing but violence, and Riony wasn't sure whether the dragonlords and dragonriders were much different. Maybe violence was needed.

Maybe the Rebel Riders were just what they needed.

Riony didn't know exactly what good they might bring, whether they would help or hurt them, but she already knew they weren't the heroes she read about.

Chapter Nine

Being outside in the open left Kess on edge. She glanced at the sky every other second, between keeping her eyes on Riony and sharpening new bone knives.

After a week cooped up inside, with nothing but bickering between the Rebel Riders, Eslinde, and Riony's groups as winter rains hammered the ground above, the first day of sun seemed like a good reason for a day out.

Riony had stopped complaining about Kess shadowing her, which Kess figured was progress. As long as she wasn't going to be expelled from the group, as long as she could be left to do what she needed to do to keep Riony safe, Kess was happy. That was all she needed.

Or at least, that's what she told herself, as she watched Riony move through a sword training sequence with her massive crystal blade. *Unlit.* And Kess's chest felt like it was being squeezed between dragon claws.

Riony caught Kess tracking her movements and frowned at whatever she saw on her face. "If I only use it with the float magic on, I'm going to get soft."

Kess could only nod and watch the strength in each swing, the tension in Riony's arms and shoulders, the tight grip on the hilt, the twitch of Riony's lips and nose as she pushed through.

Heat flushed through Kess and sweat prickled over her neck where a lump had formed and refused to dislodge.

That sun is too bright today for winter clothing. It's just the heat. It's not how impossibly razing beautiful she is. Get a grip.

Kess had already moved off Griskin. His dark fur soaked in the sunlight, and he lay on his belly beside her, panting. Kess leaned her back against a cool block of stone.

Two dragons patrolled overhead, one of the riders—*Zeina, ugh*—who Kess wasn't sure she trusted, and Yensen, who had earned her trust by his unflinching loyalty to Eslinde during their escape.

The patrol shifts had been going well, and Kess had even flown a few on her own, after a little more instruction from Dashiel on landing safely.

No signs yet that the king and his search had narrowed down their location to Eslindekeep.

But it was decided that there wasn't a lot of use knowing an attack was incoming if they couldn't get Dracuni away quickly or safely. Another few weeks of growth and she wouldn't fit through the gateways anymore.

Dracuni needed to learn how to fly. And despite the risk of leaving the base, that training couldn't be done underground.

The half-built walls of the keep made a perfect practice ground, and Dracuni was currently perched on a section beside Shiff, both flapping their wings, Dracuni carefully mimicking Shiff's movements. Dashiel and Vance stood on the unfinished wall as well, calling out instructions.

Eslinde lounged on Viska below, keeping the gold dragon's wing stretched out, so that when Dracuni jumped, and fell, there was a soft landing.

Kess was surprised that Riony wasn't staying closer beside Dracuni to keep her safe. But from the way Kess's eyes weren't the only ones on Riony as she moved through her display of strength with her massive sword, she figured Riony's message to them all was clear.

Aishena and Benjin also trained nearby, and a yelp of celebration from the boy cut the air. Aishena was down, if only for a second, and up again fast enough to put her brother on his back as he preened and paraded his win.

Even Lyrrin remained separate, sitting on her own to the side on a stacked pyramid of stone blocks, hunched over and working on something small in her hands as she often did.

Shadows broke the bright glare of sunshine as the two dragons on patrol came in to land. Time to swap for the next shift.

Norallei and Thallan were already bringing their dragons out of the base and waved a signal to the incoming riders as they took off.

Zeina and her aqua seasong dragon, Gleem, hit the ground first. Gleem had a Bovin between her teeth, the massive beast old and boney, but big enough to feed all the dragons for a while.

The warrior woman didn't seem happy with the quarry, though. She leaped to the ground, her face darkened with a scowl. She flicked her head toward her dragon who nodded in reply and moved off toward the underground entrance without her.

Kess wondered what that would be like, to have the mental connection and communication with a dragon that a bond brought.

When Yensen brought his dragon to a stop, Zeina marched up to him.

"Where were you? You were meant to remain patrolling above the keep while I went farther out to hunt and check on nearby enclaves. That's the plan you and your princess set up. You'd think you could follow it."

Yensen's long eyes narrowed, and in a flat voice, he replied, "I was following game to hunt. I apologize that I ended up following it too far."

Zeina gestured to the empty mouth and claws of Ambri.

"I didn't say it was a fruitful hunt," Yensen muttered.

Riony paused mid swing and strode across to Zeina's side. "What's going on?"

Zeina's body swayed toward Riony's as though drawn like a magnet, and her expression softened. "Thankfully nothing. Thankfully you all weren't ambushed while this royal lapdog here abandoned his post. I thought grayglim were meant to be reliable."

"Yensen is," Kess called over.

The grayglim caught her eye and gave her a grateful nod.

She added, "And we need more food. If he had a chance to hunt, it was good he took it."

Zeina scoffed, but her attention was off Yensen now and on Riony.

She lazily rested an arm on Riony's shoulder. "I think we should take him off the patrol roster. Do you want to replace him?"

Yensen rolled his eyes and guided Ambri away into the base.

Riony laughed nervously. "Oh, I don't know the first thing about flying."

Zeina's voice dropped lower. "I could teach you. I'd love to take you for a ride, whenever you like."

Riony's cheeks matched her hair. Her eyes flickered, a flashing glance over to Kess, who turned around to pat Griskin and pretend not to be listening in. But it was hard not to. The semicircle of walls surrounded them like an amphitheater and all sound within carried.

Riony murmured, "Okay, so, you need to be careful how you phrase things around me. I have misread situations and been disappointed in the past."

Zeina's voice was a deep rustle of dried leaves. "I won't disappoint you. I could not disappoint you *right now*, if you like."

Moving away, Zeina trailed her arm off Riony's shoulder and tilted her head for Riony to follow as she disappeared into the base.

Kess shot a look at Aishena, who didn't seem concerned at all about Zeina's blatant flirting or the starstruck look Riony returned the Rebel Rider.

The Hjelzahn girl had finished her training and joined Dashiel on the wall beside Dracuni. A jolt of shock passed through Kess to see Aishena laughing at something Dashiel had said. Laughing? Kess didn't think the woman had more than one emotion.

Even Benjin, a few steps away, was staring open-mouthed at the sight.

Riony took a step to follow Zeina, and Kess's heart caught in her throat.

Then another figure came jogging out of the base entrance, a skip in her step as hazel hair tumbled around her neat and new delver's armor.

"Nisk? What are you doing here?" Riony met her with a tight hug.

Niskina pulled out of the hug and raised her eyebrows at Riony's still flushed cheeks.

"I got your message about moving the gateway, and the Rebel Riders actually being *the* Rebel Riders, and I was going to reply with a note, but thought I'd just come through and give you my report in person, since you've moved the gateway here."

"I'm pretty sure our note also said that the gateways could run out of charge and would need to be used less." Riony had sent their last message through when the gateway was still at the shrine, before they brought it to the base. It hadn't been used since then.

Niskina waved that away. "By then we had also moved the depths gateway up into the undercity. I was getting ready to start using it all the time, setting up trade with the shrine enclaves. I suppose we're going to have to use the one down the hill instead now. But it is good to know rather than find out."

"And it is good to see you, but this will have to be the last time," Riony said.

Kess hoped so. Niskina still looked at her as though she were the vilest scum to walk the earth. Kess knew enough of her own guilt. She didn't need another reminder.

"Of course." Niskina nodded distractedly and craned her neck, taking in everyone there and waving to the others. "So, where are they? I saw Zeina on my way out, and oh my stars, *Riony*! But where is *he*?"

Riony chuckled and pointed to the distant end of the empty field allocated to the dragonkeep, where Kess had sent Jaym to hunt his pocket-hawk, far away from Riony. He cut a fine, heroic silhouette in the distance, and Niskina sighed melodramatically.

"I know we're not using the gateways again now except for emergencies. But wanting to sleep with a Rebel Rider counts as an emergency, right?" Niskina looked longingly toward Rider Jaym.

"I would scold you but I'm feeling a very high level of emergency myself." Riony also had her eyes locked on the entrance to the base.

From it, the Alderkin stepped out into the light as well, squinting at the sun.

"Zeina?" Niskina pointed to Riony's still red cheeks. "Were you ... did I interrupt something?"

"Hopefully something that can be picked up again soon." Riony shook herself and focused on Niskina. "Come on, let us know what you came to say."

Niskina gave Riony a long knowing smile. "Only a couple of things to report. We've been hearing rumors of some dragonlords leaving Elundrae entirely, by ship."

"Leaving?" Aishena stepped in to join them. There was a hard edge to her voice. "Do we know which families?"

The Alderkin had reached them now too, standing a little to the side to listen. Eslinde, still on Viska, had propped herself up to give the report her attention as well. Even Jaym meandered back their way. Only Lyrrin remained focused on her own activity.

Kess climbed back onto Griskin, moving to intercept Jaym before he brought his little bird close to Riony again.

"No. We only know the 'rats from a sinking ship' impression that the stories are giving." Niskina grimaced. "And there's worse news. A couple of the gateways, from shrines that we haven't taken Dracuni to for the longest, have gone dark."

Riony frowned deeply and lifted her sword over her shoulder to sheath it. "So soon? I thought they would last longer. How is the gateway in the depths still working but the others are running out of charge already?"

After a few shared glances between the Alderkin, Shael spoke up. "It's the living dead. When they move around the shrines, they drain the magic faster through the barrier protection magic. This happened to us as well during the war. Anywhere the living dead were nearby, magic disappeared for us, too fast, once the unicorns were gone."

"What can we do?" Riony asked.

"It's too much of a risk taking Dracuni through to any of the shrines to recharge them now," Aishena said.

"I can send out messages," Niskina offered. "Get any communities at risk of losing their protection to move along to enclaves where Dracuni has been more often and more recently."

"Have you heard from Myrwa? Are they okay?" Riony's voice was strained with worry.

Kess lingered behind her for a moment, wishing she could protect Riony from even the hurt of such worry.

"They're fine. All good for now. I did invite them to the undercity to keep everyone safe there, but Kellae said she wasn't letting her brother and baby grow up underground. None of them wanted to."

Riony's shoulders drooped. "Yeah, I get that."

"It's not so bad," Niskina said. "You could all come and join us. Even in the last week, we've been able to organize so much. The delvers have taken me back in and I'm also working with other groups. But having you there could help so much. And I'd love to have you with me. Well … not all of you."

Niskina met Kess's eyes. Kess turned away.

Riony's voice followed Kess as she moved away from the conversation. "I'd love to, but I think we're safer here, especially with Dracuni. At least there's only a handful of people I have to keep an eye on here, rather than the entire undercity."

Am I still one of the people she needs to keep an eye on?

Kess tried to swallow the feeling away, but it felt stuck in her dry throat.

Stalking Griskin forward, Kess stepped into Jaym's path. He greeted her with a charming smile and stroked a finger down his hawk's neck. It cheeped, and Kess smiled softly at it. The sleek dark-eyed bird of prey was beautiful.

Jaym angled to watch the conversation continuing behind them.

"Who's the newcomer?" he asked.

"An ally," Kess replied. "From the undercity. To where she's returning soon."

He watched Niskina with smiling eyes, especially when she noticed he'd come closer and was fluttering long lashes his way. "Such interesting allies you have."

Niskina stepped away then, giving Jaym one last long, lingering glance before leaving. But his attention had turned to Dracuni.

"This one still can't fly? Rather strange for its age."

"Is it?" Kess sidestepped Griskin to put herself between Jaym and the unidragon.

He moved as well, keeping assessing eyes on Dracuni. "What breed is she? I haven't seen anything like her before."

"She's wild born." Kess remembered Eslinde saying she wasn't as good at lying as she thought she was, so she tried to keep to the truth, a truth that wouldn't raise any further suspicions. "No idea of the father. A seasong mother, but one that wasn't typical either. So we don't know."

"Hmm. A mystery then." Jaym shrugged, then moved as though to join Riony and Aishena where they chatted behind Kess.

"No. Take that bird of yours away. I told you before to keep your distance."

Jaym laughed and scratched the bird's cheeks and it leaned into his fingers. "But why? My little hawk? How could anyone be frightened of her?"

Kess growled. "It doesn't matter. What matters is that you keep it away from Riony or you'll lose the arm you use to perch your bird."

Only smiling wider, Jaym lifted his free hand in surrender. "Yes, Mestra!"

He offered a mocking salute, then jogged off toward the base entrance.

"It's inspiring, you know," a soft voice murmured from Kess's side.

She turned to find Dashiel there, smiling with closed lips and a slight sadness to their eyes. "What is?"

Dashiel leaned in and whispered, "How protective you are of her."

They indicated Riony with their eyes.

"It's what she deserves. The least she deserves."

Kess had spoken with Dashiel about how she and Riony knew each other a couple of nights ago during a quiet moment. Dashiel had broached the subject by asking which of the people in their life now were ones who wanted to kill Kess. Just so they could be prepared.

Kess explained she couldn't be sure but did explain the different relationships with each of them.

Staring across at Riony now, Dashiel sighed. "You know ... I do like you, Kess."

Kess choked on her words. "Like me? Like ... how like?"

Dashiel shrugged, smile growing. Their voice remained low. "But I really didn't realize the level of competition I was up against. I can't compete with her."

Opening her mouth, Kess found she didn't know what to say. Because no, nobody, in Kess's eyes, could match Riony. She was all Kess could think of, all she dreamed of, all she wanted to look at, all she wanted ... All she wanted.

Dashiel's lips twisted up cheekily. "Maybe I'll compete with you for Riony."

Kess scoffed. "You're senseless if you think I have any part in that contest. No, but you would be up against Rider Zeina. And maybe Aishena. Good luck."

"Aishena Hjelzahn." Dashiel turned glittering eyes toward the grayglim woman. "Impressive rivals indeed. Do you think I'd have a chance?"

Kess smirked, but before she could reply, a strange, tortured roar split the air.

Dracuni lifted her head high, her cry piercing the air. Then Shiff echoed her.

Kess turned Griskin toward them, but there was no sign of their distress. Nothing attacked them, there was no ambush, no invaders.

"Dracuni?" Riony bellowed, racing toward the unidragon.

Dracuni leaped down from the wall recklessly, the ground cracking beneath her where she landed. Her body swayed strangely as she stalked across the field.

Shiff followed, gliding down and prowling the same direction.

Viska remained motionless, glittering gold like a statue.

Eslinde, in Viska's saddle, yelled, "I don't know what happened."

"Shiff? What is it?" Dashiel called out. "She's not replying. She feels so ... I don't know, defensive?"

Riony chased to catch up with the smaller dragons. "Dracuni isn't responding either. What are they doing?"

Both dragons growled, eyes wild and furious.

Ahead of them, right in line of their path, Lyrrin sat on her stack of stones, eyes wide and shaking.

Chapter Ten

Lyrrin wanted to toss the stupid crystal down from the stack of stones she was sitting on and shatter it on the ground.

If it was to work for you, it would sing to you.

Lyrrin grunted through gritted teeth. The ten-stroke rune did sing to her. At least a little. Maybe she just wasn't listening hard enough.

She just had to keep trying, and then she could show the Alderkin that she was like them. But she'd been sitting under the blazing sun, and although the air was crisp, the heat had built up under the heavy hood she wore.

She tossed it back, glaring out across the field. Niskina was there, and as much as it was nice to see her, Lyrrin couldn't offer more than a frustrated wave. Riony and the others were all busy flirting with each other like idiots. Lyrrin didn't understand why all of them had been so silly lately.

Even the rustle of bantam ferrets scurrying around in the weedy brush that poked out between paving and unfinished foundations didn't brighten Lyrrin's mood.

Dracuni still hadn't learned to fly either, so at least Lyrrin wasn't the only one failing.

No. I'm not failing today.

It took countless more attempts before Lyrrin traced down the last curved line of the rune, and the crystal lit up in a deep green.

She was about to leap down from her perch and run to show everyone what she'd done—whatever it was—when Dracuni and Shiff roared and charged toward her, and everyone was yelling.

And the Alderkin's eyes all turned toward Lyrrin.

"The dragon summoning rune, she's activated it!" Shael said.

Lyrrin gasped, scrubbing her trembling fingers speedily across the rune surface, trying to remember the sequence she'd just worked out to deactivate the magic again.

It took three tries as Dracuni and Shiff breathed down on her, teeth bared, before the glow of magic went out.

Everyone stared at her. But at least they were all okay. At least she'd deactivated it before anything bad had happened.

Neither young dragon seemed ready to harm her, but they were drawn in, compelled, fierce with determination. Lyrrin continued to shake.

A dragon summoning rune? What did that even mean? What were the dragons going to do?

Only Dracuni and Shiff had come toward her. Viska remained where she was, with Eslinde seated on top.

Lyrrin opened her mouth to apologize, to ask the Alderkin what she'd just done, but another roaring howl carried through the air.

One that didn't come from their dragons nearby. Not from any of the dragons within the base. Not from the two on patrol, high above.

Another dragon swooped in, drawn in, screaming and furious.

A dusky purple etherdart. The same dragon that had filled Lyrrin's nightmares for weeks as Kife and Kess relentlessly pursued them from its saddle.

"Sparks, no!" Riony screamed, rushing to Dracuni's side.

"There's no rider on him!" Kess circled Griskin around, out of the path of the incoming beast.

"As much of a relief as that is, I still never wanted to see that dragon again and it doesn't exactly look friendly."

The purple dragon scanned across the ground and all the targets before him. Then like an arrow through the air, he shot toward Viska.

"Watch out!" Vance scrambled down the half-formed wall, racing for his dragon.

Shiff moved to follow, but eyeing the full-grown dragons again, backed up and hid behind an outcrop of wall.

Eslinde twisted in the saddle, reaching to control the gold dragon, but Kife's etherdart was already upon them.

The purple crashed down over Viska's head, pinning her to the ground beneath long talons. Dusky wings swept and fluttered, keeping his balance as he clawed viciously against the tamed dragon's skull.

One of his wingtips swiped across Viska's back, catching Eslinde in its path and flinging her off the saddle and across the field. She screamed through the air. The sound cut off as she thumped to the ground.

Lyrrin cried out in her stead. Hands on the crystals at her belt, she moved to help, but Dracuni, herself again, blocked her path, keeping her away from the wild dragon attacking Viska.

Caught between Viska and Eslinde, Vance growled almost as loud as the dragons, then ran for Lyrrin's mother.

Kife's etherdart howled and grumbled, claws raking into golden scales, and then leaning down to close sharp teeth around Viska's forehead. The tamed dragon whimpered and twitched, unable to defend herself.

Purple light streaked through the field as Riony charged in, sword glowing bright.

Lashing his head back, a spray of blood followed the etherdart's clenched snout. Within its teeth was a sharp spike of metal. The taming stake.

Viska slumped. Blood poured from the open wound on her forehead.

The purple dragon spat the spike, and it clattered on the ground, a streak of crimson on the gray stone.

"Get away from her!" Riony bellowed, swinging her sword warningly through the air at the wild dragon.

Hissing, the purple turned all his attention to her. The spark of flame glittered between the dragon's teeth.

Lyrrin whimpered, fighting against Dracuni who had her hood grasped in a claw. Viska, Eslinde, Riony … was her mistake going to cost all of them?

She couldn't throw far enough to get any of her crystals there to help.

The dragon's mouth opened, and Riony was knocked sideways by the heavy flank of a leaping wolf.

Kess and Griskin stood in Riony's place, glaring wordlessly up into the dragon's fiery maw.

"Kess!" Riony spat from where she lay sprawled across to the side, being dragged farther out of fireball range by Aishena.

Benjin bounded on his toes beside them, as though ready to race in too, but a sharp word from his sister kept him back.

Kess lifted her chin, daring. "I watched you hatch and I freed you. Don't make me your enemy."

The purple's mouth slammed closed again, eyes narrowing over Kess. And then Kess gasped, clutching at her head and slumping over Griskin.

"Get out of the way," Dashiel yelled. "The patrol is coming in!"

Thallan and Norallei, on their bronze and white dragons, were diving down from the clouds above. And from the entrance to the base, Zeina, on Gleem, Jaym on his red dragon, and Samor on his flamesong rushed out.

The purple's head whipped around to take in his enemies, then he bellowed out an earth-shaking roar. Hot air blasted over Kess and Griskin, gusting their hair and fur. The dragon spun in place, tail flicking out. It struck Kess across the chest, sending her off the wolf and rolling across the ground.

The purple etherdart took off, swirling the dust behind it, speeding away from the riders coming in.

Riony was back on her feet, breathing heavily as she watched the purple flee for a few seconds before turning her eyes toward Lyrrin. There was so much disappointment in her expression it made Lyrrin crumble.

Then Riony was in action again.

She took a few steps toward Kess. "Are you—"

"Fine … Winded …" Kess wheezed as she lifted herself on her elbows.

Griskin rushed to her. He licked her face, whining.

"Eslinde?" Riony yelled across the field.

Lyrrin couldn't see where her mother had fallen, behind stacks of rusted steel. She held her breath.

"I've got her," Vance called back. "She's coming around."

Dracuni had let Lyrrin go, but she couldn't seem to get her feet to work.

Her eyes were on the golden dragon, lying with the hole in her head, blood still tricking out. Dashiel was beside her, pressing their hands to the wound.

"Viska's still alive. But won't be for long," the pain in their voice was eye-watering.

Aishena rushed over beside them, lending her help to stem the bleeding. Shiff emerged from her hiding spot and scampered worriedly at Dashiel's side.

With two matching *thwumps*, Thallan and Norallei landed beside the other Rebel Riders.

"What happened?" Thallan asked, eyeing the wounded dragon. "We had our eyes on the horizon, but that dragon came out of the nearby woods, got to you before we could. Was it some kind of ambush?"

"It was something," Riony growled, stalking up to the Alderkin. "What was that? A dragon summoning rune?"

Yrik set his face firm and didn't reply.

Shael stepped between them, her icy-blue hair shimmering in the sunlight. "It's magic only meant for use in protecting unicorns."

Riony swung her arm in the direction the purple dragon fled. "Then why did it send that dragon into a dragon murdering rage?"

Shael pressed her hands together before her face, then opened them palm outward. "I do not know. It is only meant to summon nearby dragons to a location, when a unicorn was under threat, so they could protect it."

Benjin gave the sky a thoughtful look. "That's what happened at the first taming, isn't it? Why a dragon was there, after Yeonard Draekhan attacked the unicorn?"

Shael bowed her head silently.

"Is that why Gleem, Hux, and Shani just went over all strange?" Zeina stroked her dragon's neck.

"Our steeds had no change," Thallan said from the back of the bronze dragon.

Priyune flicked a withering look his way. "It has no effect on tamed dragons, they have no mind to compel."

"Dracuni says she felt like she had to go to the source of the call, that she couldn't fight it. It scared her to lose control like that," Riony said.

"It should not have happened. The child shouldn't have invoked the magic," Yrik muttered.

Lyrrin's eyes filled with hot tears.

Riony pointed her finger aggressively toward the Alderkin. "Don't you dare blame this on her. Aren't you supposed to be teaching her? You wouldn't even tell her what the stone did."

Lyrrin held the unlit crystal so tight that it bit into her palm. If she'd known, would she have kept trying, just to prove she could?

I just wanted to show them I could do it, that the crystals sang to me too. But if they'd told me, if they shared it with me because I'm Alderkin like them, I would have had nothing to prove.

And now Viska was mortally injured and Lyrrin's mother hurt.

Yrik caught her eye, the sapphire hue shared between them, then he looked down at his feet.

"Viska's fading," Dashiel's voice broke.

Their hands were slick with crimson. The wounds all around Viska's forehead were too large for them to hold together.

Looking to Riony, Dashiel pleaded, "Is there anything we can do for her?"

Dracuni sidestepped closer and closer to Viska, lilac eyes tilted in worry.

Riony dropped her sword and jogged over beside the unidragon. "No. I *know*. But ..."

Lyrrin didn't need to hear Dracuni's mind-speak to understand. Dracuni wanted to help. Dracuni always wanted to help.

But all the Rebel Riders were watching.

Still lying on her back, Kess struggled up into a sitting position. Her voice came out broken and husky, "No. Eslinde ..."

"It sounds like Eslinde's okay. And maybe Viska will get through this on her own?" Riony offered, her voice high and desperate.

Dashiel growled, "She has a gaping hole in her brain, and she's almost gone."

Dracuni snorted at Riony, then pushed past her to stand beside Viska. The gold dragon's head was half as big as the smaller dragon, and broken scales were scattered around the ground between splatters of blood.

Riony cursed under her breath and ran back to grab her sword. She muttered, "And of course all our new witnesses are on their dragons right now too."

Lyrrin took in the scene, as Aishena and Benjin moved in beside Riony. Kess was clawing her way back up onto Griskin.

Finding her feet again, Lyrrin rushed over to her sister's side. She pulled a flash crystal from her belt, ready just in case. She wondered about throwing it then and there, hiding what the riders were about to see. But she couldn't explain that, couldn't explain how Viska would magically be healed afterward.

Thallan squinted at the scene before him. "What's going on? What's your dragon doing?"

Riony cricked her neck. "Something that we're not going to have any issue from you about, agreed?"

Dracuni lifted a talon and raked it over the back of her other hand. She raised it to press against Viska's cheek.

Hobbling toward them, supported by Vance, Eslinde gasped. "No, wait!"

Then Viska glowed. Dracuni's healing blood absorbed into her and flushed through her like moonlight spilling between clouds, shining out through her wounds and the gaps of her scales.

And a swirling shadow drifted from the skies, floating down over the golden dragon. She stirred.

Lyrrin swallowed. Now they had a newly wild dragon at their backs, and five awestruck riders facing them.

Five more people who knew about Dracuni's blood.

Chapter Eleven

Riony and her companions formed a line between the newly untamed gold dragon and the Rebel Riders who were staring aghast at what they'd just witnessed.

"I'm sorry," Lyrrin whispered.

Riony bumped an elbow against her sister's shoulder. "It's not your fault, you couldn't have known."

Also sorry, Dracuni thought, slinking up behind Riony.

"It's okay. You did what you had to, to save Viska. Now we just have to see what this lot think of it." Riony tightened her grip on the hilt of her sword and addressed the riders. "Everyone's going to be calm and make good decisions about this, right?"

If the five riders on their dragons chose to attack them then and there, Riony didn't like their odds. But Aishena and Benjin stood prepared to fight, and Lyrrin had a flash crystal ready.

Their presence settled Riony. With them at her side, she felt as though she could face anything, and even having Kess lurking at her shoulder with a throwing knife in each hand didn't detract from that.

Riony swallowed, as she felt the shocking realization that Kess's presence actually added to her sense of comfort and confidence.

She took my place in front of Kife's dragon.

For all Kess's promises and words, for all her little shows of loyalty, Riony still hadn't truly believed that Kess had meant it. That she wasn't still a selfish little gremlin plotting foul deeds.

But that moment with Kife's dragon was life or death. Kess had, without hesitation, put herself and Griskin in Riony's place when a fiery death was the likely outcome.

That wasn't some game or manipulation.

Kess had been ready to die to protect Riony.

What do I sparking do with that?

Kess still breathed unevenly and rubbed at the place on her chest where the tail had struck.

Under the heat of the sun and the crisp winter breeze, Riony felt feverish. She shook off all the confusing thoughts and feelings of that revelation and focused on the situation before her.

Still, as she glared up at the Rebel Riders, it made a world of difference knowing—*really* knowing—that Kess's blades were meant for her enemies and not for her.

Thallan stared back at Riony, taking his time in his own thoughts, but no doubt very different ones.

Finally, he said, "Your dragon bleeds silvernix?"

"So what if she does?" There was no point denying it with the way Viska had been magically healed in clear sight. "Do I need to also see what you bleed?"

The golden dragon raised herself gingerly off the ground, her head swaying.

Vance and Dashiel closed in on her cautiously, speaking to her in soft words and trying to keep the dragon's attention. But the snap of terse words between Riony and Thallan caused Viska's yellow eyes to narrow on them. She growled wildly.

Eslinde leaned heavily against a block of stone to the side. "Inside, all of you! You're going to overwhelm Viska."

Dracuni nudged Riony on the shoulder. **She's right. Viska knows those two, but she's really confused. She needs space.**

Riony's nose twitched, and she gestured to the riders. "You first."

Zeina's expression was intense, but she gave Riony a single nod and led the way, in quiet conversation with her aqua seasong.

The four other riders followed after only a short hesitation and a barked command from Thallan.

Once the riders and their dragons had disappeared into the entrance, Riony gestured for her friends and the Alderkin to follow.

Lyrrin hung back, her eyes on Eslinde.

"I'm fine, really." Eslinde offered a smile with a smudge of blood on her lip. "Go inside with your sister."

The princess tilted her head as she looked to Riony.

Leave Lyrrin outside with a newly re-wilded dragon or bring her in with me to face people who might want to kill us for Dracuni?

Riony wasn't sure either which was the best option, but she nodded to Eslinde and pulled her sister along with her.

Benjin glanced back at Viska and the Zarram siblings before stepping into the tunnel. "Why did he do that? Why did Kife's dragon pull Viska's stake out?"

"Is it because he was summoned?" Lyrrin asked in a small voice.

She still held the summoning crystal tight in one hand and flash stone in the other, as though her hands had fused closed around them.

The Alderkin shared glances and then shrugs that were some of the more human motions Riony had seen them make.

Yrik caught up to Lyrrin in a few long strides and spoke with his head slightly bowed. "The summoning magic lured the purple dragon in, but it wasn't the cause of the violence. The dragon chose that himself."

Lyrrin turned wide eyes up toward him. "Are you sure? None of the other wild dragons have wanted to pull other dragon's stakes out."

"Maybe because none of those other wild dragons have experienced being tamed before themselves," Aishena said thoughtfully.

"You think he was trying to help? But he was so violent." Lyrrin's voice trembled.

A cold stone of old pain shifted heavily inside of Riony. "Maybe he didn't know whether pulling the stake out would cure or kill Viska, but maybe it didn't matter. Maybe he thought even death was preferable to enslavement."

Silence followed them the rest of the way into the base. They reached the stables where the riders were settling their dragons in. The purple glow of Riony's sword merged with the orange light of the torches crackling along the walls.

There should have been two dragons still on patrol, but with Kife's etherdart still out there and Viska currently a liability, nobody seemed willing to take their dragons up again right now.

Yensen came in after them. His silky hair was disheveled, awoken from a rest after his night, then morning shift. "What happened?"

Riony gave him a quick rundown, and with a nod, he rushed off to check on Eslinde.

Thallan guided his bronze dragon into a stall and left it there, sitting dully. "You can put that giant sword of yours away, girl. We aren't going to fight you for your dragon."

Riony deactivated the rune but kept the sword in her hands.

Thallan shook his head roughly. "But don't think we aren't annoyed you kept this from us. All the bickering about what we could do, how we were going to untame enough dragons instead of killing them, while there you were sitting on the means to do what needs to be done."

Is that what I am? The means to an end? Dracuni sat down close to Riony, her tail tucked tightly around her.

No, Riony thought firmly.

Then to Thallan, she asked, "If our roles were reversed, and you had Dracuni, would you have told us?"

Thallan's mouth opened, then closed. He lifted his chin and huffed. "We'll never know, I suppose."

Jaym strolled over, sighing as he looked over Dracuni. "All that silvernix ..."

"Back it up," Riony snapped.

Jaym froze, grinned, and took two large steps back. His pocket-hawk was currently nowhere in sight, and Riony hoped it stayed that way.

He sighed audibly. "It's just incredible, though! And she's alive, hasn't withered away like the unicorns in captivity did. You've got all the silvernix you could ever want."

"She's not in captivity and no, we haven't. Dracuni's blood is her own. How she uses it and when is up to her. She belongs to herself."

Samor reached a hand up to stroke the cheek of his black and gold flamesong. "As she should."

Jaym shrugged, which caused a smoky huff of disapproval from his dragon, followed by a flurry of apologies from Jaym.

Zeina leaned up against Gleem's aqua scales. "I suppose I'd feel the same way if it were Gleem with the precious blood."

Thallan and Norallei seemed less convinced. The leader and his partner stood shoulder to shoulder, the Taen woman on edge like a petite bodyguard at his side.

Glancing back, almost guiltily at his tamed dragon, Thallan scoffed. "It's one thing to look after your steeds, but it's another to put the feelings of a wild beast ahead of the salvation of our world."

"Using the resource is worth thinking about," Norallei added. "We need all the help we can get."

"And instead, we're losing dragons." Thallan gestured toward the exit. "If you had the silvernix, you should have put Viska's stake back in too. Now she's gone."

Dracuni tossed her snout up and huffed. *Viska isn't gone. She's waking up, for the first time since she was a baby. She's confused and hurt. But she recognizes the two who raised her.*

Riony translated that along, and the three riders with wild dragons were in instant agreement. Their own dragons were agitated, eager, and worried, huddled together in silent communication.

Kess stepped Griskin forward to be beside Riony rather than behind. "Vance and Dashiel had spoken a number of times about wanting to untame Viska. I'm sure this isn't how they wanted it to happen, but I don't know if anyone would have been willing to put the spike back in again."

"We'll see how that plays out when those riders out there get roasted," Thallan scoffed.

Through the huge, arched doorway, Eslinde limped in, supported by Yensen. She waved away any concern. "Nobody has been roasted yet. If anyone can get Viska under control again, it's the Zarrams."

"What are we even doing here? Why did you bring us in, when you have all these resources"—Thallan flung one arm toward Dracuni and another toward the Alderkin—"but refuse to share them, refuse to even use them yourself."

A deep, angry heat rose within Riony, scorching her mouth dry. "Use them for what? Going out and waging war on the king and the curse and every other dragonrider in the land? There are times for fighting back and times for protecting what's important. I'm just trying to protect what we have."

In a low, mocking voice, Jaym said, "And you suggested we were the ones acting like dragonlords."

Eslinde's gaze was painfully disappointed. "For how long? How long can we look after only what is important to us when the rest of the world burns?"

I could ... if it would help everyone—

"No!" Riony snapped.

Her head swirled with visions of Dracuni bleeding, stuck with knives, tied to bottles and drained. All for the cause. All to save a world and the dragon enslaving people in it who weren't doing a thing to save themselves.

Thallan watched her for a long moment, then in a voice like one would use to calm a wild animal, he said, "I'm not going to push you, because I can see that trying to use Dracuni against her will is a sure way to set you against us, and we don't want that."

Thallan sounded terrifically begrudging on that point. Zeina, however, nodded earnestly.

"So we aren't using Dracuni, but what if there was another one?" Jaym asked.

Riony squinted in confusion. "Another what?"

He waved a hand in Dracuni's direction. "Unicorn ... dragon thing? How did you come across this one, anyway?"

Pushing away her anger, Riony said, "I didn't just come across her. She was changed, in her egg, by silvernix."

"That's what you did?" Kess coughed a harsh laugh. Then looking at the ceiling, she muttered in barely a whisper, "Typical sympathetic fool."

Between Riony and Aishena, they explained the situation with the broken dragon eggs.

Dracuni's feelings washing through to Riony had an edge of heartbreak. She knew the story already, but it was never a fun one to recount. For Dracuni to hear again about her dead siblings. About her mother's rejection.

"I only ended up keeping Dracuni, and finding out about her blood, because her own mother attacked and disowned her because she was different," Riony concluded.

At her side, Kess turned her face away, hiding it behind her hair, and Griskin stepped back.

Having listened with great interest, Thallan asked, "If you made her, couldn't we make more?"

More like me? Dracuni blinked her large eyes.

Riony threw her hand up in the air. "Oh, there's a good idea. We've got one creature that the Dragon King would pursue us to the ends of the earth for. Why don't we have more of those? That's got to be the answer!"

Eslinde, however, perked up from where she leaned heavily against Yensen. "No, no, it might be worth considering."

Riony gaped. "Is it? How fair is that for the creatures you create? I didn't mean for this to happen to Dracuni, for her very blood to be something people would hunt her for, would kill for."

The Alderkin had moved forward into the conversation, circling around where Dracuni sat.

Priyune spoke with the cadence of a poet. "How can it be right to create a life knowing that is the fate you've given it? That it will be seen only as a resource to be coveted?"

Shael tutted. "Seems like the very way humans ended up where they are currently."

Eslinde tilted her head. "Cruel as it may seem, having more living creatures with silvernix blood is an opportunity we can't ignore."

Aishena leaned in, speaking just for Riony. "It has its issues, but if there were more unidragons, smaller ones, that the Dragon King didn't know about, we could keep the shrines activated without risking Dracuni."

Riony's chest heaved. All she had done and suffered to protect Dracuni seemed to crash over her at once, a weight set against every life she'd tried to save and improve by giving them shelter at those shrines. Shrines that would soon have no magic left to keep them safe.

She only wanted to protect people, protect lives. Her shoulders slumped.

She didn't know what to do.

Thallan, however, spoke with a confidence as though he had already made his plans. "One of our other groups who keep to the west have eggs at the moment. They've been focused on trying to breed more dragons into our cause. I'm sure they could spare one for us to try."

"It's worth trying," Eslinde said. "At least then we'll know if the process is repeatable and can plan accordingly."

"It won't be a long trip to collect an egg," Zeina said, like a peace offering. "We can also gather the food we need along the way to bring back as well."

At Riony's shoulder, Aishena whispered, "You could go with them again, make sure they aren't plotting against us. We can keep Dracuni safe here."

Riony ran a hand down her face. She pictured Myrwa, and Kellae, and the baby Riony had helped bring into the world. If they could create even one more unidragon, who could keep the magic of the shrines alive a little longer, wasn't that worth it?

Mouth dry, Riony nodded her agreement. Although the way the others were already planning the journey, she wasn't sure they needed it. Eslinde and the Rebel Riders moved away to the meeting room, with Lyrrin chasing after, checking on her mother after the fall she had.

The Alderkin drifted away together, and Aishena and Benjin followed.

Kess hovered for a moment. She turned to Riony as though about to say something. Riony's own mouth opened, words of thanks for what Kess had done sticking in her throat. A raw graze marred Kess's cheek below the constellation of dark spots and the shadows of bruising spread on her jaw.

Anything Riony had meant to say came out as a rough grunt.

Kess flinched, barely perceptibly, nodded once, and left.

Riony dropped down onto her haunches and leaned her forehead into Dracuni's side. "Why has everything become so hard?"

Dracuni didn't answer, but the emotions she shared with Riony were laden with sadness.

"Because you're trying to do everything yourself to keep everyone safe."

The voice startled Riony, who thought she was alone except the dragons. She looked up to see Yensen there.

Razing, sneaky grayglim.

"How quickly everything turned dangerous today. I wasn't even there ..." Yensen's gaze went toward where Eslinde had gone, and his hands clenched into fists. "And it wasn't even a trained dragon. Just some wild beast causing chaos. What if it had been one of the Dragon King's riders?"

Riony sighed and stood back up. "Believe me, I thought it was when I first saw it and all of those what-ifs are still burning holes in my head."

Yensen walked by the stalls with the tamed dragons and watched the untamed ones moving freely together farther down the stables. "Such as, what if you were gone, and those of us remaining here were besieged, trapped with Dracuni?"

"That's what the gateway is here for."

Yensen strode to Riony's side, his mouth and eyes strained with worry. "But what if there's no one here who knows how to open it? I want you to teach me how. If the rest of you are gone on some mission, I want a way to keep everyone safe here too. To keep Eslinde safe."

Riony swallowed, shaken at seeing the stoic grayglim expressing emotion. "It won't happen. We'll make sure there's always someone here who can use the gateway."

Another layer to the hay, lamb, wolf, farmer riddle. A lamb that knows the gateway rune. Riony's head hurt.

"It would be easier if more of us knew how to do it. It would be safer. Teach me."

"I can't. That's not my knowledge to share." Now that the Alderkin were with them, and what Lyrrin had told her about them and her father, it didn't seem right to be sharing something that wasn't hers.

Yensen laughed bitterly. "The Alderkin aren't going to teach me. They are as closed off and unsharing as the tales always said."

After the events of the morning, Riony couldn't argue. But keeping the shrine rune secret was about more than just respect to the Alderkin. It was about keeping the way of fleeing with Dracuni safe among Riony and those she trusted.

She said, "We haven't even shared the gateway rune with our friends living at the shrines."

Yensen's eyes narrowed and he looked over Riony in a way that made her want to shrivel away to nothing.

"I feel as though if you truly cared for them, you would have, as if you truly cared for Eslinde. Keeping that knowledge secret is only leaving all of us in danger."

Chapter Twelve

The aqua dragon cut to the right so swiftly Riony lifted from the saddle. She hung in the air, her brain sending desperate signals to her body to *grab something, grab on to something now before you fall to your death!*

A strong arm snaked around her middle, pulling her back into the seat. Zeina leaned in, pressing up close to Riony's back and speaking into her ear.

"I've got you. Don't panic."

"Who's panicking?" Riony replied in a high, panicked voice.

The rushing air whipped her hair around her face as they rose higher into the clouds at a blistering pace. The flickers of red around her flight goggles looked like licks of flame.

While Gleem wove and spun in the air, nearby Samor flew his immense flamesong dragon. Aishena and Kess rode with him, and Thallan was on his bronze dragon along with Norallei. Both glided calmly through the smoke-tinted sky on their way back to Eslindekeep.

Their mission had been surprisingly quick and easy. Half a day's flight out to find the other Rebel Rider group, a short conversation in which Thallan convinced them to relinquish one of their soon-to-hatch eggs, and some hunting on the way home. A refreshing lack of betrayal or infighting.

Riony was pleased.

The hardest part had been leaving Eslindekeep to start with. Kife's purple dragon had remained hanging around and ambushed Thallan's tamed dragon on their way out.

They'd left it behind after a short chase, but there were worries that it would be there waiting for them again when they returned. They were going to have to be more careful with their tamed dragons.

At least Jaym had stayed behind with his wild dragon to do patrols. Viska still wasn't allowing a rider but wasn't showing signs of aggression and had given in to pleas to move inside.

The second hardest part of the trip was when Zeina convinced Riony to fly up front.

A growl rumbled through the aqua dragon's neck and through Riony.

"I don't think your dragon likes me!" Riony yelled over her shoulder.

Through the layers of armor between the two of them, Riony felt Zeina chuckle.

"She likes you just fine. Just relax. Gleem knows what she's doing."

"But to counter that, I *don't* know what I'm doing."

"You're doing fine. Gleem's not some tamed dragon who's going to drop out of the sky if you stop giving her direction. You just need to get used to being in the rider's seat. So you can ride Dracuni one day, if she ever gets off the ground."

They dove then, shooting down in a way that felt like the whole world was coming up to smack Riony in the face. She yelped, and Gleem rumbled again.

She's doing this on purpose!

The way Zeina pulled Riony in closer, she wondered if they both were, and she flushed hot all over in a way that warded off all the chill of the winter flight.

Thanks to the dragon summoning rune, she hadn't managed to follow Zeina that day to find out just how not-disappointed she might have been.

And as much as she wanted to know, Riony had to admit to herself she was palm-sweatingly nervous about the entire situation.

Zeina was a *Rebel Rider*, and stories or not, Riony could easily believe the audacious woman had known plenty of romantic encounters.

While Riony's only experience came down to a few fumbling kisses. One with a girl in the village she'd grown up in after leaving Heithorn estate, another with a young man in the undercity—just in case, but no—and her first kiss. The one with Kess, that had somehow been so terrible it left everyone in tears.

But 'so terrible it left everyone in tears' perfectly described most of Riony and Kess's relationship.

At least until everything had changed. Riony wasn't sure what their relationship was now, what she wanted it to be, or if she could ever get over all of the *terrible* and *tears* of their past.

Riony glanced across to where Kess rode on the black and gold dragon nearby, and Kess was already looking back. Riony turned away.

The way Kess had watched her recently felt … different. Lyrrin's voice reentered her head, saying *I think she likes you.*

Riony shivered. *That selfish gremlin only likes whatever gets her closer to what she wants.*

Riony just didn't know anymore what that was.

Gleem curved beneath her, angling up as though ready to loop around entirely upside down.

Riony cried, "You do know this is only the third time I've ever been in the sky?"

Zeina leaned back a little. "Really? I would have thought …"

She clicked her tongue and Gleem promptly evened out, coming back up into a soothingly smooth glide.

"Sorry, the way you were taking it, I thought you'd been up more. It took me a dozen times flying before I didn't feed the birds with the contents of my stomach. Do you want to switch places and I'll take over again?"

Riony laughed. "I think we all know you're already in control here."

All of the riders with untamed dragons could speak with them much the same as Riony could with Dracuni. They'd explained that only a person the dragon has bonded with can hear them speak, which is why most humans thought dragons were mindless beasts for so long.

Zeina didn't need to nudge and command her dragon into action the way riders with tamed dragons did. Gleem flew freely on her own, any discussion about where and how she flew was silent between her and Zeina.

Until recently, Riony had thought Dracuni was unique in her ability to communicate. But learning that all dragons spoke to bonded humans and each other left her wondering about the old Rolanian myth, that dragons were born from the tortured souls of the dead who got lost on their path to the stars.

Riony had loved listening to her mother sharing those stories at bedtime with her and Lyrrin, and after all that had changed, all she'd learned since, those stories now felt so childish. But childish in a way that she longed for and wished she could capture again in a world that now felt so hard.

"How long have you been with Gleem?" Riony asked around the lump in her throat.

"I found her as a hatchling when I was fifteen. Her mother had been downed by a patrol of dragonriders out near the dragonlord estate I was indentured to. And all of a sudden I found myself on the run with her."

Riony turned and smirked. "I know a little something about that. Sounds like an adventure."

Zeina beamed back. "It's quite the story. I could tell you all of it, if you like. Maybe … tonight? Come to my room."

Riony had mistaken words and looks for flirtation in the past, but there was no mistaking the raw hunger in Zeina's gaze.

Heat flushed Riony's cheeks, and she cleared her throat. "Yeah. That sounds"—another throat clearing—"good."

Riony had already been anxious to get back, worried about those she'd left behind. Normally, Aishena would be there to keep everyone safe, but she came along on the mission when Lyrrin and Benjin demanded that they wanted to look after Dracuni themselves.

Not allowing it would be an insult to their capability. They had been adamant, in the way preteens excelled at.

The level of trust for Eslinde and her group had grown as well, so the only person Riony wasn't sure of yet that was left behind was Jaym, and of all the Rebel Riders, he seemed the most harmless. Apart from his bird.

Lyrrin's heartbeat transferring through the paired crystals was steady, but Riony knew she'd remain worried until she saw them all again.

And Zeina's proposal only added another layer of anxiety to returning home.

The heavy beat of wings sounded loudly as Thallan and Samor brought their dragons in close by Gleem's side.

Aishena signaled and gestured down to the dry and cracked plains below.

A swath of darkness lay across the ground, undulating like ink spilling in slow motion, with two red glowing points—eyes like burning coals within a form of dripping gloom.

The shadow dragon.

It roared, and the air seemed to ripple and distort. A sharp pang of anguish ached through Riony and her eyes watered.

Now that she knew what the being was, what had created it, the sadness it emanated broke her heart even more.

Its roar also broke the hard-baked dirt beneath it, as long dead creatures clawed their way up through the ground.

"Glad we're up here," Zeina muttered.

Riony nodded and was about to turn away when she noticed more movement, from beneath where the shadow dragon's wings gusted as it raised itself away into the sky.

Small figures, insect-like from their distance, moved in a scattered pattern. People, running from the raised revenants. Leaving behind carts and belongings.

Riony's flesh pinched all over with goosebumps. She scanned the horizon to get her bearings.

They weren't far from one of the shrine enclaves. One that had run out of magic.

They must be traveling to find somewhere safe. Because we've been hiding. Keeping Dracuni away.

"We have to go help them," Riony said.

Zeina's expression was grim, but she nodded and made a few hand gestures to Thallan.

Thallan shook his head as he swiped a signal with his arm.

"He says we're going to continue on," Zeina translated.

"No, we sparking aren't. There are people down there. I'm going to help, one way or another." Riony pulled her sword from its sheath and activated the float rune.

Staring down, she set her jaw. She hadn't ever fallen quite that far before but had made some big jumps with the float rune and was fairly confident the magic would cushion her landing.

Catching Aishena's eye, Riony pointed down, hoping she was understood. The Hjelzahn girl nodded and began barking orders toward Samor, with Kess backing her up. The quiet giant of a man hunched over, beset.

Zeina grabbed Riony's arm. "You want to risk getting ripped up by revs to save a handful of people? Our plans are bigger than that, and we need to stay in one piece if we're going to save the world. We're safe up here and should stay safe."

Riony tugged free of her grip. "And you'd be okay with just flying past and letting all those people die?"

"No, but—"

"But what? They can't stay safe up on dragon wings. Take me down lower or I'm taking myself down lower." Riony swung one of her legs around to sit sideways in the saddle, ready to jump.

"Fine," Zeina snapped, and Gleem snorted a huff and dove. "But you know my dragon's a seasong, right? She's got no fire attack to burn those revs."

"That's fine," Riony snapped back. "I have my own."

Gleem swooped in low, where the tree line would have been, if there were anything more than the odd charred stick and scratchy bush covering the ground.

Riony swiped her finger along the second rune on her sword, and pink flames cracked up the blade.

Then she jumped.

Winter-frosted mud cracked under Riony's boots as she landed.

A baby-faced woman screamed as Riony appeared before her, sword blazing. She screamed again when she turned from the strange, burning, sky-fallen woman back toward the gnashing human revenant that had been chasing her.

"Duck!" Riony yelled.

The woman squealed a third time as she crouched down below grasping claws and the swing of a solid crystal sword, swirling with flames.

Riony hit the rev straight through the head, knocking the age-bleached skull into the air. But the undead abomination kept moving.

The headless body took a twitching step forward, and Riony rammed her sword through its tattered rib cage. The remnants of ancient flesh smoldered, then caught alight.

Angling her sword up and putting all her strength into the motion, Riony cut the rev through the middle, shattering its chest into jagged, burning chunks, then brought it smashing back down again to cleave through between its hips.

Disturbingly, the pieces of destroyed rev still moved, but there wasn't much it could do split in twain.

Riony stretched a hand for the woman and pulled her back to her feet. "Find somewhere to hide."

The woman stared back, wide-eyed and panting. "Where?"

Taking in a view of the battlefield, Riony had to concede it had been a dumb suggestion.

The plains were flat and almost bare as far as the eye could see. There was no cover, nowhere to hide, and the revenants were everywhere. The people dodged around them, running back and forth between carts and abandoned belongings.

A gust of wind stirred up dried grass and broken sticks as the other dragons came in close, but no undead-cleansing fire followed. The humans and revs on the ground were all too closely mixed.

Many riders wouldn't consider that a reason not to burn everything in their quest to destroy revenants, but the Rebel Riders didn't start raining fire on everyone and that raised their esteem in Riony's eyes.

A boar revenant ran for Riony. She spun to the side, thrusting her flaming blade into its flank as it charged by. She was still extracting her sword from the juddering remains when the flightless carcass of a massive carrion bird lunged for her, twiglike wings flapping as though it still had feathers.

The hooked beak struck for Riony's neck, then a flash of charcoal fur rushed by and it was gone.

Bones cracked and splintered in Griskin's jaws.

Shimmering gold and blue dragonrider armor came into view as Aishena twirled through the fray to Riony's side, athames slicing glowing arcs through the air as she went.

"You decided to join me!" Riony called over.

"Of course. Watch you back, tamebrain!"

Riony whipped around to see another human revenant dashing her way. Then two pale darts swished through the air. A bone dagger hit into each of the revs hip joints. The revenant's steps became stiff and awkward, slowing it down to a jolting march.

Still, it reached rotten claws for Riony, until another volley of daggers hit its shoulders, and its arms dropped like a lifeless puppet.

Riony's sword made short work of finishing off the incapacitated creature.

Kess and Griskin appeared at Riony's side. The wild girl's black-and-white hair had been detangled during her time spent with a princess, but the gusting air from circling dragons gave her a windswept look.

It paired with a fierce expression and flush of pink on her cheeks as her chest rose and fell, staring back at Riony.

As Riony realized she'd been staring in return.

"Are you okay?" Kess asked, frowning at her apparent dumbfoundedness.

Riony nodded mutely.

Aishena, moving in from ahead, raised her eyebrows at Kess. "Nice trick with the knives."

"Are you kidding me?" Riony huffed. "Nice trick? Do you know how long it took you to start complimenting me, and you're already impressed by her?"

Aishena's expression returned to normal and she shrugged. "It was impressive."

"It's not enough to clear these revs, though," Kess said. "We need fire. And even that might not keep them down."

"I have an idea about that," Aishena replied, casually stamping a heel onto a small slithering snake skeleton. "I've already shared it with the riders. They're ready. We've got to let everyone here alive know to drop to the ground at the same time. And hold on."

Riony nodded once and got moving. She didn't need the details—if Aishena planned it, she trusted it. And they didn't have any more time to spare. Screams of pain sounded from all around and the three of them, even with their impressive tricks, weren't enough to save everyone there.

Dodging between ravenous undead, Riony vaulted up onto an abandoned cart and waved her flaming sword in the air.

She hollered out the instructions twice, hoping everybody heard through their panic and screaming.

Aishena and Kess both called out the same instructions from their positions as well, and on the count of three, bodies dropped to the muddy ground all across the field.

Okay, so far so good ... Except, across to one side, a young girl, smaller than Lyrrin, was still running. A ghastly bear revenant galloped after her.

To the side of the carnage, Zeina brought Gleem in to land, and the dragon's chest lifted, puffing up as it prepared to breathe.

"Oh sparks."

Riony leaped across the field, coming down on top of the running girl. She brought both of them crashing to the ground. The girl screamed and whimpered beneath her. The revenant bear thumped down on top of them both.

And Gleem breathed.

It was like a hurricane being birthed from the dragon's maw and spreading across the land. So much more powerful than Dracuni's starved mother had been when her breath had flung Riony across the ice cave.

Riony dug her fingers into the dirt as air blasted over them. Revenants, unable to fathom what was happening, didn't slow their chase or hold on. They cartwheeled in the wind like tumbleweed away from the prone humans.

And once they were clear of the people, the fire hit.

Thallan brought his bronze etherdart sweeping over them, shooting fireballs at individual revs that were thrown beyond the main group.

But where the majority of the boney blights landed in a tangled mass, there was Samor and his flamesong.

Riony had never seen a flamesong breathe fire before.

When it did, she could feel the heat scorching her face from across the field. A constant raging jet of flames erupted around the revenants. The glow of fire lit the dragon's gold and black scales from within, all across her chest and neck, as though the inferno was more than it could contain.

Even with the intensity of that burn, some revenants still moved within it.

But between the rushing air blasting the revenants back and the roaring inferno they hit on the other side, the revenants were mostly gone.

Once the last few stubborn revenants were blown away, Gleem could stop and the humans could make a clear run for it. But there were a few revs that managed to hold on.

Like the bear. On Riony's back.

Its claws dug into Riony's armor, and the weight of its ragged bones threatened to squash the child beneath them both. Riony pressed up onto her elbows to give the girl space, and the wind caught beneath her, threatening to tear her free from her grip on the ground.

Huge teeth clamped down, crunching Riony's backplate and yanking at it with a growl. She cried out at the pressure as it pulled, ripping the leather straps free. The mangled steel clattered down beside them as the bear snapped again.

Fabric tore as it took a mouthful of her padded shirt and ripped it free. The chill of the air blasting over them cut across her bare back.

She had to move, do something, or the rev was going to kill her with its next bite.

Riony roared as she pressed her body upward and to the side, taking the weight of the skeletal bear with her. A curved claw scraped down her arm as they twisted together in the air, then the bear lost its grip and tumbled away from her in the wind.

But up off the ground, the air caught Riony as well. She reached out, dragging her fingers through the mud but not finding any purchase.

"Whoa, no, no, no!"

Air buffeted her on all sides as she flipped and rolled, skidding straight toward the burning wall of dragonfire.

Chapter Thirteen

Kess stared into the flames, aghast, as the heat intensified.

"More wood?" she asked.

Riony had an old, half-burnt trunk over one shoulder, then dropped it onto the bonfire. "Yup. It must be *bigger*!"

"Bigger! Bigger!" Lyrrin chanted as she threw a bundle of sticks in as well.

The orange light glittered over Dracuni's scales as she and Shiff sat side by side, watching.

Kess thought considering how close Riony had been that afternoon to being cooked alive, she might have shied away from flame. But she built the bonfire with utter, fearless glee.

Kess had only caught Riony with seconds to spare. She and Griskin raced across the field when they saw Riony tumbling toward the flamesong's fiery breath. Kess swung off her saddle to grab her, falling free herself in the wind.

She grasped Riony's hand, then Griskin grabbed Kess's boot in his mouth, and the three of them held tight to each other and the ground until Gleem stopped gusting a tornado around them.

Sitting to the side as every Rolanian in their group threw anything that would burn onto the growing fire, Kess rubbed her ankle. But her heart ached more.

Every time she closed her eyes, she was met with a vivid image of Riony's bare back, where the rev had ripped her armor away.

Of the crosshatch of old scars wrinkling her skin.

The one time Kess had struck Riony herself, she never even broke the skin. But it didn't matter. She might as well have inflicted every single wound Riony had suffered.

Kess had never seen the results of those beatings before. The painting of cruelty made indelible upon Riony's skin. Now, it was all Kess could see.

Once the threat of being blown into dragonflame had passed, Riony had helped Kess back up onto Griskin and then thanked her. Actually thanked her. With her words.

It was an act that shattered something inside Kess, and it had been hard for her not to break down crying then and there. She didn't want or expect or deserve gratitude, not from Riony. That wasn't why she was doing any of it.

Maybe, *maybe* if she saved Riony's life one thousand more times, she might feel as though she had come close to repaying the debts of all her mistakes. Beyond that, Kess doubted she could ever do enough to be worthy of Riony's *gratitude*.

But right now, Riony was still alive and even seemed happy, and Kess would do anything to keep things that way.

They hadn't managed to outright kill many of the revs, which was concerning considering the flamesong firepower applied, but they had managed to keep them burning and at bay long enough for the people to get their belongings and escape.

They considered that a win, and an air of celebration filled their camp as the bonfire grew.

Stars twinkled down from a clear, crisp night sky like a blanket of diamonds. Dashiel loped over to Kess, brushing their hands down from soot and smelling like woodsmoke.

"It's looking pretty good, isn't it?"

"Does it need to be so big?" Kess asked, wary of drawing attention to their location.

"Of course it does. It's Midwinter's Eve! Don't worry. There'll be fires all over Elundrae tonight." Dashiel grinned, and the light of the fire glowed through their blond hair. "I'm glad you got back in time for this."

Kess nodded, as though she understood, but Midwinter's Eve was a Rolanian custom, and one she'd never experienced. Taens considered the longest night of the year a more solemn affair.

Once, when she was little, she saw the slaves on Heithorn estate building a similar bonfire for their celebration. Her father sent one of their riders on a dragon out into the field. They destroyed the fire and all the decorations the slaves had made from fabric scraps and straw.

Kess didn't understand why. Their celebration wasn't going to hurt anyone.

Her father told her otherwise. "If we let them have one thing, they will think themselves capable of more. They might start to think they don't need us, our protection. They might think they could organize against us. They can't forget who they belong to."

Kess never did see a Midwinter's Eve celebration after that.

"What ... do we do with this?" Kess gestured weakly toward the fire.

Dashiel beamed. "Oh, you'll see. It's a lot of fun. I haven't done this in years. Not since my father banned it."

Their smile faded then.

Kess's voice came out rough. "I know you didn't exactly choose to leave your home and that things ended badly there, but I'm glad you are free to be who you want to be now."

Dashiel's shoulders lifted. They looked out over the fire again, watching Riony and Aishena, who were arguing about how much of their fuel reserves were going toward the bonfire. Riony had taken up the chant of *bigger, bigger*.

Dashiel returned smiling eyes to Kess. "I'm glad I ended up here, too."

Kess grinned crookedly. "So, how have you found life out here in the big bad world, after growing up as a spoiled dragonlord?"

Dashiel's jaw dropped in mock indignation, but their eyes remained smiling.

"What? I'm asking from experience." Kess laughed wryly. "I know there are still some things I miss."

Dashiel raised both hands as though weighing something between them. "Some burning sticks out in the middle of nowhere or going to parties at the Dragon King's palace ...?"

"Dash!" Vance called out. He was dragging in a very large log he'd found somewhere. "Give me a hand with this."

"Never mind. This is going to be amazing." Grinning again, Dashiel ran off.

Across the paved area, Aishena and Benjin were staring at the fire with as much confusion as Kess. Eslinde moved around, cheerily handing out bowls of steaming curry. The Alderkin took the food gratefully and Eslinde remained to speak with them.

Gleem lay resting near the fire, taking up all the space on that side, and the other two wild dragons were up on patrol with Samor and Jaym.

Kife's purple dragon had been seen again on their return that afternoon, making another attempt on Thallan's bronze etherdart, so they kept all the tamed dragons inside. The purple dragon didn't seem interested at all in the wild dragons.

The Rebel Riders who weren't on patrol were on their way out of the base tunnel, carrying with them the dragon egg they'd retrieved.

Thallan placed it down on a cube of cut stone. "We're ready to make our attempt."

The bonfire was abandoned as everyone grouped around to watch. Kess climbed back onto Griskin and moved in closer as well.

Dracuni rested her head over Riony's shoulder, and Riony patted her cheek.

Warily, she said, "We never did agree on where you were getting your silvernix from."

"We have our own," Thallan replied gruffly. "How big did you say the crack was?"

The man drew his sword, aiming the pommel toward the head-sized egg. Riony explained, and he struck the shell.

The sound of it cracking echoed in the silence. Aishena flinched and turned away. He hit it one more time, splitting it down the middle so the inner membrane was visible.

Lyrrin gasped, and Riony pulled her in beside her. "It'll be okay."

"Here's hoping it is," Thallan said and opened a tiny vial of iridescent fluid.

"Here's hoping for more than okay," Norallei added, dark eyes gleaming in the firelight.

Thallan grunted in agreement, and he let the drop fall onto the egg.

A shimmer of moonbeam glow grew from within the broken shell, brightening as the immature creature inside wriggled and squirmed.

Kess turned away from the magical illumination, watching Riony instead. Imagining how she'd done the same for Dracuni's egg, after the others had been smashed beyond hope.

Remembering how she'd left Riony there to die when she could have saved her but had been too hurt, too angry, too selfish in the moment.

When Riony glanced her way, hand around the acorn pendant, Kess wondered if Riony was remembering the same thing.

With one final crackling tear, the shell fell open entirely, and the hatchling within mewled, fighting its way free of the membrane.

Everyone drew a collective breath. The Alderkin drew symbols in the air as they often did. Some form of prayer, Kess assumed.

The hatchling's scales were velvety and a bright silver, brushed with the light tint of rainbow hue. Just like Dracuni's.

It had a few horns around its head, and one central one too, like Dracuni's.

Less fur, but still a small tuft at the end of its tail. Like Dracuni.

"Did it work?" Riony asked in a hushed tone.

"Only one way to find out." Thallan turned his sword in his hands with one swift motion and ran the blade across the hatchling's thigh.

The baby dragon bleated a scream.

Lyrrin matched it. "No! What are you doing?"

She ran forward, throwing her arms around the dragonling.

Driven by furious impulse, Kess's hands squeezed around Griskin, pushing him forward in a pounce to put them between the man and the hatchling.

Thallan raised his hands and scowled back. "Calm down. How else were we supposed to know if it worked?"

He held up the sword, tilting the blade in the low light. A soft line of red ran along its edge. "Which it didn't anyway, by the looks of it."

"You didn't have to be so violent about it," Kess growled. "It's a newborn."

Sneering at his sword, Thallan lowered it. "Some violence is necessary."

Lyrrin made low, comforting sounds to the hatchling and worked on dabbing the red blood away from its wound.

"What a waste," Norallei said flatly.

"We did everything right though." Zeina kicked a rock, then turned toward Riony. "Was there anything else? Anything different the first time?"

Shrugging, Riony moved closer to the hatchling, looking it over. "Lyrrin had scratched a few patterns into the vial, after moving to the undercity and seeing runes for the first time. I didn't think much of them at the time, but now that we know what she is ..."

Eslinde gave the Alderkin a hopeful look. "Could the magic have worked that way?"

Yrik, Shael, and Priyune whispered between each other in their language for a moment before Yrik shook his head. "We don't know of any runes which would work that way. Do you remember what you drew?"

Lyrrin's lips pulled in. "No. It was years ago. I didn't know proper runes then. I just liked how they looked and drew my own."

"The vial is gone, too," Riony added.

"Regardless, it shouldn't work on glass either," Yrik said.

Thallan sheathed his sword with a harsh thrust. "So it may be impossible to replicate! That would have been nice to know before spending silvernix on *this*."

He gestured to the diminutive, floppy hatchling. Smaller still than Dracuni had been when Kess first saw her. "It's not worth the resources to be raising another hatchling right now, not something so small and strange."

Kess's finger's tensed, and Griskin growled.

Thallan raised his voice. "Am I wrong? The thing has taken on only the worst aspects of a unidragon, and even this one still can't fly."

"Shh!" Lyrrin snapped. "You're scaring him. Can't you feel how scared he is?"

Riony's eyes closed and she swore softly.

Zeina released a breath that grew into a chuckle. "Well, Thallan, it looks like it's not your choice anyway what becomes of the hatchling. He's bonded with the little one."

"Bonded?" Lyrrin gasped.

Zeina smiled. "Pretty easy to do when a newborn has been hurt and you're the first creature to comfort him. Thallan might have realized that if he'd ever bonded with a hatchling himself."

Riony groaned a long sigh. "Didn't I say no more pets?"

Kess's heart raced, and she kept her face turned away from the group around the hatchling.

Was it so easy to bond with a dragonling?

And she'd missed yet another chance. Because her first instinct was to attack, rather than comfort. Because she had as much violence within her as the man she'd rebuked.

As much as Kess knew now that there were more important things than having her own dragon, knowing that the thing she had spent most of her life yearning for had been right there and she didn't get it, left her shaking with overwrought feelings.

It doesn't matter. I am by Riony's side, and I've been allowed to fly among friends. That's enough. That's so much more than I deserve.

She swallowed away the ache inside her that longed for more.

Thallan gave the baby dragon a long, disappointed stare, then marched off in a huff, Norallei close at his back.

Dashiel helped Lyrrin take the newborn hatchling inside, followed by Dracuni, Shiff, and the Alderkin. Vance, Benjin, and Zeina returned to the fire.

Eslinde sounded tired as she said, "Another unidragon could have helped our cause so much. If we had a way to keep the shrine enclaves activated, you'd never have had to risk yourselves as you did for those travelers today."

"Sharing how to use the gateways would have helped save those people too," Yensen said. "They could have traveled to another enclave when there were signs theirs was failing."

Aishena and Riony moved into the conversation.

Riony pulled her coat tighter around her. She'd changed into an untorn shirt when they'd returned and wore no armor now. Away from the fire where they were, the chill was biting.

She sighed. "It could be worth sharing, but I feel like the Alderkin would be angry about that."

"We may have to risk angering them," Aishena replied. "Niskina's last message sounded worried about the enclaves, not just for them running out of magic. They've been using the gateway down the hill from the undercity to trade and grow the settlements, but it seems to be attracting dragonrider attention."

Kess was about to leave, when Riony called over, "What do you think?"

"What do I ... think?" Kess blinked back in surprise.

"Do we share the gateway rune with everyone? As someone who we only escaped from because we could use the gateways and you couldn't, I feel like you might have some insight." Riony smirked, but there didn't seem to be any malice in her tone.

She wants my opinion? Kess desperately wanted to give one that made Riony happy, to show she was on her side, but as she opened her mouth, she knew she owed Riony the truth.

"The gateways were the only thing that kept you out of our reach. And we were just two idiots with one dragon. With the Dragon King after you, the risk is so much more. The priority now is to keep Dracuni safe."

Which then keeps Riony safe, Kess thought.

"And if the wrong people found out how to use the gateways, we'd have no hope." Kess held Riony's gaze as she spoke. "But what is hope for us could be the condemnation of others. If you decide to share the knowledge, I'm behind your decision."

Riony's forehead wrinkled, and her mouth worked into a faint smile.

"Come on!" Zeina yelled from near the fire. "The moon is up! It's time!"

A full grin broke over Riony then and she rushed away to Zeina's side. Everyone followed, leaving Kess alone and cold at the edge of the firelight.

Griskin whined softly as Kess rubbed his ears. He fidgeted beneath her as he often did when he'd spent all day inside or strapped to a dragon's back.

"Alright, boy. Go for a run." She pushed herself off his back and sat down against the block of stone that still had the dragon egg remains on top.

Griskin licked her face once, then bounded away across the empty roads and flat foundations of Eslindekeep, chasing rodents in the dark.

From this angle, the fire had two large peaks like burning columns, with a gap between. Kess inhaled sharply as Riony ran straight into the flames.

With one large leap, Riony passed through the gap in the fire and landed on the other side, whooping and laughing.

Zeina was the next to follow, and soon everyone was taking turns jumping through the flames. Even Aishena and Benjin had a go.

A low, long note reverberated through the air, lifting in a slow warbling melody. It took a moment for Kess to realize the sound came from Gleem.

She sat there, mesmerized by the singing dragon.

No seasongs in captivity ever sang. Even in all the time Kess had tracked Dracuni's mother, she'd never sung. The sound was beautiful and sad all at once.

"Hey! Are you going to have a go?" Riony jogged up to Kess's side, face flushed and breathing heavily.

"A go?"

"It's tradition for Midwinter's Eve. Jump through the fire, be cleansed and reborn through an act of courage. It's a whole thing. You should do it."

"I would, but ..." Kess's eyelids fluttered as she stared back blankly. She gestured to her legs.

"I mean on Griskin, of course." Riony looked around for where the wolf had gone.

"No! It might singe his fur. Absolutely not."

Riony scoffed. "You ran him toward dragonfire this very afternoon."

"That was different. I'd never risk him for something frivolous."

A cheer went up from around the fire as Eslinde landed her first jump through the flames and stumbled into Vance's awaiting arms.

Even the princess is doing it. Kess stared at the ground.

Riony turned as though to leave, then turned back again. She ran a hand through her hair and frowned, struggling with something. Her wild red locks weren't tied back in the usual thin pigtail she wore and they curled around her neck.

She shifted her weight from one foot to the other a couple of times, then made a sound between a sigh and a groan.

"Alright. Come on, then." She leaned down to Kess with her arms out.

Kess balked. "What are you doing?"

Riony paused where she was. "Unless you *don't* want to jump through fire, like some kind of fire-hating non-courageous non-jumper."

"If that was meant to provoke me it was a terrible attempt. The quality of your insults has dropped drastically."

"It's a lot harder to rip you up with words when you aren't being the living incarnation of nastiness." Riony shrugged. "So do you want to jump or not?"

Kess exhaled slowly. She could see in the deep furrows in Riony's forehead that her offer was costing her something. That carrying Kess for any reason was something that probably sickened her.

But still she stood there, arms out, waiting.

Still, she had followed a wolf across the blighted land to save someone who had hurt her, whom she hated.

She just couldn't help herself from helping others.

"Okay."

"Okay, then." Riony brought her arms down around Kess's shoulders and legs and scooped her up with ease.

Kess's chilled limbs pressed against Riony's warmed chest, and she wondered if the woman could feel how fast her heart was beating. She swallowed down the way Riony's touch made her lips gasp and her eyes water from an overwhelm of raw emotions.

Dashiel whistled and cheered as they approached the fire, and before Kess knew it, Riony was running.

She kept Kess held tight in her arms, and the flicker of heat grew hotter, and then they were jumping, passing between the pillars of fire.

There was a moment where they hung in the air, free from gravity and surrounded by the glow of flames, and all Kess could feel was warmth and the press of Riony's body and the air imprisoned in her lungs.

Golden light touched the outline of Riony's neck and cheeks, sheened in sweat, and lit her hair up as bright as the flames themselves.

They hit the ground on the other side with a thud and Riony stumbled, giggling as she readjusted to account for Kess's weight, bringing them back upright at the last moment.

They breathed in time with each other, and for a moment, their eyes locked, and it felt as though Riony pulled Kess a little closer.

Then she leaned over to put Kess down beside a stone block where a couple of bowls and cups had been left.

"And not singed at all." Riony half smiled.

Kess wanted to disagree. It felt as though she were burning all over.

She just swallowed and said with a crackly voice, "Thank you."

She expected Riony to leave her alone again then, but instead, Riony pulled off her coat, grabbed a bowl of half-eaten curry and rice, and sat down against the rock beside Kess.

"I need a rest to cool off a bit," Riony said breathily.

Over at the fire, Aishena and Dashiel seemed to be taking turns, one-upping each other and measuring how far they could jump each time.

Kess glanced at Riony as the woman scooped food into her mouth with her fingers. The dark lines of the tattoo on her arm contrasted with the gleam of firelight highlighting her skin.

Clearing her throat twice before her words would work, Kess asked, "What does it mean? Your tattoo."

A sad smile lifted on Riony's lips.

"My mother." She pointed to the four rings.

"Aishena's brother." She pointed to the two blades.

"Niskina's father." She pointed to the candle.

"We all got the same tattoo. Sharing our pain." She returned to eating.

"Niskina too? I thought it was something special, between you and Aishena."

Riony side-eyed Kess.

"Because of your relationship." Kess blushed.

"My relationship with Aish is the same as with Nisk. We're family. That's what this tattoo means. Why we all have it. But they chickened out of getting the other ones."

"You have more?"

Riony smirked. "Not any you'll be seeing."

Kess's breath rattled between the chill of the stone at her back and the warmth of the fire before her.

Aishena was taking another jump while Dashiel goaded her from the side. She vaulted through the flames with the elegance of flight, landing a body's length farther than where Dashiel marked their best attempt. Dashiel howled with faux outrage.

"I wouldn't mind …" Kess licked her dry lips. "If you and Aishena were together. She's someone who would be worthy of you."

Riony choked on her food. "I'm sorry. In what world do you think I need your approval for who I'm with?"

Kess lifted one shoulder in a casual shrug. "Maybe you do need it considering you've spent so long with someone like Aishena and *haven't* gone there."

Riony dropped her bowl on the ground, staring at Kess. Then laughter burbled out, shaking her chest. "You are full of surprises lately."

"Got to keep you on your toes." Kess returned the smile but couldn't keep the sadness out of it as she watched Aishena and Benjin celebrating her win.

"You know, I met the Hjelzahns once before, when I was very young." Kess lowered her eyes, drawing aimlessly in the dirt as the memory returned. "My parents took me to their dragonkeep while chasing a cure for my legs."

"I don't remember that," Riony said.

"It was before you came to me. We went to Hjelzahnkeep's palace to meet an experimental surgeon in the Hjelzahn's employ who said he was interested in my special case. He spoke of all the wonders his surgery could achieve beyond what silvernix alone could do. We had been so hopeful."

Riony leaned her head back, then rolled it Kess's way. "I already know this story doesn't end in a happily ever after. But I'll admit I'm a little scared about how it gets there."

Kess scrubbed out the lines she'd drawn. "It turned out when he said surgeon, he meant that he was employed as a torturer. He was interested in me because he wanted to learn how he could inflict my disability onto others."

Riony exhaled a breath that puffed into mist around them. "What? Why?"

"People who were immobile but could still feel every pain? I was perfect in his eyes. And the way he learned was by cutting into people."

Riony didn't say anything then, only stared at Kess with a deep furrow between her brows and those indescribable eyes.

"Four times he butchered me, then healed me with silvernix, only to open me up again, exploring my bones and muscles and sinew with his instruments. He used no sedative. He wanted to see every effect upon me while he worked."

Kess took a trembling breath and closed her eyes, only to see the scars on Riony's back. She opened them again, shaking her head to clear it.

"I was … I don't know, five? Six years old at the time? My parents stopped him when it became clear he was only working to his benefit and wasn't going to fix me. I still have nightmares sometimes … that I'm back there."

Riony slumped slightly, moving in so that her shoulder touched Kess's. "I'm sorry that your parents were such utter, deplorable shits."

"Me too."

"Stars, how did we survive that place?" Riony stared up at the sky.

Kess waited until she looked down again, and she held Riony's gaze. "You survived because you're strong. I only survived because I latched on to your strength. And I'm sorry. I'm sorry that I hurt you. I'm sorry I let anyone ever hurt you."

Riony's head shook in the smallest motion, and she opened her mouth.

Then Zeina strolled by in front of them. The beautiful warrior woman had her hair out of its normal braids, and the deep-brown locks curled around golden eyes that watched Riony with a heavy warmth. She tilted her head ever so slightly as she gave Riony a pointed look, then headed away into the base entrance.

Riony's throat pumped as she swallowed. She moved as though to get up.

Kess nodded to herself and stared at the ground.

Leaning forward, Riony pulled her coat back on and shivered, then settled back in beside Kess. "Have you eaten tonight?"

Unable to speak, Kess shook her head.

"I'll get you something."

"I don't need—"

"I know," Riony said firmly. "But isn't it nice sometimes to let other people look after you anyway? Like the way you've had my back lately. I appreciate that and I just ... I wanted to—"

A cloaked figure dashing out of the base entrance cut off Riony's words.

Aishena called out, "Niskina?"

Riony was on her feet in seconds, running to meet the woman. Kess whistled for Griskin.

Niskina grasped Riony for support. She gasped out her words around heaving breaths. "Myrwa's enclave ... they're being attacked!"

CHAPTER FOURTEEN

Riony's sword glowed in one hand while Aishena helped buckle the side straps of the scale mail vest she'd thrown on.

"It'll do," Riony snapped, pushing past her toward the gateway.

"*Riony*," Aishena scolded back.

With Riony's own armor ruined earlier that day, and in the rush, the chest armor was all she had over her clothing. It was ill-fitting and without proper padding, but Myrwa's enclave was under attack *right now* and there wasn't any time.

"I was going to join them for Midwinter's Eve." Niskina spoke between gulping breaths. "When I went through, it was chaos. I got a couple of kids out who were hiding in the shrine building, then came right away for help."

Weapons were grabbed and they all assembled near the gateway, attaching what armor they could in the moments they had.

You should have more armor on. Dracuni's thoughts felt like a hailstorm of worry.

"Open it," Riony ordered Benjin, who waited with his crystal-studded staff near the activation rune.

He glanced to Aishena for confirmation, then the gateway magic flickered and glowed. He selected the symbol for Myrwa's shrine, and the light turned red.

It took a moment for Riony to realize what she was seeing through the shimmering window.

The glow of fire.

She ran.

The hot sting of smoke met her eyes and lungs as she broke through to the other side. Half the shrine structure around the gateway had been smashed away, opening it to the destruction.

The ground crunched beneath Riony's feet as she ran on, the footsteps of Aishena, Dashiel, Vance, Niskina, and the Rebel Riders fanning out behind her. Kess and Griskin bounded away through the smoke.

A charred, acrid stench clogged each breath, and Riony threw an arm up in front of her face as a burst of embers flew at her.

Everything was on fire. Riony pushed through between the burning shelters, scanning for movement. There was only fire, and a single, gurgling scream that cut off before Riony could trace it.

"Where are they? Where is everyone?"

Her foot hit a lump and she stumbled. A burnt log, she thought at first. But it was too soft.

Bile stung her throat as the body became clear. Seared beyond recognition, their face was blackened and blistered. But someone Riony had known.

She had been looking to the skies and at eye level for any attackers or survivors. But as she turned her eyes to the ground, she saw the people who were missing.

Bodies smoldered amid the roaring flames. Everywhere Riony turned were faces and bodies and clothing she recognized. Emra, with her pretty doe eyes. The gaunt man she'd carried when they first ran from the revenant army together.

Kellae. Her legs burned away and body curled around two smaller ones. All gone.

Riony's face crumpled and twisted and she bellowed wordlessly.

Aishena appeared beside her, then barked through the smoke, "Keep the kids away!"

At the collapsed shrine, Eslinde and Yensen held Lyrrin and Benjin in place. Dracuni was squeezing her way through the gateway as well.

"No, go back!" Riony yelled.

I want to help too. I could save people.

Riony's knees felt ready to give way. She wasn't sure there was anyone left to save.

"Myrwa?" Riony cupped her hands around her mouth, calling the woman's name again and again.

Through a gust of smoke, Kess appeared on Griskin.

"There are some survivors hiding out in the forest. Not many. I saw two." Her words were crackly and forced. "They wouldn't come with me."

Griskin whined and licked his paws.

"Myrwa? I haven't seen her."

Kess's lips pulled in and she shook her head.

As everyone converged beside Riony, faces grim, it was clear nobody had found any more survivors.

Niskina let out an animalistic wail. "I should have stayed. I should have tried to get more people out. But I couldn't see, couldn't get out of the shrine … There was no one else nearby, only fire …"

"It looks like it was already almost over by the time you arrived," Aishena said. "The few you saved might have been the last."

Riony took another step and it crackled beneath her feet, crunching in an all too familiar way. She bent down, brushed her hand through the ash, and came upon something sharp.

She sifted it out in her fingers. Broken glass. Shards of shattered glass, all over the ground.

There was no reason for it to be there, no reason but one.

"Kife." The word was a guttural growl.

Glass collected from the nearby factory.

Did he scatter it before or after he killed everyone? Riony couldn't fathom the cruelty either way.

She held up the shard and it glinted in the flames. "This is a message from *your brother*."

Kess turned two shades paler. "He … he knows the enclaves are important to you."

Hit with an awful realization, Riony had to fight back the urge to be sick. She ran back to the gateway.

What is it? Dracuni moved out of her way, but even from a distance Riony was sharing every heart-aching, anguished emotion with the unidragon.

She couldn't reply. Her fingers trembled as she activated the gateway again and chose the symbol for another enclave at random, smashing her palm against it.

The gateway rippled and glowed—flaming red.

"It's all of them! They're attacking all of them!"

Eslinde covered her mouth with her hands.

Through the rippling image, she saw movement. The flap of dragon wings. People running through the hazy red light.

There was still time.

Aishena grabbed Riony by the back of her armor as she tried to charge through. "We have to get to as many shrines as we can, as fast as we can."

"What do you think I'm trying to do?" Riony shook her grip off.

"We have to be smart about it if we want to save as many people as possible." She stepped up onto a fallen stone and pointed between everyone. "Three rescue groups. Bring the Alderkin through, one with each group to run the gateways. Riony with Yensen and Kess. Vance with Dash and Thallan. Benjin, you're with me and Norallei."

"I want to help too, I can," Lyrrin said, then was pulled in closer to Eslinde.

Aishena shook her head. "We need a place to bring and heal survivors. Eslinde, Lyrrin, and Dracuni will go back to Eslindekeep. Dracuni?"

Dracuni nodded forcefully. ***I'm going to help.***

Aishena couldn't hear her, but the intent was clear. "Eslinde is going to tell everyone that she's using her royal supply of silvernix to heal people, so we don't get questions. Lyrrin, you're going to help Dracuni provide the silvernix where it's private and safe."

"And us?" Zeina asked, pointing to herself, Jaym, and Samor.

"Get your dragons in the air and to the any shrines you can reach. Try to clear off the attacking dragons. We aren't going to be able to keep everyone at Eslindekeep with us, so Niskina, you're going back to the undercity to prepare."

Benjin pushed Riony out of the way and reset the gateway to Eslindekeep, and the riders with wild dragons rushed through, followed by Dracuni at a slower, squeezing speed.

Riony's every muscle twitched and ached, needing to move, to take action. She couldn't even think clearly through what Aishena was saying, whether any of it would work, be safe, or if anything could ever be right ever again after what she'd just seen.

They're dead. They're all dead.

"Are we all set?" Aishena called across the remaining group.

"No." Yensen stepped closer to Eslinde. "I'm going back to Eslindekeep too. I have to make sure Eslinde and Lyrrin stay safe."

Riony found herself nodding, but Aishena swiped a hand through the air, cutting off the request.

"We need our best fighters out there protecting people and helping survivors escape. You're with Riony." Aishena's tone was final.

Yensen's jaw set, but Eslinde put a hand on his arm. "We'll be fine, Yen. Stay with Riony. That's an order."

But what if they're not fine? What if someone gets to them while I'm not there?

A buzzing hum of emotions built in Riony's skull.

How, how am I going to keep everyone safe?

Riony's mouth was dry, her voice harsh from the smoke. "Kess, will you stay back with them?"

"You ... don't want me with you?" Kess's face pinched in the way it did when she was fighting down emotions.

Riony shook her head. "I need someone I can trust to keep Lyrrin and Dracuni safe. Can I trust you?"

"You can," Kess said firmly.

"What about you?" Niskina asked, looking between Riony and Yensen. "It will just be the two of you."

"We'll be fine," Riony replied.

Kess locked eyes with her, nodded once, then followed Eslinde and Lyrrin through the gateway.

The Alderkin came through then, and the magical passageway to Eslindekeep closed and reopened again to a fiery scene. Dashiel, Vance, and Thallan went through with Priyune.

Riony held her breath as they opened the gateway again. Maybe it had just been that one other enclave ...

But as the magic rippled again, more fire shone through. She and Yensen stepped through. Yrik went with them, remaining at the gateway as Riony and the grayglim ran out into the flaming devastation.

It was like Myrwa's enclave all over again. Everything burned, including bodies on the ground. But here there was movement. Here there were still screams.

Here, Riony could fight back.

Silhouetted through the smoke, an armored figure raised a sword to strike a body beneath them. Riony barreled forward, colliding with the dragonrider and bringing them down beneath her. She held her sword, glowing purple in one hand, but struck down hard with her bare fist against the man's face again and then again. Her knuckles cracked and split, and the rider fell still.

Seeking her next target, she caught her breath when dragons became visible through the haze. But they were grounded. Stationary. Sitting around the edges of the camp beside the standing stones.

She could see their riders, all off their tamed steeds, wandering through the burning enclave to finish off anyone their dragonfire had missed.

Everything was red through Riony's eyes, and her blood felt molten in her veins.

Whimpering behind her shot her around. The young man there, who had almost been ended at the blade of the rider, stared at Riony's feral expression.

She blinked at him, then snapped, "Get to the gateway!"

He ran, and Riony rose to her feet in time to block the swing of an incoming sword. She swept her blade around, roaring as she brought it hammering across the rider's helmeted head.

She struck with the flat of her sword. Some part of her, deep inside, cringed away from killing. But it was almost entirely lost within the mindless rage boiling through her. When the rider collapsed beneath her assault, she didn't know whether he was alive or dead.

She stalked up and down between the burning huts like a beast of prey, cutting down the few dragonriders who strayed into her path, finding survivors to be even fewer.

Each body she stepped over, she checked for signs of life with trembling fingers. Each one who proved too still for life left a scar on her heart like a hot brand.

Ahead of her, the smoke parted briefly, and a rider stood there, motionless, staring at Riony. Her eyes streamed from the sting of smoke, and she wiped them with the back of her arm to clear them. The man's dark hair was braided thickly along the top of his head, and he laughed in a gut-twisting, familiar way.

"Kife!" Riony roared.

He laughed even louder and stepped back into the haze.

Riony ran for him. Smoke blew so thickly across her path that she couldn't see.

"Yensen? Over here! We have to catch him!"

Riony pushed farther through, chasing around the back of a burning hut.

"Yensen! Where are you?"

No reply.

Rounding the corner, Riony's face was met with the swing of a burning block of wood.

Sparks sprayed around her, singeing her eyes and hair. She choked on the puff of ash and stumbled back. Her body crashed into another, scale mail clattering against scale mail. Arms came up and grabbed her under the shoulders, pinning her to her captor.

The dragonrider in front of her—not Kife—kicked her sword from her hand.

Hot liquid ran from her stinging nose, and she tasted blood. "Yensen!"

She flexed her shoulders, pulling forward to free herself of the grapple. The rider holding her grunted. A woman. She held tight.

Sparks. Where's Kife?

A searing gust of wind blew around them and the sound of dragon wings beat through the dark night above.

"How'd we miss this one with our burn?" the rider in front of her said.

Sword in one hand and charred wood in the other, he swung the wood like a bat into Riony's stomach. The flexible scale mail offered little protection for the blunt blow.

Riony wheezed and spat blood at the rider. "The same way you're going to miss your asses when I've beaten them clear off you."

"The only thing coming off is that rider armor you've stolen." The man angled his sword point above her shoulder, slipping it under the straps of the vest. "How dare you wear it, peasant?"

With a tearing slice, he cut through and the scale mail fell free from Riony's shoulder on that side, slumping and clattering over her chest.

"Come on, finish her off. The others are leaving." The female rider readjusted her hold.

"Yeah, yeah." The rider aimed his sword forward lazily, as though Riony were any of the defenseless civilians they'd just been murdering.

He pressed the tip against her unprotected chest where the armor had fallen away, then lunged.

She wrenched to the side, and the sword thrust across her instead of through. The edge scraped along her exposed collarbone. She overestimated the female rider's hold on her and turned too far, pulling out of the rider's grasp and putting her arm into the slicing sword.

The blade bit deep into her bare bicep.

The rider swore and readjusted their attack.

Gritting her teeth, Riony ducked the next swing, scooping her own sword up in the same motion. Grasping it in both hands, Riony stalked toward the riders, face and body dripping with blood.

The woman took one look at her and bolted, disappearing into the smoke.

A mad ringing in Riony's ears blocked out all other sound. The clash of her sword against the man's. His cries as she cut through his armor, knocking him to his knees. The useless pleas rambling from his lips as he crawled backward away from her.

Riony only saw a monster. How was he any better than the revs she smashed to pieces? How was the thing in front of her different than those cruel beings of destruction? *They killed them. They burned them all as though they were nothing.*

Riony's whole face was wet as she raised her sword for a final blow.

The ringing sound shifted, cleared. The buzzing tone resolved into a long, high-pitched scream. Riony's chest heaved, scorched dry from smoke, and she turned away from the cowering rider.

The fury that overwhelmed her iced over as a toddler, hair smoking, staggered toward her, arms up. Their face was blackened with soot.

And Riony remembered why she was there.

Jamming her sword away in its sheath at her back, she gathered the child in her arms.

"It's okay. It's okay, I've got you." Riony glanced back at the rider, reassured to find him gone.

All the dragons were airborne now, and Riony expected to run from another volley of dragonfire. Then an even larger dragon came diving in through the dark sky, scattering the riders. There was a flicker of gold scales between others so dark they were lost in the night. Samor and his flamesong, Shani.

Riony steadied her breath. She'd missed her chance at Kife, but there was still more to do.

"Amma. *Ammaaaaaaa.*" The infant sobbed, pointing a chubby finger toward the burning hut.

Holding the infant close to her, Riony moved sideways, shielding the child from the radiant heat as she moved to the remains of the structure.

A body lay in the doorway. Riony squatted down and felt for a pulse on the blond woman's wrist. Still alive, but no amount of shaking would rouse her.

Riony dragged her away from the flames, balancing the squirming child in her other arm. "Yensen! Where are you?"

Still, he didn't come.

"Stars, damn it," Riony muttered. Her sliced arm throbbed, and every part of her head felt like it had been assaulted by lightning hornets.

With a pained grunt, she placed the child down for long enough to haul the mother over one shoulder, then pulled the child back in with her bleeding arm again and brought them all up to standing.

She carried them both back to the gateway.

Yrik, waiting there, activated the magic when he saw her approach.

"Where's that depths-cursed grayglim?" she growled.

"He took a survivor through a while ago."

"Why hasn't he come back yet?"

The shimmering window of the gateway glowed the cool blue of crystal light, and as though summoned, Yensen stepped through. His sweeping eyes were narrowed and lips thin.

Kess followed close behind on Griskin.

When she saw Riony in front of her, her eyes traveled up and down Riony, taking in the dripping blood and bodies she carried, and her face pinched in violently.

Despite all the raging heat inside and out, Riony shivered. "What happened, is everyone—?"

"They're fine. Everyone's okay. We came back to help you." Kess's words trembled slightly. "We should have come sooner."

Movement on Riony's shoulder startled her. The woman there shifted, then moaned. Then in a rush she began struggling.

"Slow down, it's alright!" Riony bent forward and put her on her feet.

The woman wobbled, unsteady. She coughed desperately, but when she saw her child, she straightened and pulled the infant into her arms.

Wiping the blood off her mouth with the back of her good arm, Riony tilted her head to the woman. "There are people to help you through there. Can you walk?"

Nodding, the mother stroked her baby's ashy hair. "Thank you."

Her steps were faltering, but she made it through. Yrik closed the portal after her.

Even before the woman had left, Kess was at Riony's side, binding the gash in her arm with a bandage. "This will have to do until we go back. I'm assuming that's not yet."

"No. I still heard more survivors. The riders were chased off before they could get everyone." Riony didn't mention Kife as she stared at the careful work of Kess's fingers as she tied the bandage.

Yensen grunted, then dashed away to continue the search.

Kess's hand lingered on Riony's arm.

Riony's breathing became hard. "You're … You're supposed to be looking after Lyrrin and Dracuni, that's what I asked you to do."

Kess flinched slightly. "Aishena and Benjin are with them now. They cleared the smaller camps already. When we realized you were alone … They agreed to stay so I could find you."

"Why was I alone? What was Yensen doing?"

"He came through with a survivor, but then he went to get a dragon. He said you needed more air support. But we knew Samor was already coming this way, so I made the grayglim come back through with me."

Riony frowned, her head still spinning with a sickening mix of grief and rage. Why would Yensen think she needed air support? To catch Kife?

Kess licked her lips and her voice cracked. "Was that okay? I know you told me to stay with Lyrrin and Dracuni. I'm sorry. I just …"

The air sighed out of Riony. "No. That's okay. It's … good you're here. We still have a lot to do."

Riony only said the words out of some sense of wanting to offer comfort to anyone she could when everything had been razed all around them.

But as she and Kess worked together to clear the rest of that enclave, then moved to the next and the next, Kess's presence at her back was the only thing that kept Riony from falling apart.

The cool light of early morning filled the sky by the time they stumbled back to the gateway and Yrik informed them that there were no more shrines left to go to. They'd saved everyone they could save.

Yensen went back to Eslindekeep then, where everyone else was gathering to recover.

"I'm going back to Myrwa's first," Riony said as Kess moved to follow the grayglim.

Her voice came out jittery. She didn't want to ask. She couldn't speak the words aloud. But she didn't want to go alone.

But she didn't need to ask.

"I'm with you." Kess bowed her head in a slow nod and stepped back from the gateway.

Yrik waved to the passage through to Eslindekeep. "We should go back. I'm worried how much we've used the gateways tonight. They might not last much longer. I don't want to be stuck out here."

"You go. I can get us where we need to be." Riony patted him on the shoulder. "Thank you."

The Alderkin paused, then scribed a symbol in the air and pressed his hand to Riony's shoulder as well, before disappearing through the portal.

Riony closed it after him, then reopened the way to Myrwa's.

Only low fires and hot coals remained of the earlier inferno.

Riony moved through them slowly on legs aching with fatigue. She worked systematically, checking every body within the ring of the standing stones. Kess remained at her back, silent, as a spill of orange light swathed the sky.

The bloodred-tinted sun came up over the mountains, reflecting over the smoky clouds, as Riony found what she was looking for but wished she'd never find.

A single, aged arm, reaching out from below the fallen wall of the destroyed shrine.

Riony held Myrwa's cold hand as daylight spread over them. She pulled the beautiful, wise woman's shawl free and clutched it to her face as though to dry tears.

But no tears came. They had all been burned away.

All that was left was pure blood-and-ash-stained rage.

Chapter Fifteen

The impact jarred through Riony's forearm and up the bone to her shoulder, aching deep in contrast to her knuckles that had long since gone numb. She ignored the pain and struck out again. Her lips twisted mirthlessly as the thin sheet of metal buckled and dented beneath her blows.

The storeroom—the farthest from anyone else in Eslindekeep that Riony could find—was dark. Only a trembling glow from a torch in the hall outside reached in to where Riony pummeled the steel crates with her fists.

A shadow passed between her and the flame and Riony's entire body tensed.

She didn't turn around. "What is it? Did something happen?"

"No. Everyone is fine." Kess's voice was low and cautious. "Are you … okay?"

Every nerve inside Riony hummed, refusing any truth in Kess's words.

Everybody *wasn't* fine.

Myrwa was dead. Kellae, dead. Her brother and child, dead. Hundreds dead.

And any moment could bring more death. And Riony couldn't work out how to be strong enough to save everybody.

"I'm *fine*," Riony spat back. She struck out again, her fist hitting the metal crate like a gong. "I'm just training. *Alone.*"

How long had she been there? She couldn't even remember. It felt like forever since the burning enclaves, but at the same time the images filling her head were so fresh and new she could be seeing them for the first time.

On return to Eslindekeep, she'd made her way down a whole extra level to where narrow corridors led to an empty dungeon and more storage. She went as far as she could go without leaving the underground base. She didn't want anyone to see her like this.

Trust razing Kess and her wolf to find her.

"Okay." Kess and Griskin's shadow that cast over Riony shifted.

Loosing a shrieking grunt, Riony cracked her knuckles against the crate again. She blinked weary eyes at her hands. They looked so dark.

Covered in blood, it soaked into every joint and stuck to the layer of ash Riony hadn't cleaned away. She hadn't healed, hadn't changed, hadn't washed, hadn't slept, hadn't eaten. The scale mail vest hung crooked over her, clattering as she stared at her trembling hands.

"Kess?" Her voice was a broken, tiny plea.

The shadow returned.

Riony remained still, her back to the wolf and creature who rode him. Her chest heaved as her fury rekindled.

"Why did you listen to me? Why did you stay with Eslinde and Lyrrin instead of helping save people?"

"I ... I wanted to do what you needed of me."

"You shouldn't have! Whatever this pledge of yours is, it's stupid." And Riony was stupidest of all for letting herself use it, for trying to take what she wanted from Kess instead of what should have been done.

Guilt burbled in Riony, shaking her words. "You could have saved more people. You and Griskin, you're fast and deadly. If you were there, we could have gotten to Kife. We could have stopped him!"

We could have cut him through to the core and pulled every pain of vengeance from him for killing them, for killing them all. Riony wanted to scream the words, but they stuck in her throat.

"He was there?"

Riony turned, locking Kess in her burning gaze. "Sparking *Kife.* You brought him into this! How did you ever think letting a sadist like him know about Dracuni was a good idea? Biggest mistake of your life, Kess, with no small competition."

Kess's shoulders shook but she didn't look away. "I know. I'm sorry."

Riony roared, "Sorry doesn't cut it! Kife killed all of those people because of you! And I couldn't save them!"

Griskin lowered his head and growled.

Kess ran a hand over his ear, hushing him. "I know. All of this is on me. Not you."

Riony's lips pulled away from her teeth, feral. She wanted Kess to argue, to fight back. She wanted someone to scream at her in return and blame her in the same way the voices in her head did.

How dare Kessara Heithorn look me in the eye and just ... take the blame?

It made Riony feel as though there was something deeper within Kess's confession of guilt, that her admissions were easy because they were covering something far worse.

And that the something far worse was something Riony couldn't guard against or anticipate because she just wasn't smart enough to handle any of this.

Riony's body gave in, and she slumped, her back clattering against the metal crate behind her. She slid down to the ground.

"I can't deal with your games, Kess. I can't. Not now." Riony pressed her palms against her eyes.

Griskin padded closer.

Kess's voice was low and thick. "I won't ask you to trust me. I know trust is something earned. All I can do is continue trying to earn it from you."

Riony laughed dryly. "And I'll be the idiot giving you a chance right up until you stab me in the back. Why can't I ever be smart about things?"

"Do you know what I've noticed?" Kess climbed down from Griskin in slow, cautious motions and sat against the crate beside Riony.

"How you never could respect personal space?"

Kess rolled her eyes in the gentlest way Riony had ever seen. "How every time you talk about yourself not being smart, it's when what you're really being is *compassionate.* Giving me another chance was your compassion. Coming back for me and facing a nightmare of conglomerated revs was your compassion. Not stupidity."

"It can be both."

"No." Kess leaned in, a bright fervor in her eyes. "Your compassion is not just smart, it's *powerful*. It affects those around you in ways you don't even comprehend. It's why everybody looks to you for your strength and guidance and love."

Riony let her head hang between her knees, shaking it.

"Do you remember, at Heithorn estate, when the barn cat got burned by Kife's dragon?" Kess asked.

Riony convulsed, the memory an unwanted sting among the fresher memories of fiery death.

Kess continued. "I was sad for the creature, but thought it was the way it was and there was nothing that could be done. But you … you fought for it. You would have pulled the sun from the sky to save a barn cat if you could have."

"I was just a dumb kid." Riony's voice was heavy with pain.

"Your compassion inspired me. I spent that whole afternoon sneaking around, wearing my hands and gown raw crawling through the estate on my own, trying to find where my parents kept the silvernix."

Riony lifted her head and gave Kess a long, questioning look. "You did? But the cat …"

Kess's expression hardened. "I didn't find it in time. I never told you because I was ashamed of having failed … of my uselessness."

Riony swallowed a sob that pushed through her throat. She had been the one who had spent the day wailing and crying to her parents. Kess, the girl she always thought of as a cruel, selfish gremlin, was the one who had taken action, as futile as it had been.

She was still staring at Kess, unable to shift her eyes. And there was pain there, hidden beneath the hard pinch of her expression.

Feigning a light tone, Riony said, "Probably for the best. Can you imagine the whipping I would have had if your parents discovered silvernix missing and the cat magically healed? One I wouldn't have survived, I'm sure. All I'm hearing right now is that my stupidity inspires further stupidity."

Kess tutted. "Then you're not listening."

"Then I'm deaf and dumb."

"Stop it."

Silence fell over them. Griskin grumbled and curled up beside Kess and she stared at the floor with some deep, ferocious thoughtfulness.

Riony watched her mutely as the chill of the room cooled her fury and burning muscles.

"I'm sorry," Kess said. "For our life together back then. For ever treating you as though I owned you. For all the cruelty you suffered because of me."

There had been so many nights when she was young when Riony had lain awake, dreaming of the day Kessara would profess her apologies to her and how she would laugh and laugh in the girl's face when she did.

Riony's voice shivered out. "You were only a child. And you didn't exactly have it easy either."

"It's no excuse."

Riony shrugged. "It does mean a lot, though. That you've grown into someone who can acknowledge the harm you've done."

"And how do you think I got here? You. Only you. How else could I have ever learned kindness except from the only person who has shown it to me, even in the face of my dreadful selfishness?"

Kess reached a hand forward as though to touch Riony, but pulled back again and pressed it to her chest. "You are a beacon, and we around you just moths, fated to follow your radiance in the hopes we could ever one day glow as bright."

Riony felt heat creep up her neck. "Overly dramatic, Kess."

Kess ignored the interruption. "You change me in ways I never dreamed I could be worthy of. You inspire people."

Anger rose in Riony again and she wrapped her arms around her middle. The scale mail points bit into her bare skin.

"Maybe I wish I didn't. I *inspired* those people to live around the shrines, to build homes there. I told them they would be safe there." The words growled out. "How many died because of *me*?"

Kess shook her head. "You lost friends out there last night, didn't you?"

"I lost family. I lost people who trusted me and paid for it." A great tearing pain filled Riony's chest, and she squeezed her arms tight as though holding herself together.

"I'm so sorry. It's not your fault, but I know you can't believe it right now. I can't imagine how much it hurts."

Kess frowned, watching Riony's dry eyes and the ragged breaths spilling from her lips. "This is different though, to last time. When you ... I mean, at the waterfall. I thought you'd lost someone then ..."

"You *were* there. I knew it." Riony turned on Kess, facing her fully. "Why ...?"

Her voice stuttered out, remembering just how broken and vulnerable and *naked* she had been.

"You could have killed me then and there, and I couldn't have done a thing to stop you. Why didn't you?"

"Do you think me so dishonorable?"

Riony's gaze roamed over Kess's pale face. "I did."

Kess's head bowed, a sad motion of agreement, as though she felt the same about who she used to be. Then tentatively she asked, "What happened that day, that left you so ... hurt?"

Hurt? Kess chose a kind word. More like destroyed. Shattered. Ripped right in half in a way that still didn't feel mended.

"Are you intent on bringing up every painful memory for me right now?"

"I'm sorry. You don't have to answer."

Riony scrubbed her hands over her face as a sharp sting ran between her nose and eyes.

But she found the words coming out anyway. "It was my amma. It was my dead mother. She'd risen as a revenant and ..."

Kess drew a sharp breath and covered her mouth with one hand.

Riony laughed, harsh and hysterical. "Oh, it gets worse. Dracuni managed to heal her, but not really. Only in body, not in soul. So I got to watch her die in front of me. A second time."

Despite her efforts to pass it off as the world's most tragic joke, Riony's voice shook with sobs by the end of her sentence, and she barely got the last words out.

A tentative touch of chilled fingers pressed to her shoulder. Kess's hand, small and gentle, imbued with a crushing weight of comfort that cracked Riony right through.

With a strangled sob, Riony's arms lashed out and wrapped around Kess. Choking on her tears, she drew the girl's body into her own, right onto her lap. Kess let out a tiny yelp but remained still as Riony squeezed her as though she were a childhood doll that could ease all her suffering with a tight enough embrace.

Riony cried. She couldn't cry like that around anyone else, but with Kess, with all the pain they'd shared between them already, it didn't feel so hard.

And Kess made not a single other sound or movement until Riony could breathe again.

Snuffling into Kess's shoulder, Riony spoke wetly. "Sometimes I ... I wish the guest, Eslinde, never came to Heithorn estate. That I hadn't stabbed that guard, hadn't taken Lyrrin. And me and my parents would still have been slaves, but I would have still *had them*."

Kess's hips shifted, pressing into Riony's thighs, but she didn't attempt to push free of the cage of Riony's arms. Instead, she lifted her own hands, placing them around Riony's back.

"It wouldn't have worked out. We'd all have died to the revs along with my parents."

The ruins of the estate when they'd last been there had been scattered with the remains of all those who hadn't survived that attack.

Had Kess seen the bodies of her parents too?

"I'm sorry you lost them that way. That's how I lost mine, the first time."

"Eylin and Farrad were good people. It's their loss that should be mourned. My parents can get razed in life and in death."

Riony huffed in surprise. "You remember their names? You couldn't even remember mine for most of your life."

"I was being willfully spiteful. I'm sorry. I won't ever call you that awful epithet again. I'll only call you what you wish to be called."

Riony's fury had eased in the warmth of their embrace, but her heartbeat still hammered as she remembered Kess bowing low, stumbling over how to address Riony for her pledge. "It's Eyfarr. That's my last name now. Lyrrin and I made it when we stopped being Uf'Heithorn."

"I like that," Kess whispered. "Maybe I need to change my name too. I'm not sure I ever was a Heithorn. If you think things were bad while you were around, they got far worse for me once you were gone."

"Oh, I'm sorry," Riony scoffed. "How dare I emancipate myself and my family from slavery and a death sentence?"

Kess's forehead dropped onto Riony's shoulder. "If anything, you should have far sooner. I only mean that your absence made it clear you were the only good thing in my life."

A shiver rattled up Riony's back. She didn't know how to take this new version of Kess, so forthright and earnest.

But truthfully, Kess had always been forthright and earnest when it came to the things she cared about. She would tell anyone who would listen with her full heart how she would be the best dragonrider in the world one day, no matter how her claims were met with scorn.

Riony only had to believe that the thing Kess cared about had shifted.

Do I? And if I do, does that mean I'm the thing Kess now cares about above everything else?

Her closeness to Kess and press of their bodies together suddenly felt awkward. Riony swallowed roughly but didn't move.

"I'm not sure how good I ever was or what good I've ever done," Riony whispered. "All the mistakes I've made … Even my compassion, that you're saying is my strength, has only screwed me up at every turn."

If she hadn't saved Kess in the cave, Brishan might still be alive, they could have stayed in the undercity, never suffered the losses of everyone in the enclaves. But Riony found she couldn't speak that weight onto Kess's shoulders.

Instead, she said, "We shouldn't have freed Kife's dragon. If it wasn't lurking around, attacking the tamed dragons, Thallan and Norallei could have gone out by air and stopped more of the attacks. Every good thing I try to do comes back to hurt me."

Kess stiffened in Riony's hold, and then she slowly pulled away.

Riony's grasp involuntarily tightened for a second before she let go. Cold air rushed into the space Kess had been.

Eyes averted, Kess reached a hand for Griskin and he came to her.

"Then it's clear I'm failing at doing all I need to do to protect you." She half turned back to Riony. "Will you be okay?"

Riony nodded dumbly.

Kess pulled herself up onto the wolf's back and left.

Riony remained frozen in place for a long while, breathing through another short round of tears. The dark chill of the room felt so much deeper than before. Composing herself, Riony cleaned her hands off as well as she could, wincing at the deep splits on her knuckles, then wandered back toward the main living area.

She was met by Yensen, waiting within a passageway. His eyes narrowed over her face, and Riony wondered how swollen it must look.

"Are you well?" he asked with stilted care.

"I'd be a whole lot weller if I hadn't been left alone out there last night."

Yensen lowered his eyes and bowed. "Forgive me. I felt I had to return to Eslinde to ensure her safety."

"And why did you *feel* that strongly enough to abandon your orders?" Riony figured the newcomers might not consider Aishena to be higher ranking than them, but she sure did.

The grayglim tilted his head, silky black hair curtaining the sides of his face. He sounded apologetic as he replied, "Because I don't trust Kessara Heithorn."

Riony's blank stare became a chuckle, and she began moving again. "Man, are you late to the party. I'm not even sure the party is still going."

Yensen walked at her side. "I've seen how she's manipulated herself into your favor, but I beg you to remain wary. Has she told you how she had a private meeting with the Dragon King not long before our escape?"

Riony's steps faltered. "No, but—"

"I fear they created a plot then, one that we have all been playing our parts out in since."

Riony picked up her pace as though she could leave Yensen and his accusations behind. "That doesn't make sense."

Yensen kept up without any sign of effort. "Doesn't it? Who knew the most about you and your connection to the shrine enclaves, specifically to Myrwa and how important they were to you?"

Pain bloomed fresh in Riony's chest, and she wrinkled her nose. Timelines and motivations flashed through her head. Had the Dragon King already known about Dracuni, the enclaves, everything, before she and Kess escaped Zarram dragonhold that night?

The riders who came for them then, maybe they'd waited for Kess to take a dragon and followed her, all part of the plan. When that didn't work out, Kess could have arranged the attacks on the enclaves, somehow. She'd been out flying patrols alone once or twice, could have taken a dragon and sent messages.

Riony's stomach roiled, and she shook it off. "No. Kess is smarter than that. If she'd really been plotting to hurt us, she'd have struck the undercity, not the enclaves. And thankfully that refuge is still safe from the dragonlords. The attacks last night were all Kife."

"You admit she's clever but underestimate the level of plotting she's capable—" Yensen cut off as figure marched toward them.

Aishena had her hands at the athames on her belt and her expression was dark. The torches along the corridor flickered from her brisk pace.

"Aish? What is it?" Riony jogged to meet her.

Aishena's lips pulled in. "It's Kess."

Riony and Yensen's gaze locked.

Aishena continued. "She's stolen the Zarrams' orange dragon and left."

Riony's heart froze into a solid stone.

Chapter Sixteen

Kife's untamed dragon was on Kess faster than she expected. She'd barely gotten Ambri into the air before the purple etherdart came shooting out of the nearby woods toward them.

"Come on, then. Let's do this."

Her heartbeat thundered as she aimed Ambri into the sky as fast as the orange dragon could fly. But it had been thundering like that for every second since Riony pulled her into her grieving embrace. The simple thrill of chasing dragons through biting winter air was a relief to her enflamed emotions.

The bright burst of fire gusted over Kess's shoulder, and she gasped away from it. The purple was on their tail, mouth snapping. Kess angled her dragon sharply away before the jagged maw could close on Ambri's wing.

Waves and waves of wailing anger washed over Kess and she felt faint with the disconcerting inability to distinguish her own feelings from those invading her.

She'd experienced similar the other times she'd been near the purple dragon since he was freed. He had screamed wordlessly in her mind when he'd been untamed and when she'd placed herself between him and Riony.

Dragons only communicated with those they were bonded with, but Kess wouldn't fool herself into thinking this was communication. The blare of anger and upset felt more like a psychic attack.

She didn't know what it meant. She only knew the dragon was furious, and ready to take that anger out on her.

He snapped at the orange dragon again.

As agile and free as he was, Kess wasn't sure she and her modest ability to control the tamed dragon were going to be enough to escape his attacks. But she had to try. She had to fix at least one thing for Riony.

At least I didn't bring Griskin into this.

Samor was out on patrol on his flamesong, and once Kess spotted the silhouette of them in the distance, she took Ambri and the purple dragon the other direction. She wanted to keep everyone else out of this as long as she could.

The faint echo of shouting rose from far below. Tiny figures emerged from the tunnel to Eslindekeep. Only one could be identified at this distance by the bright glow of her red hair.

She's going to be angry. I should have explained myself.

But Kess knew if she had, she'd never have gotten away with Ambri.

With her eyes off the purple, Kess almost missed the claws angling for Ambri's head. She pulled away at the last moment. With teeth gritted, she leaned into the orange scales, pushing the dragon to fly faster, higher and higher.

The air felt thin up there, and the ground so, so far down.

They were above the purple dragon now, and Kess held her breath, awaiting the perfect moment. There. She was directly over Kife's dragon, flying in line as it came up toward them.

And Kess was no longer afraid to fall.

She gave Ambri one final order to glide in slow circles and then dropped from the saddle.

She kept her eyes open as she fell, the flight goggles protecting them as she aimed herself as best she could. Three heartbeats passed of nothing but the air whipping through Kess's hair and clothes and pummeling her ears and then came the hard impact against purple scales.

Too high near the dragon's head, Kess narrowly avoided skewering herself right through with one of his horns. She twisted and slid between the double row of spikes down its neck. Both her arms flung out, grasping for purchase.

She'd just gotten her hands around one of those spines and brought herself into a sitting position on the dragon's shoulders when he was upon the orange dragon again.

"No!" Kess commanded, wrenching the spike she held to her left with all her strength.

Kife's dragon turned, his stomach clipping the orange's wings, and he roared, inside and out.

A violent buck of his shoulders left Kess gasping as she lifted into the air, fingertips slipping along to the tip of the spike. She clutched on to the very end and pulled herself back in, thumping onto the purple scales again as the bucking continued.

His emotions ached through her, clearer than ever as she pressed herself to his back. *Angry. Angry. Angry.* And also, deeper, *Hurt.*

Kess screwed her eyes closed at the barrage.

She screamed over the wind. "I'm sorry. You should be angry! You have been hurt. I should have saved you, right at the very beginning. When you first hatched and I wished you were mine. I should have kept you safe from Kife and all his cruelty."

A shiver of recognition intertwined with the violent feelings. The purple gave another, smaller wriggle of his shoulders in his attempts to dislodge his unwelcome rider.

His scales shimmered in the midday light. They had brightened since he'd been freed. Still dusky in tone, but not the dulled cloudy gray they had become under Kife's ownership.

"I shouldn't have freed you from the taming when I did. You should have always been free, to have the life you deserved right from the start."

From the start. The words seemed to echo back at Kess with another wave of recognition. The dragon growled.

"From the start," Kess said again.

In the gap of time between Kife's cruelty in choosing the dragon Kess had wanted, and before the dragonhandler had come through to tame it, Kess had sat with the purple hatchling, telling him all about the life they would have had together if he were her dragon.

And after he had been tamed until Riony had come and found her there late at night, Kess had sat beside the hatchling and cried tears she couldn't explain, because the vibrant life she'd sensed in the newborn dragon, that had attracted her to it, felt as though it had all gone away.

The dragon's bucking and squirming stilled. The violent levels of anger reduced to a simmering rage.

"Do you ... do you remember me?"

The purple hissed suddenly and veered as two swift shapes shot their way. The red of Hux and aqua of Gleem cut through the air.

A growl rippled down the purple etherdart's neck to Kess.

From Gleem's back, Zeina waved the hand signals for, "Are you okay?"

Kess waved her own in return. "Back off, I've got this."

Gleem keened and flicked her snout toward the purple, who responded with bared teeth and low grumble. ***Confusion. Disdain ... Envy.***

The sensations tugged at Kess's nerves.

Zeina shrugged, pulling Gleem in to glide a respectful distance below. Hux came up and over them, carrying Jaym and Dashiel.

As they passed, Dashiel cupped both hands near their face and mouthed, "Wow."

They continued upward to rescue the riderless orange dragon.

Kess shook her head at Dashiel's awe. She felt no more accomplished than a flea on a wolf's back.

She'd come into the air with the goal of somehow convincing this creature to stop attacking them, but now she wanted so much more for it.

Her heart ached with every version of her life where she'd made better choices. Where the magnificent creature beneath her had never had his freedom and soul stripped away for so many years.

"I didn't know then what I know now. I wasn't someone then who could have made the right choice, who had the power to save you even if I did." Kess ran her hands over the purple scales.

"But when the chance came to me to free you, I'm glad I did. It's one of the few things I've done that I'm proud of."

She leaned in, pressing her forehead to the back of the dragon's neck. "So please don't make me regret it by continuing to attack us."

The storm of emotions blowing through Kess had cleared of anger now. Only the hurt remained within Kife's dragon ...

No. Kess refused to think of him as that anymore. Kife had never named him, never seen him as anything more than a simple tool.

Kess had once thought of a name for him, in the moment she'd seen the hatchling for the first time. It had just come to her and felt so right.

What was it again?

Lyomir. *That was it.* The memory of the name reverberated in Kess's mind. That's what she would call him now.

Lyomir ducked and wove away from the two Rebel Riders' dragons who coasted through the air on each side at a safe distance. The orange dragon descended quickly toward Eslindekeep with Dashiel in control.

Lyomir snarled their way but didn't try to chase the tamed dragon again.

Kess still breathed a little easier once they were both away and safe underground again.

Now she just needed to get herself safely on the ground again.

"Lyomir, will you stop attacking us?"

The purple dragon loosed a long, snarling growl, and Kess braced to be thrown off his back. And then …

I'll stop.

Kess's breath stuck. Those were words. Kess hadn't been sure before, the way the thoughts had echoed her own. But those were words coming to her from the dragon. Begrudging, seething, irritable words.

Her eyes welled up and she couldn't wipe them because of the goggles.

To hear a dragon speak even once was a sun-born blessing greater than Kess had ever known. Even if the tone sounded like Lyomir hated Kess and everything about the situation right to his fiery core.

She leaned against his scales. "And if there's anything, anything I can do for you, I will. If there's any way I can help you through your pain, I want to."

As I learn to work through mine too.

They were slowly coming to land. The bare flat slabs of Eslindekeep were blocked out like a chessboard beneath them. It was through no effort on Kess's part, but rather the guidance of Gleem and Hux.

Both the seasong and etherflame were significantly larger than the etherdart, and Kess wondered whether anything she'd said or done had an impact on Lyomir or if he was just playing nice to avoid aggression from them.

They landed in the icy sludge that was all that remained from a light dusting of snow that morning. And then, as to make a point of what he thought of having a human on his back, Lyomir gave one whiplike buck and threw Kess off. She landed with a squelch in a puddle.

With one final growl, Lyomir rushed fluidly into the air again with a powerful flap of his wings and flew out of sight.

Kess levered herself up off her back with a groan as footsteps raced her way. A shadow cut the glare of the high sun as Riony bent over her and pulled her free of the mud.

"What were you thinking?" Every feature on Riony's face blazed with fury.

But her hands were gentle as they brought Kess up into her arms. Griskin had reached them as well, circling and prowling beside them, but Riony continued to carry Kess herself.

"I wanted to solve a problem for you."

"By killing yourself?"

"I'm still alive, aren't I?"

"I have no sparking idea how."

The sounds of Gleem and Hux coming to land whomped behind them.

Kess ringed one hand around her other wrist and rubbed it. She'd strained it somewhere along the way. She wouldn't be surprised if her entire body ached tomorrow.

Under Riony's glare, she tried to explain herself. "I only took Ambri out to lure the purple dragon in. I needed a way to get to him, attempt to communicate with him."

"I saw. I thought … Why did you even think you could do that?"

Kess shrugged. "The day Lyrrin used the dragon summoning rune, I felt something. His emotions. I knew he wasn't just attacking mindlessly. He was hurting. I thought if I could do something, it might lessen the hurt for him and for you."

She could still feel that pain, even now. Although the dragon had flown out of view, she could still feel the lingering touch of his emotions within her. She knew he remained nearby.

Riony's jaw clenched. "You didn't … You don't have to risk yourself for me like that."

They marched toward the tunnel entrance. Eslinde, Yensen, and Aishena stood there, waiting and watching, a range of scolding and concerned expressions across their faces. Riony took Kess straight past them.

There was a waver in her step, the kind of slight stagger that came from exhaustion, but she kept Kess held tight in her bandaged arms.

Dashiel jogged up the tunnel to join them. "Kess? Kess! That was incredible! You just flew on a wild dragon. Do you know how few people have done that?"

"And who do you razing think we are?" Zeina barked as she and Jaym strolled up beside them.

Dashiel's full lips pouted. "You know what I mean. A full-grown wild dragon, not one she's bonded with. Not that you aren't impressive in your own right, of course."

"Of course." Zeina gave Dashiel a sly wink.

"So are we going to have a problem with the purple again? Or did our fierce little wolf rider scare him off?" Jaym eyed Kess as though he were ready to write her up into one of his stories.

"He said he'll stop."

Dashiel's steps bounced. "He spoke to you? Are you bonded?"

"No. No, I don't think it was like that, at all." Kess flicked at some of the mud on her leg.

Zeina and Jaym shared a look but said nothing else.

They reached an intersection as the tunnel split off into the various chambers and private rooms. Riony stopped, seeming unsure where she was going and why she was taking Kess along with her. Griskin grumbled and yapped, nudging up against Riony's side.

"You can put me down now," Kess said softly.

Blinking a couple of times, Riony nodded vaguely and placed Kess onto Griskin's saddle.

"I'm … going to check on Dracuni," Riony stumbled the words out and turned away.

Kess wanted to tell Riony to get some rest, to look after herself. Dracuni was weakened from the blood spent on the injured the night before, but she was okay. She knew Riony wasn't going to listen to her, though.

Which is why Kess strengthened her resolve to do anything she could to lighten Riony's load.

If Lyomir stopped attacking them as he said, that was one small problem solved. But only one of many so much larger.

What if we can't solve the others?

Kess didn't know what that would mean. Only that Riony wouldn't give up. She'd never give up. Even if it killed her.

Chapter Seventeen

Riony dropped into the saddle behind Zeina, adjusting the tightness of the strap she'd just added around her wrist.

"This is utter foolishness," Eslinde's strained voice came from below.

The silver-haired princess skirted around Gleem as though she could block the dragon's way.

"It's been decided." Riony didn't look at her or any of the others they were leaving behind.

She focused instead on triple-checking her weapons and new armor were all in order. Being kitted head to toe in the blue and gold scale mail from Eslinde's supplies rather than her dinted and rusty hodge-podge of reclaimed steel armor had been one of Aishena's requirements for agreeing to the mission.

The only variation to the gleaming scales was the faded, dried-blood red of Myrwa's shawl, tied around her waist. A reminder of why she was doing this.

"I never decided it," Lyrrin snapped back. "You can't just go and attack a *dragonkeep*! That's ... utter foolishness."

Riony flicked an annoyed gaze Lyrrin's way. Siding with Eslinde instead of her, now?

She probably wouldn't have liked this even if Eslinde wasn't here, a deeper voice of reason told Riony. But Riony wasn't in a mood to listen to reason. Reason could go die in a ditch.

Turning her eyes back to her armor, she muttered, "Utter foolishness would be letting Kife and the Dragon King and all those riders who burned the enclaves think they can do that with no consequences."

So, you're going to be as violent as them? Dracuni sat across the space, tail flicking. Riony ignored her.

"It's been a while since we bit back," Thallan said from atop his bronze dragon. "We let the dragonlords grow too bold. But with more numbers now, it's as good a time as any to attack."

He pushed his tamed dragon into motion and headed out of the stables first. Yensen rode with him, glowering. He'd wanted to remain with Eslinde again, but Riony insisted. She had a plan for him.

Norallei followed, with Kess riding as her second. Griskin remained behind. They had no intention of being out of the air until they came home triumphant.

"I don't know why you want to attack at all." Lyrrin's voice grew higher. "How is that going to protect anyone? I thought that's what we did."

Riony's eye twitched as Jaym walked through with his pocket-hawk on his arm and climbed onto Samor's dragon behind him.

"Did we? Did we protect Myrwa and Kellae? We haven't protected *anybody*. Nothing we did made a difference. Nothing is going to end the dragonlords cruelty unless we make it stop. And *you* ..." Riony turned to face Eslinde. "I thought you'd be all for this. Didn't you want us on the offensive? Taking out the Dragon King himself?"

"Ready?" Zeina asked softly.

You shouldn't go. Dracuni snorted. **Not without me.**

Riony ignored the unidragon again. Even if Dracuni could fly, there was no way Riony would bring her along. That would be *utter foolishness.*

Riony nodded to Zeina, and Gleem carried them out of the stables. Dashiel and Aishena followed on Ambri.

Jaym sighed in a dramatic way. "I doubt Yeonard Draekhan will be there today for us to assassinate, most unfortunately, but taking out even a few tamed dragons should weaken the shadow dragon, so that's something."

Eslinde jogged to keep up beside them. "It's not so much the method as the timing and the target. Striking Gerichkeep is a distraction, a bait you are taking. The attacks on the enclaves were clearly on purpose to draw us out and look what is happening!"

Eslinde waved her arm at the five dragons in a line, making their way along the long corridor to the exit.

"If they planned to draw us out, we were drawn out that night and they didn't take their advantage." Riony blinked for too long, and flashes of fire and bodies filled her vision. "I don't believe there was any plan greater than Kife's cruelty."

"I think there was more," Kess said. She spoke with a heavy thickness of guilt. "The dragonlords couldn't allow the enclaves to keep thriving."

Riony knew how the enclaves were thought of. Dens of criminals and cannibals. The riders probably thought they were doing the right thing exterminating everybody.

Kess continued. "They couldn't allow a place where people could live freely outside of the keeps, without the control and ownership of masters, without needing the protection of dragons. It was a threat to their power, and they will destroy anything that threatens their power."

Riony twisted around in her seat, holding Kess's gaze. She had easily agreed to come along, but these days Kess might jump into a vat of molten glass if Riony asked her to. She didn't seem happy about it, though. Deep lines of concern wrinkled her narrow face.

Am I making a mistake?

All voices of doubt were buried beneath a haze of anger and memories falling like ash.

Daylight temporarily blinded Riony as the dragons moved outside. The five formed a rough circle, awaiting the order to go.

Eslinde moved into the center, turning on the spot as she pleaded with them. "If our enemies seek to crush us, then all the more reason to play it safe for a while."

Lyrrin stood beside her, fingers clenched around the paired heart stone hanging from a string at her neck. "You could at least take me with you! You know I can help. I'm sick of sitting back here, feeling your heart straining through battle, unable to do anything! You have no idea how that feels!"

Eslinde's hand went out almost reflexively and pulled Lyrrin closer to her.

Riony checked her sword was secure one last time. "You haven't flown on a dragon before and you aren't starting now."

Dracuni, remaining in the shadow of the tunnel, said nothing else, only watched Riony with sorrowful eyes.

Riony's jaw twitched.

She turned away from those on the ground and addressed the ones riding with her. "We have to take a stand."

"You don't." Eslinde's voice had become soft. "You're just a child—"

"Hiding away while the world burns is what dragonlords do," Riony raised her voice.

Vance joined Eslinde. He placed a hand on her shoulder, but it seemed not so much in support as consolation. Riony nodded to him. He was their best rider remaining behind with Jaym's dragon—who they'd been assured had agreed to allow Vance as a rider.

"We're not going to keep hiding while others suffer. We're taking the fight to those causing the suffering."

"Hear! Hear!" Zeina bellowed.

Thallan gave Riony a slow, firm nod, then flew into the air.

Samor's face remained grim, but behind him, Jaym thumped a fist to his chest, saluted Riony, then they were next off the ground.

Moments later they were all flying far above Eslindekeep, and Riony fought off a shiver, feeling as though she'd left her heart behind.

The dragons arranged in a V-shaped formation, with Thallan at the lead, and glided northeast toward Gerichkeep.

It had been chosen as their target for three reasons.

First, it was a smaller keep and would have fewer defenses.

Second, it was a long way away from other dragonkeeps, so it would take a while before backup arrived.

And third, the reason that had warmed Riony to the plan, the riders who had attacked Myrwa's enclave wore Gerich's colors.

Riony and her team took the flight there easy, making sure not to tire the dragons before the attack.

Eslinde had provided what information she had on the keep in their earlier planning stages, before it became clear they were moving from planning to doing.

Gerichkeep had twenty-five dragonriders in their ranks, now twenty-three after Samor and Shani took out two during the attacks on the enclaves.

Riony had balked at the madness of going five against twenty-three, but it was likely only a few riders would be on patrol when they first struck, with a few more sitting in preparation for if they were needed. Most wouldn't even be in the rider's dragonhold.

They could take down the ones in the air fast and not get overwhelmed by more as they came out in waves. At least, that's how Thallan said it was when they used to harry keeps.

"Besides, most of the kids they put on dragons these days are only trained to burn revs from the air. They have no idea how to handle attacks from other riders," Jaym had added.

Checking over her sword and armor for the dozenth time, Riony stifled the anxiety jittering through her nerves.

In front of her, Zeina shifted suddenly, then yelled back to Riony, "Behind us and up."

Riony looked over her shoulder, squinting through the ashy air. A dusky shape followed at a distance.

Kife's sparking dragon.

Riony wasn't sure how she felt about the thing. It was a reminder of all she'd suffered while Kess and Kife had hunted them, and Viska was still out of action thanks to it.

But after the stunt Kess had pulled, however she'd managed to communicate with the purple dragon, it had no longer attacked the tamed dragons within their group.

"Is it going to be a problem?" Riony asked.

Zeina shook her head. "Gleem doesn't think so. The poor thing is confused, mostly. Angry, but not sure who to be angry at."

Riony bit her lip. "As long as it doesn't take any more of that anger out on us."

They settled into silence for the rest of the flight. Zeina didn't chat or flirt or invite Riony to her bed again since the two times Riony hadn't followed through.

Maybe she would when they got home again, triumphant after the mission.

Riony wasn't even sure she wanted that anymore.

If they got home again.

It felt far too soon when Thallan signaled Gerichkeep was within sight. They lifted higher into the sky then, hiding within the smoke-tainted clouds in order to get closer without causing alarm too soon.

Riony counted four dragons out on patrol. It seemed like a lot for a smaller keep, based on the information Eslinde provided.

But Riony didn't doubt they could deal with four tamed beasts.

They were almost directly over the keep when one of Gerich's riders changed course suddenly, aiming their way.

Across their five dragons, Riony's companions signaled their readiness and dove from the clouds.

Zeina hung back slightly as Samor and Norallei brought their dragons into a swift chase with two of the keep's riders. All four of Gerich's riders wore her colors—green and black—and even their dragons stayed on theme as well, foresty toned treedarts and etherdarts.

Thallan and Dashiel took their dragons even farther down, shooting fast right to the rooftops of the dragonkeep, to the large open flight deck of the rider's dragonhold.

They unloaded their cargo of the two grayglims there and took off again.

Riony held her breath as Yensen and Aishena disappeared from view. That part had been Riony's contribution to the plan. She wanted the grayglims to hit the riders in their barracks before they had a chance to reach their dragons.

Even Yensen, who'd been arguing blue in the face that he wanted to remain with Eslinde, had turned around at the proposal. He'd agreed it was a good plan and could make the whole mission work.

"Do I have to kill them?" Aishena had asked.

"They didn't think twice about killing innocent people at the enclaves," Riony reminded her.

Aishena had stared back with her stony expression and midnight eyes.

Riony flinched first. "Do what you think is best."

"I will."

Now, Riony just hoped Aishena would make it out of there alive.

Samor had already taken down one rider and turned his massive flamesong to another. Norallei's white shimmerdart, Iffyr, sped circles around it as well, and thin white blades flashed through the air. One of Kess's daggers hit the target and another rider fell.

Zeina evaded sharply as a bolt of flame shot by. A grass-green dragon chased close behind.

Riony grunted. "Quit running. The thing is half Gleem's size."

A moment later there was no need, as Thallan and Dashiel brought their dragons back into the battle, chasing the spring-toned dragon off.

A small speck flew from Jaym's wrist toward the fourth rider, hitting them in the face in a puff of feathers. The rider's cries carried across the sky as the small hawk ripped at their goggles and face.

Riony stared, horrified at the bird.

The harassed rider's dragon veered sideways, dropping the rider right off its back.

"One of Jaym's favorite tricks," Zeina said.

"Wow. I hate it." Riony shuddered and looked away. "But that's four down already."

From the city below, a cacophony of bells sounded. The alarm was well and truly raised.

"By the stars ..." Zeina waved her arms in broad signals to the other riders. "Ten more! Ten coming out now!"

"What? There shouldn't be that many!" Riony followed the woman's gaze and confirmed the numbers.

Maybe they had been wary of retaliation after all. Maybe they were ready and waiting for this attack that had been lured in, like Eslinde had said.

Aishena and Yensen must not have been able to stop that wave. Riony only hoped they could stop the next.

She bared her teeth at the incoming dragons.

If they want a fight, that's exactly what we came for.

Dashiel cut Ambri right across Gleem's path as three of the new riders went after them. They ducked and wove through the air, leading those three away. Norallei and Thallan brought their two dragons close, flying them in a matching evasion pattern as Kess downed the first of the ten new attackers.

Samor and Shani didn't run. He and his massive dragon barreled headfirst toward the largest two of the incoming riders.

"Not scared of much, are they?" Riony laughed out the words.

"Yeah, well." Zeina's tone was flat. "Neither of them has cared much about anything in life since they both lost their partners."

Riony's breath stuck. "Oh."

She didn't have long to dwell on that, though, as a speckled green and black treedart crashed into Gleem's back, claws first.

Gleem roared a high-pitched cry as the smaller dragon grasped onto her hips and began climbing up toward Riony and Zeina.

"I've got it!" Riony yelled and unsheathed her sword.

With one hand she activated the float rune and then quickly buckled the hilt to the end of the strap she'd attached to her wrist. She wasn't dropping her weapon midair ever again.

Riony ducked a thin dart of fire as she shifted around into a crouched position. Wind buffeted her on all sides as Gleem's wings beat hard. Trying to stand still was harder than remaining in motion so she could adjust to the movement of flight.

She stood up and marched toward the small dragon climbing Gleem's back.

The rider on the speckled dragon wore an astonished expression as though that were the last thing they expected to see.

Surprise jolted Riony too.

She's so young.

Riony swung her sword toward the rider, but the girl was already backing their treedart off Gleem. They pulled back awkwardly, jarring sideways to dodge the sword, and the rider yelped as she lost grip of her dragon.

Her scream as she fell free entirely pierced right through Riony. The tamed treedart, without instruction, continued its awkward sideways flutter and followed the falling girl toward the ground below.

Riony's breath came hard, and her nerves rattled. She returned to the seat behind Zeina as they dove suddenly beneath another attack.

There were still eight after them, and they were staying in groups, keeping the Rebel Riders on the back foot.

Yensen and Aishena better keep any more riders from coming out or we're done.

Both of Gleem's wings snapped in beside her chest as Thallan and Norallei flew down each side with a Gerichkeep rider close after them. Riony followed Kess with her eyes as Norallei's dragon went past. The intensity in her expression seemed filled with pain, and the scream of the young rider who fell echoed in Riony's mind again.

She hadn't even touched the girl, but Riony knew her death was going to haunt her for a long time.

How many had Kess killed directly with her knives? How much did it cost her each time? What had Riony asked of her?

Bile burned the back of Riony's throat.

That's what we came here for, isn't it? To fight? To kill?

Some violence is necessary.

Thallan and Norallei's dragons separated then, and the two riders diverted all attention to Norallei. They were almost on her and Kess when a dark shape came rushing down from the clouds.

Kife's purple etherdart screamed a roar as he grasped one of the small dragon's head within his talons. They wrestled midair, and the rider was thrown moments before the purple pulled the smaller dragon's taming stake free.

Riony gasped. They had no silvernix to complete the untaming, even if they could get to the groundward tumbling dragon in time. It didn't have a chance.

The purple spun on one wing and aimed next for Norallei's dragon, and Riony yelled wordlessly for Zeina to turn their way.

But Kife's dragon didn't attack Iffyr. He went instead for the next rider chasing after them.

Well, damn. That might help turn the tables a bit.

Swooping back up again, Zeina headed Gleem up into the ashy clouds.

"What are you doing?" Riony yelled.

"There's too many of them!"

"There wouldn't be if you'd actually attack!"

They were too far away from the rest of the battle, and none of the riders had followed them up there, meaning all the remaining riders were focused on the rest of their group. Another two chased Norallei and Kess again, sending a volley of fireballs their way.

Riony's head filled with fire again. Burnt bodies. Burnt friends. Riony shook off a disturbing vision of Kess lying still in ashes.

Nerves jangled through Riony. Zeina was being too cautious, and Riony had run out of patience.

Dashiel brought Ambri not far beneath Gleem as they tried to shake the enemy on their tail. And Riony didn't hesitate to take her chance.

She launched herself toward the dark-green dragon chasing Ambri. With her glowing sword in hand, she came down fast, but not bone-breakingly so, right between the dragon's wings.

She didn't let the rider turn around, didn't want to see their face. She struck hard, batting the rider with the flat of her sword across the back of the head. They slumped in the saddle and the dragon spiraled, spinning groundward.

Grunting and breathing in sharp pants, Riony leaped again. Norallei's shimmerdart was the next closest island in the air, and Riony landed on Iffyr's outstretched wing as he glided by. She ran lightly along the thick leather.

"What are you ...?" Norallei snapped in shock.

"Be careful!" Kess reached out an arm almost as though to catch Riony as she ran across the dragon's back and sent herself flying toward the treedart chasing after them.

Riony overshot her jump to the small dragon and struck her sword out at the last moment, catching the dragon's pale-green wing. It sliced through the membrane without slowing Riony's momentum at all.

The resistance of sword through leather was enough to jerk the hilt out of Riony's hand, but she caught onto the strap and pulled it back into her palm before gravity took her entirely.

Still, she was falling, with no other dragon in her path.

I guess I'm going to see just how far I can fall with this float magic.

As the wind rushed up around her, Riony had a clear view down to the dragonkeep below, where a gleaming shimmerdart came racing out of the dragonhold faster than a shooting star.

Thallan took his dragon after it, but it was far too fast.

Riony's vision filled with aqua scales and she thumped onto Gleem's back.

"What kind of stunt was that?" Zeina rasped and swore under her breath a long string of curses. "Never mind. That messenger dragon was our cue to finish up and get out of here before reinforcements come in."

Zeina began signaling to Thallan, and him back.

"No, we're not done here," Riony growled.

Someone else had taken out another two riders. Only three remained. If they could rid Gerichkeep of all its riders, all those who had rained fire on Myrwa's enclave, Riony would call it a good day.

Zeina smacked her hands down onto the front of her saddle and yelled both at Thallan and Riony. "Stars! We're done! We should go before things get worse!"

Thallan signaled what Riony had learned was a negative and pointed toward the remaining three riders.

Riony grinned viciously and her lips trembled.

Zeina only grunted and Gleem curved to join Dashiel and Ambri in chase of a fast etherdart.

A shrieking roar scraped through the air. A larger Gerichkeep rider had latched their dragon onto the wild purple's neck from above. They twisted and wrestled, but the talons of the green etherdart were latched tight.

Norallei and Kess swooped in on the white shimmerdart, snapping at the air near the attacker's wings. As they flew a tight loop to come after them again, the Gerichkeep rider backed off, letting the purple go.

Iffyr's second pass looped around again, white blades flicked through the sky like the shimmer of flying fish.

One hit the rider. He fell from his saddle and his dragon lurched, wings twitching wildly in a way that left it tumbling from the air, blocking Iffyr's path. With less than seconds to spare, Norallei pushed her dragon down in an attempt to dodge the falling beast.

Riony's breath caught. *No. Go over. OVER.*

The weight of the mindless dragon crashed across Iffyr's back, wings tangling against wings with a whipping crack.

A moment later the dragons separated again. And another body fell.

"No!" Riony cried. She grasped Zeina's back. "Quick, that way!"

She knew they were too far away. Everyone was too far away.

The white shimmerdart had carried two small women with dark hair wearing the same blue and gold armor, and from this distance Riony couldn't tell whether it was Norallei or Kess who was falling.

The remaining rider seemed dazed, injured, but quickly regained control of the tamed dragon.

Riony held her breath as it dove and caught the falling body in its talons.

Samor brought his flamesong in a moment later and then continued through to beside Gleem.

"It's Norallei," he bellowed across the gap of air.

Riony found herself able to breathe again. But then—

Samor shook his head with a dreadful finality.

Dead? Riony's hand clenched around the acorn at her neck.

Zeina shrieked. "We should have gone! We should already be gone, all of us ..."

Riony kept staring at the shimmerdart circling below. Norallei and Kess had been sitting as close as Riony and Zeina were now. It could have been either of them. It had been so close ...

The last of the Gerichkeep riders was gone and Thallan brought his bronze dragon up into a smooth glide beside them.

"Thallan," Zeina's voice broke over the word.

"I know," he barked back. "It doesn't change the plan."

"But ... *Norallei*! She's ... you ..." It sounded as though Zeina was crying.

Thallan stared back, still and grim. "Norallei would want us to finish this. We're winning. The grayglims have kept the remaining dragonriders grounded. We should push our advantage now. We could burn down the whole keep!"

"That wasn't part of the plan. Riders only," Riony said, but her voice had become small, too small to carry across the noise of flight.

"No," Jaym bellowed from behind Samor. "We're done. We're leaving."

With a dully sad look, Samor nodded. He signaled to Dashiel, who nodded in reply.

Ambri loosed three loud, piercing wails on Dashiel's command, and they dove together toward the dragonhold. Thallan sneered at the other Rebel Riders but turned his dragon to follow.

With the end of their attack signaled, Riony kept her eyes on the building below and as far away as possible from Kess and the dragon she rode and the body that dragon carried. And she waited to see the grayglims emerge, ready to be picked up so they could leave.

Come on, Aish. Time to get out of here.

Riony had given them clear instructions. Don't go too far in. Stay close to an exit so they could leave as soon as the signal was given. But as Thallan and Dashiel circled the dragonhold, it felt like an eternity, and neither Yensen or Aishena came out.

Then there was movement. On a balcony on the far side, Yensen stepped out into view, carrying Aishena, limp in his arms.

CHAPTER EIGHTEEN

Riony cradled Aishena's body as they rode behind Dashiel back toward Eslindekeep. The moment she'd seen Aishena slumped in the grayglim's arms, she'd leaped from Zeina's dragon, far and fast enough that her knees felt like they were ready to pop right out of their sockets.

She was trying to rub the pain out of them as Aishena finally stirred.

"Hey, welcome back," Riony said softly.

Aishena's face scrunched and she groaned.

"She's awake?" Dashiel asked.

"She just reached for her weapons so I'd say that's a good sign." Riony made a hushing sound and wrapped her free hand around Aishena's fingers that were clasped around an athame.

Her other arm remained supporting Aishena against her chest.

"Where are we?" Aishena's voice was woozy and drawling.

"Yensen found you unconscious and got you out."

"Mmph." Aishena reached a trembling hand to her windblown hair, touching tentatively around her head and wincing.

Riony pulled her a little closer. "Careful, just stay still. We'll get you back and I'm sure Dracuni will make you all better."

She'd already checked Aishena's wounds. One growing lump on the back of her head from a blow that thankfully didn't break the skin, and a graze on one cheek—probably where she'd fallen.

Having had her own head cracked like an egg before, Riony didn't feel much relief from Aishena being awake. She wanted Aishena healed, and cursed herself that she didn't bring silvernix with them.

It still felt wrong to her, somehow, asking Dracuni to bleed into a bottle for them. Probably because she knew Dracuni would do it, and once they started asking that of her, where would they stop?

"I'm fine," Aishena mumbled. "Must have gotten blindsided by one of the riders in the barracks. Surprised they didn't finish me when I was down considering what I'd done to their friends."

The sky seemed touched by fire as sunset fell early over the end of the short winter's day. They would be back at Eslindekeep soon, and Riony looked forward to being somewhere warm and out of the relentless cold wind. She couldn't stop shaking.

"What did you do to their friends?" she asked gently.

"Made sure they couldn't get into the air. They should live though, if that's what you're asking, depending on how soon they are treated. Although they won't be flying for some time depending on what treatment is spent on them."

Riony felt a low swell of sadness fill her chest, thinking about those who silvernix wouldn't have the chance to save. Up ahead, Kess flew Norallei's tamed shimmerdart alone, Norallei's body still carried within its claws.

She felt a pang of bitter gratefulness that Iffyr was a tamed dragon, that he wouldn't be mourning his rider too.

"You did good, keeping them from joining the fight. We would have been ruined if more riders showed up."

Aishena scoffed, then winced. "I'd have done better if I wasn't unconscious so long. I thought I'd cleared my area. I don't know where my attacker came from."

"I'm just glad you're still here with us, thanks to Yensen. How would we replace you if you died? How could we ever find someone as hot as you to fill that hole? Impossible."

A thin smile spread on Aishena's lips. "Are we back to this again? Must I once more crush your hopes of a relationship?"

Riony rolled forward and bent to rest her forehead against Aishena's. "No. You know how I feel about you. We're family."

And I almost lost you. Like the Rebel Riders lost Norallei.

Zeina, Samor, and Jaym flew in a tight group farther ahead. Thallan hung back behind everyone. Riony knew he and Norallei were in some sort of relationship, but they were private about it. She was glad at least Yensen was with Thallan on his dragon in case he needed someone.

Riony wasn't scared of taking risks herself, but seeing other people suffer the consequences left her questioning whether the entire mission had been a mistake.

"Almost there. Hold on," Dashiel said from up front, and they descended toward the blocky slabs and bare ground of Eslindekeep.

There was some maneuvering and tense communication as Samor and Jaym received Norallei's body midair so that Kess could land.

Dashiel got Ambri to the ground first and headed them toward the tunnel into the base.

"Can you look after Aishena for a moment for me? I want to check on the others." Riony shifted Aishena into a more upright position.

"I'm okay," Aishena said, sitting at a slight angle.

Dashiel pulled Aishena closer to them, holding her with one arm to help keep her from slipping off. "I've got her."

"Thanks." Riony jumped down and opened the entrance for them.

The heavy doors slid open, and Eslinde stood there waiting.

Riony hesitated as the princess cast shrewd eyes over those who returned, and those who hadn't. "Casualties?"

Blood rushed away from Riony's face as she choked on Norallei's name.

"I'm surprised there weren't more," Eslinde said coldly.

A spark of anger warmed within Riony. "The mission was a success, overall. We cleared fourteen dragons and more riders from that keep."

"And one of our friends is dead. You call that a success?" Eslinde gestured to where Gleem and Shani were landing in the clearing where they had the bonfire on Midwinter's Eve.

"Fourteen dragons," Riony said again. "And only one—"

"You're prepared to lose someone every time you launch an attack? Only the blessed sun knows how you've kept Lyrrin alive so long with that approach."

Riony's hands curled into fists.

Eslinde lifted her chin, staring up at Riony unflinchingly. "Who, exactly, are you prepared to lose next?"

Riony's words caught in her throat, and then Thallan came through on his dragon, pushing Riony and Eslinde apart as he took himself, Yensen, and his dragon straight into the base.

Riony tried to get his attention but was thoroughly ignored in a way that felt like a hot knife to the gut. Eslinde turned and followed them into the dark tunnel.

Fuming, Riony returned her attention to the Rebel Riders.

Samor carried Norallei's broken body down from his flamesong over his shoulder, then laid her gently on the ground.

Parts of the small Taenish woman were bent in the ways they shouldn't have been and her head hung limp.

Zeina came to stand beside Samor and Jaym. Her face was drawn in a long frown and her eyes sharp. They flashed toward Riony as she approached, followed by a small shake of the head.

Riony's steps faltered. She wasn't welcome.

Do they blame me?

It had been Thallan who had suggested retaliation, who mentioned how they could do some damage to a dragonkeep the way they used to.

But it had been Riony who ran with the idea of attacking the keep and riders. Who pushed for it until everyone who needed to be was on board.

She stood there, separated from the tight huddle of Rebel Riders as the night darkened and then grew suddenly bright as Shani breathed her powerful flamesong breath.

No pyre for Norallei. She would have a rider's funeral of dragonfire.

Kess appeared on Griskin by Riony's side. She hadn't even noticed Kess take Iffyr away into the base and return with her wolf.

Staring into the blazing fire, Riony whispered, "Was it all a mistake? Should we have never attacked the keep?"

Kess turned shadowed eyes her way. "What happened wasn't your fault. You had a good plan. Everybody involved knew the risks. We all considered it worth it."

The gentle wariness in Kess's tone made Riony's hackles rise.

"Don't bovinshit me, Kess. Of anybody, I don't want you telling me what I want to hear." Riony pointed toward the burning body. "That was almost *you*."

Kess held her stare, chin set as though she were going to argue. Then she exhaled deeply and rubbed where a deep bruise was forming around one wrist.

"You inspire people, Riony. With your compassion and desire to protect others."

"You've done this speech already," Riony growled.

"But you aren't the only inspiring person around here," Kess continued, undeterred. "People like Thallan, they inspire people too. But they inspire people to violence."

Riony shook her head, still feeling like she was being coddled. "The mission was my idea."

"Inspired by who? No. I recognize people like him because I grew up surrounded by them." Kess turned away to face the fire. The flame flickered in her eyes and glowed across her spotted cheekbone.

Her voice became faraway and dreamlike. "I grew up torn between a family that knew only violence and cruelty, and you and the resilient kindness you showed when you had every right not to. Torn on who to become, caught between all those confused desires and loyalties."

The depth of emotion, of thinly concealed fury merged with longing, had Riony transfixed. She watched Kess's lips as she spoke.

"I only wish I'd chosen kindness sooner. If I could start over, I would have chosen you, and the kindness you inspire, right from the start, over any dragonrider or dragonlord or Dragon King in the land."

Kess turned back to her then, eyes like burning stars. "That's the Riony I love. Not the one that the violence and cruelty of others is creating."

A weak crackle of sound emerged from Riony's throat as her breath cut off midway.

Of all the words that might have come out of Kessara Heithorn's mouth, Riony never expected those. Even with Kess's recent turnaround in attitude, Riony would have found it more likely for her to say, 'excuse me while I go and feed Griskin to a dragon' or 'you know what, you're right about Aishena being the hottest in the land.'

But Kess had used the words *Riony* and *I* and *Love* in a combination that made Riony's head ring like a struck bell. And Kess said it like it was the simplest, easiest thing, as natural as breathing.

Sparks. What the sparking WHAT?

She wanted to throw back something about how a vile little gremlin such as her shouldn't use words she didn't understand, but she could only stare back as some great and terrible emotion released and unfurled within her chest like a blossom from beneath snow.

Kess didn't wait for any kind of reply. She bowed her head and left, slinking away on Griskin into the base.

Riony remained shaken and numb in the winter night as she watched Zeina and Samor and Jaym console each other and the funeral fire burned down, and then she stumbled her way in to sleep on the floor beside Dracuni.

Her dreams were all of death and fire and Kess.

Big sister, wake up.

Riony groaned as Dracuni nudged her with a claw. "What is it?"

"Vance saw smoke while out on patrol." Eslinde's voice came from somewhere above.

Riony's eyes felt swollen, and she peeled them open to squint at the princess. "So it's a normal day in Elundrae."

"A large tower of smoke, from the direction of Gerichkeep," Eslinde clarified.

Pulling herself up into a sitting position on her thin blanket, Riony stretched out sore muscles in her arms. "What? Why? We explicitly didn't leave the place burning."

"We don't know. Vance was on patrol all night and the other riders are mourning. So Dashiel and Kess are preparing to go and see what is happening. I was hoping you'd go with them. Keep them safe."

Riony nodded, her exhausted mind still trying to catch up.

You need more rest. Stay. You don't have to take orders from her.

Riony patted her on the end of her snout. "I know. But I do want to make sure everyone stays safe. And I want to see what this smoke business is about."

Riony had dumped her armor around the floor of the stables beside her when she'd gone to sleep, so she scooped up just the basics. She put them on and met Kess and Dashiel beside Ambri as they prepared for the three of them to go.

The trip back to Gerichkeep was fast as they didn't need to conserve energy this time.

And the pillar of smoke was clear from the moment they were in the air. They followed it like a beacon. The dark column rose swaying into the sky, thick and clogged with ash, and then rained those burned-out embers across the land.

Dashiel kept Ambri up high within that smoke at first, hidden in case of any other riders on wing.

But they were alone in the sky. Coming down closer to the dragonkeep, the source of the billowing blackness was clear. The entire city was ablaze. Between the glowing patches of flame, the streets churned with dark shapes.

"Revs," Kess called out, pointing.

"What? How did they—?" Riony choked on her words.

The revs got in because there was nothing left to keep them out. Revs could, given the chance, scale a dragonkeep's walls. It was up to the riders protecting the keep to burn them before they went over the top.

But Gerichkeep had just lost most of its riders.

"There are so many." Dashiel's voice was low, awed with fear. "I'd heard rumors of a revenant army, but I never thought ... I didn't think it would be like *this*."

Riony shivered. She'd seen something like it before, the night Kellae gave birth, and when they had flown to find the Rebel Riders, but even then, it wasn't that many. Had it just been growing and growing all this time?

Kess half turned around to Riony behind her. "Even if the keep had all its riders, they might not have withstood—"

"Don't." Riony swallowed hard. "Is anyone down there still alive? Can we save anyone?"

She pulled a seeing stone from her belt pouch and activated it but couldn't bring herself to look. She handed it forward to Kess.

Kess took a few seconds to get the angle right on the clear crystal, then scanned over the city below.

"I don't think so. I can only see revs and fire."

Their fingers touched as Kess handed the crystal back.

Dashiel shook their head. "The fires must have been from people's attempts to stop the revs, from what remaining dragons there were. But the revs don't seem to care."

Riony felt a wave of sickness, imagining all of those people in their last moments, trying to fight the revs back with fire only to find that they wouldn't burn.

Her heart broke into a separate piece for every soul that had been lost in the keep below.

"A messenger dragon got out. Why didn't it bring help from other keeps?" Kess asked.

The words warbled emptily in Riony's mind. She was unable to make sense of anything anymore through the morass of grief and pain.

Dashiel circled them around to the far side of the keep, where the main road went off to the east. Like ants swarming over abandoned cake, revenants poured out of the dragonkeep, creating a thick blanket on the ground as the army headed east.

Now one dragonkeep's worth of corpses larger again.

Riony feared for anything in its path.

Chapter Nineteen

Lyrrin held the silvernix-changed hatchling on her lap, stroking his soft scales. Her sister's room, where she waited, was practically bare. Bags remained unpacked to one side of the simple cot that looked like it hadn't been slept in once. The mattress was cold and firm beneath Lyrrin.

A few items of armor and clothing lay strewn around from hasty changes. Many of them crusted with dried blood.

Lyrrin wiped her nose and squeezed Elumon closer.

"Lyrrin?"

She startled, and Elumon's emotions matched hers, sending a streak of **scared, scared** through her head.

She whispered, "Hush, it's just big sister."

Riony stood frozen in the doorway. "Are you here to say 'I told you so' as well?"

Lyrrin had heard Riony tell the others the fate of the dragonkeep. She'd also seen the crushed spirit and exhaustion in the dark lines and red stain around Riony's eyes.

"I'm not."

"I wouldn't blame you if you were." Riony unbuckled the vest of scale mail and dropped it unceremoniously to the floor.

"I'm *not*," Lyrrin repeated. "But maybe if you'd listen to me—"

"I know, okay? I know things aren't going well. I know I'm screwing everything up. But I don't know what to do." Riony leaned her back against the wall and clasped her hands behind her head, squeezing it between her arms.

Lyrrin bit her lip. Things had been going so well for a while. Lyrrin had been so happy spending time with Eslinde and the Alderkin and all her friends and family at the base, that it had been easy to forget the problems of the outside world.

Up until the enclaves were attacked. Lyrrin could hardly fathom that all those people they knew were gone. She couldn't look too closely at that truth or the pain it caused, or she began feeling like the world was broken right through and could never be better.

But she could see how Riony couldn't look away. How her sister took on every weight and trouble of the world as though they were her fault.

Lyrrin knew it wasn't Riony's fault though. That lay only on those who caused the harm. Those who attacked the enclaves. The revenants who brought down the keep. Only those causing the harm could take that blame.

She cleared her throat softly. "Do you know how jealous I was of you and Dracuni?"

Riony shook her head, still pressed between her arms. "You don't need to be. Dracuni loves you, and you've spent almost as much time raising her as I have."

"But you bonded with her. You can speak with her. And I used to get so upset that I couldn't share that connection."

Riony slumped a little farther down the wall. "I'm sorry."

"But now I have Elumon—"

"You decided on a name?"

"Yes, Elumon Opalscales."

The hatchling blinked up to Lyrrin and thrummed happily at the sound of his name.

Riony raised her eyebrows. "Not Sir Elumon Opalscales?"

"Why would he be a sir? Now stop interrupting me for once!"

Elumon had a full stomach, but still sleepily chewed on one of Lyrrin's thumbs with his gummy mouth. She patted him and sighed.

"Now that I have Elumon, I've started to understand how big of a responsibility it is. And Elumon doesn't even have silvernix blood, but I'm still worried about him *all the time*."

Riony's arms dropped to her sides, and she huffed wryly. "You're good with animals. You'll be fine."

"Shush!" Lyrrin snapped. "You're still not listening. Come and sit down and be quiet for once."

Lyrrin shuffled over and patted the spot on the mattress beside her.

Riony grumbled under her breath, "Been spending lots of time with the princess I see."

But she still slouched across the room and sat beside Lyrrin.

Facing her sister, Lyrrin locked her with a serious stare. "What I'm saying, is that I know you have so many responsibilities, and you're doing your best to look after all of them. But even with good intentions, things can go wrong."

Riony shivered, but her mouth remained firmly closed.

Softening her voice, Lyrrin said, "You couldn't have known the revenants were going to attack the dragonkeep."

Riony shook her head as though fighting the words, but they came out in a rush. "But if we hadn't weakened their defenses, they might have been able to keep the revs out."

"And if they hadn't attacked the enclaves first, you wouldn't have weakened their defenses," Lyrrin countered.

"And they might not have attacked the enclaves if we weren't in hiding," Riony's voice went higher.

"How far back do you want to keep chasing the blame? All the way back to the first taming? There would be no revenants at all if the king hadn't begun taming dragons. Or perhaps we go back earlier? Was it the Alderkin's fault? Or maybe unicorns fault for the very blood they were born with?"

"That's ridiculous."

Lyrrin gestured wildly with her hands at the point floating between them.

Sleepy. Be still. Elumon grumbled and tucked his head under his tail.

Lyrrin calmed herself and said, "Of course it's ridiculous. So why are you happy to take the blame back just so far that it lands on you?"

Riony shook her head and stared at the floor. "Because I can't keep making mistakes that hurt people."

"And it's because you feel that way that I know you're a good person. Because you care. About all those people. About everyone." Lyrrin grasped her sister's hand in hers and squeezed it gently in her sharp fingers.

"Caring doesn't keep people alive." Her voice came out husky and broken. "And fighting back … I don't know if I can …"

Lyrrin reached her other hand to Riony's as well. Elumon snorted, disturbed by her movement, and hopped off her lap to go and sniff Riony's discarded armor.

Lyrrin watched him, still unable to believe he was hers, that they were bonded, that his egg had been brought in by Rebel Riders who had become their friends.

She could hardly believe, even now, that her mother was here with her, and an Alderkin family, and all these people who had come together to help Dracuni and Elundrae.

She offered her sister a gentle smile. "I wish we could fix the world just by making friends. And I still think we can, in a way. We were, with the enclaves."

Riony flinched as though struck but remained silent.

"*They weren't a mistake.* The mistake was that we didn't realize that there are people and forces out there who don't want the world to change, and who are going to do anything to stop us. And those are the ones we need to fight back against."

"It hasn't helped. I don't know …"

Lyrrin pulled Riony's hand in tighter. "Sometimes we do have to fight. And kick the asses of everyone who gets in our way. And nobody is better at that than you. And I know it's a big responsibility. That's why we're going to change the world *together*."

Riony's hand squeezed back, and she finally looked up and met Lyrrin's gaze. "Big dreams, bold deeds, right?"

It hurt Lyrrin to see how much pain filled her sister's eyes. But there was still fire there too. She smiled and nodded. "Big dreams, bold deeds."

***

"If we left when I signaled it, we'd still have Norallei." Zeina's voice carried through the meeting room. She stood, leaning with both hands palm down on the table, staring down Thallan on the other side.

Eslinde had called the meeting, after giving the riders some time to grieve, but it seemed those few days weren't enough to cool tempers. Riony could see the raw pain in all of them, except Samor who as always held his feelings close.

"You pushed it too far, old friend. As you always do." Jaym sat beside her, hunched in his chair.

Thallan's battle-worn features had roughened over the last few days. His neatly trimmed beard grew long and patchy and his hair hung unbraided. He paced behind Riony's chair.

But he seemed to take no worry in his companion's words. "Too far? Look at the win we've struck. Not just a dozen or so dragons, but an entire keep, gone."

"A win?" Riony balked at the word, one she'd come so close to using with Eslinde herself.

She'd called it a success. But time and the fall of the entire keep had stolen that word from her mouth.

"Thousands were lost in that keep. Families. People who loved and cared for one another," Eslinde spoke with the ringing eloquence of restrained emotion.

"Dragonlords," Thallan spat. "Our enemy. And the enemy to our land. So many have now been removed, will no longer keep taming dragons for their factories or defenses. This *is* a win."

Zeina dropped into her chair, mouth hanging open. "But we lost Norallei. Don't you even care?"

"Don't you dare assume how I feel." Thallan paused his pacing to glare across the room where everyone had gathered except the Zarram siblings who were on patrol.

Riony glanced to Aishena on her one side and Lyrrin on the other. She couldn't assume how Thallan was feeling, but she could imagine too clearly her own reaction if she lost someone she loved.

She'd almost lost Aishena. And it had been a close call for Kess.

That's the Riony I love. A jolt rattled down her spine like an icy avalanche at the memory of the words.

She turned, casting a surreptitious glance over her shoulder. The table had been filled by the time Kess arrived, and she remained on Griskin, by the wall at Riony's back. Pale eyes met hers from the shadows, and Riony hastily turned away again.

Thallan batted a hand in the air and paced again. "Beyond any pain, I refuse to have her loss count for nothing. If anything, we should ramp up attacks. We defeated fourteen dragons with ease. Do that a few more times and surely that would weaken the shadow dragon noticeably. Isn't that what we want?"

Silence. Benjin opened and closed his mouth a few times without finding his words. The Alderkin leaned toward each other, whispering in their language.

Riony locked eyes with Eslinde for a moment, and then she stood slowly, facing Thallan.

"We were lucky to only lose one during our attack of Gerichkeep. How many are you willing to lose each time?"

His fiery expression didn't waver. "As many as necessary."

Riony moved to block his pacing and hold his attention. "We hardly have the numbers as it is! Which of us should die next?"

Thallan moved around her, waving her away. "Any sacrifice is worth destroying our enemy!"

Sparks, was this how I sounded? Riony was mortified, and anger brewed in her, twitching the tendons in her hands.

Thallan paused his pacing again, turning to Riony with a dark fervor in his eyes.

"Don't you see? We could have the upper hand if we keep the pressure on. We could follow the revenant horde and weaken any keep in its path. The revs would do the work for—"

Riony's fist cracked against Thallan's nose.

Chairs scraped around the room as everyone shot to their feet.

Thallan stumbled backward, more shocked than hurt. "How dare you?"

"You're lucky I held back," Riony growled. "What you're saying, what you're planning, it's not okay, and it's not going to happen. We will fight when we need to, but we will not get drawn into the kind of rampant cruelty the dragonlords deal out."

Aishena, Kess, Lyrrin, and Benjin lined up beside Riony. Yensen had Eslinde and the Alderkin moved into a corner and behind his guard.

A twinge of scolding emotion reached Riony from Dracuni in the stables.

Are you punching people?

Only those who deserve it.

Thallan scowled back at Riony, flicking his chin toward the other Rebel Riders for support.

Riony shook out her hand and pulled it into a fist again with the crack of knuckles. "Do we have an understanding? Or do you need me to hit you hard enough that you understand that unnecessary violence isn't the answer?"

Zeina and Jaym strolled over, almost warily. They moved to join the group standing beside Riony.

Only Samor stood beside Thallan.

The leader of the riders breathed heavily as he looked Zeina and Jaym up and down. "You'd stand with them? Those you've only known a few weeks?"

Jaym shrugged and shook his head at Samor. "I'm more surprised you're sticking with him. Sam ... after everything. After it was Thallan's plans that got Gerlinda killed."

Samor folded his arms, looming behind Thallan. "We stuck together then. We stick together now. This is all I have left. And it's all Thallan has left now too. Taking out as many dragonlords as possible in the time we have left sounds good to me."

Zeina's face remained still and fierce, but her eyes glistened. "I will not put myself nor Gleem into another of your suicide missions."

Jaym nodded. "Not Hux either. They have their own say in this too, unlike your dragon."

Thallan's jaw twitched. "So we are separating, then. Fine. Samor and I will go and find one of our other groups that might be more worthy of action."

"Oh no. I don't think that's going to be possible." Eslinde stepped out from behind her grayglim.

"What do you mean? I'm sure our true friends will take us in." Thallan seemed genuinely confused.

"I mean that we can't exactly allow those who know about Dracuni to leave and go about their own business." Eslinde's expression was apologetic, but firm.

Riony's lips shifted into an *O* shape. Eslinde was right, and as usual at least a full step or two ahead of Riony.

Thallan's lips turned up on one side. "What are you going to do? Imprison us here?"

"If we must." Eslinde bowed her head. "Or we could stop the infighting and come to an agreement again."

Thallan barked a laugh. "Yes, tell me how you will imprison us and then how you'd like to be agreeable again in the same breath."

Kess moved forward on Griskin and whispered in Riony's ear, "Something is happening. Griskin hears people in the base."

"What?" Riony wished she'd brought her sword with her. "Everyone, quiet!"

There was a muttering of continued argument before the intensity of Riony's glare silenced everyone.

Then she heard it too. Whimpering. Crying. Stumbling feet.

"It's coming from the gateway." Riony moved fast, vaulting over the table to get to the exit and out into the hall. Her friends followed close behind.

The first person who wobbled out of the long shadows between torches was a teenage boy, wide-eyed and confused. He backed up against the wall and held his arms up to protect himself as Riony barreled toward him.

"Where did you come from?" She tried to sound calm and kind, but urgency raised her voice.

"The ... the undercity. It's under attack. There were dragons."

"An attack on the undercity?" Aishena repeated in a rasp.

And one bad enough that Niskina is evacuating people here.

A woman hovering over a clutch of small children tumbled up the hallway next, and Riony moved again, running for the gateway.

"Niskina?" Riony yelled as the crowd grew thicker the closer she got.

An old man stumbled past, shirt smoldering as he gasped in pain.

A surge of people pushed through the gateway as Riony reached the room, brightened by the light of the rippling magic. And then that light stuttered, faltered, then faded entirely.

Chapter Twenty

The urgency of panic overlaid Riony's movements as she traced over the rune to reopen the gateway.

"Oh, blessed sun, it's still working." Eslinde sighed from behind her as the symbols around the geode stone glowed to life.

"No, it's not." Riony pointed to the one for the undercity gateway, and it hadn't lit up like the other active options.

"My husband is still on the other side. Please open it again," a woman's voice came from the back of the crowd, and more murmurs followed with the soft crying of children.

Riony ran her hand over the sharp edge of the geode slice. "We can't. We could maybe go through to the shrine down the hill, if people can get out to there …"

"The exits were all blocked off by the riders. They have dragons, small ones, but a lot of them."

"City guard dragons, likely," Eslinde added. "Treedarts.

"What about the delvers and Niskina?" Riony turned to the crowd, seeking the wide-eyed escapees for answers.

A couple of them shrugged, but a child Riony knew from the Orphans' Den piped up. "Niskina opened the gateway for us. She was right there on the other side."

Riony grunted, then selected the symbol for the shrine down the hill from the undercity. She stepped through briefly, but it was abandoned as it had been since they'd evacuated the small enclave there on the night of the attacks.

Coming back through, she blinked as her vision went dark. A few gasps and whimpers came from the crowd, and Eslinde moved through them, comforting people.

Riony turned on the spot to find the gateway dark again.

"Did someone deactivate it?" She crouched down to trace the rune again.

"No, it just went out." Aishena stared at the crystal window, her expression grim.

Riony finished the sequence, but nothing happened. Maybe she got it wrong in her rush. She tried again. No sign of magic.

"It's run out of charge," Lyrrin said.

"Are you sure?" Yensen moved closer to Riony.

Lyrrin craned her neck, as though looking for someone.

Of their group, only the Alderkin didn't come in to where the refugees had fled. It would have been good to get their confirmation of what was happening with the Alderkin artifact, but they were keeping hidden from the newcomers.

Riony slapped her palm against the rune. There were maybe twenty or thirty people who made it through. Out of thousands. What were the dragonriders going to do to them all? To Niskina?

Aishena and Benjin whispered to each other, then approached the squirrelly boy who had known Niskina.

"Cammi, can you tell us more about what you saw?" Aishena asked.

His jaw dropped when he saw Aishena and Benjin standing before him. Using one hand to swipe his dirty-blond hair back, he stood at attention.

He delivered a report in a confident, high voice. "The dragonriders came in through the main entrances, then started rounding up delvers and anyone they thought looked dangerous. Pretty much anyone young and healthy. Someone called Kife was in charge, and he was making sure everyone knew who he was."

Riony and Kess's eyes met.

Kess shook her head warningly but didn't look away. "It's a trap. He wants us to know he's there. He wants to lure us into those horrible caves, kill us all, and take Dracuni."

"We still have to do something. They could be doing what they did in the enclaves ..." Riony's voice trailed away as her heart clenched painfully.

She shook herself and stood from where she'd knelt in front of the gateway. "If Kife is using himself as bait, I'm going to take it. The thing about bait is that even if the fish gets hooked, it's the worm that has no chance of making it out alive."

Aishena raised an eyebrow. "What do we consider our chances of the fish making it off the hook?"

Riony shrugged. "The best. Excellent. One hundred percent."

Aishena smirked. "You never were good with numbers."

"Because I put all my effort into staying alive. We can do this. We must do this. And we'll do it in a way we survive and that doesn't hand over Dracuni."

"You're determined?" Eslinde asked.

"Nothing will stop me. I'll go alone if I have to," Riony replied.

Lyrrin's lips pulled in. "No, you won't."

"Whatever you decide, I'm with you," Kess said from her side.

"Come on then, we must prepare." Eslinde gestured for them to move. "I'll see to our new guests, then join you in the meeting room. Yensen, fetch the Zarrams."

The grayglim nodded and was first to move. Riony and her friends followed, meeting the Rebel Riders where they had waited in the hall. Even Thallan and Samor had remained, watching the darkened gateway and refugees with frowns.

As they walked back to the meeting room, Aishena spoke in a clipped beat. "With the gateway out, we'll have to fly there. We won't be able to go in through the main entrances either if they are held by the Dragonriders."

A little farther down the hallway, they found the Alderkin, tucked into the shadows, having observed from a distance. They fell into the group as well.

"We'll go in through the ice cave in the mountain." Riony marched ahead, her mind racing, playing through their options.

What's happening? Dracuni's thoughts played through into hers.

Trouble. I'll explain everything soon.

You're going without me again, aren't you?

Riony pressed on, trying to ignore the pain in Dracuni's thoughts.

Aishena's face shifted only slightly, but Riony could tell she didn't like her suggestion. "We won't be able to take any dragons in that way. Even Dracuni won't fit down those tunnels."

Benjin trotted to keep up with his sister. "What about Shiff? She's still small, but even a little dragon's fire is better than nothing."

"That will be up to her and Dash," Kess said from behind.

"Elumon could come, but he's not breathing fire yet," Lyrrin added.

Riony pushed through the door into the meeting room. "Which is why he's staying here with you."

"Excuse me?" Lyrrin snapped.

Riony turned to Zeina, glancing at Jaym as well. "Will you fly us there? You only need to get us close, drop us off near the peak."

"You don't want us to join you inside?" Zeina didn't sit down, instead leaning on the back of one of the chairs.

"I want people to stay with the dragons in case we need a quick escape. We can work to clear one of the larger entrances, then signal you to come in that way."

Yensen returned then with Dashiel and Vance, talking them through what had happened.

Aishena nodded to Dashiel. "We need to get there fast, not weigh the dragons down too much. We'll take Ambri too, if that's okay."

"However we can help," Dashiel said.

Aishena took that opportunity to broach the idea of taking Shiff in.

Dashiel was already in full armor from being on patrol and paused for a moment, their face thoughtful. "Shiff is in, but I'm going with her."

Vance grunted softly. "I don't like the sounds of any of this."

Aishena nodded and looked around their group. "Jaym, will Hux let me fly with him? I want you on Ambri. We can't have a tamed dragon without a rider once we head into the depths."

Jaym gave a roguish smile. "I'm sure he could be persuaded."

Eslinde floated back into the room then, watching keenly as they planned.

"Good." Aishena nodded, then pointed around the group. "I want Benjin and myself on Hux."

Benjin quietly pumped his fist behind her.

Aishena continued. "Jaym, you can take Dashiel and Shiff on Ambri. Riony, Kess, and Griskin go with Zeina on Gleem."

"What about me?" Lyrrin's face had turned a deep red.

Aishena tilted her head slightly toward Riony. "We could take one other, if you agree."

Riony looked at her little sister for a long moment. The fierce child who had saved her life possibly more times than Riony had saved hers.

"She could—"

"You can't possibly be considering taking Lyrrin into that trap?" Eslinde placed her hands on Lyrrin's shoulders and squared up to Aishena and Riony.

Riony met her gaze. "She's capable."

Lyrrin seemed to grow visibly taller at the words.

Eslinde gaped, looking between her daughter and Riony. Her fingers were white around Lyrrin, but she began nodding slowly. "Maybe we could all go."

Yensen leaned in toward her. "You cannot. And we need people here to keep Dracuni safe. If Lyrrin is capable, then she's another capable protector who should remain here with us."

"I will stay with you as well," Vance said.

"No!" Lyrrin cried in a high-pitched whine. She tried to move closer to Riony, but Eslinde held her back.

Lyrrin's bright-blue eyes glistened with tears. "There will be enough people here with Dracuni. I should go with you. We're supposed to do things together, remember?"

Yrik took the opportunity to step into the silence. "She's right in that we should act together, but we must all act for the unidragon's well-being. None of you should be going."

"Dracuni will be fine. Our enemies don't know where we are, and it's worth going to do what we can for all those people. Sometimes we have to fight." Riony looked to Lyrrin as she spoke instead of the Alderkin.

The guilt of leaving weighed heavy on her, but Lyrrin gave a single small nod at her words. "It is worth it. Which is why I should go too."

Riony didn't want to admit the relief she'd felt when Yensen suggested Lyrrin should stay. Knowing her sister remained safe was one less thing for her to worry about.

She turned away from Lyrrin's seeking gaze and spoke to Eslinde. "I trust you will keep her safe."

"Of course," the princess replied.

Lyrrin's jaw dropped, and she let out a shriek of utter disgust. She shook Eslinde's hands off her and ran to the corner where the Alderkin stood, hiding among them.

Riony looked over the separating groups again. She didn't like taking so many of the dragons with them, especially with Dracuni still unable to fly, and Viska uncooperative.

Norallei's dragon, Iffyr, still remained, ghostlike and motionless in her stall, but nobody seemed willing to fly her or even mention her, out of respect for her lost rider.

"And you—" Riony turned to where Thallan and Samor remained, although begrudgingly, beside the other Rebel Riders. "Can we trust you to remain, just until our return? If you would stay on patrol for us while we're gone, you will be free to go after that."

Thallan folded his arms. "We are free to go now if we—"

Samor cleared his throat.

"Fine. Yes. We will do our duty here until you return. But then we part ways."

"Then we leave shortly," Aishena said.

Riony moved quickly, unable to look at Lyrrin. She left the meeting room and headed to the stables where she'd left her armor and weapons where she and Dracuni slept.

The unidragon lay with her snout on her front claws and lifted her head at Riony's approach.

I want to go too.

Riony looked away, focusing on the armor strewn around the floor. "You can't fly. How would you get there?"

Shani can carry me. She agreed.

"Shani and Samor are staying here, to keep watch here while we're away, to keep you and Lyrrin and everyone else safe." Riony pulled the scale mail vest on and began buckling it. "And what isn't safe, is taking you into a trap. You're too important."

Dracuni lifted her head and snorted roughly.

Maybe I don't want to be. Maybe I'm tired of being so important that everyone else can get hurt except for me. You always say I can make my own decisions, but then you don't let me!

"I ..." Riony froze, bent halfway to retrieve a pauldron. "I'm sorry."

She dropped the mail with a clatter and moved to kneel so she was eye to eye with the seated unidragon.

Dracuni had gotten so big, her head as long as Riony's torso. Riony leaned into her, hugging her with her shoulder just below the golden horn on her forehead.

"I wish you could have had a normal life. As normal as any of our lives could be. And I know it was my fault you were born how you were, in a way that meant you never could have that."

You didn't know this would happen. Dracuni's words seemed to thrum between them.

"Stars, you were so tiny back then. I just wanted to protect you. I couldn't bear it if you were captured. What Kife did to you last time ... it would only be the beginning."

Dracuni exhaled deeply, the warmth of her breath gusting around Riony's body.

Fine. You can go. But only if you do one thing for me.

Riony argued a little longer. She didn't like it, but in the greater scheme of all she didn't like, the gesture was small, and it made Dracuni feel better.

She spent what remaining time she had strapping on her armor and sitting with Dracuni, stroking the silky tufts of hair that emerged between the scales down her neck, trying to reassure her and herself that she would come back safe.

Then Kess and Griskin appeared in front of her. "Everyone's ready."

Riony leaned into Dracuni for one more hug. "We'll see each other soon."

We better.

When she turned around again, Kess was staring at Dracuni with an expression Riony couldn't read.

Yensen's warnings teased the edges of her thoughts, but as Riony and Kess fell into pace beside each other, Griskin's paws silent on the cold floor, Riony felt no threat.

Who would have ever believed Kessara Heithorn could change?

The idea still made Riony's insides feel strange and rattly, but she did believe it. She wanted to believe it.

If Kess could change, become someone she could trust, someone who was kind and caring, it gave Riony hope for the greater change they wished to bring to the world.

Kess fussed with the bone daggers sheathed in her bracers, but remained silent, her slim body swaying in the saddle as Griskin stalked out of the stables.

"Here." Riony reached to the side of her belt. "I want you to have this."

She thrust her arm out and kept her eyes ahead as she handed Kess the pointed shard of crystal.

"Is that ...?"

"A cutting athame. You've used it before. I'll show you how it activates on the way."

"And you want me to have it?" Kess still hadn't reached to take the crystal.

"I just thought you should have something ... a better weapon. I'd give you a return athame, but Aishena has claimed all of them. This is the only good weapon I have except my sword—especially since *somebody* made me lose my dragonguard sword."

Kess made a stuttering sound that wasn't quite a word. Riony thrust the athame handle toward her again, and finally, she took it.

"Thank you."

Riony cricked her neck and picked up her pace. "It's no big deal."

The others had their dragons outside near the entrance to the underground base. A cold wind blew over the bare roads and empty foundations of the unfinished keep. A dark smudge of soot marked the clearing nearby where Norallei's body had been burned.

It was only midafternoon, but somehow Riony already felt exhausted as she said her goodbyes to Eslinde, Vance, and Yensen.

Lyrrin and the Alderkin hadn't come out to bid the group farewell.

It's okay. We'll be back soon. Once the undercity is safe again. And Kife is dead.

Everyone else was on the three dragons that would be leaving, with Thallan and Samor already circling far above on patrol.

Kess was still tying Griskin and herself in as Riony began climbing up Gleem's aqua scales.

"Wait!"

Lyrrin's voice caused Riony to spin around.

She opened her mouth, ready to try to explain again why her sister couldn't come, but couldn't find her words. Lyrrin ran up to her, cheeks and eyes pink.

"Activate your heart stone," she demanded, tapping her chest where hers hung on a string.

Riony reached to her neck, pulling at the necklaces there, revealing the acorn pendant and the flat paired crystal. She activated it and tucked both treasures back away against her chest.

Lyrrin's small heartbeat fluttered against her own.

"And take this." Lyrrin stuck her arm out.

Riony reached for the crystal in her hand. The ten-stroke rune she'd spent so long working out, until she finally did. The dragon summoning rune.

Her voice was low with confusion and the desire not to enrage her sister any further. "What's this for?"

Lyrrin moved in close beside her, pointing at the carved lines on the crystal. "We've altered it. Me and the Alderkin. See here?"

Riony looked closer, counting out the lines. Eleven now.

"Is this going to explode?" Riony asked.

"Not everything has to explode to be useful."

"Wise words. I wonder where you heard them?" Riony smirked.

"Actually, I can't say for sure it won't explode," Lyrrin admitted.

"Wonderful."

"But we think we did it right. We've altered it so it should work on tamed dragons now." Lyrrin held Riony's hand that held the crystal, lifting it up where they both could see and gesturing to show Riony the sequence.

Riony smiled at her sister and a rush of pride made her eyes water. "Now that could be very useful. Show me again."

Lyrrin grinned back and showed Riony the sequence two more times.

Once she thought she had it memorized, Riony tucked the crystal away in a belt pouch, then bent down to crush her sister in a tight embrace.

"You will be back, won't you?" Lyrrin mumbled into Riony's shoulder. "I hate watching you leave. It always feels like it will be the last time I see you."

Riony stepped back, gave Lyrrin her most bravado-laden smirk, and ruffled the kid's blue-and-brown hair.

But as she climbed up onto Gleem behind the others and they lifted into the sky, Riony watched Lyrrin grow smaller and smaller and couldn't tear her eyes away until Eslindekeep had disappeared from sight entirely.

Chapter Twenty-One

High in the mountains above the undercity, a fresh powder of fluffy snow drifted in the brisk wind, and gray clouds lay smotheringly low, blocking the sun.

Kess kept Griskin close beside Riony. Worry seared her insides like acid and kept her face pinched into a tight frown.

They would be facing Kife today. And Kess knew exactly how cruel her brother enjoyed being.

Her hand idly touched the cutting athame in her belt as she waited for everyone to climb down from the dragons.

Nearby, Riony showed Aishena the new crystal her little sister had provided. Kess could almost see the cogs turning in the Hjelzahn woman's head, working the new resource into their plans.

Benjin stood on tiptoes to watch the information being shared as well.

From atop Gleem, Zeina was giving Riony a long look. "We'll keep out of sight and watch for your signal. Stay safe."

"Happy hunting!" Jaym called from his seat on Ambri.

Hux stalked through the snow, freely on his own. The red dragon was the first back into the sky, but soon they were all gone, high in the clouds.

"This way," Aishena said, marching toward a cliff face sheeted in ice.

Riony turned on the spot. All around them was white.

"Wasn't it that way? Nope. No, you're right." She jogged through the thick snow to catch up.

Griskin grumbled a warbling growl.

Kess leaned close to his neck and patted his ears. "Don't worry. We won't be out in the cold as long as we were last time."

"Shiff isn't enjoying the snow either," Dashiel said cheerfully.

The pale blue and purple dragon stomped grumpily at their side, hot breath streaming out in clouds. Shiff was only a little smaller than Griskin now, and the shimmerdart had been showing off how good her ball lightning breath was getting.

They reached the cliff, and Aishena ran her hands over the flow of frozen water. "It should be around here."

Riony bent down, peering through a glassy section. "Through here. It's iced up even more than before. Hang on a second."

Riony pulled her sword and looked ready to take a swing.

Kess winced. "Careful. It'll be harder than you think."

"Oh, I know. I've done this before." Riony turned her sword so the unicorn horn-shaped hilt pointed to the frozen wall.

She jabbed it deep into the ice in a few places, then spun the sword around and thrust the thicker blade between the fracture points.

It split through, and with a grunt of effort, Riony wrenched it out again, then kicked in the shattered ice until the hole was big enough for them to pass through. She sheathed her sword, never having activated its magic, and waved for Aishena to step through first.

Riony had always been strong. Kess knew that from the duties she'd been expected to perform as Kess's servant, little more than a beast of burden most of the time. As they spent so many hours together as children, Kess had seen Riony's other qualities as well, how she was so much more than a vital body.

But still, seeing just how strong Riony had gotten left Kess flushed.

Like a gentleman holding a door, Riony gestured everyone through, then followed in behind Kess.

The temperature was already warmer in the cave, sheltered from the gusting wind. Bats and owlettes overhead chittered at the intruders. Aishena and Benjin lit the way with the cyan light of glow stones, but the darkness and weight of the mountain above still seemed to crush in around Kess.

She shivered. "Didn't really want to come back to this cursed place."

Riony traced the rune on her glow stone and let it dangle in the netted pouch on her belt. "You just never saw the best parts."

"You mean swarms of cave spiders and a giant tangled conglomeration of revenants aren't highlights?"

Dashiel called back, "I thought we were only up against some riders with treedarts."

"We are," Riony confirmed. "Kess is exaggerating."

"Yes, just exaggerating," Kess said sweetly.

Riony cracked a half smile and gave Kess a small wink.

"Quiet now," Aishena hissed. "We're nearing the inhabited areas."

A hushed tension spread as they stepped from the natural caves into the Alderkin-carved tunnel through a broken wall. Griskin whined softly and licked his nose. The spores of the mushroom farms were already bothering him.

Each of their group was fully armored in Eslinde's colors and wore a plain cloak over the top. Griskin and Shiff were harder to conceal, but the undercity was large. Kess had managed to move through it before unseen, sticking to roofs and dark alleys.

As they reached the end of the tunnel and it opened out into the occupied cavern, Aishena signaled them all still, and those with glow stones deactivated their light.

From her perch on Griskin, Kess watched as a dragonrider on a dull-brown treedart stalked through an empty street. The soldier yelled when a boy stepped out of an alley, then froze at the sight of a dragon.

The guard prowled toward the child, bringing his dragon's snout right up to the boy's face. He backed up against the wall, shaking his head and crying.

Soft sounds of crystal sliding through hard leather echoed in the tunnel as Riony drew her sword.

"No," Aishena hissed back. "We can't be seen until we get to a more central area. We need to reach somewhere Lyrrin's dragon rune can get the best effect."

Riony snorted air out her nose and took a step forward.

A door opened on the street beside the dragonrider and boy, and an old woman bustled out. She grasped the boy's arm and dragged him out from under the dragon and into her home, slamming the door behind her.

The sound of the rider chuckling carried through the deserted area.

Riony still looked ready to ambush the soldier. "We should have helped."

"We need to keep as much element of surprise as we can," Aishena replied.

Once the rider had moved on, she beckoned them forward again.

"Surprise? This is a trap, remember. They know we're coming." Riony moved up beside Aishena, pointing to a narrow alleyway.

Aishena nodded and they all scurried that way. "All the more reason we need to get as close to Kife and those in command before we strike."

A thick stench of garbage filled the narrow path and things moved in the shadows ahead around a pile of refuse. Each as large as a person, the fluid forms squirmed and tumbled around each other in a pile, fighting to get to the food scraps.

"What under all the stars are they?" Dashiel whispered.

"Just cave otters. Don't worry, they won't bother us," Riony said.

At their approach, the creatures scattered. All except for one, who stood up on its hind legs, sniffed the air, and then raced toward Riony.

The collision left Riony stumbling, and the furry critter snuffled her neck as she steadied herself.

"Butterfur?" Riony gasped.

"Is that the little furry sausage that you tried to follow out of the depths?" Kess asked.

"Thought you said they wouldn't bother us," Dashiel had a hand on their sword, ready to draw.

Shiff gave the otter a low growl.

"No, but this is Sir Butterfur Spelunkychunks."

At Dashiel's blank expression, Riony continued. "He was Lyrrin's pet for a while, and no, I don't have the treats!"

Butterfur had his snout tucked under Riony's cloak and paws trying to get into her belt pouches. Whiskers twitching, he backed off, looking around behind Riony and giving each of the party a quick sniff.

He turned back to Riony with a parted mouth and a tilt to his head.

Riony frowned. "Lyrrin's not with us."

A long, low whistle from above sent the otter skittering away and the rest of them pressing further into the shadows.

Seeking the source of the sound, Kess saw shadows moving behind a gauzy curtain a few stories up.

The fabric shifted, and a familiar voice whispered down, "In here, quick. Another patrol is on the way. Bottom floor is barricaded, come in through the second."

"Was that Niskina?" Benjin whispered.

"Should have known she wouldn't let Kife's goons catch her. Let's go." Grinning widely, Riony put her hands out, fingers woven together in front of her.

Benjin stepped into them first and she boosted the boy up to the flat roof of the tiered building that had been carved from a massive stalagmite.

She helped Aishena and Dashiel reach the second floor the same way, then gave Shiff a concerned look and tried to offer her a hand climbing as well, but the small dragon managed to scramble up the limestone wall alone with a little help from sharp talons and fluttering wings.

Griskin took Kess up with a short run and bounding leap. She looked back over the edge. "You need a hand?"

"I'm good." Taking a short run up, Riony kicked up the wall and grasped the lip at the top. A satisfied, but also somehow sad smile played on her lips as she pulled herself up with the others.

The flat rooftop held a washbasin and a littering of toys. The group ducked below a line of hanging laundry, and the door ahead of them opened.

"Riony, Aish!" Niskina beckoned them in, hugging each briefly and firmly along the way. Until she got to Kess.

"What is she doing here?" Niskina snapped.

"She's here to help," Riony said, voice low as she scanned the dark interior. "And she's been doing a remarkable job of not betraying us lately. Best streak ever."

Holding Kess in her stare for a moment, Niskina finally huffed and turned away.

She muttered under her breath, "Yeah, we'll see how long that lasts."

Closing the door behind them, Niskina got moving again, taking them through the darkened room. "This way. There's more room up here."

From the walls and corners of what looked like a family home, gasps and whispering spread as their group moved through, with wolf and dragonling in tow.

"When the gateway went out, those of us who were trying to evacuate managed to get back here to hide." Niskina nodded toward the people huddling in the dark. "I wasn't sure what to do next. I'm so glad to see you all. We might have a chance now."

They reached a flight of carved stone stairs, and in a flutter of whispers, a figure stood up before them.

"Here, please take this." An older man with age-paled red hair handed something that looked like a dirty stick to Riony.

She pushed back at his hands. "No, you should keep it. I'm not hungry."

He grasped her about the wrist with wiry fingers and placed the item into her palm. "I want you to have it. I know it's not much, but you saved my life on Midwinter's Eve."

Riony blinked at the man as though trying to remember. "I did?"

A few of the other faces huddled in the shadows nodded.

"Thank you." Riony's hand closed around the brown object and she brought it to her mouth, tearing a chunk off between her teeth.

She continued following Niskina up the stairs and made a low sound in the back of her throat. "Sparks, it's good. I can't believe how much I missed this."

Kess just raised her eyebrows.

"Shroom jerky." Riony took another bite and then almost absentmindedly handed the remaining piece to Kess.

And Kess was too startled by the gesture to refuse. She nibbled on a corner of the leathery strap. It wasn't half as bad as she expected. An almost meaty texture, salty and rich. But far too fungus-flavored for Kess's liking.

She mumbled, "Not bad." And then tucked the rest away in her pocket.

Riony rolled her eyes at her. "Maybe it's an acquired taste."

They reached a room where only a few people sat, but with a short word from Niskina, they left. The curvy young woman had her tumbles of hair bundled up in a messy knot and wore the same sort of armor Riony had been wearing when they were in the depths last—soft leather covered in harnesses and steel rings.

Once they were alone, Niskina looked them over. "So, do you have a plan?"

It didn't take long to catch Niskina up on what plan they had, which made Kess worry that it wasn't enough of a plan. They explained the dragon summoning stone, although none of them knew exactly what it would do, if it worked at all after its alterations.

Niskina paced and rubbed her chin with her thumb. "Kife and his riders have taken all of Upslope and set up command on the platform overlooking Sinking Stream Lake. There are a lot of them. Even if this new rune of yours works, I just don't think we have the numbers."

"That's why we were hoping to get to Kife first, to get rid of him so the riders are without a leader." Riony's voice rattled over Kess's brother's name.

There was a day, a while ago, when Riony and Eslinde had been speaking, then Riony stormed out, glowering like a storm. When Kess asked what happened, the princess had only said she told Riony how she and Kess had met.

"Oh, is that why you're going after him?" Niskina gave Riony a skeptical glare, then shook her head. "No. The riders will have a chain of command in place. Getting rid of Kife isn't enough."

Aishena nodded at this.

Niskina continued. "We need the other delvers. I know where they are imprisoned. If we can free them, get everyone their weapons again, we could beat the invaders. As long as nobody turns on us before then."

Kess narrowed her eyes. "You think the delvers will be enough to give us the advantage? When they were imprisoned so easily already?"

Niskina took a slow, threatening step Kess's way. "They were taken by surprise. I only got away because I'm more of an honorary delver these days. I wasn't with the rest of them. The delvers will help."

"It's a good idea," Aishena agreed. "Not many in the undercity are trained the way the delvers are. They're the closest we have to a fighting force."

"So, what do we do?" Riony looked to Aishena, Niskina, and Benjin.

The Hjelzahn siblings opened their mouths at the same time, and Aishena gave way to her brother.

Benjin puffed up as he said, "Shiff is around the size of a treedart now. If we can capture one of the other riders and take their uniform, Dashiel and Shiff could disguise themselves and get through to free the delvers."

"Shiff isn't the right color," Kess muttered. "It's not going to work."

But nobody seemed to be listening to her.

They worked through a few more details, then decided they were ready to go ahead. Kess didn't feel ready.

As they moved back down through the home and out onto the rooftop again, all Kess could think about was what would happen if something went wrong? What would happen if Kife got his hands on Riony?

I can't let that happen. No matter what.

Riony led the way then, taking them at a run across the rooftops. Most of the flat-topped structures butted up against each other with only a small jump to the next. It was an easy run as the group left the side cavern which held the mushroom farms and reached the larger main cavern.

Kess wasn't clear on all the location names the others had been rattling off, but *Upslope* and *Downslope* at least were descriptive enough for her to follow. They came into the main cavern at the lower end, but not far from where the large central lake pooled in ascending tiers to the higher level.

Griskin's ears twitched, and Kess rasped, "Dragons, up ahead."

Riony slowed, bringing them to the edge of the next rooftop in a low crouch.

Below, a baker's stall was tipped on its side, loaves scattered and crushed into crumbs on the ground. A long line of men, women, and children knelt along the middle of the street.

The same rider as before on the dull-brown treedart strolled up and down beside them. "I'm getting tired of bringing your criminals in. Maybe I'll have my dragon burn you all where you are instead."

Aishena pointed to their left and whispered, "We can go around this way."

Riony didn't move.

"Riony?" Kess questioned softly.

"We wanted to capture a rider for their uniform, didn't we?" Her eyes remained locked on the man below.

"Not here." Aishena took another step, beckoning the others to follow. "It's too exposed."

A cry echoed from below. One of the kneeling men was pushed down beneath the front claw of the dragon.

Riony stood to full height.

"Riony!" Aishena, still crouching, whispered the warning.

"We're here to save people, aren't we? To save everyone we can save. That's the whole point." Riony shook her head, her jaw clenched.

"There's only one rider," Benjin offered. "We could take them, easily."

Riony gave Aishena a pleading look. "We'll still get the uniform, still go after the delvers. We'll just save who we can along the way as well. We have to."

Aishena didn't seem convinced, but another wail came from below.

The rider had his steed's mouth open, laughing as he angled it around the skull of the man beneath him. Sparks flickered around the dragon's teeth.

Riony dropped her cloak and drew her sword, lighting it up in a purple glow. She caught Kess's eye.

Without waiting for any reply, she launched off the side of the building toward the rider below.

And without a second thought, Kess followed. She was no longer afraid to fall. Not afraid to burn. Only one thing scared her now. Seeing Riony come to harm. And the fear she wouldn't be able to stop it.

Riony's elbow cracked across the rider's helmeted head before her feet hit the ground. The man swung in his saddle, falling with her the rest of the way. The blow dislodged his helmet and it flew off, rolling about in a clatter on the limestone street.

Without the rider's instructions, the treedart stilled with its mouth hanging open around the civilian's head. He whimpered once and then crawled his way free.

Riony landed easily, standing above the rider.

She glared down at him. "You can consider that a warning. But I'm brimming with the desire to continue beating you to a pulp if you feel the need to fight back."

The rider returned her glare from where he'd fallen. The wideness of surprise and insult in his eyes shifted.

They narrowed with recognition as he took in Riony's defiant stance, her glowing sword, her wild red hair. His gaze flickered to Kess at her back, mounted on her wolf. A smirk twisted his lips.

He bellowed, "Edvin! Kase! It's them. The ones the commander has been waiting for!"

Riony coiled an arm to punch the man into silence, but his voice already echoed through the street.

She turned on the spot to find two more riders emerging from the broken doorways of nearby buildings, their dragons' eyes gleaming in the low light. They spread out, forming a loose circle around Riony and Kess. A ripple of cries spread through the kneeling prisoners.

All three riders wore full armor in silver and red—the king's colors. In the air, riders normally went without helmets, wearing flight goggles only, but both the newcomers had a full head helmet and neck protection. All vulnerable parts of their body were covered.

Riony's eyebrows raised, and she glanced at Kess and the throwing daggers in her hands.

Her reputation precedes her, it seems.

A clatter of scraping and thumping behind Riony signaled the rest of her team descending to street level to join them.

"So much for just one rider." Dashiel didn't sound too upset by the change and pulled a wide, single-edged sword into one hand and a viciously pointy push dagger into their other.

"That's them alright. I'll get backup!" One of the riders broke from the circle, spurring her dragon into a sprint down the street.

"Oh no. We don't want that. Kess?"

A dagger was already flying, but the additional armor proved too effective. The bone plinked away off the rider's back.

Swearing, Riony dashed forward. She grabbed the end of the retreating dragon's tail with one hand. Then she tucked her sword under her arm and latched her other hand on to the dragon's scales as well.

The dragon kept marching forward and Riony dug her feet in against the gutter of the limestone street and strained back the other way. With a fierce growl of effort, she pulled the creature to a stop.

"What the razing—?" The female rider turned back.

With every muscle locked into the hold, Riony saw the second new rider charging toward her too late. A wide maw of pointed teeth moved in, eager to meet with her flesh.

Sailing in from the right, a wall of fur and fury hit the side of the dragon's head, sending it off target.

Riony's breath caught as she watched, and there was a moment when Kess and Griskin hung in midair, a deadly pairing, expressions sharp with fierce determination. Kess's lightning-streaked stormy hair flew back and the constellation on her cheek highlighted the icy beauty of her eyes.

Pulse pounding, Riony's own eyes widened in horror. She swore a steady stream of curses in her head as though she could scold her confused heartbeat back to normal.

Did I just find Kessara Heithorn attractive?

Her heart replied with an even larger *ka-thump* within her chest.

Oooooooh, sparks.

The full-grown gray wolf and the treedart were of similar size, and Griskin wrestled the tamed dragon's head down and away with his teeth around its neck.

The female rider pushed her steed, and the tail slipped. Riony adjusted her grip and held firm again. Sweat trickled down her neck and her muscles burned.

She glanced back, hoping for Aishena or someone to come and deal with the dragon she had by the tail. But the first rider had managed to remount and Aishena, Dashiel, Niskina, and Benjin were occupied with him.

And once that rider's attention was refocused, his victims decided it was time to escape.

Seizing their opportunity, the crowd scattered, running up and down the street. Dodging between Riony's team and the riders, they bumped and scrambled.

A lanky teen tripped over a swiping dragon's tail and slammed into Riony's side. The impact broke Riony's grip and her sword fell to the ground. It was all she could do to catch herself and the crying kid before they ended up hitting the stone street as well.

Now freed, the dragon Riony had been holding back barreled down the road, out of reach, and a moment later, out of sight.

Panting hard, Riony's lips curled. Their chance at keeping their presence quiet just rode away, and they were going to have more trouble any moment now.

A scream filled the air, and Riony hunted for the source. The first rider's dragon had its mouth clamped around Dashiel's arm. Aishena swept in like a hurricane of glowing blades, sending the rider into retreat.

Shiff hung back to the side, mouth glowing with the shimmer of lightning, but unable to get a clear shot.

A burst of fire shot through the crowd, forcing Riony to drop flat onto her stomach to dodge it.

"Careful. Our commander wants them alive." The second rider had a weighted net swinging in one hand as he faced off against Kess and Griskin.

The first rider scoffed. "Capturing them alive was a preference, not an order."

Kess held her knives but didn't send them flying against the near impenetrable armor. She and Griskin stood between her enemy and a clutch of civilians who had been cornered against a wall.

The rider threw the net. Kess met the throw with her own, daggers *thwacking* against the balled weights at the edges, redirecting them enough to tangle the net midair and send it spinning the wrong way to the ground.

Benjin and Shiff tried to move in, but a dart of fire whistled through the air from the treedart's mouth, sending them back again.

It was only two small dragons and riders, but the treedarts were nimble on the ground, harder to pin down and relieve of their riders than the flying riders of Gerichkeep were, especially while trying to keep the innocent people around them safe.

And there would be more on their way soon.

Scooping up her sword, Riony seethed with the feeling she'd made another mistake. But this one wasn't too late to fix.

Aishena had Dashiel behind her and moved as though ready to strike again. Riony ran in between her and the rider she faced, drawing his attention with a swipe of her glowing sword.

"Aish! Take the others and get out of here! I'll stay—"

"I'm not leaving you. I'm with you. Always," Kess snapped.

Huffing, Riony continued. "*Kess and I* will stay to help the remaining people. You know what you have to do."

Niskina shook her head. "Ri—"

"No, I'm not leaving these people."

The air brightened as another dart of fire flew, bursting against the wall above the heads of the huddled crowd. They crouched, crying out as sparks rained over them. Kess swatted at a singed patch of her hair as Griskin bounced side to side in front of the dragon, looking for an opening.

Drawing the summoning stone from her pocket, Riony tossed it back to Aishena.

Hissing in a low voice, she said, "Take it. We'll try to deal with this and catch up. But if we can't ... we'll be the distraction you'll need to make your plan work."

Aishena nodded, her face drawn but resolute.

Supporting Dashiel with one arm, she grabbed Niskina with the other and barked an order to Benjin and Shiff. Then the five of them ran for the shadows.

Neither of the two riders attempted to chase after them. It was clear Riony and Kess were their only targets of value.

Riony backed away from the first rider, bringing herself toward Kess. They faced the two dragons and their riders side by side.

Kess gave Riony a worried glance that made something in her chest twang sharply.

Riony forced a crooked smile. "Come on, we can take these two, easy."

Tutting, Kess turned her eyes back to their enemy. "Maybe, if you can do something smarter than throw yourself and your sword directly at your foe for once."

Riony leaned in closer and said huskily, "Are you calling me … a *one trick Pony?*"

A fierce grin spread across Kess's face. "Wouldn't dream of it."

The cruel first rider had his helmet back on. He kept one hand on his dragon, keeping it under control, and held a long rapier with his other. The second seemed to have given up on his goal of capturing them and now held a spear. Neither seemed to hold enough sense to turn around and run.

Narrowing her eyes on her opponents, Riony shrugged. "I could show you a few new moves."

Bursting into motion again, the rider with the spear rushed Riony. She dove over the swing of his long weapon and rolled to come back up to her feet, her body light with the magic of her sword.

Another *tink* as a bone blade bounced off the other rider's helmet, close to the narrow eye slit. No damage, but enough of a scare to back the man and his dragon away a few steps. Griskin pressed the advantage, snarling and snapping and the two creatures danced around each other.

That gave the people pushed into the corner enough room to run, and in a huddle of helping hands and supportive embraces, the last of them made it free.

Riony's breath grew steadier.

Just us and the riders now.

As the soldier with the spear rounded on her again, Riony took in all the details of his armor. It was almost the same as what she wore, but with the additional neck protection and helmet added as an afterthought. She could see the mismatched buckles over the top of the finer scale mail chest piece.

Riony flicked her crystal blade out, keeping the movement as precise as she could. The crystal sang as it sheered across the rider's shoulder on one side, then she spun and sliced it across on the other as well.

The tip caught under the shoulder guard, popping it off, and then the gorget fell free, leaving the rider's neck exposed.

"All yours," Riony called, ducking under a swing of the man's spear.

White bone blades passed by the side of Riony's face. They pierced the man's padded clothing, side by side above his collarbone. He juddered to a stop, wavered in his saddle, then slumped over his treedart's neck.

The tamed beast continued in its last order, turning on the spot, over and over, with no new order coming to stop it.

A short jet of fire lanced toward Kess as she pulled two new blades. Riony stepped into it, swatting the splash of flame with the flat of her sword. It licked around the edges, heating her face.

"Edvin?" Panic rose in the rider's voice as he noticed his downed companion.

In a swift movement, Riony sheathed her sword, still glowing, and rushed the distracted soldier. Using the float magic of the sword pressed at her back, she leaped across the treedart's back. As she passed the rider, she grabbed him by two fistfuls of scale mail.

She twisted her body in midair and wrenched him from his seat and slammed his body to the ground beneath hers. His helmet clanged as his head hit hard against the stone street.

He coughed one rough, wheezing breath, then stilled.

Blood welled between Riony's fingers where they remained clamped around his dragon scale armor. She gave the man a gentle shake, but he didn't move again. A glazed, bloodshot stare met hers through the thin slit of his helmet.

She jumped up to her feet, backing away until she came up against warm fur and a small body.

Spinning around, she found herself nose to nose with Kess.

"Are you …?" Kess searched Riony's face, glancing between her and the downed rider. "It's okay. Just breathe. You're okay."

"I didn't mean to …"

The circling dragon, turning around and around on the spot without its rider, drew Riony's eye. Both riders were just as dead. As all who had faced them at Gerichkeep were.

It wasn't getting any easier, knowing she had become a killer. That this was what the world had made her. That part of her wanted it, relished in paying back the pain to those who inflicted it on others. Her thoughts spiraled and collided painfully in a racket of screaming confusion.

The touch of warm fingers to her cheek drew Riony back to reality, and to Kess.

Kess held her stare. "We did what we had to."

Riony pressed her lips firmly together, took a shaky breath, and nodded once. "Come on. Let's catch up to the others."

It took one more long breath as she stared into Kess's eyes before Riony found she could move again.

When she turned away and took a step to leave, another form slithered in around the corner. A dragon, larger than any of the treedarts they just faced.

Its scales glistened with an eerie frost-like sheen.

Riony and Kess exchanged a grim look, their sides pressed together as more riders emerged, blocking both ends of the street and guarding every rooftop. There was no way out.

The white dragon strode into the space it was too large for. Its wings scraped the buildings on either side as it thumped heavy claws on the ground.

Riony tightened her grip around the hilt of her sword and pointed it at the dragon's chest. It came to a stop.

From atop the snowflame, the helmeted rider spread his arms wide in a welcoming gesture. "And here you both are."

There was no mistaking the voice of Kife Heithorn.

Riony shot a look at Kess. "Have we found ourselves at an impasse? Because I'm looking at someone who is both an imp and an ass."

Kife snapped back, "What you're looking at is your overdue ending, slave."

"You're overdue to go eat a flaming dick, Kife."

Kife's voice sounded so satisfied Riony wished she could scrub it out of his throat with a wire brush. "I knew you idiots would take the bait, but I didn't expect it to be this entertaining."

Rolling her shoulders, Riony glared back. "We always knew it was a trap. You're the one who never realized that you're a worm."

Kife pushed his snow-white dragon so that it lowered its belly to the ground and brought him close in front of Riony's eyes.

He crooned. "Oh, it was a trap alright. But it wasn't a trap *for you*."

CHAPTER TWENTY-THREE

"**W**hat do you mean, gone?"

Despite being a hushed whisper, Eslinde's voice carried over to where Lyrrin sat with Elumon, having just calmed the little hatchling to sleep. Curled up within the same stall, Dracuni lifted her head at the sounds of the conversation. It seemed both her and Lyrrin were straining to listen in.

Yensen leaned close to his princess's ear. "Thallan and Samor are nowhere within sight."

"They gave us their word they would stay on watch until the others returned. You don't think they …?" Fury flashed in Eslinde's silver eyes. Then she shook her head. "Maybe they saw something, danger they needed to go and assess or lead away? Surely, they wouldn't leave Norallei's dragon behind. Or leave us in such a precarious situation without reason."

Yensen made a noncommittal sound, eyes narrowing. "Whatever the reason, they are gone. Leaving us with only Iffyr, Dracuni, who can't and shouldn't be out flying, and Viska, who is still refusing a rider."

Vance moved away from Viska's stall, where he had been in a tense, silent conversation with the newly untamed gold dragon, as he spent most of his time recently. "Given the way she feels, we're lucky she's chosen to remain with us at all. I'll take Iffyr out on watch."

Eslinde nodded and touched her hand to his arm as he passed her to mount the white shimmerdart. "Thank you. Hopefully what you'll see is Thallan and Samor returning safe."

Vance returned a thin-lipped smile. Pushing the tamed dragon into motion, he left, followed by Yensen, sent by the princess to check on the new refugees from the undercity.

Lyrrin pressed a hand to her chest where the paired heart stone hung under her clothes. She knew she should be worried about the two Rebel Riders leaving and that they no longer had a working gateway to escape from if they ended up penned in.

But all she could think about was the pounding, rampant beat of her sister's heart.

She's fighting. She's fighting hard.

Lyrrin could only imagine what Riony might be facing, but she tried not to because it always became too terrible. She imagined her sister and friends burned in dragonfire. She imagined them rounded up and captured by an army of one hundred riders. She imagined that the altered dragon summoning rune she'd given them didn't work or, worse, backfired in some way which hurt her family.

She hadn't had time to test it, and despite reassurances from the Alderkin that it should only effect tamed dragons, exactly what it would do was unknown and created a deep well of worry in Lyrrin.

Screwing her eyes closed, Lyrrin focused on the pulse beating through the stone. It was still beating. That's what mattered.

Soft scales bumped up against her cheek.

Dracuni nudged her and made a soft thrumming sound.

"You're worried too, aren't you?" she replied, patting the unidragon's cheek.

"I'm sure it will all be okay." Eslinde floated over, back straight and smiling, but her thin fingers tangled and fidgeted in front of her.

She wore her gown today, the only one she had left her palace home with. Some days she wore the plain military uniforms available in the stores, but most often, she had remained in that same dress. The shimmering silver fabric looked more gray and flat now, as was the princess's tone.

Lyrrin's lips twisted at her mother's empty words. She had felt like this when the others had helped the enclaves and attacked the dragonkeep. Left behind to wait on news of whether those she loved survived.

But now she felt even worse. Riony and the others would be in an enclosed space, underground, with no dragons of their own but up against who knows how many others. And also up against Kife and his cruelty.

Her clawed fingers formed a fist. "You don't know that things will be okay. You don't know what Kife is like. He has no honor or goodness at all. He was more than happy to try to burn me or Benjin with his dragon's fire the first time we met!"

Eslinde knelt in front of Lyrrin and reached out to touch her cheek. "He tried to burn children? You shouldn't have even been in such a situation. How you've even remained alive, I don't know."

Lyrrin pulled away from her touch. "I'm not just a child. I was the one who saved the others that time. And now I'm not getting the chance to help at all. Not since *you* arrived."

Eslinde gasped. "I'm just trying to keep you safe."

"We're supposed to keep each other safe! That's how we've stayed alive so long, because we protect each other and trust each other. All of us."

Eslinde withdrew her hand, staring at Lyrrin with saddened eyes for a long moment. She shifted backward, sitting on her heels.

When she spoke again, her voice was low. "I'm sorry. I suppose I've never known that sort of trust. I grew up surrounded by lies and cunning."

Lyrrin swallowed her anger at the sight of her mother's pain. The few times she had tried to find out what life had been like for her as a princess, her questions had been waved away with a polite smile and a response of, "Much as you'd expect."

Eslinde's head tilted to the side, and she smiled, although without joy, her gaze on the ground.

"For a long while I thought myself clever, good at reading when someone was lying to me or not. But the truth was all I needed to do was assume everyone was lying about something, and it was always true."

When she looked back up at Lyrrin, her silver irises were flooded with a wash of tears. She reached out for Lyrrin's ungloved hands, and Lyrrin didn't pull away.

Eslinde squeezed her fingers gently in her own.

"Even now, with more allies than I've ever had at my side, I feel as though anyone could betray me at any moment and all I want is for you to be safe, for you to have a world you can live safely in. I'm sorry if I've been overprotective. But I grieved you as dead for so many years, and I couldn't bear to lose you again."

Lyrrin's nose stung with the threat of tears, and she wrinkled it. "I don't want to lose you either."

Lyrrin reached up to hug her mother, but the thump of heavy claws on stone turned her away. Vance returned on the white dragon, racing into the stables.

He slid down from the saddle with a speed that cracked his prosthetic leg against the floor, and he winced as he staggered their way. The tamed dragon remained still in the center of the wide space.

Lyrrin liked Vance. He had let her carve a little swirl of runes and patterns into the wood of his leg, even though it would do nothing.

But she didn't like the look on his face as he rushed toward them.

"There are dragons, coming in to land now."

Carefully moving Elumon's sleepy head off her lap, Lyrrin stood up. "Is it Riony and the others? Are they back already?"

Dracuni perked up at that, lilac eyes bright as she awaited the answer.

Vance shook his head and gave Eslinde a dark look.

"Thallan and Samor returned?" she asked.

Vance grunted. "No. They came in from the east, directly our way. Ten dragons with riders. I hadn't even gotten off the ground before I saw them."

"Coming in to land? Now?" Eslinde lunged to her feet.

"I've already closed and locked the outer entrance from inside."

"We've been found? How? Even if Thallan or Samor had betrayed us, surely the attack wouldn't have come so soon."

Lyrrin looked from Dracuni to Elumon to Eslinde, Vance, and Viska. They had all feared this day since they fled the first round of the Dragon King's riders. But for it to be upon them now seemed unreal.

And for it to be upon them now, while Riony was gone, left Lyrrin shaking.

Eslinde pressed her hands to her temples and then smoothed down her pale hair. "The defenses are solid. That will buy us some time. But with no gateway ... And so many more people to feed now with those who came in from the undercity."

Lyrrin said, "The others might get back soon. They might be able to chase them away."

Eslinde sent a small, fluttering smile her way, then began moving, marching for the exit of the stables room. "We must barricade the entrance, build it up even stronger, and then make a list of our food and resources, begin rationing."

Lyrrin hurried to her side. She slipped her hand into her mother's.

As they reached the door, Yensen appeared there. His expression was flat and calculating.

Eslinde gave a small sigh of relief. "Yensen, there are dragons—"

"I know." The grayglim took two large steps forward, right into Lyrrin's path.

His arm lashed around her shoulders and pulled her with him. Surprised, Lyrrin's fingers slid free from Eslinde's and she was turned around in the grayglim's rough grip.

He pinned her with her back against him and a blade pressed to her throat. "Get those hands of yours up and out in front of you, now."

Gasping, Lyrrin lifted her arms, holding them out.

"Yensen!" Eslinde shrieked his name. "What are you doing?"

"Following orders, Your Highness." He moved Lyrrin with him as he took careful steps toward the stalls holding the dragons.

Viska's golden eyes tracked them, confused and narrowed. In the middle of the room, the white dragon, tamed, gave no reaction at all.

"Orders? Who's orders? I ..." Eslinde's words trailed off and her face turned a sickly pale green.

"My orders have always come from a higher place." Yensen brought Lyrrin to a stop in front of the stall holding Dracuni and Elumon.

Dracuni growled long and low, waking the smaller dragon.

The hatchling blinked sleepy eyes, and his confusion and worry washed over Lyrrin.

Eslinde's head was shaking wildly, her usual composure completely gone. "But you've been with us all this time. You helped us escape."

"I did what had to be done to reach the target." He gave Lyrrin a sharp squeeze and she squeaked, making it clear the target he meant.

"And when it became clear there was a secondary and more important target, I did what had to be done to bide my time until both were ready to be taken. And since my plan to remove your ability to flee through the gateway worked, the time has come."

Lyrrin's fear shifted into something darker. "You did that? You had the undercity attacked, just so the gateway would run out of charge?"

The grayglim ignored her. The knife came off her throat just long enough for it to be waved Dracuni's way. "You're coming with us."

Dracuni rose up to full height, her teeth bared as she took a lunging step forward. Lyrrin edged her hands in toward her belt and the crystals it held.

But the blade was already back against Lyrrin's flesh, and it pressed closer. The bite of the sharp edge made her flinch, and she put her hands up again.

Yensen's voice above Lyrrin's head was emotionless. "Behave, both of you. And the rest of you stay back too, or the child's blood is on you."

Eslinde clutched Vance's arm for support. "Yensen, please. She's my daughter."

"She's the target and has been since I was assigned to you. Be grateful that my orders as to what to do with the target changed. Now you will let me leave with her and the silvernix dragon."

Yensen skirted around, dragging Lyrrin with him and with Dracuni following afterward. The unidragon stalked slowly, worried eyes locked on Lyrrin.

Vance and Eslinde backed away as they reached the door. Yensen leaned his head through the threshold, checking the way ahead.

And Vance rushed at them. He cleared the few steps' gap in one giant stride. Lyrrin tugged at Yensen's hold, trying to get clear, but he held tight.

Only his blade moved, flashing in the torchlight as it struck out.

Vance stilled, hanging there from the end of Yensen's arm for a moment before he stumbled backward.

"Vance!" Eslinde grasped for him, and as his weight hit hers, she fell along with him to the floor.

He groaned and curled on his side, blood pooling beneath him.

Then a larger growl overtook the room. Behind Vance, Viska loomed over him and Eslinde, golden scales shimmering and a hot glow building in her throat.

"No, she'll burn them all." Eslinde tugged at her dress, pinned beneath Vance's bulk.

Vance coughed once, then rolled onto his hands and knees. He slipped, coming back onto his stomach.

He cried out in pain, then bellowed, "Viska, no!"

The golden dragon hissed, teeth bared and eyes sharp with fury. But the glow of her flame receded.

But a rush of rage hit Lyrrin, and for a moment she wondered if it was from Viska herself. Until Elumon charged in. The hatchling snapped and bit at Yensen's ankles, small teeth pinching at the leather of his boots.

With a grumble of annoyance, Yensen kicked the dragonling away.

Pain, pain! Elumon whimpered, curling up against a wall.

Lyrrin screamed and lashed her own hands at the man. Her sharp claws met his cheek and drew four red lines along it. He glared back, unwavering as he locked her neck in his hand and aimed the tip of his bloodied blade up under her chin.

"Enough! You're only my secondary target now, child. Don't test me again!"

Eslinde sat with Vance's head on her lap, lolling lifelessly. Her shoulders shook. She was mouthing Lyrrin's name, but no sound came out.

With a harsh tug, Yensen pulled Lyrrin toward Norallei's dragon, but Viska moved between them and the tamed dragon with a warning snarl.

Yensen stilled for a moment, then muttered, "We've our own dragons waiting outside anyway."

He backed away out into the hall and barked at Dracuni to keep following them.

The unidragon's chest heaved as she trailed after them toward the exit.

Reaching the final barrier, Yensen turned to work the locks. Lyrrin looked back down the tunnel, to where Vance might die without Dracuni's help, to where the dragonling she was responsible for lay hurt. To where her mother would be left, grieving for her again.

All because she was a target? She didn't even know what that meant or why.

Figures moved in the low light at the other end of the hall. The three Alderkin, walking toward them, and then slowing as they took in the situation.

Yensen made a show of the dagger at Lyrrin's neck, and the Alderkin stilled. Then the grayglim took Lyrrin and Dracuni out into the open air, where ten dragons surrounded the entrance, awaiting them.

Chapter Twenty-Four

Through their rush to arrive at the undercity and the fighting since, Riony hadn't spared a thought for the paired crystal hanging at her chest. She had barely felt the pulse of her sister's small heartbeat below the raging drum of her own.

But as Kife's words settled over her, the flutter against her chest grew and grew, thumping in panic. The stone rattled where it hung from her necklace next to the acorn pendant.

It wasn't a trap for you.

Now she understood what it had been like for Lyrrin all those times, feeling a loved one's fear from a distance, knowing they were in danger and unable to reach them.

Riony didn't know something could hurt so much.

"What have you done?" Riony roared.

Kife touched a gloved hand to his chest. "Me? All I'm doing is collecting my reward—you two, and anything I want to do with you. Another close ally of our king, sun bless him, came up with this wonderful plan and will probably be capturing the real prize right now."

The real prize. Dracuni. *I never should have left them.*

Another close ally of the king … Riony's mind raced, trying to work out who would betray them. It could be anyone. She cursed herself for how trusting she'd been.

The hairs up the back of her neck twinged and she shot a glance back at Kess, half expecting her to declare it was her plan, then go and join her awful brother again. But Kess held firm at Riony's back.

And Lyrrin's heart beat like a trapped rabbit through the stone.

At Riony's desperate expression, Kife only laughed, a muted echo from under his helmet. The sound demolished all of Riony's restraint. She rushed at the vile man.

He shifted, bringing his dragon standing tall again, and Riony came up against the hard plates of the snowflame's chest. She dodged to the side to avoid colliding into the bulk of the beast, ducking under its trunk-like neck.

Riony knew this was a fight she couldn't win, but that last scrap of sense was buried deep under a desire to inflict a mountain of pain upon Kife for having any part in what was happening to Dracuni and Lyrrin.

There were too many dragons, too many riders, all too well armored. Fighting back was reckless and stupid and utterly a terrible idea in all ways and Kess followed Riony right into the brawl without hesitation.

Riony surged forward again. Maybe they could at least hold Kife and his riders' attention long enough for the others to free the delvers and regain control of the undercity.

She pounced to the side, stepping onto the forearm of Kife's snowflame and vaulting up its shoulder.

Her weightless leap brought her eye level with Kife, and as her sword arced toward him, his eyes widened through the narrow slit of his helmet.

Then pain shot up Riony's leg and she was tugged away, her sword tip passing a hair's breadth in front of Kife's face.

Sharp teeth clamped around her ankle and Riony was pulled from the air and thrown to the ground like a wet rag. She cried out as her back hit the street, armor clattering.

One treedart had her foot in its mouth, and another two were approaching from her sides. With her free leg, she kicked the small dragon in the snout with all her strength. Once, twice, and then its teeth slipped free, tearing along her boot as they went.

Riony rolled left as the dragon on one side snapped its jaw at her sword hand, then rolled right as the dragon on the other side bit for her shoulder. She scrambled backward, gritting her teeth at the sharp zings of pain shooting from her bleeding ankle.

Riony rose crookedly to her feet to face the three soldiers on treedarts bearing down on her. Her eyes wildly sought Kess, sought the comfort of knowing the wolf rider had her back.

But Kess was busy with her own assault.

She and Griskin were on the other side of the large snowflame and surrounded by five smaller dragons and riders. The wolf dodged and danced between the snapping jaws on all sides. Kess kept herself low to his back, churning through her supply of throwing knives in a hail of attacks.

Bone blades flew, clinked against armor, and scattered on the ground. Then one of the riders and dragons suddenly stilled, the white end of a blade protruding from the thin slit in the helmet.

That fine shot gave Kess some more room as the other riders surrounding her and Griskin hesitated and backed off.

But Kife on his snowflame did not. The white dragon's chest heaved and its head swung toward the wolf rider.

Riony's heart rammed against her chest as Kife's dragon ejected a river of white-hot liquid flame across the street where Griskin had been.

"Kess!" Riony raised an arm over her face to block the wave of heat and glare of the lightning-bright inferno.

She could only look for a moment before using her sword to block the next attack from the treedarts in front of her. She couldn't see whether those liquid flames had swallowed Kess within them. Jaws snapped the air around her and she roared ferally as she batted their snouts away, desperate to see signs of life beyond the fire.

Through the flickering burn, shadows moved. Someone screamed—a man's voice. A treedart and rider stumbled out, globs of molten liquid searing them all over, as they gurgled in pain through their last moments.

Kess had been there, right in there as well. Is she …?

The shadows shifted again, then Griskin leaped free, over the wall of shimmering white flame. Kess remained safe on his back.

Riony felt no relief. Only a heavy, suffocating realization of how much she didn't want to lose Kess and how there was still far too much risk of that happening.

Kife kept his dragon's head aimed for his sister who was pushed into a corner with a fall of limestone curtain blocking behind her.

The snowflame opened its mouth wide again, but nothing happened.

"Come on, get her!" Kife snapped, slapping his hands against the tamed dragon's neck.

It convulsed as though breathing but no more liquid flame emerged. It moved sluggishly, pain and weakness clear in the droop of its neck, wings, and shoulders. The snowflame made a wheezing, hacking sound and shook its head, spattering droplets of liquid flame across the street.

One landed on Riony's hand and seared right through the leather of the glove. She hissed, trying to wipe it away.

Kess glared up at Kife with raw disdain. "You've already burned your dragon out? You never did deserve to be a rider."

"Still a better rider than you'll ever be." Kife growled, and his dragon spun in a tight, swift circle beneath him.

The tail lashed out, swiping through the air. It caught Kess in the chest and sent her flying off Griskin. She rolled along the stone street, each bump knocking a gasping cry from her.

She tumbled to a stop right up beside the wall of fire and didn't move. The roasting heat caused thin trails of smoke to rise from Kess as she lay alongside it.

"Kess!" Riony willed Kess to move. She had to get away from there or she was going to be cooked.

Why isn't she moving? She can't be ... She's only here because of me. She's only hurt because of me.

Riony pressed her attack against the three dragons keeping her busy, trying to push past them and get to Kess. She thrust through a gap and struck one rider with her sword, but another sent a jet of orange flame her way. It scorched along the side of her head and Riony smelled burnt hair.

Griskin howled, jumping between the treedarts that penned him in, also pushing in Kess's direction.

"Kill that damned mutt already," Kife ordered lazily.

Kess stirred then, lifting onto her elbows.

She rasped. "Gris, run. Run! Go find the others."

The wolf's growl lightened to a whimper. A hot dart of fire shot his way and he skittered clear of it, gave Kess one more look, then switched direction and pounced clear over the heads of the riders on that side.

A couple of them chased him down the street.

Kess coughed and rolled herself away from the baking dragonflame. But she was down and injured, with only a few knives left on her.

The stench of singed hair filled Riony's nose, her temple and cheek hot, blobby flares of light burning in her vision. She turned in a wide swing to bring another rider off their steed, then lunged through the gap.

Dashing between swiping tails and snapping jaws, Riony reached Kess's side just as another burst of flame splashed across her back. Her scale armor heated but kept her flesh protected from the treedart's fire.

Still, the impact stunned her enough that she tripped on her injured foot. She was staggering when Kife brought his dragon around again and its tail knocked her sword from her hand. It clinked and rolled out of reach.

Riony grunted out her frustration and pain and turned around to square up against Kife and the army of dragons around her. She raised her empty hands and closed them into fists.

"What are you doing? Get out of here!" Kess hissed up from the ground.

She breathed in short, clipped breaths and blood dripped from her lips.

Riony scanned around, but there wasn't a single opening she could break through as the dragons closed in tighter. Not with her injured ankle. Not without her sword.

And even if she could, there was no way she was leaving Kess behind.

Kife lifted his helmet off, smiling down with glittering eyes at his prey. "On your knees."

Riony returned a brash smile. "I would never kneel for someone who looks like they cry when they masturbate."

With a flick of the chin from Kife, the rider closest swung the flat of his sword into the backs of Riony's legs and they folded. She cracked down onto her knees with an *oomph*.

Kife said, "Get these two in chains. We've only just begun having our fun with them."

Four riders dismounted and drew manacles from their saddlebags. One approached where Kess lay on her side, dodging a flying knife before stilling her with a swift boot to the stomach.

The other three came for Riony. She tried to stand back up but her knees had hit the stone in a way that they weren't happy about at all.

It was all she could do to land one last punch. She hit square into one rider's chest, sending him stumbling back, before the other two caught her arms and brought them in front of her.

The heavy, cold steel clicked closed around her wrists.

Riony set her jaw, glaring at the soldiers as they patted her and Kess down, taking away all remaining daggers and weapons.

Riony's eyes narrowed as she looked at the pile of discarded bone daggers on the ground. The cutting athame she'd given Kess wasn't there.

She must have it hidden somewhere. Riony tried to hide how impressed she was by that.

It was pretty easy when Kife was watching her with a smug smile and her face could only twist in disgust in response.

He flicked his head, gesturing from Riony to Kess. "You. *Carry her.*"

Riony snorted hot air from her nose. She'd carried Kess a few times recently, voluntarily even—which still felt weird. But to be ordered to do so by a Heithorn left her skin crawling.

But she feared Kess's treatment in someone else's hands more than she hated following

Kife's orders.

Groaning, Riony brought one aching knee up. She leaned over where Kess was still balled up from the kick she'd taken.

"No. You don't have to," Kess whispered.

"I know," Riony whispered back and scooped her manacled hands under Kess.

Kess had always been much smaller than Riony, even though only a year younger. But she'd always seemed too heavy when she was a weight Riony was forced to carry.

Now, as Riony lifted her in her arms, she didn't seem to weigh a thing.

Both of them tensed, sore and bloodied, as Riony brought them painfully to her feet.

Kife beamed. "Good girl, just like the dumb beast you are."

Through blood-tinted teeth, Kess said softly, "Don't listen to him."

Riony smirked. "Listen to what? I can't hear dead men."

Kife rattled out orders, sending half his troops off to find the rest of Riony's friends and the other half to march with him, flanking their prisoners.

The point of a sword at her back got Riony moving as Kife led them through the empty streets.

Riony's body hummed with the hammering of three heartbeats. Her own, Lyrrin's through the paired stone, and Kess's where they pressed together.

Every step was a lesson in how much pain she could withstand, as her knees howled and ankle stung and wrists twisted awkwardly within the sharp-edged manacles to keep Kess supported.

Riony settled into that agony, embraced it, because no matter what Kife's plans for them were, she knew it would only get worse.

Their slow parade moved out from the narrow pathways into the Grand Arch markets where stalls and carts had been upended. Broken crystals lay scattered amid a burst sack of flour and tangled fabric.

A hushed murmur came from ahead, and people came into view. A huge crowd, tightly packed into a clear area at the lower side of Sinking Stream Lake.

It seemed as though half the undercity community kneeled there, surrounded by dragons. They seemed tired and overwrought, as though they'd been trapped there under threat of dragonfire since the initial attack.

As Kife led them around the edges of the crowd and up the stairs, almost all eyes tracked Riony.

They were faces she knew. Some from her time in the undercity and those she'd helped reach the undercity from her time aboveground. Those who came here for refuge after the enclaves were attacked.

The dour-faced man from the Orphans' Den who had given Riony candy after she'd returned the stolen kids. A red-bearded man who had given Riony an extra serving of rice at Myrwa's camp. The small, craggy woman and her children who Riony had warned away from the rough settlement.

I've failed them all. None of them found safety.

It wasn't judgment, though, that filled the people's eyes. But worry. And beneath that, a simmering flicker of rage.

"I brought a little something from home. What do you think?"

Kife's voice turned Riony's attention away from the crowd, and her blood went cold.

Along the central platform—the flat-topped limestone plateau beside the tiered wall of the lake, where market-day performances were often held—stood the Heithorn estate whipping post.

The thick beam of wood was charred black up one side, but still appeared solid. Riony could imagine exactly how solid it was. She knew. She could remember. She'd bucked and pulled against that timber so many times trying to free herself from the lash of a whip, but it never granted her mercy.

"Hook them up," Kife commanded, looking like a child on a gifting day. "We are all going to enjoy the public execution of these criminals today."

Riony could only stare back. Could only hope Aishena and the others would put a stop to what was going to be a humiliating and painful death.

Kife's dragon slinked closer, and he lowered his voice. "But I think I'm going to enjoy it the most. You were always the most fun of all our slaves to whip. How you could take a lashing! And I always wondered just how many strikes it would take before you broke. Before your body simply gave in and died. Now we're going to find out."

Chapter Twenty-Five

Lyrrin lifted her chin and scowled defiantly at the king's riders surrounding the entrance to Eslindekeep's underground base. Her arms ached as she kept her hands lifted in front of her, but anytime they dropped, the blade at her neck pressed closer.

Dracuni stood back at a distance specified by the grayglim, so that he remained out of reach of her claws or bite. Her nostrils flared as she growled. But Lyrrin knew there was little the unidragon could do from that distance. Her breath did not burn; it only healed.

Low clouds darkened the day and a light fall of snow left Lyrrin chilled. She wasn't dressed to be outside. She had her hooded coat on, but no shoes, and hadn't been wearing her gloves for a while. Her fingers already ached from the cold, and she didn't know what Yensen intended to do with her next.

The grayglim marched forward, his grip ironclad on Lyrrin's arm.

"I have the ones our king wants. All has gone as promised," he announced.

One of the riders, with intricately braided black hair and dark, calculating eyes, replied, "Not quite. You said there would be no dragons left here when we came in, but we had to lure off a couple that were on patrol with two of our own. I thought grayglims were supposed to be better than allowing a mistake like that."

Yensen stilled, and his voice had the brittle sharpness of someone unable to believe their authority would be challenged. "My plan has still succeeded. You'd have had no luck digging our quarry out of its hole without me."

The rider, sitting atop a huge yellow dragon, only huffed. He squinted at Dracuni. "What sort of strange dragon is that anyway?"

"One our king will be pleased to receive. Now, give me your steed."

The two men locked gazes for a long moment, then the rider sniffed lazily and climbed down from the saddle. "Of course. I'll ride with another."

One of the other riders tossed Yensen some flight goggles, then Yensen yanked Lyrrin toward the yellow dragon.

He was really going to take her away. Away from her friends, her mother, from any chance of seeing Riony return safe from whatever was making her heart beat a manic percussion.

Yensen pulled the knife away and readjusted his hold, grasping Lyrrin under the armpits to push her up onto the dragon's saddle.

"No!" she shrieked.

Feral panic ignited within her and she bucked and screamed, writhing in his grip. She arched her back and kicked her feet into Yensen's legs. His hold didn't falter.

She cried, her voice raw with desperation, "Dracuni, run! Fly! You've got to get away!"

Dracuni spread her wings and ran. Penned in as she was by the ring of larger dragons, there was nowhere to go, and her wings flapped helplessly, unable to catch the wind. She remained grounded, panting and cowering between the larger beasts.

Ignoring her struggles, Yensen hoisted Lyrrin onto the dragon and secured her in front of him on the saddle. He took the reins and signaled the dragon to take off. With a powerful beat of wide, leathery wings, the dragon lifted from the ground.

Hovering there amid a swirl of snowflakes and dust, the yellow beast snatched Dracuni in its talons, lifting her effortlessly along with them. Dracuni whined and her tail whipped, but she was pinned within the cage of claws.

Yensen leaned over Lyrrin from behind and undid her belt. He pulled it free with a sharp tug, then tossed it and all of the crystals it contained away into the air.

Lyrrin wriggled but his hold on her remained firm. He grasped her with one hand as he pulled his goggles on with the other.

"There's nowhere for you to run now, child. Stop squirming. Consider yourself lucky you're wanted alive."

Lyrrin growled, "You're the one who'll be lucky to be alive when Riony finds out what you've done. She's going to smash you into jelly!"

Around them, the other nine dragons lifted from the ground as well, following them skyward.

"Best if you give up hopes of seeing your sister again now. I doubt she'll survive the trap laid for her."

Lyrrin refused to believe that, and the man's assumption only made her angry. "A trap you helped lay! We trusted you. How could you?"

"I'm following my king's orders, and there is no higher honor. I only remained with Eslinde so that if and when she ever found you again, I could finish the job of killing her child."

She tried to stay strong, but knowing her death had been wanted for so long wasn't a good feeling.

She whimpered, "Why?"

Yensen pulled a length of cord from a pocket and bound Lyrrin's wrists together, then fastened them to the front of the saddle. "Because you're a half-breed abomination that the king wanted erased."

Tears reappeared in Lyrrin's eyes, freezing there in the blast of the icy wind. She felt chilled right through in her thin clothes as they ascended higher.

With Lyrrin secure, Yensen took the reins again. "But after I reported back about the silvernix dragon, the king had me watching you both and holding my cover. Lucky for you he decided having someone who could perform Alderkin magic but pass as human was more valuable than cleaning up Eslinde's mess."

Lyrrin wrenched at her bound hands, trying to curl her sharp fingers into the twine, but she was stuck fast. They had lifted directly upward toward the gray clouds, and Eslindekeep was a small stamp of patchwork beneath them.

Yensen turned the yellow dragon to the east, when something flashed far below.

A golden streak, bursting at speed from the base tunnel.

Viska emerged and rushed into the sky, roaring with fury. Dracuni cried a sad yelp in return.

Yensen swore, then muttered, "I didn't think that sulking beast would be a problem."

"Looks like you made her angry." Wind buffeted Lyrrin's eyes, making it hard to see, and she squinted, tracking the shooting-star of golden scales.

Not just Viska, but Viska with riders. They shot vertically toward them, closing space quickly. Five figures rode together along her back.

Lyrrin's heart jolted with the spark of hope.

Unless any of the undercity refugees could fly, that was Vance, Eslinde, and the Alderkin. Considering Viska hadn't even allowed Vance to ride her since she was untamed, Lyrrin doubted it could be anyone else.

Vance is okay!

Lyrrin didn't know how but was happy to see him still alive and able to fly, and they were coming after her.

Yensen gestured a few signals to the other king's riders, and they peeled off from their positions around the grayglim's dragon, heading back toward Viska. Yensen pushed the yellow to fly faster and kept to their eastward heading.

Lyrrin angled around to watch behind them, holding her breath.

Viska's golden scales blazed against the pale backdrop. She roared as the riders reached her, blocking her path. The sky became a tangle of tails and wings, weaving, darting, chasing.

Viska had the advantage. She was fast and nimble and able to react with her own mind, compared to the slower tamed dragons that relied on orders from their riders. But with nine versus one, Viska was harried from every angle, unable to break through.

A burst of bright light cut through the battle, and two riders backed off.

Flash stones. The Alderkin are helping!

The battle of dragons shimmered and swirled in the air like colorful flags buffeted by wind. Viska flamed, catching a rider off guard and sending them spiraling. Then another rider caught Viska's tail in their dragon's claws, pulling her away from the group.

Another bright flash of a midair explosion went off. A burst stone shattered, showering the air with ember-hot shards. It echoed like thunder and Viska broke free.

But all the while Yensen took Lyrrin and Dracuni farther and farther away.

Then, from the horizon, two more dragons appeared. Thallan, riding his bronze etherdart Brunzell, and Samor on his black and gold flamesong Shani, dove into the fray.

Brunzell moved at an incredible speed and reached the battle first, his shooting fireballs scattering the enemy.

Lyrrin smiled. The Rebel Riders hadn't abandoned them. They'd only been led away by the king's riders, who they must have defeated. And they'd come back to help. But her smile faltered as Samor and Shani joined the fight as well.

The flamesong unleashed her massive torrents of flame against the king's riders, taking three of them out in one blast. Both riders and dragons fell to the earth, burning. Lyrrin gasped, mouth hanging open, the horrific sight scorched into her eyes.

The sky was clearer now, and the two new riders had balanced the battle, but neither of them seemed interested in pursuing Yensen.

They focused their attack on the king's riders.

Only Viska separated out, chasing after the yellow dragon, bringing the fight with her.

The crisp air filled with the smell of smoke and charred flesh and Yensen grunted, pushing the yellow to fly faster, but with its burden of Dracuni, it seemed to have reached its limit.

One of the swifter king's riders caught up to Viska again, causing the gold dragon to loop around and backtrack to get away from a volley of fireballs.

Yensen turned to watch too then, a grim look on his face as a woman's scream reached them through the air.

Lyrrin bit her lip, and Yensen sucked in a sharp breath too.

He had spent so long pretending to be working to keep the princess alive, maybe he cared more than he thought?

"It's not too late to turn around. We could go back, help them. They would forgive you," Lyrrin said.

Yensen's reply was dry and rough. "They made their own decision to come after us into the fight. They will face the consequences."

Lyrrin wrenched her arms against where they were tied, trying to break free so she could show the grayglim some of his own consequences, but the bindings remained tight. Her fingers grew cold and numb.

Viska flew like a streak of lightning, leading the dragon on her tail in a race through the clouds.

Come on, come on! You can beat them.

Thallan and Brunzell kept occupied trading blasts of fireballs between them and the king's riders, and Samor and Shani had been forced downward by a pair of blue dragons working together.

In a move more elegant than any of the tamed dragon's could achieve, Shani arched upward in a full loop, coming up over the battle and back in behind her pursuers, catching them in her enormous jet of flame.

But one of Thallan's combatants had broken off from his group and snuck up behind them.

Lyrrin gasped as a fireball struck directly onto Shani's back, between her wings. The black and gold scales came away singed, but otherwise unhurt.

But Samor, who had been riding on that back, fell.

His arms and legs waved limply as his body tumbled in the air, trailing smoke, and Shani dived for him. The flamesong dragon caught her rider in her claws.

There was a moment of stillness as Shani glided clear of the rest of the battle.

Then Shani roared. The sound filled the air, a terrible wailing howl of grief that seemed to reach from horizon to horizon. It started low, then turned high and pitiful with the pain of mourning.

Lyrrin let out her own small whimper, her mouth open and eyes watering.

Then Shani's roar changed again, growing stronger, and she launched herself back into the center of the battle. There were four king's riders remaining, swerving between Brunzell and Viska, and Shani brought herself to hover in the middle.

She bellowed a deep, painful, grumbling sound, and her chest seemed to expand. She barked that noise again, growing larger, glowing brighter, the shimmer of flames showing around her neck and chest but not emerging from her throat.

Viska seemed to understand what was coming and turned to flee. But too slow.

Shani exploded.

Lyrrin's mouth snapped wide open and her whole face stung with the anguish of what she'd just seen. The explosion was blinding, a churning mass of rushing flame that filled the sky and blew apart clouds. Even from their distance away, the shock wave smacked Lyrrin like a physical blow.

And somewhere within that explosion was Viska and those she carried.

CHAPTER TWENTY-SIX

Kess had become so still in Riony's arms that she had to look down to see if she was still breathing.

Kess stared back with eyes round and pale as a full moon. Filled with a kind of fear Riony had never seen the stubborn young woman express before.

"Hey, it's okay," Riony whispered through a half smile. "This isn't my first time, you know. I'm an old hand at this. I'll be fine."

Kess's head shook in a small jittery motion.

The intensity of Kess's expression made Riony frown. "Don't worry. I'll handle it as long as I have to handle it. You just focus on being ready when the others show up to save the day."

"No." Kess's voice trembled, and her breath came fast. "I can't see you hurt like that again. I won't."

Riony's mouth opened to reply, but her throat felt like it had been clogged by her heart. She managed a weak, "Kess ..."

Then a soldier pulled Kess out of Riony's arms. Riony tried to hold on, but her manacled wrists had no purchase and had left her fingers deadened.

Two more soldiers came up behind Riony and grabbed her arms, lifting them up to hang the manacles over one of the steel hooks at the top of the post.

She resisted, straining against them, and they shoved her face-first into the whipping post. Her shoulders twisted badly as the familiar click of the locking bolt slid home. Then they released their grip on her, knowing there was nowhere she could go.

Riony tested the hold of her bonds, tugging with all her strength. She was bigger now, older, stronger than the last time she'd been bound to that post. But it remained just as solid. The wooden beam had been mounted onto a heavy steel plate beneath them, and Riony tried to rock the entire construction, but it stayed steady.

On the opposite side, the soldier who had taken Kess struggled as she snarled and writhed in his arms, her legs hanging limp beneath her. He ended up using the full length of his body to pin Kess against the post as he lifted her arms high to hook her to the post.

Once she was attached, she remained hanging with her face pressed against the charred timber. Her feet wobbled weakly but couldn't support her weight.

Riony stretched around to the side to move closer.

Kess's cheeks were red from anger and black from soot and she stared blankly at the crowd as though she were already gone.

Riony wanted to touch her chin, lift her face up and look into those piercing eyes so much that her bound hands ached.

"Hey, Kessara, look at me. We're going to be okay. I can take whatever your weak-ass brother has in mind. I'll bet you his noodle arms simply fall right off long before I break."

Kess remained still and didn't look up. And murmurs arose from the watching crowd.

Riony followed her gaze then. Over the lip of the platform, across the lake below, through the middle of the crowd, another parade of dragonriders approached.

They had three prisoners in tow. Niskina, Dashiel, and Benjin.

So much for our escape plan. Riony swore long and loud, inside her own head only so as not to give Kife the satisfaction of her panic.

He watched her with shrewd pleasure regardless. Riony glared back. They didn't have Aishena yet. Griskin and Shiff were still out there somewhere too. Riony refused to give up hope while she was still breathing.

Kife climbed down from his dragon. He landed lightly and strode to the edge of the platform, right beside the whipping post. Small pieces of limestone crystal from the plateau's lip crunched as he put one boot onto it.

"People of the caves." He addressed the crowd in a booming voice. "My riders and I have come to liberate you from the fear you've lived in all these years."

As he spoke, the soldiers who had locked them to the post pulled daggers and were working them between all the joins and buckles of Riony and Kess's chest armor. Riony's body jostled as the last fastening was cut and her scale mail clattered to the ground at her feet.

Next, they cut away her under-padding. Soon she was left in just a shirt that had been drenched in sweat from the earlier fight and now clung cold to her skin.

Kess's armor and gambeson followed shortly after, and the soldiers took it away.

Kife continued. "We will free you from the fear of the world above, of the shadow dragon and revenant curse, and fear of dangerous criminals such as these two here."

He swung an arm back toward Riony and Kess where they were bound.

Kife paused as though expecting some kind of reaction, but the crowd remained silent.

"They aren't buying your bovinshit, Kife." Riony leaned back casually, creating a triangle between her arms, body, and post.

Kife unsubtly ignored her and raised his voice again. "We are here to turn this place from a mess of cowering pitiables, into a flourishing city, under the protection of dragonriders and the wing of our Dragon King himself. You will become great under our care and under our control."

A solitary voice in the crowd booed, loud and sharp. Dragonriders at the perimeter of the group descended upon the woman and dragged her away.

Mutters and whimpering spread, then was silenced again as Kife yelled, "You will see there is no room for dissent. You will see exactly what happens to those who go against me and my rule, and you will learn who is in control."

Kife reached an arm straight out to one side, palm up and waiting.

"Are you hoping for someone to hand you a spine, a heart, or some other vital organ you're missing?" Riony heckled, eyeing his pants pointedly.

Kife kept his arm out and his smile broad. "I did consider gagging that big mouth of yours, but I so look forward to hearing you scream."

A soldier approached carrying a lash. Riony's skin shivered into rough goosebumps at the sight of it. The whipping post Kife had brought from home, but the lash was something new.

Back at Heithorn estate, they had always used simple leather whips. Enough to welt and sometimes tear the skin. Enough to make the recipient wish to never feel that pain again.

But the knotted, hooked lash of stiff hide being placed into Kife's hand was something altogether different.

Riony wondered if it was Kife's own design. She wondered whether he'd whipped anyone else with it before, and whether they survived. She wondered how much it was going to hurt.

"It's fine. I can do this. Don't worry." She whispered the words toward the beam of wood in front of her, but it wasn't clear whether she spoke them to Kess or herself.

Kife stepped up behind Riony, arm lifted.

"I enjoyed it, you know." Kess's voice rang strong and clear from the other side of the post.

Kife stilled. "Enjoyed what?"

"Freeing your dragon." Kess sighed out the words. She shifted her torso and leaned her side into the post, lifting her head. "Just as I enjoyed freeing your pretty slave back at Skaellakeep."

"What are you doing?" Riony whispered, but Kess ignored her.

Kife's forehead creased, then he shook his head in dismissal and raised his arm higher.

A wild chuckle emerged from Kess. "How she ran when I gave her the option to! I think that was when I realized that you and I are more alike than I ever imagined."

"We are nothing alike!" Kife snapped. He took a lurching step her way.

"But, brother, we are," Kess crooned the words, with all the sly, nasty energy she used to hold. "Because no human or creature would ever want to remain by your side unless forced to. Because in the end, even as able-bodied as you are, you're even more unwanted than *I* am."

Kife bared his teeth and air hissed out between them. He straightened up and marched over behind his sister. "I'll show you exactly how unwanted you are."

Riony's indrawn gasp was only halfway through her throat when the lash hit. It cracked across Kess's back with a blistering sound.

The broken, wailing scream that followed felt like it split Riony deeper than the lash could have. Her mouth opened as though the cry were her own, then she bit it closed, teeth grinding against each other.

"No! What are you doing?" she growled through her locked jaw. "It's meant to be me."

Riony had been prepared for a beating. She'd been prepared for it for half her life. To bleed at the hands of others had become her normal and for all she wished she could live free of pain, she could *handle* it. She was used to it.

But when she'd thought feeling Lyrrin's panic through the paired stone and being so far away was a torture greater than she'd ever known, she hadn't imagined this. Seeing the pain that should have been hers inflicted onto someone else. Someone she cared about.

Unable to make it stop.

Kife pulled back the knotted lash and struck again. Droplets of red sprayed across the air.

Kess's scream was lost under the roaring that filled Riony's ears. White-hot fury scorched her every nerve ending. She bucked against her bindings like a wild animal.

"Somebody do something!" Riony shrieked desperately toward the crowd.

She sought her friends, lined up at the front of the crowd below, bound in their own heavy manacles. Niskina's face had gone pale, watching with her jaw set. Benjin looked away. Dashiel cried.

Everyone else's expressions were a mix of the same. Some eyed the dragons surrounding them warily.

"Do something!" Riony pleaded again. "There are more of you than there are of them. You can stop this! Somebody stop this!"

Kife lifted his arm again. Kess's body heaved with sobs that were more like short, rasping screams.

"Don't do it, Kife. Touch her again and you are dead!" Riony bellowed, straining against her bonds.

He smiled in reply. "Why ever would I stop? As though you have anything to offer me other than this beautiful display. And this is so much better than I'd originally planned. Far more entertaining."

He struck again, and Kess's neck arched back, her face turned up to the cavern ceiling and mouth open in a silent scream.

Riony screamed in her place, and hot tears spilled as Kess's head lolled down against the post.

"Stop, please stop," Kess whimpered.

"Ah, the begging begins already." Kife toyed with the lash, inspecting the bloodied ends. "I knew you wouldn't last long. But let's keep going anyway."

He raised the lash, and Kess screamed before it even hit, then the sound shifted into a low moan.

Riony couldn't feel or think anything anymore except blurring, burning, roaring rage. She was barely aware of the feral grunts she made and the wild thrashing of her body.

Kess's voice was a screaming whisper. "Please. No more. I'll do anything. Anything."

Kife laughed. "Then keep on begging."

"I can do more!" Kess rushed the words out. "I have something more valuable to offer."

Scoffing, Kife brought the lash swinging toward her again.

"I know how they made Dracuni. I know how to make more!" The words flew from Kess's mouth faster than the lash.

Kife pulled back at the last moment.

Riony stilled, blinking the fury from her eyes. "Kess?"

Kife's eyes shot to Riony, assessing her, then back to his sister. He moved closer to the whipping post, standing between the two of them.

With his voice low, he said, "More? You can make more? Tell how."

Kess wobbled where she hung from the hook, her face wet with tears and spattered red. "I will. Once you free me. Please. It hurts."

What is she doing? We never worked it out. Not really. Unless she's just desperate enough to lie, or unless she has some other plan. Riony's mouth had gone dry and all she could do was stare between the Heithorn brother and sister and pray to all the stars far above them that Kess wasn't betraying her again.

Kife tutted. "Four lashes? I'm disappointed that's all it took to have you giving up such wealth of knowledge. I'm disappointed to share our family name."

"Then free me *and* promise me a place as a dragonrider. You know that's all I want. All I've ever wanted."

Riony's blood turned cold at Kess's words, and all the fight left her.

Kess didn't meet her eyes as she continued. "Promise me that, then I will tell you. Then you will have more, be richer than any lord or king in the land."

Rubbing his thumb over his chin, Kife paced. "No, no, that seems too easy. You've always had too much of a soft spot for this redheaded beast. If I'm going to believe you've turned on her again, I need a show of loyalty from you before you can rejoin the winning side, sis."

"I'll do anything," Kess replied.

Riony knew what Kife was going to ask before he spoke. She and Kess locked eyes, a swirl of unspoken emotions pleading through red-rimmed lashes and determined, steady gaze.

Kife dangled the cruel lash in the air, letting it swing. Crimson painted the ends and dripped onto the pale limestone below.

"You never had the guts to whip your slave yourself. You're going to make up for that today."

CHAPTER TWENTY-SEVEN

Kess closed her eyes for a few seconds, breathing through the pain of her shredded back.

Her flesh felt on fire and blood soaked what remained of her shirt, pooling around to the front. The lashing was both harder and easier than she'd expected. Harder for it being a different kind of pain than she'd ever known before, like fire and ice at war within her flesh. But easier because she wasn't watching it being inflicted on Riony.

She'd done her best to balance appearing to break at a realistic moment, while not being so hurt she couldn't move. But considering her brother's low estimation of her, she may have been able to stop even sooner and have him believe she couldn't take any more.

The agony far greater than her raw back was how Riony was looking at her.

"You miserable, backstabbing goblin! I can't believe you'd turn on me *again*." Riony gave one sudden wrench against the hook, her face contorted with anger. "Actually, yes, I can. It's exactly the kind of thing a traitorous, malignant pest like you would do."

Kess's expression twisted into the sneering mask she'd worn most of her life. "I'll do anything I have to do to get what I want. You'd have learned that by now if you weren't such a tame-brained beast."

She loaded her words with bitterness, drawing on all her pain from every cruelty and heartbreak in her life to give them unquestionable sincerity.

She needed Kife to believe everything she said. And if Riony believed it too, it was a price Kess was willing to pay. It was a small cost, when what she planned to do had the biggest price of all.

Kife's broad smile showed he was lapping up every moment, as though watching his favorite stage play.

He stepped up onto the small platform with the whipping post and reached up to where Kess's heavy manacles were hooked. The soldier hadn't bothered locking the bolt in place for her as they had for Riony. Kess couldn't stand tall and lift the chains off the metal loop herself.

All eyes were on them as Kife hauled Kess up by the wrists and released her from the solid beam. The crowd below seemed confused, muttering between themselves. And at the front, Riony's friends had no confusion. Niskina and Benjin looked ready for murder.

But it was Dashiel's expression that cracked Kess's heart in two. Wide-eyed and unbelieving, their head shook. Kess wanted to shout out, to explain herself, to banish the look of disappointment that cut deeper than Kife's lashings.

But she kept her expression set. They would all know her true intentions soon enough. And then it would be too late.

I just hope this works.

Kess had gone through dozens and dozens of plans and ideas and hopes in her mind since they were captured. She wanted to use the cutting athame, still hidden behind her belted waistband, to cut Riony free. But there was no way she could reach up high enough for that once her hands were free.

Aishena was still unaccounted for. And as terrifyingly skilled as the young woman was, Kess doubted she could take on all of the soldiers and their dragons alone. Kess hoped that, at best, Aishena would save Riony and her friends.

At least Griskin is already free.

All of Kess's planning came down to one final idea. One action she could take.

She could get rid of Kife, once and for all.

Her brother let her fall from the hook, and she folded roughly down to the ground. The motion pulled at her torn skin and she gasped in pain.

Riony wrenched at the whipping post again, making the metal sheet the beam was bolted to rattle.

Kife then pushed the handle of the lash into Kess's hands and dragged her by the arm around to behind Riony.

He looked at where Kess hunched over on her side on the ground and up at Riony's back. "We might need to bring a chair in for her!"

A chuckle rippled from the soldiers nearby.

Kess took a deep breath. *At least once Kife's gone, his cruelty will be gone with him.*

Maybe whoever is next in command will end this public display, treat their prisoners better, give Aishena more of a chance to free everyone. Kess knew it was a slim hope, but she had to hold on to something.

She knew it was worth it, either way, to remove Kife. As one of only two enemies who knew about Dracuni, he had to go. And since she was the one who told him, she would make that happen.

Kess's hands felt heavy in the manacles. Good. She dropped the lash, and the chain hanging between her wrists clattered as she moved her fingers toward her waistband. She flinched at the sound, but a sudden roaring covered her actions.

She froze, seeking the source of the howling, mourning screams that seemed to echo from every direction.

Every dragon in the room had lifted their heads, wailing horribly.

Every *tamed* dragon. Kess scanned across the crowd and toward the back she saw a figure slinking through the shadows, lit by a sickly yellow-green glow from something in their hand.

The dragon summoning crystal. Aishena had activated it.

The result wasn't exactly as anticipated. The dragons weren't moving Aishena's way as the wild dragons had. But it was certainly doing something.

The dragons' distressed cries sounded so much like those of the shadow dragon that it left Kess shaking.

"What's going on? Get those dragons under control!" Kife barked.

A nearby rider called back, "It's not reacting to any commands!"

Kife took a step away, and Kess panicked. She needed him to remain close. She had to act fast.

Grasping for the athame at her belt, she fumbled it and it clattered loudly onto the metal square of the whipping platform below her.

Kife spun around, glaring down at it and her.

"Oh dear. Did you think you were going to catch me off guard with that little toothpick?"

Smirking, he bent down to where it lay, plucking it out of her weakly grasping fingers.

And Kess smiled back in return.

She flung both arms upward so fast that it made the wounds on her back ignite with agony, then dropped the chain around Kife's neck.

He swore and pushed back to his feet, taking her with him as she clung tight around his shoulders with her manacled hands.

"Let go of me, you useless wretch!"

He wavered on his feet as her weight unbalanced him, lurching to the side. Kess arched her back, swinging as much of her weight the same way, taking them both toppling over the lip of the limestone platform.

"Kess! *Kess*!" Riony's cries chased them from above.

And they fell, down the drapery of the limestone slope and into the lake below. The ice-cold water slapped against Kess's back, blinding her with pain, and she put everything she had into remaining conscious, keeping her grip.

The water was cloudy from churning silt. Kess wasn't sure how deep it was. It just had to be deep enough. Her brother kicked and writhed against her, but his own armor and the weight of Kess's body and chains fought against his efforts. They both went deeper, deeper, into the milky blue pit.

Stars filled Kess's closed eyes and her lungs swelled to bursting, but she kept her arms locked around her brother's fighting body.

She could do this. For Riony. To remove Kife as a danger from her life forever, she'd do anything. As her consciousness darkened, this seemed the easiest thing of all to do.

All she had to do was keep holding on. And sink.

***

Riony's shoulders strained as she angled to see over the lip of the platform to the lake below where Kess and Kife had just vanished.

"Kess?" Her cry was lost under the warbling screams of the dragons around the cavern.

Riony's face burned hot against cold streaks of tears.

Raze it, Kess. What did you do?

There was movement all around, cries and murmurs reaching through the periphery of Riony's vision and hearing, but all she could do was stare at the cloudy water below, where nobody re-emerged, where no reply came.

Riony tried to lean farther out, to see the edge of the lake closest to the drop from above. Maybe Kess had resurfaced there, out of her line of sight. But with her hands pinned above her head, she couldn't reach far enough.

"This depths-cursed, sparking post!" Riony kicked unhelpfully at the solid beam and rattled her cuffed hands against her bonds.

She still hasn't come up. I have to get to her.

In desperation, Riony wrapped her fingers around the chain between her manacles, then leaned back and put her feet up against the beam of wood. She stretched her entire body out, pulling against the metal hook she was attached to, every muscle from head to toe screaming with effort.

The smallest bend in the weld holding the hook to the metal top casing rekindled her resolve, and she bellowed wordlessly, wrenching against her bonds. The steel groaned and warped and Riony's arms felt as though they did the same.

And then with a final crack, the hook snapped free.

Riony fell backward, hitting the ground and rolling from the momentum. She curled up and brought her knees under her, coming up into a crouching position.

The cries from below grew louder. No longer whimpering murmurs, but a chorus of confident, rousing shouts.

"She's free!"

"Move, now."

"Come on, together."

Breathing heavily, Riony watched the crowd below as she rose to her feet.

And they rose too.

Only a few at first. Faces Riony recognized. People she knew. People she had helped.

But more quickly followed, building like a wave of bodies. The fierce determination on every face made Riony's heart swell.

The dragonriders, still trying to get their screaming dragons to respond, were caught unawares as the first of the crowd reached them. They were swarmed. Dragged from their steeds, they disappeared beneath the surge of bodies.

A flash at the corner of her eye turned Riony from the scene below and she leaned back to dodge an incoming swing of a sword. The few soldiers on foot who had guarded around the platform came for her.

Sparks flew as Riony blocked another strike with the chain between her wrists.

She yelled at them, "Back off! I don't sparking have time for this!"

Riony could swim well enough, but not with her hands chained. Not if she was trying to carry another body as well. The cutting athame Kess had dropped lay just behind the line of guards. If she could just get to it, then get to the water ...

Riony's pulse hammered.

It's been so long already.

Riony clasped her hands together as one and brought them and the heavy manacles hammering down over a guard's helmeted head. He stilled, swaying, and she kicked him in the chest, sending him bodily into the soldier next to him. Both went down.

In the breathing space that followed, Riony shot a look over the lake again, and the rioting population beyond. No movement in the water.

"Kess, come on, come back."

At the front of the crowd, Aishena came into view, her own glowing yellow athame brandished in one hand. In a flurry of elegant strikes, she downed the final guard beside Niskina, Dashiel, and Benjin, then freed them from their chains.

Riony lunged sideways to avoid being skewered by a sword, then ran across the platform to the nearest edge.

She stood tall and screamed, "Aish! I need help!"

"I'm coming!" The young grayglim woman vanished into the crowd again.

An almost gleeful growl came from behind Riony, and Shiff burst through into the middle of the remaining guards, snapping at their legs.

Griskin followed, leaping on soft paws toward the now abandoned whipping post. He sniffed around it, but his eyes and nose were running. Turning his face up, he looked desperately toward Riony.

"I'll get her. I'm going to get her!"

Aishena appeared by Riony's side, cropped hair swinging around her chin as she scanned for nearby threats. Shiff and Griskin had the closest guards at bay.

Riony held her arms out in front of her. "Quick!"

Aishena nodded once and sliced so swiftly through the cuffs of steel Riony thought she'd take her hands right off along with them and wasn't sure at that point she even cared as long as it was fast.

But the manacles were cut away with careful precision and clinked onto the ground.

Riony touched her fingers briefly to Aishena's shoulder, turned away, and dove off the high platform into the lake below.

The cold touch of the meltwater hit Riony like a slap to the face and she aimed her body down, kicking her aching legs hard until she reached the silty bottom. She swung her arms all around, finding nothing. A current pulled at her—the lake's waters flowing from this reservoir along to the next—and she worried how far Kess might have been drawn along.

But she didn't have enough breath to find out. She pushed off the bottom, speeding desperately to the surface to draw in air again.

She turned on the spot in the milky water, hoping to see that Kess had somehow returned on her own, as she gulped three deep breaths, then went under again.

Back and forth she swam, her body screaming from exertion as her armored legs weighed her down, and no other body met her searching fingers.

Again, she emerged to breathe.

Her face scrunched up and she squeezed her sodden hair in her hands. "No. No, no, no!"

Something approached her through the water, and Riony spun around to meet it, splashing water in her wake.

She wished to see Kess's face, but instead, a furry snout pushed up to sniff at her cheek.

She blinked water from her eyes, staring at the cave otter as her breaths heaved. She swiped a hand to push Butterfur away.

"Kess?" she cried desperately, as though her voice alone could bring her back from the watery depths. "Kess!"

Butterfur returned, undeterred, sniffing and nipping at Riony's shirt as his long, silky body sluiced through the water.

Riony lifted a hand again in frustration and then through her panic came a moment of clarity.

Her voice stuttered. "Kess ... *Kess has the treats.*"

The otter rolled in the water, sniffed once, then duck-dived away in a flash.

Riony clamped her mouth closed, holding back the gut-wrenching sobs that were building in her chest. Shaking her head, she gasped a frustrated breath and prepared to dive again, when a shadowed shape rose in the water toward her.

A pale face, veiled in a tangle of dark and light streaked hair broke the surface.

Riony cried out wordlessly. She splashed closer, and the top of Butterfur's head emerged as well, then his snout, biting closed around a mouthful of shirt. Kess's thin arms hung heavy on one side, hands heavy in the manacles, and the milky water around her tinted pink.

Riony clutched the unresponsive girl to her chest and leaned back, kicking toward the nearest shore as Butterfur followed, digging around one of Kess's pockets.

Riony's fingers pressed into the mangled flesh on Kess's back and she flinched, clenching her teeth.

"I'm sorry. I'm so sorry," she whispered, but there was no reply.

There was no sign Kess felt any pain, or anything at all.

Reaching the bank, Riony hauled herself out of the water, then pulled Kess up after her. The body was a dead weight, slumping bonelessly. Riony fell into a sitting position, shaking all over.

All around, fighting continued. But the sounds were muted in Riony's ears. Even when cheers went up in the crowd, they sounded like a distant humming.

She adjusted Kess's lifeless body and drew her onto her lap.

Riony pushed the matting of wet hair off Kess's face. Her skin was cold and still.

"Kess? Come on. I know you're tougher than this. I know you're still with me. You said you'd be with me, always."

Riony grasped for the string around her neck. Fishing the acorn pendant and heart stone from under her shirt, she yanked on the string, breaking it. Tucking the pulsing crystal back against her chest again, Riony took the acorn in trembling fingers and pulled it open.

Inside, in a small glass vial procured from Eslindekeep's stores, was the gift Dracuni had forced on her before she left.

A gift she now thanked all the stars she took.

She let the silvernix drop onto Kess's cheek. As she waited for it to take effect, wishing and praying that it would take effect, that it wasn't too late, she lifted Kess closer.

Cradling her in one arm, she pressed her forehead to Kess's. "Come on. You can't leave me. Not now. Now when ..."

A shimmering light sparkled through Riony's wet eyelashes. She sobbed in relief as that glow built, growing stronger, and Kess's body jerked and twitched in her arms. Riony held tight as Kess's lungs expelled water and torn skin knitted closed and the small body seized and gasped in pain.

Kess *gasped*. Kess *breathed*. And that was all Riony wanted to hear.

As pale eyes opened and stared up at Riony's, there was a moment of confusion. And then a flurry of words.

"Forgive me. I was never going to hurt you. I'd never whip you, ever again. I was only pretending to betray you again to get free, to get close enough to Kife so that—"

"I know." Riony cupped Kess's cheek and pressed a thumb to her lips. "I'm not that big of a *tame-brained beast*, you know. I knew all along. Kind of nice to see you tricking someone who isn't me for once. Although I wish I knew what you really had planned."

"You knew? You trusted me?" This seemed to break something inside Kess more than the lashing had, and fat tears toppled from her eyes.

"Not actually dumb, remember? Just caring."

Kess's still shackled hands came up together, fingers still icy cold, and clutched around where Riony's were against her face. "I'd have done it anyway, even if you hated me for it. It's okay. It's okay if you hate me, as long as you're safe."

There was a soft ache to Kess's voice. A dreaminess, as though none of this were true, as though she couldn't believe she were still there and alive, that the fingers she squeezed within hers were real.

Riony pulled her closer again, pressing her cheek to Kess's.

Her lips moved against Kess's ear. "I ... I don't hate you."

An avalanche of sobs overtook Kess then, shaking them both with their ferocity, and Riony kept her held in their embrace as though they were the only two people in the world.

Two soon became three, as the warm bulk of Griskin's fur settled down against them. He whined softly, pressing his forehead against Kess's back.

Then another cheer went up, louder this time as the fear and fury and water had all drained from Riony's ears.

"The last rider is down!" Benjin's voice rang out over the crowd.

The dragons had stopped screaming at some point. Riony wasn't sure when. The effect the altered summoning stone had on them hadn't lasted long. Riony and her friends alone wouldn't have stood a chance defeating the soldiers without the help of the people of the undercity.

Butterfur sat on the bank a little way down, gnashing open-mouthed on the saturated piece of mushroom jerky he'd extracted from Kess's pocket.

And the creatures of the undercity too.

Niskina could be heard through the chattering of triumph, giving orders about what to do with the dragonrider prisoners and any remaining soldiers out within the city. Riony hadn't seen any other delvers around. Aishena must have never reached them. But everyone seemed to look to Niskina as a leader.

Dashiel came sliding down the slick limestone bank toward Riony and Kess.

"Is she okay? Oh, stars." Their approach slowed as they took in how Riony and Kess held each other.

"I'm okay." Kess wiped her face, now very red, and sat up, shifting out of Riony's lap.

"Wow. That was … I can't believe we did it! I mean, not that I did a lot, but look. We, they, everyone stood up against the dragonriders and won." Dashiel beamed.

Despite the smile, their face was pale, and they cradled one bloodied arm close to their chest.

"Yeah, I suppose we did." Riony wasn't sure either just how much she'd done.

You inspire people.

Riony found herself staring at Kess's lips as though she spoke the words again, but they were still.

Relief for the undercity being freed lasted only a moment for Riony. A cold, aching heaviness struck her, as though one of the mammoth stalactites from the ceiling above had cracked off and crushed her.

She clutched for her chest, panting with fear.

Halfway to climbing onto Griskin, Kess stilled. "What is it?"

Riony's hands closed around the paired heart stone, knuckles white and fingers cutting against the sharp edges.

It had gone entirely still.

Chapter Twenty-Eight

The sky roiled with fire. A single mammoth ball of it, hissing and crackling where Shani had been moments before.

Lyrrin couldn't take her eyes off it. The sheer horror of it, of that poor dragon, driven to such a grave act by grief. Of the fear her mother, her Alderkin family, and her friends had also been caught in the explosion. That she might have just lost them all in one instant.

But as she watched, neck craned to look around Yensen, she noticed that Yensen also had his eyes locked on the tragic inferno.

Their dragon continued to glide forward, Dracuni still caught in its claws below. But Yensen was distracted.

And she couldn't waste that moment.

Lyrrin glanced down at where her belt usually was, with its array of crystals ready to blind or explode at a moment's notice. But it was long gone. And her hands were still bound together at the wrist and tied to the front of the saddle.

There was only one thing she had left.

She crumpled over, hunching onto her hands, wailing for her mother. The kind of bratty, tantrummy cry she'd recently outgrown.

Yensen ignored her, pointedly continuing to look away.

With her chest leaning over her bound hands, she plucked her fingers around her neck until one hooked on the string there, and she pulled the heart stone free. It jumped in her hands, beating so hard from her sister's heartbeat that it almost bounced free and fell from her grip.

Lyrrin clutched it hard with one hand and brought one of her sharp claws against it with the other, covering the action with her leaning body.

She paused. What to draw? She'd never tried recreating the paired heart rune. She'd never seen much point in creating more. There were only so many heartbeats she wanted to keep track of at one time, and feeling Riony's from a distance generally brought her more worry than comfort.

So she'd also never tested the rune with any others.

"What are you doing?" Yensen grumbled.

Lyrrin flinched and rushed out two quick runes. Her pointed nail screeched over the crystal surface.

Yensen grabbed the back of her shirt, pulling her up. His hands thrust to either side of her, grasping for the crystal in her hands. She ran her finger over the runes.

Light. Burst.

Lyrrin had considered using light and burn but didn't want to cause the kind of explosion that might send her or Dracuni falling from the sky. It was already risky enough adding her flash combination to an untested rune.

Riony's heart beat faster and wilder than Lyrrin had ever felt it, and the glow of the crystal built.

"Let go of that! What have you done?"

Lyrrin locked her fingers around the flat slice of translucent stone as Yensen tried to pry it free.

The light pulsed, flashing in time to the heartbeat, growing bright and strong, then brighter and stronger. Lyrrin squeezed her eyes closed and her eyelids flashed red, black, red, black as the blinding light shone right through.

Yensen leaned away, grunting, then forward again and the hard strike of blunt metal smashed against Lyrrin's fingers.

She cried out, and the crystal slipped free. She opened her eyes to try to grasp it again, but it was already out of reach of her tied hands.

The stone spun, flashing like a falling star as it tumbled from the sky. The power of its glow burned a wavering line into Lyrrin's vision, but she could still see around the edges.

Yensen, on the other hand, rubbed watering eyes with the palms of his hands, cursing. He held a dagger in one of them. He must have looked directly at the stone in order to strike it free from her grip.

Blinded. But not for long.

Lyrrin wrenched at the rope around her hands, wriggled and kicked in the saddle, but she remained stuck. But her thrashing seemed to send confusing signals to the tamed dragon they rode on.

It veered from their smooth glide, twisting sideways and flying a full, horizontal circle. Maybe if she could move the right way, she could make the dragon turn back toward Viska.

Riony should have let me fly with some of the riders before. I could have seen what to do.

But her movements did something, and that was all she had. Emboldened, Lyrrin leaned forward as far as she could, thrusting her hands through the rope so they stuck farther out up front. She pushed and slapped at the dragon's neck, wherever she could reach.

A short puff of fire emerged, then the dragon ascended higher.

"Stop it!" Yensen grasped the back of Lyrrin's neck in a painful pincer grip and pulled her back.

Lyrrin twisted in the saddle, bringing her legs up for a final, reckless kick against the dragon's neck.

And Dracuni screamed.

No. Lyrrin's chest squeezed with the fear that she'd made the dragon crush her friend. But as she looked over the edge of the saddle, through the blurring streaks in her vision, she saw something almost as bad.

Dracuni was falling.

The dragon had let go, and Dracuni tumbled in a spiraling rush through the air.

"No!" Lyrrin yelled aloud.

"What did you do?" Yensen turned his head side to side, blinking unseeing eyes.

Dracuni howled again, more distant, and Yensen grunted.

He leaned over Lyrrin, taking control of the dragon again. He aimed the beast in the rough direction of the screaming unidragon and pushed it into a dive.

Lyrrin wriggled, jabbing her shoulders into the grayglim. Even without his sight, he was gaining on Dracuni simply from following her cries.

"You've got to fly! Dracuni, put your wings out. Stretch them out!" Lyrrin shouted with her whole chest.

Dracuni yelped again, passing through a low puff of cloud. Her wings fluttered and tangled around her spinning body. And then she pushed them out.

One diaphanous wing caught the air but the other crumpled against the pressure, twisting up at a painful angle.

"Keep trying! You can do it," Lyrrin yelled. "Straight out, nice and strong!"

Pale scales glittered in the dim light as Dracuni turned over and over again. The ground came up fast beneath her and Yensen's dragon came down from above.

The unidragon's wings thrust out and wavered. Held, then failed. Thrust out again, billowed in the wind, and Dracuni stabilized.

"Good work! Now flap! Go! Get out of here!" Lyrrin's eyes flooded with tears and her mouth split in a fierce, proud smile.

With her eyes on Dracuni, making small careful motions of her shimmering wings, Lyrrin almost missed the oncoming field of grass and rocks.

She shrieked, high-pitched, "We're going to hit the ground!"

Yensen swore and adjusted his hand movements, and their dragon arched and swooped upward, skimming the earth, then rising back into the sky.

"Where is it? Where did the silvernix dragon go?" Yensen yelled in Lyrrin's ear.

Dracuni wasn't far below them now, flapping her small wings frantically and hovering in a wobbly way. But as she remained silent, and Yensen's red eyes still searched blindly, she could have been anywhere.

"Gone! Flown away. You can't catch her."

Yensen brought their dragon to a slow glide. He rubbed his eyes again.

Dracuni's lilac eyes met Lyrrin's and her nostrils flared. Her wings pumped harder, moving their way, but even with all her effort, their own dragon's gentle soaring took them farther away.

Lyrrin shook her head fiercely. She mouthed the words, *No. Go!*

She wished once more she could communicate with Dracuni in her mind. Even at the now vast distance, Lyrrin could still feel a small tug of emotion from Elumon, twanging inside her.

Am I ever going to see him again? What will he do without me?

Lyrrin tried to send comforting emotions back to the hatchling. But all she could do for Dracuni was shake her head and hope the unidragon could read lips.

"Is that it? Over there?" Yensen squinted at Lyrrin and then in the direction she was looking.

His vision is clearing.

Dracuni still hovered, struggling to stay airborne. Not moving closer, but not fleeing either. She was an easy target for a larger, faster dragon, even with a half-blinded rider.

Yensen turned their dragon back around. They had glided a fair distance away, but at full speed they would close that gap quickly.

Then another dragon appeared through a gust of gray cloud, rushing their way. Glinting gold against the ashy sky.

"Viska!" Lyrrin yelled, bouncing in the saddle.

She breathed deeply and leaned into the chilled wind, trying to see the faces of all who rode with her, to know they were still okay.

Yensen grumbled, eyes twitching as he wiped them dry again and looked between the shimmer of silver and sparkle of gold in the sky.

Behind Viska, two more dragons appeared. Thallan riding Brunzell, and one remaining king's rider. They dodged and chased each other in swirling arcs, all coming their way.

Muttering under his breath, Yensen leaned over Lyrrin again and pushed their dragon around, turning it away from the others and building its speed again.

He's running?

Lyrrin twisted her wrists within the rope, but it remained tight. Viska was moving a lot slower than she had before and wasn't gaining on them. They were going to leave them all behind.

Lyrrin turned in the saddle as far as she could, trying to keep her eyes on the others. "No! Just let me go. You've lost. Dracuni's gone. You didn't get what you wanted. Let me go!"

Yensen pushed her shoulder out of his way. "Quiet!"

Lyrrin turned to the other side. Viska had caught up to Dracuni now and hovered beside her, assisting the struggling unidragon. They were so far away now they were just small, bright smudges in the air.

Lyrrin hadn't been able to see if Viska still carried everyone she had before.

She tried to use her most convincing voice as she pleaded, "You don't need me. Please. Just give up, give me back to them. Before it's too late."

"It's already too late." Yensen kept his eyes forward, on the eastern horizon. "We'll be lucky if the king doesn't take both our heads for failing to bring the silvernix dragon in after all this time, because of you."

"Then don't take me to him! Take me back to Eslinde. It doesn't matter what you've done. If you just take me back, we can work it all out." Lyrrin thought that might be a lie.

Still, they had forgiven Kess and brought her in as a friend, after all she had done. But at that moment Lyrrin hated the grayglim so much she couldn't make it sound true regardless.

"No. There'll be no other opportunity for me now. But at least I still have you. You might have been the secondary target, but my king still wants you. So that's where I'm taking you."

Lyrrin's voice broke. "To the Dragon King himself?"

Yensen's voice remained strong and low. "You're going to meet your grandfather. And pray that he decides you're worth keeping when you stole from him the prize he wanted most."

Lyrrin shivered. The blasting, icy wind felt as though it went straight through her. Her eyes watered from straining to stay open against it, and her eyelashes felt frosted. Hunching forward again, she wished she still had the heart stone to cling to as she tried to stay warm.

She ached as though she'd been punched in the belly.

She'd only just found her mother. Only just found the truth of who she was and met people like her. And now she was being taken away from everyone she loved to meet family that she never wanted to know.

RIONY couldn't even remember how she'd gotten from the edge of the lake back to the platform with the whipping post. She gave it a single, resentful glance, then kicked at the chest armor that had been cut off her. The buckles were all ruined. It wasn't going back on.

I'll have to find something else. Or just go without.

Everything blurred in an anxious haze.

Riony didn't know what was happening. She only knew she had to get to her sister as fast as possible.

The crystal could have run out of charge. Or she left it behind somewhere. It doesn't mean her heart has stopped.

Please let it not mean that.

Riony's chest felt hollow without the additional pulse beating beside it. But almost as though to fill that space, more worry and fear and guilt flowed in.

Her own ... and more? Even from such a vast distance, she shared those emotions with Dracuni. She had to get to them both.

What do I need? Armor. Sword ...

"Kess?" Riony turned on the spot, her mind whirling with worry.

Where did she go? The last time Riony saw her was a few moments ago when she'd explained how the paired crystal had stopped beating.

"I'm here," said Kess from her side. She carried Riony's sword, rested across both her arms.

Griskin panted from the run he'd just been on to retrieve it.

Behind them, Aishena bandaged Dashiel's arm as Shiff stood guard, and Benjin helped Niskina round up the defeated soldiers and catch up the newly freed delvers on what was happening.

Riony stared at her sword in Kess's hands for a long few seconds. Had she asked Kess to get it? She couldn't remember.

"Thank you." She grasped the hilt and took the still lit but fading weapon.

She hadn't been to a shrine with it in a while, and the charge seemed to be running out. After quickly deactivating it, its true weight returned.

Riony winced as she took a step back.

"Your ankle ..." Kess said.

"It's fine." Riony leaned heavily on her other leg.

Her skin had swollen around the puncture holes from the dragon bite, tight inside her leather boot, and it throbbed hotly. But there was nothing to be done. Unless someone else had a precious family heirloom squirreled away in an acorn, Riony doubted there was a single drop of silvernix in the undercity.

Riony leaned on her sword like a crutch. "We'll head out the top way, flag down Zeina and Jaym, and get to Eslindekeep as quick as we can, then …"

Another surge of emotion hit Riony. The same soup of worry, guilt, and fear from before, but stronger now, enough to make her guts ache and eyes water. How was she feeling Dracuni so intensely from so far away?

Big sister? Big sister!

Riony frowned. "Dracuni?"

"Dracuni?" Niskina echoed as she, Aishena, Benjin, and Dashiel joined them.

We're coming. Where are you?

Riony's eyes widened. "She's nearby. We have to get to one of the entrances."

"Stoneshield Gate is closest." Niskina raised her voice and gestured to the milling people in that direction. "Clear a path!"

The crowd parted, and Riony broke into a loping, uneven sprint.

Griskin could have moved faster, and with her pounding ankle, Riony was sure Aishena, Benjin, and even Dashiel with their injured arm could have all moved faster than her. But they all kept pace, even Shiff at the back. Niskina remained behind.

Beyond the market area where the community had been gathered, the streets through Upslope were clear, and they reached the tunnel exit quickly.

Riony had never been out that way before, a passage normally reserved for delvers only, and she hadn't been one long enough for such perks. Soon the huge stone doorways loomed into sight, carved into an imposing shield design surrounded by crystals.

A couple of treedarts sat idly beside the gate, unresponsive due to their riders having been taken away. Aishena split off to an alcove at the side and worked the opening mechanism. The deep, gravelly grinding of stone against stone reverberated through the tunnel, and daylight cut through the dusty air.

I'm here, Dracuni. Can you hear me? Riony stepped out onto the rocky plateau, staring up at the low storm clouds that were tinted orange in the few gaps the afternoon sun reached.

"She's flying!" Benjin shouted and jumped once on the spot.

Riony followed his gaze and saw three dragons descending. Viska, Iffyr, and Dracuni. *Flying!*

Three others emerged from behind the snowy peak, red, orange, and aqua. Zeina and Jaym with their dragons plus Ambri, following the others in.

"What happened? Why did they come here?" Aishena asked, her expression grave.

Riony! The word was like a sob in Riony's mind, and then no more words followed, only torrents of crushing sadness.

Riony squinted to see the faces of the riders. Benjin had lost his crystal-encrusted staff when he was captured and it hadn't been returned to him yet, and none of them had a seeing stone on them, so they had to stand and wait as the dragons landed.

Dracuni came in first, a little too fast. Her claws clattered on the stones as her momentum tumbled her all the way along the plateau and right up to Riony's side.

Eslinde landed next on Iffyr, with the hatchling, Elumon, holding onto her lap. Viska had scorch marks down an entire side and one wing was torn. She carried Vance and the Alderkin. Only two of them. Yensen was missing as well. No Thallan. No Samor.

And no Lyrrin.

"Where is she?" Riony planted her feet firmly apart to avoid crumbling.

Dracuni bowed her head and closed her lilac eyes. Her sides pumped like bellows, gasping deep breaths.

Silence only followed.

"WHERE IS SHE?"

Eslinde slid from the white shimmerdart dragon. She clutched Lyrrin's hatchling against one shoulder and landed heavily on the rocky ground. Elumon pushed out of her hold and jumped down, running over to hide between Dracuni and Shiff.

The princess took a few wavering steps toward Riony and then dropped down onto her knees. "I'm sorry. It's all my fault. Yensen ... he betrayed us."

Eslinde's face was swollen and red, dripping with tears.

Riony spoke through a mouth that felt filled with ash. "Is she ... did she ...?"

Vance approached Eslinde, standing above her. "The grayglim took her. Alive."

Riony's hand pressed against her chest, feeling the crystal below her shirt. "The paired heart stone stopped a while ago."

Dracuni lifted her head, and the sounds of her thoughts were laced with sorrow. *She used it. Blinded the rider with it so I could get away. But I couldn't fly well enough to help her too.*

Riony's legs could have been made of chalk, ready to crumble to dust, and she leaned onto Dracuni's neck, holding her for both comfort and support.

But she was alive?

She was alive, and he took her away. I'm sorry.

"It's not your fault." Riony squeezed her tight.

"It's not. It's mine." Eslinde's voice cracked, and she bent forward, placing her forehead on the ground. "I won't ask your forgiveness, because I won't ever forgive myself for bringing a traitor with me."

Vance crouched beside Eslinde and put an arm over her shoulders. "We tried to catch up and get Lyrrin back, but with Viska injured, there was no chance. It was all we could do to get away safely."

The two Rebel Riders had landed now as well, and Jaym and Zeina looked at the charred golden dragon.

Zeina asked, "And the others?"

Vance shook his head. "All lost. With Eslindekeep compromised, we took Iffyr and Elumon and fled here. The refugees at the keep will make their way on foot to the nearest still active shrine."

All lost? Riony turned her eyes away from where Eslinde's thin shoulders shook. Behind her, Yrik and Priyune held each other, missing their third. Shael was gone. Thallan and

Samor too. Zeina and Jaym shared heavy expressions.

Riony's fingers drifted over Dracuni's scales, and she stepped away. Hobbling forward, she reached down to Eslinde, pulling the princess reluctantly to her feet.

"We're going to get her back, okay? Our little spitfire is a survivor."

Eslinde squeezed Riony's fingers in hers, and fresh tears fell in heavy, fat drops.

Kess was giving Eslinde a sharp, scrutinizing stare. "You lost an earring, princess."

Riony noticed it then, how the spiraling silver jewelry dangled only on one side.

Eslinde's face crumpled, then reformed into an expression of solemnity. "We almost lost Vance, too."

Dashiel jogged to their brother. "What happened? You look fine. Is that *blood*?"

Vance patted Dashiel on the back and gave a more thorough rundown of Yensen's trap and what they had been through.

The fear and worry surging from Dracuni had eased now, but the guilt only grew stronger.

Little sister saved me. And I couldn't save her.

Riony shared in the heartbreak. Her sister had been taken away, and she knew that in every logical way, saving Dracuni came first and was the most important thing, but it didn't make the loss of Lyrrin hurt any less.

She wished she could go back and make different decisions but didn't know what she would change.

We did the right thing, helping free the undercity, helping save those people. Riony couldn't make herself choose between all of them and her family, even hypothetically.

She couldn't work out where the line fell, between what was right for the world and what she was willing to lose for that cause.

She would give up her life for all those around her, all who had become her family, and at the same time didn't want any of them to give up theirs.

With so much at stake, with so much against them, loss was inevitable.

But Riony refused to lose her sister.

Scanning across the faces of those around her, she knew they would stand with her. Aishena and Benjin stood side by side, with fierce, determined expressions. Dracuni had brought Elumon in closer, and she and Shiff both calmed the distraught hatchling.

The Rebel Riders looked eager for vengeance, and the Alderkin would protect Dracuni no matter what. Eslinde, Vance, and Dashiel looked to Riony expectantly.

And Kess sat on Griskin, close to Riony's shoulder, willing to do anything for her.

Between them all, they had six dragons and something to fight for.

Riony called out, "Is everyone ready to move? If we follow right away, we'll have an advantage of surprise. And the quicker we can get Lyrrin back, the better."

Eslinde's head shook in a wobbly way. "Yensen is taking her to my father, to the king. They're probably already there."

"Then that's where we are going too."

I'm ready. Dracuni took a step forward, chest still heaving and wings heavy at her sides.

Riony looked the unidragon over. "You can stay here with the Alderkin and recover."

I can fly again. I want to go too.

"I'm not sure if any of us are going anywhere," Aishena said, her eyes on the eastern horizon. "Look."

Riony turned, and for a moment she couldn't quite work out what she was seeing. Something like a strange flock of birds, but distant and too large to be birds, but too many to be anything else … surely.

It couldn't be dragons. Not that many of them. Not hundreds of them.

But as much as Riony willed the truth away, dragons they were.

And they were coming directly toward the undercity, fast.

"Everyone inside, quick! Dragons too!" Aishena yelled.

Riony's head shook. *No. We need to go after Lyrrin.*

But there was no point in speaking those words. She knew there was no way forward as the sky between her and her sister had become a wall of flying beasts.

And as the dragons were within sight of them now, so were they within sight of the incoming dragons. A dozen broke ahead of the rest, shooting their way at a terrifying speed.

Despite Aishena's order, everyone had remained frozen.

"Go." Riony gave Eslinde a gentle push, and then yelled at Dracuni, "Inside, now!"

But little sister …

I know.

They all moved. Vance supported Eslinde, and Dracuni and Shiff herded Elumon in front of them. The larger wild dragons followed after their riders, and the two tamed dragons were brought in by Aishena and Dashiel.

The Alderkin stared up in heartbroken awe at the opened doorway to a home they had been separated from for so long, then stepped inside as well.

Riony and Kess remained until the rest had made it inside, as the dragons above were close enough that their wing beats thundered like drums.

"Come on," Kess urged with a gentle press of her hand to Riony's shoulder.

Her face scrunched up and she shook her head heavily, then allowed herself to be guided inside.

The heavy stone doors of the undercity closed behind them, cutting off the roar of the first dragon to land where they had just been standing.

They were safe inside, for now. But those doors felt like a tomb closing them into their graves alive. With the full force of the Dragon King's army imprisoning them from outside.

CHAPTER THIRTY

L yrrin's teeth chattered as Yensen marched her through the immense hallways of the Dragon King's palace. Her eyes bulged, both in fear and in awe.

She'd never set foot in a dragonkeep city before, let alone seen anything as grand and daunting as this place. She'd grown up in makeshift huts and limestone rooms small enough she and her sister were always stepping on each other.

The brutal vastness of the glossy, gilded space she walked through was overwhelming.

Slick black tiles reflected a strange, cold blue glow from the lamps. Sculptures of dragons in fierce, violent poses lined the hall. Their eyes seemed to follow Lyrrin's every move and made her feel small and vulnerable.

The floor gleamed like a polished mirror, every slapping step of her bare feet echoing in the cavernous space.

They passed by other guards and servants on duty, who cast curious looks their way, but nobody challenged what Yensen was doing with her, why the grayglim was pushing a trembling child along beside him.

He had pulled her hood over her blue hair and thrown a cloth over her bound hands, but that was more to hide her fingers than the fact she was bound up like a hostage.

A large glass and steel window framed the next intersection, offering a view out over the capital city, with all its jutting towers, shadowed by the high protective walls in the distance. The sun had nearly set.

Are the others okay? Does Riony know what happened to me by now? Will she come for me?

Riony probably would, but Lyrrin wasn't sure she wanted her to. Her sister would fight her way across half the kingdom if she had to. But here, in the slick marble hallways surrounded by high walls and guards and grayglims and dragonriders, Lyrrin feared what would become of anyone who tried to rescue her.

But she hadn't yet given up on trying to rescue herself.

Her eyes darted around, taking in the high ceilings adorned with chandeliers that sparkled like icy stars and the long corridors that seemed to stretch into infinity. She felt like a mouse in a maze, trying to spot a way out before the trap was sprung.

Lyrrin's heart pounded as they approached a grand pair of double doors, and Yensen whispered to the guard standing before them.

With a nod, the guard moved to open the entryway.

Lyrrin tried to steady her breathing, but the chill rattling her bones from their recent flight and the fear of what lay ahead made it impossible.

Her pace slowed, and she tried to turn back, but Yensen held her shoulder in an iron grip, as unyielding and cold as the palace itself.

The doors swung open, revealing the vast throne room beyond. Lyrrin's breath hitched as she took in the sight of the Dragon King.

He sat still as a statue, silver hair woven into an intricate net of braids that hung down to his waist. A large hooked nose gave him a commanding, predatory appearance emphasized further by the sharp, toothlike crown on his head.

To the side of his throne stood a young woman. Almost a match to Eslinde, but with black hair, streaked only with a few long lines of silver.

The look she gave Lyrrin as she was pushed in front of them was withering, as though Yensen had thrown the carcass of a mangled rat at her feet.

As they neared the throne, Lyrrin's stomach tightened. She couldn't help but glance at the grayglim, wondering if there was any trace of humanity left beneath his stony exterior. But his expression remained blank.

He'd long since stopped talking to her, refusing to even acknowledge her pleas or bargains.

Only the tremor in his fingers betrayed any emotion. *Is he scared too?*

The Dragon King turned then, casting terrifying eyes over Lyrrin and Yensen. They sparkled in all the wrong ways.

"I'm told you flew in alone, without the dragon I asked you to bring me." His voice filled the chamber in a way that made Lyrrin want to clutch her ears to block them.

Yensen knelt at the foot of the throne, tugging on Lyrrin to force her to do the same.

"Your Majesty, the dragon escaped in the last moments, due to the explosion of a rebel flamesong dragon." There was no pleading in the grayglim's voice, only a statement of fact.

Lyrrin shot him a glance, though, because it wasn't the whole truth. He had left out the part that it was her actions that helped Dracuni escape.

Lyrrin lifted her bowed head slightly so she could peer up at the king from under her hood. He looked younger than Lyrrin expected, but she'd heard the tales of how he had become immortal through the copious amounts of silvernix he used.

He glared with those strange darkly bright eyes. "It would be an understatement to say I'm disappointed. After so long waiting for you to set your trap, all the resources spent, for you to return empty-handed now is unforgivable."

Unforgivable. Is Yensen going to be punished? Executed?

A deep, angry part of Lyrrin hoped for it.

Yensen only bowed lower, as though he'd already accepted this was his fate, and Lyrrin's eyes stung.

What was it Aishena used to say? *I am the hand and must act as the voice commands.* Lyrrin had seen how even an unfinished grayglim training left Aishena acting as though that was all she was. A tool for someone else's control, and the Dragon King was the one who controlled all the grayglims.

Yensen was nothing but a tool, utterly loyal to a king who seemed ready to discard him for his failure, and Lyrrin suddenly found herself scared for his life and what her life might become without him, there in a place where he was the only familiar face she had left.

Her voice felt scratchy and small in the echoing chamber. "He brought me in. I wouldn't call that empty-handed."

Yensen flashed her a confused look from the corner of his dark eyes.

Both the king and the woman beside him also turned to her then and Lyrrin flinched under their gaze.

"Are you even sure this is the right child? She looks … almost normal," the woman said.

On her streaked hair, she wore a fine crown of thin silver and gold braided around what seemed to be a real dragon tooth at the front.

Is she the queen? Is she Eslinde's mother?

Yensen reached over and pulled Lyrrin's hood back and removed the cloth covering her hands.

The queen gagged as though she'd seen something horrific and fanned her face with one hand. "Why is it still alive? It should have been destroyed the moment you found it."

"Calm yourself, Vellira." The king raised a hand her way, holding it still in the air between them. "It was my decision to bring the half-breed in alive. Since Eslinde ran off with my other precious resources, I had to take something precious back. Stand, grayglim."

Yensen stood.

"You said in your reports this child can carve runes into crystal?"

Yensen flashed a dark look toward Lyrrin. She remained on her knees, unsure whether she should, or could, stand again.

He nodded once. "That she can."

"And she can, given the right costuming, pass as human," the king continued. "That will make things easier."

"My love, please," Queen Vellira knelt at the side of the throne, hanging on to the armrest on one side and staring up with pleading eyes. "You can't consider keeping this abomination. It never should have lived. We must erase our daughter's mistake before any more learn of it."

It. Abomination. Mistake. A face-flushing fury rose within Lyrrin. That woman was her *grandmother*. Her own grandmother wanted her dead, because of something Lyrrin had no way of changing about herself.

Lyrrin wanted to argue, to tell them she wasn't just some thing to be erased, but overwhelming emotions left her mute.

Vellira continued in a sweet, pleading tone. "We can recapture the Alderkin when your army captures that other rare dragon you're so interested in. You can keep those monsters for whatever you need them for, keep them locked up and hidden away as before, but don't keep this *thing*."

Yeonard Draekhan turned toward his wife, cupping her cheek in his hand. His head swayed in small motions as though considering, and then he nodded.

Lyrrin's shaking stopped as her body turned even colder.

The king opened his mouth to speak again, but Yensen's voice came out faster.

"I hadn't been able to include the information in a report yet, but it was the child's actions that created the … rare dragon. She may be able to assist in breeding more." There was an edge of panic in his words that hadn't been there before.

The king stilled, eyes widening slightly, and then he withdrew his hand from the queen's cheek.

"You know how it was created?" The king's voice lowered but seemed to boom even louder.

Yensen's lip twitched but he remained standing at attention and spoke clearly. "Partially."

"And this child knows the rest?" Yeonard Draekhan stood then. He loomed tall, backlit by the crackling blue lamps along the wall.

Yensen didn't confirm or deny the king's assumption. He locked eyes with Lyrrin, his expression urgent, and flicked his chin up.

Lyrrin rose shakily to her feet as the Dragon King strode toward her.

Staring down with narrowed eyes, he grasped her chin, his strong fingers in a pincerlike grip, and made her face him. "You will share with me what you know, child. We could become great allies, you and me, if you obey me. And you will obey me. For I am your king, and we are family."

Lyrrin knew her continued existence relied on being useful to this man. On being obedient. She knew even if he allowed her to live that he could make that life as difficult and painful as he wished.

But for the king to command her obedience with the mention of *family* fired up every rebellious nerve inside her. Family was love. Family was protecting one another. Family was what Lyrrin had just been wrenched away from.

Lyrrin glared at the Dragon King through stinging, hot eyes. "We are *not* family."

SECRET OF THE
DRAGON
CROWN
SELINA A FENECH
BOOK SIX OF THE
SHADOW
DRAGON SAGA

CHAPTER ONE

The Dragon King's fingers squeezed around Lyrrin's jaw, digging into her soft flesh. She tried to pull away, but he held firm in a way that could crack bone.

Still shivering from the cold flight there, she held his gaze and it made her shudder harder. There was something wrong about his stare, with those bottomless black irises and silver-bright pupils. It curdled her stomach and brought the sting of tears.

"Don't think you are so special that I will tolerate your disobedience, child." The tips of his fingers clenched. His voice rattled her insides and thundered around the walls of the empty throne room.

Lyrrin could feel her skin bruising.

Beside her, Yensen kept his eyes forward, as though nothing was happening at all. Over near the throne, the queen cast furtive looks their way and remained so still she didn't even seem to be breathing.

No one is going to help me. Lyrrin wanted to keep defying the man but was already regretting her words that had made him angry. She had to be smarter.

Tilting her chin up so high it stretched her throat, the king asked, "Are you going to cooperate or should I have this grayglim dispose of you here and now?"

Through gritted teeth, Lyrrin mumbled, "I can't tell you what I know if you break my jaw."

He didn't let go. "Of course you can. What I break can be fixed. As many times as we have to until you learn your place. But there'll be no need for that, because you're going to cooperate, aren't you?"

A sharp zing of terror cut through Lyrrin's stomach. Teary and tired, she nodded once. It was barely a movement at all, locked in the king's grasp, but he would have felt it.

He released her, and she gasped in relief. Her head flopped forward and a tear splashed free.

Stalking back to the throne, Yeonard Draekhan flicked a hand toward his wife. "Leave us."

The queen bobbed a curtsy once, then strode briskly to the door without questioning the order. The tight angle of her shoulders looked like fear to Lyrrin.

The king leaned back in the throne, as though resting after a leisurely stroll. He addressed Yensen. "Tell me how the hybrid creature was made."

The grayglim cleared his throat and went over everything, the entire story of how Riony had healed the broken dragon egg with the vial of silvernix Lyrrin had decorated.

The king kept Lyrrin locked in his terrible gaze. "What runes did you carve on the glass?"

"I don't remember." Her voice came out small and breathy, scared she'd be seen as not cooperating again.

But it was only the truth. All she remembered was that she'd just learned about the magical runes in the undercity and was so enchanted with them that she wanted to draw her own ones on the silvernix vial to make it pretty and protected and magical too.

But whatever I did, Riony wouldn't have known what it was, how to activate it, or even known there was something to activate.

The king didn't look happy with her answer.

She shot a pleading look toward Yensen, but his only response was a slight narrowing of his eyes.

She rambled. "The markings I carved probably didn't do anything anyway. It was years ago when I did them and I didn't even know how to use any runes back then. And my sister didn't activate the rune when she used the silvernix."

Lyrrin's thoughts raced, going over the details. Riony may not have activated it when she used it, but had Lyrrin, when she'd carved the runes? Could it have affected the silvernix then?

"So the carvings may have had nothing to do with the process." Lyrrin's grandfather looked at her as though she were a disappointing plate placed in front of him at lunch.

Stay useful. Stay cooperative. Don't give him too much. Don't let him work out how to get more unidragons.

Lyrrin's head hurt. Maybe the carvings did have nothing to do with it. They were on glass, not crystal, and how could it have had any magical charge for it to work?

Maybe it was something else entirely, to do with Dracuni's parents or that specific batch of silvernix?

Lyrrin chewed her lips and settled her thoughts. It didn't matter that she didn't know how to make more unidragons. All she had to do was keep the king thinking she did and keep him busy trying ways that weren't going to work until she could escape.

"The carvings must have done something," Lyrrin said confidently. "Because we tried making another hybrid with just an egg and silvernix and it didn't work."

Elumon. I hope he's okay.

Lyrrin's chest ached with a strange hollowness at being away from the hatchling.

The king didn't reply, only pierced her with an assessing gaze.

Overwrought, Lyrrin turned to Yensen. "Tell him. Tell him we did."

Her voice strained up into a high-pitched whine as the grayglim didn't even look at her. He opened his mouth but the king spoke first.

"Stop looking to him for assistance, child." Yeonard reclined further into his throne. "He is not your friend or ally or anything other than my loyal hand, as every grayglim is."

Lyrrin's lips pulled in and she kept her eyes on Yensen.

He had betrayed Eslinde for the king, but Lyrrin also knew not every grayglim was totally loyal. Brishan had abandoned his duties to be with Niskina's mother.

And there was also Lady Hjelzahn. She'd become the wife of a Hjelzahn heir, although she had remained a grayglim afterward too, so it was unclear where her loyalties lay, even before she became possessed and killed him and two of her children. Maybe she wasn't a good example.

Still, Lyrrin was only asking Yensen to confirm what was true, not commit treason. "Yensen, please tell him how we couldn't make another unidragon."

Yensen's jaw tightened. "It is true, my king. The dragonling created in the test did not have silvernix blood."

"Grayglim," Yeonard Draekhan scratched the side of his hooked nose. "Take one of your knives and pierce the palm of your hand with it. All the way through."

"Yes, my king."

Lyrrin's jaw dropped. "What? No!"

Yensen moved fast. His right hand swished across his belt and he plucked a slim dagger from a sheath. The blade flashed in the flickering blue light as he raised it, then brought it down into the palm of his other hand. There was a sickening tearing sound as the blade went through right to the hilt.

"Why? Why did you do that?" Lyrrin shrieked, both at Yensen and the man smirking down from his throne.

The Dragon King rose and strolled casually toward them. "Because the grayglim knows whom he serves, the only person he serves. Because he understands unfailing loyalty. And because you, my granddaughter, need to know that I have *hundreds* of grayglims just as loyal, all willing to do anything for me."

Yensen's jaw tensed and a sheen of sweat spread over his forehead, but he made no other movement. Lyrrin couldn't take her eyes off his hand, the blade going through it, the trembling twitch of his fingers, and the blood dripping onto the floor.

The king had ordered it, and he had done it, without hesitation … I have no friends here.

All of the shuddering cold and curdling fear and stinging nausea within Lyrrin met and merged in a rush of sickness in her throat.

She knew she could swallow it away. She could …

But maybe she didn't want to.

Heaving forward, Lyrrin emptied the contents of her stomach onto the Dragon King's boots. The splatter of her vomit echoed in the stark throne room.

The king inhaled sharply through his nose and glared at her in horror.

He raised a hand. His fingers, each ringed in ornate gold rings studded with multiple glassy gems, clenched into a fist, then opened flat again.

Lyrrin wiped her mouth and put on her smallest, most childlike voice. "I'm sorry. Blood makes me sick. I think I might …"

She made a convulsing motion with her chest and the king stepped back.

"Get her out of here. Now!"

Lyrrin did her best not to smile. It had been only a small act of rebellion, maybe, but one she was getting away with.

"My king?" Yensen asked, as though unsure the order was for him, despite him being the only other person in the room.

"I want you watching her. She's your responsibility."

Yensen nodded once, then pulled the dagger from his hand as quickly as he'd put it there. His face was pale. "Where do you wish her kept?"

Lyrrin made a gagging sound and puffed her cheeks.

Stepping back again, the king's face twisted. "I don't care, just take her away. Tomorrow we'll begin trials for creating more hybrids. I'll need to get more silvernix. We'll need more than we have on hand here, so deal with getting her cleaned up before then."

Yensen bowed, then grasped Lyrrin by the back of the neck with his uninjured hand and steered her briskly to the exit.

They pushed out through the doors, with Lyrrin trotting to keep up with Yensen's long strides. Two more grayglims flanked the doorway, and Yensen gestured to one who fell in beside him. They whispered together for a moment, then the other grayglim split off again, hurrying down another hallway.

Yeonard Draekhan's booming voice, yelling for servants, echoed all the way to Lyrrin as Yensen pushed her around another corner and they began climbing steps.

She sighed in relief to be away from that awful man, whom she never wanted to consider her grandfather. Now she just had to get herself all the way free.

"Where are you taking me?" Lyrrin asked.

"Eslinde's chambers. They are secure." Yensen removed his hand from her neck.

Despite being released, there wasn't anywhere for Lyrrin to go other than up or down, and she doubted she'd have much luck simply running for it. Her legs felt weak and wobbly.

The thought that they were going to her mother's room also drew curiosity from Lyrrin. She wanted to see that space, find something of her mother's to hold on to. So she kept going up the stairs.

Yensen drew a black strip of fabric from a pouch and bandaged his hand.

"Does it hurt?" Lyrrin asked.

Yensen gave her a flat stare and returned to his work.

"Sorry. Of course it does." Lyrrin grunted in disgust. "I can't believe he made you do that! I can't believe you did that!"

Yensen tied off the fabric, pulling it taut with his teeth. "I'm grateful to my king that he spared me after my failure."

"Don't be grateful to him! That was cruel. Him choosing awful pain instead of instant execution isn't something to be grateful for."

They reached the top of the stairs, and Lyrrin groaned to see another long hallway lined with arched niches ahead of them and more stairs beyond. The palace was huge. Who needed this much space?

"He is my king, and yours." Yensen nudged her shoulder to keep her moving. "We are both lucky to be alive, and you haven't been harmed. As long as you behave, it will be fine."

Lyrrin snorted. "I am *not* going to behave. And you shouldn't either for someone who makes you stab yourself. Did Eslinde ever make you stab yourself? I doubt it."

Yensen didn't reply. His expression was as stony as ever, but his silky black hair hung messily and there was tension around his eyes, giving him a pained, haunted look.

Is he thinking about her? Did he ever really care for Eslinde?

They continued on in silence. The passage was lined with statues of angry-looking people posing with weapons, looming out of each arched alcove. Lyrrin sneered at them and the harsh, cold stone all around. There was no warmth there. No plants or animals, no pets or personal touches of a home lived in and loved. The whole place felt lifeless.

A pang of sadness hit Lyrrin as she remembered the small two-room dwelling she and Riony had shared in the undercity, with its soft blankets and broken door and often some critter or another Lyrrin had tempted in with food.

Is Riony still in the undercity now? Did she and the others manage to help? Are they okay? Do they know what happened to me yet?

Lyrrin wished she still had her heart stone, to feel her sister's heartbeat again.

At the top of the next flight of stairs, Yensen pushed a door open, and then pushed Lyrrin inside. He reached to a strange toggle on the wall, and with a click the room illuminated.

"Servants with food and clean clothing are on their way. Don't do anything stupid. *Behave*," he said.

Lyrrin stuck her tongue out at him.

He closed the door, locking it between them.

Lyrrin stared at the solid doorway as she took a few deep breaths and then turned around.

Eslinde's room … No, Eslinde's *chambers*. Lyrrin hadn't expected how big they would be, how many rooms were involved. There were four doorways splitting off from the vast central living area she'd stepped into, a space draped in books along every wall, like a waterfall of tomes all around, spilling out from the shelves in piles on the ground.

Only a few other pieces of furniture occupied the space. A small table with two chairs beside a large window at one end, and a lounge and armchairs—Lyrrin hadn't seen those before but knew about them—around another low table, covered in books. A patch on the floor near there had a dark stain marring the polished tiles.

Lyrrin scurried over to the lounge and pulled a blanket from it. She draped it over her chilled shoulders and brought it up to her face. It smelled like her mother.

Pulling it tight around her, she quickly checked the other rooms, looking for weapons or exits. The first she tried was too dark to see into.

Lyrrin noticed another one of the toggle switches near the door. She tentatively flicked it, and light crackled from the lamp fittings in the same eerie blue of the rest of the palace. It was cooler than the cyan glow of the Alderkin light stones.

Inside was a bathroom. So different to those in the undercity, with hot spring water running perpetually into stone baths, filling the air with steam. This one was cold, with a shining steel tub and metal pipes and taps.

But it contained no windows or exits, so Lyrrin moved on. Behind the second door was a storage closet. The third was a room even more filled with books than the living area, creating a maze across the floor. Lyrrin flicked the toggle, but the lights in there didn't work.

A large window on the other side brightened the room with the last dull purple light of day. Lyrrin made her way there, growing eager as she saw the balcony beyond the glass.

The massive window had a door built in, and Lyrrin grinned when she pushed and it swung open easily.

Her smile faded, though, as she stepped out onto the balcony, so, so far above the ground below with nothing on the slick marble walls to climb down. Someone would have to be desperate to try to get down from there.

Against the dusk-bruised sky, something massive moved, flying off to the northeast. A dragon, bigger than she'd ever seen. Its wings seemed to stretch from one side of the city to the other, four times as big as any dragon Lyrrin had known. Bigger than the shadow dragon itself.

A dragon that big could swallow someone whole.

Cold wind gusted against Lyrrin's face. She pulled the blanket closer again and went back inside. The fourth and final room was the bedroom. Her mother's bedroom. Lyrrin traced around the walls, hoping for some secret doorway to reveal itself, as she avoided the desire to crawl into the massive bed in the center of the space and curl up and cry.

She followed the boundary all the way around and back out of the room and to the front door again, dragging her fingertips along the wall as she went. Nothing but slick, streaky marble all the way, with no seams or buttons revealing a concealed escape route.

The texture only changed when she reached the front door, where ornate carvings surrounded the threshold. And as her fingers passed over a section of them, she felt the stone there sing.

Lyrrin stopped, blinked, and backtracked. She ran her fingers and eyes over the area, heart pounding. Within the swirling lines and intricate patterns a different sort of design became clear.

Alderkin runes.

She touched the symbol hesitantly, feeling how it sung to her, a reverberation deep in her chest.

Alderkin runes on ... crystal? It had to be charged crystal for it to hum like that, but it looked just like the surrounding stone. Lyrrin leaned closer and saw the careful layer of paint and the edges of the carved section.

Prying her sharp fingers into the gap, Lyrrin grasped the crystal and pulled.

The long, thin shaft slid from the wall. Beyond the painted cap, the transparent quartz glowed softly. A cavity in the middle held a small vial of silvernix.

"Sparks, yes!" Lyrrin whispered breathily.

There was a crystal she might be able to work with and silvernix to keep her safe. They felt like a gift from her mother, waiting there for her, to give her hope, to give her a chance to get free.

She examined the rune. She'd never seen one like it before, so she wasn't sure what she could do with it.

I'll work it out soon enough.

But what she wasn't sure of was how the crystal was still charged. They were a long, long way from any shrines there.

Lyrrin remembered Shael's words when they had been talking about the standing stones and how they charge the crystals.

There's only one way that works without—

Her mother knows already. Alleem worked it out for her, to keep her safe.

Lyrrin dropped down to the floor, cradling the crystal on her lap. She turned it in her hands, and along the bottom was a line of swirling shapes. Alderkin writing. Lyrrin wished she knew what it meant.

Did my father make this? For Eslinde?

All her plans to carve that length of crystal into pieces and test out rune combinations shattered as surely as if she'd pelted the stone onto the floor. She couldn't do it. She couldn't destroy what might be the last thing in the world her father had left behind.

She had so little of anything left of those she loved. Riony and Eslinde and Dracuni and Aishena and Benjin and Elumon and Niskina and everyone who had become her friends and family felt a world away from her and suddenly all she wanted was to be squeezing her doll she'd left in the undercity tight in her arms as Riony squeezed tight around her.

I'm going to see her again. I'm going to get out of here.

But even the voice in her head sounded weak and scared and all the pain and fear of the day hit her like the smack of a dragon wing.

Because how could she stay strong in this awful, lifeless place, all alone? How could she stay safe around a man who would make even those loyal to him stab themselves through their hand?

How could she survive against that sort of cruelty and power?

Chapter Two

The silken plates of Dracuni's scales jolted against Riony's back.

Teetering on the edge of sleep, Riony woke with a start, her heart cracking into a sprint as she was hit by Dracuni's fear and her own all at once. She grasped around nearby until her fingers closed on the hilt of her crystal sword, heavy and uncharged.

She scrambled blindly to her feet. "What is it? What's wrong?"

Riony scrubbed the palm of her free hand into her bleary eyes, trying to clear them. The unfamiliar room was lit by a single glow stone, left activated because Dracuni didn't like the complete darkness the caves otherwise provided. Lyrrin never used to like it either.

Elumon slept on a blanket on the other side of the tiled floor, undisturbed. Cool air from the open vent nearby blew the frayed edges of Myrwa's shawl that was draped over Riony's shoulders, tickling her bare arms. Nothing else moved.

The unidragon's flanks heaved with gasping, sobbing breaths. ***Nightmare. I'm sorry.***

The tension in Riony's sword hand eased, but her heart hadn't gotten the all clear message yet, still rattling hard. "Same as usual? Flying?"

Yes. Flying. Falling … The fear rushing into her from Dracuni changed to a deep aching shame and sadness. ***Losing little sister.***

Riony turned around and leaned into Dracuni's neck, holding her and stroking a hand over her pale rainbow scales.

"It's not your fault. It's okay."

A truth and a lie. Riony didn't blame Dracuni at all. But it wasn't okay.

Lyrrin was gone.

It had been over a week since they'd sealed themselves into the Alderkin depths with an army of dragonriders outside. Over a week since Lyrrin had been taken away.

Over a week since Riony or Dracuni had managed any semblance of proper sleep, until Niskina and Aishena had ordered them home at midday to take a nap before they passed out on their feet.

Riony wasn't sure what time it was, but the low murmur of the sounds of the undercity rumbling through the stone walls suggested everyone else was still awake.

Dracuni's lilac eyes glimmered with the reflected cyan glow, her eyelids drooping heavily.

Ruffling the tuft of hair above her horn, Riony sighed.

"Come on. Back to sleep. You need it."

Riony expected resistance, but Dracuni's head lowered down to the ground and her eyes squeezed closed, pressing loose a tear. It didn't take long for the exhausted unidragon to fall asleep again with Riony stroking her eye ridges and whispering calming words.

But Riony's own hopes of sleep had once again been lost.

She left her sword beside Dracuni and tiptoed out of the room. Now that the panic of startling awake was gone, Riony knew they were safe in there. Only approved people could get in. The chambers she'd been given were deep within the Delver's Circuit.

These huge razing chambers.

Riony had originally wanted to go home to her tiny apartment at the top of Dragonwing Tower, but Dracuni wouldn't fit in there. So she'd gotten what she'd wanted for so long. The spacious, rich home of a delver. Fully furnished, the chambers even had proper beds, a large dining table, and lounges. Riony hadn't even seen a lounge since leaving Heithorn estate.

Every inch was beautifully decorated, the doors and walls carved with flowing organic patterns. Everything from the plumbing to the ventilation, hot and cold, all worked. No sticky door mechanisms there.

She was neighbors to the Hjelzahns, with enough room for Dracuni and Elumon and Sir Butterfur and all the pets Lyrrin could want, and it all felt cold and empty because Lyrrin wasn't there with her.

Out in the large living area, the air was muggy, steamed by the hot spring bath at one end of the room. Riony rolled her braies up to the knees and stepped into the scalding water, then sat down on the edge.

"I don't have any treats," she said, as Butterfur sluiced through the pool toward her, sniffing around her thin undershirt.

The cave otter looked up at her, then looked over her shoulder on one side, then the other, as he often did. Searching for someone who wasn't there.

Butterfur twitched his snout accusingly, then swam off, disappearing into a pipe that a creature his size had no right fitting through.

Riony scooped a handful of water and splashed her face, then swiped through her hair. Or what was left of it. It had grown long in their time aboveground, the deep red picking up gold highlights from being under the sun. But one too-close puff of dragonfire burned away half of it.

Riony had raggedly cropped the rest herself. Zeina promised her she was still hot, but even that praise hadn't stirred anything in Riony.

Her toes tingled in the steaming water as she pulled the heart stone from where it hung beneath her shirt, now missing its other half.

She sat there staring at it, willing it to miraculously burst to life again and show her that Lyrrin's heart still beat. In a haze of exhaustion, she thought she might have done it when there was a low thump and a dull grinding sound.

But it was the entrance door rolling open behind her.

She half turned, squinting at the strange silhouette quietly stalking in, backlit by the corridor's lighting.

"Sparks," Riony growled low under her breath.

The last person she wanted to see or be alone with.

Ever since coming back to the undercity, since the fight against the riders ... since the whipping post ... Riony found she couldn't look at Kess. Holding her gaze on the wolf girl was like staring at the sun. A strange, dizzying, deeply scarring sensation.

She simply couldn't do it. Every time Kess was around or within view, a churning pressure seemed to fill Riony like a pot boiling over, if the pot also lost all emotional coherence and ability to think straight. Which would make sense because it was a pot. But Riony found the experience overwhelming.

So she'd been making sure she saw Kess as little as possible.

The way Kess also eschewed eye contact made Riony think she'd noticed the avoidance.

Kess cleared her throat. "Sorry. I thought you were sleeping. I was just going to drop these off and go."

Riony lifted her gaze from the ground to see Griskin, Kess's legs, and an overflowing woven basket balanced on those legs. She lowered her eyes quickly again.

"Drop what off?"

"Your belongings."

"I don't have ..."

The clink of glass and rustle of blankets from within the basket cut off Riony's words. Griskin sniffed and whined as he brought Kess closer.

"Someone else had moved into your old place. But one of your neighbors kept these for you, in case you came back." Kess lowered the basket down in front of her.

Riony's shoulders slumped as she saw the familiar woven blanket, carefully folded on top, spotted with burn holes. Her nose wrinkled as she moved it aside to find neatly stacked glass jars filled with dried herbs, crystals with experimental runes carved on them, and an old straw doll with an age-dulled red ribbon.

With the threat of the siege, not enough food to feed the dragons they and the defeated riders had brought underground, the Alderkin vanishing, and Eslinde locking herself away, utterly heartbroken, Riony had been too busy to check what had become of her old home.

Or too scared to go back there without Lyrrin. To hold these remnants of their old lives when Riony was so far away from holding Lyrrin herself ... It hurt like a knife in the heart.

"Thanks," she choked out, staring at Griskin's feet.

The wolf snuffled and pawed at his nose.

"It's nothing." Kess and Griskin turned away.

Riony reached into the basket, grasping a cold glass jar in her hand. Her head spun as the smell of wild animal and honeyed wilderness that Riony had come to associate with Kess drifted across to her. Kess and the wolf were almost at the door again when a sound that was barely a word stuttered desperately from Riony's mouth.

"Wait," she managed to say more clearly. "I ... can put something together for the pup. To help him with the fungus allergy."

They padded back silently to her side. "Do you have what you need?"

"Yeah, I should. Tried to always have the supplies around for if Lyrrin had a flare-up." Riony's throat closed over her sister's name.

She lifted her legs from the water and turned around to face the basket completely, leaning over and digging through, bringing the jars out and lining them up beside her.

She only needed two herbs for the mix, three for best results.

She found the genjermint quickly, but the blue pine was being more elusive. Her search revealed a half-filled jar of hennan and her thoughts shuddered to a stop as she remembered applying the muddy paste made from it to Lyrrin's hair to darken away the bright-blue tone.

If only I could have disguised all of us, somehow. Kept Dracuni hidden from everyone. I've made so many mistakes.

She closed her eyes to force away the tears. In her moment of hesitation, Kess moved closer and slid down from Griskin to sit on the ground beside the basket.

Riony took a shaky breath, found the herbs she needed, then turned around again so she wasn't facing Kess. With her back to the pool, she worked on pulling corks from the jars and sniffing them to make sure they were still potent enough.

Kess murmured, "I have ..."

A quick glance to the side showed Kess holding one hand in front of her, clasped closed around something small. She was way too close and Riony's body felt hot and disjointed the way it had when she'd poisoned herself with corpsefoot.

She grimaced and almost dropped a jar.

Kess withdrew her hand and Riony heard a belt pouch clasp open and closed. "I should go. You need to sleep."

No kidding. But it wasn't going to happen. Riony hadn't told anyone, but she'd been having nightmares too.

Every time she closed her eyes, she saw the faces of the people she'd killed, the burning enclaves, the destroyed keep, the whipping post. Only keeping busy had kept those visions away, but she was being betrayed by her body's physical desperation for rest.

Her hands had stilled on the jars and her eyes were unfocused.

Kess spoke softly. "I'll go. I'll come back later when it's ready, or you could give it to someone else to pass on to me."

Kess shifted, and Riony dared to look at her back as she moved to remount Griskin. She swallowed hard.

"Are you ... okay?" Riony felt awful that whatever was going on inside her meant she hadn't checked on Kess after what she went through.

Kess stopped and turned back. "Me?"

Riony flicked her eyes to look at the ground again. She busied her hands with mixing the three herbs she needed into the emptiest jar.

"After ... what Kife did. After almost drowning."

"I'm fine. You used silvernix on me. I'm completely healed."

"But are you *okay*?"

Silence stretched out between them. Riony couldn't be sure, because she refused to look, but it felt as though Kess moved closer.

Kess asked, "What would you give for what is most important to you?"

"Don't answer my question with another question. I'm too tired for mind games."

"No. I really want to know."

Rolling her eyes, Riony begrudgingly thought about it. Then she decided not to think and just let her mouth take over and trust its truth.

"My life. If I knew that giving my life would change this world in a way that mattered, I wouldn't hesitate." Riony's eyes filled with tears that didn't fall as she suddenly felt as though her small life was so insignificant in the face of all she wanted, all she hoped to save, the scale of what she faced.

Her head dropped forward, shaking. "I want Lyrrin back more than anything, but there is so much more to consider now, so many more lives at risk that I feel like I could save if I just push a little harder."

"Push any harder and you'll destroy yourself."

"We all destroy ourselves for something. All that matters is that we choose a worthy cause to destroy ourselves for."

The only sound in the room was Kess's trembling breath, then she whispered, "That's how I feel too. Whatever I suffer, whatever I've been through, it's worth it."

Riony flinched as a hand came near her face, brushing along the flame-cropped hair. She snatched the wrist from the air, tight in her own, and instinctively turned as though toward danger and came face-to-face with Kess.

Kess froze, eyes round like prey, but not without defiance. Mouth parted, nostrils flared, cheeks red. "I'm sorry."

Her hand tugged, trying to move away again, but Riony didn't let go.

Their gazes met and Riony's world swirled down to nothing but those icy-blue eyes staring back into hers.

The overwhelming sensation flooded her. The tingling pressure squeezed her heart and rushed up her spine and spread across her scalp and blurred her vision with the heat of emotion.

Riony's breath stuttered, and her fingers flexed, opening and closing around Kess's wrist as though trying to let go but held in place by an unseen force. Once, twice, three times she tried to release, then her grasp locked tight and pulled, bringing Kess into her.

Their lips crushed together.

Riony pressed her mouth against Kess with an all-consuming need, and for a heartbeat, Kess was frozen, motionless under her touch. Then the kiss was returned with a frantic yearning that sent Riony mindless.

Releasing Kess's wrist, she tangled both hands into Kess's stormy hair and drove her whole body into the kiss. The smaller body beneath her crumpled, falling back under her assault and together they thumped onto the floor, lips still joined.

Riony felt the sharp inhale of air into Kess's mouth and she chased that breath.

When Riony opened Kess's mouth with hers, pressing deeper, Kess arched up against Riony's chest. Riony slid her hands under the small of Kess's back and pulled her in tight with all her strength, needing her closeness as though any distance between their bodies wounded her very soul.

Kess released a gasping, songlike whimper that made Riony's heart beat so hard she felt ready to pass out. She pressed her mouth over the cry with a low moan.

Hot air gusted over the back of Riony's neck, followed by a vicious, rumbling growl.

Riony froze. The only movement she made was the shaking from her frantic breath and rampant pulse. She slowly lifted her hands and lips away from Kess in surrender as bared teeth pressed against her skin.

Kess stared up wild-eyed at Riony and the wolf at her neck.

"Gris! It's okay. She's … she's not hurting me."

The wolf growled again but backed away enough for Riony to move without fear that she was about to be decapitated by wolf bite. She sat up, kneeling straddled across Kess's thighs, breathing like she'd been fighting for her life.

Sparks. What did I just do?

"I didn't?" Riony's mouth went dry. "I didn't hurt you, did I?"

"No, not at all." Despite the words, Kess looked utterly devastated.

Eyes glistening, lips and cheeks flushed. Riony had rarely seen her like that, her emotions so clear and vulnerable on her face.

What did I just do? And why did Kess let me?

Riony felt horrified that Kess's pledge somehow extended to *this*. Allowing Riony to do that to her, even if she didn't want to.

I pledge my life to you and your cause. For whatever good it can provide you.

Where was the boundary? Riony was a world away from knowing what she wanted right now but she didn't want *that*.

"Sorry. I'm sorry. That wasn't right. I shouldn't have." Riony shifted onto her haunches and reached to help Kess up.

Griskin growled again. He shoved into the space in front of Riony, pushing her back onto her rump as he nudged Kess to sit up, licking her face.

Is she okay? What did I just do?

The boiling-over sensation still ran rampant throughout Riony. The way Kess had kissed her back … She had, hadn't she? She hadn't just imagined it?

What sort of love had Kess meant back when she'd said, "That's the Riony I love?"

And was that also what this overwhelming feeling was?

What did I just do? And why do I so badly want to do it again?

Kess, red-faced and chest heaving and eyes averted, climbed onto the still growling wolf's back. "I should go."

Riony nodded drunkenly from her seat on the floor. She spotted the jar of mixed herbs beside her, knocked on its side but unspilled. She recorked it and thrust it up toward Kess.

"Here."

Kess reached for it. Their fingers touched and it felt like a bolt of lightning. Riony bit her tongue to keep quiet as every part of her wanted to tell Kess to stay. Even if it meant being mauled by a wolf.

Confused and ashamed and drowning in a kind of wanting she'd never experienced before, Riony watched Kess leave.

When the door closed, she flopped backward onto the ground. Her head fell over the lip of the pool, lolling into the warm water, and she swore loudly. For an aching hazy-sweet moment, all she could think about was the kiss.

That kiss. With Kessara Razing Heithorn. *That kiss.*

And then all her other worries returned in the crush of a landslide.

CHAPTER THREE

Ambushed. Again.

Kess and Griskin stepped out of Riony's room to find Niskina waiting for her in the hallway. The curvy woman leaned against the wall and swung her poleaxe lazily like a pendulum in front of her.

"If you're here to warn me away from Riony again, then …"

Then Kess didn't know what.

A few moments ago, she would have said it didn't matter because Riony was already avoiding her like she'd avoid a plague-ridden pile of manure.

Until she *wasn't*.

Until she was doing something entirely different than avoiding.

Kess's hands shook with the thud of her fired-up pulse and her cheeks felt hot as her mind relived the kiss in a loop. She let it. She never wanted to forget how every touch felt, every press of skin to skin, the curve of Riony's mouth under hers.

Kess's lips had become a reliquary, haunted by the sensation of Riony's kiss.

Brushing back her tumbling hair, Niskina narrowed her eyes on Kess. "Are you okay? You look sick."

"I'm fine," Kess snapped.

Hiding the heat in her face behind her hair, she pushed Griskin onward down the passageway. "I'm late getting to scouting for the day."

"I'll walk with you, then." Niskina fell in beside her.

Griskin growled, and Kess shushed him, rubbing his ears.

Niskina widened the gap. "What's got him all riled up?"

Hands in my hair, around my waist, falling back under Riony's weight.

Kess swallowed. "Nothing. Did you want something?"

"I've been wanting to talk to you. Alone. But haven't found the chance."

They'd all been busy since the siege began, working to make sure the undercity was safe.

The Alderkin had done some magic to block the main entryways to the depths before they disappeared, but there were other barricades and defenses that had to be built in case the army of dragons outside managed to dig their way in.

Kess's main job had been regular trips out through the hidden mountain exit to spy down on those keeping them imprisoned, then reporting her findings to the others.

Which Kess had made sure was the only time she spent around Niskina and the guilt her presence evoked in her.

She sighed. "Here we are, alone. Get to the threats already."

They moved through the quiet hallways of Delver's Circuit, the private tunnels carved between the exclusive homes there, but would soon be out onto the busy streets of Upslope.

Kess hoped Niskina wouldn't try to murder her before then.

Niskina frowned slightly, and her full lips popped open. "No threats. I just wanted to say … ugh. Look. What you did for Riony, taking that whipping instead of her … I've seen her scars. She has so many scars. And I know Ri is the type who would have taken more, but it means the world that she didn't have to."

Kess nodded, muted by the depths of her agreement.

Niskina snorted and shook her head. "And I still can't believe it was *you* who saved her from that!"

"I live to defy people's expectations, I guess."

Niskina grew solemn and her words rambled. "Aish has been telling me things. And after what you did to Kife too, well, I know he deserved it in every way, but he was your brother. And still you didn't hesitate to do what had to be done."

Kess pressed her eyes closed for a moment, rocking gently in the darkness as Griskin kept them moving forward.

Kife. Her brother. The last of her family, gone. For the better, and even the wolf she rode on was more family than any of them had ever been, but that didn't reduce the pain that rebounded within her chest as though she were hollow inside.

Kife's body had been recovered the day of his death by a competent swimmer, to make sure the water reservoirs weren't tainted. He was burned without ceremony.

Kess opened her eyes. "And I'd do it again. I meant my pledge."

Niskina reached out, grasping Kess around the arm and bringing her and Griskin to a stop. "I know. I can see it now. You really have changed. I'm sorry I didn't believe you before."

Niskina's touch was gentle and warm. The touch of a friend. A touch Kess had so rarely felt.

She blinked rapidly to clear the wash of salt water on her eyes. "I'm sorry too. I'm sorry that I didn't change sooner. I'm sorry you lost your father because of me."

Niskina's nose flushed pink, and she fluttered her eyelids too. "We don't know what would have happened, even if you were on our side. We don't know … I decided to redirect my ire toward Lady Hjelzahn for now, although apparently she's possessed or something?"

"You could blame the shadow dragon, then," Kess offered.

Niskina half smiled and held out a hand.

Kess reached back, shaking it, offering a nervous, thin-lipped smile. Silently, they both turned and continued on together.

Leaving the guarded exit of Delver's Circuit, the bustling hum of the undercity loudened, and Griskin sniffled.

Kess looked numbly at the jar clutched in her hand, trying to focus on the *here and now* and not the *there and Riony's kiss*. She dug around her pockets for a handkerchief.

Niskina cleared her throat, but her voice still came out low with concern. "So, how was she? How's Riony feeling?"

Feeling our bodies pressed together, feeling the warmth of Riony's skin through her thin shirt.

The glass jar slipped in Kess's fingers. She fumbled, catching it at the last moment.

"She's upset … tired. I think she's too tired to be thinking straight."

That had to be it. Why what happened, happened. Riony was just exhausted and overwhelmed and seeking comfort from the closest body.

Kess was sure Riony didn't like her, in *any* particular way. Riony only allowed her to be around, only done what she'd done to help her because she would have done that for almost anyone. It was just who she was.

That moment together … Kess couldn't assume it meant anything.

No matter how real it felt. *How it felt …*

Niskina hummed agreement. "I know losing Lyrrin is hitting Riony hard, but she's not going to be able to do anything if she doesn't take a break and look after herself. Do you know how hard I had to bully her to even take a few hours to go and catch up on some sleep?"

Sleep she wasn't getting, even before my visit.

"We all destroy ourselves for something," Kess whispered.

"Huh?"

Kess shook her head. "Riony would do anything, give everything for others. That's why she needs us. She can save the world, but we're here to save her."

Niskina hummed again in thoughtful agreement.

Kess uncorked the jar and a bright, cool fragrance emerged.

She shook some of the herbal mix into the handkerchief on her lap and recorked the rest for later. Knotting the corners into a neat bundle with a piece of string, she then leaned forward and tied it to the front harness of Griskin's saddle.

The scent wafted around them.

Passersby gave her and her wolf space, stepping away as they saw them and Niskina coming through. Niskina received respectful nods and even a salute or two, with wary glances reserved for Kess.

When Kess and Griskin had explored the undercity the first time, the richer areas of Upslope had been quiet and sparsely populated. Exclusively for delvers—which Kess had recently learned about—and others with the money or means to separate themselves from the masses packed in Downslope.

Not anymore. Upslope was as densely filled as the rest of the undercity. The town square area beside the long curtain of stone that ran across the cavern had become a training ground, where Aishena, Zeina, Benjin, and some delvers were teaching melee combat to anyone willing.

Overhead in the gaps between the towering stalagmite apartments and the dripping stalactites far above, dragons flew. All the smaller treedarts that remained after the invading riders were defeated had been gathered up, and the even more daring undercity volunteers were receiving training from Vance, Dashiel, and Jaym on how to fly.

And the dragons too big to fly easily in that space, Viska, Gleem, Hux, and Ambri, were attracting even more people in to where they were being housed on the Upper Flats, just to see them.

Kess and Niskina reached the top of the flowstone steps, and an arm raised above the crowd nearby, waving them down. The people parted, revealing Jaym, grinning a dazzling, crooked smile. His pocket-hawk, Teeka, perched on his shoulder, preening the man's golden blond curls.

Cute little thing. But also another thing that I will protect Riony from. Even Riony's name in her thoughts made Kess feel ready to combust like dragonfire again.

Niskina stilled, waiting for the Rebel Rider to reach them.

But she kept her eyes on Kess and narrowed them suspiciously. "Riony didn't say anything to you, did she? Do anything odd?"

Kess choked. "What do you mean?"

"I'm just worried she's secretly plotting a one-woman rescue mission again, like when she went off after you."

Kess frowned. Would Riony do that? She'd gone after Kess; of course she'd go after Lyrrin. Although Riony only had to get through Kife to reach Kess, for all she knew when setting out. Rescuing a captive of the Dragon King was something else entirely.

"If she is, why would she tell me about it?" Kess asked.

"I think she opens up to you more than the rest of us sometimes."

"She probably cares less what I think about her."

"Maybe." Niskina didn't sound convinced. "You better not be in on letting her endanger herself. You've been acting weird ever since you came out of her room and—"

"Look at these two majestic heroines!" Jaym reached them, arms wide in greeting.

Kess exhaled her relief as her heart continued to race and her mind kept reliving every touch shared between her and Riony. Acting weird was the least of her concerns. She felt lucky she hadn't keeled over on the spot from the intensity of her feelings.

Niskina scoffed at the Rebel Rider. "You're such a flatterer. But you know it doesn't work if you do it to everyone."

"Oh, I think it still works." He winked at her and then turned and gave Kess another, even more conspiratorial wink.

Niskina rolled her eyes, but a grin grew across her lips.

Jaym leaned in and looped a finger around one of the steel rings on Niskina's leather harness vest. "You and I have that meeting to get to, the one before the other meeting with everyone else later."

"So many meetings." Niskina sighed dramatically, still grinning. "If I must."

A rough voice barked from nearby, "If it's such a struggle for you, let someone who's capable take charge!"

The neatly coifed man stood flanked by two others, looking more like bodyguards than companions. His silver tunic was spotless and lay under a glow stone that had been fitted into a decadent gold necklace.

It wasn't the first time Niskina and the others had been challenged for the work they were doing in the undercity. Generally by people who all looked much like this man.

They were few and far between, but tensions were rising with the dragon army outside and risk that they might get *inside*. But people were coming together too, helping each other, learning how to defend each other.

Dracuni had also decided she wanted to help. She'd seen people suffering and argued with Riony for days before Riony agreed to bottle her blood.

And so the ill and injured were offered access to the silvernix supplies 'belonging to the benevolent princess' who had come to the undercity. Kess thought it was a good idea. They needed as many healthy bodies as possible for what might come next. And Dracuni's blood helped so many.

But still, some people weren't happy.

Niskina raised her eyebrows at the man. "I'm not in charge, for starters. I'm doing the work I can to be of service. And I'm sure I remember you were happy with the services I offered the undercity when I was able to get crystals recharged."

The glowing crystal pendant swung as the man huffed. "That was before you brought in all the riffraff, letting them into Upslope."

"There was space there, and people need a place to live." Niskina shrugged.

The man stepped closer, his brown skin deepening red. "And now people are saying you're going to start rationing food?"

A crowd was building, watching the exchange. Rowdy voices muttered their agreement as the man yelled into Niskina's face.

Kess slipped a dagger from where it was sheathed on her bracer and turned Griskin around for a better angle, preparing to take on the mob that was forming.

Niskina huffed, hands on her hips. "We're *under siege*, if you haven't noticed. The undercity is fairly self-sufficient, but there are so many more people here now."

The crowd surged, grumbling and arguing. Kess tensed, prepared to fight.

Jaym raised his voice, calling like a town crier over the crowd. "People who were saved from the terrible massacre of Midwinter's Eve by this very brave young woman right here! That night ... you wouldn't believe the horrors we were witness too."

A hush fell over the surrounding people and their eyes turned to him.

Jaym lowered his voice, melodious and solemn. "Some of you know. Oh yes. Some of you were there. You, maybe? Or you?"

He pointed vaguely into the crowd, not at anyone particular. A few people still grumbled but were hissed into silence by those around them.

Kess's fingers loosened around the bone knife. Jaym had the crowd transfixed.

Hopping up onto a step, the Rebel Rider's voice carried over the audience. "Some of you weren't there, but you've heard the tales from those who survived. And how did they survive? Only through the actions of the heroic beauties here before you."

Kess's eyes widened at being included. But the glances her way weren't the kind she was used to. They were curious and awed. Some of them were openly reverential. The man leading the assault sputtered as the crowd jostled him and his cronies away.

Niskina sidled over beside where Kess watched Jaym spin his tale about the night the enclaves were attacked, with all his embellishments, especially about Niskina's role in the heroics. He made it sound like a grand legend of old, a far cry from the tragic, messy atrocity that it was.

Smirking, Niskina whispered, "Yep, he's as good orally as he is in print."

The man's words worked like magic, soothing the crowd and clearly raising both Niskina and Kess in their estimations.

But Kess's own estimations of herself had dropped. When presented with a problem, she had as ever been ready for violence, but Jaym had found another solution.

Jaym finished his story and the crowd dispersed, a new energy humming through them. A positive energy.

Niskina folded her arms and lifted her chin at the man. "Does this mean you're going to write me into one of your stories?"

His grin in return was broad and hungry. "Maybe, but we'll need some more to write about first. Now ... that meeting?"

Niskina nodded a farewell to Kess and followed Jaym away down the street.

Kess watched for a moment, taking in all the faces around her.

Would she have taken lives if things had turned nasty? Added more marks to all the others tallied in her brutal past? She was a killer.

She'd even killed her own brother.

Sighing, Kess slid her bone dagger away and urged Griskin on again, heading to the passageway up into the mountains.

The scent of the herbal parcel thickened again as they moved, and Kess's heart felt heavy. The intoxication of the kiss had worn off, and only questions that felt as though they were traps designed to maim her remained.

Did the kiss mean anything? Of course not.

Could it happen again? Of course not.

Did Riony actually care for her?

How could someone like her ever love a killer like me?

Back at Eslindekeep, Lyrrin had talked about how they don't attack, they protect. Kess had liked that. The kid was smart. Hopefully smart enough to survive the Dragon King's captivity.

In her time surviving aboveground, Kess had done anything she had to do to protect herself. She'd done it for so long that she'd gotten too used to it. She'd become hard and vicious and deadly in defending herself and only herself.

She had more to protect now, could be someone who protected instead of attacked. She had been that for Riony, and she would continue to be. No matter what.

Griskin moved through the cave and reached the iced-over waterfall. Kess used the cutting athame Riony had given her to clear the hole that had closed over since her last trip out.

She'd volunteered them for the task of scouting since she knew the mountain range well from her time stalking the mother dragon. She knew where she could go to get a good view down over the entrances of the depths, and she doubted anyone without their own wolf to ride would be able to make their way to that peak.

Stepping out into the blistering winter winds, a strange sensation washed over Kess. She squinted at the smoky skies that rained ash onto the snow and made the alpine landscape muddy and gray.

She'd had that feeling every time she'd come out of the depths. A strange mix of longing and anger and shame which felt basically the way Kess usually felt, but still somehow unfamiliar.

Nothing moved in the sky, so Kess pulled a pale blanket from a saddlebag and threw it over her back. Griskin crunched upward through the snow.

The leather delver armor that she'd been given was warm and chosen because it didn't glint in the sun the way the golden scale mail from Eslindekeep did. But Kess still preferred to cover herself entirely, lest even the small metal rings on the harness catch the eye of one of the riders below.

It was a hard climb to the highest peak. Rocks skidded beneath Griskin's paws as he leaped them from narrow ledge to narrow ledge.

They settled on a rocky outcrop, backs to a cliff, and looked down. Kess squinted through the seeing stone Riony had loaned her.

Just doing the same as they've been doing every day.

The majority of the dragon army were camped on the slopes below, tents and dragons alternating in a pattern around the entrances. A few flew patrols, far closer to the ground than even Kess's perch.

There was always a team of five or six dragons at the Alderkin depth gates, trying to force their way inside. They burned and clawed and dug, but so far the stone of the gates, and whatever the Alderkin had done to it, held strong.

The strange sensation tugged on Kess's senses again. Closer.

"I know you're there!" Kess yelled into the wind. "Show yourself!"

A trickle of ice and pebbles cascaded down the rock face.

Above Kess, a large shape moved, casting a shadow over her. Claws appeared, clutching the top of the cliff, and a dusky purple head snaked down. Griskin whined, his back foot slipping from the narrow ledge before he caught himself.

Kess rubbed a hand on his neck to reassure him. "If Lyomir wanted to roast us, he would have done it by now. He's had plenty of opportunities, following us around up here. Haven't you?"

The dragon huffed. ***Maybe ... I wanted ... to get closer first.***

The words came through slow and disjointed, as though the dragon were still finding his voice after so long without one. But those words, slicing into Kess's mind so clearly, made her gasp.

"You're close enough now," Kess challenged.

The etherdart's eyes narrowed as he moved even nearer, taking in Kess and her wolf with an eager curiosity that washed from him to her. He didn't speak again. Or burn them alive.

"Why did you follow us here?"

From the very first day they had rushed to the undercity to defend it against Kife, Lyomir had followed them. At a great distance and out of sight, but Kess had sensed his presence. As she had every time she'd come out scouting.

You ... interest me. Compel me. Lyomir closed his hazy green eyes in a slow blink as though he didn't like that fact one bit. *You make me hear ... song.*

The echoing, gravelly voice in Kess's head hummed four notes.

Kess cringed, suddenly embarrassed. "I sang to you. After you were born. Before you were tamed. *Close your eyes, and dream so deep, while dragons sleep, while dragons sleep.*"

A Rolanian lullaby. The only one Kess had known at the time, learned from Riony. Kess's parents had never sung to her.

Lyomir sighed deeply and the hot air warmed Kess's face. *My memories, thoughts ... all chaos.*

"I'm sorry." Kess had no idea what it would feel like, living through being tamed, then waking up again after so long.

Lyomir's head shook in a shiver and his teeth bared. Kess braced herself. Then his eyes met hers.

But I see you in the chaos. Singing. Freeing me. Joining me in the air.

"I see it too," Kess whispered desperately.

Since Kess had first flown on Lyomir in her attempt to stop him attacking their tamed dragons, she had longed to fly with him again, dreamed of sharing the sky with him.

She'd felt a connection between them, but it was one so raw and delicate that she feared even examining it would make it vanish.

But as they spoke, his words inside her felt like strands of thread weaving into her soul, tying them together. She could feel his every shift in emotion and how they were reacting to hers. The sensation dizzied her as it all accumulated into a single resounding thought.

We're bonded.

A deep thrumming sound reverberated in Lyomir's throat. Kess's fingers trembled, and she reached up. Lyomir balked, pulling away.

Kess exhaled roughly, a wry smile on her face. Bonded maybe, but the purple etherdart radiated only the barest tolerance for her.

I'll take it.

Kess lowered her hand, and Lyomir moved closer again. He sniffed at her, then Griskin, making the wolf growl softly.

"Now that we're on speaking terms at least, is there anything you need? Are you safe out here, from all the dragons down the hill? I can't get you into the caverns below through the tunnel I came out. It's too small. But I'll be out here often."

Lyomir's head tilted side to side. *I ... owe ... to you.*

"You don't owe me a thing."

You freed me.

It was the Taenish way, to owe and repay debts. How Kess had been raised. And then there was Riony, willing to give anything for those she cared about and everyone else, never asking anything for it. Something Kess was getting used to. Something she preferred.

"I only returned to you what was taken from you unjustly. I only made things right."

Lyomir watched her steadily with his huge eyes, her own image reflected within them, so small.

Kess straightened up as she stared back.

Small, but mighty. More than anyone had ever expected her to be.

With the kiss from Riony still burning on her lips and the voice of a dragon in her mind, Kess felt capable of anything. And she knew if she didn't want Riony sneaking off to go and save Lyrrin on her own, something had to be done about it.

"You owe me nothing." Kess squared her shoulders and stared up at Lyomir. "But … There's something important I need to do. Somewhere I have to go. Not as payment or as a master's command. It is for you to choose."

My choice? Hmph. Lyomir's eyes narrowed, looking out at the gray skies around them, then back to Kess.

From her heart, she asked, *Will you fly with me again?*

CHAPTER FOUR

The heavy stone rolled toward Riony, pressing her between it and the doorframe. She grunted and matched its pressure, pushing back the other way. All the muscles in her back and arms coiled and strained.

"I know you're—mmph—in there!"

Putting her shoulder against the stone, she forced the gap wide enough for her to stumble through into the dismal room beyond. Only a small, single glow stone lit the space, half lost within a mess of blankets, clothing, and dishes of old food scattering the floor. The smell wasn't great.

"Go away," a feeble voice called from somewhere buried beneath it all.

Catching her breath, Riony grumbled, "You can't hide in here forever."

"I can, if you simply leave me be."

"Yeah, I'm not going to do that."

Riony stomped across the space, clattering the ceramic plates in her wake. She grabbed a handful of woven wool and pulled it up to reveal Eslinde curled up beneath.

The princess's hair was tangled, a cloudy haze of silver around old, loosened braids, and her eyes were puffy and bruised as though she'd cried and not slept in equal amounts. She tried to grab the blanket back, but Riony wrenched it off her and tossed it clear.

Eslinde made a pitiful sound and turned her face away.

Exhaling deeply, Riony lowered herself down to sit next to her, pushing aside a barely touched bowl of mushroom stew. She wondered who had been delivering the princess food. Probably Vance.

"Listen, I'm sorry, really. I wish I could leave you be. I wish I could let you get through this however you need to get through this. Stars, I wish I could be in here wallowing with you. But there is so much to do, and we are drowning out there. We need you."

Eslinde looked honestly shocked. "Why? I am a curse. I can be of no help to anyone."

"Because, as you dared to point out to me once, we are just children. And we've got a whole lot of people looking to us for solutions to a whole depths-damned siege that's happening right now, and we could really use the advice of someone who might know a little bit more about politics and warfare and all of this sort of thing. Someone maybe like a princess."

Eslinde groaned and rolled over the other way.

Riony put a hand on her shoulder. The woman was small, thin-boned much like Lyrrin, but she'd lost more weight recently.

"I know how you feel. Believe me. I want Lyrrin back as much as you."

A sob racked through her small body. "Then I have hurt you as well. I brought a traitor in and lost my daughter. Again. All those around me are destined to suffer or betray me.

I can trust nobody."

Riony made a rude noise. "You can trust me. You can trust Kess. And Vance and Dashiel. And Aishena and Benjin. And Niskina."

Eslinde made a similarly rude noise, sandwiched between silent sobs.

"*And* most of all, you can trust Lyrrin. You know how clever she is, how brave she is. She's probably running circles around her captors, giving them more trouble than they bargained for. You can trust her ability to survive."

The soundless tears ceased, and Eslinde looked up at Riony from the side of her eye. "Do you really think so?"

The words had originally been meant only as a comfort to Eslinde, but as Riony challenged their meaning within her, she found she had no hesitation. "Yeah, I do."

Lyrrin would survive. She'd fought and outwitted slavers and dragonriders and undead. Riony just wished she knew how long her sister would have to survive without her, before they could rescue her, somehow.

She had been trying to work out a way that she could go, but none of her plans came close to being even as good as the worst ideas she'd ever had.

Riony squeezed Eslinde's shoulder. "But I don't know if *I'm* going to survive the complexities of organizing a community of refugees into a defensive force while keeping the peace during a siege. This isn't what I'm built for. I'm only built to hit things with a sword and look hot."

Eslinde slowly rolled into a sitting position, then looked up and held Riony's gaze. "I think you are capable of far more than you think."

A sudden soft, warm feeling in Riony's chest surprised her. It was so close to how she'd felt when her amma would praise her for being able to identify herbs correctly during their studies together that it left her flooded with complex emotions.

She shrugged bashfully. "We'd still really appreciate your input, though. There's a meeting in ten minutes in my room. It's right around the corner. Will you be there?"

Eslinde's eyes shimmered, red-rimmed, and her lips pulled into a tight line. Then she nodded once.

"Do you … need any help cleaning up?" Riony offered awkwardly.

Eslinde's back straightened and there was a spark in her eye. "Who is the child here?"

Riony rubbed her chin, thinking about it. "Does that mean you're taking over and I can lock myself in a room for a week? Because I'm down for that swap."

Eslinde scoffed. "You wouldn't even if you could."

Riony wasn't sure whether Eslinde would actually show, but she was the first one there. Her face had been washed, her hair pulled back into a neat bun, and the dress which she had seemed to have worn since they arrived at the undercity had been changed out for a neat and simple military uniform brought from Eslindekeep.

She gave Riony a grateful but still sad smile and took a seat at the long dining table that ran down along one side of the living area. The Alderkin-made chairs were high-backed, inlaid with agate and crystal with finely woven cushions.

Eslinde was dwarfed by them, and despite the richness of the room being beyond anything Riony had ever known, she felt as though they were all children playing tea parties rather than people who could manage the scale of issues they faced.

How are we going to get through this?

Eslinde was quickly joined by Aishena, Benjin, and Niskina. And then Dashiel, Vance, Jaym, and Zeina arrived. They were all surprised to see the princess there and greeted her happily.

"Where's Kess?" Eslinde asked, edged with concern.

Riony was wondering the same thing. She hadn't seen Kess since the day before, and her nerves had been strung tight at the thought of seeing her again after that. Maybe Kess was now avoiding her.

Ouch. That thought hurt.

As though meeting a challenge, her mind offered up other ideas for why Kess wasn't there that hurt even more.

What if something happened to her? What if she's hurt? What if she's never coming back?

Riony dropped into her seat, suddenly lightheaded.

Aishena seemed less worried. "She's late. We should start without her. We have a lot to go over."

Riony glanced to the front door once more, willing it to open, before turning to the others. Dracuni and Elumon were curled up across the room on the other side of the softly steaming pool. Pangs of hunger came from Dracuni, and Lyrrin's hatchling had become lethargic without a regular stream of food.

Vance, Dashiel, and Jaym began their report on how the rider training was going, and a twinge of embarrassment joined the other emotions Riony was sharing with Dracuni.

Dashiel had taken her to practice flying that morning, but Dracuni returned early, sullen and silent.

Riony directed her attention to the unidragon, extending her thoughts.

Did you get to do some flying?

The space is too small. With sharp rocks everywhere. Her thoughts were laced heavily with shame and fear.

She'd only flown that one other time. The time she still had nightmares about.

I'm sorry I was busy this morning. What if next time I go with you?

Fly together?

Yeah. What do you think?

Riony's shoulders dropped as the unidragon's overwhelming emotions calmed.

I'd like that.

Dashiel's voice pulled Riony back to the meeting. "It won't matter if we have everyone flying like masters if the dragons are all too weak from hunger to do anything."

"So I might have thought of a way to deal with the food issue," Riony said. She lifted both hands in front of her, framing her words. "Cave spiders."

"*Cave spiders*?" Zeina cringed back in her chair. "Stars, I hate it down here."

Dashiel had gone an off-green color. "Wait. Is that a type of food down here? I thought the street vendor was teasing me. What did I razing eat?"

Aishena shook her head. "It's one thing catching the occasional spider for a snack—"

Dashiel turned sideways to bend over and put their head between their knees. "I'm going to be sick."

"—but it would take the delvers weeks of chasing around, picking the creatures off to get enough to feed the dragons." Aishena patted Dashiel on the back in a *there-there* motion.

"Except I know where to find a whole heap of spiders all in one place. Remember where I got my sword?" Riony had shared the tale of her and Kess's adventures through the depths with her friends before, but it was clear they thought she was grossly exaggerating.

Aishena frowned thoughtfully. "How many are we talking about?"

"Enough for all the dragons to have a solid feed." Riony leaned back, folding her arms. "Not an easy mission, though. We'd have to get past the revenant conglomerate. But I can lead the way. I know what it's like down there."

"I want to see the rev king!" Benjin said, far too eagerly.

Eslinde watched the entire exchange, aghast. "You're going to try catching enough *cave spiders* to feed the dragons, after fighting a ... a *rev king*? This is your plan?"

Riony walked her fingers in the air. "I'm kind of hoping we can just sneak past it. I don't want to see that mountain of bones again."

Eslinde rubbed her forehead. "Blessed sun, maybe it is good I'm here."

Vance chuckled wryly.

"If it's as bad as you said down there," Aishena sounded skeptical, "you'll need a bunch of good fighters with you. Some of the ones we're training are ready."

"Ready?" Zeina barked a laugh. "Ready to sometimes land a decent blow on an unmoving training pole. If the things I've seen the vendors selling are spider legs—and I will be thanking my ancestors tonight that I haven't eaten any—"

Dashiel made a gagging sound.

"Then those blighted things are *big*."

Niskina rolled her eyes. "They aren't even venomous."

The sound of the door rolling open shot Riony up in her seat. Her heartbeat became frantic with a mix of relief and embarrassment and something else even stronger as Kess rode in on Griskin.

"You're late," Aishena snapped. "And why are you *wet*?"

Kess ignored her, riding right up beside Riony. Her dark hair was flattened to her scalp and sopping wet, and all her clothing glistened with water. Griskin remained dry, except for where Kess dripped on him. She carried something long and thin on her lap.

Kess laid the item reverentially onto the table in front of Riony. It took a long moment before Riony could tear her gaze away from Kess to see her dragonguard sword lying before her.

Riony gaped at it. She touched her fingers lightly to the cold, slick steel, to be sure it was really there. Around the table the others whispered in confusion between themselves. They didn't know what that sword was. What that sword *meant.*

How for all their talk of perilous missions and rev king's and cave spiders, that small, incredible, wolf-riding girl had just faced them all alone and returned with something Riony had thought was gone forever.

And Riony found she didn't care one bit about that piece of metal that used to mean so much to her. She cared far more that Kess had risked her life for it.

I could have lost her.

"What were you thinking? Going down there alone?" Riony surged up to her feet. "Why would you do that?"

Kess didn't flinch. She raised her chin and said firmly, "I went to recover your sword because I wanted to prove that I can retrieve things that are important, no matter how impossible it may seem."

Riony wanted to yell at her, to scream that she didn't need to keep proving herself, didn't need to continue her pledge or put her life second to it. Riony didn't want any of that. She just wanted Kess.

She wanted Kess.

Unsteady on her feet, Kess's next words knocked Riony right back into her chair.

"Because I'm going to go and get Lyrrin back for you."

Riony could only gape at her.

Eslinde's head shook, and her voice trembled. "How?"

Riony's ears felt clogged and eyes blurred as Kess explained her plan. How the purple dragon had followed them, was outside the siege and willing to fly Kess to the capital. How Kess knew some of the layout of the palace, enough to find her way around. How Griskin would help sniff Lyrrin out.

How she was prepared to leave immediately.

Kess no longer looked at Riony, pitching her scheme to the rest of the table. "It makes sense that it's me who goes. Alone."

Riony felt as though she could choke on her heartbeat. "What? No! You're not going alone. And if anyone is going to get Lyrrin back, it should be me. I should go too."

Niskina sucked in a breath through her teeth. "It does sort of make sense for Kess to go. She sounds like our best chance to save Lyrrin. And we need you here."

Riony slapped her hands on the table. "You just want her gone because you don't like her."

Niskina glared back. "It's not like that. Just think for a moment. It's a good plan."

Aishena gave Riony a pitying look. "She's right. It is a good plan. Kess should do this."

"Aish," Riony pleaded.

The stern young woman locked Riony with a stare that seemed to look right into her soul, understanding every part of her.

She nodded gently. "But I don't think she should go alone. Chances of success will be higher if Benjin and I go with her."

Benjin silently pumped a fist.

Dashiel, who had recovered from their nausea, cleared their throat. "If you're taking more volunteers, I'd like to go too. I know the city inside out and much of the palace too. I can help."

"If you're going, I'm going," Vance said.

"Not this time, brother. You and Jaym need to stay and keep up the training without me."

"You just want to get away from the cave spiders," Aishena said.

"Stop," Dashiel replied, swallowing hard.

Kess shook her head. "It's too dangerous. I'm going alone, and I'm going now."

Aishena gestured to Benjin and they both rose from their chairs. "It is dangerous, which is why we're coming. We'll go and prepare now."

The two of them were out of the room before Kess could argue again, with Dashiel following quickly after.

Eslinde looked around the table. "I should go too. I want to go. I know the palace better than anyone."

Kess, already looking put out, shook her head fiercely. "I'm sorry, princess, but you don't have the skill set for this mission. The Hjelzahns and Dash will, I suppose, be helpful."

"Then let me go too," Riony grumbled again through gritted teeth.

Niskina leaned forward across the table and pulled Riony's hands into hers. "I know you're desperate to get Lyrrin back, but we need you to lead the mission to feed the dragons. And Dracuni needs you here. You can't leave her alone, not with an army outside trying to reach her."

Riony felt torn into three pieces as she looked between Dracuni and Kess and into her heart where she held Lyrrin. She was desperate to get her sister back, but she could also see clearly now how desperate she was to keep Kess by her side.

A great, dreadful clarity about just how she felt for Kess hit her like the beat of a dragon wing.

All her attention turned to Kess and the bright daring of her eyes and the scatter of spots across her cheek and the soft pink of her lips.

In a husky, low tone, Kess said, "Trust this to me. Let me do this for you."

Riony reached for the hilt of the sword lying on the table before her. She clutched the dragonscale patterned metal tight, feeling the familiar shape of it in her palm.

"I can't talk you out of this, can I?" Riony murmured back.

Kess searched her face. "Why would you want to?"

The whole table fell silent, awaiting the answer. Heat flushed up Riony's neck and all her words failed her.

Jaym clapped his hands together, breaking the spell.

He spoke joyfully. "We have successfully planned two missions today! Two! Better progress than most of our meetings, I have to admit. I'm feeling good about this."

He slid his seat back, signaling the end of the meeting. Vance hurried away, and Niskina gave Kess a long look and single nod before Jaym slung an arm over her shoulders and they left together with Zeina, arguing about the quality of undercity food.

Eslinde spoke softly with Kess for a long moment while Riony remained trapped in place, caught within the gravity of her feelings.

She didn't want Kess to go. Kessara Heithorn. The wretched gremlin. The person Riony would have once put high on her list of most deserving a painful and humiliating death. She wanted Kess there, with her, right beside her and even closer.

Riony wasn't sure what Eslinde saw in her face as she approached their conversation, but the first heir stepped away, leaving Riony and Kess alone.

Face-to-face again, Riony still couldn't find her words. What could she say? Would Kess stay if she begged her to? And what would that mean for Lyrrin?

Stomach churning, Riony lifted one hand up between them. Kess tilted her head as she looked at it, then grasped it with her own. There was a soft tremor there, and she tensed as Riony stepped closer. Her legs pressed up against Griskin's flank. With their hands gripped tight between their chests, Riony pressed her forehead to Kess's.

The uneven panting of Kess's breath merged with Riony's.

"Come back to me, okay?" Riony whispered.

"I will. I'll bring Lyrrin back for you."

Riony shook her head, forehead wobbling against Kess's. Riony turned her head to the side and their cheeks touched.

"You too. I need you to come back to me too. Do you understand?"

Kess pulled away, the corner of her lips brushing Riony's as she did. Mouth parted, she frowned at Riony as though she didn't understand at all but nodded anyway.

With her free hand, Riony grasped one of her string necklaces and pulled it off over her head. The acorn pendant dangled as she reached over Kess and placed it around her neck.

Kess's eyes widened into bright pools.

"We're ready." Aishena's voice cut through from the doorway. "The sooner we leave, the better."

She, Benjin, and Dashiel were armored and carrying packs.

Eslinde pushed back in and wrapped Kess in an embrace, and Riony farewelled the others.

Then everyone was gone, leaving Riony alone with Dracuni and Lyrrin's hatchling. On wobbly legs she went and flopped onto the ground between them.

She patted Elumon down the back of his maned neck, so much liked Dracuni's. "Lyrrin will be back with you soon. I hope."

He blinked at her and made a sad croaking noise.

Riony leaned back into Dracuni, seeking the warmth and comfort of her silky scales. It all felt like too much, understanding how she felt about Kess only to have to say goodbye. She wanted to chase after her, do the reckless thing that old Riony wouldn't have hesitated to do.

But she understood more now, about the world, and responsibility. She knew protecting Dracuni, keeping Dracuni fed and alive, was more important than anything else, even her own heart.

Dracuni turned her neck around and laid her head on Riony's lap with a soft sigh.

"You've been quiet. Are you happy Kess is going too?"

No. She is a friend now. I've just been thinking.

"What about?"

The depths. The spiders. The bone monster. Other things.

Riony could feel her worrying about it all like a weight in her stomach.

"It was pretty scary for you last time we were down there, wasn't it? We'll be more prepared this time. I'll be fine."

Dracuni snorted. *Actually, I had an idea. Something to help with the meat problem.*

"Yeah?"

Yeah. But you're not going to like it.

Chapter Five

Yensen held Lyrrin in place with a firm hand on her shoulder, right in front of the maw of a dragon with teeth as long as Lyrrin stood tall.

She fought her fear. The dragon was tamed, it shouldn't—*wouldn't*—act without orders. *But what if it does get orders?*

She knew as soon as they walked onto the flight deck that the immense silver and gold dragon could only belong to the Dragon King. That it was the same one she'd seen flying through the darkening sky on her first night in the palace.

And if she displeased the man, she could be dragon food within seconds.

Yensen had already given her his daily warning, about how their king was good and kind and just and would remain that way as long as Lyrrin behaved for him. Lyrrin held serious doubts. Good, kind, and just people didn't become cruel when someone misbehaved.

For now, though, the king was occupied with other matters.

A stream of servants loaded metal crates and fabric-wrapped furniture onto the back of the dragon, overseen by the queen.

The dragon—an etherflame probably, but Lyrrin was still getting used to identifying dragon types—had its head and body lowered, and staircases on wheels were rolled up beside it. It didn't have the normal cap of a taming spike in the center of its head, but instead, a polished length of wood emerged from just above one eye.

The end of a spear. It was the first tamed dragon. No wonder it was so big. It was over eighty years old.

Eighty years enslaved to that man. Poor thing.

One servant climbing the stairs fumbled the crate she carried, and it slipped, clattering in her hands as she caught it again before it crashed to the ground.

The queen howled, "If you drop that, I will have you flayed strip by strip and your ribbons hung out for the birds!"

The king only kept half an eye on the loading work. Before him, a man in a very simple but tidy gray tunic delivered a report in a long monotonous string. They both stood beside a small table that seemed to be a temporary office desk, strewn with papers, quills, and a small chest.

Whether Yensen had brought her in too early or the messenger's delivery had taken too long, nobody paid any attention to her as their continued their work.

Lyrrin strained to listen to the report but found the queen's business far more interesting than glassworks production numbers (lower than expected) and defenses at the king's external factories (weakened, with so many dragons away under other orders).

There was so much furniture, ghostly and bumpy in its protective shrouds, getting stacked and roped onto the back of the dragon, but the palace itself hadn't seemed any barer for the lack of it. How did they have so much? And where were they taking it?

The Dragon King had a whole additional private palace along with his one here in the capital. Eslinde had shown it to Lyrrin on a map once. It lay on the coast to the northeast.

Maybe they were moving things there. But Lyrrin also remembered Niskina's reports of dragonlords packing all their precious belongings and fleeing Elundrae entirely.

The messenger's tone changed to one more somber, drawing Lyrrin back.

"Dastmyr, Salix, and Skaellakeep have been breached."

"All three?" Yeonard Draekhan sounded more skeptical than concerned. "Small breaches, perhaps."

The messenger seemed to shrink, and his voice wavered. "Overrun, my king. There weren't enough riders left to defend them, and the numbers of undead have risen dramatically."

"My heirs?"

With a bowed head, the messenger delivered his news as though his head was on the executioner's block, and they were his final words. "Unknown. Presumed dead."

"Hmm," the king grumbled without any emotion.

That was all? Lyrrin studied the man with ferocious eyes. Three of his children could be dead, and all it got from him was a polite grunt?

The king turned back to the messenger, and Lyrrin expected him to say something about his heirs, about all the people lost in those keeps along with them, about any plans to do something about it.

He said, "Any updates from the undercity siege?"

Lyrrin held her breath. Not what she was expecting, but news from the undercity was something she desperately wanted too. She leaned in closer.

The messenger seemed equally confused about the change of subject.

He stuttered, "The rider army you've sent are trying all they can, but the entrances haven't yet been penetrated."

Yes! Lyrrin smiled grimly. She didn't know for sure whether Riony and her friends were still okay, but she assumed they must be within the undercity, with Dracuni, if the Dragon King was trying so hard to get in. And failing.

Yeonard Draekhan's awful eyes turned on Lyrrin then, and she hid her smile a second too slow. He dismissed the messenger, and the man bowed stiffly and skittered away in obvious relief.

All the pressure of the Dragon King's attention fell on Lyrrin, and goosebumps prickled over her with the fear of what that attention would bring.

Because it was clear he wasn't happy.

The queen came to her husband's side and seemed to notice Lyrrin's presence for the first time as well.

She looked her up and down, mouth twisted. "Well. Our little grandchild cleaned up well. It almost looks sweet. If I didn't know what it really was."

Lyrrin offered her most saccharine smile in return, fluttering her lashes over her startling blue eyes—the one thing that the flurry of servants who had cleaned and dressed her couldn't change.

They had forced her into a chair and covered her scalp with a horrible stinking gunk, so different to the earthy paste Riony used to dye her hair.

Lyrrin didn't want her hair changed. She'd become proud of the shimmering blue color that was growing in, that it was *her* hair, her family's hair, undisguised, for once in her life. Now it was a harsh black. She hated it.

She also hated the horrible, dull gray dress they wrestled her into. It was too tight around her chest and draped too long over her feet, tripping her up.

The servants had looked at her pointed nails and planned to try to trim them, but Yensen explained she needed them for the work she was to do for the king.

Instead, they found new gloves for her, fancy silk ones. The tips of Lyrrin's nails already pierced through the fragile seams.

But she passed as fully human.

Strange that was how she had to appear when the qualities the king wanted from her were from her Alderkin side.

"She appears well, and yet she continues to defy me," Yeonard Draekhan said in his booming tone.

"I'm not—"

"All ten of the first batch of trials failed. Ten vials of silvernix wasted. Ten hatchlings wasted."

Lyrrin turned cold from scalp to toes. The hatchlings ... he didn't ...

"I tried—"

"Did you?"

The disappointment in his tone actually hurt.

"I told you I don't know how I did it before. I tried all the runes I know, and some combinations. That was trying. What else could I do?"

"Do it the way you did before. Stop stalling, stop trying to trick me. I need you to make this work. The land needs you to make this work. How many people must die because we don't have the resources to tame enough dragons to defend against the shadow dragon's blight?"

The queen hovered nearby, her forehead wrinkled ever so slightly as she listened, but she didn't question anything.

Lyrrin did, though. The fire of defiance burned through her at the king's words. How dare he blame any of that on her? The keeps were falling because they weren't defended, because the Dragon King had moved all the riders he could find to the undercity.

"You know the shadow dragon's curse will only get worse if you keep taming more dragons," Lyrrin challenged back. "You know all those people could be saved and the curse ended, if you just stop fighting against those of us who are trying to do exactly that!"

"You have too much of your mother in you," Yeonard said. "With the same ridiculous dreams. Elundrae as we know it cannot exist without tamed dragons."

He turned away to the portable desk and picked up the small chest there. "And we must have the means to continue making more."

He pushed the chest into Lyrrin's hands.

She already knew what was inside. The first ten vials had been delivered and returned in that same jeweled box. But she opened the lid anyway to see the line of glittering bottles laid out on velvet within.

"I expect this next round of trials to succeed, or there will be consequences."

Lyrrin's mouth puckered. He could expect all he wanted. It wasn't going to work.

But he hadn't punished her for failing the first time. He still believed she could do it. He still thought she was valuable to him.

Running her fingers over the vials, Lyrrin decided she was feeling bold enough to test just how valuable he considered her.

She stroked the gloved tips of her fingers over the teardrop-sized glass, holding the precious silvernix. She'd hoped she could use some to do her own tests when they had been delivered to Eslinde's rooms the first time, but she had been watched the whole time she had them, the vials counted in and out.

"I can do my best, that's all I can promise," Lyrrin said, and then she let the chest tumble from her fingers.

She feigned an attempt to catch it, juggling it in the air and flinging the vials out all around. Yensen, the king, and queen, all started forward in their own attempts to save the precious contents. But the rain of glass already clinked and cracked onto the ground.

Lyrrin gasped dramatically. "I'm so sorry! These gloves, they make me so clumsy."

She stepped around in a circle, acting flustered and bending to collect the now empty chest. The last couple of intact vials crunched beneath her shoes and she spread a trail of shimmering unicorn blood across the floor in her wake, making it unclear which spots were broken vials, and which were her footprints.

As she stood back up, the king stood over her, his arm mid swing.

"You stupid creature!"

The back of his knuckles cracked against her cheek, filling her head with ringing pain. She shrieked in outrage, her temper flying free of the bonds of her good sense, and she swung her clawed hand back in response.

Her nails, poking through the tips of her gloves, scratched across the king's upper arm. They cut through the weave of his tunic, into his skin. Blood stained through the frayed fabric.

Lyrrin froze, staring at what she'd done. Her cheek ached and ears rung with her pounding heartbeat and a triumphant voice crowed within her at the knowledge the king's blood brought.

He's just a man. And he can bleed.

But she'd also just attacked the king, and he looked ready to murder her.

His fist was raised, but before he could strike, hands grabbed Lyrrin from behind and dragged her out of reach.

Yensen held her tight, restraining her arms and panting out his words. "My king, forgive me that I didn't protect you from this creature sooner."

The king glared from Lyrrin to the silvernix spoiling on the floor. The bright shimmer was fading as it lay on the streaked, glossy marble.

Taking a slow, threatening breath, he lowered his fist. Moving his thumb within his fingers, he crushed something then wiped the palm of his hand directly over the bloodied area on his arm.

And then he glowed. Lyrrin had seen her sister glow like that more times than she'd have liked. She knew what it meant.

Scowling at the wound, as though the torn and stained clothing were a bigger issue than the injury Lyrrin had given him, he wiped his hand clean on a handkerchief his wife hastily passed him. As he worked it around the rings on all his fingers, Lyrrin's eyes widened.

Was every one of the silvery gems on those rings a dose of silvernix?

The Dragon King could bleed, but not for long.

"Take it back to its rooms," he muttered to Yensen. "I'll send more silvernix soon. And maybe I'll send something else too. Something to encourage the wild beast to behave. My late son Hjelzahn had a man in his employ who is very skilled at getting results out of people who are being defiant. A man very good with his tools."

Lyrrin kept her mouth squeezed shut. She didn't trust herself to say anything else that wouldn't get her into more trouble, and luckily Yensen kept her hands pinned behind her as well.

Both she and the grayglim sighed in relief when the king turned away and left.

As the fury that had fired up Lyrrin cooled, the throbbing in her cheek grew stronger, and she licked her lips, finding them split and bloody. But as she rubbed the fabric of her glove around her fingers, feeling the small bumps inside, she knew it was worth it.

The queen seemed locked in place, her chest rising and falling in short breaths. Yensen bowed to her and tugged on Lyrrin to move her away.

"How dare you?" The queen gasped her words, scandalized to breathlessness. "How dare you strike the king?"

Lyrrin pulled out of Yensen's grasp. "He hit me first."

The queen's cheeks darkened as though they were as bruised as Lyrrin's. "But you never *strike back*!"

Yensen grew very still at Lyrrin's side, but Lyrrin was twitchy with fury.

"He should never have hit me to start with!" She had expected consequences, possibly even worse ones, for destroying the silvernix. Even if it was seen as an 'accident.'

But she was still angry that it had happened. It was still wrong.

She shook her head in confusion at the woman. "How could you marry someone like that? Someone who hits children?"

Queen Vellira's back straightened and her streaked black-and-white hair swished behind her. "Of course I had to—wanted to marry him. He's *the king*."

Lyrrin stared at her grandmother. It felt absurd to call her that. She barely looked older than Eslinde. How young had she been when she married the king? When he halted her aging with silvernix as he had halted his own?

Servants still moved around behind them, casting surreptitious glances at the royal quarrel.

The queen stepped closer to Lyrrin, her voice a threatening hiss. "He is our king, and if you keep defying him, he *will* bring his torturer in, whether you're a child or not."

Torturer? Is that what he meant by the man with the tools?

Lyrrin tried to keep her voice strong, but it broke over her words. "I didn't think you cared."

"I don't." Vellira dropped the words like a blow, then turned her back on Lyrrin. "It's only that your failure is Eslinde's failure which in turn is my failure, and failure isn't tolerated. The king will only accept disappointment so many times before there are consequences, no matter how important you think you are to him."

She placed both hands on her stomach as though she might throw up.

Lyrrin looked at the side of the woman's face, the blotchy pink and pale skin. Was she sick? Surely if the king was spending so much silvernix on trying to make more unidragons, he'd have enough for his wife.

"I'm sorry I broke the silvernix," Lyrrin said gently, carefully. "It was a terrible accident. I know how rare and precious it is. There mustn't be much left."

"The king still has plenty."

Lyrrin smirked at how easily the queen offered the information.

She pushed a little further. "Are you sure? Have you seen it yourself?"

Yensen grasped her arm, squeezing a warning.

The queen shrugged a shoulder. "Only the king has access to the main supply."

"But you must have seen somethi—"

Yensen tugged Lyrrin backward sharply. "Your Majesty, I will remove this creature from your presence now."

Vellira half turned but didn't look at them. "Please do."

With a shove in the center of her back, Yensen moved Lyrrin at a fast pace across the flight deck.

She craned her neck back, staring at her grandmother, the massive, mindless dragon, and the stacked-up furniture, and a frown wrinkled her face.

"You're pushing your luck," Yensen hissed to her once they were in the corridor outside.

A hysterical chuckle escape Lyrrin's bleeding lips. "Am I? What have I done wrong? I'm trying my best, doing what the king wants. You know that I don't know how to do it, so what do you expect to happen?"

Yensen scoffed and gave her another nudge. "You can fool the others, but I know that wasn't an accident."

Lyrrin pulled her gloved hand closed in panic, and her footsteps stumbled and caught on the hem of her dress. Yensen caught her by the back to keep her upright.

He kept her in that grip and bent to whisper in her ear as some servants passed by.

"You're foolish to be prying into things you shouldn't. Getting rid of all that silvernix just to get information on the king's supply was a transparent ploy."

The tightness in Lyrrin's chest eased. She was happy for Yensen to think that was all she was doing.

"I'm the foolish one?" she asked. "You're the one pledging your loyalty to a man who hits children. Who threatened me with his torturer."

Yensen's face grew stony, and he looked straight ahead up the stairs.

Lyrrin wasn't going to let him ignore her. "And it's not just me, either. How many children died in the attacks on the enclaves? How many people are dying in the keeps that are unprotected because all *your king* cares about is getting Dracuni?"

"He's doing what is most important in the long-term. He needs Dracuni to repair this world. I trust his plan."

Lyrrin made a rude noise. "I trust he's a cruel old man who has no value for life other than his own anymore."

They reached the entrance to Eslinde's chambers, and Yensen opened the door and tried to push Lyrrin in.

She turned on him, pleading with her eyes. "Eslinde trusted you. She believed in you, cared for you. You could still be out there right now, helping them, making a real difference in the world. If you'd just help me ..."

He pushed her again, sending her stumbling back, and slammed the door between them.

"Fine. *Fine,*" Lyrrin seethed under her breath. "I don't need you anyway."

Muttering curses under her breath, she hurried to the room with the large balcony window and floor filled with books. Even though she knew Yensen couldn't see her, even if he was peering through the keyhole, she still ducked down behind a large stack of tomes as she carefully peeled her silk glove off.

The soft tinkle of glass sounded as three tiny vials landed in the palm of her other hand.

That was all she'd dared take, pushing them up into the holes at the ends of her gloves before dropping the others. That was all she'd dared allow missing as she obscured how many other vials were smashed on the floor.

Three vials. That was plenty to do some tests of her own. Three vials of silvernix ... but no crystals.

She hadn't worked out yet how she was going to get her hands on crystal. The only one she had was the locking rune, but she didn't want to ruin it with her experiments. Being able to lock her prison from within could also come in useful.

The runed crystal had been made by her pabba for Eslinde. She couldn't bring herself to carve it up, even for her escape.

Besides, she had another idea she wanted to test.

She crouched down beside the towering window and picked one of the diamond-shaped panes close to the floor. The hazy orange light of a smoky midday streamed into the otherwise unlit room. With her bare fingers, she began carving a line around the edge of the glass.

It had to work ... Lyrrin didn't know what she'd carved on the glass holding the silvernix that created Dracuni, but she knew now that runes on glass worked as well as on crystal.

The king's first trials had also been Lyrrin's first trials. She had carved every rune she knew and carefully activated them. The one with the light symbol lit up like a tiny glowfly. The burn rune vial warmed.

There wasn't enough surface area for them to do much, like the tiny shard crystals she'd cut from larger stones when she was low on resources. But it worked.

"And now I'll see if it works on something bigger."

The pane popped free. It was a decent size, larger than her splayed hand. She cut a second, as the chilled winter wind from outside whistled in, making her shiver from the cold and anticipation.

Once she had two panes laid out on the tiled floor, she considered her options and decided to play it safe. She carved a light symbol onto one. The glass made soft, screeching sounds under her nails, and she kept checking over her shoulder as she worked, but nobody burst in to see what she was doing.

Just to be sure, Lyrrin wailed some fake sobs to cover the noise.

The next step she wasn't so sure about. She tried resting one of the vials on the glass the way the vial on the locking rune crystal sat on it.

She traced the rune to activate it.

Nothing.

She tried setting all three vials on the glass. Nothing She sat and waited a few minutes in case it needed time to charge. Still nothing.

Maybe it needs direct contact when it's glass instead of crystal?

She knew silvernix spoiled quickly when it wasn't encased in dragonglass. But just how encased did it have to be?

She carefully pulled the stopper from one vial and released the shimmering drop onto the middle of the unmarked glass, then as quickly as she could, she sandwiched the runed pane over the top.

The opalescent fluid squeezed and spread between them, creating a mirror. It didn't reach to the edges and spill. It remained sparkling and moonlit.

Holding her breath, Lyrrin traced her fingers over the rune.

And the dim room lit up bright with a soft cyan glow.

Biting back a yelp of delight, Lyrrin bounced in place where she sat. She held the diamond of sandwiched glass over her head in triumph.

It worked. It worked, it worked, it worked!

Lyrrin's mind whirled with the possibilities. She had magic again. She had power again. She could make her escape. She sat there for a few long moments, enjoying the familiar cool glow.

As she brought her finger back to the rune to deactivate it, she frowned.

Was it dimmer than before?

"Already?" she whispered.

She hastily traced the rune again and the light went out. Holding the glass in front of the window, she angled it back and forth in the light. The silvernix still glittered, but it had dulled noticeably.

It wasn't fully enclosed. The gaps all around the edge seemed to be allowing the silvernix to spoil. Not immediately, but far too fast.

Without access to larger bottles or a way to seal the edges with glass, Lyrrin wasn't sure what to do. She hadn't been allowed any glass drinkware, not allowed anything sharp, as though she were a dangerous criminal.

The flat panes were all she had.

She activated the light rune again, and the air rushed out of her at how much dimmer it was already. She doubted it would last another few minutes.

She had magic again, but it didn't last long.

And she only had two more vials of silvernix available to make her escape.

Chapter Six

The red glow of fire brightened the ground far below. Sunset had passed recently, and smoke filled the dusky sky, sharp in Kess's lungs.

"What's down there? Can you take us lower to see?" Kess called to Lyomir.

He didn't reply. He had kept a sullen silence ever since finding out he wasn't flying only Kess and Griskin, but also Aishena, Benjin, and Dashiel as well. He had allowed it, but he clearly wasn't happy about having other humans riding him.

He stretched his wings out to glide down slowly.

"That's Tjollaskeep," Aishena said from further along the purple dragon's spine.

Lyomir hadn't allowed any saddles, so each of them had roped themselves in between the double row of spikes down his back. Griskin was carefully tied between Kess and Aishena, with Benjin and Dashiel at the back. Except for the wolf, they were all kitted out in dark leather delver armor and flight goggles.

Although the scale armor they had from Eslindekeep would have offered more protection, wearing shimmering rider armor in Eslinde's colors didn't seem the most covert option.

As they grew closer, the walled city spread beneath them. A couple of buildings burned, the last embers smoldering like red eyes in the dark. But mostly the keep was simply empty. Unlit. Lifeless.

"Maybe they evacuated?" Dashiel said.

Kess shivered. Dragonkeeps were meant to be impenetrable. A safe haven from the undead blight. Protected by their massive walls and dragonfire. But Kess had seen Gerichkeep fall to the revenant army. She'd prayed that it was an anomaly, that something had gone wrong there that could never go wrong again.

Seeing another dragonkeep broken and abandoned shook Kess to her core.

All the people flying with her were also once dragonlords too, raised to believe in the strength of their defenses against the undead. The tense silence suggested they all felt the same way about what they saw.

They flew on to the east, and the full moon rose red above them, ringed in a ghostly glow from the ever-present haze.

"Look," Dashiel said, voice cut short with emotion.

Under the bloody moonlight, the ground churned with motion. The revenant army, marching onward. Uncountable in its multitudes.

"Ardahnkeep is just ahead," Aishena said. "They're heading right for it."

"It'll be protected, though, won't it?" Dashiel asked. "I mean, it's *Ardahnkeep*."

The shape of the city appeared, silhouetted on the horizon like a jagged tooth. The firstborn heir's dragonkeep, formed around the old Rolanian capital, and second biggest city in Elundrae.

Although Ardahn himself had died long ago, his descendants kept the dragonkeep in high regard as equally populous and flourishing as the capital.

"I don't know," Aishena replied. "From the numbers of dragons besieging the undercity, Eslinde thinks the king has drawn riders from every keep to be there. Maybe not all of them, but Ardahnkeep isn't going to have much more protection than their walls."

"Which doesn't help much when some of those revs down there are flying." Kess urged Lyomir onward with her thoughts, eager to be away from the ocean of undead below.

They flew high, where the air was chilled and thin, and between them and the ground there were large shapes hovering over the rev army, worn wings beating unevenly.

"Can we help them? The people in Ardahnkeep?" Benjin asked.

Aishena's voice replied, hushed, "I don't think us and one dragon are going to turn the tides for them in any meaningful way."

Kess frowned. She'd also come to this painful conclusion.

They needed to push on. They needed to fulfill their mission and get back safe with Lyrrin, and then they could work to do more toward breaking the curse.

They couldn't let the Dragon King hold access to someone with so much knowledge of Alderkin magic and Dracuni. If he found a way to use Lyrrin's knowledge to tame more dragons, things would only get worse.

But most of all, Kess needed to bring Lyrrin back for Riony.

Kess lifted a hand to touch the lump beneath her leather armor where the acorn hung.

I need you to come back to me too. Do you understand?

The way Riony had pulled her close, forehead pressed against hers ... It was just the same as how she farewelled Aishena and the rest of her friends and family.

It warmed Kess beyond measure to think that maybe she had raised herself in Riony's esteem to that same level. But still her greedy heart wanted more. It yearned for how that kiss had made her feel.

Not just tolerated, not just friend, or even family, but *wanted*. Wanted in the kind of crushing, all-consuming, too-much way that Kess had always wanted things, a way that she sometimes thought only she knew.

The way she felt about Riony in return.

Benjin cleared his throat as they passed over Ardahnkeep and continued onward.

"Do you think Hjelzahnkeep is okay?" His voice had grown deeper recently, but now it rose high, breaking over the words.

"I'm sure it is. It hasn't been in this army's path," Aishena replied in a tone far gentler than she usually used.

They all grew silent again.

Kess directed Lyomir, skirting out over the water, along the shoreline of Grand Hofen. When she'd asked this favor from him, she'd explained all about where they needed to go and what they needed to do. He'd somewhat uncomfortably told her he didn't know the land, didn't know where anything was. He had no real memories of the places he'd been while tamed.

All recollections of his life existed as though through a grease-smeared lens, dulled and gray, lacking clarity or emotion or anything other than the ability to follow orders.

So he allowed Kess to guide him with her thoughts and gentle touches of her hands to his neck. It mirrored how she rode Griskin, how she would give him direction, but he would choose whether he would follow it, and how.

It wasn't long before Draekhanhelm loomed before them.

Lyomir swooped in low then, coming in over the soft waves of the harbor. Ocean spray fell across Kess's face, salty on her lips. The dragon's wings remained still and silent as they glided up over the keep's walls and between the tallest of the buildings.

Kess was on alert for dragonriders on guard spotting them, no matter how elegantly stealthy the purple etherdart moved through the dusk. But no dragons appeared.

They flew over unguarded streets that were mostly quiet, but some were lit by torchlight and pounded with the angry chants of crowds.

Not even any city guards on treedarts emerged to deal with the unrest.

"Well, that was easy," Benjin said. "I thought we were going to have to fight our way into the keep."

"Don't jinx us," Kess hissed back.

"He's right though." Dashiel's expression was drawn tight, scanning the air around them. "There should have been at least a couple of riders with eyes on any unscheduled arrivals. But this place is entirely unguarded."

Benjin pulled his crystal-studded staff and looked through a clear section at the end. "The Dragon King wouldn't have sent all his riders away, surely. He wouldn't leave all these people defenseless."

"The rev army isn't quite on their doorstep yet. Maybe the riders that are still here are taking a night off," Dashiel offered.

"Let's hope so." Kess guided Lyomir up a little higher, out of the cover of the buildings. "The palace is just up ahead. Be ready."

The dark stone blocks and spires of the palace rose skyward in their path. The last time Kess had flown in, she'd been too panicked to really take in the scale of the structure.

The bulk of the palace formed a half-circle shape, like archways tipped flat and stacked unevenly upon each other, creating deep gaps where courtyards lay. Along the curved top, towers jutted upward. The whole thing was reminiscent of the Dragon King's crown.

Lyomir moved in silently, and Kess looked for somewhere he could drop them off. They didn't want to risk landing in a flight deck.

Then swift, dark wings cut through the sky. A black-and-white dragon rose in front of them.

Kess swore, and Lyomir's surprise and anger also slammed into her.

Silent, brainless thing!

She could feel his strong urge to continue forward, to clash with that dragon and pull its taming stake free.

Kess pushed back with her own thoughts and feelings. *Turn, turn away!*

They hovered there, dragon facing dragon, as Lyomir growled.

Metal glinted on the back of the black-and-white dragon as the rider brought something to their mouth. A piercing whistle blew. Within seconds, two more smaller dragons emerged from a flight deck on the upper levels of the palace.

"It looks like not all of the city was left unguarded," Benjin said almost matter-of-factly.

"I told you not to jinx us!" Kess replied.

Lyomir turned then, looping sharply to the side and downward. Kess's stomach lurched, and Griskin whined behind her.

Three more pips from the whistle blew, then the king's rider was after them.

Lyomir's wing membrane rippled and fluttered as they skimmed one high wall of the palace, then they were shooting along a wide street, low to the cobblestones.

Kess angled around to keep an eye on their pursuer. The black-and-white dragon was close behind them, close enough to hit them with their breath. But nothing came.

Black and white ... what breed is that?

Seasongs had black scales. Snowshimmers were regularly white, but never black. Dracuni's seasong mother had been silver and black, but this dragon was too small to be purely seasong.

"Is that a seashimmer?" she yelled back to Dashiel.

"Yeah, weird choice for a rider."

Kess hadn't seen that hybrid breed before. They were generally only used in ice production.

"They must have scraped the bottom of the barrel to be riding that thing," Aishena said. "Its cold breath is useless against revs."

"It is fast, though." Kess tugged the end of a throwing knife, then pushed it back into the sheath.

The rider was within range, but she didn't have to take their life. She just had to get away from them. Narrowing her eyes, she scanned their path ahead. The seashimmer may be fast, but all of its reactions relied on signals from its human rider.

Kess leaned forward, both hands flat against Lyomir's scales. She cleared her mind of everything except their connection, the feeling of oneness it brought.

Okay, we're going to lose these clowns. You know what to do. I'll spot for you.

Lyomir lifted straight up, wings gusting out and bringing them to a sudden stop. Benjin cried out as he slipped sideways, dangling from his rope. Dashiel caught him and hauled him back up.

The black-and-white dragon shot past them, then far down the wide street and corrected to come after them again.

Kess spotted a dark gap between buildings ahead, and without more thought than that, Lyomir turned that way. With wings tucked close, he dove down the narrow alley, beneath covered walkways that cut from building to building above them.

Kess leaned right, and he whipped the same way, pumping his wings hard as he broke across a wide square, then behind a building lined with columns.

Two more sharp turns within the city streets, and Kess could no longer hear their pursuer. She brought Lyomir to a stop under the cover of a large arched gateway. The two smaller dragons from the palace circled high above, but none were coming directly for them.

"Nice flying." Dashiel looked flushed and worked to tighten the ropes holding them in place.

Kess patted the purple scales. "It was all Lyomir. I knew he was an incredible dragon from the moment he was born."

The dragon's sides were heaving with deep breaths, and there was a slight thrum of pride washing through from him to Kess. He snorted grumpily.

"We're not going to be able to get into the palace by air, it seems," Aishena said. "We're going to have to work out another way in. On foot."

Kess wrinkled her nose. She'd hoped it would have been faster and easier than that, hoped she would be back by Riony's side again soon. But nothing was ever that easy.

She reached back to Griskin, ruffling the fur around his neck. He tail thumped happily, as it always did the moment they were no longer in the air anymore.

Aishena watched the surrounding streets with narrowed eyes. "We need somewhere to hide out. We need to let those guards give up their search before we attempt to breach the palace."

Dashiel winced. "I know a place. Zarram dragonhold is just around the corner from here. I don't know what state it will be in, whether anyone will be there …"

"It's worth checking out." Kess undid the ropes tying her in place, then turned around to work on Griskin's. "Lyomir, will you be able to fly out of here without trouble from those other riders?"

The purple dragon huffed as though even the question was an insult. Kess could have sworn he rolled his green eyes.

She half smiled and climbed onto Griskin, then all of them got down from the dragon's back and onto the street.

Lyomir peered out from under the gate's archway, stretching his wings. *I'll stay close. Call when you need me.*

He didn't wait for any kind of reply. Air gusted around Kess and ruffled Griskin's fur as the purple dragon took off and disappeared into the night sky, with the king's riders chasing after him.

Stay safe. Kess sent her thought to Lyomir like a wish, already missing him.

Even though she knew that with a dragon no longer on their team, it was her own chances of getting in to save Lyrrin and out again safely that had dropped dramatically.

CHAPTER SEVEN

The mountain of conglomerated revenants rumbled up the slope, bones clattering on the stone in a horrific percussion. Glowflies filled the air, fleeing in a hum of shooting light.

Riony ran ahead, leading it after her.

She huffed deep breaths between bellowing over her shoulder, "Come on, you mess of tangled tailbones. You remember this dance. Come and get me!"

A chorus of roars replied.

"Now!" She reached the summit and dropped, skidding between Dracuni's legs.

And the unidragon breathed.

It was so much larger than last time. A storm cloud of silver flame burst through the cavern and across the charging monster.

But it had the same effect.

The rev king's advance faltered, slowed, then came to a juddering stop as the bright shimmer of fire spread across it and through all the gaps between its bony mass.

A wet, crackling sound filled the air as the revenants' roars became screams. Human and animal and cries that sounded like neither echoed through the cavern.

Over the glowing bones, organs and flesh reformed, bodies long dead surged with life as they were healed with the power of Dracuni's magic.

Riony squeezed her eyes closed and turned away as all those creatures, those poor animals who had once died and were brought back undead, had their bodies returned only to remain dead.

Dracuni had been right. She didn't like it at all.

But it was a good idea. It would create meat for the dragons and get rid of all those revs in one blow.

Behind the unidragon, Vance swore in a rough, awed voice. "It's working. It's actually working!"

"Greaaaat," Riony mumbled, trying to hold back the rise of sickness that heated through her chest as she got to her feet.

Amma. She could still feel the bony claws of her dead mother's hands ripping into her skin, still see her mother's soft face reforming, piece by piece under Dracuni's fire, only to fall still again. It hurt less now. But 'less' was still enough to make Riony want to curl into a ball.

Niskina squeezed between the tunnel wall and Dracuni in order to reach Riony. Her lips turned down, and she wrapped Riony in a hug. Riony leaned into her. She wanted Lyrrin or Aishena or Kess—*sparks, I want Kess?*—to seek that comfort from, but they were all gone. Niskina also knew, though, what this meant to Riony. She squeezed her hard.

Farther back in the tunnel, Jaym eyed the entangled mass of skeletons and corpses spilling across the cavern in front of them under Dracuni's continuing flame. "That is quite the magic trick. But I don't think we're going to get as much meat out of this as we'd hoped."

Riony half turned in Niskina's arms, glancing for a moment but unable to keep her eyes on the scene for long.

Jaym was right. The revs that were less degraded, that had even a little skin clinging to their skeletons, regrew more flesh, but those that had been picked clean by the spiders twitched and moaned, then fell still without healing.

Riony moved out of the embrace and patted Dracuni's neck. "That's enough."

The stream of fire slowed, then sputtered out. The unidragon made a wheezing sound, and her head slumped.

"You okay?"

Yeah. Just ... tired. Really tired.

Her legs shuddered and folded beneath her, and her flanks heaved with labored breaths. "Whoa, easy." Riony helped support Dracuni's bobbing head.

I'm okay. Just feeling weak. Need to rest.

"Some food will help her recover quicker if she's anything like a snowflame," Vance said softly. "Which she seems to be, with how much flaming affects her. The flame's fuel must be being drawn directly from her bloodstream."

Riony gestured to the renewed corpses. "Given its effect, I'd say that's a good bet."

Vance moved closer, examining Dracuni's eyes and snout. "You said her mother was a seasong, though? She couldn't be all seasong, or she wouldn't flame at all. I would have said she had a snowflame father, but considering they're a human raised and tamed breed, I don't know how that could have happened."

Dracuni's worry leached into Riony's senses. *Don't snowflames have shorter lives if they breathe too much?*

"You're okay. I'm sure that just hit you hard because you were already hungry. And we're not going to need you to use your flame again anytime soon." Riony patted her mane, then clarified to Vance, "She's worried about how long snowflames live."

Vance bent over to look Dracuni in the eye. "One big burn can use up a snowflame entirely if pushed too far. Next time, keep to smaller, controlled puffs when possible so that you're keeping a gauge on how you feel in between."

Dracuni's nerves settled, and she gave a small nod.

"Watch yourself!" Niskina barked.

Riony spun around to find the skeleton of a bear dragging itself weakly across the ground toward her. Its back half had reformed with the dead weight of skin and organs, but the regenerating magic hadn't worked on its front half. The rev slowly clawed her way.

Given a few more minutes, it could have taken a chunk out of her leg if she'd kept her back to it. Now, Riony was ready to put it out of its misery.

She drew her dragonguard sword in one hand. Her crystal sword was with her as always, sheathed on her back. But as it was out of charge, she figured she'd change things up. Her old sword felt so familiar in her grip, but also so strange in how lightweight and flexible it was compared to the weapon she'd become used to.

She brought it cracking down through the back of the bear's spine bones, close to the skull, and the bones fell apart, lifeless on the floor.

Niskina pushed past her and hammered her poleaxe down on another still twitching rev.

"Here you go." Riony grabbed the meaty back leg of the bear and dragged it close to Dracuni. "Eat up, I guess?"

The unidragon sniffed the meat with equal amounts of distrust and starved appetite. The flesh was new and fresh and smelled fine, and after a tentative bite, Dracuni flushed with happy feelings as she joyfully devoured the rest.

Riony turned away. Meat was meat, but this whole situation still felt kind of icky.

In the spill of entangled skeletons and reformed corpses, a few revs still clung to the last vestiges of animation, and Riony, Niskina, and Vance moved through and made sure they were all put to rest.

Riony paused beside one, waiting to watch whether it burst back to life again as the revs aboveground now regularly did, but it stayed dead. Maybe they were too far away from the shadow dragon's call down there to have been made stronger in that way.

"Looks like we'll have enough to give all the dragons one decent meal from this." Vance poked at the pile with his boot as though checking for any more signs of life.

"And if we need more, we now have a clear path through to the nightmare of spiders beyond," Riony added joyfully.

Niskina poked Jaym playfully as he cringed at the mention of spiders.

She looked over Riony, still with a flicker of sympathy in her expression. "We can finish up down here. Now that Dracuni has done her thing, we can bring others in to finish the work. You don't need to be around all this."

Riony squeezed Niskina on the shoulder in thanks. The whole experience down there left her feeling as though a snake was coiling around in her stomach. She was also eager to hear if there was any news yet from the rescue team.

It's only been a day. Stop freaking out.

Dracuni finished her food and was standing again on shaky legs. Her stomach rumbled.

Riony raised her eyebrows. "All good?"

I feel even hungrier than I did before.

"Come on. The others will bring you some more meat soon, but you've got to go and rest now."

The two of them made the slow journey back through the tunnels to the collapsed section, where delvers had set up ropes and pulleys and a platform big enough for Dracuni to ride on. Riony pulled one of the ropes, ringing a bell far above, and before long they were slowly edging their way up the deep hole.

At the top, Riony passed on the message that it was clear for more helpers to go down and help with the meat collection. She had no way to explain to the delvers and volunteers working with the dragons exactly how all those fresh carcasses appeared down there.

It was the best they could do to make sure no one saw Dracuni use her flame and keep the source of the meat between a small group of more trusted workers.

The corridor leading back to the main cavern held an odd, nostalgic feeling. The swirling, floral engravings that decorated the neatly carved limestone and the temperate air, suffused with cyan light and just a hint of fungal scent, all felt like home.

Riony had ventured out through this same tunnel the day she found the dragon nest and had run through it blindly on the day she and Kess had been washed away into the depths. She had snuck in through it on the day they'd defeated Kife, and she'd come back there to be alone and cry after finding out Lyrrin had been taken.

Today, she and Dracuni walked in tired silence, and as they came to the end of the tunnel, Eslinde stood waiting for them, flanked by two tall, robed figures.

Riony knew who they were, and it made her itchy with anger.

"Oh, *now* you decide to finally pop up again?"

Priyune and Yrik had the grace to bow their heads lower.

Eslinde returned a fire-bright glare. "Riony, listen. They have returned with something to share."

"Maybe they could have shared a bit more earlier on? Like before Lyrrin got taken? Maybe that would have helped?"

Dracuni bumped her shoulder. **Be nice. She was their family too.**

Not like she was ours. Riony knew she was being unreasonable. She was also hurting.

"We are sorry for our absence." Priyune stepped forward and drew a symbol in the air with her long fingers. "But we were working. We had much to do with only four hands, and we don't yet know whether it has worked."

"Please let us show you." Yrik gestured for her to follow.

Riony remained where she was. "Dracuni needs to rest."

Eslinde moved close and looped her arm around Riony's. "Dracuni needs to be there for this too. Come. You'll like it."

Riony snorted air through her nose but sighed her agreement. She expected to continue out of Whisperwind Passage, but the Alderkin led them all back in and around a couple of short turns into a circular chamber.

"Oh ..." Riony mumbled as the large geode slice sitting in the center of the space came into view.

Niskina had moved the gateway up from the depths, but since it was out of charge, nobody had really bothered checking on it since then.

"*Oh*," she said again, taking in the ring of massive standing stones around the edge of the room, apparently freshly carved from crystal-streaked limestone. "Is that ... are they going to work?"

Yrik bowed apologetically. "We don't know. We had no access to core crystals of the size that would have been used for shrines in the past. But we hope there is enough crystal within these stones to work."

Priyune tilted her head to Dracuni, who hovered at the entrance, one front paw lifted in hesitation. "We will know shortly."

"Go on, go in," Eslinde encouraged.

Dracuni stepped into the circle. There was no immediate feedback, no visual sign or sound that indicated anything was working the way shrines normally did.

But when Riony followed Dracuni into the ring formed by the stones, a zing of energy tickled up the back of her neck.

"Try the gateway," Riony said in a hushed breath.

Yrik bowed low before the oval crystal, bending to place his forehead against the base before tracing the rune. A small, wavering glow built within the symbols around the edge of the gateway. Yrik selected one, and the gateway shimmered to life.

Dracuni trilled with excitement. Eslinde let out a yelp of celebration, and the Alderkin both raised their hands and drew a wide, swirling shape with them.

Riony grasped the sides of her head in her hands and let out a long breath.

This is huge. They had a working gateway again. They could get people out of the siege.

But where could they send them that was safe?

"Dracuni, can you fit through?" Riony eyeballed the size of the unidragon compared to the gateway.

The last time she'd fit through was the night of the enclaves attacks, and it was a tight squeeze then. As she moved up to the crystal now, she couldn't even wriggle her front shoulders through.

She backed out again, looking bashful.

"This is still good, though. This means a lot. If people want to leave the siege, they can. And ..." Riony's eyes popped wide.

She wrestled her crystal sword free from its sheath on her back and held it in front of her. Quickly skimming her finger over the rune, the blade glowed purple and the weight floated away.

"Yes, yes, yes!" She kissed the glowing crystal. "Oh, I've missed you!"

And not just her sword. All of the used-up crystals throughout the undercity could be brought in and recharged. There would be enough light and warmth and weapons for everyone.

Riony walked over to Yrik and Priyune. She wasn't sure of Alderkin etiquette and hoped she wasn't overstepping as she pulled them both into an embrace with an arm each.

"Thank you. This is going to change everything."

She was startled when they held her back just as tight.

"You were right. We should have shared more, sooner. And if we had done so, we might have saved my granddaughter, your sister." Yrik's gravelly voice rumbled near her ear.

He pulled back and looked at her with eyes so similar to Lyrrin's. "After suffering that loss, after seeing how far into death our land has fallen, we have made our decision. We will share everything now. Any of our magic that can assist, we will give it, in order to keep what we can of the world alive, human and otherwise."

Riony offered them a sad smile. Fishing for the string around her neck, her heart clenched, thinking of the other string, now gone along with Kess.

I hope she's okay, that she hasn't needed the silvernix in that acorn.

At the end of the remaining string, the flat slice of crystal hung. The remaining unpaired heart stone.

"Here. You should have this back."

Priyune lifted both hands together to receive it and then clasped it close to her chest. "I'll return it to the warrior's tomb."

"Yeah … just maybe wait until we clear out the spiders down there first."

Riony looked at the gateway again. A few more of the shrine symbols around the outside had gone dark since the last time she'd seen a working gateway.

"The shrine just down the hill is still active. We could send scouts out that way to check on the situation outside. I don't like not knowing what's happening out there," Riony said.

Without Kess and Griskin, they hadn't had anyone game enough to climb the frozen mountain peak to bring back a report.

"You may not need to travel so far," Yrik replied. "We used to have a way to oversee our exits without needing to go outside."

Eslinde's eyes remained on the shimmering gateway, a slight crease between her pale eyebrows. "That sounds useful indeed."

Yrik deactivated the rune at the base of the oval crystal. "It will take time to recreate, though. It's a complicated array of runes. The previous setup was destroyed when the battle for this deemfret was lost."

As though snapped out of a spell, Eslinde turned to them, blinking rapidly. "If only we could have done this at Eslindekeep …"

Priyune and Yrik shared a long look between themselves and whispered tersely in their own language.

Then Yrik bowed. "We didn't have the resources then, even if we had the will. But there was a way we could have kept the gateway there active, and we will live with the guilt for what could have been if we'd shared that knowledge earlier."

Priyune placed both hands palm outward in front of her face. "There is a way to keep crystals charged without shrines. Aleem discovered it in his work for the unicorn slayer."

Holding her strange stance, as though hiding behind her own hands, she explained how bottled unicorn blood kept close to crystals could keep them charged.

"Stars." Riony shook her head and moved closer to Dracuni. "I can understand why you didn't want anyone to know that bit of information."

More reasons people will want my blood. Wonderful. The unidragon's head was lowered, exhaustion drooping her eyelids.

"We did not want to use Dracuni that way," Priyune said it like an apology and lifted her hands higher. "It would have taken more than a few drops to keep a crystal that size charged."

Eslinde watched as Riony rested a hand on the unidragon's neck. "Even if the gateway had still been working then … Yensen was clever. He had me so thoroughly tricked. I'm sure he would have just found some other way to get what he wanted."

"He had us all tricked." Riony circled around the nearest standing stone, brushing her hand over the sharply carved limestone.

Lightning-bright zigzags of clear calcite shot through the milky stone. She noticed how the rough surface formed into a repeating pattern, scratched with fine lines she'd never noticed on the time-worn crystals surrounding shrines aboveground.

Every part of the massive stones was covered in hair-fine runes, barely visible in the low light. It must have taken the two Alderkin every waking moment since they got there to create them.

And they had achieved their goal. They had a working gateway again.

Riony's breathing grew ragged with the rampant energy that filled her.

I could go after Lyrrin, catch up to the others.

She moved toward the gate as though she could leave right away and then stopped. Perhaps in the past, she would have.

Now, all the working pieces of what lay before them turned more clearly in her mind. She had no way of contacting the rescue party to meet up with them again. She didn't have Griskin with her this time to help her get into the capital dragonkeep, to help sniff her way to her goal. There were more revs than ever.

It was impossible, and as much as she didn't want to care, as much as she wanted to be the Riony again who threw herself mindlessly at impossible things, she knew there was something greater she had to put her strength behind now.

Dracuni.

She had to be protected, for all she could provide the world. This humming circle of magic they stood in was proof of that. It was going to mean so much to the undercity community.

Riony couldn't run into a trap and leave Dracuni behind. Not even to save Lyrrin.

She was going to have to trust Kess's promise that she would bring her sister home. That they would both come home.

I do. I trust her. Came the thought Riony never would have thought she would think.

Riony turned back to face the gateway, narrowing her eyes.

No, she couldn't travel through it to chase after Lyrrin. But it could be used for other things.

Chapter Eight

Kess hugged the shadows with Griskin, avoiding streetlights as they moved through the quiet nighttime of the city. She wasn't sure how recognizable she'd be to anyone who may peer out a window, seeing as she was riding on her wolf, but she was sure there would be those in the capital who still believed she was the heir slayer.

"This way." Dashiel adjusted their backpack and took the lead, hurrying down the quiet stone street.

Around another corner, the streets became familiar to Kess. The last time she'd seen them they had been filled with floodwater and rioters. Soon they reached the front entrance to Zarram dragonhold and found it scorched and barricaded closed.

Aishena thumbed one of the athames at her belt. "I don't think we're getting through that."

"But on the good side, it doesn't look like anyone else has been getting through there either." Dashiel almost sounded cheerful, but their eyes were sad. "Let's see if we can get in through the back."

They hurried up the street. Only moonlight and the occasional streetlamp lit their way. The clatter of metal startled them all. A couple of cats that could fit in the palm of a hand circled an old milk can.

The gate to the stockyard came within view. It was bent and broken but chained closed in an upright position. Dashiel reached it first and gave it a shove. It rattled but didn't open.

Aishena pulled her athame and it lit up yellow as she traced the rune. She sliced through the links, and they pushed the whining metal open just far enough to squeeze through.

No bovin brayed and no stream washed down the pathway as they made their way down to the building this time, but still …

"This all feels too familiar," Kess said. "What are the chances someone has fixed that drop gate of yours?"

"I don't think it's going to be a problem." Dashiel pointed.

The external gate was still down off its hinges where Riony had left it, and the heavy metal internal gate had been propped up on a pile of splintered furniture. There was enough room beneath to crawl under.

They went one after another into the darkness beyond, keeping a wary eye on the heavy gate above. Once they were inside and away from any prying eyes, Aishena activated a glow stone at her belt.

Griskin sniffed at footprints in the dirt there and growled softly.

"I'm less sure now that this place is unoccupied," Kess said.

"It doesn't exactly look like somebody else has moved in. This is a mess." Dashiel's expression darkened, and Aishena moved closer beside them.

Inside, scorch marks marred the walls and litter was strewn along the corridor. Kess pushed the nearest doorway open, checking inside.

"Is that room secure?" Aishena asked.

Kess couldn't see everything in the dark chamber, but Griskin wasn't bristling, so she nodded.

Aishena touched fingertips to Dashiel's arm. "Stay here. Benj and I will do a sweep to make sure we're alone. Kess, look after Dash."

"What makes you think I'm the one who needs looking after?" Dashiel called toward Aishena as she walked away.

She threw back, "Because you don't have a wolf."

Dashiel shrugged. "I suppose that's a fair point."

Kess opened her own mouth to argue. She and Griskin could have the building cleared far faster than the other two. But Aishena rounded the corner up ahead, the paired blades she always carried strapped to her pack but never used glinting before she and Benjin disappeared.

Kess activated her own glow stone and turned to Dashiel to suggest they do their own scouting, when she noticed how pale their face had become.

They had moved into the room, kicking dully at the papers strewn across the ground, blackened and crisp. Cabinets along the walls had been wrenched open, doors hanging askew and anything of value cleared out. A couple of low cots were piled near the entrance, out of place in what seemed to be a storeroom.

Dashiel dropped down to sit on one of them and soot puffed out.

"I'm sorry," Kess said. "It must be hard, being here."

"I think the hardest part is that I never thought I'd come back here. That I'd never have to see it like this." Dashiel half smiled at her. "And that it doesn't hurt nearly as much as I feel it should. Does that make me a terrible person?"

Kess brought Griskin closer, and the wolf settled down on his stomach so that Kess was closer to Dashiel's level. "Coming from someone who watched their own home burn to the ground as well, I actually understand exactly what you mean."

Dashiel nodded eagerly. "It's just a place, and one with so many conflicting memories. Home came with me when I left. Home was Vance and Shiff, Eslinde and Viska."

That Kess didn't understand. She'd been flung from her home with nothing.

Dashiel watched Kess's faltering expression with a frown. "And you. You're family now, too."

A rush of warmth filled Kess, watching Dashiel's kind, eager eyes. She remembered the first time they'd met after the taming ceremony, how easily Dashiel had accepted her, befriended her, taken her flying, and held her when she broke down crying afterward.

Before then, nobody but Riony had ever treated Kess with that care. Dashiel had shown her what friendship could be, outside of the complications Kess and Riony's relationship held.

"You are too good for this world," Kess said through a fierce grin. "Now stop it. I'm meant to be cheering you up, not the other way around. Although it may be a mission I'm woefully inadequate for."

Dashiel glanced toward the door. "Listen, I don't mind a little overprotective energy. But I don't need looking after. Wolf or no wolf. Now, let's work on our plan so we can show Aishena that we're half as good at this stuff as she is."

Kess snorted, reminding herself instantly of Lyomir, then dug around in her saddlebags for the map of the palace Eslinde had given them.

The princess had drawn it up in a hurry herself and chased after them to hand it over before they'd left.

It was rough but had notes on potential entrances, guardrooms and grayglim lodgings, and places prisoners may be kept. Kess held the parchment flat between her and Dashiel.

"Our first problem with moving around on foot is that we're all kind of recognizable," Dashiel said. "Me, the rare Rolanian dragonlord, you and your wolf. And the Hjelzahn children half the kingdom and one possessed grayglim have been hunting for."

Kess didn't know what Lady Hjelzahn was doing now. She just hoped she was doing it far, far away. "So we'll need disguises. We can fit in as commoners or beggars around the city while we work out how to get into the palace. After that, we're going to need something more."

"I'm not sure Aishena and Benjin are going to pass as commoners or beggars at the moment."

"Maybe we should have gotten them to dye their hair before we left. It's gotten very pale." Kess cursed her hurry to leave so fast and that she'd brought the others with her.

The Hjelzahn siblings' hair was its natural silver tone again, a clear mark of their royal lineage. Kess's own hair, streaked through with long strands of white from all the silvernix her parents had spent on her in her youth also stood out, but still had enough black that the telltale brightness could be hidden more easily.

Dashiel smiled softly, some color returning to their cheeks. "I do like Aishena with her silver hair though."

Kess closed the map in her hands. "Oh, really?"

"Okay, I like her either way." Dashiel's tone was dreamy. "Have you seen how good she is at ... pretty much everything?"

"Well, yes," Kess admitted sourly. "Does this mean you're no longer competing for Riony's affections?"

Dashiel rasped a laugh. "I think that competition is over."

Kess's heart kicked up its pace as though she were staring down a sword point. Over? Was Riony with Zeina? Someone else? What had Kess missed?

"What do you mean?"

Dashiel leaned in close and gestured at her with both hands.

Kess shook her head, frowning.

This made Dashiel laugh harder. "Stars, Kess. Have you not seen the way she was looking at you after she pulled you from that lake, and honestly every moment since?"

Kess had only noticed how Riony had been trying hard *not* to look at Kess since pulling her from the lake. She'd noticed the avoidance, the sharp tension in Riony's shoulders and lips whenever Kess came too close.

"What way? Is she angry at me?"

Dashiel broke into laughter so hard tears squeezed from the corners of their eyes.

Kess wanted to reach out and shake them. "What do you mean, Dash?"

"I feel improper even being in the same room as that look. If that look could be bottled, it'd be worth more than silvernix. That look, Kessara."

Heat flushed through Kess. "*What look*?"

She had no more time to force an answer because Griskin rumbled a warning growl and surged up to his feet.

"What is it?" Dashiel drew their sword and dagger.

Footsteps approached, more than two sets. The door swung open and Aishena stepped in, dragging a tied-up line of three prisoners behind her. Benjin followed at the back, staff glowing red and held high.

Aishena gave the thin silk rope a tug. "We found this lot camping out in the living chambers upstairs. Otherwise, the place is empty. What should we do with them?"

The bound people cowered from the heat of Benjin's staff and the wolf in front of them. There was a brown-skinned teenager close to Benjin's age who hadn't yet lost the soft cheeks of childhood, a bronze and freckled woman, and an older man with a stooped back and bushy hair who stood protectively in front of them.

"Azri, is that you?" Dashiel lowered their weapons.

The man squinted over the wolf's back. "Dashiel? I thought you were dead!"

"I've just been gone for a while." Dashiel stepped around Griskin and clasped the man's hands. "It's okay. Let them go. I know them."

Aishena maintained her hold on the end of the rope. "They've *seen us*."

"Azri and his family worked here, for my family. We can trust them. They're good people."

Aishena's nose twitched, but she brought the end of the rope in and worked on the knots binding each of her captive's wrists together.

With his hands free again, Azri bowed to Dashiel. "I'm sorry we've been living here without permission, my lord. Nobody else would hire us after everything."

Dashiel grasped his shoulders, urging him back up. "I'm sorry, and don't worry. You can stay here. We're just ... visiting."

The woman and teen were freed, and the teen's eyes remained wide and locked on Griskin. The mother equally seemed frozen in fear by the wolf.

They must know the city well. They could help us get disguises too. A couple of growls from Griskin and they'd give us the clothing off their own backs.

Kess sighed inwardly. That was how she used to work, when faced with smugglers and slavers. She hated that it was still her first instinct.

She brushed her hands over Griskin's ears to settle him. He lowered down again onto his belly and panted happily.

"He's not going to hurt you."

"*Is he a wolf?*" the teen whispered dramatically.

Kess smiled in what she hoped was a friendly way. "He's a good boy. You're safe."

Kess pulled a loaf of the brown root-flour bread from the undercity out of her bag and broke it, handing half toward the three newcomers. Dashiel, Aishena, and Benjin followed her lead, sharing supplies they had brought.

Azri bowed. "Thank you."

Kess shrugged. "That's okay. You'll all need your strength for when the rev army reaches the capital."

"The what?" the woman balked, choking on her first mouthful.

Kess frowned. "The revenant army? That's marching this direction?"

Blank looks were returned.

Aishena added, "The one that has destroyed more than a couple of dragonkeeps in its path already?"

The family looked at them like they were crazy.

"You haven't heard anything about it?" Dashiel asked gently. "Nobody has said anything?"

Azri shook his head. "A friend who works for another dragonlord had some crazy gossip about why their lord was leaving for Elgartha, but nobody believes it. There's been no news in the daily sheets."

Kess and Dashiel shared a look. They didn't know. The whole general population didn't know what was coming for them. It was being kept quiet.

Dashiel ran through everything that had been happening, the size of the revenant horde, and the destruction left in its wake.

Azri scoffed. "The Dragon King will protect us if there are any revenants around. Keeps cannot fall."

His wife shoved him in the shoulder. "It's been weeks since I've received a letter from my sister at Gerichkeep. What if they're right?"

"We're right. We've seen it with our own eyes," Dashiel said.

Azri's mouth turned down. "All the riders are away at the moment. The skies have been so empty. What can we do? What do we do if the revenants get in?"

Kess remembered the inferno that had become of Gerichkeep when those remaining there had tried to fight back. "Hide. You should hide. Don't try to fight back or burn them. They don't burn anymore."

"*They don't burn?*" the teen whispered, aghast.

Kess continued. "When the revenants reach the city, get somewhere secure that you can barricade yourselves into."

"The flamesong stalls here would work well," Dashiel added.

Kess nodded. "Stock up with as many supplies as you can to last as long as you can before having to come out. Start now."

Azri shifted side to side on his feet, glancing at the door.

"Yes, *now* now," Kess confirmed.

Azri bowed once more to Dashiel, eyes wide, and then herded his family to the door.

"And spread the word. Tell everyone you can to do the same," Kess called after them.

Benjin thumped the end of his staff on the ground and deactivated the burn rune. "We're just going to let them go? They were my first prisoners."

Aishena patted him on the top of the head.

Dashiel's mouth was pulled thin. "Do you think it's going to make any difference? If the revs get into the capital?"

Kess pictured the swarming masses of undead they'd seen heading this way. And if Ardahnkeep fell first, the army could be twice as big again when it got there.

There was no point telling people like Azri and his family to fight back. Not when the revs wouldn't burn, wouldn't stay dead. There was nowhere else for them to run.

Hiding made the most sense. But Kess wasn't sure it would help at all while the rest of the city was defenseless.

The pocket-hawk keened, the shrill whistle cutting through the low hum of industrial clatter and braying of bovin. Riony flinched as the bird appeared in a flutter before her.

"Relax." Niskina reached her arm out horizontally, creating a perch for Teeka to land.

Riony cringed at the beady-eyed creature. "I wish Jaym hadn't brought that thing along. It's a bad omen."

"Only to you with your weird bird issues. I think she's cute, and she's also part of our plan." Niskina pulled a small scrap of blue fabric from the bird's beak. "The others are ready."

Riony adjusted her crouched position on the ground behind the scrubby bushes, eying the high-walled factory ahead. Her hands were sweaty with anticipation. She dusted them in the ashy dirt and tried to focus on what they were about to do.

It had been over a week since the Alderkin had gotten the gateway in the depths active, and since Kess and the others had left to find Lyrrin.

Stars, what is taking them so long? I should have gone with them.

More than a couple of times, Riony almost charged off through the gateway to go after them. But the people of the undercity needed her. The hungry dragons needed her. Dracuni needed her.

The last big meals of revs and spiders didn't last long, especially for the younger, still growing dragons. And what Dracuni got back barely covered the energy she'd expended in flaming the rev king.

So Riony came up with a plan to get more meat.

She glanced behind her. Her heart panged at not seeing Kess there at her shoulder, or any more familiar faces.

Instead, she addressed a team of strangers—delvers and new recruits from the undercity. "Remember to leave the dragonrider guards to us. Stick to those on the ground."

They nodded as one, watching Riony intensely. A crystal slab provided by the Alderkin hung on each of their torsos like badly made chest armor. Their gazes settled heavily on Riony, filled with expectation and awe.

Sparks. What tamebrain put me in charge? Riony still wasn't used to being looked at as the leader, even if it was just for this mission. She hoped she'd prepared everyone well enough.

Niskina scratched the palm-sized raptor around the neck, then gave her a piece of red fabric. Teeka took it in her beak and launched back into the sky. "Not long now."

Jaym, Zeina, and Vance led the second team, coming in from the back of the large compound.

There was no gate or ground level entrance into the glass factory ahead, since all transit in and out was done by dragons. There were only walls that jutted two stories high all around the interior buildings and smokestacks that belched smoke in long columns.

The whole place was as large as Heithorn estate, with dormitories, living areas, and its own stockyard of bovin to feed the working dragons within. After Riony had the idea to raid factories' food supplies to feed their own dragons, Eslinde helped with a list of options for factories still running outside of keeps. And there were plenty to choose from.

Niskina leaned closer to Riony and whispered, "How are you going to celebrate when we get home after our heroic mission? Do you and Zeina have plans?"

Riony's palms felt slick again. "Um … we're not …"

"What? You have a Rebel Rider, right there, who seems perfectly willing. Isn't that the dream? Why aren't you on that?" Niskina assessed Riony's wincing expression. "Stars, girl. Jaym and I have been going at it since day one of him getting to the undercity!"

Riony blinked a couple of times. "Wait, is that what all the *meetings* have been?"

Niskina smirked and bumped her shoulder against Riony's. "I love you, but you can be slow to catch on sometimes. Is that the issue with Zeina? Are you not getting her cues? 'Cause I'll do you a favor and tell you right now that she wants you bad."

Riony pressed her hands into the ground, staring at the dry dirt. "No, it's more that maybe I'm not as into her as I thought I'd be. That maybe … maybe I'm into someone else."

"Aishena? I thought you'd learned your lesson with her already. When she's not interested, she's not interested."

Riony swallowed hard. "Someone *else* else."

Niskina's eyes remained locked on Riony for a long, silent moment.

Then Niskina shrugged lightly. "Kess … isn't that bad."

Riony huffed a relieved breath. "Wow. That's high praise from you."

"I mean, you could do better."

Despite Niskina's playful smirk, a defensive anger flared inside Riony. "I'm not so sure I could. Kess is …"

Riony's mouth went dry under the weight of all that Kess was to her, all she'd become. All the qualities and strengths held within that one body that she could now see so clearly since the bitter veil of hatred had been pulled away.

All they had survived together, because of each other. All Riony would be willing to suffer just to continue having Kess at her side. All the dragonflame-bright emotions within her that burned at being apart and at imagining being together again.

"She is the star my heart reaches for." Riony exhaled the words roughly.

Niskina's eyebrows crept upward, a soft smile forming on her lips.

Riony coughed. "Also, she's hot … and stuff."

"Then I hope you and your star are reunited soon. Now, let's get to work." Niskina pointed upward.

Jaym's pocket-hawk circled above in the clear winter's day sky. It was time to move. Niskina gave the signal to the ten others waiting behind them.

A moment later, Riony had her glowing sword in her hand, rushing forward on light feet, leading her team toward their target ahead. A purple glow shone from each of their crystals, and as the stone fortifications rose up in front of them, they jumped.

As a group they soared high over the scorched ground surrounding the factory, arcing toward the top of the wall.

Riony's feet planted onto the stone walkway first. She turned back, making room for those following her.

Niskina landed, wide-eyed and gasping. "Sparks, these float runes are fun."

The team landed lightly all around. One middle-aged man with a rust-toned beard flew high, his trajectory taking him up over the other's heads instead of onto the wall. Riony thrust out a hand, catching him around the ankle. With a quick tug, she had him down on the wall with the rest of them.

"You good?" she asked.

He brushed himself off and stood tall. "I swear this is shorter than what we'd practiced."

Riony chuckled quietly. "Love your enthusiasm."

Across the other side of the facility, the soft glow of purple shimmered through the midday air. Less obvious than if they'd come at night, but they were still plenty visible to the guards standing watch at the ends of the fortification walkway.

Riony directed three of her team that direction as the guards reached for the alarm bell. The metal clanged as Riony, Niskina, and the rest of the team dropped down the other side of the wall into the factory yard.

Riony had scouted the area three times that week in preparation for the raid. She knew there would be guards on the walls. She knew they would sound the alarm.

She'd counted out the eight guards and twenty slaves, the one overseer, and two dragonriders. Without a ground entrance and with all their own dragons stuck in the undercity, they were never going to get in less detected than they just had. So they just brought double the numbers.

Riony's team swarmed down through the stockyard, running between the pawing bovin, upset at the intrusion into their pen. As guards came into view, running out of the buildings at the sound of the bell, her team split into groups of two and three to set upon them.

Vance and the Rebel Riders' team would be doing the same, coming in from the other side.

Riony kept on straight ahead, rushing the central tower in long strides, ignoring the guards and smaller scuffles around her. Her targets were larger.

The first of the dragons appeared from an open archway at the top of the tower. A yellow etherflame. Its rider yelled something lost under the growing clatter of battle.

Riony sheathed her sword, still lit, onto her back, and pounced like a cat onto the side of the tower. She grasped a protruding waterspout and swung around it, throwing herself higher. Her fingers latched on to a window ledge, and she kicked up again, her float rune carrying her.

Her hand slipped on the next hold and her chest hammered. But she had to reach the dragonriders before they roasted the teams below.

Go, go, go. She dug her toes and fingers into the vertical stone and scrambled skyward as the yellow dragon emerged and spread its wings. As it dropped from its perch to glide over the grounds below, Riony pushed off the tower with both feet, sending herself flying for its rider.

The woman wasn't nearly as surprised by Riony's airborne attack as she deserved to be. She pulled a short sword in time to smack it weakly across the blue and gold scale armor Riony wore. Dodging to avoid a better aimed second blow, Riony skidded down the dragon's back, between its beating wings.

Steadying her feet against the beast's spine, she drew her sword. A shadow fell over her, and she only had a split second to drop out of the way of the second dragon's snapping maw. The smaller bronze etherdart shot over them, circling around to come up behind Riony again.

The goggled rider smiled viciously as their dragon bore closer.

Riony braced, turning to face the approaching beast with her sword drawn. "Easy to feel superior while you're hiding behind all those scales and teeth. Come down here and fight me one-on-one!"

The dragon's mouth opened, aimed right for her.

A dart of red-brown feathers shot in from the side, colliding with the rider's head. Riony ducked under a bronze wingtip as the dragon swerved away.

The pocket-hawk screeched as she clawed into the rider's face, her wings out, fluttering as the man tried to swat her away. Blinded by the bird, his dragon slammed into a chimney, wings tangling as it and its rider tumbled to the ground.

Okay, maybe I don't hate the bird entirely.

The diminutive hawk circled again, her head angling around and beady eyes on Riony. *She still creeps me out, though.*

Riony shook off the near-dragon-bite adrenaline and turned back to the rider she shared a dragon with. The woman's attention was off Riony now, bringing the yellow etherflame down over the stockyard below where Riony's team fought the guards. The dragon's chest swelled.

"You'd burn all of them, friend and foe, wouldn't you?" Riony barked.

The woman spun around, reaching for her sword again. But Riony already had her fist colliding with the woman's temple. Her flight goggles flew off as her head snapped away from the blow.

She slumped in her saddle.

And now here I am, up in the air with a whole dragon to manage.

The yellow dragon was still following through on its signal to burn. Riony stepped over the unconscious rider and slapped her hands over the dragon's neck, poking and prodding until the dragon lifted its head away from the people below, releasing a jet of flame into the air in front of them.

The heat blew back over Riony as the dragon continued to glide onward, out over the facility walls and away from the others.

Riony had sat in on a couple of lessons that Vance and Zeina gave to the new undercity riders. She hoped it would be enough to get the dragon under control and back where she needed to be. She shifted her position, pressing more purposefully against the dragon's scales.

Riony let out a whoop as the dragon circled, turning toward the factory again. Soon they were approaching the walls where Zeina stood, waving up at her.

"A little help?" Riony yelled down as she passed over.

With a running jump, the Rebel Rider came flying her way. Riony caught her with an outstretched hand.

"Need me to get you back on the ground?" Zeina grinned.

The rider who was slumped between them groaned, and Riony pulled a rope to quickly lash her hands before she regained her senses.

"Me, not so much. The dragon, yes." Riony shuffled around, letting Zeina in front.

"Happy to handle it for you." Zeina's eyes glittered.

Riony patted Zeina on the shoulder, grasped her sword tight, and jumped down to the nearest roof. Her eyes darted around, taking in their progress.

The two dragons were dealt with. The second team had met up with the first, working on bringing together and binding up all eight guards. Jaym and Vance were dragging the overseer kicking and cussing out of a building to the side. Slaves watched in small huddles around the yard and through doorways, whispering excitedly together. One spotted Riony, pointing to her as though he knew her.

From her perch on the roof, Riony could see the stores at the back, mountains of white sand and other minerals in heaps mined from the neighboring quarry. Down through the high windows of the long building in the center of the grounds, a dozen juvenile etherflames were chained into small cages beside glowing red furnaces.

The bovin in the stockyard, disturbed by the clashing humans, cowered in one corner, braying, despite being twice as tall as any of the creatures that had scared them.

Riony jumped down beside Niskina, who was bent over the man with the rusty beard. "We all good? All clear?"

"Sure are. And just one injury." As Niskina straightened up, the man glowed.

He sputtered as the silvernix did its work, hands clutched over red wetness at his side. "Sorry, got a bit too carried away. Again."

"Lucky the princess has been so giving with the silvernix she brought from the capital," Niskina said, eyes on Riony.

"Yeah, lucky."

It wasn't clear whether anyone was believing their lie about where the influx of silvernix had been coming from recently. Dracuni had been offering more and more of her blood to others, healing those in the undercity who needed it, making sure there was a supply for those going on risky missions.

Without the food she needed to replenish, it had been weakening her a lot.

"I'm sure the *princess* will be really grateful in return for the food we bring back,"

Riony said.

Vance already had the team moving. A slave showed them to a building on the side where carcasses of freshly slaughtered bovin hung. They loaded as much as they could into a cargo crate for Zeina to take to the nearby gateway with the yellow dragon.

Coming to join Riony and Niskina, Vance said, "The people here want to come and join us in the undercity. Jaym has gone to see if the bronze dragon is still good to fly as well, then we'll get all the people and meat out of here and call it a good day."

Riony bent over to help up the healed man. "Our fresh recruits did really well. They're going to be off running raids without us in no time."

The man turned red around his beard. "We couldn't have done this without you. You took down those dragonriders! You …"

Overcome, the man made a series of swishing, exploding noises, his hands gesturing wildly.

Riony shrugged and patted her sword. "I've just had more practice with this. You'll be taking down dragons yourself soon."

"This was also all your plan," Niskina told Riony. "Don't sell yourself short. You'll be giving Aishena competition for strategy if you keep this up."

"I'm not sure my plan was that well thought out. I'm not sure what we're supposed to do now with all of this lot." Riony gestured to the tied-up guards and remaining bovin.

Niskina and Vance discussed the logistics of getting the rest of the bovin out, whether they could get them through the gateway to the undercity alive for future use. The guards they'd leave behind. Someone would fly in to check on the factory and find them at some point.

Riony turned to face the building holding the working dragons inside, her mind chewing over a thought that had been with her since she first started planning the raid.

She—and Jaym's bird—had taken down two more riders and their tamed dragons that day. After the dragons were used to help carry out what they needed, those dragons would be freed. They had a couple more doses of silvernix with them for that purpose.

The riding dragons were one thing, but there were another dozen tamed dragons inside, locked in cages.

All of which could be untamed, far more easily than taking down those with riders one at a time. When Eslinde had helped her find a target for this raid, she'd shown her locations of factories all over Elundrae.

If they could gain control of each the way they had this facility, they could free dozens and dozens of dragons at a time. They could work toward the numbers of untamed dragons needed that might make an impact on the shadow dragon's curse.

Riony's chest felt heavy, and she shivered as her sweat chilled on her skin.

They could do it. They might finally be able to make a difference. But every untamed dragon required more of Dracuni's blood.

Chapter Ten

Lyrrin pushed the carefully stacked pile of books over in an avalanche, frantically kicking the last few out of the way. The section of wall hidden behind them had deep score marks in the stone from her nails, marking out a rough circle just large enough for Lyrrin to squeeze out of.

Or she hoped it would be, once it broke through to the other side. Which had to happen now.

The torturer was on the way.

She gave the stone a push, but it was still firmly attached, despite the hours and hours of work she'd put into carving the escape route. She needed something more to get through to the other side.

The handle of the entrance door turned and rattled.

"It's locked!" a deep, unfamiliar voice yelled from the other side.

It sure is.

Lyrrin had made sure of it the moment she'd overheard that the torturer had arrived. The rune lock her father made for Eslinde worked well, sealing up every entrance to the chambers.

Lyrrin ran for the nearby window and popped out two panes she had cut free and set back into place earlier. She carved her rune into one and placed a drop of silvernix sandwiched between the glass.

Back at the carved wall, she traced the rune again and it lit up yellow. She'd have to work fast before the charge ran out. She only had one vial of silvernix left after that.

Pushing the point of the diamond panes toward where she'd already carved, the cutting rune magic pressed into the stone like toes into sand. She pushed until there was no more resistance, breaking through the other side, and then ran it around the whole circle.

The front door shuddered loudly as something large smashed against it.

"Open this door immediately!" the deep voice yelled.

"How has she locked it?" another grumbled.

"I'll keep trying to get through. You go and get help."

Neither was Yensen. Her ever-present warden was only rarely off duty for short breaks.

Would he let he torturer take me, if he was here?

No matter how the guards hammered on the door or jammed things into the keyhole, the magical lock held. Lyrrin focused on her cutting. The golden glow faded with just a hair's breadth of stone left uncut.

She grunted shrilly and tossed the used-up glass aside. It shattered where it landed.

"What's going on in there?" The door shook again.

Lyrrin leaned back on her elbows. She hitched up her gray dress and kicked at the cut section with both feet. The shock of hitting the stone jarred up through her bones. She struck out again.

Crack. The cut section shifted. Leaning forward, Lyrrin pushed the polished marble with her hands and wriggled it through and out the other side. She tentatively put her head through the hole.

She didn't know exactly what she'd find there, only that from her observations of the palace layout, there was something through that wall other than a long drop down.

A chilled, narrow hallway lay beyond, illuminated by torches that sputtered from the winter wind howling through open slit windows in the walls.

Some kind of secret passage? Or was this where the servants appeared and disappeared from? Lyrrin rarely saw them moving around the main corridors. Whatever it was, it continued in both directions, turning a corner and dropping down stairs to the left. Hopefully to a way out.

Lyrrin squeezed the rest of her body through the hole, cursing at her gown as it caught beneath her. Once on the other side, she checked on the final vial of silvernix and two pieces of blank glass she had wrapped in a scarf in her pocket, and then ran. The thumping at Eslinde's chamber door chased after her.

Down on the next level, doorways began appearing along the passage. Lyrrin tried one, cracking it open carefully. The clang of pots, crackle and spit of cooking, and hum of working voices came from beyond. She shut the door quickly and ran on.

She'd seen so little of the palace, and the place was huge. These tunnels felt like a maze within a maze.

Where do I go?

A doorway up ahead caught her eye. Made of a heavier metal, with the dark stain of damp footprints marking the ground around it.

Lyrrin gave it a hesitant push and found the dull purple of evening light and sappy scent of freshly pruned hedges beyond. A courtyard, wide and geometrically trimmed, and empty.

The garden was walled in on all sides, but it still felt like *outside.* That gave Lyrrin hope.

She tried to sneak through the shadows beside hedges and keep out of sight, but the polished pebbles there made a terrible crunching sound, so she moved back to the middle of the stone path and tried to walk casually as though she were meant to be there.

Two stories of windows looked down onto the courtyard, cold blue lighting shining from within, and a bell tower stood at one end, shooting up into the star-spotted evening sky.

An old memory surfaced, of the much smaller bell tower in the village she and Riony had grown up in, the sound of the bell marking time throughout the day, or used to warn of any signs of a revenant attack. Lyrrin hadn't heard any bells ring since she came to the palace.

From the window right at the top, a dark silhouette peered down at her.

Lyrrin gasped and ran again.

Arched entrances stood on three of the four walls of the courtyard, and Lyrrin had picked one at random. She reached it and peered inside. Two palace guards marched in time up the hallway within, their neat, quilted armor rustling with each step. Jolting back, Lyrrin ran for the entrance on the other side of the garden, her heart pounding.

She startled again when faced with more figures, but these didn't move. They were the statues she had seen before lining corridors in the castle. She recognized the one holding a long spear overhead from when she'd been taken to Eslinde's chambers.

If that way leads to where I was, maybe the other way might get me out of here.

Running on soft feet, she paused again at the next intersection, checking to see if it was clear. She sighed as the hallway lay empty beyond, leading to another stairway down. A spark of hope warmed her, and she stepped forward again.

A hand landed on her shoulder.

"What is this? An heir, wandering all alone?"

The voice chilled Lyrrin right through. She spun around, staring up into the merciless, dark eyes of Lady Hjelzahn.

Lyrrin backed away from Aishena and Benjin's creepy mother and hit the wall behind her. She reached for her pocket where the glass and silvernix were held.

In a flash of steel, the tip of a blade pressed against Lyrrin's hand until she stilled again and raised those bare hands in front of her.

Lyrrin stared up the length of the sword to the statuesque woman beyond. "Are you going to kill me?"

She only questioned it because Lady Hjelzahn didn't immediately strike her down, as Lyrrin thought she might. Instead, her dark eyes flickered and eyebrows knit.

"Who are you?" she asked.

"I'm Lyrrin Eyfarr," she said, without hesitation.

"Eyfarr?" Lady Hjelzahn lifted her blade, making Lyrrin tilt her face up to avoid it.

The woman wore full grayglim armor, the shadowy scales muted in the cool light. With her dark skin and sweeping eyes, she looked so much like her daughter, except for her black hair pulled back into one single long braid and the inhuman coldness her presence exuded.

She inspected Lyrrin with a scrutinizing glare. "I saw you, in the caves with my children. But now you're here? How? Why?"

What had been a calculating, murderous look in Lady Hjelzahn's expression now showed hesitation, confusion.

Lyrrin pushed her lower lip out, letting it tremble, hoping to leverage that confusion, if not draw out some sympathy. "I don't want to be here. I'm being kept prisoner by the king. I'm trying to get away."

The grayglim's eyes seemed to look right through her. "You're born from the blood of the king. You're one of them."

"I'm not like them," Lyrrin grumbled.

"You are an heir. I can *feel* it. I can feel how you have to die. But you are also ... something else." The tip of the blade dropped a fraction.

"You can feel it?" Lyrrin lowered her hands, and the woman didn't react.

Her eyes became glassy. "It's all I feel. All I can think about, all I care about. I wait and watch for any opportunity to kill those who enslaved the dragons, as though if I kill all of you I could ... I could stop feeling so sad."

She shook her head and brought the sword tip up against Lyrrin's sternum.

Lyrrin ran her words fast. "No! I don't have to die. You don't have to kill me. Please listen. You're possessed by the spirit of the shadow dragon. That's why you're being driven to kill heirs. It's not who you really are. You could fight it."

The corner of the grayglim's mouth twitched.

"Every one of you must die." Lady Hjelzahn breathed the words like a prayer and plunged the sword into Lyrrin's middle.

Lyrrin's eyes popped wide. A sickening, flame-laced agony exploded through her.

"No!" The voice that screamed wasn't her own.

Lady Hjelzahn hissed and extracted her blade from Lyrrin's flesh in a swish of movement that hurt as greatly again in reverse. The world turned blotchy and dim.

Pounding footsteps grew louder. Lady Hjelzahn ran the other way, vanishing into the shadows. Lyrrin panted pained breaths, and her legs gave way beneath her.

Scale armor rattled as an arm caught her. Yensen swore under his breath as he inspected her wound. His dark hair hung loose around his face.

Other figures, blurred in Lyrrin's vision, moved around him.

He barked, "You two, continue pursuit."

More movement and thundering steps. Lyrrin's mouth remained open, locked in a silent scream.

A grayglim Lyrrin didn't know bent over them, looking more irritated than concerned. "How did she get out? She was locked in her chambers. That's why we came for you."

"Go quick. Inform the king. We need silvernix. I'll take her there directly." Yensen rose up to his feet in a smooth motion, but even that made Lyrrin whimper, feeling cut in two.

Silvernix. I have silvernix! Lyrrin opened her mouth to tell Yensen where it was. She couldn't even feel her own hands to find it herself. She just wanted this hurting to stop. From her stomach to her ribs, everything felt seared and slippery and wrong.

Then she clamped her mouth shut again. *It's my last vial. My last chance.*

Yensen said he was taking her to silvernix. She could wait. She could make it.

Would she make it? It was hard to think.

Then they were moving, and the jostling of Yensen's swift steps blinded Lyrrin with pain.

"You're going to be okay." Yensen held her cradled tight to his chest. His voice was low and surprisingly gentle. "Our king will have silvernix for you."

Fear chilled Lyrrin. What if he didn't? He'd been using so much on the trials and often said he had to collect more.

Her words gurgled, "Will ... he ...?"

"The palace always has a supply. The king never lets it run low."

Light and dark flashed in Lyrrin's hazy vision and fire and ice warred within her, making her shiver and sweat. She coughed and tasted blood.

Yensen cursed again. "How is that blighted woman still here? I told the king Kverra Hjelzahn was the Heir Killer in my missives, but nothing seems to have been done about it. Idra the First was found dead last week during her visit, and the king is still allowing Prysha the First to stay at the palace, for her supposed *safety*."

He was rambling like Lyrrin had never heard before. Even through her agony, Lyrrin heard the change in Yensen's tone. How *my* king had become *the* king.

"But I never thought she would go after you. I never thought you'd be out of your chambers alone." His voice cracked with worry.

For her? Or because he would be the first person punished if the king's precious half-Alderkin was lost. Lyrrin struggled to grasp the last thin strands of her consciousness as those thoughts whirled within her.

They turned a sharp corner and galloped down a flight of stairs in a way that made Lyrrin wish she'd given up her own vial of silvernix to have avoided the pain.

"Let us through!!" Yensen snapped.

They came up against a barred gate. The metal was formed into twining thorned vines that crawled and grew in Lyrrin's wavering vision. It blocked the width of the corridor. Two guards stood at ease within, in front of another solid metal door.

"Only approved persons can enter the royal silvernix chamber."

Yensen grunted. "The king will approve this. He will want this girl to live."

"If it is our king's wish, we can escort the silvernix with you to be used in his presence."

Lyrrin stopped shivering. She didn't feel the pain so much now. Her eyelids just felt heavy. She felt much better. She was okay ... she just wanted to sleep.

"We don't have that much time. Let us through!"

The guards remained still. Not even a bleeding child in Yensen's arms moved them to break their orders.

Then with a sliding kick of their feet, they drew to attention.

"Let me see her." The king's face appeared in front of Lyrrin, and he grasped her chin, looking down with incandescent eyes.

Lyrrin wanted to swat him away so she could sleep, but her hands weren't responding. None of her body seemed to be there anymore. Everything was hazed and dim. At least three more grayglims surrounded the king, then six, then three, swimming in her vision.

Yeonard Draekhan snapped, "Open it."

There was a rustle of movement and a clang as the gate swung before them. Lyrrin bumped in Yensen's arms as they stepped through, waiting again as the two guards each moved to a slot in the wall on either side of the solid door in front of them.

"Hurry," Yensen whispered, too low for anyone but Lyrrin to hear.

Mechanisms turned and there was the grinding of metal, and they were moving again. Into darkness at first, and then with a click the room illuminated.

Or perhaps Lyrrin had died and fallen into a haunted land of death.

Skeletons surrounded her. She let out a weak wail. Arms squeezed around her a little tighter. Yensen still carried her, hurrying her toward shelves carved of the same dark, streaked stone that most of the palace was made from.

"Do it," commanded the king.

Lyrrin's eyes fluttered as something cool and wet touched her cheek.

A harsh white glare filled the space, cutting across the strange shapes all around her. The light came from her, rushing out from every part of her bare skin, streaming from her hands, mouth, eyes, blinding her. Her hearing filled with the hum of a thousand glowflies.

It hurts. Stars, it hurts! Riony had never told her that being healed with silvernix was an agony as great as the original wound.

Lyrrin screamed. Her body twisted and twitched from the pain of closing the hole through her middle. She felt every reconnection of flesh, from her navel through all the intricate parts of her insides and along the line of her back.

Her body surged as all the blood she'd washed Yensen and the floors of the palace with was renewed within her.

The light faded. She was left gasping and lightheaded, as she stared with clear eyes at her scarlet sodden dress and the long rip in its middle.

Her hearing cleared as well, to voices speaking over her head.

"It was Lady Hjelzahn, my king. She continues to be a danger to you and your heirs. If you'd let me—"

"You'll leave her be." The king turned away, running a finger along the stone shelf in front of him.

It was tall as the king and as narrow as a hand's breadth, carved with intricate designs up the sides. A second shelf stood close by like its twin in the center of the domed room. Each held a single vial on each tier, except for where one was now missing. Less than a dozen in total.

A small supply kept on hand, brought in from wherever else the king kept the rest.

Yensen asked, "Kverra Hjelzahn ... You want nothing done?"

"Yes. Apart from this little inconvenience, she has proven useful."

Inconvenience? Lyrrin scowled.

Yensen hadn't yet attempted to put her on her feet, despite how she wriggled in his arms, fully revived. This space horrified her, made her want to run.

She hadn't been dreaming when she saw skeletons before.

The walls of the chamber were lined with skulls and bones, stacked and laid out into a hypnotic pattern.

Of all the skeletons Lyrrin had seen raised and walking, she'd never seen these. The white bones held a faint opalescent shimmer. The long skulls had a spiraling golden horn in the center of the forehead.

Unicorns. Dozens and dozens of unicorns.

There were some different skulls too, set alone on plinths that looked like broken standing stones from shrines. The skulls seemed human, but sharper.

Lyrrin brought her fingers to her own chin and cheekbones, wondering if her skull was like that too.

The room was filled with terrible trophies, from the remains of those the king had defeated to the broken standing stones, to the slice of geode gateway, broken in half, arching across the two shelves.

Lyrrin shivered, then glared at the monster that was her grandfather. "Lady Hjelzahn told me she wants you and all your heirs dead. How is that useful?"

The king didn't look at her. He locked eyes with Yensen instead. "They've all been plotting against me, you know. All of the Firsts. Ulfren and his razed cult of sun-mad worshippers was the worst. Do you know how much work it has been managing that mess? Far easier dispersing them now that he's gone."

Yensen's arms around Lyrrin stiffened but he made no other reaction.

"The First heirs were *your children*," Lyrrin said.

"One can always have more children. Sometimes it's good to start again fresh." Yeonard Draekhan turned to Lyrrin then, looking over her as though she were nothing. An inconvenience. "Now leave. This isn't a place for you."

Yensen moved without hesitation, carrying Lyrrin from the silvernix chamber. She lifted her head to look over his shoulder, staring at the king. He watched her in return as he closed the heavy steel door between them.

His group of grayglims waited for him outside. Yensen spoke with one of them in a brief whisper. What Lyrrin could hear sounded more like a string of code words than anything she could understand.

He kept his tight grip on her as he left them and marched swiftly down the long hall.

"I can walk now," she said.

"I'm sure what you really want to do is *run*." The grayglim made no effort to put her back on her feet.

Lyrrin folded her arms over her sticky dress and pouted. "Wouldn't you if you were in my place? The king is going to use his torturer on me, and I just got *stabbed*!"

"It wouldn't be like this if you cooperated. If you gave the king what he wants."

"A unidragon?"

Yensen shushed her with a hiss, despite them being the only people in the corridor.

"And what do you think the king will do once he has one?"

Yensen's expression shifted from anger to something more fervent. "He will repair our land! He will have enough silvernix to heal everyone, make all the dragonkeeps safe again. It will be humanity's fresh start."

Lyrrin scoffed. "I don't think that's what he meant when he said that. This is a man who doesn't even care about his own family. What makes you think he isn't going to keep all a unidragon gives him for himself?"

Yensen took Lyrrin up a flight of stairs, not half as gently as he'd carried her down them. "You kept Dracuni to yourselves."

"For her safety," Lyrrin snapped back. "Was there ever a time when someone needed healing and it didn't happen? Was there ever a time any of us could have helped people and didn't?"

Yensen's lips grew thin. He turned down a wider hallway that Lyrrin didn't recognize, lined with thin, pointed windows.

He seemed so close to cracking, so Lyrrin kept pushing. "The queen said the king still has plenty of silvernix hidden away somewhere. If the king was going to save our land, to do all these things you hope from him, why hasn't he started already?"

Yensen's mouth twitched.

"He talks of having more children as though they're just a resource to be made and spent. The way he treats me as well. Do you honestly think he's going to care more about the rest of the world?"

"He is our king," Yensen parroted as he often did, and his expression closed off.

He approached a wall and pressed something there, making a section of it swing away. He took her into a darker, rougher tunnel.

A dank smell made Lyrrin's nose wrinkle. "This isn't the way back to Eslinde's rooms."

Yensen huffed. "Rooms you've clearly discovered a way out of. I'd be a fool to take you back there."

A small chamber opened ahead, and Yensen finally put Lyrrin down to stand beside him. He kept one hand ringed like a shackle around her wrist as he struck a flint beside a torch, lighting it ablaze.

A small dungeon lay ahead of them, gated with a grid of iron, with a short corridor of cells beyond. One side was a mess of warped metal and cracked stone, as though an explosion of some kind had ripped it to pieces. But a solid door with small, barred window on the other side of the passage remained whole.

Yensen dragged Lyrrin to it. "This kept your Alderkin family secure for decades. It should keep you out of trouble until you've done what is needed."

"And then?" Lyrrin challenged him, standing straight with the full length of her blood-sodden dress on display.

"Then ..." Yensen's mouth twitched. "I'm sure the king will still find you useful."

He closed and locked the door, plunging Lyrrin into darkness.

Only a small flicker of flame reached through the barred window, and Lyrrin's eyes worked hard to adjust. The ground was uneven and crunchy under her soft shoes and the drying blood all over her left her feeling itchy and cold.

All the warmth of hope her earlier escape attempt had filled her with was long gone, replaced now with a deep, sinking sadness.

This is how my father and the other Alderkin lived for so long?

The space was small, claustrophobic. There was no daylight. No glass.

She reached into her pocket and unwrapped the scarf. She sighed when she found the two pieces of glass and vial of silvernix still whole.

But the walls and door were far too thick to cut through with her final dose of silvernix. She'd have to think of something else.

There was a shuffle of movement outside.

"That was quick," Yensen said.

A gruff, haughty tone answered. "Our king wants you relieved. We'll be guarding the cell as our friend here does his work."

What work? Lyrrin frowned and pushed closer to the door to listen.

A tense silence followed.

"Those are the king's orders?" Yensen's voice was clipped.

"He wants results, and he doesn't trust you anymore to get them."

Silence again, only broken by Lyrrin's heavy breaths as her stomach churned and fingers trembled.

My late son Hjelzahn had a man in his employ who is very skilled at getting results out of people who are being defiant. A man very good with his tools.

"Yensen?" Lyrrin whispered into the door, pleading, hoping.

A single set of footsteps marched away.

The door opened. Lyrrin stumbled back away from it, heart thumping like a trapped rabbit.

A very average man with neat black hair and tidy gray tunic stood at the cell's threshold, rimmed in the orange glow of the torchlight. He had soft cheeks and square chin and wore glasses that reminded Lyrrin of Yoskar.

A leather bag hung heavy in one of his hands, jangling as he shifted it.

He looked Lyrrin up and down, eyes moving over her clawed hands, her bright eyes, the blood soaking her dress. And he smiled widely, showing all his teeth.

CHAPTER ELEVEN

Griskin's ears twitched, flicking forward, alert. Kess felt every movement and tension in the wolf's neck, translating it like a second language.

Someone was coming their way.

"Shh. Hide!" she rasped to the others.

Aishena tried a door to her side, but it was locked. Dashiel frowned back the way they'd come. They couldn't go that way. They barely slipped past three guards who marched into that courtyard after them. Benjin slipped closer behind his sister.

The cold stone floor of the palace seemed to absorb every sound, but the silence felt more oppressive than comforting. The corridor stretched long and empty ahead, lamps flickering with a bluish light that cast the guard's shadow on the wall as she rounded the corner toward them.

"Behind the statues." Kess barely breathed the words, gesturing with her hands to get the message across.

Aishena, Dashiel, and Benjin ducked into an alcove each. The sculptures of golden warriors barely concealed their forms as they huddled behind them, trying to become invisible. Only Aishena managed it seamlessly.

Kess urged Griskin into their own alcove. He bumped the gilt figure as he wedged in behind it. Kess held her breath as it teetered and rocked, then stabilized. The large wolf was too big for the space, unable to hide behind the statue like the others.

It got them out of direct view down the hallway, but they'd be obvious to anyone walking past.

The guard's footsteps grew louder, reverberating off the stone walls.

Turn around, go a different way, Kess wished silently.

As the guard drew closer, Kess radiated with tension, her hand hovering over her throwing knives. The guard's shadow loomed down the hall. Kess pulled a bone blade free. The guard was only a few steps away.

Peeking from behind the golden biceps of the ancient Taen warrior, Kess prepared her shot. Blue light flickered off the guard's bare face and neat braids.

She's barely older than me. Kess's stomach churned.

But if the guard saw them hiding there, she could raise the alarm, and it would all be over.

Kess had to act. But maybe, maybe she didn't have to kill anyone today.

Hand whipping out like a striking snake, Kess threw her blade. It went wide, behind the young woman, and cracked into the glass bulb covering a lamp. Broken shards hailed to the floor and the guard yelped.

Halted mid-step, the guard turned toward the mess. The bone blade lay farther down the hallway, and Kess eyed it, hoping the guard wouldn't see it too. Hoping she wouldn't have to kill the girl after all.

The guard leaned over and kicked at the fallen debris. "Ugh, I hate these dragonflame lights! Someone has to clean this razing mess up."

With a huff, she returned back the way she came.

Once she was out of earshot, Kess and the others emerged from their hiding places.

"That was too close," Aishena said. "This is foolish, trying to sneak around a palace with a huge wolf. Maybe we should go on alone."

The three others wore padded silver and black guard gambesons but unless castle guards had started riding wolves, there wasn't much point in Kess wearing the uniform. She remained in delver armor.

"As though your disguises are going to work for anyone who sees you up close. Any one of us is going to set off alarms if we're spotted."

Kess gestured to Aishena's row of crystal athames along her belt and twin grayglim blades strapped to her back, then Benjin, carrying his crystal-studded staff and looking barely into puberty, and then Dashiel, with clearly Rolanian features.

"*And* you two are the ones with bounties still on you. You could easily be recognized." Kess continued down the hallway, checking the intersection up ahead to make sure the guard was gone.

It had taken too many days to find a way into the palace. Aishena had done the majority of the reconnaissance trips alone, timing the guards' shifts, and stealing uniforms. But despite Aishena's solo journeys into the palace, she hadn't been able to find Lyrrin. That was when they decided to all go together.

"We just need to keep our faces hidden." Aishena hurried to catch up. "How are you going to keep Griskin hidden?"

"I can't exactly leave him behind," Kess said flatly. "Besides, he's the one who's going to find Lyrrin for us."

Griskin grumbled softly and sniffed at the polished floor.

Kess smirked. "And I think he's got her scent."

Aishena's mouth was a hard line, but she nodded and let Kess take the lead. They rushed along the cold hallways, letting Griskin follow his nose. Kess held him back at each intersection, letting Aishena clear it first.

It was such a different experience, gliding down those long passages on Griskin's swift feet, compared to the hard and squeaking wheeled chair Kess had last traveled those spaces on before.

At the next corner, Aishena paused, ducking down and running her fingers over the floor. She held them up, marked red.

"Blood?" Dashiel asked.

Griskin sniffed at it, whining.

Benjin looked from the wolf to the red stains dripping all the way up the hall. "Is it Lyrrin's?"

Kess didn't want to answer. Her heart pounded with the fear that they were too late.

That she had failed Riony.

"The blood's still wet," Aishena said. "We should move fast."

They took off at a run, Griskin chasing along the trail of blood. They no longer checked corners before they rounded them. Every second counted.

Two guards fell into their path, freezing as they were met with their strange group. Griskin pounced upon one, knocking him to the floor. Aishena vaulted over the other, landing behind her and cracking an elbow into the back of her neck, making her drop, boneless.

Dashiel and Benjin dragged the two woozy guards into a shadowed corner, and Griskin sniffed ahead. The messy trail of blood went one way, but Griskin seemed torn between that and a second direction.

Kess took the chance to get her bearings. She didn't know what was down the corridor where the blood trail went, but she had been the other way before.

"This way," she hissed, and they set off at a run again.

Every moment of the night when Eslinde had led Kess down into the hidden dungeon to meet the Alderkin was clear in Kess's memory. It wasn't a time she'd easily forget.

When they reached the room with the secret door, Aishena said, "I've already checked, she's not down there."

It was one of the first places Kess had instructed Aishena to look.

"She might not have been down there before, but I think she is now." Kess pointed to a smear of blood on the stone that opened the passage.

Griskin also still had Lyrrin's scent, eager to rush down the dark tunnel.

Voices and the orange flicker of torchlight came from ahead. Kess and her team slowed their pace, drawing weapons. The dungeons were at a dead end. They were going to have to fight through the guards down there.

In the dimly lit chamber outside the cells, three guards clad in heavy armor stood scattered around the room, chatting in low voices. The air hung thick with the scent of damp stone and faint whimpers echoed from beyond.

Griskin growled low in his throat.

Lyrrin.

Kess signaled with a sharp nod, and her team moved as one. Aishena was the first to strike, slipping into the shadows with the grace of a seasoned predator. She crept behind the nearest guard, clamped a hand over the man's mouth, then shoved his head against the nearby stone wall. The guard went limp, sliding to the floor.

The second two guards drew alert, scrambling for their weapons.

Before he could draw his sword, Benjin had the next man stumbling backward at the end of his burning hot staff. The red glow trailed through the dim air, reflecting in the man's terrified eyes as he tried to dodge away from the unfamiliar magic.

As he cowered back, Benjin raised the staff and cracked it down. The guard sprawled beneath the blow.

Kess and Griskin took on the third guard. As Dashiel rushed in on one side, the wolf swerved around behind the man and snapped at his ankles, pulling his feet out from under him. Dashiel crouched over the squirming guard and knocked him on the temple with the pommel of their push dagger.

Kess scanned the room to ensure no one else was left standing.

A man called from one of the cells beyond. "What's going on out there?"

The voice caused a shiver of familiarity through Kess.

Benjin was first to where the sound had come from, the only closed cell. "The door's locked."

Aishena and Dashiel began searching the downed guards.

An anxious shiver had built within Kess. She couldn't wait for the keys. She needed to get that door open now.

Pulling the cutting athame Riony had given her, she activated it and attacked the heavy door, trying to cut through. The enchanted crystal carved and sliced, but the cell door was solid.

"Got the key!" Dashiel ran in beside her, ducking beneath Griskin to turn the lock.

The moment he was out of the way, Kess hissed, "Griskin, go!"

Understanding, the wolf reared back and pushed the door in with his front paws. It swung hard, clattering against the stone wall. Inside, a single torch lit the space.

The man in the middle of the cell, looking very neat and clean-faced, turned to the intrusion. He held a long, barbed blade in one hand.

A curious smile widened his lips. "Kessara Heithorn?"

Kess reeled back in her saddle. She almost turned and fled, faced with this man, this monster, who haunted her nightmares. Who had once taken joy in carving her open time and time again. A bag of familiar tools sat open at the man's feet.

Kess's throat jammed closed as fear overtook her every nerve.

Then she saw Lyrrin in the back corner of the cell, shivering and drenched in blood, and her fear burned away.

A child. She's just a child!

Fury tore through Kess, heating her eyes and snorting out in sharp breaths. The torturer must have noticed her murderous change of expression. He raised the barbed blade, brandishing the wicked point toward Griskin.

Kess growled more ferociously than the wolf. Her fingers tightened around the weapon already in her hand. Her arm and eyes and fingers worked in concert, fluid and instinctual. She knew her target, she threw the blade, she didn't hesitate.

This was one life she wouldn't question taking.

Golden light shot like a falling star across the room.

As the monster of a man stood there gulping, with no blade jutting from his chest, Kess thought she'd somehow missed. The athame clattered to the stone floor.

With a bewildered expression, the man raised his hands over where his heart should have been, and they came away bloody from a hole that went right through.

He fell to his knees, then awkwardly backward onto the filthy floor, and didn't move again.

Kess tried to breathe, to still the shake in her hands, as Aishena and Dashiel came up behind her.

"Sparks. What is *he* doing here?" Aishena's voice held an edge of terror the young woman usually never showed.

"He's never going to do any of his evil work again, that's what," Kess said.

"You ... how do you know about him?" Aishena frowned, locking eyes with her. "Oh, Kess ..."

Kess blinked away the threat of tears and turned back to Lyrrin. She reached for the acorn at her neck. "Are you okay? Did he touch you?"

Lyrrin stared at them all, mouth dropped wide. "No. No. He only just got here."

"You're covered in blood!" Benjin took off his guard jacket and handed it to her.

Lyrrin put it on, the oversized fabric puffy around her.

She craned her neck to look behind where they all stood in the doorway. "It's from something else. I'm fine. Where's—?"

"Riony had to stay with Dracuni. She sent us, and we're going to get you back to her," Kess said.

Lyrrin frowned but nodded.

From far overhead, a clanging bell rang.

Dashiel picked up Kess's cutting athame and handed it back to her. "And we really need to be getting out of here, right now."

Kess offered for Lyrrin to ride on Griskin with her, but Lyrrin insisted she was fine. Far shorter than the rest of them, she still managed to keep up as they ran.

Back in the main hallways of the palace, the sounds of marching boots echoed from every direction. Kess led the way, hurrying them back along the route they'd come in. They were almost back at the courtyard that led through to their exit when three grayglims appeared as though from thin air, blocking their path.

"The other way, go!" Aishena hissed.

They sprinted together down the corridor and a flight of stairs, the grayglims close behind. Another area Kess wasn't familiar with.

They passed a huge floor-to-ceiling window which looked out over the city and skidded to a stop when faced with another group of two grayglims and half a dozen castle guards, led by Yensen.

Kess's lip curled as her head swiveled back and forth. They were penned in.

CHAPTER TWELVE

Kess reached for the knives in her bracers, calculating how many grayglims she might manage to drop before they were overwhelmed.

Lyrrin stepped in front of her, waving directions. "Back to the window!"

Kess pounced Griskin toward the glass, pressing close to peer out. The drop was sheer, running down the full height of the palace walls. "You think we should jump?"

Lyrrin's face screwed up. "What? No! Do you have a death wish? You and Riony ... I swear."

"You can't get out that way." Yensen stepped to the front of the circling guards and grayglims. "Return Lyrrin to us, and we will make your deaths swift."

"Don't you mean *or* we will make your deaths swift?" Dashiel laughed nervously.

"No," Yensen said.

Kess pulled a throwing knife for each hand, and Aishena, Benjin, and Dashiel all drew their weapons too.

Lyrrin had one of her hands in her pocket but took a small step away from the window toward Yensen. "You don't have to do this. You know you're not on the right side. I know you know it!"

The grayglim sneered in response.

"Don't bother with him," Kess said. "He's made his loyalties clear."

"No." Lyrrin stamped a step closer to the grayglim. "People can change. People can be forgiven. You of all people should believe that too, Kess."

Kess's heart panged sharply, and her expression softened before she shook it off.

"No. Not everyone deserves that. Not the kind of person who would leave a child alone with that monster and his tools," Kess growled the words, directing them at the grayglim she had once trusted, once fought beside. "Do you have any idea what the Hjelzahn's torturer would have done to her?"

Yensen held Kess's stare for a long, silent moment. His chest lifted and fell in a visible breath, and he drew two swords. "Take them."

The grayglims at his side burst into motion. Kess tensed, pushing Griskin in front of Lyrrin and bringing her hands up to throw her blades.

Then a tearing sound cut the air and the charging grayglim fell face-first to the floor in a clatter of smoke-toned scale armor.

Kess blinked, unsure what had happened. Neither she, Aishena, Benjin, or Dashiel had moved from their holding positions.

But then she saw the source of the attack. Yensen held one sword lunged forward, reddened with his companion's blood. In the moment of confusion, as cries went up from the other grayglims and guards, he struck out with his second sword, toppling a guard to his left.

Chaos erupted. The remaining four grayglims and five guards broke into action, swinging to down Yensen and the palace invaders. With one grayglim down and Yensen, possibly, on their side, they were in a better position than before.

But four was still far more grayglims than Kess felt comfortable facing, and as the clash of combat grew louder, she knew more would be on the way.

Aishena and Benjin pushed through the chaos with their glowing Alderkin weapons. An athame went skidding across the floor, leaving a burning trail as a grayglim disarmed Aishena of it.

She should be using her long blades! She's at a disadvantage with the daggers. Why doesn't she use her swords?

Kess had to dodge her own attackers, ducking under swinging blades as Griskin pounced between guards and grayglims.

Dashiel had Lyrrin behind them, backing up against the window. One of the grayglim approached, catlike, batting almost playfully at them with the tip of their sword.

Kess looked for an opening to reach them. Dashiel was a fine fighter, but not at take-on-a-grayglim-solo level. She threw her knives, teeth clenched as she felled two guards.

Yensen and Aishena had dropped a couple of guards as well, but now that the element of surprise was gone, the grayglims weren't so easy to defeat.

Behind Dashiel, Lyrrin had turned to the window, running her sharp nails over it.

Maybe she's decided jumping is preferable after all.

The sharp scrape of her claws on the glass rang through the air and Griskin whined, pulling his ears back. As he cringed from the sound, he missed a step, and the length of a grayglim's blade sank deep into his neck.

Kess wailed in horror as the wolf dropped beneath her. "No. *No!*"

More knives found their way into her hands, and she flung them—one, two, three, four, five—into the chest and face of the grayglim above her. He froze, mid-swing, wavering on the spot.

Rough, gurgling sounds came from Griskin's throat. He lay on his side, pinning one of Kess's legs beneath him. The final castle guard stepped in beside the still wavering grayglim and swung his sword down at Kess in a swishing blow.

"Kess!" Aishena moved in, knocking the stumbling pin-cushioned grayglim the rest of the way down with a bash from her shoulder.

The other guard turned the swing of his sword away from Kess to meet Aishena instead, and they clashed blow for blow above Kess and Griskin, yellow and red light streaking from Aishena's athames.

Kess turned away, ignoring the fight. She reached an arm around Griskin's neck, feeling for the wound. "Come on, boy, you're okay. You're going to be okay."

Air wheezed from his throat and the hot metallic tang of blood filled the air. Kess knew he wasn't going to be okay, not on his own. But she could save him.

She tore the acorn pendant off and pulled it open. She knew Riony had given it to her in case she needed it to save Lyrrin, Aishena, Benjin, Dashiel, or maybe, *maybe* even herself. But there was no way she wasn't going to use it to save Griskin.

Kess pushed Griskin's fur apart and applied the precious drop of fluid to his skin.

"Get down!" Lyrrin's voice cut through the fighting.

The girl dropped to her belly on the ground, and everyone who knew what she was capable of followed her orders in an instant. Aishena, Benjin, Dashiel, and even Yensen all hit the floor.

Kess couldn't pull her leg free from Griskin as light glimmered from beneath his thick fur and he twitched and howled. So she simply threw herself over his back as best she could to protect him from whatever Lyrrin had set off.

The grayglims and remaining guard were unable to understand that when this small girl gave you an order, you followed it. They stood, unsure, confused at their opponents' strange behavior.

Behind where Lyrrin lay, a swirl of Alderkin runes had been etched in the glass, covered in a film of shining liquid. The whole window glowed and rattled. Cracks cut across the surface like lightning.

In an explosion of tinkling sound, the glass burst outward. Shards flew across the corridor, skewering the standing grayglims and guard. Kess gasped as sharp points jabbed through her leather armor, sinking into her back. She kept her arms around Griskin, covering him as the healing light faded.

As the last clinking of falling glass faded, bodies dropped.

"Is that all of them?" Lyrrin's voice sounded small, a little ill but determined.

"How did you *do that*?" Benjin was first on his feet, staring between Lyrrin and the field of broken glass all around with his mouth wide open.

Dashiel helped Lyrrin to her feet, and Yensen stood beside them. Lyrrin offered the grayglim a tentative smile.

"You two okay over there?" Aishena called over to Kess from where she'd sheltered in a doorway.

Griskin yawned with a soft yelping sound and rolled off his side, bringing Kess up with him as he stood. The warmth of blood trickled down her back from sharp points of pain.

But all she cared about right now was that Griskin was okay.

She rubbed his ears. "Yeah, we're good."

Aishena sheathed her athames. "Then we need to— *Watch out!*"

There was movement beside Lyrrin. Yensen's arms shot out, grabbing her and pulling her in.

"What are you—?"

"Stop him!"

Everyone yelled at once. Kess brought Griskin across the space in one huge leap, ready to put the traitorous grayglim down for good.

There was a tearing squelch as a blade sank into skin, and Yensen fell.

Kess blinked at the scene before her, trying to work out who had gotten to him first.

Then she saw another grayglim, punctured with glass shards but still breathing, up on his knees, his sword thrust into Yensen's chest. Right where Lyrrin had been standing a second before. The blade slid deep into Yensen's side, between the scales of his armor.

"No!" Lyrrin cried out, trying to support Yensen as he staggered, crumpling over her. Dashiel and Benjin grasped him from either side, adding their strength to halt his fall.

The other grayglim pulled his arm back to strike again. His eyes glowed white from within a face painted red from a hundred cuts. Then Griskin was on him, teeth around the back of his neck.

Crunch. The wolf tossed the man's limp body from his mouth.

"Do we have any more silvernix?" Lyrrin kneeled at Yensen's side. Her cheeks were slick with tears as she leaned over, pressing her hands to the gaping wound on the man's chest. "I only had one left, which I used on the window."

Aishena, Dashiel, and Benjin shook their heads.

"I don't have any more. I'm sorry." Kess brushed a hand over the sticky blood in Griskin's fur, her nose wrinkled. The wolf tensed, ears pricking up.

"We have to go," Kess said, straining to hear what Griskin had already noticed. Footsteps, pounding their way.

"Leave me. Go while you can," Yensen groaned.

"We're not leaving you!" Lyrrin shook her head, then looked around at the rest of them. "We can't leave him. He helped us. He saved me. I know where they have silvernix. We can go there."

"No!" Yensen snapped. "They will trap you in there if you try."

Kess swore as the footsteps grew louder. "Get him up onto Griskin with me. Quick! We need to get out of the palace."

Aishena and Dashiel got their arms under the grayglim, and he cried out roughly as they lifted him. Kess shifted backward in her saddle so there was room for him in front of her, wincing as pain lanced through the wounds in her own back.

Is there glass still in me? It feels like it.

Every lift of Yensen's limbs and body as the others positioned him onto the wolf left him gasping between stubborn refusals.

"You shouldn't ... just leave me ..."

"Go, go!" Kess ordered as the shadows of approaching figures filled the other end of the hall.

Yensen slumped over Griskin's neck, and Kess helped keep him from falling off as they raced through the palace, the others running at their side. Yensen's breaths labored and sputtered, and when Kess put a hand to his neck to steady him, his skin felt cold.

Kess's lips curled as her heart raged between disgust and sympathy. She wanted to hate him for how he'd betrayed them. She did hate him, as much as she hated who she once was.

Softly, she said, "Just hold in there, okay? We'll get you fixed up as soon as we're out of here."

Yensen's head shook, either in denial or because he didn't have the strength to steady it as Griskin ran. "You ... would help me? After what I've done?"

"I know what it is to have made mistakes. Terrible mistakes that should never have been forgiven." Kess furrowed her brows as blood spurted from Yensen's side. "You're not a bad person, Yensen. You were loyal, above all. You were just loyal to the wrong cause."

Yensen bowed over farther, resting entirely over Griskin's neck. "If you ... if you had more silvernix ... you would have, wouldn't you? You would have used ..."

Kess still held the empty acorn pendant clasped in one fist. She could never regret saving Griskin. She just wished Riony had given her enough to do more.

It had stunned her that Riony had given her any at all. They had always been so against bleeding Dracuni into bottles. Now that Dracuni allowed it, how did they stop from asking for too much? How did they say no to taking her blood when it could have meant saving more lives?

Kess tried to swallow all the aching questions away as she also swallowed away the pain in her back. "We're almost out. Come on, I know you're tough. You can make it."

Yensen didn't reply. Griskin pounced out into the dark courtyard, and the grayglim slipped in the saddle, falling sideways.

"Whoa, whoa!" Kess grasped at his armor, trying to catch him.

Aishena moved in quick, getting under the man and propping him back up. She held him for a moment, looking into his face, then turned to Kess.

Her lips pulled thin, and she shook her head.

"What is it?" Lyrrin skidded to a stop on the gravel up ahead.

"We tried. I'm sorry," Kess said.

She and Aishena worked together to move the lifeless body off Griskin's saddle. Lyrrin remained in place, her clawed hands flexing and eyes glistening.

Again, in a softer voice, Kess said to Yensen, "We tried. I'm sorry."

The grayglim's blank eyes stared back up at her.

"Someone's up there!" Benjin called from across the courtyard, pointing to the tall tower that rose high above them. "They're watching us."

"We really, really, really need to go now," Lyrrin said.

Kess turned, her head heavy with sorrow and dulled by her own pain. "Now you're in a hurry? Why? They're all the way up there."

"Because if that's who I think it is, it's Kverra Hjelzahn," Lyrrin replied.

Aishena grew very still. "How do you know?"

Lyrrin gestured to all the blood on her gown. "We ran into each other earlier tonight. I think that's where she's been hiding out, keeping watch for her victims."

"Then move, move!" Kess urged Griskin into a run again. They were across the courtyard when she realized Aishena wasn't following.

Her cropped silver hair swung around her chin as she stared up at the tower and the silhouette within.

"I'm not coming." Aishena's dark eyes glimmered in the low light. "I need to go and see my mother."

Chapter Thirteen

The blood on Lyrrin's dress had dried like a crackly leather. Facing the woman who spilled that blood again wasn't high on the list of things she wanted to do.

"The rest of you go, get Lyrrin out safely." Aishena checked over her weapons and stretched her shoulders. "I'll catch up when I can."

Benjin thumped the end of his staff on the ground. "No way. If you're going after Mami, I'm coming too."

"Wait, wait, wait. You can't be serious." Dashiel looked between Aishena and the exit from the courtyard that would get them out of the palace. "I feel as though we should be avoiding the near-immortal grayglim who wants the majority of people here dead."

Aishena gave her head a swift shake. "A near-immortal grayglim who has been stalking the king and heirs for years all across Elundrae? If our goal is to also remove the Dragon King, she could be useful. Think about what she might know."

Lyrrin squinted back up at the tower. The silhouetted shape in the window had vanished. Hidden again in the shadows, always lurking, always watching.

Just what has she seen?

"Do you think you can capture her?" she asked Aishena. "Alive?"

Aishena went still, her head slightly bowed. "Either I do, or I put her down for good."

"Can you do it alone?"

"Maybe." She seemed pained to admit her doubt.

"With us helping?"

Aishena looked around the group. "A much better chance."

"Then I'm going too," Lyrrin said and joined Aishena and Benjin.

Dashiel sighed and jogged back to them as well. "As long as we can be fast about it. Just a reminder that we have a palace worth of guards chasing after us."

Aishena offered them a thin smile.

"Kess, are you in?" Lyrrin called out.

Over on the wolf, Kess blinked woozily. She winced as she straightened up in her saddle and nodded. "Griskin can help us find her."

The rumble of footsteps in the distance pulled Lyrrin's attention. "Let's move."

The wolf dashed ahead first, and Kess checked the exit out of the courtyard that led to the tower. The leather armor on her back glistened wetly in the low light and was torn in a few places. But Lyrrin had seen the glow of silvernix come from Kess during the fight, hadn't she? It had all been a blur in the corner of her eye as she'd worked on her runes, then sheltered from the explosion they brought.

"This way." Kess and Griskin led them at a run along the corridor.

Aishena ran shoulder to shoulder with Benjin, muttering quickly to him. They reached a locked doorway and Aishena sliced their way through with her cutting athame.

Inside, the small base of the tower was dusty and disused. A few old chairs sat stacked and neglected by one wall beside a coiled rope and some gardening tools. A narrow staircase traced the outside edge of the square tower, with stone balustrades edging the gap all the way up the center.

Aishena wiped the dust over the first step with her fingers. "No footprints."

"She's up there," Kess replied as Griskin sniffed the air.

That was when Lyrrin noticed how much of a trail they were leaving. Drops of blood and tacky red footprints had followed them into the tower. Benjin closed the door, then took one of the chairs and propped it behind the handle, but anyone on their trail would still know exactly where they went.

Aishena and Benjin took the lead, taking the stairs two at a time, with Dashiel close behind.

Kess put an arm out, holding Lyrrin back. "Stick close to me. I need to get you safely back to Riony."

Lyrrin's face scrunched up at her sister's name. An awful anger and sadness burbled inside her that Riony wasn't there.

She came to save Kess. Why not me?

Kess watched her with furrowed brows. "She wanted to come for you. She *really* wanted to. In her just-about-to-go-and-do-something-stupid way. That's why we came to get you for her. So she could stay and look after Dracuni. So they could stay safe."

They moved together up the stairs, following the others at a jog—fast for Lyrrin, slow for Griskin.

Lyrrin remembered when the wolf had stalked brazenly into their campsite one night. They had all drawn weapons, expecting an attack from the evil girl they thought had stabbed Riony in the back and left her for dead.

All of them except for Riony.

When it was clear the wolf was alone, that he was trying to get Riony to go with him, the argument about what to do had lasted for days. Nobody else thought it was a good idea to follow Griskin. Nobody else thought it was worth finding out what happened to Kess, worth helping her if she was still alive.

Only Riony.

She doesn't care for Kess more than me. She had to go after Kess because she was the only one who would.

And there was Lyrrin, with four friends who had come to save her, and save her sister and Dracuni from danger at the same time.

Lyrrin pushed her anger away. "Thank you for coming to help me. And for protecting Riony, in all the ways you do."

Kess kept her eyes on the stairs in front of them. "It's what she deserves."

As they ascended the staircase, the air grew cooler, the stone walls narrowing around them. The sound of the wind became more pronounced, slipping through small openings in the tower.

Lyrrin huffed, winded from the run. "Well, you deserve more too. I hope Riony is finally being a bit nicer to you now."

Kess went pale, yet her cheeks were splotchy red.

"Are you okay?"

The clash of weapons echoed through the tower. Lyrrin and Griskin broke into a faster run.

"She's here!" Aishena yelled from a flight up.

Ahead, the stairs led to a small landing where a wooden door stood flung open. Lyrrin rushed through into a cobweb-strewn belfry. The room was stark, with high, narrow windows that allowed shafts of moonlight to pierce through the gloom.

Benjin grabbed for Lyrrin as she stepped in, pulling her to cover behind a solid beam.

Aishena and her mother battled across the room, weaving between bells and ropes that lay discarded across the floor. Lady Hjelzahn's gaze was cold and unyielding. Her twin blades gleamed in the dim light as they flitted through the air in swirling attacks.

The woman's older swords, taken from her in their earlier battle, remained strapped on Aishena's back, untouched, as she fought back with her glowing athames.

Lyrrin searched the space with her eyes for a weapon. She patted down her clothing. She had nothing left to use. Dashiel skirted around the edges of the square room, sword and dagger drawn. Griskin stepped forward, growling.

"Don't engage!" Aishena ordered.

They held positions, eyes on the battle.

The clash of crystal against steel rang out as Aishena met her mother's strikes with her own, each blow fierce and desperate to keep her at bay.

"You never beat me before, and you won't now," Lady Hjelzahn drawled, as though the assault took no effort at all to ward off.

Lyrrin could see the strain on Aishena's face, focused in total concentration. Her athames flashed, red and yellow, barely able to keep her mother's longer twin swords held back.

Kverra's blade caught Aishena's shoulder, slicing through her guard uniform and drawing a line of crimson across her skin. Aishena hissed but didn't falter. She hit back lightning fast, slicing through the tip of one of Kverra's blades with a swift strike of her cutting athame.

The metal clattered to the ground, leaving Lady Hjelzahn with half the reach on that side. But with a sharp twist of her wrist, she disarmed Aishena of the yellow crystal, sending it skittering across the floor.

Beside Lyrrin, Benjin rolled his shoulders, then turned away from the duel to face her. He thrust the crystal-studded staff out toward Lyrrin.

"Here. Take this."

"What? Why?" Lyrrin's fingers closed around the wood she had carved.

In the center of the space, Aishena dropped into a crouch. "Now!"

Benjin took a deep breath and rushed into the fray. With a fluid motion, he vaulted over his sister, drawing the swords from her back in the same movement and launching himself at Kverra. The clash of the two sets of twin blades sent sparks flying, then the tear of armor and flesh came as Benjin landed his first strike.

Kverra stumbled backward as his assault was joined by Aishena's. Her mask of indifference slipped into wide-eyed shock and then teeth-bared anger as the red athame sizzled across her cheek.

With a feral snarl, she kicked Benjin in the chest, sending him rolling back, but that only gave an opening for a white bone knife to fly in from Kess's hand, puncturing into the woman's neck. It didn't slow her down at all.

"This isn't working!" Lyrrin shouted, frustration lacing her voice.

No matter how they wounded the woman, she just kept moving.

Aishena's eyes flashed with determination. "It is. Trust me! Do as I say, when I say it! Lyrrin, you're up. Push her back. We need fire!"

Heart pounding, Lyrrin nodded. The weight of Benjin's staff in her hands grounded her, and she spun it in her fingers to bring the crystal with the burn rune toward her. Scratching over it quickly, she added in a float symbol and activated them both.

The crystal sung under her fingers, feeling like the home she'd been missing.

Pink flames bloomed around the stone, bursting outward. Lyrrin charged forward, staff held out. Aishena and Benjin cleared a path for her, and she pushed through between them, thrusting the magical flames at the possessed woman's chest.

Kverra dodged backward across the cluttered space toward the entrance.

The fire roared, crackling over the gray armor and Kverra's neck and face. The room filled with the smell of burned hair. Then the staff was struck by the pommel of two swords, knocking it away in a move that jarred Lyrrin's arms. The end of the staff smacked against a nearby bell, clanging loudly.

"Dash! Get Lyrrin!" Aishena commanded.

An arm wrapped Lyrrin from behind, pulling her backward as two blades flashed down toward her face. Dashiel's broadsword blocked the blow, and everyone around Kverra scattered back.

With bare hands, Lady Hjelzahn patted away the flames smoldering across her chest and neck. Her armor hung crookedly, some of the straps burned loose, but there were no injuries showing beneath.

Lyrrin watched in disbelief. "It didn't do anything, she's—"

"Kess, hip joints, now!" Aishena yelled.

From the shadowed corner of the room, two blades flew out, one after the other. They each struck deep into Lady Hjelzahn's hips. She snarled, trying to take a step forward, but her legs moved awkwardly.

Aishena moved in front of her, pressing her back with lashing arcs of her red athame. In faltering steps, Lady Hjelzahn wobbled in retreat, warding off every blow with her swords, but unable to dodge and maneuver. She backed up against the wooden door and it creaked on its hinges.

"Benj, swords!" Aishena cried.

Without hesitation, he threw them to her. She dropped her athame and snatched the weapons from the air. With a roar, Aishena drove both swords into Lady Hjelzahn's shoulders and out the other side, pinning her to the wooden doorway. No blood poured from the wounds.

The woman twitched and bucked against the steel blades, shrieking as she found herself caught tight.

Lyrrin's chest heaved as she stared at the grayglim, pinned in place like a butterfly, defiance burning in her eyes despite the blades through her flesh. "Is that it? Is she trapped?"

"I will kill you. I will kill all of you! You all have to die." Lady Hjelzahn brought her swords up, able to move from the elbows down only.

Aishena kicked the weapons from her hands. Panting hard, she watched her mother with dark, intense eyes.

Kess, looking paler and more drawn than before, rode up beside her. "That's one way to stop her."

"A little trick I learned from you," Aishena replied.

Kverra's voice went cold and low. "Conniving and unfair numbers? This isn't how I trained you, Aishena. A grayglim would face me one-on-one with honor. Free me, and we will finish this duel properly."

Aishena's angular shoulders raised up around her neck and she winced.

Her mother's inhuman voice rose louder. "I am your mestra! You are the hand and must do as I command."

With a heavy sigh, Aishena's expression steadied, and she locked eyes with her mother. "I'm not going to fight you again. The blow will come hard enough when you understand all you have done."

Kverra snarled. She twisted her torso, pressing left and right as though she could cut right through her own shoulders to get free.

Aishena pulled a parcel from her belt pouch. "I brought this along, in case we needed it. Hopefully whatever is possessing you isn't immune to morass mercy."

Kess flinched away as Aishena pushed the fabric parcel up to her mother's face. She writhed and struggled, cursing through the wad of cloth and herbs. But after a torturously long moment, Lady Hjelzahn, Heir Killer, fell still.

Lyrrin released a long sigh of relief. "You did it!"

"We did it." Aishena put the parcel away, brushing her hands off.

She watched the woman for a long moment, then her shoulders dropped heavily. "Come on, let's get her tied up, then get us all out of here."

Benjin turned away quickly, keeping his eyes averted from where his mother's body hung from the door. He gathered up his sister's athames and brought them back to her, and Dashiel brought some rope over. Once Kverra was thoroughly bound, they worked together to pry the swords free. Aishena's hands shook around the hilts of the extracted weapons, and she quickly passed them on to Benjin.

Lyrrin waited beside Kess, who was slumped over Griskin's neck.

"It's nice to work as a team, isn't it?"

Kess smiled back weakly. "Yeah. It is."

Lyrrin's own smile faltered as she took in Kess's unfocused eyes and blue lips. "Are you sure you're okay?"

"I'll be fine as long as ..." Kess stilled.

Griskin growled, his ears flattening back. A moment later, Lyrrin heard it too. Footsteps, many of them, thundering up the stairwell below.

Dashiel ducked out the doorway, then back in again, pushing the door closed behind them. "Safe to say, we've been found."

"How many?" Benjin swung the twin blades in his hands.

Dashiel's expression was one of utter desolation. "All of them?"

Lyrrin's fingers tightened around the staff she still held. Her gaze ran over it, cataloging the crystals she had available, what options she had. She could still fight, but Kess looked on the edge of passing out, and Aishena and Benjin were sheened in sweat and still catching their breath from their recent efforts.

The drop from the narrow windows was steep and far. There were no other exits from the disused bell tower. No way out. They were trapped.

Chapter Fourteen

Kess closed her eyes and took a deep breath, willing her consciousness not to topple off the precipice into darkness. Pain radiated in throbbing waves from multiple points on her back.

She felt worried, deeply worried, in a way she didn't usually feel. She had been so close to getting Lyrrin out, getting her back to Riony. She didn't want to fail.

When she opened her eyes again, the others were all working to block the belfry door. Aishena and Dashiel had their shoulders up against a bell larger than them. It scraped disharmoniously across the floor as they pushed it toward the door.

Lyrrin and Benjin dragged some of the larger coils of rope across, dropped them into a heavy pile around the bell, then ran back to get more.

As they loaded a couple more smaller bells, crates, and ropes onto the barricade, the door rattled violently. Aishena and Dashiel leaped forward to add their weight to the blockade.

Loud thumping and shouting reverberated through to them and the wood of the door strained.

"Even if this holds, we can't stay in here forever," Dashiel groaned, back pressed against the door.

Lyrrin held up the crystal staff and pointed it toward one of the windows. "I have a float rune on here now, but it's only small. It might only get a safe landing for one or two of us if we have to jump."

Kess pulled her cutting athame and ran the yellow crystal around one of the upright wooden beams.

She called to the two kids, "Come and catch this. Dash, they might need your help."

Once the top was cut through, she indicated for Griskin to lower himself down, then bent over to cut through the bottom. Curving her back that way forced out a whimper, and starbursts of pain obscured her vision. The wounds from the glass shards were worse than she'd originally thought, or at least had become worse since, with every movement she'd made.

The athame cut through, and the three beside her caught it, taking it over to wedge against the door.

As Kess winced through the agony of straightening back up again, more waves of worry reached her.

They were different than usual. They weren't her worries.

Lyomir?

No reply came, but she could feel his presence, distantly. He said he would stay close. He must be around the keep somewhere. Could he feel her too?

"There's one way out of here," Kess said. "By dragon."

"Do you think you can get Lyomir to come for us? Here?" Dashiel shuffled the beam, getting it positioned at a forty-five-degree angle against the door.

"I'm not sure. But I don't know what else we're going to do." Kess wiped cold sweat off her forehead.

"Try to call him." With the beam in place, Aishena warily moved away from holding the door as well.

The barricade held, and the rattling and thumping from the other side quieted down.

Lyrrin angled her ear toward the door. "What are they doing? Do you think they've given up?"

A booming crack made her jump away. A thin split ran up the middle of the door. A few seconds later, the echoing thud hit again. The top hinge popped from the wall.

Dashiel sighed. "Sounds like somebody found a battering ram."

"Keep loading the barricade," Aishena ordered, working to cut a second beam down. "And Kess, get Lyomir here, now!"

"I'll try." Kess reached out with her senses and thoughts calling toward her bonded dragon.

Lyomir? Can you hear me? Can you find me?

She pictured the tower they were in, how it had looked from outside. To reach them, Lyomir would have to fly right over the palace and into the couple of remaining dragonriders still on guard.

No words came back to Kess, only a strong surge of annoyance, like a growling *harrumph* in her head.

Kess found herself shivering. What if he didn't come for them? What if he decided they weren't worth fighting his way in for?

The crack of splintering wood cut the air. One of the planks of the door snapped and a thick column of metal, shaped like a fist at the end, pushed through. One more strike, and the vertical plank broke free, slivers of sharp wood hanging around the edges.

A guard moved into the hole, pushing an arm and shoulder through. Aishena struck out with a swift sequence of blows, forcing the man to retreat again. The battering ram slammed into the door again.

Kess moved to the window, glaring at the long drop down. If Lyomir didn't come, they might have to jump. As injured as Kess already felt, she wasn't sure she'd survive that fall. It was getting harder and harder for her to even keep her eyes open.

Lyomir, we need you. I need you.

A deeper, angrier growl filled her head. The strength of the emotion made Kess gasp. He was close.

A burst of flame lit the night sky outside. A human scream merged with the shriek of a dragon, and a massive shape walloped against the tower, shaking the walls, then crashed to the ground below.

Dark wings flashed through the air. ***Puny tamed beast.***

"It's him, he's here!" Kess called to the others.

They rushed to join her at the window. Lyomir circled above, and another dragon lay smoldering in the courtyard below.

"We need to get out there so he can reach us. We've got to get up onto the roof." Aishena stepped onto the sill of the narrow window, angling out over the drop and looking up. "We're going to have to climb."

Benjin thumb-pointed to his unconscious mother. "What are we going to do with her?"

Aishena frowned. "Can Griskin carry her?"

Kess nodded with a matching frown. He could but getting out through the narrow window and up onto the roof with them both would be a feat Kess wasn't confident of.

Aishena jumped back in and waved Dashiel to her side. Together they lifted Lady Hjelzahn and draped her face down over Griskin, behind Kess. Aishena pulled some thin cave-silk rope from her belt and lashed the woman in place.

Benjin and Lyrrin were already halfway out the window. A purple glow came from one of the crystals on Lyrrin's staff, which stuck out over her shoulder. The length was wedged down the back of her gown.

"The ledge is really narrow. Watch your step." Aishena stepped out beside them.

She clung to the side of the window as she helped boost the children up out of sight. One of Lyrrin's feet slipped and dangled down over the top of the window. Aishena climbed up behind her and the sounds of them scrambling onto the roof echoed down.

Dashiel waved a hand questioningly toward Kess.

"You go first," she replied, punctuated by the crack of another plank on the door splitting through.

Dashiel stepped out confidently, as though striding along the back of a trusted dragon. Aishena's hand appeared, reaching down from above. Dashiel grabbed it and was hoisted up.

"Come on, Gris," Kess moved them to the window again and pushed him forward.

He stepped up with both front paws, pushing his head through the narrow space. Kess tried to push him farther, and he whined softly. The door tore open again like rippling thunder.

Wincing, Kess climbed up his neck, pushing away his thick fur so she could see around him. The ledge on the other side was barely a palm's-width across. Enough for a human to stand on with just their toes. A wolf of Griskin's size would have far more difficulty.

"You can do it. Just keep your claws dug in." Kess urged him forward again.

He stepped over the sill, straddling it with his stomach. His front paws skidded and scraped against the exterior wall, unable to find purchase against the narrow ledge.

"Raze it!" Kess pulled back, bringing him off the window and back into the belfry.

"Kess?" Dashiel called from above.

She turned Griskin so she could lean sideways out the window. Dashiel's face watched down from over the roof's edge.

"Get Aishena to throw down more rope. I'll tie Kverra on. You're going to have to pull her up."

"What about you?"

"I'm not leaving Griskin." Kess groaned as she pulled herself back inside and reached for the knots holding the possessed grayglim onto the wolf's back.

With the cacophonous clatter of broken wood and tumbling bells, the remains of the door burst apart. Kess's hands reached instead for her knives as grayglims and guards flooded into the room. They spread out into the space, gauging the situation, taking in the one girl on her wolf confronting them.

At least this will be one epic way to go out. Kess gave Griskin's ears a rub for good luck and felt satisfied that she'd succeeded in one last thing for Riony.

Lyrrin was out. Lyrrin was saved. She had done that.

She only wished she could also see Riony again.

Roaring worry filled her, but she steadied herself through her pain and sent her first two knives flying.

Only one hit its mark, sending the grayglim tripping sideways as he grasped his bleeding neck. He collapsed on the ground and the whole tower shuddered as though he had weighed as much as a giant.

"What—?"

An avalanche of slate tiles and stone crushed down over the approaching guards. Griskin dodged back, and Kess flung an arm up in front of her face as shattered chunks hailed around her.

I won't let you die, small fool.

A purple claw thrust down through the collapsing roof, tearing the hole in it wider. Dust filled the air and Kess choked on it, but it wasn't the dust that made her eyes sting with tears.

Lyomir's teeth came within view, mouth open and roaring into the hole he'd torn through the tower roof. To reach Kess.

Griskin bounded forward over the shifting debris and struggling bodies of the guards beneath it. The roof had fallen at an angle, and the wolf ran up it to the dragon waiting above.

Aishena, Dashiel, and the kids were already on the dragon's back, tying themselves in place. Griskin looped around behind the dragon, using his spine as a ramp to climb up and join the others.

They were met with a multitude of arms, catching Kess as she slumped sideways from her saddle, getting Griskin secured, moving Kverra off the wolf and into a better position.

Kess gasped and panted, pain and adrenaline warring over every short breath as Lyomir's wings *whumped*, lifting them into the sky. He moved with such swift power that it took Kess's breath away all over again.

"There's another rider behind us," Aishena warned.

Lyomir snorted.

They sped across the spires and roofs of the city like a fleeting shadow. The palace dragonrider followed, falling farther and farther behind.

Kess folded forward where she sat, pressing trembling hands against the purple scales beneath her.

Thank you.

A growl thrummed through Lyomir's neck. **Maybe try not getting into so much trouble in the first place.**

Kess huffed a laugh, then whimpered as something sharp cut deeper into her skin. **You're hurt.**

You're not. Griskin's not. Lyrrin's not. I'm calling that a good day.

They sailed over the high dragonkeep walls and out over the surrounding scorched grasslands. Lyrrin watched the trailing dot behind them through the clear crystal on her staff, then gave a whoop so loud it made everyone else on the dragon jump.

"They've turned around! We did it! We got away!" She flung herself in a hug around Aishena, who tolerated it with a grimace and awkward pat on the head. "I can't wait to see Riony and Dracuni and Elumon and everyone again!"

Kess's chest tightened at Riony's name with a longing pull, as though her heart had been bound in rope and was being pulled away.

Riony. I hope she's safe. I hope she … I hope she wants to see me again.

"Thank you!" Without warning, Lyrrin wrapped her arms around Kess next.

"Ah!" Kess grunted as pain lanced through her.

Lyrrin pulled back quickly, turning her palms upward to reveal them red where she'd touched Kess's back. "Is this your blood?"

Aishena and Dashiel's heads both swung her way.

Kess winced apologetically. "I think I have a bit of glass in me."

Lyrrin gasped and covered her mouth. "Oh no! I'm sorry!"

"It's not your fault. Your magic saved us."

"*A bit of glass?*" Narrowing her eyes, Aishena switched places with Lyrrin, shuffling down between the spines of the dragon. "Let me see."

Kess shook her head. There wasn't much they could do up there on the dragon's back.

She opened her mouth to say as much when Dashiel snapped, "Don't make us hold you down."

"She's as bad as Riony." Aishena tutted and pushed against Kess's shoulder.

Sighing, Kess leaned forward and submitted her back for inspection.

A bright cyan glow lit up and Aishena's fingers prodded none too gently around the tears in the leather. She hissed under her breath and tentatively tugged at one of the shards. Kess bit off a yelp. Griskin pressed his snout against her face and licked her cheek.

"That one's deep," Aishena murmured. "It'll be better to leave them in for now or you're only going to bleed more. Stay still, I'll bandage around them."

Kess remained in place. She wasn't sure she could move again if she wanted to. Every breath brought a thousand daggers of agony. Aishena pulled a long strip of bandage out and got to work.

Benjin stayed farther down the dragon's back, close to Kverra. He watched his mother warily, but there was also a sad softness to his expression. Her old twin blades he had wielded lay across his lap. Lyrrin moved down in slow shuffles to his side.

She presented the crystal staff to him. "Thanks for letting me use it."

Benjin didn't reach out to take it back. "You know, I think you should keep it."

Lyrrin's lips turned down. "What? Why?"

"I know you made it for me, and that means a lot. But the crystals, the staff … it was always more Yoskar's thing."

Aishena reached under Kess's stomach, passing the bandage through and bringing it around and around her middle, pulling it tight in a way that left Kess drenched in the fevered sweat of pain.

"And I always wanted to be like Yoskar, for such a long time," Benjin continued, eyes on his sister. "But not so much anymore."

Smiling, he turned back to Lyrrin. "Besides, you can do way cooler things with those crystals than I can."

Lyrrin half smiled and pulled the staff in to hug it against her chest.

Aishena tied off the bandage. "Just hold on. Lyomir is fast. It won't be long until we're back in the undercity."

Back where there was silvernix. Back with Riony.

Kess's eyes drooped closed.

When she opened them again, there was light. A shell-pink stretch of sky lay above her, tainted with blotches of gray clouds.

She felt cold to her core, and her tongue felt thick and dry. "How … long?"

A hand was wrapped around hers, hot to touch against her icy fingers.

Dashiel said, "Shh, rest. We're almost there."

Kess tried to sit up to see where they were. No part of her body wanted to move right.

Dashiel held her down with a hand on her shoulder. "*Rest.* I don't want to face Riony if you don't make it."

Lyomir rumbled beneath them, the leathery flutter of his wings the only other sound as they beat hard. The heave of his chest had all his passengers rising and lowering with him. The worry Kess had felt before continued to fill her head.

Don't overdo it. You've been flying all night.

Don't tell me what to do, little fool.

"There's something happening up ahead!" Lyrrin yelled from nearby.

Kess turned her head to see her sitting up in front, using the seeing stone on the staff to look down over snowy mountains below. She handed the staff to Aishena, who immediately bristled.

"What is it?" Kess asked.

"A battle. The siege dragons, they're all over the place, fighting."

"Fighting who?" Kess pushed Dashiel's hand away and sat up with a wailing groan. Her whole body had seized up during the night and she felt weak and shivery.

"It's hard to see what's going on. It's chaos." Aishena handed the staff back to Lyrrin.

Kess shook her head, and her heart pounded. "A battle at the undercity entrance can only mean one thing. The siege has broken. Either they've gotten in, or Riony and the undercity riders have come out. We have to go and help."

Lyomir veered away. ***We should go around this mess. I'm taking you back to the other entrance.***

Taking me back to the other entrance won't help me at all if Dracuni has been caught. We're going to help them.

Aishena gave Kess a long, assessing look, then glanced around at Dashiel, Lyrrin, and Benjin. "None of us are in any condition to join the fight."

But Kess heard the uncertainty hidden in her tone. She straightened up further. "And what happens if we don't?"

"We have to help," Lyrrin said.

Aishena squinted back toward the battle. "Fine. We can at least go a bit closer to see what's happening."

Kess gave her a grateful nod. *Lyomir?*

The purple etherdart snorted loudly. But he turned back toward the battle.

Lyrrin squinted through the seeing stone as they drew closer. "I can't see anyone familiar. It's just a bunch of dragonriders fighting a bunch of dragonriders. I can't see Riony or Dracuni or any of our friends."

"Are you sure? Absolutely sure? They aren't already downed?" Kess asked.

"I'm sure," Lyrrin replied.

As close as they were now, Kess could see most of the dragons were larger breeds, none of the smaller treedarts the new undercity riders would be flying, none flying with the fluid motions of the untamed Viska, Gleem, or Hux. The battle had slowed, with a number of dragons flying away in every direction, fleeing the conflict, and others returning to the ground.

"What are they doing?" Benjin leaned around from near the back.

Aishena said, "I don't know. But if they don't have our friends, we need to get out of here before they see us."

Too late. Lyomir put on a burst of speed, taking them diving.

Behind them, four matching red etherflames swooped after them, having come in from behind while they were distracted.

The sudden drop wrenched Kess against the rope she was tied to the dragon with, and she screamed as she dropped again onto his scaled back, pushing one of the shards in her skin deeper.

Lyomir loosed a rough, frustrated growl, slowing his retreat.

I'm okay. Just get us out of here. Kess could barely think the words clearly through the fiery sting. Could he feel her pain along with her thoughts and emotions, the way she felt his?

But even through his worry for her, Kess could sense how exhausted he was too. He'd been flying his fastest all night, for her.

The red dragons caught up fast, coming up around them on every side. Their riders didn't direct their dragons to claw or bite or flame, but they harried Lyomir from the sides, the back, and above, forcing him down, down, down.

The side of the mountain came up toward them, bright with snow and dotted in dark rocks. Lyomir landed hard, skidding across the icy surface, sending a spray of cold powder over them all.

Lyrrin, Dashiel, Aishena, and Benjin had their weapons in their hands already and cut through the ropes holding them in place on the purple dragon's back.

Kess reached for her throwing knives, but her vision swam, and her fingers felt frozen and numb. She blinked, trying to clear her sight.

Around them, the four red dragons landed lightly. Lyomir growled turning on the spot, penned in. And on each dragon sat a rider wearing Yeonard Draekhan's colors.

CHAPTER FIFTEEN

Dracuni swerved right, wings pulled in after a rushing burst of speed. Riony pressed close to the unidragon's neck and the opalescent hair of Dracuni's mane tickled her face as she kept her eyes on upcoming challenges.

"To the right again, between those stalactites."

It's too narrow.

"It's fine. You can do it. Just like the last one."

If I miss and knock you off …

"You'll catch me." Riony smirked. "Go on, it'll be good practice. The flying through that gap part, I mean, not the knocking me off part."

Dracuni sighed but aimed the direction Riony suggested. Riony felt the thrill in Dracuni's emotions as they zipped between the narrow rock formations, a hair's breadth away from scraping the stone.

Riony let out a whoop. "That was amazing! You're getting so much better."

Dracuni didn't answer, but a ripple of pride transferred through her senses.

Riony let her own pride rush back in return. They'd practiced relentlessly in those tight quarters, and it was paying off.

Still, the lure of open skies teased at the back of her mind—a stretch of endless blue where Dracuni could truly soar, without the looming rock and constant need to pivot at the last moment. Without being hunted for what she was.

Would she ever have that freedom?

For now, the undercity training was invaluable. They were learning to adapt, to maneuver through confined spaces—skills that might mean the difference between life and death in battle.

They wove through the forest of long, jagged limestone draping from the undercity's cavern ceiling. The air was cool and still up there, and Dracuni's scales were warm beneath Riony, riding without a saddle. The unidragon's wings beat steadily, the ripple of air over the diaphanous membrane an inspiring sound.

Riony patted Dracuni's neck. "I still can't believe how big you've gotten. I remember when you fit in my backpack, so tiny and cute."

I just remember being hungry and Butterfur stepping on me.

"Listen, some mistakes were made, but we survived." Riony huffed a laugh. "Sparks, that little furry sausage has grown so big now too."

Do you think little sister will be bigger when we see her again?

Riony's smile faded. "She's only been gone a week or so."

It feels like longer.

"I know." Riony missed her sister keenly, like a gaping wound in her chest that only bled more for also missing Kess and everyone else she cared for. "We'll have her back soon. I'm sure we will."

They better all be back soon. They better all be safe.

They banked left around a particularly sharp turn, heading down over the Grand Arch markets, and passing another rider out training on one of the tamed treedarts. The markets hummed below, and faces turned up to watch them.

But more were focused on a commotion on the main street that people were rushing toward. A whistle sounded—the signal to call in defenses. Riony's pulse quickened.

"Down there, quick. We need to see what's going on."

Dracuni angled her wings, gliding downward. Riony strained her eyes to pick out details. Niskina was there, taking charge of the situation. Something was definitely wrong.

Dracuni landed on a low rooftop beside the market, and Riony jumped down between a couple of stallholder's carts. She pushed through the crowd, wishing she had a weapon with her.

Niskina's voice carried to her as she went. "The mountain entrance has been revealed to the enemy. Get up there now and get it sealed! It has runes prepped for closure. You know what to do."

A small squad of delvers moved off at a jog, passing Riony as she reached Niskina.

"Sorry about that, but it was important that I got in as fast as I could. For a few reasons," a boyish voice said.

"What's happened? How—?" Riony's voice cut off the moment she saw Benjin.

The young boy's shorn silver hair sparkled in the cyan light. He wore an armored uniform that was too large for him and was crusted with dried blood.

Tracking where her gaze fell, he said, "It's not my blood. Also, don't freak out when you see Lyrrin. I mean, it was her blood, but she's okay."

"What? Lyrrin? You got her? Where is she?" Riony turned a full circle, her heart thumping its way up into her throat as she scanned her surroundings.

Beside them, Niskina sent more delvers running in all directions with orders.

Once she faced Benjin again, he shook his head, brows furrowed. "They're outside the Shield Gate entrance. We got caught on our way back. The riders who captured us sent me in to let you know. They want to talk."

Riony's skin chilled. "Captured? Is everyone okay?"

Benjin winced slightly. "So far. Kess is injured."

The air huffed out of Riony like she'd been struck in the chest.

Niskina gestured to them both to follow her, leading them away from the crowd of onlookers. "They want to talk? About what? They just want to lure us out so they can finally take Dracuni."

"I'm not so sure," Benjin said. "Things were crazy out there. The riders were all fighting each other! Like an insurrection or something. Except I'm not sure which side won or what they were fighting about."

They moved around a corner to a quieter street. Dracuni perched on the rooftop above, watching down with concern.

"It doesn't matter." Riony was jangly and tense all over, her fingers twitching and back strained.

Lyrrin was there, just outside. And Aishena, Dashiel, and Kess … Kess was injured.

Riony closed her hands into fists. "It doesn't matter what they were fighting about or if it's a trap. I'm going out there and getting our family back."

"They've returned? Where's Lyrrin?" From one end of the street, Eslinde rushed toward them, guided by a delver. She carried her gown scooped up in front of her as she ran.

From the other end, the Alderkin approached, cloaked and hooded and with their own delver escort.

Benjin caught them up in a flurry of words. He finished with, "Whatever we do, we really have to hurry. We … also brought someone else home with us too."

Riony raised her eyebrows at that.

Niskina said, "I want everyone back safe too, but we can't risk the safety of the entire undercity for it."

Eslinde's face was set in flat lines of determination. "I'm getting my daughter back, one way or another."

"We'll use the gateway," Riony said, her mind racing the way her feet longed to. "Travel to the nearest shrine downhill and go up to meet with the riders that way."

Benjin shook his head. "That's half a day's hike. I'm not sure we have that much time."

Riony's mouth felt gummed up and her heart rioted.

It was Niskina who asked gently, "How injured is Kess?"

Benjin paled and shook his head.

"Then we're going out, through Shield Gate." Riony turned to Yrik and Priyune. "Can you clear the way, get it open quickly?"

Yrik bowed his head. "We can. But we may have another option. We have been working on the runic arrangement needed to view outside our gates. It will allow you meet with those outside without risking yourself."

"I'm not worried about myself right now!" Riony snapped.

Niskina put a calming hand on Riony's shoulder. "Then worry about Dracuni. If we open the gate and they force their way in, it will be war in here, with Dracuni the prize."

Riony turned her face up, and Dracuni looked back down at her, a heartsick pain shared between them.

She let a long breath out through her nose and addressed Yrik. "Okay, if you say we can meet with them with your magic, then let's do that. But I also want one of you getting the gate cleared and ready to open so we can bring the others in as soon as possible."

Yrik traced his finger through the air. "I'll get it done. I will make this mountain sing to bring Lyrrin home."

"Dracuni, go with him. I want you at the gate, ready." Riony didn't want to say what she needed to be ready for. She still hated asking for Dracuni's blood.

But Dracuni simply nodded once and took to the air again.

They split up, with Yrik leaving toward Shield Gate with a handful of delvers, and Riony, Eslinde, Niskina, and Benjin following Priyune.

The Alderkin woman's shoulders hunched and her long fingers were dusty and seemed worn from use. The Alderkin had followed through with their promise, working tirelessly in any way the people of the undercity needed.

Broken services were repaired, new crystals were carved. They had provided all the float runes requested for the raid on the glass factory and other upcoming missions. If anything, Riony was worried they were working too hard.

Maybe they all were. But when the alternative was admitting defeat and the collapse of all good in their world, how could they stop?

Priyune led them through to an empty chamber close to where the gateway crystal and new shrine was housed.

Within it, the central space had been cleared, and five long, thin crystals stood around the edge, like spears jutting from the ground.

"Wait beyond the circle," Priyune directed, moving to the nearest crystal. She started at the bottom, tracing a long and complicated sequence of runes up the shaft. "Once the view of outside appears, you can step in."

"What will it do? Is this like a gateway?" Eslinde asked.

Priyune moved along to the next crystal. "Not quite. You will see the second location as though through a gateway, and you will step into it as though through a gateway, but it will only project your image there. You will physically remain within this room."

Riony twitched, bouncing on the balls of her feet, her whole body still wanting to run. "As long as it gets us out there so we can talk those depths-damned riders into giving our people back, I don't care how it works."

Niskina side-eyed her. "Pity the fool who stands between you and your star."

Priyune moved around, activating each crystal rod in turn. As she traced over the final runes of the fifth, the air between them shivered and shifted, forming a vision of a rocky plateau. Three riders in the king's colors paced there, ghostlike and hazy around the edges. They argued with no sound.

Behind them, close to the farthest boundary of the crystal arrangement, sat a huddle of bodies. Two lay prone and lifeless.

Heart jolting, Riony took a hurried step forward.

Priyune blocked her path. "Once you are within the array, they will see you and hear you, and you will hear them. Don't move too far once you are in, or you will step out again. You are not really there. Don't try to touch anything."

Riony nodded, although the words had floated through her head without finding purchase. She could only focus on the people lying on the rocky ground.

The features of all the figures were too fuzzy to identify. But there was nobody in that group she wanted to lose.

"I'm ready," Eslinde said, stepping beside Riony.

The princess clasped Riony's hand, and her fingers trembled. They stepped together into the vision, with Niskina and Benjin at their back.

"Razed skies!" A female rider whose limbs seemed carved from tree trunks startled at the sight of them. She cast her gaze over Riony's shoulder and back again a couple of times. "How did you ... did the gate open?"

Riony glanced around. Behind her, the cavern chamber had vanished, replaced instead with the exterior of Shield Gate.

And in front of her, the land and sky extended out to the horizon. Figures became whole and details cleared.

Kess's purple dragon lay at the edge of the plateau, snout bound in rope and seething, and Griskin lay at his feet, bound so thoroughly he lay motionless on his side.

The three king's riders gawked at Riony's sudden appearance.

Aishena and Dashiel also watched, wide-eyed. They knelt with their hands bound in front of them. Lyrrin wasn't one of the bodies on the ground. She stood beside the others, her face and dress darkened with the rust of old blood, but she bounced and beamed brightly when she saw Riony.

It was Kess who lay face down, lifeless. So limp, the captors hadn't even bothered tying her up.

"What did they do to her?" Riony growled.

Benjin gripped her arm from behind as though to keep her in place. "It wasn't them."

Every nerve in Riony twinged with the desire to run to Kess. To feel for her pulse, her breath, to scoop her up and make sure she was okay. But she couldn't do any of those things. Not yet.

It took Eslinde hissing "Is that *Kverra Hjelzahn*?" for Riony to turn her attention away from Kess to the second body lying motionless.

Benjin replied, "Mami? Yeah."

Riony's eyes popped wide. "Okay, that's a surprise you could have mentioned."

Benjin shrugged. "Well, everyone's going to get a surprise if the morass mercy we used on her wears out before we get her somewhere secure."

Eyebrows creeping even farther up her forehead, Riony nodded. "Right. Yes."

With clenched teeth, she turned her attention back to the riders who had formed up in a line before them. They all still wore bewildered expressions but weren't making any aggressive actions.

Gesturing to the gate behind her, Riony said, "We have more ways to get in and out than you know."

"So it seems. All the more reason this siege has been a farce from the beginning." The bulky woman scowled, but the ire was directed to the sky behind her, not at Riony and her companions.

"Call me Lerris." She stepped forward, one hand out as though expecting Riony to shake it.

Riony remained still. "Are we friends? Because friends don't hold their friends' loved ones hostage."

Lerris continued scowling, but Riony suspected it may just be how she looked. "No, not friends. Although I hope we can become allies."

She made an expansive gesture to the downward slope of the mountain and land beyond. Where tents and dragons had once filled the space, the remnants of a battle now marred the landscape. Fires spotted the ground and more than one downed dragon lay in the rocky snow around the entrance.

In the far distance, dragon silhouettes as small as birds were fleeing, and while there were still far more dragons and their riders sitting in wait for orders around them than Riony enjoyed seeing, it was half the numbers there had once been.

"What happened out here?" Eslinde asked.

Lerris inclined her head. "The right decision was made. One it seems you came to some time ago, your highness."

"Can we skip the formalities and get to the point?" Riony's eyes were back on Kess, willing her to move, to show any sign of life across the distance.

Lerris's eyebrows drew in. "The point is that dragonkeeps are falling. Entire dragonkeeps! All those here who fought today on our side have lost homes that we weren't there to protect because we were *here*. Here chasing some flippant desire of the man we once called our king, while the people suffer!"

Eslinde's hand in Riony's tightened.

Her voice was breathy. "How many keeps?"

Lerris shook her head, and her mouth opened but no sound emerged. She took a moment and cleared her throat.

"Too many. But we refuse to lose any more. No matter the orders. No matter old loyalties. The revenant army marches upon the capital, left defenseless. Those who refused to join our side have been chased back there, but from all reports I've heard, that won't be enough. We need more. We need every dragon we can get."

Riony took a step forward, challenging the woman's personal space. "Great. So go, then! Go and leave us and our friends who look like they are bleeding out in the dirt!"

Lerris glanced back at Kess as well. "Her injuries aren't our doing. And you can have her back, you can have them all back, if you agree to join us in the battle against the revenant army when the time comes."

Riony's eyes narrowed to slits. "Holding my injured family hostage isn't a good start along our road toward working together."

The rider folded her barrel-sized arms across her chest. "How else could we have brought you out to speak with us? We found a way and we used it. You have power in your ranks that we need."

Eslinde asked, "What do you need us for?"

"We know there are dragons in there, a lot of them. The ones the king sent with that upstart Heithorn jerk who suddenly gained his favor."

"One upstart jerk who is no longer with us," Riony said.

Lerris's lips curled up into what might count as a smile. "We've also heard stories that you're allied with the Rebel Riders. And we know you have Dashiel on your side, and Vance Zarram, two of the best riders I've ever trained, and whom I'm glad to see survived the destruction of their hold."

Dashiel straightened up proudly. "Lerris was my mestra as I trained to be a rider. She's a good person, and what she's saying is true. We saw the army. We saw how little the capital is prepared."

"Dash. She's tied you up," Riony said.

Dashiel shrugged. "Well, yes. But what she's saying still deserves consideration."

Riony chewed her lip. Every instinct in her told her not to trust dragonriders. This had to be some kind of trap, and she hated how reasonable the woman sounded.

Eslinde gave her hand another squeeze. "I know of Mestra Lerris too. She is honorable. And we will, someday soon, have to face my father and the curse that plagues our land. One way or another. Better we do it with all these people by our side as well."

Lerris remained front and center, with two younger men by her side. Riony tried to gauge their expressions, looking for any indication of malice.

If anything, they just seemed exhausted and as worried and wary as Riony.

Riony lifted her chin at the riders. "So if we agree to help you, then what?"

"Then we will leave you and your friends alone until the time comes and we call for you. And we will trust that you will come to our aid. I've heard tales of your honor as well."

Behind the riders, Lyrrin gave a small, hopeful nod, and Kess remained still. The people Riony loved were all there in front of her and yet felt a million worlds away. And all it took to get to them was forging an alliance with their enemy.

She looked to Eslinde, who returned a steely expression and nodded.

"Yes." Riony rattled all over with desperation. "Yes, we will help when the time comes."

With a grand flourish of her arm, Lerris signaled the riders waiting below. In an instant, they began taking to the air, one after another.

Riony watched in disbelief. They were really leaving.

"Go, go quick and get the gate open," Eslinde whispered back to Niskina and Benjin.

The three riders before them were turned away, making further signals to some closer riders. The next time Riony glanced behind her, Niskina and Benjin were gone, vanished from sight.

Eslinde spoke in a regal tone, "So, we agree to work together to face our true enemy, the shadow dragon's curse and the revenants it raises. And you will not try to encroach upon the undercity in any way before the time comes for us to fight side by side?"

Lerris snorted. "There's nothing in that dank cave we want. Whatever the king was so keen to capture, he can go get it himself. We're done with his orders."

One of the men at her side pulled a blade and marched back toward the prisoners. Riony bit her tongue bloody with worry, but the man simply cut through the bindings holding each of them.

As he turned his knife toward Kverra Hjelzahn's ropes, Aishena snapped, "If you want to live, don't touch those."

Lerris watched as they were all freed, including wolf and dragon, both growling and grumbling, then turned back to Riony. "They're all yours."

Lyrrin was first to move. She ran for Riony, arms out.

Riony balked, taking a step back and shaking her head vehemently. Lyrrin frowned but stilled before she attempted to wrap herself around Riony and go right through, revealing their illusion.

Riony wanted to hold her sister so badly, and as much as the Alderkin's spell had facilitated the negotiations, it wasn't facilitating getting Riony and her loved ones reunited in the way Riony longed for.

Aishena and Dashiel moved together to lift Kess gently onto Griskin's back.

"Is she ...?" Riony called over, keeping her feet planted.

Dashiel shook their head. "She needed urgent treatment hours ago, but she's holding on."

That's my girl. Hold on.

"See to your companions. I do hope they will all be well, and I apologize for delaying them." Lerris approached a red dragon seated at the edge of the plateau and hauled herself up onto its back. Her scowl shifting into something sadder. "You will hear from us again ... I fear far too soon."

The moment Lerris and her two companions were in the air, Riony called out to the others, "The gate will be opening in a moment. We have to go, but we'll meet you inside!"

"What? Why?" Lyrrin reached for Riony, and her hand passed right through.

"That's why."

Lyrrin's bright-blue eyes sparkled as she waved her hand through Riony's middle in awe.

Riony swatted her uselessly back. "Stop that. It's weird."

Eslinde brushed a ghostly hand across Lyrrin's cheek. "We won't be long."

Aishena shouted from where she stood over Kverra Hjelzahn's body. "You better not be. Because I lost my morass mercy in our escape, and I think my mother is waking up."

CHAPTER SIXTEEN

The race from the illusion crystals to Shield Gate was a blur of frantic, pounding feet, interspersed with apologizing to those Riony collided with in her haste. By the time she reached the undercity exit, her pulse pounded like crashing waves in her ears, and she'd left Eslinde far behind in the streets of the undercity.

Yrik stood before the looming double doors of stone, hands pressed deep into a hole cut into the shield shaped relief. A glow of magic shone around his wrists as he worked on the enchanted mechanisms within the gate.

"He's opening it now." Benjin hovered on tiptoes near the Alderkin's shoulder, watching him work and breathing hard from his own run there.

Niskina acknowledged Riony, then joined the delvers waiting there. With a few quiet orders, they left.

Riony knew why. They didn't need any more witnesses to Dracuni's power.

The unidragon sat to the side, tail flicking and eyes worried.

Lyomir is being very loud about Kess.

Riony nodded. Her heart was also.

The stone doorways groaned and scraped, bringing the yellow of early morning light in to merge with the cyan glow of the undercity. Griskin was first through, bolting straight to Riony, whom he had gone to for aid once before and turned to again now as Kess lay limply over his neck.

He whined as Riony moved to his side. She ran her hands over the stupid gremlin's clammy, far too cold skin, the tacky blood, the sharp points of glass poking out of her back below padding and bandages.

"Sparks, Kess. What did you do to yourself?" Riony breathed the words and thought after them, *for Lyrrin. For me.*

Riony had a vial of silvernix on her that Dracuni demanded she always carry now, but before she could reach it, the unidragon moved in beside her. She scratched the tip of her snout, then pressed it to Kess's cheek.

Kess jerked upright as starlight exploded from her. Riony caught her as she screamed and gasped through the pain of being healed. Her torso twitched and arched, and an awful squelching sound came from her back. Long shards of glass twisted and cut through her skin as the magic tried to expel them but the bandages held them in.

Riony grasped for the gauze, wrenching it between her fisted hands and tearing it off. Five long daggers of glass slithered their way out of Kess's back, then fell and shattered on the cavern floor. With a high, gasping cry, Kess slumped forward again, and Riony was there to catch her. Kess's face rested against Riony's neck as she gasped deeply.

"It's okay. You're going to be okay." She cradled the back of Kess's head in one hand and whispered into her hair as the light faded and their breathing steadied together. A deep ache filled Riony's chest and arms, an all-consuming desire to hold Kess like that forever.

Kess shifted in her embrace. "Ri—"

"Ow!" Riony yelped.

She backed away from Kess, who was sitting up on her own now, blinking at Riony as though woken from a dream.

"You're here this time!" Lyrrin stood at Riony's side, poking her with a sharp finger. "And you cut your hair!"

Lyrrin, safe and happy and with her again. Riony bent over the small girl, then straightened back up with her trapped in a tight embrace, lifting her off her feet.

"Little moon. I'm so glad you're back. I'm sorry I didn't come to get you myself."

"It's okay. I understand." Lyrrin nuzzled into Riony and then pushed away. "Gross. You're so sweaty!"

Riony put her sister back on her feet. "And you're covered in smelly blood. Are you going to tell me about that?"

"Are you going to tell me how you were a ghost a minute ago?"

"Ask your grandfather."

Aishena hollered over them, "Reunions later! We need to deal with this, now!"

She and Dashiel charged in, carrying Kverra Hjelzahn between them. The woman was bound around her hands and feet, but her eyes were open, and she was wrestling against her bonds.

Lyomir followed after, huge eyes locked on Kess. Kess gave him a small smile, and the dragon huffed grumpily and turned back around.

"Deal with what?" Breathing hard, Eslinde jogged up the tunnel, having finally caught up. Her eyes landed on Lady Hjelzahn. "Oh, blessed sun."

Vance followed at the princess's side and continued running straight to Dashiel, catching their sibling in a clapping embrace.

"Amma!" Lyrrin squealed.

Eslinde met the charging child on her knees and was toppled onto her back by her momentum.

"And I get a poke in the ribs. But fine, I guess," Riony muttered.

Tsking, Aishena shouted, "I said reunions later! I can't hold her on my own!"

Kverra snarled, "You won't be able to hold me for long at all."

A chill ran down Riony's back at the woman's voice, so hollow and cold.

Riony hurried to join Aishena in keeping the grayglim woman pinned. The ropes around the woman's ankles had loosened with her writhing and Riony held her feet down onto the tunnel floor.

"Weird you're complaining about reunions when you're the one who brought your murderous possessed mother home." Riony hissed as the woman bucked harder, giving no sign of easing up. "Also, it's so good to see you again."

"I have a plan." Aishena pressed all her weight down on the woman's shoulders, having to dodge as she angled her head around, trying to bite her. "And it's good to see you too."

Niskina stood as still as a statue at their side, glaring down at the woman who had killed her father. "And what exactly is your plan? Because I hope you've brought her in for justice."

"I've lost as much and more to this woman's hands as you. And if by justice you mean revenge, then yes, if my plan doesn't work, we will have no option but to end this mockery of life she's living." Aishena's silver hair swung around her chin as she bowed her head. "But first ... first I want to try to heal her."

"Heal her ... how?" Riony asked.

With an unspoken apology softening her eyes, Aishena said, "When your mother was healed ... it seemed to me that whatever compulsion the shadow dragon had over her was severed."

"Whatever happened to my amma then, she didn't survive it."

"Because she was long dead already. I don't think my mother ever fully died, that the curse somehow made its way inside her when she was knocked down. She is still Kverra Hjelzahn *and* something more, something controlling her. And if we heal her, maybe we can break that connection."

Crouching by his sister's side, Benjin's eyes widened hopefully. "Do you really think it will work?"

Aishena's face crumpled in a display of emotion she so rarely let slip. Her mouth moved but made no sound and she shrugged.

"It's worth a try." Riony looked questioningly to Dracuni.

The unidragon was already moving closer. ***It's okay. Now that I'm bigger, it's only a little cut.***

You'll let me know if it's ever too much, if we're ever asking too much from you.

Dracuni brought her claw up to her nose again, her opalescent moonlight scales glimmering in the cyan light. Each cut she made on herself for others healed quickly, but recently there had been so many that faint scars were showing around the softer scales and skin on her snout and forearms.

She touched her silvernix blood to Lady Hjelzahn. The woman lit up bright but didn't writhe or scream as the healing worked through her body, the way Riony knew could hurt so keenly.

As the magic worked through Lady Hjelzahn, Riony's gaze drifted upward, away from her and to the beautiful young woman on the wolf, keeping to the shadows away from everyone else. She had a bone knife in each hand, in a way that once would have had Riony running. But Kess kept sharp, wary eyes on the grayglim woman.

The light faded.

"Did it work?" Benjin asked.

Kverra lay still beneath them, midnight-dark eyes darting from person to person around her.

Riony and Aishena released their hold on her, backing away.

With a smooth, easy motion, Lady Hjelzahn bent at the waist and sat up, her wrists and ankles still tied. "I feel ... better. I feel clearer, healed as though from some long illness."

Benjin beamed, but Aishena blocked him from moving any closer. She squatted down in front of her mother and grasped the long, whiplike braid of black hair at the nape of her neck.

Turning the woman's face side to side, Aishena peered into her eyes. "It didn't work. She's still possessed."

"Are you sure?" Eslinde asked.

"I know my mother. This is something else." With a slow sigh, Aishena activated her cutting athame. "Niskina will get her wish after all."

Niskina had both hands over her mouth. "Oh, Aish ... I didn't want this."

Riony wanted to argue, to give her friend hope, but she could see it too. That same, inhuman emptiness she felt when she looked into the woman's dark eyes. It hadn't left. She hadn't changed.

"I am your mother and your mestra! Stop being foolish and untie me."

Aishena only shook her head as though it weighed as much as the world.

Lady Hjelzahn growled at them and wrenched at her bonds again.

Staring at the lethal weapon glowing in her hands, Aishena spoke flatly, "I assume beheading would have to put her down once and for all?"

"I'll take the children away," Eslinde said hurriedly.

"No!" Benjin snapped. "I'm staying. No matter what."

"I'm sorry. I really thought it would work," Aishena whispered and lifted her blade.

Riony's chest squeezed around her heart. It wasn't fair for them to lose their parents again and again. For Aishena and Benjin to have had lost their father and siblings, then had to flee from their own mother who wasn't their mother anymore. Only to lose her again now, like this.

It wasn't fair that Riony had to watch her own mother die, clawed apart in the hands of the curse's creatures, only to have her come back and die again. Riony's fists clenched, nails digging into her palms at the memory.

It wasn't ...

Riony's eyes widened, and she lurched forward, grabbing Aishena by the shoulder and pulling her back. "It was different! With my amma. It was different. It wasn't just silvernix, it was Dracuni's flame."

Aishena's flat look of determination faltered, and her knuckles were white around the hilt of her crystal blade. "Do you think it will make a difference?"

Riony helped Aishena back to her feet, and they moved away. "We should try, just in case."

Riony thought to Dracuni, *Will you do this for us?*

Of course. But I am feeling hungry again.

I'll get you more to eat really soon. Just a short burst, the way Vance said.

Dracuni moved in front of Lady Hjelzahn, who stared the dragon down fearlessly, although she backed up in small wriggles until she hit the wall.

"You're going to burn me? Fine, burn me, take my head. You cannot stop me, and you cannot stop what is coming for all of you. I will—"

Dracuni flamed. A short puff that started and stopped so quickly that the silvery fire came out like a bursting cloud.

It surrounded Kverra, blocking her from view as the flickering flame and bright light glared. Gasping breaths grew louder and faster, culminating in a single, heart-piercing shriek.

Then the healing flame and light were gone.

Kverra leaned with her back pressed hard into the wall behind her, her eyes open so wide that all the whites around her dark irises were visible. She stared from Aishena to Benjin, back and forth in a flutter, then her face scrunched in on itself and she fell sideways.

Her mouth opened in a silent scream, and her body curled up, shaking with heavy sobs.

"Is this a good sign or a bad sign?" Riony asked.

Aishena stepped over the shuddering woman, who made no further attempt to pull free of her bonds or attack her daughter.

Through Kverra's racking cries, the soft rhythm of hushed words escaped. Over and over. "What have I ... what have I done? What have I... What have ... What have I done?"

"I never in my life saw my mother cry." There was no emotion in Aishena's voice, only something deeply tired and final. "But that is her."

Chapter Seventeen

Riony didn't particularly enjoy hearing the story of where all the blood on Lyrrin came from, how Yensen died, or how the Dragon King, Lyrrin's own grandfather, had called a torturer to use on her.

Eslinde was white-faced and drawn at the stories as well. She spoke more to herself than the others. "Oh, Yensen … What a waste my father makes of good people."

Riony shook her head, awed. "Stars, I'm so sorry I couldn't be there for you. But I'm so proud of how you kept yourself alive."

"I learned from the best," Lyrrin said from above where she rode on Riony's shoulders.

She had only been gone for less than two weeks, but she still seemed somehow heavier. Older.

Riony squeezed her legs. "Let's not make this a 'who can survive near-death most often' competition, though, okay?"

Tell her I'm proud too! Tell her I'm sorry too, that I couldn't save her. From where she followed behind, the jittery waves of the unidragon's guilt and shame washed over Riony with almost overpowering strength.

Reaching their new front door in Delver's Circuit, Riony bent over and put her sister down.

"Dracuni has nothing to be sorry for and is proud of you too." She pushed the square stone button, and the stone door rolled open.

"Elumon!" Lyrrin cried as the doorway cleared.

The little hatchling danced there, hopping back and forth on anxious claws, expecting Lyrrin's arrival. He had gotten larger in the time Lyrrin had been away, growing fast the way Dracuni did in her early days.

Lyrrin giggled as the dragonling licked her face with a long split tongue. "I know!"

She held his head cupped in her hands and nodded along to a long and silent conversation between them. "I missed you too."

"He's not the only one," Riony said with a flick of her chin.

Lyrrin's gasp could have used up all the air in the room as there was a splash from the pool and slap of wet running footsteps.

"Butterfur! You're so big!"

The cave otter, balancing on back legs and tail, was taller than Lyrrin now. He nuzzled his whiskered snout all over Lyrrin's face as she squealed.

He dropped to all fours again and circled around Lyrrin twice, sniffing anything that might have been a pocket. With a huffing bark, Sir Butterfur Spelunkychunks slithered on his belly back to the pool again.

"Oh no. I should have brought some treats home for him." Lyrrin looked devastated.

Riony chuckled. "Don't worry, he gets plenty of food. Come on, go inside."

"Is this our new place? It has a pool! And furniture!" Lyrrin beamed up at her. Her hair had been darkened to a glossy black, and it made her bright-blue eyes stand out against her pale skin.

Only Eslinde followed in behind Riony, Lyrrin, and Dracuni.

With it being decided that Lady Hjelzahn was no longer a threat, she was left with her children. Aishena and Benjin half carried the broken woman away to deal with the fallout of her curse as a family.

After a few more brief reunions, everyone else split off as well. Vance and Dashiel, arms over each other's shoulders, went one way, and Niskina, wet-faced yet calm, left on her own. Yrik gave Lyrrin a number of long, very human hugs before letting her go, remaining behind to seal the gateway again, just in case.

Riony didn't notice when Kess left. She only noticed her absence like a spike through her heart when she found her gone. There was so much more she wanted to say to her …

She hadn't even had time to thank her for bringing Lyrrin home safe.

And now Riony was waylaid under a ceaseless barrage of a moment-by-moment rundown of Lyrrin's adventures. And she savored every bit of it because her sister was home with her again.

"And I think she's pregnant," Lyrrin said with the sort of wired, buzzing enthusiasm only a child who'd had a night filled with far too much excitement and zero sleep possessed.

She zigzagged around the room like a ricocheting ball, looking at each chair and lounge and carving on the wall and dipping her hands into the pool, then patting Elumon again, then playing with the doorways to the adjoining rooms.

"Who?" Riony asked.

"The queen, of course! Some of the things she and the king were saying made me think it. Like they didn't care at all if the other heirs were all getting killed one way or another, how they were going to have more."

Eslinde tutted. "Who else was killed, did they say?"

Lyrrin gaped, but her mouth continued at full speed. "I'm sorry, they're your brothers and sisters, aren't they? I kind of keep forgetting that you're part of that family because you're not like them at all. I really didn't like the king, but it was still kind of interesting there. They said a lot of interesting things. Things that gave me ideas."

"I've had some ideas while you were gone too. We've got a lot to talk about." Riony pulled Lyrrin to a stop with another hug. "And I'd love to hear all your ideas, but for now, how about getting cleaned up and resting? Benjin said you were flying all night."

"He *always* exaggerates. It was maybe only half the night, and before that was capturing Lady Hjelzahn, and before that was when I tried to escape on my own and this happened." Lyrrin gestured to her blood-stained dress. "Wow, was that really just last night? Feels like forever ago!"

Eslinde brushed a hand through her hair. "Which is why you really need to get some rest."

"I'm not tired!" Lyrrin snapped, instantly teary.

Eslinde shot a worried look at Riony.

Riony returned a wry smile. *Welcome to caring for an overtired child.*

There was a knock at the door, which Riony had left open as an invitation for the other reunion Riony longed for. She spun around, eager to see Kess there.

Zeina stood tall within the doorframe. "Can I talk to you for a moment? Sorry to interrupt."

"That's okay." Riony gave Lyrrin a smile, and then checked with Eslinde. "Do you think you can manage this?"

Eslinde gave Riony a fearful look.

Grinning toothily, Riony backed away. "I won't be gone long. There are some clean clothes in that room and there's food through there, in the cold chest."

"*We have a cold chest?*" Lyrrin's eyes bugged wide, and she bolted, Eslinde chasing after.

Riony met the Rebel Rider at the door, and they stepped outside together.

The well-lit hallway was short, off the main looped path of Delver's Circuit. There was only one other round doorway down that hall, directly across from them, that led to the Hjelzahn's chambers.

I hope they're doing okay.

Zeina folded bare, muscled arms across her chest and smiled in a way that would have left Riony in a puddle on the floor not long ago. "Your friends really did it. Rescued the girl right from under the Dragon King's nose. I'm impressed."

"Yeah, me too."

Riony had spent every day since the others had left on the mission with a deep, nagging icy feeling in her gut. A sickening worry that none of them would make it home again. That she'd lose Aishena, Benjin, Dashiel ... that she'd lose Kess, when Kess had come to mean so much to her.

That feeling hadn't left yet. Not entirely. It seemed to pull at her insides, desperate to see Kess again, to prove that she was really there, prove it with her eyes and with her hands, as though physical touch was the only thing that could relieve her worry that none of this was real.

Zeina raised dark eyebrows at Riony's heating cheeks. "And the siege is over?"

Riony cleared her throat. "Word travels quickly."

"Niskina gave me the rundown already, about your deal with the riders." Zeina leaned a hip against the wall. "Which is why I'm here. Gleem is desperate to get out of this cave, and now that we can, I thought I could go and do something useful."

Riony blinked, trying to comprehend through her overstimulated brain.

Zeina continued. "If things are that bad out there, we're going to need more numbers. I know it's not the army we need, but I can go and bring in the other Rebel Riders. There are two other small groups, four in each."

Eight more riders. It wasn't many, in the scheme of things. But Riony's brain had been stewing on something, burbling away between all the other excitement of the day.

She chewed her lip, thinking. "Are their dragons tamed or wild?"

"Wild, all except one which was a rescue."

"Get them to untame it, if they're willing." Riony pulled her vial of silvernix from her pocket and pushed it into Zeina's hand.

"You think it's a good idea? That I should go?" Zeina frowned over her golden eyes.

"It is. And I thought you wanted to?"

"I do ..." Zeina wet her lips. "Unless you want me to stay."

Oh ... sparks. Riony had so rarely been in the position of needing to let someone down gently. Let alone *a Rebel Rider.* She struggled for words, gaping.

A movement at the end of the hallway where it intersected with the main loop drew Riony's attention away. The shadowed form of Kess stalking past on Griskin.

Heart picking up to a gallop, Riony took one step that way before she'd even noticed her actions. She shook her head, turning back to Zeina.

"Sorry. I ... um ..."

Zeina followed her line of sight as Kess disappeared around the corner again.

"Don't worry. I get it." She huffed a sigh. "She is impressive, after all. Listen, just promise that if things don't work out with her, you'll consider me again."

Riony offered the stunning woman a brash smile, her feet already leading her away backward. "Are you calling me a quitter?"

Zeina barked a laugh. "You? Never."

Riony turned and sprinted down the hall. There was no sight of Kess from the intersection as the tunnel curved away sharply, and Riony bolted along it, running up behind the wolf and girl around the next corner.

"Kess!"

She swung around, her pale eyes flashing. "What is it? Is everything okay?"

Her hands were already moving to where she kept her knives, as though Lady Hjelzahn were about to emerge from the shadows and slit their necks.

Riony stopped by Griskin's side, in line with where Kess sat in her saddle.

"Everything's fine. I just wanted"—Riony's eyes locked on Kess's lips and she swallowed hard—"to talk to you."

"About?" Kess tucked her flight tangled hair behind one ear, and Riony's gaze traced every touch of the motion.

Sparks. Was she always this beautiful?

Riony replied, "I don't know, maybe about how you almost just died saving my sister for me?"

Kess smiled crookedly. "Is this supposed to be you thanking me?"

"I'm getting to that! Stars ..." Riony took a step closer, her thighs pressing into Griskin's fur as she searched Kess's face, trying to translate every change of expression and what it might mean. "I just wanted to make sure you're okay first. You were hurt. Badly."

"I'm better now, thanks to Dracuni."

"But you *were hurt.* What happened to the silvernix I gave you?"

"I used it on Griskin."

Riony coughed a bewildered laugh. "And you called me a sympathetic fool for saving Dracuni in her egg."

"You wouldn't have done it for Griskin?" Kess tilted her head judgmentally.

"You know I'd do anything for the big pup."

Growing serious, Kess leaned closer, her words a low hush. "And I'd do anything for you."

"Sparks, Kess. I don't want you as a bodyguard. And it's hurting me more seeing you kill yourself trying to be." Riony stepped closer again, one leg on either side of Kess's hanging in her saddle.

She brought a hand up and cupped Kess's spotted cheek. "I just *want you*."

Kess's breath caught audibly. "You want me?"

Breathing labored, Riony leaned in, her nose brushing Kess's. "I need you. I ... *raze it all* ... can I just kiss you now?"

Kess's answer came back on a breath that warmed Riony's face. "Please."

A fraction closer, and their lips brushed each other's.

Then with a desperate grunt, Riony fell upon Kess like a starved animal. Her hands grasped around Kess's waist, fisting into the blood-stained leather and pulling her closer. Kess's own hands reached back, clawing into Riony's back through her shirt. They each kissed the other as though they might die if they stopped.

Griskin rumbled a warning growl.

Riony's lips remained over Kess's. "Go on, bite me. I don't care."

She lifted Kess from her saddle, turning her to face her fully, then pressed back into the kiss until Kess was caught between her and the wall.

Riony kissed her with every ache of longing she'd endured during their time apart, and Kess returned it with a yearning strength that seemed so much more.

In a gasping gap as they drew breath, Kess whispered, "Is *this* you thanking me?"

"I haven't even started thanking you. This is all for me."

Kess chuckled, a soft, gentle laugh that felt like a rare and precious gem.

Riony lost herself in the hazy pleasure for a long moment, where nothing in the world existed beyond Kess's lips against hers. She placed a flutter of soft kisses over the corners of her mouth, then delved deeper, enjoying Kess's whimper in response.

"Riony?" Eslinde's voice, panicky and high, echoed down the corridor, breaking them apart. "Are you there? Are you coming back?"

Riony groaned, rolling her neck to look toward her chambers. She ran her fingers down Kess's arms, then squeezed her hands.

"I have to go back." She didn't want to let go. "Come with me. Come and stay with me."

"Riony? Where are youuuuuuu?" Lyrrin's voice followed, unnaturally piercing and edged with upset.

Kess, breathless and flushed, shook her head. "Go. You need to be with your family."

Riony turned away and her heart panged deeply, pulling her back to Kess. "You're my family too. I want you with me."

"REEEEE-OH-NEEEEEEEEEE!" The echo of Lyrrin's cry pummeled the tunnel walls.

"Sparks." Riony winced dramatically.

"It's okay. I understand." Kess squeezed Riony's hands with trembling fingers and then let go.

Riony's nose scrunched up with the effort needed to turn away. Every part of her screamed with the need to pull Kess into her arms again.

But she had other responsibilities to put first, always, above what she wanted, or needed. Maybe, one day, things would change. But with all the threats still surrounding her and those she loved she wasn't sure that day would ever come.

CHAPTER EIGHTEEN

Lyrrin had a map of Elundrae laid out on the main table of her chambers, and all the guests she'd invited in sitting around it, and it was getting later and later into the evening and Riony still wasn't back.

The front door held all Lyrrin's attention as she glowered at it, willing it to open.

Food soon? Elumon asked from under her chair.

Soon, Lyrrin thought back, trying to stop her frustration and worry also reaching the hatchling.

Eslinde leaned over and said in a gentle voice, "I'm sure she's fine. The factory raids simply take as long as they take."

Niskina stifled a yawn. "She's been on one every day for weeks now. She's an expert liberator of dragons at this stage."

Beside her, Jaym reclined in his chair. Today's raid was the first he and Niskina hadn't also joined, citing the excuse that they were too sparking exhausted, thanks, and needed a break.

Dracuni, also tired from all of the blood she'd been providing recently, was resting in her own room nearby.

Everyone was working so hard. Since returning, Lyrrin had been with Riony every moment she wasn't out on raids, which wasn't much.

Lyrrin didn't like how hard Riony had been pushing herself, but she understood why. If they had any chance of weakening the shadow dragon's curse, of weakening the revenant army before it reached the capital, they had to untame as many dragons as possible, as quickly as possible.

A couple more seats along the table, Priyune and Yrik whispered together briefly in their own language. Across the other side, Lady Hjelzahn sat with a hunched back, her face bowed and hidden under a now loose tangle of black hair, covering her face like a waterfall. Aishena and Benjin sat stiffly on either side of her like wardens beside a prisoner more than children beside their mother.

The room fell silent again as an awkward tension built.

"Maybe I could serve some food while we wait," Eslinde offered.

Food? Elumon's head popped up near Lyrrin's lap.

With a soft, grinding noise, the circular doorway rolled open.

Lyrrin shot up to her feet. "Finally!"

Riony froze in the doorway, her face smudged in soot and blood. "What's going on? Were you having a party while I wasn't home? Because first of all, rude, and secondly, you need more friends your own age."

"We're having a meeting, remember? I told you this morning. About my plan."

Nodding once in a wobbly, exaggerated motion, Riony said, "Right. Yes. Your plan. Sorry we're late."

Sighing, she stepped inside, with Kess following in on Griskin close to her shoulder, looking equally haggard and battle worn. There was a seat left for each of them across the ornate, carved crystal table from each other. Riony leaned her sword beside her chair and winced as she sat down. Kess slid from Griskin's back into her chair without her usual elegance, landing with a thump.

Riony eyes were glued to Kess's ever motion. "You probably don't need to be here for this. You should go and rest. You need it."

"Like you can talk," Kess's gaze also remained on Riony. "I'll sleep when you sleep."

Riony's nostrils flared and her eyes sparkled with an intensity Lyrrin couldn't quite read.

"You know, I will go and get some food. I'm sure these two are hungry after their mission." Eslinde rose and fluttered to the kitchen.

"Bring a knife to cut this tension with too," Niskina whispered not so quietly to Jaym.

"All went well, then?" Aishena asked. Although she'd only been on a few raids, she sounded as tired as the rest of them.

Without looking away from Kess, Riony replied, "Aside from one dragon who decided to take its years of captivity out on us, just perfect."

Benjin shot his sister a look. "We should be helping more."

Aishena's gaze flickered between him and their mother. "We have other things to look after right now."

"It's okay, we've got it covered." Riony did part her eyes briefly from Kess, frowning at Lyrrin. "I'm surprised you haven't been asking to come along."

"I would, if you'd like me to." Lyrrin straightened up in her chair, a flush of pride over her cheeks that Riony was now considering her someone who could be invited on missions.

I hope that means she agrees to my plan.

"But I'm plenty busy here too." She grasped her crystal-studded staff, once Benjin's, and showed off three new runed stones embedded into it. "Yrik and Priyune have been teaching me so much! I learned five new runes this week. Five!"

Eslinde returned with a platter piled with cold rope-worm slices, golden goat cheese, and root flour flatbread.

"Right here, thank you very much," Riony patted the table in front of her.

Elumon skittered under the table to assault Riony with pleading hatchling eyes. Eslinde handed the platter over, then returned to her seat.

She smiled sadly at the staff in Lyrrin's hand. "I do love seeing what you create with the crystals. The way you carve runes reminds me of your father's handwriting. He used to write poetry for me in Alderkin."

Lyrrin pouted back. She had seen one rune carved by her father, and the curves of his lines had the familiar shape of her own. "I wish I could have met him."

Eslinde smiled more, scrunching up her eyes as they glimmered wetly. "Me too. Now, let's get to your plan."

With one hand, Riony piled food indiscriminately onto a large piece of bread, then pushed the remaining platter across the table to Kess. Before taking her first bite, Riony also flicked a slice of rope worm under the table, and happy emotions zinged from Elumon to Lyrrin.

As the two of them ate, the rest of the group looked to Lyrrin.

Her worry had shifted to nervousness, now faced with all these people waiting to hear her plan. She wrung her hands in front of her.

"Go on," Eslinde whispered.

"I was thinking ... I had the idea ..." Lyrrin cleared her dry throat. "When we were talking about removing the Dragon King, one of the reasons it would be better if he was gone was because he's the only person who knows where his main supply of silvernix is kept. But what if he wasn't?"

Faces all around watched her silently, the only sound Riony's chewing.

Lyrrin continued. "If we could find his stash and take it from him, we would take almost all of his power. And also, we'd be able to use that silvernix for untaming all the factory dragons, and more, instead of relying on Dracuni all the time."

Eslinde's smile faltered. "That would be amazing ... but the location the king keeps his silvernix has been sought by many for decades, with no luck."

Jaym reached for the platter, poked at it with a frown, then pushed it away again. "We gave it a good crack a couple of times, for the same strategic reasons. But alas, no secret hoard of silvernix was found."

Turning from the Rebel Rider to the heir-killing grayglim, then the Alderkin and the King's own daughter, Lyrrin said, "But we know more now. Between what all of us here know about him and Elundrae, we've got the best chance ever."

"Where would we even start?" Niskina asked.

Lyrrin stood up so that she could reach over the large map in front of her, pointing out locations. "When I was at the palace, the king said he needed to get more silvernix than they had on hand, and that night I saw him flying his dragon to the northeast, which would take him to his private palace."

Jaym folded his arms and shook his head sympathetically. "One of the first places we checked. Searched the place top to bottom while he wasn't there."

Priyune straightened in her chair, eyebrows raised. "All the way to the bottom? Are you sure? There is a deemfret under where the unicorn slayer built his detestable structure."

That perked Benjin up. "A deemfret? Do you mean an Alderkin depths, like this one?"

"Not quite the same," Yrik said. "It's far smaller. A solely sacred space rather than one built for community. A place of crystal as dark as the night sky, unlike anywhere else in these lands."

Jaym sucked air through his teeth. "*That* we did not find."

Eslinde had paled, and her hands tightened on the arms of her chair. "Alleem never mentioned it. I've been there plenty of times too and never saw any sign of it."

Lyrrin stabbed the location on the map with her finger. "And if you didn't find it, who's to say the silvernix isn't there? The king could be keeping the silvernix underground in the deemfret."

Priyune let out a weak wail, as though even the concept of the unicorn blood being stored in their holy space stung her. She leaned into Yrik, both whispering in distraught tones to each other.

Everyone else held expressions that had changed from skeptical to warily enthusiastic.

Except for Riony, who was chewing her lip and still staring at Kess. One of her legs bounced, fidgeting rampantly.

"Riony? What do you think?"

"Hmm?" She blinked at Lyrrin. "Yeah, finding the silvernix would be good."

"That's not ..." Lyrrin sighed gruffly, shaking her head at Riony. She had to forgive her sister. She was clearly exhausted to distraction.

Turning instead to the once-murderous grayglim, Lyrrin lowered her voice as though calming an animal. "Lady Hjelzahn?"

The woman flinched slightly. "I no longer deserve that title."

"Kverra," Lyrrin corrected. "Did you see anything? Do you remember anything from your time ... following the king and heirs around? Anything that might help us?"

"My ..." Kverra's voice broke, and she remained hunched over, not looking at any of them. "Aishena has explained to me what is happening in our land, why our king no longer deserves my loyalty. I find it all hard to believe ..."

Her voice dropped, husky and wavering. "But my own actions over the past years defy belief far more. I have spent my days obsessed with killing the king, my king, and all his bloodline, and now I am expected to continue working against him? I don't ... I don't know how to believe what I feel and see anymore."

"But if you saw anything—"

Lyrrin cut off as Aishena gave a sharp shake of her head. She noticed then how Kverra's shoulders were shaking violently.

"I'm sorry. I think we should go." Aishena pushed to her feet, and Benjin followed, throwing Lyrrin an exaggerated apologetic expression.

The two of them supported their mother from the room.

Lyrrin sighed and dropped back into her chair. "I really thought she might know something that could help."

Eslinde's smile had returned. "You've already done so well. Bringing us all together like this to share information. I think you might really be onto something."

"Well, that brings me to the next point," Lyrrin said, trying to sound older than she was. "I want to lead this mission."

That got Riony's attention, finally.

Eslinde also gasped softly, "Lyrrin ..."

"Before you say anything, remember how many times my plans and my magic saved us. I can do this, really." Lyrrin firmed up her jaw, staring them both down.

"No." Riony shook her head, drowsily awed. "You're right. I'm sure you can. But we can do it together."

Lyrrin winced. "I don't think we can. You can't come on this one."

Riony leaned back in her chair, smirking. "Oh, so *you're* excluding *me* now? Is that how it is?"

"Given your own plan, and your promise to Mestra Lerris, and the need to keep Dracuni safe, you and all our best dragonriders need to stay here. Same with Yrik and Priyune—this deemfret and the people here need them. I'll still take help, of course. Aishena and Benjin, probably; they were amazing when they came to rescue me before."

"And me. I'll go," Eslinde said, reaching for Lyrrin's hand. "I know my father's private palace. I've spent time there."

"You've really thought this all through, haven't you?" Riony pushed her chair back and came to stand beside Lyrrin.

With a firm jaw, Lyrrin rose to face her, prepared to continue defending her plan.

But Riony bent over, bringing Lyrrin into a hug. "I think it's a really solid plan."

"Thank you," Lyrrin said, muffled by Riony's shoulder. "I'm sure it won't be nearly as dangerous as what we've faced before."

"Don't jinx it." Riony backed away, giving Lyrrin's hair a quick ruffle.

"Well, it seems we have a lot of preparations to manage." Eslinde stood as well, watching her daughter a little teary-eyed.

Lyrrin grabbed her sister's hand and swung her arm back and forth with enthusiasm. "I still have more details I want to go through. Will you help?"

"Of course, little moon."

"We'll be off, then," Niskina said.

"Glad I could help, although I'm not sure I entirely did." Jaym chuckled and offered Lyrrin a small salute. He caught up to Niskina and they exited shoulder to shoulder.

Yrik turned his hand Lyrrin's way, curving it through the air in an elegant gesture. "We'll take our leave too. We have much to do."

He and Priyune followed the others out.

Kess was still in her chair, watching Riony like a child might watch a beloved toy dropped in a stream drifting out of reach.

She whistled softly, bringing Griskin to her side. "I'd better get going too."

Riony returned an equally strange expression to Kess, cheek twitching and chest heaving.

"Actually," Eslinde said brightly, "I was thinking that maybe Lyrrin could have a sleepover with me tonight? If that's okay?"

"A *sleepover*?" Lyrrin wheezed. "Can I?"

Riony's jaw dropped as a breath rushed out of her. She answered with her eyes on Kess, who had frozen in her chair, hands on Griskin's saddle.

"Um. Yeah. Sure. That would be okay with me."

"Wonderful. Come on, let's go now. I want to keep planning with you, since I'm on your team." Eslinde's eyelashes fluttered at Riony, and she smiled as she put a hand on Lyrrin's back, ushering her out.

"Elumon! Come on. He can come too, right?"

The hatchling loped across the room to follow them.

"Of course."

Lyrrin beamed up at her mother. It was still a concept she was getting used to, having a mother again. Riony's amma, growing up, had been Lyrrin's as well in every way, and Riony had cared for her as much as any mother would since then.

But having Eslinde around was different. Lyrrin was so excited to get to know everything about her, to share all of both their lives they'd missed out on experiencing together.

I hope we stay up all night talking!

She glanced back to wave to Riony as they reached the door, beaming from the successful evening, only to find her sister with an expression that looked desperately distraught. She was stalking toward Kess in a way that looked almost murderous.

"Is she ... okay?" Lyrrin asked, her smile dropping.

Eslinde pressed her hand into the middle of Lyrrin's back, pushing her into the hallway. "She's fine."

"She's not angry at me for wanting to have a sleepover, is she?"

"No, I don't think so." Eslinde chuckled and closed the door behind them.

Chapter Nineteen

Kess woke from sleep like crawling out of a thick, warm syrup that pulled back against her every time she tried to reach consciousness.

She wasn't even sure why she was fighting it.

I want to stay like this forever.

She lay on her side under a cloudy tangle of blankets. Riony's body was curled around her from behind and warm like the touch of summer sun, one heavy arm draped over Kess's middle.

Riony was so rarely stationary. She seemed perpetually in motion, rolling her shoulders or shifting from leg to leg as though her body feared the concept of stillness. To have her there, so comfortable, so trusting in Kess's company that she was completely at rest, was such a deep, aching honor that it made tears well in Kess's eyes.

The gentle inhale and exhale of Riony's sleeping breaths were sweeter than a love song.

She's really here. Really here, with me.

With the lack of natural light in Riony's bedroom it was almost impossible to tell what time of day it was, but Kess's body clock roused her as equally as the exhaustion of the previous week and late night fought to pull her back to slumber.

Kess's heart had awakened to Riony's touch as well, pattering quickly in a way that would be hard to calm again.

Sleep or not, Kess was content to lie there in that moment for as long as she could. She reached down to shift one of her legs into a more comfortable position, and Riony's arm instantly tensed. Then both arms snaked around Kess and pulled her tight to her chest.

"Don't go," Riony mumbled into Kess's hair.

"I'm not going anywhere." Kess closed her eyes as an electric energy thrummed through her at being in Riony's embrace. "I'm sorry I woke you."

"Am I awake?" Her voice was thick and soft with sleep. "Let me check."

A warm kiss pressed to Kess's bare shoulder where her undershirt had slipped down. Riony sighed heavily around the second kiss before planting the third.

Kess forgot how to breathe. "Yeah. You seem awake to me."

"I don't know. Pretty sure I'm dreaming."

Kess couldn't disagree. Everything felt dreamy and soft-edged and unreal.

Because how could she have this? How could she exist in this moment of raw, peaceful joy? It felt like the moment of calm before the nightmare takes over the knife twists.

She'd never known a time when the knife didn't cut away her happiness. A shiver of dread overtook Kess's body. Already overwrought with emotion at everything about her current situation, she couldn't suppress it.

Riony's drowsy kisses along her back grew more forceful, and she crushed Kess tight to her again.

Then she stopped and ran a hand down Kess's arm. "You're shaking. Are you okay?"

"Yes …" Kess squeezed her eyes closed. "No."

Riony shuffled behind her, lifting up onto one elbow and leaning over her. "What's wrong?"

There was no judgment in Riony's expression, no annoyance or anything other than concerned care, and it only made Kess shiver harder.

How could I deserve this?

She wanted to make an excuse, to flee, but had no easy way out. Griskin had been closed out the night before. They were alone in what was now Riony's bedroom. Alderkin finery woven like liquid from cave silk in blues and purples was mismatched with an earthy collection of worn and singed blankets.

A well-loved doll with a red ribbon sat on a chair beside the bed, and although there was another bedroom in those chambers for Lyrrin, Kess was sure the young girl slept in this room with Riony most nights, as they must have for years in the smaller apartment they'd had before.

Riony waited patiently, and Kess steeled herself. Even if she didn't deserve this, she owed her courage to Riony. She owed her truth.

Kess worked to find her words. "Doesn't it scare you? *Having* anything. Happiness, friends, family, love. Aren't you terrified it will all be taken away?"

"Only every razing moment."

Kess rolled onto her back, staring up into Riony's multihued, ineffable eyes. Riony, who had grown up with her loving parents and still had her sister and friends who would do anything for her. She had lost so much but still had so much more she could lose.

Kess asked huskily, "How do you handle it?"

"Badly, mostly, and with as much inappropriate and ill-timed humor as possible." Riony smirked, but then her smile softened, and she lowered herself down, propping her head up on a fist. "I wish I could tell you it was easy, but I can tell you it's worth it, to have those things in your life."

Kess rolled over onto her side again, facing Riony. Her fiery-red hair was trimmed short all around one side where it had been burned, but a mop of unruly curls still tumbled over her face.

She had always been the most beautiful thing Kess had ever known, right from the day her parents had cruelly gifted Riony to her as a slave. There was no way to ever leave all of the injustice and trauma of their past behind, but the way Riony watched her now felt new.

It wasn't with the feigned respect of a belligerent slave, or pity, mere tolerance, or outright hostility. Not any of the ways Riony had once looked at her.

Kess's trembling eased, and her breath grew steadier again.

Riony's free hand found Kess's, toying with her fingers. "Is that what's worrying you? Not me? I didn't do anything wrong?"

"Never."

Riony lowered her eyes, her lashes shadowing them. "Really? Because I'll openly admit I am brand new to all of this. Outside of the theatre of my own mind and reading Rebel Riders, I mean."

"You haven't been with anyone else like this before?" Kess shook her head, confused. "*You?*"

"Thank you for the expression of shock. But nope."

"Me either." Heat flushed from Kess's collarbones to her cheekbones. "Was it ... okay for you?"

"Okay? *Okay?*" Riony dropped Kess's hand, her expression aghast as she sat fully upright.

"You made me question if I'd ever understood the word pleasure before. You made sounds come out of me I didn't even know were *in* me. You made me feel like I was filled with exploding starlight. Sparks, Kess. The slightest touch from you makes me dizzy with how much I love you."

Kess's thoughts blanked out entirely as though her head just took a great blow. "You ... love ... me?"

Riony lifted one shoulder. "What do you think we're doing here?"

Seeking comfort or relief or simple recreation? Kess had a hundred excuses in her mind for why Riony had turned to Kess the way she had recently. She'd never assumed love. She couldn't ... even if it was the reason she'd said yes in return.

The time they had spent together, the closeness and kisses and bare vulnerability was one thing, but to hear those words, *those words* from Riony ...

Kess's mind flared back to life with a surge of frantic emotion and she sat up to face Riony.

"I love you too. I've loved you for so long, longer than I could ever admit, because I never knew love. I couldn't perceive it, couldn't *accept* it. And when I finally realized ... I've caused you so much suffering. I don't deserve to love you and could never, ever deserve for you to love me in return."

Riony's head tilted as though she were considering this. "But I do."

"But I've hurt you. In so many ways. My selfishness, my family, my mistakes I've made while pursuing my foolish dreams."

Riony frowned yet smiled at the same time, soft and determined. "But I do."

Kess's voice rose higher. "But I have so much blood on my hands. I'm not a hero like you. I looked after myself and only myself for too long. I would have torn this land and every heart in it apart for what I wanted, and I still would, only I have learned to *want* better. But I've done too much to be loved."

Riony leaned forward into Kess's space. "But. I. Do."

"But I'm ..." Kess's words broke off.

I'm not enough. I couldn't ever be enough.

Riony brushed a hand across Kess's cheek, smearing wetness there. "Do you think you can talk me out of this? Stars, Kess. All the things you're saying are all the reasons I *do* love you."

Kess scoffed in a way that was almost a sob. "Maybe you're the one who doesn't understand love, because they aren't good things."

"That you're a survivor? That you're driven? Forthright and passionate? Sly, confident, and effortlessly capable?" Riony leaned her forehead onto Kess's. "And *especially* how overly dramatic you are."

More tears spilled from Kess's eyes as she laughed. "You're the one who just said *filled with exploding starlight*."

"No drama. Just facts."

Kess leaned away from Riony, chewing her lip and giving her an assessing look. "Might be something that needs to be tested again, for accuracy."

Riony huffed a breath and lunged onto Kess, knocking her back onto the bed with a giggling yelp.

Their hands were tangled beneath each other's clothing, and their mouths hot and raw from kissing when someone pounded at the door.

"Hey, you two!" Niskina's voice bellowed from outside. "Hate to interrupt whatever's going on in there which isn't obvious at all, but you're going to be late for today's mission."

"Sparks, already?" Riony groaned.

She lifted herself off Kess into a plank above her and yelled over her shoulder, "We're not here."

"Did you really think that was going to work?" Niskina replied, muffled through the stone.

Riony sighed, leaning down again and hiding her face in Kess's neck. "Just one day. I want just one day off before we either save the world or die trying."

"We could barricade the door," Kess offered.

"Give me your cutting athame and I'll make sure it never opens again."

"Sounds good to me. Although, we'll eventually starve."

Riony pressed a long kiss to Kess's neck. "We'll die happy."

Niskina pounded on the stone again. "Also, this wolf of yours is real upset at being locked out here!"

Riony and Kess sighed as one.

"Fine," Riony yelled. "We're getting up. But we're not happy about it."

There was some incoherent muttering from the other side of the door, drifting off as Niskina left.

The bed was a low platform of stone, softened by a quilted mattress. Kess shuffled to the edge and dropped her legs over, looking around for her clothes, armor, and weapons that were strewn on the floor amongst Riony's.

"Let me fix that up for you." Riony moved behind her, running fingers through her tangled hair. "Considering I'm the one who messed it up."

Riony's nails combing against Kess's scalp and pulling the hair into braids made goosebumps rise over her skin. It had once been one of Riony's duties as Kess's carer, to braid her hair. Her hands still moved surely with the muscle memory, and the feeling of it brought a swell of mixed emotions rushing into Kess.

She murmured, "I can do it. You don't have to."

"Listen. Anything that means I get to keep touching you, I'm all in." Riony continued twining the hair into neat braids. "I can also help you with your leg exercises, if you'd like. I think I remember how."

In an even smaller voice, Kess echoed, "You don't have to."

Riony stopped then. She reached around and cupped Kess's chin, turning her to look back. Her expression was serious. "You know people who love each other do things for each other. No bargaining or debts. You know that, right?"

"I'm ... still getting used to it."

Riony shook her head, and one hand traced lines over Kess's shoulder where her undershirt had fallen away. "You did this for me. You took these scars for me."

Kess hadn't seen the marks left from her brother's whipping herself but had been told they were there by Dashiel who had checked on her back on that night. Thin, barely there, white lines that the silvernix had closed, but not soon enough to be unmarred.

Kess met Riony's eyes. "That was different."

"How?"

"You already have too many."

Riony didn't say anything but began placing kisses across all the places she'd traced.

"We're never getting out of here if you start that again."

"It's very, very hard to stop."

"I know." Kess turned all the way around, catching Riony's kisses with her mouth.

A deep warmth of unfamiliar emotion consumed Kess.

Happiness.

Pulling back for a breath, Kess said, "Do you remember when we went to Heithorn estate to rescue Dracuni, and before lifting me onto the dragon you told me you were going to give me everything I ever wanted?"

Riony's lips quirked under Kess's. "I do say a lot of dumb things, don't I?"

"But you have. You have given me everything I ever wanted. I never thought this sort of happiness could be mine, and it's all because of you."

Riony pulled Kess off the edge of the bed and back onto the covers and into her arms.

Kess laughed. "So we're choosing *die happy*?"

Riony's voice was a lazy growl. "You always used to say to me that you'd watch me die one day."

Kess pulled back, frowning. "I'm sorry I did that. It wasn't what I meant, really. I think, even back then, I just always hoped that we'd be together that long."

Riony pouted. "Aw! But also, you know that's the worst possible way of expressing that sentiment."

Kess ran her nose up Riony's cheek and pressed a kiss to the corner of her lips. She felt Riony shiver under her touch. "I hope I've improved since then at expressing my sentiment."

"You have indeed."

It was at least another hour before they emerged from Riony's bedroom, still groggy and red-cheeked. The happiness that filled Kess felt as though it could burst her rib cage with the sheer immensity of it.

Riony loves me.

But further down, in the pit of her stomach, a chill grew as they once again picked up their weapons.

Even yesterday's mission had some close calls. How much longer could their luck last? Would it end on today's mission, or tomorrow's? Or the next?

Despite all of Riony's reassurances, Kess still found it hard to believe she deserved any of this, which made her fear even stronger that it was all going to be taken from her soon.

Chapter Twenty

Dragons fought in the distance. Tiny silhouettes swirling around each other, puffing bright flame. Riony kept her eyes on them from the plateau outside of the undercity.

Don't you dare get any closer.

Since the siege broke, a few riders still loyal to the Dragon King had tried to return to their mission of capturing Dracuni. Mestra Lerris and those on her side had so far kept them away.

Eslinde walked up beside Riony, dressed in full blue and gold scale mail, her thin blade at her hip. "I think Lerris got the better numbers and riders when she led her mutiny. It bodes well for the battle to come."

Riony hummed grumpily. "A battle they will have us to help with too, thanks to their neat bit of extortion."

Eslinde kept her eyes on the distant aerial combat. "Extortion or not, wouldn't we have tried to help anyway? Knowing one of the last and biggest sanctuaries for human life in our land was under threat? We have to take a stand at some point, and if not then, when? When there is nothing left to save?"

"Just because you can make lots of good points doesn't mean I have to be happy about it. I know it's inevitable. I know it's what we have to do if anything in this world is going to change."

Riony looked around the plateau and everyone there, thinking about all they'd given, all they might still give. Waiting just out of sight inside the entrance tunnel with the Alderkin, Dracuni had given the most lately. The number of scars of bloodletting on her were multiplying rapidly.

Viska and Ambri, gold and orange, sat nearby as Lyrrin and her team said their goodbyes. Viska was alert, focused on Vance in silent conversation, and Ambri, still tamed, sat still and unthinking. Nobody knew just how long this mission would take, so supplies and packs were loaded onto the dragons.

They could be gone hours, days, weeks. They could be gone forever.

"But I still hate that other people let it get to this point and that I and those I love have to fight and die for other people's mistakes and wrongs." Riony gestured to where Lyrrin was saying goodbye to Niskina and Dash. "Where my sister, your daughter, is about to fly into danger even now."

"I'll be with her this time. I'll do everything I can to keep her safe," Eslinde said.

Aishena, Benjin, and their mother were also leaving with them. The hatchling, Elumon, was going too, since Jaym recommended it would be best for his and Lyrrin's bond that they remained together.

It was a strong group, but Riony still worried.

Riony turned to Eslinde and held out a hand. "Look after yourself too. Everyone comes home safe, okay?"

Eslinde brushed the hand aside and stepped in to hold Riony tight. "Same goes for you."

Riony returned the embrace, and when Eslinde pulled back, she smiled and tucked Riony's flop of hair behind one of her ears in a way that was so similar to how her own mother once had that it left a lump in her throat. Oblivious to Riony's swell of emotions, Eslinde turned away to say goodbye to Vance.

Lyrrin ran in toward Riony then, and Riony knelt down to catch her in a hug. "All ready for your big mission?"

"Could you make that sound any more patronizing?" Lyrrin scoffed. "But yes, I think we are."

Riony squeezed her tight. "You're going to do great. I love that you're going to be the one who steals your grandfather's ill-gotten riches from him."

"That might have been part of the reason why I planned all of this." Lyrrin chuckled wickedly.

Letting her go enough that she could look into her bright-blue eyes, Riony swallowed hard. "Before you leave, there's something I wanted to tell you."

Lyrrin assessed Riony's serious expression. "It's not bad news, is it? Why would you save bad news for right now?"

"Not bad news. Good news? I suppose? More like ... something I want your approval on." Riony hesitated, then swallowed again. "It's about me and Kess."

Lyrrin stared back. "Are you two fighting again? You looked so angry at her the other night."

Riony flushed red. "No. We're together."

"Together how?" Lyrrin asked.

"As a couple."

"A couple of what?"

Riony huffed. "We're together *romantically*."

"Oh!" Lyrrin seemed to consider this, then pulled a face. "You and her? Really?"

Riony's heart sank. She wasn't sure what she'd do if Lyrrin didn't approve of the relationship. "You don't like her?"

Lyrrin looked over Riony's shoulder to where Kess waited near the undercity entrance. "No, she's okay, and I love Griskin. I just thought you hated her."

Not long ago that had been true. "Feelings have changed, and it was a surprise to me too how much everything has changed."

"Romantically ... With like, kissing and everything?" Lyrrin's face scrunched up with disgust. "I could see you were looking at her differently, like an intense sort of way, but I didn't know what it meant. All you older lot look at each other like that all the time ..."

Shaking her head, she looked to where Vance and Eslinde were saying a long goodbye, eyes locked longingly on each other despite the tense distance between them.

Lyrrin gasped scandalously. "Them too? It's them too, isn't it?"

Riony had seen it before, the simmering emotions underlying Vance and Eslinde's interactions, but nothing had ever seemed to come of it.

"Maybe they need a sleepover arranged for them too," Riony muttered.

"What?"

"Nothing." Riony poked Lyrrin until she turned back around to face her, then gave her one more hug. "Now, I know you've got everything planned, but be careful, okay? Check in through gateways when you can."

"I don't think we'll be gone that long. I'm sure the silvernix is at the king's private palace, and we have everything we need to get in. This is going to be the quickest mission ever, better than any of yours." Lyrrin squeezed Riony once, then backed away to go and say goodbye to Dracuni and the Alderkin.

"Always has to be a competition with her," Riony murmured as Dashiel and Aishena walked over.

"Are you sure I shouldn't be going with them?" Dashiel looked to Aishena with harrowing puppy dog eyes.

Riony refused to be swayed. "We need all the best riders with us. That means you and your brother."

Kess had offered that morning as well to go with Lyrrin and keep her safe for Riony, and Riony had to point out that she and Lyomir were among their best riders too, which left Kess very thoughtful and red-faced.

"I might argue I'm one of our better riders too," Aishena smirked but was distracted by her mother moving past to load a saddlebag onto Viska, and her expression turned steely again.

The woman had cleaned herself up greatly since the last time Riony had seen her. She wore her full grayglim armor, and her hair was back in its long whiplike braid.

Riony raised her eyebrows. "You're sure taking her is a good idea?"

"She's a grayglim first, regardless of anything else. If put to task, she will perform." Aishena lowered her voice then, fidgeting with the guard armor she wore, stolen during their last mission. "Mostly though ... I don't trust leaving her behind alone. She is ... a threat to herself."

"I'm sorry things haven't worked out better for you and your family." Riony moved in, clasping the stern young woman around the shoulders and pressing her forehead to Aishena's.

Aishena grasped Riony's arm in return. "She needs time. We all do."

"Then I hope you all get that time."

As Lyrrin, Aishena, Benjin, Eslinde, and Kverra mounted the two dragons, waved one more time, and took flight, Riony continued wishing all of them would have more time.

Niskina patted her on the back. "I'm sure they'll be okay. We've all survived worse. And look on the bright side ... at least you have your bedroom to yourself for a while now."

Smirking, Niskina backed away, returning into the undercity, joined by Vance and

Dashiel. They passed Kess along the way, who waited at the entrance for Riony.

A great roaring wave of love filled Riony, as it always did now when she looked at Kess and saw Kess returning that look.

Riony had imagined being in love, had longed for it for most of her life. She'd crushed hard on more beautiful girls than she could count. But something had always gotten in the way of any romance growing, so she had only ever gotten as far as dreaming.

She never thought it would feel like *this*. This insatiable inferno of need and the desire to fulfill her love's needs in return.

She never thought it would be with and for Kessara Heithorn.

But that fire was quelled by the chill of fear for those who had just left.

Riony sighed. Letting her shoulders roll back with a long exhale, she stared at the retreating dragons in the distance. The soft shifting of dirt underfoot heralded Griskin and Kess appearing beside her.

Kess said nothing, asked for nothing. Only remained waiting beside Riony as they watched until Viska and Ambri vanished from sight.

Riony leaned into Kess then, her head on Kess's shoulder. It still left her dumbfounded how this wild girl who was once her tormentor always seemed to know exactly what Riony needed.

But what Riony needed most was to not lose anyone else she loved, and that was feeling more and more impossible with what was coming.

Apummeling gust of icy wind sent Dracuni barrel-rolling through the air.

"Whoa. Get your wings out. Steady!" Riony clung tight to the tumbling unidragon.

With a crack like wind hitting sails, Dracuni's wings caught the air again, leveling them out and slowing them down.

Sorry. I didn't expect that.

"Yeah, wind is a thing outside of caves. That's why we're out here, so you can get used to it," Riony replied.

She didn't return into the undercity with the others after Lyrrin left. She needed some space with her feelings, and Dracuni also needed practice flying in the open skies. As the distant dragon battle had ended and all seemed quiet, the two of them took flight over the white-topped mountains.

They remained wary as they skimmed around one tall peak. Snow disturbed in their wake glittered in an icy stream.

I understand the concept of wind. It was just stronger than I expected.

"And you're even stronger. You're doing amazing." Riony patted the opalescent mane down Dracuni's neck.

The unidragon had proven to be fast and agile in their practice, more than anyone had expected after her slow start to flying. But her endurance was still lacking. Whether it was because she had to work harder to fly than other dragons or whether she was already tired from the bloodletting, Riony wasn't sure.

Even now, Dracuni's flanks heaved with strained breaths. The wind picked up, howling and battering against them both.

Riony recognized the landscape beneath them and called out, "Come on. Let's take a break. Land down there."

Is it safe? Dracuni's ever-present, underlying worry laced her thoughts.

"There's no one else around. Except Kess and Lyomir."

The purple dragon and Kess kept their distance, circling high above, keeping watch over them while still giving them space.

Reluctantly, Dracuni landed in the thick snow, and Riony jumped down beside her, boots crunching as she sank down to her calves.

She shivered, rubbing her bare arms. She was dressed for the temperate atmosphere of the undercity, not for being out flying or trudging through the snow, but there was something she wanted to see.

"Come on, this way."

Where are we going? Dracuni gave another nervous glance at the sky.

"I wanted to show you where you came from." Riony followed the slope down, scanning the drifts of sparkling white for the entrance to the ice cave.

Where I was made ...

The sadness in those words landed hard on Riony. "I'm sorry."

You saved my life. You didn't know what that would mean for my future.

It didn't make Riony feel much better.

How could Dracuni ever be able to live freely, when her own blood put a target on her?

So much about the upcoming battle relied on Dracuni and would only put her under even greater threat. Even if they saved the capital and ended the curse, Dracuni would continue to be at risk for all her life.

The mouth of the cave appeared, half-buried behind a soft drift of snow. The two of them pushed inside and the howling wind cut off.

Staring around the cave, Dracuni's lilac eyes glistened. *Sometimes I wonder if I should cut my horn and my mane. It would help me stand out less.*

Riony's chest contracted with sadness. That Dracuni would have to change herself to remain safe felt wrong. But maybe it was something Riony should have done far earlier. She'd disguised Lyrrin to keep her safe. But she also knew how hard that had been on her sister.

"The nest was a bit farther in," Riony said, leading the way.

Dracuni took a step, and her leg slipped from under her, wobbling before she steadied again.

"You okay?"

Just tired.

"You've been giving too much blood lately. We should slow down."

We don't even have enough for the plan yet.

Dracuni's steps were timid and shaky, and her chest heaved, still catching her breath from the flight. Her eyes seemed dimmer than they usually did.

Riony shook her head. "It's too much. If we don't have enough, then we don't have enough. Even if we can't heal all the untamed dragons."

As though you aren't giving everything to the cause? Wouldn't give everything? I'm doing this because I want to. Dracuni snorted. *Because why should it be dragons who are the ones to suffer and die to fix what humans did?*

"They shouldn't. But if it's between you and them—"

Then we choose them. Just because they've been enslaved doesn't make them any less. Without the spike in their brain, they would be as intelligent and feeling as I am. I'm going to do everything I can to help them survive this.

Dracuni locked eyes with Riony. Her pale rainbow-sheened scales seemed to glow in the cool light of the ice cave. Riony leaned in and hugged the unidragon around her snout, patting her on the cheek.

"You're right. I just wish it didn't cost you so much."

Dracuni's thoughts held a hint of smugness. *We all have to decide at some point what is worth destroying ourselves for.*

Riony flinched and backed away. "Were you ... did you hear all of that?"

Dracuni huffed something like a laugh.

"You didn't! What else did you hear?" Riony acutely remembered the desperate, awkward, but passionate kiss that had followed that conversation.

Dracuni's eyes narrowed cheekily, and she wandered away, farther into the cave. *You asked for little sister's approval, but not mine?*

"I was getting to it ..." Riony muttered, chastened as she hurried after.

Dracuni glanced at her over her shoulder. *I approve. I haven't really seen you happy much. But this makes you happy. That's good.*

Riony pressed a hand to her chest, wondering just how much of her happiness and love overflowed to Dracuni for her to feel it too.

"I am happy, and I feel so loved. And just imagine what all our lives and this world could have been if we'd all felt happy and loved from the beginning."

Dracuni nudged the tip of her nose to Riony's cheek.

They reached the place the nest had been, but the area was filled with blown-in snow, melted in patches on the outcrop of warm earth that emerged there.

Only a few old shards of broken egg remained. Riony kicked around through the snow and muck for a while, but the tiny vial that had held the silvernix that created Dracuni couldn't be found. She continued searching a bit longer, so there was time for Dracuni to rest more fully before they took to the air again.

The moment they stepped back outside, a red dragon was visible, flying in toward the undercity entrance.

Mestra Lerris.

Riony and Dracuni flew swiftly down to meet with her, and Kess and Lyomir landed close behind them.

The bulky woman didn't bother dismounting from her dragon. Her face was drawn, pulled tight around her mouth and eyes. She called across the plateau to Riony and Kess.

"The revenant army has reached the capital. It's time."

Riony inhaled sharply. "Now?"

"Now. The undead already attempt to breach the walls. They came upon the city faster than expected in the last stretch. The shadow dragon flies with them, driving them to a frenzy."

Riony's heart hammered. Lyrrin and the others had only just left. They weren't ready. Even with Dracuni's insistence to do so, they hadn't yet bottled enough blood for what would be needed in the battle. Riony had wanted a dose of silvernix in the hands of every dragonrider out there, and they weren't even close.

Mestra Lerris turned her dragon sideways, as though already preparing to fly back the way she'd come.

She yelled with a harried urgency, "My riders have all received the crystals you supplied for them. I have a higher confidence that they will be able to stay on their dragons than you seem to have, but we are grateful. But do we also have you? Will you follow through on your promise and join us now?"

"Are the revs burning?" Kess called from her seat on Lyomir.

Lerris's expression stretched tighter. "They aren't yet staying dead."

Stars, no. Something inside Riony seemed to crumple and die.

With everything they'd done, with all the missions, all those factory dragons untamed, and still there was no sign of the shadow dragon's curse ending, or even weakening.

Maybe it can't be. Maybe it can't be reversed at all.

Riony pressed her hands to Dracuni's scales and pulled herself together. "We're with you, either way."

The mestra nodded once and was in the air again a second later.

Riony's heart beat like war drums, signaling the fight about to begin. One they had no hope of winning if the revenants still didn't burn.

There was still the backup plan, the final, apocalyptic gambit only for use if it came down to a situation where survival was already unlikely. Because if that plan worked, it would likely be the last thing any of them ever did.

Chapter Twenty-One

Lyomir growled beneath Kess as the battle came within view.

Uncountable corpses in ashy gray and earthen reds formed an ocean, crashing against the walls of Draekhanhelm. Hundreds of dragons flew above, evading and clashing with flying revenants while also attempting to burn those on the ground. Their flaming breaths were no more than small sparks of light, consumed by the mass of the horde. Sputtering candles in the darkness.

The living corpses of massive carrion birds and bats, down to smaller pocket-hawks and owlettes swarmed the skies. Any revenant whose wings were still intact enough to fly.

Above and below, everything swirled—a living storm cloud of smoke and fire, chaos and corpses. And flying above, casting a dark pall over everything beneath, flew the shadow dragon itself.

"I think the technical term for that," Riony yelled from nearby on Dracuni, "is a shit show."

Kess couldn't disagree.

After receiving Mestra Lerris's news, the undercity team rallied fast. They were armored and armed and in the air with the speed their drills had trained them for.

Niskina and the Alderkin remained behind, preparing for the aftermath of the battle, whatever that might be. Griskin had fretted when Kess took off without him, but considering what they were flying into, she preferred he stayed safe. She wasn't intending on leaving Lyomir's back anyway.

Kess still felt strange wearing delver's armor. She had become so used to her ratty leathers over the years. She'd been offered rider's scale mail from Eslinde's supplies like most of the others wore, but she preferred the flexibility of the delver armor and the anchor points on the harness for tying herself to the saddle.

It also felt strange to have a large, flat slab of runed crystal strapped to her back, the way everyone in their group except for Riony had.

In the front of their team, Jaym flew on Hux, and Vance rode Kife's left behind snowflame. It could no longer breathe its liquid fire without risking its life, but it could still fly well, and Vance preferred Viska go with Lyrrin and Eslinde to keep them safe.

Dashiel had taken Norallei's white dragon, Iffyr, with Shiff flying beside, still too small to carry a rider, but able to assist. And behind them the thirty-odd newly trained riders followed on treedarts.

Kess frowned at the battle they approached. Their numbers weren't even close to enough to make a difference.

The main mass of the fight filled the fields to the west of the dragonkeep, lit by the orange light of late afternoon, but the revenant army had the walls entirely encircled.

There are so many of them.

Vance signaled from up ahead, and he, Dashiel, and Jaym took the new riders with them directly into the fight. Kess raised a hand to signal back, and she and Riony split off, avoiding the aerial warfare and heading over the city.

Spotting a flat-topped building that looked clear, Kess caught Riony's attention and pointed to it.

Riony frowned back. "I should stay with you and the others."

"You know that you shouldn't. That's not the plan. You and Dracuni need to stay safe for later," Kess yelled over the gusting wind.

Jaw set tight, Riony adjusted her flight goggles, then turned away. Myrwa's shawl was tucked around her neck, one end fluttering behind her, the dull red looking like blood in the afternoon light. She and Dracuni glided down and landed on the crenelated tower top.

Kess circled twice, watching the skies around them for threats, then she and Lyomir flew to join the fight.

"Are you ready?" Kess spoke the words aloud and pushed them through her mind connection to her dragon as well.

Brave little one, don't question me. Lyomir growled and picked up speed.

Coming back over the city walls, Lyomir swooped low, sending a roiling fireball at the revenants climbing the steel and stone. The flame exploded as it hit, sending a handful of undead creatures toppling down into the masses below.

Kess stared, aghast, as the hole Lyomir had burned in the revenants' ranks closed over instantly. Even if the revs that were hit died, it made less impact than plucking a hair from a giant's head or a single star from the sky.

A mourning hopelessness filled her. She wasn't sure how much was from the immensity of the task before them or the effect of the shadow dragon itself, circling above.

Still, she didn't slow, didn't turn around. They were there to make a difference. She wasn't giving up.

Kess braced as Lyomir flew them into the thick of battle. A burst of orange flame came from the left and Lyomir swerved away from it, then under the lunging claws of a haggard plains eagle.

For each dragonrider in the sky there seemed to be a dozen or more undead creatures assaulting them. Kess couldn't spot Dashiel, Vance, or Jaym among the mess. She could barely see what was right in front of her.

The nearest rider had a massive carrion bird locked in chase with them, and Kess turned Lyomir to assist. The rider wore the king's colors, but that didn't matter anymore. The only fight now was between life and death.

Kess leaned close over Lyomir's purple scales as he shot in fast. With a thunder-crack crunch, he caught the undead bird in his jaws. Mangy feathers burst from the creature, gusting in the wind over Kess. With a wide swing of his head, Lyomir threw the crushed body of the creature away, into the path of a smaller swarm of flying creatures, scattering them.

Even with its bones shattered and feathers torn, the carrion bird rev continued flapping and squalling hideously as it fell to the ground.

Kess and Lyomir passed ahead of the rider they'd cleared the tail of, and the woman signaled her gratitude.

A swell of pride filled Kess, and something that tasted almost like hope. Grinning fiercely, Kess opened herself to Lyomir's thoughts and feelings and shared all of hers in return. They wove through the battle as one.

To the left, Kess would think, and Lyomir would act almost faster than thought. The thrill of their connection, the speed of their flight, each life they saved by snatching away the hunting revenants, filled Kess with a deep satisfaction.

This was it. This was what she'd always dreamed of, to be a dragonrider, fighting the undead scourge with her peers. It was bittersweet, to have this moment, when the chances of surviving beyond it felt so low.

But now she had this, she had Lyomir, and Riony, and she was doing what she had always known deep in her bones that she was made for. She wasn't giving it up. She would do everything she could to survive and to keep everything that had been so hard won.

Below her, two riders in Skaella's red and blue were caught in a midair wrestle with something huge, bigger than the treedart-sized carrion birds.

Blessed sun ... it's a dragon. A revenant dragon!

Kess had never seen one before, in all her years aboveground. Whether it was because dragons themselves often burned up when they were downed or some other reason, the shadow dragon hadn't seemed to raise them before.

Another sign the curse has only worsened? Kess shuddered.

The dragon had dark, rotten flesh with scales still holding on only in patches. Tears in its wings fluttered in the wind, but otherwise it was whole, and massive.

Lyomir snarled. ***Abomination. We will destroy it.***

They dove, spear like through the sky. Afternoon sun glinted on Lyomir's purple scales, and Kess's braids whipped behind her. Lyomir landed on the back of the death-blackened dragon rev and sank his claws in. Then he barrel-rolled.

Kess held tight, prepared for it, but the speed still stretched and strained the leather strap buckling her to her saddle. The undead dragon below roared, torn away from the others it was attacking. In the outer arc of his spiral, Lyomir released the creature, sending it flying.

Steadying out again, Kess came up between the two riders in red and blue. Their faces registered shock as they took her in, looking over her to Lyomir and his lack of taming spike, and Kess was shocked in return to see she recognized them.

The two riders who had been partying with Kife the night she found him to ask for help to hunt Dracuni. Kess couldn't remember their names. But it was clear they recognized her too.

The woman offered her a nod and a salute. Kess lifted her arm to return the gesture, when a burning eagle crashed down over the rider, sending her tumbling to the earth in a spray of ashes and sparks.

Kife's other friend went after her on his dragon.

Kess had to duck under the cloud of scorched feathers, and as she came clear on the other side, the revenant dragon was there again, coming back toward her.

Kess felt Lyomir's urge to dive under the revenant, and she pushed back hard.

Over, over! Panic filled her, remembering Norallei's fate.

At the last second, Lyomir twisted upward, cutting in between the deathly dragon's wings. It turned, unnaturally fast, and was right on their tail, bearing down fast.

Dive now, away from the army. We need to get somewhere clear if we want any chance of outrunning this thing.

Lyomir dropped suddenly, sending Kess lifting in her saddle. She held tight, teeth gritted as the army of land-bound revs came up toward them. Flying away from the city, Lyomir veered north to where the air and ground were clearer. The undead dragon screeched a rattly roar as it snapped at his tail.

It was easily as fast as Lyomir and it would never tire, never slow down.

We need to get behind it. We've got to ground it.

I will tear the thing to pieces.

Lyomir lifted, bringing his body up vertically with wings out wide to break the wind. The undead dragon shot beneath him, then he and Kess lunged downward, onto the undead dragon's back.

Lyomir got all four claws clutched around the ragged corpse, and the rev twisted and whipped its head back, trying to bite him in return. Its wings beat awkwardly without their full range of movement.

Lyomir snapped his teeth around one and bit clear through the bony structure. With a squeeze of his claws, he ripped the other wing free from the shoulder. He roared with triumph, and then in pain, as the rev landed its own bite into one of his front legs.

The weight of both dragons had them plummeting, and the ground flew toward them. Kess could feel Lyomir cursing through their thoughts as he tried to pull free from the revenant's teeth.

Crush it! "Crush it!" Kess screamed, inside and out, as hitting the ground became imminent.

Lyomir stretched all four legs out in front of him with the revenant within them and used his wings to slow their descent as much as possible.

They still hit hard, skidding across charred plains with the revenant beneath them. Ash and dirt plowed up around them, choking Kess. She jolted roughly in the saddle, and there was a snap as the leather strap buckling her in snapped. She clung tight to Lyomir's neck.

Somewhere in the landing, Lyomir and the dragon were freed from each other's hold, and he pumped his wings once, twice, bringing them out of the dust cloud.

Are you okay? Kess's heart pounded in her throat.

Lyomir growled, and Kess could feel his pain. **Merely a scratch.**

Kess leaned out over his side to look down. The undead dragon lay in a twisted mess, black scales and limbs scattered in the long trail their landing had left.

And yet it still moved.

What will it take to stop these things?

Lyomir brought them higher again, with great effort. They'd been in the fight mere moments and he was already injured and exhausted.

Kess shook her head as she looked down over the ocean of undead before them. It washed up like a tide against the walls of the capital, surging higher and higher. Soon, they would spill into the city itself.

And the shadow dragon circled lazily overhead.

A chill of mourning filled Kess as she watched the battle they moved to rejoin. The riders were all working so hard, but the revs still weren't dying by fire, didn't seem to be able to be put down at all. They weren't making any impact on the army.

Raze it all. This is an awful stalemate at best, and a slow death at worst.

Kess knew what had to be done. There was no choice left.

Call to Hux and Shiff. Tell them to retreat, bring Vance too if they can find him. We'll meet at Riony's location.

I can keep fighting.

I'm sure you can. But it doesn't matter if that fight gets us nowhere.

Grumbling, Lyomir took them through the thinner edges of the battle, skirting around and back over the city. As they came in toward the tower, Dashiel arrived from the other side on Iffyr, Shiff leading them in, and Vance trailing as well on his dragon. Jaym and Hux were farther back, the red dragon burning their way clear of a flock of undead birds.

Riony paced like a stalking wildcat on the flat tower top, glowing sword in hand and Dracuni at her back, sitting patiently. When she saw them incoming, she moved back to give them room.

Lyomir landed in the center of the roof beside Riony, and Iffyr and Shif landed perched on the crenelated edge.

Kess took a moment to catch her breath and brush ash off her armor, and Riony ran to her.

"Are you hurt? What's happening?" She looked up from the ground, so much smaller for once from Kess's high vantage point.

"Nothing's happening, which is the problem. Nothing is dying, nothing undead, anyway." Kess wanted to climb down to her, to hold her, but there was no time. She couldn't even reach her hand from her saddle.

Vance arrived then, taking up a perch on the other side of the tower, the stone cracking under the snowflame's claws. There was no space left for Hux to land. He circled above.

I will let them know our plans, Lyomir thought to Kess.

Vance adjusted his position on the saddle, shaking out one of his arms. "Why did you call us back in?"

"Were you managing to make any difference out there?" Kess asked in return.

He shook his head roughly. "Saved a few of our greener riders' lives, but if you mean in number of revs we actually stopped, I don't think we were doing a damned thing."

Kess took a deep breath and turned back to Riony. "It's time we use the summoning rune."

"Already? Are you sure?" Dashiel blanched, making a smudge of blood over their cheek stand out starkly.

Riony looked equally uncertain. "If this works the way we hope it will, we could lose every tamed dragon out there. Which, in case you forgot, is *every dragon,* except ours here."

Kess looked over the battle again, at all the riders who had abandoned their loyalty to the king in order to do the right thing, at all the riders who had remained loyal, but were out there fighting for their lives and others now anyway, at all the new and not nearly experienced enough riders they had brought from the undercity.

They could all die. Their dragons could all die.

They had prepared their own undercity riders as well as they could for this outcome. Kess had been amazed at how much Dracuni had given, how much the Alderkin had given, to make sure everyone had a chance to survive, but still, it was only a chance. And all the riders who weren't on their side that morning didn't even have that.

Kess sighed. "We can't stop the revenants as is, and this is our last chance. We have to weaken the shadow dragon if we want any hope to stop this army before it adds everybody in the capital below to its numbers. Whether this works or not, there's nothing else we can do."

Riony's head swayed almost drunkenly. The self-doubt in her eyes hurt Kess physically, and she had to clutch her saddle with white knuckles to stop from throwing herself down to hold her.

Riony's voice wavered as she asked, "And if it doesn't work? If the curse can't be reversed at all?"

Vance growled. "Then we are condemning every single rider and dragon here."

"They're already dead if we don't." Kess's eyes stayed pinned on Riony. "This is our only hope. This is what you've worked so hard for, to make this happen. Because you do believe it has a chance. Keep believing."

Riony's nostrils flared and her eyes glimmered wetly, but she reached to her belt pouch and drew out the summoning stone. Not the one they had taken to the undercity, altered to make tamed dragons unresponsive.

A new one, freshly carved by the Alderkin with the original summoning rune.

"Big dreams, bold deeds." After a long, steadying breath, Riony traced the rune, and the stone lit up in a rich green, like an unburned forest. She held it aloft over her head.

Beneath Kess, Lyomir stiffened and growled, head swinging sharply toward the crystal. Shiff and Dracuni followed, each of the wild dragons mesmerized by it, eyes locked and chests heaving and claws digging into the rooftop's stone as the magic drew their focus. Hux flew down from above, clinging to the side of the tower to get closer.

Lyomir? Kess called to him through their connection.

There was no reply, only a sense of urgency, need, command.

Dashiel looked from Shiff to the skies over the city. "How long is this going to take?"

Kess was about to reply when she followed Dashiel's gaze. From the direction of the palace, a small group of dragons flew their way. Three of normal size in red and white, led by one immense silver and gold beast.

The Dragon King.

Riony gave a forced laugh. "You don't think they're coming to help with the battle, do you?"

"Nope," Kess whispered, because nobody needed to hear it.

The king and his team's trajectory was clear. They were flying straight toward the tower. Straight for Dracuni, who remained stunned senseless by the summoning rune's power.

"The revs are scaling the walls." Lyrrin lowered her seeing stone. She didn't want to watch anymore.

Nasty creatures, Elumon thought. He had flown on his own for a while but was currently resting on Viska's back.

Lyrrin sat in her own saddle behind Eslinde, with Viska flying them carefully northeast toward the king's private palace, which took them within view of the capital and the army of revenants that marched upon it. The living corpses had moved so fast, like an avalanche of undead pouring across the ground.

When they first saw how close the army was to Draekhanhelm, Eslinde had even suggested they turn back, to warn the others, to help them as they would surely be entering that battle soon. But the rest of them agreed it was more important they continue on their mission.

And more important than ever that they find the king's silvernix, and fast.

Aishena, Benjin, and their mother flew on Ambri, just behind Viska.

Thin wisps of white hair, pulled free from a tight bun by the wind, whipped around Eslinde's flight goggles. "Are your sister and the others there yet?"

"I can't tell; we're too far away now. But there are a lot of dragons in the sky."

Elumon pressed his snout under Lyrrin's arm from behind, then snaked his neck around to look up at her.

Big dragon friends are coming. I hear them.

Lyrrin closed her eyes for a moment and the visions of the massive undead army, of all the human and animal revenants roaring for human blood, remained burned in her mind.

You worry?

Yes. I worry. We have to get the silvernix. They're going to need it.

"This is good, in a way." Eslinde turned around in her saddle to face Lyrrin. "All defenses will be sent to the capital. The private palace should be less guarded than usual."

Lyrrin chewed her lip. "Do you think the king will leave it completely unguarded, though, if the silvernix is there? Even if nobody else knows where it is, the king must keep some guards around."

Or maybe he just relied on it being secret. Everything the Rebel Riders could tell her about their time searching the place suggested minimal staff and security even in normal times.

Lyrrin's stomach churned. Something didn't feel right.

"We're going to be fine. We've got your magic and what almost amounts to three grayglims with us." Eslinde measured up Benjin with her eyes. "Maybe two and a half."

Lyrrin tried to smile in return but her lips twitched crookedly. Something nagged at the back of her thoughts.

Don't worry. I help too. Elumon tucked himself in at her side and put his head on her lap. His emotions felt just as worried and fearful as her own.

Lyrrin patted him distractedly.

Eslinde's brow furrowed, and she tilted her head. "How do you feel about having Lady Hjelzahn with us, after what she did to you?"

"What, stabbing me?" Lyrrin dismissed it with a wave of her ungloved hand. "She was possessed then. I don't think she's going to do it again. I'm more worried about her for Benjin and Aish."

"Do you think she's a threat to them?"

"No, I just don't think they quite got their mother back the way they wanted."

Despite having their mother with them and no longer trying to kill anyone of Draekhan bloodline, they'd all been sadder since.

Eslinde remained quiet for a long moment, looking over her shoulder at the Hjelzahn family on the dragon behind them. "I had a talk with Kverra …"

Lyrrin waited, and Eslinde paused for another long few seconds before continuing.

"She told me she doesn't know how to be a mother again, after everything she's done. She is mourning her husband, a son, and a daughter as though their deaths were fresh, deaths that were by her hand, even if not by her heart."

Lyrrin couldn't imagine how that must feel, to know you'd done something terrible, but against your own will. Nobody blamed Kverra herself, not really, but all of the hurt still remained.

Eslinde's voice grew softer, barely carrying over the wind. "She also told me she wasn't sure she ever knew how to be a mother. When her husband told her he wanted Aishena trained to be a grayglim too, Kverra had to stop being her mother entirely and become her mestra instead. She doesn't know how to be what her children need right now."

Lyrrin shrugged. "But it's easy. They just need her. I know she's sad right now and maybe that's making them all sad, but they just need her to be there."

Eslinde's face scrunched up as though in pain, and smoothed again.

Lyrrin glanced back at the Hjelzahns. Aishena rode up front, controlling the tamed dragon, with her mother behind and Benjin at the back. It seemed they rode in silence, but every few seconds, Aishena would turn back to check on her family.

Lyrrin said, "When I first met Lady Hjelzahn, in the depths, I could see how much Aishena wanted to trust her, how much she wanted her mother to be there for her."

Eslinde turned away to face their heading. She adjusted her flight goggles, wiping beneath them. "I feel as though it's rare for mothers to be everything they wish to be for their children. And even when so much is out of our control, it's too easy to feel as though we can never be forgiven for that."

Lyrrin's own eyes flushed wet as she watched the tense angles of her mother's thin frame. She leaned forward in her saddle and hugged around her waist from behind, pressing her cheek to Eslinde's back.

"I forgive you, for not being there when I was growing up. If you need that. But I was never angry at you. It was never your fault, and you came and found me as soon as you could. You left your kingdom behind for me!"

A restrained sob shook through Eslinde, and she half turned again, holding Lyrrin in return. "And I would do it again. You are *everything* to me. You have all your father's magic and wisdom, all of Riony's fire and temerity, all of the kindness and joy of the parents who raised you."

"And all of *your* courage and cleverness," Lyrrin squeezed her amma tight.

Eslinde laughed brightly. "Do you think so?"

"Of course!"

Eslinde kissed the top of her head. "Then we have everything we need to succeed."

Lyrrin smiled, but the worry nagging at her returned. The winter air was cool, and even a blazing afternoon sun didn't take the chill off as they flew, and it seemed to sink deep into Lyrrin's bones. In the distance, a high single spire emerged from the smoky haze. The Dragon King's private palace, Draekhan's Rest.

We're almost there. This has to work.

Elumon, put out at having had to move when Lyrrin hugged Eslinde, had curled up behind her again.

He lifted his head suddenly. **Something ... calls ...**

Beneath the saddles, Viska shivered strangely, then growled, long and low. Without warning, she turned sharply, back the way they'd come.

"Viska? Viska!" Eslinde yelled, but the golden dragon made no response.

"They've activated the summoning stone ... already?" Lyrrin gasped.

Elumon stretched out his neck, holding his horned head high.

Lyrrin prepared to throw herself bodily on the hatchling if he looked like he was going to take flight.

Are you okay? You aren't tempted to go?

It calls, but not for me.

Lyrrin sighed. Yrik had assured her that the summoning stone only summoned fully grown wild dragons. At no point in the past was it ever useful to them to summon hatchlings, and they would have considered it cruel to do so.

But they were still on Viska, being drawn in by the magic.

Aishena brought Ambri, tamed and unaffected by the call, around beside them. She yelled over the wind, "We need to get you off Viska, or you're going to end up back at the battle!"

Eslinde looked between the two dragons, then at the ground far below. "Oh, blessed sun."

Aishena called out, "I'm bringing Ambri in as close as I can."

"Maybe we should have made float runes for all of us too," Lyrrin mumbled through her fear.

With slow and careful movements, Aishena brough Ambri in from behind and above, laying the orange dragon's head and neck along one side of Viska's back, between her wings and close to Lyrrin's saddle.

Benjin and Kverra lashed cave silk ropes around them, then climbed down onto Viska's lower back, just at the start of her tail.

"Come down to us, Highnesses. We will help you up," Kverra called, clutching tight to her rope and swaying between the spines of the dragon's back.

"I'm right behind you," Eslinde said to Lyrrin with an encouraging nod.

Lyrrin brought her legs in beneath her and shifted around in her saddle. She didn't mind so much being up high on a dragon when she was seated comfortably and strapped in, but undoing the rope that secured her left her hands trembling.

Elumon stood beside her. ***I can fly, but I'll walk with you.***

Thank you. Lyrrin placed an arm around his neck and rose up to stand.

The dragon's spine ramped down like a path between a twin row of spikes, but fear trapped Lyrrin's feet.

Come on. It's only a few steps away.

She lifted one foot and stumbled awkwardly forward, clutching Elumon for stability. Gusts of air rocked the dragons like rowboats in a storm, threatening to tip Lyrrin over the edge.

Eslinde caught her by the back of her coat when she staggered too far to the left and brought her back to the middle again. Viska's golden scales shone like a second sun in the afternoon light, and Lyrrin felt dizzy as she slipped down the last couple of steps and into Kverra's waiting arms.

"Easy now. I'll boost you up. Ready?" Lady Hjelzahn's voice was commanding and even, but without the unearthly cold it had once held.

Lyrrin nodded once, then was lifted beneath her armpits up onto Kverra's shoulders. From there, Aishena reached down and pulled her the rest of the way up onto Ambri.

Heart pounding, Lyrrin dropped into one of the saddles and clutched it with rattling fingers. A moment later, Elumon flew behind her.

That was fun!

"Sure. Fun for those who have wings."

A scream pierced the air from below, making Lyrrin jolt upright. Viska was diving. With no warning, the golden dragon dropped out from beneath Ambri and the people standing on her back. The saddles all tugged to the side with the twang of rope.

"Amma!" Lyrrin leaned out from her saddle, and Aishena caught her, holding her from going too far.

She could see hands, clasped not far below, holding on to the dragon's side. A dark-skinned head with shorn white hair. Benjin.

"Where are the others?" Aishena bellowed as she reached down to haul him up.

Lyrrin's eyes followed the second rope, pulled taut, down, down ...

Kverra Hjelzahn swung at the end of it, with Eslinde caught around the waist.

Lyrrin gasped. "We have to pull them up!"

Benjin had reached the saddles, and once he secured himself, both he and Aishena grasped the remaining rope and pulled. But the angle lay wrong, making the spinning weight of the two women below hard to drag up.

Lyrrin tore open the pouch at her belt, dragging out two of the largest crystals she'd brought with her. Unmarked ones, ready for any contingency. She scratched out the symbols in a hurry—a float rune on each—and activated them.

She held them out to Elumon. "Can you take these down to them? One to Eslinde first, then to Kverra."

The hatchling cowered. *Me?*

Lyrrin could feel his fear woven between her own so the two were hard to distinguish. *Please, you're the only one who can.*

Elumon gave a solemn nod and grasped a purple glowing crystal in each of his front claws, then swooped down off Ambri's back. ***What if I can't? What if I can't?***

Lyrrin wasn't sure those thoughts were meant to reach her, but the hatchling's worried repetition came through clearly.

Eslinde and Kverra were spinning wildly at the end of the rope, and Kverra was using both hands and all her strength to keep a hold of Eslinde.

It took a few tries before Elumon could get close enough for Eslinde to reach. He would fly forward, then back out fearfully again as a leg almost smacked across his face. And it took longer again before Eslinde snatched the float crystal from him.

Benjin let out a whoop of celebration, but Lyrrin still held her breath.

The crystals were small. Only enough to reduce their body weight a little. But as Eslinde held her crystal, Kverra was able to readjust her hold on her, freeing up one of her arms. She caught the second crystal Elumon brought in to them.

"Pull!" Aishena ordered as soon as both women had a crystal in hand.

She and Benjin tried again, and the rope slid upward, reeling Eslinde and Kverra in. Elumon remained flying beside them, nudging them with his nose to keep them stable.

It felt like two long lifetimes before Eslinde and Kverra were on top of Ambri, panting as though they'd been drowning.

Eslinde crawled into the saddle beside Lyrrin and the two of them held each other fiercely.

Elumon landed behind them, shaking all over.

Lyrrin gave the hatchling a warm smile. *You saved them. Thank you!*

I saved them? His thoughts were still clouded with worry, but a tinge of pride broke through.

From over Eslinde's shoulder, Lyrrin thought she saw Benjin and Aishena move to embrace their mother as well. But then Aishena reached past her mother and brought Benjin up into the front saddle with her.

When Kverra sat in the middle saddle, Eslinde slapped a weary hand on to her shoulder.

"I am in your debt," she said.

Kverra shook her head, braided hair swinging. "Your highness, it is my duty."

"Duty or otherwise, I'm glad to have you here with us. I think we all are."

Aishena brought Ambri circling around in a slow glide back toward the private palace again.

She cast a quick glance over her shoulder. "We will be glad if we all stay alive for the rest of our mission."

"I am sure that will be the most excitement we'll see." Eslinde handed the float crystal back to Lyrrin, but Lyrrin refused it.

"Hold on to it, just in case."

Eslinde huffed a small laugh. "Well, the private palace isn't far ahead. We'll be back on the ground soon."

The nagging worry awakened in Lyrrin again. "Did you ever look for the silvernix there?"

"Not myself. I was never interested to find it. Some of the other heirs did, though. Ylva had a few times and never found anything. But they didn't know what we know."

"Kverra? Did you ever spend time there? See anything?" Lyrrin asked warily from how her questioning had gone last time.

Lady Hjelzahn remained stoic, with only her voice betraying her with a crack of emotion. "I did stalk the king there, a number of times, in my ... attempts to kill him."

A muscle in her jaw jumped. "But he was never alone, thank the sun's blessing. He would oversee mining that was being done there, but never alone. He didn't even fly his dragon there alone. He always brought grayglims with him."

Lyrrin's mind raced. It didn't make sense. If the Dragon King was the only person who knew where the silvernix was, then he'd have to be alone when he went there.

"Was there *anywhere* you ever saw him alone?"

"If there was, he wouldn't still be alive," Kverra said flatly. "There was only one place he ever went into entirely alone, and it was always too heavily guarded from the outside."

Lyrrin's eyes popped wide. There was only one place. A place she had seen him remain alone in.

She called out over the gusting wind in a rush, "We're going the wrong way!"

Riony scanned the horizon all around, seeking any sign that the summoning stone had worked. Apart from keeping Dracuni, Lyomir, Shiff, and Hux lured in by its compulsion, there weren't yet any signs of other wild dragons approaching.

What if they've already moved too far away and aren't coming?

Only the Dragon King on his massive dragon, followed by three more, were flying toward them fast.

"We have to get Dracuni out of here." Riony still clutched the summoning stone in one hand and hauled herself hastily onto the unidragon's back.

But Dracuni didn't respond to her urgency to leave.

Kess leaned over Lyomir's neck, looking equally worried. "I don't think any of our dragons are moving while the summoning stone is activated. They can't think about anything else."

"Then deactivate it!" Jaym yelled from the side of the tower where Hux clung, hanging vertically.

His pocket-hawk flittered around the red dragon, making Riony flinch away. She was glad she hadn't been asked to go out into the aerial battle with the revs before. *So many birds. Ew.*

Dashiel brought the tamed shimmerdart they rode in close and extended an arm out to Riony. "If we deactivate it too soon, the wild dragons won't come all the way into the battle. But we can still keep away from the king. Throw me the crystal."

Riony did without hesitation. "What are you going to do?"

Catching the glowing green stone, Dashiel shrugged and half smiled. "The dragons will follow it, right? So let them follow it."

The white dragon's wings thrust down powerfully, sending it and Dashiel shooting into the sky. A second later, Dracuni jolted forward, launching off the tower as well and into pursuit.

Riony shot a glance over her shoulder. Kess and Lyomir, Jaym and Hux, and Shiff on her own were all flying after the summoning stone as well. Vance, on Kife's old snowflame, went the other way toward where the Dragon King and his riders weren't far behind.

He must be trying to buy us some time. It was foolish, though. The snowflame couldn't breathe fire anymore. Kife had burned it out with misuse.

Vance and the white dragon rushed headlong at the pursuers, weaving like an eel through water as the first gust of fire from the king's massive silver and gold etherflame burst around them. One of the three riders with the king broke off, chasing Vance, but the rest remained on target.

There wasn't much Riony could do other than hold on tight. Dracuni and the other mesmerized dragons chased after Dashiel and the crystal as though their lives depended on it. And maybe they did.

And all their lives were in Dashiel's hands.

Come on, keep us away from the king, just a little longer.

Dashiel led them on a winding chase through the city, skirting between towers fluidly, bringing the trail of wild dragons behind them. The king's huge beast barreled after them, less agile but unstoppable. It hit a spire, sending shattered stone crashing down onto the streets below, and it didn't even slow down.

They were away from the larger battle with the revenants, but some of the flying undead had crossed the walls and circled around, flying down to pick off any human foolish enough to still be outside.

Dashiel kept them moving at a dizzying pace, and the Dragon King remained close behind, his dragon's wings beating like rhythmic thunder. *Fwoomp, fwoomp, fwoomp.*

Dashiel must have decided to change tact, lose the larger mass of the king's dragon with an uphill climb as they all shot higher at a steep angle toward the ashy clouds above.

A swarm of undead bugs hit Riony and she swatted them away as they picked at the skin of her face and tried to dig through her armor. Clearing the air again, she squinted out to the horizon. More flying revs? Or …

A dark shape flew straight at her, dropping in from above. The living corpse of a carrion bird, as big as a Dracuni, claws outstretched as it aimed for Riony.

Terror zinged through her limbs and her face twisted in disgust. She dropped sideways in her saddle, hanging out to the side by her fingernails, to avoid the collision. The flash of sharp beak and rotten feathers as it shot past left Riony shuddering.

Gross, gross, gross!

Then a short, sharp yelp came from below her, followed by a longer scream in an all too familiar voice.

"Kess!"

Riony whipped around in time to see the carrion bird rip Kess from her saddle. Lyomir didn't even blink, continuing after the summoning stone.

The revenant flapped hard as it angled its head around, trying to peck at the prey it had captured. Its beak clacked against the float rune on Kess's back, then ripped it free. The unactivated stone hurtled sickeningly down. Kess cried out again, dangling and twisting in the revolting creature's grasp, so high above the city below.

A hum of fury and fear roared through Riony.

She gritted her teeth, gave Dracuni one final concerned look, then she jumped.

Riony plunged toward Kess, dodging Lyomir as he flew up past her, making the air swirl and buffet against her. Through her flight goggles, Riony could see Kess swing her glowing yellow cutting athame. But even if she could strike a blow that would kill the awful thing, it would only leave Kess falling faster.

In a burst of ashy feathers, Riony hit the revenant. The impact sent all three of them spinning through the air.

The rev's wings whipped hard, now with twice the burden, trying to keep them all airborne but caring more about tearing its prey apart than falling. Heart pounding and hating every second, Riony grasped at the horrible creature's body, climbing around it until she could reach Kess in its claws beneath.

"Riony?" Kess gasped.

"Fancy … meeting you … here," Riony ground out between panting breaths and gritted teeth.

She wrapped one arm around Kess, and with the other, she wrestled against the scaly gray legs that were dug into Kess's delver armor. Riony pulled one claw free, which then lashed out and scratched her across the face. Pain lanced over Riony's forehead, and her flight googles were pulled free, falling out of reach.

The cutting athame flashed, parting the bird from its other foot, and then Riony and Kess fell again.

"Riony!"

Kess's hair whipped in Riony's face as she kept her clutched tight against her chest.

"Activate my sword! Can you reach it?" Riony screamed over the rushing air and lifted Kess higher over her shoulder.

The rooftops of the city below raced toward them. Riony's hands shook as she held Kess, terrified more of losing her grip than what awaited them on the ground below if Kess couldn't reach the rune.

"Got it!" Kess yelled, and a purple glow illuminated around them. Their descent slowed, but not by enough. With the weight of both of them and the speed they were already moving, Riony guessed they'd just downgraded from imminent death to immense pain.

A dark, red-tiled roof came up beneath them. Riony angled her legs toward it and held Kess cradled in both arms.

Tiles cracked as they hit, and a horrific crunch came from Riony's first leg to land. It buckled beneath her and the second leg twisted awkwardly and she did everything she could not to crush Kess as they went rolling over each other across the roof.

The pain hit before they came to a stop in a clatter of ceramic shards. Redness blurred Riony's vision from the blood in her eyes.

Hissing air through her teeth instead of screaming, Riony lay on her back, her crystal sword still glowing and uncomfortable beneath her.

She reached an arm out for where Kess had come to a stop beside her. "Kess? Kessara!"

Hands found hers. "Stay still!"

She's okay. She made it. The words pounded in time to her heartbeat.

"Are you hurt?" she asked through a whimper.

Broken roof tiles clinked and clattered away as Kess shifted closer. "Am *I* hurt. Am *I* hurt? You absolute maniac. You didn't even … and it was a *bird* … and … I would slap you for doing something so foolish if your pain wasn't the sole cause of my own."

"I wasn't losing you. No matter what." Riony grinned weakly. "Of course I'd fall for a girl like you."

Kess's hands moved around Riony, brushing rubble off, and at least once, pulling a piece out from where it was jammed into her armor. "Stop using all your energy on being so razing charming, or I may still slap you."

"Weird way to propose. But yes."

"I'd say you were delirious, but you're just being you." Kess tsked and brushed a finger through Riony's hair before her hands moved away again.

Riony rolled off her sword and onto her side. Pressing up onto one elbow with a groaning wince, she worked to wipe the blood from her eyes. Across the other side of the city, the smudgy shapes of dragons continued their chase.

Kess leaned over her, pushing her back onto the roof with a hand on her sternum. "I said, stay still."

"I need to get back to Dracuni."

"I know. But you're not going anywhere like this. Your legs are bending in unnatural ways."

"Are you flirting … with me …?" A wave of pain engulfed Riony and her words petered out.

A soft kiss brushed over one of Riony's cheeks, and a hand cupped the other. In a gentle voice, Kess whispered, "Stay. Still."

And then the familiar coolness of silvernix dropped onto Riony's forehead.

As the magic kicked in, Riony bucked upward as far as the sword strapped beneath her allowed. She cried out and Kess caught her, holding her through the pain. Light exploded around them, shimmering from Riony's skin as Dracuni's bottled blood wrought her whole again with a violence equal to the fall that had broken her apart.

Riony pressed her face to Kess's, foreheads and noses squashed together as though they could merge into one and then lips followed, kissing over a closed mouth scream drenched in starlight.

Because the pain was nothing, nothing at all, if it meant Kess was still there with her.

As the glow faded, the two of them remained panting, mouth to mouth.

"You need to get back to Dracuni," Kess whispered.

"Yeah." Riony stretched her legs out, testing them and glad to find them both still whole.

She rolled sideways to unpin her sword from beneath her, then rose to her knees.

Scrubbing her eyes clear, she gave Kess a long look, making sure she wasn't secretly injured as well. Some of the leather of her delver armor had been torn, but there was no sign of blood pooling. Kess's flight goggles lay on the roof beside her, along with the dismembered bird claw. *Yuck.*

In Kess's hand was her spent vial of silvernix.

Riony moved to pick Kess up, but Kess shook her head.

"I'll only slow you down. I'll be fine here, and once the summoning stone is done with, Lyomir will come for me. But you need to go and help Dracuni, now!"

Riony grunted, turning between Kess and the distant dragon chase. The king was right on top of Dracuni and the others. Dashiel was doing their best to keep away, but that was all they could do. They had no other defenses, and Vance hadn't returned to help either.

Riony drew her sword into one hand and gave Kess a pained look.

"Go," Kess urged.

Riony threw herself back toward Kess, catching her in a long, bruising kiss, forcing into that moment every hope and wish and dream that the two of them would somehow make it out of this, that this wouldn't be the last time they touched, the message that Riony loved her with a depth greater than the darkest caves and higher than any dragon flew.

Each of them had only been rationed a single dose of silvernix each. Riony slipped hers into her hand, then pressed it into Kess's. "Stay alive for me. I'm not losing you. Not today, not ever."

Then they broke apart, and Riony ran.

She skidded down the slope of the broken tiled roof and launched off the edge, flying high over the rooftops below with the power of her sword's float rune and her own strength.

The shapes and layout of the city below were so unfamiliar, but years of navigating the undercity roofscape had made that method of travel second nature. She bolted across flat ridges and kicked off tower walls, keeping her footing as she spotted the next safe landing and leaped forward again.

The float rune kept her moving fast, gliding over the ghost-town streets of the capital, where only the occasional flicker of movement passed beneath. Humans still seeking shelter and the flying revenants who had moved in to hunt.

Even those revs are ripping through everything they can find. If the rest of them get in …

Riony searched the skies again as the battle around the walls raged.

Dashiel was bringing Iffyr and the following dragons swooping down again. They weren't far ahead, and Riony tensed, sprinting faster. One of the smaller dragons along with the king was shooting down like an arrow at Dracuni.

Catapulting herself off a rooftop, Riony arched through the air and intercepted the rider with a knee to the face.

The man swung in his saddle from the blow. He wore grayglim armor, and a sharp curse word betrayed his surprise, but that didn't stop him from getting a dagger into his hand and bringing it up to where Riony clung on to him.

She fell backward onto the dragon's neck to dodge the strike, and the tamed dragon jolted, confused by the apparent jumble of orders. The grayglim readjusted, bringing the dragon from its dive into a flat glide, then he drew a second, longer blade.

From on her back, Riony kicked out both feet into the man's chest before he could swing his sword her way. He lifted from his seat, knocked into an uncontrollable somersault down the length of the dragon and off the end of its tail.

Riony scrambled upright again and into the saddle. She sheathed her still glowing sword onto her back and pivoted around to gauge the current situation.

The tamed dragon beneath her was continuing on with its last command, taking her away from the chase with Dracuni and the king and out into the larger battle again. Riony poked at the creature's neck the way she'd been taught, but the red and white dragon didn't respond.

"Sparks, turn around!" Riony yelled.

Had it been trained differently somehow? The dragon wasn't responding to anything Riony had been instructed on in the event she found herself alone on a tamed dragon again. But Dashiel had said not all dragons were taught to respond to the same orders. Different trainers had different methods.

She was only getting farther and farther away from Dracuni, who still had the king and one other rider chasing her.

I could go back over the rooftops again … Riony looked down, her eye caught by movement.

A flood of revenants spilled over the keep's walls and through the streets below. Panic filled Riony as she got her bearings.

Where was Kess? Where did she leave Kess? She spotted the rooftop. It wasn't far from there, and a horde of revenants plowed that way. And Kess didn't have Lyomir, she didn't have Griskin. She was trapped.

Riony roared, trying to physically turn the dragon's neck to change its direction.

A shadow darkened Riony, and she braced for the attack of another flying revenant.

The blow didn't come. The attacker instead smashed down onto the tamed dragon's head, a writhing bundle of green scales and leathery wings, screeching in wild fury.

CHAPTER TWENTY-FOUR

The first few wild dragons were visible on the horizon as Aishena flew Ambri toward the capital. By the time Lyrrin could hear the battle raging around the keep, the sky was filled with scores of untamed dragons brought in by the summoning crystal.

The calling has stopped now, Elumon informed Lyrrin.

She nodded, a little dazed. The summoning stone had done its job. The others must have deactivated it once all those wild dragons were close enough.

Lyrrin was awed at the sheer number of them. *Riony did so much over the last few weeks, untamed so many dragons in factories around the capital!*

This was good and bad.

It was good because the plan was working exactly the way they had hoped it would. All the recently untamed dragons were drawn in, and they were behaving the same way Lyomir had when presented with tamed dragons. They were attacking and trying to pull the taming stakes from their kin.

It was also bad, because the plan was working exactly the way they had hoped.

And because Ambri was still tamed.

There were easily as many newly wild and wrathful dragons as there were tamed ones with riders, and they were throwing themselves into a wrestling, midair battle with each one they could catch. Piercing shrieks cut through the sounds of beating wings and screaming riders.

Flying revenants tangled within the chaos as colorful dragons swirled and chased each other, and the shadow dragon loomed far overhead, circling like the promise of death to all below.

In the middle saddle, Kverra Hjelzahn stared up at the creature, her expression blank, dark eyes edged red with emotion.

Lyrrin pulled her own gaze away from the mourning spirit and back to the battle ahead. She watched, her jaw dropping, as they flew closer.

"Riony will be fine. She's on Dracuni; the untamed dragons shouldn't go after her." Eslinde, still in the saddle with Lyrrin, gave her a squeeze around the shoulder. But a deep frown cut a line between her eyebrows.

Vance was on a tamed dragon, and so was Dashiel. Lyrrin didn't need Eslinde to say it to know that's what she was thinking. Or about their own risk on Ambri.

"I'm going to have to take us through that if we want to reach the palace," Aishena yelled over her shoulder.

"Do you think you can?" Eslinde held Lyrrin a little tighter.

"Do you want to turn around?" Aishena shot back.

"No, we need to do this," Lyrrin replied.

"Then we're going to find out." Aishena's angular shoulders lifted up around her silver hair as she leaned closer to Ambri and brought them into the battle.

So many creatures. Elumon tucked in close behind Lyrrin, shivering.

Lyrrin braced as Ambri suddenly flung left, almost tossing her from her saddle. Snapping dragon teeth filled her vision, then were gone just as fast, replaced with the flutter of fetid feathers. A flock of undead birds trailed across their path, and Benjin sliced three of the smaller ones from the sky with his twin blades to clear them away from Aishena.

Lyrrin knocked a final one away from her and Eslinde with her crystal staff.

It didn't fall, just swirled around in the air behind them, then sought a new target.

There are still so many revs. Aren't they burning yet? Lyrrin turned her face upward to the shadow dragon. Thin streams of inky darkness swirled down from the entity like reversed smoke, seeking dragons whose spikes had been torn free.

One etherflame, head bloodied and body limp, fell from the sky directly in front of them, and Aishena swerved Ambri steeply to avoid hitting it.

Across to the right, another dragon lit up brightly as their rider used their provided dose of silvernix on it, preventing it from dying midair from the open wound in its brain. A second, smaller glow of purple lit up as that rider then bailed with their float stone from the dragon's back as it roared furiously.

But only the riders who had come with them from the undercity had silvernix and knew what to do with it. None of the other riders were prepared for this assault. Lerris's team had been given float runes, but didn't know why, didn't know what was coming.

They had argued for days about whether or not they could trust them with the plan and the silvernix needed to save their dragons, but it hadn't mattered anyway. There wasn't enough time to provide Dracuni's blood to them all.

That's why we have to find the king's supply. Now.

The palace came within sight, the half-circle structure of it looking like a broken jaw lying in the middle of the keep. Aishena brought them lower, cutting through the streets and around towers to lose a massive dark-red flamesong on their tail.

The ground below churned, streets filled with revenants of all shapes and sizes, charging and tumbling over each other as they encroached into every part of the keep, seeking human blood. They skittered over rooftops and piled against doorways and gates until the sheer mass of them crashed through.

Screams echoed up from within buildings.

Eslinde watched in horror and turned Lyrrin's face away from it when she saw that she was watching as well.

"Flight deck is up ahead," Aishena barked. "Hold tight, we're coming in fast!"

Another dragon emerged from the cavernous entrance, blue and white, rushing toward them, spear like. Aishena turned Ambri, but the other dragon also turned away, fleeing past them.

The blue and white dragon angled out toward the harbor. The flamesong that had been tailing Ambri turned on it and snatched it from the air within its claws. It brought the blue and white dragon, and its riders, crashing down beneath its weight onto a rooftop below.

Eslinde swiveled around to watch with a gasp. "That was Prysha's dragon … my sister …"

"Nothing we can do. Hold on!" Aishena ordered again, and the orange ash-tinted sunlight vanished as they went into the flight deck.

The vast polished stone floor screeched beneath Ambri's claws as they skidded down the length of the space. Lyrrin thrust forward, bumping into Kverra's back, and Elumon tumbled against Lyrrin's as Eslinde tried to hold them all steady.

They all lurched forward again as Ambri came to a complete stop.

"You did it! We made it!" Lyrrin cheered, pulling off her flight goggles.

"I won't ever question your flying again," Eslinde sighed the words out.

"Or anything else, I should hope," Aishena muttered as she slipped from her saddle and leaped gracefully to the ground.

Kverra remained silent as she followed, but a small half smile appeared on her lips, vanishing as fast as smoke dispersed in the wind.

Eslinde brushed Lyrrin's darkened hair back from where it had stuck to her temples around the goggles.

They had no more time to recover from the flight or landing as their presence raised a rally of cries in the flight deck.

Ambri had stopped a fair distance into the space, not far from where a mid-sized silver and red dragon was being loaded up with luggage.

A half dozen grayglims stood guard around a dark-haired woman in their midst. The queen.

Her utterly repulsed expression as she stared back showed she had identified those on the orange dragon in return. "What are *you* doing here?"

Eslinde helped Lyrrin down from the dragon, then stared back at her mother, hard-eyed. "We're not packing up and running, which it seems is what you're doing."

Hissing her disgust, the queen waved both arms as though shooing animals.

Addressing her grayglims, she snapped, "Go on, get them! Clear these intruders out of our way!"

The six grayglims broke into motion, rushing their way.

"You know the drill," Lyrrin called out, lobbing a crystal toward the gray-armored guards in an underarm throw.

Eslinde, Aishena, Benjin, and Kverra closed their eyes, and Elumon covered his face with a wing as the flash stone burst with bright light in front of the charging grayglims. Lyrrin's vision glowed red through her eyelids, and she waited for it to fade before looking again.

Queen Vellira cried out, covering her streaming eyes with both hands, and the guards slowed their approach, faces grim as their gazes searched blindly for their opponents.

Elumon crouched into a pouncing pose but shuffled backward behind Lyrrin rather than forward. *I fight?*

The little hatchling's inner voice was tinged with fear.

No, leave it to the others.

Aishena, Benjin, and Kverra danced in between the grayglims with deadly silence. The hilts of swords and unlit athames cracked into vital places—knees, sternums, the backs of heads—and grayglims fell in a tumble.

Five were down, when the sixth, panicked at the sound of falling bodies, lashed out with a wild thrust of his sword. It was luck alone that meant Aishena had her back in line with the attack.

"Watch out!" Benjin yelled.

Aishena spun toward the threat, then a body collided with her side, pushing her away from the thrusting blade. The length of the sword instead clinked against scale mail and sank into Kverra's stomach.

"Mami!" Aishena gasped the word and downed the final guard with a cracking blow to his jaw.

Lyrrin ran to join Benjin and Aishena as they dropped beside their fallen mother.

"What's happening?" Vellira cried, turning around blindly. "Do you have them?"

"No. We have you." Eslinde stepped in front of the queen, tapping the point of her thin epee against her chest until she stilled.

Kverra had both hands clutched over her stomach. As Aishena pried them away, Lyrrin expected to find the wound clean and dry, the way Kverra's body had been while she was possessed, only half alive and unbleeding.

But as fingers were drawn back, a spill of red oozed from the deep wound.

Aishena hissed. "I was going to parry that blow. *You* should have been able to parry that blow. What were you thinking?"

Kverra turned her face to the side, jaw tensed.

Aishena grasped her mother's chin, turning her back, not gently.

Her voice trembled as it rose, loud enough to echo within the flight deck. "Did you think you could go out in some heroic moment and be absolved of all your guilt? All you would have done was take yet another member of our family from us!"

Kverra's dark eyes flashed, and her head shook with small motions of denial.

Aishena's expression grew cold and still again. "We all have silvernix with us. You're not dying today, as much as you may have wanted to."

Benjin was already rummaging through his belt pouch.

"Don't use your own. Save it. We have some more available right here," Eslinde called over.

She stepped closer to the queen and brought a hand to the golden necklace hanging over her collarbones. With a quick tug, she tore it free and tossed it over to Aishena.

Kverra coughed, and a small splatter of blood sprayed. She choked on her words. "I'm ... sorry."

Aishena examined the necklace, then pulled free a small vial from within the gem-encrusted pendant. "Don't be sorry. Just *be here*. For us."

Benjin put his arm around Aishena as she applied the silvernix to their mother, and the woman's dark skin shimmered with light.

Vellira inhaled in outraged. "That was mine!"

Lyrrin remained kneeling beside the healing woman and yelled back at the queen, "You shouldn't be using it anyway if you're pregnant."

Vellira's eyes narrowed and her back went ramrod straight. "You think I am?"

"Surely, you wouldn't be, given there were meant to be no more first heirs, even before me." Eslinde circled the woman who barely seemed older than her, trailing the point of her blade after her. "Or did you and Fadda decide it was time to start out fresh?"

"My husband makes his own decisions. If he or others think I am pregnant, all the better for me to be included in his decisions." Vellira shrugged carelessly as she eyed Eslinde's sword. "Your king, our Dragon King, will be back soon, and you will suffer for mistreating me when he returns."

Eslinde stilled then and shared a worried look with Lyrrin. "Where is he now?"

"He has taken his dragon to help with the battle."

Lyrrin scoffed. There was only one thing out there the king cared about.

Dracuni.

Please don't let him catch her.

Vellira continued, haughtily. "But he will be coming back for me soon, so he can protect me when we leave, together."

The glow of the silvernix healing Kverra faded, and Aishena and Benjin helped their mother back to her feet.

"Leave to where?" Kverra straightened but didn't push out of her children's hold. She locked eyes with the queen. "All the years I gave to being a grayglim warden, to protecting the Draekhan line, only to see now this is all you are ... Cowards who would flee their people when things are most dire."

"We are not cowards! We are only doing what is sensible."

Lyrrin imagined her grandfather, out within that mess of revenants and wild dragons and other riders, and Riony and Dracuni, and all the damage he had done or could yet do to the world and those Lyrrin loved.

All he had ever shown any care for was finding his new source of silvernix, of maintaining his health, youth, power. But also that of his wife. The only other thing Lyrrin had seen him care for.

Standing up, Lyrrin called Elumon to her side and nodded to Eslinde. "We have to keep moving. Bring her with us. She could be useful if the king does return."

Eslinde quirked an eyebrow, but acquiesced, giving her mother a small shove on the shoulder to get her moving. She led the way at a swift march into the corridors of the palace.

The queen huffed petulantly. "Where are you taking me? What are you even doing here?"

"We've come to take all of my grandfather's silvernix," Lyrrin declared.

Vellira loosed a cackling chuckle. "And you think it's here? Don't be ridiculous. He doesn't keep more than a small supply in the palace at any time."

"You're right," Lyrrin agreed. "He doesn't keep it all here. But we are in the right place."

Lyrrin had explained her thoughts on where to go to Eslinde and the others on the flight, and Eslinde had agreed it was promising. The only place the Dragon King was ever alone. A room well-guarded and barred, where only a few select people had ever stepped within.

A room which held broken remnants of Alderkin magic that may not have been as broken as first appearances suggested.

They hurried for the silvernix chamber, Eslinde leading them confidently through the long glossy corridors of dark stone.

The palace was empty of the usual bustle of guards and nobles, and as Lyrrin became familiar with where they were, she took the lead. They rounded the next corner, and in the eerie cold light of the dragon-powered lamps, a mixture of strangely shaped figures shambled at the other end of the hall.

Low growls filled the air, and clacking, skeletal heads swiveled their way.

The revenants had reached the palace.

Chapter Twenty-Five

Riony clung to the saddle of the red and white dragon she'd commandeered as it pinwheeled out of control. The tamed dragon wasn't responding to any of her commands. Even if she could work out how to ride the thing, her efforts were entirely hampered by the wild dragon wrapping itself around her dragon's head.

The gold-green treedart was one Riony remembered from one of her factory missions. Most of the dragons they'd untamed were etherflames, etherdarts, and flamesongs—good firebreathers used for smelting.

But one glass factory had a whole team of treedarts that were being used to haul sand from an adjoining quarry. It had infuriated Riony, seeing the powerful creatures being used that way. Tamed and enslaved, just to be beasts of burden.

The treedart didn't appear to recognize her or care one bit that there was a human clinging to the red and white dragon it attacked.

It only seemed to care about ridding that tamed dragon of the spike that kept it enslaved.

Which is great. Just great. Exactly what we were hoping for. Except I wasn't meant to be on a tamed dragon when it was happening.

She didn't even have a dose of silvernix anymore to heal the poor red and white dragon with once the treedart got its stake out, and she wasn't looking forward to falling down into the revenant army below along with it.

Dizziness swirled through Riony as they continued circling in a horizontal corkscrew and it was all she could do to hold on. Her flight goggles had been lost earlier, and the bitter, cold wind left her eyes watering. She wiped them clear.

All around, more dragons arrived. Dozens and dozens. Riony had counted their efforts with the factory dragons at around one hundred freed, and it seemed as though almost that many had responded to the summoning stone.

Dashiel must have deactivated it when they saw it had worked, because the wild dragons weren't all flying the same way toward it. They were careening throughout the battle in every direction, seeking their targets.

Riony stared, aghast. *Whose tamebrain idea was it to bring one hundred wild and angry dragons bent on ripping the taming stakes from their kin into the most tame-dragon dense area in the land?*

Oh right, it was mine.

It had seemed like a good idea, at first. What better way to quickly untame dragons en masse than recruiting dragons to do it for them?

But the reality of it was a bloodbath.

Spatters of dragon blood rained over Riony as the green treedart shrieked. The red and white dragon finally stabilized. Riony sighed with relief, then ducked as a ball of fire shot over her head.

She shook off the dizziness and tried to get her bearings. If the summoning stone was no longer activated ...

Dracuni? Riony cried loud in her mind.

Where are you, big sister?

Green wings flapped, clipping Riony's shoulder as the treedart flew away, and Riony realized why her dragon had stopped spinning. A deep hole showed in the middle of its forehead, and it hung limply in the sky for another moment before its wings crumpled in and they plummeted together.

I'm on a red and white dragon, near the walls, going down fast!

Riony clung to her glowing sword, looking for a place to jump to safety, but the sky was a riot of tangled dragons and revenants.

I see you!

Dodging beside a whopping flamesong, Dracuni burst into view, racing after the falling dragon and Riony. With three long steps across the red and white scales, Riony leaped high into the air.

Dracuni ducked beneath her, and Riony caught her saddle as she came over the top.

Getting herself properly seated, Riony patted Dracuni's neck. "Nice catch."

Sorry I didn't come sooner. One of the king's riders was still chasing me.

Riony checked behind them. "Nobody there at the moment. I think you lost them. But we should deal with that dragon ahead of us. I couldn't heal it. I don't have my silvernix anymore."

Why? What did you do to yourself this time?

"Nothing. I gave it to Kess." Riony shied away from the details.

With a surge of determination, Dracuni dove fast toward the red and white dragon. As she came up behind it, the unidragon huffed a short burst of silvery fire, lighting the injured beast up just as it crashed down into the revenants below.

Hopefully they soften its landing. Revenants rarely went after dragons and animals. Only humans. With the hole in its head healed, the red and white would have a good chance of surviving.

"Where's Lyomir?" Riony yelled over the rush of flying, worried to her core about someone else's chances of surviving.

Flew away fast when the summoning stopped calling us.

Did he get to Kess? Has he got her?

I can't hear him now. Too many voices.

"Sparks," Riony grunted.

They were out within the main battle now, far from the rooftops of the keep where Riony had left Kess. *I should have brought her with me. I never should have let her go.*

Riony wanted to ask Dracuni to take her there, to go back and make sure that the revs crawling through the city hadn't found Kess, but she couldn't. She knew their place was right there, within the heart of the chaos.

It was the only reason Dracuni had been brought into the battle at all.

To save as many dragon lives as they could.

Gritting her teeth, Riony pulled her focus away from the deep ache in her heart toward the work before them. She scanned the messy skies.

"That way, the yellow etherflame!"

Dracuni shot toward the falling dragon, catching it in a short puff flame.

It revived quickly, wings swishing wildly as it got the air back under it again. Another two dragons followed in quick succession as Dracuni pitched up and down through the air between them.

A familiar purple and icy-blue treedart came in beside them, followed by a white shimmerdart.

Dashiel waved, beaming from its back. "You're okay!"

Riony gave a casual salute in return. "Thank you for keeping Dracuni okay, too."

"And Kess?"

Swallowing hard, Riony kept her eyes away from the keep and the revenants crawling all over it. "Survived the fall. Fine the last I saw her. Where are the others?"

"Vance and I have mostly been playing keep-away with the wild dragons. Luckily, the Dragon King also backed off when the wild dragons came in. A heap of them went straight after his dragon." Dashiel pointed out over the harbor where the silver and gold monstrosity circled.

A couple of smaller dragons still harried it, like owlettes trying to bring down a bovin. The tamed dragon moved almost with the speed and precision of those who could control their own actions. Riony figured that synergy between beast and rider must have come with eighty odd years of the king flying it.

Its head swiveled fast, snapping efficiently at its attackers, catching them in its teeth.

"Haven't seen Jaym since the summoning rune stopped. I was over the city a moment ago. The revs have reached the palace. The whole city is filled with them. If they don't start burning soon ..."

"Then we're all totally boned." Riony didn't bother yelling that loud enough for Dashiel to hear.

She still held on to the tiny scrap of hope that this madness was going to work. That all the dragons around them being forcibly untamed would be enough. Enough to finally weaken the shadow dragon's curse.

All throughout the sky, dragons were lighting up with the healing power of silvernix. That alone filled Riony with pride and awe that those from the undercity who had been entrusted with Dracuni's blood for that very purpose actually followed through.

Everyone there knew exactly how high the stakes were.

And with each healed dragon, another curling shadow was threaded free from the shadow dragon above.

Riony could still feel the heavy weight of the entity's mourning, trying to infect her.

The glow of float runes from riders having to bail from newly wild dragons also peppered the battle.

They had provided those crystals to every rider they could, undercity and Mestra Lerris's riders alike. They would be saved from falls, but that didn't help them a whole lot when they were falling into an army of revenants below.

A purple glow of a falling rider passed in front of them.

Dashiel signaled their goodbye. "I'll catch that one. Good luck!"

"Stay safe!" Riony and Dracuni turned the other way, racing toward another wounded dragon.

A giant bat revenant screeched, coming for Riony as Dracuni puffed her healing breath again. Lighting up her sword with the burn rune, Riony swatted the horrible creature away. Its dry, leathery wings caught alight, and it fell away in a trail of smoke.

Riony watched as carefully as she could through stinging eyes, trying to tell whether the revenant was falling because it had expired from the burning or whether it just didn't have enough wing left unburned to remain airborne.

As Dracuni healed another dragon and another, Riony's chest tightened over her thumping heart. There were so many to heal. All of Mestra Lerris's team and all the dragons from riders still loyal to the king didn't have silvernix or any idea what was happening and why.

They were the ones who most needed Dracuni's help, but it also meant with every breath of healing flame, Dracuni was exposing herself and what she could do to everyone who could see.

There was no coming back from this.

The next dragon Dracuni healed was a familiar snowflame.

"Vance?" Riony yelled.

She could see no sign of him falling alongside the snowflame. Riony craned around, checking all the nearby dragons and revenants Dracuni dodged through. A flash of gold streaked by.

Viska's back. Dracuni's thoughts were edged with exhaustion.

Lyrrin and Eslinde aren't with her? Riony panicked, worried they'd activated the stone too soon and brought the others back along with the golden dragon.

No. Just Viska. She has Vance.

Dracuni was breathing hard, her wingbeats arrhythmic and weak.

Riony ran a hand down her neck, finding it feverish. "We can stop whenever you need to. You've already saved so many."

Dracuni snorted. ***What would you say if I said that to you?***

Riony scrunched her nose and then steeled herself. "That there are still so many more to save. Just ... small puffs, okay? Conserve your strength."

Dracuni raced on to heal her next target. Riony caught glimpses of Hux and Jaym a couple of times, catching falling riders. She still had yet to see Kess and Lyomir.

Riony lost count of how many more dragons Dracuni revived. The unidragon moved sluggishly, her eyelids drooping over lilac eyes. Riony clenched her teeth over her words of worry, wishing she could infuse the unidragon with her own energy, her own life, the way Dracuni had so often done for her.

Riony felt Dracuni's guilt and pain as she didn't reach a sunflower yellow dragon she was heading for in time and it crashed hard to the ground below.

There were too many obstacles in the air, and the more tired Dracuni got, the harder it was to navigate.

A flock of smaller revenants blocked their way ahead. Dracuni tried to swerve but her wings faltered, struggling to hold a glide let alone the push needed to switch directions at speed. Riony brought her sword up, ready, when a swirling vortex of air cleared their path.

"Hey! You miss me?" Zeina swept in across their path on her shining aqua seasong.

Riony grinned from ear to ear. "Took your razing time!"

Zeina waved behind her, where more Rebel Riders swooped along on a colorful mix of dragons. "And it looks like we got here just in time. This is a shit show."

"Right?" Riony laughed, but it came out more like a sob.

"What do you need?" Zeina asked.

Riony needed Dracuni to be at full health, full energy again, to not have expended so much of herself. But she couldn't do anything about that. Zeina had left before they'd distributed silvernix, so she wouldn't have any.

"The riders on tamed dragons need help, and we need these skies to be clear of revs."

"We'll see what we can do." Zeina lifted one arm into the air, swirling it, then pointing in a gesture to the other Rebel Riders.

Each rode a wild, untamed dragon, unbothered by the factory dragons as they formed a V-shaped wedge in front of Dracuni, with Zeina at the lead. Gleem released her gusting breath again, knocking both revenants and dragons clear.

Then the formation split up, fanning out from Dracuni, plucking flying revenants and falling riders from the smoky air.

Tamed and untamed dragons still tussled fiercely all around them, but the battle cleared enough for Riony to identify where the dragons who most desperately needed healing were.

"You ready to go again?" Riony lay a hand on Dracuni's opalescent scales.

Only a faint sensation of affirmation returned as Dracuni followed Riony's direction to the next target.

She managed to heal almost a dozen more, then her wings started to slip in the air like fingers grasping a soapy ledge, lacking the strength to hold air beneath them.

"It's okay, it's okay." Riony's voice lifted in panic.

She deactivated the flame on her sword, leaving only the float rune active. But if Dracuni fell, that magic would offer little help.

Dracuni's thoughts came to Riony only in drifts of blurred exhaustion, a sensation of fading away.

As she cast around for a friendly face to call in assistance from, she caught a glimpse of red and white behind them. "Sparks, really?"

The king's rider chased toward them. Riony cursed at the loyalty of the rider to persist in their mission, even given the utter chaos around them.

"We've got a tail again. We need to move!"

Dracuni shuddered, letting out a whimper that solidified into a roar, and she stretched her wings with painful effort. But they didn't hold.

"Sparks," Riony hissed.

The king's rider was still a way off but had clearly spotted them and was coming in as directly as they could through the battle.

Riony leaned over Dracuni, pressing her forehead to the back of Dracuni's neck. *I know you can do this. Come on. Just a little bit more, then you can rest.*

The unidragon stretched her wings again, and they held, just enough to glide. Riony used her own body weight, leaning out from the saddle to help turn them, aiming back into the thick of the battle, hoping to find one of their companions for help within.

But the king's rider gained.

A bristle of emotion shivered down the unidragon's neck and into Riony.

Dracuni lifted her head, seeking.

"What is it?"

Familiar ... voice ...?

Blinking her watering eyes clear, Riony squinted at a large shape coming in beside them, her heart rampaging with the hope of seeing Gleem, Hux, Viska, or any friendly dragon at their side.

Instead, it was one of the larger wild dragons. It flew calmly and apparently wasn't driven to maim the tamed dragons like the others were. It hovered curiously at Dracuni's side.

Riony thought it was a flamesong at first, based on the size.

But as she took in its colors and patterns, she realized it wasn't one of the dragons she'd untamed at all. It was a seasong, silver, with a few flecks of black.

"It's your amma ..." Riony exhaled the words huskily.

A deep pang of emotion rang back from Dracuni.

A long, low growl rumbled from the seasong in return. Riony kept her sword clutched tight in one hand warily. The last time she'd seen the mother dragon, it had tried to kill both her and Dracuni. And she was no longer emaciated and weak as she had been then.

Dracuni's wings fluttered, and she and Riony dropped suddenly, sending Riony's stomach up into her throat before they stabilized again. The seasong rumbled a growl, head flicking their way, sniffing at the air with flared nostrils.

Dracuni thrummed, then opened her mouth to release a stuttering, whimpering song.

Tears filled Riony's eyes. *You can sing?*

The mother dragon growled and then returned the sound, just two humming notes of the haunting melody. And then the snap of dragon teeth behind them broke off the sound.

The king's rider had reached them.

"Come on, we need to get out of here!" Riony yelled over the wind, but she could feel within her own bones how drained Dracuni was. It was a miracle they hadn't already fallen from the sky.

The silver and black seasong swung her head around to the pursuers, eyes narrowed. Then she roared so loudly it should have blasted the clouds from the sky.

In a fluid motion like twirled ribbon, she curved up and over Dracuni, then set upon the king's rider and his tamed beast. The smaller etherdart's wings crumpled within her claws.

Riony watched in awe for a moment, then Dracuni dropped again, farther this time, before her wings caught the air with a wet-fabric clap.

I'm ... sorry. Dracuni's thoughts seemed hollow, echoing into Riony like a sound from the distance depths of a cave.

Riony's hair whipped into her eyes, and she clung to Dracuni. "It's okay. It's going to be okay."

The unidragon's wings gave again. They were so close above the revenant army now that Riony could hear the clack of their bones as hundreds of claws and teeth reached up toward them.

A dark shadow dropped down in front of them, faster than Dracuni's faltering fall. The shadow dragon. Riony clenched her teeth against the anguished cry its presence made her want to loose.

The cursed mass of dragon souls bellowed a thunderous roar, and Riony held her breath as she watched and waited, hoping ...

Please don't work. Please be weakened.

The ground beneath churned.

The first new revenant to rise was the red and yellow dragon Dracuni hadn't reached in time. Purple lights spotted through the masses as downed riders revived as murderous undead. Flickering orange trails of smoke rose from revenants who had been burned and continued to march on.

Riony's heart dropped into an icy well.

And Dracuni dropped again. Riony clung to her, patting her neck through tears.

It's okay. You did so well. So well. You saved so many lives.

There was no response from the unidragon as they crashed down into the sea of monstrous undead.

Chapter Twenty-Six

Skeletal claws and ragged, rotten flesh skidded on the polished floor of the palace corridor as the revenants charged toward Lyrrin and her team. The human and animal corpses formed a thick wall, like a flood of gray water rolling their way, glinting with sharp teeth and pale, dead eyes.

Elumon's fear spiked though Lyrrin so strongly she had to clutch the nearby wall to stop from falling over.

Queen Vellira stood frozen in the revenant's path. "They've made it to the palace? How? It's impossible."

"If you had any idea what was going on out there, you wouldn't be so surprised." Eslinde grabbed her by the elbow and tugged her onto the nearby stairs. "Move! Everyone! We need to get to the silvernix chamber."

Lyrrin's attention snapped away from the raging creatures' approach. The silvernix chamber was just down the stairs. She hopped down the first few, only to find Elumon didn't follow. His moonlight wings fluttered as he trembled.

Come on, we'll be safe down there. We can lock them out.

With a small yelp, he bolted down the stairs, almost bowling her over on the way.

The little hatchling had never seen revenant up close before. Lyrrin wanted to reassure him that they probably wouldn't hurt him, but she didn't know for sure and didn't want to test it. Either way, the creatures were terrifying.

Aishena, Benjin, and Kverra brought up the rear as they all galloped down the wide flight of stairs, coming up to the barred gateway below.

Lyrrin had been faint with pain and blood loss the last time she'd been there. She remembered there'd been guards waiting within to open this gate, then the more solid door beyond it. But no guards remained on duty now, whether they'd been called to some other tasks or simply fled.

Eslinde reached the gate first and grasped on to the bars, giving it a hard shove. It rattled, remaining closed.

"It's locked!"

Elumon circled around Lyrrin's feet, panting. **We're trapped. We're trapped!**

"I might be able to pick it, but it takes time," Kverra said.

"We don't have time." Aishena pulled an athame in each hand, pointing to the top of the stairs, where the first, fastest revs had reached.

She lit up the yellow blade and slashed down through the lock, cutting the latch.

With a kick to the gate, it swung open.

"Go, go!" Eslinde herded everyone through.

They crowded into the small space between the gate and the solid vault-like doorway, designed just for a couple of guards at a time. Aishena and Kverra slammed the gate closed as the revenants tumbled down the stairs toward them.

"We can't lock this again!" Kverra said.

Aishena leaned her shoulder to the bars, pulled a coil of cave silk rope from her belt and began lashing the gate closed. A canine-shaped revenant bounded down the last few stairs, smashing against the metal. It snapped yellowed teeth at Aishena's arm as she reached through the bars to loop the rope again.

Aishena screamed as its jaw locked around her wrist. Kverra barged in beside her, thrusting both arms through the bars. She grunted with effort as she wrestled the revenant's mouth open.

The quilted guard armor Aishena wore tore through as she wrenched her hand away. Blood dripped around her fingers.

Kverra finished lashing the rope and backed away from the bars as the rest of the revenants crashed against them. Spindly arms of sinew and bone clawed through, trying to reach them.

"That's not going to hold for long," Aishena said.

"Are you okay? Do you need silvernix for that?" Benjin hovered around his sister.

Aishena cradled her bleeding wrist. "It's not going to matter either way unless we get through to the next room soon."

Eslinde stood near one of the two keyholes on either side of the door, running her fingers over it with a distraught look. "It requires two keys, turned together, of which we have neither."

"I could cut through again," Aishena offered.

Eslinde shook her head and knocked on the solid metal. "Try, but the latch mechanism is deep within the door."

"Move aside," Lyrrin ordered, then put a hand out for Aishena's cutting athame. "Can I have that for a moment?"

Aishena handed the blood-smudged crystal over. The bars behind them shuddered and rattled as the revenants scrambled to reach them.

Lyrrin activated the cutting athame and plunged it straight into the middle of the metal door, creating a thin, deep hole. She then pulled a long, finger-sized crystal from her belt, activated it, and jammed it in.

Eslinde leaned in to see what she was doing, and Lyrrin pushed her back away. A popping explosion made the metal door clang and groan, and dark energy consumed all the internal cogs and mechanics within the lock into a swirling void. Air howled and sucked in, ruffling Lyrrin's hair, and then the small crystal ran out of charge and the magic cleared.

Eslinde gaped. "That ... The Alderkin taught you *that*?"

"I wanna know how to do that," Benjin grumbled.

Lyrrin pushed the door, and it swung freely, the entire locking innards obliterated. "A pretty powerful combination, isn't it!"

Eslinde helped open the heavy door wider and hurried through. "I'd say. I'm happy they've been teaching you, although I have to admit I'm a little concerned they taught a child how to do *that*."

"I'll only use it for good." Lyrrin smiled with narrowed eyes. "And maybe the occasional prank."

The bars behind them rattled again, weld points groaning and snapping. The whole thing was going to come off the walls before the rope tying the gate snapped.

"Quickly," Eslinde called from inside the silvernix chamber.

Lyrrin urged Elumon to go in, then followed. He seemed equally terrified of the creepy ossuary ahead as he was the revenants and kept so close to her that he risked tripping her. Aishena, Benjin, and Kverra followed in, pushing the heavy door closed behind them.

The structure of the metal had remained solid after Lyrrin's magic, only a bit bent in places, but there would be no way to lock it again.

"Get whatever you can to barricade it." Kverra pointed to the stone pillars holding skulls and the heavy stone shelving in the center of the space.

"Not the shelves," Lyrrin said. "Don't touch them."

A great smash and clatter came from the other side of the door, ringing like broken bells, and revenants roared. They were through the gate. The force of their bodies struck the inner door, rattling it. Aishena and Kverra put their shoulders into holding it as Benjin wedged bones and unicorn horns beneath it to jam it closed.

"Float rune," Benjin yelled from beside one of the low display pillars.

Kverra tossed him the crystal Lyrrin had carved for her earlier, and he activated it. Holding it and the heavy stone together, he lifted the plinth enough to drag it over to the door, propping it against the metal.

Eslinde did the same with another block of stone. "That might hold them for a little while, but it sounds like they are tearing right through the metal on the other side. I hope you're right about there being a way out of here."

Want out too. Don't like it here. Elumon tucked his head under a wing.

Lyrrin bit her lip. She hoped she was right too.

The round room otherwise had no visible doors or windows, only walls covered with intricately arranged bones and unicorn skulls.

Lyrrin moved into the center of the domed chamber where the two narrow shelves stood, arched over the top with the broken remains of a gateway geode.

She'd been too unwell to really consider the doorway-like structure the last time she'd been in there, to really look at it. The geode oval was broken in half, but the shelves it sat on were made of a dark, glossy stone, struck through with lightning streaks of pale crystal.

Could they work the same way as other crystals?

Lyrrin had seen the stones the Alderkin had created the new shrine with in the undercity. They weren't pure crystal either, but rather limestone with crystal veins.

Stepping between the shelves, carvings along the inner sides became clear. Delicate swirls that felt familiar to Lyrrin, almost like looking at her own handwriting, lined up both edges of the twin shelves and along the floor between them.

"Look! There are runes," Lyrrin cried.

She kneeled down, running her fingers over a larger one on the floor where a gateway's main activation rune usually sat.

Eslinde rushed to her side. She gasped when she saw it. "I never ... I never came in here. I hate this room so much. If I'd seen this ..."

"The king probably counted on nobody who knew what runes looked like coming in here." Lyrrin frowned as she looked over the carvings. "I don't know what this bit is, though. It's not normal magical runes."

Eslinde's face scrunched with emotion. Her voice came out small, almost lost under the clamor of revenants trying to beat their way inside. "It's Alderkin language."

"Can you read it?"

Eslinde shook her head, but it didn't seem like a denial. "Not all Alderkin writing. But I can read this. It's something Alleem used to write for me, on every message we shared."

Lyrrin's breath caught. "What does it say?"

Eslinde brushed her fingers over the words as though caressing a lover's cheek. "Love beyond barriers. Although, that is a poor translation of the true meaning. In Alderkin, this word's meaning encompasses not just physical boundaries, but time, emotions ... life and death."

A tear splashed down from the tip of Eslinde's nose onto the glossy stone.

Lyrrin's eyes stung with the threat of her own tears. She already knew that the carvings there must have been done by her father. She'd heard how the Dragon King had taken him away, forced him to work and share his magic, tried to get him to share gateway magic.

His last words were that he'd never shared it. That he found another way.

Lyrrin swallowed the emotions away. She had work to do.

She examined the carvings of the main rune. The Alderkin had assumed the king wanted gateway magic in order to use it to move around the kingdom, to rule it even more fully, to have that power for himself along with all his others.

Then Lyrrin started thinking maybe he wanted the gateway magic for something else. A way for him, and only him, to reach his main supply of silvernix.

And he set it up in a place where he always kept just enough silvernix stocked on the shelves to keep the magic charged. I should have known earlier!

"It's close to the usual gateway rune, but a bit different here," Lyrrin pointed to where the strokes were changed.

"Can you activate it?" Eslinde asked as she wiped her cheeks.

Benjin rushed over from where his sister and mother guarded the entrance. "You'd better! That door is coming off its hinges. Hurry!"

With a nod, Lyrrin ran her fingers over the lines cut into the stone. The song was muffled, dull compared to runes carved on pure crystal. But it was there.

She tried the normal sequence, running her long-nailed fingers up around the main lines, down through the central V line, then up and around, but nothing happened. She tried a variation. Nothing. The thundering crashes at the metal door and roaring from beyond overwhelmed the song from the stone, and she wasn't sure where she went wrong.

"Cover my ears for me?"

Eslinde's eyebrows wrinkled in confusion, but she placed a palm over each of Lyrrin's ears.

Taking a deep breath, Lyrrin tried again.

This has to work. Riony, Dracuni, and the others need us. They need us to get the silvernix for them. Pabba, let me hear the song you created.

Lyrrin moved her fingers slowly, letting the sounds of the stone hum through her, listening deep within. She trailed her fingertip over the final line, and magic lit up in front of her.

Benjin let out a whoop, and Eslinde gasped.

Lyrrin looked up, seeking any symbols they could select for their destination. But there were none. The gateway had opened already, only a single location available.

A gloomy chamber was half-visible through the wavering magic.

The metal of the door wailed like a vengeful spirit, buckling in on one side, and grasping claws thrust through.

Aishena and Kverra backed away to join the others at the magical portal.

A human revenant pushed its head through the broken door, teeth gnashing.

Eslinde turned Lyrrin's shoulders, pushing her toward the gateway. "Wherever this leads has to be better than here. Go!"

Elumon? Come on. Lyrrin waited as the hatchling came quivering to her side again, and they stepped through together. All the others rushed after, as the metal door crashed down behind them, revenants tumbling into the silvernix chamber. They were on their feet in seconds, racing for the humans.

Lyrrin held her breath as she traced the rune on the other side, and the gateway closed, cutting them off. Darkness surrounded her. She scrambled for the light stone on her belt and activated it within its netted bag. Cyan light spilled out, revealing the familiar layout of an Alderkin shrine. But not any of the ones Lyrrin had visited in her travels so far.

The gateway in front of her had been changed. The usual rune was carved out, replaced with the altered one that only paired it with the shelf structure in the palace. Her father never revealed the magic of gateways to the king, only this one, different way.

There were gasps and mutterings behind her, and as Lyrrin turned to see the rest of the space, her own jaw dropped.

The stone walls of the shrine building had been hollowed with long niches—shelves filled with hundreds of bottles of silvernix, maybe thousands.

Elumon sniffed hesitantly at the shimmering glass.

"I never thought he'd still have so much," Eslinde exhaled the words in a rush.

"Blessed sun. We really found it. I can't believe it." Kverra shook her head.

"*Lyrrin* really found it," Benjin said.

"I couldn't have without everyone's help, without what everyone knew." Lyrrin blinked a few times, making sure she was really seeing what she was seeing. There'd be enough silvernix there for every injured dragon and rider. If they could get back to them in time.

"Gather up the silvernix quickly." Aishena shook out empty cloth bags and handed them around.

Kverra and Eslinde began plucking the vials and carefully filling the bags.

Aishena grabbed a nearby bottle, and a moment later her dark skin glowed. She groaned and shook out her injured hand.

Benjin had circled the space, then went to look out the doorway. He came back in notably paler. "We still have a problem."

The silvernix collection paused as they all went to see outside. Everything was shadowed, even outside the building, as though night had fallen early. As Lyrrin squinted out beyond the ring of standing stones, the reason for the thick darkness became clear.

The shrine was entirely encompassed with a writhing mass of inky black magic and revenants.

"The first taming …" Lyrrin whispered. "We're at the shrine where the first taming happened."

They'd seen it once from a distance. A beshadowed, cursed place. The revenants gurgled and growled all around, not just encircling the ground where the standing stones created a protective barrier, but also climbing above them, as though over a glass dome. Only the odd patch of sky showed between them.

Benjin offered a wry half smile. "At least the revs can't get in."

The sheer mass of bottled silvernix stored there no doubt had something to do with that. Keeping the shrine and its protective barrier active.

Lyrrin's own lips puckered. "Yeah, but we can't get out, either."

"How are we going to get the silvernix back to the others?" Eslinde's shoulders slumped. "We can't go back to the palace. And if this is the site of the first taming, we're almost on the other side of Elundrae …"

"Lyrrin could adjust the gateway!" Benjin said, bouncing with enthusiasm at his idea. "Make it go to one of the other ones, somewhere safe."

Aishena shook her head. "Safe for us, but there aren't any close enough to the capital, and we'd be on foot. We wouldn't be able to get all of this where it needs to be in time."

Benjin wasn't deterred. "Then we send Elumon. He could fly from somewhere closer, carry at least some silvernix with him?"

Elumon whimpered and ducked behind Lyrrin. ***Not on my own!***

"It would still be a really long way." Lyrrin turned away from the cursed shadows surround them, stepping back into the shrine.

Cyan light twinkled off the carefully stored bottles of precious fluid. They had more silvernix than anyone could ever need, enough to save everyone, but no way to get it to them that was safe.

Lyrrin ran her hands over the geode crystal, thinking about the shelves of stone that formed the doorway on the other side, the room now flooded with undead. An idea started to form. Utterly reckless. Unlikely survivable.

Riony would approve ... if it were anyone but Lyrrin doing it.

"Maybe it's time we stop trying to be safe ..." she whispered, mostly to herself.

Louder, she said, "Keep loading up all the silvernix, and fill one bag for Elumon to carry. I'm going to open the portal back to the palace, and he's going to carry the silvernix to the others from there."

Eslinde shook her head, pale eyebrows drawn tight together. "That room is filled with revs. They'll set upon us the moment the gateway opens!"

Lyrrin was already picturing what would happen when the magic connected them to that room again. Would they even have a chance to push Elumon through before the revs flooded them? Would they have a chance to fight back? Would they be able to close the gateway again?

Lyrrin pushed away her fear. "It's our best chance of getting silvernix to the others. They used the summoning stone. You know what that means. There are going to be a lot of people and dragons out there who need this. Dracuni included."

The five of them stood in silence for a long moment.

"You're right," Eslinde said finally. "It's what we should do."

Elumon stared up wide-eyed, inhaling sharply through his nose. ***No. No, I don't want to go alone.***

His fear stabbed through Lyrrin's mind like a cutting athame. She knelt down beside him, cupping his snout in her hands and locking eyes with him.

I know it's scary. I'm scared too.

Elumon's nostrils flared, and he whimpered.

I'll do everything I can to make sure you'll be safe. And that we will too. And what we're doing here ... it could save so many others too. It could save Dracuni, big sister, all our friends.

You're always brave. Always easy for you. I'm always scared.

Lyrrin half smiled. *You know that's not true. You can feel how I feel. I'm always scared too. I just have to act brave so Riony and Eslinde let me do things.*

Elumon snorted, and his eyelids snapped closed and open again.

"Will he do it?" Eslinde asked gently.

Lyrrin brushed her thumbs over the hatchling's cheeks. Her own little dragon, bonded to her. She wished she could take away all his fear, but she knew he had to learn how to manage it himself. So she just waited for his response.

With a big inhale of breath that puffed out his chest, Elumon nodded once.

Smiling beneath wet eyes, Lyrrin brought him in for a hug. "Aishena, Benjin, Kverra, they'll all keep the revenants off you and me while you get away."

Lyrrin looked to the others for confirmation, and they all nodded.

"I can't say how long we'll keep that many revs at bay, especially if they aren't burning. But we'll do what we can," Aishena said.

Getting back to her feet, Lyrrin stared at the gateway, imagining the room beyond. "I have an idea that might help. But we have to open the gateway again. We have to try this. We need to get the silvernix to the others ... no matter what."

Dracuni came to a plowing stop amid the revenant army. The crackle and crunch of bony bodies beneath her was louder than a roaring waterfall. Splinters of osseous matter hailed everywhere. Dirt stained black from decades of dragonfire stirred up all around, choking and blinding Riony as she clung to the unidragon's neck.

Not even the pain of the landing channeled through from Dracuni to Riony. She had become so used to sharing her mind with the unidragon's emotions that now without them she felt empty inside.

Opalescent scales slipped under Riony's sweaty hands as she felt for life.

"Come on, you're going to be okay." *You have to be.*

A faint thud of a heartbeat still tapped under the scales, but there was no other response.

A growl rumbled from Riony's side. The revenants were undeterred by the dragon crash-landing in their midst. She barely had time to lift her sword, angling the flat edge like a shield as the first of them hit.

Decayed, yellowed claws lashed through the settling dust as undead clambered carelessly over Dracuni to reach their human prey.

"Get off her!" Riony roared.

Wiping grit from her eyes, she swung the thick crystal blade in a wide arc. Glowing purple light trailed after it and one human revenant's head was separated from its neck with a satisfying crack.

Looking around from her perch atop Dracuni, Riony was struck with a gut-clenching terror. An endless mass of undead swarmed her way.

They wouldn't hurt Dracuni themselves. Revenants only went after humans. But that didn't mean many other terrible things couldn't happen to Dracuni if Riony left her there and tried to escape.

As though Dracuni had sent that thought through, urging her to flee, Riony snapped back, "I'm not leaving you!"

Dracuni's head lay on its side in the dirt, eyes closed. Her chest lifted in weak, fluttering breaths.

A horrifically small human revenant scrambled up Dracuni's back, and Riony balked, skidding down the unidragon's neck to the ground away from it. She smashed her sword ahead of her like a battering ram, clearing a path to beside Dracuni's head.

If all the revenants were coming after her, she couldn't let them climb all over Dracuni to get to her. She positioned herself with Dracuni's head to her back and prepared for the next surge of ravenous undead.

Just hold them off until someone comes to help.

Riony batted a scaly white-eyed dreer away, then pivoted to block the grasping claws of more human revenants, both skeletal and far, far too fresh.

A charging bovin revenant crashed into all of them from the side. Its thick-boned skull hammered Riony's shoulder and cheek before she could roll away from it. She came back up onto one knee.

Her heart pumped at a raging pace. She spat dirt and blood. Her face and arm heated from the blow, and she was rolling her shoulder socket to confirm she hadn't lost any motion when a weasel revenant skittered up her back and sank sharp teeth into her neck.

She snatched it in one hand, throwing it off her.

Revenants tumbled in from every direction and crushed over her, burying her in gnashing teeth and scratching claws that poked through her armor and ripped at her face. Riony swung her sword in wild, cutting arcs, cracking through bodies indiscriminately and desperately.

The area cleared for just long enough for Riony to draw a breath that ached all the way down. She managed to get back up to her feet, and then the undead hit her again. A revenant latched on to one of her arms and she wrenched it free. She just had to keep fighting, just had to keep swinging, keep the revenants off her and Dracuni, just a little longer.

Someone had to have seen her and Dracuni go down. Someone had to come for them. Zeina, Vance, Dashiel, Jaym …

Kess. Where are you?

Daring a look back at the sky, there was still no sign of the purple dragon and his rider.

Riony's chest squeezed around her panting breaths, caught in the fear that when she'd left Kess on that rooftop, it was the last time they'd ever see each other.

Something sharp stabbed into Riony's back, piercing the armor. Searing pain and the trickle of warm blood followed. She spun blindly and smashed her sword down like a hammer on an anvil over the tusked revenant before it struck again.

The wound was just over her left hip, and her leg wobbled beneath her. She grunted, steeling herself and standing strong as every part of her body screamed.

Then the beat of wings above made the breath in her throat catch.

A white dragon. Iffyr! With Dashiel still riding.

"We're here! Here!" Riony's voice cracked around the words, lost in the roaring battle.

But still the shimmerdart swooped their way and Riony laughed with relief.

The undead assault on her didn't slow, and she backed up closer to Dracuni, waiting and hoping for the shimmerdart to come in and rescue them. If Dashiel was still on the tamed dragon, then they still had their silvernix with them, unspent.

Would it be enough to revive Dracuni? Get them airborne and out of this cesspit of frenzied bone and rotten flesh?

Riony chose to believe it would. Her arms felt heavy and solid as stalagmites as she swung her sword again and again.

Then the shrieks of fighting dragons came from above, and her heart frosted over. A wild flamesong had Iffyr in its claws, wrapping the smaller shimmerdart entirely and wrenching at its taming spike.

Dashiel dangled from the tip of one wing, being flung side to side in the midair wrestling match.

Shiff flew close, darting back and forth, but unable to get through the whirlwind of tails and wings to reach Dashiel. The three dragons and Dashiel went over the capital's high walls, crashing downward into the city on the other side.

"Sparks, no!" Riony wailed.

The stickiness of blood spread across her lower back and every swing of her blade tugged on throbbing wounds all across her body. Blood trickled down one side of her face and the muscles in her arms stung so fiercely she wasn't sure how much longer she could keep fighting.

Above, the battle still raged between tamed dragons, wild dragons, and flying revenants. But the sky seemed clearer now. Whether that was due to newly untamed dragons leaving the area entirely or dying, Riony wasn't sure. A wishful part of her hoped it was because there were fewer undead in the skies.

Then at least her friends still up there on their dragons had a chance.

If they were still up there.

Dragonfire, in shooting darts, fireballs, and streams of flame, made the world glow orange and red. There was more than before … what were they doing?

Like a meteor crashing to earth, a burning ball of carrion bird hurtled down into the revenants in front of Riony. It smashed apart in a spray of flaming feathers, catching the undead around it on fire as well.

Riony shielded herself as sparks blew across her face. She turned away to keep off the next creature attacking her.

But then she shot a glance back again.

The carrion bird revenant wasn't moving. It wasn't getting up again, feathers or not, to scratch its way across the field to tear into Riony.

It was down. It was dead. It burned and it stayed dead.

Heart pounding, Riony fumbled exhaustion-locked fingers over the burn rune on her sword. It lit up in combination with the float rune, creating flickering hot-pink flames all up the blade.

Muscles screaming from overuse, Riony put her whole body into her next swing, smashing through the wall of undead in front of her. Desiccated flesh and aged bone smoldered and caught alight, and a line of revenants went down with a shrieking roar.

It's working. It's working! The revs are burning again. Do you hear that, Dracuni? We did it. You did it.

Riony sobbed from wonder and relief and the ragged exhaustion of her aching limbs and pain of the jagged scratches in her flesh.

The revs were burning. They were dying by fire and staying dead.

Casting watering eyes upward, Riony sent a thank you to all the factory dragons who had come in and untamed their kin, to all the riders who had risked their lives to heal their untamed dragons, to the stars watching down from above.

They'd done it.

They'd untamed enough dragons to make a difference. Finally.

Even if this was the end for her, for Dracuni, they had weakened the curse enough that there would be hope for those left behind. Some may survive. That was something. That had to be enough.

Distracted in that moment, Riony missed the next attack. Snapping jaws crushed around Riony's waist, long fangs digging in between the scales of her armor.

She roared with pain, bringing her flaming sword around to knock the revenant off her.

It gurgled a scream as it backed away from the burning sword, angling around to strike again from the other side.

The large, four-legged predatory creature was so mangy Riony couldn't tell what it had once been. It snapped at her again, catching her wrist as Riony tried to dodge a snarling human skeleton.

For every revenant she struck down with fire, a hundred more were there to take its place, and everything hurt. Sweat mixed with blood and ash and ran into Riony's eyes, smearing the world into a gray and red nightmare.

Her heart and lungs were ready to give up and Riony trembled all over from overworked muscles and exhaustion. And the revenants kept coming.

A flapping sound came through the turmoil, small and distant, barely louder than the thudding pulse within her own ears.

Could it be Dashiel? Did Iffyr get free, or maybe Shiff? Riony shot a look over her shoulder, desperate with hope.

"*Elumon?*" Riony gasped.

The small hatchling's wings worked hard to keep it up as it flew unevenly overhead, carrying a loaded sack in his claws.

"How did you ...?" Riony grunted as claws lashed down her cheek, and she turned her focus back to the fight around her, burning the next line of revenants away with a wavering, clumsy swing.

The momentum of the attack sent her broken body tumbling, and she cracked down onto one knee.

Elumon was there, carrying something.

It has to be silvernix. They found it. Lyrrin found it!

Riony didn't know what was going on, why he was alone, how the hatchling had flown all the way there from the private palace so fast.

Had she been fighting for that long? It felt like forever.

"Here! Down here, quick!" she bellowed into the air above, waving her flaming sword in a circle to get his attention.

The hatchling pivoted, changing direction and dropping down their way.

The small pale dragon looked so much like how Dracuni did when she was younger, and a hot sting of tears scrunched Riony's face.

A human revenant grappled her from one side, pinning her sword arm to her body as it tried to chew through the armor at her shoulder, crunching scales and leather in its stinking maw.

On her knees, Riony braced as another skeleton grabbed her from the other side. Her fist cracked against its face, but it was on her again a moment later.

Elumon flew closer. The little thing looked terrified, hovering over Riony.

She wished she could communicate with him, the way she could with Dracuni. But she had to hope he could just hear her anyway and cooperate.

"Dracuni first," Riony gasped out in a scream as the revenant chewing her shoulder moved up to her neck. "DRACUNI FIRST! HEAL HER, NOW!"

There was a startling, tearing sound at her neck and pain exploded through Riony, blurring out everything else.

All she could think was *get to Dracuni. Heal her.*

Dracuni needed to be saved. But it was so long since Riony had been able to spare a glance her way, she didn't even know if the unidragon was still breathing.

Claws dug deep into the back of her scalp and a heavy weight of bodies crushed over her, pushing her down onto her stomach. She tried to fight them off, but every limb was weighed down, heavy with exhaustion and sticky with hot blood.

More and more revenants covered over her, all trying to reach through and dig into her skin and pull her to pieces, creating a thick mass over her, squashing the air from her lungs and blocking out all light above, leaving Riony drowning under the churning wave of undead.

Chapter Twenty-Eight

"There's more over there." Kess leaned over Lyomir's neck to the right, leading him toward the huddle of humans in the alleyway below.

They were backed into a dead end, and a horde of revenants stampeded their way, a tornado of snarling jaws and scrambling limbs.

With a gruff snort of air, Lyomir swooped low, catching on to the side of the building with one claw above the screaming people, lowering the other leg over their heads and down between them.

Kess called from her saddle, "Get on!"

The people jumped up onto Lyomir's talons, clutching around his leg in a tangle, all holding on to each other and the dragon as he lifted them into the air again.

With the humans cleared, Lyomir blasted a fireball down into the space. It hit the incoming revenants, the fire rolling along between the stone walls of the narrow street.

Kess watched, grinning viciously as the revenants burned. They crumpled under the scorching heat and didn't move again.

Riony's reckless plan had worked. Finally. *Finally.*

Another burst of screams came from the rescued people below as flames licked around them, but Lyomir flew them clear. He turned sharply, heading toward the high, glossy stone tower in the center of the palace where they'd left all the other survivors they'd plucked from the chaos below.

The sloped roof was perilous but still safer than being on the ground among the revs. Lyomir hovered above it as the newest batch of rescues climbed off, assisted by those below, all clinging to each other to keep anyone from toppling off the steep edge.

The tower was tall enough and smooth-walled enough that it would be safe for a while longer. Depending on when the battle turned. If it ever would.

The revs were burning, but few riders remained in the air who could do that, and there were so, so many revenants.

Kess gave a worried glance over all the people there. Both civilians fished out from within the city and riders with float runes thrown from their newly untamed dragons. They wouldn't fit many more on.

Most of the city was clear of people, and Kess hoped it was because they were all hiding, like Kess had told them to do. But enough people had either not heard the message, not listened to it, or were caught out to keep Kess busy saving them from the revs.

Kess and Lyomir had been scooping people up nonstop since he'd found her on the rooftop where Riony had left her.

They hadn't even had a chance to get back into the main battle. Kess saw Riony fly by on Dracuni once, but it was a while ago. Her mouth was dry and heart felt raw with worry.

"Up again. Let's see who else we can find."

How many more? Lyomir thought back like a groan.

"All of them."

We can't save them all, little thing.

"But we're going to try. Come on. You're not saying you're tired, are you?"

Lyomir scoffed in a gust of smoky air and took them high above the city.

The sky over the battle surrounding the walls was clearer, and down within the roiling field of undead, something large lit up bright.

Probably another tamed dragon being healed after its stake was removed. But it was already down on the ground, which meant its rider would need help.

Kess tapped Lyomir on the neck to signal their heading, and he shot that way with a gusting beat of his wings.

Kess squinted through her flight goggles as the light below dimmed, and her heart flung itself into her throat, cutting off her breath.

Dracuni.

"Faster! Go faster!" Kess cried.

The unidragon lay within a mass of bodies. Many weren't moving, scattered around the dragon and still smoking. But in front of Dracuni, a pile of revenants squirmed and fought over something like a flock of gulls over a fish out of water.

No, no, no. Riony! It couldn't be anyone else drawing the revs fury. Only Riony would be so razing stupid to have stayed there with Dracuni amid all of that.

Faster. Faster! Kess pleaded. She couldn't see Riony herself within the piling bodies. If she was under there ... they weren't going to reach her in time.

Lyomir pushed faster anyway, and as they swooped down, Dracuni stirred. The unidragon lifted up tall, wailing a growling, sorrowful cry, and then she breathed.

Silver flame rushed over the mound of revenants in front of her. Agonized, inhuman cries filled the air and the undead twitched and writhed under the blast of healing magic.

Kess held her breath as Lyomir brought them down, crashing over the revenants on the other side of the reforming mountain of corpses and silver fire.

"Riony? Riony!" Kess yelled. She wished she could leap down from Lyomir's back and search through the butcher's yard below to find the woman she loved more than anything else. To find her alive.

She's underneath. The little bright one said.

Kess's blood turned cold.

Dracuni's flaming ended, and she heaved deep breaths, legs wobbling beneath her. On her back, Elumon clutched on to her saddle, cowering and wings trembling.

Kess stared wide-eyed and numb at the pile of bodies as tall as Lyomir. "We have to get her out ... She ... she ..."

Kess's worries filled her head with screams. Would Dracuni's flame have reached Riony under there? Would it even matter if she was crushed again? Was she even still alive to have been healed?

The army of revs roared all around them and it was nothing compared to the roaring of Kess's own heart.

Lyomir turned on the spot, sending a quick succession of fireballs out into the approaching army around them. It blasted the revenants back, creating a clearing around them ringed in fire.

Kess shifted to the side to climb off Lyomir, and he shrugged a shoulder roughly, pushing her back into the saddle.

Stay. It's dangerous.

With a snap of his jaws, he picked up the top layer of corpses and flung them away. Dracuni worked on the other side, dragging bodies off the pile with her teeth and claws.

Together the dragons dug down through the smoking mound, fast at first, and then more carefully as they got closer to the bottom layers, to the ground and what lay beneath.

Kess flung her flight goggles off so she could wipe her eyes.

As the charcoal-stained dirt below came into view, so did the glint of gold and blue scale mail and a vibrant flop of red hair.

"Riony!" Kess squealed her name and launched herself off Lyomir's back.

He gave a warning growl but didn't stop her that time.

She slipped down his shoulder, landing on soft bodies of healed revenants. Panting hard through clenched teeth, Kess crawled swiftly over to Riony's side.

Dracuni cooed songlike sounds, nudging her nose against Riony's shoulder. The scale mail and padding below had been torn clear away there and across her middle and around her neck. The bare skin beneath was slick and red but whole, no gaping wounds showing.

Still, Riony didn't move.

Kess fell on top of Riony, grasping her face in both hands and pressing a salty kiss over her forehead. The ground all around was muddy with spilled blood.

"Wake up. Come on. You can't leave me now. Not now. We did it. The revs are dying. You broke the curse. You saved us, and you need to be here to see what you've done."

The sounds of more fireballs being shot out to keep the revenants back roared over Kess's shoulder, but she could only look at Riony's closed eyes, her crimson-spattered cheeks, searching for any sign of life.

Kess bared her teeth in an effort to fight off tears. "I love you. Don't leave me."

A soft, low groan parted Riony's lips. Her voice came out rough and scratchy. "Not ... going ... anywhere."

Kess sobbed in relief.

Riony's eyes remained closed. Her shoulder shifted as though trying to lift her arm, and she grunted and lay still again. "Sparks. I feel like I've been entirely pulled apart and put back together again."

Kess peppered her cheek with teary kisses. "I think you were, you razing, tame-brained maniac."

Overhead, Dracuni grumbled and huffed as though in agreement.

Riony smirked. "Glad you're okay too, Dracuni. Also, like you can talk."

Finally, she opened her eyes, lids peeling back slowly, and she grunted as she raised a wobbling hand.

"I was worried about you." Her fingers brushed over Kess's lips. "Is it over? Did we win? Did I kill all the revs? I feel like I killed a lot."

Kess laughed and eyed the smoldering bodies around them and the still flaming sword lying to Riony's side. "You took down a few."

"*A few?*"

"Don't worry. I'll make sure you get your 'killed the most revs single-handedly' prize later." Kess's eyes were locked with Riony's, her insides roaring with relief that she was still with her. "Just a few hundreds of thousands still to clear up and we're done."

Lyomir sent out another volley of fireballs. All around, the crackle of fire echoed and a gust of smoke made Kess's eyes sting.

"Is that all?" Riony winced as she sat upright. "Back to work, then."

Kess held her shoulders, helping to steady her, and Riony slumped forward, resting her forehead on Kess's shoulder.

"Take a breather. You're exhausted. Lyomir is keeping the revs off us."

Riony's head shook, rolling against Kess. "The battle isn't over until a bard writes an epic ballad about it."

"I'll get Jaym to work on that." Kess wrapped her arms around Riony, feeling her warm and tacky with drying blood.

Riony lifted her head, tilting it toward Dracuni in silent conversation.

What is it? Kess directed to Lyomir.

A tamed dragon with your human friends is coming in. Little bright one hears his bonded child. Lyomir flicked his snout skyward.

Kess followed the direction, seeing an orange dragon coming their way.

Kess hadn't thought much of Elumon's presence there a moment ago. The hatchling was the least of her concerns while Riony was buried under bodies. But she turned her eyes to him again where he sat atop Dracuni.

His wings fluttered with excitement as Ambri got closer and he had a cloth sack beneath his claws, filled with clinking glass.

A bag full of silvernix? They'd found it. Lyrrin and the others must have found the king's supply.

"How did they ...?"

Riony squinted. "Not sure. Dracuni is trying to pass on what Elumon is saying, but the kid is way too overexcited to be making much sense. But he's guiding Lyrrin here."

The orange dragon glided in, circling once before coming to land in the cleared area around Dracuni. Aishena rode up front with Benjin, Eslinde, and Lyrrin at the back, and Kverra Hjelzahn was in the middle, holding a sixth passenger beside her.

Her dark hair was coiffed in intricate braids to highlight the white streaks in the front, her fine gown wrinkled, and she glared petulantly.

"You stole yourself a queen?" Kess raised her eyebrows.

Eslinde climbed down the dragon's side. She held up a bag, heavy with vials. "Her and more."

Kverra Hjelzahn pushed the queen down next, and Eslinde clamped a hand on her mother's shoulder.

Riony said, "Lyrrin's grandmother? Can't say it's a pleasure."

The queen snarled and looked away, then seemed to take in the horde of revenants around them and her face blanched.

Groaning all the way up, Riony got to her feet, stretched, then loped over to help Lyrrin down from the dragon's back. Benjin jumped down beside them.

Aishena remained in the saddle, directing the tamed dragon around and burning a rush of incoming revs. "There are still tamed dragons in the sky and others downed we might be able to help. Are you okay here?"

Riony nodded once. "Go. Dashiel and Iffyr went down over the wall, that way, not long ago. Do what you can."

Aishena's dark eyes glinted, her chest heaved, and she took Ambri speeding back up into the air, Kverra going with them.

Kess remained on the ground. Her thundering pulse, brought on from the fear Riony had been lost, was only just easing, when the news of Dashiel sent it racing again. She began making her way back to Lyomir, pulling herself up onto his back. Riony had been right before; there was still so much to do.

Riony had Lyrrin scooped in a crushing hug, and when she put the girl down, her blue eyes were wide with disgust as she looked over Riony's shoulder at all the bodies of revenants around them.

"What happened here?"

Riony shrugged. "You know, the usual. What about you? How did you get back so fast from the private palace?"

"We didn't go. I realized the king didn't keep the silvernix there. He kept his access to it here in the capital palace." Lyrrin's voice was high and clipped with excitement.

Kess paused as she reached the saddle, looking back. "The one that was filled with revenants?"

Benjin bounced, making the twin swords at his hips jangle against his armor. "Lyrrin got us out! She worked out how she could use the very stone the palace was made from like crystals."

Lyrrin smiled bashfully. "Well, they already sort of were crystal, partially. The pale streaks in the marble held enough crystal to channel the magic. That was how my father made the gateway for the king, so I didn't really work it out myself. I just did what Alleem had done."

Kess shook her head, not quite following the rambling children.

Benjin crowed, "She made the whole floor one giant magic crystal by carving a rune on it! A burn rune!"

Lyrrin shrugged modestly. "It was lucky we had all the bottled silvernix to charge it up."

"It roasted every rev all the way along! Like PHWOOSH! So much fire! I think I lost my eyebrows!" Benjin lifted his arms in the air, mimicking an explosion.

Eslinde laughed softly. "It was deeply terrifying. But it cleared the way back to Ambri."

The hatchling jumped down from Dracuni's back then, pale wings fluttering, and he ran up to Lyrrin.

She crouched beside him, smiling. "But we sent Elumon ahead, because we weren't sure at first it was going to work."

"I'm glad you did," Riony said. "He arrived just in time."

Kess settled herself in her saddle and wiped the remnants of tears off her face. "We should get moving again. Get all that silvernix where it will do some good and—"

Lyomir tensed beneath her, and a vast shadow flashed over them through the clouds of smoke.

"No!" Riony cried, running toward Dracuni.

A massive silver and gold shape dropped over the unidragon, grasping her in talons like scooping her in a net. Dracuni bleated, squirming in the king's dragon's hold as it lifted skyward again.

"Let her go!" Riony roared.

Yeonard Draekhan, the Dragon King, turned his enormous dragon around to face all those below him, and flame flickered in its mouth.

"We have Vellira! We have your wife!" Eslinde's voice boomed over the scrambling sounds of Riony running for her sword and Lyomir growling beneath Kess.

Eslinde grasped the queen by her shoulder and pushed her in front of them all, beneath the silver and gold dragon's jagged, old teeth.

"Give Dracuni back, and you can have her," Eslinde yelled.

Vellira's expression brightened, and she reached both arms up toward her husband.

The threat of flaming ended, and the dragon's mouth closed. From atop the saddle, the Dragon King peered down at his wife and daughter with a cold, hard expression. Something akin to disappointment.

Then he turned his dragon around and flew away, taking Dracuni with him.

"My king? My king!" Vellira cried out.

"Dracuni!" Riony scooped her sword up, but the long wings of the dragon had already lifted them far out of reach.

"Up here, quick!" Kess called to her, and Riony came running.

Vellira's head was shaking, her face scrunched in denial. "No. No! My king, you're taking me with you. You have to take me with you!"

She shook off Eslinde's hold on her, running after the flying dragon, stumbling over the bodies littering the ground.

Riony jumped, landing heavily onto Lyomir's back behind Kess.

But Kess's eyes were on the queen's mad rush. "Watch out. Catch her!"

The woman was running blindly into the surrounding mass of revenants.

Eslinde charged a few steps after her mother, but Lyrrin grabbed her hand, pulling her back. A surge of revenants braved the wall of flame around the clearing as the queen drew near, the lure of her human flesh too strong.

They burst through, the first undead creatures burning and collapsing around the screaming woman, but their bodies smothered the flames the fell on, clearing a gap and more poured over them. They dragged the shrieking woman down and her screams cut out.

Eslinde yelped a gasp and pulled Lyrrin in, turning her head away from the sight. Benjin stood in front of them, both swords drawn.

Lyomir snarled, shooting another fireball toward where the revs were breaking through.

Lyrrin turned her head while staying within Eslinde's arms. Her vibrant eyes glimmered with tears but her expression was firm.

She yelled up to Kess and Riony. "Go! Go and get Dracuni!"

"What about you?" Riony yelled back, her eyes locked on the king's escaping dragon.

"Viska's coming in. We'll be okay. Go!" Lyrrin cried with her full chest.

Kess glanced back at Riony for confirmation.

Riony held her flaming sword low in one hand, as though too tired to lift it properly. Her blood-smeared face was crumpled, and she turned a pained look from her sister to Kess and nodded.

Kess joined her thoughts with her dragon. *Go. Go fast. You can catch up to them, can't you?*

Lyomir growled in reply. He stretched his purple wings wide, breaking into a running start so fast he churned up the dirt and bodies beneath him. They cut into the air at a dizzying speed.

The shape of the king's dragon was already small, far ahead in the dimming sky. Yeonard Draekhan flew out over the water, away from the harbor. Away from the capital. Away from Elundrae itself. Leaving all the devastation behind.

CHAPTER TWENTY-NINE

Riony crouched behind Kess as Lyomir sped them across the water after the Dragon King and Dracuni, every muscle in her body strained.

Even with having been healed by Dracuni's flame, Riony's limbs all ached down to the bone from exhaustion and also probably also from being crushed under the hundreds of revs that had died reformed on top of her.

She shook out her arms, stretched her shoulders, and clenched her jaw, trying to will enough energy to return. Lyomir was gaining on the massive silver and gold beast the king rode, and she *would* get Dracuni back. She could feel the unidragon's fear from there, stabbing into her heart.

I'm coming. It's going to be okay.

"What's your plan?" Kess's voice blew to Riony on the smoky wind.

She pointed with her glowing purple sword. "I'll hack that dragon's legs right off if I have to."

Kess drew the cutting athame Riony had given her from where it was concealed in her armor and handed it back. "You get Dracuni free. Lyomir and I will try to keep the king and dragon busy."

Riony stared at the body-warmed crystal knife in the palm of her hand. The day she'd found it was the same day she first saw Dracuni's egg. She closed her fingers around it so tight the chipped edges dug into her skin, then she tucked it away safely.

Kess pulled her flight goggles off from where they were sitting atop her head. "Have these too. You're going to need them more than me."

Riony took them gratefully since hers were long gone and she was going to have to get over to the king's dragon somehow. She didn't want to be squinting into the wind while she launched herself through the air.

She wiped her eyes as clear as she could from the dust and tears and blood and yanked the goggles on. Holding her breath, she looked over her shoulder to where her sister, Eslinde, and Benjin had been left behind.

A wall of fire surrounded them, offering some protection from the revs, and Vance and Viska had been close, but Riony's heart still rattled with the fear of leaving her loved ones behind in the middle of all those monsters.

Air rushed out of Riony's mouth in relief as she saw the golden dragon on the ground, collecting her family, but that relief faded fast as a red and white dragon and king's rider swooped toward Riony from the side.

"Watch out," she called to Kess and Lyomir.

The purple dragon banked hard as the snowflame sent a jet of liquid fire their way. The two dragons spiraled around each other, and Kess sent a couple of blades flinging toward the rider. They clinked off the grayglim's armor. The snowflame angled over them, forcing Lyomir down and away from the chase toward the king.

Swooping low, Lyomir skimmed the waves of the harbor with one wingtip as he came back around. The king's rider stayed close on his tail, matching every move.

"We're not losing this guy easily." Kess narrowed her eyes as she watched behind them. "And he's slowing us down."

Riony hefted her sword up, glaring at the king and his dragon up ahead. "Just get me close."

Kess nodded, and Lyomir dived toward the white-caped sea. He sped down so fast that Riony had to cling tight to Kess to avoid being left behind, and then the dragon's wings shot out and they catapulted back up high into the air. Leathery wings pumped hard and icy, salt-spray wind whistled around them.

The burst of speed brought them up behind the king's massive dragon. Dracuni hung within its claws, her tail and head and one wing hanging free from the cage of talons. She squirmed and bleated.

Big sister! It's too tight. I can't get out.

I'm coming to get you.

Be careful.

Me? Always.

Dracuni's emotions surged unchecked through Riony. All her desperation and anger and worry for Riony washed through like a burning tide, leaving Riony's exhausted mind dizzy.

As Lyomir came up higher, over the gold and silver tail, Riony put one hand on Kess's shoulder, squeezed, didn't want to let go, then did.

She jumped, careening through the air. Jumping, and falling, had become second nature to her, and she angled her body, bringing her feet around and bending into the landing.

Riony's muscles screamed in protest as she landed hard on the shimmering scales of the king's dragon, and for a moment, her exhaustion, the gusting wind, and the combining emotions of Dracuni's hope and fear all threatened to overwhelm her. She slipped, landing on hands and knees, grasping on to the back of the king's saddle to avoid tumbling off the dragon's back entirely.

Are you okay?

I made it. Just one old man to deal with and I've got you.

Dracuni's emotions surged again, but the bitter edge of fear had gone. Now there was only the warmth of hope, of love, of trust shared between them.

Riony let that power run through her, warming and revitalizing her body. She shook her head, steeling herself.

The Dragon King turned to her with cold precision, his silver-bright and midnight-dark eyes gleaming unnaturally as they landed on Riony.

His voice boomed. "*Who are you?*"

Riony rose to her feet, holding her sword out like a challenge. "Hi. We've never met.

But you've tortured and killed so many of my loved ones that I really feel as though we're close, you know?"

His eyes narrowed, and intricate silver braids whipped in the wind.

Riony lifted her chin at him. "Now let go of my dragon and I might go easy on you."

"You've made a mistake, ridiculous child," he drawled. "I have not ruled this land for eighty years by being weak."

In a languid motion, the king stood up on his saddle, drawing a gleaming steel sword.

Riony scoffed. "Mine's bigger."

The king swung at her, neat and practiced and so fast Riony almost missed it. She deflected the strike with her crystal blade, but the king was already bringing another blow around toward her middle, where her armor had been torn away.

She had to jump backward to avoid being gutted. She slipped down the dragon's spine and grabbed one of its spikes to steady herself.

Sparks, he's good.

Even with the training Aishena had given her, Riony realized the disadvantage she was at. What was a year of lessons compared to decades and decades of practice?

Riony considered simply running, climbing down the dragon's side and cutting Dracuni free. But while ever this cruel monster of a man before her lived, Dracuni would never be safe. And as the king marched down the dragon's spine toward her, it was clear he didn't intend to let her go either.

"You're the one who created this creature, who has kept it from me." He tilted his head as he looked her up and down, lips curled.

"And I'm the one who's going to beat your ass until you learn you can't just take anything you want."

Riony rushed him, barreling in so recklessly toward the man it caught him off guard. He dodged sideways and Riony pulled her swinging blade after her, connecting a hit. The blow struck his shoulder, sending silver and red scales from his armor clattering away, cutting right through.

The king scowled, glaring at the swell of blood staining his skin. He slapped one hand against the hilt of his sword. The rings he wore clacked against the metal, and he lit up with the glow of silvernix. The wound was sealed before Riony's eyes.

The light hadn't even faded before the tip of the king's blade caught Riony under the chin, leaving her jaw stinging and bloody.

She had no silvernix left to heal every blow. She should have taken some from the stolen supplies, but the urgency to fly after Dracuni was too great. Pain was something Riony was familiar with though. She'd take as many hits as she had to, would keep fighting through all of it, to save her Dracuni.

She raged, throwing everything she had left against the man. Swing after swing she met his sword, but every time she got a blow through, the crack of breaking glass and glow of silvernix followed. Every time the king struck her, she bled more.

He carefully targeted the torn away gaps in her armor, jabbing the point of his sword into her belly, slicing across her shoulder, nicking her neck.

Desperation flared in Riony's chest. Her arms shook, weaker with every swing. Her breath came in ragged gasps. Every muscle in her body burned hotter than dragonflame. She smashed her sword toward the king again, only to have it deflected with an effortless parry.

Back across the water, Lyomir still clashed with the king's grayglim. The rest of the battle was far behind, the city and all the people and revenants warring within just a smoky smudge on the horizon. Nobody else was coming to help.

I can't stop now. I can't give up. I won't.

The king would run out of silvernix eventually. He *had* to.

With a roar, Riony flung herself at him again, blades clashing in a flurry of strikes. The king's movements were smooth and easy, while each of Riony's felt like dragging her limbs through quicksand. Her body wanted to give out, but she kept pressing, pushing through every ounce of pain and exhaustion.

She landed a hit on his thigh, her sword biting deep. The blow sent the king reeling, and he fell onto his knees, then back. Another crack came from his rings, and he growled as the silvernix took effect.

But Riony wasn't going to wait for him to heal again. She stepped over him, bracing against the howling wind, raising her sword to strike.

"Carve! Ten point, left, upper!" Yeonard Draekhan bellowed, eyes flashing.

Riony hesitated. "What?"

The dragon's shoulders shifted, sending Riony scrambling backward to rebalance. Then its head came whipping around at a terrifying speed, jaws wide.

A sharp snap echoed through the sky as its teeth clamped down, right where Riony had been standing a moment ago. She would have been swallowed whole if she hadn't fallen back.

But that wasn't much consolation as the dragon still managed to catch on to her leg.

Pain shot through her like wildfire, and she screamed, feeling bone grind beneath the dragon's crushing teeth. Her sword fell from her hand, clattering uselessly against the beast's spine and dropping off into the waves below.

No!

The world spun and darkened at the edges.

A great, wailing scream was torn from Riony's throat as the dragon whipped its head forward again, taking her with it. She hung like a rag doll from its mouth, her left leg from the knee down trapped between immense, crushing teeth.

Dracuni's fear spiked, and the world burned bright.

Riony cried out as the unidragon's flame flickered around her in a puff. The healing magic stung as it closed the multitude of bleeding wounds across Riony. It tried to fix the splintered bones and shredded flesh of her leg, but the limb remained trapped in the dragon's bite, crushing it again as swiftly as it healed, trapping Riony in a repeating loop of agony that shattered her senses.

Roaring through gritted teeth, Riony fought to stay conscious. She couldn't stop.

She couldn't give in.

Dangling upside down, Riony was in line with where Dracuni was trapped in the dragon's claws. From somewhere above, the king laughed and called another strange order to his dragon.

Riony braced, reaching wildly for her sword before the creature swallowed her whole. *It's gone. My sword is gone.*

The gold and silver scales of the dragon's jaw shimmered in the fading sunset as it opened. And then smashed closed again.

Riony shrieked as pain lanced through her. The dragon's jaw chomped again and again in a mechanical chewing action.

A terrible thought turned Riony's insides cold. *He's toying with me. He's going to let his dragon chew on me as long as he can.*

Dracuni keened a songlike cry. A puff of healing flame gusted around Riony again as she felt herself fading, the magic renewing her just enough to feel every crushing bite acutely again.

And still the dragon chewed, breaking bones as fast as they healed.

Stars swirled across Riony's vision, and sickness swelled through her. She heaved breaths to stay conscious. Blood ran down her leg, her stomach, splattered on her face.

Stop. Dracuni, stop! I have to get free. You're only going to use yourself up otherwise.

But you're hurting, you're hurting! The panic cut deep into her thoughts.

Riony wished she had the wherewithal to keep her emotions and pain in check, to stop sharing them with Dracuni, but it was all she could do to not simply scream and scream and scream.

I have to get free.

Riony blindly patted around her pockets and withdrew the cutting athame with trembling fingers. Her vision blurred as she traced the rune, fumbled it, then finally got the sequence right.

Roaring with effort, Riony folded at the waist, bringing herself up. She pressed her hands against the scaly lips of the massive creature. Saliva and blood hung in strings all around as she grabbed on to the lower lip with one hand to hold herself up. With the other, she slashed with the cutting athame at the dragon's teeth.

The aged, yellow fangs her mangled leg was pinned between were already jagged and broken from decades of use, but each was as thick as a tree trunk. The glowing athame cut long, crisscrossed gashes through them.

Riony swung from the motion of flight and her vision darkened and she couldn't hit the same place twice to cut deep enough to free herself.

A combined scream and sob of frustration ripped from her.

Let me heal you again. Let me!

No. No! Riony could already feel how weak the use of the flame had made Dracuni. She'd expended so much since using it on the pile of revenants.

Riony clung on to the dragon's lower jaw, panting through bared teeth, tears filling the tight seal inside her flight goggles. Her head shook as she realized what she had to do.

No. Don't heal me yet, she thought to Dracuni. *Soon. You'll know when.*

Her fingers trembled as she drew a steadying breath. She knew what she had to do. If she didn't act, she wasn't going to last much longer anyway. She had one last chance to get free. And she had to, to save Dracuni, to see all those she loved again. She *had to.*

For Dracuni and the world and what Dracuni meant to the world.

She had to.

Riony looked up to the sky, bruised by dusk and smoke, hoping to see her ancestors, her parents in the stars to give her strength. But the rallying reply to her wishes came from within her.

A warmth, a tugging pull of powerful love.

All the support and strength she needed came from the love she had for those around her, Lyrrin, Aishena, Benjin, Niskina, Eslinde, Dashiel, Vance, Zeina, Jaym, Dracuni, and Kess. And the love they gave her in return. She would do anything for them.

Anything.

Riony brought Myrwa's shawl up from her neck, filling her mouth with the fabric and biting down. Then she swung the cutting athame again.

And plunged it down through the flesh above her knee.

Bile rushed up her throat and searing pain sent her reeling as the crystal sank through like a knife through mist. Skin, bone, skin again. Riony's skin flushed hot and cold all over and her hands shuddered as agony blinded her.

The athame slipped from her grasp. Her leg ... what was left of it, fell from the dragon's mouth.

Her body swung free heavily, jarring her, and she felt her grip on the dragon's jaw slipping as well.

In a roaring cry, Dracuni's flame engulfed her. Riony's fingers slid over wet scales as the magic worked down her leg like molten metal through her veins, knitting torn flesh and regrowing bone. The wound closed, neat and round over a partially reformed knee, and then the pain ended.

Riony's hands scrambled for purchase, clinging to the mouth of the creature as though it were a life raft while it continued to chew on the parts of her that were left behind.

Your leg! What did you do?

What I had to do.

I'm sorry.

It's not your fault.

Even though the pain ended, Riony's head swam with exhaustion. She felt every bit as chewed up and spit out as she was. She had no weapons left. And if she fell ...

We're finishing this. One way or another. I'm not stopping until you're free.

Dracuni trilled sadly, her tufted tail and loose wing struggling futilely against the giant dragon's talons.

It was a long way up to get on top of the dragon's head again and then a risky path down its neck to reach the king. Maybe she could try to throw herself over to Dracuni instead, but she'd lost the cutting athame.

Turning her face upward, Riony prepared herself to climb.

The dragon continued chewing, and above one of its dull eyes, a polished length of wood jutted out.

The tale of the first taming, the mural in the undercity, flashed through Riony's mind. How Yeonard Draekhan had thrown a spear at the dragon summoned by the Alderkin after he'd murdered a unicorn. The spear covered in silvernix. It was still in there, just like a taming spike.

Riony knew what she had to do. She flung her first arm up, clasping fingers around the ridge over the dragon's upper lip.

Do you have another healing breath in you?

Dracuni's thoughts had grown dim since she healed Riony's amputation. ***I think ... one more?***

That's all we need. Be ready.

Riony groaned as she reached her other arm up beside the first, dragging her body over the dragon's mouth. Her fingers cramped and were slick with sweat and dragon spit.

Stars, I can barely hold on.

She brought one foot up onto the dragon's bottom lip and tried to bring the other up to meet it. She slipped as her phantom leg, only air, failed to hold her.

"Sparks!" She pressed herself to the dragon's snout to stop from falling.

Dracuni yelped.

I'm okay. This is just going to take some getting used to.

Teeth bared, she climbed again. She clung from her fingertips onto the dragon's nostril ridge, edging her way up. Cringing, she got one foot into the corner of the dragon's eye. It didn't react, didn't even blink as she hoisted herself over its eyelid.

But then it stopped chewing.

"How did you ...?" The king's voice boomed her way, outraged. "Skyward, buck!"

The dragon's head flicked upward. Riony's foot slipped, and her body flung sideways as she clung tight to the creature's eyelid. She grinned viciously as the motion brought her higher. She let go as the dragon nodded its head down again, rising up over its eye ridge and landing beside the spear.

She knelt there, unevenly on mismatched legs, both hands wrapped around the aged, polished wood as the dragon's head flicked up again.

Keeping her fingers wrapped tight, Riony wrenched at the spear. The brittle wood crackled in her grasp, sliding with a slow, painful suction. Riony leaned backward, putting her whole body into the motion as the dragon bucked up and down, trying to throw her off.

"Come on, come on!" Riony screamed over the whipping wind and whomp of massive wings.

And the spear slipped free.

Now! Riony rolled down the dragon's snout, grasping for purchase as her final pull left her unbalanced. The dragon bucked again, and she tumbled into the air over its head, then slammed down onto her back between its eyes.

A gust of silver fire hit the massive dragon from below.

Riony stared up at the sky as the dragon stilled, and a long, winding ribbon of black smoke rushed down toward them. It passed right through her, and then the dragon roared.

The sound rumbled beneath Riony like sky full of thunder.

"No, no!" the king yelled. He slapped his hands over the dragon's back, yelling a stream of commands.

The dragon was no longer listening.

Riony rolled onto hands and knees, staring with a vicious smile down the dragon's neck toward the man.

The dragon's head flung upward sharply again. With the spear dislodged, Riony had nothing to hold on to, and she was sent flying high above.

Riony held her breath, eyes narrowed, fingers still wrapped tight around the spear she'd pulled free. She arched up, body weightless for a moment at the summit. Then she angled around, targeting her landing.

Falling had become so easy for her.

Riony steadied the spear as she plummeted down again. The Dragon King stared back from his saddle, mouth open in horror as his newly wild dragon writhed beneath him, and Riony came crashing down over him.

The tip of the spear hit him in the center of his chest, plunging right through the armor, and out the other side.

The ageless man howled, pressing up to his feet and stumbling backward down the dragon. "You can't … you can't kill me. Nothing can kill me."

Sprawled on the dragon's neck where she landed, Riony smirked up at him. "Anything can seem impossible until it happens. And I've always had big dreams."

Silver light burst from the king's skin again as he used another dose of silvernix. He gurgled as the spear shifted around his healing organs but remained skewered through him. He cracked another ring, pushing against the end of the spear, trying to force it out of him as the light glowed again.

The dragon swerved sharply. The king stumbled, slipped. He rolled, clattering down the length of the dragon's back and off the end of its tail.

Riony clung to his saddle, her breath panting like sobs as the king screamed and cursed as he fell into the air, silvernix making him glow like a falling star.

With that much silvernix, he could survive the spear … Could he survive the fall too? Riony pushed herself upright. She wanted to get to her feet, to dive after the man and make sure he didn't make it, even if she went with him, but her single leg scrambled uselessly beneath her.

The silver and gold dragon roared again. The sound was filled with fury and vengeance, like the wails of newborn life combined with the power of the ocean, so loud Riony's ears ached.

The beast veered suddenly, diving after the king. Riony cried out, wrapping herself around the saddle to hold on. What was the monstrous creature doing?

Whatever it wanted. Riony swallowed hard. She and Dracuni had to get out of there.

Dracuni?

No reply came.

Are you okay? Dracuni?

The silver and gold dragon's massive jaws hinged open as they came up behind the falling king. The teeth slammed closed around the man who had kept it enslaved for eighty years. Bone crunched and blood sprayed up over the dragon's snout.

Riony's eyebrows raised. She was fairly certain there was no surviving that.

She wiped her goggles clean with her palms, casting her gaze around frantically. *Dracuni?*

Off the side of the dragon, back the way they'd come, a pale body tumbled in the air. Dropped. Falling. Unconscious.

"Dracuni!" Riony screamed.

She kicked off the back of the dragon with her one leg, rolling headfirst into the air. Salty wind ripped at her as she sped downward, trying to reach the unidragon in time. She had no float rune, no silvernix. She had nothing left.

But she couldn't lose Dracuni too.

CHAPTER THIRTY

The ring of fire surrounding the clearing dimmed, smothered by the undead surging around it. Lyrrin's feet felt stuck to the ground as a rotting bovin and far too fresh human corpses, bloodied and blistered, broke through and raced toward her.

She'd never been as brave as Riony. She'd fight when she had to, but the shivering underlayer of fear never went away.

Now, Elumon's fear added to it as he wove around behind her shins, stepping out boldly, then backing away again in repetition.

You've done so well. You saved Dracuni and Riony! And we're together again now. I'll keep you safe.

Want to keep you safe too.

Lyrrin's heart warmed. She smiled in the face of fear.

Maybe it's time you try out that flame of yours.

Elumon growled softly and emerged again from behind her, raising his head. Lyrrin eyed the approaching revenants and grasped her staff, activating the burn rune on it.

Benjin moved beside her, twin swords raised. "I don't suppose your magic works on metal too? I could really go for some flaming blades right now."

"I don't think we've got time to test that at the moment. But let's try it later."

"Vance!" Eslinde's strained scream came as she drew her thin blade in one hand and used the other to pick up the bag of silvernix beside Elumon.

"We've got you!" Vance's voice yelled from above.

Air gusted around them so furiously it almost blew Lyrrin to the ground. Viska's golden wings arched over their heads, turning the world a warm yellow as the setting sun shone through the thin membrane. Lyrrin coughed as dust and ash and the smell of death swirled all around. A revenant growled close by.

A bright silvery flash shot across Lyrrin's grayed-out vision.

Elumon, did you—?

Then the world was engulfed in sun-bright gold as a jet of fire roared overhead. Viska blasted the approaching revenants with a relentless, charring burn.

"Climb up, quick!" Vance called.

Eslinde grasped Lyrrin's hand and brought her to the dragon's shoulders, giving her a boost.

Lyrrin scrambled the rest of the way. Viska still had multiple saddles from their earlier flight toward the private palace and she climbed in behind Vance, then reached down to help pull Benjin up and into the saddle beside her. Elumon flew up and landed behind them.

"I'm on, go!" Eslinde called from below, still clinging to Viska's scaly arm.

Vance leaned sideways to grab both of her arms as the golden dragon thrust her wings down, taking them off the ground.

The moment they were in the air, Lyrrin turned her eyes the direction the Dragon King had flown, trying to track where he'd taken Dracuni and where her sister and Kess were.

But a darker shape blocked the view.

A heart-wrenching sadness hit Lyrrin as the shadow dragon descended down over them. It came so close a sweep of its umbrous wing passed right over Viska, washing them all in inky shadows and darker grief.

Elumon tucked his head in under her arm, whimpering.

Benjin sobbed beside her, swatting at the tears on his face. Lyrrin let hers flow. She kept her bright eyes on the swirling, living darkness that formed the cursed entity.

All those dragons, all their spirits, separated from their bodies, tangled together and mourning. She reached out a hand, her blue tipped nails brushing the last wisps of black that trailed over them.

"I'm sorry," she whispered, as salty tears dripped into her mouth.

Riony had untamed so many dragons on her missions recently, and so many more had been untamed that day. Lyrrin felt good at how many they had healed, how many dragons could live their life freely again. Whether they'd broken the curse from doing that or not, it was good to have helped them.

But the curse had been weakened. The revs could be stopped with fire again—Lyrrin had worked that out in the palace—and even the size and bulk of the shadow dragon had decreased. She could see the threads of darkness weaving it together now, fraying and bare in sections around a single, larger core.

As the shadow dragon touched the ground, everyone on Viska held their breath. As it lifted its head and roared, Eslinde whispered a prayer to the sun and a repetition of, "Please, please, please ..."

Lyrrin watched the field of corpses in the clearing below, burned by Riony's sword and dragonfire.

The shadow dragon's cries echoed all around, its grieving sound rattling through Lyrrin's bones, calling, calling the dead. Calling for their vengeance. Calling for their aid.

But they didn't rise again.

The roaring continued, growing louder, as the shadow dragon turned on the spot, whiplike tail swishing like a ribbon of smoke behind it.

Again and again it called, and the dead didn't respond.

"It worked ... It worked," Eslinde rasped. She made a sound between a laugh and a sob and leaned into Vance's side. He wrapped an arm around her, pressing a kiss to the top of her head.

With one final sky-rending scream, a large curl of shadow tore from the cursed creature, right from its middle, and flew out toward the harbor where Riony and the Dragon King had flown.

What's happening out there? Lyrrin chased it with her eyes.

Tiny dragon-shaped smudges moved in the distance. Lyrrin turned her staff around, reaching for the seeing stone at the top.

"Look," Benjin said, pointing below with one of his swords.

The shadow dragon had stilled, grown quiet. So much smaller and less substantial than before, it rose back into the air, wafting past Viska and vanishing into the dusky sky above. Not gone, not entirely, not until every last dragon was freed. But it had lost its power.

"Now we just have to clean up the rest of the revs!" Benjin cheered.

"Hmm, easy." Vance leaned over, looking down at the patchy landscape of undead and fire beneath them. "Where's Dash? I haven't seen them in a while."

Eslinde pointed toward the walls of the capital. "They went down over the city. Aishena and Kverra went after them a while ago."

"On Ambri?" Vance growled, shooting a worried glance that way.

Viska aimed her path at the city.

"No, we have to go after Riony!" Lyrrin traced over the rune on the seeing stone. "We have to help get Dracuni back."

"The king took her. We have to stop him getting away," Eslinde added with a gentle touch to Vance's shoulder.

With teeth bared, he shook his gaze away from the city and nodded.

Lyrrin brought the seeing stone up in front of her eyes.

"What's happening?" Eslinde asked.

Through the magnifying crystal, it took a moment to pinpoint the action in the expanse of sky over the sea.

Lyrrin gasped, as the first thing she saw was Dracuni falling. Her shimmering, moonlight-toned body was limp, lifeless. Lyrrin scanned around, spotting Riony, also falling, just above her. There was no glow of purple magic around her.

Lyrrin tried to explain what she was seeing but only a panicked squeak came out.

Then there was a flash of purple through the seeing stone.

Lyomir, with Kess on top, diving toward the falling bodies. She couldn't see the king or his dragon; she could only track as the bodies of Dracuni and Riony and Lyomir went down toward the ocean below.

Viska turned again suddenly, and Lyrrin lost her target.

"They ... they're ..." she stammered.

"Look out!" a familiar voice yelled from nearby.

Orange scales streaked past in front of them, forcing Viska to turn again to avoid a collision. Ambri sped by, with Shiff close behind, a trail of a dozen wild dragons chasing after.

The tamed orange dragon had a crowd of people clinging to her back. Lyrrin recognized Aishena, Kverra, and Dashiel, along with Mestra Lerris. The others wore dragonrider armor in a range of colors.

Viska joined the chase, speeding in between the wild dragons at the end. The gold dragon growled and snapped the air toward them in warning, making them back off.

Lyrrin turned, trying to get a clear view of the harbor again. *Riony ... Elumon, can you hear Dracuni? Can you hear Lyomir?*

Elumon remained silent for a long moment. ***Only Lyomir. He says they're coming back.***

Lyrrin's heart flopped in her chest with a burst of relief. *Are they all okay?*

Elumon looked up from under her arm with large lilac eyes but didn't answer.

Viska wove left, then a sharp right, making Lyrrin focus on the chase in front of them. She cast her gaze over the battle.

The skies were almost clear now. All the flying revs were gone, and the only dragons with riders still on them were wild ones and Ambri. Many newly wild dragons were disappearing over the horizon, but some remained, hovering in a bewildered state or chasing anything that moved with wrathful fury.

The factory dragons that had come in had few targets left. Many of them had also spent their energy and anger, and they rested, perched on the keep walls or were long gone as well.

Those still with vengeance to spare were chasing Ambri, one of the only tamed dragons left in the air.

Viska wove between them, growling fiercely as she checked them with bumps of her neck. The dragons grumbled back, but Viska was larger than most of them. A few smaller treedarts bowed their heads and dipped away from the chase quickly. A flamesong at the head of the chase didn't give up so easily, even as Viska nipped at its tail and wings.

From each side, more dragons approached. Hux, brilliant red, and Gleem, glowing aqua in the dusk. The wild dragons still had their bonded riders, and both had also picked up a few extra passengers along the way.

The three wild dragons pinned the flamesong between them in the air, muscling into its space. Gleem rumbled a long, warning sound, and the flamesong clicked its teeth at her. When Hux joined in as well, yelping a harsh retort, the flamesong slowed, cowed.

With the last of the pursuers turning away, Viska rose over the top, flying past the flamesong to join Ambri up ahead.

"Viska and the others are explaining things to the wild dragons," Vance said. "Convincing them to stop attacking any remaining tamed dragons."

Lyrrin turned around to watch the flamesong following Hux and Gleem, as a few of the other smaller dragons joined them as well, flying lower over the revs.

Vance pointed. "They've agreed to help burn the revs."

The flamesong swooped, loosing a massive stream of fire across the field below. The fire consumed everything beneath, where revenants swarmed along the base of the keep walls. The metal sheeting over the massive stone walls glowed in startling reds and oranges as plumes of smoke darkened the falling night.

"Thanks for the backup," Aishena called over as they drew near. "I wasn't sure I was going to be able to lose all those dragons."

Dashiel grinned from the saddle behind her. "I didn't doubt you for a moment."

"We wouldn't have ended up with so many after us if Dashiel and Shiff weren't playing hero, gathering up riders who'd gone down in the streets. Took a while to extract everyone."

Aishena pointed to all the other riders clinging to Ambri.

Mestra Lerris shared the back saddle with Kverra, but many other riders hung on between the spikes down the orange dragon's spine.

"Sounds like Dash," Vance grumbled.

Beside Ambri, Dashiel's pale blue and purple dragon did a little loop in the air.

"Are there any more that need help?" Eslinde asked.

"I used my last silvernix on Iffyr," Dashiel called over. "But with what Aishena brought, I think we got the last surviving dragons and riders we could see in that area."

Mestra Lerris shook her head fiercely. "You lot are mad, utterly mad, for what you did! I thought at first the wild dragons were part of the shadow dragon's curse worsening ... And then Dashiel explained."

Eslinde said, "I'm sorry we didn't share the plan with you sooner."

The riding master's eyebrows pulled tight over her eyes, darkening her expression. "We lost many today. So many good riders, because they weren't prepared."

Lyrrin cast her eyes down to the ground below, to where Hux, Gleem, and the wild dragons moved over the keep walls and through the city, burning the revenants in the streets. How many had died that day? How many people would be waiting for family that would never come home?

She glanced again toward the harbor, where Lyomir slowly returned, silhouetted by the last rays of sun.

"But many were saved too, by that strange dragon of yours. The one the king wanted all along. And now I can see why." Mestra Lerris shook her head again. "I see why you couldn't trust us with that information earlier. And blessed sun, your plan worked. The revs are burning. The revs aren't rising again. They have been stopped."

But was the cost too high? Lyrrin found tears in her eyes. After so long protecting Dracuni's secret, now every rider in the sky that day saw her magic. A shiver of fear ran through Lyrrin, wondering what that was going to mean.

And there was still so much to do.

Still more dragons to untame. And what would become of Elundrae with so many wild dragons released upon the land?

The curse was broken, and it took so many lives. So many died.

But now, at least, they would stay dead.

Eslinde held Mestra Lerris's gaze across the gap between their dragons, until the muscled rider offered a salute, and she returned it.

"Where are Dracuni and the others?" Aishena asked.

Lyrrin wiped her eyes and pointed out over the harbor. "Elumon said they're coming back but won't say anything else."

Vance frowned. "Viska says the same, that they're on the way, but won't say any more."

From Ambri, Aishena's eyebrows dropped, and she turned the orange dragon sharply toward the water. Viska followed as they sped toward the harbor.

As they crossed over the city, human figures were emerging, gathered on rooftops to avoid the last of the revenants and the fire. They must have been hiding during the earlier attack, like Kess had told them to do. Her warning had saved a lot of lives.

Lyomir flew toward them, crookedly, one wing ripped.

Something large hunched behind Kess, but it wasn't clear what. It might have been Riony. Lyrrin couldn't see Dracuni. She leaned out to one side, trying to see past those in front of her and around the purple dragon, to see if Riony and Dracuni were flying behind.

The purple etherdart glided down roughly toward the long flat stone of a wharf, and Viska, Shiff, and Ambri mirrored him. They landed on the pier, and no additional dragons appeared behind Lyomir.

"Where's Dracuni?" Lyrrin's voice squeaked out, barely a whisper.

From behind Kess, Riony's head lifted, her red hair bright in the gloom of dusk. Her eyes searched over those in front of her, softening as she saw Lyrrin and Eslinde, and then her expression dropped as she turned to Ambri, seeing Lerris and the other riders there.

She looked exhausted, worn down, and she slouched down behind Kess again.

"Riony needs help!" Kess yelled from Lyomir's saddle.

"Coming!" Aishena was down from Ambri in a flash, rushing in a sprint to the purple dragon. Lyrrin slid down from Viska as well, running up behind her.

Riony moved, slipping unsteadily down the dragon's side to the ground.

Aishena gasped as she caught her, steadying her by getting under her shoulder.

Lyrrin's run faltered as she approached, stumbling to a stop. Her sister leaned her weight on Aishena, standing on only one leg. Her armor was torn and bloodied all over, and a clean, healed stump hung at the end of one thigh.

"Riony!" Lyrrin burst into movement again, hurrying to her sister.

She clutched for Riony's other side, and her sister swayed her way, wobbling beneath her touch, and then fell forward, despite Lyrrin and Aishena's attempts to catch her.

They all fell, sprawling on the ground beside each other.

"You reckless tamebrain," Aishena whispered, brushing back Riony's hair tenderly as she knelt beside her.

Riony remained face down, on hands and knee. Her whole body shuddered with grief and Lyrrin wrapped her in a speechless embrace.

"What happened?" Eslinde's armor clattered as she joined them.

All the others moved closer, surrounding Aishena and Lyrrin as they tried to lift Riony again. Her head shook, and only a rough wail escaped her throat.

Eslinde looked up to Kess for answers. "Did the king get away with Dracuni?"

Kess leaned over from her saddle, shoulders slumped and face grim. "No. Riony untamed his dragon. The king is gone. His dragon is gone. But Dracuni ... she was already so weak, after everything. And we didn't have any silvernix left."

Lyrrin felt hot tears spilling and her head shook, angry at what Kess was saying. "What do you mean? Where is she?"

Riony rose up on one trembling knee and covered Lyrrin in a crushing, sobbing embrace. "She didn't make it. Dracuni's gone."

Chapter Thirty-One

Riony still wasn't used to the artificial leg Vance had helped her get. Her thigh ached, and she leaned heavily on the crutches she'd been using while adjusting. The crutches made more people stare at her than if she disguised the loss of her leg entirely.

She didn't care. Let them look. Let them see what she'd lost. She was proud of what she'd done, and she'd do it again in a heartbeat.

But standing for long periods had become painful.

Standing before Dracuni's funeral pyre was even more painful again.

The neatly formed stack of timber had been built on the grand balcony of the palace, overlooking the public square below. Dracuni's body lay on top, scales shimmering so vividly in the afternoon light.

In the few days since the battle, word had spread about how the curse had been broken, how the city had been saved. Soon everyone knew how the strange, magical dragon who had saved them hadn't survived, how her body had been retrieved from the sea.

And now it seemed most of the city crowded into the square below to watch the funeral.

As it should be, Riony thought.

Nerves rattled her as she approached the pyre. Eslinde handed her a flaming torch, and with a deep breath, Riony thrust it into the tinder at the base.

The fire took quickly, flickering around the still body of pale, opalescent scales lying on top. They didn't cover Dracuni's body with a shroud. It was important she was seen.

"In our battle against the curse of death that plagued our land for too long, there were many heroes." Eslinde stood before the fire, her voice strong and resonant as she spoke to those watching below.

Riony stepped back in line with her friends, Lyrrin on one side and Kess, sitting atop Griskin, on the other.

Aishena, Benjin, and their mother were on the other side along with the Zarram siblings. Farther away, a tier down, was Mestra Lerris and all the dragonriders who had survived. Jaym, Zeina, and the Rebel Riders stood with them. The glow of the fire made the scale armor they all wore shine a flickering gold.

Eslinde swept her arm around, gesturing to Riony and all those in line with her. "Heroes who we would not have seen victory without. Many who gave so much to make our victory possible. Many who gave everything."

"Sparks." Riony grunted as a fat tear spilled over one cheek.

Griskin shuffled closer, his fur pressing against her crutch. Kess wrapped her hand around Riony's. Lyrrin, dry-eyed, tsked.

A guard came along the row, handing out lit candles to each of them.

The pyre roared, flames engulfing Dracuni's motionless form in a solid wall.

"We farewell one of our greatest heroes here today. A dragon, born by a unique miracle with the magic needed to break the curse, and the brave and kind heart needed to give herself entirely to that cause."

Riony breathed deep as her tears came fast, dropping one after another down her cheeks and splattering on the dark marble floor.

Eslinde raised her candle. "We send our love with her as she rises to find her way home in the sky, with those who've gone before. Let the lights held by our ancestors, sparkling above, guide her. We send our love to those who hold their own candle in the sky and wait for us, those left behind."

Below in the quiet crowd, flickers of light spread as candles were lit. A few at first, then more. Sparkles of light filled the square like a sea of stars.

It had been Eslinde's idea to give Dracuni a Rolanian funeral, rather than the Taen one most royalty or riders received. In Rolanian myth, dragons were creatures of tragedy, born from the angry souls of the dead who lost their way on their path to the sky.

To see Dracuni honored as a soul who would sit with her ancestors above, to see the crowd of people below holding light for her, filled Riony's chest to bursting.

Riony sniffled hard, awed by the beauty and sadness of the moment. The tears kept coming, and she leaned into Kess, crying on her shoulder.

She whispered the final words as Eslinde spoke them aloud to the audience. "Keep your candles burning bright. We will be together again."

Soon, Riony thought.

A tickle of worry washed over Riony.

I'm fine.

Are you crying?

Of course I'm crying. It's your funeral. Shush!

Riony turned back to the fire. The flames roared and crackled, heating her face as she stared, no longer able to see Dracuni within.

Eslinde turned and nodded to Riony, signaling her to leave. Swinging her crutches around, Riony limped away from the funeral, her friends falling into single file behind her as Eslinde remained to present medals to the surviving dragonriders.

Pushing through into the palace, Riony moved faster, dropping the mourning act. Elumon waited just inside, and Lyrrin skipped along with him as they hurried down a flight of stairs and into a private room below.

The Alderkin met them at the door. "How did it look?"

"Perfect." Riony smiled, wiping away the last remnants of tears. "The flames have covered Dracuni now. I think it's safe to end the illusion."

Five thin spears of crystal stood around the edges of the room, where all furniture had been cleared away. Dracuni lay motionless in the middle of the space, in the exact pose the vision of her on the pyre had appeared.

She cracked one eyelid open. ***I can move again?***

Yrik and Priyune traced over the symbols on the ring of crystals, and the glow of magic dulled away.

"Now you can," Riony said, stepping in and giving Dracuni a hug as she rose up.

Dracuni fluttered her wings and stretched out a back leg. ***I got a cramp.***

Riony chuckled. "It was worth it. I think everyone bought it. The dragon with the silvernix blood and healing breath is gone. Nobody will be hunting you anymore. You're free."

Kess stalked up beside them on Griskin. "She'll be free once the unidragon really is no more. Now that the illusion is over, we need to get to work, before anyone catches a glimpse of her."

Riony eyed the clippers, cutting athame, and pots filled with dye at the edge of the room. When Dracuni left this room again, she would no longer look like herself.

"I hate having to change you, just so you can live freely," Riony whispered.

I don't mind. Everybody changes. You changed, so you could live. Dracuni bent down and jabbed Riony's wooden leg with her horn.

Aishena, Benjin, and Kverra Hjelzahn handed out the tools, and Dashiel and Vance came in as well, closing the door after them.

Only the people in that room, plus Eslinde, Jaym, Zeina, and Niskina back in the undercity, would know that Dracuni lived. People Riony trusted. People who would do anything for Dracuni. Family.

Benjin poked at the dark gooey substance in the dye pot he held. "The rumors and stories going through the city after the battle were wild. So many people saw Dracuni's healing flame. Even when we worked on spreading the news Dracuni was gone, there were people saying they were going to steal her bones or her horn."

"That's so mean! And gross!" Lyrrin said.

"If anyone does poke around, they'll find the remains of the other dragon we hid within the pyre," Dashiel said. "I think we found a really good size match from the bodies after the battle."

"And a horn from the king's skeleton collection," Kess added. "It's a good plan. It's going to work."

Lyrrin picked up a pair of clippers and snipped them menacingly at her sister. "Yeah, only it would have been really nice to have known about your plan earlier! I can't believe you let me think Dracuni was dead!"

Riony held up her hands and backed away. "There wasn't any time to tell you! We only made the plan out on the water, after Kess caught us."

Riony's heart stuttered at the memory. She'd really thought for a while that Dracuni was gone, until Kess healed her with the dose of silvernix Riony had given her. But that was the moment Riony had decided maybe it was better if Dracuni didn't go back with them.

Lyrrin punched her hard in the arm. "You still could have told me sooner!"

"I wanted to, but we had an audience as soon as we got back. We had to sell it."

Lyrrin punched her again.

"Ow! Kess, save me!"

Kess raised an eyebrow. "I'm not getting on her bad side. That kid practically burned half the palace down."

Elumon wriggled in between the sisters, tilting his head at Lyrrin. His horn had already been trimmed a couple of days ago, just in case anyone decided he was more like Dracuni than he was.

Lyrrin huffed at the hatchling and put her hands on her hips. "Don't you start. I know you and the other dragons were in on it as well!"

"Speaking of selling it, you sure cried a lot for a funeral you knew wasn't even real," Aishena teased.

Riony pulled a rude face at her. "It might not have been real, but that doesn't mean it wasn't true."

She turned toward Dracuni, cupping her large head on both sides. "Everything Dracuni did for the world, how much of a hero she is, how proud I am of her, and how close she really did come to sacrificing everything … All of that was true."

Tears brimmed in Riony's eyes again. "With or without her horn, she's magical."

Dracuni sniffled and bumped the tip of her snout against Riony's face. *I learned how to be a hero from the best.*

Aishena really is excellent at everything she does.

I mean you, you big tamebrain.

Smirking, Riony wrapped her arms around the unidragon's head, hugging her tight.

I always wanted to be like you. Strong. Caring. Selfless. Dracuni paused after her last thought, then added bashfully, *Although it was nice to see such a big party being held for me.*

Riony backed up. "Did you peek?"

Just once!

Riony tutted. "Besides, it wasn't a party, it was a funeral. But yes, it was nice to see so many people there for you."

Only having heard part of the conversation, Kess frowned and shrugged. "My father always said more people will go to a funeral than a birthday party because most people would like me better dead than alive."

"Wow," Riony said. "Your parents were the worst."

"No argument there," Kess replied.

Lyrrin, having forgotten her earlier ire, gasped, her eyes wide. "Wait, when is Dracuni's birthday?"

Birthday? Dracuni thought, confused.

Riony's face scrunched up as she tried to work out the dates. "We missed it. Her first birthday would have been back when we were at Eslindekeep."

"Oh no!" Lyrrin looked more devastated than any recent events had caused. "*We missed it?* We need to do something for her!"

"You know what? We should," Riony agreed.

Birthdays were the last thing on Riony's mind during that time. Even now, as the world felt like it had taken a collective sigh of relief after the shadow dragon's curse was weakened, it had been hard for Riony to shake off her anxiety and alertness the trials of the last year and longer had set in her.

It felt as though she'd been running for her entire life. Fighting for her entire life. Trying to keep herself and those she loved alive.

She couldn't believe it had been over a year since she first saw Dracuni's egg, since she first felt Dracuni's thoughts and emotions merging with her own.

She never could have known back then where she'd be now.

Riony smiled as she picked up the cutting athame. "But first, we have a little bit more work to do. It's time for a change."

Dracuni nodded, bowing her head.

A wave of bittersweet emotion filled Riony from inside and out. She wished Dracuni could be free without having to hide herself, just as she wished Lyrrin and the Alderkin could too.

Riony had kept Lyrrin safe most of her life by disguising her, and now she'd do the same for Dracuni.

They all deserved to live in a world where they could be themselves without fear or threat. But the world wasn't quite there.

Not yet.

Riony would keep those she loved safe until it was.

With horn and hair trimmed, and scales dyed to a rich, midnight black, Dracuni flew over the palace. The smoke of the battle still tainted the air, leaving it tangy and thick.

Riony could feel the unidragon's trepidation at being so visible, out in the sky where so many eyes in the city could see her.

But Riony encouraged her out anyway. She wanted Dracuni to experience her freedom, to know she was safe.

They flew together silently for a while over the ruins of the city, where people were working to clean up ashes and rubble. Heads turned upward to watch—there were so few dragons in the skies now.

Hux, Gleem, and the other Rebel Riders with wild dragons kept up patrols, making sure the newly untamed dragons didn't cause trouble, and burning any final revenants that had been missed.

But nobody recognized Dracuni. Nobody tried to chase them or catch her.

And after a while, Dracuni's worry tipped over into joy.

"There they are." Riony pointed to a courtyard in the higher levels of the palace.

They landed in the neatly trimmed, if slightly scorched garden. Lyrrin balanced a big bundle of candles in one arm, salvaged from supplies from the earlier funeral. She'd been coerced into wearing a dress at the funeral but had since changed into a simple top, pants, and her own hooded coat, hood pulled back.

"We're all ready. You're just in time!" she sang.

Riony hadn't had a chance to change, but as part of her plan to help Dracuni feel confident they were safe, and strip some of her own defenses, she'd taken off her outer layer of armor she'd worn for the funeral. The chilly air left her bare arms prickling, but it felt good.

Aishena, startlingly, had changed into a dress. A very simple gray slip with gold braiding around the neckline that hung expertly over her angular form.

Riony did a double take. "I'm sorry, but who allowed you to look so good in a dress, on top of everything else?"

"Did I ever need anyone's permission?" Aishena asked back, deadpan.

Riony chuckled as she slipped down from Dracuni's back. She landed awkwardly on her artificial leg, stumbling forward.

Kess brought Griskin into her path, catching her. As she helped Riony get her balance again, she sighed. "I had been hoping I'd see you in a dress."

Riony smirked and leaned in closer, muttering into Kess's ear. "I'm just looking forward to when I can get you out of yours."

She ran a finger over the embroidery down the side of Kess's gown. The skirts were hitched up around the saddle, revealing leather pants beneath.

A giddiness had filled Riony, born from joy and relief that left her feeling lightheaded, and she reveled in it. She ducked in and kissed Kess's neck.

The soft gasp Kess released could have knocked Riony flat on her back if she wasn't being supported in her arms. Kess's embrace tightened and she kissed the cropped hair at Riony's temple.

"Stars, I love you." Riony exhaled roughly and pressed her lips over Kess's.

"Would you two stop already, we're waiting!" Lyrrin yelled.

Riony and Kess broke apart, smiling and flushed.

"Birthday. Right. That's what we were doing." Riony limped over to join the others where Lyrrin had them all sitting on the paving in a semicircle around Dracuni.

Everyone had found neat formal clothing somewhere, leaving Riony feeling shabby in her undershirt and chausses. But as they all smiled and teased as she took a seat on the ground, she knew nobody cared. All that mattered was that they were together.

Dashiel lit Aishena and Benjin's candles for them, and then Aishena turned and lit her mother's from her own. The Alderkin still wore their long cloaks and hoods, needing them to move about the palace unrecognized, but sat beside the others, chatting amiably.

Eslinde and Vance had trays of food in front of them, covered in metal domes. Elumon sniffed around them and Eslinde shooed him away. "Later!"

Dracuni settled down, watching everyone around her, bright-eyed and happy.

"Has everyone got a candle?" Lyrrin asked.

"Except for Dracuni." Riony smiled as her sister organized everything.

They'd only had a couple of birthdays in the undercity after their parents were gone, but Riony always tried to hold them the way her amma and pabba had taught her, and Lyrrin remembered well.

Her little sister moved around Dracuni, flustered for a moment, before placing the candle on the ground in front of her. "That will have to do."

Do I need to do anything? Dracuni sniffed at the small flame.

Riony adjusted her artificial leg into a more comfortable sitting position.

As she looked at the candle in her hands and the people around her, her giddiness changed into something more somber.

Addressing everyone, she said, "In Rolanian tradition, when someone grows a year older, we remember those we've lost. And we ask them to watch over the person whose birthday it is for another year."

Dashiel leaned closer to Vance, bumping shoulders. "Do you remember doing this when we were young? It's been so long since Pabba allowed it."

Vance nodded sadly.

Riony held up her candle. "Dracuni, do you want to go first? Who do you want to remember?"

The unidragon tilted her head, thinking. The dyed black scales made her lilac eyes startlingly bright.

My siblings, lost before they were born. I hope they are watching me.

Riony took a trembling breath and relayed her message to the others.

Aishena bowed her head.

"I remember my parents, Eylin and Farrad. They would have loved you, Dracuni." Riony hugged one arm around herself, wrapping her hand over her tattoo of the rings, swords, and candle.

Kess had climbed down from Griskin and sat beside her. She slid an arm around Riony's waist.

With a heaving breath, Riony continued. "We also remember Myrwa, Kellae and her brother and baby ... all our friends lost that night."

A tremor of sadness from Dracuni joined with her own.

Wiping at her face, Riony indicated for someone else to take a turn.

Eslinde cleared her throat, her silver eyes shining. "We remember the brave riders Thallan, Norallei, and Samor. We remember Shael and her bold kindness."

The Alderkin bowed their heads and together drew a synchronized pattern in the air before them.

Benjin's voice broke as his words jumped out. "Yoskar ... We remember Yoskar. And Fadda and Neif."

Kverra Hjelzahn's face crumpled, and Aishena and Benjin caught her in an embrace.

Over her mother's head, Aishena said solemnly, "Brishan. Jonna. Caed. Daymora.

Honorable delvers and friends."

Riony's head hung heavily as each name struck her heart. She let tears fall, for all they'd lost, every one of them. Vance and Dashiel didn't mention their father much, but Riony could see their grief now in how they held each other's hands.

Lyrrin lifted her candle hesitantly, eyes averted and voice low. "I ... I remember Yensen."

"*We* remember Yensen," Riony echoed, nodding to her sister.

Lyrrin smiled tearily back.

A silence fell as they all looked up to the stars and remembered the people they had lost along the way.

Dracuni rose up, dark scales glistening like the night sky, and her chest expanded. Opening her mouth, she sang. A deep, lingering note filled with sadness and longing that reverberated around the candlelit courtyard. Then the tone lifted into a melodious trill.

I feel stronger, Dracuni thought, awed.

Riony smiled at her part seasong, all magical dragon friend. *That's those above we've remembered watching over you. That's the power of their love. And ours.*

Everybody raised their candles one last time, before placing them all in the center of the circle, letting them burn down.

Eslinde opened up the trays of food, sharing around sweet buns and sliced fruit, and a few pieces of meat for Dracuni and Elumon.

"That was beautiful," Kess said, staring at the candles with an intense expression.

"Yeah, it was kind of cool," Benjin agreed. "Taens just give presents."

Riony laughed. "Really?"

Aishena and Eslinde and the Zarrams all nodded.

I could have had presents? Dracuni snorted.

Taking a big bite of cake, Riony spoke with her mouth full. "Maybe we'll do that next year."

They remained in the courtyard together for a while, sharing food and laughing and crying and laughing again. As the night grew darker and air grew colder, people drifted away to their beds.

Soon only Kess and Riony remained, tucked in together against Griskin's fur to keep warm as they stared up at the moon.

"What do you want to do now?" Kess asked.

Riony turned to face her and waggled her eyebrows.

"I mean with your life. With your freedom. With this world that you saved."

"Saving the world really was a group effort. There's no way it would have turned out so well on my own. Much like what I want to do with you."

Kess pursed her lips and gave Riony a hard look. "Would you stop deflecting for once?"

Riony pouted and leaned back against Griskin's side again. Buying time, she reached overhead and scratched his back. The wolf's tail thumped on the ground happily.

"I've kind of been avoiding thinking about it," Riony finally admitted after Kess refused to break.

"Why?" Kess's voice had become small.

"Because I don't know what I want to do. I've spent so much of my life just … surviving. Doing whatever I had to do to keep myself and those I love alive. I never really thought about the future. Never really thought I'd have one."

A dark emotion flashed over Kess's features, scrunching up her face. "I'm sorry."

Riony shook her head, turning to look at Kess, her shimmering ice-blue eyes and spots like stars over her cheekbone and white-streaked charcoal hair. "I know there's still no guarantee, there's still danger, but these last few days, for the first time in a long time, it feels like I have a life ahead of me."

It felt strange, saying it out loud. Riony swallowed the feeling away, trying to be as forthright and brave with her wants as the woman in front of her. "I have some ideas … But I don't want to rush into it. I want to spend some time first just … breathing."

Kess seemed to echo that with a deep breath of her own, one that released with an expression like heartbreak. "Whatever you want. You deserve any future you want."

Riony reached for one of the salt-and-pepper braids beside Kess's face, wondering how she'd fallen so deeply in love with this wild, passionate woman who had once been so cruel. But as she stared at Kess's beautiful face, knowing all they had been through together, for each other, it didn't seem so strange at all.

"Of every future I could want, of all the futures there could be, I want mine to be with you."

Kess's expressions brightened, her nose still scrunched as though in disbelief. "You do?"

Riony smirked, leaning in to kiss Kess's neck. "You promised you'd watch me die one day. I'm holding you to it. And I'm not planning on dying anytime soon."

Chapter Thirty-Two

Lyrrin paced up and down the side of the long table she'd arranged to be brought into one of the palace's flight decks. It was laden with trays of flatbreads and dips and jugs of spiced drinks. Eslinde carried in another tray, arranging it between the others.

"Why aren't they here yet?" Lyrrin huffed.

Eslinde surveyed the spread, then took a seat with a tired sigh. "It's still early. Everyone will be here soon."

"Why can't they be here now? It's been weeks since I saw Riony." Lyrrin kicked the leg of the chair next to Eslinde's.

Eslinde tutted softly. "It was only last week. Riony visits as often as she can. And we both agreed it would be good for Riony to have some time for herself."

Lyrrin pouted. She had agreed that it seemed like a good idea, and it also meant she could spend a lot more time with Eslinde, but she didn't realize she'd miss Riony so much. Even with frequent visits, it wasn't the same as the years they'd spent side by side, inseparable.

She sighed. "I know. But she has to come today, because I did so much to prepare for her birthday!"

"She'll be here," Eslinde said.

Lyrrin paced around the table again to where Elumon was sniffing at the food. He'd grown a lot in the last few months, almost as big as Griskin, but not quite big enough for Lyrrin to fly safely on yet. According to the Zarrams anyway.

But Lyrrin was small too, and she and Elumon had been on a couple of small flights around the palace.

Can you hear Dracuni yet? Are they on the way at least?

Not yet. A sense of longing came with the thought.

Lyrrin knew he missed Dracuni as well. She rubbed a hand over the stub where his horn had been trimmed down. At a casual glance it looked like a scar from a taming spike removal. A lot of dragons had those now.

As he'd gotten bigger, the tufts of hair he'd been born with had been replaced with scales, and apart from his opalescent rainbow tone, he looked just like any other dragon.

The flight deck was otherwise empty of dragons. All tamed dragons in the palace and city had now been freed. Even the dragons that had been powering the palace's strange electric lights were gone. Lamps were now fitted with Alderkin glow stones, giving off their familiar cyan shine.

The polished cavernous room that opened out to the sky at one end echoed with Lyrrin's pacing footsteps. It had been strange at first for Lyrrin, living in the palace where she'd once been held prisoner.

But after the battle, as dragonlords and remaining riders and advisors clamored for leadership within the rubble, it soon became clear that Eslinde was the last remaining first heir still alive. All others had been lost to Lady Hjelzahn, when their keeps fell, or when trying to flee the revenant hordes that day.

Between Eslinde's claim to the throne, her ownership over the king's silvernix supply, and the backup of the few riders still with dragons, all others vying for control soon backed down.

But there had still been *so many meetings* since. Lyrrin was tired of them, and the way her mother looked as she poured herself a drink, she figured Eslinde was as well.

Lyrrin paced back and took a seat beside her, smiling in a way that crinkled her eyes. "This should be fun for everyone."

Eslinde smiled back. "I think so too. It's a lovely idea."

Wingbeats at the end of the flight deck had Lyrrin springing back out of her seat again, hopefully looking for Riony and Dracuni.

A red dragon came in to land, wind rustling the tablecloth.

"Oh, it's just them," she said a little too loud.

"Happy to see you too, little spitfire," Niskina called down the length of the vast room.

She climbed down from Hux and Jaym followed. His pocket-hawk flittered around, then landed amid the red dragon's crown of spikes, preening herself. Hux moved away from the entry to where food and drink had been put out for the incoming dragons.

"Are we the first here?" Jaym asked as he reached the table.

"Yes," Lyrrin muttered.

Eslinde stood and greeted them both with a hug, and Niskina walked past Lyrrin with a wrapped bundle under one arm. She ruffled a hand through Lyrrin's undyed hair.

Both she and Jaym wore rider's armor, dusty and marred from use.

Lyrrin straightened her hair again and patted down the dress Eslinde had encouraged her to wear. Most around the palace and city still wore Taenish grays, but Eslinde had some more colorful dresses made and Lyrrin didn't hate them. She wore a blue one today that matched her eyes.

Niskina hid her parcel under the table and sat down. "Zeina sends her apologies. She's caught up with Gleem and the others trying to manage a group of wild dragons that have been taking their anger out on a town out west."

"You both look like you've been busy too," Eslinde said.

Niskina glanced down at her dirty armor and windswept locks, then over at Eslinde, in a pristine gown with silver hair coifed in an elegant bun. "We didn't have a chance to stop and change. There's a lot to do out there."

Niskina had been on the wing with Jaym and the Rebel Riders since the battle at the capital. As soon as news reached the undercity that the revenant curse was weakened, people began hesitantly moving aboveground again.

With the shrines being recharged by Dracuni, communities were springing up all around Elundrae, living under the sun and sky and stars.

There were still plenty living in the undercity, but Niskina thought she wasn't needed there as much anymore.

She helped herself to some food, swiping flatbread through a plate of dip and oil. "There are a few dragonlord holdouts in the north where the revenant army didn't pass through. We're working through them at the moment, convincing them to hand over their dragons."

Jaym leaned on the table beside her and grinned roguishly. "One way or another."

Niskina gave him a gentle eye roll. "Mostly with diplomacy. Sure, some of them are angry and don't want to give up their wealth and power, but none of them can deny the change in the land since the curse has weakened."

It had only been a few days ago that Eslinde had called Lyrrin out onto their balcony, staring up at the sky with wide-eyed wonder. Lyrrin hadn't been sure what she was looking at, at first, because the sky was clear.

Then Lyrrin saw it too. *The sky was clear.* No ash fell. No smoke grayed out the sun. The sky was *blue*, a glowing, vibrant azure, with thin streaks of white cloud.

Eslinde gave Jaym a glittering smile. "I've heard your words are doing far more than your aerial battle skills anyway. The new Rebel Riders tales you've been putting out to explain to everyone what happened, and why the dragons were freed, have been doing a good job spreading the word."

Jaym took a seat beside Niskina, draping an arm around her and winking. "What can I say? I've found new inspiration."

Eslinde looked toward the patch of open blue at the end of the flight deck. "I think we all have."

Niskina raised her glass to that, then sighed. "One problem we keep running into is actually *because* of how good things are getting. The last few dragonlords are saying that since things are better, they should be allowed to keep their dragons."

"Of course they can keep dragons," Eslinde said, gesturing to Hux at the other end of the deck. "If those dragons are wild and agree to it."

Niskina nodded. "That's what we told them too. Every last dragon is getting untamed. It's only fair."

Pouring himself a drink, Jaym looked up and down the long, empty table. "This isn't just for us, is it? Who else is coming?"

"The usual," Eslinde replied. "Although Yrik and Priyune are away traveling at the moment and can't make it."

The Alderkin had built a shrine within the palace, as they had at the undercity. Once it was completed, they took their leave, traveling around Elundrae to repair broken shrines and looking for any signs of other Alderkin survivors.

They came back to visit about as often as Riony did, and they sounded quietly hopeful the last time they were there.

It had been good having a gateway in the palace. Lyrrin had gone back to visit the undercity a couple of times. She missed Butterfur, as she'd been unable to lure him through the gateway to the palace with her. He was too busy swimming through the pools of the undercity and raiding bins with his family.

That was where he should be. With family. But she still liked to visit and give him treats sometimes.

Dracuni's coming! Elumon perked up, flushed with excitement. His next message was more of a grumpy afterthought. ***And Lyomir.***

Lyrrin turned to the end of the flight deck to see the two dragons flying in side by side—Dracuni still dyed midnight black, stark beside Lyomir's dusky purple.

They glided down onto the open end of the deck, with nobody on their backs.

"Where's Riony? And Kess?" Lyrrin asked.

Dracuni says they're walking in. They wanted to see some of the city.

"*Walking?*" Lyrrin balked. "They're going to be late!"

Dracuni trotted up the rest of the flight deck, frolicking around Elumon as he reared up to greet her. Lyomir huffed and remained at the end near the entrance.

"Who's going to be late?" Benjin came running in from the palace side entrance. "Are we late?"

Aishena and Dashiel followed him in.

"Riony and Kess are *walking*," Niskina said.

"Of course they are," Aishena replied.

"You're right on time," Eslinde said, standing to greet them all.

Lyrrin joined them as well, giving each a hug.

She backed away from Benjin with a grimace. "Why are you so sweaty?"

He grinned. "Came straight from training so we wouldn't be late."

"I tried to tell him there was time to change. The guest of honor isn't even here yet." Aishena's silvery locks swung loose around her brown face. She and Dashiel both wore neat, casual clothing.

"You could have changed. You should have changed." Lyrrin wrinkled her nose teasingly.

"Just because you're a princess who can spend her days relaxing doesn't mean we all can." Benjin only grinned more as he wafted his shirt.

"I have been very busy with my rune research and experiments!"

Benjin's silvery hair had been growing out as well and he smoothed it back. "Which is why I need to train hard to be your official grayglim warden. Not that you need a bodyguard. But so I can be around all the time when you're doing more awesome magic! I want my flaming blades!"

Lyrrin offered him a smile of truce and ushered him over to the seat beside hers. She liked the idea that he was going to stay around. Since the battle, it felt like a lot of them had drifted off different ways. But the Hjelzahns all remained at the palace with Eslinde and Lyrrin.

Although Hjelzahn the First had died, Hjelzahnkeep was one of the few not to fall to the revenant horde, but Kverra, Aishena, and Benjin were still many generations and many heirs away from being necessary there.

Lady Hjelzahn had returned to her role of training grayglims, although whether it was on Eslinde's instruction or a change in heart in general, her lessons were far less intense than before, according to Aishena.

When Eslinde asked Aishena to also take a role teaching, it had left her dumbstruck for a while before she agreed.

"I want a new type of grayglim than before. Ones who can use their wisdom and instinct to make the right choices, beyond their loyalty. I can't think of anyone better suited to bestow that learning than you," Eslinde had said, causing Aishena to blink rapidly, then excuse herself.

The uneven footsteps of an artificial leg swung Lyrrin around again, only to see Vance walking in.

Eslinde popped up out of her seat, thin hands smoothing down her dress. She rushed over to greet Vance, and the two of them hugged awkwardly.

Benjin leaned closer to Lyrrin and whispered, "Are those two still—?"

"Acting clueless about each other's feelings?" Lyrrin whispered back. "Yes. I'm working on it."

Lyrrin knew her mother was still grieving for Alleem, even after all this time, and she didn't really understand the allure of romance that had seemed to spread through their group like a plague. But in the past few months, Lyrrin had seen how happy Riony's relationship with Kess made her.

And she wanted that for her mother as well. There hadn't been a lot of time lately to get Eslinde and Vance alone together since Eslinde spent so much time with Lyrrin. Maybe Lyrrin just needed a night away ...

She gasped, outraged by a realization.

The sleepover!

As Vance reached the table, Viska, Shiff, and Ambri glided in together onto the flight deck. They greeted Dracuni, Hux, Lyomir, and Elumon fondly.

Ambri had been one of the first dragons to be untamed after the battle, once everything had settled down. It was done with both Zarrams and other wild dragons around her, to be there for her as she awoke. As usual, she was angry at first. She left, wanting her freedom, but often returned to spend time with Viska and Shiff.

Vance and Dashiel had been taking care of all the dragons that needed untaming, trying to give them a positive experience as they awoke again, finally freed. They'd taken over the king's dragonhold, working with riders and breeders who were interested in building relationships with untamed dragons, the way the Zarrams had.

"Riony's still not here?" Vance looked at the people already seated.

A grumbling of 'noes' came from around the table.

Lyrrin looked to Elumon for an update, but the dragons were too busy in discussions of their own.

Vance sat down heavily beside Eslinde. "And I thought I was late."

"You are," Eslinde said with a slight smile as she offered him a drink.

"My apologies. I wanted to check on some of the bovin herds we've released onto the plains. It took a bit longer than expected."

"How are they?" Eslinde asked with far greater interest than Lyrrin thought the topic deserved.

"Doing well. Grazing and moving about as though they'd never been penned. Maybe a third are already missing, but that was expected with so many hungry dragons around now. We're working on increasing numbers soon."

Niskina smiled at the news. "We've been seeing some reach the north as well. And more dreer and other animals moving around too. And green ... so much green! Grass and forests are all sprouting again."

Jaym leaned back in his chair and put his feet up on the table. "Been ages since the last time we've seen any revs. People are still hesitant to leave the safety of the shrines for now, though."

Lyrrin straightened in her chair. "Do you think when the revs are all gone, Riony and Dracuni won't need to travel around so much to keep the shrines charged?"

Getting some time for herself wasn't the only reason Riony was regularly away. She and Dracuni made frequent stops at the shrines, ostensibly checking in on the settlements there, but really to keep the shrine's protective barriers active.

"Maybe," Eslinde replied. "Although the shrines are also needed to recharge the Alderkin crystals the communities are using too."

Lyrrin slumped a little. "I suppose."

They had discussed trying to hide small bundles of the king's silvernix supplies at each shrine to keep them activated, but they weren't sure it would be safe.

Niskina shrugged. "Riony said the shrines seem to be lasting longer between visits, with less revenants around to drain them. So I don't know how busy our missing heroes have really been."

"What's this about missing heroes?" Riony stepped in through the nearby entrance, flushed and short of breath. "Do you think they mean us?"

Kess padded in on Griskin beside her. "They might mean you."

Riony grinned. "I think they mean us."

"Finally!" Lyrrin shot from her chair and grabbed her sister's hand, dragging her at a run back to the table.

Riony limped behind her. "Whoa, slow down! Do you know how many stairs I just walked up?"

"Then you should have flown in and not been late!" Lyrrin pushed her down into the seat beside hers.

Riony readjusted her leg, then undid her belt, hanging it and her dragonguard sword on the back of her chair. She wore a loose tunic that left her arms bare, like she always preferred, but the fabric was clean and new, not like the old tatty clothing she'd worn for years.

"Did you enjoy your *walk*?" Niskina asked with a smirk.

Riony wiped a hand over her forehead, brushing back the flop of red hair. It had grown out just long enough to have a tiny braid at the back again.

"Yes, actually. It was nice to spend some time walking with Kess. I enjoyed seeing more of the city."

Niskina raised her eyebrows.

Riony tsked and shook her head at Kess. "These people, always with their minds in the gutter."

Niskina threw a scrap of flatbread at Riony.

Kess slid into the seat beside Riony, and Griskin bounded away to take a big drink from one of the dragon's troughs. "It was good, though. The city has really rebounded after the battle."

Riony leaned her cheek on one hand, looking at Kess. "Maybe we could stay in one of the buildings by the harbor for a while. It's nice down there."

Jaym scoffed. "Look at these two, on holiday while the rest of us are working so hard."

"Yeah, it's pretty sweet." Riony grinned toothily and reached for some food.

Lyrrin slapped her hand. "Presents first! We've been waiting so loooong."

"Presents?" Riony asked.

Dashiel and Vance shared a sharp look with each other.

Lyrrin sighed. "It's your birthday, remember? And we're doing it Taen style this time! Surprise!"

Lyrrin reached down under the table and dragged out a long heavy parcel wrapped in red cloth.

Riony helped her haul it up the rest of the way, frowning at Kess. "Were you in on this?"

Kess smiled back with narrowed eyes. "Maybe."

"Open it, open it!" Lyrrin squealed.

Riony barely had the first bit of cloth unwound, but Lyrrin couldn't contain her excitement.

"I made it for you myself. I mean, Yrik and Priyune also helped a bit, but it was mostly me, since the glass magic doesn't seem to work for them. But they taught me what I needed to do to harden it all enough to make it work and fuse together the different materials. And there are some new runes on there too!"

Riony's jaw dropped as the final fabric fell away.

She rose from her seat, bringing the hefty sword of glass and dark crystal with her. The high polish and facets gleamed in the cyan light as she turned it side to side in front of her face. Along the shaft of the blade, enclosed droplets of silvernix shimmered. Riony stared, open-mouthed, her head shaking.

As Riony said nothing, Lyrrin grew nervous. "Do you like it? I know how much the one you lost meant to you, and I know I can't really replace it, but I thought you might like this anyway. Do you?"

Riony traced the float rune, and the blade lit up purple. "This is ... this is the second most beautiful thing I've ever seen in my life."

"Second?" Lyrrin pouted.

Kess frowned as well. "It's much nicer than the other sword was."

"Never said it wasn't." Riony put the weapon down beside her chair and grabbed Lyrrin up in a big hug. "I can't wait for you to show me what the other runes on this do."

"Maybe not at the dinner table," Eslinde said. She leaned over from the other side and held a scroll of paper out for Riony. "This is from me."

Riony put Lyrrin back down in her seat. She cracked the wax seal and unrolled the parchment, frowning at a wall of tiny handwriting.

"Um ... thanks. What is it?" she said.

"An official declaration. That I, as heir to the Draekhan throne, affirm you as one of my daughters."

Riony continued to hold the parchment, staring at it as her breath came heavy.

Eslinde's pale cheeks flushed pink. "I hope that's not too presumptive of me. But you are already a sister to my daughter. I felt there was nothing more I wanted than for all of us to be family."

Lyrrin held her breath, waiting for Riony's response. Eslinde had run the idea past her a while ago, and Lyrrin loved it. But she also knew how Riony felt about her parents she'd lost before.

Riony's face scrunched up. Her voice came out huskily. "Thank you. I'm ... I'm honored."

Eslinde shook her head. "No. I am."

Benjin huffed. "How are we expected to compete with those presents?"

Aishena rolled her eyes as she pulled a satin bag from beside her and tossed it over the table. "I'm not calling you princess."

Riony grinned as she caught the lumpy bag. Tugging the drawstring open, she gasped. "No way!"

"What is it?" Lyrrin knelt up on her chair to try to see through the bag's opening.

"No way!" Riony repeated, pulling a couple of shiny red apples from the bag. She grinned and tossed one back to Aishena.

"Thanks, but I had apples just a few weeks ago." Aishena's eyes glittered as she handed the apple to Benjin.

Riony barked a laugh.

"Apples?" Vance asked.

Eslinde shrugged, looking equally bewildered. Lyrrin laughed too, thrusting her arm into the bag to steal one.

"It's the thought that counts," Aishena said.

Riony gleefully handed apples around to everyone at the table.

Kess held hers in front of her. "I don't get it."

Dracuni wandered over from the end of the flight deck, sniffing at the empty bag and nudging Riony with her snout.

"You remember them too? They were your first meal." Riony and Dracuni spent a moment, locked in private, silent conversation, before Riony turned back to the others, taking a big bite from her apple.

At the other end of the table, Vance and Dashiel wore matching frowns.

Dashiel blurted, "We weren't told we were doing presents. We thought we were doing the candle thing again."

Riony just laughed again. "That's okay. I wasn't expecting anything."

"I'm sure I told you about this," Aishena said.

Dashiel rubbed a hand through their blond curls. "Maybe? I get a bit distracted when you're around."

Aishena smiled wickedly in return.

"Gross," Riony smirked. "You know, even Dracuni got me something."

Dashiel turned a deep red. "I'm so sorry. I'll make it up to you."

Lyrrin looked between Riony and Dracuni. How had a dragon Riony spent most of her time with manage to get a present? "What did she get you?"

"News, from her mother." Riony smiled as she chewed around the core of her apple, right down to the seeds. "She has a new clutch of eggs."

Lyrrin bounced in her chair.

"That is happy news," Aishena said with only sadness in her voice.

Riony nodded to her solemnly.

"More baby dragons?" Lyrrin squealed. "Will they visit?"

"I don't know about that," Riony said. "Maybe."

A short silence fell, as Niskina and Kess held a staring competition across the table. Then Niskina stood up and handed Riony her wrapped gift.

"Ours first. So we can show up whatever she got you." Niskina gave Kess a sly look.

"This isn't a competition." Riony took the parcel.

"We'll see." Kess returned the sly look, relaxing back into her chair.

Lyrrin waited impatiently as Riony undid the ties and pulled back the fabric. She was a little disappointed to see a book inside.

Niskina grinned and sat back in her chair, leaning shoulder to shoulder with Jaym. "It's every chapter of the Rebel Riders in existence, all bound together. Including the most recent stories featuring the popular new redheaded character."

Riony gasped and clutched the book to her chest. "Okay. You two win."

"You haven't even opened mine yet," Kess said.

"Every chapter, Kess. Every. Chapter."

"Fine. As long as I can read them, too." Kess shrugged, pulling a tiny bundle of satin from her pocket, holding it out. "Here."

All around the table, chairs squeaked as everyone leaned in to see what was in the palm-sized pouch as Riony worked it open.

Kess spoke softly. "While we've been traveling, Riony has midwifed at a few births. It's been amazing to see … her skill, knowledge, gentleness in aiding mothers and newborns through their labor. She's been incredible."

Riony's frantic tugging at the small parcel stilled as it fell open and her eyes glistened with a flood of tears. "Kess …"

Five silver rings lay on the black satin, sparkling like stars.

Kess bowed her head. "They aren't the same ones handed down through your family. But you still deserve them, to recognize the five generations of women in your line who have brought life into this world. You more than any other."

Riony heaved a deep breath, and her hand closed tight around the rings. She turned to Kess, lunging forward to kiss her deeply.

"I still think our present was the best," Niskina muttered.

"No chance. I got her *a sword*!" Lyrrin yelled back.

Riony and Kess broke apart, laughing, and Riony slipped the five rings onto the fingers of one hand.

Lyrrin grabbed her sister's shoulders, physically turning her back toward her, telling her about all the new magic she'd learned and what the sword could do. They ate together, and Riony wiped a bit of dip off Lyrrin's chin as she talked.

People moved around the table, chatting with each other and sharing food and flicking through the new chapters of the Rebel Riders, arguing and laughing about the details.

Benjin showed Niskina how much taller he'd gotten, and Kess moved a few seats down to chat with Dashiel, both giggling.

Eslinde moved around from the other side of the table to join Lyrrin and Riony. "This has been a lovely night. You did well organizing it."

"She's always been the brains of the group," Riony replied.

They shuffled their seats closer as Lyrrin slumped sleepily in her chair.

Lyrrin hadn't grown much in the last few months. Not shooting up the way Benjin or the dragons were.

She still felt so small compared to everyone else, but as she sat there between Riony and Eslinde, she felt okay with that.

She knew now who and what she was and where she belonged. And she loved that place.

Lyrrin pulled Riony and Eslinde in closer, cuddling up between them, happy she was still small enough to do so.

Chapter Thirty-Three

Kess waited at the party until almost everyone was gone. Even Riony had left a while earlier, due to her leg being sore from their long walk through the city.

But Kess remained behind, waiting until she was sure she could be alone with Lyrrin.

As Eslinde and Vance cleared the table, Lyrrin sat farther away with Elumon. Kess took Griskin over beside her, lowering the wolf down so she was closer to the girl.

Lyrrin looked up, yawning. "You had such a nice present for Riony."

"You too." Kess swallowed.

She'd always struggled to talk to Lyrrin. She'd started their relationship with so much anger and jealousy that this girl had been loved by Riony when she hadn't been. She wasn't sure why Riony entrusted this task to her.

Clearing her throat, she reached out a closed hand. "Riony and I have a present for you, too."

Lyrrin looked at Kess's clenched fingers. "Really? Is that how Taen birthdays work?"

"No. This is something special, just for you."

Lyrrin reached out her clawed fingers, and Kess placed a tiny empty vial into her palm.

"You found it!" Lyrrin held up the bottle in front of her, staring in awe at the markings in the glass.

Kess nodded, speaking quietly. "When I was scouting during the siege, I took Griskin to look for it. He sniffed it out of the snow pretty quickly."

Kess had almost given the vial to Riony right after finding it. Then she saw how shattered Riony was, having lost Lyrrin. Then Riony had kissed her. Then Kess had left to rescue Lyrrin.

There was always so much to worry about.

"I only told Riony I had it recently, after the battle."

Lyrrin's blue eyes sparkled, enthralled by whatever she was seeing in the minute scratched lines.

Kess half smiled. "Riony asked me to hold on to it since then. But we talked tonight and think you should have it. It makes sense since you created it. Also, I think Riony just doesn't want the responsibility of deciding what to do with it. But she trusts you to decide."

Lyrrin's hand closed around the vial and she nodded. "I'll keep it safe."

Kess returned a torn expression. It was a big responsibility to be handing to a child. But she'd seen what that child could do and knew she had a heart as big as Riony's.

"Thank you." Kess turned Griskin away.

"Thank you!" Lyrrin called after her. "For making Riony happy. I've liked you being around. Although you could have been nicer sooner."

Kess huffed a laugh. "Rub it in, why don't you?"

Lyrrin stuck her tongue out as Kess waved good night.

At the far end of the flight deck, Lyomir raised his head. ***I can eat her for you if you'd like.***

Kess chuckled. She loved her grumpy dragon so much.

Good night, Lyomir.

Kess stalked on Griskin down the long corridors of the palace. It was late, and only muffled voices sounded here and there through closed doors around her. She balanced Riony's new sword, book, and declaration scroll on her lap. The apples were all gone.

The massive palace was fuller than it had ever been, with Eslinde opening the doors to people who had lost homes during the battle, but Riony and Kess still had a room set aside for them for when they visited.

Just as they had a home in the undercity. And in the new enclaves around the shrines, all over Elundrae. They had a home anywhere they were together.

Griskin brought Kess into the modest living area of their chambers. The doorway to the bedroom beyond was open, and Riony lay on the covers of the bed.

Her artificial leg was off, dropped carelessly on the floor, and she held one hand up in the air over her face, admiring the shine of silver on her fingers.

Riony noticed Kess come in and called out, "Should I get my tattoo redone to add another ring?"

Kess opened the balcony doors, looking up at the risen moon. It was cool and white, a color Kess was still getting used to. It had always been a bloody orange before from the smoky skies.

Then Kess brought Griskin into the bedroom and beside the bed. "I don't know, will it fit in?"

Riony sat up and turned her arm for Kess to appraise the existing tattoo, flexing noticeably.

Kess smiled. "Yeah, it'll fit."

Riony reached out, taking her presents off Kess. "Thanks for bringing these up for me. My leg's giving me trouble again."

"Can't relate." Kess climbed off Griskin onto the bed beside Riony, and the wolf padded away back to the living room to sit in the open air of the balcony.

Riony snorted a laugh. She admired her new sword for a moment, then propped it up against her side of the bed. The declaration from Eslinde was placed reverentially on the nightstand. She kept the book on her lap, flicking through the pages. "Taens might have some okay customs."

Kess just smiled as she moved beside Riony to rub the knotted muscles in her thigh. She'd never received much in the way of gifts from her family. Her birthday was generally forgotten, until it was used as an excuse to banish Kess from her home. With Riony already gone by that point, there'd been nothing at Heithorn estate she missed.

Kess hadn't known until recently why Riony and her family had left, fleeing with Eslinde's newborn, but as much as Kess had felt abandoned at the time, it still made sense.

Why wouldn't they want to leave that awful place?

She'd just wished Riony had taken her with them, even though she knew part of what Riony had been fleeing was her. Riony had never been happy in that awful place either. She never could have been.

But now ... Kess was in awe, seeing Riony so joyful, so relaxed. Surrounded by family and love, but no longer crushed under the weight of responsibility to keep them all alive. It was beautiful in a way that ached.

And I get to be part of that.

It still didn't feel real sometimes. Kess had Riony, Griskin, Lyomir, and a home with people who loved and respected her. The world was healing, and she'd played a role in making that happen. She'd been able to be so much more than the dragonrider hero she once dreamed of being.

She had more than she could have ever wanted.

And it was nice to sleep in a soft bed sometimes too.

Although, the way Riony was looking at her, she wasn't sure either of them would be getting much sleep that night.

"Did you see the kids in the city?" Riony leaned back on her elbows.

"Which ones?"

Riony watched her with an intensely soft stare. "The ones riding on other kids' backs as they crawled around, howling like wolves. Because you should have seen their faces when *they* saw *you*."

Kess's hands stilled on Riony's thigh. "I was wondering why they were staring ... I thought ..."

"That they'd all just seen their hero?"

Kess shook her head. Back when she'd imagined herself as a dragonrider, she'd wanted it to prove that she could be as good, or better, than other riders. To win the approval of those who'd always hated her. At some point, that dream no longer seemed important.

Kess was so used to people looking at her with pity, disgust, or as though she were invisible, she hadn't even imagined that the kids playing in the city idolized her.

"Do you really think that was why?"

Riony shrugged one shoulder. "Or, I don't know, maybe they were all stunned by your beauty. I wouldn't be surprised. My new sword came second for a reason."

Kess pictured the scene again in her mind with the new context. The scramble of children playing in the still charred stone streets, acting out a battle as their favorite heroes. Heroes who looked like them.

"I also saw more than a couple of kids with toy peg legs and big stick swords. I thought they were pretending to be pirates."

"*Pirates?*" Riony knuckled Kess in the ribs, making her squeal.

Kess dodged out of the way. "Are you jealous there were more kids pretending to ride wolves than there were pretending to be you?"

Riony pillowed her arms behind her head. "No. Maybe. Wolves are cool, okay? I can't compete with that."

"Lucky for you it's not a competition." Kess leaned back onto the bed beside Riony.

"It was sort of weird to see, though. And there was a market stall selling acorn pendants!" Riony shook her head, laughing. "Maybe we should ask Jaym to stop writing so many details about us."

Kess doubted the children they saw had been reading the Rebel Riders chapters. "I think it's more than that. The story has spread, taking on a life of its own. People know what you did."

"What we did," Riony corrected sternly.

"What me and some pirate did."

Riony gasped in mock outrage and lunged forward, tackling Kess around the waist and pinning her down from above. "Kessara, you always did know how to go right for the heart."

"Yours was the only heart I ever wanted."

They stared at each other for a long moment, breaths coming short, and Riony grew solemn.

"No matter what stories spread about us, we'll always know the truth. What we went through, what we sacrificed, what we lost. What we almost lost." Riony traced a finger around Kess's neck, along the string where the original acorn pendant still hung.

Kess tucked a strand of red hair back behind Riony's ear. "How brave and honorable you remained, every step of the way."

"And hot. Don't forget hot."

"Never."

Riony sat up, flicking through the pages of her bound volumes again. "Jaym hasn't even come close to capturing the true magic and greatness of what we've done."

Kess waited, eyebrows quirked. Riony just stared back sweetly.

"You mean sex, don't you?"

"I mean the sex." Riony nodded.

Kess let out a bright giggle. "And yet you're the one who thought I was being literal when I suggested we *go for a walk* before getting to the party tonight."

She greatly enjoyed the dumbfounded look that hit Riony.

"Wait … you meant …?"

Kess just stared back sweetly.

Riony's eyes softened, filled with longing. "I guess we've got to make up for lost time then."

She chucked the Rebel Riders tome behind her onto the side table. It thumped beside the scroll declaring Riony as part of the royal family.

The corner of Kess's mouth lifted. "So, do you want me to call you Princess now? Your Highness? Milady?"

Riony snuggled in beside Kess, wrapping her arms around her. "You can call me whatever you want."

Kess raised her eyebrows questioningly.

Riony nuzzled closer. "Even *that*. It's kind of grown on me, now that things are different. Funny how you can love something you once hated. I wouldn't mind being your Pony again."

Kess shook her head. "I promised you I'd never call you that again."

Riony backed away slightly, frowning. "I don't remember that."

"I might have made the promise to a hallucination ... but it still stands. Besides, I don't think I could take all the jokes it would open up."

"Aw, but I have so many. *So many.*"

"Never again," Kess teased, and then Riony kissed her on the side of the neck, and all her other thoughts fell away, and all she felt was warm and loved and filled with hope for the future.

Two days ago, while passing by the shrine that had once been Myrwa's enclave, Riony and Kess had seen the shadow dragon.

It was so much smaller than before, barely as big as a treedart.

They watched it for a while, flying behind it on Dracuni and Lyomir, as its wispy form glided through the clear blue sky. It landed here and there, calling its haunting cry, but nothing crawled out of the ground at its command.

The rush of grief the being's presence caused had also lessened. But Kess still grieved for it anyway. She knew now the creature had never been to blame, that it was only a creation of the greed of humans, taming and enslaving dragon spirits.

It was hard to tell how many tamed dragons there still were in Elundrae, but it wouldn't be much longer before the shadow dragon would be gone for good.

Did the shadow dragon think? Feel? Did it want to end? Did all of the broken pieces that formed it long to be back in the bodies they'd been driven from?

Kess found she held hope for the cursed entity, because of her own experiences. That if a creature so evil, so irredeemable, and so hated could find healing, then surely the shadow dragon could too.

She knew that all those broken pieces could find their place once more and be whole, and happy, and even loved.

THE END

GLOSSARY

Including pronunciation guide

CHARACTERS

Riony Eyfarr (Ree-OH-nee AY-far) – Rolanian, Daughter of Eylin and Farrad, born when servants to the Gyrstein Dragonlords, then sold on as a family to the Heithorn Dragonlords, and since living as fugitive slaves. Trained as a midwife and herbalist. Sword enthusiast.

Lyrrin Eyfarr (Li-rin AY-far) – Daughter of "The Guest", an unknown dragonlord woman, and an unknown father. Taen and Elgarthan? Has some unusual features. Likes animals and magic.

Kessara Heithorn (Kess-AH-ra High-thorn) – From the once wealthy Heithorn dragonlords with strong dragon riding traditions, estranged. Taen. Rides a wolf.

Kife Heithorn (K-eye-f High-thorn) – Elder brother to Kessara, dragonrider. Taen.
Dracuni (Drak-YOU-nee) – Unique hybrid between unicorn and dragon, created from the use of silvernix on a broken dragon egg, and something more?

Griskin (Griss-kin) – Large gray wolf, male, for some reason abides Kess's company.

Aishena Hjelzahn (AYSH-ena Hyel-zarn) – Delver, Middle sibling of three (remaining), fifth generation heir, grayglim in training. Taen.

Benjin Hjelzahn (BEN-jin Hyel-zarn) – Youngest sibling of three (remaining), fifth generation heir. Taen.

Kverra Hjelzahn (Kv-errar Hyel-zarn) – Grayglin warden and wife to Vori Hjelzan, fourth generation heir to the Dragon King. Taen.

Yeonard Draekhan (Yeh-nard DRAKE-arn) – Dragonking, ruler of Elundrae. Taen. First to tame a dragon.

Eslinde Draekhan (Ez-Lind-eh DRAKE-arn) – Last of the dragon-king's first generation heirs.

General

Alderkin (ALL-der-kin) – a secretive and powerful race of elven humanoids. Masters of rune crystal magic. Extinct.

Alderkin Depths – Massive underground cities once inhabited by the Alderkin. There are five known Alderkin Depths across Elundrae.

Alderkin Runes – Magical symbols carved into crystal items, which, when somehow charged, allow for a range of magical functions. The runes must be traced in the right sequence and direction of strokes in order to be activated and deactivated.

Alderkin War – A twenty-year war between the Alderkin and the Dragon King's forces, ending thirty years prior to the events in these books. Prompted by the human's slaughter of unicorns, and the Alderkin's attempts to protect them.

Athame (Ah-Thahm-Ay) – A dagger of varying size, made from crystal, and powered by various Alderkin runes for utility or combat.

Breachers – Undercity dwellers who brave the aboveground world to scavenge resources, highly dangerous but sometimes required.
Delvers – Undercity dwellers who brave the dangers of the Alderkin depths to salvage useful artifacts to be sold in the undercity. A risky but lucrative profession.

Dragon Glass – Glass manufactured with the use of dragon's fire to melt the base ingredients.

Dragon guards/riders – Those trained to ride dragons, generally for combat purposes. Either born to or hired by Dragonlord families who own the dragons.

Dragonhold – A building with multiple facilities for dragon keeping and raising, including hatchery, stables, and training areas.

Dragonkeeps – Walled in cities protected by dragons. The Dragon King has built and gifted a dragonkeep to each of his first generation heirs.

Dragonlords – Those who have the riches and resources to own their own dragons. Not necessarily royalty.

Elgarthans – A sea-faring race, pale skinned, they will visit and trade with Dragonkeeps for the riches of steel and glass provided through dragon labor, but rarely remain in Elundrae due to the dangers.

Elundrae (Ell-Un-Dray) – The continent in which the story takes place. Nearest neighboring country being Elgartha, across the seas to the East.

Rebel Riders – Title of a popular serial fiction, published and distributed in chapters.

Revenant/Rev/Shadow Revenant – Any undead creature raised by the Shadow Dragon's curse. Generally defeated by fire or dismemberment.

Rolanians – Once ruling large cities throughout Elundrae, most Rolanian settlements were destroyed as the Shadow Dragon curse spread through the land. As very few Rolanians became dragonlords, they had to buy into protection from those who had dragons, often at the cost of their own freedom. Generally presenting with a warm array of darker skin tones, and hair ranging from blonde, through reds and browns.

Shadow Dragon – a cursed and mysterious creature of smoke and sadness that brings the undead blight to the land of Elundrae. Wherever the Shadow Dragon touches ground, the dead rise.

Silvernix – Unicorn blood. Miraculous healing qualities, a single drop can cure a body from near death. Can only be stored in dragon glass, otherwise loses potency within minutes. Opalescent liquid.

Taens – Generally dark-haired and light-to-mid-brown skin-tones, Taens were once a warrior like clan of horse-riders, taking residence through the north-west of Elundrae. When the Dragonking rose to power, Taens became favored and more likely to become dragonlords, and soon became the dominant race across the land.

Taming – The ceremony in which all dragons are subjected to in order to be domesticated, similar to a lobotomy. Performed not long after birth on dragons bred in captivity. Utilizes silvernix in the process.

Undercity – A human settlement, established in the large upper cavern of the Central Alderkin Depths, as a refuge from the dangers of the aboveground world.

Unicorns – Ethereal, horned horse-like creatures. Driven to extinction in the race for the riches of their blood.

Tree Dart
Sea Song
Snow Shimmer
Ether Flame

Dragons
Natural subspecies

Etherflame – Plains dragons. Golds and reds, large size. Fire breathing for clearing grasslands/cooking herds, and big wings for hovering. Blood itself is flammable and is aerosolized in breath weapon. Most common dragonrider mount.

Seasong – Sea dragons. Silvers, greens, blacks, largest size, big lungs creates big surge of air/sound to stun schools of fish, and bigger mouth for feeding. There are tales they once sang, but never have in captivity or once tamed. Mostly used for interbreeding and beasts of burden.

Snowshimmer – Mountain dragons. Whites-blues, medium-sized, fast build for snatching up rare prey. Big talons, lightning breath attack, rare and solitary. Used in industry for power and interbreeding.

Treedart – Forest dragons. Yellows, browns, purples, camouflaged scales. Smallest type, with concentrated fire bolts for individual prey. Considered pretty basic by breeders and dragonlords, mostly used for interbreeding. Main/only dragon still in the wild because of size.

Interbred selective breeding species

Etherdart – Etherflame/Treedart cross. Medium size, tough but slow, big fireballs. A basic combat dragon.

FlameSongs – Etherflame/Seasong cross. Largest size, high-capacity fire-breathers, used mostly for industrial uses, not used as mounts because they can spontaneously explode.

Seashimmer – Seasong/Snowshimmer cross. Large size, cold, icy breath used in ice making and food storage industry.

Shimmerdart – Snowshimmer/Treedart cross. Small size, with small ball lightning darts, dangerous for single targets but not great against mass undead, bred for speed as scouts/communications/assassinations.

Snowflame – Snowshimmer/Etherflame cross. Medium-large size, white "liquid" fire, fast, considered a great dragonrider mount, but short lifespan as breath weapon deteriorates their health fast.

Treedart/seasong – don't interbreed successfully.

Herbs

Carrowmy – culinary.

Corpsefoot – used for contraception, dangerous in high doses.

Genjermint – sleeping tea.

Hennen – for hair dye.

Morass Mercy – powerful sedative with bad side effects.

Plumeberry – tart, seedy berries, poison detox.

Shillgrue – to condition leather.

Tinctoria – for hair dye.

Weftweed – a sticky (both in appearance and sap production) antiseptic.

Animals

Bantam Ferrets – Mouse sized ferrets.

Bovin – A large (twice human height) buffalo or yak style creature, docile, used to be in large herds that supported wild dragons. Moved into farming for captive dragons.

Carrion Birds – Massive scavengers with a cry like a wolf's howl.

Cave Otters – A large sized otter with specially adapted claws that allow them to climb sheer walls easily, pale colors to match limestone surroundings.

Cave Spiders – Head-sized spiders, nonvenomous.

Dreer – Deer with Armadillo like scales, that grow as large as giraffes. Also popular prey for wild dragon populations in the past.

Glowflies – firefly-like bugs, finger sized, live in large swarms and light up when disturbed.

Mouse Deer – Cat sized deer with fangs.

Olm – Just like real olm, but larger than human size and carnivorous.

Owlettes – Cave dwelling owls that feed on small rodents and insects within the caves, the size of a small hand.

Rope Worms – Just a worm, but much larger. Delicious when fried.

ALDERKIN RUNES

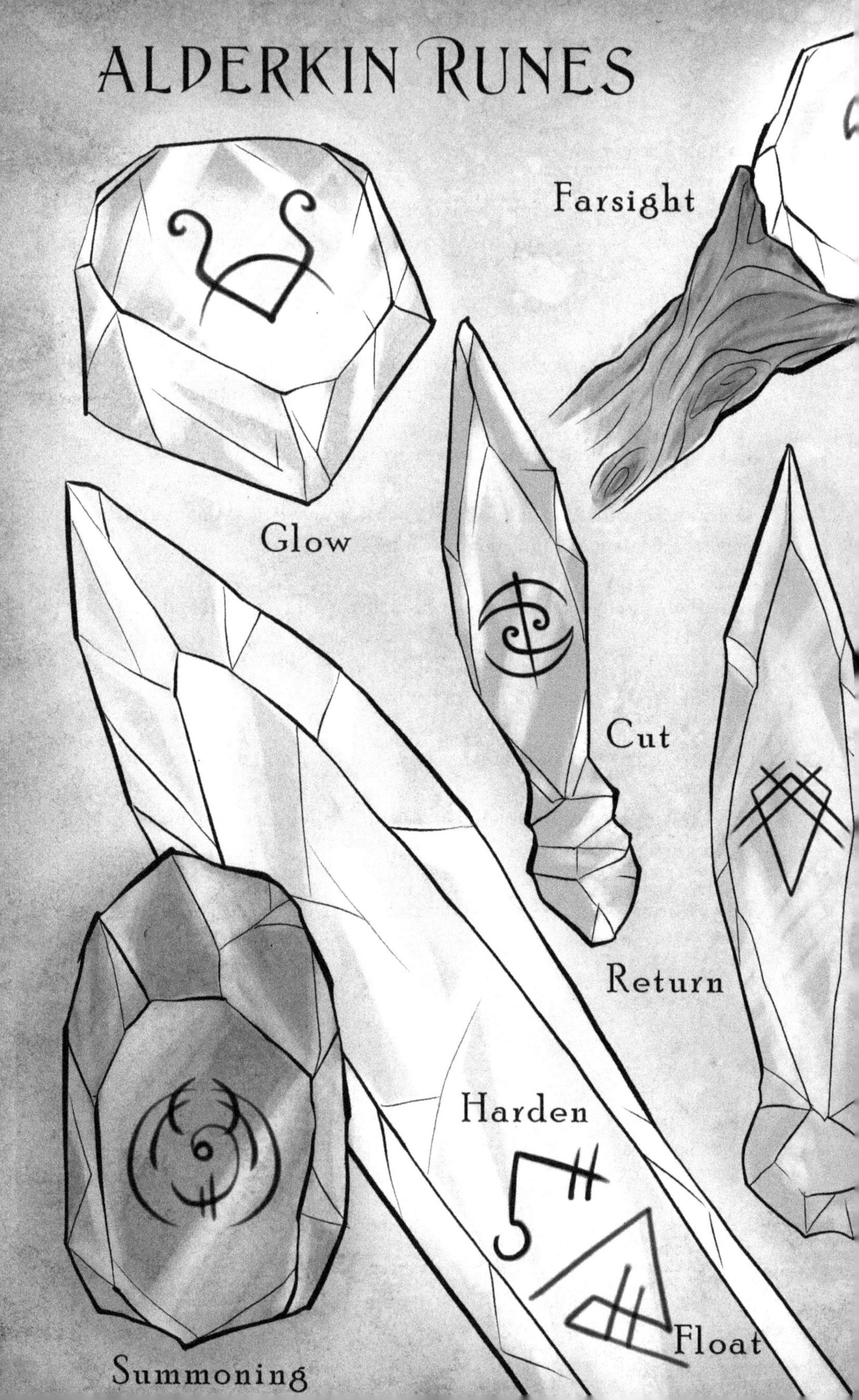

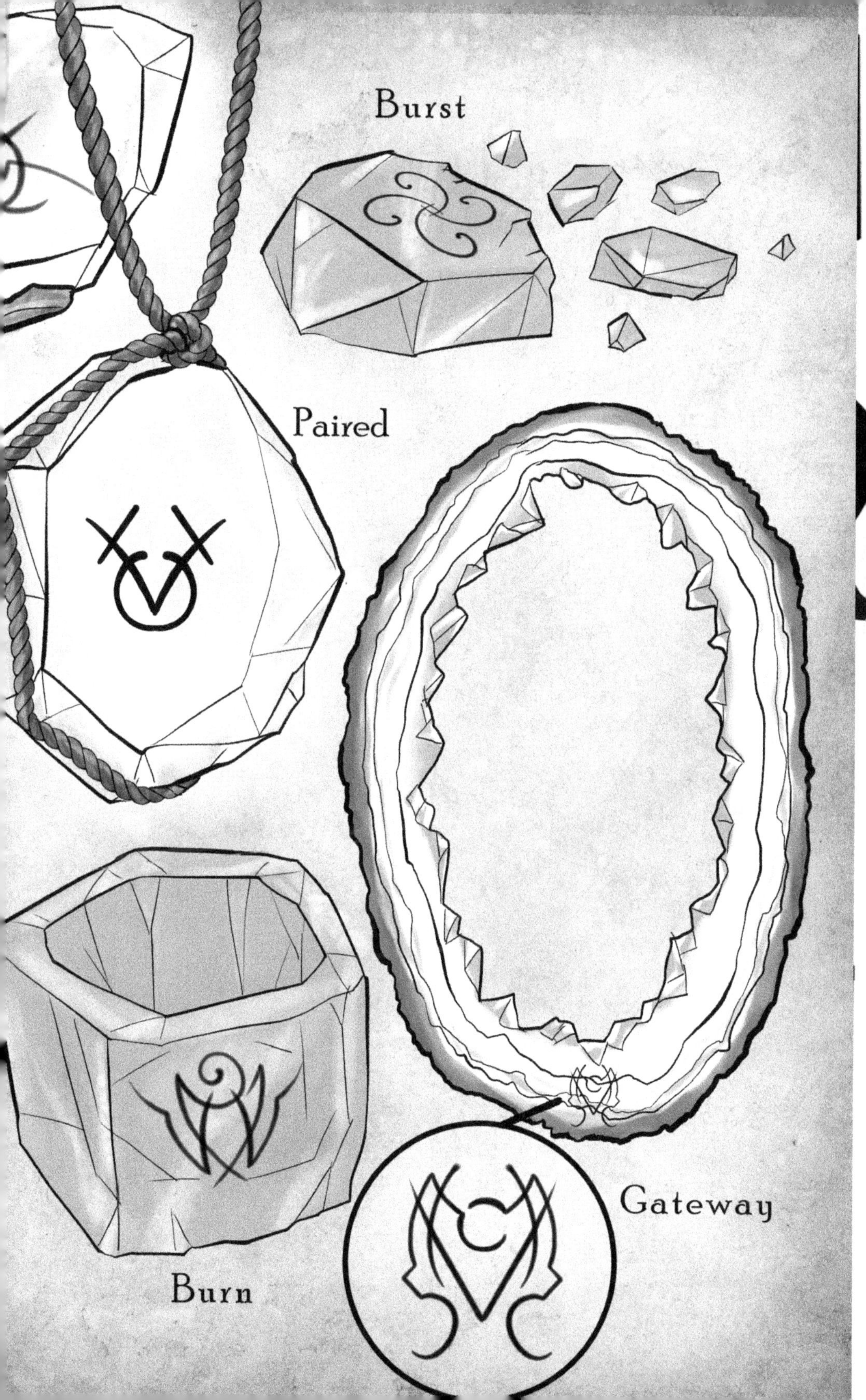

Burst
Paired
Burn
Gateway

About the Author

Professional daydreamer, Selina A. Fenech writes "adorably dark" Epic and Urban Fantasy for teens and adults. Filled with sweet and quirky characters, laugh out loud moments, and perilous adventures, her magical worlds are perfect for readers who love daring twists and happily ever afters.

A cancer survivor determined to live life to the fullest, she is an escape room enthusiast, avid gardener, foodie and self-proclaimed geek, residing in Australia.

In addition to literature, Selina applies her unique take on the dichotomy of light and dark as a professional fantasy artist working under the name Selina Fenech and has published many illustrated books, oracle decks, and colouring books.

Find Out More About Selina

OFFICIAL WEBSITE: www.selinafenech.com

Memory's Wake Trilogy

A modern girl lost in and hunted in a fairy tale world.
An illustrated young adult portal fantasy with Arthurian
and Victorian themes.

Empath Chronicles

Teenagers with superpowers fueled by emotions ... what
could go wrong? A young adult superhero romance.

More Books by Selina A Fenech

Beshadowed

You have been lied to. Werewolves, vampires, ghosts ... they aren't what you think. What is really lurking in the dark? A spooky urban fantasy.

Fairy Tale Wishes

Enchanting and inclusive standalone fairy tale retellings.